The heir to the magnificent English trading company, the Noble House
... the direct descendant of the first Toranaga Shōgun battling to usher
his country into the modern age ... a beautiful young French woman
forever torn between ambition and desire.... Their lives intertwine in
an exotic land newly open to foreigners, *gai-jin,* torn apart by greed,
idealism, and terrorism. Their passions mingle with monarchs and
diplomats, assassins, courtesans and spies. Their fates collide in James
Clavell's latest masterpiece set in nineteenth-century Japan—an un-
forgettable epic seething with betrayal and secrets, brutality and hero-
ism, love and forbidden passions....

JAMES CLAVELL'S

GAI-JIN

*the long-awaited sixth novel in his
magnificent Asian Saga*

Please turn the page for more extraordinary acclaim ...

JAMES CLAVELL'S

GAI-JIN

A Novel of Japan

A Dell Book

Published by
Dell Publishing
a division of
Bantam Doubleday Dell Publishing Group, Inc.
1540 Broadway
New York, New York 10036

U.S ISBN: 0-440-21680-X

Canadian ISBN: 0-440-21809-8

Reprinted by arrangement with Delacorte Press

Printed in the United States of America

Published simultaneously in Canada

May 1994

10 9 8 7 6 5 4 3 2 1

RAD

This novel is for you,
whoever you are,
with deep appreciation—for
without you, the writer part of
me would not exist. . . .

GAI-JIN,
meaning foreigner, is set in Japan, in 1862.

It is not history but fiction. Many of the happenings did occur according to historians and to books of history which, of themselves, do not necessarily always relate what truly happened. Nor is it about any real person who lived or is supposed to have lived, nor about any real company. Kings and queens and emperors are correctly named, as are a few generals and other exalted persons. Apart from these I have played with *history*—the where and how and who and why and when of it—to suit my own reality and, perhaps, to tell the real history of what came to pass.

THE ASIAN SAGA
so far consists of:

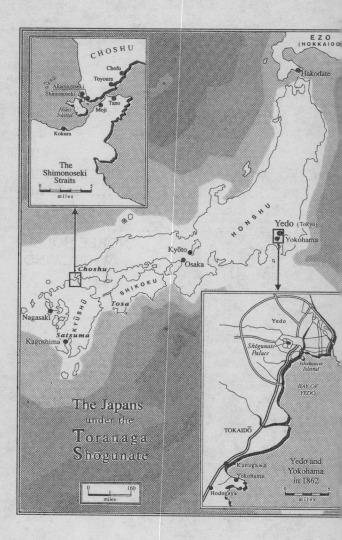

Map of Japan in 1862

BOOK ONE

1

YOKOHAMA

14th September 1862:

THE PANIC-STRICKEN GIRL WAS galloping full speed back towards the coast, half a mile ahead, along footpaths that led precariously through the rice swamps and paddy fields. The afternoon sun bore down. She rode sidesaddle and though normally expert, today she could hardly keep her balance. Her hat had vanished and her green riding habit, the height of Parisian fashion, was ripped by brambles and speckled with blood, tawny fair hair streaming in the wind.

She whipped the pony faster. Now she could see the tiny hovels of the Yokohama fishing village clustering the high fence and canals that enclosed the Foreign Settlement and spires of the two small churches within and knew, thankfully, in the bay beyond were British, French, American and Russian merchantmen and a dozen warships, both steam and sail.

Faster. Over narrow wooden bridges and canals and irrigation ditches that crisscrossed the paddy and swamps. Her pony was lathered with sweat, a deep wound on his shoulder and tiring rapidly. He shied. A bad moment but she recovered, and now she swerved onto the path that led through the village to the bridge over the encircling canal and to the main gate and the samurai guard house, and Japanese Customs House.

The two-sworded samurai sentries saw her coming and moved to intercept, but she charged through them into the wide main street of the

Settlement proper on the seafront. One of the samurai guards rushe
for an officer.

She reined in, panting. "*Au secours . . . à l'aide,* help!"

The promenade was almost deserted, most of the inhabitants a
siesta or yawning in their countinghouses, or dallying in the Pleasu
Houses outside the fence.

"Help!" she called out again and again, and the few men sprea
along its length, British traders and off-duty soldiers and sailo
mostly, some Chinese servants, looked up startled.

"God Almighty, look there! It's the French girl . . ."

"What's amiss? Christ, look at her clothes . . ."

"Cor, it's her, the smasher, Angel Tits, arrived couple of week
ago . . ."

"That's right, Angelique . . . Angelique Beecho or Reecho, som
Frog name like that. . . ."

"My God, *look at the blood*!"

Everyone began converging on her, except the Chinese who, wis
after millennia of sudden trouble, vanished. Faces began to appear i
windows.

"Charlie, fetch Sir William on the double!"

"Christ Almighty, look at her pony, poor bugger will bleed to deatl
get the vet," a corpulent trader called out. "And you, soldier, quick, ge
the General, and the Frog, she's his ward—oh, for God's sake, th
French Minister, hurry!" Impatiently he pointed at a single-story hous
flying the French flag. "Hurry!" he bellowed. The soldier rushed off
and he trundled for her as fast as he could. Like all traders he wore a to
hat and woolen frock coat, tight pants, boots, and sweated in the sui
"What on earth happened, Miss Angelique?" he said, grabbing he
bridle, aghast at the dirt and blood that speckled her face and clothe
and hair. "Are you hurt?"

"*Moi, non* . . . no, I think not but we were attacked . . . Japanner
attacked us." She was trying to catch her breath and stop shaking, stil
in terror, and pushed the hair out of her face. Urgently she pointe
inland westwards, Mount Fuji vaguely on the horizon. "Back there
quick, they need—need help!"

Those nearby were appalled and noisily began relaying the hal
news to others and asking questions: Who? Who was attacked? Ar
they French or British? Attacked? Where? Two-sword bastards agaii
Where the hell did this happen . . . ?

Questions overlaid other questions and gave her no time to answe
nor could she yet, coherently, her chest heaving, everyone pressin;

loser, crowding her. More and more men poured into the street putting
n coats and hats, many already armed with pistols and muskets, a few
with the latest American breech-loading rifles. One of these men, a
ig-shouldered, bearded Scot, ran down the steps of an imposing two-
tory building. Over the portal was 'Struan and Company.' He shoved
is way through to her in the uproar.

"Quiet, for God's sake!" he shouted, and in the sudden lull, "Quick,
ell us what happened. Where's young Mr. Struan?"

"Oh, Jamie, *je* . . . I—I . . ." The girl made a desperate effort to
ollect herself, disoriented. "Oh, *mon Dieu*!"

He reached up and patted her shoulder like a child, to gentle her,
doring her, like all of them. "Don't worry, you're safe now, Miss
Angelique. Take your time. Give her some room, for God's sake!"
amie McFay was thirty-nine, chief manager of Struan's in Japan.
"Now, tell us what happened."

She brushed away the tears, her tawny hair askew. "We . . . we were
ttacked—attacked by samurai," she said, her voice tiny and accent
leasing. Everyone craned to hear better. "We were . . . we were on the
. . on the big road . . ." Again she pointed inland. "It was there."

"The Tokaidō?"

"Yes, that's it, the Tokaidō . . ." This great coastal trunk toll road, a
ittle over a mile west of the Settlement, joined the Shōgun's forbidden
apital, Yedo, twenty miles northwards, to the rest of Japan, also
orbidden to all foreigners. "We were . . . riding. . . ." She stopped
nd then the words poured out: "Mr. Canterbury, and Phillip Tyrer and
Malcolm—Mr. Struan—and me, we were riding along the road and
hen there were some . . . a long line of samurai with banners and we
vait to let them pass then we . . . then two of them rush us, they wound
Mr. Canterbury, charge Malcolm—Mr. Struan—who had his pistol
ut and Phillip who shout me to run away, to get help." The shaking
egan again. "Quick, they need help!"

Already men were rushing for mounts, and more guns. Angry shouts
egan: "Someone get the troops . . ."

"Samurai got John Canterbury, Struan, and that young chap Tyrer—
hey've been chopped on the Tokaidō."

"Christ, she says samurai have killed some of our lads!"

"Where did this happen?" Jamie McFay called out above the noise,
urbing his frantic impatience. "Can you describe the place where this
appened, exactly where?"

"By the roadside, before Kana . . . Kana something."

"Kanagawa?" he asked, naming a small way station and fishing

village on the Tokaidō, a mile across the bay, three odd miles b
coastal road.

"*Oui*—yes. Kanagawa! Hurry!"

Horses were being led out of the Struan stables, saddled and ready
Jamie slung a rifle over his shoulder. "Don't worry, we'll find then
quickly. But Mr. Struan? Did you see if he got away—if he wa
hurt?"

"*Non*. I saw nothing, just the beginning, poor Mr. Canterbury, he . .
I was riding beside him when they . . ." The tears flooded. "I did no
look back, I obeyed without . . . and came to get help."

Her name was Angelique Richaud. She was just eighteen. This wa
the first time she had been outside the fence.

McFay jumped into the saddle and whirled away. Christ Almighty
he thought in anguish, we haven't had any trouble for a year or more
otherwise I'd never have let them go. I'm responsible; Malcolm's hei
apparent and I'm responsible! In the Name of God, what the hel
happened?

Without delay, McFay, a dozen or so traders, and a Dragoon office
with three of his lancers found John Canterbury on the side of th
Tokaidō, but viewing him was more difficult. He was decapitated an
parts of his limbs were scattered nearby. Ferocious sword cuts wer
patterned all over his body, almost any one of which would have been
death blow. There was no sign of Tyrer and Struan, or the column o
samurai. None of the passersby knew anything about the murder, wh
had done it, or when or why.

"Would the other two have been kidnapped, Jamie?" an America
asked queasily.

"I don't know, Dmitri." McFay tried to get his brain working
"Someone better go back and tell Sir William and get . . . and bring
shroud or coffin." White-faced, he studied the passing crowds, wh
carefully did not look in his direction but observed everything.

The well-kept, beaten earth roadway was massed with discipline
streams of travellers to and from Yedo, which one day would be calle
Tokyo. Men, women and children of all ages, rich and poor, al
Japanese but for an occasional long-gowned Chinese. Predominatel
men, all wearing kimonos of various styles and modesty, and man
different hats of cloth and straw. Merchants, half-naked porters
orange-robed Buddhist priests, farmers going to or coming from mar
ket, itinerant soothsayers, scribes, teachers and poets. Many litters an
palanquins of all kinds for people or goods with two, four, six or eigh

bearers. The few strutting samurai amongst the crowds stared at them balefully as they passed.

"They know who did it, all of them," McFay said.

"Sure. *Matyeryebitz!*" Dmitri Syborodin, the American, a heavyset, brown-haired man of thirty-eight, roughly clothed and a friend of Canterbury, was seething. "It'd be goddam easy to force one of them." Then they noticed a dozen or so samurai standing in a group down the road, watching them. Many had bows and all Westerners knew what adept archers samurai were.

"Not so easy, Dmitri," McFay said.

Pallidar, the young Dragoon officer, said crisply, "Very easy to deal with them, Mr. McFay, but ill-advised without permission—unless of course they attack us. You're quite safe." Settry Pallidar detailed a dragoon to fetch a detachment from the camp, with a coffin, the American visibly irritated by his imperiousness. "You'd better search the nearby countryside. When my men arrive they'll assist. More than likely the other two are wounded somewhere."

McFay shuddered, motioned at the corpse. "Or like him?"

"Possibly, but let's hope for the best. You three take that side, the rest of you spread out and—"

"Hey, Jamie," Dmitri interrupted deliberately, hating officers and uniforms and soldiers, particularly British ones. "How about you and me going on to Kanagawa—maybe someone in our Legation knows something."

Pallidar disregarded the hostility, understanding it, well acquainted with the American's fine service record. Dmitri was an American of Cossack extraction, an ex–cavalry officer of the U.S. Army, whose grandfather had been killed fighting the British in the American War of 1812. "Kanagawa is a good idea, Mr. McFay," he said. "They should certainly know what big procession of samurai passed through and the sooner we find out who the culprit is the better. The attack must have been ordered by one of their kings or princes. This time we can peg the bastard and God help him."

"God rot all bastards," Dmitri said pointedly.

Again the resplendently uniformed Captain did not provoke but did not let it pass. "Quite right, Mr. Syborodin," he said easily. "And any man who calls me a bastard better quickly get himself a second, a pistol or sword, a shroud and someone to bury him. Mr. McFay, you'll have plenty of time before sunset. I'll stay here until my men return, then we'll join the search. If you hear anything in Kanagawa, please send me word." He was twenty-four and worshipped his regiment. With barely concealed disdain he looked at the motley group of traders. "I suggest the rest of you . . . gentlemen . . . begin the search, spread out but stay in visual contact. Brown, you go with that group and search those woods. Sergeant, you're in charge."

"Yessir. Come on, you lot."

McFay took off his coat and spread it over the body, then remounted. With his American friend he hurried northwards toward Kanagawa, a mile away.

Now the dragoon was alone. Coldly he sat on his horse near the corpse and watched the samurai. They stared back. One moved his bow, perhaps a threat, perhaps not. Pallidar remained motionless, his sabre loose in its scabbard. Sunlight sparked off his gold braid. Pedestrians on the Tokaidō hurried by silently, afraid. His horse pawed the ground nervously, jingling the harness.

This isn't like the other attacks, the lone attacks, he thought with growing anger. There's going to be hell to pay, attacking those four, a woman amongst them, and killing an Englishman so foully. This means war.

A few hours ago the four of them had ridden out of the main gate, past the Customs House, casually saluted the samurai guards who bowed perfunctorily, and trotted leisurely inland along meandering paths, heading for the Tokaidō. All were expert riders, their ponies nimble.

In Angelique's honor, they wore their best top hats and riding clothes, and were the envy of every man in the Settlement: one hundred and seventeen resident Europeans, diplomats, traders, butchers, shopkeepers, blacksmiths, shipwrights, armorers, adventurers, gamblers and many ne'er-do-wells and remittance men, most of them British, the clerks Eurasian or Chinese, a few Americans, French, Dutch, Germans, Russians, Australians and one Swiss; and amongst them three women, all matrons, two British, wives of traders, the last a madam in Drunk Town, as the low-class quarter was called. No children. Fifty to sixty Chinese servants.

John Canterbury, a good-looking, craggy-faced British trader acted as their guide. The purpose of the excursion was to show Phillip Tyrer the way by land to Kanagawa, where meetings with Japanese officials took place from time to time; it was well within the agreed Settlement area. Tyrer, just twenty-one, had arrived yesterday from London via Peking and Shanghai, a newly appointed student interpreter to the British Legation.

This morning, overhearing the two of them in the Club, Malcolm Struan had said, 'May I come along, Mr. Canterbury, Mr. Tyrer? It's a perfect day for sightseeing; I'd like to ask Miss Richaud to join us—she hasn't seen any of the country yet.'

'We'd be honored, Mr. Struan.' Canterbury was blessing his luck. 'You're both welcome. The ride's good though there's not much to see—for a lady.'

'Eh?' Tyrer had said.

'Kanagawa's been a busy post village and stopover place for travellers to and from Yedo for centuries, so we're told. It's well stocked with Teahouses, that's what most brothels are called here. Some of them are well worth a visit, though we're not always welcome like at our own Yoshiwara across the swamp.'

'Whorehouses?' Tyrer had said.

The other two had laughed at his look. 'The very same, Mr. Tyrer,' Canterbury had said. 'But they're not like the doss houses or brothels in London, or anywhere else in the world; they're special. You'll soon find out, though here the custom is to have your own doxy, if you can afford it.'

'I'll never be able to do that,' Tyrer said.

Canterbury laughed. 'Maybe you will. Thank God the rate of exchange favors us, oh my word! That old Yankee Townsend Harris was a canny bastard.' He beamed at the thought. Harris was the first American Consul-General appointed two years after Commodore Perry had forced the opening of Japan to the outside world, first in '53, then '56 with his four Black Ships—the first steamers seen in Japanese waters. Four years ago, after years of negotiating, Harris arranged Treaties later ratified by major Powers that granted access to certain ports. The Treaties also fixed a very favorable rate of exchange between silver Mex—Mexican silver dollars, the universal coin of exchange and trade in Asia—and Japanese gold *oban,* whereby if you changed Mex for *oban* and later exchanged them for Mex, you could double or triple your money.

'An early lunch, then off we go,' Canterbury said. 'We'll be back in good time for supper, Mr. Struan.'

'Excellent. Perhaps you'd both join me in our company dining room? I'm giving a small party for Mademoiselle Richaud.'

'Thank you kindly. I trust the tai-pan's better?'

'Yes, much better, my father's quite recovered.'

That's not what we heard in yesterday's mails, John Canterbury had thought worriedly, for what affected the Noble House—the nickname

by which Struan and Company was known the world over—affected
them all. Rumor is your old man's had another stroke. Joss. Never
mind, it's not often a man like me gets the chance to chat to a real tai-
pan-to-be, or an angel like her. This's going to be a great day!

And once en route, he became even more affable. "Oh, Mr. Struan,
you . . . are you staying long?"

"Another week or so, then home to Hong Kong." Struan was the
tallest and strongest of the three. Pale blue eyes, long reddish brown
hair tied in a queue, and old for his twenty years. "No reason to stay,
we're in such good hands with Jamie McFay. He's done a sterling job
for us, opening up Japan."

"He's a nob, Mr. Struan, and that's a fact. Best there is. The lady will
leave with you?"

"Ah, Miss Richaud. I do believe she'll return with me—I hope so.
Her father asked me to keep an eye on her, though temporarily she's the
French Minister's ward while she's here," he said lightly, pretending
not to notice the sudden gleam, or that Tyrer was deep in conversation
with Angelique in French, which he himself spoke hesitantly, and
already under her spell.

Don't blame him, Canterbury, or anyone, he thought, amused, then
spurred forward to give the others room as the path ahead became a
bottleneck.

The terrain was flat but for bamboo thickets, though it was wooded
here and there—the trees already autumn-tinged. There were many
duck and other game fowl. Paddy fields and rice swamps were being
cultivated intensively, and land reclaimed. Narrow pathways. Streams
everywhere. The stench of human manure, Japan's only fertilizer, ever
present. Fastidiously, the girl and Tyrer held scented handkerchiefs to
their noses, though a cooling breeze came off the sea to take away most
of the stink and the dregs of summer's humidity, mosquitoes, flies and
other pests. The far hills, densely forested, were a brocade of reds and
golds and browns—beech, scarlet and yellow larch, maples, wild rho-
dodendrons, cedar and pines.

"It's beautiful there, isn't it, Monsieur Tyrer? A shame we can't see
Mount Fuji clearer."

"*Oui, demain, il est là! Mais mon Dieu,* Mademoiselle, *quelle
senteur.*" What a smell, Tyrer replied happily in fluent French—an
essential language for any diplomat.

Casually Canterbury dropped back alongside her, neatly displacing
the younger man. "Are you all right, Mademoiselle?"

"Oh, yes, thank you, but it would be good to gallop a little. I'm so happy to be outside the fence." Since she arrived two weeks ago with Malcolm Struan on the bimonthly Struan steamer she had been closely chaperoned.

And quite right too, Canterbury was thinking, with all the riffraff and scum of Yokohama, and let's be honest, the odd pirate sniffing around. "On the way back you can take a turn around the racetrack if you like."

"Oh, that would be wonderful, thank you."

"Your English is just wonderful, Miss Angelique, and your accent delightful. You were in school in England?"

"La, Mr. Canterbury." She laughed and a wave of heat went through him, the quality of her skin and beauty exhilarating. "I've never been to your country. My young brother and I were brought up by my aunt Emma and uncle Michel, she was English, and refused always to learn French. She was more a mother than an aunt." A shadow crossed her. "That was after my mother died birthing my brother, and Father left for Asia."

"Oh, sorry about that."

"It was a long time ago, Monsieur, and I think of my darling aunt Emma as Mama." Her pony tugged at her reins. She corrected him without thought. "I was very lucky."

"This's your first visit to Asia?" he asked, knowing the answer and much more, wanting to keep her talking. The snippets of information about her, gossip, rumors, had sped from smitten man to smitten man.

"Yes, it is." Again her smile lit up his being. "My father's a China trader in your Colony of Hong Kong. I'm visiting him for the season. He's a friend of Monsieur Seratard here, and kindly arranged this visit for me. You may know him, Guy Richaud, of Richaud Frères?"

"Of course, a fine gentleman," he answered politely, never having met him, knowing only what others had told him: that Guy Richaud was a philandering, minor foreigner who had been there for a few years, scratching a living. "We're all honored that you're visiting us here. Perhaps I may host a dinner in your honor, at the Club?"

"Thank you. I will ask my host, Monsieur Seratard." Angelique saw Struan glance back, up ahead, and she waved gaily. "Mr. Struan was kind enough to escort me here."

"Really?" As if we didn't know, Canterbury thought, and wondered about her, how you could catch and hold and afford such a treasure, wondered about the brilliant young Struan who could afford it, wondered too about rumors that the struggle for dominance between Struan's and their major trading rival, Brock and Sons, was rising again, something to do with the American civil war that had started last year.

The pickings are going to be huge, nothing like a war for business, both sides already going at each other like maniacs, the South more than a match for the Union . . .

"Angelique, look!" Struan reined in, pointing. Ahead a hundred yards, down the small rise, was the main road. They came up beside him.

"I never thought the Tokaidō would be this big, or so crowded," Phillip Tyrer said.

Except for a few ponies, everyone was on foot. "But . . . but where are the carriages, or tumbrils or carts? And more than that," she burst out, "where are the beggars?"

Struan laughed. "That's easy, Angelique. Like almost everything else here they're forbidden." He shifted his top hat to a more jaunty angle. "No wheels of any sort are allowed in Japan. Shōgun's orders. None!"

"But why?"

"It's one sure way of keeping the rest of the population in order, isn't it?"

"Yes, indeed." Canterbury laughed sardonically, then motioned towards the road. "And add to that, every Tom, Dick or Mary there, high or low, has to carry travel papers, permission to travel, even to be outside their own village, same for princes or paupers. And notice the samurai—they're the only ones in all Japan who can carry weapons."

"But without proper stagecoaches and railways, how can the country possibly work?" Tyrer was perplexed.

"It works Japan style," Canterbury told him. "Never forget Jappers have only one way of doing things. Only one. Their way. Jappers are not like anyone else, certainly not like Chinese, eh, Mr. Struan?"

"Indeed they are not."

"No wheels anywhere, Miss. So everything, all goods, food, fish, meat, building supplies, every sack of rice, stick of wood, bale of cloth, box of tea, keg of gunpowder—every man, woman or child who can afford it—has to be carried on someone's back—or go by boat, which means by sea 'cause they've no navigable rivers at all, so we're told, just thousands of streams."

"But what about the Settlement? Wheels they are allowed there, Mr. Canterbury."

"Yes, indeed they are, Miss, we've all the wheels we want though their officials bitched like bloody . . . sorry, Miss," he added quickly, embarrassed. "We're not used to ladies in Asia. As I was saying, Japper officials, they're called Bakufu, they're like our civil service, they argued about it for years until our Minister told them to get f— to, er, to forget it because our Settlement was our Settlement! As to beggars, they're forbidden too."

She shook her head and the feather on her hat danced merrily. "It sounds impossible. Paris, she is . . . Paris is filled with them, everywhere in Europe, it's impossible to stop the begging. *Mon Dieu*, Malcolm, what about your Hong Kong?"

"Hong Kong's the worst," Malcolm Struan said, smiling.

"But how can they forbid begging and beggars?" Tyrer asked, perplexed. "Mademoiselle Angelique is right, of course. All Europe's a begging bowl. London's the richest city in the world, but it's inundated."

Canterbury smiled strangely. "There're no beggars because the Almighty Tycoon, the Shōgun, king of the lot, says no begging, so it's law. Any samurai can test his blade on any beggar at any time—or on any other bugger . . . pardon . . . or anyone else for that matter so long as he's not samurai. If you're caught begging you're breaking the law, so it's into the slammer, prison, and once there, the only penalty's death. That's law also."

"None other?" the girl said, shocked.

" 'Fraid not. So Japanners are untoward law-abiding." Again Canterbury laughed sardonically and looked back at the twisting road, halting abruptly half a mile away at a wide shallow stream that every person had to ford or be carried over. On the far bank was a barrier. There, they bowed and presented papers to the inevitable samurai guards.

Bloody bastards, he thought, hating them but loving the fortune he was making here—and his lifestyle that centered around Akiko, now his mistress of a year. Ah yes, luv, you're the best, most special, most loving in all the Yoshiwara.

"Look," she said. On the Tokaidō they could see groups of passersby had stopped and were pointing in their direction, gaping and talking loudly above the ever present hum of movement—hatred on many faces, and fear.

"Pay no attention to them, Miss, we're just strange to them, that's all, they don't know better. You're probably the first civilized woman they've ever seen." Canterbury pointed north. "Yedo's that way, about twenty miles. Of course, it's off limits."

"Except for official delegations," Tyrer said.

"That's right, *with permission,* which Sir William hasn't got once, not since I've been here and I was one of the first. Rumor has it that Yedo's twice as big as London, Miss, that there's over a million souls there and fantastic rich, and the Shōgun's castle the biggest in the world."

"Could that be a lie, Mr. Canterbury?" Tyrer asked.

The trader beamed. "They're powerful liars, that's the God's truth, Mr. Tyrer, the best that have ever been, they make the Chinee seem the Angel Gabriel. I don't envy you having to interpret what they say, which sure as God made periwinkles won't be what they mean!" Normally he was not so talkative but he was determined to impress her and Malcolm Struan with his knowledge while he had the opportunity. All this talking had given him a vast thirst. In his side pocket was a thin silver flask but he knew, regretfully, that it would be bad manners to swig some of the whisky in front of her.

"Could we get permission to go there, Malcolm?" she was saying. "To this Yedo?"

"I doubt it. Why not ask Monsieur Seratar'?"

"I shall." She noticed that he had pronounced the name correctly, dropping the 'd' as she had taught him. Good, she thought, her eyes drawn back to the Tokaidō. "Where does she end, the road?"

After a curious pause, Canterbury said, "We don't know. The whole country's a mystery and it's clear the Jappers want to keep it that way and don't like us, any of us. They call us *gai-jin,* foreign persons. Another word is *I-jin,* meaning 'different person.' Don't know the difference 'cepting I'm told gai-jin's not so polite." He laughed. "Either way, they don't like us. And we are different—or they are." He lit a cheroot. "After all, they kept Japan closed tighter than a gnat's . . . closed for nigh on two and a half centuries until Old Mutton Chops Perry bust her open nine years ago," he said with admiration. "Rumor says the Tokaidō ends in a big city, a kind of sacred city called Keeotoh, where their chief priest—called the Mikado—lives. It's so special, and sacred, we're told the city's off limits to all but a few special Japanners."

"Diplomats are allowed to travel inland," Tyrer said sharply. "The Treaty permits it, Mr. Canterbury."

The trader eased off the beaver topper of which he was inordinately proud, mopped his brow and decided that he would not let the young man spoil his air of bonhomie. Cocky young bastard, with your hoity-toity voice, he thought. I could break you in two and not even fart. "It depends how you interpret the Treaty, and if you want to keep your

ead on your shoulders. I wouldn't advise going outside the agreed
afe area. That's a few miles north and south and inland, whatever the
reaty says—not yet, not without a regiment or two." In spite of his
esolve, the swell of the girl's full breasts under the green form-fitting
acket mesmerized him. "We're penned in here but it's not bad. Same
t our Settlement at Nagasaki, two hundred leagues westwards."

" 'Leagues'? I don't understand," she said, hiding her amusement
nd pleasure at the lust surrounding her. "Please?"

Tyrer said importantly, "A league is approximately three miles,
Mademoiselle." He was tall and lithe, not long out of university, and
esotted by her blue eyes and Parisian elegance. "You, er, you were
aying, Mr. Canterbury?"

The trader tore his attention off her bosom. "Just that it won't be
much better when the other ports are opened. Soon, very soon we'll
aave to break out of them too if we're to really trade, one way or
'other."

Tyrer glanced at him sharply. "You mean war?"

"Why not? What are fleets for? Armies? It works fine in India,
China, everywhere else. We're the British Empire, the biggest and best
hat's ever been on earth. We're here to trade and meanwhile we can
give them proper laws and order and proper civilization." Canterbury
ooked back at the road, soured by the animosity there. "Ugly lot,
aren't they, Miss?"

"*Mon Dieu,* I do wish they wouldn't stare so."

" 'Fraid you just have to get used to it. It's the same everywhere. As
Mr. Struan says, Hong Kong's the worst. Even so, Mr. Struan," he said
with sudden esteem, "I don't mind telling you what we need here is our
own island, our own Colony, not a rotten, smelly mile strip of festering
coast that's indefensible, subject to attack and blackmail at any moment if it weren't for our fleet! We should take an island just like your
granddad took Hong Kong, bless him."

"Perhaps we will," Malcolm Struan said confidently, warmed by
the memory of his famous ancestor, *the tai-pan,* Dirk Struan, founder
of their company and main founder of the Colony twenty-odd years
ago in '41.

Without being aware of what he was doing, Canterbury slipped out
his small flask, tipped it back and drank, then wiped his mouth with the
back of his hand and slid the flask away. "Let's go on. Best I lead,
single file where necessary, forget the Jappers! Mr. Struan, perhaps
you'd ride alongside the young lady, and Mr. Tyrer, you keep the rear."
Very pleased with himself, he spurred his pony into a brisk walk.

As Angelique came alongside, Struan's eyes crinkled in a smile.
had been openly in love with her from the first moment he had seen
four months ago in Hong Kong, the first day she arrived—to take
island by storm. Fair hair, perfect skin, deep blue eyes with a pleasi
upturned nose in an oval face that was in no way pretty but possesse
strange, breathtaking attractiveness, very Parisian, her innocence a
youth overlaid with a perceptible, constant, though unconscious sen
ality that begged to be assuaged. And this in a world of men with
eligible wives, without much hope of finding one in Asia, certai
never like her. Many of the men rich, a few of them merchant princ
"Pay no attention to the natives, Angelique," he whispered, "they
just awed by you."

She grinned. Like an Empress, she bowed her head. "*Merci, Mo
sieur, vous êtes très aimable.*"

Struan was very content and now, very sure. Fate, joss, God threw
together, he thought, elated, planning when he would ask her fathe
permission to marry. Why not Christmas?

Christmas will be perfect. We'll marry in the spring and live in t
Great House on the Peak in Hong Kong. I know Mother and Fath
already adore her; my God, I hope he really is better. We'll give a hu
Christmas party.

Once on the road they made good progress, taking care not
impede traffic. But, whether they liked it or not, their unexpect
presence—the vast majority of incredulous Japanese had never se
people of this size and shape and coloring, particularly the girl—alo
with their top hats and frock coats, stovepipe trousers and riding boo
and her boots and riding habit and top hat with its saucy feather, a
riding sidesaddle, inevitably created traffic jams.

Both Canterbury and Struan watched those on the road carefully
the oncomers swirled past, around them, though always giving way
their progress. Neither man sensed or expected any danger. Angeliq
kept close, pretending to ignore the guffaws and gaping and the occ
sional hand that tried to touch her, shocked at the way many m
carelessly tucked up their kimonos, exposing their skimpy loinclot
and ample nakedness: 'Dearest Colette, you'll never believe me,' s
thought, continuing the letter she would complete tonight to her be
friend in Paris, 'but the vast majority of the legions of porters on t
public highway wear ONLY these tiny loincloths that hide almo
nothing in front and *become a thin string between the buttocks behin*
I swear it's true, and I can report that many of the natives are qu
hairy though most of their parts are small. I wonder if Malcolm . .

She felt herself flush. "The capital, Phillip," she said, making conversation, "it is truly forbidden?"

"Not according to the Treaty." Tyrer was vastly pleased. Only a few minutes and she had dropped the Monsieur. "The Treaty arranged for all Legations to be in Yedo, the capital. I was told we evacuated Yedo last year after the attack on ours. Safer to be at Yokohama under the guns of the fleet."

"Attack? What attack?"

"Oh, some madmen called *ronin*—they're some kind of outlaw, assassins—a dozen of them attacked our Legation in the middle of the night. The British Legation! Can you imagine the gall! The devils killed a sergeant and a sentry . . ."

He stopped as Canterbury swung off the roadway and reined in and pointed with his riding crop. "Look there!"

They halted beside him. Now they could see the tall, thin banners held aloft by the ranks of samurai tramping around a bend towards them, a few hundred yards ahead. All travellers were scattering, bundles and palanquins hastily thrown to the ground, well out of the way, riders dismounting hurriedly, then everyone knelt on the sides of the roadway with heads bowed to the packed earth, men women children, and stayed motionless. Only the few samurai remained standing. As the cortege passed, they bowed deferentially.

"Who is it, Phillip?" Angelique asked excitedly. "Can you read their signs?"

"Sorry, no, not yet, Mademoiselle. They say it takes years to read and write their script." Tyrer's happiness had evaporated at the thought of so much work ahead.

"It is the Shōgun perhaps?"

Canterbury laughed. "No chance of that. If it was him they'd have this whole area cordoned off. They say he has a hundred thousand samurai at his slightest beck. But it'll be someone important, a king."

"What shall we do when they pass?" she asked.

"We'll give them the royal salute," Struan said. "We'll doff our hats and give him three cheers. What will you do?"

"Me, *chéri*?" She smiled, liking him very much, remembering what her father had said before she had left Hong Kong for Yokohama: 'Encourage this Malcolm Struan, but with care, my little cabbage. I have already, discreetly. He would make a marvelous match for you, that's why I advocate this sightseeing trip to Yokohama, unchaperoned, providing he escorts you in one of *his ships*. In three days you're eighteen, time you were married. I know he's barely twenty and

young for you, but he's smart, the eldest son, he'll inherit the Nobl
House in a year or so—it's rumored his father, Culum, the tai-pan,
much sicker than the company publicly allows.'

'But he's British,' she had said thoughtfully. 'You hate them, Pap
and say we should hate them. You do, don't you?'.

'Yes, little cabbage, but not publicly. Britain's the richest country
the world, the most powerful, in Asia they're king, and Struan's th
Noble House—Richaud Frères are small. We would benefit im
mensely if we had their French business. Suggest it to him.'

'Oh, I couldn't, Papa, that would be . . . I couldn't, Papa.'

'You're a woman now, not a child, my pet. Beguile him, then he wi
suggest it himself. Our future depends on you. Soon Malcolm Strua
will be the tai-pan. And you—you could share it all. . . .'

Of course I would adore such a husband, she thought. How wis
Papa is! How wonderful to be French, therefore superior. It's easy t
like, perhaps even to love this Malcolm with his strange eyes an
young old looks. Oh, I do so hope he asks me.

She sighed and turned her attention to the present. "I will bow m
head as we do in the Bois to His Majesty, the emperor Louis Napoléo
What is it, Phillip?"

"Perhaps we'd better turn back," Tyrer said uneasily. "Everyon
says they're touchy about us near their princes."

"Nonsense," Canterbury said. "There's no danger, never has been
mob attack—this isn't like India, or Africa or China. As I said, Japar
ners are mighty law-abiding. We're well within the Treaty limit an
we'll do as we always do, just let them pass, raise your titfer politely a
you would to any potentate, then we'll go on. You're armed, M
Struan?"

"Of course."

"I'm not," Angelique said a little petulantly, watching the banner
that now were barely a hundred yards away. "I think women shoul
carry pistols if men do."

They were all shocked. "Perish that thought. Tyrer?"

Feeling awkward Tyrer showed Canterbury the small derringer. "I
was a going-away present from my father. But I've never fired it.'

"You won't need to, it's only the lone samurai you have to watch
the ones or twos, the anti-foreign fanatics. Or the ronins," then adde
without thinking, "Not to worry, we haven't had any trouble for a yea
or more."

"Trouble? What trouble?" she asked.

"Nothing," he said, not wanting to concern her and trying to cover the slip. "A few attacks by a few fanatics, or two, nothing important."

She frowned. "But Monsieur Tyrer said there was a mass attack on your British Legation and some soldiers were killed. That's not important?"

"That was important." Canterbury smiled thinly at Tyrer who read the message clearly: you're a bloody idiot to tell a lady anything of any importance! "But they were an isolated gang of cutthroats. The Shō-gunate bureaucracy have sworn they'll catch them and punish them."

His voice sounded convincing, but he was wondering how much of the truth Struan and Tyrer knew: five men murdered on the streets of Yokohama in their first year. The next two years two Russians, an officer and a sailor from a Russian man-of-war, hacked to death, again in Yokohama. A few months later two Dutch merchants. Then the young interpreter at the British Legation in Kanagawa stabbed from behind and left to bleed to death. Heusken, the Secretary of the American Mission, butchered into a dozen pieces while riding home after a dinner party at the Prussian Legation. And last year a British soldier and sergeant cut down outside the Consul General's bedroom!

Every murder premeditated and unprovoked, he thought, incensed, and committed by a two-sworder. Never once was any offense given—and worst of all, never once has any bastard been caught and punished by the Shōgun's all-powerful Bakufu, however much our Legation Heads screamed, and however much the Jappers promised. Our leaders are a bloody bunch of stupid bastards! They should have ordered up the fleet at once and blown Yedo to hell, then all the terror would stop, we could sleep safe in our beds without guards, and walk our streets, any streets, without fear when any samurai's nearby. Diplomats are anus eaters and this young popinjay's a perfect specimen.

Sourly he watched the banners, trying to decipher the characters. Behind the cortege, once it had completely passed, travellers picked themselves up and went on again. Those going the same way as the column followed at a judicious distance.

It felt curious to the four of them to be mounted and so high above the ragged lines of kneeling figures on both shoulders of the roadway, heads in the dust, rumps in the air. The three men tried not to notice the nakedness, embarrassed that she was there, equally embarrassed.

The ranks of samurai banner men approached relentlessly. There were two columns, each of about a hundred men, then more flags and massed ranks surrounding a black lacquered palanquin carried by eight

sweating porters. More banners and samurai followed, then mor
leading pack ponies and last a motley crowd of ladened baggag
porters. All samurai wore grey kimonos with the same insignia, thre
interlocking peonies, that was also on the banners, and straw hats tie
under their chins. Two swords in their belts, one short, one long. Som
had bows and arrows slung, a few carried muzzle-loading muskets. /
few were more elaborately dressed than others.

The columns bore down.

With growing shock Struan and the others saw what was on all th
faces, all eyes fixed on them: fury. He was the first to break the spell. "
think we'd better move farther back. . . ."

But before he or any one of them could start, a young, broad
shouldered samurai broke ranks and charged up to them, closel
followed by another man, planting himself between them and th
approaching palanquin. Choking with rage, the first man threw dow
his banner and shouted, cursing them away, the suddenness of hi
blazing anger paralyzing them. The columns faltered, then picked u
the cadence and continued passing. The kneeling people did not move
But now, over all was a great, sick silence, broken only by the sound o
marching feet.

Again the samurai cursed them. Canterbury was nearest to him
Obediently, nauseated with fear, he spurred his pony. But the turn wa
inadvertently towards the palanquin, not in the other direction. At once
the samurai jerked out his killing sword, shouted, *"sonno-joi!"* and
hacked with all his might. In the same instant the other man went for
Struan.

The blow took off Canterbury's left arm just above his biceps and
sliced into his side. The trader gaped at the stump with disbelief as
blood sprayed onto the girl. The sword whirled in another brutal arc
Impotently Struan was groping for his revolver, the other samurai
charging him, blade raised. More by luck than judgment he twisted ou
of the path of a blow that wounded him slightly on his left leg and
sliced into his pony's shoulder. The pony screamed and reared ir
sudden panic, knocking the man aside. Struan aimed and pulled the
trigger of the small Colt, but the pony reared again and the bullet went
into the air harmlessly. Frantically he tried to steady the animal and
aimed again, not seeing that now the first man was attacking from his
blind side.

"Watchouttt!" Tyrer screeched, coming back to life. Everything had
happened so fast it was almost as though he were imagining the
horror—Canterbury on the ground in agony, his pony fleeing, the girl

tupefied in her saddle, Struan pointing the gun a second time and the
killing sword arching at his unprotected back. He saw Struan react to
his warning, the frantic pony skittering at his touch, and the blow that
would have killed him was deflected somehow by the bridle or pommel
and sliced into his side. Struan lurched in his saddle and let out a howl
of pain.

This galvanized Tyrer.

He jammed in his spurs and charged Struan's attacker. The man
leapt aside untouched, noticed the girl and ran for her, sword on high.
Tyrer spun his terrified pony, saw Angelique staring at the approaching
samurai in frozen horror. "Get out of here, get help!" he screamed,
then again slammed at the man who once more twisted to safety,
recovered perfectly, and stood with his sword in attack position.

Time slowed. Phillip Tyrer knew he was dead. But that did not
seem to matter now, for in the moment's respite he saw Angelique
whirl her pony and flee safely. There was no room for Tyrer to escape,
or time.

For a split second the youthful samurai hesitated, exulting in the
killing moment, then leapt. Helplessly, Tyrer tried to back away. When
the explosion happened, the bullet thrust the man sprawling and the
sword failed, cutting Tyrer in the arm but not badly.

For a moment Tyrer did not believe that he was still alive, then he
saw Struan reeling in his saddle, blood seeping from the wound in his
side, the gun levelled at the other samurai, his frenzied pony twisting
and cavorting.

Again Struan pulled the trigger. The gun was near the pony's ear.
The explosion blew away her control and she took the bit and charged
off, Struan barely able to hold on. At once the samurai rushed after him
and this moment gave Tyrer the chance to dig in his spurs, spin away
from the road and race in pursuit, northwards.

"*Sonno-joiiii!*" the samurai shouted after them, enraged that they
had escaped.

John Canterbury was writhing and moaning in the dirt near some
petrified travellers, all of them still kneeling, heads down and frozen.
Angrily the youth kicked Canterbury's top hat aside and decapitated
him with a single blow. Then, with great care, he cleansed his blade on
the frock coat, and replaced it in its scabbard.

And all the while the cortege continued to pass as though nothing
was happening, that nothing had happened, eyes seeing everything but
nothing. Nor did any of the foot travellers move their heads from the
earth.

The other younger samurai was sitting cross-legged on the ground nursing his shoulder, using his bunched kimono to stop the flow of blood, his sword, still stained, in his lap. His compatriot went over to him and helped him up, cleansed the sword on the kimono of the nearest traveller, an old woman, who shivered in terror but kept her head pressed to the earth.

Both men were young and strongly built. They smiled at each other then, together, examined the wound. The bullet had gone right through the muscle of his upper arm. No bone touched. Shorin, the older said, "The wound's clean, Ori."

"We should have killed them all."

"Karma."

At this moment the massed samurai and the eight terrified porters carrying the palanquin began passing, all pretending the two men and the corpse did not exist. With great deference, the two youths bowed.

The tiny side window of the palanquin slid open, then closed again.

2

"HERE, MR. STRUAN, DRINK THIS," the doctor said kindly, towering over the camp bed. They were in the surgery of the British Legation at Kanagawa and he had managed to stanch most of the blood flow. Tyrer sat on a chair near the window. The two of them had arrived half an hour ago. "It will make you feel better."

"What is it?"

"Magic—mostly laudanum, that's a tincture of opium and morphine of my own devising. It will stop the pain. I have to patch you up a little but not to worry, I will use ether to put you quite to sleep."

Struan felt a sick fear rush through him. Ether for surgery was a recent innovation, much heralded, but still experimental. "I've—I've never had one or an—an operation and, and I don't . . . think . . ."

"Don't worry yourself. Anesthetics are really quite safe in the right hands." Dr. George Babcott was twenty-eight, well over six feet five and equally proportioned. "I've used ether and chloroform many times over the last five or six years, with excellent results. Believe me, you won't feel anything, and it's a godsend to the patient."

"That's right, Mr. Struan," Tyrer said, trying to be helpful, knowing he was not. His arm already had been swabbed with iodine, sewn up and bandaged and in a sling and he was thanking his luck that his wound was relatively superficial. "I met a fellow at university who told me he had had his appendix out with chloroform, and it didn't hurt a bit." He wanted to sound reassuring, but the idea of any operation—and the gangrene that all too often followed—frightened him too.

"Don't forget, Mr. Struan," Babcott was saying, masking his concern, "it's almost fifteen years since Dr. Simpson first used chloroform

23

in surgery and we've learned a lot since then. I studied under him at the Royal Infirmary for a year before I went out to the Crimea." His face saddened. "Learned a lot there too. Well, that war's over so not to worry, lovely laudanum will give you some erotic dreams too, if you're lucky."

"And if I'm not?"

"You're lucky. You're both very lucky."

Struan forced a smile through his pain. "We're lucky we found you here and so quickly, that's certain." Instinctively trusting Babcott he drank the colorless liquid, and lay back again, almost fainting from the pain.

"We'll let Mr. Struan rest a moment," Babcott said. "You'd better come with me, Mr. Tyrer, we've things to do."

"Of course, Doctor. Struan, can I get you anything, do anything?"

"No . . . no, thanks. No . . . no need for you to wait."

"Don't be silly, of course I'll wait." Nervously Tyrer followed the doctor out and closed the door. "Is he going to be all right?"

"I don't know. Fortunately samurai blades are always clean and they cut as beautifully as any scalpel. Excuse me a minute. I'm the only official here this afternoon, so now that I've done everything medically possible for the moment, I'd better act like Her Britannic Majesty's representative." Babcott was Deputy to Sir William. He ordered the Legation cutter across the bay to Yokohama to sound the alarm, sent a Chinese servant to fetch the local Governor, another to find out what daimyo, or prince, had passed through Kanagawa a couple of hours ago, put the six-man detachment of soldiers on alert, and poured Tyrer a large whisky. "Drink it, it's medicinal. You say the assassins shouted something at you?"

"Yes, it, it sounded like 'sonoh . . . sonnoh-ee.' "

"Means nothing to me. Make yourself at home. I'll be back in a moment, I've got to get ready." He went out.

Tyrer's arm was aching, with seven stitches in it. Though Babcott had been expert, Tyrer had been hard put not to cry out. But he had not and that pleased him. What appalled him were the currents of fear that continued to shake him, making him want to run away and keep on running. "You're a coward," he muttered, aghast at the discovery.

Like the surgery, the anteroom stank of chemicals, making his stomach heave. He went to the window and breathed deeply, trying unsuccessfully to clear his head, then sipped some of the whisky. As always the taste was raw and unpleasant. He stared into the glass. Bad pictures there, very bad. A shudder went through him. He forced himself to look just at the liquor. It was golden brown and the smell reminded him of his home in London, his father after dinner sitting in front of the fire with his dram, mother complacently knitting, their two servants clearing the table, everything warm and cozy and safe, and that reminded him of Garroway's, his favorite coffee house on Cornhill, warm and bustling and safe, and of university, exciting and friendly but safe. Safe. His whole life safe but now? Again panic began to overwhelm him. Jesus Christ, what am I doing here?

After their escape but still not far enough away from the Tokaidō, Struan's bolting pony had shied as her half-severed shoulder muscle gave out and Struan tumbled to the ground. The fall hurt him badly.

With great difficulty, still weak with fear, Tyrer had helped Struan onto his own pony but he had been barely able to hold the taller, heavier man in the saddle. All the time his attention was on the disappearing cortege, expecting any moment to see mounted samurai. 'Can you hold on?'

'Yes, yes, I think so.' Struan's voice was very weak, his pain great. 'Angelique, she got away all right?'

'Yes, yes, she did. The devils killed Canterbury.'

'I saw that. Are . . . are you hurt?'

'No, not really. I don't think so. Just a gash in my arm.' Tyrer tore off his coat, cursed at the sudden pain. The wound was a neat slice in the fleshy part of his forearm. He cleaned some of the blood away with a handkerchief, then used it as a bandage. 'No veins or arteries cut—but why did they attack us? Why? We weren't doing any harm.'

'I . . . I can't turn around. The bastard got me in the side. . . . How . . . how does it look?'

With great care Tyrer eased the split in the broadcloth coat apart. The length and depth of the cut, made worse by the fall, shocked him. Blood pulsated from the wound, frightening him further. 'It's not good. We should get a doctor quickly.'

'We'd . . . we'd better . . . better circle for Yokohama.'

'Yes . . . yes, I suppose so.' The young man held on to Struan and tried to think clearly. People on the Tokaidō were pointing at them. His anxiety increased. Kanagawa was nearby and he could see several temples. 'One of them must be ours,' he muttered, a foul taste in his mouth. Then he saw that his hands were covered with blood and his heart again surged with fright, then surged again with relief when he discovered that most of it was Struan's. 'We'll go on.'

'What . . . did you say?'

'We'll go on to Kanagawa—it's close by and the way clear. I can see several temples, one of them must be ours. There's bound to be a flag flying.' By Japanese custom, Legations were housed in sections of Buddhist temples. Only temples or monasteries had extra rooms or outbuildings of sufficient size and quantity, so the Bakufu had had some set aside until individual residences could be constructed.

'Can you hold on, Mr. Struan? I'll lead the pony.'

'Yes.' Struan looked across at his own mount as she whinnied miserably, tried to run again but failed, her leg useless. Blood ran down her side from the savage wound. She stood there shivering. 'Put her out of her pain and let's go on.'

Tyrer had never shot a horse before. He wiped the sweat off his hands. The derringer had twin barrels and was breech-loaded with two of the new bronze cartridges that held bullet and charge and detonator. The pony skittered but could not go far. He stroked her head for a second, gentling her, put the derringer to her ear and pulled the trigger. The immediacy of her death surprised him. And the noise that the gun made. He put it back in his pocket.

Again he wiped his hands, everything still as in a trance. 'We'd best stay away from the road, Mr. Struan, best stay out here, safer.'

It took them much longer than he had expected, with ditches and streams to cross. Twice Struan almost lost consciousness, and Tyrer only just managed to keep him from falling again. Peasants in the rice paddies pretended not to see them, or stared at them rudely, then went back to their work, so Tyrer just cursed them and pressed onwards.

The first temple was empty but for a few frightened, shaven-headed Buddhist monks in orange robes who scurried away into inner rooms the moment they saw them. There was a small fountain in the fore-court. Thankfully Tyrer drank some of the cool water, then refilled the cup and brought it to Struan, who drank but could hardly see for pain.

'Thanks. How . . . how much farther?'

'Not far,' Tyrer said, not knowing which way to go, trying to be brave. 'We'll be there any moment.'

Here the path forked, one way going towards the coast and to another temple soaring above village houses, the other deeper into the town and another temple. For no reason he chose the way towards the coast.

The path meandered, ran back on itself then went east again, no people in the maze of alleys but eyes everywhere. Then he saw the main gate of the temple and the Union Jack and the scarlet-uniformed soldier and almost wept with relief and pride, for at once they were seen and the soldier rushed to help, another went for the Sergeant of the Guard and in no time there was Dr. Babcott towering over him.

'Christ Almighty, what the hell's happened?'

It had been easy to tell—there was so little to tell.

"Have you ever assisted at an operation before?"

"No, Doctor."

Babcott smiled, his face and manner genial, his hands moving swiftly, undressing the half-conscious Malcolm Struan as easily as if he were a child. "Well, soon you will have—good experience for you. I need help and I'm the only one here today. You'll be back in Yokohama by suppertime."

"I'll . . . I'll try."

"You'll probably be sick—it's the smell mostly, but not to worry. If you are, do it in the basin and not over the patient." Again Babcott glanced at him, gauging him, asking himself how reliable this young man might be, reading his bottled terror, then went back to work. "We'll give him ether next and then off we go. You said you were in Peking?"

"Yes, sir, for four months—I came here by way of Shanghai and arrived a few days ago." Tyrer was glad to be able to talk to help keep his mind off the horrors. "The Foreign Office thought a short stay in Peking learning Chinese characters would help us with Japanish."

"Waste of time. If you want to speak it—by the way, most of us out here call it Japanese, like Chinese—if you want to read and write it properly, Chinese characters won't help, hardly at all." He shifted the inert man to a more comfortable position. "How much Japanese do you know?"

Tyrer's unhappiness increased. "Practically none, sir. Just a few words. We were told there would be Japanish—I mean Japanese—grammars and books in Peking, but there weren't any."

In spite of his enormous concern over this whole incident, Babcott stopped for a moment and laughed. "Grammars are as rare as a dragon's dingle and there're no Japanese dictionaries that I know of, except Father Alvito's of 1601 and that's in Portuguese—which I've never even seen and only heard about—and the one Reverend Priny's been working on for years." He eased off Struan's white silk shirt, wet with blood. "Do you speak Dutch?"

"Again just a few words. All student interpreters for Japan are supposed to have a six months' course, but the F.O. sent us off on the

first available steamer. Why is Dutch the official foreign language used
by the Japanese bureaucracy?"

"It isn't. The F.O. are wrong, and wrong about a lot of things. But it
is the only European language presently spoken by a few Bakufu—I'm
going to lift him slightly, you pull off his boots then his trousers, but do
it gently."

Awkwardly Tyrer obeyed, using his good left hand.

Now Struan was quite naked on the surgical table. Beyond were the
surgical instruments and salves and bottles. Babcott turned away and
put on a heavy, waterproofed apron. Instantly Tyrer saw only a butcher.
His stomach heaved and he just made the basin in time.

Babcott sighed. How many hundred times have I vomited my heart
out and then some more? But I need help, so this child has to grow up.
"Come here, we have to work quickly."

"I can't, I just can't . . ."

At once the doctor roughened his voice. "You come over here right
smartly and help or Struan will die and before that I'll thump the hell
out of you!"

Tyrer stumbled over to his side.

"Not here, for God's sake, opposite me! Hold his hands!"

Struan opened his eyes briefly at Tyrer's touch and went back again
into his nightmare, mouthing incoherently.

"It's me," Tyrer muttered, not knowing what else to say.

On the other side of the table Babcott had uncorked the small,
unlabeled bottle and now he poured some of the yellowish oily liquid
onto a thick linen pad. "Hold him firmly," he said, and pressed the pad
over Struan's nose and mouth.

At once Struan felt himself being suffocated and grabbed at the pad,
almost tearing it away with surprising strength. "For Christ sake, get
hold of him," Babcott snarled. Again Tyrer grabbed Struan's wrists,
forgetting his bad arm, and cried out but managed to hold on, the ether
fumes revolting him. Still Struan struggled, twisting his head to escape, feeling himself dragged down into this never-ending cesspool.
Gradually his strength waned, and vanished.

"Excellent," Babcott said. "Astonishing how strong patients are
sometimes." He turned Struan onto his stomach, making his head
comfortable, revealing the true extent of the wound that began in
his back and came around just under the rib cage to end near his
navel. "Keep a close watch on him and tell me if he stirs—when I
tell you, give him more ether . . ." But Tyrer was again at the basin.
"Hurry up!"

Babcott did not wait, letting his hands flow, used to operating in far worse circumstances. Crimea with tens of thousands of soldiers dying—cholera, dysentery, smallpox mostly—and then all the wounded, the howls in the night and in the day, and then in the night the Lady of the Lamp who brought order out of chaos in military hospitals. Nurse Nightingale who ordered, cajoled, threatened, demanded, begged but somehow instituted her new ideas and cleansed that which was filthy, cast out hopelessness and useless death, yet still had time to visit the sick and the needy all hours of the night, her oil or candle lamp held high, lighting her passage from bed to bed.

"Don't know how she did it," he muttered.

"Sir?"

Momentarily he looked up and saw Tyrer, white-faced, staring at him. He had quite forgotten him. "I was just thinking about the Lady of the Lamp," he said, allowing his mouth to talk, to calm himself—without letting this disturb his concentration on the sliced muscles and damaged veins. "Florence Nightingale. She went out to the Crimea with just thirty-eight nurses and in four months cut the death rate from forty in every hundred to about two in every hundred."

Tyrer knew the statistic as every Englishman knew proudly that she had really founded the modern profession of nursing. "What was she like—personally?"

"Terrible, if you didn't keep everything clean and as she wanted it. Otherwise she was Godlike—in its most Christian way. She was born in Florence, in Italy, hence her name—though she was English through and through."

"Yes." Tyrer felt the doctor's warmth. "Wonderful. So wonderful. Did you know her well?"

Babcott's eyes did not waver from the wound, or from his wise fingers as they probed and found, as he had feared, the severed part of the intestine. He swore without noticing it. Delicately he began seeking the other end. The stench increased. "You were talking about Dutch. You know why some of the Japanners speak Dutch?"

With a violent effort, Tyrer tore his gaze away from the fingers and tried to close his nostrils. He felt his stomach twist. "No, sir."

Struan stirred. At once Babcott said, "Give him more of the ether . . . that's right, don't press too firmly . . . good. Well done. How do you feel?"

"Dreadful."

"Never mind." The fingers began again, almost outside the doctor's will, then stopped. Gently they exposed the other part of the severed intestine. "Wash your hands then give me the needle that's already threaded—there, on the table."

Tyrer obeyed.

"Good. Thanks." Babcott began the repair. Very accurately. "His liver's not hurt, bruised a little but not cut. His kidney's all right too. *Ichiban*— that's Japanese for 'very good.' I have a few Japanner patients. In return for my work I make them give me words and phrases. I'll help you learn if you like."

"I'd . . . that would be wonderful—*ichiban*. Sorry I'm so useless."

"You're not. I hate doing this alone. I . . . well, I get frightened. Funny, but I do." For a moment his fingers filled the room.

Tyrer looked at Struan's face, no color now where an hour ago it was ruddy, and strong where now it was stretched and ominous, eyelids flickering from time to time. Strange, he thought, strange how unbelievably naked Struan seems now. Two days ago I'd never even heard his name, now we're bonded like brothers, now life is different, will be different for both of us, like it or not. And I know he's brave and I'm not.

"Ah, you asked about Dutch," Babcott said, scarcely listening to himself, all his attention on the repairs. "Since about 1640 the only contact Japanners have had with the outside, apart from China, has been with Dutchmen. All others were forbidden to land in Japan, particularly Spaniards and Portuguese. Japanners don't like Catholics because they meddled in their politics back in the 1600s. At one time, so legend says, Japan almost went Catholic. Do you know any of this?"

"No, sir."

"So the Dutch were tolerated because they'd never brought missionaries here, just wanted to trade." For a moment he stopped talking but his fingers continued the fine neat stitches. Then he rambled on again. "So a few Hollanders—men, never women—were allowed to stay, but only with the most severe restrictions and confined on a man-made island of three acres in Nagasaki harbor called Deshima. The Dutch obeyed any law the Japanners made, and kowtowed—growing rich meanwhile. They brought in books, when they were allowed, traded, when they were allowed, and carried the China trade that's essential to Japan—Chinese silks and silver for gold, paper, lacquer, chopsticks— you know what those are?"

"Yes, sir. I was in Peking for three months."

"Oh yes, sorry, I forgot. Never mind. According to Dutch journals of the 1600s the first of the Toranaga Shōguns, their equivalent of emperors, decided foreign influence was against Japan's interests, so he closed the country and decreed that Japanners could not build any oceangoing ships, or leave the country—anyone who did could not come back, or if they returned, they were to be killed instantly. That's still the law." His fingers stopped for an instant as the delicate thread parted and he cursed. "Give me the other needle. Can't get decent gut, though this silk's fine. Try to thread one of the others but wash your hands first and wash it when you're done. Thanks."

Tyrer was glad to have something to do and turned away, but his fingers were helpless. His nausea was growing again, his head throbbing. "You were saying, about the Dutch?"

"Ah, yes. So, warily, Dutch and Japanners began learning from the other though the Dutch were officially forbidden to learn Japanese. Ten-odd years ago the Bakufu started a Dutch language school . . ." Both men heard the running feet.

Hasty knock. The sweating Grenadier Sergeant stood there, trained never to enter while an operation was in progress. "Sorry to interrupt, sir, but there's four of the rotten little buggers coming down the road. Looks like a deputation. They's all samurai."

The doctor did not stop sewing. "Is Lim with them?"

"Yessir."

"Escort them into the reception room and tell Lim to look after them. I'll be there as soon as I can."

"Yessir." The Sergeant took one last glazed look at the table, then fled.

The doctor completed another stitch, knotted it, cut the thread, swabbed the oozing wound, and began anew. "Lim's one of our Chinese assistants. Our Chinese do most of our leg work, not that they're Japanese speakers or—or very trustworthy."

"We . . . it was the same . . . we found it was the same in Peking, sir. Dreadful liars."

"The Japanners are worse—but in a way that's not true either. It's not that they're liars, it's just that truth is mobile and depends on the whim of the speaker. Very important for you to learn to speak Japanese very quickly. We don't have even one interpreter, not of our own people."

Tyrer gaped at him. "None?"

"None. The British padre speaks a little but we can't use him; Japanners detest missionaries and priests. We've only three Dutch speakers in the Settlement, one Hollander, one Swiss who's our interpreter, and a Cape Colony trader, none British. In the Settlement we

speak a bastard sort of lingua franca called 'pidgin,' like in Hong Kong
and Singapore and the other China Treaty ports and use compradores
business intercessors."

"It was the same in Peking."

Babcott heard the irritation but more the underlying danger. He
glanced up, instantly saw into Tyrer that he was near to breaking, ready
to vomit again any second. "You're doing fine," he said encour-
agingly, then straightened to ease his back, sweat running off him.
Again he bent down. Very carefully he resettled the repaired intestine
into the cavity, quickly began to stitch another laceration, working
outwards. "How'd you like Peking?" he asked, not caring but wanting
Tyrer to talk. Better that than an outburst, he thought. Can't deal with
him till this poor bugger's closed up. "I've never been there. Did you
like it?"

"I, well . . . yes, yes, very much." Tyrer tried to collect his wits
through a blinding headache that racked him. "The Manchus are quite
subdued at the moment, so we could go anywhere we wanted quite
safely." Manchus, a nomadic tribe from Manchuria, had conquered
China in 1644 and now ruled as the Ch'ing Dynasty. "We could ride
around without . . . without any problems . . . the Chinese were . . . not
too friendly but . . ." The closeness of the room and the smell crested.
A spasm took him and he was sick again. Still nauseated, he came
back. "Sorry."

"You were saying—about Manchus?"

Suddenly Tyrer wanted to scream that he cared nothing about Manchus or Peking or anything, wanting to run from the stench and his
helplessness. "The devil with—"

"Talk to me! Talk!"

"We . . . we were told that . . . that normally they're an arrogant,
nasty lot and it's obvious the Chinese hate Manchus mortally." Tyrer's
voice was phlegmy but the more he concentrated the less he felt the
urge to flee. He continued, hesitating, "It . . . it seems they're all
petrified the Tai'ping Rebellion will spread up from Nanking and
engulf Peking, and that will be the end of . . ." He stopped, listening
intently. His mouth had a dreadful taste and his head pounded even
more.

"What is it?"

"I . . . I thought I heard someone shouting."

Babcott listened, hearing nothing. "Go on about Manchus."

"Well, the, er, the Tai'ping Rebellion. Rumor has it that more than
ten million peasants have been killed or died of famine in the last few

years. But it's quiet in Peking—of course, burning and looting the Summer Palace by British and French forces two years ago, which Lord Elgin ordered as a reprisal, also taught the Manchus a lesson they won't forget in a hurry. They aren't going to murder any more British lightly. Isn't that what Sir William will order here? A reprisal?"

"If we knew who to carry out the reprisal against we would have started. But against who? You can't bombard Yedo because of a few unknown assassins . . ."

Angry voices interrupted him, the Sergeant's English at odds with guttural Japanese. Then the door was jerked open by a samurai and behind him two others threatened the Sergeant, their swords half out of their scabbards; two Grenadiers with breech-loaders levelled stood in the passageway. The fourth samurai, an older man, came forward into the room. Tyrer backed against the wall, petrified, reliving Canterbury's death.

"*Kinjiru!*" Babcott bellowed, and everyone froze. For a moment it looked as though the older man, furious now, would pull out his sword and attack. Then Babcott whirled and faced them, a scalpel in his enormous fist, blood on his hands and apron, gigantic and diabolical. "*Kinjiru!*" he ordered again, then pointed with the scalpel. "Get out! *Dete. Dete . . . dozo.*" He glared at all of them, then turned his back on them and continued sewing and swabbing. "Sergeant, show them the reception room—politely!"

"Yessir." With signs, the Sergeant beckoned to the samurai who chattered angrily amongst themselves. "*Dozo,*" he said, muttering. "Come on, you rotten little bastards." Again he beckoned. The older samurai imperiously waved at the others and stomped off. At once the other three bowed and followed.

Awkwardly Babcott wiped a bead of sweat off his chin with the back of his hand, then continued his work, his head and neck and back aching. "*Kinjiru* means 'it is forbidden,' " he said, making his voice calm though his heart was beating violently, as it always did when samurai were near with drawn or even half-drawn swords and he had no pistol or gun in his hands, cocked and ready. Too many times he had been summoned to the result of their swords, against both Europeans and themselves—fights and samurai feuds were constant in and around Yokohama, Kanagawa and the surrounding villages. "*Dozo* means please, *dete,* go out. Very important to use please and thank you with Japanese. Thank you is *domo.* Use them even if you shout." He glanced at Tyrer who was still against the wall, shaking. "There's whisky in the cabinet."

"I'm . . . I'm all right . . ."

"You're not, you're still in shock. Take a good dose of whisky. Sip it. Soon as I'm finished I'll give you something to stop the sickness. You-are-not-to-worry! Understand?"

Tyrer nodded. Tears began streaming down his face that he could not stop and he found it difficult to walk. "What's . . . what's the matter with . . . me?" he gasped.

"Just shock, don't worry about it. It'll pass. It's normal in war and we're at war here. I'll be finished soon. Then we'll deal with those bastards."

"How . . . how will you do that?"

"I don't know." An edge came into the doctor's voice, as he cleaned the wound again with a fresh square of linen from a dwindling pile—still much sewing to be done. "The usual, I suppose, just wave my hands and tell them our Minister will give them bloody hell and try to find out who attacked you. Of course they'll deny all knowledge of the affair, which is probably right—they never seem to know anything about anything. They're unlike any other people I've ever come across. I don't know whether they're just plain stupid, or clever and secretive to the point of genius. We can't seem to penetrate their society—nor can our Chinese—we've no allies amongst them, can't seem to bribe any of them to help us, we can't even speak to them directly. We're all so helpless. Are you feeling better?"

Tyrer had taken a little whisky. Before that he had wiped the tears away, filled with shame, and washed his mouth and poured water on his head. "Not really . . . but thanks. I'm all right. How about Struan?"

After a pause Babcott said, "I don't know. You never truly know." His heart surged at the sound of more footsteps, Tyrer blanched. A knock. The door opened immediately.

"Christ Jesus," Jamie McFay gasped, his whole attention on the bloody table and the great gash in Struan's side. "Is he going to be all right?"

"Hello, Jamie," Babcott said. "You heard about—"

"Yes, we've just come from the Tokaidō, tracking Mr. Struan on the off chance. Dmitri's outside. You all right, Mr. Tyrer? The bastards butchered poor old Canterbury into a dozen pieces and left the bits to the crows. . . ." Tyrer lurched for the basin again. Uneasily, McFay stayed at the door. "For Christ's sake, George, is Mr. Struan going to be all right?"

"I don't know!" Babcott flared, his never-ending impotence at not knowing erupted as anger, not understanding why some patients lived and others less wounded did not, why some wounds rotted and others healed. "He's lost pints of blood; I've repaired a severed intestine, three lacerations, there are three veins and two muscles yet to be done and the wound closed, and Christ alone knows how much foulness has got in from the air to infect him if that's where disease or gangrene comes from. I don't know! I-don't-bloody-know! Now get to hell out of here and deal with those four Bakufu bastards and find out who did this, by God."

"Yes, certainly, sorry, George," McFay said, beside himself with worry, and shocked at the violence from Babcott who was usually imperturbable, adding hastily, "we'll try—Dmitri's with me—but we know who did it, we leaned on a Chinese shopkeeper in the village. It's damn strange, the samurai were all from Satsuma and—"

"Where the hell's that?"

"He said it's a kingdom near Nagasaki on the south island, six or seven hundred miles away and—"

"What the hell are they doing here, for God's sake?"

"He didn't know, but he swore they were overnighting at Hodogaya—Phillip, that's a way station on the Tokaidō a few miles from here—and their king was with them."

3

Sanjiro, Lord of Satsuma, eyes slitted and pitiless—a heavyset, bearded man of forty-two, his swords priceless, his blue over-mantle the finest silk—looked at his most trusted advisor. "Was the attack a good thing or a bad thing?"

"It was good, Sire," Katsumata said softly, knowing there were spies everywhere. The two men were alone, kneeling opposite each other, in the best quarters of an inn at Hodogaya, a village way station on the Tokaidō, barely two miles inland from the Settlement.

"Why?" For six centuries Sanjiro's ancestors had ruled Satsuma, the richest and most powerful fief in all Japan—except for those of his hated enemies, the Toranaga clans—and, as zealously, had guarded its independence.

"It will create trouble between the Shōgunate and gai-jin," Katsumata said. He was a thin, steel-hard man, a master swordsman and the most famous of all *Sensei*—teachers—of martial arts in Satsuma province. "The more those dogs are in conflict the sooner they will clash, the sooner the clash the better, for that will help bring down the Toranagas and their puppets at last, and let you install a new Shōgunate, a new Shōgun, new officials, with Satsuma preeminent and yourself one of a new *roju*." *Roju* was another name for the Council of Five Elders that ruled in the name of the Shōgun.

One of the *roju*? Why only one? Sanjiro thought secretly. Why not Chief Minister? Why not Shōgun—I have all the necessary lineage. Two and a half centuries of Toranaga Shōguns is more than enough. Nobusada, the fourteenth, should be the last—by my father's head, *will be the last*!

This Shōgunate had been established by the warlord Toranaga in

1603 after winning the battle of Sekigahara, where his legions took forty thousand enemy heads. With Sekigahara he eliminated all practical opposition and, for the first time in history, had subdued Nippon, the Land of the Gods, as Japanese called their country, and brought it under one rule.

At once this brilliant general and administrator, now holding absolute temporal power, gratefully accepted the title Shōgun, the highest rank a mortal could have, from a powerless Emperor—which confirmed him, legally, as Dictator. Quickly he made his Shōgunate hereditary, at once decreeing that, in future, *all* temporal matters were the sole province of the Shōgun, all spiritual matters the Emperor's.

For the last eight centuries the Emperor, the Son of Heaven, and his court had lived in seclusion in the walled Imperial Palace at Kyōto. Once a year, only, he came outside the walls to visit the sacred Ise shrine, but even then he was hidden from all eyes, his face never seen in public. Even inside the walls he was screened from all but his most immediate family by zealous, hereditary officials and ancient, mystic protocols.

Thus the warlord who had physical possession of the Palace Gates decided who went in and who came out, had de facto possession of the Emperor and his ear, and thus his influence and power. And though all Japanese absolutely believed him to be divine, and accepted him as the Son of Heaven, and descended from the Sun Goddess in an unbroken line since time began, by historic custom the Emperor and his court retained no armies, and had no revenue other than that granted by the warlord at his Gates—yearly at the man's whim.

For decades Shōgun Toranaga, his son and grandson, ruled with wise though ruthless control. Following generations loosened their hold, lesser officials usurped more and more power, gradually making their own offices hereditary too. The Shōgun remained titular head but, over a century or more, had become a puppet—but always and only selected from the Toranaga line, as was the Council of Elders. The present Shōgun, Nobusada, was chosen four years ago when he was twelve.

And not long for this earth, Sanjiro promised himself, and came back to the present problem which disturbed him. "Katsumata, the killings, though merited, may provoke the gai-jin too much and that would be bad for Satsuma."

"I do not see any bad, Sire. The Emperor wants the gai-jin expelled, as you do, as do most daimyos. That the two samurai are Satsumas will also please the Emperor. Do not forget your mission to Yedo was accomplished perfectly."

Three months ago Sanjiro had persuaded Emperor Komei, through intermediaries at the Imperial court in Kyōto, personally to sign several 'wishes' Sanjiro had suggested, and to appoint him escort to an Imperial Messenger who would formally deliver the scroll in Yedo which would ensure its acceptance—a 'wish' of the Emperor, if accepted, was difficult to refuse, sometimes. For the last two months he had led the negotiations and as much as the Elders and their Bakufu officials twisted and turned, he had dominated them and now had their written assent to certain reforms bound to weaken the whole Shōgunate. Importantly he now had their formal consent to cancel the hated Treaties, signed against the Emperor's wishes, to expel the hated gaijin and to close the land as it was before the unwelcome arrival and forced entry of Perry.

"Meanwhile, what about those two fools who broke ranks and killed without orders?" Sanjiro asked.

"Any act that embarrasses the Bakufu helps you."

"I agree the gai-jin were provocative. Those vermin had no right to be anywhere near me. My banner and the Imperial banner were in the front rank forbidding it."

"So let the gai-jin bear the consequences of their act: they forced their way onto our shores against our wishes and have the Yokohama foothold. With the men we have now, and a surprise attack by night, we could obliterate the Settlement and burn the surrounding villages easily. We could do it tonight and solve the problem permanently."

"Yokohama, yes, with a sudden attack. But we cannot get at their fleets, we cannot squash them and their cannon."

"Yes, Sire. And the gai-jin would retaliate at once. Their fleet would bombard Yedo and destroy it."

"I agree, and the sooner the better. But that would not destroy the Shōgunate and after Yedo they would go against me, they would attack my capital, Kagoshima. I cannot risk that."

"I believe Yedo would satisfy them, Sire. If their base is burnt they would have to go back aboard their ships and sail away, back to Hong Kong. Sometime in the future they may come back, but then they must land in strength to erect a new base. Worse for them, they must use land forces to maintain it."

"They humbled China. Their war machine is invincible."

"This isn't China and we are not mealymouthed, cowardly Chinese to be bled to death or frightened to death by these carrion. They say they just want to trade. Good, you want to trade too, for guns, cannon and ships." Katsumata smiled and added delicately, "I suggest if we burn and destroy Yokohama—of course, we pretend the attack is at the Bakufu's request, the Shōgun's request—when the gai-jin return, *whoever controls the Shōgunate then* would reluctantly agree to pay a modest indemnity and, in return, the gai-jin will happily agree to tear up their shameful Treaties and trade on any terms we decide to impose."

"They would attack us at Kagoshima," Sanjiro said. "We could not repel them."

"Our bay is hazardous for shipping, not open like Yedo; we have secret shore batteries, secret Dutch cannon; we grow stronger every month. Such an act of war by gai-jin would unite all daimyo, all samurai, and the whole land into an irresistible force under your banner. Gai-jin armies cannot win on land. This is the Land of the Gods, the gods will come to our aid too," Katsumata said fervently, not believing it at all, manipulating Sanjiro as he had done for years. "A divine wind, a kamikaze wind, destroyed the armadas of the Mongol Kublai Khan six hundred years ago, why not again?"

"True," Sanjiro said. "The gods saved us then. But gai-jin are gai-jin and vile and who knows what mischief they can invent? Foolish to invite a sea attack until we've warships—though, yes, the gods are on our side and will protect us."

Katsumata laughed to himself. There are no gods, any gods, or heaven, or life after death. Stupid to believe otherwise, stupid gai-jin and their stupid dogma. I believe what the great Dictator General Nakamura said in his death poem, *From nothing into nothing, Osaka Castle and all that I have ever done is but a dream within a dream.* "The gai-jin Settlement is within your grasp like never before. Those two youths awaiting judgment pointed a way. I beg you take it." He hesitated and dropped his voice even more. "Rumor has it, Sire, secretly they are *shishi*."

Sanjiro's eyes narrowed even more.

Shishi—men of spirit, so called because of their bravery and deeds—were young revolutionaries who were spearheading an unheard-of revolt against the Shōgunate. They were a recent phenomenon, thought to number only about a hundred and fifty throughout the land.

To the Shōgunate and most daimyos they were terrorists and madmen to be stamped out.

To most samurai, particularly rank-and-file warriors, they were loyalists waging an all-consuming battle for good, wanting to force the Toranagas to relinquish the Shōgunate and restore all power to the

Emperor, from whom, they fervently believed, it had been usurped by the warlord Toranaga, two and a half centuries ago.

To many commoners and peasants and merchants, and particularly to the Floating World of geishas and Pleasure Houses, shishi were the stuff of legends, sung about, wept over, and adored.

All were samurai, young idealists, the majority coming from the fiefs of Satsuma, Choshu and Tosa, a few were fanatic xenophobes, most were ronin—wave men, because they were as free as the waves—masterless samurai, or samurai who had been outcast by their lord for disobedience, or a crime, and had fled their province to escape punishment, or those who had fled by choice, believing in a new, outrageous heresy: that there could be a higher duty than that due their lord, or their family, *a duty to the ruling Emperor alone.*

A few years ago the growing shishi movement had formed themselves into small, secret cells, committing themselves to rediscover *bushido*—ancient samurai practices of self-discipline, duty, honor, death, swordsmanship and other warlike pursuits, arts long since lost—except for a few Sensei who had kept bushido alive. Lost because for the last two and a half centuries Japan had been at peace under rigid Toranaga rule that forbade warlike pursuits, where, for centuries before, there had been total civil war.

Cautiously the shishi began to meet and discuss and to plan. Swordsmanship schools became centers of discontent. Zealots and radicals appeared in their midst, some good, some bad. But one common thread joined them—all were fanatically anti-Shōgunate, and opposed to allowing Japanese ports to be opened to foreigners and foreign trade.

To this end, for the last four years, they had waged sporadic attacks on gai-jin, and begun to articulate an unprecedented, all-out revolt against the legal ruler, Shōgun Nobusada, the all-powerful Council of Elders and Bakufu that in theory did his bidding, regulating all aspects of life.

The shishi had conjured up an all-embracing slogan, *Sonno-joi*: Honor the Emperor and Expel the Barbarians, and had sworn, whatever the cost, to remove anyone in the way.

"Even if they are shishi," Sanjiro said angrily, "I cannot allow such a public disobedience to go unpunished, however merited—I agree those gai-jin should have dismounted and knelt, as customary, and behaved like civilized persons; yes, it was they who provoked my men. But that does not excuse those two."

"I agree, Sire."

"Then give me your advice," he said irritably. "If they're shishi as you say and I crush them, or order them to commit seppuku, I will be assassinated before the month is out, however many my guards—don't attempt to deny it, I *know*. Disgusting their power is so strong though most are common *goshi*."

"Perhaps that is their strength, Sire," Katsumata had replied. Goshi were the lowest rank of samurai, their families mostly penniless country samurai, hardly more than the warrior peasants of olden times with almost no hope of getting an education, therefore no hope of advancement, no hope of getting their views acted upon, or even heard by officials of low rank, let alone daimyo. "They've nothing to lose but their lives."

"If anyone has a grievance I listen, of course I listen. Special men get special education, some of them."

"Why not allow them to lead the attack on the gai-jin?"

"And if there is no attack? I cannot hand them over to the Bakufu, unthinkable, or to the gai-jin!"

"Most shishi are just young idealists, without brains or purpose. A few are troublemakers and outlaws who are not needed on this earth. However, some could be valuable, if used correctly—a spy told me the oldest, Shorin, was part of the team that assassinated Chief Minister Ii."

"So ka!"

This had occurred four years ago. Against all advice, Ii, who was responsible for maneuvering the boy Nobusada to be Shōgun, had also suggested a highly improper marriage between the boy and the Emperor's twelve-year-old half sister, and, worst of all, had negotiated and signed the hated Treaties. His passing was not regretted, especially by Sanjiro.

"Send for them."

Now in the audience room a maid was serving Sanjiro tea. Katsumata sat beside him. Around stood ten of his personal bodyguard. All were armed. The two youths kneeling below and in front of him were not, though their swords lay on the tatami within easy reach. Their nerves were stretched but they showed none of it. The maid bowed and left, hiding her fear.

Sanjiro did not notice her going. He lifted the exquisite little porcelain cup from the tray, sipped the tea. The tea's taste was good to him and he was glad to be ruler and not ruled, pretending to study the cup, admiring it, his real attention on the youths. They waited impassively, knowing the time had come.

He knew nothing about them except what Katsumata had told him: that both were goshi, foot soldiers like their fathers before them. Each had a stipend of one *koku* yearly—a measure of dry rice, about five bushels, considered enough to feed one family for one year. Both came from villages near Kagoshima. One was nineteen, the other, who had been wounded and now had his arm bound, was seventeen. Both had been to the select samurai school at Kagoshima that gave extra training, including studies of carefully chosen Dutch manuals, which he had begun twenty years ago for those showing special aptitudes. Both had been good students, both were unmarried, both spent their spare time perfecting their swordsmanship and learning. Both were eligible for promotion sometime in the future. The older was called Shorin Anato, the younger Ori Ryoma.

The silence became heavier.

Abruptly he began talking to Katsumata as though the two youths did not exist: "If any of my men, however worthy, however much provoked, whatever the reason, were to commit a violent act that I had not authorized and they remained within my reach, I would certainly have to deal with them severely."

"Yes, Sire."

He saw the glint in his counselor's eyes. "Stupid to be disobedient. If such men wanted to remain alive their only recourse would be to flee and become ronin, even if they were to lose their stipends. A waste of their lives if they happened to be worthy." Then he looked at the youths, scrutinizing them carefully. To his surprise he saw nothing on their faces, just the same grave impassivity. His caution increased.

"You are quite correct, Sire. As always." Katsumata added, "It might be that some such men, if special men of honor, knowing that they had disturbed your harmony, knowing you would have no other option than to punish them severely, these special men even as ronin would still guard your interests, perhaps even forward your interests."

"Such men do not exist," Sanjiro said, secretly delighted his counselor agreed with him. He turned his pitiless eyes onto the young men. "Do they?"

Both youths tried to maintain their direct gaze but they were overwhelmed. They dropped their glance. Shorin, the older, muttered, "There—there are such men, Sire."

The silence became rougher as Sanjiro waited for the other youth to declare himself also. Then the younger Ori nodded his bowed head imperceptibly, put both hands flat on the tatami and bowed lower. "Yes, Lord, I agree."

Sanjiro was content, for now, at no cost, he had their allegiance and two spies within the movement—whom Katsumata would be answerable for.

"Such men would be useful, if they existed." His voice was curt and final. "Katsumata, write an immediate letter to the Bakufu, informing them two goshi called . . ." he thought a moment, paying no attention to the rustle in the room, "put whatever names you like . . . broke ranks and killed some gai-jin today because of their provocative and insolent attitude—the gai-jin were armed with pistols which they pointed threateningly at my palanquin. These two men, provoked, as all my men were, escaped before they could be caught and bound." He looked back at the youths. "As to you two, you will both come back at the first night watch for sentencing."

Katsumata said quickly, "Sire, may I suggest you add in the letter that they have been ordered outcast, declared ronin, their stipends cancelled and a reward offered for their heads."

"Two koku. Post it in their villages when we return." Sanjiro turned his eyes on Shorin and Ori and waved his hand in dismissal. They bowed deeply and left. He was pleased to see the sweat on the back of their kimonos though the afternoon was not hot.

"Katsumata, about Yokohama," he said softly when they were alone again. "Send some of our best spies to see what is going on there. Order them to be back here by nightfall, and order all samurai to become battle ready."

"Yes, Sire." Katsumata did not allow a smile to show.

When the youths left Sanjiro and had passed through the rings of bodyguards, Katsumata caught up with them. "Follow me." He led the way through meandering gardens to a side door that was unguarded.

"Go at once to Kanagawa, to the Inn of the Midnight Blossoms. It is a safe house, other friends will be there. Hurry!"

"But, Sensei," Ori said. "First we must collect our other swords and armor and money and—"

"Silence!" Angrily Katsumata reached into his kimono sleeve and gave them a small purse with a few coins in it. "Take this, and return double for your insolence. At sunset I will order men to go after you with orders to kill you if you're caught within one *ri*." A *ri* was about a league, about three miles.

"Yes, Sensei, I apologize for being so rude."

"Your apology is not accepted. You are both fools. You should have killed all four barbarians, not just one—particularly the girl, for that

would have sent the gai-jin mad with rage! How many times have I told
you? They're not civilized like us, and view the world, religion and
women differently! You're inept! You're fools! You initiated a good
attack then failed to press forward ruthlessly without concern for your
own lives. You hesitated! So you lost! Fools!" he said again. "You
forgot everything I've taught you." Enraged, he backhanded Shorin in
the face, the blow savage.

At once Shorin bowed, mumbled an abject apology for causing the
Sensei to lose *wa,* to lose inner harmony, keeping his head bowed,
desperately trying to contain the pain. Ori stayed ramrod stiff, waiting
for the second blow. It left a livid burn in its wake. Immediately he, too,
apologized abjectly, and kept his throbbing head bowed, afraid. Once a
fellow student, the best swordsman amongst them, had answered
Katsumata rudely during a practice fight. Without hesitation, Katsumata had sheathed his sword, attacked barehanded, disarmed him,
humiliated him, broke both his arms and expelled him to his village
forever.

"Please excuse me, Sensei," Shorin said, meaning it.

"Go to the Inn of the Midnight Blossoms. When I send a message,
obey whatever I require of you at once, there will be no second chance!
At once, understand?"

"Yes, yes, Sensei, please excuse me," they mumbled together,
tucked up their kimonos and fled, thankful to be out of his reach, more
frightened of him than of Sanjiro. Katsumata had been their main
teacher for years, in both the arts of war and, in secret, other arts:
strategy, past, present and of the future, why the Bakufu had failed in
their duty, the Toranagas in theirs, why there must be change and how
to bring it about. Katsumata was one of the few clandestine shishi who
was *hatomoto*—an honored retainer with instant access to his lord—a
senior samurai with a personal yearly stipend of a thousand koku.

'Eeee, to be so rich,' Shorin had whispered to Ori when they had first
found out.

'Money is nothing, nothing. The Sensei says when you have power
you don't need money.'

'I agree, but think of your family, your father and mine, and grandfather, they could buy some land of their own and not have to work the
fields of others—nor would we have to work like that from time to
time to earn extra.'

'You're right,' Ori said.

Then Shorin had laughed. 'No need to worry, we'll never get even a
hundred koku and if we had it we'd just spend our share on girls and

saké and become daimyos of the Floating World. A thousand koku is all the money in the world!'

'No, it's not,' Ori had said. 'Don't forget what the Sensei told us.'

During one of Katsumata's secret sessions for his special group of acolytes he had said: 'The revenue of Satsuma amounts to seven hundred and fifty thousand koku and belongs to our lord, the daimyo, to apportion as he sees fit. That's another custom the new administration will modify. When the great change has happened, a fief's revenue will be portioned out by a Council of State, made up of wise men drawn from *any rank of samurai, high or low, of any age, provided the man has the necessary wisdom and has proved himself a man of honor.* It will be the same in all fiefs, as the land will be governed by a Supreme Council of State in Yedo or Kyōto, drawn equally from samurai of honor—under the guidance of the Son of Heaven.'

'Sensei, you said *any*? May I ask, will that include the Toranagas?' Ori had asked.

'There will be no exception, if the man is worthy.'

'Sensei, please, about the Toranagas. Does anyone know their real wealth, the lands they really control?'

'After Sekigahara, Toranaga took lands from dead enemies worth yearly about five million koku, about a third of all the wealth of Nippon, for himself and his family. In perpetuity.'

In the stunned silence that followed, Ori had said for all of them: 'With that amount of wealth we could have the greatest navy in the world with all the men-of-war and cannon and guns we could ever need, we could have the best legions with the best guns, we could throw out all gai-jin!'

'We could even carry war to them and extend our shores,' Katsumata had added softly, 'and correct previous shame.'

At once they had known he was referring to the *tairō*, General Nakamura, Toranaga's immediate predecessor and liege lord, the great peasant-general who then possessed the Gates and had therefore, in gratitude, been granted by the Emperor the highest possible title a lowborn could aspire to, *tairō*, meaning Dictator—not that of Shōgun, which he coveted to obsession but could never have.

Having subdued all the land, chiefly by persuading his main enemy Toranaga to swear allegiance to him and his child heir forever, he had gathered a huge armada and mounted a vast campaign against Chosen, or Korea as it was sometimes called, to enlighten that country and use it as a stepping stone to the Dragon Throne of China. But his armies had failed and soon retreated in ignominy—as in previous eras, centuries before, two other Japanese attempts had failed, equally in disaster, the throne of China a perpetual lodestone.

'Such shame needs to be eradicated—like the shame the Sons of Heaven have suffered because of the Toranagas who usurped Nakamura's power when the man died, destroyed his wife and son, levelled their Osaka castle, and have pillaged the heritage of the Son of Heaven for long enough! *Sonno-joi!*'

'*Sonno-joi!*' they had echoed. Fervently.

In the dusk the youths were tiring, their headlong flight racking them. But neither wanted to be the first to admit it so they pressed on until they were at the threshold of woods. Ahead now were paddy swamps on either side of the Tokaidō that led to the outskirts of Kanagawa just ahead, and to the roadblock. The shore was to their right.

"Let's . . . let's stop a moment," Ori said, his wounded arm throbbing, head hurting, chest hurting, but not showing it.

"All right." Shorin was panting as hard and hurting as much but he laughed. "You're weak, like an old woman." He picked a dry patch of earth, sat down gratefully. With great care he began to look around, trying to regain his breathing.

The Tokaidō was almost empty, night travel being generally forbidden by the Bakufu and subject to severe cross-questioning and punishment if not justified. Several porters and the last of the travellers scurried for the Kanagawa barrier, all others safely bathing or carousing at the Inns of their choice—of which there was a multitude within the post towns. Throughout the land, trunk road barriers closed at nightfall and were not opened until dawn, and always guarded by local samurai.

Across the bay Shorin could see the oil lamps along the promenade and in some of the houses of the Settlement, and amongst the ships at anchor. A good moon, half full, was rising from near the horizon.

"How is your arm, Ori?"

"Fine, Shorin. We are more than a *ri* from Hodogaya."

"Yes, but I won't feel safe until we're at the Inn." Shorin began massaging his neck to try to ease the pain there and in his head. Katsumata's blow had stunned him. "When we were before Lord Sanjiro I thought we were finished, I thought he was going to condemn us."

"So did I." As he spoke Ori felt sick, his arm throbbing like his heaving chest, his face still afire. With his good hand he waved absently at a swarm of night insects. "If he . . . I was ready to go for my sword and send him on before us."

"So was I but the Sensei was watching very closely and he would have killed both of us before we moved."

"Yes, you're right again." The younger man shuddered. "His blow almost took my head off. Eeee, to have such strength, unbelievable! I'm glad he's on our side, not against us. He saved us, only him; he bent Lord Sanjiro to his will." Ori was suddenly somber. "Shorin, while I was waiting I . . . to keep myself strong, I composed my death poem."

Shorin became equally grave. "May I hear it?"

"Yes.

> *"Sonno-joi at sunset,*
> *Nothing wasted.*
> *Into nothing*
> *I spring."*

Shorin thought about the poem, savoring it, the balance of the words and the third level of meaning. Then he said solemnly, "It is wise for a samurai to have composed a death poem. I haven't managed that yet but I should, then all the rest of life is extra." He twisted his head from side to side to the limit, the joints or ligaments cracking, and he felt better. "You know, Ori, the Sensei was right: we did hesitate, therefore we lost."

"I hesitated, he's right in that, I could have killed the girl easily but she paralyzed me for a moment. I've never . . . her outlandish clothes, her face like a strange flower with that huge nose more like a monstrous orchid with two great blue spots and crowned with yellow stamens—those unbelievable eyes, Siamese cat eyes and thatch of straw under that ridiculous hat, so repulsive yet so—so attracting." Ori laughed nervously. "I was bewitched. She is surely a *kami* from the dark regions."

"Rip her clothes off and she'd be real enough, but how attractive I . . . I don't know."

"I thought of that too, wondering what it would be like." Ori looked up at the moon for a moment. "If I pillowed with her I think . . . I think I'd become the male spider to her female."

"You mean she'd kill you afterwards?"

"Yes, if I pillowed her, with or without force, that woman would kill me." Ori waved the air, the insects becoming a pestilence. "I've never seen one like her—nor have you. You noticed too, *neh*?"

"No, everything happened so fast and I was trying to kill the big ugly one with the pistol and then she had fled."

Ori stared at the faint lights of Yokohama. "I wonder what she's called, what she did when she got back there. I've never seen—she was so ugly and yet . . ."

Shorin was unsettled. Normally Ori hardly noticed women, just used them when he had a need, let them entertain him, serve him. Apart from his adored sister, he could not remember Ori ever discussing one before. "Karma."

"Yes, karma." Ori shifted his bandage to be more comfortable, but the throbbing deepened. Blood seeped from under it. "Even so, I do not know if we lost. We must wait, we must be patient and see what will happen. We always planned to go against gai-jin at the first opportunity—I was right to go against them at that moment."

Shorin got up. "I'm tired of seriousness, and kami and death. We'll know death soon enough. The Sensei gave us life for sonno-joi. From nothing into nothing—but tonight we've another night to enjoy. A bath, saké, food, then a real Lady of the Night, succulent and sweet-smelling and moist . . ." He laughed softly. "A flower, not an orchid, with a beautiful nose and proper eyes. Let's—"

He stopped. Eastwards, from the direction of Yokohama, came the echoing report of a ship's signal cannon. Then a signal rocket briefly lit the darkness.

"Is that usual?"

"I don't know." Ahead they could just see the lamps at the first barrier. "Through the paddy is better, then we can skirt the guards."

"Yes. Better we cross the road here and go closer to the shore. They won't expect intruders that way, we can avoid any patrols, and the Inn is nearer."

They ran across the road, keeping well down, then up onto one of the paths that transversed the fields recently planted with winter rice. Suddenly they stopped. From the Tokaidō came the clatter of approaching horses and jingling harness. They ducked down, waited a moment, then gasped. Ten uniformed dragoons, armed with carbines and led by an officer, cantered out of the curve.

At once the soldiers were spotted by samurai at the barrier, who called out a warning. Others rushed from the huts to join them. Soon there were twenty lined up behind the barrier, an officer at their head.

"What shall we do, Ori?" Shorin whispered.

"Wait."

As they watched the senior samurai held up his hand. "Stop!" he called out, then nodded slightly instead of a bow, correct etiquette from a superior to an inferior. "Is your night travel authorized? If so please give me the papers."

Ori's fury soared as he saw the open insolence of the gai-jin officer who halted about ten paces from the barrier, called out something in his strange language and imperiously motioned to the samurai to open it, neither dismounting nor bowing courteously as custom demanded.

"How dare you be so rude! Leave!" the samurai said angrily, not expecting the insult, waving them away.

The gai-jin officer barked an order. At once his men unslung their carbines, levelled them at the samurai, then on an abrupt second order, fired a disciplined volley into the air. At once they reloaded and aimed directly at the guards, almost before the sound of the volley had died away, leaving a vast ominous silence throughout the landscape.

Shorin and Ori gasped. For all time guns had been muzzle-loaded with powder and shot. "Those are breech-loading rifles, with the new cartridges," Shorin whispered excitedly. Neither had ever seen these recent inventions, had only heard of them. The samurai were equally shocked. "Eeee, did you notice how fast they reloaded? I heard a soldier can easily fire ten rounds to one of a muzzle loader."

"But did you see their discipline, Shorin, and that of the horses? They hardly moved!"

Once more the gai-jin officer haughtily motioned them to open the barrier, no mistaking the threat that if he was not obeyed quickly, all the samurai were dead.

"Let them through," the senior samurai said.

The Dragoon officer disdainfully spurred forward, apparently without fear, his grim-faced men following, their guns ready. None of them acknowledged the guards or returned their polite bows.

"This will be reported at once and an apology demanded!" the samurai said, enraged with their insulting behavior, trying not to show it.

Once they had passed through, the barrier was replaced and Ori whispered furiously, "What foul manners! But against those guns what could he do?"

"He should have charged and killed them before he died. I could not do what that coward did—I would have charged and died," Shorin said, knees trembling with anger.

"Yes. I think . . ." Ori stopped, his own anger evaporating at his sudden thought. "Come on," he whispered urgently. "We'll find out where they're going—perhaps we can steal some of those guns."

4

THE ROYAL NAVAL LONGBOAT came out of the twilight and sped for the Kanagawa jetty. It was strongly built of stone and wood, unlike the others that speckled the shore, and boldly signposted in English and Japanese script: '*Property of H.M. British Legation, Kanagawa—trespassers will be prosecuted.*' The longboat was rowed briskly by sailors and crammed with armed marines. A thin band of scarlet still rimmed the western horizon. The sea was choppy, the moon rising nicely with a fair wind jostling the clouds.

One of the Legation Grenadiers waited at the end of the wharf. Beside him was a round-faced Chinese wearing a long, high-necked gown, and carrying an oil lamp on a pole.

"Oars ho!" the Bosun ordered. At once all oars were shipped, the bowman leaped onto the wharf and tied the boat to a bollard, marines followed rapidly in disciplined order and formed up defensively, guns ready, their Sergeant studying the terrain. In the stern was a naval officer. And Angelique Richaud. He helped her ashore.

"Evening, sir, Ma'am," the Grenadier said, saluting the officer. "This here's Lun, he's a Legation assistant."

Lun gawked at the girl. "Ev'nin, sah, you cumalong plenty quick quick, heya? Missy cumalong never mind."

Angelique was nervous and anxious and wore a bonnet and a blue silk hooped dress with a shawl to match that set off her paleness and fair hair to perfection. "Mr. Struan, how is he?"

The soldier said kindly, "Don't know, Ma'am, Miss. Doc Babcott, he's the best in these waters, so the poor man will be all right if it's God's will. He'll be proper pleased to see you—been asking for you. We didn't expect you till morning."

"And Mr. Tyrer?"

"He's fine, Miss, just a flesh wound. We best be going."

"How far is it?"

Lun said irritably, "Ayeeyah, no far chop chop never mind." He lifted the lamp and set off into the night, muttering busily in Cantonese.

Insolent bastard, the officer thought. He was tall, Lieutenant R.N., his name John Marlowe. They began to follow. At once the marines moved into a protective screen, scouts ahead. "Are you all right, Miss Angelique?" he asked.

"Yes, thank you." She pulled the shawl closer around her shoulders, picking her way carefully. "What an awful smell!"

" 'Fraid it's the manure they use for fertilizers, that and low tide." Marlowe was twenty-eight, sandy-haired and grey-blue-eyed, normally Captain of H.M.S. *Pearl*, a 21-gun steam-driven frigate, but now acting Flag Lieutenant to the ranking naval officer, Admiral Ketterer. "Would you like a litter?"

"Thank you, no, I'm fine."

Lun was ahead slightly, lighting their way through the narrow, empty village streets. Most of Kanagawa was silent, though occasionally they could hear boisterous and drunken laughter of men and women behind high walls that were pierced from time to time by small barred doorways. A multitude of decorative Japanese signs.

"These are inns, hotels?" she asked.

"I would imagine so," Marlowe said delicately.

Lun chuckled quietly, hearing this exchange. His English was fluent—learned in a missionary school in Hong Kong. On instructions he carefully hid the fact and always used pidgin and pretended to be stupid so he knew many secrets that had great value to him, and to his tong superiors, and to their leader, Illustrious Chen, Gordon Chen, compradore of Struan's. A compradore, usually a wellborn Eurasian, was the indispensable go-between betwixt European and Chinese traders, who could speak fluent English and Chinese dialects, and to whose hands at least ten percent of all transactions stuck.

Ah, haughty young Missy who feeds on unrequited lust, Lun thought with vast amusement, knowing lots about her. I wonder which of these smelly Round Eyes will be the first to spread you wide and enter your equally smelly Jade Gate? Are you as untouched as you pretend, or has the grandson of Green-eyed Devil Struan already enjoyed the Clouds and the Rain? By all gods great and small, I shall know soon enough because your maid is my sister's third cousin's daughter. I already know your short hairs need plucking, are as fair as your hair and much too abundant to please a civilized person but I suppose all right for a barbarian. Ugh!

Ayeeyah, but life is interesting. I'll wager this murder attack will cause both foreign devils and the Filth Eaters of these islands much trouble. Wonderful! May they all drown in their own feces!

Interesting that the grandson of Green-eyed Devil was wounded badly, and so continues the bad joss of all males of his line, interesting that the news is already rushing secretly to Hong Kong by our fastest courier. How wise I am! But then I am a person of the Middle Kingdom and of course superior.

But a bad wind for one is good for another. This news will surely depress the share price of the Noble House mightily. With advanced information I and my friends will make a great profit. By all the gods, I will put ten percent of my profit on the next horse at Happy Valley races with the number fourteen, today's date by barbarian counting.

"Ho!" he called out, pointing. The central turrets of the temple loomed over the alleys and lanes of the tiny single-story houses, all separate though clustered in honeycombs.

Two Grenadiers and their Sergeant were on guard at the temple gates, well lit with oil lamps, Babcott beside them. "Hello, Marlowe," he said with a smile. "This is an unexpected pleasure. Evening, Mademoiselle. What's—"

"Pardon, Doctor," Angelique interrupted, peering up at him, astounded at his size, "but Malcolm, Mr. Struan, we heard he was badly wounded."

"He has had quite a bad sword cut, but he's been sewn up and now he's fast asleep," Babcott said easily. "I gave him a sedative. I'll take you to him in a second. What's up, Marlowe, why—"

"And Phillip Tyrer?" she interrupted again. "Is he, was he badly wounded too?"

"Just a flesh wound, Mademoiselle, there's nothing you can do at the moment, both are sedated. Why the marines, Marlowe?"

"The Admiral thought you'd better have some extra protection—in case of an evacuation."

Babcott whistled. "It's that serious?"

"There's a meeting going on right now. The Admiral, the General, Sir William together with the French, German, Russian and American representatives and the, er, the trading fraternity." Marlowe added dryly, "I gather it's rather heated." He turned to the Royal Marine Sergeant. "Secure the Legation, Sar'nt Crimp, I'll inspect your posts later." To the Grenadier Sergeant he added, "Please give Sar'nt Crimp the help he needs, where to billet his men, etc. Your name please?"

"Towery, sir."

"Thank you, Sar'nt Towery."

Babcott said, "Perhaps you'd both follow me? A cup of tea?"

"Thank you, no," she said, trying to be polite but consumed with impatience, disliking the way the English brewed tea and offered it at the slightest provocation. "But I would like to see Mr. Struan and Mr. Tyrer."

"Of course, right away." The doctor had already judged that she was near to tears at any moment, decided she really did need a cup of tea, perhaps laced with a little brandy, a sedative and then to bed. "Young Phillip, poor chap had quite a shock I'm afraid—must have been dreadful for you too."

"Is he all right?"

"Yes, quite all right," he repeated patiently. "Come along, see for yourself." He led the way through the courtyard. The clatter of hooves and harness stopped them. To their surprise they saw a Dragoon patrol arriving. "Good God, it's Pallidar," Marlowe said. "What's he doing here?"

They watched the Dragoon officer return the salutes of the marines and grenadiers and dismount. "Carry on," Pallidar said, not noticing Marlowe, Babcott and Angelique. "Bloody bastard Japanners tried to bloody bar the road against us, by God! Unfortunately the sons of whores changed their bloody, God-cursed minds or they'd be pushing up bloody daisies and . . ." He saw Angelique and stopped, appalled. "Jesus Christ! Oh, I say, I am . . . I am most terrible sorry, Mademoiselle, I, er, I didn't realize there were any ladies . . . er, hello John, Doctor."

Marlowe said, "Hello, Settry. Mademoiselle Angelique, may I introduce plainspoken Captain Settry Pallidar, of Her Majesty's Eighth Dragoons. Mademoiselle Angelique Richaud."

She nodded coolly and he bowed stiffly. "I'm, er, most awfully sorry, Mademoiselle. Doc, I was sent to secure the Legation, in case of an evacuation."

"The Admiral already sent us here to do that," Marlowe said crisply. "With marines."

"You can dismiss them, we're here now."

"Get . . . I suggest you ask for new orders. Tomorrow. Meanwhile

I'm senior officer and in command. Senior service. Doctor, perhaps
you'd take the lady to see Mr. Struan."

Babcott had watched the two young men square up to one another
with concern, liking them both. Friendly on the surface, deadly underneath. These two young bulls will have at each other one day—God
help them if it's over a woman. "See you both later." Taking her arm,
he walked off.

The two men watched them go. Then Pallidar's chin jutted. "This
isn't a ship's quarterdeck," he hissed, "it's a job for the army, by
God."

"Bullshit."

"Are your brains lost with your manners? Why the hell bring a
woman here when Christ knows what may happen?"

"Because the important Mr. Struan asked to see her, medically it's a
good idea, she persuaded the Admiral to allow her to come tonight
against my advice, he ordered me to escort her here and send her back
safely. Sar'nt Towery!"

"Yessir!"

"I'm in overall command until further orders—show the dragoons
to quarters and make them comfortable. Can you stable their horses?
Do you have enough rations?"

"Yessir, we've plenty of room. Grub's a bit short."

"Has it ever been plentiful in this godforsaken place?" Marlowe
beckoned him closer. "Spread the word," he said dangerously. "No
fighting and if there is, it's a hundred lashes for any bastard involved—
whoever he is!"

The bar of the Yokohama Club, the biggest room in the Settlement
and thus *the* meeting place, was in uproar and packed with almost the
entire acceptable population of the Settlement—only those too drunk
to stand or the very sick were missing—all shouting in various languages, many armed, many waving their fists and cursing the small
group of well-dressed men who sat at a raised table at the far end, most
of whom were shouting back, the Admiral and General beside them
apoplectic.

"Say that again, by God, and I'll call you outside . . ."

"Go to hell, you bastard . . ."

"It's war, Wullem's got to . . ."

"Turn out the bloody army an' navy and bombard Yedo . . ."

"Flatten the f'ing capital, by God . . ."

"Canterbury's gotta be revenged, Wullum's got to . . ."

"Right! Willum's responsible, John the Cant's me mate . . ."

"Listen, you lot . . ." One of the seated men began pounding the table top with a gavel for silence. This only incensed the crowd further—merchants, tradesmen, innkeepers, gamblers, horse handlers, butchers, jockeys, seamen, remittance men, sail makers, and port riffraff. Top hats, multicolored waistcoats, woolen clothes and underwear, leather boots, from rich to poor, the air hot, stale, smoky and heavy with the odor of unwashed bodies, stale beer, whisky, gin, rum and spilt wine.

"Quiet, for Christ's sake, let Wullum speak. . . ."

The man with the gavel shouted, "It's William, for God's sake! William, not Wullum or Willum or Willam! *William* Aylesbury, how many times do I have to tell you? William!"

"That's right, let Willum speak, for Christ's sake!"

The three barmen serving drinks behind the vast counter laughed. "Proper thirsty bloody work this 'ere meeting, i'nit, guv?" one called out breezily, wiping the counter with a filthy rag. The bar was the pride of the Settlement, deliberately a foot bigger than the one in the Shanghai Jockey Club, previously the biggest in Asia, and twice as big as the Hong Kong Club's. The wall was lined with bottles of spirits, wine and beer kegs. "Let the bugger speak, for crissake!"

Sir William Aylesbury, the man with the gavel, sighed. He was British Minister in Japan, senior member of the Diplomatic Corps. The other men represented France, Russia, Prussia, and America. His temper snapped and he motioned to a young officer standing behind the table. At once, clearly prepared—as were those at the table—the officer took out a revolver and fired into the ceiling. Plaster speckled down in the sudden silence.

"Thank you. Now," Sir William began, his voice heavy with sarcasm, "if you gentlemen will all be quiet for a moment we can proceed." He was a tall man in his late forties, with a bent face and prominent ears. "I repeat, as you will all be affected by what we decide, my colleagues and I wish to discuss how to respond to this incident—in public. If you lot don't want to listen, or if you're asked for an opinion and don't give it with the minimum of expletives—we will ponder the matter in private and then, when we've decided what WILL HAPPEN, we will be glad to inform you."

A muttering resentment, but no open hostility.

"Good. Mr. McFay, you were saying?"

Jamie McFay was near the front, Dmitri beside him. Because he was head of Struan's, the largest house in Asia, McFay was the usual spokesman for the merchant-traders, the most important of whom had their own fleets of armed clippers and merchantmen. "Well, sir, we know the Satsumas are bedding down at Hodogaya in easy reach north and that their king's with them," he said, greatly concerned over Malcolm Struan. "His name's Sajirro, some name like that, and I think we sh—"

Someone shouted, "I vote we surround the bastards tonight and string the bugger up!" A roar of applause that soon trickled away amidst a few muffled curses and, "For God's sake, get on with it . . ."

"Please carry on, Mr. McFay," Sir William said wearily.

"The attack was unprovoked, as usual, John Canterbury was foully brutalized, and God only knows how long it will take Mr. Struan to recover. But this is the first time we can identify the murderers—or at least the king can and as sure as God made little apples he has the power to catch the buggers and hand them over and pay damages. . . ." More applause. "They're within reach, and with the troops we have we can peg them."

Strong cheers and cries for vengeance.

Henri Bonaparte Seratard, the French Minister in Japan, said loudly, "I would like to ask Monsieur the General and Monsieur the Admiral what is their opinion?"

The Admiral said at once: "I have five hundred marines in the fleet—"

General Thomas Ogilvy interrupted, firmly but politely, "The question applies to a land operation, my dear Admiral. Mr. Ceraturd . . ." The greying, red-faced man of fifty carefully mispronounced the Frenchman's name and used 'Mr.' to compound the insult, "we have a thousand British troops in tent encampments, two cavalry units, three batteries of the most modern cannon and artillery, and can call up another eight or nine thousand British and Indian infantrymen with support troops within two months from our Hong Kong bastion." He toyed with his gold braid. "There is no conceivable problem that Her Majesty's forces under my command cannot conclude expeditiously."

"I agree," the Admiral said under the roars of approval. When they had died down, Seratard said smoothly, "Then you advocate a declaration of war?"

"No such thing, sir," the General said, their dislike mutual. "I merely said we can do what is necessary, when necessary and when we are obliged to do it. I would have thought this 'incident' is a matter for Her Majesty's Minister to decide in conjunction with the Admiral and myself without an unseemly debate."

Some shouted approval, most disapproved and someone called out, "It's our silver and taxes wot pays for all you buggers, we've the right to say wot's wot. Ever heard of Parliament, by God?"

"A French national was involved," Seratard said heatedly above the noise, "therefore the honor of France is involved." Catcalls and sly remarks about the girl.

Again Sir William used the gavel and that allowed the acting American Minister, Isaiah Adamson, to say coldly, "The idea of going to war over this incident is nonsense, and the notion of grabbing or attacking a king in their sovereign country total lunacy—and typical high-handed Imperialist jingoism! First thing to do is inform the Bakufu, then ask them to—"

Irritably, Sir William said, "Dr. Babcott has already informed them in Kanagawa, they've already denied any knowledge of the incident and in all probability will follow their pattern and continue to do so. A British subject has been brutally murdered, another seriously wounded, unforgivably our delightful young foreign guest was almost frightened to death—these acts, I must stress, as Mr. McFay so rightly points out, *for the first time have been committed by identifiable criminals.* Her Majesty's Government will not let this go unpunished. . . ." For a moment he was drowned by tumultuous cheers, then he added, "The only thing to decide is the measure of punishment, how we should proceed and when. Mr. Adamson?" he asked the American.

"As we're not involved I've no formal recommendation."

"Count Zergeyev?"

"My formal advice," the Russian said carefully, "is that we fall on Hodogaya and tear it and all the Satsumas to pieces." He was in his early thirties, strong, patrician and bearded, leader of Tsar Alexander II's mission. "Force, massive, ferocious and immediate is the only diplomacy Japanners will ever understand. My warship would be honored to lead the attack."

There was a curious silence. I guessed that would be your answer, Sir William thought. I'm not so sure you're wrong. Ah, Russia, beautiful extraordinary Russia, what a shame we're enemies. Best time I ever had was in St. Petersburg. Even so, you're not going to expand into these waters, we stopped your invasion of the Japanese Tsushima islands last year, and this year we'll prevent you from stealing their Sakhalin too. "Thank you, my dear Count. Herr von Heimrich?"

The Prussian was elderly and curt. "I have no advice in this, Herr Consul General, other than to say formally my government would consider it is a matter for your government alone, and not the affair of minor parties."

Seratard flushed. "I do not consider—"

"Thank you for your advice, gentlemen," Sir William said firmly, cutting off the row that would have flared between them. Yesterday's Foreign Office dispatches from London said that Britain could soon become embroiled in another of the never-ending European wars, this time belligerent, pride-filled France against belligerent, pride-filled expansionist Prussia, but did not forecast on which side. Why the devil damned foreigners can't behave as civilized fellows I'm damned if I know.

"Before making a judgment," he said crisply, "since everyone of note is here and not having had such an opportunity before, I think we should articulate our problem: we have legal treaties with Japan. We're here to trade, not to conquer territory. We have to deal with this bureaucracy, the Bakufu, who're like a sponge—one moment it pretends to be all-powerful, the next helpless against their individual kings. We've never been able to get to the real power, the Tycoon or Shōgun—we don't even know if he really exists."

"He must exist," von Heimrich said coolly, "because our famous German traveller and physician, Dr. Engelbert Kaempfer, who lived in Deshima from 1690 to 1693, pretending to be a Dutchman, reported visiting him in Yedo on their annual pilgrimage."

"That doesn't prove one exists now," Seratard said caustically. "However, I do agree there is a Shōgun, and France approves of a direct approach."

"An admirable idea, Monsieur." Sir William reddened. "And how do we do that?"

"Send the fleet against Yedo," the Russian said at once. "Demand an immediate audience or else you'll destroy the place. If I had such a beautiful fleet as yours, I'd first flatten half the city and then demand the audience . . . better, I would order this Tycoon-Shōgun native to report aboard my flagship at dawn the next day, and hang him." Many shouts of approval.

Sir William said, "That is certainly one way, but Her Majesty's Government would prefer a slightly more diplomatic solution. Next: we've almost no real intelligence about what's going on in the country. I'd appreciate it if all traders would help to get us information that could prove useful. Mr. McFay, of all the traders, you should be the best informed. Can you help?"

McFay said cautiously, "Well, a few days ago one of our Jappo silk suppliers told our Chinese compradore that some of the kingdoms—he used the word 'fiefs' and called the kings 'daimyos'—were in revolt against the Bakufu, particularly Satsuma, and some parts called Tosa, and Choshu . . ."

Sir William noticed the immediate interest of the other diplomats and wondered if he was wise to have asked the question in public. "Where are they?"

"Satsuma's near Nagasaki in the South Island, Kyūshū," Adamson said, "but what about Choshu and Tosa?"

"Well, now, yor Honor," an American seaman called out, his Irish accent pleasing. "Tosa's a part of Shikoku, that's the big island on the inland sea. Choshu's far to the west on the main island, Mr. Adamson, sir, athwart the Straits. We been through the Straits there, many a time, they're not more than a mile across at the narrowest part. As I was saying now, Choshu's the kingdom's athwart the narrows, bare a mile across. It's the best, and closest way from Hong Kong or Shanghai to here. Shimonoseki Straits, the locals call it, and once we traded for fish and water at the town there but we weren't welcome." Many others called out their agreement and that they too had used the Straits but had never known that the kingdom was called Choshu.

Sir William said, "Your name, if you please?"

"Paddy O'Flaherty, Bosun of the American whaler *Albatross* out of Seattle, yor Honor."

"Thank you," Sir William said, and made a mental note to send for O'Flaherty, to find out more and if there were charts of the area, and if not to instantly order the Navy to make them. "Go on, Mr. McFay," he said. "In revolt, you say."

"Yes, sir. This silk trader—how reliable he is I don't know—but he said there was some kind of power struggle going on against the Tycoon that he always called 'Shōgun,' the Bakufu and some king or daimyo called Toranaga."

Sir William saw the Russian's eyes slit even more in his almost Asian features. "Yes, my dear Count?"

"Nothing, Sir William. But isn't that the name of the ruler mentioned by Kaempfer?"

"Indeed it is, indeed it is." I wonder why you never mentioned to me before that you had also read those very rare but illuminating journals that were written in German, which you do not know, therefore they must have been translated into Russian? "Perhaps 'Toranaga' means 'ruler' in their language. Please continue, Mr. McFay."

"That's all the fellow told my compradore, but I'll make it my business to find out more. Now," McFay said politely but firmly, "do we settle King Satsuma at Hodogaya tonight or not?"

The smoke stirred the silence.

"Has anyone anything to add—about this revolt?"

Norbert Greyforth, chief of Brock and Sons, Struan's main rival, said, "We've heard rumors of this revolt, too. But I thought it was something to do with their chief priest, this 'Mikado,' who supposedly lives in Kyōto, a city near Osaka. I'll make enquiries as well. In the meantime, about tonight, my vote goes with McFay: the sooner we belt these buggers the sooner we'll have peace." He was taller than McFay and clearly hated him.

When the cheers died down, like a judge delivering a sentence, Sir William said: "This is what will happen. First, there will be no attack tonight and—"

Cries of "Resign!" "We'll do it ourselves, by God!" "Come on, let's go after the bastards . . ."

"We can't, not without troops . . ."

"Quiet and listen, by God!" Sir William shouted. "If anyone is stupid enough to go against Hodogaya tonight he'll have to answer to our laws as well as Japanners. IT IS FORBIDDEN! Tomorrow I will formally demand—DEMAND—that at once the Bakufu, AND Shōgun, tender a formal apology, at once hand over the two murderers for trial and hanging, and at once pay an indemnity of one hundred thousand pounds or accept the consequences."

A few cheered, most did not, and the meeting broke up with a surge to the bar, many of the men already near blows as arguments became more drunken and more heated. McFay and Dmitri shoved their way out into the open air. "My God, that's better." McFay eased off his hat and mopped his brow.

"A word, Mr. McFay?"

He turned and saw Greyforth. "Of course."

"In private, if you please."

McFay frowned, then moved over the semideserted promenade along the wharfs and seafront, away from Dmitri, who was not in Struan's but traded through Cooper-Tillman, one of the American companies. "Yes?"

Norbert Greyforth dropped his voice. "What about Hodogaya? You've two ships here, we've three, and between us lots of bully boys, most lads in the merchant fleet'd join us, we've arms enough and we could bring a cannon or two. John Canterbury was a good friend, the Old Man liked him, and I want him revenged. What about it?"

"If Hodogaya was a port I wouldn't hesitate, but we can't raid inland. This isn't China."

"You afraid of that pipsqueak in there?"

"I'm not afraid of anyone," McFay said carefully. "We can't mount a successful raid without regular troops, Norbert, that's not possible. I want revenge more than any."

Greyforth made sure no one was listening. "Since you brought it up tonight and we don't talk too often, we've heard there's going to be bad trouble here soon."

"The revolt?"

"Yes. Very bad trouble for us. There's been all sorts of signs. Our silk dealers have been acting right smelly the last month or two, upping the price of bulk raw, delaying deliveries, slow on payments and wanting extra credits. I'll bet it's the same with you."

"Yes." It was rare for the two men to talk business.

"Don't know much more than that, except many of the signs are the same as in America that led to civil war. If that happens here it's going to bugger us proper. Without the fleet and troops we're bitched and we can be wiped out."

After a pause, McFay said, "What do you propose?"

"We'll have to wait and see what happens. With Wee Willie's plan I don't hope for much, like you. The Russian was right about what should be done. Meanwhile . . ." Greyforth nodded out to sea where two of their clippers and merchantmen lay in the roads—clippers still much faster back to England than steamers, paddle-driven or screw-driven . . . "We're keeping all our inner ledgers and specie aboard, we've increased our levels of gunpowder, shot, shrapnel and put in an order for two of the brand-new Yankee 10-barrel Gatling machine guns as soon as they are available."

McFay laughed. "The hell you have—so did we!"

"We heard that too, which is why I made the order, and twice as many of the new rifles than your shipment."

"Who told you, eh? Who's your spy?"

"Old Mother Hubbard," Greyforth said dryly. "Listen, we all know these inventions, along with metal cartridges, have changed the course of war—that's proved already by the casualties at the battles of Bull Run and Fredericksburg."

"Shocking, yes. Dmitri told me, said the South lost four thousand in one afternoon. Terrible. So?"

"We could both sell these weapons to the Japanners by the ton. My thought is we agree to not, and together we make bloody sure no other bugger imports them or smuggles them in. Selling Jappers steamers and the odd cannon's one thing, but not repeaters or machine guns. Agreed?"

McFay was surprised by the offer. And suspicious. But he kept it off his face, sure that Norbert would never keep the bargain, and shook the offered hand. "Agreed."

"Good. What's the latest on young Struan?"

"When I saw him an hour or so ago he was poorly."

"Is he going to die?"

"No, the doctor assured me of that."

A cold smile. "What the hell do they know? But if he did that could wreck the Noble House."

"Nothing will ever wreck the Noble House. Dirk Struan saw to that."

"Don't be too sure. Dirk's been dead more than twenty years, his son Culum's not far from his deathbed and if Malcolm dies who's to take over? Not his young brother who's only ten." His eyes glinted strangely. "Old Man Brock may be seventy-three but he's as tough and clever as he ever was."

"But we're still the Noble House; Culum is still the tai-pan." McFay added, glad for the barb, "Old Man Brock's still not a Steward of the Jockey Club at Happy Valley and never will be."

"That'll come soon enough, Jamie, that and all the rest. Culum Struan won't control the Jockey Club vote much longer, and if his son and heir kicks the bucket too, well then, counting us and our friends we've the necessary votes."

"It won't happen."

Greyforth hardened. "Mayhaps Old Man Brock will honor us with a visit here soon—along with Sir Morgan."

"Morgan's in Hong Kong?" McFay tried to stop his astonishment from showing. Sir Morgan Brock was Old Man Brock's eldest son, who very successfully ran their London office. As far as Jamie knew Morgan had never been to Asia before. If Morgan's suddenly in Hong Kong . . . what new devilment are those two up to now? he asked himself uneasily. Morgan specialized in merchant banking and had skillfully spread the tentacles of Brock's into Europe, Russia, and North America, always harrying the Struan trade routes and customers. Since the American war began last year, McFay, along with other Directors of Struan's, had been getting worrisome reports about failures amongst their extensive American interests, both North and South, where Culum Struan had invested heavily. "If Old Man Brock

nd son grace us with their presence, I've no doubt we would be
onored to give them supper."

Greyforth laughed without humor. "I doubt they'll have time, except
o inspect your books, when we take you over."

"You never will. If I have any news on the revolt I'll send word,
lease do likewise. Good night now." Overpolitely McFay raised his
at and walked away.

Greyforth laughed to himself, delighted with the seeds he had
lanted. The Old Man will be happy to harvest them, he thought,
earing them out by the roots.

Dr. Babcott trudged wearily along a corridor in the semi-darkness of
he Kanagawa Legation. He carried a small oil lamp and wore a
ressing gown over woolen pajamas. From somewhere downstairs a
lock chimed two o'clock. Absently he reached into his pocket and
hecked his fob watch, yawned, then knocked on a door. "Miss Ange-
ique?"

After a moment she called out sleepily, "Yes?"

"You wanted to know when Mr. Struan woke up."

"Ah, thank you." A moment, then the door was unbarred and
Angelique came out. Hair a little dishevelled and still drowsy, wearing
a robe over her nightdress. "How is he?"

"A little sick, and woozy," Babcott said, leading her back along the
corridor and downstairs to the surgery where the sickrooms were. "His
emperature and pulse rate are up a little, of course that's to be ex-
ected. I've given him a drug for the pain, but he's a fine, strong young
man and everything should be all right."

The first time she had seen Malcolm she had been shocked by his
ack of color, and appalled by the stench. She had never been in a
ospital or surgery before, or in a real sickroom. Apart from reading in
he Paris newspapers and journals about death and dying and illness
and the waves of plague and killing diseases—measles, smallpox,
yphus, cholera, pneumonia, meningitis, whooping cough, scarlet fe-
er, childbed fever and the like—that swept Paris and Lyon and other
ities and towns from time to time, she had had no close acquaintance
with sickness. Her health had always been good, her aunt and uncle
and brother equally blessed.

Shakily she had touched his forehead, moving the sweat-stained hair
out of his face, but repelled by the smell that surrounded the bed,
urried out.

In a room nearby Tyrer was sleeping comfortably. To her great relief

there was no smell here. She thought he had a pleasant sleeping fac
where Malcolm Struan had been tormented.

'Phillip saved my life, Doctor,' she had said. 'After Mr.—Mr. Can
terbury, I was—I was paralyzed and Phillip he flung his horse in th
assassin's path and gave me time to escape. I was—I can't describ
how awful . . .'

'What was the man like? Could you recognize him?'

'I don't know. He was just a native, young I think, but I don't know
it's difficult to tell their ages and he was the—the first I'd seen close
He wore a kimono with a short sword in his belt, and the big one, al
bloody and ready again to . . .' Her eyes had filled with tears.

Babcott had gentled her and showed her a room, gave her some te
with a touch of laudanum, and promised he would call her the momen
Struan awoke.

And now he's awake, she thought, her feet leaden, nausea welling u
inside her, head aching and filled with vile pictures. I wish I hadn'
come here. Henri Seratard told me to wait until tomorrow, Captai
Marlowe was against it, everyone, so why did I plead so ardently wit
the Admiral? I don't know, we're jus' good friends, not lovers o
engaged or . . .

Or do I begin to love him, or was I only consumed with bravado
playacting, because this whole horrid day has been like a melodram
by Dumas, the nightmare at the road not real, the Settlement inflame
not real, Malcolm's message arriving at sunset not real: *'Please com
and see me as soon as you can,'* written by the doctor on his behalf—
me not real, just playacting the part of the heroine. . . .

Babcott stopped. "Here we are. You'll find him rather tired, Made
moiselle. I'll just make sure he's all right, then I'll leave you alone for
minute or two. He may drop off because of the drug, but don't worry
and if you want me I'll be in the surgery next door. Don't tax him, o
yourself, or worry about anything—don't forget you've had a rotte
time too."

She steeled herself, fixed a smile on her face and followed him in
"Hello, Malcolm, *mon cher.*"

"Hello." Struan was very pale, and had aged, but his eyes wer
clear.

The doctor chattered pleasantly, peered at him, quickly took hi
pulse, felt his forehead, half nodded to himself, said that the patien
was doing fine and left.

"You're so beautiful," Struan said, his robust voice now just thread, feeling strange, floating yet nailed to the cot and the sweat-sodden straw mattress.

She went closer. The smell was still there as much as she tried to pretend it was not. "How do you feel? I'm so sorry you're hurt."

"Joss," he said, using a Chinese word that meant fate, luck, the will of the gods. "You're so beautiful."

"Ah, *chéri,* oh how I wish all this had never happened, that I'd never asked to go for a ride, never wanted to visit to the Japans."

"Joss. It's . . . it's the next day, isn't it?"

"Yes, the attack was yesterday afternoon."

It seemed to be difficult for his brain to translate her words into usable form, and equally difficult to compose words and say them, as she was finding it equally difficult to stay. "Yesterday? That's a life-time ago. Have you seen Phillip?"

"Yes, yes, I saw him earlier but he was asleep. I'll see him as soon as I leave you, *chéri.* In fact I'd better go now, the doctor said not to tire you."

"No, don't go yet, please. Listen, Angelique, I don't know when I'll be—be fit to travel, so . . ." Momentarily his eyes closed against a barb of pain but it left him. When he focused on her again, he saw her fear and misread it. "Don't worry, McFay will see that you're esc—escorted safely back to Hong Kong, so please don't worry."

"Thank you, Malcolm, yes, I think I should. I'll return tomorrow or the next day." She saw the sudden disappointment and added at once, "Of course you'll be better then, and we can go together and, oh yes, Henri Seratard sent his condolences . . ."

She stopped, aghast, as a great pain took him and his face twisted and he tried to double up but could not, his insides tried to cast out the foul poison of the ether that seemed to permeate every pore and brain cell he possessed but could not—his stomach and bowels already empty of everything possible—each spasm tearing at his wounds, every cough ripping more than the last with only a little putrid liquid coming out for all the torment.

In panic she whirled for the doctor and fumbled for the door handle.

"It's all right, Ange—Angelique," said the voice that she hardly recognized now. "Stay a . . . moment more."

He saw the horror on her face and again misread it, seeing it as anxiety, a vast depth of compassion, and love. His fear left him and he lay back to gather his strength. "My darling, I'd hoped, I'd hoped so very much . . . of course you know I've loved you from the first

moment." The spasm had sapped his strength but his complete belie
that he had seen in her what he had prayed for, gave him great peace. "
can't seem to think straight but I wanted . . . to see you to tell you . .
Christ, Angelique, I was petrified of the operation, petrified of the
drugs, petrified of dying and not waking up before I saw you again. I've
never been so petrified, never."

"I'd be petrified too—oh, Malcolm, this is all so awful." Her skin
felt clammy and her head ached even more and she was afraid she
would be sick any moment. "The doctor assured me and everyone that
you'll be well soon!"

"I don't care now that I know you love me, if I die that's joss and in
my family we know we—we can't escape joss. You're my lucky star,
my lodestone, I . . . knew it from the first moment. We'll marry . . ."
The words trailed off. His ears were ringing and his eyes misted a little,
eyelids flickering as the opiate took hold, sliding him into the nether
world where pain existed but was transformed into painlessness.
"Marry in springtime. . . ."

"Malcolm, listen," she said quickly, "you're not going to die and
. . . alors, I must be honest with you . . ." Then the words began
pouring out, "I don't want to marry yet, I'm not sure if I love you, I'm
just not sure, you'll have to be patient, and if I do or do not, I don't think
I can ever live in this awful place, or Hong Kong, in fact I know I can't,
I won't, I can't, I know I'd die, the thought of living in Asia horrifies
me, the stench and the awful people. I'm going back to Paris where I
belong, as soon as I can and I'm never coming back, never, never,
never."

But he had heard none of it. He was in dreams now, not seeing her,
and he murmured, "Many sons, you and I . . . so happy you love me . .
prayed for . . . so now . . . live forever in the Great House on the Peak.
Your love has banished fear, fear of death, always afraid of death,
always so near, the twins, little sister Mary, dead so young, my brother,
father almost dead . . . grandfather another violent death, but now . .
now . . . all changed . . . marry in springtime. Yes?"

His eyes opened. For an instant he saw her clearly, saw the stretched
face and wringing hands and revulsion and he wanted to shriek, What's
the matter, for God's sake, this is only a sickroom and I know the
blanket's sodden with sweat and I'm lying in a little urine and dung and
everything stinks but that's because I'm cut, for Christ's sake, I've only
been cut and now I'm sewn up and well again, well again, well
again. . . .

But none of the words came out and he saw her say something and erk the door open and run away but this was just nightmare, the good dreams beckoning. The door swung on its hinges and the noise it made echoed and echoed and echoed: well again well again well again. . . .

She was leaning against the door to the garden, gulping the night air, trying to regain her poise. Mother of God, give me strength and give that man some peace and let me leave this place quickly.

Babcott came up behind her. "He's all right, not to worry. Here, drink this," he said compassionately, giving her the opiate. "It'll settle you and help you sleep."

She obeyed. The liquid tasted neither good nor bad.

"He's sleeping peacefully. Come along. It's bedtime for you too." He helped her upstairs, back to her room. At the door he hesitated. "Sleep well. You will sleep well."

"I'm afraid for him, very afraid."

"Don't be. In the morning he'll be better, you'll see."

"Thank you, I'm all right now. He . . . I think Malcolm thinks he's going to die. Is he?"

"Certainly not, he's a strong young man and I'm sure soon he'll be as right as rain." Babcott repeated the same platitude he had said a thousand times, and did not tell the truth: I don't know, you never know, now it's up to God.

And yet, most times he knew it was correct to give the loved one hope and take away the burden of increased worry, though not correct or fair to make God responsible if the patient lived or died. Even so, if you're helpless, if you've done your best and are convinced that your best and the best knowledge are not good enough, what else can you do and stay sane? How many young men have you seen like this one and dead in the morning or the next day—or recovered if that was God's will? Was it? I think it's lack of knowledge. And then God's will. If there is a God.

Involuntarily, he shivered. "Good night, not to worry."

"Thank you." She put the bar in place and went to the window, pushed open the heavy shutters. Tiredness welled over her. The night air was warm and kind, the moon high now. She took off her robe and wearily towelled herself dry, aching for sleep. Her nightdress was damp and clung to her and she would have preferred to change but she had not brought another. Below, the garden was large and shadow-struck, trees here and there and a tiny bridge over a tiny stream. A breeze caressed the treetops. Many shadows in the moonlight.

Some moved, now and then.

5

THE TWO YOUTHS SAW HER THE moment she appeared in the garden doorway forty yards away. Their ambush was well chosen and gave them a good view of the whole garden as well as the main gate, the guard house and the two sentries they had been watching. At once they crept deeper into the foliage, astonished to see her, even more astonished by the tears coursing her cheeks.

Shorin whispered, "What's the matt—"

He stopped. A wandering patrol of a sergeant and two soldiers, the first to enter their trap, rounded the far corner of the grounds, approaching them on the path that skirted the walls. They readied, then became motionless, their black, nearly skintight clothes covered all of their bodies except their eyes and made them almost invisible.

The patrol passed within five feet and the two shishi could have attacked easily and safely from this ambush. Shorin—the hunter, the fighter and leader in battle where Ori was the thinker and planner—had selected the blind, but Ori decided they would only attack a one- or two-man patrol, unless there was an emergency or they were prevented from breaking into the armory: 'Whatever we do this time must be silent,' he had said earlier. 'And patient.'

'Why?'

'This is their Legation. According to their custom that means it is their land, their territory—it is guarded by real soldiers, so we're encroaching on them. If we succeed, we will frighten them very much. If they catch us we fail.'

From the ambush they watched the departing patrol, noting the silent, careful way the men moved. Ori whispered uneasily, "We've never seen these sort before—soldiers so well trained and disciplined. In a battle, massed, we would have a hard time against them and their guns."

Shorin said, "We'll always win—we'll have guns soon, one way or another, and anyway bushido and our courage will swamp them. We can beat them easily." He was very confident. "We should have killed that patrol and taken their guns."

I'm glad we didn't, Ori thought, deeply unsettled. His arm ached badly and though he feigned indifference he knew that he could not sustain a long sword-fight. "If it wasn't for our clothes they would have seen us." His eyes went back to the girl.

"We could have killed all three easily. Easily. And grabbed their carbines and gone over the wall again."

"These men are very good, Shorin, not ox-headed merchants." Ori kept the aggravation out of his voice, as always, not wanting to offend his friend or wound his sensitive pride, needing his qualities as much as Shorin needed his—he had not forgotten Shorin had deflected the bullet that would have killed him on the Tokaidō. "We've plenty of time. Dawn's still at least two candles away." This was approximately four hours. He motioned at the doorway. "Anyway, she would have given the alarm."

Shorin sucked in his breath, cursing himself. "Eeee, stupid! I'm stupid, you're right—again. So sorry."

Ori gave her all of his attention: what is it about that woman that troubles me, fascinates me? he asked himself.

Then they saw the giant appear beside her. From information they had been given at the Inn they knew this was the famous English doctor who achieved miracle healings for any seeking his services, Japanese as well as his own people. Ori would have given much to understand what the doctor said to the girl. She dried her tears, obediently drank what he offered her, then he guided her back into the hallway, closing and barring the door.

Ori muttered, "Astounding—the giant, and the woman."

Shorin glanced at him, hearing undercurrents that further perturbed him, still angry with himself for forgetting the girl when the patrol was nearby. He could see only his friend's eyes and read nothing from them. "Let's go on to the armory," he whispered impatiently, "or attack the next patrol, Ori."

"Wait!" Taking great care not to make a sudden movement that might be noticed, Ori lifted his black-gloved hand, more to ease his arm than to wipe the sweat away. "Katsumata taught patience, tonight Hiraga counselled the same."

Earlier when they had reached the Inn of the Midnight Blossoms, they had found to their joy that Hiraga, their friend and the greatly admired leader of all Choshu shishi, was also staying there. News of their attack had arrived.

'The attack was perfectly timed, though you could not know it,' Hiraga had said warmly. He was a handsome man of twenty-two and tall for a Japanese. 'It will be like a stick plunged into the Yokohama hornets' nest. Now gai-jin will swarm, they're bound to go against the Bakufu who won't, cannot, do anything to appease them. If only the gai-jin retaliate against Yedo! If they did that, and smashed it, that would be the signal for us to seize the Palace Gates! Once the Emperor is free all daimyos will rebel against the Shōgunate and destroy it and all Toranagas. *Sonno-joi!*'

They had toasted *sonno-joi* and Katsumata who had saved them, taught most of them and served *sonno-joi* secretly and wisely. Ori had whispered their plan to Hiraga to steal arms.

'Eeee, Ori, it is a good idea and possible,' Hiraga said thoughtfully, 'if you are patient and choose the perfect moment. Such weapons could be valuable on some operations. Personally, guns disgust me—garrote, sword or knife please me better—safer, silent, and much more frightening, whoever the target—daimyo or barbarian. I'll help. I can give you a plan of the grounds and ninja clothes.'

Ori and Shorin brightened. 'You can get them for us?'

'Of course.' Ninja were a highly secret tong of expertly trained assassins who operated almost exclusively at night, their special black clothes helping to fuel the legend of their invisibility. 'At one time we were going to burn the Legation building.' Hiraga laughed and emptied another flask of saké, the warmed wine making his tongue looser than normal. 'But we decided not to, that it was more valuable to keep it under observation. Often I've gone there disguised as a gardener or at night as a ninja—it's surprising what you can learn, even with simple English.'

'Eeee, Hiraga-san, we never knew you could speak English,' Ori said, astounded by the revelation. 'Where did you learn it?'

'Where else can you learn gai-jin qualities if not from gai-jin? He was a Dutchman from Deshima, a linguist who spoke Japanese, Dutch and English. My grandfather wrote a petition to our daimyo suggesting that one such man should be allowed to come to Shimonoseki, at their cost, to teach Dutch and English for an experimental one year, trade would come afterwards. Thank you,' Hiraga said as Ori politely refilled his cup. 'Gai-jin are all so gullible—but such foul money worshippers. This is the sixth year of the "experiment" and we still only trade for what we want, when we can afford them—guns, cannon, ammunition, shot and certain books.'

'How is your revered grandfather?'

'In very good health. Thank you for asking.' Hiraga bowed in appreciation. Their bow in return was lower.

How wonderful to have such a grandfather, Ori thought, such a protection for all your generations—not like us who have to struggle to survive daily, are hungry daily, and have desperate trouble to pay our taxes. What will Father and Grandfather think of me now: ronin, and my so-needed one koku forfeit? 'I would be honored to meet him,' he said. 'Our *shoya* is not like him.'

For many years Hiraga's grandfather, an important peasant farmer near Shimonoseki and secret supporter of *sonno-joi,* had been a shoya. A shoya, the appointed, or hereditary, leader of a village or grouping of villages with great influence and magisterial power and responsibility for tax assessments and collection, was at the same time the only buffer and protector of peasants and farmers against any unfair practices of the samurai overlord within whose fief the village or villages lay.

Farmers and some peasants owned and worked the land but by law could not leave it. Samurai owned all the produce and the sole right to carry weapons, but by law could not own land. So each depended on the other in an inevitable, never-ending spiral of suspicion and distrust—the balance of how much rice or produce to be rendered in tax, year by year, and how much retained, always an incredibly delicate compromise.

The shoya had to keep the balance. The advice of the best was sometimes sought on matters outside the village by his immediate overlord, or higher, even by the daimyo himself. Hiraga's grandfather was one of these.

Some years ago he had been permitted to purchase goshi samurai status for himself and his descendants in one of the daimyo's offerings—a customary ploy of all daimyos, normally debt ridden, to raise extra revenue from acceptable supplicants. The daimyo of Choshu was no exception.

Hiraga laughed, the wine in his head now. 'I was chosen for this

Dutchman's school, and many a time I regretted the honor, English is so foul-sounding and difficult.'

'Were there many of you at the school?' Ori asked.

Through the saké haze a warning sounded and Hiraga realized he was volunteering far too much private information. How many Choshu students were at the school was Choshu business and secret, and while he liked and admired both Shorin and Ori they were still Satsumas, aliens, who were not always allies, but frequently enemy and always potential enemies.

'Just three of us to learn English,' he said softly as though telling a secret, instead of thirty, the real figure. Inwardly alert he added, 'Listen, now that you're ronin, like me and most of my comrades, we must work closer together. I am planning something in three days that you can help us with.'

'Thank you, but we must wait for word from Katsumata.'

'Of course, he is your Satsuma leader.' Hiraga added thoughtfully, 'But at the same time, Ori, don't forget you're ronin and will be ronin until we win, don't forget we're the spearhead of *sonno-joi*, we're the doers, Katsumata risks nothing. We must—must—forget that I am Choshu and you two Satsumas. We've got to help each other. It's a good idea to follow your Tokaidō attack tonight and steal guns. Kill one or two guards inside the Legation, if you can, that will be a huge provocation! If you could do it all silently and leave no trace, even better. Anything to provoke them.'

With Hiraga's information it had been easy to infiltrate the temple, to count the dragoons and other soldiers and to find the perfect lair. Then the girl had unexpectedly appeared, and the giant, and then they had gone back inside and ever since both shishi had been staring at the garden door, glazed.

"Ori, now what do we do?" Shorin asked, his voice edged.

"We stick to the plan."

The minutes passed anxiously. When the shutters on the first floor opened and they saw her in the window both knew that a new element had come into their future. Now she was brushing her hair with a silver-handled brush. Listlessly.

Shorin said throatily, "She doesn't look so ugly in moonlight. But with those breasts, eeee, you'd bounce off."

Ori did not reply, his eyes riveted.

Suddenly she hesitated and looked down. Directly at them. Though there was no chance she could have seen or heard them, their hearts picked up a beat. They waited, hardly breathing. Another exhausted yawn. She continued brushing a moment, then put down the brush, seemingly so close that Ori felt he could almost reach out and touch her, seeing in the light from the room details of embroidery on the silk, nipples taut beneath, and the haunted expression he had glimpsed yesterday—was it only yesterday?—that had stopped the blow that would have ended her.

A last strange glance at the moon, another stifled yawn, and she pulled the shutters to. But did not close them completely. Or bar them.

Shorin broke the silence and said what was in both their minds. "It would be easy to climb up there."

"Yes. But we came here for guns and to create havoc. We . . ." Ori stopped, his mind flowing into the sudden glimmering of a new and wonderful diversion, a second chance, greater than the first.

"Shorin," he whispered, "if you silenced her, took her but didn't kill her, just left her unconscious to tell of the taking, leaving a sign linking us to the Tokaidō, then together we kill one or two soldiers and vanish with or without their guns—*inside their Legation*—wouldn't that make them mad with rage?"

The breath hissed out of Shorin's lips at the beauty of the idea. "Yes, yes, it would, but better to slit her throat and write 'Tokaidō' in her blood. You go, I'll guard here, safer," and when Ori hesitated he said, "Katsumata said we were wrong to hesitate. Last time you hesitated. Why hesitate?"

It was a split-second decision, then Ori was running for the building, a shadow among many shadows. He gained the lee and began to climb.

Outside the guard house, one of the soldiers said softly, "Don't look around, Charlie, but I think I saw someone running for the house."

"Christ, get the Sergeant, careful now."

The soldier pretended to stretch, then strolled into the guard house. Quickly but cautiously he shook Sergeant Towery awake and repeated what he had seen, or thought he had seen.

"What did the bugger look like?"

"I just caught the movement, Sar'nt, 'least I think I did, I'm not sure like, it might've been a bloody shadder."

"All right, me lad, let's take a look." Sergeant Towery awoke the Corporal and another soldier and posted them. Then he led the other two into the garden.

"It were about there, Sar'nt."

Shorin saw them coming. There was nothing he could do to warn Ori who was almost at the window, still well camouflaged by his clothes and the shadows. He watched him reach the sill, ease one of the shutters wider and vanish inside. The shutter moved slowly back into place. Karma, he thought, and turned to his own plight.

Sergeant Towery had stopped in the center of the path, and was carefully scanning the surroundings and up at the building. Many of the shutters on the upper story were open and unbarred, so he was not concerned, one of them creaking in the small wind. The garden door was locked.

At length he said, "Charlie, you take that side." He pointed near to where the ambush was hidden. "Nogger, you go opposite, flush 'em out if any's there. Keep your bloody eyes open. Fix bayonets!" He was obeyed instantly.

Shorin eased his sword in its scabbard, the blade also blackened for the night foray, then settled himself into attack position, his throat tight.

The moment Ori had slid into the room, he checked the only door and saw that it was barred, that she was still asleep, then he unsheathed his short stabbing sword and darted for the bed. It was a four-poster, the first he had ever seen, everything about it strange, its height and heavy permanence, posts, curtains, bedclothes, and for a second he wondered what it would be like to sleep in one, so high off the ground, instead of the way Japanese slept, on futons—light, square mattresses of straw—laid out at night and put away by day.

His heart was racing and he tried to keep his breathing soft, not wanting to awaken her yet, not knowing she was deeply drugged. The room was dark but moonlight came in through the shutters and he saw her long, fair hair flowing over her shoulders and the swell of her breasts and limbs under the sheet. A perfume surrounded her, intoxicating him.

Then the click of the bayonets and muttered voices from the garden . . . For a split second he was petrified. Blindly he poised the knife to end her, but she did not stir. Her breathing remained regular.

He hesitated, then padded noiselessly to the shutters and peered out. He saw the soldiers. Did they see me, or notice Shorin? he asked himself in panic.

If so then I'm trapped, but that doesn't matter. I can still accomplish what I came to accomplish and perhaps they'll go away—I have two exits, the door and the window. Patience, Katsumata always advised. Use your head, wait calmly, then strike without hesitation and escape when the moment arrives, as it always will. Surprise is your best weapon!

His stomach twisted. One of the soldiers was heading for their hiding place. Even though Ori knew exactly where Shorin was he could not pick him out. Breathlessly he waited to see what would happen. Perhaps Shorin will draw them off. Whatever happens, she dies, he promised himself.

Shorin watched the soldier approaching, hopelessly trying to fathom a way out of the trap and cursing Ori. They must have spotted him! If I kill this dog there's no way I can reach the others before they shoot me. I can't get to the wall without being seen.

Stupid of Ori to change the plan, of course they spotted him. I told him that woman was trouble—he should have killed her at the road. . . . Perhaps this barbarian will miss me and give me enough time to rush for the wall.

The moonlight caught the long bayonet in flashes as the soldier quietly probed the foliage, lifting it apart here and there to see better.

Closer and closer. Six feet, five, four, three . . .

Shorin stayed motionless, his face covering now practically masking his eyes, and held his breath. The soldier almost brushed him in passing, then went on again, stopped a moment, on a few more paces, probing again, then on again and Shorin began quietly to breathe once more. He could feel the sweat on his back but he knew he was safe now and in a few moments would be safely over the wall.

From his position Sergeant Towery could watch both soldiers. He held a cocked rifle loose in the hands, but was as unsure as they were, not wanting to give a false alarm. The night was fine, wind slight, moonlight strong. Easy to imagine shadows to be enemy in this stinking place, he thought. Christ, wish we were back in good old London town.

"Evening, Sergeant Towery, what's up?"

"Evening, sir." Towery saluted smartly. It was the Dragoon officer, Pallidar. He explained what he had been told. "Might have been a shadow, better safe than sorry."

"Better get extra men and we'll make sure that—"

At that moment the young soldier nearest the ambush site whirled on guard, his musket levelled. "Sergeant!" he called out in excitement and terror, "the bastard's here!"

Already Shorin was rushing to the attack, his killing sword on high but the soldier's training took over for that instant and the bayonet expertly held Shorin off as the others came running, Pallidar jerking out his revolver. Again Shorin pressed the attack but was inhibited by the length of the rifle and bayonet, then slipped, scrambled out of the way of the bayonet lunge and fled through the foliage for the wall. The young soldier charged after him.

"Watchiiit!" Towery shouted as the young man crashed into the undergrowth, glands now in total control propelling him to the kill. But the soldier did not hear the warning and went into the bushes and died, the short sword deep in his chest. Shorin jerked it out, quite sure there was no escape, the others almost on him.

"*Namu Amida Butsu*"—In the Name of the Buddha Amida—he gasped through his own fear, commending his spirit to Buddha, and screamed "*Sonno-joi!*" not to warn Ori but to make his last statement. Then, with desperate strength, he buried the knife in his own throat.

Ori had seen most of this but not the end. The moment the soldier had shouted and charged he had rushed pell-mell for the bed, expecting her to be startled awake, but to his astonishment she had not moved, nor had the calm tempo of her breathing changed, so he stood over her, knees trembling, waiting for her eyes to open, expecting a trick, wanting her to see him and see the knife before he used it. Then there was the wail of "*sonno-joi*" and he knew Shorin had gone onwards, then more noise. But still she did not stir. His lips came back from his teeth, his breathing strangled. Abruptly he could stand the strain no longer so he shook her angrily with his wounded arm, heedless of the pain, put the knife to her throat, ready to obliterate the scream.

Still she did not stir.

To him it was all dreamlike and he watched himself shake her again and still nothing, then suddenly he remembered that the doctor had given her a drink and he thought, One of those drugs, the new Western drugs Hiraga told us about, and he gasped, trying to assimilate this new knowledge. To make sure, he shook her again, but she only muttered and turned deeper into the pillow.

He went back to the window. Men were carrying the soldier's body out of the foliage. Then he saw them drag Shorin into the open by one of his feet like the carcass of an animal. Now the bodies were side by side, both strangely alike in death. Other men were arriving and he heard people calling from some windows. An officer stood over Shorin's body. One of the soldiers tore off the black head-covering and face mask. Shorin's eyes were still open, features twisted, the knife hilt protruding. More voices and other men arriving.

Movement within the house now and in the corridor. His tension soared. For the tenth time he made sure the door bar was secure and could not be opened from the outside, then moved into ambush behind the curtains of the four-poster, near enough to reach her whatever happened.

Footsteps and knocking on the door. Splash of light under it from oil or candle lamps. Louder knocking and voices raised. His knife readied.

"Mademoiselle, are you all right?" It was Babcott.

"Mademoiselle!" Marlowe called out. "Open the door!" More pounding, much louder.

"It's my sleeping draft, Captain. She was very upset, poor lady, and needed sleep. I doubt if she'll wake up."

"If she doesn't I'll break the bloody door down to make sure. Her shutters are open, by God!" More heavy pounding.

Angelique opened her eyes blearily. "*Que se passe-t-il?* What is it?" she mumbled, more asleep than awake.

"Are you all right? *Tout va bien?*"

"*Bien? Moi? Bien sûr . . . Pourquoi? Qu'arrive-t-il?*"

"Open the door a moment. *Ouvrez la porte, s'il vous plaît, c'est moi,* Captain Marlowe."

Grumbling and disoriented, she sat up in the bed. To his shock, Ori watched himself allowing her to reel out of bed and totter to the door. It took her a little time to pull back the bar and half open the door, holding on to it for balance.

Babcott, Marlowe and a marine held candle lights. The flames flickered in the draft. They gaped at her wide-eyed. Her nightdress was very French, very fine, and diaphanous.

"We, er, we just wanted to see you were all right, Mademoiselle. We, er, we caught a man in the shrubbery," Babcott said hurriedly, "nothing to worry about." He could see that she hardly understood what he was saying.

Marlowe pulled his gaze off of her body and looked beyond into the room. "*Excusez-moi,* Mademoiselle, *s'il vous plaît,*" he said, embarrassed, his accent tolerable, and eased past her to inspect. Nothing under the bed except a chamber pot. Curtains behind the bed this side revealed nothing—Christ, what a woman! Nowhere else to hide, no doors or cupboards. The shutters creaked in the wind. He opened them wide. "Pallidar! Anything more down there?"

"No," Pallidar called back. "No sign of anyone else. It's quite possible he was the only one and the soldier saw him moving about. But check all the rooms this side!"

Marlowe nodded and muttered a curse and, "What the hell do you think I'm doing?" Behind him the four-poster curtains moved in the slight breeze, uncovering Ori's feet in his black *tabi,* Japanese shoe-socks. Marlowe's candle guttered and blew out, and when he slid the shutter bar into place and turned back again he did not notice the *tabi* in the deep shadows beside the bed, or much of anything else, only Angelique silhouetted in the doorway candlelight hardly awake. He could see every part of her and the sight drew his breath away.

"Everything's fine," he said, even more embarrassed because he had scrutinized her, enjoying her when she was defenseless. Pretending to be brisk, he walked back. "Please bolt the door and, er, sleep well," he said, wanting to stay.

Even more disoriented, she mumbled and closed the door. They waited until they heard the bar grate home in its slots. Babcott said hesitantly, "I doubt if she'll even remember opening the door." The marine wiped the sweat off, saw Marlowe looking at him and could not resist a leering beam.

"What the hell're you so happy about?" Marlowe said, knowing very well.

"Me, sir? Nuffink, sir," the marine said instantly, leer gone, innocence in its wake. Sodding officers is all the same, he thought wearily. Mucker Marlowe's as horny as the rest of us, his eyes popped and he near ate her up, short and curlies, wot's underneath and the best bloody knockers I ever hoped to see! The lads'll never believe about her knockers. "Yessir, mum's the word, yessir," he said virtuously when Marlowe told him to say nothing about what they had seen. "Yor right, sir, again, sir, notta word from me lips," he assured him, and trailed along to the next room, thinking of hers.

Angelique was leaning against the door, trying to make sense of what was happening—difficult to put everything in order, a man in the garden, what garden, but Malcolm was in the garden of the Great House, no he's downstairs wounded, no that's a dream and he said something about living in the Great House and marriage . . . Malcolm, was he the man, the one who touched me? No, he told me he would die. Silly, the doctor said he was fine, everyone said fine, why fine? Why not good or excellent or fair? Why?

She gave up, her craving for sleep overwhelming. The moon was shining through the slats of the shutters and she stumbled through the bars of light to the bed, gratefully collapsed into the soft down mat-

ress. With a great sigh of contentment she pulled the sheet half over
her and turned on her side. In seconds she was deeply asleep.

Silently Ori slid out of his hiding place, astonished that he was still
alive. Even though he had pressed himself and his swords flat against
the wall, any proper search should have disclosed him. He saw that the
door bar was in place, the shutters barred, the girl breathing heavily,
one arm under the pillow, the other on the sheet.

Good. She can wait, he thought. First, how to get out of this trap?
The window or the door?

Not being able to see through the slats, he moved the bar back softly
and pushed one side open a fraction, then the other. Soldiers were still
milling below. Dawn was almost three hours away. Clouds building up,
drifted towards the moon. Shorin's body lay crumpled on the path like
a dead animal. For a moment he was surprised they had left his head
on, then remembered it was not gai-jin custom to take heads for
viewing or for counting.

Difficult to escape that way and not be seen. If they don't slacken
their vigilance I'll have to open the door and try inside. That means
leaving the door open. Better to go by the window if I can.

He craned out carefully and saw a small ledge below the window
that led under another window, then around the building—this was a
corner room. His excitement mounted. Soon clouds will cover the
moon. I'll escape then. I will escape! *Sonno-joi!* Now her.

Making no noise, he rearranged the bar so the shutters were slightly
open, then came back to the bed.

His long sword was still sheathed and he put it within easy reach on
the rumpled white silk counterpane. White, he thought. White sheet,
white flesh, white the color of death. Apt. Perfect to write on. What
should it be? His name?

Without haste he pulled the sheet away from her. The nightdress was
beyond his ken, alien, designed to hide everything and nothing. Limbs
and breasts, so large compared to the few bedmates he had known, legs
long and straight with none of the elegant curve he was used to from
the women's many years of kneeling-sitting. Again, her perfume. As
his eyes explored her he felt himself stirring.

With the others it had been very different. Excitement minimal.
Much banter and deft professionalism. Quickly consummated, and
usually in a saké haze to blur their age. Now there was limitless time.
She was young, and out of his world. His ache increased. And the
throb.

Wind creaked the shutters but there was no danger there, nor was

there any in the house. Everything quiet. She lay half on her stomach
A deft, soft push, and another, and obediently she moved onto her
back, her head comfortably to one side, hair cascading. Deep sigh, snug
in the embrace of the mattress. A small golden cross at her throat

He leaned over and put the tip of his razor-sharp sword-knife under
the delicate lace at the neck, lifted slightly and settled the blade against
the tension of the garment. The material parted willingly and fell away
To her feet.

Ori had never seen a woman so revealed. Or been so constricted. The
throbbing intensified like never before. The tiny cross shone. Involun
tarily her hand stirred lazily and went between her legs, resting there
comfortably. He lifted it away, then moved one ankle from the other
Gently.

6

JUST BEFORE DAWN SHE AWOKE.
But not completely.

The drug was still with her, dreams still with her, strange violent dreams, erotic and crushing and wonderful and hurting and sensuous and awful and never before experienced or so intense. Through the half-opened shutters she saw the eastern horizon blood red, weird suggestive cloud formations there that seemed to match etchings in her mind. As she moved to see them better there was a slight ache in her loins but she paid it no attention, instead letting her eyes dwell on the pictures in the sky and allowing her mind to drift back into the dreams that beckoned irresistibly. On the threshold of sleep she became aware she was naked. Languidly she pulled her nightdress around her and the sheet over her. And slept.

Ori was standing beside the bed. He had just moved out of the warmth. His ninja clothes were on the floor. And his loincloth. For a moment he looked down at her lying there, considering her a final time. So sad, he thought, last times are so sad. Then he picked up the short knife-sword and unsheathed it.

In the room downstairs Phillip Tyrer opened his eyes. His surroundings were unfamiliar, then he realized that he was still in the temple at Kanagawa, that yesterday had been terrible, the operation awful, his part despicable. "Babcott said I was in shock," he muttered, his mouth parched and bad-tasting. "Christ, does that excuse me?"

His shutters were ajar, a wind creaking them. He could see the dawn. Red sky in the morning, shepherd's warning.' Will there be a storm? He wondered, then sat up in the camp bed and checked the bandage on

his arm. It was clean, without fresh bloodstains, and he was greatly
relieved. Apart from the throb in his head and some soreness he felt
whole again. "Oh, God, I wish I'd acted better." He made an effort to
remember the aftermath of the operation but it was hazed. *I know I
cried. It didn't feel like crying, the tears flooded.*

With an effort he pushed the gloomy thoughts away. He got out of
bed and shoved the shutters open, strong now on his legs and hungry.
Nearby there was water in a jug and he splashed some on his face and
rinsed out his mouth and spat the water into the garden foliage. After
he had a little water, he felt better. The garden was empty, the air
smelling of rotting vegetation and low tide. From where he was he
could see a section of the temple walls and the garden but little else.
Through a gap in the trees he caught a glimpse of the guard house and
two soldiers there.

Now he noticed that he had been put to bed in his shirt and long
woolen underpants. His torn, bloodstained coat was over a chair, his
trousers and riding boots, filthy from the paddy, beside it.

Never mind, I'm lucky to be alive. He began to dress. *What about
Struan? And Babcott—soon I'll have to face him.*

There was no razor so he could not shave. Nor was there a comb.
Again never mind. He pulled on his boots. From the garden he could
hear the sound of birds and movement, a few distant shouts in Japanese, and dogs barking. But no sounds as in a normal town, an English
town, no morning cries of 'Hot Cross Buns-O' or 'Fresh water-O' or
'Colchester oysters, morning fresh, for sale, for sale-O,' or 'Direct
from the press, the latest chapter by Mr. Dickens, only a penny, only a
penny' or 'The *Times,* the *Times,* read all about Mr. Disraeli's great
scandal, read all about it. . . .'

Will I be dismissed? he asked himself, his stomach surging at the
thought of returning home in ignominy, a disaster, a failure, no longer a
member of Her Illustrious Majesty's Foreign Office, representative of
the greatest Empire the world has ever known. *What will Sir William
think of me? And what about her? Angelique? Thank God she escaped
to Yokohama—will she ever talk to me again when she hears?*

Oh, God, what am I going to do?

Malcolm Struan was also awake. A few moments before, some
sixth sense of danger, a noise from outside, had wakened him, though
lying here it felt as though he had been awake for hours. He lay on
the camp bed, aware of the day and the operation and that he had
been severely wounded and that the chances were that he would

die. Every breath caused a sharp, tearing pain. Even the slightest movement.

But I'm not going to think about pain, only about Angelique and that she loves me and . . . But what about the bad dreams? Dreams of her hating me and running away. I hate dreams and being out of control, hate lying here, loathe being weak when I've always been strong, always brought up in the shadow of my hero, the great Dirk Struan, Green-eyed Devil. Oh, how I wish I had green eyes and could be so strong. He's my lodestone and I will be as good as him, I will.

As always, the enemy Tyler Brock is stalking us. Father and Mother try to keep most of the facts from me, but of course I've heard the rumors and know more than they think. Old Ah Tok, more mother to me than Mother—didn't she carry me until I was two and teach me Cantonese and about life and find me my first girl?—she whispers the rumors to me, so does Uncle Gordon Chen, who tells me facts. The Noble House is teetering.

Never mind, we'll deal with them. I will. That's what I'm trained for and have worked for all my life.

He moved the blanket aside and lifted his legs to stand, but pain stopped him. Again he tried and again failed. Never mind, he told himself weakly. Nothing to worry about, I'll do it later.

"More eggs, Settry?" Marlowe said, as tall as the Dragoon officer but not as broad in the shoulders. Both were patrician, sons of serving senior officers, well formed in the face, weathered, Marlowe more so.

"No, thanks," Settry Pallidar said. "Two's my limit. Must confess that I think the cooking here is vile. I told the servants I like my eggs well-done, not phlegmy, but they've sand for brains. Actually, damned if I can eat eggs unless they're on toast, on good English bread. They just don't taste the same. What do you think's going to happen, about Canterbury?"

Marlowe hesitated. They were in the Legation dining room at the vast oak table that could seat twenty, brought from England for just this purpose. The corner room was spacious and pleasing, windows open to the garden and the dawn. Three liveried Chinese servants served the two of them. Places laid for half a dozen. Fried eggs and bacon in silver salvers warmed by candles, roast chicken, cold salt ham and mushroom pie, a side of almost rancid beef, hardtack biscuits, a dried-apple pie. Beer, porter and tea. "The Minister should ask for immediate reparations and the murderers to be handed over at once, and when there's the inevitable delay, he should order the fleet against Yedo."

"Better that we land in force—we've troops enough—and occupy the capital, remove their king, what's he called? Ah yes, Shōgun, and appoint our own native ruler and make Japan a protectorate. Even better, for them, make it part of the Empire." Pallidar was very tired and had been awake most of the night. His uniform was unbuttoned but he was groomed and had shaved. He motioned to one of the servants. "Tea, please."

The neatly dressed young Chinese understood perfectly but he gaped at him, deliberately, for the amusement of the other servants. "Heya, Mass'er? Tea-ah? Wat for tea-ah you say, eh? Wancha cha, heya?"

"Oh, never mind, for Christ's sake!" Wearily Pallidar got up and went to the sideboard with his cup and poured his own tea while all the servants guffawed hugely but silently at the insolent foreign devil's loss of face, and then continued listening attentively to what they were saying. "It's a matter of military might, old boy. And I'll tell you frankly, the General will be bloody upset about losing a grenadier to a poxy assassin dressed like Ali Baba. He'll want—and we'll all want—revenge, by God."

"I don't know about a landing—the Navy can certainly blast a path for you but we've no idea how many samurai there are, nor anything about their strength."

"For God's sake, whatever they are, or it is, we can deal with them, they're only a bunch of backward natives. Of course we can deal with them. Just like in China. Can't understand why we don't annex China and have done with it."

All the servants heard this and understood this and all swore that when the Heavenly Kingdom possessed the guns and the ships to equal the barbarian guns and ships, they would help shove barbarian noses in their own dung and teach them a lesson to last a thousand generations. All of them were handpicked by Illustrious Chen, Gordon Chen, the Noble House compradore. "You wan'ta one piecee plenty good 'ggs Mass'er?" the most courageous one said, and beamed toothily, holding more of the deliberately phlegmy eggs under Pallidar's nose. "Werry good."

Pallidar shoved the salver away in disgust. "No, thanks. Listen Marlowe, I think . . ." He stopped as the door opened and Tyrer came in. "Oh, hello, you must be Phillip Tyrer from the Legation." He introduced himself, then Marlowe, and went on breezily, "Very sorry about your bad luck yesterday but I'm proud to shake your hand. Both

Mr. Struan and Miss Richaud told Babcott if it wasn't for you they'd both be dead."

"They did? Oh!" Tyrer could hardly believe his ears. "It—it all happened so fast. One moment everything was normal, the next we were running for our lives. I was frightened to death." Now that he had said it aloud he felt better, and even better when they brushed it aside as modesty, held out a chair for him and ordered the servants to bring him food.

Marlowe said, "When I checked you in the night you were dead to the world, we knew Babcott had sedated you, so I expect you haven't yet heard about our assassin."

Tyrer's stomach reeled. "Assassin?"

They told him. And about Angelique.

"She's here?"

"Yes, and what a brave lady she is." For a moment Marlowe was filled with the thought of her. He had no favored girl at home or anywhere, just a few eligible cousins but no special lady, and for the first time he was happy about it. Perhaps Angelique will stay and then . . . and then we'll see.

His excitement picked up. Just before steaming out of his home port of Plymouth a year ago, his father, Captain Richard Marlowe R.N. had said, 'You're twenty-seven, lad, you've your own ship now—albeit a stinkpot—you're the eldest and it's time you were married. When you get back from this Far East cruise you'll be over thirty, with any luck by then I'll be a Vice Admiral and I'll . . . well, I can allow you a few extra guineas, but for God's sake, don't tell your mother—or your brothers and sisters. It's time you made up your mind! What about your cousin Delphi? Her father's service, though only Indian Army.'

He had promised that on his return he would choose. Now perhaps he would not have to settle for second or third or fourth best. "Miss Angelique raised the alarm in the Settlement then insisted on coming here last night—Mr. Struan had asked her to see him urgently—seems he's not too good, pretty bad wound in fact, so I brought her. She's quite a lady."

"Yes." A curious silence took them, each knowing the other's thoughts. Phillip Tyrer broke it. "Why should an assassin come here?"

The other two heard the nervousness. "More devilment, I suppose," Pallidar said. "Nothing to worry about, we caught the bugger. Have you seen Mr. Struan this morning?"

"I peeked in but he was asleep, hope he's going to be all right. The op was not so good and . . ." Tyrer stopped, hearing an altercation outside. Pallidar went to the window followed by the others.

Sergeant Towery was shouting at a half-naked Japanese from the far side of the garden, beckoning him. "Hey, you, come 'ere!"

The man, apparently a gardener, was well built and young and twenty yards away. He wore only a loincloth and was carrying a bundle of sticks and branches over one shoulder, some half wrapped in a dirty black cloth, while he awkwardly scavenged for others. For a moment he stood erect, then began bobbing up and down, bowing abjectly towards the Sergeant.

"My God, these buggers have no sense of shame," Pallidar said distastefully. "Even the Chinese don't dress like that—nor Indians. You can see his privates."

"I'm told they dress like that even in winter, some of them," Marlowe said. "They don't seem to feel the cold."

Again Towery shouted and beckoned. The man kept on bowing, nodding vigorously, but instead of going towards him, seemingly he misinterpreted him and obediently turned away, still half-bowing, and scuttled away, heading for the corner of the building. As he passed their window he gazed at them for an instant, then once more bent double in a groveling obeisance and hurried towards the servants' quarters, almost hidden by foliage, and was gone.

"Curious," Marlowe said.

"What?"

"Oh, just that all that bowing and scraping seemed put-on." Marlowe turned and saw Tyrer's chalky face. "Christ Almighty, what's up?"

"I—I, that man, I think he, I'm not sure but I think he was one of them, one of the murderers at the Tokaidō, the one Struan shot. Did you see his shoulder, wasn't it bandaged?"

Pallidar was the first to react. He jumped out of the window, closely followed by Marlowe who had grabbed his sword. Together they hurtled for the trees. But they did not find him though they searched everywhere.

Now it was high noon. Again the soft knock on her bedroom door, again "Mademoiselle? Mademoiselle?" Babcott called out from the corridor, his voice soft, not wanting to awaken her unnecessarily, but she did not reply. She remained standing rock still in the center of the room and stared at the bolted door, hardly breathing, her robe tight around her, her face stark. The trembling began again.

"Mademoiselle?"

She waited. After a moment his footsteps died away and she exhaled, desperately trying to stop shaking, then resumed pacing to the shuttered windows and back to the bed and back to the window once more, pacing as she had been pacing for hours.

I've *got* to decide, she thought in misery.

When she awoke a second time, not remembering the first awakening, her mind was clear and she lay in the crumpled bed linen without moving, glad to be awake, rested, hungry, and thirsty for the first, glorious cup of coffee of the day served with some crusty fresh French bread that her Legation's chef made in Yokohama. But I'm not in Yokohama, I'm in Kanagawa, and today it will be just a cup of revolting English tea with milk.

Malcolm! Poor Malcolm, I do so hope he's better. We'll return to Yokohama today, I'll board the next steamer for Hong Kong, thence to Paris . . . but oh, what dreams I had, what dreams!

The fantasies of the night were still vivid and mixed up with other pictures of the Tokaidō and Canterbury's mutilation and Malcolm acting so strangely presuming that they would marry. The imagined smell of the surgery rose in her nostrils but she fought it away, yawned, and reached for her little timepiece which she had left on the bedside table.

With the slight movement came a small pain in her loins. For a moment she wondered if it presaged an early period, for she was not completely regular, but dismissed the thought as impossible.

The timepiece read 10:20. It was inset with lapis lazuli and had been her father's gift on her eighteenth birthday, July 8th, a little over two months ago in Hong Kong. So much has happened since then, she thought. I'll be so happy to be back in Paris, in civilization, never to return, never never nev—

Abruptly she realized that she was almost naked under the sheet. To her astonishment she found that her nightdress only clung to her arms and shoulders and was totally split down the front and scrambled up behind her. She lifted the two sides in disbelief. Wanting to see better, she slid out of bed to go to the window but again felt the slight soreness. Now in the day's light she noticed the telltale smear of blood on the sheet and found a trace between her legs.

"How can my period . . ."

She began counting days and recounting them but the addition made no sense. Her last period had stopped two weeks ago. Then she noticed that she was slightly moist and could not understand why—then her heart twisted and she almost fainted as her brain shouted that the dreams had not been dreams but real and that she had been violated while asleep.

'That's not possible! You must be mad—that's not possible,' she had gasped, fighting for air, fighting for space. 'Oh, God, let this be a dream, part of those dreams.' She groped for the bed, heart pounding. *'You're awake, this isn't a dream, you're awake!'*

She examined herself again, frantically, and then again but this time with more care. She had enough knowledge to know that there was no mistake about the moisture, or that her hymen was split. It was true. She had been raped.

The room began to spin. Oh, God, I'm ruined, life ruined, future ruined for no decent man, eligible man will marry me now that I'm soiled, marriage a girl's only way to better herself, have a happy future, any future, no other way . . .

When her senses settled and she could see and think, she found herself lying across the bed. Shakily she tried to reconstruct the night. I remember bolting the door.

She peered at it. The bar was still in place.

I remember Malcolm and the foulness of his room and running away from him, Phillip Tyrer sleeping peacefully, Dr. Babcott giving me the drink and going upstair—

The drink! Oh, God, I was drugged! If Babcott can operate with these drugs, of course it could happen, of course I would be helpless but that doesn't help me now! It happened! Say I get a child!

Again panic overwhelmed her. Tears gushed down her cheeks and she almost cried out. 'Stop it!' she muttered, making a supreme effort for control. 'Stop it! Don't make a sound, don't! You're alone, no one else can help, just you, you've got to think. What are you going to do? *Think!*' She took deep breaths, her heart hurting, and tried to slam her jumbled mind into order. Who was the man?

The bar's still in place so no one could have come through the door. Wait a minute, I remember vaguely . . . or was it part of the dream before the . . . I seem to remember opening the door to—to Babcott and, and the naval officer Marlowe . . . then barring it again. Yes, that's right! At least, I think that's right. Didn't he speak French . . . yes, he did, but badly, then they went away and I barred the door, I'm sure I did. But why did they knock on the door in the night?

She searched and re-searched her mind but could not find an answer, not truly sure this had happened, the night pictures slipping away. Some of them.

Concentrate!

If not through the door he came through the window. She squirmed around and saw that the shutter bar was on the floor, below the window, not in its slots.

So whoever it was got in through the window! Who? Marlowe, that Pallidar or even the good Doctor, I know they all want me. Who knew I was drugged? Babcott. He could have told the others but surely none of them would dare to be so evil, would dare risk the consequences of climbing up from the garden for of course I would shout from the rooftops . . .

Her whole being screamed a warning: *Be careful.* Your future depends on being careful and wise. Be careful.

Are you sure that this really happened in the night? What about the dreams? Perhaps . . . I won't think about them now but only a doctor would know for certain and that would have to be Babcott. Wait, you could, you could have ruptured that tiny piece of skin in your sleep, twisting in the nightmare—it was a nightmare, wasn't it? That has happened to some girls. Yes, but they'd still be virgin and that doesn't explain the moisture.

Remember Jeanette in the convent, poor silly Jeanette who fell in love with one of the tradesmen, and allowed him, and excitedly told us all about it later, all the details. She didn't become pregnant but she was found out and the next day she was gone forever and later we learned she'd been married off to a village butcher, the only man who would take her.

I didn't allow anything but that won't help me, a doctor would know for certain but that won't help me, and the idea of Babcott or any doctor being so intimate fills me with horror and then Babcott would share the secret. How could I trust him with such a secret? If it became known . . . I have to keep it secret! But how, how can you, and what then?

I'll answer that later. First, decide who the devil was. No, first clean yourself of this evil and then you will think better. *You've got to think clearly.*

With distaste she shook off the nightdress and threw it aside, then washed carefully and deeply, trying to remember all the contraceptive knowledge she possessed, what Jeanette had done successfully. Then she put on her robe and combed her hair. Using tooth powder, she cleaned her teeth. Only then did she look in her mirror. Very carefully she examined her face. It was without blemish. She loosed her robe. So were her limbs and breasts—nipples a little red. Again she looked deep into her mirror.

'No change, nothing. And everything.'

Then she noticed that the little gold cross she had worn forever, sleeping and waking, was gone. She searched the bed carefully, then underneath and all around. It was not buried in the bedclothes or under the pillows or caught in the curtains. Last chance—hiding in the lace of the coverlet. She picked it off the floor and went through it. Nothing.

Then she saw the three Japanese characters, crudely drawn on its whiteness, in blood.

Sunlight sparked off the gold cross. Ori was holding it in his fist by the thin chain, mesmerized.

"Why did you take it?" Hiraga asked.

"I don't know."

"Not killing the woman was a mistake. Shorin was right. It was a mistake."

"Karma."

They were safe in the Inn of the Midnight Blossoms and Ori had bathed and shaved and he looked back at Hiraga with level eyes and thought, You're not my master—I will tell you only what pleases me, nothing more.

He had told him about Shorin's death and climbing into the room, that she had slept soundly and had not awakened—but no more, only that he had hidden there safely, then had taken off his ninja clothes knowing he would be intercepted and had camouflaged his swords with them, shinned down into the garden with just enough time to gather some fallen branches, to pretend to be a gardener before he was spotted and, even after recognizing the man from the road, had managed to escape. But nothing more about her.

How can I express in mortal words and tell anyone that because of her I became one with the gods, that when I had spread her wide and *saw* her I was drunk with craving, that when I entered her, I entered her as a lover and not a rapist—I don't know why but I did, slowly, carefully, and her arms went around me and she shuddered and held on though she never truly awoke and she was so tight and I held back and back and then poured forth in a way inconceivable.

I never believed it could be so marvelous, so sensual, so satisfying, so final. The others were nothing compared to her. She made me reach the stars, but that is not why I left her alive. I thought about killing her very much. Then myself, there in the room. But that would have been only selfish, to die at the crest of happiness, so content.

Oh, how I wished to die. But my death belongs to *sonno-joi*. Only that. Not to me.

"Not killing her was a mistake," Hiraga said again, interrupting Ori's thought pattern. "Shorin was right, killing her would have achieved our plan, better than anything."

"Yes."

"Then why?"

I left her alive for the gods, if there are gods, he could have said but did not. They possessed me and made me do what I did and I thank them. Now I am complete. I know life, all that remains to know is death. I was her first and she will remember me forever even though she slept. When she wakes and sees my writing in my own blood, not hers, she will know. I want her to live forever. I will die soon. Karma.

Ori put the cross into a secret sleeve pocket of his kimono and drank more of the refreshing green tea, feeling utterly fulfilled and so alive.

"You said you had a raid?"

"Yes. We are going to burn the British Legation in Yedo."

"Good. Let it be soon."

"It is. *Sonno-joi!*"

At Yokohama, Sir William said angrily, "Tell them again, *for the last time, by God*, Her Majesty's Government demands immediate reparations of one hundred thousand pounds sterling in gold for allowing this unprovoked attack and murder of an Englishman—killing Englishmen is *kinjiru*, by God! And also we demand possession of the Satsuma murderers *within three days* or *we-will-take-definitive-action!*"

He was across the bay in the small, stuffy audience room of the British Legation in Yokohama, flanked by the Prussian, French and Russian Ministers, both Admirals, British and French, the General, all of them equally exasperated.

In line opposite, seated ceremoniously on chairs, were two local representatives of the Bakufu, the chief samurai of the Settlement Guard, and the Governor of Kanagawa in whose jurisdiction Yokohama lay. They wore wide pantaloons and kimonos, and over them the broad-shouldered, winglike mantle that was belted, and two swords. Clearly all were uncomfortable and inwardly furious. At dawn, armed soldiers had hammered on the door of the Customs Houses, in both Yokohama and Kanagawa, with rifle butts and unprecedented anger, summoning the highest officials and Governor to an immediate conference at noon, the haste also unprecedented.

Between the two sides the interpreters sat on cushions. The Japanese knelt, and the other, a Swiss, Johann Favrod, sat cross-legged, their common language Dutch.

The meeting had already been in progress for two hours—English translated into Dutch into Japanese, into Dutch into English and back again. All Sir William's questions were misunderstood, or parried or needed repeating several times, delays were 'requested' in a dozen different ways to 'consult higher authorities to institute examinations and investigations' and 'Oh, yes, in Japan examinations are quite different from investigations. His Excellency, the Governor of Kanagawa, explains in detail that . . .' and 'Oh, His Excellency, the Governor of Kanagawa, wishes to explain in detail that he has no jurisdiction over Satsuma which is a separate kingdom . . .' and 'Oh, but His Excellency, the Governor of Kanagawa, understands the accused drew pistols threateningly and are accused and guilty of not obeying Japanese ancient customs . . .' and 'How many foreigners did you say were in the foreign party who should have knelt . . .' and 'But our customs . . .'

Tedious, time-consuming, and complex lectures in Japanese by the Governor, put laboriously into far from fluent Dutch and retranslated into English.

"Make it blunt, Johann, exactly as I said it."

"I have, every time, Sir William, but I'm sure this cretin isn't interpreting accurately, either what you say or what the Jappers say."

"We know that, for Christ's sake, has it ever been different? Please get on with it."

Johann put the words into an exact translation. The Japanese interpreter flushed, asked for an explanation of the word 'immediate,' then carefully delivered a polite, appropriate, approximate translation he considered would be acceptable. Even then the Governor sucked in his breath at the rudeness. The silence increased. His fingers tapped a constant, irritated tattoo on his sword hilt, then he spoke shortly, three or four words. The translation was long.

Johann said cheerfully, "Without all the *merde,* the Gov says he'll pass on your 'request' at the appropriate time to the appropriate authorities."

Sir William reddened perceptibly, the Admirals and General more so. " 'Request,' eh? Tell the bugger exactly: It's not a request, it's a demand! And tell him further: We demand an IMMEDIATE audience with the Shōgun in Yedo in three days! Three days, by God! And I'm bloody arriving by battleship!"

"Bravo," Count Zergeyev muttered.

Johann was also weary of the game and gave the words a fine-tuned bluntness. The Japanese interpreter gasped and without waiting began a flood of acrimonious Dutch that Johann answered sweetly with two words that precipitated an aghast, sudden silence.

"Nan ja?" What is it, what's been said, the Governor asked angrily, not mistaking the hostility or hiding his own.

At once, apologetically, the flustered interpreter gave him a toned-down version, but even so the Governor exploded into a paroxysm of threats and pleading and refusal and more threats that the interpreter translated into words he considered the foreigners wanted to hear, then, still rattled, listened again and translated again.

"What's he saying, Johann?" Sir William had to raise his voice above the noise, the interpreter was answering the Governor and Bakufu officials, who were chattering amongst themselves and to him. "What the devil are they saying?"

Johann was happy now—he knew the meeting would terminate in a few moments and he could return to the Long Bar for his lunch and schnapps. "I don't know, except the Gov repeats the best he can do is to pass on your request etc. at the appropriate etc. but there's no way the Shōgun will grant you the honor etc. because it's against their customs etc. . . ."

Sir William slammed the flat of his hand onto the table. In the shocked silence, he pointed at the Governor then at himself. "*Watashi* . . . me . . ." Then he pointed out of the window towards Yedo. "*Watashi* go Yedo!" Then he raised three fingers. "THREE DAYS, in a bloody battleship!" He got up and stormed out of the room. The others followed.

He went across the hall to his study, to the bank of cut-glass decanters and poured some whisky. "Anyone care to join me?" he said breezily as the others surrounded him. Automatically he poured Scotch for the Admirals, General and Prussian, claret for Seratard, and a significant vodka for Count Zergeyev. "I thought that went according to plan. Sorry it was drawn out."

"I thought you were going to burst a blood vessel," Zergeyev said, draining his glass and pouring another.

"Not on your nelly. Had to close the meeting with a certain amount of drama."

"So it's Yedo in three days?"

"Yes, my dear Count. Admiral, have the flagship ready for a dawn departure, spend the next few days getting everything shipshape, ostentatiously clear the decks for action, all cannon primed, drills for the whole fleet, and order them to be ready to join us in battle order if need be. General, five hundred Redcoats should be enough for an honor guard. Monsieur, would the French flagship care to join us?"

Seratard said, "Of course. I will accompany you, of course, but suggest the French Legation as Headquarters, and full dress uniform."

"No to the uniforms, this is a punitive mission, not to present credentials—that comes later. And no to the meeting place. It was our national who was murdered and, how shall I put it? Our fleet is the deciding factor."

Von Heimrich chuckled. "It certainly is decisive in these waters, at the present time." He glanced at Seratard. "A pity I don't have a dozen regiments of Prussian cavalry, then we could partition the Japans without a hiccup and have done with all their devious stupidity and time-wasting bad manners."

"Only a dozen?" Seratard asked witheringly.

"That would be sufficient, Herr Seratard, for all Japan. Our troops are the best in the world—of course after Her Britannic Majesty's," he added smoothly. "Fortunately Prussia could spare twenty, even thirty regiments for just this small sector and still have more than enough to deal with *any* problem we might encounter anywhere, particularly in Europe."

"Yes, well . . ." Sir William broke in as Seratard reddened. He finished his drink. "I'm off to Kanagawa to make some arrangements. Admiral, General, perhaps a short conference when I return—I'll come aboard the flagship. Oh, Monsieur Seratard, what about Mademoiselle Angelique? Would you like me to escort her back?"

She came out of her room in the late afternoon sunlight and walked along the corridor and down the main staircase towards the entrance hallway. Now she wore the long, bustled dress of yesterday, elegant again, more ethereal than ever—hair groomed and swept up, eyes enhanced. Perfume and the swish of petticoats.

Sentries at the main door saluted her and mumbled an embarrassed greeting, awed by her beauty. She acknowledged them with a distant smile and went towards the surgery. A Chinese houseboy gaped at her and scuttled past.

Just before she reached the door, it opened. Babcott came out and stopped. "Oh, hello, Miss Angelique. My word, but you look beautiful," he said, almost stuttering.

"Thank you, Doctor." Her smile was kind, voice gentle. "I wanted to ask . . . can we talk a moment?"

"Of course, come in. Make yourself at home." Babcott shut the surgery door, settled her in the best chair and sat behind his desk, swept up by her radiance and the way her coiffure showed off her long neck to perfection. His eyes were red-rimmed and he was very tired. But then that's a way of life, he thought, glorying in the sight of her.

"That drink you gave me, last night, it was a drug of some kind?"

"Yes, yes, it was. I made it fairly strong as you were—you were rather upset."

"It's all so vague and mixed up: the Tokaidō, then coming here and, and seeing Malcolm. The sleeping drink was very strong?"

"Yes, but not dangerous, anything like that. Sleep's the best cure, it would have been the best kind, deep sleep, and by Jove, you slept well, it's almost four. How do you feel?"

"Still a little tired, thank you." Again the shadowed smile and it tore at him. "How is Monsieur Struan?"

"No change. I was just going to see him again, you can come along, if you like. He's doing well, considering. Oh, by the way, they caught that fellow."

"Fellow?"

"The one we told you about last night, the intruder."

"I don't remember anything about the night."

He told her what had happened at her door and in the garden, how one robber was shot and the other spotted this morning but had escaped, and it took all of her will to keep her face clear and to stop from screaming aloud what she was thinking: you son of Satan with your sleeping drafts and incompetence. Two robbers? The other one must have been in my room when you were there then and you failed to find him and save me, you and that other fool, Marlowe, equally guilty.

Blessed Mother, give me strength, help me to be revenged on both of them. And *him, whoever he is*! Mother of God, let me be revenged. But why steal my cross and leave the other jewelry and why the characters and what do they mean? And why in blood, his blood?

She saw him staring at her. *"Oui?"*

"I said, Would you like to see Mr. Struan now?"

"Oh! Yes, yes, please." She got up too, once more in control. "Oh, I'm afraid I spilt the jug of water on the sheets—would you ask the maid to deal with them, please?"

He laughed. "We don't have maids here. Against Japper regulations.

We've Chinese houseboys. Don't worry, the moment you left the room they'll be tidying . . ." He stopped, seeing her go pale. "What's the matter?"

For an instant her restraint had left her and she was back in her room again, scrubbing and cleaning and petrified the marks would not come out. But they had and she remembered she had checked and rechecked so the secret was safe—nothing was left to show, neither moisture nor blood, her secret safe forever so long as she was strong and kept to the plan—must—and must be clever, must.

Babcott was shocked by the sudden pallor, her fingers twisting the material of her skirt. Instantly he was beside her and held her shoulders gently. "Not to worry, you're quite safe, you really are."

"Yes, sorry," she said, frightened, her head against his chest, finding the tears were flowing. "It was just, I—I was, I was remembering poor Canterbury."

She watched herself, out of herself, allow him to comfort her, utterly sure that her plan was the only one, the wise one: *nothing happened.* Nothing nothing nothing.

You will believe it until your next period. And then, if it arrives, you will believe forever.

And if it does not arrive?

I don't know I don't know I don't know.

7

Monday, 15th September:

"GAI-JIN ARE VERMIN WITHOUT manners," Nori Anjo said, shaking with rage. He was chief of the *roju*, the Council of Five Elders, a squat, round-faced man, richly dressed. "They've spurned our polite apology, which should have ended the Tokaidō matter, and now, impertinently, formally request an audience with the Shōgun—the writing is foul, words inept. Here, read it for yourself, it has just arrived."

With barely concealed impatience he handed the scroll to his much younger adversary, Toranaga Yoshi, who sat opposite him. They were alone in one of the audience rooms high up in the central keep of Yedo Castle, all their guards ordered out. A low, scarlet lacquered table separated the two men, a black tea tray on it, delicate cups and teapot eggshell porcelain.

"Whatever gai-jin say doesn't matter." Uneasily Yoshi took the scroll but did not read it. Unlike Anjo his clothes were simple and his swords working, not ceremonial. "Somehow we must twist them to do what we want." He was daimyo of Hisamatsu, a small though important fief nearby and a direct descendant of the first Toranaga Shōgun. At the Emperor's recent 'suggestion,' and over Anjo's flaring opposition, he had just been appointed Guardian of the Heir, the boy Shōgun, and to fill the vacancy in the Council of Elders. Tall, patrician and twenty-six, with fine hands and long fingers. "Whatever happens, they must not see the Shōgun," he said. "That would confirm the legality of the Treaties, which are not yet properly ratified. We will refuse their insolent request."

"I agree it's insolent but we still have to deal with it, and decide about that Satsuma dog, Sanjiro." Both were weary of the gai-jin

97

problem that had disturbed their *wa,* their harmony, for two days now,
both anxious to end this meeting—Yoshi wanting to return to his
quarters below where Koiko waited for him, Anjo to a secret meeting
with a doctor.

Outside it was sunny and kind, with the smell of sea and rich soil on
the slight breeze that came through the opened shutters. No threat of
winter yet.

But winter's coming, Anjo was thinking, the ache in his bowels
distracting him. I hate winter, season of death, the sad season, sky sad,
sea sad, land sad and ugly and freezing, trees bare, and the cold that
twists your joints, reminding you how old you are. He was a greying
man of forty-six, daimyo of Mikawa, had been the center of *roju* power
since the dictator *tairō* Ii had been assassinated four years ago.

Whereas you, puppy, he thought angrily, you're only a two-month
appointee to the Council and a four-week Guardian—both dangerous
political appointments implemented over our protests. It's time your
wings were clipped. "Of course we all value your advice," he said, his
voice honeyed, then added, not meaning it, as both knew, "For two
days the gai-jin have been preparing their fleet for battle, troops
drilling openly and tomorrow their leader arrives. What's your solution?"

"The same as yesterday, official scroll or not: we send another
apology 'for the regrettable mishap' laced with sarcasm they will
never understand, from an official they will never know, and timed to
arrive before the leader gai-jin leaves Yokohama, asking for a further
delay to 'make enquiries.' If that does not satisfy him and he or they
come to Yedo, let them. We send the usual low-level official, nonbind-
ing on us to their Legation to treat with them, giving them a little soup
but no fish. We delay, and delay."

"Meanwhile it's time to exercise our hereditary Shōgunate right and
order Sanjiro to hand over the killers for punishment at once, to pay an
indemnity, again through us, at once, and into house arrest and retirement at once. We order him!" Anjo said harshly, "You're inex-
perienced in high Shōgunate matters."

Keeping his temper and wishing he could send Anjo into immediate
retirement for his stupidity and bad manners, Yoshi said, "If we order
Sanjiro we will be disobeyed, therefore we will be forced to go to war,
and Satsuma is too strong with too many allies. There's been no war for
two hundred and fifty years. We're not ready for war. War is . . ."

There was a sudden, peculiar silence. Involuntarily both men
gripped their swords. The teacups and teapot began to rattle. Far off the

earth rumbled, the whole tower shifted slightly, then again, and again. The quake persisted for about thirty seconds. Then it was gone, as suddenly as it had arrived. Impassively they waited, watching the cups.

No aftershock.

Still no aftershock.

More waiting throughout the castle and Yedo. All living creatures waiting. Nothing.

Yoshi sipped some tea, then meticulously centered the cup in its saucer and Anjo envied him his control. Inwardly Yoshi was in turmoil and he thought, Today the gods smiled on me but what about the next shock, or the next, or the one after that—any moment now, or in a candle of time or this afternoon, or later tonight or tomorrow? Karma!

Safe today but soon there will be another bad one, a killer earthquake, like seven years ago when I almost died and a hundred thousand people perished in Yedo alone in the earthquake and in the fires that always follow, not counting the tens of thousands washed out to sea and drowned in the tsunami wave that swept unheralded out of the sea that night—one of them my lovely Yuriko, then the passion of my life.

He willed himself to dominate his fear. "War is completely unwise now. Satsuma is too strong, the Tosa and Choshu legions will become his allies openly, we're not strong enough to crush them alone." Tosa and Choshu were fiefs, far from Yedo, both historic enemy to the Shōgunate.

"The most important daimyos will come to our banner, if summoned, and the rest follow." Anjo tried to hide the effort it took him to unlock his grip on his sword, still terrified.

Yoshi was alert and well trained, and noticed the lapse and docketed it for future use, pleased that he had seen into his enemy. "They won't, not yet. They'll delay, bluster, whine, and never help us smash Satsuma. They have no balls."

"If not now, when?" Anjo's fury spilled out, whipped by his fear and loathing of earthquakes. He had been in a bad one as a child, his father becoming a torch, his mother and two brothers cinders before his eyes. Ever since, with even the slightest quake, he relived the day and smelled their burning flesh and heard their screams. "We have to humble that dog sooner or later. Why not now?"

"Because we have to wait until we're better armed. They— Satsuma, Tosa and Choshu—have a few modern weapons, cannon and rifles, we don't know how many. And several steamships."

"Sold to them by gai-jin against Shōgunate wishes!"

"Bought by them because of previous weakness."

Anjo's face reddened. "I'm not responsible for that!"

"Nor I!" Yoshi's fingers on the hilt tightened. "Those fiefs are better armed than we are, whatever the reason. So sorry, we have to wait, the Satsuma fruit is not yet rotten enough for us to risk a war that by ourselves we cannot win. We're isolated, Sanjiro is not." His voice became sharper. "But I agree that soon there must be a reckoning."

"Tomorrow I will ask the Council to issue the order."

"For the sake of the Shōgunate, you and all Toranaga clans, I hope the others will listen to me!"

"Tomorrow we will see—Sanjiro's head should be put on a spike and exhibited as an example to all traitors."

"I agree Sanjiro must have ordered the Tokaidō killing just to embarrass us," Yoshi said. "That will madden the gai-jin. Our only solution is to delay. Our mission to Europe is due back any day now and then our troubles should be over."

Eight months before, in January, the Shōgunate had sent the first official deputation from Japan by steamship to America and Europe, with secret orders to renegotiate the Treaties—the *roju* considered them 'unauthorized tentative agreements'—with British, French and American Governments, and to cancel or delay any further opening of any ports. "Their orders were clear. By now the Treaties will be voided."

Anjo said ominously, "So, if not war, you agree the time has come to send Sanjiro onwards."

The younger man was too cautious to agree openly, wondering what Anjo was planning, or had already planned. He eased his swords more comfortably and pretended to consider the question, finding his new appointment very much to his liking. Once more I'm in at the center of power. Oh, yes, Sanjiro helped put me here but only for his own vile purpose: to destroy me by making me ever more publicly responsible for all the troubles these cursed gai-jin have brought, therefore setting me up as a prime target for the cursed shishi—and to usurp our hereditary rights, wealth and Shōgunate.

Never mind, I'm aware of what he and his running dog Katsumata plan, what his real intentions are against us, and those of his allies, the Tosa and the Choshu. He won't succeed, I swear it by my ancestors.

"How would you eliminate Sanjiro?"

Anjo's brow darkened, remembering his final violent row with the Satsuma daimyo only a few days earlier.

*   *   *

'I repeat,' Sanjiro had said imperiously, 'obey the Emperor's suggestions: Convene a meeting of all senior daimyos at once, humbly ask them to form a permanent Council to advise, reform and run the Shōgunate, quash your infamous and unauthorized gai-jin agreements, order all ports closed to gai-jin, and if they don't go, expel them at once!'

'I keep reminding you, it is *only* the Shōgunate's right to set foreign policy, any policy, not the Emperor's, nor yours! We both know you've deceived him,' Anjo had told him, hating him for his lineage, his legions, his riches, and obvious, abundant good health. 'The suggestions are ridiculous and unenforceable! We've kept the peace for two and a half cent—'

'Yes, for Toranaga aggrandizement. If you refuse to obey our rightful liege lord, the Emperor, then resign or commit seppuku. You chose a boy to be Shōgun, that traitor *tairō* Ii signed the "Treaties"—it's Bakufu responsibility gai-jin are here and that is Toranaga responsibility!'

Anjo had flushed, driven almost mad by the sneering malevolence and baiting that had gone on for months, and he would have gone for his sword if Sanjiro had not been protected by Imperial mandate. 'If *tairō* Ii hadn't negotiated the Treaties and had them signed, gai-jin would have bombarded their way ashore and by now we would be humbled like China.'

'Surmise—nonsense!'

'Have you forgotten Peking's Summer Palace was burned and looted, Sanjiro-dono? Now China is practically dismembered and government out of Chinese control. Have you forgotten the British, the main enemy, were ceded one of their islands, Hong Kong, twenty years ago and now it's an impregnable bastion? Tientsin, Shanghai, Swatow now are permanent, self-contained gai-jin dominated and owned Treaty Ports? Say they took one of our islands in the same way.'

'We would prevent them—we're not Chinese.'

'How? So sorry, but you're blind and deaf, and your head's in the heavens. A year ago, the moment the latest China war was over, if we'd provoked them they would have sent all those fleets and armies against us and overrun us as well. Only Bakufu cleverness stopped them. We could not have stood against those armadas—or their cannon and guns.'

'I agree that it's Shōgunate responsibility we're unprepared, Toranaga responsibility. We should have had modern cannon and warships years ago, we have had knowledge of them for years. Didn't the Dutch advise us dozens of times about their new inventions, but you put our heads in the night buckets! You failed the Emperor. At most you could have settled for one port, Deshima—why give the American fiend Townsend Harris, Yokohama, Hirodate, Nagasaki, Kanagawa and allow them access to Yedo for their impertinent Legations! Resign and let others more qualified save the Land of the Gods . . .'

Remembering the clash made Anjo sweat, that and the knowledge that much of what Sanjiro said was right. He took a paper handkerchief from his voluminous sleeve and wiped the sweat off his brow and shaved pate and looked back at Yoshi, jealous of his bearing and good looks but mostly of his youth and legendary virility.

Not so long ago it was so easy to be satisfied, normal to be potent, he thought in sudden misery, the ever present ache in his loins reminding him. Not so long ago, easy to become erect without effort and be abundantly charged—now no longer possible even with the most desirable person, their most clever skills, or rarest salves and medicines.

"Sanjiro may consider himself beyond reach, but he's not," he said with finality. "Put your mind on it too, Yoshi-dono, our young but oh so wise Councillor, how to remove him, or your own head may be on a spike all too soon."

Yoshi decided not to take offense, and smiled. "What do the other Elders advise?"

Anjo laughed crookedly. "They will vote as I say."

"If you weren't kinsman, I would suggest you resign or commit seppuku."

"What a pity you are not your illustrious namesake and you could actually order it, eh?" Anjo got up heavily. "I'll send a reply now, to delay. Tomorrow we take a formal vote to humble Sanjiro . . ." Angrily he spun on guard as the door was jerked open. Yoshi already had his sword half out of its scabbard. "I gave orders . . ."

The flustered sentry mumbled, "So sorry, Anjo-sama . . ."

Anjo's fury vanished as a youth brushed the sentry aside and hurried into the room, closely followed by a girl, barely five feet tall, both elaborately dressed and bubbling, four armed samurai in their wake and, after them, a matron and lady-in-waiting. At once Anjo and Yoshi knelt and bowed their heads to the tatami. The entourage bowed back. The youth, Shōgun Nobusada, did not. Nor did the girl, Imperial Princess Yazu, his wife. Both were the same age, sixteen.

"That quake, it knocked over my favorite vase," the youth said excitedly, pointedly ignoring Yoshi. "My favorite vase!" He waved the door closed. His guards stayed, and his wife's ladies. "I wanted to tell you I've a wonderful idea."

"So sorry about the vase, Sire." Anjo's voice was kind. "You had an idea?"

"We . . . I've decided we, my wife and I, we, I've decided we'll go to Kyōto to see the Emperor and ask him what to do about the gai-jin and how to throw them out!" The youth beamed at his wife and she nodded in happy agreement. "We'll go next month—a State Visit!"

Anjo and Yoshi felt their minds explode, both wanting to leap forward and strangle the boy for his lack of brains. But both kept their tempers, both used to his petulant stupidity and tantrums, and for the thousandth time, both cursed the day the marriage of these two had been proposed and consummated. "An interesting idea, Sire," Anjo said carefully, watching the girl without watching, noting her concentration centered on him now and that, as usual, though her lips smiled her eyes did not. "I will put the suggestion before the Council of Elders and we will give it our full attention."

"Good," Nobusada said importantly. He was a small, thin young man, just five and a half feet, who always wore thick *geta*, sandals, to increase his height. His teeth were dyed fashionably black as Court custom in Kyōto decreed, though not here in Shōgunate circles. "Three or four weeks should be time to prepare everything." Ingenuously he smiled at his wife. "Did I forget anything, Yazu-chan?"

"No, Sire," she said prettily. "How could you forget anything?" Her face was delicate and made up in classic Kyōto Court style: eyebrows plucked and, in their place, high arching eyebrows painted on the whiteness of her makeup, her teeth dyed black, thick raven hair piled high and held in place with ornate pins. Purple kimono decorated with sprays of autumn leaves, her obi, the intricate sash, golden. Imperial Princess Yazu, stepsister of the Son of Heaven, Nobusada's bride of six months, sought for him since she was twelve, betrothed at fourteen and married at sixteen. "Of course, a decision by you is a decision and not a suggestion."

"Of course, Honored Princess," Yoshi said quickly. "But so sorry, Sire, such important arrangements could not possibly be made in four weeks. May I advise you to consider the implications for such a visit might be misinterpreted."

Nobusada's smile vanished. "Implications? Advise? What implications? Misinterpreted by whom? By you?" he said rudely.

"No, Sire, not by me. I just wanted to point out that no Shōgun has ever gone to Kyōto to ask the Emperor's advice and such a precedent would be disastrous to your rule."

"Why?" Nobusada said angrily. "I don't understand."

"Because, as you remember, the Shōgun has the sole hereditary duty to make decisions for the Emperor, together with his Council of Elders and Shōgunate." Yoshi kept his voice gentle. "This allows the Son of Heaven to spend his time interceding with the gods for all of us, and for the Shōgunate to keep mundane and common happenings from disturbing his *wa*."

Princess Yazu said sweetly, "What Toranaga Yoshi-sama says is true, husband. Unfortunately the gai-jin have already disturbed his *wa*, as we all know, so to ask my brother, the Exalted, for advice would surely be both polite and filial and not interfere with historic rights."

"Yes." The youth puffed up his chest. "It's decided!"

"The Council will at once consider your wishes," Yoshi said.

Nobusada's face contorted and he shouted, "Wishes? It's a *decision*! Put it to them if you wish, but I have decided! I'm Shōgun, you're not! I am! I've decided! I was chosen and they rejected you—all loyal daimyos did. I'm Shōgun, Cousin!"

Everyone was aghast at the outburst. Except the girl. She smiled to herself and kept her eyes downcast and thought: At last my revenge begins.

"True, Sire," Yoshi was saying, voice level though the color was out of his face. "But I am Guardian and I must advise against—"

"I don't want your advice! No one asked me if I wanted a Guardian. I don't need a Guardian, Cousin, least of all you."

Yoshi looked at the youth shaking with rage. Once I was just like you, he thought coldly, a puppet to be ordered this way or that, to be sent away from my own family to be adopted by another, or to be married, or banished and almost murdered six times and all because the gods decided I would be born the son of my father—as you, pathetic fool, were born the son of your father. I'm like you in many ways, but never a fool, always a swordsman, aware of the puppeting, and now hugely different. Now I am no longer a puppet. Sanjiro of Satsuma doesn't know it yet, but he's made me puppeteer.

"While I am Guardian, I will guard and protect you, Sire," he said. His eyes flicked to the girl, so tiny and delicate, outwardly. "And your family."

She did not meet his eyes. No need. Both knew that war was declared. "We are glad of your protection, Toranaga-sama."

"I'm not!" Nobusada screeched. "You were my rival, now you're nothing! In two years I'm eighteen and then I'll rule alone and you . . ." He pointed a shaking finger at Yoshi's impassive face, everyone appalled—except the girl. "Unless you learn to obey I'll . . . you'll be banished to the North Island forever. We-are-going-to-Kyōto!"

He swung around. Hastily a guard flung the door open. All bowed as he hurried out. She followed, then the others, and when they were alone again Anjo wiped the sweat off his neck. "She's . . . she's the source of all his . . . agitation, and 'brilliance,' " he said sourly. "Since she arrived the fool's become even more stupid than he was and not because he is fornicating himself blind."

Yoshi hid his astonishment that Anjo would make such an obvious though dangerous comment aloud. "Tea?"

Anjo nodded, morosely, jealous again of his elegance and strength. *Nobusada's not such a fool in some ways*, he was thinking. *I agree with him about you, the sooner you're removed the better, you and Sanjiro, you're both trouble. Could the Council vote to restrict your powers as Guardian or banish you? It's true you send that foolish boy mad every time he sees you—and her. If it were not for you I could manage that bitch, Emperor's stepsister or not. And to think that not only was I in favor of the marriage but I put* tairō *Ii's stratagem into place, even against the Emperor's opposition to such a match. Didn't we refuse his reluctant first offer of his thirty-year-old daughter, then his one-year-old baby, until eventually, under pressure, he agreed on his stepsister?*

Of course, the close connection of Nobusada with the Imperial family strengthens us against Sanjiro and the outside lords, against Yoshi and those who wanted him appointed Shōgun instead. The connection will be all-powerful once she has a son—that will mellow her and drain her venom. Her pregnancy is overdue. The boy's doctor will increase the dose of ginseng, or give him some of the special pills to improve the boy's performance, terrible to be so limp at his age. Yes, the sooner she's carrying the better.

He finished his tea. "I will see you at the meeting tomorrow." Both bowed perfunctorily.

Yoshi left and went out onto the battlements, needing air and time to think. Below he could see the vast stone fortifications with three encircling moats within moats and impregnable strong points and drawbridges, the walls monstrous. Within the castle walls were quarters for fifty thousand samurai and ten thousand horses, along with spacious halls and palaces for chosen, loyal families—but only Toranaga families within the inner moat—and gardens everywhere.

In the central keep, above and below him, were the most secure living areas and inner sanctum of the reigning Shōgun, his family, courtiers and retainers. And the treasure rooms. As Guardian, Yoshi lived here, unwelcome and on the fringe but also secure and with his own guards.

Beyond the outer moat was the first protective circle of daimyo palaces. These were vast, rich, sprawling residences, then circles of lesser ones, then even lesser ones, one such residence for each daimyo in the land. All had been sited by Shōgun Toranaga personally and ordered constructed to conform with his new law of *sankin-kotai*, alternative residence.

'*Sankin-kotai*,' he said, 'requires all daimyos to build at once and maintain forever a "suitable residence" under my castle walls in exact positions I have decided, where he, his family and a few senior retainers are to live permanently—each palace to be lavish, *and without defenses*. One year in three the daimyo will be allowed, and required, to return to his fief and to stay there with his retainers, but without his wife, consorts, mother, father or children, or children's children, or any member of his immediate family—the order in which daimyos leave or remain is also to be carefully regulated according to the following list and timetable . . .'

The word 'hostage' was never mentioned, though hostage taking, ordered or offered to ensure compliance, was an ancient custom. Even Toranaga himself had been hostage when a child to the Dictator Goroda; his own family had been hostage to Goroda's successor, Nakamura, his ally and liege lord; and he, the last and greatest, decided merely to extend the custom into *sankin-kotai* to keep everyone in thrall.

'At the same time,' he wrote in his Legacy, a private document for selected descendants, 'following Shōguns are ordered to encourage all daimyos to build extravagantly, to live elegantly, to dress opulently and entertain lavishly, the quicker to divest them of their fief's yearly revenue of koku which, by correct immutable custom belongs only to the daimyo concerned. In this way all will soon become debt ridden, ever more dependent on us and, more important, without teeth—while we continue to be thrifty and eschew extravagance.

'Even so, some fiefs—Satsuma, Mori, Tosa, Kii for example—are so rich that even these extravagances will leave too dangerous a surplus. From time to time the ruling Shōgun will therefore invite the daimyo to present him with a few leagues of a new trunk road, or palace, or garden, pleasure place, or temple, such amounts, times, and frequency are laid down in the following document . . .'

"So clever, so far-thinking," Yoshi muttered. Every daimyo in a silken net, powerless to rebel. But all ruined by Anjo's stupidity.

The first of the Emperor's 'requests' brought by Sanjiro to the Council—before Yoshi had become a member—was to abolish this ancient custom. Anjo and the others had prevaricated, argued and finally agreed. Almost overnight the rings of palaces emptied of all wives, consorts, children, relations and warriors and in days became a wasteland with only a few token retainers.

Our most important curb gone forever, Yoshi thought bitterly. How could Anjo have been so inept?

He let his gaze drift beyond the palaces, to the capital city of a million souls that serviced the castle and fed off it, a city crisscrossed with streams and bridges, most constructed of wood. Now there were many fires—the blossoms of earthquakes—all the way to the sea. One great wooden palace was in flames.

Yoshi noticed idly that it belonged to the daimyo of Sai. Good. Sai supports Anjo. The families are gone but the Council can order him to rebuild and the cost will crush him forever.

Forget him, what's our shield against the gai-jin? There must be one! Everyone says they could burn Yedo but not break into the castle or sustain a long siege. I do not agree. Yesterday Anjo again told the Elders the well-known story of the Siege of Malta some three hundred years ago, how Turk armies could not pry even six hundred brave knights from their castle. Anjo had said, 'We have tens of thousands of samurai all hostile to gai-jin, we must win, they must sail away.'

'But neither Turks nor Christians had cannon,' he had said. 'Don't forget Shōgun Toranaga breeched Osaka Castle with gai-jin cannon—these vermin can do likewise here.'

'Even if they did, we would have withdrawn safely to the hills long since. Meanwhile every samurai, and every man, woman and child in the land—even stinking merchants—would flock to our banner and fall on them like locusts. We have nothing to fear,' Anjo had said contemptuously. 'Osaka Castle was different, that was daimyo against daimyo, not an invasion. The enemy cannot sustain a land war. In a land war we must win.'

'They would lay waste everything, Anjo-sama. We would be left with nothing to govern. Our only course is to web gai-jin like a spider webs its far bigger prey. We must be a spider, we must find a web.'

But they would not listen to him. What's the web?

'First know the problem,' Toranaga wrote in his Legacy, 'then, with patience, you can find the solution.'

The crux of the problem with the foreigners is simply this: How do we obtain their knowledge, armaments, fleets, wealth and trade on our terms, yet expel them all, cancel the unequal Treaties, and never allow one to set foot ashore without severe restrictions?

The Legacy continued: 'The answer to all problems for OUR land can be found here, or in Sun-tzu's "The Art of War"—and patience.'

Shōgun Toranaga was the most patient ruler in the world, he thought, awed for the millionth time.

Even though Toranaga was supreme in the land, outside of Osaka Castle, the invincible stronghold built by his predecessor, Dictator Nakamura, he waited twelve years to spring the trap he had baited, and lay siege to it. The castle was in absolute possession of the Lady Ochiba, the Dictator's widow, their seven-year-old son and heir, Yaemon—to whom Toranaga had solemnly sworn allegiance—and eighty thousand fanatically loyal samurai.

Two years of siege, three hundred thousand troops, cannon from the Dutch privateer *Erasmus* of Anjin-san, the Englishman who had sailed the ship to Japan, together with a musket regiment also trained by him, a hundred thousand casualties, all his guile and the vital traitor within, before Lady Ochiba and Yaemon committed seppuku rather than be captured.

Then Toranaga had secured Osaka Castle, spiked the cannon, destroyed all muskets, disbanded the musket regiment, and forbidden manufacture or the importation of all firearms. He had broken the power of the Portuguese Jesuit priests and Christian daimyos, reallocated fiefs, sent all enemies onwards, instituted the laws of the Legacy, forbidden all wheels, the building of oceangoing ships, and had, regretfully, taken a third of all revenue for himself and his immediate family.

"He made us strong," Yoshi muttered. "His Legacy gave us power to keep the land pure, and at peace in the way he designed."

I must not fail him.

Eeee, what a man! How wise of his son, Sudara, the second Shōgun, to change the name of the dynasty to Toranaga, instead of the real family name of Yoshi—so that we would never forget the fountainhead.

What would he advise me to do?

First, to have patience, then he would quote Sun-tzu: *Know your enemy as you know yourself and you need not fear a hundred battles; know yourself but not the enemy, for every victory gained you will also suffer a defeat; know neither the enemy nor yourself and you will succumb in every battle.*

I know some things about the enemy, but not enough.

I bless my father again for making me understand the value of education, for giving me so many varied and special teachers over the years, foreign as well as Japanese. Sad I did not have the gift of tongues and so had to learn through intermediaries: Dutch merchants for world history, an English seaman to check Dutch truth and to open my eyes—just as Toranaga used the Anjin-san in his time—and all the others.

Chinese taught me government, literature and Sun-tzu's "The Art of War"; the old renegade French priest from Peking spent half a year teaching me Machiavelli, laboriously translating it into Chinese characters for me as his passport to live in my father's domains and enjoy the Willow World he adored; the American pirate marooned at Izu told me about cannon and about oceans of grass called prairies, their castle called White House and the wars in which they exterminated the natives of that land; the Russian émigré convict from a place called Siberia claimed he was a prince with ten thousand slaves and told fables of places called Moscow and St. Petersburg, and all the others— some teaching for a few days, some for months but never a year, none of them knowing who I was, and I fobidden to tell them, Father so careful and secretive and so terrible when aroused.

'When these men leave, Father,' he had asked in the beginning, 'what happens to them? They're all so frightened. Why should that be? You promise them rewards, don't you?'

'You're eleven, my son. I will forgive your rudeness in questioning me, once. To remind you of my magnanimity you will go without food for three days, you will climb Mount Fuji alone and you will sleep without covering.'

Yoshi shuddered. At that time he did not know what magnanimity meant. During those days he had almost died but achieved what was ordered of him. As a reward for his self-discipline his father, daimyo of Mito, had told him he was being adopted by the Hisamatsu family and made heir of that Toranaga branch: 'You are my seventh son. In that way you will have your own inheritance, and be of a slightly higher lineage than your brothers.'

'Yes, Father,' he had said, holding back his tears. At that time he did not know he was being groomed to be Shōgun, nor was he ever told.

Then, when Shōgun Iyeyoshi died of the spotted disease four years ago and he was twenty-two and ready and proposed by his father, *tairō* Ii had opposed him, and won—Ii's personal forces possessed the Palace Gates.

So his cousin Nobusada was appointed. Yoshi, his family, his father and all their influential supporters were ordered into severe house arrest. Only when Ii was assassinated was he freed and reinstated with his lands and honors, along with the others who survived. His father had died in house confinement.

I should have been Shōgun, he thought for the ten millionth time. I was ready, trained and could have stopped the Shōgunate rot, could have formed a new bond between Shōgunate and all daimyos, and could have dealt with the gai-jin. I should have had that Princess as wife, I would never have signed those agreements, or allowed the negotiations to go so badly against us. I would have dealt with Townsend Harris and begun a new era of careful change to accommodate the world outside, at our pace, not theirs!

Meanwhile I am not Shōgun, Nobusada is elected Shōgun correctly, the Treaties exist, Princess Yazu exists, Sanjiro, Anjo and gai-jin are battering at our gates.

He shivered. I had better be even more careful. Poison is an ancient art, an arrow by day or by night, ninja assassins in their hundreds are out there, ready for hire. And then there are the shishi. There must be an answer! What is it?

Sea birds circling and cawing over the city and castle interrupted his thought patterns. He studied the sky. No sign of change, or tempest though this was the month of change when the big winds came, and with them winter. Winter will be bad this year. Not a famine like three years ago but the harvest is poor, even less than last year. . . .

Wait! What was it Anjo said that reminded me of something?

He turned and beckoned one of his bodyguards, his excitement rising. "Bring that spy here, the fisherman, what's his name? Ah, yes, Misamoto, bring him to my quarters secretly at once—he's confined in the Eastern Guard House."

8

Tuesday, 16th September:

PRECISELY AT DAWN THE CANNON of the flagship bellowed the eleven-gun salute as Sir William's cutter came alongside the gangway. From the shore came a faint cheer, every sober man there to watch the departure of the fleet for Yedo. The wind was strengthening, sea fair, light overcast. He was formally piped aboard, Phillip Tyrer in attendance—the rest of his staff already aboard accompanying warships. The two men wore frock coats and top hats. Tyrer's arm was in a sling.

They saw Admiral Ketterer waiting for them on the main deck, John Marlowe beside him, both in dress uniform—cocked hats, gold braided and buttoned blue cutaways, with white shirts, waistcoats, breeches and stockings, buckled shoes and gleaming swords—and, immediately, Phillip Tyrer thought, Damn, how handsome and elegant yet masculine John Marlowe always is, just like Pallidar in his uniform. Damned if I have any dress clothes, or any clothes for that matter to rival them, and poor as a church mouse compared to them and not even a Deputy Secretary yet. Damn! There's nothing like a uniform to flatter a man and give him standing with a girl. . . .

He almost stumbled into Sir William, who had stopped on the top step as the Admiral and Marlowe saluted politely, ignoring him. Blast, he thought, concentrate, you're equally on duty, equally at the beck and call of the Mighty! Be careful, become part of the scenery too. Wee

Willie Winkie's been like a cat with a hornet in his bum since you reported yesterday.

" 'Morning, Sir William, welcome aboard."

"Thank you. Good morning to you, Admiral Ketterer." Sir William doffed his hat, followed by Tyrer, their frock coats tugged by the breeze. "Set sail, if you please. The other Ministers are on the French flagship."

"Good." The Admiral motioned to Marlowe. At once Marlowe saluted, went to the Captain who was on the open bridge, just forward of the single funnel and main mast, and saluted again. "Admiral's compliments, sir. Make way for Yedo."

The commands went rapidly down the line, the sailors gave three cheers, in moments the anchors were being chanted aboard and in the cramped boiler room three decks below, teams of stokers, stripped to the waist, shoveled more coal into the furnaces to another rhythmic chant, coughing and wheezing in air permanently fouled with coal dust. The other side of the bulkhead in the engine room, the chief Engineer engaged "half ahead," and the huge reciprocating engines began to turn the propeller shaft.

She was H.M.S. *Euryalus*, built at Chatham eight years ago, a three-masted, one-funnel, screw-assisted wooden cruiser frigate of 3,200 tons burthen, with 35 guns, a normal complement of 350 officers, seamen and marines—while below decks were 90 stokers and engine room staff. Today all sails were sparred and decks cleared for action.

"A pleasant day, Admiral," Sir William was saying. They were on the quarterdeck; Phillip Tyrer and Marlowe, who had greeted each other silently, hovering close by.

"For the moment," the Admiral agreed testily, always uncomfortable near civilians, particularly someone like Sir William who was his senior in rank. "My quarters are available to you, if you wish."

"Thank you." Sea gulls were dipping and cawing around their wake. Sir William studied them for a moment, trying to throw off his depression. "Thank you, but I'd rather be on deck. You haven't met Mr. Tyrer, I believe? He's our new apprentice interpreter."

For the first time the Admiral acknowledged Tyrer. "Welcome aboard, Mr. Tyrer, we can certainly use Japanese speakers here. How's your wound?"

"Not too bad, sir, thank you," Tyrer said, trying to retreat once more into anonymity.

"Good. Rotten business." The Admiral's pale blue eyes ranged the sea and his ship, his face florid and weather-beaten, with heavy jowls and a choleric roll of flesh on the back of his neck over his starched collar. For a moment he watched the smoke critically, noting its color and smell, then grunted and brushed some specks of coal dust off his impeccable waistcoat.

"Something's amiss?"

"No, Sir William. The coals we get here don't compare with Shanghai best, or good Welsh or Yorkshire coals. Too much clinker in it. It's cheap enough when we can get it but that's not often. You should insist on an increased supply, it's a major problem for us here, major."

Sir William nodded wearily. "I have but they don't appear to have any locally."

"Filthy stuff, wherever it comes from. We can't use sail today, not with this wind against us. Engine assists are perfect for this sort of exercise and close inshore maneuvers, or docking. With the best man-of-war afloat, under sails, even a tea clipper—we'd take five times as long to get to Yedo and not have enough sea room for safety. More's the pity."

Sir William was out of humor after another sleepless night and reacted instantly to the Admiral's discourtesy and stupidity telling him something that was obvious. "Really?" he said thinly. "Never mind, soon we'll have a completely stinkpot navy, no sail at all and that will be that."

Tyrer hid a smile as the Admiral flushed, for this was a sore point with naval officers and widely discussed in the London newspapers, who blithely dubbed future fleets as 'Stinkpots of various sizes, commanded by stinkpotters of various sizes, who will be dressed accordingly.'

"That won't happen in the foreseeable future and never for long-haul cruising, blockades or battle fleets." The Admiral almost spat the words out. "There's no way we can carry all the coal we need between ports and still have fighting ships. We must have sails to conserve fuel. Civilians have little understanding of naval matters. . . ." This reminded him of the present Liberal government's attack on the current Navy estimates and his blood pressure went up another notch. "Meanwhile to secure our sea lanes and keep the Empire inviolate, as a cornerstone of government policy the Royal Navy must maintain the equation of twice as many ships—wooden or ironclads, steam and sail—as the next two other navies combined, with the biggest and best engines and most modern cannon, shells, and explosives in the world."

"An admirable idea, but now out of date, not practical, and I'm afraid too rich for the Chancellor of the Exchequer and government to stomach."

"It better not be, by God." The roll of neck flesh went pink. "Mr.
Penny-pinching Gladstone better learn right smartly where his priori-
ties lie. I've said it before: the sooner the Liberals are out and the
Tories back in power the better! Not because of them, thank God the
Royal Navy still has enough ships and firepower to sink any French,
Russian or American fleets in their home waters if need be. But say
those three combine against us in the coming conflict?" Irritably the
Admiral turned and bellowed though Marlowe was close by, "Mr.
Marlowe! Signal the *Pearl*! She's out of station, by God!"

"Aye, aye, sir!" Marlowe left at once.

Sir William glanced astern, seeing nothing amiss with the following
ships, then again concentrated on the Admiral. "Foreign Secretary
Russell's too clever to be drawn into it. Prussia will war on France,
Russia will stay out, the Americans are too involved with their civil
war, Spanish Cuba and Philippines, and sniffing around the Hawaiian
islands. By the way, I've proposed we annex one or two of those
islands before the Americans do, they'd make perfect coaling stations. . . ."

Marlowe was sourly heading for the signalman, his eyes on H.M.S
Pearl, his ship, a Jason-class three-masted, single-funneled, 21-gun
screw frigate of 2,100 tons burthen, temporarily in the command of his
Number One, Lieutenant Lloyd, wishing he was aboard her and no
longer the Admiral's lackey. He gave the signalman the message,
watched him use the signal flags and read the reply before the young
man reported, "He says sorry, sorr."

"How long have you been a signalman?"

"Three months, sir."

"You'd best look up your codes, right smartly. The message said:
'Captain Lloyd of H.M.S. *Pearl* apologizes.' Make another mistake
and your balls are in the wringer."

"Yessir, sorry, sir," the crestfallen youth said.

Marlowe went back to the Admiral. To his relief the potential row
between the two men seemed to have simmered down and now they
were discussing alternative plans of action at Yedo and the long-term
implications of the Tokaidō attack. While he waited for a lull in the
conversation, he cautiously cocked an eyebrow at Tyrer—who smiled
back—wanting to be dismissed so he could ask him about Kanagawa
and Angelique. He had had to leave the same day Sir William had
arrived, three days ago, and had no first-hand information on what had
occurred since then.

"Yes, Mr. Marlowe?" The Admiral listened to the message and at once rasped: "Send another signal: report aboard my flagship at sunset." He saw Marlowe wince. "And well you might, Mr. Marlowe. Such an apology is insufficient excuse for slackness in my fleet. Is it?"

"No, sir."

"Consider who should take over your ship in his place—not you!" Admiral Ketterer turned back to Sir William. "You were saying? You don't th—" A gust crackled the rigging. Both officers looked aloft, then at the sky and all around, tasting the wind. No sign of danger yet, though both knew that the weather this month was unpredictable and in these waters storms came suddenly. "You were saying? You don't think the authorities, this Bakufu, will do what we require?"

"No, not without some form of force. At midnight I got another apology from them and a request for a month's delay so they could 'consult higher ups' and more such nonsense—my God, they can prevaricate. I sent the bloody messenger back with a flea in his ear and a curt, rather rude message to give us satisfaction or else."

"Quite right."

"When we anchor off Yedo, can we fire as many salutes as possible, create an entrance?"

"We'll make it 21 guns, a royal salute. I suppose this mission could be construed as a formal visit to their Royalty." Without turning, the Admiral rasped: "Mr. Marlowe, give the order for the whole fleet and ask the French Admiral if he would do likewise."

"Yessir." Again Marlowe saluted and rushed off.

"The plan for Yedo is still as we agreed?"

Sir William nodded. "Yes. I and my party will go ashore to the Legation—a hundred soldiers as an honor guard should be enough. The Highlanders, their uniforms and bagpipes, will be the most impressive. The rest of the plan remains the same."

"Good." Uneasily the Admiral stared ahead. "We'll be able to see Yedo when we get around that headland." His face hardened. "It's one thing to rattle a few sabres and fire off a few blank cannonades but I don't agree to bombard and burn that city—without a legal state of war."

Sir William said carefully, "Let's hope I don't have to ask Lord Palmerston to declare one, or for me to legalize one forced on us. A full report's on the way to him. Meanwhile his reply is four months away so we have to do the best we can, as usual. These murders must stop, the Bakufu must be brought to heel, one way or another. Now is the perfect time."

"Admiralty instructions are to be prudent."

"By the same post I sent an urgent message to the Governor of Hong

Kong also advising him what I planned to do and asking what reinforcements in ships and men could be available if necessary, and about Mr. Struan's condition.''

"Oh? When was that, Sir William?"

"Yesterday. Struan's had a clipper available, and Mr. McFay agreed the matter merited the most immediate haste.''

Ketterer said caustically, "This whole incident seems to be a Struan cause célèbre. The fellow who was killed hardly gets a mention—it's nothing but Struan, Struan, Struan."

"The Governor's a personal friend of the family, and the family is, er, very well connected, very important to Her Majesty's trading interests in Asia and China. Very.''

"They've always sounded like a bunch of pirates to me, gunrunning, opium running, anything for a profit.''

"Both are legal enterprises, my dear Admiral. Struan's are highly respectable, Admiral, with very important connections in Parliament.''

The Admiral was unimpressed. "A lot of ne'er-do-wells there too, by God, if you don't mind my saying. Bloody idiots most of the time, trying to cut Navy funds and our fleets—stupid when England depends on sea power."

"I agree we need the best Navy with the most competent officers to carry out Imperial policy," Sir William said. Marlowe, near the Admiral, heard the thinly veiled barb. A quick glance at the back of his superior's neck confirmed the barb had registered. He braced for the inevitable.

"Imperial policy? Seems to me," the Admiral said sharply, "the Navy spends most of its time pulling civilian and trader fingers out of their smelly holes when their greed or double-dealing takes them into messes they should never have been in in the first place. As for those bastards there," his stubby finger pointed at Yokohama on the port side, "they're the worst bunch of scallywags I've ever seen."

"Some are, most not, Admiral." Sir William's chin came out. "Without traders and trade there'd be no money, no Empire and no Navy."

The red neck became purple. "Without the Navy there would be no trade and England would not have become the greatest nation in the world, the richest, with the greatest Empire the world has ever seen, by God."

Balls, Sir William wanted to shout, but he knew that if he did, here on the quarterdeck of the flagship, the Admiral would have apoplexy, and Marlowe and every sailor within hearing distance would faint. The thought amused him and removed most of the venom that sleepless nights worrying over the Tokaidō affair had caused, and permitted him to be diplomatic. "The Navy is the senior service, Admiral. And many share your opinion. I trust we'll be on time?"

"Yes, yes, we will." The Admiral eased his shoulders, somewhat mollified, his head aching from the bottle of port he had consumed after dinner, on top of the claret. The ship was making about seven knots, into wind, which pleased him. He checked the lie of the fleet. Now H.M.S. *Pearl* was very carefully astern, with two 10-gun paddle sloops to port. The French flagship, a three-masted, 20-gun ironclad paddle frigate, was carelessly to starboard. "Her helmsman should be put in irons! She could do with a new coat of paint, new rigging, fumigating to get rid of the garlic, and a bloody good holy-stoning and their crew keelhauled. Don't you agree, Mr. Marlowe?"

"Yes, sir."

When he was satisfied all was correct, the Admiral then turned back to Sir William. "This . . . this Struan family and their so-called Noble House, is it really so important?"

"Yes. Their trade is enormous, their influence in Asia, notably in China, without compare, except for Brock and Sons."

"I've seen their clippers, of course. Beauties, and very well armed." The Admiral added bluntly, "I hope to Christ they don't try to peddle opium or guns here."

"Personally I agree, though it's not against present law."

"It is, according to Chinese law. Or Japan's."

"Yes, but there are mitigating circumstances," Sir William said wearily. He had been through the same explanation dozens of times. "I'm sure you know China will only accept cash, silver or gold, for the tea we must import, nothing else. The only merchandise they'll pay cash for—gold or silver—is opium, nothing else. It's very unfortunate."

"Then it's up to traders and Parliament and diplomats to pull their fingers out. For the last twenty years the Royal Navy has been enforcing illegal laws in Asia, bombarding China ports and cities, doing all sorts of rotten acts of war, in my opinion just to support opium—a blot on our escutcheon!"

Sir William sighed. His orders from the Permanent Under Secretary had been precise: 'For Christ's sake, dear Willie, this is the first time you'll be Minister in charge so be careful, don't make any precipitous decisions, unless they're necessary. You're astonishingly lucky: the telegraph wire has already reached Bagdad, so we can get and send messages there in an incredible seven days; add another six-odd weeks by steamer to Yokohama through the Persian Gulf, Indian Ocean via Singapore and Hong Kong, our instructions will only take an incredible two months to arrive—not the twelve to fifteen months ten-odd years ago. So if you need guidance, which you will all the time if you're wise, you're about four months off our leash, and that's the only thing that protects your neck and our Empire. Clear?'

'Yes, sir.'

'Rule number one: Handle the service Brass with velvet gloves and don't overrule them lightly, because your life and those of all Englishmen in your area depend on them. They're inclined to be boneheaded, which is excellent for obviously we need lots of these sort of fellows to go off and get killed defending our, well, Imperial policy. Do not make waves; Japan is unimportant but in our sphere of influence and we've spent considerable time and money finessing the Russians, Americans and French out. Do not foul up our Japanese nest; we've enough on our Imperial plate with rebellious Indians, Afghans, Arabs, Africans, Persians, Caribbeans, Chinese, to say nothing of the rotten Europeans, Americans, Russians, etc. My dear, dear Willie, be diplomatic and don't fuck up or else!'

Sir William sighed again, bottled his temper, and repeated what he had said a dozen times, the truth: "A lot of what you say is correct, but unfortunately we have to be practical, without tax revenue on tea the whole British economy will collapse. Let's hope in a few years our Bengal opium fields can be torched. Meanwhile we have to be patient."

"Meanwhile I suggest you embargo all opium here, all modern weapons, all modern warships, and all slavery."

"Of course I agree about slavery, that's been outlawed since '33!" Sir William's voice edged perceptibly. "The Americans have been informed long since. As to the rest, unfortunately that's up to London."

The Admiral's chin jutted even further. "Well, sir, I have certain powers in these waters. You can take it I am instituting such an embargo now. I've heard disquieting rumors about Struan's ordering rifles and cannon for sale. They've already sold these natives three or four armed steamers and the Jappers learn too fast for my liking. I will write formally by tomorrow's mail to the Admiralty to ask them to insist my orders are made permanent."

The Minister's face mottled, he planted his feet even more firmly into the deck. "An admirable idea," he said icily. "I will write by the same mail. Meanwhile you cannot make such an order without my approval and until we have a directive from the Foreign Office *the status quo remains the status quo!*"

Both of their aides blanched. The Admiral looked at Sir William, of a height with him. All officers and most men would have quailed but Sir William just stared back. "I'll . . . I'll consider what you say, Sir William. Now if you'll excuse me I have things to do." He turned and stomped off for the bridge. Weakly Marlowe began to follow. "For Christ's sake, Marlowe, stop following me like a puppy. If I want you I'll shout. Stay within shouting distance!"

"Yessir." When the man was well away Marlowe exhaled.

Sir William had exhaled too and he mopped his brow and muttered, "Awfully glad I'm not in the Navy."

"Me too," Tyrer said, amazed by the Minister's courage.

Marlowe's heart was racing, hating to be bellowed at, even by an Admiral, but he did not forget himself. "I, er . . . excuse me, sir, but the fleet's very safe in his hands, sir, and the expedition, and we all believe he's quite right about selling ships, guns, cannon and opium. Japanners are already building ships and making small cannon—this year they sailed their first iron steamship, the 300-ton *Kanrin maru* to San Francisco, crewed and captained entirely by them. They've mastered the deep. That's remarkable in such a short time."

"Yes, yes, it is." Sir William wondered briefly how the Japanese Delegation that went with this ship had fared in Washington, and what mischief President Lincoln would generate against our glorious Empire. Aren't we dependent on Confederate cotton for our Lancashire mills that are being ruined? At the same time aren't we increasingly dependent on abundant Union wheat and corn and meat and other trade? He shuddered. God damn that war! And politicians, and Lincoln. Didn't the man's inaugural speech in March include: '. . . this country belongs to the people and whenever they shall grow weary of their government they can exercise their constitutional right to amend it, or revolutionary right to dismember it or overthrow it . . .'

Inflammatory to say the least! If that idea spread to Europe! My God! Dreadful! We may be at war with them any day, certainly at sea. Must have cotton.

He was trying to collect himself, heartily relieved that the Admiral had backed down and still cursing himself for losing control. You've got to be more careful, and mustn't worry about Yedo and your stupid, arrogant decision to 'go there, by God, in three days in a battleship and see the Shōgun, by God!' as though you're Clive of India. You're not. This is your first tour of the Far East and you're a novice. Madness to put all these men at risk over a few murders, madness to risk a full-scale war. But is it?

Sorry, but no.

If the Bakufu get away with this killing, then there will be no end and we will be forced to withdraw—until allied battle fleets return to enforce Imperial wills bloodily. Your decision is correct, the manner of reaching it wrong. Yes, but it's damned difficult with no one to talk to—who you can trust. Thank God Daphne arrives in a couple of months. I never thought I'd miss her and her counsel so much. I can't wait to see her and my boys—ten months is a long time and I know the change from London's stinking pea soup fogs and gloom will make her happy and please her and it will be grand for the boys. We could use some English ladies in the Settlement, of the right sort. We'll go on trips and she will make the Legation a home.

His eyes focused on the approaching headland. Around it was Yedo and the cannonade. Was that wise? he asked himself queasily. I hope so. Then the landing and going to the Legation. You've got to do that— and prepare for the meeting tomorrow. You're alone in this. Henri Seratard's waiting for you to mess up, hoping. And the Russian.

But you're the one in charge and it's your job, and don't forget you wanted to be 'Minister' somewhere, anywhere. Indeed I did, but I never expected Japan! Damn the Foreign Office. I've never been in a situation like this: all my experience has been at the French or Russian desk in London or at the Court of St. Petersburg, odd postings wangled to glorious Paris and Monaco with never a warship or regiment in sight. . . .

Marlowe was saying stiffly, "I hope you don't mind, sir, me giving my opinion of the Admiral's position."

"Oh, not at all." Sir William made an effort to put his worry aside: I will try to avoid war, but if it is to be, it will be. "You're quite right, Mr. Marlowe, and of course I'm honored to have Admiral Ketterer in charge," he said, and at once felt better. "Our difference of opinion was over protocol. Yes, but at the same time we should be encouraging the Japanese to industrialize and to sail ships, one ship or twenty's nothing to be concerned about. We should encourage them—we're not here to colonize, but it is we who should be training them, Mr. Marlowe, not the Dutch or the French. Thank you for reminding me—the more our influence here the better." He was feeling lighter. It was rare for him to be able to talk freely to one of the up-and-coming captains and he found Marlowe impressive, both here and at Kanagawa. "Do all officers detest civilians and traders?"

"No, sir. But I don't think many of us understand them. We have different lives, different priorities. It's difficult for us at times." Most of Marlowe's attention was on the Admiral, who was talking to the Captain on the bridge, everyone nearby uneasily aware of him. The sun broke through the overcast and all at once the day seemed better. "To be in the Navy is, well, it's all I ever wanted to do."

"Your family is naval?"

At once Marlowe said proudly, "Yes, sir," wanting to add, my father's a Captain, presently in the Home Fleet—so was his father, he was Flag Lieutenant to Admiral Lord Collingwood in *Royal Sovereign* at Trafalgar—and my forebears have been in the Navy since there was one. And before that, so legend goes, they ran privateers out of Dorset where the family comes from—we've lived there, in the same house, for more than four centuries. But he said none of it, his training telling him it would sound like boasting. He just added, "My family come from Dorset."

"Mine come from the north of England, Northumberland, for generations," Sir William said absently, his eyes on the approaching headland, his mind on the Bakufu. "My father died when I was young—he was a Member of Parliament, with business interests in Sunderland and London, and dealt in the Baltic trade and Russian furs. My mother was Russian so I grew up bilingual and that got me on the first rung of the F.O. She was . . ." He caught himself just in time, astonished that he had volunteered so much. He had been going to add that she, his mother, was born the Countess Sveva, a cousin to the Romanovs, that she was still alive and once had been a lady-in-waiting to Queen Victoria. I really must concentrate—as if my family and background were any of their business. "Er, what about you, Tyrer?"

"London, sir. Father's a solicitor, like his father." Phillip Tyrer laughed. "After I got my degree at London University and told him I wanted to join the Foreign Office he almost had a fit! And when I applied to become an interpreter in Japan he told me I'd gone mad."

"Perhaps he was right, you're damned lucky to be alive and you're hardly here a week. Don't you agree, Marlowe?"

"Yes, sir. That's true." Marlowe thought the time apt. "By the way, Phillip, how is Mr. Struan?"

"Neither good nor bad was how George Babcott put it."

"I certainly hope he recovers," Sir William said, a sudden ache in his bowels.

When he had gone to Kanagawa three days ago, Marlowe had met his cutter and told him what he knew about Struan and Tyrer, about losing the soldier, the suicide of the assassin, and chasing the other one.

'Pallidar and I charged after the bugger, Sir William, but the man had just vanished. We combed the surrounding houses but nothing. Tyrer thinks they might be the two Tokaidō attackers, sir, the murderers. But he's not sure, most of them look alike, don't they?'

'But if they were the two, why should they risk going to the Legation?'

'The best we could come up with was perhaps to prevent identification and to finish the job, sir.'

They had left the wharf and hurried through the ominously deserted streets. 'What about the girl, Mr. Marlowe?'

'Seems to be fine, sir. Just shaken.'

'Good, thank God for that. The French Minister is wound up as tight as a gnat's bum about the "vile insult to honor of France and one of his nationals who is also his ward." The sooner she's back in Yokohama the better—oh, by the way, the Admiral asked me to tell you to return to Yokohama at once. We, er, we've decided to pay Yedo a formal visit in three days, by flagship. . . .'

Marlowe had felt his excitement explode. Sea or land engagements were the only real way to quick promotion and to the Admiral's bars he would have at all costs. I'll make the Old Man proud of me, and get Flag Rank long before Charles and Percy—his two younger brothers, both Lieutenants.

And now on the deck of the flagship, the sun good, the deck throbbing with the power of the engines, his excitement welled up again. "We'll be off Yedo before you know it, sir. Your entrance will be the biggest that's ever been, you'll get the murderers, indemnity and anything else you want."

Both Tyrer and Sir William had heard the excitement, but Sir William only felt chilled. "Yes, well, I think I'll go below for a minute. No, thank you, Mr. Marlowe, I know the way."

With great relief, the two young men watched him go. Marlowe checked that the Admiral was within sight. "What happened at Kanagawa after I left, Phillip?"

"It was, well, extraordinary, she was extraordinary, if that's what you were asking."

"How so?"

"About five o'clock she came down and went straight to see Malcolm Struan and stayed with him until dinner—that's when I saw her. She seemed . . . seemed older, no, that's not quite right either, not older but more serious than before, mechanical. George says she's still in some form of shock. During dinner Sir William said he'd take her back with him to Yokohama but she just thanked him and refused, said she'd first have to make sure Malcolm was all right, and neither he nor George nor any of us could persuade her otherwise. She hardly ate anything and went back to his sickroom, stayed with him and even insisted on having a cot made up there so she could be within call if need be. In fact, for the next two days, until yesterday when I went back to Yokohama, she hardly left his side and we barely spoke a dozen words to her."

Marlowe covered a sigh. "She must love him."

"That's the strange part. Neither Pallidar nor I think that's the reason. It's almost as though she's . . . well, 'disembodied' is too strong a word. It's more like she's partially in a dream and that being with him is safe."

"Christ! What did Sawbones say?"

"He just shrugged and said to be patient, not to worry, and that she was the best tonic Malcolm Struan could have."

"I can imagine. How is he, really?"

"Drugged most of the time, lot of pain, lot of vomit and loose bowels—don't know how she stands the smell though the window's open all the time." Fear washed over both of them at the thought of being so wounded and so helpless. Tyrer glanced ahead, to hide, still deeply conscious that his own wound had not yet healed, knowing it could still rot, and that his sleep had been nightmared with samurai and bleeding swords and her.

"Every time I popped by to see Malcolm—and, to be honest, to see her," he continued, "she just answered me with 'yes, no or I don't know,' so after a while I gave up. She's . . . she's still as attractive as ever."

Marlowe wondered: If Struan weren't around, would she be truly out of reach? How serious a rival could Tyrer be? Pallidar he dismissed as not in the same league—she couldn't like that pompous bugger.

"My word, look!" Tyrer said.

They were rounding the headland and they saw the vast Bay of Yedo before them, open sea to starboard, smoke from cooking fires of the sprawling city shrouding it, the landscape and overlording castle. Astonishingly the bay was almost empty of the multitude of ferries and sampans and fishing boats that normally abounded, with the few there scurrying for shore.

Tyrer was very uneasy. "Is it going to be war?"

After a pause, Marlowe said, "They had their warning. Most of us think no, not a full-scale war, not yet, not this time. There'll be incidents . . ." Then, because he liked Tyrer and admired his courage, he opened his mind to him. "There'll be incidents and skirmishes of various sizes, some of our people will get killed, some will discover they are cowards, some will become heroes, most will be petrified from time to time, some will be decorated but of course we will win."

Tyrer thought about that, remembering how frightened he had already been but how Babcott had convinced him that the first time was the worst time, how brave Marlowe had been rushing after the assassin, how ravishing Angelique was—and how good it was to be alive, young, with one foot on the ladder to 'Minister.' He smiled. Its warmth lit up Marlowe as well. "All's fair in love and war, isn't it?" he said.

Angelique was sitting in the window of the sickroom at Kanagawa, staring into space, the sun breaking through the powder-puff clouds from time to time, her heavily perfumed handkerchief to her nose. Behind her Struan was half awake, half asleep. In the garden soldiers patrolled constantly. Since the attack security had been redoubled, more troops sent from the Yokohama encampment, with Pallidar temporarily in command.

A tap on the door pulled her from her reverie. "Yes?" she said, hiding the kerchief in her hand.

It was Lim. Beside him was a Chinese orderly with a tray. "Food for Master. Missee wantchee eat, heya?"

"Put there!" she ordered, and pointed at the bedside table. She was about to ask for her tray to be brought as usual, then changed her mind, thinking it safe. "Tonight, tonight Missee food dining room. Unn'erstan, heya?"

"Unn'erstan." Lim laughed to himself, knowing that when she thought she was alone she used the kerchief. Ayeeyah, is her nose as small and delicate as her other part? Smell? What's the smell they complain of? There's no smell of death here yet. Should I tell the taipan's son that news is bad from Hong Kong? Ayeeyah, better he finds out for himself. "Unn'erstan." He beamed and left.

"Chéri?" Automatically she offered the chicken soup.

"Later, thank you, darling," Malcolm Struan said. As expected, his voice very weak.

"Try to take some," she said as usual. Again he refused.

Back once more to her seat in the window and her daydreams—about being safe at home in Paris again, in the great house of her uncle Michel and her darling Emma, the highborn English aunt who had mothered her and brought her and her brother up when her father had left so many years ago for Hong Kong, all of them surrounded in luxury, Emma planning luncheons and riding in the Bois on her prize stallion, the envy of everyone, charming the massed aristocracy and being fawned on in return, then bowing so gracefully to Emperor Louis Napoléon—Napoléon Bonaparte's nephew—and his Empress, Eugénie, and their smiling recognition.

Boxes at theatres, La Comédie Française, choice tables at Trois Frères Provençaux, her coming of age, seventeen, the talk of the season, Uncle Michel recounting his adventures at the gambling tables and the races, whispering naughty stories about his aristocratic friends, his mistress, the Countess Beaufois, so beautiful and seductive and devoted.

All daydreams, of course, for he was only a junior Deputy in the War Ministry, and Emma, English yes but an actress from a travelling group of Shakespearean players, daughter of a clerk, but neither with enough money for the outward display so necessary for Angelique in the capital of the world, for the spectacular horse, or two-in-hand and carriage that she needed so desperately to break into real society, the real upper echelon, to meet those who would marry and not just bed and flaunt and soon pass on to a younger flower.

'Please please please, Uncle Michel, it's so important!'

'I know, my little cabbage,' he had said sadly on her seventeenth birthday when she had begged for a particular gelding and the riding clothes to match. 'There's nothing more I can do, there are no more favors I can ask, I know no more arms to twist, or other moneylenders to persuade. I possess no State secrets to sell, or princes to promote. There's your young brother and our daughter to consider.'

'But please, darling Uncle.'

'I have one last idea and enough francs for a modest passage out to join your father. A few clothes, no more.'

Then the making of the clothes, all perfect, then trying them on and refitting and improving and yes, the green silk gown as well as all the others—Uncle Michel won't mind—then the excitement of the first railway journey to Marseille, steamer to Alexandria in Egypt, overland to Port Said past the first diggings of Monsieur de Lesseps' canal at Suez that all wise, informed people believe was just another stock promotion, that it would never be finished, or if it was, would partially empty the Mediterranean because those seas were higher than the seas below. Onwards, everything begged pleaded beguiled and from the very beginning correctly First Class: 'The difference is really so tiny, dear dear Uncle Michel . . .'

Sweet winds and new faces, exotic nights and good days, the beginning of the great adventure, at the end of the rainbow a handsome, rich husband like Malcolm now all spoiled because of a filthy native!

Why can't I just think about the good parts? she asked herself in sudden anguish. Why is it good thoughts dribble into the bad and then into the awful and then I start thinking about what truly happened and begin to cry?

Don't, she ordered herself, forcing away the tears. Behave. Be strong!

You decided before you left your room: nothing happened, you will act normally until your next period arrives. When it begins—*it will begin*—then you are safe.

But if . . . if it doesn't?

You won't think about that. Your future *will not* be torn asunder, that wouldn't be fair. You will pray and you will stay close to Malcolm, and pray for him too, and act the Florence Nightingale, and then perhaps you will marry him.

She glanced at him over the handkerchief. To her surprise he was watching her.

"Is the smell still so awful?" he asked sadly.

"No, *chéri*," she said, pleased the lie sounded more sincere each time and required less effort. "Some soup, yes?"

Wearily he nodded, knowing that he must have some nourishment but whatever he consumed would inevitably be retched out of him and tear the stitches, within and without, and the pain that followed would unman him again, much as he tried to contain it. *"Dew neh loh moh,"* he muttered. The curse was Cantonese, his first language.

She held the cup and he drank and she wiped his chin, and he drank a little more. Half of him wanted to order her away until he was up and about again, the other half terrified she would leave and never return. "Sorry about all this—I love your being here."

For a reply she just touched his forehead gently, wanting to leave, needing fresh air, not trusting herself to speak. The less you speak the better, she had decided. Then you will not be trapped.

She watched herself minister to him and settle him and all the while let her mind drift to ordinary happenings, to Hong Kong or to Paris, mostly Paris. Never would she allow herself to dwell on that night's wake-sleep dream. Never during the day, too dangerous. Only at night when the door was safely barred and she was alone and safe in bed could she release the dam and permit her mind to voyage where it would. . . .

A knock. "Yes?" Babcott strode in. She flushed under his gaze. Why is it I think he can always read my thoughts?

"Just wanted to see how both my patients are doing," he said jovially. "Well, Mr. Struan, how are you?"

"About the same, thank you."

Dr. Babcott's sharp eyes noticed that half the soup had gone but there was no vomit yet to clear up. Good. He held Struan's wrist. Pulse rate jumpy but better than before. Forehead still clammy, still a temperature, but that's also lower than yesterday. Dare I hope he will actually recover? His mouth was saying how improved the patient was, that it must be the ministrations of the lady, nothing to do with him, the usual. Yes, but so little else to say, so much up to God, if there's a God. Why do I always add that? If.

"If you continue to improve I think that we should move you back to Yokohama. Perhaps tomorrow."

"That's not wise," she said at once, frightened she would lose her haven, her voice harsher than she had wanted.

"Sorry, but it is," Babcott said kindly, wanting at once to calm her, admiring her fortitude and concern over Struan. "I wouldn't advise it if there was a risk, but it would be wise, really. Mr. Struan would have much more comfort, more help."

"*Mon Dieu,* what else can I do? He mustn't leave, not yet, not yet."

"Listen, darling," Struan said, trying to sound strong. "If he thinks I can move back, that would be good, really. It would free you and make it easier."

"But I don't want to be free, I want us to stay here, exactly as it is now without . . . without any fuss." She felt her heart pumping and she knew she was sounding hysterical but she had not planned for a move. Stupid, you're stupid. Of course there would have to be a move. Think! What can you do to prevent it?

But there was no need to prevent anything. Struan was saying that she should not be concerned, it would be better to be back in the Settlement, she would be safer and he would be happier and there were dozens of servants and suites of rooms in the Struan Building, that if she wished she could have the suite next to his and she could stay or leave, just as she wished, with constant access by day or by night. "Please don't worry, I want you to be content too," he assured her. "You'll be more comfortable, I promise, and when I'm better I'll . . ."

A spasm took him and used him.

After Babcott had cleaned up and Struan was once more drugged asleep, he said quietly, "It really would be better for him there. I've

more help, more materials, it's almost impossible to keep everything
clean here. He needs . . . sorry, but he needs stronger aid. You do more
than you can imagine for him, but certain functions his Chinese
servants can do better for him. Sorry to be blunt."

"You don't have to apologize, Doctor. You're right and I understand." Her mind had been racing. The suite next to Malcolm's will be
ideal, and servants and fresh clothes. I'll find a seamstress and have
beautiful dresses made, and be correctly chaperoned and in
command—of him and of my future. "I only want what's best for
him," she said, then added quietly, needing to know, "How long will
he be like this?"

"Confined to bed and fairly helpless?"

"Yes, please tell me the truth. Please."

"I don't know. At least two or three weeks, perhaps more, and he
won't be very mobile for a month or two after that." He glanced at the
inert man a moment. "I'd prefer you didn't say anything to him. It
would worry him unnecessarily."

She nodded to herself, content and at ease now, everything in place.
"Don't worry, I won't say a word. I pray he'll get strong quickly and
promise to help all I can."

As Dr. Babcott left her he was thinking over and over, My God, what
a wonderful woman! If Struan lives or dies, he's a lucky man to be
loved so much.

9

THE 21-GUN SALUTE FROM EACH OF the six warships, anchored off Yedo, that had accompanied the flagship echoed and re-echoed, all personnel in the fleet excited and proud of their power and that the time for restitution had come.

"Thus far and no further, Sir William," Phillip Tyrer exulted, standing beside him at the gunnel, the smell of cordite heady. The city was vast. Silent. The castle dominant.

"We'll see."

On the bridge of the flagship the Admiral said quietly to the General, "This should convince you that our Wee Willie's just a little popinjay with delusions of grandeur. Royal salute be damned. We'd better watch our backsides."

"You're right, by Jove! Yes. I'll add it to my monthly report to inform the War Office."

On the deck of the French flagship, Henri Seratard was puffing his pipe and laughing with the Russian Minister. "*Mon Dieu*, my dear Count, this is a happy day! The honor of France will be vindicated by normal English arrogance. Sir William is bound to fail. Perfidious Albion is more perfidious than ever."

"Yes. Disgusting that it's their fleet and not ours."

"But soon your fleets and ours will have replaced them."

"Yes. Then we're secretly agreed? When the English leave, we take Japan's North Island, plus Sakhalin, the Kuriles and all islands linking it to Russian Alaska—France the rest."

"Agreed. As soon as Paris gets my memorandum it will surely be ratified at the highest level, secretly." He smiled. "When a vacuum exists, it is our diplomatic duty to fill it. . . ."

* * *

With the cannonade a great fear exploded over Yedo. All remaining skeptics joined the masses clogging every road and bridge and lane, fleeing with the few possessions they could carry—of course no wheels anywhere—everyone expecting that bursting shells and rockets they had heard of but had never witnessed would any moment rain fire and their city would burn, burn, burn and them with it.

"Death to gai-jin," was on every lip.

"Hurry . . . Out of the way . . . Hurry!" People were shouting, here and there in panic, a few crushed or shoved off bridges or into houses, most stoically plodding onwards—but always away from the sea. "Death to gai-jin!" they said as they fled.

The exodus had begun this morning, the moment the fleet had weighed anchor in Yokohama harbor, though three days earlier the more prudent merchants had quietly hired the best porters and removed themselves, their families and valuables when rumors of the *unfortunate incident*—and the resulting foreign uproar and demands—had flashed through the city.

Only the samurai in the castle and those manning the outer defenses and strong points were still in place. And, as always and everywhere, the carrion of the streets, animal and human, who slunk and sniffed around the lockless houses, seeking what could be stolen and later sold. Very little was stolen. Looting was considered a particularly hideous crime and, from time immemorial, perpetrators would be pursued relentlessly until caught and then crucified. Any form of stealing was punished in the same fashion.

Within the castle keep, Shōgun Nobusada and Princess Yazu were cowering behind a flimsy screen, their arms around each other, their guards, maids and court ready for instant departure, only awaiting the Guardian's permission to leave. Everywhere in the castle proper, men were preparing defenses in depth, others harnessing horses and packing the most valuable possessions of the Elders for evacuation, with their owners, the moment shelling began or word was brought to the Council that enemy troops were disembarking.

In the Council chamber at the hurriedly convened meeting of the Elders, Yoshi was saying, "I repeat, I don't believe they'll attack us in force, or sh—"·

"And I see no reason to wait. To go is prudent, they will start shelling any moment," Anjo said. "The first cannonade was their warning."

"I don't think so, I think it was just an arrogant announcement of their presence. There were no shells in the city. The fleet won't shell us and I repeat, I believe the meeting tomorrow will take place as planned. At the meet—"

"How can you be so blind? If our positions were reversed and you commanded that fleet and possessed that overwhelming power, would you hesitate for a moment?" Anjo was stark with rage. "Well, would you?"

"No, of course not! But they are not us and we not them and that's the way to control them."

"You are beyond understanding!" In exasperation Anjo turned to the other three Councillors. "The Shōgun must be taken to a safe place, we must go too to carry on the government. That's all I propose, a temporary absence. Except for our personal retainers, all other samurai will stay, the Bakufu stays." Once more he glared at Yoshi. "You stay if you wish. Now we will vote: the temporary absence is approved!"

"Wait! If you do that the Shōgunate will lose face forever, we'll never be able to control the daimyos and their opposition—or the Bakufu. Never!"

"We are just being prudent! The Bakufu remains in place. So do all warriors. As Chief Councillor it's my right to call for a vote, so vote! I vote Yes!"

"I say No!" Yoshi said.

"I agree with Yoshi-san," Utani said. He was a short, thin man with kind eyes and spare visage. "I agree, if we leave we lose face forever."

Yoshi smiled back, liking him—daimyos of the Watasa fief were ancient allies since before Sekigahara. He looked at the other two, both senior members of Toranaga clans. Neither met his eyes. "Adachi-sama?"

Finally, Adachi, daimyo of Mito, a rotund little man, said nervously, "I agree with Anjo-sama that we should leave, and the Shōgun of course. But I also agree with you that then we may lose even though we gain. Respectfully I vote No!"

The last Elder, Toyama, was in his middle fifties, grey-haired with heavy dewlaps and blind in one eye from a hunting accident—an old man as ages went in Japan. He was daimyo of Kii, father of the young Shōgun. "It bothers me not at all if we live or die, nor the death of my son, this Shōgun—there will always be another. But it bothers me very much to retreat just because gai-jin have anchored off our shore. I vote against retreat and for attack. I vote we go to the coast and if the jackals land we kill them all, their ships, cannon, rifles notwithstanding!"

"We don't have enough troops here," Anjo said, sick of the old man and his militancy that had never been proved. "How many times do I have to say it: we do not have enough troops to hold the castle and stop them landing in strength. How many times do I have to repeat, our spies say they have two thousand soldiers with rifles in the ships and at the Settlement, and ten times that number in Hong Kong an—"

Yoshi interrupted angrily, "We would have had more than enough samurai and their daimyos here if you hadn't cancelled *sankin-kotai*!"

"That was at the Emperor's request, given in writing and presented by a Prince of his Court. We had no option but to obey. You would also have obeyed."

"Yes—if I'd taken delivery of the document! But I would never have accepted it, I would have been away, or would have delayed the Prince, any one of a hundred ploys, or bartered with Sanjiro who instigated the 'requests,' or told one of our Court supporters to petition the Emperor to withdraw the requests," Yoshi's voice snapped. "Any petition from the Shōgunate must be approved—that's historic law. We still control the Court's stipend! You betrayed our heritage."

"You call me a traitor?" To everyone's shock Anjo's hand tightened on his sword hilt.

"I say you allowed Sanjiro to puppet you," Yoshi replied without moving, calm on the surface of his skin, hoping that Anjo would make the first move and then he could kill him and have done with his stupidity forever. "There is no precedent to go against the Legacy. It was a betrayal."

"All daimyos other than immediate Toranaga families wanted it! The consensus of Bakufu agreed, the *roju* agreed, better to agree than to force all daimyos into the camp of the outside lords to challenge us at once as Sanjiro, the Tosas and Choshus would have done. We would have been totally isolated. Isn't that true?" he said to the others. "Well, isn't it?"

Utani said quietly, "It's certainly true I agreed—but now I think it was a mistake."

"The mistake we made was not to intercept Sanjiro and kill him," Toyama said.

"He was protected by Imperial Mandate," Anjo said.

His old man's lips curled from his yellow teeth. "So?"

"All Satsuma would have risen up against us, rightly; the Tosa and Choshu would join in and we'd have a general civil war we cannot win. Vote! Yes or no?"

"I vote for attack, only attack," the old man said stubbornly, "today on any landing, tomorrow at Yokohama."

From far off came the skirl of bagpipes.

Four more cutters were heading for the wharf, three packed with Highland Infantry to join others already formed up there, drums beating and bagpipes wailing impatiently. Kilts, busbies, scarlet tunics, rifles. Sir William, Tyrer, Lun and three of his staff were in the last boat.

As they came ashore, the captain in charge of the detachment saluted. "Everything's ready, sir. We've patrols guarding this wharf and the surrounding areas. Marines will take over from us within the hour."

"Good. Then let's proceed to the Legation."

Sir William and his party got into the carriage that had been ferried and manhandled ashore with so much effort. Twenty sailors picked up the traces. The captain gave the order to advance and the cortege marched off, flags waving, soldiers surrounding them, a resplendent, six-feet-eight drum major to the fore, Chinese coolies from Yokohama nervously dragging baggage carts in the rear.

The narrow streets between the low, one-story shops and buildings were eerily empty. So was the inevitable guard post at the first wooden bridge over a festering canal. And the next. A dog charged out of an alley, barking and snarling, then picked itself up and scuttled away howling after a kick lifted it into the air and sent it sprawling ten yards. More empty streets and bridges, yet their way to the Legation was tortuous because of the carriage and because all streets were only for foot traffic. Again the carriage stuck.

"Perhaps we should walk, sir?" Tyrer asked.

"No, by God, I arrive by carriage!" Sir William was furious with himself. He had forgotten the narrowness of the streets. At Yokohama he had privately decided on the carriage just because wheels were forbidden, to further ram home his displeasure to the Bakufu. He called out, "Captain, if you have to knock down a few houses, so be it."

But that did not become necessary. The sailors, used to handling cannon in tight places below decks, good-naturedly shoved and pushed and cursed and half carried the carriage around the bottlenecks.

The Legation was on a slight rise in the suburb of Gotenyama, beside a Buddhist temple. It was a two-story, still uncompleted structure of British style and design inside a high fence and gates. Within three months of the Treaty's signing, work had begun.

Building had been agonizingly slow, partially because of British insistence on using their plans and their normal building materials such as glass for windows and bricks for bearing walls—which had to be brought from London, Hong Kong or Shanghai—constructing foundations and the like, which Japanese houses did not normally possess, being of wood, deliberately light and easy to erect and repair because of earthquakes, and raised off the ground. Most of the delays, however, were due to Bakufu reluctance to have any foreign edifices whatsoever outside Yokohama.

Even though not fully finished, the Legation was occupied and the British flag raised daily on the dominant flagpole, which further incensed the Bakufu and local citizens. Last year occupation was temporarily abandoned by Sir William's predecessor when ronin, at night, killed two guards outside his bedroom door, to British fury and Japanese rejoicing.

'Oh, so sorry . . .' the Bakufu said.

But the site, leased in perpetuity by the Bakufu—mistakenly, it had been claimed ever since—had been wisely chosen. The view from the forecourt was the best in the neighborhood and they could see the fleet drawn up in battle order, safely offshore, safely at anchor.

The cortege arrived in martial style to take possession again. Sir William had decided to spend the night in the Legation to prepare for tomorrow's meeting and he bustled about, stopping as the Captain saluted. "Yes?"

"Raise the flag, sir? Secure the Legation?"

"At once. Keep to the plan, lots of noise, drums, pipes and so on. Pipe the retreat at sunset, and have the band march up and down."

"Yes, sir." The Captain walked over to the flagstaff. Ceremoniously, to the heady skirl of more pipes and drums, once more the Union Jack broke out at the masthead. Immediately, by previous agreement, there was an acknowledging broadside from the flagship. Sir William raised his hat and led three resounding cheers for the Queen. "Good, that's better. Lun!"

"Heya, Mass'er?"

"Wait a minute, you're not Lun!"

"I Lun Two, Mass'r, Lun One come 'night, chop chop."

"All right, Lun Two. Dinner sunset, you make every Mass'er shipshape never mind."

Lun Two nodded sourly, hating to be in such an isolated, indefensible place, surrounded by a thousand hidden, hostile eyes that everyone carelessly dismissed, though nearly all must sense. I'll never understand barbarians, he thought.

*   *   *

That night Phillip Tyrer could not sleep. He lay on one of the straw mattresses atop a ragged carpet on the floor, wearily changing his position every few minutes, his mind unpleasantly crossed with thoughts of London and Angelique, the attack and the meeting tomorrow, the ache in his arm, and Sir William who had been irritable all day. It was cold with a slight promise of winter on the air, the room small. Windows with glass panes overlooked the spacious, well-planted back gardens. The other mattress bed was for the Captain but he was still making his rounds.

Apart from sounds of dogs foraging, a few tomcats, the city was silent. Occasionally he could hear distant ships' bells of the fleet sounding the hours and the throaty laughter of their soldiers and he felt reassured. Those men are superb, he thought. We're safe here.

At length he got up, yawned and padded over to the window, opened it to lean on the sill. Outside it was black, the cloud cover thick. No shadows but he saw many Highlanders patrolling with oil lamps. Beyond the fence to one side was the vague shape of the Buddhist temple. At sunset after the bagpipes had beat the retreat and the Union Jack had been ritually pulled down for the night, monks had barred their heavy gate, sounded their bell, then filled the night with their strange chanting: *"Ommm mahnee padmee hummmmm . . ."* over and over again. Tyrer had been calmed by it, unlike many of the others who shouted catcalls, telling them rudely to shut up.

He lit a candle that was beside the bed. His fob watch showed it was 2:30. Yawning again, he rearranged the blanket, propped himself up with the rough pillow and opened his small attaché case, his initials embossed on it—a parting gift from his mother—and took out his notebook. Covering the column of Japanese words and phrases he had written out phonetically, he muttered the English equivalents, then the next page, and the next. Then the same with the English and said aloud the Japanese. It pleased him every one was right.

"They're so few, I don't know if I'm pronouncing them correctly, I've so little time, and I haven't even begun to learn the writing," he muttered.

At Kanagawa he had asked Babcott where he could get the best teacher. 'Why not ask the padre?' Babcott had said.

He had, yesterday. 'Certainly, my boy. But can't this week, how about next month? Care for another sherry?'

My God, can they drink here! They're sozzled most of the time and certainly by lunch. The padre's useless, and smells to high heaven. But what a stroke of luck about André Poncin!

Yesterday afternoon he had accidentally met the Frenchman in one of the Japanese village shops that serviced their needs. These lined the village main street that was behind High Street, away from the sea and adjoined Drunk Town. All the shops appeared to be the same, selling the same kinds of local merchandise from food to fishing tackle, from cheap swords to curios. He was searching through a rack of Japanese books—the paper of very high quality, many beautifully printed and illustrated from woodblocks—trying to make himself understood to the beaming proprietor.

'*Pardon, Monsieur,*' the stranger had said, 'but you have to name the type of book you want.' He was in his thirties, clean-shaven, with brown eyes and brown, wavy hair, a fine Gallic nose and well dressed. 'You say: *Watashi hoshii hon, Ing'erish Nihongo, dozo*—I would like a book that has English and Japanese.' He smiled. 'Of course, there aren't any, though this fellow will tell you with abject sincerity, *Ah so desu ka, gomen nasai,* etc.—Ah, so sorry I have none today, but if you come back tomorrow . . . Of course he's not telling the truth, only telling you what he thinks you want to know, a fundamental Japanese habit. I'm afraid Japanese are not generous with the truth, even amongst themselves.'

'But, Monsieur, may I ask, then how did you learn Japanese—obviously you're fluent.'

The man laughed pleasantly. 'You are too kind. Me, I'm not, though I try.' An amused shrug. 'Patience. And because some of our Holy Fathers speak it.'

Phillip Tyrer frowned. 'I'm afraid I'm not Catholic, I'm Church of England, and, er, and an apprentice interpreter at the British Legation. My name is Phillip Tyrer and I've just arrived and a bit out of my depth.'

'Ah, of course, the young Englishman of the Tokaidō. Please excuse me, I should have recognized you. We were all horrified to hear about it. May I present myself, André Poncin, late of Paris. I'm a trader.'

'*Je suis enchanté de vous voir,*' Tyrer said, speaking French easily and well though with a slight English accent—throughout the world, outside of Britain, French was the language of diplomacy, and lingua franca of most Europeans, therefore essential for a Foreign Office posting—as well as for anyone considering themselves well educated. In French he added, 'Do you think the Fathers would consider teaching me, or allowing me to join their classes?'

'I don't believe any actually give classes. I could ask. Are you going with the fleet tomorrow?'

'Yes, indeed.'

'So am I, with Monsieur Seratard, our Minister. You were at the Legation in Paris before here?'

'Unfortunately no, I've only been to Paris for two weeks, Monsieur, on holiday—this is my first posting.'

'Oh, but your French is very good, Monsieur.'

'Afraid it's not—not really,' Tyrer said in English again. 'I presume you are an interpreter too?'

'Oh, no, just a businessman, but I try help Monsieur Seratard sometimes when his official Dutch-speaking interpreter is sick—I speak Dutch. So you wish to learn Japanese, as quickly as possible, eh?' Poncin went over to the rack and selected a book. 'Have you seen one of these yet? It's Hiroshige's *Fifty-three Stages on the Tokaidō Road*. Don't forget the beginning of the book is at the end for us, their writing right to left. The pictures show the way stations all the way to Kyōto.' He thumbed through them. 'Here's Kanagawa, and here Hodogaya.'

The four-color woodblock prints were exquisite, better than anything Tyrer had ever seen, the detail extraordinary. 'They're marvelous.'

'Yes. He died four years ago, pity, because he was a marvel. Some of their artists are extraordinary, Hokusai, Masanobu, Utamaro and a dozen others.' André laughed and pulled out another book. 'Here, these are a must, a primer for Japanese humor and calligraphy, as they call their writing.'

Phillip Tyrer's mouth dropped open. The pornography was decorous and completely explicit, page after page, with beautifully gowned men and women, their naked parts monstrously exaggerated and drawn in majestic, hairy detail as they joined vigorously and inventively. 'Oh, my God!'

Poncin laughed outright. 'Ah, then I have given you a new pleasure. As erotica they're unique, I have a collection I'd be glad to show you. They're called *shunga-e,* the others *ukiyo-e*—pictures from the Willow World or Floating World. Have you visited one of the bordellos yet?'

'I . . . I, no . . . no, I—I, er, haven't.'

'Oh, in that case, may I be a guide?'

Now in the night, Tyrer remembered their conversation and how secretly embarrassed he had been. He had tried to pretend he was equally a man of the world, but at the same time kept hearing his father's grave and constant advice: 'Listen, Phillip, Frenchmen are all vile and totally untrustworthy, Parisians the dregs of France, and Paris without doubt the sin city of the civilized world—licentious, vulgar, and French!'

Poor Papa, he thought, he's so wrong about so many things, but then he lived in Napoleonic times and survived the bloodbath of Waterloo. However great the victory, it must have been terrible for a ten-year-old drummer boy, no wonder he will never forgive or forget, or accept the new Era. Never mind, Papa has his life and as much as I love him, and admire him for what he did, I have to make my own way. France is almost an ally now—it's not wrong to listen and learn.

He flushed, remembering how he had hung on André's words— secretly ashamed of his avid fascination.

The Frenchman explained that here bordellos were places of great beauty, the best of them, and their courtesans, the Ladies of the Floating World, or Willow World as they were called, easily the best he had ever experienced. 'There are degrees, of course, and streetwalkers in most towns. But here we have our own Pleasure Quarter, called Yoshiwara. It's over the bridge outside the fence.' Again the pleasant laugh. 'We call it the Bridge to Paradise. Oh, yes, and you should know that . . . oh, excuse me, I interrupt your shopping.'

'Oh, but no, not at all,' he had said at once, aghast that this flow of information and rare opportunity would cease, and added in his most flowery and honeyed French, 'I would consider it an honor if you would care to continue, really, it is so important to learn as much as one can and I'm afraid the people I associate with, and talk to, are . . . regretfully, not Parisian, mostly stodgy and without French sophistication. To return your kindness perhaps I may offer you some tea or champagne at the English Tea House, or perhaps a drink at the Yokohama Hotel—sorry, but I'm not a member of the Club yet.'

'You are too kind. Yes, I would like that.'

Thankfully he beckoned the shopkeeper, with Poncin's help paid for the book, astonished it was so inexpensive. They went into the street. 'You were saying about the Willow World?'

'There's nothing sordid about it, as with most of our brothels and almost all those elsewhere in the world. Here, as in Paris, but more so, the act of sex is an art form, as delicate and special as great cuisine, to be considered and practiced and savored and thought of as such, with no . . . please excuse me, no misguided Anglo-Saxon "guilt." '

Instinctively, Tyrer bridled. For a moment he was tempted to correct him and say that there was a vast difference between guilt and a healthy attitude towards morality and all good Victorian values. And to add that, regretfully, the French had never possessed any distinction with their leaning towards loose living that seduced even such august nobles as the Prince of Wales who openly considered Paris home ('*a source of grave concern in the highest English circles,*' the *Times* glowered, '*French vulgarity knows no end, their wretched display of wealth and outrageous innovative dances, like the cancan where, it is reliably reported, the dancers deliberately do not and are even required not to wear any undergarments whatsoever*').

But he said none of it, knowing he would only be parroting more of his father's words. Poor Papa, he thought again, concentrating on Poncin as they strolled the High Street, the sun pleasing and the air bracing, with the promise of a fine day tomorrow.

'But here in Nippon, Monsieur Tyrer,' the Frenchman continued happily, 'there are marvelous rules and regulations, both for clients and the girls. For instance, they're not all on show at one time, except in the very low-class places, and even then you can't just go in and say, "I want that one." '

'You can't?'

'Oh, no, she always has the right to refuse you without any loss of face on her part. There are special protocols—I can explain in detail later if you wish—but each House is run by a madam, called mama-san, the *san* being a suffix meaning mistress, madam or mister, who prides herself on the elegance of her surroundings and her Ladies. They vary, of course, in price and excellence. In the best, the mama-san vets you, that's the right word, she considers if you are worthy to grace her House and all it contains, in substance whether or not you can pay the bill. Here a good customer can have a great deal of credit, Monsieur Tyrer, but woe betide you if you do not pay or are late once the bill is discreetly presented. Every House in all Japan will then refuse you every kind of entrance.'

Tyrer had guffawed nervously at the pun.

'How word passes I don't know, but it does, from here to Nagasaki. So, Monsieur, in certain ways this is paradise. A man can fornicate for a year on credit, if he so desires.' Poncin's voice changed imperceptibly. 'But the wise man buys a lady's contract and reserves her for his private pleasure. They are really so—so charming and so inexpensive when you consider the enormous profit we make on the money exchange.'

'You, well, that's what you advise?'

'Yes, yes, I do.'

They had had tea. Then champagne at the Club where André was clearly a well-known and popular member. Before they parted, André had said, 'The Willow World deserves care and attention. I would be honored to be one of your guides.'

He had thanked him, knowing he would never take advantage of the offer. I mean, what about Angelique? What about, what about catching one of the vile diseases, gonorrhea, or the French disease that the French call the English disease and the doctors call syphilis that George Babcott mentioned pointedly abounds, under any name, in any Asian or Middle Eastern Treaty port, '. . . or any port for that matter, Phillip. I see lots of cases here amongst the Japanese, not all European related. If you're that way inclined, wear a sheath, they're not safe, not much good yet. Best you don't, if you know what I mean.'

Phillip Tyrer shuddered. He had had only one experience. Two years ago he had become boisterously drunk with some fellow students after their finals, in the Star and Garter public house on Pont Street. 'Now's the time, Phillip, old boy. It's all fixed, she'll do it for tuppence, won't you, Flossy?' She was a bar girl, a bawdy of about fourteen, and the tumble had taken place hurriedly, sweatily, in a smelly upstairs cubbyhole—a penny for her and a penny for the publican. For months afterwards he was petrified he was poxed.

'We have more than fifty Teahouses, as they're called, or Inns, to choose from in our Yoshiwara, all licensed and controlled by the authorities, more going up every day. But take care, go nowhere in Drunk Town.' This was the unwholesome part of the Settlement, where the low-class bars and rooming houses clustered around the only European brothel: 'It's for soldiers and sailors and seamen, and for the riffraff, ne'er-do-wells, remittance men, gamblers and adventurers who congregate there, on sufferance. Every port acquires them because we have no police yet, no immigration laws. Perhaps Drunk Town's a safety valve but unwise to visit after dark. If you value your pocket book and your privates don't take them out there. *Musuko-san* deserves better.'

'What?'

'Ah, a very important word. *Musuko* means son, or my son. *Musuko-san* literally means Honorable Son, or Mr. My Son, but in the patois, cock or My Honorable Cock, pure and simple. Girls are called *musume*. Actually the word means daughter, or my daughter, but in the Willow World, vagina. You say to your girl, *'Konbanwa, musume-san.'* Good evening, *chérie*. But if you say it with the twinkle she knows you mean, How is it? How is your Golden Gully, as Chinese sometimes call man's passage to paradise—they are so wise, the Chinese, because the sides certainly are lined with gold, the whole nourished by gold and only opened with gold, one way or another . . .'

Tyrer lay back, his notebook forgotten, brain churning. Almost before he realized it, the little book of *ukiyo-e* that he had hidden in his briefcase was open and he was studying the pictures. Abruptly he replaced it.

No future in looking at dirty pictures, he thought, consumed with disgust. The candle was guttering now. He blew out the flame, then lay back, the familiar ache in his loins.

What a lucky man André is. Obviously he has a mistress. That must be marvelous, if even half of what he says is true.

I wonder if I could get one too? Could I buy a contract? André said many here do, and rent private little houses in the Yoshiwara that can be secret and discreet if you wish: 'It's rumored all the Ministers possess one, Sir William certainly goes there at least once a week—he thinks no one knows but everyone spies him and laughs—but not the Dutchman who's impotent, according to rumor, and the Russian who openly prefers to sample different Houses. . . .'

Should I risk it, if I could afford it? After all, André gave me a very special reason: 'To learn Japanese quickly, Monsieur, acquire a sleeping dictionary—it's the only way.'

But his last thought before sleep overwhelmed him was: I wonder why André was so kind to me, so voluble. Rare for a Frenchman to be so open with an Englishman. Very rare. And strange that he never mentioned Angelique once . . .

It was just before dawn. Ori and Hiraga, again in all-encompassing ninja clothes, came out of their hiding place in the temple grounds overlooking the Legation and ran silently down the hill, across the wooden bridge and into an alley, down it and into another. Hiraga led. A dog saw them, growled, moved into their path and died. The deft short arc of Hiraga's sword was instantaneous and he hurried onwards with the blade unsheathed, hardly missing a step, ever deeper into the city. Ori followed carefully. Today his wound had begun to fester.

In the lee of a hut on a protected corner, Hiraga stopped. "It's safe here, Ori!" he whispered.

Hastily both men slipped out of their ninja clothes and stuffed them into the soft bag Hiraga carried slung on his back, replacing them with nondescript kimonos. With great care Hiraga cleansed his sword using a piece of silk cloth, carried for that purpose by all swordsmen to protect their blades, then sheathed it. "Ready?"

"Yes."

Again he led onwards into the maze, surefooted, staying under cover where he could, hesitating at every open space until he was sure they were safe, seeing no one, meeting no one, then pressing on, heading for their safe house.

They had been watching the Legation since early morning, the bonzes—the Buddhist priests—pretending not to notice them, once they were sure the two men were not thieves and Hiraga had identified himself and their purpose: to spy on the gai-jin. All bonzes were fanatically xenophobic and anti-gai-jin, to them synonymous with Jesuit, still their most hated and feared enemy. 'Ah, you are shishi, then you are both welcome,' the old monk had said. 'We have never forgotten Jesuits ruined us, or that the Toranaga Shōguns are our scourge.'

From the middle of the fifteenth century to the early sixteenth, Portuguese alone knew the way to Japan. Papal edicts had also given them exclusivity to the islands, and Portuguese Jesuits the sole right to proselytize. Within a few years they had converted so many daimyos to Catholicism, therefore naturally their retainers, that Dictator Goroda had used them as an excuse to massacre thousands of Buddhist monks at that time militant, dominant in the land and opposed to him.

The *tairō*, Nakamura, who inherited his power, expanded it immensely, and played off bonze against Jesuit with honey, persecution, suffering and killing. Then came Toranaga.

Toranaga, tolerant of all religions, though not of foreign influence, observed that all converted daimyos had initially fought against him at Sekigahara. Three years later, he became Shōgun and two years after that he resigned in favor of his son, Sudara, but kept actual power—an old established Japanese custom.

During his lifetime he leashed Jesuits and Buddhists severely, and eliminated or neutralized the Catholic daimyos. His son, Shōgun Sudara, tightened the curbs and his son, Shōgun Hironaga, finished the plan laid down so carefully in the Legacy where he formally outlawed Christianity from Japan on pain of death. In 1638, Shōgun Hironaga destroyed the last Christian bastion at Shimabara, near Nagasaki, where a few thousand ronin, thirty thousand peasants and their families were in rebellion against him. Those who refused to recant were crucified or put to the sword immediately as common criminals. All but a handful refused. Then he turned his attention to the Buddhists.

Within days he was pleased to accept the gift of all their lands, and so fettered them.

'You are welcome, Hiraga-san, Ori-san,' the old monk had said again. 'We are for the shishi, for *sonno-joi* and against the Shōgunate. You are free to come or go as you please. If you want help, tell us.'

'Then keep a tally of the numbers of soldiers, their comings and goings, what rooms are occupied and by whom.'

The two men had waited and watched throughout the day. At dusk they put on their ninja clothes. Twice Hiraga moved closer to the Legation, once he scaled the fence to experiment and reconnoiter but quickly retreated unseen when a patrol almost trod on him.

'We'll never get in by night, Ori,' he whispered. 'Or by day. Too many troops now.'

'How long do you think they'll stay?'

Hiraga smiled. 'Until we drive them out.'

Now they were almost at their safe house, an Inn that lay to the east of the castle. Dawn was near, the sky lighter and cloud cover thinner than yesterday. Ahead the street was deserted. So was the bridge. Confident, Hiraga hurried onto it, skidded to a stop. A Bakufu patrol of ten men stepped out of the shadows. At once both sides went into attack-defense positions, hands on their sword hilts.

"Come forward and give me your identification papers," the senior samurai called out.

"Who are you to challenge anyone?"

"You see our badges," the man said angrily, stepping onto the wooden slats of the bridge. The remainder of his men spread out behind him. "We are warriors of Mito, 9th Regiment, guardians of the Shōgun. Identify yourselves."

"We have been spying on the enemy stockade. Let us pass."

"You look like thieves. What's in that bag on your back, eh? Identification!"

Ori's shoulder was throbbing. He had seen the telltale discoloration but had hidden it from Hiraga, and the pain. His head ached but he knew instantly he had nothing to lose and an admirable death to gain.

"Sonno-joi!" he bellowed suddenly, and hurled himself at the samurai on the bridge. The others backed off to give them room as Ori hacked with all his might, recovered as the blow was deflected and again attacked, feinted, and this time his blow was true. The man was dead on his feet, then crumpled. At once Ori darted for another man who retreated, went for another who also retreated. The ring of men began to close.

"Sonno-joi!" Hiraga shouted, and rushed to Ori's side. Together they stood at bay.

"Identify yourselves!" a young warrior said, unimpressed. "I am Hiro Watanabe and do not wish to kill or be killed by an unknown warrior."

"I am shishi from Satsuma!" Ori said proudly, adding an alias as was their usual custom, "Riyama Takagaki."

"And I from Choshu, my name Shodan Moto! *Sonno-joi,*" Hiraga shouted, and hurled himself at Watanabe, who retreated without fear, as did the others nearby.

"I've never heard of either of you," Watanabe said through his teeth. "You're not shishi—you are scum." His rush was parried. Hiraga, a master swordsman, used his assailant's strength and speed to catch him off balance, sidestepped and cut under the opposing sword into the man's unprotected side, withdrew and in one continuous movement sliced into the man's neck, decapitated him as he toppled to the ground, ending once more in perfect attack position.

The silence was profound. "Who did you study under?" someone asked.

"Toko Fujita was one of my Sensei," Hiraga said, every part of him ready for the next killing.

"Eeeee!" This was one of Mito's revered sword masters, who had been killed in Yedo's earthquake of '55 when a hundred thousand also perished.

"They are shishi, and men of Mito do not kill shishi, their own kind," one of the men said softly. *"Sonno-joi!"* Warily, this man moved aside a pace, not sure of the others, his sword still ready. They looked at him, then at one another. Opposite him another man moved. Now there was an inviting, narrow path between them, but all swords stayed poised.

Hiraga readied, expecting a trick, but Ori nodded to himself, his pain forgotten, victory or death the same to him. Taking his time, he cleansed his blade and sheathed it. Politely he bowed to both the dead men and strode through the narrow passage, looking neither right nor left nor backwards.

In a moment Hiraga followed. Equally slowly. Until they turned the corner. Then they both took to their heels and did not stop until they were well away.

10

THE FIVE BAKUFU REPRESENTA-
tives came leisurely into the Legation forecourt in their palanquins.
They were an hour late and preceded by samurai with banners bearing
their official emblems and surrounded by guards. Sir William stood at
the top of the wide steps that led to the imposing entrance. Beside him
were the French, Russian and Prussian Ministers—their aides, Phillip
Tyrer and others of the Legation staff to one side—and an honor guard
of Highlanders with some French soldiers Seratard had insisted upon.
Admiral Ketterer and the General had remained aboard, in reserve.

Ceremoniously the Japanese bowed, Sir William and the others
raised their hats. Ritually they conducted the Japanese to the large
audience hall, trying to restrain their amusement at their outlandish
costumes: small black lacquered hats set square on their shaven pates
and tied elaborately under their chins, the vast shouldered overgar-
ments, multicolored ceremonial silk kimonos, voluminous pantaloons,
thong sandals and shoe socks split between the toes—*tabi*—fans in
their belts and the inevitable two swords. "Those hats aren't big
enough to piss in," the Russian said.

Sir William sat in the center of one line of chairs with the Ministers,
Phillip Tyrer on one end to balance the delegation. The Bakufu took
the opposite row, interpreters on cushions in between. After lengthy
discussion they agreed on five guards each. These men stood behind
their masters and eyed each other suspiciously.

Following strict protocol, the adversaries introduced themselves.
Toranaga Yoshi was last: "Tomo Watanabe, junior official, second
class," he said, pretending a humbleness he did not feel, and took the
lowest position at the end of the row, his clothes less elaborate than

145

those of the others who, with all guards, had been commanded on pain
of punishment to treat him as the least important official here.

He settled himself, feeling strange. How ugly these enemies are, he
was thinking, how ridiculous and laughable with their tall hats, outlandish boots and ugly, heavy black clothes—no wonder they stink!

Sir William said carefully and simply: "An Englishman has been
murdered by Satsuma samurai . . ."

By five o'clock European tempers were frayed, the Japanese still
polite, smiling, outwardly imperturbable. In a dozen different ways
their spokesman claimed that . . . so sorry, but they had no jurisdiction
over the Satsuma, or knowledge of the murderers or any way to find
them, but yes, it was a regrettable affair, but no, they did not know how
to obtain reparations, but yes, under some circumstances reparations
might be sought, but no, the Shōgun was not available, but yes, the
Shōgun would be pleased to grant an audience when he returned, but
no, not in the foreseeable future, but yes, we will immediately petition
for an exact day, but no, it could not be this month because his present
whereabouts are not known for certain, but yes, it would be as soon as
possible, but no, the next meeting and all meetings should not take
place in Yedo, but yes, in Kanagawa, but so sorry, not this month,
perhaps next, but no, so sorry we do not have authority. . . .

Every point had to be translated from English to Dutch to
Japanese—as usual to be discussed at length by them—then pe-
dantically resubmitted into Dutch into English with an inevitable
homily, and ever polite requests for explanations on the most trivial
point.

Yoshi found the whole proceeding vastly interesting, never having
been near gai-jin en masse or attended a meeting where unequals,
astonishingly, discussed policy and did not listen and obey.

Three of the other four were genuine though unimportant Bakufu
officials. All had used false names, a normal custom when dealing with
aliens. The imposter, who secretly spoke English, sat beside Yoshi. His
name was Misamoto. Yoshi had ordered him to remember everything,
to tell him discreetly of anything important not translated accurately,
otherwise to keep his mouth shut. He was a felon under sentence of
death.

When Yoshi had sent for him the day before yesterday, Misamoto
had at once prostrated himself, shaking with fear.

'Get up and sit over there.' Yoshi pointed with his fan to the edge of
the tatami platform on which he sat.

Misamoto obeyed instantly. He was a small man with slitted eyes and long, grizzled hair and beard, the sweat running down his face, his clothes coarse and almost rags, hands callused and his skin the color of dark honey.

'You will tell me the truth: your interrogators report that you speak English?'

'Yes, Lord.'

'You were born in Anjiro in Izu and have been to the land called America?'

'Yes, Lord.'

'How long were you there?'

'Almost four years, Lord.'

'Where in America?'

'San Francisco, Lord.'

'What is San'frensiska?'

'A big city, Lord.'

'Just there?'

'Yes, Lord.'

Yoshi studied him, needing information quickly. He could see that the man was desperate to please but at the same time frightened to death, of him and of the guards who had hustled him in and shoved his head to the ground. So he decided to try a different approach. He dismissed the guards and got up and leaned on the windowsill, looking at the city. 'Tell me, quickly, in your own words what happened to you.'

'I was a fisherman in the village of Anjiro in Izu, Lord, where I was born thirty-three years ago, Lord.' Misamoto began at once— obviously the tale told a hundred times before. 'Nine years ago I was fishing with six others in my boat, a few *ri* offshore, but we were caught in a sudden storm that quickly became a great one and we were blown before it for thirty days or more, eastwards, out into the great sea, hundreds of *ri*, perhaps a thousand, Sire. During this time, three of my companions were washed overboard. Then the sea became calm but our sails had been ripped to pieces and there was no food and no water. The three of us fished but caught nothing, there was no water to drink . . . One of us went mad and jumped into the sea and began to swim to an island he thought he saw and drowned quickly. We saw no land or ship, just water. Many days later the other man, my friend Ishii, died and I was alone. Then one day I thought I had died because I saw this strange ship that went along without sails and seemed to be on fire, but it was just a paddle steamer, American, going from Hong Kong to San Francisco. They rescued me, gave me food and treated me as one of them— I was petrified, Lord, but they shared their food and drink and clothed me. . . .'

'This American ship took you to this San place? What happened then?'

Misamoto told how he had been put with a brother of the Captain of this ship, a ship's chandler, to learn the language and do odd jobs until the authorities decided what to do with him. He lived with this family for about three years, working in their shop and in the port. One day, he was taken before an important official called Natow who questioned him closely, then told him he was to be sent with the warship *Missouri* to Shimoda to be an interpreter for Consul Townsend Harris who was already in Japan negotiating a Treaty. By this time he wore Western clothes and had learned some Western ways.

'I accepted happily, Sire, certain I could be helpful here, especially helpful to the Bakufu. On the ninth day of the eighth month of the year 1857 by their counting, five years ago, Sire, we hove to off Shimoda in Izu, my home village not far north, Sire. The moment I was ashore I obtained permission to leave for a day and set off at once, Lord, to report to the nearest guard house to find the nearest Bakufu official, believing I would be welcome because of the knowledge I had got. . . . But the barrier guards would not . . .' Misamoto's face twisted with anguish. 'But they wouldn't listen to me, Sire, or understand. . . . They bound me and dragged me to Yedo. . . . That was about five years ago, Lord, and ever since I've been treated like a criminal, confined like one though not in prison and I keep explaining and explaining I'm not a spy but a loyal man of Izu and what had happened to me . . .'

To Yoshi's disgust, tears began streaming down the man's face. He cut the whimpering short. 'Stop it! Do you or do you not know it is forbidden, by law, to leave Nippon without permission?'

'Yes, Lord, but I th—'

'And do you know under the same law, if broken, whatever the reason, whoever he or she is, the lawbreaker is forbidden to return on pain of death?'

'Oh, yes, Sire, yes—yes I did but—but I did not think it would include me, Sire, I thought I'd be welcomed and valuable and I'd been blown out to sea. It was the storm th—'

'A law is a law. This law is a good law. It prevents contamination. You consider you have been treated unfairly?'

'Oh, no, Lord,' Misamoto said hastily, wiping his tears away, with even greater fear, bowing his head to the tatami. 'Please excuse me, I beg your forgiveness, please ex—'

'Just answer the questions. How fluent is your English?'

'I . . . I understand and speak some American English, Sire.'

'Is that the same as the gai-jin here speak?'

'Yes, Sire, yes, more or less—'

'When you came to see the American Harris were you shaven or unshaven?'

'Unshaven, Sire. I had a trimmed beard like most sailors, Sire, and let my hair grow like theirs and tied into a pigtail and knotted with tar.'

'Who did you meet with this gai-jin Harris?'

'Just him, Sire, just for an hour or so, and one of his staff, I don't remember his name.'

Once more Yoshi weighed the dangers of his plan: to go to the meeting disguised, without Council approval, and to use this man as a spy, to overhear the enemy secretly. Perhaps Misamoto is a spy already, for gai-jin, he thought grimly, as all his interrogators believe. Certainly he's a liar, his story far too smooth, his eyes too cunning, and he's like a fox when off guard.

'Very well. Later I want to know everything you have learned, everything and . . . do you read and write?'

'Yes, Lord, but only a little in the English.'

'Good. I have a use for you. If you obey exactly and please me, I will review your case. If you fail me, however slightly, you-will-wish-you-had-not.'

He explained what he wanted, assigned him teachers, and when his guards had returned Misamoto yesterday clean-shaven, his hair dressed like a samurai's, and wearing the clothes of an official with two swords though these were false and without blades, he had not recognized him. 'Good. Walk up and down.'

Misamoto obeyed and Yoshi was impressed how quickly the man had learned an erect posture as the teacher had shown him, not the correct, normal servile attitude of a fisherman. Too quickly, he thought, convinced now that Misamoto was more, or less, than he wanted others to see.

'You understand clearly what you are to do?'

'Yes, Sire, I swear I won't fail you, Sire.'

'I know, my guards have orders to kill you the instant you leave my side, or become clumsy, or . . . indiscreet.'

"We'll stop for ten minutes," Sir William said wearily. "Tell them, Johann."

"They ask why." Johann Favrod, the Swiss interpreter yawned.

"Pardon. Seems they think they've discussed all the points etc. etc,
that they'll carry back your message etc. etc. and meet again at Kanagawa with the reply from on high etc. etc. in about sixty days as
suggested earlier etc. etc."

The Russian muttered, "Let me have the fleet for a day, and I'll
solve these *matyeryebitz* and this whole problem."

"Quite," Sir William agreed, adding in fluent Russian, "Sorry, my
dear Count, but we're here for a diplomatic solution, preferably." Then
in English, "Show them where to wait, Johann. Shall we, gentlemen?"
He got up, bowed stiffly, and led the way into a waiting room. As he
passed Phillip Tyrer he said, "Stay with them, keep your eyes and ears
open."

All the Ministers headed for the tall chamber pot that was in the
corner of their anteroom. "My God," Sir William said thankfully.
"Thought my bloody bladder would pop."

Lun came in leading other servants with trays. "Heya, Mass'er. Tea-
ah, sam'wich-ah!" He jerked a disdainful thumb towards the other
room. "All same give monkees, heya?"

"You'd better not let them hear you say that, by God. Perhaps some
of them speak pidgin."

Lun stared at him. "Wat say, Mass'er?"

"Oh, never mind."

Lun went out laughing to himself.

"Well, gentlemen, as expected, progress zero."

Seratard was lighting his pipe, André Poncin beside him, carelessly
pleased with Sir William's discomfiture. "What do you propose to do,
Sir William?"

"What's your advice?"

"It is a British problem, only partially French. If it was entirely mine
I would have already settled it with French élan—on the day it happened."

"But of course, *mein Herr,* you would need an equally fine fleet,"
von Heimrich said curtly.

"Of course. In Europe we have many, as you know. And if it was
Imperial French policy to be here in strength as our British allies, we
would have had one or two fleets here."

"Yes, well . . ." Sir William was tired. "It's clear that your collective advice is to be tough with them?"

"Rough and tough," Count Zergeyev said.

"*Ja.*"

"Of course," Seratard agreed. "I thought that's what you had already in mind, Sir William."

The Minister munched on a sandwich and finished his tea. "All right. I'll close the meeting now, reconvene for ten tomorrow, with an ultimatum: a meeting with the Shōgun within a week, the murderers, the indemnity or else—with, er, of course your joint approval."

Seratard said, "I suggest, Sir William, given it might be difficult for them to deliver a meeting with the Shōgun, why not keep that for later until we have reinforcements—and real cause for a meeting with him. After all, this exercise is a show of force to correct an evil, not to implement Imperial policy, yours or ours."

"Wise," the Prussian said reluctantly.

Sir William pondered the reasons behind the suggestion but could find no fault or hidden hazard. "Very well. We'll demand an 'early meeting' with the Shōgun. Agreed?"

They nodded. "Excuse me, Sir William," André Poncin said pleasantly, "may I suggest that I tell them your decision—for you to begin the meeting and then close it at once would be somewhat of a loss of face. Yes?"

"Very wise, André," Seratard said. As far as the others knew, Poncin was just an occasional trader with some knowledge of Japanese customs, a smattering of Japanese, a personal friend and occasional interpreter. In reality Poncin was a highly regarded spy employed to uncover and neutralize all British, German, and Russian endeavors in the Japans. "Eh, Sir William?"

"Yes," Sir William said thoughtfully. "Yes, you're right, André, thank you, I shouldn't do it myself. Lun!"

The door opened instantly. "Heya, Mass'er?"

"Fetch young Mass'er Tyrer quick quick!" Then to the others, "Tyrer can do it for me. As it's a British problem."

When Phillip Tyrer returned to the other reception room overlooking the forecourt, he went up to Johann with as much dignity as he could muster. The Bakufu officials paid no attention and continued chatting, Yoshi slightly apart. Misamoto was beside him—the only one not talking. "Johann, give them Sir William's compliments and tell today's unsatisfactory meeting is adjourned and they are to reconvene tomorrow at ten for what he expects will be a satisfactory conclusion to this unwarranted affair: the murderers, the indemnity and a guaranteed, early meeting with the Shōgun or else."

Johann blanched. "Just like that?"

"Yes, exactly like that." Tyrer was also tired of the shilly-shallying, constantly reminded of John Canterbury's violent death, Malcolm Struan's serious wounds and Angelique's terror. "Tell them!"

He watched Johann deliver the short ultimatum in guttural Dutch. The Japanese interpreter flushed and began the lengthy translation as Tyrer studied the officials carefully without appearing to do so. Four were attentive, the last was not, the small man with narrow eyes and callused hands that he had noticed earlier—all other hands were well groomed. Again this man began whispering to the youngest and most handsome official, Watanabe, as he had been doing from time to time all day.

Wish to God I could understand what they were saying, Tyrer thought irritably, more determined than ever to do whatever was necessary to learn the language quickly.

As the shocked and embarrassed interpreter finished there was a silence, broken only by the sucking in of breath though all faces remained impassive. During the translation he had noticed two glance surreptitiously at Watanabe.

Why?

Now they seemed to be waiting. Watanabe dropped his eyes, hid behind his fan and muttered something. At once the narrow-eyed man beside him stood awkwardly, and spoke briefly. Relieved, they all got up and, without bowing, silently trooped out, Watanabe last, except for the interpreter.

"Johann, they really got the message this time," Tyrer said happily.

"Yes. And they were very plenty pissed."

"Obviously that's what Sir William wanted."

Johann mopped his brow. He was brown-haired and medium height, thin, strong with a hard, lined face. "The sooner you're interpreter the better. It's time I went home to my mountains and snows while I've still got my head intact. There're too many of these cretins, they're too unpredictable."

"As the interpreter, surely you have a privileged position," Tyrer said uneasily. "The first to know."

"And the carrier of bad news! They're all bad news, *mon vieux*. They hate us and can't wait to throw us out. I made a contract with your Foreign Office for two years, renewable by mutual consent. The contract, she is up in two months and three days and my English is going to hell." Johann went to the sideboard near the window and took a deep draft of the beer he had ordered instead of tea. "No renewal, whatever the temptation." He beamed suddenly. "*Merde,* that's the problem about leaving here."

Tyrer laughed at his pixy look. "*Musume?* Your girl?"

"You learn fast."

In the forecourt the officials were getting into their palanquins. All gardening activity had stopped, the half dozen gardeners kneeling motionless with heads to the earth. Misamoto was waiting beside Yoshi, conscious that any mistake and he would not be standing erect, desperately hoping he had passed the first test. Somehow or another I'll be useful to this bastard, he was thinking in English, until I can get back aboard an American ship and paradise and tell the Captain how I was kidnapped off Harris's staff by these poxy scum. . . .

He looked up, froze. Yoshi was watching him. "Lord?"

"What were you thinking?"

"I was hoping I'd been of value, Sire. I . . . Look out behind you, Sire!" he whispered.

André Poncin was coming down the steps, heading for Yoshi. Instantly his guards were a protective screen. Unafraid, Poncin bowed politely and said in fair though halting Japanese: "Lord, excuse please, can give message from my Master, French High Lord, please?"

"What message?"

"He say please perhaps you like see inside steamship, engine, cannons. Asks humbly invite you and officials." Poncin waited, saw no reaction, except an imperious wave of the fan in dismissal. "Thank you, Lord, please excuse me." He walked away, sure he had been right. On the first step he noticed Tyrer watching him from the audience room window, bit back a curse, and waved. Tyrer waved back.

When the last samurai left the forecourt the gardeners carefully resumed their work. One of them shouldered his spade and limped away. Hiraga, his head swathed with a filthy old cloth, his kimono ragged and dirty, was happy with the success of his spying. Now he knew how and when and where the attack tomorrow should take place.

Once more safe in his palanquin en route back to the castle— with Misamoto, at his orders, sitting at the far end—Yoshi let his mind roam. He was still astonished at their ill-mannered dismissal, not furious like the others, just patient: revenge will be taken in a manner of my own choosing.

An invitation to see the engines of a warship and to go over one? Eeee, an opportunity not to be missed. Dangerous to accept but it will be done. His eyes focused on Misamoto who was staring out of a slit window. Certainly prisoner Misamoto has been useful so far. Stupid of interpreters not to translate accurately. Stupid of the Russian to threaten us. Stupid for them to be so rude. Stupid of the Chinese servant to call us monkeys. Very stupid. Well, I shall deal with them all, some sooner than others.

But how to deal with the leaders and their fleet?

"Misamoto, I have decided not to send you back to the guard house. For twenty days you will be housed with my retainers and continue to learn how to behave like a samurai."

Misamoto's head was on the floor of the palanquin at once. "Thank you, Lord."

"If you please me. Now, what will happen tomorrow?"

Misamoto hesitated, petrified: the first rule of survival was never to carry bad news to any samurai, to say nothing, volunteer nothing, but if forced, to tell anyone only what you think he wants to hear. Unlike *there,* America, paradise on earth.

The answer's obvious, he wanted to shout, falling back into his habit of thinking in English—the only thing that had kept him sane all the years of his confinement—if you saw how they treat each other in the gai-jin family I lived with, how they treated me, sure a servant, but even so like a man, better than I ever dreamed possible, how every man can walk tall and carry a knife or gun, 'cepting most black men, how impatient they all are to solve a problem to hurry on to the next—if necessary by fist or gun or cannonade—where most everyone's equal under their law, and there are no stinking daimyos or samurai who can kill you when they wish. . . .

Yoshi said softly, reading him: "Answer me truthfully, always, if you value your life."

"Of course, Lord, always." Petrified, Misamoto did as he was told blindly. "So sorry, Lord, but unless they get what they want, I think they'll—they will level Yedo."

I agree, but only if we're stupid, Yoshi thought. "Can their cannon do that?"

"Yes, Lord. Not the castle but the city would be fired."

And that would be a stupid waste of Toranaga resources. We would only have to replace them all, peasants, artisans, courtesans and merchants to service us as usual. "Then how would you give them a little soup but no fish?" Yoshi asked.

"Please excuse me, I don't know, Lord, I don't know."

"Then think. And give me your answer at dawn."

"But . . . yes, Lord."

Yoshi leaned back on his silk cushions and focused his mind on yesterday's meeting of the Elders. Eventually Anjo had had to withdraw the order to evacuate the castle, for without a clear majority the order would be invalid—so he, as formal Guardian, had forbidden the Shōgun's departure.

I won, this time, but only because that stubborn old fool, Toyama, insisted on voting for his insane attack plan, thus neither for me or against me. Anjo is right: the other two normally vote with him against me. Not because of merit but because I am who I am—the Toranaga who should have been Shōgun, not that stupid boy.

Because Yoshi was safe in his palanquin, alone but for Misamoto who could not know his inner thoughts, he allowed his mind to open the compartment marked Nobusada, so secret, so volatile, so dangerous, and permanent.

What to do about him?

I cannot contain him much longer. He's infantile and now in the most dangerous claws of all, those of the Princess Yazu: Emperor's spy and fanatic against the Shōgunate who broke her engagement to her adored childhood playmate, a handsome and very eligible Prince, the Shōgunate who forced her into permanent exile from Kyōto and all her family and friends and into a marriage to a weakling whose erection is as limp as a banner in summer and may never give her children.

Now she has schemed this State visit to Kyōto to kowtow to the Emperor, a masterstroke that will destroy the delicate balance of centuries: Authority to subdue the whole Empire is granted by Imperial Edict to the Shōgun, and his descendants, who is also appointed Lord High Constable. Therefore orders issued by the Shōgun to the country are its laws.

One consultation must lead to another, Yoshi thought, *and then the Emperor rules and we do not. Nobusada will never realize it, his eyes clouded by her guile.*

What to do?

Again Yoshi went down the well-trodden but oh-so-secret path: *he is my legal liege lord. I cannot kill him directly. He is too well guarded unless I am prepared to throw away my own life with the deed which, at the moment, I am not. Other means? Poison. But then I would be suspect, correctly, and even if I could escape the bonds that surround me—I'm just as much prisoner as this Misamoto—the land would be plunged into a never-ending civil war, gai-jin will be the only gainers,* and worse I would have betrayed my oath of allegiance to the Shōgun, whoever he is, and to the Legacy.

I have to let others kill him for me. The shishi? I could help them, but to help enemies committed to your own destruction is dangerous. One other possibility. The gods.

He permitted himself a smile. *Good luck and bad luck,* wrote Shō- gun Toranaga, *fortune and misfortune are to be left to Heaven and natural law—they are not things that can be got by praying or worked by some cunning device.*

Be patient, he heard Toranaga saying to him. Be patient.

Yes, I will be.

Yoshi closed that compartment until the next time and again consid- ered the Council. What shall I tell them? Of course by now they will know I met the gai-jin. I will insist on one absolute rule in future: we must send only clever men to these meetings. What else? Certainly about their soldiers, gigantic, with their scarlet uniforms and short skirts and enormous feathered hats, every man with a breech-loading gun, shining with care, as cherished as any of our blades.

Shall I tell them that these enemies are fools, who have no finesse and can be ruled through their impatience and hatreds—Misamoto told me enough to conclude they are as fractious and hate-ridden as any daimyo? No, this I will keep to myself. But I will tell them tomorrow our Delegation will fail unless we devise a delay gai-jin will be happy to accept.

What should that be?

"That messenger, Misamoto," he said idly, "the tall man with the big nose, why did he speak like a woman, using women's words? Was he a half man—half woman?"

"I don't know, Sire. Maybe he was—they have many aboard ship, Sire, though they hide it."

"Why?"

"Don't know, Sire, difficult to understand them. They don't talk openly about fornication as we do, of the best position or if a boy is better than a woman. But about speaking like a woman: in their language men and women, they all speak the same, I mean they use the same words, Sire, unlike Japanese. The few sailors I met who could speak some words of our language, men who'd been to Nagasaki, they spoke the same as the big nose did, because the only people they speak with are whores, learning our words from our whores. They don't know our women speak different from us, that men, Sire, use different words, as civilized persons should."

Yoshi hid his sudden excitement. Our whores are their only real contact, he thought. And they all have whores, of course. So one way to control them, even attack them, is through their whores, female or male.

"I will not order my fleet to bombard Yedo without a formal written order from the Admiralty, or Foreign Office," the Admiral said, his face flushed. "My instructions are to be circumspect, like yours. We are NOT on a punitive mission."

"For God's sake, we have had an incident that must be dealt with. Of course it's a punitive mission!" Sir William was equally angry. The eight bells of midnight sounded, and they were in the Admiral's quarters aboard the flagship at the round table, the General, Thomas Ogilvy, the only other person present. The cabin was low, large and heavy-beamed, and through the stern windows the riding lights of other vessels could be seen. "Again, I believe without force they will not budge."

"Get the order, by God, and I'll budge them." The Admiral refilled his own glass with port from the almost empty cut-glass decanter. "Thomas?"

"Thanks." The General held out his glass.

Trying to contain himself, Sir William said, "Lord Russell has already given us instructions to press the Bakufu for damages, twenty-five thousand pounds, over Legation murders, the Sergeant and Corporal last year—he will be even more incensed over the current incident. I know him, you don't," he added, exaggerating for effect. "I won't receive his approval for three months. We must obtain satisfaction now or the murders will continue. Without your support I cannot maneuver."

"You have my full support, short of war, by God. Bombarding their capital commits us to war. We're not equipped for that. Thomas? You agree?"

The General said carefully, "To surround a village like Hodogaya and eliminate a few hundred savages and put a minor native potentate into chains is a lot different than trying to secure this vast city and invade the castle."

Witheringly, Sir William said, "Then what about your 'no conceivable operation that the forces under my command cannot conclude expeditiously'!"

The General reddened. "What one says in public, as you well know, bears little relation to practice, as you well know! Yedo is different."

"Quite right." The Admiral drained his glass.

"Then what do you propose?" The silence grew. Suddenly the stem of Sir William's glass snapped between his fingers, and the others jumped, unprepared. "Damn!" he said, the destruction somehow diminishing his rage. Carelessly he used the napkin to mop up the wine. "I'm Minister here. If I find it necessary to make it an order and you refuse to obey, which of course you have a right to do, I will ask for your immediate replacement, of course."

The Admiral's neck went purple. "I have already put the facts before the Admiralty. But please don't mistake me: I am more than ready to seek vengeance for the killing of Mr. Canterbury and the attack on the others. If it's Yedo, I merely require the written order as I have said. There's no hurry, now or in three months, these savages will pay as we require, with this city or a hundred others."

"Yes, they will, by God." Sir William got up.

"One more piece of necessary information before you go: I cannot promise to stay at this anchorage much longer. My fleet is unprotected, the sea bottom dangerously shallow, weather promises to worsen, and we're safer at Yokohama."

"How much longer is safe?"

"A day—I don't know, I've no control over weather, which this month is irascible, as you're aware."

"Yes, I'm aware. Well, I'll be off. I require you both at the ten o'clock meeting ashore. Kindly fire a salute at dawn when we break out the colors. Thomas, please land two hundred dragoons to secure the area around the wharf."

"May I ask why two hundred more men?" the General asked quickly. "I've already put a company ashore."

"Perhaps I may wish to take hostages. Good evening." He closed the door quietly.

The two men stared after him. "Does he mean it?"

"I don't know, Thomas. But with the Honorable, impetuous William bloody Aylesbury you never know."

In deep darkness another detachment of heavily armed samurai came out of the main castle gate, ran silently across the lowered drawbridge, then over the bridge that spanned the wide moat heading for the Legation area. Other companies were also converging. More than two thousand samurai were in place, with another thousand ready to move in when ordered.

Sir William was plodding up from the wharf with his guard, an officer and ten Highlanders, through the deserted streets. He was depressed and tired, his mind on tomorrow, trying to conceive a way out of this impasse. Another corner and another. At the end of this street was the open space that led up to the Legation.

"My God, sorr, look there!"

The space was crammed with silent samurai, motionless and watching them. All heavily armed. Swords, bows, spears, a few muskets. A slight noise and Sir William's party glanced around. The road back was blocked with massed, equally silent warriors.

"Christ," the young officer murmured.

"Yes." Sir William sighed. This could be one solution, but then God help every man jack of them—the fleet would respond instantly. "Let's go on. Have your men ready to fight if need be, safety catches off."

He led the way forward, not feeling brave, just out of himself somehow, observing himself and the others as if above the street. There was a narrow path between the samurai, an officer at the head. As Sir William came within ten feet, the man bowed politely, equal to equal. Sir William watched himself raise his hat with equal politeness, and walk on. The soldiers followed, rifles in hands, fingers on triggers.

All the way up the hill. Same silence, same watching. All the way to the gate. Massed samurai, motionless. But none in their forecourt. The forecourt and gardens were filled with Highlanders, armed and ready, others on the roof and at the windows. Soldiers opened then locked the gate after him.

Tyrer and all the rest of the staff were waiting in the foyer, some in nightclothes, some part dressed, and they crowded around him. "My God, Sir William," Tyrer said for all of them, "we were petrified they'd captured you."

"How long have they been here?"

"Since about midnight, sir," an officer said. "We had sentries at the bottom of the hill. As the enemy arrived, these lads gave us warning and fell back. We'd no way to warn you or signal the fleet. If they wait till dawn we can hold this place until more troops arrive and the fleet opens up."

"Good," he said quietly. "In that case I suggest we all go to bed, leave a few men on guard, and let the rest turn in."

"Sir?" The officer was perplexed.

"If they wanted to do us they would have done so already without the silent treatment and ballyhoo." Sir William saw them all staring at him and he felt better, no longer depressed. He started up the stairs. "Good night."

"But, sir, don't you think . . ." The words trailed off.

Sir William sighed wearily. "If you wish to keep the men on duty, please do so—if it will make you happier."

A sergeant hurried into the foyer and called out, "Sorr, they're all leaving! The wee buggers are scarpering."

Glancing out of the landing window, Sir William saw that, sure enough, the samurai were melting into the night.

For the first time he became afraid. He had not expected them to disappear. In moments the path down the hill was clear and the space below empty. But he sensed that they had not gone far, that every doorway and nearby street would be crammed with enemies, all waiting confidently to spring the trap.

Thank God the other Ministers and most of our lads are safe aboard. Thank God, he thought, and walked on up the stairs with a step firm enough to encourage those watching him.

11

Thursday, 18th September:

THE INN OF THE FORTY-SEVEN Ronin was in a dingy alley not far from Yedo castle, set back from the dirt roadway, and almost hidden behind a high, ill-kempt fence. From the street the inn appeared drab and nondescript. Inside it was lush, expensive, the fence solid. Well-groomed gardens surrounded the sprawling single-story building and its many isolated one-room bungalows were set on low pilings and reserved for special guests—and privacy. The inn's patrons were well-to-do merchants, but also it was a safe house for certain shishi.

Now, just before dawn, it was peaceful: all patrons, courtesans, mama-san, maids, servants sleeping. Except the shishi. Quietly they were arming themselves.

Ori sat on the veranda of one of the little houses, his kimono down around his waist. With great difficulty, he was replacing the bandage over the wound on his shoulder. The wound was fiery red now and angry and agonizingly sensitive. His whole arm throbbed and he knew a doctor was urgent. Even so he had told Hiraga it was too dangerous to fetch one or to go to one: 'I might be followed. We cannot risk it, too many spies and Yedo is Toranaga sanctuary.'

'I agree. Go back to Kanagawa.'

'When the mission is over.' His finger slipped and brushed the festering sore and a pain stabbed deep to his innards. There's no hurry, a doctor can lance it and remove the poison, he thought, only half

161

believing it. Karma. And karma if it continues to rot. He was so absorbed that he did not hear the ninja slide over the fence and creep up behind him.

His heart twisted with fright as the ninja clapped a hand over his mouth to prevent any outcry. "It is *me*," Hiraga whispered angrily, then released him. "I could have killed you twenty times."

"Yes." Ori forced a smile and pointed. Amongst the bushes was another samurai, the arrow in his bow poised. "But he's on guard, not me."

"Good." Hiraga greeted the guard and, mollified, pulled off his face mask. "Are the others inside and ready, Ori?"

"Yes."

"And your arm?"

"Fine." Ori gasped and his face twisted in pain as Hiraga's hand snaked out and grabbed his shoulder. Tears seeped from his eyes but he remained silent.

"You're a liability. You cannot go with us today—you will go back to Kanagawa." Hiraga stepped onto the veranda and went inside. Greatly dispirited, Ori followed.

Eleven shishi were seated on the fine tatami, armed. Nine were Hiraga's compatriots from Choshu. Two newcomers were from the Mori patrol that had let them pass yesterday, later to desert and beg permission to join them.

Hiraga sat, tiredly. "I could not get within two hundred paces of the temple or the Legation, so we cannot fire it and kill Lord Yoshi and the others when they arrive. Impossible. We must ambush him elsewhere."

"Excuse me, Hiraga-san, but are you certain it was Lord Yoshi?" one of the Mori men asked.

"Yes, I'm sure."

"I still cannot believe he would risk coming out of the castle with a few guards just to meet some stinking gai-jin, even disguised. He is too clever, surely he would know he is the supreme target for shishi, except the Shōgun, bigger even than the traitor Anjo."

"He is not clever. I recognized him, I was close to him once in Kyōto," Hiraga said, secretly not trusting either of the Mori samurai. "Whatever his reason, he could risk the Legation once without guards, not twice. Surely that is why the area is awash with Bakufu samurai. But tomorrow he will be outside the castle again. It is an opportunity we cannot miss. Could we mount an ambush somewhere? Anyone?"

"Depends on the number of samurai with the cortege," a Mori samurai said. "*If* a meeting is held as the gai-jin want."

"If? Would Lord Yoshi try a stratagem?"

"I would, if I were him. They call him the Fox."

"What would you do?"

The man scratched his chin. "I'd delay, somehow."

Hiraga frowned. "But if he goes to the Legation as yesterday where would he be the most vulnerable?"

Ori said, "Getting out of his palanquin. The gai-jin forecourt."

"We can't get there, even with a suicide rush."

The silence gathered. Then Ori said quietly, "The nearer to the castle gates the safer his captains would feel, therefore the fewer their immediate guards and the less their vigilance, coming out . . . or going back in."

Hiraga nodded, satisfied, and smiled at him and motioned to one of his compatriots. "When the House wakes, tell the mama-san to fetch Ori a doctor, secretly and quickly."

Ori said at once, "We agreed it is not safe."

"An asset must be protected. Your idea is perfect."

Ori bowed his thanks. "Better I go to the doctor, *neh*?"

In first light Phillip Tyrer half ran half walked towards the wharf with two Highlanders, a sergeant and a private in tow. 'Good God, Phillip, two guards are more than enough,' Sir William had said a moment ago. 'If the Jappers intend mischief our entire garrison won't be sufficient to protect you. The message has to be delivered to Ketterer and you're it. 'Bye!'

Like Sir William he had had to pass through the hundreds of silent samurai who had returned just before dawn. No one molested him or even seemed to acknowledge his presence other than with a quick flick of their eyes. Ahead now was the sea. His pace quickened.

"Halt, who goes there, or I'll blow yor bloody head off," a voice said from the shadows, and he skidded to a stop.

"For Christ's sake," Tyrer said, palpitating with fright. "Who the hell d'you think it is, it's me with an urgent message for the Admiral and General."

"Sorry, sir."

Quickly Tyrer was in a cutter being rowed briskly towards the flagship. He was so glad to be out of the Legation trap he could almost weep and urged the oarsmen on faster, then went up the gangway two rungs at a time.

"Hello, Phillip!" Marlowe was officer of the watch on the main deck. "What the devil's up?"

"Hello, John, where's the Admiral? I've an urgent dispatch for him from Sir William. The Legation's surrounded by thousands of the bastards."

"Christ!" Anxiously Marlowe led the way down a gangway, then aft. "How the hell did you get out?"

"Just walked. They let me through their ranks, didn't say a bloody word, not one of them, just let me through. I don't mind telling you I was scared fartless—they're everywhere, except inside our walls and down by our wharf."

The Marine sentry outside the cabin door saluted smartly. " 'Morning, sir."

"Urgent dispatch for the Admiral."

At once the voice slashed through the door: "Then for God's sake Marlowe, bring it in! Dispatch from whom?"

Marlowe sighed, opened the door. "Sir William, sir."

"What the hell's that idiot done n—" Admiral Ketterer stopped seeing Tyrer. "Oh, you're his aide, aren't you?"

"Apprentice interpreter, sir, Phillip Tyrer." He handed him the letter. "Er, Sir William's compliments, sir."

The Admiral tore the letter open. He was wearing a long flannel nightgown and tasselled sleeping hat and thin-rimmed reading glasses and he pursed his lips as he read:

I consider it best to cancel your appearance at the meeting today, as well as the General and the other Ministers. We are totally surrounded by hundreds, if not thousands of heavily armed samurai. Thus far they have done nothing hostile, or prevented anyone from leaving, yet. Certainly they have the right to put their own troops where they wish—perhaps it's just a bluff to unhinge us. For safety, however, I will handle the Bakufu alone, if they appear as demanded. (If this occurs I will run up a blue pennant and will endeavour to keep you advised of developments.) If the Bakufu do not appear I will wait another day or two, then may have to order an igno-minious withdrawal. In the meantime, if you see the flag hauled down it will mean they have overrun us. You may then take whatever action you see fit. I am, Sir, yr obedient ser-vant. . . .

Carefully the Admiral reread the letter, then said decisively, "Mr. Marlowe, ask the Captain and General to join me here at once. Send the following message to all ships: 'You will instantly go to action stations. All Captains to report aboard the flagship at noon.' Next, send a signal to the Ministers asking them to be kind enough to join me here as soon as possible. Mr. Tyrer, get yourself some breakfast and be ready to carry back a reply within a few minutes."

"But, sir, don't you think—"

The Admiral was already bellowing at the closed door. "Johnson!"

Instantly his orderly opened the door. "Barber's on his way, sir, your uniform's freshly ironed, breakfast's ready the moment you're at table, the porridge's hot!"

Ketterer's look fell on Marlowe and Tyrer. "What the devil are you waiting for?"

At Yokohama the Struan cutter—the only steam engine, propeller-driven small boat in the Japans—swung against their wharf, wind brisk with a slight swell to the grey sea under the overcast. Jamie McFay climbed nimbly up the steps, then hurried along its length heading for their two-story building dominating the High Street. It was barely eight o'clock but he had already been out to meet the bimonthly mail ship that had arrived with the dawn, to collect mail, dispatches and the latest newspapers that his Chinese assistant began to load into a cart. Clutched in his hand were two envelopes, one opened the other sealed.

" 'Morning, Jamie." Gabriel Nettlesmith intercepted him, stepping out from a small group of sleepy traders waiting for their boats. He was a short, roly-poly, untidy, smelly man, reeking of ink and unwashed clothes and the cigars that he smoked perpetually, editor and publisher of the *Yokohama Guardian,* the Settlement's newspaper, one of the many in Asia that Struan's owned, openly or secretly. "What's amiss?"

"Lots—be kind enough to join me for tiffin. Sorry, can't stop."

Even without the fleet at anchor the harbor was already busy with cutters plying to and from the half a hundred merchantmen, others clustering around the mail ship, still others heading for her or coming back. Jamie was the first ashore, a matter of principle with him and a business expedient where prices of essential items, always in short supply, could fluctuate wildly depending on the mails. Hong Kong to Yokohama direct by mail steamer took about nine days, via Shanghai, about eleven, weather permitting. Mail from home, England, took eight to twelve weeks, weather and piracy permitting, and mail day always an anxious time, joyous, awful or in between but ever welcome, waited for and prayed for nonetheless.

Norbert Greyforth of Brock and Sons, Struan's main rival, was still a hundred yards offshore, sitting comfortably amidships, his oarsmen pulling hard, watching him through his telescope. McFay knew he was being observed but it did not bother him today. The bugger will know soon enough if he doesn't know already, he thought, feeling uncommonly frightened. Frightened for Malcolm Struan, the Company, himself, for the future and for his *ai-jin*—love person—who waited equally patiently in their tiny Yoshiwara house across the canal, outside the fence.

He increased his pace. Three or four drunks lay in the gutter of High Street like old sacks of coal, others scattered here and there down along the seafront. He stepped over one man, avoided a raucous group of inebriated merchant seamen staggering for their boats, ran up his steps into the large foyer of Struan's, up the staircase to the landing and down the corridor that led to suites of rooms the whole length of the godown.

Quietly he opened a door and peered in.

"Hello, Jamie," Malcolm Struan said from the bed.

"Oh, hello, Malcolm, 'morning. I wasn't sure if you'd be awake." He closed the door behind him, noticed that the door to the adjoining suite was ajar, and went over to the huge teak fourposter that, like all the furniture, came from Hong Kong or England. Malcolm Struan was pasty-faced, and drawn, propped on pillows—the boat trip back from Kanagawa yesterday had drained more of his precious strength, even though Dr. Babcott had kept him sedated and they had made the journey as smooth as possible. "How are you today?"

Struan just peered up at him, his blue eyes seemingly faded and set deeper into their sockets, shadows underneath. "Mail from Hong Kong's not good, eh?" The words were flat, and gave McFay no way to break it easily.

"Yes, sorry. You heard the signal gun?" Whenever the mail ship came within sight, it was the custom for the Harbor Master to fire a cannon to alert the Settlement—the same procedure all over the world, wherever there were Settlements.

"Yes, I did," Struan said. "Before you tell me the bad, close her door and give me the chamber pot."

McFay obeyed. The other side of the door was a drawing room and beyond that a bedroom, the best apartment in the whole building and normally reserved exclusively for the tai-pan, Malcolm's father. Yesterday at Malcolm's insistence and her happy compliance, Angelique had been installed there. At once the news had rushed around the Settlement, feeding other reports and rumors that *their* Angelique had become the new Lady of the Lamp, and the betting odds on that she was Struan's in more ways than one, every man wanting to be in his bed.

'You're mad,' McFay had told some of them at the Club last night. 'The poor fellow's in terrible shape.'

Dr. Babcott interrupted, 'He'll be up and about before you know it.'

'It's got to be wedding bells, by God!' someone said.

'Drinks on the house,' another called out expansively, 'Good-oh, we'll have our own wedding, our first wedding.'

'We've had lots, Charlie. What about our *musumes*?'

'They don't count, for God's sake, I mean a real church wedding— and a right proper christening an—'

'Jumping Jehovah, are you implying one's in the oven?'

'The rumor's they was like stoats on the ship coming here, not that I blame him . . .'

'Angel Tits weren't even feeanced then, by God! Say that agin', impugg'ning 'er 'onor, and I'll do you, by God!'

McFay sighed. A few drunken blows and broken bottles, both men had been thrown out to crawl back within the hour to an uproarious welcome. Last night, when he had peeped in here before going to bed himself, Malcolm was asleep and she was nodding in a chair beside the bed. He awoke her gently. 'Best get some proper sleep, Miss Angelique, he won't wake now.'

'Yes, thank you, Jamie.'

He had watched her stretch luxuriously like a contented young feline, half asleep, hair down around her bared shoulders, her gown high waisted and loose, falling in folds that the Empress Josephine had favored fifty years before and some Parisian *maisons de couture* were trying to reintroduce, all of her pulsating with a male-attracting life force. His own suite was along the corridor. For a long time he had not slept.

Sweat soaked Struan. The effort of using the chamber pot was vast with little to show for all the pain, no feces and just a little blood-flecked urine. "Jamie, now what's the bad?"

"Oh, well, you see . . ."

"For Christ sake, tell me!"

"Your father passed away nine days ago, same day the mail ship left Hong Kong direct to us, not via Shanghai. His funeral was due three days later. Your mother asks me to arrange your return at once. Our mail ship from here with news of your—your bad luck won't arrive in Hong

Kong for another four or five days at the earliest. Sorry," he added lamely.

Struan only heard the first sentence. The news was not unexpected and yet it came as violent a slash as the wound in his side. He was very glad and very sad, mixed up, excited that at long last he could really run the company that he had trained for all his life, that for years had been hemorrhaging, for years held together by his mother who quietly persuaded, cajoled, guided and helped his father over the bad times. The bad was constant and mostly due to drink, which was his father's medicine to cushion blinding headaches and attacks of Happy Valley ague, *mal-aria*, *bad air*, the mysterious killing fever that had decimated Hong Kong's early population but now, sometimes, was held in abeyance by a bark extract, quinine.

Can't remember a year when Father wasn't laid up at least twice with the shakes, for a month or more, his mind wandering for days on end. Even infusions of the priceless cinchona bark that Grandfather had had brought from Peru had not cured him, though it had stopped the fever from killing him, and most everyone else. But it hadn't saved poor little Mary, four years old then, me seven and forever after aware of death, the meaning of it and its finality.

He sighed heavily. Thank God nothing touched Mother, neither plague nor ague nor age nor misfortune, still a young woman, not yet thirty-eight, still trim after seven children, a steel support for all of us, able to ride every disaster, every storm, even the bitter, perpetual hatred and enmity between her and her father, godrotting Tyler Brock . . . even the tragedy last year when the darling twins, Rob and Dunross, were drowned off Shek-O where our summer house is. And now poor Father. So many deaths.

Tai-pan. Now I'm tai-pan of the Noble House.

"What? What did you say, Jamie?"

"I just said I was sorry, Tai-pan, and here—here's a letter from your mother."

With an effort Struan took the envelope. "What's the fastest way for me to get back to Hong Kong?"

"*Sea Cloud,* but she isn't due for two to three weeks. The only merchantmen here at the moment are slow, none due for Hong Kong for a week. Mail ship would be the fastest. We could get her to turn around right smartly but she's going via Shanghai."

After yesterday, the idea of an eleven-day voyage, more than likely with bad seas, even typhoon, horrified Malcolm. Even so, he said,

"Talk to the captain. Persuade him to go direct to Hong Kong. What else's in the mails?"

"I haven't been through them yet, but here . . ." Greatly concerned with Struan's sudden pallor, McFay offered the *Hong Kong Observer.* "Nothing but bad, I'm afraid: The American civil war's picking up steam, seesawing with tens of thousands of deaths—battles at Shiloh, Fair Oaks, dozens of places, another at Bull Run with the Union army the loser and decimated. War's changed forever now with breech-loading rifles and machine guns and rifled cannon. Price of cotton's gone sky high with the Union blockade of the South. Another panic on the London Stock Exchange and Paris—rumors that Prussia will invade France imminently. Since the Prince Consort died in December, Queen Victoria still hasn't appeared in public—it's rumored she's pining to death. Mexico: we've pulled our forces out now it's apparent nutter Napoleon III's determined to make it a French domain. Famine and riots all over Europe." McFay hesitated. "Can I get you anything?"

"A new stomach." Struan glanced at the envelope clenched in his hand. "Jamie, leave me the paper, go through the mails, then come back and we'll decide what to do here before I leave . . ." A slight noise and they both glanced back at the adjoining door that now was half open. She was standing there, elegant peignoir over her nightdress.

"Hello, *chéri,*" she said at once. "I thought I heard voices. How are you today? Good morning, Jamie. Malcolm, you look so much better, can I get you anything?"

"No, thank you. Come in. Sit down, you look wonderful. Sleep well?"

"Not really, but never mind," she said, though she had slept wonderfully. Her perfume surrounding her, she touched him sweetly and sat down. "Shall we breakfast together?"

McFay dragged his attention off her. "I'll come back when I've made the arrangements. I'll tell George Babcott."

When the door had closed, she smoothed Struan's brow, and he caught her hand, loving her. The envelope slipped to the floor. She picked it up. A little frown. "Why so sad?"

"Father's dead."

His sadness brought her tears. She had always found it easy to cry, to make tears almost at will, seeing from a very early age their effect on others, her aunt and uncle particularly. All she had to do was to think of her mother who had died bearing her brother. 'But Angelique,' her aunt would always say tearfully, 'poor little Gerard is your only brother, you'll never have another, not a real one, even if that good-for-nothing father of yours remarries.'

'I hate him.'

'It wasn't his fault, poor lad, his birth was ghastly.'

'I don't care, he killed Maman, killed her!'

'Don't cry, Angelique. . . .'

And now Struan was saying the same words, the tears easy because she was truly sad for him. Poor Malcolm to lose a father—he was a nice man, nice to me. Poor Malcolm trying to be brave. Never mind, soon you'll be well and now it's much easier to stay, now that the smell has gone, most of the smell has gone. A sudden spectre of her own father came into her mind: 'Don't forget this Malcolm will inherit everything soon, the ships and power and . . .'

I won't think about that. Or . . . or about the other.

She dried her eyes. "There, now tell me everything."

"Nothing much to tell. Father's dead. The funeral was days ago and I have to go back to Hong Kong at once."

"Of course at once—but not until you are well enough." She leaned forward and kissed him lightly. "What will you do when we get there?"

In a moment he said firmly, "I'm heir. I'm tai-pan."

"Tai-pan of the Noble House?" She made her surprise seem genuine, then she added delicately, "Malcolm, dear, terrible about your father, but . . . but in a way not unexpected, no? My father told me he had been sick a long time."

"It was expected, yes."

"That is sad but . . . tai-pan of the Noble House, even so. Please may I be the first to congratulate you." She curtseyed to him as elegantly as to a king, and sat back again, pleased with herself. His eyes watched her strangely. "What?"

"Just that you, you make me feel so proud, so wonderful. Will you marry me?"

Her heart missed a beat, her face flushed. But her mind ordered her to be prudent, not to hurry, and she pondered whether to be as grave as he was grave, or to release the exploding exuberance she felt at his question and her victory and to make him smile. "La!" she said brightly, teasing him, fanning herself with a handkerchief. "Yes, I will marry you, Monsieur Struan, but only if you . . ." A hesitation and she added in a rush, "Only if you get better quickly, obey me implacable, cherish me hugely, love me to distraction, build us a castle on the Peak in Hong Kong, a palace on the Champs-Elysées, fit out a clipper ship as a bridal bed, a nursery in gold, and find us a country estate of a million hectares!"

"Be serious. Angelique, listen to me, I'm serious!"

Oh, but I am, she thought, delighted that he was smiling now. A gentle kiss but this time on the lips, full of promise. "There, Monsieur, now don't taunt this defenseless young lady."

"I'm not taunting you, I swear to God. Will-you-marry-me?" Strong words but he did not have the strength to sit up yet or reach out to bring her closer. "Please."

Her eyes still teased. "Perhaps, when you're better—and only if you obey me implacable, cherish me—"

"Implacably, if that's the word you want."

"Ah, yes, pardon. Implacably . . . etceteras." Again the lovely smile. "Perhaps yes, Monsieur Struan, but first we must get to know each other, then we must agree to an engagement, and then, *Monsieur le tai-pan de la Noble Maison*, who knows?"

Joy possessed all of him. "Then it's yes?"

Her eyes watched him, making him wait. With all the tenderness she could muster, she said, "I will consider it seriously—but first you must promise to get well quickly."

"I will, I swear it."

Again she dried her eyes. "Now, Malcolm, please read your mother's letter, and I'll sit with you."

His heart was beating strongly and the elation he felt took away the pain. But his fingers were not so obedient and he had trouble breaking the seal. "Here, Angel, read it to me, will you please?"

At once she broke the seal and scanned the singular writing that was on the single page. " 'My beloved son,' " she read aloud. " 'With great sadness I must tell you your father is dead and now our future rests with you. He died in his sleep, poor man, the funeral will be in three days, the dead must cherish the dead and we, the living, must continue the struggle while we have life. Your father's Will confirms you as heir, and tai-pan, but to be legal the succession has to be done with a ceremony witnessed by me and Compradore Chen in accordance with your beloved grandfather's Legacy. Settle our Japanese interests as we discussed and return as quickly as you can. Yr devoted Mother.' " Tears filled her eyes again because of a sudden fantasy that she was the mother writing to her son.

"That's all? No postscript?"

"No, *chéri,* nothing more, just 'your devoted mother.' How brave of her. Would that I could be so brave."

Oblivious to everything except the portent of these happenings, she gave him the letter and went to the window that looked out onto the harbor and, drying her eyes, opened it. The air was fresh and took away the sickroom smell. What to do now? Help him to hurry back to Hong Kong away from this foul place. Wait . . . will his mother favor our marriage? I don't know. Would I if I was her? I know she didn't like me, the few times we met, so tall and distant, though Malcolm said she was that way with everyone outside family. 'Wait till you get to know her, Angelique, she's so wonderful and strong . . .'

Behind her the door opened and Ah Tok came in without knocking, a small tea tray in one hand. "*Neh hoh mah,* Mass'r," good day, she said with a beam, showing the two gold teeth of which she was very proud. "Mass'r slepp good, heya?"

In fluent Cantonese, Malcolm said, "Stop speaking gibberish."

"Ayeeyah!" Ah Tok was Struan's personal amah who had looked after him since he was born and a law unto herself. She hardly acknowledged Angelique, her concentration on Struan. Stout, strong and fifty-six, wearing the traditional white smock and black trousers, the long queue hanging down her back signified that she had chosen amah as her profession and had therefore sworn to remain chaste all her life and so never to have children of her own that might divert her loyalty. Two Cantonese manservants followed with hot towels and water to bathe him. Loudly, she ordered them to close the door. "Mass'r bar'f, heya?" she said pointedly to Angelique.

"I will come back later, *chéri,*" the girl said. Struan did not answer, just nodded and smiled back then stared again at the letter, lost in thought. She left her door ajar. Ah Tok grunted disapprovingly, shut it firmly, told the other two to hurry up with his bed bath, and handed him the tea.

"Thank you, Mother," he said in Cantonese, using the customary honorific for such a special person who had cherished and carried and guarded him when defenseless.

"Bad news, my son," Ah Tok said—the tidings had rushed through the Chinese community.

"Bad news." He sipped the tea. It tasted very good.

"After you have bathed you will feel better and then we can talk. Your Honorable Father was overdue his appointment with the gods. He's there now and you are tai-pan, so the bad has become good. Later this morning I'll bring some extra-special tea I've bought for you that will cure all your ills."

"Thank you."

"You owe me a tael of silver for the medicine."

"A fiftieth part."

"Ayeeyah, at least half."

"Ayeeyah, a twentieth part, Mother." With hardly any thought he bargained automatically, but not unkindly, "And if you argue I'll remind you you owe me six months' wages paid in advance for your grandmother's funeral—her second."

One of the servants chortled behind her but she feigned not to notice. "If you say so, Tai-pan." She used the title delicately, the first time she had ever said it to him, watching him, missing nothing, then snapped at the two men sponging and cleaning him carefully and efficiently: "Hurry up with your work. Does my son, the tai-pan, have to endure your clumsy ministrations all day?"

"Ayeeyah," one of them unwisely muttered back.

"Take care, you motherless fornicator," she said sweetly in a dialect Struan did not understand. "Just get on with it and if you nick my son while shaving I'll put the Evil Eye on you. Treat my son like Imperial jade or your fruit will be pulverized—and don't listen to your betters!"

"Betters? Ayeeyah, old woman, you come from Ning Tok, a turtle-dung village famous only for farts."

"A tael of silver says this civilized person can whip you five out of seven times at mahjong this evening."

"Done!" the man said truculently even though Ah Tok was an accomplished player.

"What's all that about?" Struan said.

"Servants' talk, nothing important, my son."

When they had finished they gave him a fresh, crisp night shirt. "Thank you," Struan said to them, greatly refreshed. They bowed politely and were gone.

"Ah Tok, bolt her door, quietly."

She obeyed. Her sharp ears heard the rustle of skirts in the adjoining room and she resolved to increase her vigilance. Nosey, foreign devil toad belly whore with her Jade Gate so hungry for the Master a civilized person can almost hear it salivating . . .

"Light the candle for me, please."

"Eh? Are your eyes hurting you, my son?"

"No, nothing like that. There are safety matches in the bureau." Safety matches, the recent Swedish patent, were usually kept locked

away as they were highly sought after, therefore had a ready sale and
therefore had a habit of disappearing. Petty theft was endemic in Asia.
Uneasily she used one, not understanding why they would not light
unless the side of their special box was struck. He had explained why
but she only muttered about more foreign devil magic.

"Where do you want the candle, my son?"

He pointed at the bedside table within easy reach. "Here. Now leave
me for a little while."

"But, ayeeyah, we should talk, there is much to plan."

"I know. Just wait outside the door and keep everyone away until I
call."

Grumbling, she walked out. So much talk and bad news had exhausted him. Nonetheless, painfully he balanced the candle on the side
of the bed, then lay back a moment.

Four years ago on his sixteenth birthday his mother had taken him to
the Peak to speak privately: 'Now you are old enough to learn some
secrets of the Noble House. There will always be secrets. Some your
father and I keep from you until you become tai-pan. Some I keep from
him, and some from you. Some I will now share with you and not with
him, or your brothers and sisters. Under no circumstances are these
secrets to be shared with anyone. Anyone. You promise before God.'

'Yes, Mother, I swear it.'

'First: perhaps one day we may need to give each other personal or
dangerous information in a private letter—never forget, anything in
writing may be read by alien eyes. Whenever I write to you I will
always add, P.S. I love you. You will do the same, always, without fail.
But if there is *no* P.S. I love you, then the letter contains important and
secret information, from me to you or you to me only. Watch!'
Shielding the paper she had prepared, she lit some safety matches and
held them under the paper, not to fire it but to almost scorch it, line by
line. Miraculously, the hidden message appeared: *Happy Birthday,
under your pillow there's a sight draft for ten thousand pounds. Keep it
secretly, spend it wisely.*

'Oh, Mother, there is? There really is, ten thousand?'

'Yes.'

'Ayeeyah! But how do you do it? The writing?'

'Take a clean quill or pen and write your message carefully in a
liquid I will give you, or milk, and let it dry. When you heat the paper as
I did, the writing will appear.' She used another match and gravely lit a
corner of the paper. In silence they watched it burn. She ground the

ashes to dust under her tiny high-booted foot. 'When you're tai-pan, trust no one,' adding strangely, 'even me.'

Now Struan held her sad letter over the candle's flame. The words came into view, no mistaking her handwriting:

Sorry to tell your father died raving, besotted with whisky. He must have bribed a servant to sneak it in again. Much more to tell in person. Thank God he's out of his misery but it was the Brocks, my cursed father and my brother Morgan, who give us no peace and caused his strokes—the final one came just after you left when we discovered details, too late, of their secret Hawaiian coup against us. Jamie has a few details.

For a moment he stopped reading, sick with rage. Soon there'll be a reckoning, he promised himself, then read on:

Beware of our friend Dmitri Syborodin. We discover he's a secret agent for that revolutionary, President Lincoln, not the South as he pretends. Beware of Angelique Richaud . . .
    His heart twisted with sudden fright: *Our Paris agents write that her uncle Michel Richaud went bankrupt shortly after she left and is now in Debtors' Prison. More facts: her father keeps very poor company, has very substantial gambling debts, and secretly boasts to intimates he'll soon represent all our French interests—received your letter of the 4th recommending this, presume at her instigation—he won't, he's insolvent. Another of his "secrets": you'll be his son-in-law within a year. Of course, ridiculous, you are far too young for marriage, and I could not conceive of a worse connection. Singly or together they are out to snare you, my son. Be circumspect and beware of feminine guile.*

For the first time in his life he was furious with his mother. Shakily, he shoved the paper into the flame, held it while it burned then pulverized the ash to nothingness, smashed the flame out and sent the candle skittering and lay back nauseated, heart pounding, all the time his mind shouting; how dare she investigate Angelique and her family without asking me! How dare she be so wrong! Whatever sins they committed Angelique is not to blame. Mother of all people should know the sins of the fathers are not to be blamed on the children! Wasn't my beloved grandfather much worse, wasn't he a killer and not much more than a pirate, as her father still is? She's a bloody hypocrite! It's none of her business who I marry. It's my life and if I want to marry Angelique next year I will. Mother knows nothing about Angelique—and when she knows the truth she'll love her as I do—or else, by God! She . . .

"Oh, Christ," he gasped as pain ripped him apart.

12

McFAY LOOKED UP FROM THE
piles of letters, documents and journals littering his desk. "How is
he?" he asked anxiously as Dr. Babcott came in and closed the door.
The office was spacious, facing the High Street and the sea.

"It was a stomach seizure of some kind, Jamie. To be expected, I'm
afraid, poor chap. I dressed his wound—he'd torn a few stitches. I gave
him a draft of laudanum." Babcott rubbed his eyes, red-rimmed with
fatigue, his frock coat heavy and frayed at the sleeves and stained, here
and there, with chemicals and dried blood. "Not much more I can do
for him at the moment. What's the latest from the fleet?"

"Status quo: the fleet's at action stations, Legation's still surrounded, the Bakufu are supposed to appear soon."

"What happens if they don't?"

McFay shrugged. "I've had orders to get Malcolm back to Hong
Kong as soon as possible—very important for him. I can get him on the
mail sh—"

"I absolutely forbid it," Babcott said, with more anger than he
intended. "That would be stupid and highly dangerous, highly dangerous. If they got into a storm, which is likely this time of the year . . .
well, severe and prolonged vomiting would tear the repairs apart—
which would kill him. No!"

"Then when will it be safe?"

The doctor glanced out of the windows. Whitecaps out past the
headland, none in the bay. Sky overcast. He weighed his helplessness
against his knowledge. "At least a week, perhaps a month. God knows,
Jamie, I don't."

"If you were to go on the mail ship, would that help?"

177

"For Christ's sake, no! Didn't you hear me clearly? No. No! He's not to move. Nine days on a ship would kill him."

McFay's face closed. "What are Malcolm's chances? Really. It's very important I know."

"Still good. His temperature's more or less normal and there's no sign of any festering." Babcott rubbed his eyes again and yawned. "Sorry, didn't mean to snap at you. Been up since midnight patching the results of a sailor-versus-soldier Drunk Town brawl, and a dawn emergency in the Yoshiwara, had to sew up a young woman who tried to cut herself into the next world." He sighed. "It would help to keep him as calm as possible. I'd say his bad news probably brought on the attack."

The knowledge and implications of Culum Struan's death and therefore Malcolm's new status as tai-pan—of vital and immediate concern to all their rivals—had rushed through the Settlement. In Brock's, Norbert Greyforth had interrupted a meeting to open the first bottle of champagne from the case he had had kept chilled against this day for many weeks—chilled in their new, and highly profitable, ice house next door to their godown. 'Best news we've had in years,' he chortled to Dmitri, 'and I've another twenty cases for the party I'm throwing tonight. A toast, Dmitri!' He raised his cut glass, the best Venetian that money could buy. 'Here's to the tai-pan of the Noble House: out with the Old, out with the New, by God, and may they be bankrupt within the year!'

'I'll drink with you, Norbert, but to the success of the new tai-pan, none of the rest,' Dmitri said.

'Open your eyes to reality. They're the old, we're the new—once they had guts when Dirk Struan was alive but now they're weak, McFay's weak—why, with his enthusiastic help and a little persuasion on the night of Canterbury's murder we could have roused the whole Settlement, the fleet, the Army, we'd have captured this bugger Satsuma king, hanged him, and be living happily ever after.'

'I agree. John Canterbury's going to be revenged, one way or another. Poor bastard,' Dmitri said. 'You know he left me his business?' Canterbury's was one of the smaller trading houses, specializing in the export of silk cloth, and particularly cocoons and silkworm eggs, a highly lucrative trade to France where the silk industry, once the best in the world, had been decimated by disease. 'John always said he would but I never believed him. I'm his Executor too—Wee Willie gave me the deed before he left.'

'Samurai are all bastards, no reason to murder him like that. What about his *musume*? Old John was besotted with her. She's carrying, isn't she?'

'No, that was a rumor. In his will he asked me to take care of her, give her money to buy her own shack. I went to see her but her mama-san, Raiko, that old bat, she told me the girl had gone back to her village but she'd send on any money. I paid over what John had said, so that was that.'

Thoughtfully Norbert finished his wine and poured more and felt better. 'You should take care of yourself too,' he said, keeping his voice down, judging the time ripe. 'You've the future to think of, not a few rolls of cloth and worm eggs. Consider the Great Game, the American game. With our contacts we can buy any amount of British, French or Prussian armaments—we've just signed an exclusive deal to represent Krupp's in the Far East—at better prices than Struan's can give you, have them delivered in Hawaii for transshipment to . . . to wherever, no questions asked.'

'I'll drink to that.'

'Whatever you want, we can get cheaper and faster.' Norbert refilled their glasses. 'I like Dom Pérignon, it's better than Tatt—that old monk knew about color and sugar, and the lack of it. Like Hawaiian sugar,' he added delicately, 'I hear it's going to be so pricey this year to be almost a national treasure, for North or South.'

Dmitri's glass stopped in midair. 'Meaning?'

'Meaning, just between us, Brock and Sons have the lock on this year's crop, meaning that Struan's won't have so much as a hundred-pound sack, so your deal with them won't happen.'

'When's this going to be common knowledge?' Dmitri's eyes slitted.

'Would you like to be part of it? Our deal? We could use a trustworthy agent for the States, North and South.'

Dmitri poured for both of them, enjoying the touch of the chilled glass. 'In return for what?'

'A toast: to the demise of the Noble House!'

Throughout Yokohama other toasts were being quaffed at the rare tidings of Culum's death and the succession of a new tai-pan, and in boardrooms throughout the Far East, and elsewhere, that traded with Asia. Some toasts were celebratory, some vindictive, some toasted the succession, some cursed all Struan bones to the devil, some prayed for their success, but all men of business considered how the news would affect them, for, like it or not, Struan's was the Noble House.

In the French Legation Angelique clinked glasses, sipped the champagne warily, her glass cheap and barely adequate, like the wine. "Yes, I agree, Monsieur Vervene."

Pierre Vervene was the Chargé d'Affaires, a tired, balding man in his forties. "The first toast requires a second, Mademoiselle," he said, raising his glass again, towering over her, "not only prosperity and long life to the new tai-pan, but to the tai-pan—your future husband."

"La, Monsieur!" She put down her glass, pretending to be cross. "I told you that in confidence because I'm so happy, so proud, but it must not be mentioned out loud, until he, Monsieur Struan, makes it public. You must promise me."

"Of course, of course." Vervene's tone was reassuring but he had already mentally drafted the dispatch he would rush to Seratard aboard their flagship at Yedo the moment she left. Clearly there were innumerable political ramifications and opportunities that such a liaison would create for France and French interests. My God, he was thinking, if we're clever—and we are—we can control the Noble House through this young strumpet with nothing to recommend her except a fairly pretty face, delectable breasts, an overripe maidenhead and buttocks that promise her husband a wanton vigor for a month or two. How the devil did she snare him—if what she says is really true. If it is . . .

Merde, the poor man must be insane to settle for this baggage, with no dowry and disreputable lineage, to be the mother of his children! What incredible luck for that odious swine, Richaud, now he'll be able to redeem his paper. "My sincerest congratulations, Mademoiselle."

His door swung open and the Legation's Number One Boy, an elderly, rotund Chinese dressed in linen coat, black trousers and black skullcap and laden with mail, barged in. "Heya, Mass'r, all same mail-ah, never mind!" He plonked the letters and packages on the ornate desk, gawked at the girl, and belched as he left.

"My God, these foul-mannered people are enough to drive one mad! A thousand times I've told that cretin to knock first! Excuse me a moment." Quickly Vervene leafed through the letters. Two from his wife, one from his mistress, all postmarked two and a half months ago: Both asking for money, I'll wager, he thought sourly. "Ah, four letters for you, Mademoiselle." Many nationals sent their mail in care of their nearest Legation. "Three from Paris and one from Hong Kong."

"Oh! Oh, thank you!" She brightened seeing that two were from Colette, one from her aunt, the last from her father. "We're such a long way from home, no?"

"Paris is the world, yes; yes, it is. Well, I expect you'll want some

privacy, you can use the room across the hall. If you'll excuse me . . ."
Vervene motioned at his heaped desk, his smile self-deprecating.
"Affairs of State."

"Of course, thank you. And thank you for your good wishes, but
please, not a word. . . ." She swept out graciously, knowing that within
hours her marvelous secret would be common knowledge, whispered
from ear to ear. Is that wise? I think so. Malcolm did ask me, didn't he?

Vervene opened his letters, scanned them, quickly saw they both
asked for money but no other bad news, at once put them aside to read
and enjoy later and began the dispatch for Seratard—with a secret
copy for André Poncin—delighted to be the bearer of good tidings.
"Wait a moment," he muttered, "perhaps it's like-father-like-daughter
and just the usual exaggeration! Safer to report it as *a few minutes ago
Mademoiselle Angelique whispered in confidence that . . .* then the
Minister can make up his own mind."

Across the hall, in a pleasant antechamber that faced the small
garden off the High Street, she had settled herself expectantly. Colette's first letter gave her happy news of Paris and fashion and affairs
and their mutual friends so delightfully that she raced through it,
knowing she would reread it many times, particularly tonight in the
comfort of her bed when she could savor everything. She had known
and loved Colette most of her life—at the convent they had been
inseparable, sharing hopes and dreams and intimacies.

The second letter gave more exuberant news, ending about her
marriage—Colette was her own age, eighteen, already married a year
with one son: *I am pregnant again, dearest Angelique, my husband is
delighted but I am a little fretful. As you know the first was not easy
though the Doctor assures me I will be strong enough. When will you
return? I cannot wait . . .*

Angelique took a deep breath and looked out of the window and
waited until the twinge had passed. You must not leave yourself open,
she repeated to herself, near tears. Even with Colette. Be strong,
Angelique. Be careful. Your life has changed, everything changed—
yes, but only for a little while. Do not be caught unawares.

Again a deep breath. The next letter shocked her. Aunt Emma wrote
the awful news of her husband's fall and: *now we are destitute and my
poor poor Michel languishes in Debtors' Prison with no help in sight!
We've nowhere to turn, no money. It's terrible, my child, a nightmare . . .*

Poor darling Uncle Michel, she thought, weeping silently, a shame
he was such a bad manager. "Never mind, dear darling Aunt-Mama,"

she said aloud, filled with a sudden joy. "Now I can repay all your kindnesses, I'll ask Malcolm to help, he'll certainly . . ."

Wait! Would that be wise?

While she pondered that she opened her father's letter. To her surprise the envelope contained only a letter, without the expected sight draft she had asked for, on money brought with her from Paris and deposited in the Victoria Bank, money that her uncle had generously advanced to her—on the solemn promise that she must not tell his wife and that her father would instantly repay the loan the moment she reached Hong Kong, which he told her he had done.

> *Hong Kong, September 10. Hello, my little cabbage, I hope that all is well and your Malcolm idolizes you as I do, as the whole of Hong Kong does. It's rumored his father is at death's door. I will keep you advised. Meanwhile I write in haste as I leave for Macao on the tide. There's a wonderful business opportunity there, so good that I have temporarily pledged the money instruments you left in safekeeping and will invest for you as* an equal partner. *By the next post I will be able to send you ten times what you wanted and tell you the wonderful profit we have made—after all, we have to think of your dowry, without which . . . eh?*

Her eyes could not read on, her brain in turmoil. Oh my God! What business opportunity? Is he gambling all that I have in the world?

It was nearly two o'clock and McFay was weary, his stomach empty, his mind filled with gloom. He had written a dozen letters, signed half a hundred chits, paid dozens of bills, checked the previous day's books, which showed trading was down, found that all goods ordered from America were either cancelled, held up or offered at increased prices, all business with Canada and Europe equally affected in some degree by the American civil war. No good news either in any dispatches from Hong Kong—a lot of bad from their branch in Shanghai, though Albert MacStruan, the power there, was doing a sterling job. My God, he thought, it'd be a catastrophe if we have to evacuate Shanghai, with all our investments there.

The city was again in turmoil and the three foreign concessions under British, French and American control beset with rumors that armies of rebel irregulars of the immense Tai'ping Rebellion, based in and around Nanking—a major city southwards they had captured nine years ago and used as a capital—were again on the move. The clipping from the *Shanghai Observer* read:

Two years ago when our valiant force of British and French troops, ably assisted by the local mercenary army, organized and paid for by our merchant princes, both European and Chinese, under the command of the gallant American soldier of fortune, Frederick Townsend Ward, drove off the rebels for a thirty-mile radius, we all presumed the threat was put away forever.

Now eyewitnesses report an irresistible army of half a million rebels, with some European officers, have massed to come against us, and another half million will again stab north for Peking. Their opposing Manchu armies are unreliable and helpless, their Chinese levies mutinous, so this time we will not survive. It is hoped that Her Majesty's Government will prevail on the Manchu authorities to appoint Captain Charles Gordon to command of Mr. Ward's force, grievously wounded in action, and to the position of overall command of Manchu training. Your correspondent believes this will be, as usual, too little too late.

We need a fully equipped British Army stationed in China, permanently—nervousness in India over the recent, dreadful Indian Mutiny of native sepoys notwithstanding. Business continues to be disastrous with the price of silk and tea at an all-time high. Famine conditions exist in most areas within five hundred miles . . .

More depressing news from home. Monumental rains had washed out the harvest and famine was expected in Ireland and other areas—though not like the Great Potato Famine when hundreds of thousands died. Vast unemployment in Scotland. Destitution in Lancashire with most cotton spinning mills silent, including three owned by Struan's, because of the Union embargo on Southern cotton and blockade of all Southern ports. With Southern cotton England had supplied cloth to the world. A Struan clipper ship crammed with teas, silks and lacquer inbound London had been lost. In the stock market Struan's was down badly, Brock's up with the successful arrival of the first of the season's teas.

Another letter from his fiancée of five years, Maureen Ross, more bad: . . . *when am I to arrive? Have you sent the ticket? You promised this Christmas would be the last to be apart . . .*

"It can't be this Christmas, lassie," he murmured with a scowl, much as he liked her. "Can't afford it yet, and this isn't the place for a young lady."

How many times had he written and told her, knowing that really Maureen and her parents wanted him to work for Struan's in England or Scotland or better still to leave 'that infamous company and work at home like a normal man,' knowing that really he wanted her to break off the engagement and to forget him, knowing that most British wives soon hated Asia, loathed Asians, abominated the Pleasure Girls, raged against their ready access, despised the food, moaned for 'home' and family, making their husbands' lives a permanent misery.

Knowing, too, that he enjoyed Asia, loved his work, adored the freedom, treasured their Yoshiwara and would never happily go home. Well, he thought, not until I retire.

The only good in the mail were the books from Hatchard's in Piccadilly: a new illustrated edition of Darwin's explosive *On the Origin of Species,* some Tennyson poems, a newly translated pamphlet by Karl Marx and Friedrich Engels called *The Communist Manifesto,* five copies of *Punch,* but most important of all another edition of *All the Year Round.* This was the weekly started by Charles Dickens, and contained the fourteenth installment of *Great Expectations*—to be published in twenty parts.

In spite of all that he had to do, McFay, like everyone else who had received a copy, locked the door and consumed the installment rapaciously. When he read the last line, 'to be continued next week,' he sighed. "What the devil will Miss Havisham do next, evil old bitch? Reminds me of Maureen's mother. Hope to God it all works out for Pip. Somehow or other it has to! Hope to God good old Dickens gives us a happy ending. . . ."

For a moment he was bemused, lost in admiration of the man and his marvelous range of stories, from *Oliver Twist* more than twenty years ago, through *Nicholas Nickleby, David Copperfield* and a dozen others to the riveting *Tale of Two Cities.* Dickens is the greatest writer in the world, no doubt about it.

He got up and stood at the window, watching the sea and sending good thoughts to the fleet at Yedo and to the mail ship that need not now be diverted but would continue on her regular route to Shanghai instead of direct to Hong Kong with Malcolm Struan, worrying about him and the future that somehow quickly became mixed up with Pip and Miss Havisham, wondering how Pip would extract himself from the mess he was in and would the girl fall in love with him.

Hope so, poor lass. What about my lassie, Maureen? It's time I had a family . . .

A knock. "Mr. McFay. May I see you a moment?" It was Piero Vargas, his assistant.

"Just a moment." Feeling a little guilty he put the copy under the pile, stretched and opened the door.

Piero Vargas was a handsome, middle-aged Eurasian from Macao, the tiny Portuguese enclave, forty-odd miles west of Hong Kong, set like a pimple on a slip of Mainland China and occupied since 1552. Unlike the British, the Portuguese considered Macao equal to the mother country and not a colony, encouraged their settlers to intermarry with Chinese, and accepted Eurasian offspring as nationals, allowing them permanent access to Portugal. British intermarriage was greatly discouraged, though many had families. Their offspring, however, were not accepted in Society. By custom those born in Shanghai took their father's name, in Hong Kong their mother's.

Ever since the British came to China, they had contentedly employed the brightest Macaoans as shroffs—money changers—and compradores, who, of necessity, spoke English as well as dialects of Chinese. Except the Noble House. Their compradore was the enormously wealthy Gordon Chen, the illegitimate son of their founder, Dirk Struan, by one of his many mistresses, though not the last, the fabled May-may.

"Yes, Piero?"

"Sorry to interrupt, senhor," Piero said, his English liquid and sweet-sounding. "Kinu-san, our silk supplier, asks for a personal interview with you."

"Oh, why?"

"Well, it's not really for him but for two buyers who arrived with him. From Choshu."

"Oh?" McFay's interest picked up. Almost two years of tentative probes from the daimyo of Choshu, the fief far to the west on the Straits of Shimonoseki, had produced some very important business last year, authorized by the Head Office in Hong Kong and arranged by them: a 200-ton paddle steamer with a very private cargo—cannon, shot and ammunition. Paid for promptly in gold and silver, half in advance, half on delivery. "Bring them in. Wait, better I see them in the main reception room."

"Sí, senhor."

"Is one of them the same fellow as last time?"

"Senhor?"

"The young samurai who spoke a little English?"

"I did not take part in the discussion, senhor, I was on leave in Portugal."

"Ah, yes, now I remember."

The reception room was big, with seating for forty-two at the oak table. Matching sideboards and tallboys for silver plate and glass fronted display cases, gleaming and well kept, some with arms. He opened one of them, took out a belt and holstered pistol attached. He buckled the belt around his waist, making sure the pistol was loaded and loose in the holster. It was always his custom when meeting samurai to be as armed as they were. 'A matter of face,' he told his subordinates, 'as well as safety.' As a further prop he leaned the Spencer rifle against a chair, and stood by the window, facing the door.

Vargas came back with three men. One was middle-aged, fat, unc-tuous and swordless, Kinu, their silk supplier. The other two were samurai, one young the other in his forties though it was difficult to tell. Both short, spare, hard-faced and armed, as usual.

They bowed politely. McFay noted that both men had instantly seen the breech-loader. He returned the bow in kind. *"Ohayo,"* he said. Good morning. Then, *"Dozo"*—please—indicating the chairs oppo-site him, a safe distance away.

"Goo'd morning," the younger said without a smile.

"Ah, you speak English? Excellent. Please sit down."

"Speak 'ritt're," the youth said—the l's sounding like r's because there was no 'l' sound in Japanese, v's being equally awkward. For a moment he spoke to Vargas in Fukenese, their common Chinese dia-lect, then the two men introduced themselves, adding they had been sent by Lord Ogama of Choshu.

"I am Jamie McFay, chief of Struan and Company in Nippon, and am honored to see you." Again Vargas translated. Patiently Jamie went through the obligatory fifteen minutes of enquiries after their daimyo's health, their own health, his health and that of the Queen, the outlook in Choshu, in England, nothing particular, everything bland. Tea was served and admired. At length the young man came to the point.

With great care Vargas kept the excitement out of his own voice. "They want to buy a thousand breech-loaders with a thousand bronze cartridges per gun. We are to name a fair price and deliver within three months. If within two months, they will pay a bonus—twenty percent."

Outwardly, McFay was equally calm. "Is that all they wish to buy at the moment?"

Vargas asked them. "Yes, senhor, but they require a thousand rounds per rifle. And a steamship of small size."

McFay was counting the huge potential profit, but more so he was remembering his conversation with Greyforth, and the well-known hostility of the Admiral and General, supported by Sir William, to any sale of any armaments. Remembering the various murders. And Canterbury hacked to pieces. And that he himself did not approve of the sale of armaments, not until it was safe. Would it ever be safe with such a warlike people? "Please tell them I can give them an answer in three weeks." He saw the pleasant smile vanish from the younger man's face.

"Answer . . . now. No three week."

"Not have guns here," McFay said slowly, directly to him. "Must write Hong Kong, Head Office, nine days there, nine days back. Some breech-loaders there. All rest in America. Four or five months minimum."

"No unner'stand."

Vargas interpreted. Then there was a conversation between the two samurai, the merchant answering their questions with fervent humility. More questions to Vargas, politely responded to. "He says very well, he or a Choshu official will return in twenty-nine days. This transaction is to be secret."

"Of course." McFay looked at the youth. "Secret."

"*Hai!* Sek'ret."

"Ask him how the other samurai, Saito, is." He saw them frown, but could read nothing from their faces.

"They don't know him personally, Senhor."

More bows and then Jamie was alone. Lost in thought, he put the gun belt back into the case. If I don't sell them the guns, Norbert will—whatever the morality.

Vargas returned, very pleased. "An excellent possibility, senhor, but a big responsibility."

"Yes. I wonder what Head Office will say this time."

"Easy to find out, senhor, quickly. You don't have to wait eighteen days, isn't Head Office upstairs?"

McFay stared at him. "I'll be damned, I'd forgotten! Difficult to think of young Malcolm as tai-pan, our ultimate decider. You're right."

Running feet approached, the door opened. "Sorry to butt in," Nettlesmith said, puffing from his exertion, his grubby top hat askew. "Thought you'd better know, just got word the blue signal flag went up the Legation mast a few minutes ago . . . then came down and went up again, then came down to *half mast* and stayed there."

Jamie gaped at him. "What the devil does that mean?"

"Don't know, 'cepting that half mast usually means a death, doesn't it?"

Greatly perturbed, the Admiral again trained his binoculars on the Legation flagpole, the other men on the quarterdeck, his Captains from the rest of the fleet, Marlowe, the General, French Admiral, and von Heimrich equally concerned, Seratard and André Poncin pretending to be. When the lookout had given the alarm half an hour ago, they had all hurried on deck from the lunch table. Except the Russian Minister: 'If you want to wait in the cold, very well, damned if I am. When word comes from the shore, yes, no or war, please wake me. If you start shelling I'll join you. . . .'

Marlowe was watching the roll over the Admiral's collar, despising him, wishing he were ashore with Tyrer, or aboard his own ship, the *Pearl.* At noon the Admiral had replaced the temporary captain with a stranger, a Lieutenant Dornfild, disregarding his advice. Bloody old bastard, look at the way he fiddles so bloody pompously with his binoculars—we all know they are highly expensive and issued to Flag Rank only. Bloody old—

"Marlowe!"

"Yessir."

"We'd better find out what the devil's going on. You go ashore . . . no, I need you here! Thomas, would you please be good enough to send an officer to the Legation? Marlowe, detail a signalman to go with the detachment."

At once the General jerked his thumb at his aide who hurried off, closely followed by Marlowe. Seratard pulled his heavy great coat closer against the chill of the wind. "I'm afraid Sir William has boxed himself in."

"I remember you giving your opinion this morning," the Admiral said curtly.

The meeting he had called with the Ministers had been noisy and had brought forth no solution, except Count Zergeyev's: immediate and massive force. 'Which, my dear Count,' he had pointed out sourly at once, 'we don't have now if it's necessary to follow up a simple bombardment to seize the city and surrounds.'

Ketterer pursed his lips and glared at Seratard, the dislike mutual. "I'm sure Sir William will find an answer, but I tell you frankly, by God, if I see our colors struck, Yedo goes up in smoke!"

"I agree," Seratard said. "A matter of national honor!"

Von Heimrich's face hardened. "Japanners are not stupid—like some people. I cannot believe they will disregard the force we have now."

The wind picked up suddenly, crackling some of the spars aloft, sea greyer, clouds greying. All eyes went to a black squall line on the eastern horizon. The squall was heading shorewards, threatening their exposed anchorage.

"Marlowe, send a . . . *Marlowe!*" the Admiral bellowed.

"Yessir?" Marlowe came running.

"For God's sake, stay within hailing distance! Signal all ships: 'Prepare to stand out to sea. Should conditions deteriorate rapidly, on my command take individual action and rejoin at Kanagawa as soon as conditions permit.' You Captains get back to your ships while you've the weather." They rushed off, glad to be away.

"I will get back to my ship too," the French Admiral said. "*Bonjour, messieurs.*"

"We'll come with you, Monsieur Admiral," Seratard said. "Thank you for your hospitality, Admiral Ketterer."

"What about Count Alexi? He came with you, didn't he?"

"Let him sleep. Better for the Russian bear to sleep, *n'est-ce pas?*" Seratard said coldly to von Heimrich, both of them knowing full well Prussia's secret overtures to the Tsar to remain neutral in any confrontation, to allow Prussia to expand in Europe to satisfy an open state policy: the creation of a German nation of German-speaking peoples with Prussia its spearhead.

Marlowe, hurrying for the signalman, saw his ship, the *Pearl,* neatly at anchor and was worried about her, loathing not being aboard and in command. Uneasily he glanced seaward again, gauging the squall line, the weight of blackening clouds, the smell and the taste of the salt on the wind. "That bugger's going to be a sod."

In the Legation audience room Sir William, flanked by a Scots officer, Phillip Tyrer and guards sat coldly facing three Japanese officials who were leisurely seating themselves, their guards behind them: the grey-haired Elder, Adachi, daimyo of Mito, the mock samurai, Misamoto the fisherman, and last, a short, big-bellied, Bakufu official, secretly fluent in Dutch, whose covert assignment was to report in private to Yoshi on the meeting and the behavior of the other two. As usual, none had used their correct names.

Five palanquins had arrived yesterday, with the same ceremony though an increased number of guards. Only three were occupied, which Sir William had found curiously disturbing. This, added to heightened samurai activity during the night around the temple and Legation, prompted him to send a partial alarm signal to the fleet by half-masting the pennant that he hoped Ketterer would understand.

Outside in the forecourt, Hiraga, again disguised as a gardener, had been equally perturbed—even more so that Toranaga Yoshi was not amongst the officials. This meant the attack plan so carefully poised to ambush Yoshi near the castle gates on his return had to be called off. At once he had tried to melt away, but samurai irritably ordered him back to work. Seething, he obeyed, waiting his chance to escape.

"You're two and a half hours late," Sir William said icily as an opening salvo. "In civilized countries diplomatic meetings are on time, not late!"

Immediate and flowery apologies of no consequence. Then the usual obligatory introductions and sugary compliments and aggravating politenesses, and over an hour of back and forth, of demands calmly deflected, ponderous arguments, delays requested, astonishment where none was merited, questions needing to be repeated, facts dismissed, the truth disregarded—alibis, explanations, rationalizations, excuses, all courteously delivered.

Sir William was about to explode when, with great formality, the Elder, Adachi, produced a sealed scroll, handed it to their interpreter who handed it to Johann.

Johann's own weariness dropped away. "*Gott im Himmel!* It's under the seal of the *roju.*"

"Eh?"

"The Council of Elders. I'd recognize the seal anywhere—it's the same as Ambassador Harris got. You better accept it, formally, Sir William, then I'll read it aloud if it's in Dutch, which I doubt." He stifled a nervous yawn. "Probably just another delaying tactic."

Sir William did as Johann suggested, hating to be so confined and having to rely on foreign mercenary interpreters.

Johann broke the seal and scanned the document. His astonishment was open: "It's in Dutch, by God! Skipping all the titles, formal language, etc., it says: *The Council of Elders, having received what appears to be a just complaint, apologizes for the dereliction of its subjects and wishes to invite the honored Minister of the British and other accredited Ministers to meet the Council thirty days from now, in Yedo, when the formal complaint will be presented, the matter discussed, acted upon, and an indemnity for said just complaint agreed. Signed . . . Nori Anjo, Chief Minister.*"

With a supreme effort, Sir William kept his erupting relief bottled. This unbelievable reprieve gave him the face-saver he desperately needed, and now if he could finesse them just a little further . . . To his sudden fury, out of the corner of his eye, he noticed Tyrer smiling broadly. Without looking at him he hissed, "Stop smiling, you bloody idiot," and in the same breath added harshly, "Johann, tell them they will have my reply in three days. Meanwhile I want an immediate indemnity, in gold, in three days, for ten thousand pounds sterling for the families of the Sergeant and Corporal murdered in this Legation, last year, and already demanded four times!"

When this was translated, he saw consternation on the face of the elderly man. Another lengthy conversation between him and the Bakufu official.

Johann reported wearily, "The old fellow dismisses this with their usual: that that 'unfortunate occurrence' was by a Legation staff employee who then committed seppuku—suicide. It's not the Bakufu's fault at all."

Equally tiredly, Sir William said, "Give them back the usual, by God: that they appointed him, they insisted we employ him, so they are responsible—and he only committed suicide because he was badly wounded in the murder attempt on my predecessor and liable for immediate capture!" Trying to push away his tiredness, he watched the two officials talking with their interpreter, and the third man listening as he had done all afternoon. Perhaps he's the one with real power. What happened to the other men from yesterday, particularly the younger man—the one André Poncin accosted as he left. What is that devious bastard Seratard up to?

The freshening wind caught a loose shutter and jolted it against the window. One of the sentries leaned over the lintel and hooked it back in place. Not far offshore was the fleet, the ocean a deep grey now and whitecapped. Sir William noticed the looming squall line. His anxiety for the ships increased.

Johann said, "The old fellow asks, will you accept three thousand?"

Sir William's face went red. "Ten thousand in gold!"

More talk, then Johann mopped his brow. "*Mein Gott,* ten it is, to be paid in two installments at Yokohama, ten days from now, the balance the day before the Yedo meeting."

After a deliberately dramatic pause, Sir William said, "I will give them my answer in three days if it's acceptable."

Much sucking in of breath, a few more wily attempts to change the three days to thirty, to ten, to eight, all of which were stonewalled and refused. "Three."

Polite bows and the Delegation was gone.

Once they were alone, Johann beamed. "That's the first time we made any progress, Sir William, the very first time!"

"Yes, well, we'll see. Just don't understand them at all. Obviously they were trying to wear us down. But why? What's the good of that? They already had the scroll so why the devil didn't they hand it over in the beginning and have done with all their cursed time wasting? Bunch of bloody idiots! And why send two empty palanquins?"

Phillip Tyrer said brightly, "Seems to me, sir, that's just one of their characteristics. To be devious."

"Yes, well, Tyrer, come with me, please." He led the way to his private office and when the door was closed he said angrily, "Didn't the F.O. teach you anything? Are you totally without brains? Don't you have enough sense to have a poker face at diplomatic meetings? Are your brains addled?"

Tyrer was in shock at the venom. "Sorry, sir, very sorry, sir, I was just so pleased at your victory I cou—"

"It wasn't a victory, you idiot! It was just a delay, albeit heaven sent!" Sir William's relief that the meeting was over and had, against his expectations, achieved much more than he could have wished for, fuelled his irritability. "Are your ears filled with mildew? Didn't you hear the 'what appears to be a just complaint'—that's the biggest hole they could ever leave, by God! We achieved a delay, that's all, but it happens to suit me perfectly and if the Yedo meeting takes place in thirty days I'll be astounded. The next time DON'T let your feelings show, for God's sake, and if you ever become an interpreter . . . you just better learn Japanese quickly or you'll be on the next boat home with a note on your record that will get you a posting to Esquimoland for the rest of your life!"

"Yes, sir."

Still steaming, Sir William saw the young man staring at him stoically and wondered what was different about him. Then he noticed his eyes.

Where have I seen that look before—the same, almost indefinable strangeness that young Struan also had? Ah yes, of course, now I remember! In the eyes of the young soldiers coming back from the

Crimea, the untouched as well as the wounded—allied or enemy. War had torn the youth out of them, torn out their innocence with such obscene speed that forever after they were changed. And it always shows not in their faces but in their eyes. How many times was I told: before the battle a youth, a few minutes or hours later, an adult—British, Russian, German, French, or Turk the same.

I'm the idiot, not this young chap. I'd forgotten he's hardly twenty-one and in six days he's almost been murdered and been through as violent an experience as any man can have. Or woman, by Heaven! That's right, there was the same look in the girl's eyes too. Stupid of me not to realize it. Poor girl, isn't she barely eighteen? Terrible to grow up so fast. I've been so lucky.

"Well, Mr. Tyrer," he said gruffly, envying him—that he had come through his baptism of fire bravely, "I'm sure you'll be all right. These meetings are, well, enough to try the patience of Job, eh? I think a sherry is in order."

Hiraga had had great difficulty escaping from the garden through the circles of samurai, and sneaking back to the Inn of the Forty-seven Ronin. When he reached it, long overdue, he was shocked to discover the assassination party had already left for the ambush.

Ori said helplessly, "One of our people reported that the Delegation had come out of the castle exactly as yesterday, banners as yesterday, that there were five palanquins as yesterday, so we presumed Lord Yoshi would be in one."

"Everyone was supposed to wait."

"They did, Hiraga, but if . . . if they hadn't left when they did they would never be in place in time."

Rapidly Hiraga changed into a cheap kimono and collected his weapons. "Did you see the doctor?"

"We, the mama-san and I, we thought it too dangerous today. Tomorrow will be fine."

"I'll see you in Kanagawa then."

"Sonno-joi!"

"Go to Kanagawa! Here you're a hazard!"

Hiraga slipped over the fence and went by back alleys and little-used paths and bridges, circling for the castle. This time he was lucky and avoided all patrols.

Most of the daimyo palaces outside the castle walls were deserted. Using cover well, he picked his way from garden to garden until he reached the burnt-out wreckage of what had been the daimyo's palace destroyed during the earthquake three days ago. As planned, his shishi friends were gathered for the ambush near the broken main gate that fronted the main pathway to the castle gate. There were nine of them, not eleven.

"Eeee, Hiraga, we'd given you up!" the youngest, the most excited, whispered. "From here we'll kill him easily."

"Where are the Mori samurai?"

"Dead." His cousin, Akimoto, shrugged. He was the oldest amongst them, a burly twenty-four. "We came by separate ways but I was near them and the three of us ran into a patrol." He beamed. "I fled one way, they another. I saw one take an arrow and go down. I never knew I could run so fast. Forget them, when will Yoshi pass by?"

Their disappointment was vast when Hiraga told them their prey was not in the cortege. "Then what shall we do?" a tall, very handsome youth of sixteen asked. "This ambush is perfect—half a dozen important Bakufu palanquins have gone by with hardly a guard around them."

"This place is too good to risk for no special reason," Hiraga said. "We'll leave one at a time. Akimoto, you firs—"

The shishi on guard whistled a warning. Instantly, they went deeper into cover, eyes pressed to openings in the broken fences. An ornate, covered palanquin with eight half-naked bearers and a dozen samurai banner guards was thirty-odd yards away, heading leisurely for the castle gate. No one else was in sight, either way.

Instant recognition of the emblem: Nori Anjo, head of the Council of Elders. Instant decision, *"Sonno-joi!"*

With Hiraga in the lead they rushed as one man to the attack, slaughtered the front two ranks of guards and hurtled for the palanquin. But in their excitement they had misjudged by a few seconds and that allowed the remaining eight guards, hand-picked warriors, to recover. In the frantic melee, the bearers squealed with fright, dropped their poles and fled—those who escaped the first violent onslaught—and this gave Anjo the moment he needed to slide the palanquin's far door open and roll out as Hiraga's sword went through the soft wood to impale the cushion where he had been a second before.

Cursing, Hiraga jerked the sword out, whirled in defense as he was menaced from the back, killed the man after a searing clash of swords, then leaped over the poles for Anjo who had scrambled to his feet, his sword out and now covered by three guards. Behind Hiraga, five of his friends were duelling with the other four samurai, one shishi was already dead, one helpless on the ground mortally wounded, and another, screaming with bloodlust, misjudging his adversary, slipped on the body of a sobbing bearer, and took a terrible cut in his side. Before his assailant could recover, a shishi slashed at the guard with total ferocity and the samurai's head rolled in the dust.

Now it was seven against six.

At once Akimoto broke off his fight and rushed to support Hiraga who had hurled himself at Anjo and his three guards and was being overwhelmed. Feinting brilliantly, Hiraga forced one of the guards off balance and impaled him, withdrew and darted to one side to draw off the other two, giving Akimoto the opening he needed to dispatch Anjo.

At that moment there was a warning shout. Twenty castle guards had rounded the corner fifty yards away and were charging to Anjo's support. The barest hesitation from Akimoto gave a guard time to parry the ferocious blow that would have killed Anjo, allowing him to scramble and flee towards the reinforcements. Now the shishi were completely outnumbered.

No way to get Anjo! No way to overcome!

"Retreat!" Hiraga shouted, and, again as one man, the maneuver rehearsed many times, Akimoto and the remaining four broke off their duels and charged back through the damaged main gate, Hiraga last— the badly wounded youth, Jozan, hobbling after them. Momentarily the guards were thrown into confusion. Then they collected themselves and, heavily reinforced, hurtled in pursuit while others intercepted Jozan, at bay, sword high, reeling, blood pouring from his side.

Akimoto was leading the pell-mell retreat through the damaged castle, their line of pullback already well reconnoitered. Hiraga was rearguard, the enemy gaining on him. He waited until he reached the first barricade where Gota waited in ambush to support him, stopped suddenly and the two of them whirled to counterattack, chopping and hacking viciously, mortally wounding one man, forcing the next to fall and bring down another. Instantly they fled again, leading the enemy deeper into the maze.

Almost stumbling, they rushed through the next narrow gap in the half-burnt wall where Akimoto and another waited in a second ambush. Without hesitation these two cut down the first of the attackers, screaming "Sonno-joi" while the remainder, stunned by the suddenness of the assault, halted to regroup. When they gave their battle cry and jumped over the body of their comrade through the bottleneck, Akimoto, Hiraga, and the others were nowhere to be seen.

At once the samurai fanned out and began a meticulous search, the sky filled with nimbus clouds and menacing.

In front of the burnt-out main gate, Anjo was now surrounded by guards. Five of his men had been killed, two were badly wounded. The two dead shishi had already been beheaded. The young shishi was helpless on the ground, one leg almost severed and he was holding on to it in agony, trying to stick it back together. Jozan was huddled against a wall. Rain began.

The samurai standing over the youth said again, "Who are you? What's your name, who sent you, who's your leader?"

"I've told you, shishi from Choshu, Toma Hojo! I was leader! No one sent me. *Sonno-joi!*"

"He's lying, Sire," a panting officer said.

"Of course," Anjo said, seething. "Kill him."

"Respectfully request he be allowed to commit seppuku."

"Kill him!"

The officer, a big, bearlike man, shrugged and went over to the youth. With his back to the Elder, he whispered, "I have the honor to act as your second. Stretch your neck." His sword sang in the air as he dealt the single blow. Formally he lifted the head by its topknot, presenting it to Anjo.

"I have seen it," Anjo said, following correct ritual, at the same time choked with rage that these men had dared to attack him, dared to frighten him half to death—him, Chief of the *roju*! "Now that one— he's a liar too, kill him!"

"Respectfully request he be allowed to commit seppuku."

Anjo was about to rave at him to kill the attempted assassin brutally or commit seppuku himself when he sensed the sudden collective antagonism of the samurai around him. The usual fear permeated him: whom do I trust? Only five of these men were his personal guards.

He pretended to consider the request. When his fury was contained, he nodded, turned and stomped off towards the castle gates in the increasing rain. His men went with him. The remainder circled Jozan.

"You can rest a moment, shishi," the officer said kindly, wiping the rain from his own face. "Give him some water."

"Thank you." Jozan had prepared for this moment ever since, with Ori and Shorin and others four years ago, he had sworn to 'honor the Emperor and expel the foreigners.' Summoning his waning strength, he groped to his knees, and was horrified to realize he was petrified of dying.

The officer had seen the terror, had expected it and quickly came forward and squatted beside him. "Do you have a death poem, shishi? Tell it to me, hold on, do not give way, you are samurai and this is as good a day as any," he said softly, encouraging the youth, willing the tears to stop. "From nothing into nothing, one sword cuts your enemy, one sword cuts you. Shout your battle cry and you will live forever. Say it: *Sonno-joi . . . again . . .*"

All the time he had been preparing himself. With a sudden fluid movement, he stood erect and whirled his sword from the sheath—and the youth into eternity.

"Eeee," one of his men said with admiration. "Uraga-san, that was marvelous to see."

"Sensei Katsumata of Satsuma was one of my teachers," he said throatily, his heart pounding like never before, but pleased that he had performed his duty as a samurai correctly. One of his men picked up the head by its topknot. The rain became tears, washing away the real ones. "Clean the head and take it to Lord Anjo for viewing." Uraga glanced at the castle gates. "Cowards disgust me," he said, and walked away.

That night, when it was safe, Hiraga and the others sneaked out of the cellar that had been located in advance. By different routes they slipped away for their safe house.

It was overcast and black, wind strong with spattering rain. I will not feel cold, I will not show discomfort, I am samurai, Hiraga ordered himself, following the pattern of training in his family ever since he could remember. Just as I will train my sons and daughters—if my karma is to have sons and daughters, he thought.

'It's time you married,' his father had said a year ago.

'I agree, Father. I respectfully request you change your mind and allow me to marry my choice.'

'First, it is the duty of the son to obey the father; second, it is the father's duty to choose the wives of his sons and husbands of his daughters; third, Sumomo's father does not approve, she is Satsuma and not Choshu, and last, however desirable, she is not suitable. What about the Ito girl?'

'Please excuse me, Father, I agree my choice is not perfect but her family is samurai, she is samurai trained and I am possessed by her. I beg you. You have four other sons—I have only one life and we, you and I, we both agree it is to be devoted to *sonno-joi* and will therefore be short. Grant this to me as a lifetime wish.' By custom such a wish was a most serious request and meant that, if granted, it precluded asking for any other, ever.

'Very well,' his father had said gruffly. 'But not as a lifetime wish.

You may be affianced when she is seventeen. I will welcome her into our family.'

That was last year. A few days later he had left Shimonoseki, supposedly to join the Choshu regiment in Kyōto, actually to declare for *sonno-joi* and become ronin—and put his secret four-year adherence and training to use.

Now it was Ninth Month. In three weeks Sumomo became seventeen but now he was so far outside the law there was no chance of safe return. Until yesterday. His father had written: *Astonishingly, our Lord Ogama has offered a pardon to all warriors who openly embraced* sonno-joi *and will restore all stipends if they return at once, renounce the heresy and again swear allegiance to him publicly. You will take advantage of this offer. Many are returning.*

The letter had saddened him, almost destroying his resolve. 'Sonno-joi is more important than family or even Lord Ogama, even Sumomo,' he had told himself over and over. 'Lord Ogama cannot be trusted. As to my stipend . . .'

Fortunately his father was relatively well off compared with most, and, because of his shoya grandfather, had been promoted to *hirazamurai,* the third rank of samurai. Above were senior samurai, hatomoto and daimyo. Below hirazamurai were all others—goshi, *ashigaru,* rural samurai, and foot soldiers, who were of the feudal class but below samurai. As such his father had had access to lower officials and the education of his sons was the best available.

I owe him everything, Hiraga thought.

Yes, and obediently I worked to become the best pupil in the Samurai School, the best swordsman, the best at English. And I have his permission and approval and that of the Sensei, our chief teacher, to embrace *sonno-joi,* to become ronin, to lead and organize Choshu warriors as a spearhead for change. Yes, but their approval is secret, for if known, surely it would cost my father and the Sensei their heads.

Karma. I am doing my duty. Gai-jin are scum we do not need. Only their weapons to kill them with.

The rain increased. And the tempest. This pleased him, for it made interception less likely. The beckoning bath and saké and clean clothes kept him warm and strong. That the attack had failed did not concern him. That was karma.

Ground into him by his teachers and heritage, until it was a way of life, was the certainty that enemies and traitors were everywhere. His steps were measured, he made sure he was not being followed, changed direction without logic and, whenever possible, explored ahead before moving.

When he reached the alley his strength drained out of him. The Inn of the Forty-seven Ronin and its surrounding fence had vanished.

All that remained was emptiness and the reeking smell and smoking ashes. A few bodies, men and women. Some decapitated, some hacked to pieces. He recognized his comrade shishi, Gota, by his kimono. The mama-san's head was on a spear thrust into the ground. Attached was a sign: *It is against the law to harbor criminals and traitors.* The official seal below was of the Bakufu, signed by Nori Anjo, chief of the *roju*.

Hiraga was filled with surging fury but it was icy and merely added more layers to that already within. Those cursed gai-jin, he thought. It is their fault. Because of them this happened. We will be revenged.

13

Sunday, 28th September:

MALCOLM STRUAN CAME OUT OF sleep slowly. His senses probed, testing. He had always known much about mental pain, losing two brothers and a sister; the anguish caused by his father's drunkenness and ever increasing rages; from impatient teachers; from his obsessive need to excel because one day he would be *the* tai-pan; and from his nagging fear he would be inadequate however much he prepared and trained and hoped and prayed and worked by day and by night, every day and every night of his life—no real childhood or boyhood like others.

But now as never before he had to test the level of his awakening, to plumb the depth of what physical pain he had to endure today as today's norm, disregarding the sudden, blinding spasms that arrived without warning or logic.

Just a throbbing ache today but better than yesterday. How many days from the Tokaidō Road? Sixteen. Sixteenth day.

He allowed himself to become more awake. Truly better than yesterday. Eyes and ears open now. Room steady in the early light. Clear sky, light wind, no storm.

Two days ago the storm had ceased. It had blown for eight days at typhoon strength, then vanished as quickly as it had arrived. The fleet standing off Yedo had scattered the first day, seeking safety at sea. Alone of all the warships, the French flagship had disengaged early, just making it back safely to Yokohama. No other ships had returned.

200

No need to worry yet, but everyone watched the horizon uneasily, hoping and praying.

During the gales here at Yokohama a merchantman had been blown ashore, some buildings damaged, many cutters and fishing boats lost, havoc wrought in the village and Yoshiwara, many tents in the military encampment on the bluff blown away but no casualties there, or in the Settlement.

We were more than lucky, Struan thought, concentrating on the central problem of his universe. Can I sit up?

A tentative, awkward attempt. Ayeeyah! Pain, but not too bad. With both arms he pushed further and now he was erect, his hands braced behind him.

Bearable. Better than yesterday. Waiting a moment, then leaning forward, carefully taking his weight off one arm. Still bearable. Weight off both arms. Still bearable. Taking care he pulled the bedclothes off and cautiously tried to swing his legs to the floor. But he could not, the stabbing pain too great. A second try, again failure.

Never mind, I'll try later. He lowered himself as gently as he could. When his weight was off his waist and on his back he sighed with relief. "Ayeeyah!"

'Patience, Malcolm,' Babcott had said every day at every visit—three or four times daily.

'Sod patience!'

'Quite right too—but you really are doing fine.'

'And when can I get up?'

'Now, if you wish—but I wouldn't advise it.'

'How long?'

'Give it a couple of weeks.'

He had cursed openly but in many ways he was glad for the reprieve. It gave him more time to consider how he was going to deal with being tai-pan, with his mother, with Angelique, with McFay and pressing business problems.

'What about the guns for Choshu?' McFay had asked a few days ago. 'It'll be a huge, continuing business.'

'I've an idea. Leave it with me.'

'Norbert will have sniffed these Choshus out long since and he's bound to make them an undercutting offer.'

'The hell with Norbert and Brock! Their contacts are not as good as ours, and Dmitri, Cooper-Tillman and most of the other American China traders are on our side.'

'Except in Hawaii,' McFay said sourly.

In the last mail, ten days ago—no further news since then and the bimonthly steamer not expected for another five days—Tess Struan had written: . . .

> The Victoria Bank has betrayed us. I believe they have been secretly supporting Morgan Brock in London with lavish letters of credit. With these, he has secretly bought out or bribed all our Hawaiian agents, cornering the whole sugar market, excluding us totally. Worse, though I've no proof, it's rumoured he has close contacts with the Rebel President Jefferson Davis and his cotton plantation owners, proposing to barter the whole crop against cotton futures for English mills—a deal that would make Tyler and Morgan the richest men in Asia. THIS MUST NOT HAPPEN! I am at my wit's end. Jamie, what do you suggest? Give this dispatch to my son with the same urgent request for help.

'What's your suggestion, Jamie?'

'I don't have one, Mal . . . Tai-pan.'

'If the deal's done the deal's done and that's the end of it. Say it is, could we intercept the cotton somehow?'

McFay had blinked. 'Pirate it?'

Struan had said levelly, 'If need be. Old Man Brock would, he has in the past. That's one possibility, the cotton will all go in his ships. Second: our Navy breaks the Union blockade and then we can all get all the cotton we want.'

'It could, if we declare war on the Union. Unthinkable!'

'I don't agree. For God's sake, we should come in on Davis's side, Southern cotton's our lifeblood. Then they'll win, otherwise they won't.'

'Agreed. But we're equally dependent on the North.'

'How do we take away his ships? There must be a way to break the chain. If he can't move the cargo he's bankrupt.'

'What would Dirk do?'

'Go for the jugular,' Malcolm had replied at once.

'Then that's what we have to find . . .'

Where and what is it? he asked himself again, lying quietly on the bed, willing his brain to work clearly on this problem and all the others. Angelique? No, I'll think about her later—but I know I love her more every day.

Thank God I can write letters now. Must write to Mother again, if anyone should know the jugular it's her; isn't Tyler Brock her father and Morgan her brother, but how dare she sneer at Angelique's family? Should I write to Angelique's father? Yes, but not yet, there's time enough.

So much other mail to catch up on, books to order from England, Christmas not so far away, the Jockey Club Charity Ball in Hong Kong, Struan's annual Ball to think about, meetings today: Jamie at least twice, Seratard this afternoon—what does he want? What else is planned for today? Phillip's coming to chat again after breakfast . . . wait a minute, no, not today. Yesterday Sir William ordered him back to Yedo, to prepare the Legation for the meeting with the Council of Elders in twenty days.

'Will the meeting really take place, Sir William?' he had asked when the Minister had visited him. With the fleet no longer protecting the Legation, and extensive though not overtly hostile samurai activity all around them, after a few face-saving days Sir William had considered it prudent to return to Yokohama, ostensibly to prepare for the delivery of the indemnity money.

'I think so, Mr. Struan. Perhaps not punctually, but yes, the ceremonial will happen approximately then and we will have taken a real leap forward. If they produce the first payment of 5,000 pounds as promised . . . well, that will be a very good indication. By the way, I understand you've a steamer due to leave today for Hong Kong, could I prevail upon you to allow one of my staff and some urgent mail to go with her—my wife and two sons are expected soon and I have to make plans.'

'Of course, I'll mention it to McFay. If you want a berth on any of our ships to meet them, just say the word.'

'Thank you—I was planning two weeks' vacation when they arrive. One gets hidebound, cooped up here, don't you think? Miss the bustle of Hong Kong, that's quite a city though damned if the people at Whitehall appreciate it! Plenty of good roast beef, some cricket or tennis, the theatre or opera, and several days at the races would be most welcome. When will you return?'

When?

News of our Tokaidō disaster would have arrived almost a week ago, presuming the mail ship weathered the storm. Mother will have had a fit though showing nothing to outsiders. Will she come here on the first available ship? Possibly, but there's HQ to look after—and Emma, Rose and Duncan. With Father dead, me not there, eighteen days is too long for her to be away. Even if she's already aboard there's at least another three or four days to prepare my defenses. Strange to consider her a possible enemy; if not enemy no longer friend. Perhaps she's friend after all; she always has been, however distant, always attending Father with little time for us.

'Hello, my son, how could I ever be your enemy?'

He was astonished to see her standing by the bed, his father also, and this was strange because he remembered his father was dead but it did not seem to matter—quickly out of bed without hurt and chatting with them happily in the cutter crossing Hong Kong harbor, storm clouds everywhere, both of them listening deferentially and approving his clever plans, Angelique sitting in the stern, her dress diaphanous, breasts beckoning, uncovered now, his hands there and lower, all uncovered now, her body writhing against his, hands caressing his face . . .

"Malcolm?"

He awoke with a start. Angelique was beside the bed, smiling at him, peignoir blue silk rich and discreet. The dream vanished, except the threat and promise of her body, ever pulsating in his subconscious. "I . . . oh, I was dreaming, my darling, but it was about you."

"Oh, yes? What?"

He frowned, trying to recollect. "I don't remember," he said, smiling up at her, "except that you were beautiful. I love your gown."

She pirouetted gaily to show it off. "The tailor you asked Jamie to arrange made it! *Mon Dieu,* Malcolm—me, I think he is marvelous—I ordered four dresses, I hope that's all right . . . oh, thank you!" She bent down to kiss him.

"Wait, Angelique, wait, just a second. Look!" Carefully he raised himself, dominating the pain, took both supporting hands away and held them out to her.

"That's *wonderful, chéri,*" she said, delighted, catching his hands. "Ah, Monsieur Struan, I think I'd better take care to be chaperoned all the time now, and never be alone with you in your bedroom."

Smiling, she stepped closer, carefully put her hands on his shoulders, allowed his arms to go around her and kissed him. Her kiss was light, promising and avoided his need for more. Without guile she kissed his ear, then straightened, allowing his head to rest against her breast, the intimacy pleasing her—and him very much. Soft silk there, with that uncanny, irreplaceable, special warmth.

"Malcolm, did you really really mean what you said about wanting to marry me?" She felt his arms tighten and the wince of pain.

"Of course, I've told you so many times."

"Do you think, do you think your parents, pardon, your mother, she will approve, yes? Oh, I do hope so."

"Yes, oh yes, she will, of course she will."

"May I write to Papa? I would like to tell him."

"Of course, write when you wish, I will write too," he said throatily, then, swamped by her affection, his need overcoming his discretion, he kissed the silk, then again, harder, and almost cursed aloud as he sensed her retreat before it happened. "Sorry," he muttered.

"No need for 'sorry' or any Anglo-Saxon guilt, my love, not between us," she said gently. "I want you too." Then, following her plan, switched her mood, entirely in control, her happiness infectious. "Now I will be the nurse Nightingale."

She plumped the pillows and began to make the bed neater. "Tonight is a French dinner hosted by Monsieur Seratard, tomorrow night he has arranged a soiree. André Poncin is giving a piano recital of Beethoven—I prefer him so much to Mozart—also Chopin and a piece by a young man called Brahms." A church bell began, sounding the call to early service, almost immediately to be joined by others, sweeter and more melodious, from the Catholic church. "There," she said, helping him lie back comfortably. "Now I will go for my toilette and return after Mass when you are toiletted."

He held her hand. " 'Bathed.' You're wonderful. I love y—" Abruptly their eyes went to the door as someone tried the handle. But the bolt was on.

"I did it when you were asleep." She chuckled like a little girl playing a game. Again the handle moved. "Servants always come in without knocking, they need to be taught lessons!"

"Mass'er!" the servant called out. "Tea-ah!"

"Tell him to go away and come back in five minutes."

Struan, caught up in her pleasure, shouted the order in Cantonese, and they heard the man go off grumbling.

She laughed. "You must teach me Chinese-speaking."

"I'll try."

"What's 'I love you'?"

"They don't have a word for love, not like us."

A frown went across her face. "How sad!"

She slipped over to the door, unbolted it, blew him a kiss, and vanished into her own suite. Her bolt slid home.

He watched the door, aching. Then he heard the bells change, becoming more insistent, reminding him: Mass!

His heart twisted. Didn't think about that, that she was Catholic. Mother's diehard Church of England, twice on Sundays, Father as well, us too, in procession, along with every other decent family in Hong Kong.

Catholic?

Doesn't matter, I . . . I don't mind. I've got to have her, he told himself, his healthy, hungry throbbing ache pushing the pain away. "I must."

That afternoon the four perspiring Japanese porters put down the iron-banded chest, watched by three Bakufu officials of no import, Sir William, interpreters, an officer from the army accounting department, the Legation shroff, a Chinese, and Vargas, to check him.

They were in the main Legation reception room, the windows open and Sir William was hard put not to beam. Laboriously one of the officials produced an ornate key and unlocked the chest. Within were silver Mexican dollars, a few tael bars of gold—about an ounce and a third in weight—and some of silver.

"Ask why the indemnity isn't all in gold as agreed?"

"The Official says they could not obtain the gold in time but these are clean Mex and legal currency, and will you please give him a receipt." 'Clean' coins meant those that were unshaved, or unclipped, a common practice, and sloughed off onto the unwary.

"Begin counting."

Happily his shroff tipped the contents onto the carpet. At once he spotted a clipped coin, Vargas another and another. These were put to one side. Every eye stayed on the carpet, on the neatly stacked, growing piles of coins. Five thousand pounds sterling was an immense sum when the salary of a full-time interpreter was four hundred a year and pay your own lodgings, a shroff a hundred (though a good percentage of everything that passed through his hands would somehow stick there), a servant in London twenty pounds a year and all found, a soldier five pennies a day, a sailor six, an Admiral six hundred pounds a year.

The counting was quickly done. Both shroffs checked the weight of each small bar of gold twice, then the weight of each of the stacks of chipped coins, then used an abacus to calculate the total against the current rate of exchange.

Vargas said, "It comes to four thousand and eighty-four pounds, six shillings and seven pence farthing, Sir William, in clean coin, five hundred and twenty pounds in gold, ninety-two pounds sixteen in clipped coins for a grand total of four thousand, six hundred and ninety-seven pounds, two shillings, and seven pence farthing."

"Sorry, eight pence, Mass'er." The Chinese bowed and nodded his head, his pigtail long and thick, making the slight, face-saving adjustment as agreed in advance with Vargas, deciding that the amount that his Portuguese counterpart had deducted for their fee, two and a half percent, or one hundred and seventeen pounds, eight shillings and sixpence between them, was less than what he would have maneuvered, but passable for half an hour's work.

Sir William said, "Vargas, put it back in the chest, give them a receipt with a note that the underpayment will be added to the last installment. Johann, thank them, and say we will expect the full amount, in gold, in nineteen days."

Johann obeyed. At once the other interpreter began a long statement. "They now ask for an extension, sir, and—"

"No extension." Sir William sighed, dismissed the others and prepared for another hour, closing his ears until he was astonished to hear Johann say, "They've suddenly come to the point, sir: it's the Yedo meeting, sir. They ask that this be delayed another thirty days to make it fifty days from now . . . the exact words are: the Shōgun will return from Kyōto then and he has informed the Council of Elders to advise the Foreign Ministers that he would grant them an audience on that day."

To give himself time to think, Sir William called out, "Lun!" Lun appeared instantly. "Tea!"

Within seconds the trays arrived. And cigars, snuff and pipe tobacco. Soon the room was filled with smoke and everyone coughing and all the time Sir William was considering options.

First and foremost, I'm probably dealing with low-level officials, so anything agreed will be subject to further negotiation. Next, in any event the fifty days will surely extend into two months, even three, but if we have an audience with the Ultimate Power, of course under British leadership, we will have taken a lasting step forward. Actually, I don't mind if the delay goes to three, even four months. By then I'll have Lord Russell's approval for war, reinforcements will be en route from India and Hong Kong, the Admiral will have his damned authority, and we'll have the forces to invest, hold and fortify Yedo if we have to.

I could say, let us have the meeting as planned and then the Shōgun meeting. That would be best, but I feel they won't go against the mystical Shōgun's wishes and somehow they'll wheedle and twist and mesh us again.

Johann said, "The spokesman says, as that's agreed, we will bid you farewell."

"Nothing is agreed. A thirty-day extension is not possible for many reasons. We have already arranged a date for the Council of Elders that will take place as planned and then, ten days later, we will be pleased to meet the Shōgun."

After an hour of sucked-in breaths, aghast silences, blunt Anglo-Saxonese, Sir William allowed himself to be whittled down and got his compromise position: The meeting with the Council of Elders to take place as planned, and the meeting with the Shōgun twenty days after that.

Once alone again with Sir William, Johann said, "They won't abide by it."

"Yes, I know. Never mind."

"Sir William, my contract's up in a couple of months. I won't renew."

Sir William said sharply, "I can't do without your services for at least six months."

"It's time to go home. This place is going to be a bloodbath soon and I've no want to have my head on a spike."

"I'll increase your salary by fifty pounds a year."

"It's not the money, Sir William. I'm tired. Ninety-eight percent of all the talk is *Sheisse*. I've no patience now to sift the kernel of wheat from the barrel of dung!"

"I need you for these two meetings."

"They'll never take place. Two months odd, then I'm off, the exact day is on the paper. Sorry, Sir William, but that's the end, and now I am going to get drunk." He left.

Sir William went across the hall to his office window and searched the horizon. It was nearing sunset now. No sign of any of the fleet. My God, I hope they're safe. Must keep Johann somehow. Tyrer won't be ready for a year at least. Who can I get that I can trust? God damn it!

Light from the dying sun illuminated the sparsely furnished room, not enough to see by so he lit an oil lamp, adjusting the wick carefully. On his desk were neat piles of dispatches, his edition of *All the Year Round*—long since read from cover to cover, with all the newspapers from the last mail ship, several editions of *Illustrated London News* and *Punch*. He picked up the advance copy of Turgenev's *Fathers and Sons* in Russian sent to him by a friend at the Court of St. Petersburg, amongst other English and French books, started to read it, then, distracted, put it aside and began the second letter of the day to the

Governor of Hong Kong, giving details of today's meeting, and asking for a replacement for Johann. Lun came in silently, closing the door.

"Yes, Lun?"

Lun came up to his desk, hesitated, then dropped his voice. "Mass'er," he said cautiously, "hear trou'bel, trou'bel soon Yedo Big House, big trou'bel."

Sir William stared up at him. Big House was what the Chinese servants called their Yedo Legation. "What trouble?"

Lun shrugged. "Trou'bel."

"When trouble?"

Again Lun shrugged. "Whisk'y water, heya?"

Sir William nodded thoughtfully. From time to time Lun whispered rumors to him with an uncanny knack of being right. He watched him pad over to the sideboard and make the drink, just as he liked it.

Phillip Tyrer and the kilted Captain were watching the same sunset from an upstairs window of the Legation at Yedo, the usual groups of samurai stationed outside the walls and in all approaches up the hill. Dark reds and orange and browns on the empty horizon mixed with a strip of blue above the sea. "Will the weather be good tomorrow?"

"Don't know much about the weather here, Mr. Tyrer. If we were in Scotland I could give you a wee forecast," the Captain, a sandy-haired, thirty-year-old ramrod, laughed. "Rain with scattered showers . . . but, och ay, it's no' so bad."

"I've never been to Scotland, but I will on my next leave. When do you go home?"

"Maybe next year, or the year after. This is only my second year." Their attention went back to the square. Four Highlanders and a sergeant plodded up the hill through the samurai and entered the iron gates, returning from a routine patrol to the wharf where a detachment of marines and a cutter were stationed. Samurai were always in attendance, standing around, sometimes chatting, or in clusters near fires that they lit if it was cold, movement constant. No one, soldier or Legation employee, had been prevented from leaving or entering, though all had passed through intense, always silent scrutiny.

"Excuse me, I'll see the Sergeant, make sure our cutter's there, in case, and close down for the night. Dinner at seven as usual?"

"Yes." When he was alone Tyrer stifled a nervous yawn, stretched and moved his arm to ease the slight ache there. His wound had healed perfectly, no longer any need to use a sling. I'm bloody lucky, he thought, except for Wee Willie. Damn the man for sending me here,

I'm supposed to be training to be an interpreter, not a dogsbody. Damn damn damn. And now I'll miss André's recital that I was so looking forward to. Angelique is certain to be there.

Rumors of her secret betrothal had rushed around the Settlement like a foehn wind—unsettling. Hints dropped to her or to Struan had brought forth neither denial nor confirmation, nor even a clue. In the Club the betting was two to one that it was a fact, twenty to one that the marriage would never take place: 'Struan's as sick as a dog, she's Catholic and you know his mum, for God's sake, Jamie!'

'Taken! He's better every day and you don't know him like I do. Ten guineas against two hundred.'

'Charlie, what odds you give me that one's up the spout?'

'Oh, for God's sake!'

'Angel Tits ain't a doxy, for Chris' sake!'

'A thousand to one?'

'Done, by God . . . a golden guinea!'

To Tyrer and Pallidar's disgust, the odds and bets, ever more personal and detailed, changed daily. 'The buggers here are a lot of guttersnipes!'

'You're right, of course, Pallidar. A scummy lot!'

With intense speculation going on about Struan and Angelique, there was more about the extent of the storm and the fleet, worse that it might be in dire trouble, and doom generally. Japanese merchants were more nervous than usual too, whispering rumors of insurrections all over Japan against or for the Bakufu, that the mystical Mikado, supposed high priest of all Japanese, who held sway in Kyōto, had ordered all samurai to attack Yokohama.

'Poppycock, if you ask me,' the Westerners told one another, but more and more guns were purchased and even the two trader wives slept with a loaded weapon beside their beds. Drunk Town was rumored to be an armed camp.

Then, a few days ago, an act of war: an American merchantman, storm battered, had limped into Yokohama. In the Shimonoseki Straits, inbound from Shanghai for Yokohama with a cargo of silver, ammunition and arms, then onwards to the Philippines with opium, tea and general trade goods, she had been fired upon by shore batteries.

'The devil you were!' someone called out over the explosion of anger in the Club.

'You're goddam right we were! And us as peaceful as a buttercup! Those Choshu bastards were mighty accurate—what crazy bastard sold them goddam cannon? Blew off our top t'gallants before we knew what was happening and could take evading action. Sure, we returned their fire but we've only a couple of stinky goddam five-pounders that'd not give a body much cause to hiccup. We counted as many as twenty cannon.'

'My God, twenty cannon and expert gunners could easily close Shimonoseki, and if that happens we're in dead trouble. That's the quickest and only safe way here.'

'Ay! The Inland Waters are a must, by God!'

'Where the hell's the fleet? They could go and knock out those batteries! What about our trade?'

'Ay, where's the fleet, hope to God she's safe!'

'And if she's not?'

'Charlie, we'll just have to send for another. . . .'

Stupid people, Tyrer thought, all they can think of is send for the fleet, boozing and money.

Thank God the French Admiral brought back André with him. Thank God for André even though he's volatile and strange but that's only because he's French. Thanks to him I've already two exercise books crammed with Japanese words and phrases, my daily journal's chockablock with an abundance of folklore, I've a rendezvous with a Jesuit when we're again in Yokohama. Such marvelous progress and so important for me to learn quickly—and that's without even thinking about the Yoshiwara.

Three visits. The first two guided, the third alone.

'André, I just can't tell you how much I appreciate all the time you've given me, and all the help. And as to tonight, I can never repay you, never.'

That was after the first visit.

Nervous, flushed, sweating, almost tongue-tied but pretending to be manly he had followed André out of the Settlement at dusk, joining the jovial crowds of men Yoshiwara bound, passed the samurai guards, politely raising top hats and receiving perfunctory bows in return, across the Bridge to Paradise towards the tall gates in the enclosing wooden fence.

'Yoshiwara means Place of Reeds,' André said expansively, both of them well lubricated with champagne that in Tyrer's case had only increased his foreboding. 'It was the name of a district in Yedo, a reclaimed swamp, where the first ever, fenced bordello area was decreed and built by Shōgun Toranaga two and a half centuries ago. Before that, bordellos were scattered everywhere. Since then, so we're told, all cities and towns have similar enclosures, all of them licensed and tightly controlled. By custom, many are called Yoshiwara. See those?'

Above the gate, a series of Chinese characters were etched elegantly into the wood. 'They mean, *Lust is pressing, something must be done about it.*'

Tyrer laughed nervously. Many guards inside and outside the gate. Last night when André had volunteered to escort him—they were in the Club then, drinking—he had mentioned a trader had told him the guards were there not just to keep the peace but mostly to keep the whores from escaping, 'So they're really all slaves, aren't they?' To his shock he had seen Poncin flush angrily.

'*Mon Dieu,* don't think of them as whores or call them whores as we understand the word. They're not slaves. Some are indentured for a number of years, many sold by their parents at an early age, again for a number of years, but their contracts are Bakufu approved and registered. They're not *whores,* they're Ladies of the Willow World and don't forget it. Ladies!'

'Sorry, I . . .'

But André had paid no attention. 'Some are geishas—Art Persons—those trained to entertain you, sing and dance and play silly games and are not for bedding. The rest, *mon Dieu,* I've told you, don't think of them as whores, think of them as Pleasure Women, trained to please, trained over many years.'

'Sorry, I didn't know.'

'If you treat them properly they'll give you pleasure, almost any kind you want—*if they want to*—and if the money you give is correct. You give them money, which has no significance, they give you their youth. It's an odd bargain.' André had looked at him strangely. 'They give you their youth and hide the tears you cause.' He quaffed his wine and stared at the cup, abruptly maudlin.

Tyrer remembered how he had quietly refilled their glasses, cursing himself for breaking the feeling of easy friendship, to him valuable friendship, swearing to be more cautious in future and wondering why the sudden fury. 'Tears?'

'Their life isn't good, but even so it isn't always bad. For some it can be marvelous. The most beautiful and accomplished become famous, they're sought after by even the most important daimyo—kings—in the land, they can marry in high places, marry rich merchants, even samurai. But for our Ladies of the Willow World who are just for us gai-jin,' André had continued bitterly, 'there's no future but to open another house here, to drink saké and employ other girls. *Mon Dieu,* treat them all properly, because once they're here they're polluted in the eyes of all other Japanese.'

'Sorry. How awful.'

'Yes, no one understan—' A burst of drunken laughter from the men around drowned him for a moment, the Club filled, raucous and steaming. 'I tell you these cretins don't care or give a damn, none of them, except Canterbury, he did.' André had looked up from the dregs of his drink. 'You're young and unsullied, here for a year or two and seem willing to learn, so I thought . . . there's so much to learn, so much good,' he had said suddenly, and left.

That was last night and now they were within the Yoshiwara gate, André took out his small pistol. 'Phillip, are you armed?'

'No.'

André gave the pistol to the unctuous attendant who gave him a receipt and put it with many others. 'No weapons are allowed within the fence—the same in all Yoshiwaras, even samurai must give up their swords. *On y va!*'

Ahead of them now, on either side of the wide street and alleys leading off it, were lines of neat little houses, many for eating or just small bars, all built of wood with verandas and oiled paper shoji screens, and raised off the ground on low pilings. Everywhere color and sprays of flowers, noise and laughter, and lanterns, candles and oil lamps. 'Fire's a huge hazard, Phillip. This whole place burned down the first year but within the week was booming again.'

All the Houses bore individual signs. Some had open doors and sliding shoji windows. Many girls were in them, ornately or demurely dressed in kimonos of varying quality, depending on the standing of the House. Other girls were promenading, some with colorful umbrellas, some attended by maids, paying little or no attention to the gawking men. Intermixed were vendors of all kinds, and swarms of maids shouting the virtues of the Houses in versions of pithy, raucous pidgin, and sounding over everything the happy banter of potential customers, most of whom were recognized and had their favored places. There were no Japanese except for guards, servants, porters and masseurs.

'Never forget, Yoshiwaras are a place for joy, the pleasures of the flesh, eating and drinking as well, and that there's no such thing as sin in Japan, original sin, any kind of sin.' André laughed and led the way through the typically well-ordered crowd, except for a few brawling drunks who were quickly and good-naturedly pulled apart by huge, expert bouncers, at once to be sat on stools and plied with more saké by the ever attentive maids.

'Drunks are welcome, Phillip, because they lose count of their money. But don't ever pick a quarrel with a bouncer, they're fantastically good at unarmed combat.'

'Compared to our Drunk Town this place is as well disciplined as the Regent's Promenade at Brighton.' A boisterous maid caught Tyrer's arm and tried to pull him into a doorway. 'Saké, heya? Jig jig plenty good, Mass'er . . .'

'Iyé, domo, iyé . . .' Tyrer burst out—no, thank you, no—and hurriedly caught up with André. 'My God, I had to really tug to get away.'

'That's their job.' André turned off the main street through a passageway between dwellings, down another, stopped at a seedy door set into a fence, a grubby sign above, and knocked. Tyrer recognized the characters that André had written for him earlier: House of the Three Carp. A small grill slid back. Eyes peered out. The door opened and Tyrer stepped into a wonderland.

Tiny garden, oil lanterns and candlelight. Glistening grey stepping stones in green moss, clusters of flowers, many small maples—blood-red leaves against more green—pale orange light coming from the half-obscured shoji. Little bridge over a miniature stream, waterfall nearby. Kneeling on the veranda was a middle-aged woman, the mama-san, beautifully attired and coiffured. 'Bonsoir, Monsieur Furansu-san,' she said, put both her hands on the veranda and bowed.

André bowed back. 'Raiko-san, konbanwa. Ikaga desu ka?' Good evening, how are you? 'Kore wa watashi no tomodachi desu, Tyrer-san.' This is my friend, Mr. Tyrer.

'Ah so desu ka? Taira-san?' She bowed gravely. Awkwardly Tyrer bowed, then she beckoned them to follow her.

'She says Taira is a famous old Japanese name. You're in luck, Phillip, most of us go by nicknames. I'm Furansu-san—the nearest they can get to Frenchman.'

Taking off their shoes so as not to dirty the very clean and expensive tatami, then sitting awkwardly cross-legged in the room, André Poncin explained the tokonoma, the alcove for a special hanging scroll and flower arrangement, changed daily, guiding him to appreciate the quality of the shoji and woods.

Saké arrived. The maid was young, perhaps ten, not pretty but deft and silent. Raiko poured, first for André and then Tyrer, then herself. She sipped, André drained the tiny cup and held it out for more. Tyrer did the same, finding the taste of the warm wine not unpleasant but insipid. Both cups were immediately filled and drained and refilled. More trays and more flasks.

Tyrer lost count but soon he was enveloped with a pleasing glow, forgot his nervousness and watched and listened and understood almost nothing the other two said, just a word here and there. Raiko's hair was black and shining and dressed with many ornate combs, her face thick with white powder, neither ugly nor beautiful just different, her kimono pink silk with interweaving green carp.

'A carp is *koi,* usually a sign of good luck,' André had explained earlier. 'Townsend Harris's mistress, the Shimoda courtesan the Bakufu arranged to distract him, called herself Koi, but I'm afraid it didn't bring her luck.'

'Oh? What happened?'

'The story told amongst courtesans here is that he adored her and when he left he gave her money, enough to set herself up—she was with him for about two years. Shortly after he returned to America, she just vanished. Probably drank herself to death or committed suicide.'

'She loved him that much?'

'They say that in the beginning when the Bakufu approached her she adamantly refused to go with a foreigner—an unheard-of aberration, don't forget he was the first ever to be actually allowed to live *on Japanese soil.* She begged the Bakufu to choose someone else, to allow her to live in peace, said she would become a Buddhist nun, she even swore she would kill herself. But they were equally adamant, begging her to help them solve this problem of gai-jin, pleading with her for weeks to be his consort, wearing her down by what means no one knows. So she agreed and they thanked her. And when Harris left they all turned their backs on her, Bakufu, everyone: Ah, so sorry, but any woman who has gone with a foreigner is tainted forever.'

'How awful!'

'Yes, in our terms, and so sad. But remember, this is the Land of Tears. Now she is legend, honored by her peers and by those who turned their backs, because of her sacrifice.'

'I don't understand.'

'Nor do I, nor any of us. But they do. Japanese do.'

How strange, Tyrer thought again. Like this little house and this man and woman, chattering half in Japanese, half in pidgin, laughing one with another, one a madam the other a customer, both pretending they are something else. More and more saké. Then she bowed and got up and left.

'Saké, Phillip?'

'Thanks. It's quite nice, isn't it?'

After a pause, André said, 'You're the first person I've ever brought here.'

'Oh? Why me?'

The Frenchman twisted the porcelain cup in his fingers, drained the last drop, poured some more, then began in French, his voice soft and filled with warmth, 'Because you're the first person I've met in Yokohama with . . . because you speak French, you're cultured, your mind is like a sponge, you're young, not far off half my age, eh? You're twenty-one, and not like the others, you're untainted and you'll be here for a few years.' He smiled, spinning the web tighter, telling only part of the truth, molding it: 'Truly you're the first person I've met who, *alors,* even though you're English and actually an enemy of France, you're the only one who somehow seems to merit the knowledge I've acquired.' An embarrassed smile. 'Difficult to explain. Perhaps because I've always wanted to be a teacher, perhaps because I've never had a son, never married, perhaps because soon I have to move back to Shanghai, perhaps because we've enemies enough and perhaps . . . perhaps you could be a firm friend.'

'I would be honored to be your friend,' Tyrer said at once, enmeshed and under his spell, 'and I really do think, I really have always thought we should be allies, France and Britain, not enemies and—' The shoji slid back. Raiko, on her knees, beckoned Tyrer. His heart surged.

André Poncin smiled. 'Just follow her, and remember what I told you.'

As in a dream Phillip Tyrer got up unsteadily and padded after her, down a corridor, into a room, across it and along a veranda, into another empty room where she motioned him in, closed the shoji, and left him.

A shaded oil lamp. Charcoal brazier for warmth. Shadows and darkness and patches of light. Futons—small square mattresses—laid out as a bed on the floor, a bed for two. Downy coverlets. Two *yukatas,* wide-sleeved, patterned cotton gowns for sleeping in. Through a small door a bathhouse, candle-lit, tall wooden tub filled with steaming water. Sweet-smelling soap. Low, three-legged stool. Diminutive towels. Everything as André had foretold.

His heart was beating very fast now and he pushed his mind to remember André's instructions through the saké haze.

Methodically, he began to undress. Coat, waistcoat, cravat, shirt, woolen vest, each article meticulously folded and nervously placed in a pile. Awkwardly sitting, then pulling off his socks, reluctantly his trousers and standing up once more. Only his woolen long johns remained. Weaving a little, then an embarrassed shrug and he took them off and folded them, even more carefully. His skin prickled into goose bumps and he walked into the bathhouse.

There was water from the barrel as he had been told and spilled it over his shoulders, the warmth pleasant. Another and then the sound of the shoji opening and he glanced around. 'Christ Almighty,' he muttered.

The woman was beefy with huge forearms, her yukata brief, nothing under except a loincloth and she strode purposefully towards him with a flat smile, motioned him to squat on the stool. In absolute embarrassment he obeyed. At once she noticed the healing scar on his arm and sucked in her breath, said something that he could not understand.

He forced a smile. 'Tokaidō.'

'*Wakarimasu.*' I understand. Then, before he could stop her she poured water over his head—unexpectedly and not part of his forewarning—and began soaping and washing his long hair, then his body, her fingers hard, expert and insistent, but taking care not to hurt his arm. Arms legs back front, then offering him the cloth and pointing between his legs. Still in shock he cleansed those parts, meekly handed the cloth back. 'Thank you,' he muttered. 'Oh, sorry, *domo.*'

More water took away the last of the soap and she pointed to the tub. '*Dozo!*' Please.

André had explained: 'Phillip, just remember that, unlike with us, you have to be washed and clean *before* you get into the bath, so others can use the same water—which is very sensible, don't forget wood is very expensive and it takes a long time to heat enough—so don't piss in it either, and don't think of her as a woman when you're in the bathhouse, just a helper. She cleans you outside, then inside, no?'

Tyrer eased himself into the tub. It was hot but not too hot and he closed his eyes, not wanting to watch the woman making the bath tidy. Christ, he thought in misery, I'll never be able to perform with her. André's made a vast mistake.

'But . . . well, I, er, don't know how much I, er, pay, or do I give the girl the money first or what?'

'*Mon Dieu,* you should never actually give money to any girl, anywhere, that's the height of bad manners, though you can barter savagely with the mama-san, sometimes with the girl herself, but only after tea or saké. Before you leave you'd put it discreetly in a place she would see it. In the House of the Three Carp, you give no money, it's a special place—there are others like it—only for special customers, one of which I am. They'll send you a bill, two or three times a year.

But listen, before we go there you have to swear by God that you'll pay the bill the moment it's presented, and that you will never, never introduce anyone else there or talk about it.'

So he had sworn and promised, wanting to ask how much but not daring to. 'The, er, bill, when does that come?'

'When it pleases the mama-san. I told you, Phillip, you can have pleasure the year round on credit, under the correct circumstances—of course, I'm surety for you. . . .'

The warmth of the bath water permeated him. He hardly heard her bustle out and then, later, bustle back again.

'Taira-san?'

'*Hai?*' Yes?

She was holding up a towel. Curiously lethargic, he climbed out, his muscles drowsed by the water, and let her dry him. Once more the special places he did himself, finding it easier this time. A comb for his hair. Dry starched yukata and she motioned him towards the bed.

Again panic surged through him. Shakily he forced himself to lie down. She covered him, folded back the other coverlet and again left.

His heart was thundering but lying down felt marvelous, the mattress soft and clean and sweet-smelling, feeling cleaner than he had felt for years. Soon he was calmer and then the shoji opened and closed and he was filled with utter relief but no longer calm. The half-seen girl was tiny, willowy, pale yellow yukata, hair long and cascading. Now she was kneeling beside the bed. '*Konbanwa, Taira-san. Ikaga desu ka? Watashi wa Ako.*' Good evening, Mr. Taira. Are you well? I am Ako.

'*Konbanwa, Ako-san. Watashi wa Phillip Tyrer desu.*'

She frowned. 'F . . . urri . . . f.' She tried to say Phillip several times but could not, then laughed gaily, said something he did not understand, ending with Taira-san.

He was sitting up now, watching her, heart pounding, helpless, not attracted by her, and now she was pointing to the other side of the bed. '*Dozo?*' Please, may I?

'*Dozo.*' In the candlelight he could not see her clearly, just enough to think that she was young, he estimated about his own age, that her face was smooth and white with powder, teeth white, red lips, hair shiny, nose almost Roman, eyes narrow ellipses, her smile kind. She got into the bed and settled herself, turned and watched him. Waiting. His shyness and inexperience paralyzed him.

Christ, how do I tell her I don't want her, don't want anyone now, that I can't, I know I can't and it won't . . . it won't tonight, it won't and

I'll disgrace myself and André . . . André! What can I tell him? I'll be a laughingstock. Oh, Christ, why did I agree?

Her hand reached out and touched his cheek. Involuntarily he shivered.

Ako murmured sweet sounding words of encouragement but inside she was smiling, knowing what to expect from this child of a man, well prepared by Raiko-san: 'Ako, tonight is a rare moment in your life and you must remember every detail to regale us with at first meal. Your client is a friend of Frenchy, and unique in our world—he's virgin. Frenchy says he is so shy you will not believe it, that he will be frightened, will probably weep when his Honorable Weapon fails him, he may even wet the bed in his frustrated excitement, but do not worry, dear Ako, Frenchy assures me you can deal with him in the normal way, and that you've nothing to worry about.'

'Eeee, I'll never understand gai-jin, Raiko-san.'

'Nor I. Certainly they are all peculiar, uncivilized, but fortunately most are pleasantly rich, it's our destiny to be here so we must make the most of it. Very important, Frenchy says this one is an important English official, potentially a long-term customer so make him experience the Clouds and the Rain, one way or another, even if . . . even if you have to use the Ultimate.'

'Oh ko!'

'The honor of the House is at stake.'

'Oh! I understand. In that case . . . Somehow I will.'

'I have every confidence, Ako-chan, after all you have almost thirty years' experience in our Willow World.'

'Is he like Frenchy in his tastes, do you think?'

'That he enjoys his back part tickled, and occasionally Pleasure Pearls? Perhaps you should be prepared but I asked Frenchy directly if the youth had leanings towards liking men and he assured me no. Curious that Frenchy chose our House to initiate a friend, instead of the others he now frequents.'

'The House was not to blame, never. Please, don't think about it, Raiko-chan. I am honored that you have chosen me, I will do everything necessary.'

'Of course. Eeee, when you think that the Steaming Stalks of gai-jin are usually much larger than civilized persons, that most gai-jin fornicate satisfactorily though without Japanese vigor, flair and urge to plumb the limits, except for Frenchy, you would think they would be happy fornicators like normal persons. But they are not, they have so many cobwebs in their heads that somehow fornication is not our

Most Heavenly Pleasure, but some kind of secret, religious evil. Weird.'

Experimenting now, Ako moved closer and caressed his chest, then shifted her hand lower and was hard put not to laugh out loud as the youth jerked with fright. It took her a few moments to compose herself. 'Taira-san?' she murmured.

'Yes, er, *hai,* Ako-san?'

She took his hand and placed it inside her yukata on her breast, leaned over and kissed his shoulder, forewarned to be careful of the wound in his arm that a courageous shishi had given him. No reaction. Moving against him closer. Whispering how utterly brave, how strong and manly, how fulsome the maid had described him and his fruit. All the while patiently caressing his chest, feeling him shiver but still no passion. Minutes passed. Still nothing. Her concern grew. Fingers soft as butterflies and yet still he lay inert—hands, lips, everything. Gently caressing, careful to circle, no real intimacy yet. More minutes. Still nothing. Her dismay mounted. Fear that she might fail overlay her dismay. Touching his ear with her tongue.

Ah, a slight reward: her name spoken throatily and his lips kissing her neck. Eeee, she thought, and relaxed and put her lips around his nipple. Now it's only a matter of time to explode his virginity to the skies, then I can order some saké and sleep till dawn and forget that I am forty-three and childless, and only remember that Raiko-san rescued me from the sixth-class House that my age and lack of beauty had relegated me to.

Tyrer was idly watching the samurai in the Legation square, the sun touching the horizon, his mind increasingly beset by Ako, then two nights later, Hamako. Then Her.

Fujiko. The night before last.

He felt himself hardening and eased that part more comfortably, knowing that now he was inexorably caught in that world, the Floating World where, as André had told him, living was only for the moment, for pleasure, drifting with never a care like a blossom in the current of a calm river.

'It's not always calm, Phillip. What's she like, Fujiko?'

'Oh, er, haven't you seen her, don't you know her?'

'No, I only told Raiko-san the sort of girl you might like, the accent being on "sleeping dictionary." How was she?'

He had laughed to cover his complete embarrassment and disquiet at being asked such a personal question, so directly. But André had given him so much that he wanted to be 'French' and forthright, so he put aside his misgivings that a gentleman should not discuss or disclose such personal information. 'She . . . she's younger than I am, small, tiny in fact, not—not pretty in our terms, but she's astonishingly attractive. I think I understood her to say that she was new there.'

'I meant in bed, how was she? Better than the others?'

'Oh. Well, there was, er, well, no comparison.'

'Was she more vigorous? Sensuous? Eh?'

'Well, yes, er, dressed or undressed, incredible. Special. Again I can't thank you enough, I owe you so much.'

'De rien, mon vieux.'

'It's true. Next time . . . next time you'll meet her.'

'Mon Dieu, no, that's a rule. Never introduce your "special" to anyone, least of all a friend. Don't forget, until you set her up in your own place, with you paying the bills, she's available for anyone with the money—if she wants.'

'Oh. I'd forgotten,' he had said, hiding the truth.

'Even if she's set up she could still have a lover on the side if she wants. Who's to know?'

'I suppose so.' More anguish.

'Don't fall in love, my friend, not with a courtesan. Take them for what they are, pleasure persons. Enjoy them, like them but don't love them—and never let them fall in love with you. . . .'

Tyrer shivered, hating the truth, hating the idea of her being with another, and bedding as they had bedded, hating that it was for money, hating the ache that was in his loins. My God, she really was so special, lovely, liquid, a sweet chatterbox, gentle, kind, so young and only in the House for such a short time. Should I set her up? Not should, could I? I'm sure André has his own place with his special friend though he's never said, nor would I ever ask. Christ, how much would that cost? Bound to be more than I could afford. . . .

Don't think about that now! Or her.

With an effort he put his attention on the garden below but the ache remained. Part of the Highland detachment were assembling around the flagstaff, the trumpeter and four kettledrummers already in position for the lowering of the flag. Routine. The motley group of gardeners were collecting by the gate to be counted and then dismissed. They grovelled their way through the gates and through the samurai and were gone. Routine. Sentries closed and bolted the iron gates. Routine. Drums and trumpet sounding as the Union Jack was slowly lowered— no sun sets on the British flag was British law throughout the world.

Routine. Most of the samurai marching away now, leaving only a token force for the night. Routine.

Tyrer shivered.

If everything's routine why am I so nervous?

The Legation gardeners trooped into their dormitory hovel that adjoined the other side of the Buddhist temple. None of them met Hiraga's gaze. All had been warned that their lives, and the lives of all their generations, depended on his safety.

'Beware of talking to strangers,' he had told them. 'If the Bakufu find you've harbored me your reward will be just the same, except you will be crucified, not killed cleanly.'

With all their abject protestations that he was safe, that he could trust them, Hiraga knew that he was never secure. Since the Anjo ambush ten days ago, most of the time he had been at their Kanagawa safe house, the Inn of the Midnight Blossoms. That the attack had failed and all but one of his companions killed was karma, nothing else.

Yesterday a letter had arrived from Katsumata, the leading, though clandestine, Satsuma shishi, now in Kyōto: *Urgent: in a few weeks, Shōgun Nobusada will create an unheard-of precedent by coming here to pay the Emperor a state visit. All shishi are advised to gather here at once to plan how to intercept him, to send him onwards, then to take possession of the Palace Gates.* Katsumata had signed his code name: Raven.

Hiraga had discussed what to do with Ori, then decided to return here to Yedo, determined to act alone to destroy the British Legation, furious that the Council of Elders seemed to have been bamboozled and neutralized by the gai-jin. 'Kyōto can wait, Ori. We've got to press home our attack on the gai-jin. We must infuriate them until they bombard Yedo. Others can deal with the Shōgun and Kyōto.' He would have brought Ori but Ori was helpless, his wound worse, with no help from any doctor. 'What about your arm?'

'When it's unbearable, I'll commit seppuku,' Ori had said, his words slurred from the saké he was using to dampen the pain—the three of them, he, Ori and the mama-san, having a final drink together. 'Don't worry.'

'Isn't there another doctor, a safe one?'

'No, Hiraga-san,' the mama-san, Noriko, said. She was a tiny woman of fifty, her voice soft. 'I even sent for a Korean acupuncturist and herbalist, both friends, but the poultices have been no value. There's the giant gai-jin . . .'

'You're stupid,' Ori shouted. 'How many times must I tell you? This is a bullet wound, one of their bullets, and they saw me at Kanagawa!'

'Please excuse me,' the mama-san said humbly, her head to the tatami, 'please excuse this stupid person.' She bowed again and left, but in her secret heart she was cursing Ori for failing to be a true shishi and not committing seppuku while Hiraga was here, the most perfect second a man could wish for, and so lessen the awful danger surrounding her and her House. News of the fate of the Inn of the Forty-seven Ronin had rushed fifty *ri* and beyond—an outrageous retribution to kill all patrons, courtesans and servants and to spike the head of the mama-san.

Monstrous, she thought, inflamed. How can a House forbid any samurai entrance, shishi or not? In olden days samurai killed much more than today, yes, but that was centuries ago and mostly only when it was merited and not women or children. That was when the law of the land was just, Shōgun Toranaga just, his son and grandson just, before corruption and dissipation became a way of life for descendant Shōguns, daimyo and samurai alike, who for a century and more have spread their rapacious taxations over us like pus! The shishi are our only hope! *Sonno-joi!*

'Anjo must die before we die,' she said fervently when Hiraga had at length returned safely two days after the attack. 'We've been petrified you'd been caught and burnt with the others. It was all done on Anjo's orders, Hiraga-san, on his orders—in fact he was returning from the Inn when you attacked him near the castle gates, he had personally ordered and witnessed the executions, leaving men there in ambush in case all you shishi returned unawares.'

'Who betrayed us, Hiraga?' Ori had asked.

'The Mori samurai.'

'But Akimoto said he saw them engulfed and killed.'

'It must have been one of them. Did anyone else escape?'

'Akimoto—he hid out in another Inn for a day and a night.'

'Where is he now?'

Noriko said, 'He's occupied—shall I send for him?'

'No. Tomorrow I will see him.'

'Anjo must pay in blood for the Inn—that's against all custom!'

'He will. So will the roju. So will Shōgun Nobusada. And so will Yoshi.'

In his private quarters high up in the castle keep, Yoshi was composing a poem. He wore a blue silk kimono and sat at a low table, an oil lamp on it and sheets of rice paper, brushes of different thicknesses, water to soften the block of jet ink that now had a tiny, inviting pool in the hollowed-out center.

Twilight was becoming night. From outside the hum of Yedo's million souls was ever present. A few houses on fire as usual. From the castle below the comforting, muted noise of soldiers, hooves on cobblestones, an occasional throaty laugh wafting upwards with the smoke and smells of the cooking fires through the decorative, bowman openings in the vast walls, not yet shuttered against the night chill.

This was his inner sanctum. Spartan. Tatamis, a tokonoma, the shoji door in front of him so positioned and lit that he could see the shape of any figure outside but no one there could look within.

Outside this room was a larger anteroom with corridors leading off it to sleeping quarters, empty at present except for retainers, maids and Koiko, his special favorite. His family—his wife, two sons and a daughter, his consort and her son—were all safe and heavily guarded in his hereditary, fortress castle, Dragon's Tooth, in the mountains some twenty *ri* northwards. Beyond this antechamber were guards and other rooms with other guards, all sworn to his personal service.

His brush dipped into the ink pool. He poised the point over the delicate rice paper then wrote firmly:

> *Sword of my fathers*
> *When in my hands*
> *Twists uneasily*

The writing was in three short, flowing vertical lines of characters, strong where they should be strong and soft where softness would enhance the picture that the characters made—never a second chance to refine or change or correct even the slightest fault, the texture of the rice paper sucking in the ink at once to become indelibly a part of it, varying the black to grey depending how the brush was used and the amount of water therein.

Coldly, he scrutinized what he had done, the placement of the poem and the whole picture that the shades of black calligraphy made within the expanse of white, the shape and the fluid, obscured clearness of his characters.

It's good, he thought without vanity. I cannot do better yet—this is almost to the limit of my capability, if not at the limit. What about the meaning of the poem, how it should be read? Ah, that's the important question, that's why it is good. But will it achieve what I want?

These questions prompted him to review the shocking state of affairs here and at Kyōto. Word arrived a few days ago that there had been a sudden, bloody but successful coup there by Choshu troops who had thrown out Satsuma and Tosa forces who had, for the last six months, held power there in an uneasy truce. Lord Ogama of Choshu now commanded the Palace Gates.

At the hastily convened meeting of the Council tempers had flared, Anjo almost frothing with fury. 'Choshu, Satsuma and Tosa! Always those three. They're dogs who must be crushed! Without them everything would be in control.'

'True,' Yoshi had said, 'I tell you all again we must order our troops in Kyōto to put down the rebellion at once—whatever the cost!'

'No, we have to wait, we have insufficient forces there.'

Toyama, the old man, wiped his grizzled chin and said, 'I agree with Yoshi-dono. War is the only way, we must declare Ogama of Choshu outlaw!'

'Impossible!' Adachi had said querulously, for himself and the last Elder. 'We agree with Anjo, we cannot risk offending all daimyos, encouraging them to mass against us.'

'We must act at once!' he had repeated. 'We must order our troops to retake the Gates, put down the rebellion.'

'We have insufficient forces,' Anjo had said stubbornly. 'We will wait. Now is not the time.'

'Why won't you listen to my advice?' By now Yoshi was so angered that it almost surfaced. He had contained it with an effort, knowing that to rave and lose his temper would be a fatal error and turn them all permanently against him. Wasn't he the youngest, the least experienced but the most qualified, with the most influence amongst daimyos, who could, if he wished, alone amongst the Elders, raise his standard and pitch the whole country into civil war as had existed for centuries before the Shōgun Toranaga? Were they not all jealous and spitting when he was appointed Guardian and an Elder by Imperial 'request' without consulting them, by whomever the Son of Heaven was manipulated? 'I know I'm right. Wasn't I right about the gai-jin? I'm right about this.'

The plan he had conceived to remove the gai-jin and their fleet from Yedo to gain time to deal with their own internal problems had been a perfect success. It was so simple: 'With great ceremony and feigned humility we give the gai-jin a pittance of a ransom, propose a future meeting with the Council which will be delayed and further delayed or cancelled, or even staged with puppets if need be, implying at the last

moment, when their patience is at an end, that a meeting with the
Shōgun when he returns is to be arranged—which can also be delayed,
renegotiated and delayed and will never happen, or even if it does
sometime in the future, it will produce nothing we do not wish.

'We gained some of the time we needed, and discovered a permanent way of dealing with them: use their impatience against them, give
them "promises" and lots of soup but no fish, or at the most a few
rotting pieces we don't need or want. They were satisfied, their fleet
sailed away into the storm and perhaps under the sea. None have
returned yet.'

Old Toyama said, 'The gods aided us with that storm, again their
Divine Wind, *kamikaze* wind, as they did against Kublai Khan's invad-
ing hordes centuries ago. When we expel them it will be the same, the
gods will never forsake us.'

Adachi had been preening himself. 'It's true I carried out our plan to
perfection. The gai-jin were as docile as a fifth-rate courtesan.'

'Gai-jin are a sore that will never heal while we are weaker in
military power or wealth,' Anjo said irritably, wringing his hands.
'They are a sore that will not heal—not without burning it out, and we
cannot do that yet, not yet, not without means to build ships and make
cannon. We cannot be diverted and order troops to take the Gates, not
yet. They are not the immediate enemy, nor Choshus, the immediate
enemy is *sonno-joi* and shishi dogs.'

Yoshi had noticed how very much Anjo had changed since the
assassination attempt: now he was far more irascible, stubborn, his
resolve weakened though his influence over the other Elders had not. 'I
don't agree but if you think we have insufficient forces let us order a
general mobilization and let us finish the outside lords and any who
join them!'

Toyama said, 'War is the only way, Anjo-sama, forget shishi, forget
gai-jin for the moment. The Gates—first we must repossess our hereditary rights.'

Anjo had said, 'We will, at the right time. Next: the Shōgun's visit
will go forth as planned.'

Over his further protests Anjo had again carried the vote, three to
two, and in private had added malevolently, 'I told you, Yoshi-dono,
they will always vote with me, shishi will never succeed against me,
nor will you, nor will anyone.'

'Even Shōgun Nobusada?'

'He . . . he is not an enemy and he takes my advice.'

'And the Princess Yazu?'

'She will obey . . . she will obey her husband.'

'She will obey her brother, the Emperor, until she dies.'

To his shock Anjo had said with a twisted smile, 'You propose an accident? Eh?'

'I propose nothing of the sort.'

Yoshi felt chilled, afraid the man was becoming too dangerous to leave alive, already too powerful to neutralize, too farsighted, supported by a swarm of cohorts ready and able to swallow him up. . . .

A silhouette was approaching the door, almost noiselessly. Without thinking his right hand went to his long sword that lay beside him even though he was sure he recognized her. The figure knelt. Delicate knock.

"Yes?"

She slid the door back smiling, bowed and waited.

"Please come in, Koiko," he said, delighted with this unexpected visit, all his demons vanishing.

She obeyed, closed the door and ran over to him, her long, multipatterned kimono sibilant, knelt again and pressed her cheek to his hand, at once noticing the picture poem. "Good evening, Sire."

He laughed, and gave her a tender hug. "To what do I owe this pleasure?"

"I missed you," she said simply. "May I see your poem?"

"Of course."

As she studied his work, he studied her, a constant pleasure for him in the thirty-four days she had been here within the castle walls. Extraordinary clothes. Pure eggshell skin, shining raven hair that, when loosed, would reach to her waist, delicate nose, her teeth left white as were his and not blackened in Court fashion.

'Stupid!' his father had said to him as soon as he could understand. 'Why should we blacken our teeth just because it's a Court custom started by an Emperor centuries ago whose teeth were old and rotting, who therefore decreed that dyed teeth were superior to having teeth like animals! And why use paints for our lips and cheeks as some still do because another wanted to be a woman and not a man, pretended to be one, and courtiers imitated him-her to curry favor.'

Koiko was twenty-two years old, *Tayu*, the highest possible grade of geisha in the Willow World.

Hearing whispers about her and curious, some months ago he had sent for her, enjoyed her company and then, two months ago, had ordered her mama-san to submit a proposal for her services. Correctly the proposal had gone to his wife to deal with. His wife had written from Dragon's Tooth, their castle home:

Beloved Husband, I have today concluded satisfactory arrangements with the mama-san for the Tayu Koiko of the House of Wisteria. Sire, we considered it is better to have her exclusivity than a first option on her services, and also safer as you are surrounded by enemies. At your whim the contract is renewable monthly, payment monthly in arrears to ensure that her services are maintained to the very high standard you should expect.

Your Consort and I are pleased that you have decided to have a toy, we were and are continually most concerned for your health and safety. May I compliment you on your choice, it is rumored that Koiko is rare indeed.

Your sons are well and happy, and your daughter and myself. We send our everlasting loyalty and long for your presence. Please keep me closely advised as I must direct our Paymaster to set aside funds . . .

Correctly his wife had not mentioned the amount, nor would it concern him, for that was a prime wifely function: to manage and guard the family wealth and pay all bills.

Koiko looked up. "Your poem is flawless, Yoshi-chan," she said, and clapped her hands, the 'chan' an intimate diminutive.

"You're flawless," he said, hiding his pleasure at her judgment. Apart from her unique physical attributes, she was renowned in Yedo for the quality of her calligraphy, the beauty of her poems, and her shrewdness in art and politics.

"I adore the way you write, and the poem, it is superb. I adore the complexity of your mind, particularly why you chose 'when' and not perhaps 'now,' and 'twists' when a lesser man could use 'moves' or the more blatant 'stirs,' which would give it sexual overtones. But the placement of your final word, the final 'uneasily'—ah, Yoshi-chan, how clever to use that word last, an underneath word, perfect. Your creation is superb and can be read a dozen ways."

"And what do you think I'm saying?"

Her eyes lit. "First tell me if you intend to keep it—to keep it openly, secretly or to destroy it."

"What is my intention?" he asked, enjoying her.

"If you keep it openly, or pretend to hide it, or pretend it's secret, you plan it to be read by others who, one way or another, will inform your enemies, as you want."

"And what will they think?"

"All but the cleverest will presume that your resolve is weakening, your fears are beginning to overrun you."

"And the others?"

Koiko's eyes lost none of their amusement but he saw them pick up an added glint. "Of your chief adversaries," she said delicately, "Shōgun Nobusada would interpret it that in your inner mind you agree with him that you are not strong enough to be a real threat, and he'll happily postulate it will become easier and easier to eliminate you the longer he waits. Anjo would be consumed with envy at your prowess as a poet and calligrapher and would sneer at the 'uneasily,' believing it to be unworthy and ill chosen, but the poem would obsess him, worrying him, particularly if it was reported as a secret document, until he would have eighty-eight inner meanings all of which would increase his implacable opposition to you."

Her openness dazzled him. "And if I kept it, secretly?"

She laughed. "If you wanted to keep it secret, then you would have burnt it at once and never shown it to me. Sad to destroy such beauty, so sad, Yoshi-chan, but necessary to a man in your position."

"Why? It's just a poem."

"I believe this one is special. It is too good. Such art comes from deep wells within. It reveals. Revelation is the purpose of poetry."

"Go on."

Her eyes seemed to change color as she wondered how far she dared go, always testing intellectual limits—to entertain and excite her patron, if that was his interest. He noticed the change but did not discern the reason.

"For example," she said easily, "to the wrong eyes it could be construed that your innermost thought was really saying: 'The power of my ancestor namesake, Shōgun Toranaga Yoshi, is within my grasp, begs to be used.' "

He watched her and she could not read his eyes. Eeee, he was thinking, all his senses shrieking danger. Am I so apparent? Perhaps this lady is too perceptive to keep alive. "And the Princess Yazu? What would she think?"

"She's the cleverest of all, Yoshi-chan. But then you know that. She would realize the meaning instantly—if you have a special meaning." Again her eyes could not be read.

"And if as a present to you?"

"Then this unworthy person would be filled with joy to be given such a treasure——but in a quandary, Yoshi-chan."

"Quandary?"

"It is too special, to give or to receive."

Yoshi took his eyes off her and looked at his work very carefully. It was everything he desired, he could never duplicate it. Then he considered her, with equal finality. He watched his fingers pick up the paper and hand it to her, closing the trap.

Reverently she received the paper with both hands and bowed low. Intently she scrutinized it, wanting the whole of it to be put indelibly in her memory as the ink on the paper. A deep sigh. Carefully she held the corner near the oil flame. "With your permission, Yoshi-sama, please?" she said formally, looking at him, eyes steady, hand steady.

"Why?" he asked, astonished.

"Too dangerous for you to leave such thoughts alive."

"And if I refuse?"

"Then, please excuse me, I must decide for you."

"Then decide."

At once she lowered the paper into the flame. It caught and flared up. Deftly she twisted it until only a tiny scrap was still burning, the ash still in one piece, carefully balanced it on another sheet until the flame died. Her fingers were long and delicate, fingernails perfection. In silence they folded the paper containing the ashes into an ogami and put it back on the table. The paper now resembled a carp.

When Koiko looked up again her eyes were filled with tears and his affection went out to her. "So sorry, please excuse me," she said, her voice breaking, "But too dangerous for you . . . so sad to have to destroy such beauty, I wanted so very much to keep it. So very sad but too dangerous . . ."

Tenderly, he took her in his arms, knowing that what she had done was the only solution, for him, and for her, awed by her insight in discerning his original intent: that he had planned to hide it, designed to be found and passed on to all those she named, particularly the Princess Yazu.

Koiko's right, I can see that now. Yazu would have seen through my ploy and read my real thoughts: that her influence over Nobusada must vanish, or I am a dead man. Isn't that just another way of saying 'Power of my ancestor . . .' But for Koiko I might have put my head on their spike!

"Don't cry, little one," he murmured, sure now that she could be trusted.

And while she allowed herself to be gentled and then warmed and then to warm him she was thinking within her third heart, her most secret heart—the first for all the world to see, the second only opened to innermost family, the third never never never revealed to anyone—in this secret place she was sighing silently with relief that she had passed another test, for test it surely was.

Too dangerous for him to keep such treason alive, but much more dangerous for me to have it in my possession. Oh yes, my beautiful patron, it is easy to adore you, to laugh and play games with you, to pretend ecstasy when you enter me—and godlike to remember that at the end of each day, every day I have earned one koku. Think of that, Koiko-chan! One koku a day, for every day, for being part of the most exciting game on earth, with the most exalted name on earth, with a young, handsome, astonishing man of great culture whose stalk is the best I have ever experienced . . . and yet at the same time to earn more wealth than any, ever before.

Her hands and lips and body were responding adroitly, closing, opening, opening further, receiving him, guiding him, helping him, an exquisitely fine-tuned instrument for him to play upon, allowing herself to brink, pretending ecstasy perfectly, pretending to plunge again and again but never plunging—too important to retain her energies and wits, for he was a man of many appetites—enjoying the contest, never hurrying but always pressing forward, now teetering him on the crevasse, letting him go and pulling him back, letting him go, pulling back, letting go in a seizure of relief.

Quiet now. His sleeping weight not unpleasant, stoically borne, careful not to move lest she disturb his peace. Well satisfied with her art, as she knew he had been with his. Her last, most secret, exhilarating thought before drifting into sleep was, I wonder how Katsumata, Hiraga and their shishi friends will interpret 'Sword of my fathers . . .'

14

KYŌTO

Monday, 29th September:

A FEW MILES SOUTH OF KYŌTO IN twilight, a vicious rearguard skirmish was in progress between fleeing Satsuma troops and Choshu forces of Lord Ogama who had recently seized control of the Palace Gates from them. The Satsuma sword master, Katsumata, the secret shishi, supported by a hundred mounted samurai, was leading the fight to protect the escape of Lord Sanjiro and their main Satsuma force a few miles southwards. They were heavily outnumbered. The country was open, wind blustering with a heavy stench of human manure from the fields and above an ominous buildup of storm clouds.

Again Katsumata led a furious charge that broke through the forward ranks towards the standard of the Choshu daimyo, Ogama, also mounted, but they were forced back bloodly, with heavy losses as reinforcements rushed to protect their leader.

"All troops advance!" Ogama shouted. He was twenty-eight, a heavyset angry man wearing light bamboo and metal armor and war helmet, his sword out and bloodied. "Bypass these dogs! Go around them! I want Sanjiro's head!"

At once aides rushed off to relay his orders.

Three or four miles away, Lord Sanjiro and the remnants of his force were hurrying for the coast and Osaka, twenty-odd miles away, to seek boats to carry them home to the South Island of Kyūshū, and the safety of their capital, Kagoshima, four hundred sea miles southwest.

In all there were about eight hundred fighters, well equipped and fanatic samurai desperate to rush back to join the fight, still smarting from their defeat and being forced out of Kyōto a week ago. Ogama had staged a sudden night attack, ringing their barracks and setting fire to the buildings, abrogating the solemn agreements between them.

With many losses the Satsumas had fought their way out of the city to the village of Fushimi where Sanjiro angrily regrouped, Choshu detachments dogging them. 'We are trapped.'

One of his captains said, 'Lord, I propose an immediate counterattack, towards Kyōto.'

Katsumata said emphatically, 'Too dangerous, too many troops against us, they will overwhelm us. Sire, you will alienate all daimyos and further frighten the Court. I propose you offer Ogama a truce—if he allows an orderly withdrawal.'

'On what grounds?'

'As part of the truce you accept that his forces will be custodians of the Gates—his forces, not the Tosa, and that will sow further dissension between them.'

'I cannot accept that,' Sanjiro had said, shaking with rage that Ogama had duped him. 'Even if I did he will not consent, why should he? We are in his grasp. He can piss all over us. If I were him I would fall on us here before midday.'

'Yes, Lord, he will—unless we forestall him. We can by this ruse, he's not a real fighter like you—his troops are not filled with zeal like ours, nor are they as well trained. He only succeeded against us because he fell on us by night in a filthy betrayal. Remember, his alliance with the Tosa is precarious. He must consolidate his hold of the Gates and has insufficient troops to meet every problem for the next few weeks. He has to organize and get reinforcements without provoking opposition. And soon the Bakufu must come back in force to take back the Gates as is their right.'

By Toranaga Edict, all daimyos visiting Kyōto were limited to five hundred guards, all of whom had to live under severe restrictions in their own fief barracks, built by decree without defenses. The same Edict allowed Shōgunate forces to number more than all the others together. Over the centuries of peace the Bakufu had allowed these laws to languish. In recent years, Tosa, Choshu and Satsumas daimyos—depending on personal strength—had twisted the bureaucracy to increase their numbers until forced to send the added warriors home.

'Ogama is not a fool, he will never let me escape,' Sanjiro said. 'I would spike him if I had him trapped.'

'He is not a fool, but he can be manipulated.' Then Katsumata dropped his voice. 'Added to the Gates, you could agree that, if or when there is a Convention of Daimyos, you would support his claims to head the Council of Elders.'

Sanjiro exploded, 'Never! He has to know I would never agree to that. Why should he believe such nonsense?'

'Because he is Ogama. Because he has fortified his Shimonoseki Straits with dozens of cannon from his not-so-secret, Dutch-built weapons factory and believes therefore, rightly, he can stop gai-jin ships from using it at his whim, yet still be safe against them. That he alone, he thinks, can put into practice the Emperor's wish to expel the gai-jin, that he alone can restore the trappings of power to the Emperor—why shouldn't he claim the big prize, *tairō*—Dictator?'

'The Land will be torn apart before that.'

'The last reason he would welcome a possible truce is because, Sire, never before has he possessed the Gates—isn't he an upstart, a usurper, isn't his line ordinary,' Katsumata said with a sneer, 'not ancient or exalted like yours. A further reason: he will accept the truce you offer because you will offer it to be permanent.'

In the rumble of astonished, angry opposition, Sanjiro had stared at his counselor, astounded at the vast range of concessions Katsumata proposed. Not understanding, but knowing Katsumata too well, he dismissed the others.

'What is behind all this?' he asked impatiently. 'Ogama must know any truce is only good until I am safe behind my mountains where I will mobilize all Satsuma and then march on Kyōto to repossess my rights, avenge the insult and take his head. Why such nonsense from you?'

'Because you are in mortal danger like never before, Sire. You are trapped. There are spies amongst us. I need time to organize boats in Osaka, and I have a battle plan.'

At length Sanjiro had said, 'Very well. Negotiate.'

The negotiations had so far lasted six days.

During this time Sanjiro placidly stayed at Fushimi, but with spies on all roads to and from Kyōto. As a measure of mutual trust, Sanjiro had agreed to move into a less defensible position, and Ogama had withdrawn all but a token force athwart the escape route. Then both waited for the other to make a mistake.

With supreme power in Kyōto, however tenuous, Ogama, supported by more than a thousand samurai, seemed to be content to tighten his grasp on the Gates, cultivating daimyos and, more particularly, courtiers who were sympathetic. These Ogama persuaded to approach the Emperor, asking Him to 'request' the immediate resignation of Anjo and the Council of Elders, to convene a Convention of Daimyos who would be given the power to appoint a new Council of Elders—with himself as *tairō*—who would rule until Shōgun Nobusada became of age, and at one stroke replacing all Toranaga adherents in the Bakufu.

To Ogama's delight he was told the news of his cannon's firing on gai-jin ships had greatly pleased the Emperor, and that, together with Sanjiro's proffered truce and extraordinary concessions, had further bolstered his influence at Court. 'The truce is accepted,' he had imperiously told Katsumata yesterday. 'We will ratify the agreement, seven days from now, here in my headquarters. Then you can retire to Kagoshima.'

But this morning had come the astonishing word of Shōgun Nobusada's proposed visit. At once Sanjiro sent for Katsumata. 'What could possess Anjo and Yoshi to agree? Are they mad? Whatever happens they lose.'

'I agree, Sire, but this makes your position even more dangerous. With Ogama holding the Gates, therefore access to the Emperor, any enemy of Ogama's is an enemy of the Emperor.'

'Obvious! What can I do? What do you suggest?'

'Immediately send Ogama a letter suggesting a meeting in three days to discuss the ramifications of the visit—he must be as astonished as any daimyo. Meanwhile, tonight after dark we implement the battle plan.'

'We can't escape without Ogama knowing, there are spies all around us, and his troops within easy distance. The moment he hears we're breaking camp he will fall on us.'

'Yes, but we leave the camp exactly as it is, taking only our weapons—I can outmaneuver him, I know him.'

Angrily Sanjiro had said, 'If that is so why didn't you sniff out the surprise attack, eh?'

Oh, but I did, Katsumata could have said, but it suited me better that Ogama temporarily holds the Gates. Didn't we escape his trap without much trouble? Ogama will never be able to deal with the Court, hostile daimyos, the Tosa, Shōgun Nobusada's visit or the Princess Yazu—not that Nobusada will arrive. Ogama will be held responsible for his death also.

'So sorry, Sire,' he had said, pretending an apology, 'I am finding out why your spies failed you. Heads will roll.'

'Good.'

Soon after dark Katsumata sent specially trained men who quietly decimated the unsuspecting Choshu troop spying on them. Then, following Katsumata's battle plan, except for him and his hundred cavalry, Sanjiro and the regiment hurried south with orders to leave a hundred men every three *ri* to join up with him as he fell back, following them. Confidently Katsumata settled into ambush across the Kyōto road. He was sure that he could survive until dawn, enticing the Choshu into a running fight, when they would probably break off the fight and return to Kyōto to reinforce their position there, leaving only a token force in pursuit. Rumors were rife that Ogama's alliances were already falling apart, the rift widened by lies spread by Katsumata's covert allies.

He had been astonished to find Ogama leading the chase and that they had caught up with them so quickly. Karma.

"Attack!" Katsumata shouted, and again he whirled his horse from feigned flight. At once his seemingly scattered cavalry joined into violent phalanxes and burst through their opponents who were sent reeling back in disorder, the cold, wet air heavy with the smell of sweat and fear and blood burning his nostrils. Men died to the left and right, his and theirs, but he fought his way through and now the path was almost clear to Ogama but once more he was foiled so he broke off and fled—really retreated this time—those alive following him. Of the hundred only twenty remained.

"Bring up our reserve! Five hundred koku for Katsumata's head," Ogama shouted, "a thousand for Lord Sanjiro!"

"Sire!" One of his most experienced captains was pointing upwards. Unnoticed in the excitement, the storm clouds had taken most of the sky and threads reached out for the moon. "So sorry, but the road back to Kyōto is difficult and we don't know if those cunning dogs have another ambush waiting."

Ogama thought a moment. "Cancel the reserve! Take fifty horsemen and harry them to death. If you bring me either head, I will make you a general, with ten thousand koku. Break off the battle!"

Instantly his captains hurried away, shouting orders. Ogama sourly peered into the gathering dark where Katsumata and his men had vanished. "By my ancestors," he muttered, "when I'm *tairō*, Satsuma will be a Choshu protectorate, the Treaties will be cancelled and no gai-jin ship will ever pass my Straits!" Then he turned his horse and, with his personal guards, spurred gladly for Kyōto. And destiny.

That same evening in the French Legation at Yokohama the party and recital Seratard had arranged in Angelique's honor was a great success. The chef had surpassed himself: fresh bread, platters of stewed oysters, cold lobster, shrimps and prawns, baked local fish spiced with ginger and garlic served with leeks from his own garden, and tarte aux pommes, the dried apples from France only used on special occasions. Champagne, La Doucette, and a Margaux from his home village of which he was very proud.

After dinner and cigars, great applause had heralded André Poncin, an accomplished though reluctant pianist, more applause after each piece, and now, almost midnight and after three encores, there was a standing ovation as the last lovely chord of a Beethoven sonata died away.

"Marvelous . . ."

"Superb . . ."

"Oh, André," Angelique said breathlessly in French from her place of honor near the piano, her mind cleansed of the lurking misery by his music. "It was beautiful, thank you so very much." Her fan fluttered charmingly, eyes and face perfection, new crinoline over hooped petticoats, low-cut, shoulders bare, the fine green silk cascading in gathered tiers accentuating her wisp of waist.

"*Merci*, Mademoiselle," Poncin replied. He got up and raised his glass, his eyes barely veiled. "*À toi!*"

"*Merci*, Monsieur," she said, then once more turned back to Seratard, surrounded by Norbert Greyforth, Jamie McFay, Dmitri and other traders, everyone in evening dress with ruffled silk shirts, vivid waistcoats and cravats—some new but most old, crumpled and hastily pressed because she was to be there. Some French army and naval officers, uniforms heavy with braid, dress swords added to the unaccustomed splendor, British military equally like peacocks.

Two of the other three women in the Settlement were in the crowded, oil- and candle-lit room, Mabel Swann and Victoria Lunkchurch. Both stout, in their early twenties and childless, wives of traders, both cross-eyed with jealousy, their husbands tethered sweatily beside them. " 'Tis time, Mr. Swann," Mabel Swann said with a sour sniff. "Yus. Prayers n'bed with a nice English cup of tea."

"If you're tired, my dear, you an Vic—"

"Now!"

"Thee, too, Barnaby," Victoria Lunkchurch said, her Yorkshire accent as heavy as her hips, "and put dirty thoughts out of thy head, lad, afore I belt thee proper!"

"Who me? Wot thorts?"

"Those thorts, thee'n that foreign baggage there, may God forgive thee," she said with even more venom. "Out!"

No one missed them or knew they had left. All were concentrating on the guest of honor, trying to get nearer, or if they were within the circle, to stop being elbowed out.

"A splendid evening, Henri," Angelique was saying.

"It's only because of you. By gracing us you make everything better." Seratard mouthed gallant platitudes while he was thinking, what a pity you're not already married and therefore ripe for a liaison with a man of culture. Poor girl to have to endure an immature bovine Scot, however rich. I would like to be your first real lover—it will be a joy to teach you.

"You smile, Henri?" she said, suddenly aware that she had better be careful of this man.

"I was just thinking how perfect your future will be and that made me happy."

"Ah, how kind you are!"

"I think th—"

"Miss Angelique, if I may be so bold, we're having a race meet this Saturday," Norbert Greyforth broke in, furious that Seratard was monopolizing her, disgusted that the man had the rudeness to speak French, which he did not understand, detesting him and everything French, except Angelique. "We're—there's going to be a new race, in, er, in your honor. We've decided to call it the Angel Cup, eh, Jamie?"

"Yes," Jamie McFay said, both of them Stewards of the Jockey Club, equally under her spell. "We, well, we decided it will be the last race of the day and Struan's are providing prize money: twenty guineas for the cup. You'll present the prize, Miss Angelique?"

"Oh, yes, with pleasure, if Mr. Struan approves."

"Oh, yes, of course." McFay had already asked Struan's permission, but he and every man within hearing wondered about the implications of that remark, though all bets against an engagement were off. Even in private, Struan had given him no clue though McFay had felt duty bound to report the rumors.

'None of their rotten business, Jamie. None.'

He had agreed but his disquiet increased. The captain of an incoming merchantman, an old friend, had slipped him a letter from Malcolm's mother asking for a confidential report: *I wish to know everything that has happened since this Richaud woman arrived in Yokohama, Jamie. Everything—rumour, facts, gossip—and I need not stress that this is to be a serious secret between us.*

Bloody hell, Jamie thought, I'm committed by holy oath to serve the tai-pan whoever he is and now his mother wants . . . but then a mother has rights, doesn't she? Not necessarily, but Mrs. Struan has because she's Mrs. Struan and, well, you're used to doing what she wants. Haven't you done her bidding, her requests and suggestions, for years?

For the love of God, stop fooling yourself, Jamie, hasn't she truly been running Culum and Struan's for years, and neither you nor anyone has ever wanted to face the fact openly?

"That's right," he muttered, shocked by the thought he had been afraid to bring to the front of his mind. Suddenly uncomfortable, he hastily covered his lapse, but everyone was still concentrating on Angelique.

Except Norbert. "What's right, Jamie?" he asked under the buzz of conversation, his smile flat.

"Everything, Norbert. Great evening, eh?" To his great relief, Angelique diverted them both.

"Good night, good night, Henri, gentlemen," she said over general protests. "I'm sorry but I must see my patient before I sleep." She held out her hand. With practiced elegance, Seratard kissed it, Norbert, Jamie and the others awkwardly and before anyone else could volunteer, André Poncin said, "Perhaps I may escort you to your home?"

"Of course, why not? Your music transported me."

The night was cool and overcast but pleasant enough, her woolen shawl decoratively around her shoulders, the bottom ruffle of her wide, hooped skirt dragging carelessly in the dirt of the wooden sidewalk—so necessary during the summer rains that transformed all roads into bogs. Only one small part of her mind dragging with it.

"André, your music is wonderful—oh, how I wish I could play like you," she said, meaning it.

"It's only practice, just practice."

They strolled along towards the brightly lit Struan Building, speaking companionably in French, André very aware of the envious glances of the men streaming across the street to the Club—boisterous, packed, and inviting—warmed by her, not with lust or passion or desire, just with her company and happy chattering that hardly ever required an answer.

Last night at Seratard's "French" dinner in a private room in the

Yokohama Hotel, he had sat beside her and found her youth and seeming frivolity refreshing; her love and knowledge of Paris, the restaurants, theatres, the talk of her young friends, laughing about them and strolling or riding in the Bois, all the excitement of the Second Empire filling him with nostalgia, reminding him of his university days and how much he, too, missed home.

Too many years in Asia—China and here.

Curious this girl is so much like my own daughter. Marie's same age, birthdays the same month, July, same eyes, same coloring . . .

He corrected himself: *Perhaps* like Marie. How many years since I broke with Françoise and left the two of them in her family pension, near the Sorbonne, I boarded in? Seventeen. How many years since I last saw them? Ten. *Merde,* I should never have married, Françoise enceinte or not. I was the fool, not her, at least she remarried and runs the pension. But Marie?

The sound of the waves took his vision to the sea. A stray gull cawed overhead. Not far offshore were the riding lights of their anchored flagship and that broke the spell, reminding him and concentrating his mind.

Ironic, this slip of a girl now becomes an important pawn in the Great Game, France versus Britain. Ironic but life. Do I leave it until tomorrow, or the next day, or deal the cards as we agreed, Henri and I?

"Ah," she was saying, her fan fluttering, "I feel so happy tonight, André, your music has given me so much, has taken me to the Opéra, has lifted me until I can smell the perfume of Paris. . . ."

In spite of himself he was beguiled. Is it her, or because she reminds me of what Marie might have been? I don't know, but never mind, Angelique, tonight I'll leave you in your happy balloon. Tomorrow is soon enough.

Then his nostrils caught a suggestion of her perfume, Vie de Camille, reminding him of the phial he had acquired from Paris with such difficulty for his *musume,* Hana—the Flower—and sudden rage swept away his impulse to kindness.

There was no one within hearing distance, most of the High Street empty. Even so, he kept his voice down. "Sorry to tell you, but I've some private news you should have. There's no way to break it easily but your father visited Macao some weeks ago and gambled heavily, and lost." He saw the swift pallor. His heart went out to her but he continued as he and Seratard had planned. "Sorry."

"Heavily, André? What does that mean?" The words were barely audible and he saw her staring at him wide-eyed, rigid in the lee of a building.

"He has lost everything, his business, your funds."

She gasped. "Everything? My funds too? But he can't!"

"Sorry, he can, and has. He's within the law. You're his daughter, an unmarried woman—apart from being a minor—he's your father with jurisdiction over you and everything you possess, but of course you know that. Sorry. Do you have other money?" he asked, knowing she did not.

"Sorry?" She shivered and fought to make her mind work clearly, the suddenness of knowing that the second of her great terrors was now a reality and common knowledge tore asunder her carefully, self-generated cocoon. "How—how do you know all this?" she stammered, groping for air. "My—my funds are mine . . . he promised."

"He changed his mind. And Hong Kong's a village—there are no secrets in Hong Kong, Angelique, no secrets there, or here. Today a message arrived from Hong Kong, couriered from a business partner. He sent the details—he was in Macao at the time and witnessed the debacle." He kept his voice friendly and concerned as a good friend should be, but telling only half the truth. "He and I, we own some of your father's paper, loans from last year and still unpaid."

Another fear slashed into her. "Doesn't . . . my father doesn't pay his bills?"

"No, I'm afraid not."

In anguish she was thinking of her aunt's letter and knew for certain now that her uncle's loan had not been repaid either and he was in jail because . . . perhaps because of me, she wanted to shout, trying to keep her balance, wishing this was all a dream, oh God, oh God what am I going to do?

"I want you to know if I can help, please tell me."

Abruptly her voice became shrill. "Help me? You've destroyed my peace—if what you say is true. Help me? Why did you tell me this now, why why why when I was so happy?"

"Better you should know at once. Better I tell you, than an enemy."

Her face twisted. "Enemy, what enemy? Why should I have enemies? I've done nothing to anyone, nothing nothing noth—" The tears began flooding. In spite of himself, he held her for a moment, compassionately, then put both hands on her shoulders and shook her.

"Stop it," he said, letting his voice sharpen. "My God, stop it, don't you understand, I'm trying to help you!" Several men were approaching on the other side of the street but he saw that they were weaving and concerned only with themselves. No one else nearby, only men making for the Club well down the street behind them, he and she

protected by the building's shadow. Again he shook her and she
moaned, "You're hurting me!" but the tears ceased and she came back
to herself.

Partly to herself, he thought coldly, this same process repeated a
hundred times before with varying degrees of twisted truths and violence, with other innocents he needed to use for the betterment of
France, men so much easier to deal with than women. Men you just
kicked in the balls or threatened to cut them off, or stuck needles . . .
But women? Distasteful to treat women so.

"You're surrounded by enemies, Angelique. There're many who
don't want you to marry Struan, his mother will fight you every way
she—"

"I've never said we were going to be married, it . . . it's a rumor, a
rumor, that's all!"

"*Merde!* Of course it's true! He's asked you, hasn't he?" He shook
her again, his fingers rough. "Hasn't he?"

"You're hurting me, André. Yes, yes he's asked me."

He gave her a handkerchief, deliberately more gentle. "Here, dry
your eyes, there's not much time."

Meekly she obeyed, began to cry, stopped herself. "Why're-
yousoawfulllll?"

"I'm the only real friend you have here—I'm truly on your side,
ready to help, the only real friend you can trust—I'm the only friend
you have, I swear it, the only one who can help you." Normally he
would add fervently, I swear by God, but he judged her hooked,
reserving that for later. "Better you hear the truth secretly. Now you've
time to prepare. The news won't arrive for at least a week, that gives
you time to make your betrothal solemn and official."

"What?"

"Struan's a gentleman, isn't he?" With an effort he covered the
sneer. "An English, sorry, a Scottish, a British gentleman. Aren't they
proudly men of their word? Eh? Once the promise is public he can't
withdraw whether you're a pauper or not, whatever your father has
done, whatever his mother says."

I know, I know, she wanted to scream. But I'm a woman and I have
to wait, I've been waiting and now it's too late. Is it? Oh, Blessed
Mother, help me! "I don't . . . don't think Malcolm will blame me for
my father or—or listen to his mother."

"I'm afraid he has to, Angelique. Have you forgotten Malcolm
Struan is a minor too, however much he's tai-pan? His twenty-first
birthday's not till May next year. Until then she can put all sorts of

legal restraints on him, even annul a betrothal under English law." He was not completely sure of this but it sounded reasonable and was true under French law.

"She could put restraints on you too, perhaps take you to court," he added so sadly. "Struan's are powerful in Asia, it's almost their domain. She could have you hauled into court—you know what they say about judges, any judges, eh? She could have you dragged before a magistrate, accuse you of being a coquette, a deceiver, just after his money or worse. She could paint a nasty picture to the judge, you in the dock and defenseless, your father a gambling, bankrupt ne'er-do-well, your uncle in Debtors' Prison, you penniless, an adventuress."

Her face became haggard. "How do you know about Uncle Michel? Who are you?"

"There are no tricks, Angelique," he said easily. "How many French citizens are in Asia? Not many, none like you, and people like to gossip. Me, I'm André Poncin, China trader, Japan trader. You've nothing to fear from me. I want nothing but your friendship and trust and to help."

"How? I'm beyond help."

"No, you're not," he said softly, watching her carefully. "You love him, don't you? You would be the best wife a man can have, given the chance, wouldn't you?"

"Yes, yes of course . . ."

"Then press him, beguile him, persuade him any way you can to make your betrothal public. I can guide you perhaps." Now, at last, he saw that she was really hearing him, really understanding him. Gently he delivered the coup de grace. "A wise woman, and you are as wise as you are beautiful, would get married quickly. Very quickly."

Struan was reading, the oil lamp on the table beside his bed giving enough light, the door to her room ajar. His bed was comfortable and he was engrossed in the story, his silken nightshirt enhancing the color of his eyes, his face still pale and thin with none of its former strength. On the bedside table was a sleeping draft, his pipe and tobacco and matches and water laced with a little whisky: 'Good for you, Malcolm,' Babcott had said. 'It's the best nighttime medicine you could have, taken weak. Better than the tincture.'

'Without that I'm awake all night and feel dreadful.'

'It's seventeen days now since the accident, Malcolm. It's time to stop. Really to stop, not good to rely on medicine to sleep. Best we stop it for good.'

'I tried that before and it didn't work. I'll stop in a day or two. . . . '

Curtains were drawn against the night, the room cozy, the ticktock of the ornate Swiss timepiece peaceful. It was almost one o'clock, and the book, *The Murders in the Rue Morgue,* was one that Dmitri had loaned him this morning saying: 'Think you'll like it, Malc, it's what they call a detective story. Edgar Allan Poe's one of our best writers—sorry, was, he died in '49, the year of the Gold Rush. I've a collection of his books and poems if you like this one.'

'Thanks, you're very kind. Good of you to drop by so often. But why so glum today, Dmitri?'

'News from home is bad. My folks . . . it's all bad, Malc, all mixed up, cousins, brothers, uncles on both sides. Hell, you don't want to hear about that. Listen, I've lots of other books, a whole library in fact.'

'Go on about your family, please,' he had said, the pain of the day beginning. 'Really, I'd like to hear.'

'All right, sure. Well, when my granddaddy and his family came over from Russia, from the Crimea—did I tell you our family were Cossacks—they settled in a little place called Far Hills in New Jersey, farmed there till the War of 1812—my granddad was killed in it—great place for raising horses, too, and we prospered. The family stayed in New Jersey mostly, though two of his sons moved south, to Richmond, Virginia. When I was in the army, oh, fifteen-odd years ago—it was just the Union Army then, not North or South. I joined the cavalry and stayed for five years, spent most of my time in the South, South and West, the Indian Wars if you could call them that. Spent part of the time in Texas, a year while it was still a republic, helping them blow off their Indians, then a couple after she joined the Union in '45, we were stationed out of Austin. That's where I met my wife, Emilie—she also comes from Richmond—her pa was a colonel in Supplies. My, that's pretty country around Austin, but more so all around Richmond. Emilie . . . Can I get you anything?'

'No, no thanks, Dmitri, the pain will pass. Go on, will you . . . talking, your talking helps me a lot.'

'Sure, all right. My Emilie, Emilie Clemm was her name—she was a distant cousin of Poe's wife, Virginia Clemm, which I didn't find out till later but which's why I've a collection of his works.' Dmitri had laughed. 'Poe was a great writer but a bigger drunk and cocksman. Seems like all writers are bums, drunks and/or fornicators—take Melville—maybe that's what makes them writers, me I can't write a letter without sweating. How about you?'

'Oh, I can write letters—have to, and keep a journal like most people. You were saying about this Poe?'

'I was going to tell you he married Virginia Clemm when she was thirteen—she was also his cousin, imagine that!—and they lived happily ever after but not very if what was reported in the newspapers and gossip was true—he was a randy son of a bitch though she didn't seem to mind. My Emilie wasn't thirteen but eighteen and a Southern belle if ever there was one. We were married when I got out of the army and joined Cooper-Tillman in Richmond—they wanted to expand into armaments and ammunition for export to Asia, which I'd learned a lot about, that and shooting Indians and horse trading. Old Jeff Cooper figured that guns and other goods outward bound from Norfolk, Virginia, would go well with opium up the China coast, silver and tea inbound to Norfolk—but, you know Jeff. Cooper-Tillman and Struan's are old friends, eh?'

'Yes, and I hope it remains so. Go on.'

'Nothing much more, or everything. Over the years, others in the family moved down South and spread out. My ma was from Alabama, I have two brothers and a sister, all younger than me. Now Billy's with the North, New Jersey 1st Cavalry, and my little brother Janny—named after my granddaddy, Janov Syborodin, Janny's cavalry too, but with the 3rd Virginian, Advance Scouts. It's all crap—those two know crap about war and fighting and they'll get themselves killed, sure as hell.'

'You . . . are you going to go back?'

'Don't know, Malc. Every day I think yes, every night yes and every morning no, don't want to start killing family whatever side I'm on.'

'Why did you leave and come to this godforsaken part of the world?'

'Emilie died. She got scarlet fever—there was an epidemic and she was one of the unlucky ones. That was nine years ago—we were just about to have a kid.'

'What rotten luck!'

'Yes. You and me, we've both had our share. . . .'

Struan was so concentrated in his mystery book that he did not hear the outside door to her suite softly open and close, nor the lightness of her tiptoeing, nor notice her peer in for an instant, then disappear. In a moment there was an almost imperceptible click as her inner, bedroom door closed.

He looked up. Now listening intently. She had said that she would look in but if he was asleep she would not disturb him. Or if she was tired she would go straight to bed, quiet as a mouse, and see him in the morning. 'Don't worry, darling,' he had said happily. 'Just have a good time, I'll see you at breakfast. Sleep well and know I love you.'

'I love you too, chéri. Sleep well.'

The book was resting in his lap. With an effort he sat upright and swung his legs over the side of the bed. That part was just bearable. But not getting up. Getting up was still beyond him. His heart was pounding and he felt nauseated and lay back. Still, a little better than yesterday. Got to push, whatever Babcott says, he told himself grimly, rubbing his stomach. Tomorrow I'll try again, three times. Perhaps it's just as well. I'd want to stay with her. God help me, I would have to.

When he felt better he began to read once more, glad for the book, but now the story did not absorb him as before, his attention wandered, and his mind started to intermix the story with pictures of her about to be murdered, and corpses, him rushing to protect her, other glimpses becoming ever more erotic.

At length he put the book away, marking the place with a page she had given him, one from her journal. Wonder what she writes in it, knowing her to be as diligent as anyone. About me and her? Her and me?

Very tired now. His hand reached for the lamp to turn the wick down, then stopped. The little wineglass with sleep in it beckoned. His fingers trembled.

Babcott's right, I don't need it anymore.

Firmly he doused the light and lay back and closed his eyes, praying for her and his family and that his mother would bless them, and then for himself. Oh, God, help me get better—I'm afraid, very afraid.

But sleep would not take him. Turning or trying to gain comfort hurt him, reminding him of the Tokaidō and Canterbury. Half asleep half awake, his mind buzzing with the book, the macabre setting and how would it finish? Adding all kinds of pictures. And more pictures, some bad, some beautiful, some vivid, every little movement to get more comfortable bringing blossoms of pain.

Time passed, another hour or minutes, and then he drank the elixir and relaxed contentedly, knowing that soon he would be floating on gossamer, her hand on him, his hand on her, there on her breasts and everywhere, hers equally knowingly, equally welcomed, not only hands.

15

Friday, 3rd October:

JUST AFTER DAWN ANGELIQUE GOT out of bed and sat at her dressing table in the bay windows overlooking the High Street and harbor. She was very tired. In the locked drawer was her journal. It was dull red leather and also locked. She slid the little key from its hiding place, unlocked it, then dipped her pen in ink and wrote in it, more as a friend to a friend—her journal these days seemed her only friend, the only one she felt safe with:

'Friday, 3rd: another bad night and I feel ghastly. It's four days since André gave me the terrible news about Father. Since then I have been unable to write anything, to do anything, have locked my doors and "taken to my bed" feigning a fever, apart from once or twice a day going to visit my Malcolm to allay his anxiety, closing the door to everyone except my maid who I hate, though I agreed to see Jamie once, and André.

'Poor Malcolm, he was beside himself with worry the first day when I did not appear nor would open my door, and insisted that he be carried on a stretcher into my boudoir to see me—even if they had to break down the door. I managed to forestall him, forcing myself to go to him, saying that I was all right, it was just a bad headache, that, no, I did not need Babcott, that he was not to worry

about my tears, telling him privately that it was just "that
time of the month" and sometimes the flow was great
and sometimes my days irregular. He was embarrassed
beyond belief that I had mentioned my period! Beyond
belief! Almost as though he knew nothing about this
female function, at times I don't understand him at all
although he's so kind and considerate, the most I've ever
known. Another worry: in truth, the poor man is not
much better and daily in so much pain I want to cry.'

Blessed Mother, give me strength! she thought. Then there's the
other. I try not to worry but I'm frantic. The day approaches. Then I'll
be free from that terror, but not from penury.
   She began to write again.

'It's so difficult to be private in the Struan building,
however comfortable and pleasant, but the Settlement is
awful. Not a hairdresser, not a ladies' dressmaker (though
I have a Chinese tailor who is very adept at copying what
already exists), no hat maker—I haven't yet tried the
shoemaker, there's nowhere to go, nothing to do—oh,
how I long for Paris, but how can I ever live there now?
Would Malcolm move there if we married? Never. And if
we don't marry . . . how can I pay for even a ticket home?
How? I've asked myself a thousand times without an
answer.'

Her gaze left the paper and went to the window and to the ships in
the bay. I wish I were on one of them, going home, wish I'd never come
here. I hate this place . . . What if . . . If Malcolm doesn't marry me I'll
have to marry someone else but I've no dowry, nothing. Oh God, this
isn't what I'd hoped. If I managed to get home, I've still got no money,
poor Aunt and Uncle ruined. Colette hasn't got any to lend, I don't
know anyone rich or famous enough to marry, or far enough up in
society so I could safely become a mistress. I could go on the stage but
there it's essential to have a patron to bribe managers and playwrights,
and pay for all the clothes and jewels and carriages and a palatial house
for soirees—of course you have to bed the patron, at his whim not
yours, until you are rich and famous enough and that takes time, and I
don't have the connections, or have any friends who do. Oh dear, I'm
so confused. I think I am going to cry again. . . .

She buried her face in her arms, the tears spilling, careful not to make too much noise lest her maid hear her and start wailing, creating a scene as on the first day. Her nightdress was cream silk, a pale green dressing gown around her shoulders, hair tousled, the room masculine, the curtained four-poster huge, this suite much bigger than Malcolm's. To one side was the anteroom that adjoined his bedroom, a dining room off it that could seat twenty with its own kitchen. Both those doors were bolted. The dressing table was the only frivolity, she had had it curtained with pink satin.

When the tears stopped, she dried her eyes and silently studied her reflection in the silver mirror. No lines, some shadows, face a little thinner than before. No outward change. She sighed heavily, then began to write again:

'Crying simply doesn't help. Today I MUST talk to Malcolm. I simply must. André told me the mail ship is already one day overdue and the news of my catastrophe is bound to arrive with it—why is it English call a ship *she* or *her*? Her. I'm terrified Malcolm's mother will be aboard—news of his injury should have reached Hong Kong on the 24th, which gives her just enough time to catch this mail ship. Jamie doubts she would be able to leave at such short notice, not with her other children there, her husband dead just three weeks and still being in deepest mourning, poor woman.

'When Jamie was here, the first time I've ever really talked to him alone, he told me all sorts of stories about the other Struan's—Emma is sixteen, Rose thirteen and Duncan ten—most of them sad stories: last year two other brothers, the twins, Robb and Dunross, seven, were drowned in a boating accident just off a place in Hong Kong called Shek-O where the Struans have lands and a summer house. And years ago when Malcolm was seven, another sister, Mary, then four, died of Happy Valley fever. Poor little thing, I cried all night thinking of her and the twins. So young!

'I like Jamie but he's so dull, so uncivilized—I mean gauche, that's all—he has never been to Paris and only knows Scotland and Struan's and Hong Kong. I wonder if I could insist that if . . .' She crossed that out and changed it to '*when* we're married . . .' Her pen hesitated.

'Malcolm and I will spend a few weeks in Paris *every year*—and the children will be brought up there, of course as Catholic.

'André and I were talking about that yesterday, about being Catholic—he's very kind and takes my mind off problems as his music always does—and how Mrs. Struan was Calvinist Protestant, and what to say if that ever came up. We were talking softly—oh, I am so lucky he is my friend and forewarned me about Father— suddenly he put his fingers to his lips, went to the door and jerked it open. That old hag Ah Tok, Malcolm's amah, had her ear to it and almost fell into the room. André speaks some Cantonese and told her off.

'When I saw Malcolm later in the day he was abject in his apologies. It's unimportant, I said, the door was un- locked, my maid was correctly in the room, chaperoning me, but if Ah Tok wants to spy on me, please tell her to knock and come in. I confess I've been distant and cool to Malcolm and he goes out of his way to be extra pleasant and calm me, but this is how I feel, though also I must confess André advised me to behave so until our be- trothal is public.

'I had to ask André, had to, I'm afraid, ask him for a loan—I felt awful. It's the first time I've ever had to do it but I'm desperate for some cash. He was kind and agreed to bring me twenty louis tomorrow on my signature, enough for incidentals for a week or two—Malcolm just doesn't seem to notice that I need money and I didn't want to ask him. . . .

'I really do have an almost permanent headache, trying to plan a way out of the nightmare. There is no one I can really trust, even André, though so far he has proved his worth. With Malcolm, every time I start the speech I have rehearsed, I know the words will sound forced, flat and dreadful before I begin so I say nothing.

' "What is it, darling?" he keeps saying.

' "Nothing," I say, then after I've left him and re- locked my door, I cry and cry into my pillow. I think I shall go mad with grief—how could my father lie and cheat and steal my money? And why can't Malcolm give me a purse without my having to ask, or offer some so that I can pretend to refuse and then accept gladly? Isn't that a husband's or fiancé's duty? Isn't it a father's duty to protect his beloved daughter? And why is Malcolm waiting and waiting to make our betrothal public? Has he changed his mind? Oh God, don't let that happen. . . .'

Angelique stopped writing, tears beginning again. One dropped on to the page. Again she wiped her eyes, sipped some water from a tumbler, then continued:

'Today I will talk to him. I must do it today. One good piece of news is that the British flagship came back into the harbor safely a few days ago to general rejoicing (we are really quite defenseless without warships). The ship was battered and had lost a mast, to be closely followed by all other vessels, except a 20-gun steam frigate called *Zephyr,* with over two hundred aboard. Perhaps it's safe, I hope so. The newspaper here says that fifty-three other seamen and two officers died in the storm, the typhoon.

'It was terrible, the worst I have ever known. I was terrified, by day and by night. I thought the whole building would be blown away, but it is as solid as Jamie McFay. Much of the native quarter vanished, and there were many fires. The frigate *Pearl* was damaged, also losing a mast. Yesterday a note came from Captain Marlowe: I have just heard that you are sick and I send my deepest and most sincere condolences, etc.

'I don't think I like him, too haughty though his uniform makes him very glamorous and accentuates his manhood—which tight breeches are of course supposed to do, just as we dress to show our breasts and waists and ankles. Another letter arrived last evening from Settry Pallidar, the second, more condolences, etc.

'I think I hate both of them. Every time I think of them I'm reminded of that hell called Kanagawa and that they did not do their duty and protect me. Phillip Tyrer is still in the Yedo Legation but Jamie said he had heard Phillip was supposed to be coming back tomorrow or the day after. That's very good because when he does I have a plan th—'

The dull echoing roar of a cannon made her jump and pulled her attention to the harbor. It was the signal gun. Far out to sea another cannon answered. She looked beyond the fleet to the horizon and saw the telltale smoke from the funnel of the arriving mail ship.

Jamie McFay, a briefcase heavy with mail under his arm, guided a stranger up the main staircase of the Struan Building, sunlight flooding through tall and elegant windows of glass. Both wore woolen frock coats and top hats though the day was warm. The stranger carried a small case. He was squat, bearded, ugly and in his fifties, a head shorter than Jamie though wider in the shoulders, an unruly thatch of long grey hair sprouting from under his hat. They went down the corridor. McFay knocked gently. "Tai-pan?"

"Come in, Jamie, door's open." Struan gaped at the man, then said at once: "Is Mother aboard, Dr. Hoag?"

"No, Malcolm." Dr. Ronald Hoag saw the immediate relief and it saddened him though he could understand it. Tess Struan had been vehement in her condemnation of the 'foreign baggage' she was sure had her hooks into her son. Hiding his concern at Malcolm's loss of weight and pallor, he put his top hat beside his bag on the bureau. "She asked me to see you," he said, his voice deep and kindly, "to find out if I could do anything for you and to escort you home—if you need escorting." For almost fifteen years he had been the Struan family doctor in Hong Kong and had delivered the last four of Malcolm's brothers and sisters. "How are you?"

"I'm . . . Dr. Babcott has been looking after me. I'm . . . I'm all right. Thanks for coming, I'm pleased to see you."

"I'm pleased to be here too, George Babcott is a fine doctor, none better." Hoag smiled, his small topaz eyes set in a creased and leathery face, and continued breezily, "Filthy voyage, the tail of the typhoon caught us and we almost foundered once, spent my time patching up sailors and the few passengers—broken limbs mostly. Lost two overboard, one a Chinese, a steerage passenger, the other some sort of foreigner, we never did find out who he was. The Captain said the man just paid his fare in Hong Kong, mumbled a name. Spent most of the time in his cabin, then came on deck once and, poof, a wave caught him. Malcolm, you look better than I expected after all the rumors that flooded the Colony."

Jamie said, "I'd best leave you two together." He put a pile of letters on the bedside table. "Here's your personal mail, I'll bring your books and newspapers later."

"Thanks." Malcolm watched him. "Anything important?"

"Two from your mother. They're on top."

Dr. Hoag reached into his voluminous pockets and brought out a crumpled envelope. "Here's another from her, Malcolm, later than the others. Best read it, then I'll have a look at you, if I may. Jamie, don't forget about Babcott."

Jamie had already told him that Babcott was in Kanagawa for a clinic this morning and that he would send the cutter for him the moment they had seen Malcolm. "See you later, Tai-pan."

"No, best wait a moment, Jamie." Struan opened the letter Hoag had given him and began to read.

When Jamie had reached the main deck of the mail ship, Dr. Hoag had met him, told him that he had all Struan mail ready so they could leave at once, and in answer to his immediate question, and relief: 'No, Jamie, Mrs. Struan's not aboard, but here . . . here's a letter from her.'

It read simply: *Jamie, do whatever Dr. Hoag asks and send me detailed, confidential reports by every mail.*

'You know what it says, Doc?'

'Yes, hardly necessary but then you know the lady.'

'How is she?'

Hoag thought a moment. 'As usual: imperturbable outwardly, inwardly a volcano. One day it has to explode—no one can keep such sadness contained, so many tragedies, no one. Even her.' He had followed Jamie down the gangway, eyes everywhere. 'Must say I'm pleased to have the chance to visit Japan—you're looking very fit, Jamie. This posting certainly agrees with you. Let's see, it's almost a year, isn't it, since your last leave? Now tell me everything, first about the murderous attack . . . then about Miss Richaud.'

By the time they reached shore, Dr. Hoag knew all that Jamie knew: 'But, please,' he added uneasily, 'please don't mention to Malcolm what I've told you about Angelique. She's a wonderful person, she's had a terrible time too, I really don't think they've bedded, the secret betrothal is hearsay but he's smitten—not that I blame him, or anyone in Asia for that matter. I hate the idea of sending Mrs. Struan secret reports, for obvious reasons. Anyway, I've written one, a watered-down version, and it's ready to go when this ship turns around. My loyalties must be to Malcolm first and foremost, he's tai-pan.'

Now watching Malcolm Struan lying there, reading the letter Hoag had given him, seeing the wan face and listless body, he began to wonder. And to pray.

Struan looked up. His eyes narrowed. "Yes, Jamie?"

"You wanted me to do something?"

After a pause Malcolm said, "Yes. Leave a message at the French Legation—Angelique's there, she said she was going to wait for her mail—say an old friend has arrived from Hong Kong that I'd like her to meet."

McFay nodded and smiled. "Done. Send for me when you want anything." He left them.

Uneasily Struan watched the door. Jamie's face had been too open. Trying to regain his calm, he went back to the letter:

> *Malcolm, my poor dear son, Just a short note in haste as Ronald Hoag leaves at once for the mail ship I held up so he could catch it, and you can have the best care. I was aghast to hear about those swine and that they had attacked you. Jamie reports that this Dr. Babcott has had to operate—please write by any express mail you can and come home quickly so we can care for you properly. I send my love and prayers, as do Emma, Rose and Duncan. P.S. I love you.*

He looked up. "So?"

"So? Tell me the truth, Malcolm. How are you?"

"I feel dreadful and I'm afraid I'm going to die."

Hoag sat in the armchair and steepled his fingers. "The first is understandable, the second not necessarily accurate though very easy—very, very easy and very, very dangerous to believe. Chinese can 'makee die,' can think themselves into death even though healthy—I've seen it happen."

"Christ, I don't want to die, I have everything to live for. I want to live and get well so much I can't tell you. But every night and every day at some time the thought hits me . . . it hits like a physical blow."

"What medicine are you taking?"

"Just some stuff—laudanum's in it—to help me sleep. The pain's rotten and I'm so uncomfortable."

"Every night?"

"Yes." Struan added, half apologetically, "He wants me to stop taking it, says I've . . . I should stop."

"Have you tried?"

"Yes."

"But haven't stopped?"

"No, not yet. My—my will seems to forsake me."

"That's one of its problems—however valuable and beautiful it is."
He smiled. "Laudanum was the name first given by Paracelsus to this
panacea. Do you know Paracelsus?"

"No."

"Neither do I," Hoag said with a laugh. "Anyway, we passed the
name on to this tincture of opium. Pity that all derivatives are habit
forming. But then you know that."

"Yes."

"We can wean you off it, that's no problem."

"It's a problem, I know that too, and that you still don't approve of
our opium trade."

Hoag smiled. "I'm glad you made that a statement, not a question.
But then you don't approve of it either, no China trader does but you're
all trapped. Now, no economics, no politics, Malcolm. Next, Miss
Richaud?"

Struan felt the rush of blood in his face. "Now you bloody listen
once and for all time: whatever Mother says, I'm old enough to know
my own mind and can do what I want! Clear?"

Hoag smiled benignly. "I'm your doctor, Malcolm, not your mother.
I'm also your friend. Have I ever failed you, or any one of your
family?"

With a visible effort Struan shoved away his anger but could not still
his racing heart. "Sorry, sorry, but I . . ." He shrugged helplessly.
"Sorry."

"That's not necessary. I'm not trying to interfere in your private life.
Your health depends on many factors. It seems she's a major one.
Hence my question. I ask for medical reasons—not family reasons. So,
Miss Angelique Richaud?"

Struan wanted to sound manly and calm but could not contain his
frustration and burst out, "I want to marry her and it's driving me mad
lying here like a . . . lying here helpless. For Christ's sake, I can't even
get out of bed yet, can't pee or . . . can't do a God-cursed thing, can't
hardly drink or eat or anything without it hurting like hell. I'm going
mad and much as I try I don't seem to be getting better . . ." He
continued ranting until he weakened. Hoag just listened. Eventually
Struan stopped. He mumbled another apology.

"May I take a look at you?"

"Yes . . . yes, of course."

With great care Hoag examined him, put his ear to his chest to listen
to his heart, looked in his mouth, took his pulse, peered at the wound
and smelt it. His fingers probed the stomach walls, searching for the

organs beneath, the extent of the damage: "Does that hurt . . . This . . . Is it easier here?" Every little push caused Malcolm to groan. At length, Hoag stopped.

Struan broke the silence. "Well?"

"Babcott has done a very good job with what would have by this time killed a normal man." Hoag's words were measured and full of confidence. "Now we will try an experiment." Gently he took Struan's legs and helped him to sit on the side of the bed. Then, his arm around Malcolm's shoulders, taking most of the weight with his surprising strength, he helped him stand. "Careful!"

Struan could not stay upright by himself, but he had the impression of standing and this encouraged him. After a moment or two Hoag settled him in the bed again. Struan's heart was thumping from the pain but he was greatly satisfied. "Thanks."

The doctor sat back in the armchair and gathered his own strength. Then he said, "I'm going to leave you now, got to get myself organized. I would like you to rest. After I've seen Babcott I'll come back again. We'll probably come back together. Then we'll talk. All right?"

"Yes. And . . . Thanks, Ronald."

For an answer Hoag just patted him on the arm, picked up his belongings and left.

Once alone, the tears seeped down Struan's cheeks and these happy tears took him in sleep. When he awoke, he felt rested, for the first time refreshed, and he stayed without moving, glorying in the fact that he had stood up—with help, yes, but he had been on his feet and made a beginning, and that now, now he had a real ally.

From where he lay, slightly turned on his left side, he could see out of the window toward the sea. He loved the sea and hated it, never at ease on it, fearing it because it was uncontrollable and unpredictable like on the sunny day when the twins and the Bosun rowed offshore a hundred yards or so and a wave came and overturned the boat and a current took them down, all of them swimmers, the twins like fish, but all gone except the seaman. The shock devastated him and almost killed his father. His mother stayed in one of her walking comas, saying repeatedly: 'The will of God. We must go on.'

Won't think about my brothers, or Dirk Struan, he told himself, glad to be safe ashore. But our past is bound to the sea, inexorably, and our future. Isn't our ultimate strength in our clippers and steamers—and China?

Japan's a small market, interesting but small, never to be compared with China. We can make money here certainly—selective armaments and ships and British skills will make a bundle. I'm going to tell Jamie to conclude the Choshu order. Let them kill themselves and the quicker the better. Sir William's weak-kneed dillydallying, waiting for London's approval to war is stupid. If it were up to me I would order them to hand over the murderers, to pay up at once or tomorrow a state of war would exist between us, and the first act would be to stamp out Yedo. I will never, never forgive the bastards!

The horizon beckoned. Soon I must go back to Hong Kong to take charge. A week or so. No hurry. Plenty of time.

What's the time now?

There was no need to turn and look at the clock, the angle of the sun told him it was about noon and he thought that normally he would order lovely rare roast beef and Yorkshire pudding, with rich gravy and roast potatoes, a bowl or two of diced roast chicken with fried rice and mixed vegetables, and other Chinese dishes that Ah Tok would make and he enjoyed—however much his mother and brother and sisters decried as tasteless, without nourishment, probably poisonous and only fit for heathens. . . .

A slight sound. Angelique was curled up in the armchair, dwarfed by it, her face tearstained, and more unhappy than he had ever seen her.

"Christ, what's the matter?"

"I'm—I'm ruined." Her tears began again.

"For God's sake, what're you talking about?"

"This, it was in today's mail." She got up and handed him a letter, tried to speak, couldn't. The sudden movement he made to take it twisted him and he barely managed to stop crying out.

The paper was green, like the envelope, dated Hong Kong, 23rd Sept., the letterhead Guy Richaud, Richaud Frères, and in French, which Struan could read adequately:

Darling Angelique, In haste. The business deal I told you about did not turn out very well, my Portuguese Macao partners cheated me so I lost heavily. All my present capital has vanished and you may hear lies spread by enemies that I am unable to make new banking arrangements so the company is in the hands of Receivers. Don't believe them, the future is bright, never fear, everything is in hand. This letter goes by tomorrow's mail ship. Today I have passage on the American steamer, Liberty, for Bangkok, where I am promised new financing from French Sources. *I will write from there, in the meantime, I am your devoted Father.*

   P.S. By now you will be aware of the sad but expected news about Culum Struan. We have just heard about the vile Japper attack on Malcolm. I hope he's not badly hurt, please wish him well and give him my hopes for a quick recovery.

Struan's mind was in a turmoil. "Why are you ruined?"

"He's . . . he took all my money," she whimpered, "stole all my money and lost that as well, he's a thief and now—now I've nothing in the world. He stole all that I have, oh Malcolm, what am I going to do?"

"Angelique, Angelique, listen!" She seemed such a waif, so melodramatic, that he almost laughed. "For goodness' sake, listen, that's no problem. I can give you any money you wa—"

"I can't accept money from you," she cried out through her tears. "That's not right!"

"Why not? Soon we'll be married, won't we?"

The crying stopped. "We . . . we will?"

"Yes. We'll—we'll make the announcement today."

"But Father, he's . . ." She sniffed tearfully like a child. "André told me he was sure that there was no business deal in Macao or anywhere and never was. It seems Father was a gambler and must have gambled it all away. Father had promised, he had promised Henri, Henri Seratard, he would stop, and pay his bills. . . . Everyone knew but me, oh Malcolm, I never knew, I feel so terrible I could die, Father stole my money, he swore to keep my money safe!" Another burst of crying and she ran over to him and was on her knees beside the bed, her head buried into the counterpane. Tenderly he stroked her hair, feeling very strong and in command. The door opened and Ah Tok strode in.

"Get out," he bellowed. *"Dew neh loh moh!"* She fled.

Genuinely frightened, Angelique cowered deeper into the covering. She had never known his anger. He caressed her hair. "Don't worry, my darling, don't worry about your father, I'll see what we can do to help him later, but now you mustn't worry, I'm looking after you," his words ever more tender. Her sobbing lessened, the vast weight off her now that she had told him the truth and given him the news before he heard it from others—and that he *did not* seem to care.

André's a genius, she was thinking, exhausted with relief. He swore that this would be Malcolm's reaction: 'Just be honest, Angelique, tell

Malcolm the truth, that you didn't know your father was a gambler, that this is the first you've heard about it and you're shocked beyond words, that your father has stolen your money—important you use the words "stolen" and "thief"—tell the truth, show him his letter and with the right amount of tears and tenderness this will bond him to you forever.'

'But André,' she had said miserably, 'I daren't show him Father's letter. I daren't, his postscript sounds so awful—'

'Look! Without the second page the postscript just says, *my hopes for a quick recovery*. Perfect! The second page? What second page? There, it's torn up and never existed.'

André's nimble fingers glued the last shred of the reassembled second page into place. "There, Henri," he said, and pushed it across the desk. "Read for yourself." It had taken him no time at all to rebuild the page from the pieces he had seemingly thrown carelessly into his wastepaper basket.

They were in Seratard's office, the door locked. The page read:

> ... *and hope, as we discussed, you can position an early betrothal and marriage* by whatever means necessary ... *He is the catch of the season and vital for our future, yours particularly. Struan will permanently solve Richaud Frères. Never mind that he is British, too young or whatever, now he's tai-pan of Struan's and can assure us of a smooth future. Be adult, Angelique,* do anything necessary *to bond him to you because your future is presently threadbare.*

"That's not so terrible," Seratard said uneasily, "just a father's panic advice, reaching for straws. Struan is without doubt a wonderful catch for any girl and Angelique ... who could blame a father?"

"That depends on the father. This, if used at the correct time in the correct way, is another weapon over her, therefore over the Noble House."

"Then you think the poor girl will be successful?"

"We must work to make it so. Now that we've this evidence to use, if necessary, we must assist her as a matter of policy." André's lips were a thin cold line. "Not that I think she's a poor girl. She's the one who's prepared to snare him by *any means necessary*. Eh?"

Seratard sat back in the red leather chair. His office bureau was tatty except for a few oils of modern, little-known French painters, Manet amongst them, that he collected cheaply through a Paris agent from time to time. "What's she doing but reacting to a young man's love?" He shoved the paper back. "I don't like these methods, André. They're distasteful. You encouraged the girl into the morass of half-truths by telling her to give him half the letter."

"Machiavelli wrote, 'It is necessary for the State to deal in lies and half-truths, because people are made up of lies and half-truths. Even princes.' And certainly, by definition, all Ambassadors and politicians." André shrugged. Carefully he folded the letter. "Perhaps we won't have to use it, but it's good to have it because we represent the State."

"Use it, how?"

"The fact that she tore it up and . . ."

"She didn't," Seratard said, shocked.

"Of course," André said coldly. "But it's her word against mine and who wins that contest? The fact that she tore up the second page and only showed Struan the first should be enough to damn her in his eyes. This gives him a perfect excuse to annul any promise of marriage 'as he had been deceived.' His mother? If she knew about this she would concede us all sorts of concessions to gain possession of it, if he insists on marrying Angelique, against her advice."

"I don't like blackmail."

André flushed. "I don't like lots of methods I'm obliged to use for our, I repeat, *our* purposes." He put the page with the fine writing into his pocket. "Circulated in society or published, with the details, this document would destroy Angelique. In a court it would damn her. Perhaps it only shows the truth: that she is just an adventuress, in conspiracy with her father who is—who is at best a gambler and soon to be bankrupt, like her uncle. As to encouraging her, I only tell her what she wants to know and say. To help her. It's her mess, not mine or ours."

Seratard sighed. "Sad. Sad that she is embroiled."

"Yes, but she is, isn't she, to our advantage?" André's lips smiled but not his eyes. "And yours personally, Monsieur? Judiciously used this would guarantee her into your bed, would it not, if your undoubted charm failed, which I doubt."

Seratard did not smile. "And you, André? What are we going to do about Hana, the Flower?"

André looked at him abruptly. "The Flower is dead."

"Yes. And under such strange circumstances."

"Not strange," André said, his eyes suddenly flat as a reptile's. "She committed suicide."

"She was found with her throat cut, with your knife. The mama-san says you spent the night with her as usual."

André was trying to work out why Seratard was probing now. "I did, but this is none of your business."

"I'm afraid it is. The local Bakufu official sent a formal request for information yesterday."

"Tell him to kill himself. Hana, the Flower, was special, yes, she was mine, yes. I paid the very top pillow price for her, but she was still only part of the Willow World."

"As you said so rightly, people are made up of lies and half-truths. The complaint reports that you had a violent row with her. Because she had taken a lover."

"We had a row, yes, and I wanted to kill her, yes, but not for that reason," André muttered, choked. "The truth is . . . the truth is she did have some clients. Three—in the other House, but this was . . . this was before she became my property. One of them . . . one of them gave her the pox. She gave it to me."

Seratard was aghast. *"Mon Dieu, syphilis?"*

"Yes."

"Mon Dieu, you're sure?"

"Yes." André got up and went to the sideboard and poured some brandy and drank it. "Babcott confirmed it a month ago. No mistake. It could only have been her. When I asked her about it, she . . ."

He was seeing her again, looking up at him in the little house within the walls of the House of the Three Carp, a little frown on the perfect oval of her face. She was just seventeen and five feet tall.

'*Hai, gomen nasai,* Furansu-san, spot, like yours, but year 'go, mine *sukoshi,* rittle, *hai,* rittle, Furansu-san, *sukoshi,* no bad, go 'way,' she said gently with her sweet smile in her usual mixture of Japanese and bits of English, her l's always like r's. 'Hana tell mama-san. Mama-san say see doctor, he say no bad. No bad spot but because just begin pillow and I small. Doctor say pray at shrine and drink medicine, ugh! But few week all gon'way.' She added happily. 'All gon'way year ago.'

'It hasn't "gone away"!'

'Why anger? No worry. I pray at Shinto shrine like doctor say, pay priest many taels, I eat'—her face crinkled with her laugh—'eat nasty medicine. Few week all gone.'

'It hasn't gone. It won't. There's no cure!'

She had looked at him strangely. 'All gon', you see me, my body, all, how many time, *neh*? Of course all gon'way.'

'For Christ sake, it hasn't!'

Another frown, then she shrugged. 'Karma, *neh*?'

He had exploded. Her shock was vast and she put her head to the tatami and pitifully began to beg his pardon, 'No bad, Furansu-san, gon'way, doctor say, gon'way. You see same doctor soon, all go'way. . . .'

Outside their shoji walls he could hear footsteps and whispers. 'You have to see the English doctor!' His heart was thundering in his ears and he was trying to speak coherently, knowing that going to a doctor, any doctor, was useless and that though sometimes the ravages could be arrested, perhaps, as sure as the sun would dawn tomorrow, the ravages would one day arrive in force. 'Don't you understand?' he had shrieked. *'There's no cure!'*

She just stayed bowed, shaking like a brutalized puppy, saying monotonously, 'No bad, Furansu-san, no bad, all go'way . . .'

He dragged himself back and looked again at Seratard. "When I questioned her about it she said she had been cured, a year ago. She believed it, of course she believed she was cured. Me, oh yes, I was screaming and asked her why she hadn't told Raiko-san and she mumbled something about, What was there to tell, the doctor said it was nothing and her mama-san would have told Raiko-san if it had been important."

"But this is terrible, André. Did Babcott see her?"

"No." Another swallow of brandy but he felt none of its customary bite, then said in a rush, desperate to tell someone at last, "Babcott told me the pox . . . he told me an early poxed woman can appear to be without blemish in every way, that she won't always pass it on, not every time you bed, God knows why, but it's inevitable she will sometime if you continue with her and once a sore appears you're lost, though after a month or so the sore or sores go away and you think you're safe but you're not!" Now the vein in the center of André's forehead was knotted and pulsating. "Weeks or months later there's a rash, this's the second stage. It's strong or weak depending on only God knows what and sometimes brings hepatitis or meningitis and stays or goes away, the rash, depending on Christ knows what. The last stage, the horror stage, appears anytime—anytime—months up to . . . up to thirty years later."

Seratard took out a handkerchief and wiped his brow, praying that he would be spared, thinking about the frequent times he visited the

Yoshiwara, about his own *musume* that now he kept for himself alone but could never guarantee had no other lover. How can you prove or disprove that if there's collusion with the mama-san when they're only interested in fleecing you? "You had the right to kill her," he said grimly. "And the mama-san."

"Raiko wasn't responsible. I'd told her none of the girls here, anywhere in the Yoshiwara, were ones I wanted. I wanted someone young, special, a virgin or almost one. I begged her to find me a flower, explaining exactly what I wanted, and she did and Hana-chan was everything I wanted, perfection—she came from one of the best Houses in Yedo. You can't imagine how beautiful she is, was . . ."

He remembered how his heart had leapt the first time Raiko had shown her to him, chattering with other girls in another room. 'That one, Raiko, in the pale blue kimono.'

'I advise stay with Fujiko or Akiko or one of my other ladies,' Raiko had said. When she wanted, her English was good. 'In time I will find you another. There little Saiko. In a year or two . . .'

'That one, Raiko. She perfect. Who is she?'

'Her name is Hana, the Flower. Her mama-san say the pretty little thing was born near Kyōto, bought by her House when three or four for training as geisha.' Raiko smiled. 'Luckily, she's not geisha—if geisha, she would be not on offer, so sorry.'

'Because I gai-jin?'

'Because geisha is for entertainment, not pillowing, and, Furansu-san, so sorry, truly difficult to appreciate if not Japanese. Hana's teachers were patient, but she could not develop the skills so she was trained for the pillow.'

'I want her, Raiko.'

'A year ago she was old enough to begin. Her mama-san arranged the best pillow prices, of course only after Hana had approved the client. Three clients only have enjoyed her, her mama-san says she is fine pupil, and only allowed to pillow twice weekly. Only mark against her, she was born in the Year of the Fire Horse.'

'What that mean?'

'You know we count time in cycles of twelve years, like the Chinese, each year with an animal name, Dragon, Snake, Cockerel, Bull, Horse and so on. But each also has one of the five elements: fire, water, earth, iron, wood that vary, cycle by cycle. Ladies born in Year of Horse, with the fire sign, are thought to be . . . unlucky.'

'Not believe superstitions. Please say price.'

'She is a pillow Flower beyond price.'

'The price, Raiko.'

'To the other House, ten koku, Furansu-san. To this House, two koku a year, and price of house of her own within my fence, two maids, all the clothes she wants, and parting gift of five koku when you no longer require her services—this sum to be deposited with our Gyokoyama rice merchant-banker, at interest which, until time of parting, is yours—all to be in writing, signed and registered with Bakufu.'

The sum was huge by Japanese standards, extravagant by European counting even with the rate of exchange heavily weighted in the European's favor. For a week he had bartered and had managed to reduce the price only a few sous. Every night his dreams drove him onwards. So he had agreed. With due ritual seven months ago she had been presented to him formally. She agreed to accept him formally. They both signed formally. The next night he had pillowed and she was everything he had dreamed. Laughing, happy, enthusiastic, tender, loving. "She was a gift of God, Henri."

"Of the devil. The mama-san too."

"No, it wasn't her fault. The day before I received Hana, Raiko told me, formally—it was also on the deed of payment—that the past was the past, she promised only to cherish Hana as one of her own girls, to make sure Hana was never seen by other men and remained mine alone, *from that day onwards*."

"Then *she* killed her?"

André poured another drink. "I . . . I asked Hana to name the three men, one of them is my murderer, but she said she couldn't—or wouldn't. I—I smashed her around the face to force it out of her and she just whimpered and didn't cry out. I would have killed her, yes, but I loved her and . . . then I left. I was like a mad dog, it was three or four o'clock by then and I just walked into the sea. Maybe I wanted to drown myself, I don't know, don't remember exactly, but the cold water gave me back my head. When I got back to the House, Raiko and the others were in shock, incoherent. Hana was crumpled where I left her. Now in a mess of blood, my knife in her throat."

"Then she committed suicide?"

"That's what Raiko said."

"You don't believe it?"

"I don't know what to believe," André said in anguish. "I only know I went back to tell her I loved her, that the pox was karma, not her fault, not her fault, that I was sorry I said what I said and did what I did, that everything would be as before except, except when it became . . . became obvious we would suicide together . . ."

Henri was trying to think, his own brain addled. He had never even heard of the House of the Three Carp before rumors of the girl's death had rushed through the Settlement. André's always been so secretive, he thought, correctly so, and he's right, it was none of my business—until the Bakufu made it official. "The three men, did this Raiko know who they were?"

Numbed, André shook his head. "No, and the other mama-san would not tell her."

"Who is she? What's her name? Where is she? We'll report her to the Bakufu, they could force it out of her."

"They wouldn't care, why should they? The other House—it was a meeting place for revolutionaries, Inn of the Forty-seven Ronin, a week or so ago it was burned to the ground and her head stuck on a spike. Holy Mother of God, Henri, what am I going to do? Hana's dead and I'm alive. . . ."

16

Early that afternoon Dr. Hoag was in the cutter heading for the Legation wharf at Kanagawa. Babcott had sent word that he could not leave Kanagawa, as he was operating in his clinic there but would return as soon as possible: *... sorry, it can't be until late tonight, probably not until tomorrow morning. You're more than welcome to join me here if you wish but be prepared to stay the night, as the weather is changeable ...*

Waiting on the wharf was a Grenadier and Lim, who wore a white coat, loose black trousers, slippers and small skullcap. As Hoag came ashore Lim yawned a token bow. "Heya, Mass'er, Lim-ah, Numb'r One Boy."

"We can stop pidgin coolie talk, Lim," Hoag said in passable Cantonese, and Lim's eyes widened. "I am Medicine Doctor Wise Enlightened." This was Hoag's Chinese name—the meaning of the two characters nearest to the Cantonese sound of 'hoh' and 'geh'—selected out of dozens of possibilities for him by Gordon Chen, the Struan compradore, one of his patients.

Lim stared at him, pretending not to understand, the usual and quickest way to make a foreign devil lose face who had the impertinence to dare to learn a few words of the civilized tongue. Ayeeyah, he thought, who's this gamy fornicator, this putrid red devil mother-eater with the neck of a bull, this toadlike monkey who has the gall to speak in our tongue with such a foul superior manner ...

"Ayeeyah," Hoag said sweetly, "also I have many, very many dirty words to describe a fornicator's mother and her putrefying parts if a man from a dog-piss, dung-heap village gives me an eyelid of cause—like pretending not to understand me."

"Medicine Doctor Wise Enlightened? Ayeeyah, that's a good name!" Lim guffawed. "And never have I heard such good man-talk from a foreign devil in many a year."

"Good. You will soon hear more if I am again called foreign devil. Noble House Chen selected my name."

"Noble House Chen?" Lim gawked at him. "Illustrious Chen who has more bags of gold than an oxen has hairs? Ayeeyah, what a fornicating privilege!"

"Yes," Hoag agreed, adding not quite the truth, "and he told me if I have any dung-mixed troubles from any person of the Middle Kingdom—be he high or low—or not the at-once service a friend of his must expect, to mention the vile fornicator's name on my return."

"*Oh ko,* Medicine Doctor Wise Enlightened, it is indeed an honor to have you in our humble dung-heap house."

Dr. Hoag felt he had achieved greatness, blessing his teachers, mostly grateful patients, who had taught him the really important words and how to deal with certain persons and situations in the Middle Kingdom. The day was pleasant and warm and the look of the small town pleased him, the temples he could see over the rooftops, fishermen trawling the inland waters, peasants everywhere in the paddy, people coming and going and the inevitable stream of travellers on the Tokaidō beyond. By the time they reached the Legation with Lim's overtly attentive support, Hoag had a fairly good picture of what the situation was in Kanagawa, today's number of Babcott's patients, and what to expect.

George Babcott was in his surgery, assisted in the operation by a Japanese acolyte, a trainee appointed by the Bakufu to learn Western medicine, the anteroom outside crowded with villagers, men and women and children. The operation was messy, a foot amputation: "Poor fellow's a fisherman, got his leg trapped between the boat and the wharf, should never have happened, too much saké, I'm afraid. When I'm through we can discuss Malcolm. Did you see him?"

"Yes, no hurry. It's good to see you, George, can I help in any way?"

"Thanks, I'd appreciate that. I'm all right here but if you could sift through the mob outside? Those who are urgent, those who can wait. Treat any you want. There's another 'surgery' next door though it's little more than a sickroom. Mura, give me the saw," he said in studied English to his assistant, and accepted the tool and began to use it. "Whenever I have a surgery here it gets hectic. In the cabinet there are the usual placebos, iodine, etc., usual medicines, painkillers, bitter cough mixtures for the sweet old ladies and sweet ones for the angry."

Hoag left him and looked over the waiting men, women and children, astonished with their orderliness, patience, the bows and lack of noise. Quickly he established none had smallpox, leprosy, measles, typhoid or cholera or any of the other infectious diseases or plagues that were endemic in most of Asia. More than a little relieved he began to question them individually and met with grave suspicion. Fortunately, one was an elderly itinerant Cantonese letter writer and soothsayer, Cheng-sin, who could also speak some Japanese. With his help—after being introduced as the Giant Healer's Teacher—and a promise of an especially good, new modern medicine to ease his hacking cough, Dr. Hoag began a second surgery.

Some had minor ailments. A few were serious. Fevers, illnesses, dysentery and the like, some he could diagnose, some he could not. Broken limbs, sword and knife cuts, ulcers. One, a young woman, in great pain, heavily pregnant.

His practiced eye told him the birth, her fourth, would be bad and that most of her trouble was caused by marrying too young, working the fields too long and carrying too much. He gave her a small bottle of opium extract. "Tell her when her time is come and the pain is bad to drink a spoonful."

"Spoonful? How big, Honorable Wise Enlightened?"

"A normal-size spoon, Cheng-sin."

The woman bowed. *"Domo arigato gozaimashita,"* she muttered as she left, pathetic in her thanks, both hands trying to carry the weight of her belly.

Children with fevers and colds and hookworm, sores but not nearly as bad as he had expected, no *mal-aria*. Teeth generally good and strong, eyes clear, no lice—all patients astonishingly clean and healthy compared with similar villagers in China. No opium addicts. After an hour he was happily in his stride. He had just finished setting a broken arm when the door opened and a well-dressed, attractive young girl came in hesitantly and bowed. Her kimono was blue patterned silk, the obi green, hair dressed with combs. Blue sunshade.

Hoag noticed Cheng-sin's eyes narrow. She answered his questions and spoke even more persuasively though clearly quite nervous, her voice soft.

"Medicine Doctor Wise Enlightened," Cheng-sin said, his speech punctuated with the permanent, dry cough that Hoag had diagnosed instantly as terminal consumption. "This Lady say her brother need important help, near death. She beg you to accompany her—house is nearby."

"Tell her to have him brought here."

"Unfortunately afraid to move him."

"What's the matter with him?"

After more questions and answers, which to Hoag sounded more like bargaining than anything else, Cheng-sin said, "Her house only one or two street outside. Her brother is . . ." he coughed as he searched for the word, "sleep like dead man, but alive with mad talk and fever." His voice became more honeyed. "She afraid move him, Honorable Medicine Doctor Wise Enlightened. Her brother samurai, she say many important persons very happy if you help brother. I think she say truth."

From Hong Kong newspapers Hoag was acquainted with the importance of samurai as the absolute ruling class in Japan, and that anything that would gain their confidence, and thus their cooperation, would assist British influence. He studied her. At once she dropped her eyes. Her nervousness increased. She appeared to be fifteen or sixteen and her features quite unlike the villagers, lovely skin. If her brother's samurai so is she, he thought, intrigued. "What's her name?"

"Uki Ichikawa. Please to hurry."

"Her brother's an important samurai?"

"Yes," Cheng-sin said. "I accompany you, not be fear."

Hoag snorted. "Afraid? Me? The pox on fear! Wait here." He went to the surgery, opened the door quietly. Babcott was heavily involved extracting an abscessed tooth, his knee on the youth's chest, the distraught mother wringing her hands and chattering. He decided not to disturb him.

At the gates the Sergeant of the Guard politely stopped them and asked where he was going. "I'll send a couple of my lads with you. Better safe than sorry."

The girl tried to dissuade them from bringing soldiers but the Sergeant was adamant. At length she agreed and, more nervously, led the way down one street, into an alley, into another and then another. The villagers they passed averted their eyes and scuttled away. Hoag carried his doctor's bag. Over the rooftops he could still see the temple, and was reassured, and glad for the soldiers, knowing it would have been foolhardy to go without them. Cheng-sin plodded along, a tall staff in his hand.

This young lady's not all she pretends to be, Hoag thought, not a little excited by the adventure.

Into another alley. Then she stopped at a door set in a tall fence and knocked. A grille opened, then the door. When the burly servant saw the soldiers he started to close it but the girl imperiously ordered him to desist.

The garden was small, well kept but not extravagant. At the steps to the veranda of a small shoji house, she slipped out of clog shoes and asked them to do the same. It was awkward for Hoag, as he wore high boots. At once she ordered the servant to help him and was obeyed instantly.

"You two best guard here," Hoag said to the soldiers, embarrassed by the holes in his socks.

"Yes, sir." One of the soldiers checked his rifle. "I'll just look around the back. Any trouble just shout."

The girl slid back the shoji. Ori Ryoma, the shishi of the Tokaidō attack, lay on the futons, the sheet soaking, a maidservant fanning him. Her eyes widened seeing Hoag and not Honorable Medicine Giant Healer, as she had expected, and she backed away as he came in ponderously.

Ori was unconscious, in a coma—his swords on a low rack nearby, a flower arrangement in the tokonoma. Hoag squatted on his haunches beside him. The youth's forehead was very hot, face flushed, dangerously high fever. The cause was quickly apparent as Hoag pulled away the bandage on his shoulder and upper arm. "Christ," he muttered, seeing the extent of the puffy, poisonous inflammation, the telltale smell and black of dead tissue—gangrene—around the bullet wound.

"When was he shot?"

"She not know exactly. Two or three weeks."

Once more he looked at the wound. Then, oblivious of all the eyes focused on him, he went out and sat on the edge of the veranda and stared into space.

All I need now is my fine Hong Kong hospital and fine operating equipment, my wonderful Nightingale nurses, together with a barrel of luck, to save this poor youth. Fucking guns, fucking wars, fucking politicians . . .

For God's sake, I've been trying to patch up gun mutilations all my working life, failing most of the time—six years with the East India Company in bloody Bengal, fifteen years in the Colony and Opium War years, a volunteered year in the Crimea, the bloodiest of all, with the Hong Kong Hospital Detachment. Fucking guns! Christ, what a waste!

After he had sworn his rage away he lit a cheroot, puffed, then discarded the match. At once the shocked servant rushed forward and picked up the offending object.

"Oh, sorry," Hoag said, not having noticed the pristine cleanliness of the path and surrounds. He inhaled deeply, then dismissed everything from his mind except the youth. At length he decided, began to throw his butt away, stopped and gave it to the servant who bowed and went to bury it.

"Cheng-sin, tell her I'm sorry but if I operate or not I think her brother will die. Sorry."

"She says, 'If die, is karma. If no help, he dies today, tomorrow. Please to try. If he dies, karma. She ask help.'" Cheng-sin added softly: "Medicine Doctor Wise Enlightened, this youth important. Important try, heya?"

Hoag looked at the girl. Her eyes gazed back at him.

"Dozo, Hoh Geh-sama," she said. Please.

"Very well, Uki. Cheng-sin, tell her again I can't promise anything but I'll try. I will need soap, lots of hot water in bowls, lots of clean sheets, lots of sheets torn into swabs and bandages, lots of quiet and someone with a strong stomach to help me."

At once the girl pointed at herself. "Sōji shimasu." I will do it.

Hoag frowned. "Tell her it will be very unpleasant, much blood, much stink, and ugly." He saw her listen intently to the Chinese, then reply with evident pride, "Gomen nasai, Hoh Geh-san, wakarimasen. Watashi samurai desu."

"She say, 'Please to excuse, I understand. I am samurai.'"

"I don't know what that means to you, pretty young lady, and I didn't know women could be samurai, but let's begin."

Hoag found out quickly that one characteristic of samurai was courage. Never once did she falter during the cleaning operation, cutting away the infected tissue, releasing the foul-smelling pus, flushing the wound, blood pulsing from a partially severed vein until he could stanch the flow and repair it, swabbing and swabbing again—the big sleeves of the maid's kimono into which she had changed rolled up and fastened out of the way, and the scarf with which she had tied back her hair, both soon soiled and reeking.

For an hour he worked away, humming from time to time, ears closed, nostrils closed, every sense engrossed, repeating an operation he had done a thousand times too often. Cutting, sewing, cleaning, bandaging. Then he had finished.

Without haste he stretched to ease his cramped back muscles, washed his hands and took off the now bloody sheet he had used as an apron. Ori was balanced on the edge of the veranda as a makeshift table, he standing in the garden against it: 'Can't operate on my knees easily, Uki,' he had said.

Everything he had wanted done she had done without hesitation. There had been no need to anesthetize the man, whose name, he was told, was Hiro Ichikawa; his coma was so deep. Once or twice Ori cried out, but not from pain, just some devil in his nightmare. And struggled, but without strength.

Ori sighed deeply. Anxiously Hoag felt his pulse. It was almost imperceptible, so was the breathing. "Never mind," he muttered. "At least he has a pulse."

"Gomen nasai, Hoh Geh-san," the soft voice said, *"anata kanga-emasu, hai, iyé?"*

"She says, 'Excuse me, Honorable Wise Enlightened, you think yes or no?' " Cheng-sin coughed. He had spent the time well away from the veranda, his back towards them.

Hoag shrugged, watching her, wondering about her, where the strength came from, where she lived and what would happen now. She was quite pale, her features stark but still dominated by an iron will. His eyes crinkled with a smile. "I don't know. It's up to God. Uki, you number one. Samurai."

"Domo . . . domo arigato gozaimashita." Thank you. She bowed to the tatami. Her real name was Sumomo Anato, she was Hiraga's wife-to-be, and Shorin's sister, not Ori's.

"She asks what should she do now?"

"For her brother, nothing at the moment. Tell the maid to put cold towels on his forehead and keep bandages soaked with clean water until the fever goes down. If the . . . once the fever's gone—I hope before dawn—the youth will live. Perhaps." And what are the odds, was usually the next question. This time it did not happen. "Well, I'll go now. Tell her to send a guide for me early tomorrow morning . . ." If he's still alive, was in his mind, but he decided not to say it.

As Cheng-sin translated he began to wash his instruments. The girl beckoned the manservant and spoke to him. *"Hai,"* the man said, and hurried away.

"Medicine Doctor Wise Enlightened, before you go Lady say sure to want bath. Yes?"

Dr. Hoag was on the point of saying no, but found himself nodding yes. And he was glad that he did.

In the gloaming Babcott sat on the Legation veranda enjoying a whisky, exhausted but pleased with his surgery. There was a good smell of the sea on the breeze that touched the garden. As his eyes strayed involuntarily to the shrubbery where the black-clothed assassin had been caught and killed three weeks ago, the temple bell began tolling and the distant deep-throated chant of the monks sounded: *"Ommm mahnee padmee hummmmm . . ."* He looked up as Hoag plodded up towards him. "Good God!"

Hoag wore a patterned, belted yukata, white shoe-socks on his feet and Japanese clogs. Hair and beard combed and freshly washed. Under his arm was a large straw-covered cask of saké and he was beaming. " 'Evening, George!"

"You look pleased with yourself, where have you been?"

"The best part was the bath." Hoag put the cask onto a sideboard, poured a stiff whisky. "My God, the best I've ever had. Can't believe how good I feel now."

"How was she?" Babcott asked dryly.

"No sex, old man, just scrubbed clean and dunked in damn near boiling water, pummelled and massaged and then into this garb. Meanwhile all my clothes were washed and ironed, boots cleaned and socks replaced. Marvelous. She gave me the saké and these . . ." He fished into his sleeve and showed Babcott two oval-shaped coins and a scroll covered with characters.

"My God, you've been well paid, these are gold oban—they'll keep you in champagne for at least a week! The Sergeant told me you were on a house call." They both laughed. "Was he a daimyo?"

"Don't think so, he was a youth, a samurai. Don't think I helped him much. Can you read the scroll?"

"No, but Lim can. Lim!"

"Yes, Mass'r?"

"Paper what?"

Lim took the scroll. His eyes widened and then he reread it carefully, and said to Hoag in Cantonese: "It says, 'Medicine Doctor Wise Enlightened has performed a great service. In the name of Satsuma shishi, give him all help he needs.' " Lim pointed at the signature, his finger trembling. "Sorry, Lord, the name I can't read."

"Why are you frightened?" Hoag asked, also in Cantonese.

Uneasily Lim said, "Shishi are rebels, bandits hunted by the Bakufu. There're bad people even though samurai, Lord."

Impatiently Babcott asked, "What's it say, Ronald?"

Hoag told him.

"Good God, a bandit? What happened?"

Thirstily Hoag poured another drink and began describing in detail the woman, the youth and wound and how he had cut away the dead tissue. ". . . seems the poor bugger got shot two or three weeks ago and—"

"Christ Almighty!" Babcott leapt to his feet as everything fell into place, startling Hoag who spilt his drink.

"Are you bonkers?" Hoag spluttered.

"Can you find your way back there?"

"Eh? Well, well yes, I suppose so but what—"

"Come on, hurry." Babcott rushed out, shouting, "Sergeant of the Guard!"

They were loping down a back alley, Hoag leading, still in his yukata, but now wearing his boots, Babcott close behind, the Sergeant and ten soldiers following, all of them armed. The few pedestrians, some with lanterns, scattered out of the way. Above was a fair moon.

Hurrying faster now. A missed turning. Hoag cursed, then doubled back, got his bearings and found the half-hidden mouth to the correct alley. On again. Another alley. He stopped, pointed. Twenty yards ahead was the door.

At once the Sergeant and soldiers charged past him. Two put their backs to the wall on guard, four slammed their shoulders into the door, bursting it off its hinges and they poured through the gap, Hoag and Babcott after them. Both carried borrowed rifles easily, expert in their use, a common skill and a necessity for European civilians in Asia.

Along the pathway. Up the steps. The Sergeant hauled the shoji open. The room was empty. Without hesitation he led the way into the next room and the next. No sign of anyone in any of the five interconnecting rooms or kitchen or little wooden outhouse. Out again into the garden.

"Spread out, lads, Jones and Berk go that way, you two over there, you two that way and you two guard here, and for Chrissake, keep your 'kin eyes open." They went deeper into the garden in pairs, one guarding the other, the lesson of the first assassin well learned. Into every nook. Around all the perimeter, safety catches off.

Nothing. When the Sergeant came back he was sweating. "Sweet fanny adams, sir! Not a bloody whisper, nothing. You sure this is the right place, sir?"

Hoag pointed to a dark patch on the veranda. "That's where I operated."

Babcott cursed and looked around. This house was surrounded by others but only roofs showed above the fence and no windows overlooked this way. Nowhere else to hide. "They must have left the moment you did."

Hoag wiped the sweat off his brow, secretly glad that she had slipped away and was not trapped. After he had left for the bath he had, regretfully, not seen her again. The maid had given him the money and scroll, both neatly wrapped, and the cask and told him her mistress would send a guide for him tomorrow morning and thanked him.

About her brother, now, he was ambivalent. The youth was just a patient, he was a doctor and wanted his work to succeed. "Never occurred to me the youth might have been one of the assassins. It wouldn't have made any difference, not to the operation. At least now we know his name."

"A thousand oban to a bent button it was false, we don't even know if the youth was her brother. If he was shishi as the scroll said, it's bound to be false and anyway, being devious is an old Japanese custom." Babcott sighed. "I can't be certain either it was the Tokaidō devil. Just a hunch. What are his chances?"

"The move wouldn't have helped." Hoag thought a moment, so squat and froglike against the immense height of Babcott, neither of them conscious of the difference. "I checked him just before I left. His pulse was weak but steady, I think I got most of the dead tissue away but . . ." He shrugged. "You know how it is: 'You pays your money and you takes your chances.' I wouldn't bet much money he'll live. But then, who knows, eh? Now, tell me about the attack, the details."

On the way back Babcott related all that had happened. And about Malcolm Struan. "He worries me, but Angelique's just about the best nurse he could have."

"Jamie said the same. I agree there's nothing like a beautiful young lady in a sickroom. Malcolm's lost a devilish lot of weight—and spirit—but he's young and he's always been the strong one in the family, after his mother. He should be all right so long as the stitches hold. I've every confidence in your work, George, though it'll be a long haul for him, poor lad. He's very taken with the girl, isn't he?"

"Yes. And reciprocated. Lucky fellow."

They walked in silence a moment. Hoag said hesitantly, "I, well, I presume you know his mother is completely opposed to any form of liaison with the young lady."

"Yes, I've heard that. That creates a problem."

"Then you think Malcolm's serious?"

"Head-over-heels serious. She's quite a girl."

"You know her?"

"Angelique? Not really, not as a patient, though, as I said, I've seen her under terrible stress. You?"

Hoag shook his head. "Just at parties, the races, socially. Since she arrived three or four months ago she's been the toast of every ball, and rightly so. Never as a patient, there's a French doctor in Hong Kong now—imagine that! But I agree she's stunning. Not necessarily an ideal wife for Malcolm, if that's his bent."

"Because she's not English? And not wealthy?"

"Both of those and more. Sorry, but I just can't trust the French— bad stock—it's in their makeup. Her father's a perfect example, charming, gallant on the surface and scallywag just below and through and through. Sorry, but I wouldn't select his daughter for my son when he's of age."

Babcott wondered if Hoag knew that he was aware of the scandal: while young Doctor Hoag was with the East India Company twenty-five–odd years ago in Bengal, he had married an Indian girl, against convention and the open advice of his superiors and had consequently been dismissed and sent home in disgrace. They had had a daughter and a son and then she had died—the London cold and fog and damp almost a death sentence to someone of Indian heritage.

People are so strange, Babcott thought. Here's a fine, brave, upstanding Englishman, a great surgeon, with children who are half Indian— so socially not acceptable in England—complaining about Angelique's heritage. How stupid, and even more stupid to hide from the truth.

Yes, but don't you hide from it either. You're twenty-eight, lots of time to get married, but will you ever find a more exciting woman than Angelique anywhere, let alone in Asia where you will spend your working life?

I won't, I know. Fortunately Struan will probably marry her, so that's that. And I will support him, by God! "Perhaps Mrs. Struan is just being protective, like any mother," he said, knowing how important Hoag's influence was with the Struans, "and just opposed to him getting entangled too young. That's understandable. He's tai-pan now and that will take all of his energies. But don't mistake me, I think Angelique is quite a young lady, as courageous and fine a mate as anyone could want—and to do a good job Malcolm will need all the support he can get."

Hoag heard the underlying passion, docketed it and left the matter there, his mind suddenly back in London where his sister and her husband were bringing up his son and daughter, as always hating himself for leaving India, bowing to convention and so killing her, Arjumand the lovely.

I must have been mad to take my darling into those foul winters, dismissed, broke, with no job and having to start all over again. Christ, I should have stayed and battled the Company, eventually my surgical skills would have forced them, forced them to accept me and would have saved us . . .

The two sentries left on guard saluted as they passed. In the dining room dinner was laid for two. "Scotch or champagne?" Babcott asked, then called out, "Lun!"

"Champers. Shall I?"

"I've got it." Babcott opened the wine that waited in the Georgian silver ice bucket. "Health! LUN!"

"And happiness!" They clinked glasses. "Perfect! How's your chef?"

"Fair to awful but the quality of our seafood is good: shrimps, prawns, oysters and dozens of different kinds of fish. Where the devil's Lun?" Babcott sighed. "That bugger needs stick. Swear at him, will you?"

But the butler's pantry was empty. Lun was not in the kitchen. Eventually they found him in the garden beside a pathway. He had been decapitated, his head tossed aside. In its place was the head of a monkey.

"No, Lady," the mama-san said, very afraid. "You cannot leave Ori-san here tomorrow, you must leave at dawn."

Sumomo said, "So sorry, Ori-san will stay until—"

"So sorry, since the attack on Chief Minister Anjo, the hunt for shishi is intense, rewards for information are to the sky, with death for anyone, *anyone in a house harboring them.*"

"That order's for Yedo, not here in Kanagawa," Sumomo said.

"So sorry, someone has talked," the mama-san said, lips tight. Her name was Noriko and they were alone in her private quarters in her Inn of the Midnight Blossoms, both kneeling on purple cushions, the room candle-lit, a low table with tea on it between them and she had just returned from an angry meeting with the rice merchant moneylender who had raised the interest rate on her mortgage from thirty to thirty-five percent, pleading the dangerous state of the realm. Motherless dog, she thought, seething, then compartmentalized that problem to deal with the more dangerous one before her. "This morning we heard that Enforcers are—"

"Who?"

"Enforcers? They're special, interrogating Bakufu patrols, men without mercy. They arrived in the night. I expect to be visited. So sorry, at dawn he must go."

"So sorry, you will keep him until he is well."

"I-dare-not! Not after the Inn of the Forty-seven Ronin. Enforcers know no mercy. I don't want this head spiked."

"That was in Yedo, this is Kanagawa. This is the Inn of the Midnight Blossoms. So sorry, Hiraga-san would insist."

"No one insists here, Lady," Noriko said sharply. "Even Hiraga-san. I have my own son to think of, and my House."

"Correctly. And I have my brother's friend and Hiraga's ally to think of. Also the face of my brother to remember. I am empowered to settle his debts."

Noriko gaped at her. "All Shorin's debts?"

"Half now, half when *sonno-joi* rules."

"Done," Noriko said, so unbalanced with the windfall she never expected to collect that she failed to bargain. "But no gai-jin doctors, and only a week."

"Agreed." At once the girl reached into her sleeve for the purse in a secret pocket. Noriko sucked in her breath seeing the gold coins. "Here are ten oban. You will give me a receipt and his detailed account, the balance of the half we have agreed, when we leave. Where can Ori-san be safe?"

Noriko cursed herself for being so hasty, but having agreed, now it was a matter of face. As she considered what to do she studied the girl in front of her, Sumomo Anato, younger sister of Shorin Anato, the shishi, the Wild One—the boy she had initiated into the world of men so many years ago. Eeee, what lust, what vigor for one so young, she thought with a pleasant though untoward ache. And what a memorable courtesan this girl would make. Together we could earn a fortune, in a year or two she would marry a daimyo, and if she's still virgin what a pillow price I could get! She's every bit as beautiful as Shorin had said, classical Satsuma—according to him samurai in every way. Every bit as beautiful. "How old are you, Lady?"

Sumomo was startled. "Sixteen."

"Do you know how Shorin died?"

"Yes. I will be revenged."

"Hiraga told you?"

"You ask too many questions," Sumomo said sharply.

Noriko was amused. "In the game we play, you and I, though you are samurai and me mama-san, we're sisters."

"Oh?"

"Oh, yes, so sorry, the very serious game of trying to cover for our men, to shield them from their bravery, or stupidity, depending on which side you are, risking our lives to protect them from themselves merits trust on both sides. Trust of blood sisters. So, Hiraga told you about Shorin?"

Sumomo knew that her position was tenuous. "Yes."

"Hiraga is your lover?"

Sumomo's eyes slitted. "Hiraga is . . . was affianced to me before he . . . before he left to serve *sonno-joi*."

The mama-san blinked. "A Satsuma samurai allows his daughter to be betrothed to a Choshu samurai—whether shishi or not, ronin or not?"

"My father . . . my father did not approve. Nor my mother, though Shorin did. I did not approve their choice for me."

"Ah, so sorry." Noriko was saddened, knowing too well that that meant continual pressure, confinement in their house, or even worse: "Are you outcast from your family?"

Sumomo stayed motionless, her voice remained calm. "A few months ago I decided to follow my brother, and Hiraga-san, to spare my father that shame. Now I am ronin."

"Are you mad? Women cannot become ronin."

"Noriko," Sumomo said, gambling. "I agree we should be blood sisters." A stiletto appeared in her hand.

Noriko blinked, not having seen where it had appeared from. She watched as Sumomo pricked her finger and offered her the knife. Without hesitation she did the same and they touched fingers, mixing their blood, then bowed gravely. "I am honored. Thank you, Sumomo-san." Smiling, the mama-san returned the knife. "Now I am a tiny bit samurai, yes?"

The knife slid back into the sleeve sheath. "When the Emperor regains all his power, HE will make those deserving it, samurai. We will petition for you, Hiraga-san, Ori and I."

Again Noriko bowed her thanks, loving that idea but sure it was beyond possibility and that she would never live to see the unthinkable happen: the day the Toranaga Shōgunate ceased to be. "On behalf of all my line, thank you. Now saké!"

"No, thank you, so sorry, but Sensei Katsumata made women in his class forswear saké, telling us it would forever blunt our skills and spoil our aim. Please, where is Hiraga-san?"

Noriko, watched her, hiding her smile. "Katsumata, the great Sensei? You studied under him? Shorin told us you could use sword, knife and *shuriken*. Is that true?"

With dazzling speed Sumomo's hand went into her obi, came out with a shuriken and hurtled the small, razor-sharp, five-bladed circle of steel across the room to *thwakkk* viciously into the exact center of a post. She had hardly moved.

"Please, where is Hiraga-san?" she asked gently.

17

YEDO

THAT NIGHT HIRAGA LED THE SIlent charge up and over the stockade of a daimyo's palace in the second ring outside the castle walls and rushed through the gardens for the back entrance of the mansion, the night lit by a halfhearted moon. All six men wore the same short, black, night-fighting kimonos without armor for speed and quiet. All had swords, knives and garrotes. All were Choshu ronin Hiraga had summoned urgently from Kanagawa for tonight's raid.

Around the mansion the sprawling compound of barracks, stables and servants' quarters that would normally house five hundred warriors and the daimyo's family and servants was eerily empty. Only two sleepy sentries were at the back door. These men saw the raiders too late to sound an alarm and died. Akimoto stripped one of his uniform and put it on, then dragged the bodies into the undergrowth and rejoined the others on the veranda. They waited, motionless, listening intently. No warning shouts or they would have abandoned the attack at once.

'If we have to retreat, never mind,' Hiraga had said at dusk when the others had arrived in Yedo. 'It's enough that we can penetrate so close to the castle. Tonight's purpose is terror, to kill and spread terror, to make them believe no one and no place is beyond reach of us or our spies. Terror, in and out quickly, maximum surprise and no casualties. Tonight's a rare opportunity.' He smiled. 'When Anjo and the Elders cancelled *sankin-kotai,* they dug the Shōgunate's grave.'

'We fire the palace, Cousin?' Akimoto asked happily.

'After the kill.'

'And he is?'

'He's old, grey hair and little of it, thin and small, Utani, the *roju* Elder.'

They all gasped. 'Daimyo of Watasa?'

'Yes. Unfortunately I've never seen him. Anyone?'

'I think I'd recognize him,' the eighteen-year-old youth said, a bad scar running down the side of his face. 'He's scrawny, like a diseased chicken. I saw him once in Kyōto. So tonight we send an Elder onwards, eh, a daimyo, eh? Good!' He grinned and scratched at the scar, a legacy from the unsuccessful Choshu attempt to seize the Palace Gates in Kyōto last spring. 'Utani won't be running anywhere after tonight. He's mad to sleep outside the walls and let it be known! And without guards? Stupid!'

Joun, a seventeen-year-old, always the cautious one, said, 'Excuse me, Hiraga-san, but are you sure this isn't a trap baited with false information? Yoshi is called the Fox, Anjo worse. We've heavy prices on our heads, eh? I agree with my brother, how could Utani be so stupid?'

'Because he has a secret assignation. He's a pederast.'

They stared at him blankly. 'Why should he want to keep that secret?'

'The youth is one of Anjo's intimates.'

'*So ka!*' Joun's eyes glittered. 'Then I think I would keep that secret too. But why should a pretty boy give himself to someone like Utani when he already has a powerful patron?'

Hiraga shrugged. 'Pay, what else? Nori's a miser, Utani lavish— aren't his peasants the most taxed in all Nippon? Aren't his debts to the sky? Isn't he known for consuming gold oban like grains of rice? Soon, one way or another, Anjo will leave this earth. Perhaps this pretty boy thinks Utani will survive and the risk is worth it—Utani has influence at Court, eh? Koku! Why not, his family's probably destitute and drowning in debt—aren't almost all samurai, below hirazamurai rank, at poverty level?'

'True,' they all agreed.

'That's been true since the fourth Shōgun,' the eighteen-year-old said bitterly, 'almost two hundred years. Daimyos take all the taxes, sell samurai status to stinking merchants, more and more every year, and still they cut our pay. Daimyos have betrayed us, their loyal retainers!'

'You're right,' Akimoto said angrily. 'My father has to hire himself out as a farm laborer to feed the rest of my brothers and sisters. . . .'

'Ours has only his swords left, no house, just a hut,' Joun said. 'We're so deep in debt from Great-grandfather's time we can never repay the loans. Never.'

'I know how to settle those filthy money worshippers: cancel their debts or kill them,' another said. 'If daimyos sometimes pay off their debts like that, why not us?'

'A fine idea,' Akimoto agreed, 'but it would cost you your head. Lord Ogama would make an example of you, in case his own lenders stopped advancing money against—what is it now—against four years' taxes ahead.'

Another said, 'My family stipend hasn't changed since Sekigahara, and the cost of rice up a hundred times since then. We should become merchants or saké brewers. Two uncles and Elder Brother have given up their swords and done that.'

'Terrible, yes, but I've thought of it too.'

'Daimyos betrayed all of us.'

'Most have,' Hiraga said. 'Not all.'

'True,' Akimoto said. 'Never mind, we'll choose our own daimyo when we've expelled the barbarians and broken the Toranaga Shōgunate. The new Shōgun will give us enough to eat, us and our families, and better weapons, even some of the gai-jin rifles.'

'He'll keep them for his own men, whoever he is.'

'Why should he, Hiraga? There'll be enough for everyone. Don't the Toranagas hoard five to ten million koku yearly? That's more than enough to arm us properly. Listen, if we're split up in the dark, where do we regroup?'

'The House of Green Willows, south of Fourth Bridge, not here. If that's too difficult, hide somewhere and make your way back to Kanagawa. . . .'

Now on the veranda, listening carefully for danger, enjoying the sensation, Hiraga smiled, his heart beating well, feeling the joy of life and approaching death, every day nearer. In a few moments we move again. Action at long last . . .

For days he had been in the temple beside the English Legation, waiting impatiently for an opportunity to fire it but always too many enemy troops, foreign and samurai. Each day acting the gardener, spying, listening, planning—so easy to kill the tall barbarian there who escaped the Tokaidō attack. Astonishing that only one barbarian was killed out of the easy target of three men and a woman.

Ah, Tokaidō! Tokaidō means Ori and Ori means Shorin, and they mean Sumomo who is seventeen next month and I will not consider my father's letter. I will not! I will not accept Ogama's pardon if I have to recant *sonno-joi*. I will follow its lodestone to whatever death it steers.

Just me alive now. Ori is dead or will die tomorrow. Shorin gone. And Sumomo?

Last night tears had wet his cheeks, tears from the dream that she was in, her bushido and fire and perfume and body beckoning and lost to him forever. Impossible to sleep, so he sat in the Lotus seat, the Buddha position, using Zen to fly his mind to peace.

Then this morning, a gift of the gods, the furtive, coded message from Koiko's mama-san about Utani, who had heard it, equally secretly, from Koiko's maid. Eeee, he thought gleefully, I wonder what Yoshi would do if he knew our tentacles reached out even to his bed, even around his balls?

Confident now they were still undetected, he jumped up and went to the door, used his knife, sliding the bar back. Inside quickly. Akimoto stayed on guard in the sentry's uniform. The others followed Hiraga noiselessly up the stairs towards the women's quarters, the route already given to him. Everything was lavish, best woods, finest tatamis, purest oiled paper for shoji and most fragrant oils for lamps and candles. Turning a corner. The unsuspecting guard stared at him blankly. His mouth opened but no sound came out. Hiraga's knife had stopped it.

He stepped over the body, went to the end of the corridor, hesitated a moment to get his bearings. Now a cul-de-sac. Either side were walls of sliding shoji, rooms behind them. At the end just one, bigger and more ornate than all the others. An oil lamp burned within, also in some of the other rooms. A few snores and heavy breathing. Silently he motioned for Todo and Joun to follow and the others to guard, then went forward again like a night-hunting beast. The sound of heavy breathing increased.

A nod to Joun. At once the youth slipped past him, crouched at the far door then, at another sign from Hiraga, slid the shoji open. Hiraga leapt into the room, then Todo.

Two men were prone on the exquisite silk quilts and futons, naked and joined, the youth spread, the older over him, clutching him and thrusting, panting and oblivious. Hiraga stood over them, reared his sword on high and with two hands gripping the hilt drove the point through the back of both bodies just above the heart, burying it into the tatami floor, impaling them.

The old man gasped and died instantly, his limbs quivering beyond death. The youth clawed impotently, unable to turn, unable to move his trunk, only his arms and legs and head but, even so, he still could not twist enough to see what had happened nor could he understand what had happened, only that his life was somehow seeping away as all his body opened. A howl of terror gathered in his throat as Todo leapt forward and twined the garrote to choke it back—just too late. Part of the cry hung in the now fetid air.

Instantly he with Hiraga whirled for the door, all senses frenzied. Hiraga with knife poised. Todo, Joun and those in the corridor with swords raised, hearts pounding, all ready to charge, flee, fight, rush, die, but battle and die proudly. Behind Hiraga the delicate hands of the youth tore at his neck, his long, perfect and painted nails gouging the flesh around the wire. The fingers shuddered and stopped and fluttered and stopped and fluttered. And were still.

Silence. Somewhere a sleeper stirred noisily, then returned to sleep. Still no alarms or warning shouts. Gradually the raiders wrenched themselves from the brink, numbed and sweat-stained. Hiraga signalled the retreat.

At once they obeyed except for Joun who ran back into the room to recover Hiraga's sword. He straddled the bodies but with all his strength he could not pull the sword out or ease it out. Hiraga waved him away, tried himself and failed. On a low lacquered sword stand were the weapons of the dead men. He picked one up. At the door he looked back.

In the clean, steady light of the oil lamp the two bodies seemed like a single monstrous, multilegged human-headed dragonfly, the crumpled quilts its gorgeous wings, his sword a giant silver pin. Now he could see the face of the youth—it was quite beautiful.

Yoshi was strolling on the battlements, Koiko beside him; he was easily a head taller than her. A chill was on the small wind and the smell of the sea at low tide. He did not notice it. Again his eyes flicked from the city below to the moon and he watched it, brooding. Koiko waited patiently. Her kimono was the finest Shantung with a scarlet under-kimono and her hair, loosed informally, fell to her waist. His kimono was ordinary, silk but ordinary, and swords ordinary, ordinary but sharp.

"What are you thinking about, Sire?" she asked, judging it time to dispel his gloom. Though they were quite alone she kept her voice down, well aware that nowhere within the castle walls was really secure.

"Kyōto," he said simply. As quietly.

"Will you accompany Shōgun Nobusada?"

He shook his head though he had already decided to go to Kyōto before the formal party—the deception habitual.

Somehow I must stop that young fool and become the sole channel between Emperor and Shōgunate, he had been thinking, his mind assaulted with the difficulties surrounding him: the madness of this state visit, Anjo whose hold over the Council had forced approval, Anjo with his hatred and plotting, the trap I'm in here in the castle, the multitude of enemies throughout the land, the chief of them Sanjiro of Satsuma, Hiro of Tosa and Ogama of Choshu who now holds the Gates *that are our birthright*. And added to all of those and waiting to pounce like salivating wolves are the gai-jin.

They have to be dealt with, permanently. The boy Nobusada and the Princess have to be neutralized, permanently.

The permanent solution for the gai-jin is clear: in any way we can devise, whatever the sacrifice, we must become richer than them, and better armed. This must be secret national policy, now and forever. How to achieve this? I do not know yet. But as policy we must flatter them to sleep, keep them off balance, using their foolish attitudes against them—and employ our superior abilities to cocoon them.

Nobusada? Equally clear. But he's not the real threat. It's her. I don't have to worry about him but her, Princess Yazu, she's the real power behind him, and in front.

The sudden mental picture of her with a penis and Nobusada the receiver made him smile. It would make a wonderful *shunga-e*, he thought, amused. *Shunga-e* were erotic, many-colored woodcuts so popular and prized amongst Yedo's traders and shopkeepers that they had been proscribed by the Shōgunate for a century or more as too licentious for them, the lowest class, and too easy to be used as lampoons against their betters. In Nippon's immutable hierarchy, instituted by the *tairō*, Dictator Nakamura, then made permanent by Shōgun Toranaga, first were samurai, second farmers, third artisans of every kind, and last, despised by all, merchants: 'leeches on all other labor,' the Legacy called them. Despised because all others needed their skills and wealth—most of all their wealth. Particularly samurai.

So rules, certain rules, could be eased. Thus in Yedo, Osaka and Nagasaki where the really rich merchants lived, *shunga-e*, though officially outlawed, were painted, carved and merrily produced by the best artists and printmakers in the land. In every epoch, artists vied with each other for fame and fortune, selling them by the thousands.

Exotic, explicit, but always with gargantuan genitalia, hilariously out of all proportion, the best in perfect, moist, and mobile detail. Equally prized were *ukiyo-e* portraits of leading actors, the constant meat of gossip, scandal, and license—actresses were not permitted by law, so specially trained men, *onnagata,* played female roles—and, above all, prints of the most famous courtesans. "I would like someone to paint you. It's a pity Hiroshige and Hokusai are dead."

She laughed. "How should I pose, Sire?"

"Not in bed," he said, laughing with her, unusual for him to laugh, and she was pleased with the victory. "Just walking along a street, with a sunshade, green and pink, and wearing your pink and green kimono with the carp of woven gold."

"Perhaps, Sire, instead of a street, perhaps in a garden at dusk catching fireflies?"

"Ah, much better!" He smiled, remembering the rare days of his youth on summer evenings when he was released from studies. Then he and his brothers and sisters and friends would go out into the fields and hunt fireflies with gossamer nets and put the tiny insects into tiny cages and watch the light miraculously pulse on and off, composing poems, laughing and larking with no responsibilities, and young. "Like I feel with you now," he muttered.

"Sire?"

"You take me out of myself, Koiko. Everything about you."

For answer she touched his arm, saying nothing and everything, pleased with the compliment, all her mind concentrated on him, wanting to read his thoughts and needs, wanting to be perfect for him.

But this game's tiring, she thought again. This patron is too complex, too farsighted, too unpredictable, too solemn and too difficult to entertain. I wonder how long he will keep me. I begin to hate the castle, hate confinement, hate the constant testing, hate being away from home and the ribald laughter and chatter of the other ladies, Moonbeam, Springtime, Petal and most of all my darling mama-san, Meikin.

Yes, but I glory being in the center of the world, adore the one koku a day every day, exult that I am who I am, handmaiden to the most noble lord who is really just another man and, like all men, a fractious little boy pretending to be complicated and who can be controlled by sweets and spanking as always, and who, if you are clever, decides to do only what you have already decided he may do—whatever he believes.

Her laughter trilled.

"What?"

"You make me joyous, filled with life, Sire. I shall have to call you Lord Giver of Happiness!"

Warmth pervaded him. "And so to bed?"

"And so to bed."

Arm in arm, they began to leave the moonlight. "Look there," he said suddenly.

Far below, one of the palace mansions had caught fire. Flames began gushing upwards, then clouds of smoke. Now, faintly, they could hear fire bells and see ants of people milling around, and soon lines of other ants forming to join the fire to the water tanks: *Fire is our greatest hazard, not woman,* Shōgun Toranaga had written in his Legacy with rare humor. *Against fire we can be prepared, never against woman. All men and all women of marriageable age will be married. All habitations will have tanks of water within easy reach.*

"They will never put it out, will they, Sire?"

"No. I suppose some fool has knocked over a lamp or candle," Yoshi said, his lips tight.

"Yes, you are right, Sire, the clumsy fool," she said at once, gentling him, sensing an unexpected anger in him—and not knowing why. "I am so glad you are in charge of fire precautions in the castle so we can sleep safely. Whoever did it should be talked to severely. I wonder whose palace it is."

"It's the Tajima residence."

"Ah, Sire, you continue to amaze me," Koiko said with touching admiration. "How wonderful to be able to distinguish one palace from another amongst the hundreds so quickly, and from so far away." She bowed to hide her face, sure it was the Watasa and that now daimyo Utani must be dead and the raid successful. "You are wonderful."

"No, it is you who are wonderful, Koiko-chan." He smiled down at her, so sweet and tiny and observant and dangerous.

Three days ago his new spy, Misamoto, ever anxious to prove his worth, had reported the rumors circulating in the barracks about the tryst of Utani and the pretty boy. He had ordered Misamoto to allow the secret to be overheard by Koiko's maid, who was certain to whisper it to either her mistress or their mama-san or both, *if* other rumors were true: that this same mama-san, Meikin, was an avid supporter of *sonno-joi,* and that clandestinely she allowed her House to be a meeting place and sanctuary for shishi. The news would be passed to shishi who would instantly react at such a marvelous opportunity for a major kill.

For almost two years his spies had kept her and her House under surveillance, both for this reason and because of the growing stature of Koiko.

But never once had the merest scrap of evidence appeared to support the theory and condemn them.

Ah, but now, he thought, watching the flames, Utani must be dead if the palace is fired and now I have real evidence: a whisper planted in a maid has borne evil fruit. Utani was—is—a coup for them. As I would be, even more so. A small shudder touched him.

"Fire frightens me," she said, misinterpreting the shudder, wanting to give him face.

"Yes. Come along, we'll leave them to their karma." Arm in arm they walked away, Yoshi finding it hard to conceal his excitement. I wonder what your karma is, Koiko. Did your maid tell you and you told her to tell the mama-san and are part of the chain?

Perhaps, perhaps not. I saw no change in you when I said Tajima instead of Watasa, and I was watching very carefully. I wonder. Of course you are suspect, always were suspect, why else should I choose you, doesn't this add spice to my bed? It does, and you are everything your reputation promised. Truly I am more than satisfied, so I will wait. But now it is easy to trap you, so sorry, even easier to extract the truth from your maid, from this not-so-clever mama-san and from you, pretty one! Too easy, so sorry, when I close the trap.

Eeee, that will be a hard decision because now, thanks to Utani, I have a secret and direct line to the shishi, to use to uncover them, destroy them or even to use them against my enemies, at my whim. Why not?

Tempting!

Nobusada? Nobusada *and his Princess*? Very tempting! He began to laugh.

"I am so happy you're so happy tonight, Sire."

Princess Yazu was in tears. For almost two hours she had used every practice that she had ever read or seen in pillow books to excite him and though she had succeeded in making him strong, before he could achieve the Clouds and the Rain he had failed her. Then, as usual, he had burst into tears, raving in a paroxysm of nervous coughing that it was her fault. As usual the tempest vanished quickly, he begged forgiveness, falling asleep nestled close to kiss her breasts, suckling a breast, curled in her lap.

'It's not fair,' she whimpered, exhausted and unable to sleep. I must

have a son or he is as good as dead and so am I, at the very least so
shamed that I will have to shave my head and become a Buddhist nun
. . . *oh ko, oh ko* . . .

Even her ladies had not been able to help. 'You're all experienced,
most of you married, there must be some way to make my Lord a man,'
she had shouted at them after weeks of trying, both she and they aghast
that she had lost her temper. 'Find out! It is your duty to find out.'

Over the months her court had consulted herbalists, acupuncturists,
doctors, even soothsayers to no avail. This morning she had sent for her
chief Matron. 'There has to be a way! What do you advise?'

'You are only sixteen, Honored Princess,' the Matron had said on
her knees, 'and your Lord sixteen an—'

'But everyone conceives by that time, far earlier, almost everyone.
What's the matter with him, or with me?'

'Nothing with thee, Princess, we have told you many times, the
doctors assure us that nothing with thee is wr—'

'What about this gai-jin doctor, the giant I've heard about? One of
my maids told me it's rumored he does miracle cures of all kinds of
ailments, perhaps he could cure my Lord.'

'Oh, so sorry, Highness,' the woman had burst out, appalled, 'it's
unthinkable that he or you would consult a gai-jin! Please have patience, please. Cheng-sin, the marvelous soothsayer, told us patience
will surely—'

'It could be done secretly, fool! Patience? I've waited months!' she
had shrieked. 'Months of patience and still my Lord hasn't yet the
glimmerings of an heir!' Before she could stop herself she had slapped
the woman's face. 'Ten months of patience and ill advice is too much,
you miserable person, go away! Go! GO AWAY FOREVER!'

All day she had planned for tonight. Special dishes that he liked
were prepared, well seasoned with ginseng. Special saké laced with
ginseng and powdered rhinoceros horn. Special perfumes, heavily
aphrodisiac. Special prayers to the Buddha. Special supplications to
Amaterasu, the Sun Goddess, grandmother of the god Niniji who
came down from Heaven to rule Nippon who was great-grandfather
of the first mortal Emperor, Jinmu-Tenno, founder of their Imperial
Dynasty, twenty-five centuries ago—and therefore her direct ances-
tress.

But all had failed.

Now it was in the black time of the night and she wept silently, lying
on her set of futons, her husband asleep on his beside her, not happy in
sleep, a cough now and then, his limbs jerking, his sleeping face not

unpleasing to her. Poor silly boy, she thought, anguished, is it your karma to die heirless like so many of your line? *Oh ko, oh ko, oh ko! Why did I allow myself to be talked into this disaster, out of the arms of my beloved prince?*

Four years ago when she was twelve, and with the delighted approval of her mother, last and most favorite consort of her father, Emperor Ninko, who had died the year she was born, and with the equally delighted and necessary acquiescence of the Emperor Komei, her much older stepbrother who had succeeded him, she was happily affianced to a childhood playmate, Prince Sugawara.

That was the year the Bakufu formally signed the Treaties that opened Yokohama and Nagasaki, against Emperor Komei's wishes, the majority of the Court, and the outspoken advice of most daimyos. That was the year *sonno-joi* became a battle cry. And the same year the then *tairō*, Ii, proposed to the Prince Advisor that the Princess Yazu marry the Shōgun Nobusada.

'So sorry,' the Advisor said. 'Impossible.'

'Very possible and highly necessary to bond the Shōgunate to the Imperial Dynasty and bring further peace and tranquility to the land,' Ii had said. 'There are many historical precedents when Toranagas have agreed to marry Imperials.'

'So sorry.' The Advisor was effete, elaborately dressed and coiffured, his teeth blackened. 'As you well know Her Imperial Highness is already engaged to be married as soon as she reaches puberty. As you well know, too, the Shōgun Nobusada is also engaged to the daughter of a Kyōto noble.'

'So sorry, engagements of such illustrious persons are a matter of state policy, in Shōgunate control and always have been,' Ii said. He was small, portly and inflexible. 'Shōgun Nobusada's engagement, at his own request, has ceased.'

'Ah, so sorry, how sad. I heard it was a good match.'

'Shōgun Nobusada and Princess Yazu are the same age, twelve. Please advise the Emperor, the *tairō* wishes to inform him the Shōgun will be honored to accept her as wife. They can marry when she is fourteen or fifteen.'

'I will consult the Emperor but, so sorry, I am afraid your request will not be possible.'

'I certainly hope the Son of Heaven will be guided by Heaven on such an important decision. The gai-jin are at our gates, the Shōgunate and Dynasty must be strengthened.'

'So sorry, the Imperial Dynasty needs no strengthening. As to the

Bakufu, obedience to the wishes of the Emperor would surely improve the peace.'

Ii said harshly, 'The Treaties had to be signed. The barbarian fleets and weapons can humble us whatever we say publicly! We-are-defenseless! We were forced to sign!'

'So sorry, that is the problem and fault of the Bakufu and Shōgunate—Emperor Komei did not approve the Treaties and did not wish them signed.'

'Foreign policy, any temporal policy, such as the marriage I so humbly suggest, is the absolute province of the Shōgunate. The Emperor'—Ii chose his words carefully—'is preeminent in all other matters.'

' "Other matters"? A few centuries ago, the Emperor ruled as was custom for millennia.'

'So sorry, we do not live a few centuries ago.'

When Ii's proposal, considered by all those opposed to the Bakufu as an insult to the Dynasty, became known there was a general outcry. Within a few weeks shishi had assassinated him for his arrogance and the matter lapsed.

Until two years later when she was fourteen.

Though not yet a woman Imperial Princess Yazu was already an accomplished poetess, could read and write classical Chinese, knew all the court rituals necessary to her future, and was still enamored of her prince and he of her.

Anjo, needing to enhance the prestige of the Shōgunate, increasingly under threat, again approached the Prince Advisor who repeated what he had already said. Anjo repeated what Ii had already said but added, to the astonishment of his adversary, 'Thank you for your opinion but, so sorry, Imperial Chancellor Wakura does not agree.'

Wakura was in his forties, a man of high court rank though not of the nobility who, from the beginning, had assumed leadership of the xenophobic movement amongst middle-ranking nobles opposed to the Treaties. As Chancellor, he was one of the few who had Imperial access.

Within days Wakura sought an interview with the Princess. 'I am pleased to tell you that the Son of Heaven requests you agree to annul your engagement to Prince Sugawara and marry Shōgun Nobusada instead.'

Princess Yazu almost fainted. Within the Court an Imperial request was a command. 'There must be some mistake! The Son of Heaven

opposed this arrogant suggestion two years ago for obvious reasons.
You are opposed, so is everyone—I cannot believe the Godhead would
ask such a hideous thing.'

'So sorry, but it is not hideous and it is asked.'

'Even so, I refuse—I refuse!'

'You cannot, so sorry. May I explain th—'

'No, you may not! I refuse, I refuse, I refuse!'

The next day another interview was requested and refused, then
another and another. She was equally inflexible. 'No.'

'So sorry, Highness,' her Chief Matron said, very flustered. 'The
Imperial Chancellor again requests a moment to explain why this is
asked of you.'

'I will not see him. Tell him I wish to see *my brother*!'

'Oh, so sorry, Highness,' the Chief Matron said, appalled, 'please
excuse me but it is my duty to remind you the Son of Heaven has no
kith or kin once he has ascended.'

'I . . . of course, please excuse me, I know. I'm—I'm overwrought,
please excuse me.' Even within the Court only the Emperor's wife,
consorts, mother, children, his brothers and sisters, and two or three
Councillors, were allowed to look him in the face without permission.
Outside of these few intimates it was forbidden. HE was divine.

Like all Emperors before him, from the very moment Komei had
completed the rituals that mystically joined his spirit to that of the
recently deceased Emperor, his father, as his father had joined with his,
and he had with his in unbroken line back to Jinmu-Tenno, he had
ceased to be mortal and became a Deity, the Keeper of the Sacred
Symbols—the Orb and Sword and Mirror—the Son of Heaven.

'Please excuse me,' Yazu said humbly, appalled at her sacrilege.
'I'm sorry I . . . Please ask the Lord Chancellor to petition the Son of
Heaven to grant me a moment of his time.'

Now, through her tears, Yazu was remembering how, many days
later she was on her knees before the Emperor and his ever present
multitude of courtiers, heads bowed, she hardly recognizing him in his
formal swirling robes—the first time she had seen him for months. She
had begged and pleaded in a litany of weeping, using the necessary
Court language hardly understood by outsiders, until she was spent.
'Imperial Highness, I do not want to leave home, I do not want to go to
this foul place Yedo, the other side of the world, I beg leave to say we
are the same blood, we are not Yedo upstart warlords . . .' And had
wanted to screech, We are not descended from peasants who do not

speak properly, dress properly, eat properly, act properly, cannot read or write properly and stink of *daikon*—but she dared not. Instead she said, 'I beg you, leave me be.'

'First: please go and listen carefully and calmly as befits an Imperial Princess to what the Lord Chancellor Wakura has to say.'

'I will obey, Imperial Highness.'

'Second, I will not allow this against your will. Third, return on the tenth day, then we will talk again. Go now, Yazu-chan.' It was the first time in her life that her brother had called her by the diminutive.

So she had listened to Wakura.

'The reasons are complicated, Princess.'

'I am accustomed to complications, Chancellor.'

'Very well. In return for the Imperial betrothal, the Bakufu have agreed to the permanent expulsion of all gai-jin and to cancel the Treaties.'

'But Nori Anjo has said this is impossible.'

'True. At this time. But he has agreed at once to start modernizing the army and at once to build an invincible navy. In seven, eight, perhaps ten years he promises we will be strong enough to enforce our will.'

'Or in twenty or fifty or a hundred years! The Toranaga Shōguns are historic liars and not to be trusted. For centuries they have kept the Emperor confined and usurped his heritage. They are not to be trusted.'

'So sorry, now the Emperor is persuaded to trust them. In truth, Princess, we have no temporal power over them.'

'Then I would be a fool to give myself as hostage.'

'So sorry, but I was going to add that your marriage would lead to a healing between Emperor and Shōgunate, which is essential to the tranquility of the State. The Shōgunate would then listen to Imperial advice and obey Imperial wishes.'

'If they became filial. But how would my marriage bring that to pass?'

'Would not the Court, through you, be able to intervene, even to control this youthful Shōgun and his government?'

Her interest had quickened. '*Control?* On behalf of the Emperor?'

'Of course. How could this boy—compared with you, Highness, he a child—how could this boy have any secrets from you? Of course not. Surely the Exalted's hope is that you, his sister, would be his go-between. As wife of the Shōgun you would know everything, and a remarkable person such as yourself could soon have all the threads of Bakufu power within your hands, through this Shōgun. Since the third

Toranaga Shōgun there has never been a strong one. Would you not be perfectly placed to hold the real power?'

She had thought about that for a long time. 'Anjo and the Shōgunate aren't fools. They would have deduced that.'

'They do not know you, Highness. They believe you are only a reed to be twisted and shaped and used at their whim, just like the boy Nobusada, why else did they choose him? They want the marriage, yes, to enhance their prestige, certainly to bring Court and Shōgunate closer. Of course, you, a girl, would be their pliant puppet, to subvert Imperial will.'

'So sorry, you ask too much of a woman. I do not want to leave home, nor give up my Prince.'

'The Emperor asks that you do this.'

'Once again the Shōgunate is forcing him to barter, when they should just obey,' she had said bitterly.

'The Emperor asks that you assist to make them obey.'

'Please excuse me, I cannot.'

'Two years ago, the bad year,' Wakura continued in the same measured way, 'the year of famines, the year Ii signed the Treaties, certain Bakufu scholars were searching history for examples of deposed Emperors.'

Yazu gasped. 'They would never dare—not that!'

'The Shōgunate is the Shōgunate, they are all-powerful at the moment. Why shouldn't they consider removing an obstacle, any obstacle? Did he not, his *wa* destroyed, even consider abdicating in favor of his son, Prince Sachi?'

'Rumor,' she burst out, 'that cannot be true.'

'I believe it was, Imperial Princess,' he said gravely. 'And now, in truth, He asks, *please will you help him?*'

Beyond herself, she knew whatever she said, it would always return to the 'ask.' No way out. In the end she would have to comply or become a nun. Her mouth opened for the final refusal but it never happened. Something seemed to sever in her mind and, for the first time, she began thinking by a different process, no longer child but adult, and this gave her the answer. 'Very well,' she said, deciding to keep her own counsel. 'I will agree, providing I continue to live in Yedo as I have lived in the Imperial Palace . . .'

That conversation had brought her to this night's silence, broken only by her weeping.

Yazu sat up in the bed and wiped her tears away. Liars, she thought bitterly, they promised me, but even on that they cheated. A slight sound from Nobusada and he turned in his sleep. In the lamplight without which he could not sleep he looked more boyish than ever, more like a younger brother than a husband—so young, so very young. Kind, considerate, always listening to her, taking her advice, no secrets from her, everything that Wakura had foretold. But unsatisfying.

My darling Sugawara, now impossible—in this lifetime.

A shiver went through her. The window was open. She leaned on the lintel, hardly noticing the mansion below that was gutted and smoldering, other fires spotted here and there throughout the city, moonlight on the sea beyond—smell of burning on the wind, dawn lightening the eastern sky.

Her secret resolve had not changed from that day with Wakura: to spend this life wrecking the Shōgunate who had wrecked this lifetime, to rip away their power by any means, to return that power to the Godhead.

I will destroy as they destroyed me, she thought, far too wise now to even whisper it down a well. I begged not to come here, begged not to have to marry this boy, and though I like him, I loathe this hateful place, loathe these hateful people.

I want to go home! I will go home. That will make this life bearable. We will make this visit whatever Yoshi does or says, whatever anyone does or says. We will go home—and we-will-stay-there!

BOOK TWO

18

Monday, 13th October:

IN BRILLIANT MIDDAY SUNSHINE ten days later, Phillip Tyrer sat at a desk on the veranda of the Yedo Legation contentedly practicing Japanese calligraphy, brush and ink and water, surrounded by dozens of filled and discarded pages of rice paper, astonishingly inexpensive here compared with England. Sir William had sent him to Yedo to prepare for the first meeting with the Elders.

His brush stopped abruptly. Captain Settry Pallidar and ten equally immaculate dragoons were riding up the hill. As they came into the square the samurai there, many more than before, parted to allow them access. Slight, stiff bows acknowledged by a slight, stiff salute, clearly a newly established protocol. Redcoat sentries, many more than before, opened the iron gates and closed them after the troops had clattered into the high-walled forecourt.

"Hello, Settry," Tyrer called out, running down the main steps to greet him. "Good God, you're a sight for sore eyes, where the devil did you come from?"

"Yokohama, old boy, where else? Came by boat." As Pallidar dismounted, one of the gardeners, hoe in hand, was already hurrying in a half-bowing run to hold the bridle. When Pallidar saw him, his hand went to his holster. "Get away!".

"He's all right, Settry. He's Ukiya, one of our regulars and always very helpful. *Domo, Ukiya*," Tyrer said.

299

"Hai, Taira-sama, domo." Hiraga put on a vacant smile, his face half obscured by the coolie hat he wore, bowed and did not move.

"Get away," Pallidar repeated. "Sorry, Phillip, but I don't like any of the buggers near me, particularly with a bloody hoe in his hand. Grimes!"

Instantly the dragoon was there and he shoved Hiraga away roughly, taking the bridle. "Hop it, Jappo! Piss off!"

Hiraga obediently bobbed his head, kept the vacuous grin in place and moved away. But he stayed within easy listening distance, bottling his desire to avenge the insult instantly—with the razor-sharp hoe, the small stiletto hidden in his hat or with his iron-hard hands.

"Why on earth come by boat?" Tyrer was saying.

"To save time. Patrols report extra Jappo barricades all along the Tokaidō and traffic jams all the way from Hodogaya to Yedo, worse than Piccadilly Circus on the Queen's birthday, making everyone more nervous than usual. Have a dispatch from Sir William, he's ordering the Legation closed and you and your staff back—I'm your escort for 'face.' "

Tyrer stared at him. "But what about the meeting? I've been working like the devil to get everything ready."

"Don't know, old boy. Here."

Tyrer broke the seals on the official letter:

P. Tyrer, Esq., British Legation, Yedo: This is to inform you I have agreed with the Bakufu to postpone the meeting from October 20th to Monday, November 3rd. To save unnecessary expense in troops, you and your staff will return immediately with Captain Pallidar.

"Three cheers! Yokohama here I come."

"When do you want to leave?"

"Immediately, the Great White Father says, immediately it will be. Can't wait. How about after lunch? Come and sit down. What's new in Yokopoko?"

"Not much." As they strolled up to the veranda and easy chairs, Hiraga moved under the lee and continued hoeing.

Pallidar lit a cheroot. "Sir William, the General and Admiral had another bash at the local governor and Bakufu, swearing they would have his guts for garters if they didn't produce Canterbury's murderers

—and now Lun's, pretty bloody awful, what? All they got was the usual fawning and, Ah, so sorry, we're watching all roads, all paths to catch them, so sorry for delays and inconvenience! Oh, says Sir William, then you know who they are? Oh no, says the Jappos, but if we check all papers and watch everyone, perhaps we'll find them, we do everything possible, please to help by being more careful of revolutionaries. A lot of balls! They could catch them if they wanted. They're liars."

"Terrible about Lun. Ghastly! I went into shock. Sir William almost had a stroke. Still no sign of how the murderers got into our place at Kanagawa?"

"Nothing, any more than last time." Pallidar had noted the many pages filled with practice characters but did not comment. He loosened his collar. "The Corporal left in charge was demoted and he and the other two given fifty lashes for dereliction of duty. Stupid not to be sharp after the other attack. But why the monkey's head?"

Tyrer shuddered. "Sir William thinks it was because Lun jeered at their Delegation, called them 'monkeys' and it was their form of revenge."

Pallidar whistled. "That means at least one of them, unbeknownst to our people, secretly understands English—or at the very least pidgin."

"We came to the same conclusion." With an effort Tyrer threw off his fear. "To hell with that, I'm delighted to see you. What else is new?"

Pallidar was idly watching Hiraga. "The General believes there's more to the increased barricades and native troop movements than meets the eye. The traders say their Jappo contacts whisper that all roads out of Yedo are strangled and that the real reason's civil war's brewing. Damn nuisance not knowing. We should be moving around like the Treaty allows, should be finding out for ourselves—the General and Admiral agree for once we should operate here like in India, or anywhere else, send out patrols or a regiment or two to show the flag, by God, and contact some of the discontented kings to use them against the others. Do you have a beer?"

"Oh, of course, sorry. Chen!"

"Yes, Mass'r?"

"Beeru chop chop," Tyrer said, not at all sure his friend's militancy was the correct approach. The foreman of the gardeners came nearer and stood in the garden below and bowed deeply. To Pallidar's surprise Tyrer bowed back though his bow was slight. *Hai, Shikisha? Nan desu ka?* Yes, Shikisha, what do you want?

With even more astonishment Pallidar listened as the man asked something, Tyrer replied fluently and their conversation went back and forth. At length the man bowed and left. *"Hai, Taira-sama, domo."*

"My God, Phillip, what was all that about?"

"Eh? Oh, old Shikisha? It was just that he wanted to know if it was all right for the gardeners to prepare the garden in the back. Sir William wants fresh vegetables, cauliflower, onions, brussels sprouts, baking potatoes and . . . what's the matter?"

"You're really speaking Jappo then?"

Tyrer laughed. "Oh, no, not really, but I've been cooped up here for ten days with nothing to do so I've been swotting and trying to learn words and phrases. Actually, though Sir William read me the Riot Act about pulling my finger out, I'm enjoying it immensely. I get a tremendous charge out of being able to communicate." Fujiko's face leapt to the forefront of his mind, communicating with her, the hours spent with her—the last time ten days ago when he had returned to Yokohama for a day and the night. Hooray for Sir William, tonight or tomorrow I'll see her again, wonderful.

"Wonderful!" he said without thinking, beaming. "Oh," he added hastily, "oh, er, yes, I enjoy trying to speak and read and write it. Old Shikisha's given me lots of words, mostly work words, and Ukiya." He pointed to Hiraga who was gardening industriously, always within distance, not knowing that 'Ukiya' was an alias and just meant 'gardener.' "He's helping me with writing—jolly intelligent fellow for a Japanese."

During a writing lesson yesterday, he checked rumors he had heard, he asked him with signs and words Poncin had given him, to write the characters for 'war,' *senso,* and 'soon,' *jiki-ni.* Then he combined his crudely written attempts as 'War, in Nippon, soon. Please?'

He had seen a sudden change and surprise. *'Gai-jin toh nihon-jin ka?'* Foreigners and Japanese?

'Iyé, Ukiya. Nihon-jin toh nihon-jin.' No, Ukiya, Japanese and Japanese.

The man had laughed suddenly and Tyrer had seen how good-looking he was and how different from the other gardeners, wondering why he was seemingly so much more intelligent than the others, though, unlike the British equivalent worker, most Japanese could read and write. *'Nihon-jin tsuneni senso nihon-jin!* Japanese are always fighting Japanese,' Ukiya had said with another laugh, and Tyrer laughed with him, liking him even more.

Tyrer grinned at Pallidar. "Come on, what's new? Not business, for goodness' sake—Angelique."

Pallidar grunted. "Oh, are you interested in her?" he asked flatly, greatly savoring the joke inside himself.

"Not at all." Tyrer was equally flat, equally teasing, and they chuckled together.

"Tomorrow's the engagement party."

"Lucky Malcolm! Thank God I'm released, marvelous! I'd hate to miss that party. How is she?"

"As pretty as ever. We had her as guest of honor at the mess. She arrived looking like a goddess, escorted by the frog Minister, pompous ass, and that André Poncin chap—don't like either of them. It was—"

"André's rather nice actually—he's helping me a lot with my Japanese."

"Perhaps he is but I don't trust him. There's a long article in the *Times* about the coming European conflict: France and probably Russia against Germany. We'll be dragged in again."

"That's one war we can do without. You were saying?"

An immense grin. "It was a terrific evening. Had one dance with her. It was smashing. A polka—danced my heart out. Close up, her—well, without being disrespectful, I have to say her bosoms are like milk and honey and her perfume . . ." For a moment Pallidar was reliving that heady moment, the center of attention on the hastily constructed dance floor, gorgeous sparkling uniforms, she the only woman present, candles and oil lamps and the Guards Band playing lustily, dancing on and on, the perfect couple, everyone else consumed with jealousy. "Don't mind admitting I envy Struan."

"How is he?"

"Eh? Oh, Struan? Slightly better so the story goes. I haven't seen him but they say he's out of bed. I asked Angelique and she only said he's much better." Another beam. "The new doctor, Dr. Hoag, their family doctor, has taken over. I hear he's pretty damn good." Pallidar finished his beer. Another appeared from the ever attentive Chen, smiling and round and a pattern of Lim, equally a plant, and also a distant cousin of the Struan compradore. "Thanks." Pallidar sipped it appreciatively. "Damn good beer."

"It's local. Ukiya says Japanese've brewed it for years, the best from Nagasaki. I imagine they copied some Portuguese beer centuries ago. What else's new?"

Pallidar looked at Tyrer thoughtfully. "What do you make of Hoag's assassin story? The operation and mysterious girl?"

"Don't know what to think. I thought I recognized one of them, remember? The fellow was wounded in exactly the same place. Everything adds up. Pity you and Marlowe didn't catch him. Ironic if one of our side cured him, so that he can murder more of us." Tyrer dropped his voice, always servants nearby and soldiers. "Between you and me, old boy, Sir William's sending for more troops and ships from Hong Kong."

"I'd heard the same. It'll be war soon, or we'll have to intervene if they start fighting amongst themselves . . ."

Hiraga was listening carefully as he weeded and hoed, and though he missed many words he caught the marrow and their news confirmed his own, increasing his worries.

After setting the Utani mansion on fire, he and his friends had reached their nearby safe house without incident. Todo and others wanted to return to Kanagawa as soon as the barriers opened at dawn, and left. He, Joun, and Akimoto decided to remain in hiding at separate dwellings, to await an opportunity to attack the Legation.

That same dawn with eerie, unprecedented speed the Bakufu doubled the barriers on the Tokaidō, and extended their grasp on all four main trunk roads as well as all roads, paths and even tracks leading out of Yedo. With stepped-up surveillance, this effectively locked them in, along with all shishi and other antagonists throughout the capital.

Four days ago the mama-san Noriko sent a letter from Kanagawa, saying that with all the increased, hostile activity, this was her first opportunity, relating about Ori and Sumomo and the gai-jin doctor, and ended:

Still no sign of Todo and the other two shishi—they have vanished without trace. We know they passed the first barrier but nothing more. We fear they were betrayed and you are betrayed. Escape while you can. Ori is much stronger every day, his wound still clean. I have sent him to safety near Yokohama—the last place the Bakufu will expect him to go. Your Lady refuses to leave without your order—send it at once for I fear that my House is being watched. If we are attacked seek word from Raiko, the House of the Three Carp at Yokohama. News of Utani's assassination speeds throughout Nippon, and terror with it. Sonno-joi!

He began to write a reply but her messenger was very afraid. 'Getting here was terrible, Hiraga-san. Barrier guards are ordering everyone to strip completely—men, women, even children—in case messages are hidden in loincloths. It happened to me, Sire.'

'Then how did you escape?'

The messenger pointed to his bottom. 'I enclosed the letter in a small metal tube, Hiraga-san. I do not want to risk that again, some guards are very wise in the ways of smugglers. Please trust me with a spoken message.'

'Then give your mistress my thanks and hopes and tell Sumomo-san to report to Shinsaku at once.' Hiraga had used his father's private name that only she would know, and would therefore be sure the order to return home had come from him. He paid the man. 'Be careful.'

'Karma.'

Yes, karma, Hiraga thought, and began to concentrate again on the foreign words, glad that Ori was alive, enjoying the joke that indeed a gai-jin had saved Ori to kill more gai-jin, as he himself would kill these two. During their retreat, during the confusion of leaving I could do it, if not both then one of them, whoever is the first target. Eeee, all gods, if you exist, watch and guard Sumomo. Good that she resisted her parents, good she journeyed to my parents' home in Choshu, good she came to Kanagawa, more than good that she dares to join me in battle—she will be a worthy mother to my generations, if that is my karma. Therefore much better she goes home to safety. Better she is in Choshu far from danger . . .

His ears caught the word 'Shimonoseki.' The gai-jin officer was talking volubly and seemed quite excited, and though most of the words were lost, Hiraga gleaned that cannon had fired on some ships in the Straits, had killed some sailors, and that all gai-jin were furious because the Straits were essential to their shipping.

Yes, it is, Hiraga thought with grim amusement, which is exactly why you will never have *our* Straits. With the cannon we have even now we can close them and keep them closed to any barbarian fleet— and soon our Dutch built and designed armament factory will be casting sixty-pounders, completing three a month, with gun carriages!

The tide has turned in our favor at long last: Lord Ogama of Choshu, alone of all daimyo, obeys the Emperor's wish to attack and expel the gai-jin; correctly he and Choshu troops firmly hold the palace gates; Katsumata is gathering all shishi to ambush and destroy the Shōgun, unbelievably winkled out of his lair, on the way to Kyōto; and now our grip tightens on the gai-jin's citadel, Yokohama . . .

Abruptly all attention in the forecourt went to the barred and guarded gates as shouting erupted. Hiraga's stomach turned over. A samurai officer at the head of a patrol under the banners of the Bakufu, and personal insignia of Toranaga Yoshi, was loudly demanding entrance, the redcoated soldiers telling him, as loudly, to go away. Just behind him, bound and battered and cowed, was Joun—his shishi comrade.

A bugler sounded the alarm. All troops inside the walls rushed to action stations, some with half-buttoned uniforms and hatless but all with rifles, full magazines and bayonets, all gardeners were on their knees, heads into the earth—Hiraga, caught off guard, remained standing for a moment then hastily followed suit feeling totally naked. Warriors, massed in the square, began collecting ominously.

Shakily Tyrer got to his feet. "What the devil's up?"

With studied slowness Pallidar said, "I suppose we'd better find out." He got up leisurely, saw the Captain in charge of the Legation guards at the doorway queasily opening his holster. " 'Morning, I'm Captain Pallidar."

"Captain McGregor. Glad you're here, yes, very glad."

"Shall we?"

"Yes."

"How many troops do you have here?"

"Fifty."

"Good, more than enough. Phillip, nothing to worry about," Pallidar said to reassure him, outwardly calm but his adrenaline circulating strongly. "You're ranking official, perhaps you should ask him what he wants. We'll escort you."

"Yes, yes, very good." Striving to appear calm, Tyrer put on his top hat, straightened his frock coat and walked down the steps, all eyes on him. The dragoons watched only Pallidar, awaiting his orders. Five yards from the gate Tyrer stopped, the two officers just behind him. For the moment all that he could think of was that he wanted to urinate. In the silence he said haltingly, *"Ohayo, watashi wa Taira-san. Nan desu ka?"* Good morning, I am Mr. Tyrer, what you want please?

The officer, Uraga, the big bearlike man who was at the shishi ambush of Anjo outside the castle, glared at him, then bowed and held the bow. Tyrer bowed back but not quite as low—as André Poncin had advised—and said again, *"Good morning, what you want please?"*

The officer had noted the less than respectful bow and exploded in a rush of Japanese that totally swamped Tyrer, whose dismay mushroomed. So did Hiraga's, because the officer was asking for immediate permission to search the Legation and grounds, and to interview all Japanese there at once because it was probable shishi assassins and revolutionaries were amongst them: *"Like this one,"* he finished angrily, pointing at Joun.

Tyrer searched for the words. *"Wakarimasen. Dozo, hanashi wo suru noroku."* I don't understand, please to speak slowly.

"Wakarimasen ka?" You don't understand? the officer said with exasperation, then raised his voice, believing like most people when talking to a foreigner that loudness made his words clearer and more understandable, and repeated what he had said, the guttural language sounding even more threatening, and ended with, *"It won't take much time and please understand it is for your own protection!"*

"So sorry, not understand. Please you to speak English or Dutch?"

"No, of course not. It should be clear to you. I only want to come in for a little while. Please open the gates! It's for your protection! Look, your gates! Here, I will show you!" He stepped forward, grasped one of the bars and rattled the gates loudly, everyone inside shifted nervously, many safety catches came off and Pallidar ordered loudly, "Safety catches on! No firing without my order!"

"I don't know what the hell he's talking about," Tyrer said, a chill sweat running down his back. "Except it's obvious he wants us to open the gates."

"Well, we're not bloody doing that, not to that armed rabble! Tell him to go away, that this is British property."

"This. . . ." Tyrer thought a moment, then pointed at the flagstaff and Union Jack, *"this English place . . . no to enter. Please to go!"*

"Go? Are you mad. I have just explained, this is for your own protection. We have just caught this dog and we are sure another is here or hiding near here. OPEN THE GATES!"

"So sorry, not understand . . ." Helplessly Tyrer looked around as more Japanese words surrounded him. Then his eyes focused on Hiraga not far away. *"Ukiya, come here,"* he called out in Japanese. *"Ukiya!"*

Hiraga's heart almost stopped. Tyrer shouted at him again. With pretended terror, after a stumbling, grovelling run, Hiraga put his head in the dirt at Tyrer's feet, his rump towards the gate, his coolie hat covering most of him.

"What man say?" Tyrer asked.

With much feigned shaking, all senses razor-edged, Hiraga replied softly, *"He's a bad man . . . he wants to come in, to . . . to steal your guns."*

"Ah, yes, come in. Why?"

"He . . . he wants to search."

"No understand. What mean 'ser'ch'?"

"Search. He wants to look at your house, everywhere."

"Yes, understand come in. Why?"

"I told you, to search—"

"You, gardener," the officer shouted, and Hiraga jerked as anger flowed over him. For the first time in his life, out there at the center of attention, on his knees in front of a gai-jin, knowing that under his hat he wore a rough turban, if that was taken off it would reveal the shaven pate and topknot of a samurai, he was suddenly sick with fear.

"You, gardener," the man shouted again, rattling the gates, *"tell the fool I only want to search for assassins—shishi assassins!"*

Desperately Hiraga said softly, *"Taira-sama, the samurai wants to come in, to look at everyone. Tell him you are leaving, then he can come in."*

"No understand. Ukiya, go there!" Tyrer pointed at the gates. *"Say go away, nice go away!"*

"I cannot. I cannot," Hiraga whispered, trying to get his mind working and overcome his nausea.

"Phillip," Pallidar said, the sweat staining the back of his uniform. "What the devil's he trying to tell you?"

"I don't know."

Tension soared as the officer battered the gates again, once more demanding entrance, his men began to surge forward and grip the bars to assist him. Goaded into action, Pallidar went closer. Coldly he saluted. Equally coldly the man bowed. Then, slowly Pallidar said, "This is British property. You are ordered to leave in peace or accept the consequences."

The officer stared at him blankly then, again, with words and actions, told him to open the door—and quickly.

"Go away!" Without turning his back Pallidar called out, "Dragoons only! Prepare volley!"

Instantly the ten dragoons rushed forward in unison, formed two ranks just in front of the gates, in unison the front rank knelt, all ten safety catches came off, shells went into the breech and they aimed. In the sudden silence Pallidar slowly unbuckled his holster. "Go away!"

Abruptly the officer laughed and his laugh was taken up in the square. There were hundreds of samurai there and he knew thousands were nearby and tens of thousands within reach. But none of them had seen the carnage that a few stalwart, disciplined British soldiers could cause with their fast and easy-to-fire breech-loaders.

As quickly as the laughter arose, it died. Both sides waited for the inevitable first move. Frantic expectation swept everyone: This'll be to the death, *shikaru-beki*, Christ Almighty, *Namu Amida Butsu* . . .

Hiraga sneaked a quick look up at Tyrer, saw the blank helplessness and cursed, knowing that any second the officer must order the attack to save face amidst the rumbling animosity outside. Before Hiraga could stop himself, his self-survival mechanism decided to gamble and he heard himself whisper in English—never once before had he made any indication to Tyrer he could speak the language, "P'rease to trust—p'rease say words: *Shusho . . . doz*—"

Tyrer gaped. "Eh? Did you say 'trust'? Eh?"

Committed now, heart thundering and hoping that the two officers nearby were so concentrated on the outside they would not overhear him, Hiraga whispered haltingly, his pronunciation only fair, 'l's' impossible for him. "P'rease quiet. Danger! Pre'tend words yours. Say *Shusho, dozo shizuka ni . . .* say words!" Sick with fear he waited then, sensing that samurai tension outside was at the breaking point, hissed in English again, as an order: "Say-words-now! Now! *Shusho . . . dozo shizuka ni . . .* quick!"

Almost out of himself Tyrer obeyed. *"Shusho, dozo shizuka ni . . ."* parroting the words exactly and those following, not knowing what he was saying and endeavoring to put into perspective that this gardener could speak English and that this was not a dream. Within seconds he saw that the words were having an effect. The officer shouted for quiet. Tension was lessening in the square. Now the officer listened intently to him, occasionally saying, *"Hai, wakatta"*—Yes, I understand. Tyrer's courage flooded back and he concentrated on Hiraga and the Japanese. The words ended quickly with *"domo."*

At once the officer launched into a reply. Hiraga waited until it had ended. "Shake head," he whispered. "Say *Iyé, domo,* bow quick-quick, back house. Order me go too."

More controlled now, Tyrer firmly shook his head. *"Iyé, domo!"* he said importantly, and in awed silence, the center of the world, he stomped back towards the house, stopped in sudden confusion, turned and called out in English, "Ukiya! come along . . . oh, Christ," searched frantically for the Japanese word, found it and beckoned him: *"Ukiya, isogi!"*

With the same grovelling run Hiraga obeyed. At the top of the steps so that only Tyrer could hear, stooping abjectly, his back to all eyes he said, "P'rease order o'rr men, now safe. Inside house quick p'rease."

Obediently Tyrer called out, "Captain Pallidar, order the men to stand down, it's, er, it's quite safe now!"

Once inside the Legation, out of sight, Tyrer's ashen relief turned to anger. "Who are you, what the devil did I say, eh?"

"Exp'rain 'rater, Taira-san. Samurai want search, you, o'rr men, want take guns," Hiraga said, stumbling over the words, not yet recovered from his own fear. He stood erect now, looking him straight in the eyes, not as tall but as sweat-stained, knowing he was not yet out of the trap. "Captain very anger, want guns, taking guns, want searching for . . . for Bakufu enemy. You say him, 'No, Captain, *kinjiru*, forbidden searching. Today I and men 'reave here, then you search. Not now, *kinjiru*. We keep weapons when 'reave. *Kinjiru* forbidden stop us. Thank you. I now prepare go Yokohama.' "

"That's what I said?"

"Yes. P'rease now outside again, order me, gardeners back to work angri'ry. Word *hatarake*," Hiraga said queasily. "We speak 'rater, in secret, you me, yes?"

"Yes, but not alone, with an officer present."

"Then no speak, so sorry." Hiraga assumed his grovelling posture and backed out of the room, the exchange having taken only a few seconds, and once more dropped to his knees before Tyrer, rump towards the forecourt.

Unsettled, Tyrer stepped out into the light. He saw that everyone was still waiting. "Captain Pallidar, and, er, Captain McGregor, stand the men down, then please join me for a conference. *Hatarake! Ikimasho!* Get to work! Hurry up!" he shouted at the gardeners who obeyed at once. Thankfully Hiraga fled to the safety of the garden, muttering to the gardeners to cover him, officers and sergeants started shouting orders and the world began again.

Oblivious of everything, Tyrer stood on the veranda watching Hiraga, undecided, aghast that obviously he was a spy at the same time blessing him for saving them.

"You wanted us?" Pallidar said, breaking his reverie.

"Oh! Oh, yes . . . please follow me." He led them into his office, closed the door, and told them what he had said.

Both congratulated him. "Damned impressive, Phillip," Pallidar said. "For a moment I was sure we were going to have a showdown and Christ knows what would have happened then. Too many of the buggers really—eventually they would have overrun us. Eventually.

Of course the fleet would have revenged us but we would have been pushing up daisies and that's a pretty bloody boring thought."

"More than a bit boring," Captain McGregor muttered then glanced at Tyrer. "What do you want us to do now, sir?"

Tyrer hesitated, astonished that neither had heard Hiraga's English, but pleased with his newfound stature—it was the first time McGregor had called him 'sir.' "We'd best obey Sir William. Order everyone to pack up and . . . but without making it look like an ignominious retreat, can't let them have our guns—what cheek!—or let them think we're running away. We'll march out with, er, with bands and pomp."

"Perfect, after we've ceremoniously run down the flag."

"Fine! Well, I'd better . . . I'd better make sure all dispatches are boxed, etc."

Captain McGregor said, "May I suggest, sir . . . I really think you've earned a large glass of champagne—I do believe we've a few bottles left."

"Thank you." Tyrer beamed. "Perhaps we . . . let's Splice the Mainbrace." This was the traditional naval phrase for issuing a ration of rum to all hands. "Also we should all have tiffin first—show them we're not going to be hurried."

"I'll get it organized right away," McGregor said. "Damn clever to think of getting that gardener to help with the words, some of them sounded quite English. But why did they want to search the Legation?"

"To find . . . to search for Bakufu enemies."

Both men stared at him. "But there aren't any Jappos here, except gardeners, if that's what they meant."

Tyrer's heart surged as this at once pegged Ukiya but Pallidar was saying, "You're not really going to allow them to search our Legation, are you? Surely that would create a dangerous precedent."

At once his bonhomie vanished, for of course Pallidar was right. "Damn, didn't think of that at the time!"

McGregor broke the silence. "Perhaps . . . perhaps before we leave, sir, you could invite the samurai officer to walk around with us, inspect the Legation, nothing wrong with inviting him. He can inspect the gardeners at the same time or we could just send them off before we all leave and we lock our gates."

"A perfect compromise," Pallidar said happily.

Hiraga was weeding near a side door of the Legation, an open window nearby, dirty and sweaty, the late afternoon sun still hot. Baggage being piled in carts in the forecourt, horses groomed, some soldiers already drawn up in marching order. Sentries patrolled the circumference walls. Outside the walls massed samurai squatted under sunshades or lolled around, malevolently.

"Now!" It was Tyrer's voice from inside the room. Hiraga made sure he was not observed, ducked down into the undergrowth and quickly opened the door. Hastily, Tyrer led the way down the corridor into a room that overlooked the forecourt and bolted the door. Curtains over the closed windows filtered the sunlight. A desk and a few chairs, rolls of documents, files, and a revolver on the desk. Tyrer sat behind it and motioned to a chair. "Please sit down. Now tell me who you are."

"First, sek'ret I speak Ingerish, yes?" Hiraga remained standing, at his full height and somehow menacing.

"First tell me who you are and then I will decide."

"No, so sorry, Taira-san. I use to you, a'ready save men. Big use. True, *neh*?"

"Yes, true. Why should I keep this secret?"

"Safe me . . . you also."

"Why me?"

"Perhaps not wise have. . . . how you say, ah yes, sek'ret other gai-jin not know. I very he'rp you. He'rp 'rearn 'ranguage, he'rp about Nippon. I say you truth, you say me truth too, you he'rp me I he'rp you. What age p'rease?"

"I'm twenty-one."

Hiraga hid his surprise and smiled from under the brim of his hat, so hard to tell the age of gai-jin who all looked alike. As to the gun his enemy had placed on the table it was laughable. He could kill this fool with his hands before he could touch it. Such a simple kill, so tempting, and this a perfect place, so easy to escape from but, once outside, not so simple to escape the samurai. "Keep se'kret?"

"Who are you? Your name's not Ukiya, is it?"

"Promise se'kret?"

Tyrer took a deep breath, weighed the consequences and came up with disaster on all counts. "I agree." His heart skipped several beats as Hiraga slid the blade out of the hat brim, and cursed himself for being so reckless to put himself at so much risk. "In for a penny, in for a pound," he muttered.

"What?"

"Nothing." He watched Hiraga prick his finger, then hand him the knife.

"Now you p'rease." Tyrer hesitated, knowing what was coming, but having decided, he shrugged and obeyed. Solemnly Hiraga touched his finger to Tyrer's, mixing their blood. "I swear by gods keep sek'ret about you. You say same p'rease by Christian god, Taira-san."

"I swear by God to keep it secret about you as long as I can," Tyrer said gravely, wondering where the binding oath would take him. "Where did you learn English? A missionary school?"

"*Hai*, but I not Christian. Not safe to tell about our Choshu schools, Hiraga thought, or about Mr. Great Smell, the Dutchman, our Ingerish teacher who said he had been a priest before becoming a pirate. Truth or lie to this Taira matters not at all, he is gai-jin, a minor leader of our most powerful outside enemy and therefore to be used, distrusted, hated and killed at whim. "You he'rp es'kape?"

"Who are you? Where do you come from? Your name's not Ukiya."

Hiraga smiled and sat in one of the chairs. "Ukiya mean gardener, Taira-san. Fami'ry name Ikeda." He said the lie easily. "Nakama Ikeda, I who officer want. I twenty-two year."

"Why?"

"Because I and fami'ry, of Choshu, we fight Bakufu. Bakufu take power from Emperor an—"

"You mean the Shōgun?"

Hiraga shook his head. "Shōgun is Bakufu, head of Bakufu. He . . ." He thought a moment, then mimed a puppet on a string. "Unn'erstan'?"

"Puppet?"

"Yes, puppet."

Tyrer blinked. "The Shōgun's a puppet?"

Hiraga nodded, more confident now he was communicating, having to work hard to remember the words. "Shōgun Nobusada, boy, sixteen year, Bakufu puppet. He 'rive Yedo. Emperor 'rive Kyōto. Now Emperor no power. More two hundred year, Shōgun Toranaga take power. We fight take power from Shōgun and Bakufu, give back Emperor."

Tyrer's mind, aching with so much concentration—hard to understand this man's speech—instantly realized the far-reaching implications. "This boy Shōgun. How old please?"

"Sixteen year Shōgun Nobusada. Bakufu say what do," Hiraga said again, curbing his irritation, knowing he must be patient. "Emperor much power but no . . ." He searched for the word, could not find it so explained another way, "Emperor not 'rike daimyo. Daimyo has samurai, weapon, many. Emperor no samurai, no weapon. Can no make Bakufu obey. Bakufu have armies, Emperor not, *wakatta*?"

"*Hai, Nakama, wakatta.*" A thousand questions were jostling to be asked and Tyrer knew this man could be a well to be emptied, but it must be done cautiously and this was not the place. He saw the intense concentration on the man's face and wondered how much of what he said Nakama actually understood, reminding himself to speak slowly and as simply as possible. "How many of you fight against the Bakufu?"

"Many." Hiraga slapped at a vagrant mosquito.

"Hundreds, thousands? What sort of people, ordinary people, gardeners, workmen, merchants?"

Hiraga looked at him, bewildered. "They nothing. On'ry serve samurai. On'ry samurai fight. On'ry samurai hav weapon. *Kinjiru* other have weapons."

Tyrer blinked again. "You're samurai?"

More bewilderment. "Samurai fight. I say fight Bakufu, yes? Nakama samurai!" Hiraga took off his hat and pulled away the soiled, sweat-stained cloth that served as a turban to reveal his characteristic shaven pate and topknot. Now that Tyrer could see his face clearly, for the first time without the low-brimmed coolie hat and the first time he had really looked at him, he saw the same hard, slanting eyes of a two-sworder, and the vast difference in bone structure from villagers. "When *Shusho*, captain samurai, see me so, I dead."

Tyrer nodded, his mind amok.

"Easy me es'kape. P'rease, give so'rdier c'rothes."

Tyrer was finding it hard to keep the excitement, and dread, off his face, part of him desperate to flee, the other avaricious to have all this samurai's knowledge that could, no, would, be a major key to unlock the world of Nippon and his own future if handled correctly. Just as he was about to blurt out his agreement he remembered Sir William's previous admonition and, thankfully, took time to compose himself.

"Easy es'kape, yes?" Hiraga repeated impatiently.

"Not easy, possible. But risky. First I have to be convinced to be sure you are worth saving." Tyrer saw the sudden flash of anger—perhaps it was anger together with fear, he could not decide. Christ, samurai! I wish Sir William were here, I'm out of my depth. "Don't think I can r—"

"P'rease," Hiraga said as a supplicant, knowing that this was his only real chance to break out of the trap, but thinking, Hurry up and agree or I shall kill you and try to escape over the wall. "Nakama swear by gods he'rp Taira-san."

"You swear solemnly by your gods you will answer all my questions truthfully?"

"*Hai*," Hiraga said at once, astounded that Tyrer could be so naive

as to ask that question of an enemy or believe his affirmative answer—surely he cannot be that stupid? What god or gods? There are none.
"By gods I swear."

"Wait here. Bolt the door, only open it to me."

Tyrer put the revolver in his pocket, went and found Pallidar and McGregor and took them aside breathlessly. "I need some help. I've found out Ukiya is one of the men wanted by the samurai. It turns out he's a sort of dissident. I want to disguise him as a soldier and sneak him back with us."

Both officers stared at him. Then McGregor said, "Excuse me, sir, but do you think that's wise? I mean, the Bakufu are the legal government and if we get caught th—"

"We won't get caught. We just dress him up as a Redcoat and put him in the middle of soldiers. Eh, Settry?"

"Yes, we could do that, Phillip, but if he's spotted and we're stopped we'll be up the creek without a paddle."

"Do you have an alternative suggestion?" Tyrer said, a nervousness to his voice as his fear-excitement rose. "I want him smuggled out. Without his help we would probably all be dead and he will be extremely useful to us."

Uneasily the other two men looked at each other, then at Tyrer. "Sorry, it's too dangerous," Pallidar said.

"I-don't-think-so!" Tyrer snapped, head aching. "I want it done! It's a matter of extreme importance to Her Majesty's Government and that's the end to it!"

McGregor sighed. "Yes, sir, very well. Captain, what about mounting him?"

"As a dragoon? Ridiculous idea, a gardener won't be able to ride, for God's sake. Much better let him march, surround him with sold—"

"Fifty pounds against a brass farthing the bugger can't keep step, he'll be as obvious as a whore in a Bishop's underpants!"

Then Tyrer said, "What about if we put him in uniform, bandage his face and hands and carry him on a stretcher—pretend he's sick."

The officers looked at him, then beamed. "Good oh!"

"Even better," Pallidar said happily, "we pretend he has some foul disease, smallpox—measles—plague!" In unison they laughed.

The samurai officer and the guards they had agreed to allow within the now empty Legation followed Tyrer, McGregor and four dragoons throughout the house. Their search was meticulous, every room, every cupboard, even the attics. At length he was satisfied. In the hall were two stretchers, on each a soldier, both feverish, both bandaged, one partially, the other, Hiraga, completely—head, feet, and hands—outside his soaking uniform.

"Both very sick," Tyrer said in Japanese, Hiraga having given him the words. *"This soldier has spotted disease."*

The very mention of the words caused the samurai to blanche and move back a pace—outbreaks of smallpox were endemic in the cities but never so bad as in China where hundreds of thousands died. *"This . . . this must be reported,"* the officer muttered, he and his men covering their mouths as all believed infection and spread of the disease was caused by breathing befouled air near a sufferer.

Tyrer did not understand so he just shrugged. *"Man very sick. Not go near."*

"I am not going near him, you think I am mad?" The big man went on to the veranda. *"Listen,"* he said quietly to his men. *"Don't say a word about this to the others in the square or there may be a panic. Stinking foreign dogs. Meanwhile keep your eyes open, this Hiraga is here somewhere."*

They scoured the grounds and outhouses, the full complement of Legation staff and soldiers drawn up in the shade, waiting impatiently to begin the march down to the wharf and to the waiting boats. At last satisfied, the officer bowed sourly and stalked back through the gates, samurai massed outside, Joun still bound near the front ranks, the petrified gardeners kneeling in a row, all hats off and naked. As he approached they cowered deeper into the dirt.

"Get up!" he said angrily, disgusted that when he had ordered them to strip, not one of them had the shaven pate of a samurai, or any sword cuts, wounds or other sign of samurai status, so he had been forced to conclude his prey was still hiding inside, or had escaped. Now he was even more angry and stomped in front of Joun. "To disguise himself, the ronin Hiraga has shaved his head or allowed his hair to grow like one of those scum gardeners. Identify him!"

Joun was on his knees, broken, near death. He had been beaten and brought back to life and beaten and brought back again on Anjo's orders. "Identify this Hiraga!"

"He's . . . he's not, not there." The youth cried out as the officer's iron hard foot thudded into his most sensitive parts, then again, the gardeners shivering and terrified. "He's not . . . not there. . . ." Again the merciless blow. In desperate, helpless agony, beyond himself, Joun pointed at a youngish man who fell on his knees, screaming his innocence.

"Shut him up!" the officer shouted. "Take him before the judge, thence to prison and crucify the scum, take them all, they are guilty of hiding him, take them all!"

They were dragged away shrieking they were guiltless, the youngish man squealing that he had seen Hiraga earlier near the house and if they let him go he would show them but no one paid any attention and quickly his cries and all their cries were ended, brutally.

The officer wiped the sweat off his brow, satisfied that he had carried out his orders. He took a sip from a water bottle and spat to clean his mouth, then drank gratefully.

Eeee, he thought, and shivered. The spotted disease! A gai-jin disease brought from outside! Everything rotten comes from outside, gai-jin have got to be thrown out and kept out for all time. Angrily he watched the bands forming up, soldiers strutting, his mind on the shishi he sought.

Not possible that that gardener was a famous shishi, the Hiraga of the fight. Karma that I and my men arrived too late that day to see him and the others who escaped. Not karma, God was watching over me. If I had seen them I could not have pretended to accept the one Joun pointed out. Where is this Hiraga? He is hiding somewhere. Please God, help me.

Eeee, life is curious. I hate the gai-jin yet I believe in their Jesus God, though secretly, like my father and his father and his back to before Sekigahara. Yes, I believe in this Jesus God, the only thing of value from outside, and didn't the Jesuit Teacher Princes say Belief gives us added power and that when we had a problem to worry it as a dog worries a bone.

Hiraga is hiding somewhere. I have searched carefully. Therefore he has disguised himself. As what? A tree? What?

Inside the walls preparations for departure continued. The flag came down. Bands were playing now. Horsemen into their saddles. Stretchers into a tumbril. Gates opening, the mounted soldiers forming up, led by the gai-jin with the Japanese name, now passed and going down the hill and—

The bandages! The revelation burst in the officer's mind. There is no plague! Clever, he thought excitedly, but not clever enough! Now, do I confront them and bottle them up in one of the narrow streets? Or do I assign spies to follow him and peg him to lead me to others?

I peg him.

19

Tuesday, 14th October:

THE ENGAGEMENT PARTY WAS IN
full swing under the oil lamps that lit the crowded main hall of the
Club—the whole building taken over by Malcolm Struan and bedecked
for his party. All respectable members of the Settlement had been
invited and were present, all officers who could be spared from the fleet
and Army—and outside on the High Street patrols of both services were
ready to inhibit drunks and undesirables from Drunk Town.

Angelique had never looked more striking—crinoline, Bird of Paradise feather headdress and dazzling engagement ring. The dance was a
pulsating waltz by Johann Strauss the Younger, brand-new and just
arrived from Vienna by diplomatic pouch, which André Poncin was
playing with gusto on the piano, ably supported by a skeleton Marine
Band in full dress uniform for the occasion. Her partner was Settry
Pallidar—his selection to represent the Army had been greeted with a
roar of approval, and total jealousy.

Victoria Lunkchurch and Mabel Swann were also dancing, this time
partnered by Sir William and Norbert Greyforth, their dance cards
filled the moment the party was announced. For all their girth both
were good dancers, both wore crinolines though these could not compare with Angelique's in either richness or décolletage.

"Thee's a right rotten skinflint, Barnaby," Victoria hissed at her
husband. "Mabel and me're going to have new folderols if it costs thee
thy whole company, by God! And we wants titfers like hers, by God!"

"Wot?"

"Yes, wot! Titfers—hats!" Angelique's headdress had been the final coup de grace for both women. " 'Tis war, her against us'n." Even so their popularity overcame their jealousy, and they twirled with abandon.

"Lucky bloody bastard," Marlowe muttered, eyes only for his rival. His blue naval uniform jacket glittered with the added gold braid of an aide-de-camp, white silk trousers and stockings and black, silver-buckled shoes.

"Who?" Tyrer asked, passing by with another glass of champagne, flushed and excited with the evening and with his success in spiriting Nakama, the samurai, out of Yedo and, with Sir William's approval, into his house as a Japanese teacher. "Who's a bastard, Marlowe?"

"Get stuffed—as if you didn't know!" Marlowe grinned. "Listen, I'm the Navy's rep, I've got the next one and I'll show the bugger what's what or die in the attempt."

"Lucky devil! What is it?"

"Polka!"

"Oh, my word—did you arrange it?"

"Good God, no!" The polka, based on a Bohemian folk dance, was another recent addition to the dance floors of Europe and all the rage, though still considered risqué. "It's on the program! Didn't you notice?"

"No, never did, too much on my mind," Tyrer said happily, bursting to tell someone how clever he had been, and even more that tonight, as soon as he could, he was heading across the Bridge to Paradise and into the arms of his beloved—regretting that he was sworn to secrecy on both counts. "Dances like a dream, doesn't she?"

"Hey, young Tyrer . . ." It was Dmitri Syborodin, well oiled and sweating, a tankard of rum in his fist. "I asked the Bandmaster to throw in a cancan. Guy said I was the fifth to ask."

"My God, is he going to?" Tyrer asked, appalled. "I saw it performed once in Paris—you won't believe it, but the girls didn't wear any pantaloons at all."

"I believe it!" Dmitri guffawed. "But Angel Boobs has 'em on tonight, and not afraid to show 'em either, by God!"

"Now, look here . . ." Marlowe began hotly.

"Come on, John, he's just joking. Dmitri, you're impossible! Surely the Bandmaster wouldn't dare?"

"Not unless Malc gives him the nod."

They looked across the room. Malcolm Struan sat with Dr. Hoag,

Babcott, Seratard and several of the Ministers watching the dance floor, eyes only for Angelique as she dipped and swayed to the enchanting, daring modern music that exhilarated all of them. His hand rested on a heavy cane, the gold signet ring sparkling as his fingers moved to the beat, dressed in sleek silk evening clothes, winged collar, cream cravat and diamond pin, his fine leather boots from Paris.

"Pity he's still so disabled," Tyrer murmured, genuinely sorry, but blessing his own luck.

Struan and Angelique had arrived late. He walked with extreme difficulty, hunched over as much as he tried to remain upright, his weight on the two canes, Angelique radiantly on his arm. Dr. Hoag was with them, attentive and ever watchful. There were cheers for him and more for her and then, gratefully sitting, he had welcomed them, invited them all to partake of the feast that had been laid out on tables. "But first, my friends," he said, "please raise your glasses, a toast to the most beautiful girl in the world, Mademoiselle Angelique Richaud, my bride to be."

Cheers and more cheers. Liveried Chinese servants brought iced champagne by the case, Jamie McFay added a few words of joy and the party was on. Wines from Bordeaux and Burgundy, a special Chablis much favored in Asia, brandies, whiskies—all exclusive Struan imports—gin, beer from Hong Kong. Sides of Australian roasted beef, a few whole lambs, chicken pies, joints of cold salt pork, hams, Shanghai potatoes, baked and stuffed with roast salt pork slivers and butter, as well as puddings and chocolates, a new Swiss import. After supper had been cleared away and seven drunks removed, André Poncin took his place and the band began.

With great formality towards Malcolm, Sir William begged the first dance. Next was Seratard, then the other Ministers—except von Heimrich who was in bed with dysentery—the Admiral and the General, all of them and others taking turns with the other two women. After each dance Angelique would be surrounded by flushed and beaming faces, and then, fanning herself, she would make her way back to Malcolm's side, delightful to everyone yet completely attentive to him, every time refusing the dance, at length allowing herself to be persuaded by him: "But, Angelique, I love to watch you dancing, my darling, you dance so gracefully."

Now he was watching her, torn between happiness and frustration, frantic that he was hobbled.

'Don't fret, Malcolm,' Hoag had said this evening, wanting to calm

him, the simple act of dressing a nightmare of pain and awkwardness.
'This is the first time you've been up. It's only a month since the
accident, don't worr—'

'Tell me that once more and I'll spit blood.'

'It's not just the pain that's tearing you apart. It's the medication, or
lack of it, and today's mail. You got a letter from your mother, didn't
you?'

'Yes,' he had said in total misery, and sat on the edge of the bed, half
dressed. 'She . . . well, she's furious, never known her so angry. She's
totally opposed to my engagement, to my marriage . . . if I listened to
her, Angelique is the devil incarnate. She . . .' The words tumbled out
of him. 'She dismissed my letter, *dismissed* it and said, here read it:
*Have you gone mad? Your father's not dead six weeks, you're not yet
twenty-one, that woman's after your money and our company, she's the
daughter of an escaped bankrupt, the niece of another felon, and, God
help us, Catholic and French! Are you out of your mind? You say you
love her? Rubbish! You're bewitched. You will stop this nonsense. You-
will-stop-this-nonsense! She has bewitched you. Obviously you are in
no frame of mind to run Struan's! You are to return without that person
as soon as Dr. Hoag permits it.*'

'When I permit it. Malcolm, will you do as she says?'

'About Angelique, no. None of what she says is important, none of
it! Clearly she didn't read my letter, doesn't give a fig for me. What the
devil can I do?'

Hoag had shrugged. 'What you've already decided: you will be
engaged and in due time married. You are going to get better. You will
have lots of rest, lots of good soups and porridge and stay off the
sleeping draft and painkillers. For the next two weeks you will stay
here, then you will go back and face the'—he had smiled kindly—'the
future with confidence.'

'I'm very lucky to have you as a doctor.'

'I'm very lucky to have you as a friend.'

'Did you get a letter from her too?'

'Yes.' A dry laugh. 'I did, now that I think of it.'

'And?'

Hoag had rolled his eyes. 'Enough said?'

'Yes. Thanks.'

Now, watching her dancing, center of a universal admiration, and
lust, breasts in large part fashionably revealed, slender ankles enticing
eyes to seek further under the billowing hoops of apricot silk, he felt

himself hardening. Thank God for *that,* he thought, much of his rage evaporating, at least that's working, but, Christ, I know I won't be able to wait until Christmas. I won't.

It was nearing midnight now and she sipped champagne and hid behind her fan, fluttering it in a practiced manner, teasing those around her, then gave the glass away as though bestowing a gift, made her apologies and went gliding back to her chair that was beside Struan. Close by was an animated group of Seratard, Sir William, Hoag, other Ministers, and Poncin. "La, Monsieur André, your playing is superb. Isn't that so, Malcolm darling?"

"Yes, superb," Struan said, not feeling good at all, trying to cover it. Hoag glanced over at him.

In French she was saying, "André, where have you been hiding the last few days?" She looked over her fan at him. "If we were in Paris I would swear that you had given your heart to a new lady friend."

Poncin said lightly, "Just work, Mademoiselle."

Then, in English, "Ah, sad. Paris in the fall is especially wonderful, almost as breathtaking as spring. Oh, wait till I show it to you, Malcolm. We should spend a season there, no?" She was standing close to him, and she felt his arm go loosely around her waist, she rested her arm lightly on his shoulder and toyed with his long hair. The touch pleased her, his face handsome and clothes handsome and the ring he had given her this morning, a diamond with other diamonds surrounding it, delighting her. She glanced at it, twisting it, admiring it, wondering how much it was worth. "Ah, Malcolm, you will enjoy Paris, in season it's truly wonderful. Could we?"

"Why not, if you'd like to."

She sighed, her fingers discreetly caressing his neck, and said as though taken by a sudden thought, "Perhaps, do you think, *chéri,* do you think we could honeymoon there—we could dance the night away."

"Your dancing is a delight, Mademoiselle, in whatever city," Hoag said, sweating and uncomfortable in his overtight clothes. "Wish I could say the same for mine. May I sugg—"

"You don't dance at all, Doctor?"

"Years ago, when I was in India I did, but stopped when my wife died. She really enjoyed it so much that now I can't enjoy it at all. Marvelous party, Malcolm. May I suggest we call it a night?"

Angelique glanced up at him, her smile fading, noticed the caution on his face, looked at Malcolm and saw the exhaustion. How awful he's so sick, she thought. Damn!

"It's still early," Malcolm was saying bravely, longing to lie down, "isn't it, Angelique?"

"I must confess I really am tired too," she said at once. Her fan closed, she put it down, smiled at him, Poncin and the others, preparing to leave. "Perhaps we could slip out and let the party continue . . ."

They made their quiet apologies to those around them. Everyone else pretended not to notice them leave but in her wake was emptiness. Outside at the door she stopped a moment. "Oh la la, I forgot my fan. I'll catch you up, my darling."

She hurried back. Poncin intercepted her. "Mademoiselle," he said in French. "I believe this is yours."

"Ah, you're so kind." She accepted her fan, delighted that her stratagem had worked and that he was as observant as she had hoped. As he bent over her hand to kiss it she whispered in French, "I must see you tomorrow."

"Legation at noon, ask for Seratard, he won't be there."

She was brushing her hair in front of her mirror, still humming the last waltz she had danced. Which was the best? she asked herself. The best dance? That's easy, Marlowe and the polka, better than Pallidar and waltzes—you should waltz only with the love of your life, allowing the music to swim your head with adoration and longing, drifting you on the clouds, tingling and wanting as I am tonight, the best day of my life, engaged to a fine man and loved by him to distraction.

It should be the best day, but isn't.

Strange that I enjoyed this evening, and can act and think calmly, when already the day has passed. I'm overdue—probably with child of a rapist. This must be ended.

She was watching her reflection as though it were another person, the brushstrokes firm, titillating her scalp and head and taking away any cobwebs, astonished that she was still alive and outwardly the same after so much agony.

Curious. Every day after the first has seemed easier.

Why is that?

I don't know. Well, never mind. Tomorrow will solve the overdue though perhaps even now I shall begin in the night and there will have been no need for all the fear and crying and crying and more fear. Tens of thousands of women have been trapped like I am trapped and still have been made whole without hurt. Just a little drink and everything as before and no one the wiser. Except you and God! Except you and the doctor, or you and the midwife—or witch.

Enough for tonight, Angelique. Trust in God and the Blessed Mother. The Blessed Mother will help you, you are blameless. You are openly engaged to a marvelous man, somehow you will be married and live happily ever after. Tomorrow . . . tomorrow will begin the where and how.

Behind her Ah Soh was tidying the four-poster, picking up her stockings and underwear. The crinoline already hung on a rack with two others, and half a dozen new day dresses still wrapped in their sheaves of rice paper. Through the open window came the sound of laughter and drunken singing, and music from the Club that still showed no sign of abating.

She sighed, wanting to be back at the dance. The brush moved more vigorously.

"Miss'y wan thing, heya?"

"No. Want to sleep."

"Night, Miss'y."

Angelique bolted the door after her. The connecting door to Struan's suite was closed but unbolted. By custom, as soon as she had finished her toilet, she would knock, then go and kiss him good night, perhaps chat just a little and return again, leaving the door ajar in case he had a seizure in the night. These were infrequent now, though since he had stopped the night medicine a week ago, he was very restless, hardly sleeping, but never demanding.

Again she sat at her mirror and was pleased with what she saw. Her peignoir was silk and lacy and Parisian—a locally made copy of one she had brought with her: . . . *and you cannot believe the workmanship, Colette, or the speed of the Chinese tailor,* she had written this afternoon for tomorrow's mail ship.

Now I can get anything copied. Please send me some patterns, or cuttings from La Parisienne *or* L'Haute Couture *of the latest styles or anything wonderful—my Malcolm is so generous and so rich! He says I can order what I like!*

And my ring!!!! A diamond with fourteen smaller ones around it. I asked him how on earth he had got it and where in Yokohama and he just smiled. I really must be more careful and not ask silly questions. Colette, everything is so marvelous except I'm worried about his health. He improves so slowly and walks very badly. But his ardor increases, poor man, and I have to take care. . . . Must dress for the party now but I'll write more before the post. My everlasting love for the moment.

How lucky Colette is, her pregnancy a gift of God.

Stop! No more or the tears and terror will come back. Put the problem aside. You decided what to do, if it was or if it was not. It is, so the other plan—what else can you do?

An absent touch of perfume behind her ears and on her breasts, a slight adjustment of the lace. A gentle knock on his door. "Malcolm?"

"Come in—I'm alone."

Unexpectedly, he was not in bed but sitting in his armchair. Red silk dressing gown, eyes strange. At once some instinct put her on guard. She bolted the door as usual, and went over to him. "Not tired, my love?"

"No, and yes. You take my breath away." He held out his hands and she came closer, heart picking up a beat. His hands were trembling. He coaxed her nearer and kissed her hands and arms and breast. For a moment she did not resist, enjoyed his adoration, wanting him, and leaned down and kissed him and allowed him to fondle her. Then, the heat mounting too swiftly, she sank on her knees beside the chair, heart pounding like his, and half broke the embrace.

"We mustn't," she whispered breathlessly.

"I know but I must, I want you so much. . . ." His lips were throbbing and hot and seeking and, pushed onwards, hers responded. Now his hand was caressing her thigh, feeding more fire to her loins, and then the pleasing tormenter moved higher and higher still and she wanted more but drove herself from the ever-pressing brink and again pulled away, whispering, "No, *chéri.*" But this time he was surprisingly stronger, his other arm held her in an amorous vise, his voice and lips ever more persuasive, closer and closer but then, without thinking, he twisted too quickly and pain ripped through him. "Oh, Christ!"

"What is it? Are you all right?" she said, frightened.

"Yes, yes, I think so. Christ Almighty!" It took him a moment or two to recover, the surging pain lancing his ardor, that ache remaining, the other pain making it seem more strong. His hands still held on to her, still trembling but without strength. "Jesus, sorry . . ."

"No sorry, my darling." When, thankfully, she had recovered her own breath, she got up and poured some of the cold tea that he kept beside the bed, her loins restless and cramped and nervous, heart agitated, not wanting to stop either but must, a few more minutes and wouldn't have, must find a way to be safe, him safe, us safe—a voice shouting the litany at the forefront of her mind, 'a man never marries his mistress, nothing before marriage, everything permissible after,' pounded into her as soon as she could understand.

"Here," she murmured, giving him the cup.

She knelt and watched him, eyes closed, sweat staining his face and dressing gown. In a moment, most of her own unease and disquiet slid away. She put a hand on his knee and he covered it. "Being so . . . so close is bad for us, Malcolm," she said softly, liking him very much, loving him but not truly sure about love. "It's difficult for both of us, *chéri,* I want you too and love you too."

After a long time he said with difficulty, his voice low and hurting, "Yes, but—but you can help."

"But we can't, not before we're married, not yet, we can't, not now."

Abruptly his pain and frustration crested at having to sit all evening and endure other men dancing with her, lusting after her, while he could hardly walk where a month ago he knew he was a far better dancer than any one of them.

Why not now? he wanted to scream at her, what difference does a month or two make? For Christ's sake . . . but all right I'll accept that at marriage a proper girl must be virgin or she's a loose woman, I'll accept that a gentleman doesn't wrong her before marriage—I accept that! For the love of God, there are other ways.

"I know, we—we can't now," he said throatily, "but . . . Angelique, but please help me, please."

"But how?"

Once more words choked him: For Christ's sake, like girls in Houses do, kiss you and fondle you and finish you—do you think lovemaking is just spreading your legs and lying there like a piece of meat—the simple things these girls will do without fuss or shame and happy for you afterwards, 'Hey, you now all same good-ah, heya?'

But he knew he could never tell her. It was against all his upbringing. How do you explain to the lady you love when she's so young and artless or so selfish or just ignorant. Suddenly the truth became rancid. Something in him mutated, changed.

In a different voice he said, "You're quite right, Angelique, it's difficult for both of us. Sorry. Perhaps it would be best if you moved back to the French Legation until we leave for Hong Kong. Now that I'm getting better we must guard your reputation."

She stared at him, unnerved by the change. "But Malcolm, I am comfortable where I am, and near in case you need me."

"Oh yes, I need you." His mouth moved with the shadow of an ironic smile. "I'll ask Jamie to make the arrangements."

She hesitated, off balance, not sure how to proceed. "If that's what you want, *chéri.*"

"Yes, it's best. As you said, being so close is difficult for each of us. Good night, my love, I'm so glad you enjoyed your party."

A chill passed through her, but whether from outside or inside she did not know. She kissed him, ready to return his passion, but there was none. What had changed him? "Sleep beautifully, Malcolm, I love you." Still nothing.

Never mind, she thought, men are so moody and difficult. Smiling as though nothing were wrong she unbolted his door, blew him a tender kiss and went into her own room.

He watched their door. It was slightly ajar. As usual. But everything in their world was no longer as usual. The door and her nearness no longer tempted him. He was feeling different, somehow refashioned. He did not know why but he was very sad, very old, some instinct telling him that however much he loved her, however much he tried physically, she would never in their whole life together ever completely satisfy him.

Using his stick, he heaved himself to his feet and hobbled as quietly as he could to the bureau. In the top drawer was the small bottle of the medication that he had secreted away against nights when the idea of sleep became impossible. He swigged the last of it. Heavily, he shuffled to his bed. Gritting his teeth, he lay down and sighed as most of the pain left him. That he had consumed the last of the peace-giver did not bother him in the least. Chen, Ah Tok or any of the servants could supply him with more, whenever he wanted. After all, didn't Struan's supply part of China?

On her side of the door, Angelique was still leaning against the wall, in turmoil, unsure whether to go back or to leave well enough alone. She had heard him go to the bureau and the drawer open, but did not know why, heard the bed springs creak and his long-drawn-out sigh of relief.

It was just the pain and because we can't, not now, she thought, reassuring herself again, stifling a nervous yawn. And also because he had to sit still at the dance when he is as fine a dancer as I've ever had—wasn't it that that had first attracted me to him in Hong Kong from all the others?

Not wrong that he wants to make love—and not my fault he was hurt. Poor Malcolm, he's just overwrought. Tomorrow he will have forgotten all about it and everything will be fine—and it's better I move now, there's the other to consider. All *will* be well.

She slipped into bed and into easy sleep but her dreams were quickly peopled by strange monsters with twisted baby faces, shrieking with laughter and tugging at her, 'Mamma . . . Mamma,' writing on the sheets with her own blood that leaked from the tip of her finger she used as a pen, tracing and retracing those characters—the ones from the counterpane imprinted deeply in her mind that she had not yet had the courage to ask André or Tyrer about.

Something jerked her out of sleep. The nightscapes vanished. Uneasily awake, she glanced at the door, half expecting to see him there. But he was not and she heard, faintly, his heavy, regular breathing, so she settled back in her pillows and thought, It was the wind or a banging shutter.

Mon Dieu, I'm tired, but what a lovely time I had at the dance. And what a lovely ring he gave me.

Humming the polka and envious of John Marlowe's success, and quite sure he could have done as well, Phillip Tyrer half danced up to the door of the House of the Three Carp in the tiny, deserted little alleyway and knocked with a flourish. Here the Yoshiwara seemed to be slumbering, but not far away the houses and bars on Main Street were bubbling, the night young with the noise of men laughing and raucous singing, the occasional twang of samisen and laughter and pidgin mixed with it.

The door grille opened. "Mass'r, wat?"

"Please speak Japanese. I am Taira-san and I have an appointment."

"Ah, is that so?" the burly servant said. *"Taira-san, eh? I will inform the mama-san."* The grille closed.

As he waited Tyrer's fingers drummed on the old wood. Yesterday and last night he had had to spend all his time with Sir William, explaining about Nakama and the Legation, arranging a modus vivendi for his newfound teacher—guilty he had not revealed the vital truth that the man could speak some English. But he had sworn, and an Englishman's word was his bond.

Sir William had finally agreed 'Nakama' could be openly samurai—sons of samurai families had been attached to the French and British Legations for short periods in the past, just as Babcott had Japanese assistants. But Sir William had ordered he was not to wear or have swords within the Settlement fence. This same rule applied to all samurai, except Settlement guards under an officer on their rare, and prior-sanctioned patrols. Further that Nakama was not to dress ostentatiously or go anywhere near the Customs House or guard house, and to keep out of sight as much as possible, that if he was discovered and claimed by the Bakufu it would be his fault and he would be handed over to them.

Tyrer had sent for Nakama and explained what Sir William had agreed. By this time he was too tired for Fujiko. 'Now, Nakama, I need to send a message, and I want you to deliver it. Please write the characters for: "Please arrange . . ." '

' 'range, p'rease?'

'To fix or to make. "Please make an appointment for me tomorrow night with . . ." Leave a blank for the name.'

It had taken Hiraga a little time to understand exactly what was required of him and why. In desperation, Tyrer had found himself giving the name Fujiko and the House of the Three Carp. 'Ah, Three Carp?' Hiraga had said. '*So ka!* Give message mama-san, no mistake, arrange you see *musume* tomorrow, yes?'

'Yes, please.'

Nakama had shown him how to write the characters and Tyrer copied them, very pleased with himself, and signed the message carefully with the signature Hiraga had developed for him and now he was here at the gate.

"Come on, hurry up," he muttered—ready, willing and able.

In time the door grille opened again. By Raiko. *"Ah, good evening, Taira-san, you want us to speak Japanese, certainly,"* she said with a smile and a little bow, and followed with a flood of lilting Japanese which he did not catch, except the name of Fujiko several times, ended with, *"So sorry."*

"What? Oh, *You sorry? Why sorry, Raiko-san? Good evening, I have appointment Fujiko . . . with Fujiko."*

"Ah, so sorry," she repeated patiently, *"but Fujiko is not available this evening, and will not be free even for a short time. So sorry, but there is nothing I can do, she sends her regrets of course and, so sorry, but all my other ladies are equally occupied. Very sorry."*

Again he did not understand everything. The gist reached him. Crestfallen, Tyrer understood that Fujiko was not there, but not the reason. *"But letter, yesterday—my message man, Nakama, he bring, yes?"*

"Oh, yes! Nakama-san brought it and as I told him I thought every-

*thing would be perfect but, so sorry, it is not now possible to accommo-
date you. So sorry, Taira-san, thank you for remembering us. Good
night."*

"Wait," Tyrer shouted in English as the grille began to close, then
pleading, "you said she isn't there—here, yes? *Wait, please, Raiko-
san. Tomorrow—sorry— tomorrow, Fujiko, yes?"*

Sadly Raiko shook her head. *"Ah, so sorry, tomorrow is not possible
either, it really distresses me to have to say so. I do hope you do
understand, so sorry."*

Tyrer was aghast. *"No tomorrow? Next day, yes?"*

She hesitated, smiled, made another little bow: *"Perhaps, Taira-san,
perhaps, but, so sorry, I can promise nothing. Please ask Nakama-san
to come here during the day and I will tell him. You understand? Send
Nakama-san. Good night."*

Blankly Tyrer stared at the door, cursed bitterly, bunched his fists,
wanting to smash something. It took him a moment to recover from his
immense disappointment, then, despondently, he turned away.

Hiraga had been watching through a spy hole in the fence. When
Tyrer vanished around the corner he went back along the meandering
stone path through the garden, deep in thought. The garden was
deceptively spacious with small bungalows, always with verandas,
nestling in their own shrubbery.

But he avoided all of them, went into the shrubbery and knocked on
a panel of fence. It swung open noiselessly. The servant bowed and he
nodded and went along a path, heading for a similar dwelling. Most
Inns or Houses had secret exits and hiding places, or connections with
the one next door, and those that dared to cater to shishi paid special
attention to security—for their own safety. This part of the House of
the Three Carp was for very special guests with different cooking
facilities, maids but the same courtesans. On the veranda he kicked off
his *geta*—clogs—slid back the shoji. "What did he do?" Ori asked.

"Meekly walked away. Weird." Hiraga shook his head in wonder
and sat opposite him, nodded a brief acknowledgment of Fujiko's deep
bow. Yesterday, after delivering Tyrer's letter—with Raiko's amused
compliance he had hired Fujiko for tonight.

'May I ask why, Hiraga-san?' Raiko had said.

'Just to annoy Taira.'

'Eeee, I think he left his virginity here, with Ako. Then he tried
Mieko, then Fujiko. Fujiko made his eyes cross.'

He had laughed with Raiko, liking her, but when he saw Fujiko he was bewildered that his enemy found the girl attractive. She was ordinary, hair ordinary, everything about her ordinary except her eyes that were unfashionably large. Nonetheless he hid his opinion and had complimented Raiko that she had acquired such a flower, who looked sixteen though she was thirty-one and fifteen years a courtesan.

'Thank you, Hiraga-san.' Raiko had smiled. 'Yes, she's an asset, for some reason gai-jin like her. But please, don't forget the Taira is our client and that gai-jin are not like us. They tend to attach themselves to one lady only. Please encourage him, gai-jin are rich, and I hear he's an important official and may be here for some years.'

'*Sonno-joi.*'

'That is for you to arrange. You take their heads, but promise me not here, meanwhile I take their wealth.'

'You will permit Ori to stay?'

'Ori-san is a curious youth,' she had said hesitantly, 'very strong, very angry, very unsettled—a tinderbox. I'm afraid of him. I can hide him for a day or two but . . . but please, curb him while he's my guest? There is trouble enough in the Willow World without seeking it.'

'Yes. Have you any news of my cousin, Akimoto?'

'He's safe at Hodogaya, Teahouse of the First Moon.'

'Send for him.' Hiraga had slid a gold oban from his secret pocket. He noted how her eyes glinted. 'This will pay for any messenger, or expenses while Akimoto and Ori are here, and for Fujiko's services tomorrow of course.'

'Of course.' The coin, quite a generous payment, vanished into her sleeve. 'Ori-san may stay until I think it is time for him to move on, so sorry, then he leaves, you agree?'

'Yes.'

'Next, so sorry, shishi, but I must tell you it is very dangerous for you here. This is being sent to every barrier.' Raiko unfolded a woodcut poster, a portrait, about a foot square. Of him. The caption read: *The Bakufu offers Two Koku reward for the head of this murdering Choshu ronin who goes under many aliases, one of which is Hiraga.*

'*Baka!*' Hiraga said through his teeth. 'Does it look like me? How is it possible? I've never had a portrait painted.'

'Yes and no. Artists have long memories, Hiraga-san. One of the samurai at the fight perhaps? Unless someone closer to you is the betrayer. Bad also is that important people are seeking you. Anjo of course, but now Toranaga Yoshi.'

He was chilled, wondering if the courtesan Koiko was betrayed or was the betrayer. 'Why him?'

Raiko shrugged. 'He's the head of the snake, like it or not. *Sonno-joi,* Hiraga-san, but do not lead the Bakufu enemy here, I want my head on my shoulders.'

All night Hiraga had worried about the poster and what to do about it. He accepted a refill of saké from Fujiko. "This Taira amazes me, Ori."

"Why waste time on him? Kill him."

"Later, not now. Watching him and them, testing, trying to guess their reactions is like a game of chess where the rules keep changing constantly, it is fascinating—once you get over their stench."

"Tonight we should have done what I wanted to do: kill him and dump his body near the guard house and let them be blamed." Irritably Ori ran his right hand over the stubble already covering his shaven pate and face, his left shoulder bandaged and arm still in a sling. "Tomorrow I'll be shaved clean again and feel more like a samurai again—Raiko has a barber she can trust, but clean or not, Hiraga, this forced laziness is sending me mad."

"And your shoulder?"

"The wound's clean. It itches but it's a good itch." Ori lifted his arm about halfway. "Can't go further but I force it a little every day. It would be difficult to use in a fight. Karma. But that gai-jin Taira, if we had killed him, there would have been no risk to us or the House, you said he was so secretive he wouldn't have told anyone he was here."

"Yes, but he might have, and that's what I do not understand. They are unpredictable. They keep changing their minds, they say one thing and then do the exact opposite but not with calculation, not like we do, not like us."

"*Sonno-joi!* Killing him would have driven the gai-jin mad. We should do it the next time he comes here."

"Yes, we will, but later—he's too valuable for the moment. He will reveal their secrets, how to humble them, kill them by the hundreds or thousands—after we have used them to humble and break the Bakufu." Hiraga held out the cup again. Instantly Fujiko filled it, smiling at him. "I was even in the office of the Leader of all the Ing'erish, within five paces of him. I'm in the center of gai-jin authority! If only I could speak their language better." He was much too cautious to reveal to Ori the true extent of his knowledge, or how he had persuaded Tyrer to smuggle him out—let alone in front of this girl.

As she replenished their cups through the evening, smiling, totally attentive, never interrupting, she listened avidly though appearing not to, wanting to ask a hundred questions but much too well trained to do so. 'Just listen, smile and pretend to be dull-witted, only a toy,' mama-sans drilled into all of them, 'and soon they will tell you all you want to know without prompting. Listen and smile and watch and flatter and make them happy, only then are they generous. Never forget happy equals gold, which is your only purpose and only security.'

"In Yedo," Hiraga was saying, "this Taira was really quite brave, tonight a coward. Fujiko, what is he like in bed?"

Smiling, she hid her surprise that anyone could be so indelicate. "Like any young man, Hiraga-san."

"Of course, but what is he like? Is he in proportion—tall man, tall spear?"

"Ah, so sorry," she dropped her eyes, and made her voice humble, "but Ladies of the Willow World are directed never to discuss a client with another, whoever he is."

"Our rules apply to gai-jin? Eh?" Hiraga asked.

Ori chuckled. "You will get nothing out of her, or any of them, I tried. Raiko-san came and scolded me for asking! 'Gai-jin or not, the ancient Yoshiwara rule applies,' she said. 'We can talk generalizations, but any client particularly—*Baka-neh*!' She was really quite angry."

The two men laughed but Fujiko saw Hiraga's eyes were not laughing. Pretending not to notice, anxious to appease him and at the same time wondering how she would have to service him tonight, she said, "So sorry, Hiraga-san, but my experience is little, with young or old or in the middle. But most experienced ladies say size does not guarantee satisfaction for him or for her, but that young men are always the best and most satisfying clients."

She laughed to herself at the well-worn lie. I would like to tell you the truth for once: that you young men are the worst clients, the most demanding, the least satisfying. You're all hopelessly impatient, you've plenty of vigor, require many entries, you've puddles of essence but little contentment afterwards—and rarely generous. Worst of all, however much a girl tries not to, she can become enamored with one particular young man and that leads to even more misery, disaster and most times suicide. Old is twenty times better.

"Some youths," she said, answering without answering, "are incredibly shy, however well endowed."

"Interesting. Ori, I still can't believe this Taira just meekly turned away."

Ori shrugged. "Meek or not, he should be dead tonight and I would sleep better. What else could he do?"

"Everything. He should have kicked the door down—an appointment is an appointment and Raiko not having a substitute ready was a further insult."

"The door and fence are too strong, even for us."

"Then he should have gone into the main street and got five or ten or twenty of his people and brought them back and smashed the fence down—he is an important official, the officers and all soldiers obeyed him at the Legation. That would certainly have made Raiko kowtow for a year or more and guaranteed he would have the service he wanted when he wanted—we might have had to run off too. That is what I would have done if I were an important official like him." Hiraga smiled and Fujiko suppressed a shiver. "It's a matter of face. Yet they understand face very well. They would have defended their stupid Legation to the last man, then the fleet would have laid waste Yedo."

"Isn't that what we want?"

"Yes." Hiraga laughed. "But not when you are weaponless and grovelling like a gardener—I really felt naked!" Again a refill. Hiraga looked at her. Ordinarily, even though the girl of the evening was not particularly attractive, his normal virility and the saké would arouse him. Tonight was different. This was the gai-jin Yoshiwara, she had bedded them so was tainted. Perhaps Ori would like her, he thought, and smiled back at her for face. "Order some food, eh, Fujiko? The best the House can provide."

"At once, Hiraga-san." She hurried away.

"Listen, Ori," Hiraga whispered so no one could overhear. "There's great danger here." He took out the folded poster.

Ori was shocked. "Two koku? That will tempt anyone. It could be you, not exactly, but a Barrier guard might stop you."

"Raiko said the same."

Ori looked up at him. "Joun was an artist, a good one."

"I'd thought of that, and I've been wondering how they caught him and broke him. He knows many shishi secrets, knows Katsumata's planning to intercept the Shōgun."

"Disgusting, allowing himself to be caught alive. It is obvious we have been infiltrated." Ori handed the picture back. "Two koku would tempt anyone, even the most zealous mama-san."

"I thought of that too."

"Grow a beard, Hiraga, or mustache, that would help."

"Yes, that would help." Hiraga was glad that Ori was back in his head again, his counsel always valuable. "A strange feeling to know that this is out there."

Ori broke the silence. "In a day or two, soon as I can—I am stronger

every day—I will go to Kyōto and join Katsumata to warn him about
Joun. He should be warned."

"Yes, good idea, very good."

"What about you?"

"I am safe amongst the gai-jin, safer there than anywhere—so long
as I'm not betrayed. Akimoto's at Hodogaya, I have sent for him, then
we can decide."

"Good. You will be safer to try for Kyōto at once, before these
pictures are sent throughout the Tokaidō."

"No. Taira is too good an opportunity to miss. I will cache swords
there in case."

"Get a revolver, less obvious." Ori put his right hand inside his
yukata, moving it away from his shoulder, and scratched the bandage.

Hiraga was shocked to see the little gold cross on the thin gold chain
around his neck. "Why wear that?"

Ori shrugged. "It amuses me."

"Get rid of it, Ori—it ties you to the Tokaidō killing, Shorin and her.
The cross is an unnecessary danger."

"Many samurai are Christian."

"Yes, but she could identify that cross. It is insane to take such a
risk. If you want to wear one get another."

After a pause Ori said, "This one amuses me."

Hiraga saw the inflexibility, cursed him inwardly but decided it was
his duty to protect the shishi movement, protect *sonno-joi* and now was
the time. "Take-it-off!"

The blood soared into Ori's face. His half smile did not change but
he knew he was called. His choice was simple: refuse and die, or obey.

A mosquito buzzed around his face. He disregarded it, not wanting
to make a sudden movement. Slowly his right hand pulled the chain
away from his neck, breaking it. The cross and chain vanished into his
sleeve pocket. Then he placed both hands on the tatami and bowed low.
"You are right, Hiraga-san, it was an unnecessary danger. Please
accept my apologies."

Silently Hiraga bowed back. Only then did he relax and Ori
straighten. Both men knew their relationship had changed. Permanently. They had not become enemies, just were no longer friends,
allies always, but never friends again. Ever. As Ori picked up his cup
and raised it, toasting him, he was pleased to find his inner rage so
controlled that his fingers did not shake. "Thank you."

Hiraga drank with him, leaned over and poured for both of them.
"Now Sumomo. Please tell me about her."

"I remember almost nothing." Ori opened his fan and wafted the mosquito away. "The mama-san Noriko told me Sumomo arrived like a spirit with me on a stretcher, told her almost nothing except that a gai-jin doctor had cut me open and sewed me up again. She paid half Shorin's debts and persuaded her to hide me. During the waiting Sumomo spoke hardly at all after asking about Shorin, what had happened to him. When the messenger returned from Yedo with your message she left for Shimonoseki at once. The only news she gave was that Satsuma is mobilizing for war, and your Choshu batteries had again fired on the gai-jin ships in the Straits, turning them back."

"Good. You told her everything about Shorin?"

"Yes. She asked me seriously and then, after I told her she said she would be revenged."

"Did she leave any message or letter with the mama-san?"

Ori shrugged. "She left nothing with me."

Perhaps Noriko has one, Hiraga thought. Never mind, that can wait. "She looked well?"

"Yes. I owe her my life."

"Yes. One day she will want to collect that debt."

"Repaying her I repay you and honor *sonno-joi*."

They sat in silence, each wondering what the other was thinking, really thinking.

Hiraga smiled suddenly. "Tonight in the Settlement there was a big celebration, vile music and much drinking, it's their custom when a man agrees to marry." He quaffed his cup. "This saké is good. One of the merchants—the gai-jin you cut at the Tokaidō—is going to marry that woman."

Ori was dumbfounded. "The woman of the cross? She's here?"

"I saw her tonight."

"So!" Ori muttered as though to himself, then finished his saké and poured for both of them. A little wine spilled unnoticed on the tray. "She's to be married? When?"

Hiraga shrugged. "I don't know. I saw him and her together tonight, he walks with two canes like a cripple—your blow wounded him severely, Ori."

"Good. And the . . . the woman, what was she like?"

Hiraga laughed. "Outlandish, Ori, total buffoonery." He described her crinoline. And her hairstyle. And got up and parodied her gait. Soon both men were almost rolling on the tatamis with laughter. ". . . breasts out to here, depraved! Just before I came here I peered in a window. Men clutched her openly, she and a man clutched each other, twirling in a sort of dance in front of everyone to these horrid-sounding instruments, you couldn't call it music! kicking up her skirts so you could see halfway up, and frilly white pants to the ankles. I would never have believed it if I hadn't seen it for myself but she went from man to man like a one-sen whore and they all cheered her. The fool who's going to marry her, he just sat in a chair and beamed, imagine that!" He poured but the bottle was empty. "Saké!"

At once the door opened, a maid came in on her knees with two new flasks, poured and scuttled away. He belched, the saké getting to him. "They acted like beasts. Without their cannon and ships they are beyond contempt."

Ori glanced out of the window, towards the sea.

"What is it?" Hiraga was suddenly on guard. "Danger?"

"No, no, it was nothing."

Hiraga frowned uneasily, remembering how sensitive Ori was to outside emanations. "Do you have swords here?"

"Yes. Raiko guards them for me."

"I hate not having swords in my belt."

"Yes."

For a time they drank in silence and then the food arrived, small dishes of broiled fish, rice, sushi and sashimi, and a Portuguese dish called tempura—fish and vegetables dipped in rice flour and deep fried. Before the Portuguese arrived about A.D. 1550, the first Europeans to appear off their shores, Japanese did not know the frying technique.

When they were replete, they sent for Raiko and complimented her, refused the entertainment services of a geisha, so she bowed and left them. "You can go, Fujiko. Tomorrow, I will be here sometime after sunset."

"Yes, Hiraga-san." Fujiko bowed very low, content to be dismissed without further work as Raiko had already told her her fee was generous. "Thank you for honoring me."

"Of course, nothing that you hear or see will ever be mentioned to the Taira or any gai-jin or anyone."

Her head jerked up in shock. "Of course not, Hiraga-sama." When she saw his eyes her heart lurched. "Of course not," she repeated, her voice barely audible, bowed her forehead to the tatami and, deeply frightened, left them.

"Ori, we take a risk with that woman listening."

"With any of them. But she would never dare, nor the others." Ori used his fan against the night insects. "Before we leave we will agree on a price with Raiko to see Fujiko is placed in a low-grade house where she will be too busy to make mischief and be well away from all gai-jin, and Bakufu."

"Good. That is good advice. It may be expensive, Raiko said Fujiko is extremely popular with gai-jin for some reason."

"Fujiko?"

"Yes. Strange, *neh*? Raiko says their ways are so different from ours." Hiraga saw Ori's smile twist. "What?"

"Nothing. We can talk more tomorrow."

Hiraga nodded, drained the last cup, then got up, stripped off the starched yukata that all Houses and Inns habitually supplied their clients, and dressed again in the most ordinary kimono of a villager, rough turban and coolie straw hat, then shouldered the empty delivery basket.

"Are you safe like that?"

"Yes, so long as I do not have to uncover, and I've these." Hiraga showed the two passes Tyrer had given him, one for Japanese, one for English. "Guards on the gate and at the bridge are alert, and soldiers patrol the Settlement at night. There's no curfew but Taira warned me to be careful."

Thoughtfully Ori handed the passes back.

He tucked them in his sleeve. "Good night, Ori."

"Yes, good night, Hiraga-san." Ori looked up at him strangely. "I would like to know where the woman lives."

Hiraga's eyes narrowed. "So?"

"Yes. I would like to know where. Exactly."

"I can find out, probably. And then?"

The silence concentrated. Ori was thinking, I'm not sure tonight, I wish I was, but every time I let my mind free I remember *that night* and my never-ending surge within her. If I had killed her then that would have ended it, but knowing she's alive I'm haunted. She haunts me. It's stupid, stupid but I'm bewitched. She's evil, disgusting, I know it, but still I'm bewitched and I'm sure that as long as she's alive she will always haunt me.

"And then?" Hiraga said again.

Ori had kept all his thoughts off his face. He looked back at him levelly and shrugged.

20

Wednesday, 15th October:

ANDRÉ PONCIN BLINKED. *"YOU'RE pregnant?"*

"Yes," she said softly. "You see th—"

"That's wonderful, that makes everything perfect!" he burst out, his shock turning into a huge beam, because Struan, the British gentleman, had wronged an innocent lady, and now could not avoid an early marriage and remain a gentleman. "Madam, may I congratulate y—"

"Hush, André, no you can't and not so loud, walls have ears, particularly Legations, no?" she whispered, feeling out of herself, astounded that her voice remained so calm and she felt so calm and could tell him so easily. "You see, unfortunately, the father is not Monsieur Struan."

His smile vanished and then came back. "You're joking of course, but why the jo—"

"Just listen, please." Angelique moved her chair closer to him. "I was raped in Kanagawa . . ."

He stared at her, dumbfounded, as she told him what she thought had happened to her, what she had decided to do, how she had hidden the horror ever since.

"My God, poor Angelique, poor thing, how terrible for you," was all he managed to mutter, deeply shocked, while another piece of the puzzle fell into place. Sir William, Seratard and Struan had decided to

339

restrict news about Dr. Hoag's operation at Kanagawa to as few people as possible—keeping it particularly from Angelique, both doctors advising that to be medically wise. 'Why agitate her unnecessarily? She's upset enough about the Tokaidō affair.'

No reason yet to tell her, André thought uneasily, the irony rocking him.

He took her hand and caressed it, forcing himself to push away his own worries and concentrate on her. Seeing her there, sitting beside him in his office, so serene and demure, clear eyes and picture of innocence, only a few hours ago the belle of the best ball Yokohama had ever had, gave her story an air of total unreality. "This really happened? Really?"

She raised her hand as though taking an oath. "I swear it, by God." Now her hands were folded in her lap. Pale yellow hooped day dress, tiny orange bonnet and umbrella.

Bewildered, he shook his head. "Seems impossible."

Throughout his adult years he had been part of many such man-woman tragedies: put into some by his superiors, stumbling into a few, precipitating many, and using most if not all for the betterment of his Cause: for France—the Revolution, Liberté Fraternité Egalité, or Emperor Louis Napoleon, whoever or whatever the current vogue—and for himself, first.

Why not? he thought. What has France done for me, what will she do for me? Nothing. But this Angelique, she's either going to fall apart any moment—her serenity's unreal—or she's like some women I've known, born bad who twist truth brilliantly for their own purposes, or like some who have been pushed over the brink by terror to become a calculating, cold-blooded woman beyond her years. "What?"

"I need to remove the problem, André."

"You mean abortion? You're Catholic!"

"So are you. This is a matter between me and God."

"What about confession? You have to be confessed. This Sunday you must go an—"

"That is a matter between me and a priest, and then God. The problem must be removed first."

"That is against God's law and man's law."

"And has been done throughout the centuries since before the Flood." An edge crept into her voice. "Do you confess everything? Adultery is also against 'God's law,' isn't it? Killing's against all law too. Isn't it?"

"Who says I've killed anyone?"

"No one, but it's more than likely you have, or caused deaths. These are violent times. André, I *need* your help."

"You risk eternal damnation."

Yes, I've agonized over that with lakes of tears, she thought grimly, keeping her eyes innocent, hating him and that she had to trust him.

This morning she had awakened early and lay there thinking, reconsidering her plan, and came to realize of a sudden that she should hate all men. Men cause all our problems, fathers, husbands, brothers, sons, and priests—priests the worst of all men, lots of them notorious fornicators and deviates, liars, who use the Church for their own rotten purposes, though it is true a few are saints. Priests and other men control our world and ruin it for women. I hate them all—except Malcolm. I don't hate him, not yet. I don't know if I truly love him, I don't know what love is, but I like him more than any man I've ever known, and I understand him.

As to the rest, thank God my eyes are open at last! She was looking at André, trustful and begging. Damn you that I have to put my life in thrall to you, but thank God I see through you now. Malcolm and Jamie are right, all you want is to dominate Struan's or cause its downfall. Damnation that I have to trust any man. If only I were in Paris, or even Hong Kong, there are dozens of women I could discreetly ask for the necessary help but none here. Those two hags? Impossible! They clearly hate me and are enemy.

She allowed a few tears to appear. "Please help me."

He sighed. "I will talk to Babcott this morn—"

"Are you mad? Of course we dare not involve him. Or Hoag. No, André, I've thought it all out very carefully. Neither of them. We must find someone else. A madam."

He gaped at her again, stunned by the calm voice and logic. "You mean a mama-san?" he stuttered.

"What's that?"

"Oh . . . that's the woman, the Japanese woman who . . . who runs the local whorehouses, contracts for the services of the girls, arranges prices, allocates girls. And so on."

Her brow creased. "I hadn't thought of one of them. I did hear there's a House down the road."

"My God! You mean Naughty Nellie's . . . in Drunk Town? I wouldn't go there for a thousand louis."

"But isn't the house run by Mrs. Fortheringill's sister? The famous Mrs. Fortheringill of Hong Kong?"

"How'd you know about her?"

"Oh, my God, André, am I a foolish and bigoted Englishwoman?" she said testily. "Every European female in Hong Kong knows about Mrs. Fortheringill's Establishment for Young Ladies, though they pretend not to and never talk openly about it, or that all but the most stupid know their men visit Chinese Houses, or have Oriental mistresses. Such hypocrisy. Even you would be astonished to know what ladies discuss in the privacy of their boudoirs, or when there are no men around. In Hong Kong I heard her sister opened the House here."

"It's not the same, Angelique, it caters to seamen, drunks, remittance men—the dregs. Naughty Nellie isn't her sister, she just claims to be, probably just pays some squeeze for the use of the name."

"Oh! Then where do you go? For 'entertainment'?"

"The Yoshiwara," he said, and explained, astounded with this conversation and that he, too, could be so open.

"Do you have a special place, a special House? One where you're on good terms with the mama-san?"

"Yes."

"Excellent. Go to your mama-san tonight and get whatever drink they use."

"What?"

"My God, André, be sensible, be serious! This is serious and unless we can solve the problem I will never be chatelaine of the Noble House, so will never be able to assist . . . certain interests." She saw that this hit the mark and was further pleased with herself. "Go there tonight and ask her for it. Don't ask your girl or a girl for it, they probably won't know. Ask the *patronne,* the mama-san. You can say that 'the girl' is overdue."

"I don't know if they have such a medicine."

She smiled benignly. "Don't be silly, André, of course they have, they must have." Her right hand began straightening the fingers of her left-hand glove. "Once this problem is out of the way, everything will be wonderful, we'll be married at Christmas. By the way I decided it would be better to move out of the Struan suite until we're married— now that Monsieur Struan is gaining strength every day. I'll be moving back to the Legation this afternoon."

"Is that wise? Better to stay close to him."

"Normally, yes. Except there are proprieties, but more important, I'm sure the medicine will not make me feel pleasant for a day or two. As soon as that's over I'll decide if I should go back. I know I can rely on you, my friend." She stood up. "The same time tomorrow?"

"If I've nothing I'll send word to let you know."

"No. Better we meet here at noon. I know I can rely on you." She smiled her nicest smile.

He tingled, both because of the smile and because, whatever happened now, she was chained to him forever. "Those characters," he said, "the ones written on the sheet, do you remember them?"

"Yes," she said, surprised by the non sequitur. "Why?"

"Could you draw them for me? I might recognize them, they might have a meaning."

"They were on the counterpane, not the sheet. In—in his blood." She took a deep breath and reached over and took the pen and dipped it in the ink. "One thing I forgot to tell you. When I woke up, the little cross I'd worn since a child had vanished. I searched everywhere but it had gone."

"He stole it?"

"I presume so. But nothing else. There was some jewelry but that was not touched. The pieces were not too valuable but worth more than the cross."

The thought of her lying there in that bed, inert, the nightdress slit from neck to hem, the rapist's hand pulling away the chain, moonlight glinting on the cross, before or after, spreading her, rapidly became real and erotic and throbbed him. His eyes flowed over her as she bent over the desk, oblivious of his lust.

"There," she said, and handed him the paper.

He stared at it, the sunlight glinting on the gold signet ring he always wore. The characters did not relate in any way to anything. "Sorry, they mean nothing, don't even look Chinese—Chinese or Japanese the writing's the same." At a sudden thought he inverted the paper and gasped. "Tokaidō—that's what they mean!" The color went out of her face. "You just copied them upside down. Tokaidō ties everything together! He wanted you to know, wanted the whole Settlement to know and we would have, if you'd told anyone what had happened! But why?"

Shakily her fingers went to her temples. "I—I don't know. Perhaps . . . I don't know. He—he must be dead by now, Monsieur Struan shot him. Surely he must be dead."

André hesitated uneasily, weighing the reasons for and against. "Since we share so many secrets, and clearly you know how to keep one, sorry, but now another is necessary." He told her about Hoag and the operation. "It wasn't Hoag's fault, he had no way of knowing. It's ironic, both doctors advised against telling you, to save you anguish."

"It's because of Babcott and his opiate that I am where I am," she muttered, her voice chilling him. "The man's alive then?"

"We don't know. Hoag didn't give him much of a chance. Why would that devil want his evil known, Angelique?"

"Are there any other secrets about this horror that you know and I don't?"

"No. Why should he want everyone to know? Bravado?"

For a long time she stood staring at what she had drawn. Motionless except for her breast, which rose and fell with the regularity of her breathing. Then, without another word she walked out. The door closed quietly.

He shook his head in wonder, stared back at the paper.

Tyrer was in the small bungalow adjoining the British Legation that he shared with Babcott, practicing calligraphy with Nakama, the name by which he knew Hiraga. "Please give me the Japanese for: today, tomorrow, the day after, next week, next year, the days of the week and the months of the year."

"Yes, Taira-san." Carefully, Hiraga said a Japanese word, watched as Tyrer wrote it phonetically in roman letters. Then Hiraga wrote the characters in the space provided and again watched while Tyrer copied them. "You good student. A'ways use same order for strokes, easy, then no forget."

"Yes, I'm beginning to understand. Thank you, you're very helpful," Tyrer replied pleasantly, enjoying writing and reading and learning—and teaching him in return, noticing that Nakama was highly intelligent and a quick study. He worked through the list with him, and when he was satisfied he said, "Good. Thank you. Now please go to Raiko-san and confirm my appointment for tomorrow."

" 'Conf'rm,' p'rease?"

"Make sure of. Make sure my appointment is certain."

"Ah, understand." Hiraga rubbed his chin, already dark with an overnight stubble. "I go now conf'rm."

"I'll be back after lunch. Please be here, then we can practice conversation and you can tell me more about Japan. How do I say that in Japanese?" Hiraga gave him the words. Tyrer wrote them phonetically in an exercise book, now crammed with words and phrases, repeated them several times until satisfied. He was about to dismiss him, then, on a sudden thought said, "What's a 'ronin'?"

Hiraga thought a moment, then explained as simply as he could. But not about shishi.

"Then you're a ronin, outlawed?"

"*Hai.*"

Thoughtfully Tyrer thanked him and let him go. He stifled a yawn. Last night he had slept badly, his world upside down at Raiko's unexpected rejection.

Damn Raiko, damn Fujiko, he thought, putting on his top hat, preparing to walk down High Street to the Club for tiffin lunch. Damn learning Japanese and damn everything, my head aches and I'll never, never, never learn this dreadfully complicated language. "Don't be ridiculous," he said aloud. Of course you will, you've got Nakama and André, two very good teachers, tonight you'll have a good supper, a bottle of champagne with someone jolly, and so to bed. And don't damn Fujiko, soon you'll sleep with her again. Oh, God, I hope so!

The day was fair and the bay crowded with ships. Traders were converging on the Club. "Oh, hello, André! Good to see you, would you care to join me for lunch?"

"Thank you, no." Poncin did not stop.

"What's up? You all right?"

"Nothing's up. Some other time."

"Tomorrow?" Not like André to be so abrupt. Damn, I wanted to ask him what I should—

"I'll join you, Phillip, if I may," McFay said.

"Of course, Jamie. You look hung over, old chap."

"I am. You look the same. That was some party."

"Yes. How's Malcolm?"

"Not so hot. He's one of the things I wanted to talk about." They found a table, the room smoke-filled, airless and crowded, everyone as usual in frock coats.

They were sitting at a corner table, Chinese servants carrying trays of roast beef, chicken pies, fish pies, fish soup, Cornish pasties, Yorkshire puddings, salt pork, curries and bowls of rice for the old China Hands, plus whisky, rum, gin, porter, champagne, red and white wine and tankards of beer. Fly swats laid beside every place.

McFay used the fly whisk. "Wanted to ask you to talk to Malcolm, not at my suggestion, tell him it'd be a good idea to go back to Hong Kong as soon as possible."

"But Jamie, I'm sure he will, without my saying so. He doesn't listen to me, why should he? What's up?"

"His mother. I'm afraid now that's no secret. Don't say anything but she writes by every mail ordering me to order him back—there's not a bloody thing I can do, he just won't listen and when the news of the

party and his formal engagement reaches Hong Kong . . ." McFay
rolled his eyes. "Ayeeyah! The shit will spread from here to Yedo."

In spite of McFay's seriousness Tyrer laughed. "It already has, it's
stinky poo like never before. The Legation garden's knee-deep in a
new dressing of prime."

"Oh?" The Scot frowned and sniffed the air. "Hadn't noticed.
How's the curry?" he asked a neighbor.

"Hot, Jamie." The man, Lunkchurch, spat a piece of chicken bone
into the floor sawdust. "I'm on seconds."

Tyrer beckoned one of the waiters brushing past but the toothy youth
deliberately avoided seeing him.

"Hey, *dew neh loh moh,* waiter!" McFay shouted irritably. "Curry
plenty quick, heya!"

There was a shout of laughter and much jeering and catcalls at the
Chinese curse words from the traders and merchants, and sour looks
from the padre of the Highland Battalion who was lunching expansively with his Church of England counterpart from the Dragoons, and
their own pastor.

A plate of blood-rare roast beef was plunked down vigorously in
front of McFay. "Curry, Mass'er, plenty werry quick quick, heya?" the
young servant said, beaming.

Exasperated, McFay shoved the plate back. "This's roast beef, for
God's sake! Curry, for Christ's sake, fetch CURRY!"

"I'll have the chicken pie," Tyrer said hastily.

Grumbling, the servant went back to the kitchen and once inside the
door bellowed with laughter amidst the pandemonium there. "Noble
House 'Fay blew up like a barrel of fireworks when I shoved roast beef
under his bulbous nose, pretending I thought it was curry. Ayeeyah," he
said, holding his stomach with laughter, "I almost shat. Baiting foreign
devils is more fun than fornication!"

Others laughed with him until the Head Cook reached over and
belted him around the face. "Listen, you dirty little fornicator—and
the rest of you—don't bait Noble House foreign devils until Noble
House Chen says it is all right. Now take Noble House 'Fay his curry
quickly and don't spit in it or I'll feed you your testicles in batter."

"Ayeeyah, spitting in foreign devil food is quite ordinary, Honorable
Chief Cook," the youth muttered, his head almost off his shoulders,
then he picked up a plate of chicken pie and rushed to obey.

The plate of curry and bowl of rice banged on the table in front of
McFay. "Curry, Mass'er, you wan' heya never mind." The youth
hurried away, cursing inwardly, head aching, but still content for

though he had not dared to disobey the Head Cook, he had kept his dirty thumb in the curry all the way from the kitchen.

"Rude bastard," Jamie said. "Ten dollars to a busted flush the bugger spat in it bringing it here."

"If you're so sure, why shout at him?" Tyrer began cutting the Melton Mowbray—type pie with its thick crust.

"He needs it, they all need it, and a good kick in the backside as well." With gusto McFay began tucking into the yellowish, gruel-like chicken and potato curry, globules of fat swimming on the surface. "Next, I hear you smuggled a samurai out of Yedo who speaks some English."

Tyrer almost choked on a piece of chicken. "Rubbish!"

"Then why're you almost purple, for goodness' sake? You're talking to me, Noble House McFay! Come on, Phillip, how do you expect to keep that secret here? You were overheard." Perspiration dotted his brow from the heat of the curry, from time to time waving the flies away. "This's hot enough to fry your balls off—good though. You want to try some?"

"No, thanks."

Happily McFay continued to eat. Then, between mouthfuls, his voice hardened though he still spoke confidentially. "Unless you talk to me openly about him, old chap, in confidence—my word on it—and share everything, all his info, I'll make an announcement here and now—to him." His spoon pointed at Nettlesmith, editor of the *Yokohama Guardian,* who was already watching them interestedly. A splatter of curry fell on the tablecloth. "If Wee Willie reads about your secret first in the paper, he'll bust a gut like you've never seen."

All Tyrer's hunger had vanished. Queasily he said, "I . . . it's true we helped a dissident escape from Yedo. That's all I can say. Now he's under H.M.'s protection for the moment. Sorry, can't say any more, Official Secrets."

McFay eyed him shrewdly. "Her Britannic Majesty's protection, eh?"

"Yes, sorry. Closed mouth catchee no flies, can't say any more. Secrets of State."

"Interesting." McFay finished the plate and shouted for a second helping. "But in return I won't tell a soul."

"Sorry, I'm sworn to secrecy." Tyrer was sweating too, a way of life in Asia except during the winter and spring months, and also because his secret was known. Even so, he was pleased with the way he was handling Jamie, undoubtedly the most important of the Yokohama traders. "I'm sure you understand."

McFay nodded pleasantly, concentrating on his curry. "I understand very well, old chap. The very second I'm finished, Nettlesmith gets the exclusive."

"You wouldn't dare!" Tyrer was shocked. "State s—"

"Balderdash on State secrets," McFay hissed. "First, I don't believe you, second, even if it was we've the right to know, we're the State, by God, not a bunch of diplomat scallywags who can't fart their way out of an empty bag!"

"Now look here . . ."

"I'm looking. Share, Phillip, or read about it in the afternoon edition." McFay's beam was seraphic as he sopped up the last of the gravy with a final hunk of bread, and consumed it. He belched and pushed his chair away from the table and began to get up. "On your own head."

"Wait."

"Everything? You agree to tell me everything?"

Numbly Tyrer nodded. "If you swear to keep it secret."

"Good, but not here. My office's safer. Come on." As he passed Nettlesmith he said, "What's new, Gabriel?"

"Read the afternoon edition, Jamie. War soon in Europe, terrible in America, war brewing here."

"Just the usual. Well, see y—"

" 'Afternoon, Mr. Tyrer." Nettlesmith's canny eyes washed over him as he scratched thoughtfully then put his attention to McFay again. "I've an advance copy of the last chapter of *Great Expectations*."

Jamie shuddered to a stop, Phillip too. "I don't believe it, by God!"

"Ten dollars and the promise of an exclusive."

"What exclusive?"

"When you have one. I'll trust you." Again the shrewd eyes looked at Tyrer who tried not to wince.

"This afternoon, Gabriel? Without fail?"

"Yes, for one hour, so you can't copy it—it's my exclusive. It cost me almost every favor I have in Fleet Street to acquire—"

"To steal. Two dollars?"

"Eight, but your hour's after Norbert's."

"My last offer, eight—and I read it first?"

"Plus the exclusive? Good. You're a gentleman and a scholar, Jamie. I'll be in your office at three."

Through his open window Tyrer heard the ship's bell at the Harbor Master's office sound eight bells. His feet were propped on his desk, and he was dozing, his afternoon calligraphy exercises forgotten. No need to look at the mantelpiece clock. His brain told him it was 4:00 P.M. Now aboard ships would be the first afternoon dogwatch, a two-hour period lasting from 4:00 P.M. to 6:00 P.M., then the second from 6:00 P.M. to 8:00 P.M., thence to the normal four-hour periods until tomorrow at 4:00 P.M. Marlowe had explained that dogwatches had been invented to allow crews to be rotated.

He yawned and opened his eyes, thinking, Not much more than half a year ago, I'd never even heard of a dogwatch or been on a warship and now I'm telling time by ship's bells as easy as with a timepiece.

His mantelpiece clock chimed four. Exactly correct. In half an hour I'm to see Sir William. The Swiss can certainly make chronometers, better than us. Where the devil's Nakama? Has he run off? He should have been back hours ago. What the devil does Sir William want? Hope to God he hasn't heard about my secret. Hope he just wants more dispatches copied. Blast it that my writing's the best in the Legation, I'm supposed to be a translator not a clerk! Damn, damn, damn!

He got up wearily, tidied his work and began to wash his hands in the basin, getting the ink off his fingers. A knock. "Come in."

Behind Hiraga was a Redcoat sergeant and a soldier, both with bayoneted rifles and both angry. Hiraga was bruised, dishevelled, grey with rage and almost naked, hat gone, turban gone, his villager kimono in shreds. The Sergeant shoved him forward, bayonet ready, and saluted. "We caught 'im climbing in over the fence, sir. We 'ad the devil of a time getting 'im nice and quiet. 'E's got a pass, signed by you. Is it real?"

"Yes, yes, it is." Aghast, Tyrer came forward. "He's a guest here, Sergeant, a guest of Sir William's, and me, he's a Japanese teacher."

"A teacher, eh?" the Sergeant said grimly. "Well, tell the bugger teachers don't climb fences, don't try to run off, don't 'ave samurai 'aircuts, don't frighten people or fight like a bag full of tomcats—I've one man wiv 'is arm broke and another wiv a busted nose. Next time we catch 'im at it, we won't be so careful." Both soldiers stomped off.

Tyrer closed the door, rushed to the sideboard and brought some water back. "Here."

Hiraga shook his head, choked with rage.

"Please. Would you like saké or beer?"

"*Iyé.*"

"Please . . . well, sit down and tell me what happened."

Hiraga began pouring out an explanation in Japanese.

"*Gomen nasai, Ing'erish dozo.*" Sorry, English please.

With an effort, Hiraga changed to English and with long, seething pauses between words he said, "Many guard at Gate and Bridge. I go through swamp, go through water, over fence. These so'dier see me. I stop, bow, reach for pass, they throw to ground. Fight, but too many." Then he followed with another searing flood of Japanese venom and promises of revenge.

When the paroxysm was spent, Tyrer said, "Sorry, but it's your own fault . . ." He darted back involuntarily as Hiraga whirled on him. "Stop it!" he said angrily. "The soldier was right. Samurai frighten people! Sir William told you to be careful, so did I, we asked you to be careful."

"I was being polite, only doing what was correct!" Hiraga said in angry Japanese. *"Those ill-mannered apes fell on me, I was reaching for the pass, it was difficult to find. Apes, I'll kill them all!"*

Tyrer's heart was pounding and the sweet sick taste of fear was in his mouth. "Listen, we must solve this together, quickly. When Sir William hears about this he may throw you out of the Settlement! You and I must solve this, understand?"

"Iyé! What is 'so'rve,' please?"

Tyrer was thankful to hear the 'please' and held on to his fright. This fellow's clearly as dangerous and as violent and hotheaded as any samurai in Japan. Thank God he's not armed. " 'Solve' means to arrive at an understanding. We must solve this problem, we must, you and I, how to have you live here safely. You understand?"

" *'Hai. So desu ka! Wakarimasu.* Taira-san me we so'rve prob'rem." Hiraga curbed his rage. "P'rease, what sugg'st? Pass no good for so'dier. Men who see me, hate. How so'rve this matter?"

"First . . . first there's a good old English custom. Whenever we have to solve a serious problem. We have tea."

Hiraga stared at him blankly. Tyrer rang a bell and ordered tea from Chen, the Number One Boy who eyed Hiraga suspiciously, an ugly chopper concealed behind his back.

While they waited Tyrer sat back in his chair and solemnly stared out of the window, desperately wanting the other man to tell him about Fujiko but too well mannered to ask directly such a leading question. Damn the fellow, he was thinking, he should volunteer the info, knowing I must be anxious as hell and not make me bloody wait. Got to teach him English ways, got to teach him not to fly off the handle, the soldiers were quite right. Got to make an English gentleman out of him. But how? Then there's bloody Jamie, who's too damned clever.

After lunch he had gone with McFay to his office, was pressed to have a small brandy and then, within minutes, he found that he had told him everything.

'Och, Phillip, you're brilliant,' McFay had told him with genuine enthusiasm. 'That laddie will be a veritable gold mine if asked the right questions. Did he say where he was from?'

'Choshu, I think that's what he said.'

'I'd like to talk to him—privately.'

'If he talks to you then others are bound to find out and then the news will be . . . will be out everywhere.'

'If I know, Norbert knows, and I'll bet the Bakufu knows—they're no fools. Sorry, but there are no secrets here, how many times must I remind you?'

'All right, I'll ask him. But only if I'm present when you see him.'

'Now, that's not really necessary, Phillip, you've got so much to do. I would'na want to waste your time.'

'Yes or no!'

McFay sighed. 'You're a hard man, Phillip. All right.'

'And if I also get to read the last chapter, without charge, say tomorrow. You arrange it with Nettlesmith.'

Sharply, McFay said, 'If I have to pay the astounding sum of eight dollars, you have to contribute as well.'

'Then no interview, and I'll inform Sir William.' He smiled to himself remembering the sour look on McFay's face and then, "Cha, Mass'er, plenty quick quick" interrupted his thoughts, bringing him back to Nakama. Chen put down the tray, no longer carrying the chopper, but it was close at hand, outside the door.

Gravely Tyrer poured for both of them, added milk and sugar and sipped the scalding, iron black brew with relish. "That's better."

Hiraga imitated him. It took all of his willpower not to cry out from the heat, and to hold in what was the foulest-tasting liquid he had ever had in his life.

"Good, eh?" Tyrer said with a beam, finishing his cup. "Some more?"

"No, no, thank you. Ing'erish custom, yes?"

"English and American, yes, not French. The French—" Tyrer shrugged "—they've no taste."

"Ah, so ka?" Hiraga had noticed the slight sneer. "French not same as Ing'erish?" he asked with a pretended innocence, his fury compartmentalized for later.

"My goodness me, no, not like them at all. They're on the Continent, we're an island nation like you. Different customs, different foods, government, everything, and of course France's a minor power compared to Britain." Tyrer stirred in another spoon of sugar, pleased with himself that the man's rage seemed to have dissipated. "Very different."

"Oh, so? Ing'erish and French warred hav?"

Tyrer laughed. "Dozens of times over the centuries, and allies in other wars—we were allies in the last conflict." He told him briefly about the Crimea, then about Napoleon Bonaparte, the French revolution, and the present Emperor Louis Napoleon. "He's Bonaparte's nephew, an absolute buffoon. Bonaparte wasn't, but one of the most evil men ever born, he was responsible for hundreds of thousands of deaths. But for Wellington and Nelson and our troops he would have ruled the world. Are you understanding all this?"

Hiraga nodded. "No o'rr word, but unn'erstan'." But he had caught the gist and this turned his head upside down, though he could not fathom why a great general should be considered evil. "P'rease go on, Taira-san."

For a little while Tyrer did, then stopped the history lesson and gave him a lead: "Now to your problem. When you left the Yoshiwara those guards gave you no trouble?"

"No, pretend take vegitab'res."

"That's good. Oh, by the way, did you see Raiko-san?"

"Yes. Fujiko not possib're tomorrow."

"Oh. Well, never mind." Tyrer shrugged, dying inside.

But Hiraga saw the vast disappointment and savored it. *Sonno-joi,* he thought grimly. He had had to buy Fujiko's services himself but he did not mind. Raiko had said: 'Since you pay well, though not gai-jin prices, I agree. But he should bed her the day after. I wouldn't want him to find another . . .'

Tyrer was saying, "Nakama-san, the only real way you can be safe here is to never go out. I won't send you to the Yoshiwara anymore. You must stay here, inside the Legation."

"Better, Taira-san, I stay in vi'rrage, find safe house. Inside fence safer. Each day I come at sunup, or when you want, teach and to 'rearn. You very good Sensei. This so'rve prob'rem, yes?"

Tyrer hesitated, not wanting him off the leash but no longer caring to have him too close. "Yes, if first you show me where exactly and do not move without telling me."

In a moment Hiraga nodded and said, "I agree. P'rease, you say so'diers good me stay here and in vi'rrage?"

"Yes, I'll do that. I'm sure Sir William will agree."

"Thank you, Taira-san. Say so'diers also, if attack again I get *katana*."

"You will do no such thing! I forbid it, Sir William has forbidden it! No weapons, no swords!"

"P'rease you say so'dier, no attack p'rease."

"Yes, I'll do that but if you wear swords here you will be killed, they'll shoot you!"

Hiraga shrugged. "P'rease, no attack. *Wakatta?*"

Tyrer did not reply. *Wakatta* was the imperious form of *wakarimasu ka*: Do you understand?

"Domo." With a contained violence that Tyrer could almost smell, Nakama thanked him again and said that he would return at dawn to guide him to the safe house, and would be ready then to answer any questions that he wanted to ask. He bowed stiffly. Tyrer did the same. He walked out. It was only then that Tyrer saw the extent of the bruises over all his back and legs.

That night the wind became changeable, the sea choppy.

Out in the roads the fleet was snug at anchor and ready for sleep, the first night watch that came on duty at 8:00 P.M. already at their stations. Upwards of fifty men were in various cells for various offenses; and with varying degrees of fear six were diligently making their own cato'-nine-tails for the fifty lashes they were due at dawn for conduct prejudicial to good order and military discipline: one for threatening to break the neck of a sodomite Bosun, three for fighting, one for stealing a rum ration, and another for swearing at an officer.

Nine sea burials were scheduled for sunup.

All ship's sick bays were overloaded with sufferers of dysentery, diarrhea, the croup, whooping cough, scarlet fever, measles, venereal diseases, broken limbs, hernias and the like, routine—except for a dangerous fourteen with smallpox—aboard the flagship. Bleeding and violent purges were the recommended cures for most illnesses—the majority of doctors also being barbers—except for the lucky few patients who were given Dr. Collis's Tincture, one he had invented during the Crimea, which had cut dysentery deaths by three quarters. Six drops of the dark, opium-based liquid and your bowels began to quieten.

Throughout the Settlement everyone was preparing for dinner and the most eagerly anticipated part of the day: after-dinner conversation, discussing the day's rumors or news—thank God the mail ship's due tomorrow—enjoying the warm camaraderie and laughter over spicy scandals, the ball, tension over business problems and if war would begin, or about the latest book someone had read, a new funny story or poem another had thought up, or telling tales of storms or ice lands or desert, or journeys made to strange places throughout the Empire— New Zealand, Africa and Australia hardly explored but for coastal areas—or the Wild West of America and Canada, stories of the California Gold Rush of '49, or visits to Spanish or French or Russian America. Dmitri had once sailed the mostly uncharted western sea- board from San Francisco north to Russian Alaska. Each man told of strange sights he had seen, girls sampled or wars witnessed. Good wine and drinks and pipes and tobacco from Virginia, a few nightcaps at the Club, then prayers and bed.

A normal night in the Empire.

Some hosts specialized in chorals or poetry readings or excerpts from a coveted novel, and tonight at Norbert Greyforth's extremely private party, all guests sworn to secrecy, a special reading of the last chapter from the bootlegged copy he had had produced in his allotted hour by putting all his fifty clerks on it. 'If this leaks, the whole lot of you are dismissed,' he had threatened.

In the Club they were still discussing the previous night's ball and trying to work out how to have another. "Why not make it a bloody weekly bash, eh? Angel Tits can kick up her heels and show her knickers for me every day of the week along with Naughty Nellie Fortheringill—"

"Stop calling her Angel Tits, for chrissake, or else!"

"Angel tits she has, and Angel Tits she is!"

To jeers and catcalls the fight started, bets were taken and the two contenders, Lunkchurch and Grimm, another trader, toed the line and tried to smash each other senseless.

Almost directly across the road, on the sea side, was the large brick bungalow of the British Legation, flagpole in the courtyard, gardens, and surrounded like most important dwellings with a defendable fence. Sir William was already dressed for dinner and so was his main guest, the Admiral. Both were furious.

"The bloody bastards!" the Admiral said, his flushed face more flushed than usual, going to the sideboard to pour another large whisky. "They're beyond comprehension."

"Totally." Sir William tossed the scroll aside and glared at Johann and Tyrer who stood in front of him. An hour ago the scroll had arrived by messenger from the Japanese Governor who had sent it on behalf of the Bakufu. "Very urgent so sorry." Instead of being in Dutch as was normal, it was in characters. With Seratard's agreement, Johann had co-opted one of the visiting French Jesuit missionaries and had produced a rough copy that Tyrer at once put into correct English. The message was from the Council of Elders, and signed by Anjo:

I communicate with you by dispatch. By orders of the Shō-gun, received from Kyōto, the provisional date of the meeting in nineteen days with the roju, *and meeting the same day with the Shōgun, is to be postponed for three months as His Majesty will not return until then. I therefore send you this first, before holding a Conference as to the details. The second installment of the gift is to be delayed for thirty days. Respectful and humble communication.*

"Johann," Sir William said, his voice icy, "would you say this is unusually rude, impolite and altogether vile?"

The Swiss said cautiously, "I think that's about right, Sir William."

"For Christ sake, I've spent days negotiating, threatening, losing sleep, renegotiating until they swore on the Shōgun's head to meet in Yedo on November 5th, the Shōgun on November 6th and now this!" Sir William gulped his drink, choked and swore for almost five minutes in English, French and Russian, the others staring with admiration at the gorgeously descriptive vulgarities.

"Quite right," the Admiral said. "Tyrer, pour Sir William another gin."

Instantly Tyrer obeyed. Sir William found his handkerchief, blew his nose, took some snuff, sneezed and blew his nose again. "The pox on all of them!"

"What do you propose, Sir William?" the Admiral asked, keeping the delight off his face at this further humbling of his adversary.

"Naturally I'll reply at once. Please order the fleet to Yedo tomorrow to bombard port facilities of my choosing."

The Admiral's blue eyes narrowed. "I think we will discuss this in private. Gentlemen!" Tyrer and Johann at once began to leave.

"No," Sir William said tightly. "Johann, you can go, please wait outside. Tyrer's my personal staff, he stays."

The Admiral's neck reddened but he said nothing until the door had closed. "You know my views on bombardment very well. Until the order from England arrives, I-will-not-order-it unless I am attacked."

"Your position makes negotiations impossible. Power comes from the barrels of our cannon, nothing else!"

"I agree, we only disagree on timing."

"Timing is my decision. Good. Then kindly just order a small cannonade, twenty shells on targets of my choosing."

"Dammit, no! Am I not clear? When the order arrives I will conflagrate Japan if necessary, not before."

Sir William flushed. "Your reluctance to assist Her Majesty's policy in the most minor way is beyond belief."

"Personal aggrandizement seems to be the real problem. What do a few months matter? Nothing—except prudence!"

"Prudence be damned," Sir William said angrily. "Of course we will get instructions to proceed as I—I repeat, I—advise! It is imprudent to delay. By tomorrow's mail I will request you are replaced by an officer who is more tuned to Her Majesty's interests—and battle trained!"

The Admiral went purple. Only a few knew that in all his career he had never participated in a sea or land engagement. When he could talk he said, "That, sir, is your privilege. Meanwhile until my replacement, or yours arrives, I command Her Majesty's Forces in Japan. Good night, sir." The door slammed.

"Rude bugger," Sir William muttered, then to his surprise saw Tyrer who had been standing behind him, out of his eye line, paralyzed by the salvos. "You'd best keep your mouth shut. Did they teach you that?"

"Yessir, yes, indeed."

"Good," Sir William said, and took his agitated mind off the Gordian knot of the Bakufu, *roju* and intransigence of the Admiral for later. "Tyrer, get yourself a sherry, you look as though you need one, and you'd better join us for dinner as the Admiral has declined my invitation. You play backgammon?"

"Yes, sir, thank you, sir," Tyrer said meekly.

"While I think of it, what's this I hear about a skirmish, your pet samurai versus the British Army?"

Tyrer gave him the details and his solution, but not about his Sensei's threat to get swords, feeling ever more guilty about hiding facts from the Minister. "I'd like to retain him, of course with your approval, sir, but he is a very good teacher and I think will be most useful to us."

"I doubt that and it's more important to have no more trouble here.

No telling what the fellow will do, he could become a viper in our nest. He's ordered out tomorrow."

"But sir, he's already given me some very valuable information." Tyrer held on to his sudden distress and blurted out, "For instance he told me the Shōgun's only a boy, barely sixteen, he's only the puppet of the Bakufu, the real power belongs to their Emperor—he used the title Mikado several times—who lives in Kyōto."

"God Almighty!" Sir William exploded. "Is this true?"

It was on the tip of Tyrer's tongue to tell about the English speaking, but he managed to stop himself. "I don't know yet, sir. I haven't had time to really question him, he's difficult to bring out, but yes, I think he told me the truth."

Sir William stared at him, his mind agog with the implications of the information. "What else has he told you?"

"I've only just started and it all takes time, as you'll appreciate." Tyrer's excitement picked up. "But he's told me about ronin. The word means 'wave,' sir, they're called ronin because they're as free as the waves. They're all samurai, but outlawed for different reasons. Most of them are adversaries of the Bakufu, like Nakama, who believe they've usurped power from the Midako, sorry, Mikado, as I said."

"Wait a moment, slow down, slow down, Tyrer. There's plenty of time. Now, what is a ronin, exactly?"

Tyrer told him.

"Good God!" Sir William thought a moment. "So ronin are samurai who are either outlawed because their king has lost favor, or outlawed by their kings for crimes real or imagined, or voluntary outlaws who are banding together to overthrow the central government of the puppet Shōgun?"

"Yes, sir. He says illegal government."

Sir William sipped the last of his gin, nodding to himself, astonished and elated as he ran this all around in his mind. "Then Nakama's a ronin, and what you call a dissident, and what I'd call a revolutionary?"

"Yes, sir. Excuse me, sir, can I sit down?" Tyrer asked shakily, desperate to blurt out the real truth about the man and afraid to do so.

"Of course, of course, Tyrer, so sorry, but first get another sherry and bring me a tot of gin." Sir William watched him, delighted with him yet somehow perturbed. Years of dealing with diplomats, spies, half-truths, lies and blatant disinformation were calling up warning signals that something was being hidden from him. He accepted the drink. "Thanks. Take that chair, it's the most comfortable. Cheers! You

must be speaking very good Japanese to get all this in such a short
time," he said easily.

"No, sir, sorry, I don't, but I spend all my time at it. With Nakama,
it's, well, mostly patience, gestures, a few English words and Japanese
words and phrases André Poncin has given me, he's been tremendously
helpful, sir."

"Does André know what this man has told you?"

"No, sir."

"Tell him nothing. Nothing at all. Anyone else?"

"No, sir, except Jamie McFay." Tyrer gulped his sherry. "He knew a
little already and, well, he's very persuasive and he, well, pried it out
about the Shōgun."

Sir William sighed. "Yes, Jamie's persuasive, to say the least, and
always knows far more than he tells."

He sat back in the comfortable old leather swivel chair and sipped
his drink, his mind roving over all this priceless new knowledge,
already redesigning his reply to tonight's rude missive, wondering how
far he dare gamble and how far he could trust Tyrer's information. As
always in these circumstances, queasily he remembered the Permanent
Under Secretary's parting salvos about failure.

"About Nakama," he said. "I'll agree to your plan, Phillip . . . may I
call you Phillip?"

Tyrer flushed with pleasure at the sudden and unexpected compliment. "Of course, sir, thank you, sir."

"Good, thank you. For the moment I'll agree to your plan, but for
God's sake, be careful of him, don't forget ronin have committed all
the murders, except poor Canterbury."

"I'll be careful, Sir William. Don't worry."

"Get all you can out of him but tell no one else and give me the
information at once. For God's sake, be careful, always have a revolver
on hand and if he shows the slightest indication of violence, scream
bloody murder, shoot him or clap him in irons."

Next door to the British Legation was the American, then the Dutch,
Russian, German and last, the French, and there, in her suite that
evening, Angelique was dressing for dinner, helped by Ah Soh. In an
hour, the dinner Seratard was giving her and Malcolm to celebrate their
engagement was due to begin. Then later there would be music. 'But
don't play too long, André, say you're tired,' she had cautioned him
earlier. 'Leave plenty of time for your mission, no? Men are so lucky.'

She was glad and sad that she had moved. It's wiser, better, she thought. In three days I can move back. A new life, a new . . .

"Wat wrong, Miss'ee?"

"Nothing, Ah Soh." Angelique forced her mind away from what must soon be endured, and buried her fear deeper.

Just down the street in the best location on the waterfront, the Struan Building was well lit, as was Brock and Sons, next door, both with many clerks and shroffs still at their work. Today Malcolm Struan had moved into the tai-pan suite that was much bigger and more comfortable than the one he had been using and now he was fighting his way into his dinner clothes. "What's your advice, Jamie? Damned if I know what to do about Mother and her letters, but that's my damned problem not yours—she's giving you stick too, isn't she?"

Jamie McFay shrugged. "It's awfully difficult for her. From her point of view she's right, she only wants the best for you. I think she's worried to death over your health, you being so far away, she unable to come here. And nothing about Struan's can be solved from Yokohama, everything in Hong Kong. *China Cloud* docks in a few days from Shanghai, then a quick turn around for Hong Kong. You'll be returning with her?"

"No, and please don't bring it up again," Struan said sharply. "I'll tell you when we, Angelique and I, are leaving. I just hope to God Mother isn't on *China Cloud*—that'd be the last straw." Struan bent to pull on his boots, failed, the pain too much. "Sorry, could you? Thanks." Then he burst out, "This being like a fucking cripple is driving me over the brink."

"I can imagine." McFay covered his surprise. This was the first time he had ever heard Struan use that expletive. "I'd be the same, no, not the same, a bloody sight worse," he added kindly, liking him, admiring his courage.

"I'll be fine when we're married and all the waiting's over, everything tidy." Struan with difficulty used the chamber pot, painful always, and saw a few flecks of blood in the stream. He had told Hoag about it yesterday when it had begun anew and Hoag had said not to worry. 'Then why do you look so worried?'

'I'm not, Malcolm, just concerned. With these kinds of vicious internal wounds, any indication during the healing process should be noted . . .'

Struan finished and hobbled over to the chair by the window and sat gratefully. "Jamie. I need a favor."

"Of course, anything, what can I do?"

"Can you, well, I must have a woman. Could you arrange it from the Yoshiwara?"

Jamie was startled. "I, yes, I imagine so." Then he added, "Is that wise?"

A gust rattled the shutters and tugged at trees and gardens, clattering a few loose roof tiles to the ground, sending the rats scurrying from the piles of garbage thrown carelessly into the High Street and from the encircling turgid and fetid canal that also served as a sewer.

"No," Malcolm said.

Half a mile away from the Struan Building, near Drunk Town, in a nondescript dwelling in the Japanese village, Hiraga was lying on his stomach, naked, being massaged. The house was ordinary, the facade facing the street decrepit, a pattern of the others that lined both sides of the narrow dirt roadway, each serving as home, warehouse, and shop during the day. Inside, like many that belonged to the more substantial merchants, everything was sparkling clean, polished, cherished and expensive. It was the house of the shoya, the village elder.

The masseuse was blind. She was in her early twenties, firmly built with a gentle face and sweet smile. By ancient custom throughout most of Asia, blind people had a monopoly on the art, though there were also practitioners with normal sight. Again, by ancient custom, the blind were always quite safe and never to be touched.

"You are very strong, samurai-sama," she said, breaking a silence. "Those you fought must be dead or suffering."

For a moment Hiraga did not reply, enjoying the deep probing and wise fingers that sought out his knotted muscles and relaxed them. "Perhaps."

"Please, may I suggest, I have some special oil from China that will help heal your cuts and bruises quickly?"

He smiled. This was an often-used ploy to gain extra money. "Good, use it."

"Oh, but you smile, honored samurai! It is not a trick to get more money," she said at once, her fingers kneading his back. "My grandmother who was also blind gave me the secret."

"How did you know I smiled?"

She laughed and the sound reminded him of a lark sailing the dawn air currents. "A smile begins in many parts of the body. My fingers listen to you—to your muscles and even sometimes to your thoughts."

"And what am I thinking now?"

"About *sonno-joi*. Ah, I was right!" Again the laugh that disconcerted him. "But don't be afraid, you have said nothing, the patrons here have said nothing, I will say nothing but my fingers tell me you are a special swordsman, the best I have ever served. Clearly you're not Bakufu, therefore you must be ronin, ronin by choice because you are a guest in this house, therefore shishi, the first we have ever had here." She bowed. "We are honored. If I were a man I would support *sonno-joi*."

Deliberately her steel-hard fingertip pressed a nerve center and she felt the tremor of pain go through him and it pleased her that she could help him more than he knew. "So sorry, but this point is very important to rejuvenate you and keep your juices flowing."

He grunted, the pain grinding him to the futons yet strangely pleasing. "Your grandmother was also a masseuse?"

"Yes. In my family at least one girl in every second generation is born blind. It was my turn in this lifetime."

"Karma."

"Yes. It is said that in China today, fathers or mothers will blind one of their daughters so that when she grows up she will find employment for all her life."

Hiraga had never heard this but he believed it and was incensed. "This is not China and never will be and one day we will take China and civilize her."

"Eeee, so sorry to disturb your harmony, Lord, please excuse me, oh so sorry. Ah, that's better, again so sorry, please excuse me. You were saying, Lord . . . civilize China? As Dictator Nakamura wanted to do? Is it possible?"

"Yes, one day. It is our destiny to gain the Dragon Throne, as it is your destiny to massage and not to talk."

Again her laugh was gentle. "Yes, Lord."

Hiraga sighed as her finger released the pressure point and left a pervading, soothing glow in place of pain. So everyone knows I'm shishi, he thought. How long before I'm betrayed? Why not? Two koku is a fortune.

Getting into this haven had not been easy. When he had strode into the quarter there was an aghast silence, for here was a samurai, a samurai without swords, looking like a wild man. The street cleared except those nearby who knelt and awaited their fate.

'You, old man, where is your nearest *ryokan*—inn.'

'We don't have one, Lord, there's no need, Honored Lord,' the old shopkeeper muttered, his fear making him gabble on. 'There's no need as our Yoshiwara is nearby, bigger than most cities with dozens of places you can stay in and over a hundred girls not counting maids, three real geisha and seven trainees. It's that way . . .'

'Enough! Where's the house of the shoya?'

'There, Lord.'

'Where, fool? Get up, show me the way.'

Still enraged, he followed him down the street, wanting to smash the eyes that watched from every opening and crush the whispers in his wake.

'There, Lord.'

Hiraga waved him away. The sign outside the open shop that was filled with goods of all description but empty of people announced that this was the residence and place of business of Ichi Ryoshi, shoya, rice merchant and banker, the Yokohama agent for the Gyokoyama. The Gyokoyama was a *zaibatsu*—meaning a closely knit family complex of businesses—immensely powerful in Yedo and Osaka as rice traders, saké and beer distillers, and all-important, bankers.

He took hold of himself. With great care and politeness he knocked, squatted on his heels and began to wait, trying to dominate the pain from the beating he had taken from the ten-man patrol. At length a strong-faced, middle-aged man came out into the open shop, knelt and bowed. Hiraga bowed back equally, introduced himself as Nakama Otami and mentioned that his grandfather was also shoya, not saying where but giving enough information for him to know it was the truth and that, perhaps, as there was no ryokan to stay at, the shoya might have a room for paying guests that was not being used. 'My grandfather also is honored to have dealings with the Gyokoyama *zaibatsu*—his villages sell all their crops through it,' he had said politely. 'In fact I would like you, please, to send my pledge to them in Osaka, and would be grateful if you would advance me some cash against it.'

'Yedo is nearer than Osaka, Otami-san.'

'Yes, but Osaka is better for me than Yedo,' Hiraga said, not wanting to risk Yedo where there could be leaks to the Bakufu. He noted the cool, unafraid appraisal and hid his hatred, but even daimyos had to be careful when dealing with the Gyokoyama or their agents, even Lord Ogama of Choshu. It was common knowledge that Ogama was heavily in debt to them, with years of future revenue already pledged as security.

'My company is honored to serve old customers. Please, how long would you wish to stay in my house?'

'A few days, if it would not inconvenience you.' Hiraga told him about Tyrer and the problem of the soldiers, only because he was sure the news had preceded him.

'You may stay at least three days, Otami-san. So sorry, but you must be prepared to leave quickly in case of a sudden raid, by day or night.'

'I understand. Thank you.'

'Please excuse me but I would like an order signed by this Taira, or better the chief of the gai-jin, ordering me to open my house to you, in case or when the Bakufu arrive here.'

'I will arrange it.' Hiraga bowed his thanks and hid his irritation at the restraints. 'Thank you.'

The shoya ordered a maid to bring tea and writing materials and watched while Hiraga wrote the pledge that asked the amount be deducted from the account of Shinsaku Otami, the secret code name of his father. He signed it and sealed it with his chop, signed and sealed the receipt for Ryoshi, who agreed to advance half the amount at the usual interest of two percent per month, for the three months that would be needed to send the paper to Osaka and complete the transaction. 'Do you want the money in cash?'

'No, thank you, I still have a few oban,' he said, exaggerating, down to his last two. 'Please open an account for me, deduct the charges for my room and food. I need some clothes, swords, and could you please arrange a masseuse?'

'Of course, Otami-san. About clothes, the servant will show you our stock. Choose what you want. As to swords for sale'——Ryoshi shrugged——'the only ones I have are trinkets for gai-jin and hardly worth your trouble but you may see what I have. Perhaps I could obtain proper ones for you. Now I will show you your room and your private entrance and exit——there is a guard here, by day and by night.'

Hiraga had followed him. Never once had Ryoshi commented on his nakedness or bruises or asked any questions. 'You are welcome and honor my poor house,' he had said, and left him.

Remembering the way it was said suddenly made Hiraga's skin crawl——so polite and grave but underneath so deadly. Disgusting, he thought, disgusting that we samurai are kept in poverty by corrupt daimyos and Shōguns and Bakufu and forced to borrow from these low-class zaibatsu who are nothing but filthy, money-grubbing merchants who act as though their money gives them power over us. By all gods, when the Emperor has regained power there'll be a reckoning, merchants and zaibatsu will begin to pay. . . .

In the same instant he felt her fingers stop. "What is it, Lord?" the masseuse asked, frightened.

"Nothing, nothing. Please continue."

Her fingers obeyed, but now their touch was different and there was tension in the room.

It was an eight-mat room, the futons stuffed with down, the tatami of good quality and shojis recently renewed with oiled paper. In the tokonoma niche was an oil lamp, flower arrangement and small scroll painting of a vast landscape, its only habitation a tiny cottage in a bamboo grove, with an even tinier woman forlorn in the doorway, peering into the distance—a love poem beside it.

> *Waiting,*
> *Listening to the rain*
> *Beating on the rain*

So lonely, filled with so much hope for her man's return.

Hiraga was drifting into sleep when the screen door slid back. "Excuse me, Lord." The servant knelt and said uneasily, "So sorry, there is a low-class person outside who claims to know you, asks to see you, so sorry to disturb you, but he is very insistent an—"

"Who is he? What's his name?"

"He . . . wouldn't give a name, and he didn't ask for you by name, Lord, but kept on saying: 'Say to the samurai: Todo is the brother of Joun.'"

Instantly Hiraga was on his feet. As he slipped on his yukata, he asked the masseuse to come back tomorrow at the same time and dismissed her, moved closer to the two swords he had borrowed until the shoya could obtain better, and knelt in a defensive-attack position facing the door. "Send him here, and keep everyone else away."

The slight, dirty young peasant with a tattered kimono grovelled along the passageway and went onto his knees outside the door. "Thank you, Lord, thank you for seeing me," the youth mumbled, then looked up and beamed inanely, his front teeth missing. "Thank you, Lord."

Hiraga glowered at him, then gasped with disbelief: "Ori? But—but it's impossible!" then peered closer and saw that his tooth had just been blacked out as part of his disguise, in this light the illusion perfect. But no mistaking that Ori was no longer obviously samurai: his topknot and been cut off and all hair on the back and sides of his head roughly trimmed to the same length as the two-week stubble that covered his pate. "Why?" he asked helplessly.

Ori grinned and sat close to him. "Bakufu are looking for ronin, eh?" he whispered, keeping his voice down against ears they both knew would be listening. "I'm not less a samurai but now I can pass any barrier, eh?"

The air hissed out of Hiraga's mouth with admiration. "You are right. You are brilliant, *sonno-joi* doesn't depend on a hairstyle. So simple—I would never have thought of it."

"It occurred to me last night. I was thinking about your problem, Hiraga, an—"

"Careful. Here my name's Nakama Otami."

"Ah, so that's it! Good." Ori smiled. "I did not know what to use, hence the code."

"Have they found Todo and the others?"

"No, no, they are still missing. They have to be dead. We heard Joun was executed like a common criminal, but still don't know how he was caught."

"Why come here, Ori? It's too dangerous."

"Not like this, nor at night, and I needed to test the new Ori and to see you." Squeamishly he ran his hand over his head stubble, scratching his scalp, his face freshly shaven. "It feels awful, and dirty, somehow obscene, but never mind, now I am safe to get to Kyōto. I will leave in two days."

Hiraga stared at his head, fascinated, still bewildered by the astonishing change. "If anything makes you safe that should, except that now all samurai will take you for a common man. How can you wear swords?"

"When I need swords I will wear a hat. When I am disguised I have this." Ori slipped his good hand into his sleeve and brought out a two-shot derringer.

Again Hiraga's face lit up. "Eeee, brilliant! Where did you get it?"

"Fujiko. She sold it to me, with a box of cartridges. A client gave it to her as a present when he left Yokohama. Imagine! A low-class whore with such a treasure."

Hiraga held it carefully, weighing it in his hand, pointing it then lifting the catch to see the two bronze cartridges neatly in the barrels. "You could certainly kill two men before you were killed, if you were close enough."

"One is enough to give you time to run off and get some swords." Ori peered at Hiraga. "We heard about the soldiers. I wanted to see if you were all right. *Baka!* We will go to Kyōto together and leave this place to the dogs until we can come back in force."

Hiraga shook his head and told what really happened, then about Tyrer and discovering the enmity between the French and English, adding excitedly, "This is one of the wedges we can drive between them. We get them fighting amongst themselves, let them kill each other for us, eh? I must stay, Ori. It is only the beginning. We must learn all they know, be able to think like them and then we can destroy them."

Ori frowned, considering the reasons for and the reasons against— though he had not forgiven Hiraga for forcing him to lose face and remove her cross, he still had to protect *sonno-joi*. "In that case, if you are to be our spy, you will have to be like them in every way, and burrow into their society like a bedbug, outwardly become friends, even wear gai-jin clothes." At Hiraga's blank look he added, "Why not? That will further protect you, and make it easier for them to accept you, *neh*?"

"But why should they accept me?"

"They should not, but they are fools. Taira will be your spearhead. He can arrange it, order it. He could insist."

"Why should he?"

"Barter Fujiko."

"Eh?"

"Raiko gave us the key: gai-jin are different. They prefer to bed the same woman. Help Raiko to wrap him in their net, then he is your running dog because you are his indispensable go-between. Tomorrow tell him, even though you were furious with the soldiers, it was not his fault. With great difficulty you sneaked back to the Yoshiwara and arranged Fujiko for him for tomorrow evening and 'so sorry, Taira-sama, it would be simpler for me to arrange these trysts if I had proper European clothes to pass the barriers, and so on.' Make her available, or not, get him on her barb, and twist it. Eh?"

Hiraga began laughing quietly. "Better you stay here and not go to Kyōto, your counsel is too valuable."

"Katsumata must be forewarned. Now, the gai-jin woman?"

"Tomorrow I will find out exactly where she is."

"Good." The wind picked up and a gust passed through the house, crackling the paper in the frames and setting the oil flame dancing. Ori watched him. "Have you seen her?"

"Not yet. Taira's servants, a filthy lot of Chinese, don't speak any language I can understand so I could not find out from them, but the biggest building in the Settlement belongs to the man she is to marry."

"She lives there?"

"I am not sure but—" Hiraga stopped as an idea barreled into his head. "Listen, if I could become accepted, I could go everywhere, could find out all about their defenses, could go aboard their warships and . . ."

"And on a certain night," Ori said at once, jumping ahead, "perhaps we could capture one, or sink one."

"Yes." Both men glowed at the thought, the candle fluttering and casting strange shadows.

"With the right wind," Ori said softly, "a south wind like tonight, with five or six shishi, a few kegs of oil already planted in the right warehouses . . . even that is not necessary: we can make incendiaries and start fires in the Yoshiwara. The wind would jump those fires into the village and those would spread to the Settlement and burn it up! *Neh*?"

"And the ship?"

"In the confusion we row out to the big one. We could do it, easily, *neh*?"

"Not easily, but what a coup!"

"Sonno-joi!"

21

Thursday, 16th October:

"COME IN! AH, GOOD MORNING, André," Angelique said with a warmth that belied her anxiety. "You're very punctual. All's well with you?"

He nodded, closed the door of the small ground-floor room adjoining her bedroom that served as her boudoir in the French Legation, once more astonished that she appeared so calm and could make small talk. Politely he bent over her hand and kissed it, then sat opposite her. The room was drab with old chairs and chaise and writing desk, plaster walls with a few cheap oils by current French painters, Delacroix and Corot. "The army taught me, Punctuality is next to Godliness."

She smiled at the pleasantry. "La! I didn't know you had been in the army."

"I had a commission in Algeria for a year when I was twenty-two, after university—nothing very grand, just helping to crush one of the usual rebellions. The sooner we really stamp out the troublemakers and annex all North Africa as French territory the better." He waved absently at the flies, and studied her. "You look more beautiful than ever. Your—your state suits you."

Her eyes lost their color and became flinty. Last night had been bad for her, the bed here in the untidy, seedy bedroom uncomfortable. During the dark time her anxieties had overridden her confidence and she had become increasingly nervous about leaving her suite next to

Struan and all her comfort, so hastily. In the dawn her humor had not improved and again the all-consuming idea pervaded her: *men caused all her woes*. Revenge will be sweet. "You mean my marriage state to be, no?"

"Of course," he said after the barest pause, and she wondered, aggravated, what was the matter with him and why he was so boorish and distant like last night when the music had gone on and on, without his usual touch. He had dark rings under his eyes and his features seemed sharper than usual.

"Is anything wrong, my dear friend?"

"No, dear Angelique, nothing, nothing at all."

Liar, she thought. Why is it men lie so much, to others and to themselves? "You were successful?"

"Yes and no."

He knew that she was twisting on the spit and of a sudden he wanted to make her squirm, wanted to fan the flames to make her scream and pay for Hana.

You're mad, he thought. It's not Angelique's fault. That is true but because of her, last night I went to the Three Carp and saw Raiko and while we talked in our mixture of Japanese and English and pidgin I suddenly felt that the other had just been a rotten nightmare and that any moment Hana would appear, the laugh in her eyes, and my heart would swirl as always and we would leave Raiko and bathe together, play there, eat in private and love without haste. And when I realized the truth, with Hana gone forever, my entrails and brain crawling with spawning worms, I almost vomited. 'Raiko, got to know who three clients were.'

'So sorry, Furansu-san, I said before: her mama-san is dead, people of house scattered, Inn of Forty-seven Ronin dead.'

'There must be some way to find th—'

'None. So sorry.'

'Then tell me the truth . . . the truth, of how she died.'

'With your knife in her throat, so sorry.'

'She did it? Hara-kiri?'

Raiko had answered with the same patient voice, the same voice that had told the same story and given the same answer to the same questions a dozen times before: 'Hara-kiri is the ancient way, honorable way, the only way atone a wrong. Hana betrayed you and us, owners, patrons and herself—that was her karma in this life. There is nothing more say. So sorry, let her rest. Her fortieth day after her death day, her kami day when a person is reborn or becomes a kami has passed now. Let her kami, her spirit, rest. So sorry, not speak of her again. Now, what other thing can I do for you?'

Angelique was sitting straight in her chair as she had been taught from childhood, disquieted, watching him, one hand in her lap, the other fanned against the flies. Twice she had said, 'What do you mean, yes and no?' but he had not heard her, seemingly in a trance. Just before she had left Paris, her uncle had been the same and her aunt had said, 'Leave him be, who knows what devils inhabit a man's mind when troubled.'

'What trouble is he in, Aunt-mama?'

'Ah, *chérie,* all life is a trouble when what you earn won't pay for what is needed. Taxes crush us, Paris is a cesspit of greed and without morals, France is rumbling again, the franc buys less every month, bread has doubled in half a year. Leave him be, poor man, he does his best.'

Angelique sighed. Yes, poor man. Tomorrow I will do my best and talk to Malcolm, he will arrange to pay his debts. Such a good man should not be in Debtors' Prison. What can his debts amount to? A few louis . . .

She saw André come back into himself and look at her. "Yes and no, André? What does that mean?"

"Yes, they have such a medicine, but no, you cannot have it yet because y—"

"But why, why ha—"

"*Mon Dieu,* be patient, then I can tell you what the mama-san told me. You cannot have it yet because it cannot be taken until the thirtieth day, then again on the thirty-fifth day, and also because the drink—an infusion of herbs—must be prepared freshly each time."

His words had ripped the simplicity of her plan apart: André was to have given her now the drink or powder that he had obtained last night, she would take it at once and go to bed, saying she had the vapors. *Voilà!* A small stomachache and in a few hours, a day at the most and everything perfect.

For a moment she felt her whole world twisting but again managed to put on the brakes: Stop it! You're alone. You are the heroine whom the forces of evil have ensnared. You must be strong, you have to fight alone and you-can-beat-them! "Thirty days?" She sounded strangled.

"Yes, and you repeat it on the thirty-fifth. You must be accurate and th—"

"And what happens then, André? Is it fast, what?"

"For God's sake, let me finish. She said it's—it usually works at once. The second draft isn't always necessary."

"There's nothing I can take immediately?"

"No. There isn't anything like that."

"But this other, she said it's successful every time?"

"Yes." Raiko's answer to his same question had been, 'Nine times in ten. If the medicine does not work, there are other ways.'

'You mean a doctor?'

'Yes. The medicine usually works but is expensive. I must pay medicine maker before he will give it to me. He must buy herbs, do you understand . . .'

André concentrated on Angelique again. "The mama-san said it was effective—but expensive."

"Effective? Every time? And not dangerous?"

"Every time and not dangerous. But expensive. She has to pay the apothecary in advance, he has to obtain fresh herbs."

"Oh," she said airily, "then please pay her for me, and shortly I will repay you three times."

His lips went into a thin line. "I've already advanced twenty louis. I'm not a rich man."

"But what can a little medicine cost, André, such an ordinary medicine? It can't be expensive surely?"

"She said, for such a girl wanting such help, secret help, what does the cost matter?"

"I agree, dear André." Angelique brushed this problem aside with warmth and friendliness, her heart hardening against him for being so mercenary. "In thirty days I can pay whatever it is out of the allowance Malcolm has promised, and anyway I'm sure, *I know* you'll be able to arrange it, a good, wise man like you. Thank you, my dear friend. Please tell her it is exactly eight days from when I should have had my period. When do you get the medicine?"

"I already told you, the day before the thirtieth day. We can collect it or send someone for it the day before."

"And the—the discomfort? How long will that be?"

André was feeling very tired, uncomfortable and now furious that he had allowed himself to become embroiled, however many the potential, permanent advantages. "She told me it depends on the girl, her age, if this has been done before. If it hasn't it should be easy."

"But how many days of sickness will there be?"

"*Mon Dieu,* she didn't say and I didn't ask her. If you have specific

questions write them down and I'll try to get you the answers. Now if
you'll excuse me . . ." He got up. Instantly she allowed her eyes to fill
with tears. "Oh, André, thank you, I'm so sorry, you're so kind to help
me and I'm sorry to upset you," she sobbed, and was pleased to see him
melt at once.

"Don't cry, Angelique, I'm not upset with you, it's not your fault,
it's . . . I apologize, it must be terrible for you but please don't worry,
I'll fetch the medicine on time and help all I can, just write down the
questions and in the next few days I'll have the answers for you. Sorry,
it's . . . I've not been feeling well recently . . ."

She had pretended to comfort him and, after he had left, she weighed
what he had told her, looking out through the flyspecked curtains to
High Street, seeing nothing.

Thirty days? Never mind. I can live with the delay, nothing will
show, she was thinking over and over, wanting to convince herself.
Twenty-two more days won't matter.

To make sure she took out her diary, unlocked it and began counting.
Then she re-counted and reached the same day. November 7th. Friday.
The saint day of Saint Theodore. Who is he? I'll light candles to him
every Sunday. No need to mark the day, she thought with a shiver.
Nonetheless, she put a small cross in the corner. What about Confes-
sion?

God understands. HE understands everything.

I can wait—but what if.

What if it doesn't work or André gets sick or lost or killed, or the
mama-san fails me, or any one of a thousand reasons?

This gnawed at her. It obliterated her resolve. Real tears wet her
cheeks. Then, suddenly, she remembered what her father had once
said, years upon years ago, just before he had deserted her and her little
brother, in Paris . . .

"Yes, he deserted us," she said out loud, the first time she had ever
articulated that truth. "He did. *Mon Dieu,* from what I know now,
probably that's just as well. He would have sold us, certainly sold me
long since."

Her father had quoted his idol, Napoleon Bonaparte: "A wise general always has a line of retreat planned, from which to launch the
hammer blow of victory."

What is my line of retreat?

Then something André Poncin had said weeks ago slid into her
mind. She smiled, all her care vanishing.

*   *   *

Phillip Tyrer was putting the final touches to the draft of Sir William's reply to the *roju* in his best copperplate writing. Unlike all previous communications, Sir William was sending the original in English and a copy in Dutch, which Johann had been told to prepare.

"There, Johann, I'm done." He finished the tail of the 'B' of Sir William Aylesbury, K.C.B. with an intricate twirl.

"Scheiss in meinem Hut!" Johann beamed. "That's the best writing I've ever seen. No wonder Wee Willie wants you to copy all his London dispatches."

"Shigata ga nai!" Tyrer said without thinking. It doesn't matter.

"You're really working at it, the Japanese, eh?"

"Yes, yes, I am, and between us, for God's sake, don't tell Willie, I enjoy it immensely. What do you think of his ploy?"

Johann sighed. "With Jappos I don't think. Me, I think Jappo mealymouthing has scrambled his head."

The message read:

To His Excellency, Nori Anjo, Esq., Chief roju. *I have your dispatch of yesterday and inform you it is rejected entirely. If you do not pay the agreed installment of the indemnity for the murder of two British soldiers on time, the amount owing will be quadrupled for every day of delay.*

I am sorry to learn you are clearly not masters of your own calendar. I will correct this for you at once. I will leave for Kyōto on my flagship with an escorting squadron, twelve days from today, docking at Osaka. Then, with a mounted escort and obligatory sixty-pound cannon of our mounted Royal Artillery for royal salutes, I and the other Ministers will proceed at once to Kyōto to seek redress for you from His young Majesty, Shōgun Nobusada personally or, if he is not available, from His Imperial Highness, Emperor Komei personally, promising full royal honours with a twenty-one-cannon salute. Please inform them of our impending arrival. (signed) Her Britannic Majesty's Minister and Ambassador, Sir William Aylesbury, K.C.B. . . .

"Emperor? What Emperor?" Johann said disgustedly. "There's only the Midako, Mikado, some name like that, and he's only a kind of minor pope without power, not like Pius the Ninth, who meddles and connives and plays politics and, like all *Gottverdammt* Catholics, wants us back on the stake!"

"Come now, Johann, they're not all bad. Now English Catholics can vote and even stand for Parliament like anyone who's eligible."

"The pox on Catholics. I'm Swiss and we don't forget."

"Then why are the Pope's personal guards all Swiss?"

"They're Catholic mercenaries." Johann shrugged. "Give me the rough copy of the dispatch and I'll get to work."

"Sir Willie says you're not renewing your contract."

"It's time to move on and leave the field to younger and wiser." Johann beamed suddenly. "You."

"That's not funny. Please send Nakama in, I think he's in the garden."

"Don't trust that bastard. Best watch him, Phillip."

Tyrer wondered what Johann would say if he knew the real truth about him.

Hiraga opened the door. *"Hai, Taira-san?"*

"Ikimasho, Nakama-sensei, old chap, *hai?"* Let's go, all right? Tyrer said, beaming, still marvelling at the change.

When Hiraga had arrived at dawn this morning, gone were the dirt and rags and most of all the samurai haircut—his short hair now similar to that of almost any commoner. In his neat, starched but ordinary kimono, new sun hat hanging by its thong on his back, new *tabi* and thongs, he was like the son of a prosperous merchant.

'My God, you look terrific, Nakama,' he had burst out. 'That haircut suits you.'

'Ah, Taira-san,' Hiraga had said hesitantly, with pretended humility, following the ploy he and Ori had formulated. 'I think what you say me, he'rp me give up samurai, stop be samurai. Soon go back Choshu, become farmer 'rike grandfather, or in beer or saké factory.'

'Give up samurai? Is that possible?'

'*Hai.* Possib're. P'rease not want say more, yes?'

'All right. But it's a wise decision, congratulations.'

Involuntarily Hiraga ran his hand over his head, the close shorn sides and newness itching. 'Soon hair grows, Taira-san, same yours.'

'Why not?' Tyrer wore his hair, naturally wavy, almost to his shoulders. Unlike most he was fastidious about its cleanliness: a petti-point had hung over his bed forever, stitched by his mother, *Cleanliness is next to Godliness*. 'How are your bruises?'

'I forgotten them.'

'I *have* forgotten them.'

'Ah, thank you, I have forgotten them. Some good newses, Taira-san.' Elaborately, Hiraga had told him about going to the Yoshiwara and arranging Fujiko for tonight. 'She yours, o'rr night. Good, *neh*?'

For a moment Tyrer had been speechless. Impulsively he wrung Hiraga's hand. 'Thank you. My dear friend, thank you.' He had sat back and pulled out his pipe and offered tobacco to Hiraga who refused, hard put not to laugh. 'That's marvelous.' Tyrer's mind had jumped him ahead to their tryst, his heart throbbing and manhood conscious. 'My God, marvelous!'

With an effort he had put all those immediate, erotic thoughts aside to concentrate on the day's schedule. 'Have you arranged somewhere to stay in the village?'

'Yes. P'rease we go now, yes?'

During their walk to the Japanese quarter, always careful to keep their voices down and not speak English near any passerby, Tyrer had continued to probe Hiraga, mining diamonds, amongst them the names of the Shōgun and Emperor. At the dwelling of the shoya, he had inspected the shop and tiny drab room off it where Hiraga was supposed to be staying. Then he had brought him back to the Legation, completely pleased and reassured. 'Did you notice on the street how you were hardly noticed, even by the soldiers, now that you don't look like a samurai?'

'Yes. Taira-san. You can he'rp me, p'rease?'

'Anything, what?'

'I 'rike try to wear your clothes, become more 'rike gai-jin, yes?'

'Great idea!'

When they got back to the Legation, Tyrer hurried to see Sir William, excitedly had given him the names of the Shōgun and Emperor. 'I thought you would want to know at once, sir. Also another piece of info: I think I've understood correctly but he says all Japanese, even daimyos, have to get permission to visit Kyōto, where the Emperor lives.'

'What are daimyos?'

'That's what they call their kings, sir. But everyone, even them, they must get permission to visit Kyōto—he says the Bakufu, which is another name for the Shōgunate, like their Civil Service, are afraid to allow free access there, to anyone.' He had tried to keep calm but the words rushed out of him. 'If that's true, and if the Shōgun's there at present and the Emperor's there permanently and if all power's there—if you were to go there, sir, wouldn't that bypass the Bakufu?'

'An inspired leap of logic,' Sir William said kindly with a sigh of pleasure, already there, long before Tyrer had explained. 'Phillip, I think I will redraft the dispatch. Come back in an hour—you've done very well.'

'Thank you, sir.' Then he had told him about the 'new' Nakama and new haircut. 'My thought is that if we could persuade him into European clothes he would become more and more malleable—of course as he teaches me Japanese while I'm teaching him English.'

'Very good idea, Phillip.'

'Thank you, sir, I'll arrange it instantly. I can have the bill sent to our shroff for payment?'

Some of Sir William's good humor vanished. 'We have no excess funds, Phillip, and the Exchequer . . . Very well. But one outfit only. You're responsible the bill's modest.'

Tyrer had left hastily and now that he had finished his work on the dispatch, he was going to take Hiraga to the Chinese tailor down the road.

High Street was not crowded at this time of the day, midafternoon, most men in their countinghouses, or at siesta, or at the Club. A few drunks huddled in the lee of the wharfs, the wind still gusting. Later a football match had been arranged, Navy versus Army on their parade ground, and Tyrer was looking forward to it, but not to the meeting with Jamie McFay he had had to agree to, after the tailor's. "He's head of Struan's here, Nakama-san, somehow he'd found out about you, and that you can speak some English. He's to be trusted."

"*So ka?* Struan? The man who is to marry?"

"Oh, the servants told you about the engagement party? No, McFay's just their head merchant. Mr. Struan, the tai-pan, is the one who's going to be married. That's his building, warehouse, offices and living quarters."

"*So ka?*" Hiraga studied it. Difficult to attack or get into, he thought. Barred lower windows. "This Struan, also his woman, they stay there?"

Tyrer's mind leapt to Fujiko and he said absently, "Struan does, I'm not sure about her. In London, this building would be nothing compared to ordinary houses, thousands upon thousands. London's the richest city in the world."

"Richer than Yedo?"

Tyrer laughed. "Richer than twenty, fifty Yedos, how do I say that in Japanese?"

Hiraga told him, his sharp eyes taking in everything—disbelieving about London and most of what Tyrer was telling him as lies to confuse him.

Now they were passing the various bungalows that served as Legations, picking their way through the rubbish that was strewn everywhere. "Why different f'rags, p'rease?"

Tyrer wanted to practice speaking Japanese, but every time he started, Hiraga would answer in English and at once ask another question. Even so he explained, pointing them out: "They're Legations: that's the Russian, the American, over there's the French— that one's Prussian. Prussia's an important nation on the Continent. If I wanted to say th—"

"Ah, so sorry, you have map of your wor'rd, p'rease?"

"Oh, yes, I'd be glad to show it to you."

A detachment of soldiers approached and marched past, paying them no attention. "These men of Prush'ah," Hiraga pronounced the word carefully, "they also war against French?"

"Sometimes. They're certainly warlike, always battling someone. They've just got a new King and his chief supporter is a big tough prince called Bismarck who's trying to collect all German speakers into one great nation and—"

"P'rease, so sorry, Taira-san, not so fast, yes?"

"Ah gomen nasai." Tyrer repeated what he had said but more slowly, answering more questions, never failing to be astounded at their number and extent and range of his protégé's enquiring mind. He laughed again. "We must have an agreement, one hour about my world in English, one hour about yours in English, and then a one-hour conversation in Japanese. *Hai?*"

"Hai. Domo."

Four horsemen going out to the racetrack overtook them, greeted Tyrer and looked Hiraga over curiously. Tyrer greeted them back. At the far end of High Street by the barrier, lines of coolies with the afternoon's shipment of goods and foods began to clear through the Custom House under the watchful eye of the samurai guards. "We'd best hurry, don't want to get mixed up with that lot," he said, and crossed the road, picking his way through the horse manure, then stopped abruptly and waved. They had been passing the French Legation. Angelique was standing at her ground floor window, the curtains pulled aside. She smiled and waved back. Hiraga pretended not to have noticed her scrutiny.

"That's the lady Mr. Struan's going to marry," Tyrer said, walking on again. "Beautiful, isn't she?"

"*Hai.* That her house, yes?"

"Yes."

"Good night, Mr. McFay. Everything's locked up."

"Thanks. 'Night, Vargas." McFay stifled a yawn, continued writing his daily journal, the last job of the day. His desk was clear but for two weeks' worth of newspapers still to be read, his In tray empty, Out tray spilling over with answers to most of today's mail, and orders, bills of lading already completed and signed, ready for collection at sunup when business began.

Vargas absently scratched at a flea bite, a way of life in Asia, and put the key to the strong room on the desk. "Shall I bring you more light?"

"No, thanks, I'm almost finished. See you tomorrow."

"The Choshus are due tomorrow, about the guns."

"Yes, I hadn't forgotten. Good night."

Now that he was alone in this part of the ground floor McFay felt happier, always pleased to be on his own and always safe within himself. Except for Vargas, all clerks, shroffs and other staff had their own staircase and rooms far to the back of the godown. The communicating door between the two sections was locked nightly. Only Ah Tok and their personal servants stayed in this foresection that contained offices, the strong room where all guns, ledgers, safes with all specie in Mexican silver dollars, gold taels and Japanese coin were kept, and their living quarters on the floor above.

Mail day was always busy and a late night, tonight later than most because the moment he had got the last installment of *Great Expectations* from Nettlesmith, he had rushed upstairs and shared his allotted hour, page by relished page with Malcolm Struan, then had come down again delighted and satisfied that all had worked out for Pip and the girl and that a new Dickens epic would be announced in next month's edition.

The grandfather clock was ticking pleasantly. He wrote rapidly with a fine clear hand:

MS was enraged with his mother's letter in today's mail (Steamship Swift Wind, *a day late, one man lost overboard in storm off Shanghai, also she had to run the gauntlet in the Shimonoseki Straits, the shore batteries firing perhaps twenty rounds, without hurt, thank God!). My reply to my Mrs. S's cannonade today was honeyed (she has not yet heard about the party that will cause an explosion from Hong Kong to Java) but doubt if it will smooth any waters.*

I informed her that A had moved over to the French Legation but don't think that will mean a damn to Mrs. S, though MS was fretful all day that A hadn't visited him and again swore at Ah Tok, putting her in a filthy mood—which she passed on to all the other servants, ayeeyah!

I must record in spite of all his pain that MS is much wiser than I imagined, with an excellent grasp of business generally, and international trade, and now accepts my view that there is great potential here. We discussed the Brock problem and agreed there was nothing to be done from here but as soon as he returned to HK, he would deal with them. Again he refused to consider returning on the mail ship—Hoag fence sits and is not my ally, saying the longer Malcolm rests here, the better—a bad voyage could be traumatic.

Had a first meeting with this Japanese Nakama (that has to be an alias) who is certainly more than he pretends to be. A samurai, a ronin outlaw, who can speak some English, who would cut his hair because he has decided to give up his samurai status, who seeks to wear our clothes, has to be out of the ordinary, and watched carefully. If half of what he says is true, then we have made—through Tyrer, bless him—a major intelligence step forward. Pity that Nakama knows nothing about business, his only usable information was that Osaka is Japan's main business center, not Yedo, so all the more reason to press for the opening of that city as soon as possible. Nakama is certainly to be cultivated and . . .

There was a tap on one of the shutters. He glanced at the clock, almost ten. An hour late. Never mind, Asian time's different to our time.

Without haste he got up, slipped the small revolver into the side pocket of his frock coat, went to his private door and unlocked it. Outside were two women muffled in hooded cloaks, with a manservant. They all bowed. He beckoned the women in, gave a few coins to

the man who thanked him, bowed again and went back down the side
alley towards the Yoshiwara.

McFay relocked the door. "Heya, Nemi, you all same pretty, *neh*?"
He smiled and hugged one of them.

The girl beamed at him from under her hood, a sparkle to her, his
musume for a year and kept by him for half that time. "Heya, Jami-san,
you-ah gud, heya? This *musume* my sister, Shizuka. Pretty, *neh*?"

Nervously the other girl moved her hood aside, forced a smile. He
began to breathe again—Shizuka was as young as Nemi, as attractive
and fragrant. *"Hai!"* he said, and both were relieved that she had
passed initial scrutiny. This was the first time McFay had ever arranged
a girl for someone else. Awkwardly, he had asked Nemi to make sure
the mama-san understood the girl was for the tai-pan and therefore had
to be special. Both girls were in their early twenties, barely coming up
to his shoulder, both more at ease now though completely aware the
real hurdle had yet to be surmounted.

"Shizuka, I please you see. Tai-pan top man," he said kindly, then to
Nemi, patting his side where Struan's wound was, "She understand
about wound, *neh*?"

Nemi nodded, her white teeth sparkling. *"Hai,* I 'sp'rain, Jami-san!
Dozo, 'reave coat here, or up'stair?"

"Upstairs."

He led the way up the great staircase, well lit with oil lamps, Nemi
chattering to the new girl who was all eyes. It was his custom, from
time to time, to send for Nemi to spend the night here, the manservant
returning just before dawn to escort her back to the little dwelling he
had bought for her within the grounds of her house, the Inn of Succulent Joy. Ten gold sovereigns it had cost him for a five-year lease for
the house after days of haggling. Another ten for her contract for the
same period, plus extra for a new kimono each month, hairdressing, a
personal maid, and saké.

'But Mama-san, what if fire burn house down, heya?' he had asked,
appalled that he was agreeing to such a huge price though the extraor-
dinarily advantageous exchange rate gave them a profit of four hundred percent most months—which meant that almost everyone could
keep a pony or two, consume champagne at will, and more importantly
guaranteed that Nemi's running expenses would not amount to more
than a few pounds yearly.

The mama-san was shocked. 'Bui'd 'rike new. You pay ha'f price,
fair, *neh*?'

Nemi, present at the final negotiation, had laughed. 'P'renti fire in house, Jami-san, p'renti jig jig, *neh*?'

When McFay reached the top of the stairs he gave her another happy hug for no reason, other than she had proved to be worth every farthing, giving him so much pleasure and so much peace. On the landing was a large high-back chair. Nemi took off her cloak and hood, telling the other girl to do likewise, leaving them there. Neat and pretty kimonos underneath, hair well coiffured—chrysalis into butterfly. Pleased with himself he knocked on the door.

"Come in."

Malcolm Struan sat in his chair, a cheroot smoldering between his fingers, elegant in his dressing gown but ill at ease. "Hello, Jamie."

"Evening, Tai-pan." Both girls bowed with great deference; McFay quite unaware that almost everything about Malcolm Struan—as well as himself and most gai-jin—was common knowledge and the subject of constant and avid Yoshiwara gossip, his enormous wealth, that he had recently become tai-pan, the circumstances of his wound and now impending marriage. "This's Shizuka, she'll stay with you. The servant'll arrive just before dawn, everything as I told you. I'll knock first. She may be a bit shy but, well, no problem. This's my *musume,* Nemi. I, er, I thought it best, the first time, to bring her along to make things easier."

Both girls bowed again. "Heya, Tai-pan," Nemi said in complete control, delighted to meet him and confident with her choice. "Shizuka sister my, good *musume,* heya!" She nodded vigorously and gave Shizuka a little push. The girl went over to him, hesitantly, knelt and bowed again.

"I'll be in my rooms if you need me."

"Thanks, Jamie."

McFay closed the door quietly, went further down the corridor. His suite was tidy, masculine and comfortable. Three rooms, sitting room, bedroom, spare bedroom, all with fireplaces, and a bathroom. On the sideboard were cold cuts, fresh bread and her favorite, a freshly baked apple pie, the apples imported from Shanghai. Saké in a container of hot water, and Loch Vey whisky from Struan's own distillery that she adored.

The moment the door was bolted she stood on tiptoe and kissed him hungrily. "No see six day, first bed-u then ba'f!" she said, reversing the usual order. His heart picked up a beat though he was in no hurry.

She took him by the hand, led him into the bedroom and half pushed him onto the bed, knelt to pull off his boots and began to undress him, all the time chattering in her half-comprehensible pidgin, telling him that the Yoshiwara was abuzz with business, the Floating World prosperous, not to worry about Shizuka, she was expensive but the best, and what was this they hear about war and please we do not want war, just business, and I have a new kimono with lucky carp all over it that was, well, a little expensive, "but *ichiban,* Jami-san, you-ah 'rike veri. Bed-u!"

Obediently he got into the four-poster. The night was perfect, neither hot nor cool. She untied her obi, let the kimono fall, then her underkimono and slip. Quite naked, completely without guilt or shame about nudity like all *musume*—one of the many characteristics that set them apart, and one that McFay and all gai-jin found so astounding and enviable—she took the pins from her hair, shook it and let it fall to her waist and marched triumphantly to the bathroom and the first delight of the evening.

She sat on the toilet and reached up for the handle to the chain of the water closet and pulled. The water roared down into the porcelain bowl and, as always, she clapped her hands with glee.

The first time she had seen it she had not believed it. 'Where wat'er go?' she asked suspiciously. He had explained and drawn pictures but she still would not believe him until he had shown her the pipes and taken her into the garden where the manhole cover of the septic tank was—all pipes, water tanks, boilers, toilet bowls, hand basins, sinks, taps and the three baths imported from England, Hong Kong and Shanghai where many pieces were beginning to be manufactured for the vast Indian and Asian markets.

She had begged him to allow her to show her friends. Proudly he had agreed because this was the first such installation in all Japan, to Sir William's chagrin and Norbert Greyforth's fury, and now the pattern of the dozen or so working and nonworking copies, though not all with hot and cold water: nothing but the best and most modern, therefore British, for Struan's.

So guided tours of the privileged few to examine the Jami-san cleansing room became one of the most sought-after sights of gai-jin Yokohama, the chattering *musume* like so many exotic birds, bowing and sucking in their breaths and pulling the chain to gasps of wonder and applause.

Nemi washed her hands. With a contented sigh, she slipped under the sheets beside him.

*   *   *

Phillip Tyrer was spent and almost asleep. Fujiko bore his weight comfortably, then began to ease away.

"Iyé, matsu," *No, don't move . . . wait,* he murmured.

"I just want to fetch a towel, Taira-san. Towel, do you understand?"

"Ah, ah yes. Understand towel. You stay I get . . ."

"Oh, no, I would lose face, it is my duty. Let me go, please. . . . now do not be difficult or naughty."

She chuckled as he nuzzled her and held on but she was deft and knew her craft well and waited. Now the small room was peaceful. Outside the night was fair. Wind rustled the trees and bushes. A few drafts from around the sliding windows, not yet cold or unpleasant. Flickering oil lamp.

In a moment she slid away without disturbing his tranquility and went to the little bathroom with its high wooden tub, filled to the brim with hot water, which was on a wooden grill to allow the water to flow away when the bung was pulled out. Scented soap and chamber pot and fresh towels. Quickly she used a damp towel and dried herself.

When she came back she brought a hot towel, sponged him then dried him. All the while his eyes were tightly closed and he was near moaning with pleasure, at the same time embarrassed that she was doing it for him, not he for her. *"Ah, Fujiko-chan, you are wonderful."*

"No, it is my pleasure," she said, long over her wonder and embarrassment at the strange habits of the foreigners: that they rarely bathed, were usually consumed with shame and guilt over pillow pleasures, were astoundingly possessive and usually furious that she had other clients—stupid, what were they but clients?—or turning away, blushing, when she was undressing for their enjoyment, or covering themselves when only half naked, preferring to fornicate in the dark when everyone knew much of the thrill was to see, examine and observe, or were embarrassed purple when she attempted normal variations to prevent boredom and to prolong and increase Moments with the Gods—the time of the Clouds and the Rain.

No, gai-jin aren't like us. They almost always favor First Position with Urgency, occasionally Baiting the Hen or Cherry Blossom Time, so allowing me no opportunity to demonstrate my skills, or when, in the light, I would position myself to play with the One-Eyed Monk the many games of uplifting such as Near and Far, Over the Dragon, Springtime Planting, Stealing the Honey that even the most unpracticed youth would require and appreciate, a gai-jin would jerk away, firmly but gently pull me up alongside him, kiss my neck, hold tight and mumble incomprehensibles.

She murmured, *"Now I'll massage you to sleep."*

"Don't understand. Mess'erge?"

"Massage, Taira-san. Like this."

"Ah, now I understand. Massage, thank you."

Her fingers were gentle and wonderful and he drifted away, hardly believing his luck, proud of his performance and that she had ecstatically finished three times at least to his once—and never mind that Raiko had said that tomorrow Fujiko had to visit her village, near Yedo, to see her sick grandfather, *". . . but only for a few days, Taira-san."*

"Oh, so sorry, Raiko-san. Please, how many day 'way?"

"How many days will she be away? Only three."

"Ah, thank you. How many days will she be away?" Tyrer repeated—he had asked her and Fujiko, always to correct him.

Three days. That will give me time to recover. My God, that was the best. Wonder what will happen when the *roju* get our dispatch. I'm sure my advice's correct and that Nakama is telling the truth—God, I've a lot to thank him for, Sir William was positively beaming, and as for Fujiko . . .

Lulled by her touch, his mind began a jumble of Nakama and her and being in Japan and everything so different and learning Japanese, incessant words and phrases leaping forward untidily. The futons were hard and difficult to get used to but he was comfortable, lying on his stomach, enjoying her nearness. God, but I'm tired. Can't stand the idea of 'other clients,' he thought. Got to make her mine, just mine. Tomorrow I'll ask André to help me.

Without turning he reached back, put his hand on her thigh. Lovely silky skin.

Where was I? Oh yes, the *roju*. We'll give the buggers what-for. Bloody awful about the mail ship being fired on—we've just got to make Shimonoseki safe and if the bloody Bakufu won't do it that means taking out those batteries ourselves. Must remember to be careful about that with Nakama, mustn't forget he's from Choshu too. Could I use him as a go-between? And if the *roju* won't deal with those Satsuma devils we'll have to crush them ourselves. The bloody effrontery of the daimyo saying that he can't find Canterbury's murderers, the bastards came out of his own ranks for God's sake, I saw them hack off Canterbury's arm and the blood sprayed . . .

Her fingers froze. *"What's the matter, Taira-san?"*

Before he knew it he was hugging her, wanting to block out the Tokaidō, and then, when the trembling had stopped he lay back, pulling her with him and held on to her, the warm pliant length of her against him, loving her, so thankful to be with her, waiting for the bad to return to its recess.

She lay quiet, also waiting, not thinking about him except that once more gai-jin proved to be curious indeed, beyond understanding. It was comfortable resting against him and she was glad that the first explosion had been achieved properly, that the client was satisfied, so she could safely believe she had earned her extra fee.

When Raiko was assigning all their appointments this morning, the mama-san had told her she was putting up her rate: 'with Taira, only, because you will have extra work. Remember he could be a big fish for you, Fujiko, a long-term patron much better than Kant-er-bury-san if we're careful and if you please him. Frenchy tells me he's an important official so strive hard to please him. Only speak Japanese, no pidgin, become a teacher, encourage him, and remember he is ridiculously shy and knows nothing and never mention Kant-er-bury. We will pretend you have to go away for a few days—but do not worry, I have two clients for you tomorrow, in the afternoon a gai-jin, a civilized person at night. . . .'

With a generous patron for a year or two I could quickly pay off my debts, and life would be much better than having to take whatever client was available, she thought, then contentedly abandoned the present as she always tried to do when with a client, projecting herself into the future where she lived happily with her rich farmer husband and four or five sons. She could see their farmhouse amid their many rice fields, abundant with green shoots of winter or spring plantings, promising another rich harvest, her mother-in-law kind and pleased with her, a bullock or two tethered to a plow, flowers in the little garden and . . .

"Ah, Fujiko. Thank you, you are wonderful!"

She nestled closer and said how strong and manly he was.

"What?" he asked sleepily. One of her hands answered intimately and he twisted. *"No, Fujiko, please, first sleep. No . . . please, later . . ."*

"Ah, but a strong man like you . . ." she murmured, hid her boredom, and continued dutifully.

Ori yawned and took his eye away from the spy hole. "I've seen enough," he whispered. "Shocking."

"I agree." Hiraga kept his voice down too. "Terrible. Fujiko's performance was the worst I've ever seen. *Baka!*"

"If I was Taira I would demand my money back."

"I agree. *Baka!* She won't have him ready for hours and as for him . . . only First Position once and talk about urgency! Ten thrusts and poof, Over the Moon like a duck."

Ori had to hold his hand over his mouth to stop the laughter, then carefully he stuck little pieces of paper to cover the holes they had made in the far corner of the shoji screen. Together they slipped away into the bushes, through the secret gate in the fence, and thence to Ori's dwelling.

"Saké!"

Half asleep the maid set the tray in front of them, poured and shuffled away, still finding it difficult not to stare at their heads. They toasted each other and refilled the cups, the room small and pleasant, candle-lit, with bed futons already made up in the adjoining room. Swords were on low lacquer racks—Raiko had bent the Yoshiwara rule forbidding weapons within the walls because they were shishi, because of Hiraga's portrait and because both had swore by *sonno-joi* not use the weapons against anyone in the House, or any guest, and only in defense.

"I cannot believe Taira was taken in by her faked Moment with the Gods, Hiraga, one after another like that! Her acting was terrible. Is he that stupid?"

"Obviously." Hiraga laughed and rubbed the back and sides of his head vigorously. "Eeee, with that sized weapon he should have really made her squeal—are all gai-jin built like that?"

"Who cares—in his case it is wasted."

"No finesse, Ori! Perhaps I should get him a pillow book like a virgin bride, eh?"

"Better we kill him and them and fire the Settlement."

"Be patient, we will, there is plenty of time."

"He is a perfect target, it is another perfect opportunity," Ori said, an edge creeping into his voice.

Hiraga watched him, all warmth gone of a sudden. "Yes, but not now, he's too important."

"You said yourself if we could infuriate them enough they'd bombard Yedo and that would be wonderful for our cause."

"Yes, you are right, but we have time." Hiraga showed none of his concern, appeasing him, wanting him controlled. "Taira is answering all my questions. For instance, no one told us gai-jin fight each other like wild dogs, worse than daimyos before Toranaga—the Dutch hid that from us, eh?"

"They are all liars and barbarians."

"Yes, but there must be hundreds of bits of information like that, that will unlock the way to play them, and dominate them. We must learn everything, Ori, and then, when we're part of the new Bakufu, we will set German against Russian against Frenchman against Ing'erish against American . . ."

Hiraga shivered, remembering the little Tyrer had told him about that civil war, the battles and casualties, all the modern weapons and hundreds of thousands of armed men involved, and the unbelievable vastness of the gai-jin lands. "This evening he said the Inger'ish Navy rules the world oceans, that by their law is twice as big as the next two navies combined, with hundreds of men-o'-war, thousands of cannon."

"Lies. Exaggeration to frighten you. He and all of them want us cowed, you as much as any. He wants our secrets too!"

"I only give him what I think he should know." Hiraga belched irritably. "Ori, we've got to learn about them! These dogs have conquered most of the world—humbled China and burned Peking, and this year the French became overlords of Cochin-China and are set to colonize Cambodia."

"Yes, but the French played native prince against native prince like the British in India. This is Japan. We're different—this is the Land of the Gods. With all the cannon in the world they will never conquer us." Ori's face twisted strangely. "Even if they seduce some daimyos to their side, even then, the rest of us will slaughter them."

"Not without cannon and knowledge."

"Without cannon, yes, Hiraga-san."

Hiraga shrugged and poured for both of them. There were many shishi who shared Ori's zeal—and had forgotten Sun-tzu: *Know your enemy as you know yourself and you will win a hundred battles.* "I hope you are right, meanwhile I will find out as much as I can. Tomorrow he promised to let me look at a map of the world—he called it an 'at'ras.' "

"How do you know it will not be false, made up?"

"That is not likely, not falsifying one. Perhaps I could even get a copy, we could have it translated—and some of their schoolbooks." Hiraga's excitement picked up. "Taira said they have new skills in counting, taught in ordinary schools, and astronomy measurers called 'rong-tit-tude, 'ra-tit-ude," Hiraga pronounced the English words with difficulty, "that somehow guide them with fantastic accuracy on the oceans, a thousand *ri* from land. *Baka* that I know so little! *Baka* that I cannot read English!"

"You will," Ori said. "I never will. You will be part of our new government—I never will."

"Why say that?"

"I worship *sonno-joi,* I have already thought of my death poem, and spoken it. I told it to Shorin, the night of the attack. *Baka* that he got himself killed too soon." Ori drained his cup and poured the last drops and ordered a new flask. He looked at Hiraga narrowly. "I heard your Lord Ogama will pardon any Choshu shishi who publicly forswears *sonno-joi.*"

Hiraga nodded. "My father wrote to me about that. It means nothing to us—to Choshu shishi."

"There is a rumor that Ogama controls the Gates, excluding everyone else—even that there's new fighting between his troops and Satsumas."

"Many daimyos are misguided, from time to time," Hiraga said levelly, not liking the way the conversation was going, noticing that, in his cups, Ori was ever more quarrelsome. Tonight Raiko had again warned him that Ori was a smoking volcano. "We all agreed long ago not to be bound by the deeds or misdeeds of our hereditary leaders."

"If Ogama holds the Gates he could give back power to the Emperor and make *sonno-joi* a fact."

"Perhaps he will, perhaps he has already."

Ori drained the cup. "I will be glad to leave Yokohama. Poison is in the air. Better you come to Kyōto with me. This nest of liars may infect you."

"You will be safer on the road to Kyōto without me. Even without my hair I could be recognized."

A sudden gust tugged at the roof thatch and rattled a half-opened shutter. They glanced at it momentarily, then went back to drinking. The saké had loosened them but had not dispelled the undercurrents, thoughts of death and the net tightening around them, or of the planned ambush of Shōgun Nobusada, of Shorin and Sumomo, and most of all, *what about the gai-jin girl?* Hiraga had not yet mentioned her nor had Ori yet asked about her but both were waiting, both circling this central issue, both impatient and still undecided.

Ori broke the silence. "When Akimoto arrives tomorrow how much are you going to tell him?"

"Everything we know. He will travel to Kyōto with you."

"No, better he stays, you will need a fighter here."

"Why?"

Again Ori shrugged. "Two are better than one. Now," he said flatly, "tell me where she is."

Hiraga described the place. Exactly. "There were no bars on the windows or side door I could see." All day he had been wondering what to do about Ori—if Ori broke into the house and killed her, whether he lived or died, the whole Settlement would be in an uproar and their venom would first turn on every Japanese within reach. "I agree she is a correct target for *sonno-joi* but not yet, not while I am accepted by them and learning so many of their secrets."

"Such a perfect target should be dealt with at once. Katsumata said to hesitate is to lose. We can get those secrets out of books."

"I have already said: I do not agree."

"At the same time I kill her we fire the Yoshiwara and thus the Settlement, the three of us, and retreat in the confusion. We do it two days from now."

"No."

"I say yes! Two or three days, no more!"

Hiraga thought about that, and Ori, very carefully. Icily. Then again he decided: "It-is-forbidden."

The finality of the words washed over Ori. For the second time in as few days. Both times over *her*.

No sound in the room now. Both impassive. Outside they could hear the wind. It had dropped a little. From time to time it crackled the shoji's oiled paper. Ori sipped, seething, implacably committed but showing none of it, knowing that if both his arms were as strong as before and he was as agile as before, he would be readying to dive for his sword to fend off the attack that, unless he surrendered, was inevitable.

Never mind. In a direct fight, even if I were totally fit, Hiraga would always beat me to the first cut. Therefore he must be removed from my path in another way.

With a will to match the new enemy who was determined to thwart him, Ori vowed he would not be the first to break the silence and so lose face. Pressure between them soared. In seconds it became unbearable, now cresting . . .

Running footsteps. The shoji slid back. Raiko was chalky. "Bakufu Enforcer patrols are on the bridge and at the Gate. You must leave. Hurry!"

Both were aghast, all else forgotten. They went for their swords. "Will they come into the Yoshiwara?" Ori asked.

"Yes, in twos and threes, they have before, avoiding gai-jin but not us." Her voice trembled like her hands.

"Is there a safe way out through the paddy?"

"Everywhere and nowhere, Ori," Hiraga said for her, having examined that as a possible escape route yesterday. "The land's flat with no cover for a *ri*. If they're blocking the Gate and the bridge they'll be there too."

"What about the gai-jin area, Raiko?"

"The Settlement? They've never gone there. You mus—" She whirled, even more frightened. Both men jerked their swords half out, while a white-faced maid rushed up. "They are in the lane, making a house-to-house search," she whimpered.

"Warn the others."

The girl fled. Hiraga tried to get his brain working. "Raiko, where is your safe place, your secret cellar?"

"We have none," she said, wringing her hands.

"There must be one somewhere."

Abruptly Ori snaked over to her and she backed off, terrified. "Where's the secret way into the Settlement? Quick!"

Raiko almost fainted as he shifted his grip on his sword hilt and though not actually menaced, she knew she was near death. "I . . . into the Settlement? I—I'm not sure but—but years ago I was—was told . . . I'd forgotten," she said, trembling. "I'm not sure, but—but please follow quietly."

They stayed close to her, going deep in the bushes, careless of the branches that fought to prevent their passage, the moon still good and high between scudding clouds, the wind tugging at them. When she reached a hidden part of the fence between her Inn and the next, she pressed a knot in the wood. A section creaked open, the wooden hinges grimed and unused.

Without disturbing the carousers, she crossed this garden to the far side, through a gate into another garden and around the back, past the low, bricked, fireproof structure that served as a safe for valuables, to where the large water tanks, or wells were—the tanks part filled by rainwater, part by daily lines of water coolies.

Panting, she motioned at the wooden cover over a well. "I think . . . I think it is there."

Hiraga eased the cover aside. Crude, rusty iron bars as footholds and handholds were hammered into the mud brick walls, no sign of water below. Still frightened she whispered, "I was told it leads to a tunnel. . . . I am not sure but I was told it goes under the canal but where it comes out I do not know. I had forgotten about it. . . . I must get back. . . ."

"Wait!" Ori stepped in her way, picked up a stone and dropped it into the well. A loud plop as it hit water far below. "Who made this?"

"Bakufu, I was told, when they built the Settlement."

"Who told you about it?"

"One of the manservants—I forget who, but he had seen them . . ." They all looked over towards the main street. Angry voices there. "I have to get back . . ." She vanished the way she had come.

Uneasily they peered below. "If the Bakufu built it, Ori, it could be a trap, for people like us."

From one of the nearby houses the sound of voices cursing in English: "What the hell d'you want . . . push off!"

Ori stuck his long sword in his belt. Awkwardly because of his shoulder, he slid over the lip and began to descend. Hiraga followed, replacing the cover.

The blackness seemed ever more black, then Ori's feet hit earth again. "Careful, I think it is a ledge." His voice was strangled and echoed eerily.

Hiraga groped down beside him. In his sleeve pocket were some safety matches and he scraped one alight.

"Eeee," Ori said excitedly, "where did you get that?"

"They have them everywhere in the Legation—those dogs are so rich they just leave them around. Taira said to help myself. Look there!" In the last of the match they saw the mouth of the tunnel. It was dry and the height of a man. Water filled the well ten feet below them. In a niche was an old candle. It took Hiraga three matches to light it. "Come on."

The tunnel sloped downwards. After fifty paces or so it became wet, the floor puddled and awash in parts. Fetid water seeped down from the roughly shored roof and sides, the wood rotting and unsafe. As they went onwards the air became more rancid, breathing difficult. "We can wait here, Ori."

"No, go on."

They were sweating, in part from fear, in part from the closeness. The flame guttered and went out. Cursing, Hiraga lit it and cupped the flame, not much of the wick left or of the candle. He waded onwards, the water level rising. Still the roof sloped downwards, now the water to their hips. Ori slipped but regained his footing. Another twenty or thirty paces. Water still rising. Now to their waists, the roof not far above their heads. Onwards. Candle weakening. On again.

Hiraga was watching the candle, cursing. "Better we go back and wait in the dry part."

"No, go on until the candle goes out."

Ahead the tunnel curled into the blackness, the roof lowering to not far above the water. Nauseated, Hiraga waded forward again, the bottom slippery. More paces. The roof pressed against his head. More, and now the roof rose slightly. "Water level is going down," he said, sick with relief, wading faster, the murk stinking. Around the bend, roof higher now. Onwards. Just before the candle spluttered and died they saw dry earth and the tunnel end, a shaft leading up, another down.

Hiraga groped forward, unable to see anything. "Ori, now I am at the edge. Listen, I will toss a stone down into it." The stone took seconds and seconds ricocheting before it plopped dully. "Eeee, it must go down a hundred feet or more," he said, his stomach heaving.

"Light another match."

"I have only three left." Hiraga lit one. They could see rusty, precarious footholds leading upwards, nothing more. "How did you know Raiko knew about this?"

"It was a sudden thought. There had to be a tunnel—I would have built one if I had been them." Ori's voice was hoarse, heavy breathing. "They could be up there, in ambush. They will shove us back, or we will have to jump."

"Yes."

"Hurry up, I hate it here. Climb!"

Equally uncomfortable, Hiraga eased his long sword in his belt. Ori backed nervously, gripping his sword hilt. Abruptly the two men faced each other, near safety perhaps, but nothing solved between them.

The match guttered and went out.

In the blackness they could no longer see each other. Without thinking each had at once retreated against the tunnel wall away from the lip. Hiraga, more battle cunning, dropping to one knee, his hand on his hilt ready to slash the legs from under Ori if he attacked, listening intently for a sword sliding from its sheath.

"Hiraga!" Ori's voice rasped out of the black, well out of range, further away down the tunnel. "I want her dead. I will go after her—for *sonno-joi* and me. You want to stay. Solve the problem."

Silently Hiraga stood. "You solve it," he hissed, and at once, soundlessly, changed positions.

"I cannot. I cannot solve it, I have tried."

Hiraga hesitated, expecting a trick. "First put your swords down."

"And then?"

"Next: because she obsesses you above *sonno-joi*, you will not be armed near me in Yokohama, you will leave for Kyōto tomorrow and tell Katsumata, he is your Satsuma leader. When you return we will do it, everything as you said."

"And if I do not return?"

"Then I will do it—in a time of my choosing."

The voice grated even more. "But she could leave, escape, *neh*? What if she leaves before I return?"

"I will make sure I hear about any move and will send you word. If you cannot be here in time, I will decide. She—and her husband if by then they're married—they will only go to Hong Kong. You—or we—can follow her there." He heard Ori's heavy breathing and waited, on guard against a sudden rush, knowing he could not trust Ori while she was alive and near but this seemed to be the best plan for the moment. Killing him would be a waste. I need his wisdom. "You agree?"

He waited. And waited. Then, "Yes. What else?"

"Last: the cross, you will throw it down the well." Hiraga heard a sudden, angry intake of breath. The silence grew.

"I agree, Hiraga-san. Please accept my apologies."

Then his sharp ears heard the slight sound of cloth being moved, something went past him and then the tiny sound of metal hitting the well wall behind him, almost immediately to vanish below. Sound of swords being grounded.

Hiraga lit a match. Indeed now Ori was standing defenseless. At once Hiraga darted forward, Ori rushed back in panic but Hiraga only collected the swords. Before the match died he had had time to throw the swords also into the well. "Please obey me, Ori. Then you have nothing to fear. I will go first, wait till I call down to you."

The rungs were jagged with rust, some loose. The ascent was precarious. Then, far above, thankfully he saw the mouth of the well open to the sky, speckles of stars between clouds. Night sounds, wind and sea. Climbing again but more cautiously. It took all of his strength to ease himself up to the stone balustrade and peer around.

The abandoned well was near the canal fence, in a wasteland of weeds and derelict junk. Seashore not far off. Broken-down houses, deep potholes in the dirt roadways. Snarl of a foraging dog nearby. Raucous voices singing on the wind. Now Hiraga had his bearings. They were in Drunk Town.

22

Friday, 17th October:

In the morning light in Yedo Castle, Misamoto—the fisherman, fake samurai, and Yoshi's spy—was trembling on his knees in front of the alarmed Council of Elders, the English version of Sir William's reply shaking in his hand. Beside him cowered a Bakufu official.

"Speak up, fisherman!" Anjo, the chief Elder repeated, the audience room hushed and tense and chill. "Never mind if you don't understand all the Ing'erish words, we want to know if the Bakufu official translated the message accurately? Is that what the gai-jin message says? Exactly?"

"It's, well, yes, more or less, yes, Sire," Misamoto mumbled, so frightened he could hardly speak. "It's as the lord Official . . . more or less, Sire . . . more . . . or . . ."

"Have you seaweed for a tongue, fish offal for brains? Hurry up! Lord Toranaga says you can read Ing'erish—read!" An hour ago Anjo had been awakened by the unnerved Bakufu official who had brought Sir William's reply in Dutch and English. Hastily Anjo had convened a meeting of the Council where the official had just repeated his translation of the Dutch. "What does the paper say in Ing'erish?"

"Well, Sire, yes, it's, er . . ." Again Misamoto's voice died away, once more choked with panic.

Exasperated Anjo looked at Yoshi. "This fish head is your spy," he said with just the right amount of ice. "It was your idea to fetch him, please make him speak up."

"Tell us what the letter says, Misamoto," Yoshi said kindly, inwardly almost blind with frustration and anger. "No one is going to hurt you. In your own words. *The truth.*"

"Well, Sire, it's more or less as . . . more or less as the lord Official said, Sire," Misamoto stuttered, "but this's, this letter's, I don't know all the words, Sire, but some of them . . . well, well . . ." His face was twisted with fear.

Yoshi waited a moment. "Go on, Misamoto, don't be afraid, speak the truth, whatever it is. No one will touch you. We need the truth."

"Well, Sire, the gai-jin leader." Misamoto tried not to stammer. "He says he's going to Osaka in eleven days as the Official said, but not—not to make a—a 'Ceremonial visit' . . ." He quailed under the strength of their eyes, so terrified that now his nose was running and saliva dribbled his chin, then he blurted out, "He's not at all happy in fact he's strongly angry and he's going . . . going to Osaka with his fleet, going in force to Kyōto with cannon, sixty-pounders, and cavalry and soldiers to see the Son of Heaven and the Lord Shōgun—he's even named them, Sire, Emperor Komei and the boy Shōgun, Nobusada."

Everyone gasped, even the guards—normally impassive and not supposed to be listening. Misamoto shoved his head to the tatami and kept it there.

Yoshi pointed at the Bakufu official who blanched as all attention focused on him. "Is that correct?"

"Ceremonial visit, Sire? For your august ears that should be the correct translation . . . the barbarian wording is rude and uncouth and should, I sincerely believe, be correctly construed as a Ceremonial, State visit, an—"

"Does it say with 'cannon and cavalry' and such?"

"In principle, Sire, the lett—"

To everyone's shock, Yoshi almost shouted, "Yes or no?"

The Official swallowed, aghast that he was ordered to answer so directly, the first time in his life, and appalled that he was being challenged and ordinary rules and manners and the niceties of diplomacy were being disregarded. "I regret to inform you that, in principle, it does mention those but such an impertinence is clearly a mistake and—"

"Why did you not translate accurately?"

"For august ears, Sire, it is necessary to interpret—"

"Are those august persons named? Yes or no?"

"Their names are contained but y—"

"Are the characters of their names the correct ones?"

"It would seem, Sire, the characters appear to be c—"

"Write an exact translation of what it says at once." The raw words were said softly but the violence ricocheted off the unadorned stone walls. "Exact! Make all future communications from them, or to them, equally exact. EXACT! One mistake and your head will be on a rubbish dump. Get out! Misamoto, you did very well, please wait outside."

The two men fled, Misamoto cursing his ill luck and the day he had agreed to accompany Perry to Japan, believing the Bakufu would welcome him for his unique knowledge, would grant him a fortune— the Official swearing to be revenged on Yoshi and this lying fisherman before the Council made good the sentence that he, a wise and correct official, could not avoid.

Yoshi broke the silence, his mind working frantically to formulate the next move in the never ending conflict. "We cannot possibly allow an armed visit to Kyōto! This proves what I have been saying all along: we must have English speakers, translators we can trust—who will tell us what their foul messages really say!"

"That is not necessary," Toyama grated, his heavy dewlaps shaking with fury. "This gai-jin impertinence is insulting beyond belief, tantamount to a declaration of war. Such impertinence must be answered in blood." A rustle went through the guards. "It is a declaration of war. Good. In three or four days I will lead the surprise attack on the Settlement and finish this nonsense once and for all."

"That would be *baka*. We dare not. *Baka!*" Anjo repeated, more for the guards than anyone, easy for one to be a secret shishi admirer or *sonno-joi* adherent. "How many times must I say no attack yet, not even a surprise attack."

Toyama had flushed even more. "Yoshi-san," he said, "we could smash them and burn Yokohama, *neh*? We could, *neh*? I cannot bear the shame, it's too much!"

"You are right, of course we could destroy Yokohama, easily, but Anjo-dono is correct—we cannot get at their fleet. I suggest we continue as before," Yoshi said calmly, not feeling calm at all. "We supply them with watered soup and no fish: we offer them a meeting with the Council of Elders in thirty days, allowing ourselves to be negotiated down to eight days, delay that as long as we can."

"I will only meet those dogs on a battlefield."

Yoshi curbed his temper. "I'm sure you will do what the *roju* decides, but I propose you are represented by an imposter at this meeting: Misamoto."

"Eh?" They all stared at him.

"He'll be a perfect substitute."

Anjo said, "That stupid fisherman will never b—"

"Dressed in ceremonial clothes, taught to wear them, eight days is enough time. He looks like a samurai now though he does not act like one. Fortunately he is not stupid and he's so frightened that he will do whatever we order, and most important, he will tell the truth, which is in short supply." Yoshi saw Anjo redden. The others pretended not to notice.

"What then, Yoshi-san?"

"Next, we'll hold the meeting here in the castle."

"Out of the question!" Anjo said.

"Of course we first offer Kanagawa," Yoshi told him irritably, "then allow ourselves to agree to meet them here."

"Out of the question," Anjo said again to the agreement of the others.

"With the castle as bait we can delay again, perhaps even another month—their curiosity will consume them—and we only allow them into the outer area. Why not the castle? All the gai-jin leaders of their own free will within our grasp? We could take them hostage, their presence gives us a dozen chances to entwine them further."

They gaped at him, off balance. "Take them hostage?"

"A possibility, one of many," Yoshi said patiently, knowing he needed allies in the coming struggle. "We must use guile and silken threads and their own weakness against them, not war—until we can match their fleets."

"Until then?" Adachi spluttered. The rotund little man was the richest of them all and his Toranaga blood line equal to Yoshi's. "You really believe we have to deal with these dogs until we have fleets to match theirs?"

"Or enough big cannon to keep them off our shores. We only need a sack or two of gold and they will trample over themselves to sell us the means to blow them out of our water." Yoshi's brow darkened. "I heard a rumor that some Choshu emissaries are already trying to buy rifles from them."

"Those dogs!" Toyama spat with rage. "Always Choshu. The sooner we put them down the better."

"And Satsuma," Anjo muttered to general agreement, and looked at Yoshi. "And others!"

Yoshi pretended not to understand what his adversary implied. Never mind, he thought, the day is coming. "We can deal with all enemies, one at a time—not together."

Toyama said gruffly, "I vote we order all friendly daimyos to increase taxes at once and arm. I begin tomorrow."

" 'Advise' is a better word," Adachi said carefully, and drained his teacup. Delicate flowers decorated the lacquered trays that had been set in front of all of them. He stifled a yawn, bored and anxious to go back to bed. "Please go on with your plan, Yoshi-dono. Until we know all the details, how can we vote on it?"

"The morning of the meeting Anjo-sama will unfortunately be taken ill, oh, so sorry. As the whole *roju* is not present, we will be unable to make any binding decisions, but we will listen and try to reach a compromise. If we cannot compromise then we will, with suitable deference, agree to 'submit their desires to the full Council as soon as possible'—and delay and delay to drive them mad so they make a mistake, not us."

"Why should they agree to another delay?" Anjo asked, glad that he would not have to be nose to nose with gai-jin, distrusting Yoshi, and wondering where the trick was.

"The dogs have proved they would rather talk than fight, they are cowards," Yoshi was saying. "Though they could easily dominate us, it is clear they don't have the stomach for it."

"What if they do not agree and this insolent Inger'ish ape makes good his threat and leaves for Kyōto? What then? We cannot allow that, under any circumstances!"

"I agree," Yoshi said with great finality, and everyone tensed. "That means war—a war we must eventually lose."

Toyama said instantly, "Better to war as men than become slaves like the Chinese, Indians and all other barbarian tribes." The old man peered at Yoshi. "If they land you'll vote for war?"

"Instantly! Any attempt to land in force—anywhere—will be prevented."

"Good. Then I hope they land," Toyama said, satisfied.

"War would be very bad. I think they will talk and we can maneuver them out of this madness." Yoshi's voice became harsher. "We can if we are clever enough. Meanwhile we must concentrate on more important matters: like Kyōto and taking back control of our Gates, like the hostile daimyos, like getting enough gold to buy weapons and modernize and equip our forces—and those of our trusted allies—and not allow Choshu, Tosa and Satsuma to arm under the guise of supporting us, merely to more quickly attack us."

"The traitor Ogama should be outlawed," Toyama said. "Why don't we outlaw him and take back our Gates?"

"To attack him now would be *baka*!" Anjo told him sourly. "It would only push Satsuma and Tosa into his arms, along with other fence sitters." He shifted uncomfortably, his stomach hurting him, head hurting, and no relief from the new Chinese doctor he had consulted in secret about his constant pains. "We settle it this way: Yoshi-dono, please draft a reply to the gai-jin for approval at tomorrow's meeting."

"Certainly. But what I want to know is who is feeding our secrets to them. Who is the gai-jin spy? This is the first time they've mentioned the 'young' Shōgun and named him, and named the Emperor. Someone is betraying us."

"We will put all our spies onto it! Good. And we will meet tomorrow morning as usual, consider the draft of our reply and decide on your plan." Anjo's eyes slitted. "And to make final preparations for Shōgun Nobusada's departure to Kyōto."

The blood went out of Yoshi's face. "We have discussed this a dozen times. At our last meet—"

"His visit will go forward! He will travel by the north road, not the Tokaidō, along the coast. Safer."

"As Guardian I oppose the visit for the reasons already stated over and over—by any road!"

Toyama said, "Better for my son to be in Kyōto. Soon we will be at war. Our warriors won't be checked much longer."

"No war and no visit. Either will destroy us," Yoshi said angrily. "The moment a Shōgun kowtows, as Nobusada will, our position is ruined for all time. The Legacy states th—"

Anjo said, "The Legacy will not dominate in this."

"The Toranaga Legacy is our only anchor and cannot b—"

"I do not agree!"

Choking back his rage, Yoshi began to get up but stopped as Anjo said, "There is a last matter to decide today: the immediate appointment of the new Elder, Utani's replacement."

There was a sudden tension amongst them. Since Utani's assassination and the manner of his death—the room in which he and the youth had been impaled had not been completely destroyed in the fire—together with the failure of legions of spies and soldiers to apprehend the assassins, all the Elders had slept less comfortably. Particularly Anjo, who was still smarting from his own near assassination. Except for Yoshi, who was occasionally supported by Utani, none of the others regretted his death, or the manner of it, least of all Anjo who had been shocked to discover the identity of the paramour and loathed Utani even more for secretly stealing his occasional pleasure. "Let us vote now."

"Such an important matter should wait until tomorrow."

"So sorry, Yoshi-sama. Now is a perfect time."

Adachi nodded. "Unless the Council is at full strength we cannot make important decisions. Who do you propose?"

"I formally propose Zukumura of Gai."

In spite of his control Yoshi gasped—the daimyo was simple-minded, a kinsman and open ally of Anjo. "I have already stated my disapproval of him—there are a dozen better than him," he said at once. "We agreed on Gen Taira."

"I did not agree." Anjo smiled with his mouth only. "I merely said I would consider him carefully. I have. Zukumura is a better choice. Now we will vote."

"I do not think a vote now is wise or adv—"

"Vote! As chief Councillor it is my right to put it to a vote! Vote!"

"I vote No!" Yoshi said, and glared at the other two.

Adachi did not meet his eye, just said, "Gai have been Mito's allies since Sekigahara. Yes."

Toyama shrugged. "Whatever you want."

Yoshi slashed violently at his two opponents with the wooden sword, sweat pouring off his face, then darted back, spun and attacked again. Both men, experts, sidestepped and pressed their own attack, on orders to be victors, with failure costing them a month confined to barracks and three months' pay.

Cleverly, one man feinted to give the other an opening but Yoshi was ready and ducked under the blow and caught the man across the chest and his sword shattered with the strength of his blow—if the blade had been real it would have almost cut the man in two—eliminating him from the contest.

At once the other rushed in confidently for the kill but Yoshi was no longer where he had expected but almost floor level and hacking forward with a karate foot chop. This man groaned in agony as the iron-hard edge of Yoshi's foot crashed into his scrotum and he fell, writhing. Still enwrapped in his rage and adrenaline, Yoshi leaped at the prone man, the splintered haft of his sword ready on high, a stake to drive into the man's throat for the death blow. But he stayed the blow a hair above the man's neck, heart pumping, ecstatic with his skill and control and that he had not failed this time, victory meaning nothing. His pent-up fury was no more.

Content now, he tossed the broken haft aside and began to unwind, the exercise room bare and Spartan like the rest of the castle. All were panting from their exertions, the prone man still twisting and turning with pain. Then Yoshi was astonished to hear gentle clapping. Angrily he turned—by his custom, no one was ever invited to witness these practice sessions where the extent of his prowess could be gauged, his weaknesses could be judged, and his brutality measured—but this anger vanished also.

"Hosaki! When did you arrive?" he said, trying to regain his breath. "Why not send a messenger to tell me you were coming?" His smile vanished. "Trouble?"

"No, Sire," his wife said happily, kneeling beside the door. "No trouble, just an abundance of pleasure to see you." She bowed deeply, her riding skirt and jacket, serviceable heavy green silk, modest and travel marked, like the padded matching overmantle and wide hat tied under her chin and short sword in her obi. "Please excuse me for slipping in like this, uninvited, and not changing first but, well, I could not wait to see you—and now I am even more pleased I did for now I know that you are a better swordsman than ever."

He pretended not to be delighted, then went closer and looked at her searchingly. "Really no trouble?"

"Yes, Sire." She beamed, her adoration open. White teeth and ebony slanted eyes in a classic face that was neither attractive nor ordinary but not to be forgotten, her whole presence was one of great dignity. 'Yoshi,' his father had said nine years ago when he was seventeen, 'I have chosen your wife for you. Her blood line is Toranaga, equal to yours though from the minor branch of Mitowara. Her name is Hosaki, meaning an "ear of wheat" in the ancient tongue, a harbinger of abundance and fertility, and also a "spearhead." I do not think she will fail you in either capacity. . . .'

Nor has she, Yoshi thought proudly. Already two fine sons and a daughter, and she's still strong, always wise, a firm manager of our finances—and, rare in a wife, pleasant enough to pillow occasionally though with none of the fire of my consort or pleasure partners, particularly Koiko.

He accepted a dry towel from the man who was unhurt, and waved his hand in dismissal. The man bowed silently and helped the other, still in agony, to limp out.

He knelt near her, towelling the sweat away. "So?"

"It's not safe here, *neh*?" she said softly.

"Nowhere is safe."

"First," she said in a normal voice, "first Yoshi-chan, we will look after your body: a bath, massage and then talk."

"Good. There is much to talk about here."

"Yes." Smiling, she got up, and again at his searching look reassured him, "Truly at Dragon's Tooth all is well, your sons healthy, your consort and her son happy, your captains and retainers alert and well armed—everything as you would want. I just decided to make a short visit, on a sudden whim," she said for the listening ears, "I merely needed to see you, and to talk about castle management."

And also to bed you, my beauty, she was thinking in her secret heart, looking up at him, her nostrils filled with his masculine smell, conscious of his nearness and as always aching for his strength.

While you are away, Yoshi-chan, I can keep calm, most of the time, but near you? Ah, then that is very hard though I pretend, oh, how I pretend, and hide my jealousy of the others and behave like a perfect wife. But that does not mean that I, *like all wives,* do not feel jealousy violently, sometimes to a point of madness, wishing to kill or even better to mutilate the others, wanting to be desired and bedded with an equal passion.

"You've been away too long, husband," she said gently, wanting him to take her now, on the floor, to rut like she imagined young peasants would rut.

It was near midday with a kind wind that broomed the sky. They were within his innermost sanctum, a suite of three tatami rooms and bathing room off a corner battlement. She was pouring tea for him, elegantly as always. Since a child she had studied the tea ceremony, as he had, but now she was a Sensei, a teacher of tea in her own right. Both had bathed and had been massaged. Doors were barred, guards posted and maids dismissed. He wore a starched kimono, she a flowing sleeping kimono, her hair loosed. "After our talk I think I will rest. Then my head will be clear for this evening."

"You rode all the way?"

"Yes, Sire." The journey had been rough in fact, little sleep and changing horses every three *ri,* about nine miles.

"How long did it take you?"

"Two and a half days. I just brought twenty retainers under the command of Captain Ishimoto." She laughed. "I certainly needed the massage, and the bath. But first—"

"Almost ten *ri* a day? Why the forced march?"

"Mostly for my pleasure," she said lightly, knowing there was time enough for bad news. "But first, Yoshi-chan, tea for your pleasure."

"Thank you." He drank the fine green tea from the Ming gourd and set it down again, watching and waiting, swept up in her mastery and tranquility.

After she had poured again and sipped and set her own cup down she said softly, "I decided to come here without delay because I had heard disquieting rumors and needed to reassure myself and your captains that you were well—rumors that you were in danger, that Anjo was padding the Council against you, that the shishi attempt on him and Utani's assassination were all part of a major escalation of *sonno-joi*, that war is coming, within and from without, and that Anjo is further betraying you, and all the Shōgunate. He must be insane to allow the Shōgun and his Imperial wife to go to Kyōto to kowtow."

"All true or partially true," he said, equally quietly, and her face tumbled. "Bad news travels with the wings of a hawk, Hosaki, *neh*? It's worse because of the gai-jin." Then he told her about his meeting with the foreigners and Misamoto, the spy, then in more detail about the castle intrigues—but not about Koiko's suspected connection to the shishi: Hosaki would never understand how exciting she is and how much more exciting this knowledge makes her, he thought. My wife would only advise Koiko's immediate dismissal, investigation and punishment and give me no peace until it was done. He finished by telling her about the alien fleet at their doors, Sir William's letter and threat, and today's meeting.

"Zukumura? An Elder? That senile fish head? Isn't one of his sons married to a niece of Anjo's? Surely old Toyama didn't vote for him?"

"He just shrugged and said, 'Him or another, it means nothing, we will be warring soon. Have who you want.'"

"Then at best it will be three to two against you."

"Yes. Now there is no curb on Anjo. He can do what he wants, vote himself increased powers, make himself *tairō*, whatever stupidity he wants, such as Nobusada's stupid trek to Kyōto." Yoshi felt another tightness in his chest but put it away, glad to be able to talk openly—as much as he could ever be open, trusting her more than he could trust anyone.

"The barbarians were as you imagined them, Sire?" she asked.

Everything about them fascinated her: 'know your enemy as you know yourself . . .' Sun-tzu had been the prime learning book for her and her four sisters and three brothers, along with martial arts, calligraphy and the tea ceremony. She and her sisters also had concentrated teaching by their mother and aunts on land and financial management, together with practical methods of dealing with men of all classes, and the all-important future. She had never excelled at martial arts though she could use a knife and war fan well enough.

Everything Yoshi could remember, he told her, and also what Misamoto had said about gai-jin in the part of the Americas called California—and sometimes called the *Land of the Golden Mountain*. Her eyes narrowed but he did not notice.

When he had finished she still had a thousand questions but contained them for later, not wanting to tire him. "You help me to picture everything, Yoshi-chan, you are a wonderful observer. What have you decided?"

"Nothing yet—I wish my father was alive, I miss his counsel—and Mother's."

"Yes," she said, glad that both were dead, the father two years ago, mostly of old age aggravated by his close confinement by Ii—he was fifty-five—the mother in last year's smallpox epidemic. Both had made her life miserable, at the same time keeping Yoshi in thrall, in her opinion the father not doing his duty to the family, making bad decisions more times than not, and the mother forever being the most ill-tempered, difficult to please mother-in-law in her ken, worse to her than the wives of his three brothers.

The only clever thing they did in their whole lives, she thought, was to agree to my father's proposal of marriage to Toranaga Yoshi. For that I thank them. Now I rule Dragon's Tooth, and our lands, and they will be passed on to my sons strong, inviolate and worthy of the Lord Shōgun Toranaga.

"Yes," she said. "So sorry they are gone. I bow to their shrine every day and beg to be worthy of their trust."

He sighed. Since his mother's death he had felt in a void, more so than with his father, whom he admired but feared. Whenever he had a problem, or was afraid, he always knew he could go to her and be soothed, guided and given new strength. He said sadly. "Karma that Mother died so young."

"Yes, Sire," she said, understanding his sadness, and perfectly content for, of course, it would be the same with all sons whose first duty is to obey and to cherish their mother above everyone—all their lives. I can never fill that void any more than the wives of my sons will fill mine.

"What's your advice, Hosaki?"

"I've too many thoughts for these too many problems," she told him worriedly, her mind grappling with the mosaic of danger from every quarter. "I feel useless. Let me think carefully, tonight and tomorrow—perhaps I can suggest something that will give you a clue to what you must do, then, with your permission I'll return home the next day, one thing for certain: to further strengthen our defenses. You must tell me what to do. Meanwhile a few immediate observations for you to consider: increase the vigilance of your guards, and quietly mobilize all your forces."

"I had already decided that."

"This gai-jin who accosted you after the meeting, a Frenchman you say, I suggest you take advantage of the offer to see the inside of a warship with your own eyes, very important for you to see for yourself—perhaps even pretend to become friendly with them, then perhaps you could play them against the English, *neh*?"

"I had already decided to do that."

She smiled to herself, and lowered her voice even more. "However difficult, the sooner the better, Anjo must be removed permanently. As it is now probable you cannot prevent the Shōgun and the Princess from leaving for Kyōto—I agree she is, correctly from her point of view, the Court spy and puppet and your enemy—then you must leave secretly just after them and rush to Kyōto by the shorter Tokaidō and be there before them. . . . You smile, Sire?"

"Only because you please me. And when I get to Kyōto?"

"You must become the Emperor's confidant—we have friends in Court who will assist you. Then, one possibility of dozens: make a secret agreement with Ogama of Choshu to leave him in control of the Gates"—she hesitated as Yoshi flushed—"but only as long as he is openly allied with you against Satsuma and Tosa."

"Ogama would never believe I would keep that bargain nor would I, but we must get back our Gates whatever the cost."

"I agree. But say the final part of your pact is that if he agrees to join forces for a surprise attack on Lord Sanjiro of Satsuma at a time of your choosing, then when Sanjiro is overcome, Ogama gives you back the Gates and he gets Satsuma in return."

Yoshi frowned even more. "Very difficult to conquer Sanjiro by land when he is skulking behind his mountains—even Shōgun Toranaga did not attack Satsuma after Sekigahara, just accepted their public bows, oaths of fidelity, and curbed them with kindness. We cannot launch a sea-borne attack." He thought a moment. "That is a dream, not a real possibility. Too difficult," he muttered. "But then, who knows? Next."

She dropped her voice. "Remove Nobusada on his way to Kyōto—it is a chance in a lifetime."

"Never!" he said, openly shocked and inwardly aghast that she thought as he did or, even worse, had read his most secret heart. "That would betray the Legacy, my heritage, everything that Lord Shōgun Toranaga strived for. I have accepted him as liege lord, as I am bound to do."

"Of course you are right," she said at once soothingly, already bowing low, prepared and expecting that reaction but needing to articulate it for him. "That was *baka* of me. I completely agree. So sorr—"

"Good! Never think or say that again."

"Of course. Please forgive me." She kept her head bowed for the correct time, muttering apologies, then leaned forward and refilled his cup and sat back again, eyes downcast, waiting to be asked to continue. Nobusada should have been removed by your father, Yoshi, she was thinking calmly—I am astonished that you never realized it. Your father, and mother—who should have given him correct counsel— failed in their duty when that stupid boy was proposed against you as Shōgun by the traitor Ii. Ii shoved us all into house arrest, destroyed our peace for years, almost caused the death of our eldest son because of the months we were so closely confined that we all starved. We all knew Ii would do it long before it happened. Removing Nobusada has always been so obvious, however heretical and distasteful an action, but the only real way to protect our future. If you will not consider it, Yoshi, I will find a way . . .

"That was a bad thought, Hosaki. Terrible!"

"I agree, Sire. Please accept my humble apologies." Again her head touched the tatami. "It was stupid. I do not know where such stupidity comes from. You are right of course. Perhaps it was because I am overwrought with the dangers surrounding you. Please, Sire, will you allow me to leave?"

"In a moment, yes, meanwhile—" A little mollified he motioned for her to pour more tea, still off balance that she would dare to speak such sacrilege openly, even to him.

"May I mention one other thought, Sire, before I go?"

"Yes, provided it's not stupid like the last one."

She almost laughed out loud at the petulant, little-boy barb that did not enter even her outermost defenses. "You said, Sire, so wisely, that the most important and immediate gai-jin riddle to solve is how to sink their fleets or to keep their cannon away from our shores, *neh*?"

"Yes."

"Could cannon be mounted on barges?"

"Eh?" He frowned, deflected from Nobusada by this new tack. "I'd imagine so, why?"

"We could find out from the Dutch, they would help us. Perhaps we could build a defensive fleet, no matter how cumbersome, and anchor the barges offshore, as far out to sea as we can in strategic approaches to our important areas, like the Shimonoseki Straits, along with fortifying the mouths to all our harbors—fortunately they are very few, *neh*?"

"It might be possible," he conceded, the idea not having occurred to him. "But I don't have enough money or gold to buy all the cannon necessary for our shore batteries, let alone to build such a fleet. Or enough time or knowledge or wealth to set up our own armories and factories to make our own—or the men to run them."

"Yes, so true, Sire. You are so wise," she agreed. Then sadly, she took a deep breath. "All daimyos are impoverished and in debt—us as much as any."

"Eh? The harvest?" he asked sharply.

"So sorry to bring bad news, less than last year."

"How much less?"

"About a third."

"That is dreadful news, and just when I need extra revenue!" His fist bunched. "Farmers are all *baka*."

"So sorry, it is not their fault, Yoshi-chan, the rains were too late or too early, the sun too. This year the gods have not smiled on us."

"There are no gods, Hosaki-chan, but there is karma. Karma that there is a bad harvest—you will have to put up taxes nonetheless."

Her eyes glistened with tears. "There will be famine in the Kwanto before next harvest—and if with us, the richest rice land in all Nippon, what about the others?" The memory of the famine four years ago rushed back at them. Thousands had died, and tens of thousands in the inevitable plagues that followed. And in the Great Famine, twenty years ago, hundreds of thousands had perished. "This is indeed the Land of Tears."

He nodded absently. Then he said, his voice acid, "You will increase taxes by a tenth part, all samurai will get a tenth part less. Talk to the moneylenders. They can increase our loans. The money will be spent on armaments."

"Of course." Then added carefully, "We are better off than most, only next year's harvest is pledged. But it will be difficult to get ordinary interest rates."

He said irritably, "What do I know or care of interest rates? Make the best arrangement you can." His face tightened. "Perhaps the time has come to propose to the Council we adjust 'interest rates' like my great-grandfather."

Sixty-odd years ago the Shōgun, crushed under the weight of his father's debts, with years of future harvests mortgaged like those of all daimyos, and goaded by the ever-increasing arrogance and disdain of the merchant class, had abruptly decreed that all debts were cancelled and all future harvests debt free.

In the two and a half centuries since Sekigahara this extreme act had been promulgated four times. It caused chaos throughout the land. Suffering amongst all classes was huge, especially samurai. There was little the rice merchants, the main moneylenders, could do. Many went bankrupt. A few committed seppuku. The rest slid under cover as best they could and suffered in the general lake of pain.

Until the next harvest. Then farmers needed merchants, and all people needed rice, and so, carefully, sales were consummated and scarce—therefore highly expensive—money was loaned to them for seed and tools against the next harvest, and once more, but very humbly, money and credit was advanced to samurai, against their expected income, for living and entertainment, and silks and swords. Soon samurai overspending became endemic. With greater care moneylenders slipped back into business. Soon inducements had to be offered to them, samurai status was reluctantly proffered and gratefully purchased for some sons and everything was soon as before, with fiefs in pawn.

"Perhaps you should, Sire." She was as disgusted as he with moneylenders. "I have secret stocks of rice against famine, your men would be hungry but they will not starve."

"Good. Barter these for the guns."

"So sorry, the amount would not be significant," she told him gently, appalled with his naiveté and added quickly to divert him, "Meanwhile taxes will not produce the cash gai-jin will require."

"Then it will have to be the moneylenders," he said sharply. "Do whatever is necessary. I must have guns."

"Yes." She allowed the silence to gather, then slowly put forward a long-pondered plan: "Something you said before you left home gave me an idea, Sire. The small gold mine in our north mountains. I propose we increase the work force."

"But you have told me many times the mine is already scavenged to capacity and produces less revenue every year."

"True, but you made me realize our miners are not experts and my thought is that where there is one vein, there may be others if we had expert prospectors to seek them out. Perhaps our methods are old-fashioned. Amongst the gai-jin there may be experts."

He looked at her. "How so?"

"I was talking to Old Smelly"—this was the nickname of an old Dutchman who years ago had been a merchant at Deshima and had been enticed to become one of Yoshi's tutors and who, with the gift of maids, a youthful consort and much saké had been induced to stay until it was too late to leave. "He told me about a huge gold rush in the Land of the Golden Mountain you mentioned, only thirteen years ago, where gai-jin of all nations went to steal a fortune from the earth. Also, a few years ago there was another such gold rush in a land far to our south— he called it Van Diemen's Land. In Yokohama there must be men who took part in one or the other. Experts."

"And if they exist?" Yoshi wondered about Misamoto.

"I suggest you offer them safe passage and half the gold they discover within one year. There are many Americans and adventurers in the Settlement, so I am told."

"You would want gai-jin wandering about our lands, spying on our lands?" he asked slowly.

She shook her head then leaned forward, knowing she had his complete attention. "Once again you provided the solution, Yoshi-chan. Say you approached the most important Yokohama trader, in secret, the one you told me you thought was going to supply Choshu with rifles—I agree we must get rifles and modern cannon at all costs and prevent enemies from acquiring them. Say you offer him your gold concession, an exclusive. In return he arranges all aspects of the search and mining. You would accept only one or two unarmed prospectors, and of course they would be closely monitored. In return you are supplied immediately with so many cannon and rifles in advance, against your half of the gold found, and this merchant agrees to sell guns and cannon only to you. Never to Choshu, Tosa or Satsumas. You smile, Sire?"

"And our go-between is Misamoto?"

"Without your cleverness in discovering and training him this would not be possible." She said it with perfect deference, and sat back, secretly content, listening to his comments and her replies, knowing that he would put her plan into operation quickly, that they would somehow get some guns and never never never barter her secret rice away. Then, shortly, she could pretend to be tired and beg his permission to rest: "You should rest also, Sire, after such a marvelous though strenuous practice session. . . ."

Of course he should, a fine man like him, she thought. And once there, many judicious compliments, asking permission to massage his tired shoulder muscles, cautiously becoming more intimate, a sigh or two and quickly he would be as close as she could ever desire. As close as Koiko.

Earlier Koiko had correctly begged permission to visit her and had bowed and thanked her and said that she hoped her services had pleased the Great Lord, that she was honored to be allowed into his household for even a brief time. They had chatted for a while and then she had gone away.

Such a beauty, Hosaki thought without jealousy, or envy. Yoshi is entitled to a toy, however expensive, from time to time. Their beauty is so fragile, so transient, their life so sad, truly cherry blossoms from the Tree of Life. A man's world is so much more physically exciting than ours. Eeee, to be able to go from flower to flower without hurt or thought.

If the punishment for even a little philandering on our side was not so immediate and severe, women would consider it much more frequently. Wouldn't we? Why not? If it were safe.

Sometimes, when Yoshi is away, the thought of such enormous danger and immediate death is an almost overwhelming aphrodisiac. Foolish, for such a fleeting pleasure. Is it?

She waited, watching him, a warm glow within, adoring the game of life while his mind was abuzz with variations of the plan and how to use his creation, Misamoto.

I will start at once, he was thinking. Hosaki has a good mind and is clever at putting my ideas together. But, eeee, to articulate that about the boy was *baka* in the extreme, however correct an Act of State such an action might be. Women have no finesse.

In the Settlement this morning, just before dawn, Jamie McFay had given Nemi a final kiss and then together they walked down the corridor to Malcolm Struan's suite. He knocked gently. At once the door opened and the young girl, Shizuka, came out, eased the door closed, smiled curiously and began whispering to Nemi who took McFay by the arm and hurried him to the landing.

"What? Bad news, heya?" McFay asked nervously—he had caught a glimpse of Struan fast asleep in the huge four-poster before the door closed but all had seemed well. Nemi paid no attention to him and continued to cross-question the girl.

Exasperated, McFay said, "Nemi, what? What bad?"

She hesitated, then with an initial flood of singsong apologetic Japanese, caught herself and beamed. "No bad, Jami-san, you-ah cum Yoshiwara t'morrow, yes no?" She put on her cloak and began to go down the stairs but he stopped her.

"What bad, Nemi?" he asked suspiciously.

She stared up at him a moment, then more Japanese and pidgin that did not make sense. Finally she shrugged, "S'kr't, *wakarimasu ka*?"

"*S'kr't? Iyé*, for God's sake. What skre't, heya?"

"S'krit, Jami-san, *hai*?"

"Ah, secret, for God's sake! *Wakarimasu!* Secret what?"

She sighed with relief and beamed. "S'kret, gud! S'kret, Jami-san, Shizuka, Nemi. *Hai? Hai?*"

"*Hai*. Us keep secret. Now what?"

More incomprehensible Japanese and more pidgin as they put on their outer robes and then, frustrated because she could not explain properly or that she had to explain at all, Nemi parodied plenty of movement and whispered, "Shizuka gud, work gud o'rr night."

"Tai-pan good?"

Her eyes soared. "*Hai*, Jami-san, Shizuka gud!"

All his questions had only produced more bowing and smiles from both of them, so he had thanked Shizuka, her fee already arranged— 'tai-pan credit plenti werri gud,' the mama-san had told him. For a last time Nemi swore him to secrecy. The waiting servant took them back to the Yoshiwara.

Perturbed but not knowing why, though sure he had not been told all the truth, he had tiptoed back and stood over the bed but Struan was fast asleep, breathing peacefully, so he had left and gone to his office and worked.

Until just after ten.

"Hello, Doctor, come in, good to see you. What's new?"

Hoag's face was grim. "Ah Tok sent for me and I've just seen Malcolm, that's what's new. I wish to Christ you'd asked me first before you—oh, for God's sake, Jamie," the squat, good man added quickly, seeing him flush, "I know he asked you to arrange it, I just wish you'd thought to ask me first—I would have thought it bloody obvious it would be bloody dangerous and bloody ridiculous to try so soon after that wound with half your inside patched and near to bursting . . ." He stopped and sat down. "Sorry, but I had to let that out."

"That's all right—is it bad?"

"I don't know, some blood in his urine and plenty of pain in his loins. It seems she was very vigorous, he got carried away and when he climaxed he said his stomach spasmed with the surge and then cramped up. Poor fellow, though he's in a lot of pain now, he did tell me she was worth it."

"He said that?"

"Yes, in some detail—don't mention that I told you, eh? I've given him some painkiller so he'll sleep for an hour or two. I'll be back later." Hoag sighed and got up with a grim smile. "I had another note from Mrs. Struan, did you?"

"Yes, more of the same. Will you order him back to Hong Kong now?"

"I can't order him to do anything. He goes when he wants to go, this is the storm season, for God's sake. He's wise to stay—unless there's anything pressing in Hong Kong."

"There are dozens of reasons—that's the seat of power, there's nothing for him to do here really."

Hoag shrugged. "I agree Hong Kong would be better—I'd planned to go back with the mail ship but after last night I think I'll wait for a few more days for him."

"Take him with you, please, on the mail ship."

"I already suggested it and was told, rather impolitely, 'no.' Forget it, Jamie, it's not wrong for him to rest here and a foul sea voyage would be extremely bad for him, maybe a killer. By the way, I hear there may be another ball next Tuesday with Angel T the guest of honor."

"Malcolm didn't mention it."

"Under the auspices of Ambassador Seratard, of dubious ancestry, father of all the French. Well, I must be going—keep me advised and if Malcolm asks for a similar bout, check with me first, privately."

"All right. Thanks, Doctor"

Later Vargas knocked. "Senhor, Ah Tok says the tai-pan wants to see you."

Climbing the staircase, there was a sudden nasty twinge in Jamie's stomach, imagining himself in Malcolm's place.

"Senhor McFay!" Vargas called up from the stairwell. "Excuse me, but the Choshu samurai have just arrived, about ordering the rifles, senhor."

"I'll be right back."

McFay knocked and opened the door. "Hello, Tai-pan," he said kindly. Struan was propped in bed, his eyes strange, a flat smile on his face. "How're you today?"

"You saw Hoag?"

"Yes."

"Good, then you know she was very satisfactory and, well, thanks, Jamie. She helped tremendously though . . ." Struan laughed nervously. "Though the finish shook me up a bit. Terrific body. It was all very satisfactory but I don't think I'll need a repeat performance until I'm really better. She certainly got rid of the—the logjam." Again the short, nervous laugh. "Didn't realize, Jamie, how strong a little girl like that could be, or how much . . . you understand, eh?"

"Of course. Everything went according to plan?"

For an instant Struan wavered, then he said firmly, "Yes, better than that—I want you to double her fee."

"Certainly." McFay read the underlying anxiety and his heart went out to him. Obviously whatever happened Malcolm's deal with Shizuka was secret. If that's the way he wants it, fine. Not up to me. What's done is done. Just another secret to add to all the rest. "Glad it was all right."

"Better than all right. Did the girl say anything?"

"Only that she, er, worked hard all night, to, well, to try to please you."

A bright knock on the door and Angelique sailed in, blooming with good health, chic in a new lavender dress, parasol, feathered hat, gloves and shawl. "Hello, my love, hello, Jamie, how are you today? Oh, Malcolm, I'm so pleased to see you." As she bent over the bed to kiss Struan tenderly, "Oh, chéri, how I've missed you."

The moment the door had opened the hearts of both men stretched. McFay's nervousness soared, at once his eyes checked the bed and room to see if there were any telltale signs. But all was neat and tidy, clean new sheets and pillowcases daily—more Struan fastidiousness about cleanliness, to the point of foolishness, he thought—clean shirt every day? Ridiculous, once or twice a month more than enough but then he knew the habit had been implanted by Dirk Struan and whatever the tai-pan had decreed was law for Tess Struan and therefore her family. Struan was freshly shaved, clean nightshirt, the windows opened to the sea breeze that would carry away any trace of perfume. He began to breathe easier, then she said, "I saw Dr. Hoag," and both men almost went into spasm again.

"You poor darling," she said with hardly a pause, "he told me you'd had a bad night, poor darling, and that you won't come to Sir William's soiree this evening, so I thought I'd just drop in and sit with you until lunch."

Again, the gorgeous smile that seduced both of them and she arranged herself in the tall chair—Struan weak with love for her, at the same time sick with guilt. I must have been insane to want a whore to substitute for the love of my life, he thought, glorying in her open warmth, wanting to blurt out about Shizuka, and beg her forgiveness.

The night had begun well enough with Shizuka undressing and smiling and pressing against him, fondling and encouraging. He had touched her too, fondling and was both proud and anxious. Awkward and painful to position normally and move normally, so staying seated and beginning but not quite, then of a sudden Angelique's face and presence had swamped him, unbidden and unwanted. His manhood vanished. And as much as Shizuka had tried and he had tried, it would not return.

They rested and tried again, the ache for him awful now, overlaid with frantic, impotent rage and his need to prove himself. More groping and trying—she was well trained with hand and lips and body but nothing would create that which responded in varying degrees to lust and need, but especially to love and its indefinable mystery. Nor, whatever she did, could she or he dispel the spectre. Or conquer the pain.

At length she gave up, her young body sheened with perspiration and panting from her exertions. 'Gomen nasai, Tai-pan,' she had whispered, again and again, apologizing, but hiding her fury and almost in tears at his impotence, for she had never failed before, and was expecting him to send for servants any moment to beat her and throw her out for failure to arouse him as a civilized person would do. And more than anything, she was beset with anxiety as to how she would explain her inadequacy to her mama-san. Buddha bear witness: this man failed, not me!

'Gomen nasai, gomen nasai,' her mouth kept saying.

'It's the accident,' he mumbled, despising himself, the pain grotesque, telling her about the Tokaidō and his wounds even though he knew she would not understand the words, his frustration shattering him. When that storm had passed and his tears had passed, he made her lie beside him, had stopped her trying again and had made her understand that she would get a double fee if she kept everything secret. 'Secret, *wakarimasu ka*?' he pleaded with her.

'*Hai*, Tai-pan, *wakarimasu*,' she had agreed happily, found the medicine he required and then cradled him to sleep.

"Malcolm . . ." Angelique said.

"Yes?" Struan said at once, concentrating, his heart pounding, reminding him he had used the last of Hoag's sleeping draft and that he must ask Ah Tok to replace the mixture—for just a day or so. "I'm so pleased to see you too."

"Me too. How do you like my dress?"

"It's wonderful and so are you," he said.

"Think I'll be going, Tai-pan," McFay broke in, seeing how happy Struan had become, pleased for him though still sweating. "The Choshu reps are downstairs—all right to proceed with them?"

"As we decided. Good, thanks again, Jamie. Let me know how it goes."

"Malcolm," Angelique said quickly, "while Jamie's here . . . you remember you asked me to remind you when we were all together about my . . . the small allowance."

"Ah yes, of course. Jamie," he said expansively as she took his hand, her open pleasure casting the night into oblivion—forever, he thought happily. That night never happened! "Put my fiancée's chits against my account," he told him with a twinge of happiness at the word. "Angel, just sign chits, whatever you want, Jamie will take care of them."

"Thank you, *chéri*, that's wonderful, but please can I have some money?"

He laughed and Jamie smiled also. "You don't need any here, there's no need for cash—none of us carry money."

"But Malcolm, I w—"

"Angelique," he said, his voice firmer. "Chits are the way we pay for everything, at the Club or at any store in the Settlement, everyone does, even in Hong Kong, surely you haven't forgotten. It stops tradesmen cheating and you've a permanent record."

"But I've always had money, *chéri*, money of my own, to pay my own bills," she said with an outward show of complete honesty, "and as my father has . . . well, you understand."

"Paying your own bills? What an appalling idea. That's unheard of in good society. Now don't worry yourself," he said, smiling at her, "that's for men to do. Chits are our perfect solution."

"Perhaps French people are different, we always have cash and—"

"So do we in England and elsewhere, but in Asia we all sign chits. Whatever you want to buy just sign for it—even better we must get you your personal chop, we'll choose the perfect Chinese name for you." This was a small stamp, usually a rectangular piece of ivory or bone, the bottom of which was ornately carved with the Chinese characters that sounded like the owner's name. When pressed into an ink pad then onto paper, it would produce a unique imprint almost impossible to forge. "Jamie will arrange it for you."

"Thank you, Malcolm. But then, well, can I have my own account, *chéri*, I'm really very good at managing."

"I'm sure you are, now don't worry your beautiful head, when we're married I'll arrange it, but here it's unnecessary."

She hardly listened to herself as she entertained Struan with gossip from the French Legation, what she had read in the papers, what her friend in Paris had written about a superb residence—called 'hotel' there—on the Champs-Elysées belonging to a Countess that would soon become available and was so inexpensive, planting seeds for their glorious future, making him laugh, waiting for him to become drowsy when she would leave for her lunch at the Club with the French officers, then later to ride with them and some of the English navy officers on the racecourse, then a siesta, then to prepare for Sir William's soirée—no reason not to go but first returning to say good night to her soon-to-be husband.

Everything marvelous and terrible, most of her mind on her new dilemma: how to get cash. What am I going to do? I have to have cash to pay for the medicine, that swine André Poncin won't advance it for me, I know he won't. Damn him and damn my father for stealing my money! And damn HIM of the Tokaidō into eternal Hell forever!

Stop that and think. Remember you are on your own and you must solve your problems!

My only possession of value is my engagement ring and I can't sell that, I just can't. Oh God, everything was going so well, I'm officially engaged, Malcolm is getting better, André is helping me but the medicine's so expensive and I've no money, real money, oh God, oh God what *am* I going to do?

Tears spilled out of her eyes.

"Good God, Angelique, what is it?"

"Just that . . . just that I'm so unhappy." She sobbed and buried her head in the bedclothes. "So unhappy that—that the Tokaidō happened and you're hurt and I . . . I'm hurt too—it's not fair."

* * *

Sir William's ten-oared cutter sped through the swell in double-quick time aimed at the flagship anchored in the roads off Yokohama, her bow wave heavy. He was alone in the cabin and he stood, riding easily, in frock coat, cutaway and top hat. Sea fair, light fading in the west, the clouds already grey but with no apparent threat of storm. As she swung alongside the ship, all oars went to the vertical, he jumped onto the gangway and hurried up to the main deck to be piped aboard.

"Afternoon, sir." Lieutenant Marlowe saluted smartly. "This way, please." Past gleaming rows of cannon to the quarterdeck—the main deck and shrouds a hive of activity, cannons being secured, hawsers coiled, sails checked, smoke from the funnel—up a gangway then down another to the second gun deck, past sailors battening down and stowing gear, to the Admiral's cabin aft. The marine sentry saluted as Marlowe knocked. "Sir William, sir."

"Well, open the door, Marlowe, for Christ's sake."

Marlowe held the door for Sir William and began to close it. "Marlowe, stay here!" the Admiral ordered.

The large cabin filled the stern of the ship—many small sea windows, big table and sea chairs anchored to the deck, small bunk and toilet, large sideboard with cut-glass decanters. The Admiral and General half got up with token politeness, and sat again. Marlowe stayed at the door.

"Thank you for arriving so expeditiously, Sir William. Brandy? Sherry?"

"Brandy, thank you, Admiral Ketterer. Trouble?"

The florid-faced man glared at Marlowe. "Would you oblige, Mr. Marlowe, brandy for Sir William." He tossed a sheet of paper on the table. "Dispatch from Hong Kong."

With the usual flowery greetings, the dispatch read:

You will proceed at once with the flagship and four or five warships to the port of Boh Chih Seh, north of Shanghai (coordinates overleaf) where the main pirate fleet of Wu Sung Choi is now harbouring. A week ago a swarm of this pirate's junks, arrogantly flying his flag—the White Lotus—intercepted and sank H.M.'s mailship Bonny Sailor *in the waters off Mirs Bay, the pirate haven north of Hong Kong. The fleet here will deal with Mirs Bay—you will decimate Boh Chih Seh and sink all craft not fishing vessels if the leader, believed to be Chu Fang Choy, refuses to strike his colours and declines to surrender to Her Majesty's justice.*

When accomplished, send one ship with a report here and return to Yokohama, placing yourself as usual at the disposition of Her Majesty's servants. Show this to Sir William and please give him the enclosed. yrs., Stanshope, KCB, Governor Far East.

PS: The Bonny Sailor *was lost with all hands, 76 officers and men, ten passengers, one of whom was an Englishwoman, the wife of a trader here, a cargo of gold, opium and rice worth ten thousand guineas. Chu Fang Choy had the effrontery to have delivered to Government House a sack containing the ship's log and forty-three pairs of ears with a letter apologizing that the others could not be recovered. The woman's were not included and we fear the worst for her.*

"Bastards," Sir William muttered, with an added queasiness at the thought that, as pirates were endemic in all Asian waters, particularly from Singapore north to Peking, and the White Lotus fleets the most abundant and notorious of all, the woman could easily have been his wife who was due to arrive in Hong Kong any week from England with three of his children. "You leave on the tide?"

"Yes." The Admiral slid an envelope across the table. Sir William broke the seals:

Dear Willie, The next mail ship will bring the specie for the Legation expenses. Between ourselves, sorry, Willie, but I cannot give you any further troops at the moment, or ships. In the spring possibly. I have been ordered to return troops and ships to India where the authorities fear repetition of the Mutiny of five years ago. Added to that, the Punjab is in ferment again, pirates plague the Persian Gulf, and damned nomads in Mesopotamia have again cut the telegraph—another expeditionary force is being organized to deal with them once and for all!

How is that poor fellow Struan? Questions are bound to be asked in Parliament about 'failure to protect our nationals.'

News of your Tokaidō disaster should reach London within two weeks, their answer not for two more months. I trust they will countenance stiff reprisals, and send us the money, troops and ships to carry out their orders. In the meantime weather the storm, if there is one, as best you can. Hong Kong is seething about this attack. Struan's mother is hopping mad and all the riffraff China traders here (however rich from their foul opium trade) are up in arms, their misguided, slanted guttersnipe Press demanding your resignation. Was it ever different? as Disraeli would say! In haste, Godspeed, yrs. Stanshope, KCB, Governor.

Sir William took a large sip, hoping his face did not betray his anxiety. "Good brandy, Admiral."

"Yes, it is, my very best private stock, in your honor," the Admiral said, furious that Marlowe had given Sir William almost half a tumbler and had not used the ordinary, second grade he kept for visitors. Stupid berk, he thought, he should know better—he'll never make flag rank.

"What about going to Osaka?" Sir William asked.

"Oh, Osaka? I regret you will have to delay until I return." The smile was barely concealed.

"When will that be?" The sinking feeling became worse.

"To arrive at our destination, six or seven days depending on the winds, two or three days at Boh Chih Seh should be enough. I will have to recoal at Shanghai. Oh, I'd say I should be off Yokohama again unless fresh orders arrive in . . ." The Admiral quaffed his port and poured another. "I should be back in four or five weeks."

Sir William finished his brandy and this helped to ease his nausea. "Lieutenant, would you be so kind? Thanks."

Marlowe took his glass politely and refilled it with the Admiral's best, hiding his disgust at being a flunky and totally fed up with this aide-de-camp posting—wanting to be back on his own ship, his own quarterdeck to supervise the repairs the storm had caused. But at least I'll see some action at long last, he thought with relish, imagining the attack on the pirate haven, all guns blazing.

"Well, Admiral," Sir William was saying, "if we fail to make good our threat we will lose enormous face, the initiative, and put ourselves in great danger."

"It was your threat, Sir William, not ours. As to face, you put too much value on it, as to danger—I presume you mean to the Settlement—damn, Sir, the natives of Japan would not dare to create any major problem. They didn't really bother you at the Legation, they won't really bother Yokohama."

"With the fleet gone, we're helpless."

"Not exactly, Sir William," the General said stiffly. "The army is here in some strength."

"Quite right," the Admiral agreed, "but Sir William is perfectly correct to say the Royal Navy keeps the peace. I plan to take four warships, sir, not five, and leave one frigate on station. That should be sufficient. The *Pearl*."

Before Marlowe could stop himself, he had said, "Excuse me, sir, she's still undergoing major repairs."

"I'm so glad to know you keep abreast of the state of my fleet, Mr. Marlowe, and that you keep your ears open," the Admiral said witheringly. "Obviously *Pearl* can't go on this expedition, so you'd best report back aboard and make sure she's in first-class seagoing condition ready for any duty by sundown tomorrow or you won't have a ship."

"Yessir." Marlowe gulped, saluted and rushed off.

The Admiral grunted and said to the General, "Good officer but not dry behind the ears yet—fine naval family, two brothers also officers and his father's flag captain at Plymouth." He looked at Sir William. "Don't worry, his frigate will have stepped her mast by tomorrow and be in good order—he's the best of my captains but, for God's sake, don't tell him I said so. He'll guard you until I return. If there's nothing else, gentlemen, I put to sea right smartly—so sorry I can't join you for dinner."

Sir William and the General finished their drinks and stood up. "Godspeed, Admiral Ketterer, may you come back safely with all hands," Sir William said sincerely, the General echoing him. Then his face hardened. "If I don't get any satisfaction from the Bakufu I will leave for Osaka as planned, in *Pearl* or not, at the head of the army or not—but by God, go to Osaka and Kyōto I will."

"Best wait until I return, best be prudent, best not swear by God to undertake such an ill-advised action, Sir William," the Admiral said curtly. "God might decide otherwise."

That evening, just before midnight, Angelique, Phillip Tyrer and Pallidar left the British Legation and strolled down High Street, heading for the Struan Building. "La," she said happily, "Sir William certainly has a modest chef!"

They were all in evening dress and they laughed, for the food had been abundant English fare and especially delicious—a side of roast beef, trays of pork sausages and fresh crabs brought in on ice from Shanghai in the mail ship's ice room as part of the diplomatic pouch and therefore not subject to customs inspection or duty. These were served with boiled vegetables, roast potatoes, also imported from Shanghai, with Yorkshire pudding and followed by apple pies and mince pies with all the claret, Pouilly Fumé, port and champagne the twenty guests could drink.

"And when Madam Lunkchurch threw a crab at her husband I thought I would die," she said to more laughter but Tyrer, embarrassed, said, "I'm afraid some of the so-called traders and their wives are inclined to be boisterous. Please don't judge all Englishmen, or -women, by their behavior."

"Quite right." Pallidar was beaming, delighted that he also had been accepted as part of her escort and conscious that his evening dress uniform and plumed cap made Tyrer's drab frock coat, his old-fashioned and abundant silk cravat and top hat seem even more funereal. "Dreadful people. Without your presence, the evening would have been awful, no doubt at all."

High Street and its side streets were still busy with traders, clerks and others weaving their way home to their dwellings or strolling the promenade, the odd drunk lying by the oil lamps that lit the length of it. An occasional cluster of Japanese fishermen, carrying oars and nets, and paper lanterns to light their way, trudged up from the shore where their boats were beached, or headed down from the village for their night's fishing.

At the front door of the Struan Building she stopped and held out her hand to be kissed. "Thank you and good night, dear friends, please don't bother to wait, one of the servants can see me back to the Legation."

"Wouldn't dream of it," Pallidar said at once, taking her hand and holding on for a moment.

"I—we'd be glad to wait," Tyrer assured her.

"But I may be an hour or a few minutes, depending how my fiancé is."

But they insisted and she thanked them, and she swept past the liveried, armed night watchman, up the stairs, crinoline billowing, trailing her shawl—still caught up in the excitement of the evening and the adoration that surrounded her. "Hello, darling, just wanted to say good night."

Struan wore an elegant red silk dressing gown over a loose shirt and trousers with soft boots, cravat at his throat and he got up out of the chair, the pain deadened now by the elixir Ah Tok had given him half an hour ago. "I feel better than I have for days, my darling. A bit wobbly, but fine—how lovely you are." The light from the oil lamp made his gaunt face more handsome than ever, and her more desirable than ever. He put his hands on her shoulders to steady himself, his head and body feeling strangely light, her skin creamy and warm to his touch. Her eyes were dancing and he looked down, loving her, and kissed her. Gently at first, then, as she responded, glorying further in her taste and welcome. "I love you," he murmured between kisses.

"I love you," she replied, believing it and weak with pleasure, so happy that he seemed truly better, his lips strong and seeking and hands strong and seeking but within bounds, bounds that suddenly, deliriously, she wanted to cast aside. *Je t'aime, chéri . . . je t'aime . . .*

For a moment they stood in their embrace and then with a strength he did not know he had, he lifted her and sat again in the big, high-backed chair and cradled her in his lap, lips touching, one arm around her tiny waist, a hand quietly on her breast, the silk seeming to enhance the half-cupped warmth beneath. Wonder filled him. Wonder that here where every part of her was covered and forbidden, in the night, all was open and offered and was young, but now he was more euphoric and stimulated than he had ever been, yet at the same time controlled, no longer frantic with lust.

"So strange," he murmured, and thought, but not so strange, the pain's masked by the medicine. The rest isn't, my love for her.

"Chéri?"

"Strange that I need you so much yet I can wait. Not long but I can wait."

"Please not long, please." Again her lips sought his, nothing in her mind but him, heat welding her memory closed and worry closed and never a problem anymore. For both of them. Then the sudden sound of a nearby gunshot from outside.

Their mood shattered, she sat upright on his lap and before she knew it was hurrying for the half-open window. Below she could see Pallidar and Tyrer—damn, I'd forgotten them, she thought. The two men were looking inland, then they turned, their attention directed towards Drunk Town.

She craned out of the window but saw only a vague group of men at the far end, their bleary shouts wafted on the wind. "It seems to be nothing, just Drunk Town . . ." she said, guns and fights, even duels, not rare in that part of Yokohama. Then, feeling strange and chilled and at the same time flushed, she came back and looked at him. With a little sigh she knelt and took his hand and pressed it to her cheek, her head in his lap, but his gentleness and his fingers caressing her hair and the nape of her neck no longer drove the devils away. "I should go home, my love."

"Yes." His fingers continued their stroking.

"I want to stay."

"I know."

Struan saw himself, out of himself, the perfect gentleman, calm, quiet, helping her to her feet, waiting while she straightened her bodice and hair and draped her shawl around her. Then, hand in hand, walking slowly with her to the head of the stairs where he allowed himself to be persuaded to stay, permitting a servant to lead her below. At the door she turned once and waved a loving farewell and he waved and then she was gone.

It seemed to take him no effort to walk back and undress, letting his servant pull off his boots. Then into bed with no help at all, lying back at peace with himself and the world. Head fine, body fine, relaxed.

"How is my son?" Ah Tok whispered from the doorway.

"In the Land of the Poppy."

"Good, good. No pain for my son there."

The servant blew out the flame and then left him.

Down the High Street, the French soldier sentry, his uniform as sloppy as his manner, opened the Legation door for her. "*Bonsoir,* Mademoiselle."

"*Bonsoir,* Monsieur. Good night, Phillip, good night, Settry." The door closed and she leaned against it a moment to collect herself. The delight of the evening had vanished. In its place, the spectres were crowding for attention. Deep in thought she walked across the hall towards her suite, saw a light under Seratard's door. She stopped and, on a sudden impulse that this might be a perfect time to ask for a loan, she knocked and went in. "Oh! André! Hello, excuse me, I was expecting Monsieur Henri."

"He's still with Sir William. I'm just finishing a dispatch for him." André was at Seratard's desk, many papers spread around. The dispatch dealt with Struan's, their possible arms deal with the Choshu, and the possible help that a possible French wife might render their fledgling arms industry. "Did you have a good time? How's your fiancé?"

"He's much better, thank you. The dinner was huge, if you like to eat heavily. Ah, to be in Paris, yes?"

"Yes." My God, she's beddable, he thought, and that reminded him of the infectious vileness eating him away.

"What is it?" she asked, startled by his sudden pallor.

"Nothing." He cleared his throat and fought to control the horror. "Just out of sorts—nothing grave."

He seemed so vulnerable, so helpless that abruptly she decided to trust him again and closed the door and sat near him, pouring out her story. "What am I going to do, dear André? I can't get any cash . . . what can I do?"

"Dry your tears, Angelique, the answer is so simple. Tomorrow or the next day I will take you shopping," he said, his mind quite clear for mundane matters. "You've asked me to go shopping with you, haven't you, to help find an engagement present for Monsieur Struan. Gold cuff links with pearls, and pearl earrings for yourself." His voice saddened. "But oh, so terrible, somewhere en route back from the jewelers you lose one pair—we look everywhere but to no avail. Terrible!" His pale brown eyes held hers. "Meanwhile the mama-san has her secret payment, I will make sure the pair you 'lose' more than covers the medicine, and all costs."

"You're wonderful!" she burst out and hugged him. "Wonderful, what would I do without you?" She embraced him again, thanked him again and virtually danced out of the room.

He looked at the closed door a long time. Yes, it will cover the medicine, and my twenty louis, and other expenses if I decide, he thought, curiously unsettled. Poor little cabbage, so easy to manipulate you. You embroil yourself in deeper and deeper whirlpools. Don't you realize that now you become a thief and worse, you're a criminal planning a willful fraud.

And you, André, you are an accessory to the conspiracy.

He laughed outright, a bad twisted laugh. Prove it! Will she tell a court about an abortion, will the mama-san be witness against me? Will the court believe the story of the daughter and niece of criminals against mine?

No, but God will know and soon you will be before HIM.

Yes, and HE will know I've done much worse. And intend to do even more evil.

Tears began to stream down his face.

* * *

"Ayeeyah, Miss'ee," Ah Soh said, trying to help Angelique undress, who would not be still, again in a merry mood, her immediate problem solved. "Miss'ee!"

"Oh, very well, but do hurry." Angelique stood by her bed but continued to hum her cheery polka, the room more feminine and friendly in the oil light than during the day, the glass windows slightly ajar with the slatted shutters barred.

"Miss'ee gud time, heya?" Nimbly Ah Soh began to untie the waist straps of the crinoline.

"Good, thank you," Angelique said politely, not liking her particularly. Ah Soh was a big-hipped, middle-aged woman, a servant and not a real amah. 'But she's so old, Malcolm, can't you find me someone young and pretty who laughs!'

'Gordon Chen, our compradore, chose her, Angel. He guarantees she's completely trustworthy, she can brush your hair, bathe you, can look after your European clothes, and she's my gift to you while she's with you in Japan. . . .'

The straps loosened and the crinoline fell away, then Ah Soh did the same with the petticoat and last the vast framework of hoops of bone and metal that gave the crinoline body. Long pantaloons, silk stockings, short slip and the boned cinch and corset that made her twenty-inch waist eighteen inches and swelled her breasts fashionably. As the maid unlaced the cinch-corset Angelique let out a deep sigh of contentment, stepped out of the sea of material and flopped on the bed and, as a child would, allowed herself to be undressed completely. Obediently she raised her arms to permit the flowery nightdress to be eased around her.

"Sit, Miss'ee."

"No, not tonight, Ah Soh, my hair can wait."

"Ayeeyah, t'morro no gud!" Ah Soh brandished the brush.

"Oh, all right." Angelique sighed and scrambled off the bed and sat by the dressing table and allowed her to take out the pins and begin to brush. It felt very good. Oh, how clever André is! He makes everything so simple—now I can get all the money I need. Oh, how clever he is.

From time to time a benign sea breeze creaked the shutters. A hundred yards away, across the promenade, waves ran up the pebbled shore and departed and came again with a good sound that promised another gentle night that all in the Settlement had welcomed. The fleet had left with the light. Everyone not drunk or bedridden had watched with varying degrees of anxiety as the ships sailed off. All wished them Godspeed and a quick return. Except the Japanese. Ori was one of them and he had his eyes pressed to a crack in one of her shutters, well hidden and camouflaged by the tall camellia bushes that grew here abundantly and that Seratard, a keen gardener, had had planted.

Long before midnight Ori was in this ambush, waiting for her, time passing slowly, thinking and rethinking schemes, exhausting himself, nervously checking and rechecking that his short sword was loose in its scabbard and the derringer safe in the sleeve of his fisherman's kimono. But when he had seen her approaching the Legation in the company of the two gai-jin, all his tiredness had vanished.

For a moment he had contemplated rushing out and killing them but discarded that foolishness, knowing it was unlikely he could kill the three of them, and the sentry, before being killed himself. And anyway, he thought grimly, that would end my plan to have her once more before I die, and then to burn the Settlement. Without me to goad Hiraga he will never do it. He's too weak now—he's gai-jin infected. If Hiraga the Strong can succumb so quickly, what about others? The Emperor is right to hate gai-jin and want them expelled!

So he curbed his anger and slunk deeper into hiding, biding his time, planning for any eventuality. No way through the windows unless she unbarred them. The back door was unguarded and possible—and plenty of footholds to the next floor if it would not open. He had watched the undressing in every detail, barely two paces away, beyond the wall. Now she was being prepared for bed, the maid fussing about her mistress. His impatience became almost unbearable.

Earlier one of the mixed naval and army patrols that roamed the Settlement nightly to keep order had suddenly challenged him in a lane behind High Street. He had stopped without fear; there was no curfew nor was any part of the Settlement forbidden to Japanese, though, wisely, they kept mostly to their own quarter and chose not to tempt gai-jin temper. Unfortunately the Sergeant had rudely shoved a lantern in his face, making him jerk back, startled. The concealed short sword clattered to the ground. ''Ere, you little bastard, you knows daggers'n the like is forbidden, *kinjiru*.'

Though Ori did not understand the words, the rule and penalty were common knowledge. At once he grabbed up his knife and fled. The Sergeant fired at him but the bullet *haranggg*ed off a tile harmlessly and he leapt over a low wall to lose himself in the maze of lanes and dwellings. The patrol did not bother to give chase, just shouted a few curses after him. Carrying a knife was a small misdemeanor, worth only an immediate beating and the weapon confiscated.

Again he had waited in hiding until he could join a group of fishermen to go down to the shore, then doubled back, scaled the Legation fence and quickly found a safe place. Once there he had slumped down and began to wait.

This morning, he had pretended he was ready to leave the Yoshiwara for Kyōto as Hiraga had demanded. 'As soon as I've contacted Katsumata there, I'll send you a message,' he had said, deliberately tight-lipped. 'Make sure the girl does not escape!'

'She's the tai-pan's woman so her every step is measured and she'll be easy to find,' Hiraga had told him, as coldly. 'Watch yourself, the Tokaidō will be dangerous—Enforcer patrol and barrier guards will be very alert.'

'Better we honor *sonno-joi*, better you allow me to stay, better we burn Yokohama. Akimoto arrives today, we could do it easily.'

'We will, when you return. If you stay now you will make a mistake, the woman has turned your head and made you dangerous, to yourself, your friends and *sonno-joi*.'

'What about you, Hiraga? The gai-jin have turned you and twisted your judgment.'

'No. I tell you for the last time.'

Careless of provoking Hiraga even more, he flared, 'You saw what scum gai-jin are, drunk and revolting, fighting like beasts, carousing in the filth of Drunk Town—are these the men you want to know more of, to be like?'

'Go!'

Angrily he had collected his short sword and derringer. At Raiko's suggestion he joined the daily procession of servants leaving for Kanagawa market where the best saké and foods were purchased. With them he had passed through the Yoshiwara and Settlement barriers, the Enforcer patrol still lurking amongst the guards, making them as nervous as the villagers. Halfway to Kanagawa, the road traffic heavy, he had slipped away to the shore. There he had bribed a fisherman to row him to the far end of the Settlement, near Drunk Town, to hide him till dusk.

I am doing the correct thing, he thought with absolute conviction, the small sea wind scattering the night insects. The woman is the perfect target for *sonno-joi*. Whatever Hiraga says I may never have another chance to cast away her spell. Yes, I am in her spell. She must be a kami, a spirit, a wolf woman reborn gai-jin, no other woman could be virgin and drugged yet still be as welcoming, no other could make a man explode like I exploded, or keep me deranged with desire.

Tonight I will lay her for the second time. Then I will kill her. If I escape, karma. If I do not escape, karma. But she will die by my hand.

The sweat was running down his face and back. Once more he concentrated, watching her through the crack, so very close that, but for the wall, he could almost reach out and touch her. She climbed into bed, nightdress revealing. Now the maid turned down the oil flame to leave a warm glow of light.

" 'Night, Miss'ee."

" 'Night, Ah Soh."

Happy to be alone, Angelique snuggled down in the bedclothes, watching the flame shadows dance with the drafts, her head resting comfortably on her arm. Before Kanagawa the dark had never bothered her and she would go quickly into dreamtime to awake refreshed. Since Kanagawa her pattern had changed. Now she insisted on a night light. Sleep did not come easily. Soon her mind took her into paths of wild surmise. Her hands would stray to her breasts. Are they a little fuller than yesterday, my nipples more sensitive? Yes, yes, they are, no, it is just imagination. And my stomach? Is it rounder? No, there's no difference and yet . . .

And yet there is a vast difference, like B.C. and A.D. and at least once a day I wonder, would it be a boy or girl? Or devil, taking after the rapist father. No, no child of mine could be a devil!

Devil. That reminds me today's Friday and in two days I have to go to church and confess again. The words get no easier. How I hate confession now and loathe Father Leo, such a fat, uncouth, tobacco-smelling and lecherous old man. He reminds me of Aunt Emma's confessor in Paris—the ancient Scot, smelling of whisky, whose French was as vile as his cassock. Lucky for me that neither she nor Uncle Michel were fanatic, just ordinary Sunday Catholics. I wonder how she is, and poor Uncle Michel. Tomorrow I will speak to Malcolm. . . .

Dear, dear Malcolm, he was so nice tonight, so strong and wise and oh, how I wanted him. So glad I can talk to him, so lucky for me that Aunt Emma refused to learn French so I had to learn English. How could she possibly survive in Paris all those years speaking only English, and what possessed Uncle Michel to marry her and endure such hardship? Though I love her and him, she so dowdy, he so ordinary.

Love! That's what he would always say and she would say and that they had met when he was in Normandy one summer vacation, she an actress with a travelling Shakespearean troupe, he a junior official. It was love at first glance, they would always say, and tell how beautiful she was and handsome he was. Then running away together, married within the week, so romantic but not so happy ever after.

But we will be, Malcolm and I. Ah, yes, and I will love Malcolm as a modern wife should, we'll have lots of children, they'll be brought up Catholic, it won't matter to him, he's not fanatic either: 'I'm really not, Angelique. Of course we'll be married according to Protestant traditions, Mother will not have it otherwise, of that I'm certain. Afterwards we can have a Catholic ceremony, privately, if you wish . . .'

Never mind, even if it's secret, it's the real marriage—not like the other—the children will be accepted into Mother Church, we will all live in Paris most of the year, he will love me and I will love him and we'll make love marvelously, she thought, her heart beginning to thump pleasantly as she let her mind roam. Deeper and deeper. Then, because the evening had been wonderful and she felt wonderful and quite safe, she allowed the pleasing parts of that night's dream to return.

She could remember none of it exactly. The outrage dissolved into pictures within erotic pictures within erotic pictures. A little burning that became a pervading warmth. Knowing but not knowing. Feeling but not feeling strong arms embracing, and being possessed by a never-before-experienced sensuality and openness, head, body, life, gloriously free to abandon all restraint, to relish everything because it was . . . just a dream.

But did I awake, or almost awake, and only pretend that I didn't, she asked herself again and again, always with a shudder. I could not have responded that wantonly awake—surely not—but the dream was so strong and, in its grasp, I was driven by a tempest to want more and again more and . . .

She heard the outer door open and close and then the bedroom door latch moving and whirled to see André open the door silently and close it silently, bolt it, and lean against it, a mocking smile on his lips.

Suddenly she was afraid. "What do you want, André?"

For a long time he did not answer, then came over to the bed and stared down at her. "To . . . to talk, eh?" he said softly. "We should, eh? Talk, or—or what?"

"I don't understand," she said, understanding too well, painfully aware of the disturbing glitter in his eyes where only a few minutes before there had been only compassion. But she kept her voice reasonable, cursing herself that she had not barred the door—never a need here, always servants or Legation staff about and no one would dare enter without permission. "Please, don't y—"

"We should talk, about tomorrow and be—be friends."

"Dear André, please, it's late, whatever it is can wait until tomorrow, sorry but you've no right to come in here without knock—" In momentary panic she retreated to the other side of the bed as he sat on the edge and reached for her. "Stop or I'll scream!"

His laugh was soft and barbed. "If you scream, dear Angelique, that will bring the servants and I will unlock the door and tell them you invited me here—you wanted privacy to discuss your need for money, cash money, for your abortion." Again the mocking twisted smile. "Eh?"

"Oh, André, don't be like that, please leave, please—if someone were to see you, please."

"First . . . first a kiss."

She flushed. "Get out, how dare you!"

"Shut up and listen," he whispered harshly, and his hand caught her wrist and held it in a vise. "I can dare anything, if I want more than a kiss you'll give it to me happily or else. Without me you'll be found out, without me—"

"André . . . please let me go." As much as she tried she could not break his grip. With a twisted smile he released her. "You hurt me," she said, near tears.

"I don't want to hurt you," he said throatily, his voice sounding strange to him and he knew he was insane to be here and doing this, but he had been caught up in such sudden horror that it had overpowered his reason, his feet carrying him here of their own volition, to force her to—to what? To share his degradation. Why not? his brain was shrieking. It's her fault, flaunting her tits and blatant sexuality, reminding me! She's no better than a street slut, maybe she wasn't raped, isn't she out to trap Struan and his millions by any means? "I'm—I'm your friend, aren't I helping you? Come over here, a—a kiss isn't much payment."

"No!"

"By Christ, do it happily or I'll stop helping you and, in a day or two, I'll inform Struan and Babcott, anonymously. You want that? Eh?"

"André, please . . ." She looked around, desperate for a way to escape. There was none. He moved closer to her on the bed and reached for her breast but she pushed his hand away and began to resist and to fight and hacked with her nails for his eyes but he held her helpless as she struggled, afraid to call out, knowing she was snared and lost and would have to submit. Abruptly, there was a violent pounding on the shutter.

The suddenness ripped André out of his madness and she screamed in fright. Aghast, he leapt off the bed, rushed for the door, unlocked it and the one to the corridor, then whirled and ran to the windows, pulling them open. In seconds he had unbarred the shutters and shoved them outwards. Nothing. No one there. Nothing but bushes waving in the wind, the sound of the sea, the promenade beyond the fence empty of people.

A sentry hurried into view. "What's going on?"

"I should ask you that, soldier," André said, his heart grinding, his words tumbling over. "Did you see anyone, anything? I was passing Mademoiselle's door and heard, or thought I heard, someone pounding on her shutters. Quick, look around!"

Behind him, Pierre Vervene, the Chargé d'Affaires, a flickering candle in his hand, hurried anxiously into the room, dressing gown over his nightshirt, nightcap askew. Others began crowding the doorway, "What's going on—oh, André! What the devil . . . what's going on? Mademoiselle, you screamed?"

"Yes . . . I . . . he—" she stammered. "André was . . . he . . . someone banged on the shutters and André, well, he—"

"I was just passing her door," André said, "and rushed in—isn't that true, Angelique?"

She dropped her eyes, holding the bedclothes closer around her. "Yes, yes, that's true," she said, afraid and hating him but attempting to hide it.

Vervene joined André at the window and peered out. "Perhaps it was the wind, we have sudden squalls here and the shutters aren't exactly new." He shook one of them. Indeed it was loose and rattled noisily. Then he leaned out and shouted after the sentry. "Make a very good search and come back and report to me." Then he closed and barred the shutters, and rebolted the windows. "There! Nothing to worry about."

"Yes, yes, but . . ." Tears of relief began to well.

"*Mon Dieu*, Mademoiselle, nothing to worry about, don't cry, you're perfectly safe, no need to worry, of course not." Vervene took off his nightcap and scratched his bald pate, at a loss. Then, thankfully, he saw Ah Soh amongst the others at the doorway and motioned at her importantly. "Ah Soh, you-ah sleep here, with Miss'ee, heya?"

"Yes, Mass'er." Ah Soh hurried off to get some bedding and everyone else began to drift away.

"I'll wait with you, Mademoiselle Angelique, until she returns." The older man yawned. "Probably you were both mistaken, and it was the wind. Who would want to bang on the shutters, eh? There aren't any rotten little street urchins and guttersnipes in the Settlement to play pranks or be pickpockets, thank God! Must have been the wind, eh?"

"I'm sure you're right," André said, over his scare now, dreading that someone had been outside, watching—he had seen the crack but no other signs. "Don't you agree, Angelique?"

"I—I, perhaps yes," she said, very unsettled and not yet recovered from her fright, both because of him and because of the sudden sound. Why did it happen then? Was it someone, or just a God-given wind—truly a gift from God? Wind or not, person or not, I don't care, she decided. I don't care, I escaped, tomorrow I move back beside Malcolm, daren't stay here, mustn't stay, too close to André, too dangerous. "It sounded like someone banging, but—but I could be mistaken. It could have been a—a sudden gust."

"I'm sure it was," Vervene said confidently. "My shutters are always banging, wake me up all the time." He coughed and sat down, peering kindly at André whose face was still chalky. "No need for you to wait, my friend. You don't look very well at all, as though, Heaven forbid, you've a crisis of the liver."

"Perhaps—perhaps I have. I—I certainly don't feel very well." André glanced at Angelique. "Sorry," he said, holding her eyes, making his voice calm and soft, seemingly the old André once more, all strangeness and lust and violence vanished. "Good night, Angelique, you've nothing to be afraid of, ever. Monsieur Vervene is quite right."

"Yes . . . yes, thank you, André." She forced a smile and then he was gone. She had looked at him deeply, wanting to read the truth behind his eyes. They were friendly, nothing else. But she did not trust what she had seen. Even so, she knew that she would have to make peace with him, would accept his inevitable apologies—pretending to forget everything and agreeing the attack was a momentary madness—and would become friends again. On the surface.

She shuddered. In her innermost being she also grasped that whatever he demanded, eventually she would have to give. While he lived.

Ori was trembling, hunched down against an upturned fishing boat on the pebbled beach. Twenty yards away was the edge of the surf, the waves sibilant. "You're completely *baka*," he gasped, his fury directed totally against himself. Before he realized what he was doing he had hammered on the shutters and then, appalled at his stupidity, had rushed away, scaled the fence, found the oar he used as camouflage, shouldered it and loped across the roadway without being challenged, gai-jin voices in his wake.

Hiraga must be right, he thought, nauseated, mixed up, his heart aching in his chest, shoulder throbbing and a warm trickle of blood seeping from the tear in the wound his headlong flight had caused. Perhaps this woman really has sent me mad. Madness to pound on the shutters—what good would that do me? What does it matter if another pillows her? Why should that enflame me, make my heart roar in my ears? I don't own her or want to own her, what does it matter if another gai-jin takes her with or without violence? Some women need a measure of violence to excite them, like many men . . . ah, wait, would it have been better if she had fought me rather than welcoming me, however drugged she was—or pretended to be?

Pretended?

This was the first time such a thought had entered his mind. Some of his venom left him though his heart continued to race and the ache behind his temples did not leave. *Could* she have been pretending? Eeee, it's possible, her arms embraced me and her legs wrapped me and her body moved like no one has ever moved—all pillow partners move sensually, with moans and sighs and sometimes a few tears and, 'Oh, how strong you are, how you exhaust me, never have I had the privilege of such a man before . . .' but every client knows that these are surface words, learned by rote, part of their training, nothing more, and meaningless.

She wasn't like that, every moment had meaning for me. Whether she pretended or not doesn't matter—she probably did, women are so filled with guile. I don't care, I should not have bludgeoned the shutter like a berserk fool, revealing my presence and hiding place and probably ruining forever my chance of gaining access there again!

Again his anger burst. His fist smashed the wood of the hull. *"Baka!"* he croaked, wanting to shriek it aloud.

Footsteps on the pebbles. On guard, he slid deeper into the shadows, the moon baleful, then heard the voices of approaching fishermen, chatting one with another, and cursed himself afresh for not being more alert. Almost at once, a rough, middle-aged fisherman came around the stern of the boat and stopped. "Watch out! Who're you, stranger?" the man said angrily, readying the short mast he carried as a club. "What are you up to?"

Ori did not move, just glared up at him and at the other two who moved up beside him. One was also middle-aged, the other a youth not much older than Ori himself. Both carried oars and fishing tackle. "You do not ask those questions of your betters," he said. "Where are your manners?"

"Who're you, you're not samur—" The man stopped, petrified, as Ori leapt to his feet, the sword instantly in his hand, the blade dangerously half out of its scabbard.

"On your knees, scum, before I cut your *baka* hearts out—a haircut does not make me any less samurai!" Instantly the fishermen fell to their knees, heads to the beach and were bleating their apologies, no mistaking the authority or the way the short sword was held. "Shut up!" Ori snarled. "Where were you going?"

"To fish, Lord, half a league out to sea, please excuse us but, well, in the dark and your hair not norm—"

"Shut up! Get the boat in the water. Move!"

Once safe out to sea, now over his blinding anger, the salt air cleansing, Ori looked back at the Settlement. Lights still on in the French and British Legations, the Struan Building and the Club that Hiraga had identified for him. Oil streetlamps along the *praia*, a few windows glowing in other bungalows and godowns, Drunk Town pulsating as normal throughout the night, the gin shops never totally sleeping.

But all of his attention was on the French Legation. Why? he kept asking himself. Why should I have been so possessed with—jealousy, that's the real word. An insane jealousy. To be jealous over pillowing is *baka*!

Was it because of what Hiraga had told me: 'Taira says their custom is like ours amongst the leader class, a man does not pillow the woman he will marry before marriage . . .' which means this tai-pan will not bed her and, as she is promised, no one else has the right. Did I smash the shutters to prevent that man pillowing her—or was it to protect her?

Or was it just because I wanted no other man to enjoy her until I can again—that's even more stupid, how could I ever tell? Was it because I was the first? Does that make that pillowing different: because you have possessed her uniquely? Remember, Chinese have always believed virginity to be the most powerful aphrodisiac between Heaven and Earth. Is that why I did what I did?

No. It was a sudden impulse. I believe she is a wolf woman who must be killed—preferably after I've pillowed her once more—for me to escape her spell.

But how and when? It must be now.

Too dangerous to stay in the Settlement, or Yoshiwara. Hiraga is bound to hear I have not left. I am a dead man if he finds me. Could I risk three more days, then, if I fail to snare her, hurry off to Kyōto with Hiraga none the wiser? Safer to leave now. Which? "You, old man, where do you live?"

"Second Street, Fifth House, Lord," the fisherman said, all of them deeply afraid, long since realizing that this must be one of the ronin who were hiding in the Settlement to escape the Toranaga Enforcers.

23

Sunday, 19th October:

CHURCH BELLS WERE BECKONING the faithful on this nice crisp morning. "Not many bloody faithful in Yokohama," Jamie McFay said to Struan. McFay's shoulders and back were aching, the church and the coming service not to his liking, nothing like the austere Scottish Presbyterianism of his childhood. "Not that I'm a real churchgoer, not anymore," he said, very much on guard, unsure how Struan was going to be after their violent row the day before. "My ma's still as strict as they come, three times on Sunday!"

"Like mine, though she's Church of England," Struan agreed heavily. He walked slowly and badly, hunched over, leaning on his canes, amid groups of men converging on the church that was down the High Street and set back slightly in its own garden on a choice lot facing the sea. "The church is pretty though. Makes Yokohama permanent."

Holy Trinity, or Holy Titty as they privately dubbed it, was the pride of the Settlement. It had been consecrated last year by the Bishop of Hong Kong. The steeple was tall and the bell sweet-sounding, reminding all ex-patriots of home—so very far away. Wood and plaster and bricks from Shanghai. Neat gardens and small cemetery with only seven graves, sickness rare in Yokohama—unlike Hong Kong with its plagues and the lethal Happy Valley fever, mal-aria—all seven deaths by misadventure, except one of old age. Twenty years working in Asia were rare and men past retirement age, rarer still.

Again the bell tolled, not yet insistent, more than enough time to take their places, the Noble House pew in the first row. I need all the help I can get, Struan was thinking fervently, never devout though always a believer. I'm glad it's our church more than the other traders'.

The land and the building had been donated to the Church of England by all traders. They had enthusiastically voted the levy four hours after the Yokohama Club had opened its doors for business, the same day the Settlement was founded—at McFay's insistence and on the orders of Tess Struan, who guaranteed fifty percent of the cost. She had also pledged to provide the bell and had it cast in their new foundry in Hong Kong. When Tyler Brock heard about it, not to be outdone by his estranged and hated daughter, he had ordered a stained-glass window from London and pews of English oak.

"Sunday church's all right, once a month, Father used to say, but never in Mother's hearing." Struan smiled bleakly. "When he was younger he was as much a churchgoer as she is now . . ." He stopped a moment to gather his breath and stared out to sea. The sea was choppy, blue-grey, the sky speckled with cumulus. A dozen or so merchantmen lay snug in the roads, English predominately, one American, one Russian, yesterday's mail steamer, the French paddle steamer flagship wallowing at anchor, and the 21-gun steam frigate H.M.S. *Pearl,* still without her foremast. "Feels naked without the fleet, doesn't it?"

"Yes, it does. Not many will miss prayers today." McFay circled his head to ease the ache in his neck.

"How long do you think they'll be gone?"

"A month is my bet. . . . 'Morning, Mrs. Lunkchurch." Both raised their hats politely, Struan awkwardly, as she sailed past, bustled and bonneted, husband sweatily in tow, his face dark with bruises. "What the devil happened to him?"

"Fighting," McFay said cautiously, still trying to gauge Struan's humor—he had not seen him or heard from him since yesterday except to get a curt message this morning to join him for their walk to church. He fell into step as Struan started off again. "Seems he, Dmitri and a few others decided to visit Drunk Town last night for a Saturday night binge."

"You mean punch-up?"

" 'Fraid that was the basic idea. Dmitri, well, he said they had a grand time."

Struan noticed the sudden glint in McFay's eyes. "Ah, you were there too, Jamie?" he asked dryly, then smiled.

McFay saw the smile and was greatly relieved. "Well, yes, Tai-pan, yes, I went along ... but just to make sure Dmitri didn't get into trouble."

"Did he?" Struan asked with a sudden stab of envy.

"No, but och ay, Tai-pan, we had a grand time."

"You lucky fellow! Come on, Jamie, tell all!"

Jamie heard and saw the open friendliness and camaraderie that he had been afraid he had lost forever and beamed, his aches forgotten, angers forgotten and worries over his future. "There was a smashing cockfight at the Bull and Cock, best we've had here, they've a new ring now and a new Nagasaki beer that's better than our own Highland Dark! Two army handlers were pitted against two of our lads, Chandler Sykes and Old Bloody."

"Who?"

"He's one of our retired seamen, a master gunner, name of Charlie Bent, who paid off of *Lasting Cloud*—the same gunner who blew Wu Sung Choi's war junk out of the water for your dad, back in '43. Now he's nicknamed 'Old Bloody' as he looks after the abattoir. Well, I backed him all the way, Tai-pan, and won twenty-five pounds. Afterwards we descended on the Yokopoko Palace—that's the biggest tavern in Drunk Town, Army mostly, the Navy go to the Friar Tuck and never the twain shall meet." He laughed. "Lost a tenner at roulette, another five at dice. In no time at all there was the greatest free-for-all, traders against the rest. I think we won. Then home to bed though, er, a few repaired to Naughty Nellie's."

"You too?"

"Well, yes, but only for a nightcap, her champagne's the best and cheapest in Yokohama."

"And the girls?"

McFay laughed again. "Nothing like Mrs. Fortheringill's Establishment for Young Ladies in Hong Kong! There're about a dozen birds, most from the East End via Hong Kong, a few from Sydney in Australia, daughters of women convicts who've served their time and stayed on. They're all a bit grotty, and not to my taste." Filled with bonhomie he greeted passersby and added without thinking, "My needs are more than well looked after by Nemi." He glanced at Struan and saw the stretched face. His good humor vanished and he cursed himself for mentioning her. "You all right, Tai-pan?"

"Yes, yes of course," Struan said, abruptly filled with envy at the other man's strength and virility, not loathing him for it, just himself. "Can't bear being like this, Jamie, hate it. Hate it! Christ, it's so difficult to be patient. I've just got to, I know that." He forced a smile. "Nemi? Oh yes, she seemed a nice girl. Pretty." With a vast effort Struan tore his mind off Shizuka and his failure, his frantic need to succeed with Angelique, and to weather the shoals ahead and coming tempest his mother was bound to generate. One thing at a time. Gear yourself to get through church, then through the rest of the day until six o'clock when Ah Tok will bring you the medicine: 'Would you like a little before you go to your temple, my son?'

'No, thank you, Mother, once a day is enough. The doctor said I should be careful.'

'What do foreign devils know?'

'Ayeeyah, I'm a foreign devil.'

'Ayeeyah, yes, but you're my son. . . .'

Ah Tok's such an old biddy. But then I can trust her. No harm in a little once a day. I can quit anytime, anytime, he reassured himself. Don't need it during the day though it certainly helps. Got to decide about Mother's letter, got to write her by tomorrow's mail. Got to.

Her letter had been delivered by hand from the mail ship by special courier, inevitably a relation of their compradore, Gordon Chen. Again it had had no 'P.S. I love you.' Again the secret message had infuriated him:

Malcolm: Have you gone totally dotty? Engagement party? After I warned you? Why on earth did you totally disregard my letter and my urgent summons to return? If it wasn't for Dr. Hoag's medical report received today with the unbelievable news I would have presumed you had head injuries as well as the terrible sword wounds. I have demanded our Governor take the most stringent measures against these uncivilized beasts and bring the violators to the Queen's justice at once! If he doesn't, I warned him personally that the whole force of the Noble House will be arranged against this administration!

Enough of that. It is VITAL that you return to Hong Kong at once to make final three matters—of course I am prepared to forgive your transgression, you are still so very young, you

*have been through a terrible experience and have fallen into
the clutches of an exceedingly clever woman. I thank God
you are gaining strength every day. From Dr. Hoag's report,
thankfully you should certainly be fit enough to travel by the
time you receive this (I have instructed Dr. Hoag to return
with you and hold him personally responsible for yr safety). I
have booked passage for you both on the mail ship—not for
her, deliberately.*

*It is essential you come back QUICKLY AND ALONE: first to
formally become tai-pan. Yr grandfather left specific instructions, in writing, that MUST be complied with before you
LEGALLY become tai-pan of Struan's whatever yr father or I
leave to you by will. Before yr father died, in your absence,
my son, he made me swear what had to be sworn and that I
would swear you to these same conditions. This must be done
quickly.*

*Second: because we must decide at once how to combat
Tyler Brock's attack on us—I mentioned before that he has
the full support of the Victoria Bank and today threatens to
foreclose on our promissory notes that will ruin us if successful. Gordon Chen has suggested a solution but it is terribly
risky, may not be put to paper, and requires the tai-pan's
signature and participation. My stepbrother 'Sir' Morgan
Brock has just arrived in Hong Kong and is flaunting his
knighthood that he only acquired by persuading his heirless
father-in-law to adopt him who then, conveniently and almost at once thereafter, died.*

*Was the poor man assisted? God forgive me but I would
not doubt it. Both he and Tyler Brock openly claim that by
Christmas they will have us humbled and they will be in
possession of our Steward's box at the races in Happy Valley.
The voting for a new Steward was yesterday. As per yr
grandfather's wishes on yr behalf I again blackballed him.
God forgive me but I hate my father so much I almost become mad.*

Third: yr entrapment! I could not believe my ears about this 'engagement party' until it was confirmed. I hope by now, I pray God, yr good sense has returned and you realize what has happened to you. Fortunately of course you cannot marry without my approval and certainly not the Catholic daughter of a runaway embezzler (there are warrants out to seize him for debts). In fairness I do understand you. Gordon Chen explained how easy it would be for a youth like you to be embroiled so do not despair. We have a plan that will extract you from her toils and prove to you conclusively that she is just a—sorry, my son, but I have to be blunt—just a Jezebel.

When you marry, your wife must be English, God-fearing, never a heretic, a lady of good family, trained and at ease in SOCIETY and worthy to be your wife, bringing you a suitable dowry and qualities to assist your future. When the time comes you will have many suitable ladies to choose from.

By the same mail I have written Dr. Hoag, and also McFay expressing my shock that he allowed this engagement stupidity to happen. I look forward to embracing you in a few days. yr loving Mother

Almost at once Jamie had rushed into the room, white-faced. 'She's heard!'

'I know that. Never mind.'

'Jesus Christ, Malcolm, you can't just say never mind!' McFay spluttered, practically incoherent. He offered him the letter that shook in his hand. 'Here, read it for yourself.'

The letter, without any form of greeting, was just signed Tess Struan:

Unless you have a satisfactory explanation why you permitted my son (though he is to be tai-pan you must know is still a minor) to become engaged without first obtaining my approval—which you MUST know would never be forthcoming for such an unsuitable match, you will cease to head Struan's in Japan at the end of the year. Put Mr. Vargas in

*charge for the moment and return with my son on the mail
ship to settle this matter.*

Struan had angrily shoved the letter back. 'I'm not going back to
Hong Kong yet—I'll go when I choose.'

'Christ Jesus, Malcolm, if she orders us back then we had better go.
There're reasons th—'

'No!' he had flared. 'Understand? NO!'

'For God's sake, open your eyes to the truth,' McFay had flared
back. 'You are under age, she is running the company and has been for
years. We're under her orders an—'

'I'm not under her orders, any orders. Get out!'

'I won't! Can't you see what she asks is wise and no hardship. We
can be back here in two to three weeks, you have to get her approval
sometime, surely it's better to try now, it'll clear the air for you and
make our job easier an—'

'No! And . . . and I'm cancelling her orders: I order you. I'm tai-pan
of Struan's!'

'Christ, you must know I can't go against her!'

Struan almost faltered in his steps remembering the dreadful stab of
pain in his loins as he had thoughtlessly scrambled out of his chair to
his feet and shouted at McFay: 'You fucking listen, I remind you of
your sacred oath to serve the tai-pan, the *tai-pan,* for Christ's sake,
whoever he is, the tai-pan, not his fucking mother! REMEMBER?'

'But, don't y—'

'Who're you going to obey, Jamie? Me or my mother?' There had
been a vast chasm between them and more anger and more words, but
he had prevailed. This battle was no contest. The stipulation was
written into every document of appointment, to be signed and settled
under God's oath in accordance with their founder's instructions.

'All right, I agree!' McFay had said through his teeth. 'But I dem—
sorry, I ask the right to write to her and tell her my new orders.'

'Do that, by the mail ship, and while you're about it, tell her the tai-
pan orders you to stay here, that only I can fire you, as I will, by God, if
I have any trouble—and that if I want to get engaged, minor or no,
that's up to me.' Then he had groped back to his chair, almost doubled
up with pain.

'My God, Tai-pan,' McFay said weakly, 'she'll dismiss me whether
you like it or not. I'm finished.'

'No. Not without my say-so, it's in our bylaws.'

'Maybe. But like it or not, she can make my life and yours a misery.'

'No, you're only doing what I want. You're within Dirk's law—and that's what governs her above all else,' he said, remembering the times without number she had invoked the name of Dirk Struan to his father, or to him, or to his brothers and sisters, on a point of business or morality or on life itself. And didn't Father and Mother both say a thousand times that I was to be tai-pan after him, everyone, particularly Uncle Gordon accepting that. Any formalities can wait, she's just using that as an additional excuse to curb me—Christ, I've trained all my life for the job, I know how to deal with her and I know what's wrong here. 'I'm tai-pan, by God, and now . . . now if you'll excuse me, I—I've work to do.'

The moment he was alone he had shouted for Ah Tok.

Ayeeyah, that was one time I really needed the medicine, it works so well and saved me all that pain and anguish and gave me courage again and, later, such a happy time with Angelique. Ah, my angel, back again in her suite next door, thank God, so near and delectable and warm and near, but oh, and Christ, I wish when I thought of her the ache wouldn't begin, and that ache would not lead to the other pain and it's not yet midmorning with a boring sermon and lunch to endure—and more than eight hours until the next . . .

"Sorry about yesterday," McFay was saying. "Very sorry."

"I'm not, it brought matters out in the open and settled them," he said with a curious strength. "Now there's a real head to the company—I agree my father wasn't effective and spent most of the last few years drunk, with Mother doing the best she could, which hasn't kept us ahead of Brock's—again let's be honest, they're stronger and richer and more sound than we are and we'll be lucky to weather the current storm. Take Japan—Japan's hardly paying expenses."

"Yes, short term, but long term it will be profitable."

"Not the way you've been running it so far. Jappos are not buying any profitable goods from us. We buy silk cloth and silkworms, a few lacquer trinkets, what else? Nothing of value. They've no industry and don't seem to want any."

"True, but then China took time to open up, years. And there we've the opium, tea, silver triangle."

"True, but China's different. China's a cultured, ancient civilization. We've friends there and, as you say, a trading pattern. My point is we've got to hurry things up here to survive, or we close it down."

"As soon as Sir William sorts out the Bakufu—"

"The pox on that!" Struan's voice sharpened. "I'm tired of being stuck in a chair and sick of hearing people say we have to wait until Sir William orders the fleet and army to do its job. The next time there's a meeting with the Bakufu I want to be there—or better still you arrange a private one for me first."

"But, Tai-pan . . ."

"Do it, Jamie. That's what I want. And do it quickly."

"I don't know how that's possible."

"Ask Phillip Tyrer's tame samurai, Nakama. Better still, arrange a secret meeting then Phillip won't be compromised."

McFay had given him the information that 'Nakama' had provided. "That's a good idea," he said, meaning it, and, seeing the jutting jaw and the fire he was warmed. Perhaps at long last, he thought, here's someone who can make things happen. "I'll see Phillip after church."

"When's the next ship scheduled for San Francisco?"

"In a week, the Confederate merchantman, *Savannah Lady*." McFay dropped his voice cautiously, a group of other traders passing by. "Our Choshu order goes with her."

"Who could we trust to go with her for a special mission?" Struan asked, putting his plan into operation.

"Vargas."

"Not him, he's needed here." Again Struan stopped, his legs aching, then hobbled to the side of the promenade where there was a low wall, mostly to rest but also to keep their conversation private. "Who else? Has to be good."

"His nephew, Pedrito—he's a sharp lad, looks more Portuguese than Vargas, hardly any Chinese in his face, speaks Portuguese, Spanish, English and Cantonese—good at figures. He'd be acceptable in either the North or the Confederacy. What had you in mind?"

"Book passage for him on that ship. I want him to go with the order which we're going to quadruple, also to ord—"

"Four thousand rifles?" McFay gaped at him.

"Yes, also send a letter to the factory via tomorrow's mail ship telling them to expect him. She'll connect with the California steamer out of Hong Kong."

McFay said uneasily, "But we only got a down payment of gold to cover two hundred—we'll have to cover the whole order, that's factory policy. Don't you think we'd be overextending ourselves?"

"Some people might think so. I don't."

"Even with a shipment of two thousand—the Admiral's hysterical against importation of all arms and opium . . . I know he can't by law, "

McFay said hastily, "but if he wants he can still seize a cargo on the grounds of national emergency."

"He won't find them or hear about them until it's too late—you'll be too clever. Meanwhile draft a letter to go with the order, and a copy by the mail ship—do it yourself, Jamie, privately—asking the factory for special service on this consignment, but also to make us their exclusive agents for Asia."

"That's a fine idea, Tai-pan, but I strongly advise against upping the order."

"Make it five thousand rifles, and emphasize we'll negotiate a most attractive deal. I don't want Norbert to steal a march on us." Struan began walking again, the pain worse now. Without looking at McFay he knew what he was thinking and said, an edge to his voice, "There's no need to check with Hong Kong first. Do it. I'll sign the order and the letter."

After a pause McFay nodded. "Just as you say."

"Good." He heard the reluctance in McFay's voice and decided that now was the time. "We're changing our policy in Japan. They like killing here, eh? According to this Nakama many of their kings are ready to revolt against the Bakufu who certainly aren't our friends. Good, we'll help them do what they want. We'll sell them what they want: armaments, some ships, even a gun factory or two, in ever-increasing amounts—for gold and silver."

"And what if they turn these guns on us?"

"Once will be enough to teach them a lesson, like everywhere else on earth. We'll sell them muskets, some breech-loaders, but no machine guns, no big cannon or modern fighting ships. We're going to give the customer what he wants to buy."

Angelique knelt and settled herself in the tiny screened confessional, as best as her voluminous skirts would allow, and began the ritual, the Latin words running together as was normal for those who did not read or write the language but had learned the obligatory prayers and responses from childhood by constant repetition. "Forgive me, Father, for I have sinned . . ."

On the other side of the screen, Father Leo was more attentive than usual. Normally he listened with half an ear, sadly, sure that his penitents were lying, their sins unconfessed, their level of transgression great—but no greater than in other Settlements in Asia—and the penances he ordered were merely paid lip service, or totally disregarded.

"So, my child, you have sinned," he said in his most pleasant voice, his French heavily accented. He was fifty-five, corpulent and bearded, a Portuguese Jesuit and Believer, ordained for twenty-seven of those years and largely content with the crumbs of life he judged God permitted him. "What sins have you committed this week?"

"I forgot to ask the Madonna for forgiveness in my prayers one night," she said with perfect calm, continuing her pact, "and had many bad thoughts and dreams, and was afraid, and forgot I was in God's hands . . ."

At Kanagawa, the day after *that night*—once she had reasoned a way out of her catastrophe—she had knelt weeping before the small crucifix she always carried with her. 'Mother of God, there's no need to explain what has happened and how I've been sinned against grievously,' she had sobbed, praying with all the fervor she could gather, 'or that I've no one to turn to, or that I need your help desperately, or that obviously I can't tell anyone, even at Confession, I daren't openly confess what has happened. I daren't, it would destroy the only chance . . .

'So please, on my knees I beg you, may we have a pact: when I say at Confession: *I forgot to ask the Blessed Mother for forgiveness in my prayers,* it really means that I'm confessing and telling everything that I've told you and you've seen happen to me, together with the added little white lies I may—I will have to tell to protect myself. I beg forgiveness for asking, and beg your help, there's no one else I can turn to. I know you'll forgive me and know you'll understand because you are the Mother of God and a woman—you will understand and know you will absolve me . . .'

She could see Father Leo's profile behind the screen and smell the wine and garlic on his breath. She sighed, thanked the Madonna with all her heart for helping her. "Forgive me, Father, for I have sinned."

"Those sins don't appear to be so bad, my child."

"Thank you, Father." She stifled a yawn, preparing to accept her usual, modest penance, then to cross herself and be absolved and to thank him and to leave. Tiffin at the Club with Malcolm and Seratard, siesta in my beautiful suite next to Malcolm's, dinner at the Russian Leg—

"What kind of bad thoughts did you have?"

"Oh, just being impatient," she said without thinking, "and not content to rest in God's hands."

"Impatient about what?"

"Oh, with, impatient with my maid," she said flustered, caught unawares, "and that—that my fiancé is not as fit, is not as well as I'd like him to be."

"Ah yes, the tai-pan, a fine young man but grandson of a great enemy of the True Church. Has he told you about him? His grandfather, Dirk Struan?"

"Some stories, Father," she said, even more unsettled. "About my maid I was impa—"

"Malcolm Struan's a fine young man, not like his grandfather. You have asked him to become Catholic?"

The color went out of ` face. "We have discussed it, yes. Such a ... such a discussion   very delicate and—and of course may not be hurried."

"Yes, yes indeed." Father Leo had heard the intake of breath and sensed her anxiety. "And I agree it is terribly important, for him and for you." He frowned, his experience telling him the girl was hiding much from him—not that that would be unusual, he thought.

He was going to leave the matter there, then suddenly realized here was a God-given opportunity both to save a soul and have a worthwhile enterprise—life in Yokohama, unlike in his beloved and happy Portugal, was drab with little to do except fish and drink and eat and pray. His church was small and dingy, his flock sparse and ungodly, the Settlement a veritable prison. "Such discussion may be delicate but it must be pressed forward. His immortal soul is in absolute jeopardy. I will pray for your success. Your children will be brought up in Mother Church—of course he has already agreed?"

"Oh, we have discussed it, too, Father," she said, forcing lightness. "Of course our children will be Catholic."

"If they are not, you cast them into the Eternal Pit. Your immortal soul will be at risk as well." He was glad to notice her shudder. Good, he thought, one blow for the Lord against the Antichrist. "This must be formally agreed to before marriage."

Her heart was racing now, her head aching with apprehension that she fought to keep out of her voice, believing absolutely in God and the Devil, Life Everlasting and Eternal Damnation. "Thank you for your advice, Father."

"I will talk to Mr. Struan."

"Oh no, Father, please, no," she said in sudden panic, "that would be ... I suggest that would be very unwise."

"Unwise?" Again he pursed his lips, scratching absently at the lice that inhabited his beard and hair and ancient cassock, quickly concluding the possible coup of Struan's conversion was a prize worth waiting for and needed careful planning. "I will pray for God's guidance and that HE will guide you too. But don't forget you are a minor, as he is. I suppose, in the absence of your father, Monsieur Seratard would legally be considered your guardian. Before any marriage could be performed or consummated permission must be granted, and these and other matters settled for the protection of your soul." He beamed, more than a little satisfied. "Now, for penance, say ten Hail Marys and read the letters of Saint John twice by next Sunday—and continue to pray for God's guidance."

"Thank you Father." Thankfully she crossed herself, her palms sweaty, and bowed her head for his benediction.

"*In nomine Patris, et Filii, et Spiritus Sancti, absolvo tuum.*" He made the sign of the cross over her. "Pray for me, my child," he said with finality, ending the ritual, in his mind already beginning his dialogue with Malcolm Struan.

At dusk Phillip Tyrer was sitting cross-legged opposite Hiraga in a tiny private room in the equally tiny restaurant that was half hidden beside the house of the shoya, the village elder. They were the only customers, and this was the first real Japanese meal with a Japanese host Tyrer had experienced. He was hungry and ready to taste everything. "*Thank you invite me, Nakama-san.*"

"*It is my pleasure, Taira-san. May I say that your Japanese accent is improving. Please eat.*"

On the low table between them the maid had set many small dishes with different foods, some hot some cold, on decorative lacquered trays. Shoji screens, tatami mats, small sliding windows open to the descending darkness, oil lamps giving a pleasing light, flower arrangement in the nook. Adjoining was another private room and, outside these, the rest of the restaurant, not much more than a corridor with stools that opened to an alley that led to the street—charcoal cooking brazier, saké and beer barrels, a cook and three maids.

Hiraga and Tyrer wore loose-belted sleeping-lounging kimonos—Tyrer enjoying its unaccustomed comfort and Hiraga relieved to get out of the European clothes that he had worn all day. Both had been bathed and massaged in the nearby bathhouse. "*Please eat.*"

Awkwardly Tyrer used chopsticks. In Peking, the Embassy had advised against eating any Chinese foods: '. . . not unless you want to get poisoned, old boy. These buggers really eat dog, drink snake's bile, spoon up insects, anything, and have an astounding but universal belief, If its back faces heaven you can eat it! Ugh!'

Hiraga corrected the way to hold the sticks. *"There."*

"Thank you, Nakama-san, very difficult." Tyrer laughed. *"Will fat not get eating theses."*

" 'I will not get fat eating with these,' " Hiraga said, not yet weary of correcting Tyrer's Japanese, for he had found he enjoyed teaching him. Tyrer was an apt pupil with a remarkable memory and happy disposition—and very important for himself, a continual fountain of information.

"Ah, sorry, I won't get fat eating with these. What is, sorry, what are these foods?"

"This is what we call tempura, fish fried in batter."

"So sorry, what is 'batter'?" Tyrer listened attentively, missing many of the words but understanding the gist, just as he knew the other man would miss English words. We speak more English than Japanese, he thought wryly, but never mind. Nakama's a great teacher and we seem to have made an accommodation which is fine—without him I wouldn't be here, probably not alive, either, and would certainly never have all the face I gained with Marlowe, Pallidar and Wee Willie Winkie, let alone the invaluable intelligence he is supplying. Tyrer smiled. It pleased him to be able to think of Sir William now by his nickname when only a few days ago he had been petrified of him. *"Oh, now I understand.* Batter! *We also use batter."*

"This food to your liking, Taira-san?" Hiraga asked, switching to English.

"Yes, thank you." Whenever he could Tyrer would answer in Japanese. *"Thank for everything, massage, bath, now caml, sorry, now calm and happy."*

Some of the food he found exciting, tempura and yakitori, bite-sized pieces of chicken that were grilled with a sweet and salty sauce. *Unagi* turned out to be grilled eel with a warm sweet-sour sauce he particularly liked. *Sushi,* slivers of various raw fish of different colors and textures on a ball of rice he found difficult to swallow at first, but when dipped in a mysterious salty sauce called *soy* or *soya* they became palatable. After all, he thought, Father did advise me to try everything: 'My son, since you insist on this dramatic idea of becoming a Japanese interpreter, then I advise you to hurl yourself into their way of life and foods and so on—without forgetting you're an English gentleman with obligations, a duty to the Crown, the Empire and to God . . .'

Wonder what the Old Man would say about Fujiko. She's certainly part of their way of life. Tyrer beamed suddenly and pointed with a chopstick, *"What's this?"*

"Oh, sorry, Taira-san, it's bad manners to point with the thin end of a chopstick. Please use the other end. This is wasabi.*"* Before Hiraga could stop him, Tyrer had picked up the nodule of green paste and eaten it. At once his sinuses caught fire and he gasped, eyes watering, almost blinded. In time the conflagration passed, leaving him panting. "My Go'd," Hiraga said, copying Tyrer and trying not to laugh. "Wasabi do not eat, just put 'ritt'er—sorry, word very hard for me— just put some in the soy to make spicy."

"My mistake." Tyrer gasped, momentarily strangled. "My God, that's lethal, worse than chili! *Next time I careful.*"

"You very good for man who begin, Taira-san. And you 'rearn Japanese o'rr so quick, very good."

"Domo, Nakama-san, domo." Same with you in English. Pleased to be complimented, Tyrer concentrated on being more deft. The next morsel he tried was *tako,* sliced octopus tentacle. It tasted like slimy rubber even with a touch of soy and wasabi. *"This is very tasty, I like this very much."*

I'm starving, he was thinking. I'd like triples of the chicken, another bowl of rice, twenty more of the tempura prawns, and Hiraga eats like a baby. Never mind, I'm being entertained by a samurai, it's not a week since he helped get us out of the Yedo Legation without an international incident, not six weeks since I first met André, yet I can already talk a little Japanese, already know more about their customs than most traders who have been here since the beginning. If I can keep this up I'll be gazetted as an official interpreter in a few months and in line for the official salary: Four hundred pounds a year! Hooray, or *Banzai,* as a Japanese would say. At the present rate of exchange I can easily afford another pony but before that . . .

His heart quickened.

Before that I'll buy Fujiko's contract. Nakama's promised to help so I'll have no trouble. He promised. Perhaps we'll begin tonight—thank God, Fujiko's back from visiting her grandmother. I suppose I really shouldn't on a Sunday, but never mind.

He sighed. Between André and Nakama he had discovered that word and the marvelous way it became a panacea for all happenings, good or bad, over which you had no control. *"Karma!"*

"What, Taira-san?"

"Nothing. Food's good."

"Food's good," Hiraga mimicked him. "Good, thank you, I p'reased." He called for more beer and saké. The shoji slid back and the drinks appeared on a tray carried by a merry-faced maid who beamed at Hiraga, smiled shyly at Tyrer. With hardly a thought, Hiraga caressed her rump. *"How would you like it Over the Mountain?"*

"Eeee, you naughty man! Over Mountain? Oh, no, not me, nor Under, but I might Play the Flute for a gold oban!"

They both laughed at the sally—one gold oban being outrageously expensive, the fee a courtesan of the first class might charge for such a service. The maid poured the saké, filled Tyrer's mug and left.

"What she say, Nakama-san?"

He smiled. "So sorry, difficu't exp'rain, not words enough yet. Just joke, man-woman joke, you understand?"

"Wakarimasu. Church today, you like?" With Sir William's approval and the avid consent of the Reverend Michaelmas Tweet he had sneaked Hiraga up to the minstrel's gallery. Dressed in his new Western clothes, made to order by the Chinese tailor with his usual unbelievable speed, and beaver top hat, Hiraga had passed as Eurasian and was hardly noticed. Except by Jamie McFay who had winked discreetly.

"Church good, and your exp'rain too," Hiraga said, but inside he was still trying to sift Tyrer's information into perspective, along with the astonishing sight of all these grown men, and two revolting-looking women, singing in unison, getting up, sitting down, solemnly droning out prayers, bowing their heads to their very strange God who, after the service, Tyrer had explained was actually three people, the Father, his Son who was crucified like a common criminal, and a kami. *'So ka?'* Hiraga had said perplexed. 'So, Taira-san, woman name Madonna who not God has son God—but she not God—and she pi'rrow with kami who not God but like *hatomoto* of God with wing who not husband, husband who o'rso not God, but father is, so father of her son is grandfather, *neh?*'

'No, there was no pillowing. You see . . .'

Again he listened, eventually pretended to understand so he could question Taira about the enmity of the two churches, for he had noticed that Ori's woman was not present and had asked why. Two churches, equally powerful, constantly at war! And Ori wanted me to give up. *Baka!*

And when, head aching from concentration, he had discovered the reason for the schism—and the resulting scale of hatred and mass killings and universal wars—he knew for certain in some areas gai-jin were totally mad, but oh-so-vulnerable: the split was only because an old bonze called 'Ruther, three hundred–odd years before, had decided on a different interpretation of some minor point of dogma that had been invented by another bonze fourteen or fifteen centuries before him. This man, clearly another lunatic, had decreed, amongst other things, that poverty was to be sought, and no pillowing with women would, after death, send you forever to somewhere called Heaven, where there was no saké, no food and no women, and you were a bird.

Barbarians are beyond belief. Who could want to go to such a place? Anyone could see at once that old bonze was like any other ambitious, disgruntled fool who, after a lifetime of pretending to be chaste, just wanted to have a wife or concubine openly like any ordinary sensible bonze or person.

'Taira-san,' he had said weakly: 'Need ba'f, massage, saké, you also, then food. Fo'rrow p'rease.'

At first he had been worried that he had proffered the invitation. Now the village elder, the shoya, would discover he could speak English.

'Eeee, how wonderful to speak gai-jin, I wish I did, Otami-san!' the shoya had chortled with open admiration. 'May I tell you again that I support *sonno-joi,* and also I have assigned the cleverest of my sons to a gai-jin bonze with orders to pretend to convert to their ridiculous beliefs so he can learn their language and their ways.'

'You will make sure the servants are safe?'

'You will be protected like one of my family. For extra safety I suggest you should hire the whole restaurant and order this Taira to speak only Japanese in the bathhouse. You say he learns quickly?'

'Very.'

'Your secrets are safe with me. *Sonno-joi!*'

Hiraga smiled grimly remembering the fervor with which the shoya had echoed him, believing him not at all. I wonder what he would do if he knew of our plan to burn all Yokohama. He would shit. But before even cleaning himself he would run to the Bakufu and bash his head to the earth in his haste to serve them and betray me. *Baka!*

Tyrer was still eating voraciously. Though still hungry Hiraga toyed with his food, following accepted Japanese custom and training, of disciplining oneself to be satisfied with little, there being more hungry times than abundant, to bear cold and pain with fortitude, there being more bad days than good, more cold than warmth so best be prepared. Less is better than more. Except for saké. And fornication. He smiled. "Saké! Taira-san, *kampai!*"

This flask was soon gone. He pressed Tyrer to drink, pretending it was an important Japanese custom to toast each other. Soon Tyrer was happily telling about gai-jin wars, the extent of the British Empire, about the goods they manufactured and the amounts thereof. Because of Tyrer's sincerity—possible sincerity—and his 'I swear it's the God's truth!'—he decided to accept the information, however frightening or preposterous until proven false. An hour's study of Tyrer's school atlas and maps had truly shocked him.

"But, p'rease, how can so 'ritter country 'rike Ing'rand ru're so many?"

"Lots of reasons," Tyrer said, warm and loose and pleased with himself, and, forgetting for a moment to use simple words and ideas, he went on guilelessly, "lots of reasons, because of our superior education—superior learning, you understand?—a superior heritage, a wise and benevolent Queen and our unique and special form of government, our Parliament, which has given us superior laws and freedoms. At the same time we're blessed, we're an island fortress, the sea protects us, our fleets control the sea-lanes for trade so we've been able to develop better skills in peace and quiet, to invent and experiment, we trade more therefore we've more capital, Nakama-san, more money than anyone else . . . and we're very clever at 'divide and rule'—that's an old Roman law . . ." He laughed and finished the flask. "And, most important of all, I've told you before, we've twice the number of cannon, ships and fire power than the next two countries—half the world's ships are British, with British crews and British gunners."

So many words and ideas I don't understand, Hiraga thought, his head reeling. Romans? Who are they?

If half of what Taira says is true, no, a hundredth part, then it will take decades to catch up with them. Yes, he thought, but in time we will catch them. We are an island too. Better than them this is Land of the Gods, man for man we are tougher, stronger, better fighters, we've discipline and more courage and, most of all we must win eventually because we're not afraid to die!

Eeee, even today I can see ways to twist them that I could not have conceived a few days ago. *"Honto,"* he muttered.

" *'Honto,'* Nakama-san? The truth? What's true?"

"Just think about what you say. So much truth. P'rease, you say ear'rier . . . *Kampai!"*

"Kampai! It time visit Yoshiwara, neh?" Tyrer stifled a contented yawn, weary of questions, but feeling grand.

"I not forget, Taira-san." Hiraga hid a smile. He had already arranged that Fujiko would not be available this evening. "Finish saké, last question, then go. P'rease, you say ear'rier about machines making machines? How is possib're?"

Tyrer launched into another enthusiastic answer, saying the British were leaders in what was called the Industrial Revolution: "The steam engine, railways, steel and iron ships, spinning Jenny, seed planters, mass production, harvesters, are all our inventions, sixty-pounders, submersibles, anesthetics, new medicines, navigation—four years ago we laid the first telegraph wire across the Atlantic, a thousand leagues or more," he said grandly, deciding not to mention the cable had burnt out within a month and, soon, another had to be laid in its place. "We've invented electric generators, gas lighting . . ."

Soon Hiraga was giddy from the effort of concentration, and his desperate wish to understand everything when he understood almost nothing, but also because he could not comprehend why an official as important as Taira would answer any question an enemy would ask, for of course we are enemies.

I must learn English more quickly, I must. I will.

A gentle tap on the door and the shoji slid back. "Please excuse me, Otami-san," the maid said, "but the shoya begs a moment of your time."

Hiraga nodded briefly, told Tyrer he would return in a moment and followed the maid out into the alley that was empty and then into the busy street. The few pedestrians who appeared to notice him, bowed politely as to a merchant and not to a samurai as the shoya had ordered. Good.

The shoya was waiting in an inner room, kneeling behind the table, his arm resting comfortably on an armrest. A cat was curled beside him. He bowed. "So sorry to disturb you, Otami-san, but in case this gai-jin understands our language better than he pretends, I thought it best to speak here."

Hiraga frowned, sat on his heels and bowed back, all attention. "Yes, Ryoshi-san?"

"There are several matters you should know, Otami-sama." The strong-faced man poured green tea into little cups from the miniature iron teapot. The tea was superb, as rare as the eggshell cups, aromatic and delicate. Hiraga's foreboding increased. The shoya sipped again then took a scroll from his sleeve and spread it out. It was another copy of the woodcut poster: *The Bakufu offers two koku reward for this murdering revolutionary of many aliases, one of which is Hiraga . . .*

Hiraga picked it up, pretending this was the first time he had seen it. Noncommittally he grunted and handed it back.

The older man put the edge to the candle flame. Both watched as the paper curled and became ash, both knowing that with his new haircut and rapidly thickening stubble Hiraga's disguise was very good. "The Bakufu become fiends in pursuit of our brave shishi."

Hiraga nodded but said nothing, waiting.

Absently the shoya stroked the cat and it purred softly. "It is said Lord Yoshi is sending an emissary to negotiate with the chief gai-jin for guns. No doubt a Lord of his high rank would offer higher prices than—than Choshu emissaries." He added delicately, "Gai-jin will sell to the highest bidder."

Hiraga had heard about the Choshu samurai visiting the Noble House from Raiko—almost everyone in the Yoshiwara was aware of the negotiations—and he was sure if he knew their real names he would certainly know the men personally or their families. Only a year or so ago a stepbrother, who also had gone to the same English school in Shimonoseki, had been one of the team sent to buy the first hundred guns. Curious, Hiraga thought, that it should be to the same company owned by this tai-pan who will soon be dead, both he and his woman and this whole cesspit of evil. "Gai-jin have no honor."

"Disgusting." Another sip of tea. "In Yedo Castle there is much activity. They say the Shōgun and the Imperial Princess plan to leave for Kyōto in a week or two."

"Why should they do that?" Hiraga asked, pretending uninterest that fooled neither of them.

The older man chuckled. "I do not know, Otami-san, but it is very curious that the Shōgun should leave his lair now to travel many dangerous miles to visit the lair of many enemies when, since the beginning, he has always sent a flunky." The cat stretched and he tickled her stomach, adding thoughtfully, "The *roju* are increasing taxes in all Toranaga lands to pay for any amounts of cannon and weapons that can be bought—except by Satsuma, Tosa and Choshu."

Hiraga sensed the shoya's underlying anger, though none showed, or his own amusement: What are peasants and merchants for if not to pay taxes? "Unless the Son of Heaven can use his Heaven-granted power, the Bakufu will plunge Nippon into eternal civil war again."

"I agree."

Hiraga was thinking, I wonder how much you really agree, old man. He put that aside to ponder how to push the Bakufu and Toranaga Yoshi from their course. Akimoto should go at once to Yedo and the House of Wisteria, we haven't heard from Koiko or her mama-san for days—perhaps we should go togeth—

"Last, it seems your shishi friend, Ori-san, did not leave for Kyōto as planned," the shoya said conversationally.

Hiraga's eyes went flat, almost reptilian. The shoya suppressed a shudder. Instantly aware, the cat was erect in one smooth movement, watching warily. Hiraga broke the silence. "Where is he?"

"In that part of the Settlement where the low-class gai-jin live, drink and fornicate."

Near midnight André Poncin knocked on the door of the House of the Three Carp. At once the doorkeeper admitted him. Raiko welcomed him and soon they were drinking saké, discussing the latest news of the Yoshiwara and Settlement—she was a source of much intelligence for him as he was for her—in their usual mixture of Japanese and English.

". . . and the Enforcer Patrol searched every House, Furansu-san! As though we would hide criminals! It is against Yoshiwara rules. We know how to keep our rice bowls full: by promoting peace and avoiding trouble. Enforcers are still at the main gate, glowering at every passerby." Raiko fanned herself remembering her narrow escape and wished that she had never invited shishi to favor her House. It's time they all went elsewhere, she thought, Enforcers and shishi, however much I like Hiraga. "I wish they would go away."

"What criminals look for?" André asked.

"Traitors, ronin usually. But anyone who is against them is a traitor. Ronin, they are their usual prey."

"Bakufu? Can Bakufu be throw out? Revolution?"

She laughed softly and emptied the flask and began another. "The Bakufu are like lice in a prison—you destroy a thousand and only make room for a hundred thousand more. No, the Bakufu and Shōgunate are Nippon and with us forever."

"Tonight Taira-san here?"

She shook her head. "The girl he wanted was not available, I offered another but he refused and left. Curious, *neh*? A curious young man in many ways, though possibly a good customer. Thank you for introducing him to my poor House."

"This Japanese Sensei, teacher, samurai Taira has find—who is he, Raiko?"

"I don't know, so sorry, but I've heard he's a Yedo-man and lives in the Settlement, in the village."

"Taira-san, he talk Fujiko about him?"

"She never mentioned it, but then I did not ask her. Next time, perhaps by next time I will know, Furansu-san."

André did not believe her, but never mind, he thought, when she's ready she'll tell me. "The medicine. It arranged?"

"Of course, whatever I can do to help a favored client is my purpose in life."

He took out the pair of pearl earrings and laid them on the table. Her eyes glittered. She made no move to pick them up but he was sure she had instantly weighed them mentally, deciding on their quality, cost and resale value. "I asked to give these as present," he said pleasantly, and she smiled prettily, pretending to be overwhelmed though already aware payment would be in jewelry which could not be offered for sale in Yokohama. Her fingers trembled as she reached for them. He forestalled her, picking them up and pretending to examine them closely.

His plan for Angelique had worked perfectly. Servants from the Noble House had scoured the streets to no avail. Her anxiety and tears had been genuine, and she had whispered privately: 'Oh, André, did I do the correct thing? Malcolm was really very upset—I had no idea they were so expensive.'

'But he told you just to sign for whatever you wanted, didn't he? Not your fault that you didn't ask the price—he liked his cuff links, didn't he?'

'Yes, but André . . .'

'There will be enough left over in case it's needed—a credit against any eventuality, Angelique.'

André smiled to himself and turned his full attention to Raiko. "Value many times cost of medicine."

"The buying price, certainly. But I must send them to the Yedo or Nagasaki Yoshiwara. A difficult sale, but please do not worry, I will help you to be rid of an unwanted child."

"Not mine," he said sharply.

"Ah, so sorry, please excuse me," she said, believing him. Good, I was afraid it was his, she told herself, greatly relieved. I want no more complications with this man. "It is not my business."

"Just help for friend of friend. In Drunk Town."

"Please excuse me, so sorry."

He smiled without humor. "You know pearl. This value fifty times cost of medicine."

She kept her smile in place and her voice cooing but inside she was gnashing her teeth. "I will have them valued. Of course they are worth more than the cost of the medicine."

"Of course." He held his palm flat and she took them. The pearls were almost black, Sea Island pearls. She touched them to her teeth to feel if they were cold and carefully bit on them but they did not mar. Satisfied now that they were genuine and rich, she said lovingly, "The price, old friend?"

"Price is: all medicine, even if first time fail. What necessary if drink fail, understand? What need . . . whatever need to stop child. Yes?"

"Yes," she agreed happily, knowing this to be a marvelous bargain. "A guaranteed . . . elimination, termination."

"Plus twenty gold oban," he added, and was delighted to see her face twist with real horror though this was less than a third of what she would squeeze from the sale—the setting was of little value but he had made sure the Chinese jeweler only used the finest pearls. She groaned and cursed and they bargained back and forth, both enjoying the encounter, both knowing that the real cost of the medicine and medical advice was hardly significant to a brothel mama-san. Soon they were close to making a deal and then, of a sudden, her mood changed and she stared at him strangely, liking him, so sad for him, and thought: Should I interfere with karma?

"What?" he asked suspiciously.

"Let me think a moment, Furansu-san."

Later, in an entirely different voice, warm and soft as in the old days when he had been her first customer and had lavishly wined and dined the whole House to celebrate their opening, she said, "Since we met, much water has flowed under many bridges, lots of good times and laughter in our Floating World and, as it is in this life, also sadness and a lake of tears, not of my choosing. Suddenly I remembered the last time we bargained like this was over Hana's contract."

His face settled into a mask. "Not talk about Hana."

"Ah, so sorry, I would like to, please, because I may have a solution to her."

"There none," he said angrily. "No cure, Hana dead, Hana nothing do with pearls!"

"True. Please be calm and listen. Perhaps," she said gently, "perhaps I could find another Hana, similar, but one who already has the Chinese disease."

"Not possible," he burst out, shocked. "Disease very bad, very bad, ugly."

"Yes, near the end," she said patiently. "Many times nothing shows for years. You are not yet ugly, nothing shows with you, Furansu-san—it may be years before that happens. It depends on your karma. I should seek such a one?"

He started to speak, stopped and shook his head.

"Listen, if I could find new Hana, and then if . . ."

"Not possible!"

". . . if you approve her, and she approves you, you could be together until—until you decide . . ." Raiko shrugged. "Never mind the future, today is today and that is the rule of our Floating World. You would keep the girl here, I would build you a new house, the other naturally we destroyed, you treat her like Hana in every way, same contract price, same monthly money for clothes and lodging, and she is for you only."

Her eyes bored into him and he knew she could see into his soul, see him writhing with a frantic, sudden hope and craving to accept that which would release him from torment—the news of his karma had travelled with the speed of light, now every House barred to him, politely—oh so politely—but still barred for pillowing, only Drunk Town possible—yet be a never-ending Damocles sword over him forever. And even worse, there was no lessening of his sexual urge but a heightening, a greater obsession to pillow than before, one that had already driven him to the insanity of two nights ago with Angelique, not that he did not still desire her, he did, more than ever, and knew without a release he would try again and would not fail next time. Blessed Mother, help me, he thought, near tears, I do not want to infect her too.

"There is another possibility," Raiko was saying, her gaze curious. "We can discuss that later. Now Hana."

"Not-talk-about-Hana!"

"I have to, Furansu-san. Now. You wanted to know how she died, *neh*?" Raiko saw his eyes focus and his breathing almost stop. "After you ran out into the night and she, weeping, told me the reason, I was as shocked as you and ordered her out of the House and cursed her even though she was like my own daughter. Of course you were right and you should have killed her not just hit her before you left, you are right and of course her mama-san should have told me, and she should have told me the mom—"

"Speak, speak slow . . . more slow."

"Please excuse me but it is very hard slowly, but she should have told me the moment she knew. I was furious and left her to try to catch up with you but failed. Then one of the maids . . . it was Mieko. Mieko rushed in to say that Hana had tried to hara-kiri . . ."

Raiko was perspiring now. This was by no means the first attempted suicide she had been involved in. There had been dozens during her years as apprentice, courtesan and mama-san—she had even been born in the Willow World, her mother a specialist courtesan of the second rank. Many suicides were successful, few by the knife, most by poison or drowning, some dual suicides between lovers, the man always impoverished, even samurai. But Hana's had been the worst.

When she had rushed into the room she found the girl in agony, weeping and helpless, her neck slashed several times but no artery or vein severed and the windpipe only nicked. A little air bubbled from the cut that bled badly but not badly enough. She was crumpled on the futons, knife nearby, but her hand could not grip it and each time she tried to lift it it would slip from her grasp, all the time weeping and choking and retching, begging forgiveness and crying out, Help me . . . help me . . . help me . . .

"She was beyond all wish for life, Furansu-san," Raiko said sadly. "I've seen too many not to know. If she had lived through that attempt she would have tried again and again, without ceasing. In this world, surely in ours, there does come a time when it is good and wise to go beyond. We put animals out of misery—it is right to give the same relief to a person. So we helped her. We calmed her and cleaned her and sat her up and she had time to say, *Namu Amida Butsu,* then I held the knife to her throat and peacefully Hana fell on it. That is how she died."

"You . . . you kill . . . part . . . part kill her?"

"It was my duty as her mama-san," Raiko said simply. Again she hesitated, sighing. No need for more tears. Those had been shed long since. I have none left. How many times when I was her age, hating my life and the way I had to earn my rice, did I not contemplate the same escape, even once cutting my wrists, to be succored and saved by my mama-san who, when I was well, beat me unmercifully. But she was right, my mama-san, as I was right, because she knew I was not serious as Hana was serious, and now I cannot even remember the face of the boy she had forbidden me, only that he was a poet. "Before she died Hana asked me to apologize again for her to you. To beg your forgiveness for her."

"You . . . do you . . . forgive—forgive?"

What a strange question, she thought, startled. "That Hana was like last year's cherry blossom scattered by the wind, no need to forgive or not to forgive. Just a petal of the Willow World. She existed but did not. You understand?"

In turmoil he nodded, not comprehending all the words, but understanding what she had done and why. He hated her and blessed her, was relieved and sad and suicidal and filled with hope. "Three men, three who before me. Who?"

"I do not know, so sorry, except they were Japanese. Truly," she told him, her eyes clean, the names buried in her most secret heart, waiting to use if necessary, for or against the Bakufu. "About these," she opened her hand. The pearls glowed in the oil light, enticingly. "Let us agree that I give you one third of whatever I get from the sale, plus all medicines and whatever else is necessary. A third would be . . ." She stopped as *friend in Drunk Town* fell into place.

The medicine is for the woman who is to marry the tai-pan, she told herself excitedly. Wasn't it she who was supposed to have lost some jewelry yesterday that I thought nothing of. It must be her, the pearls confirm it . . . and if it's her, eeee, the abortion must be without his approval or knowledge or surely Jami-san would be the intermediary, not Furansu-san.

"A third would be fair," she said, and was going to add smugly, to the young gai-jin woman who is to marry the tai-pan, but seeing Furansu-san staring gloomily into his cup, decided there was no need yet to divulge she had deduced the 'who.'

Eeee, tonight has been most profitable, she thought gleefully. Knowledge of a secret abortion by such an important lady to bury, or to tell, could be extremely valuable, to the lady herself, before or after she marries, or to this tai-pan who is as rich as Adachi of Mito, before or after he marries, or even to one of his many enemies.

Next: through Hiraga I have this Taira firmly stuck to Fujiko's Jade Gate—what is it about the girl that attracts Round Eyes to her? And last but not least, the solution to Furansu-san, my precious gai-jin spy, presented herself.

Raiko wanted to shout with joy but, carefully, she retained her most modest, sincere look. "A third? Furansu-san?"

Bleakly he looked up at her, nodded his agreement.

"You have told the lady there is a risk?"

"What risk? Raiko say medicine good most times."

"It is, most times. But if the drink does not succeed, we . . . let us not worry about that now. Let us hope Buddha smiles on her and it is her karma to have an easy release, then to enjoy the good things in life." She looked at him steadily. "And you also. *Neh*?"

He stared back at her.

24

Thursday, 6th November:

DEAREST COLETTE: THE WEEKS have rushed by, and tomorrow is my special day, Angelique wrote, aglow with expectation, *I feel so good I can hardly believe it. I sleep marvelously, my cheeks are rosy, everyone compliments me and my figure is better than ever . . .* No signs, nothing, she thought. Nothing. Breasts a little tender but that's just imagination—and tomorrow all will be over.

She was sitting at the bureau in her suite facing the bay, the tip of her tongue between her lips, far too cautious to write anything that could possibly compromise her. *What a lucky omen it's his day for my new beginning.*

Tomorrow is St. Theodore's day, he's my new patron saint. You see, Colette, by marriage I become British (not English because Malcolm is Scots and part English) and St. Theodore is one of their oh-so-few saints. He became British too (he was a Greek) twelve hundred years ago and rose to be Archbishop of Canterbury . . .

Her steel-tipped pen hesitated as that name brought phantoms from the mists but she would not acknowledge them and they sank back into the depths again.

. . . that means he was like the pope of the British Isles. He reformed the Church, cast out evildoers and heathen practices, was oh-so-holy and kind, particularly to women, lived to be an astonishing eighty-eight and altogether a wonderful man of the True Church. I'm celebrating by having a special fast day, then in three days a party!

Father Leo told me about him. Ugh! I really don't like him, stinky as he is (I have to use a pomander handkerchief in the confessional—he would make you faint, dear Colette). Last Sunday I had the vapors and will certainly miss this Sunday too. Do you remember how we used to do that when we were at school, though how we avoided a scolding I'll never know.

Thoughts of Colette and school and Paris distracted her for a moment and she stared out of the window at the ocean, slate grey and stormy with a sharp wind creating seahorses that ran ashore to woosh up the beach a hundred yards away, the other side of the promenade— merchantmen at anchor, bum boats loading or unloading, the only warship, the frigate *Pearl,* resplendent with her new mast and new paint steaming for her mooring, just back from Yedo.

But Angelique did not really see any of it, her eyes beguiled by the rosy future her mind was promising. Here, in her suite, it was warm and calm with no drafts, the windows well fitting, a fire blazing in the fireplace, with Malcolm Struan dozing comfortably in a tall red velvet chair, papers, letters and invoices in his lap and scattered about his feet. The connecting door was open. Her door to the corridor unlocked. This was their new custom. Safer, both had agreed, plenty of time in the future to be private.

Some days he would arrive early and conduct his business from her boudoir until noon when he would doze a few minutes until lunch; sometimes he would stay in his own suite and some days he would hobble downstairs to the offices below. He would always say she was always welcome there but she knew that was only a politeness. Downstairs was masculine domain. She was delighted he was working— McFay had told her that since 'the tai-pan has taken charge, everyone's more diligent, we've big plans hatching and our company's humming . . .'

And so was she. No fear for the morrow. On the contrary, she was looking forward to seeing André in the evening at the Legation.

Together they had hatched an excuse and she would move back there tomorrow for three days while her rooms were repainted, and new curtains made for the windows and four-poster that she had chosen from silks in their warehouse:

'But, Angel,' Struan had said, 'we're only here for a few more weeks, the expense really isn't—'

A laugh and a kiss had changed his mind. La, I begin to love him and adore the game of getting my own way.

She smiled and began to write again:

Colette darling, I've more energy than I've ever had. Riding every day—no excursions, which makes the Settlement restricting—but lots of galloping around the racecourse with Phillip Tyrer, Settry (Pallidar), who's the best rider I've ever seen, sometimes with French and English cavalry officers, and not forgetting poor Marlowe, who is turning out to be the most dear man but not, I'm afraid, a horseman. They all left three days ago to go to Yedo where Sir William and the Ministers are having THE MEETING with the native Cabinet and their king called SHŌGUN.

Malcolm is getting better but oh, so slowly, he still walks badly but is wonderful—except on mail days (twice monthly) when he's furious with everything and everyone, even me. It's only because there are always letters from his mother (I begin to hate her) who complains bitterly that he stays here and doesn't return to Hong Kong. Three days ago was worse than usual. One of the Noble House clippers arrived, this time with another letter and a verbal summons delivered by the Captain who said: "I'd appreciate it, sir, if you could come aboard the moment we've unloaded the special cargo—our orders are to escort you and Dr. Hoag to Hong Kong right smartly . . ."

I've never heard such language, Colette! I thought poor Malcolm would have apoplexy. The Captain crumpled and fled. Again I implored Malcolm to let us do what she wants but . . . he just growled, 'We'll go when I decide to go, by

God. Don't mention it again!' Yokohama is VERY tedious, and I'd really like to return to Hong Kong and civilization.

To pass the time I have been reading everything I can lay my hands on (newspapers, apart from fashion and Paris life, are really quite interesting I was surprised to find, and they make me realize what a scatterbrain I am).

But I must prepare for all the soirees I must give for my husband, to entertain his important guests—as well as their wives. So I intend to learn about trade, opium and tea and cotton and silkworms ... But one has to be SO careful. The first time I tried to talk about an article relating to the awful state of the French silk industry (which is why Japanner silkworms are so valuable) Malcolm said, 'Don't you worry your pretty head about that, Angel ...' I could get NOT one word in even sideways, in fact he was quite irritable when I said Struan's could start a silk factory in France. ...

Oh, dearest Colette, I wish you were here, then I could pour my heart out to you—I miss you miss you miss you ...

The steel nib, set into a bone handle, began blotching. Carefully she dried it and cleaned the tip, marvelling that it was so easy, the nib again as good as new. Up to a few years ago the quill pen was commonplace and she would have had to find the special quill knife and cut a new point, splitting it to last but a page or two, whereas these Mitchell pens, mass-produced in Birmingham, would last for days and came in many sizes to please your fancy and your writing.

Behind her, Struan stirred but did not awaken. Asleep he has a tidy face, she thought. Neat and strong ...

The door opened and Ah Soh barged in. "Missee, tiffin, you wan' here or downstai', heya?"

Struan had awoken at once. "Your mistress will eat here," he said brusquely in Cantonese. "I'll dine downstairs, in our main dining room, and tell the cook the food had better be exceptional."

"Yes, Tai-pan." Ah Soh hurried off.

"What did you tell her, Malcolm?"

"Just that you'd lunch here—I'll be downstairs. I've invited Dmitri,

Jamie and Norbert." He looked at her silhouetted against the light. "You look splendid."

"Thank you. Can I join you? I'd prefer that."

"Sorry, we've business to discuss."

With a great effort he heaved himself upright and she gave him his two walking sticks. Before he took them he put his arms around her and she allowed her body to sink against him, hiding her anger that she would be cooped up again—nowhere to go, nothing to do, except to write some more or read some more and to wait. Boring boring boring.

Lun Two cut the first of the large deep-dish apple pies into quarters, slid them onto fine pewter plates, poured thick cream generously and served the four men.

"God Almighty, where the devil did you get it?" Norbert Greyforth asked, and Dmitri said over him with equal awe, "I'll be goddamned."

"The cream?" McFay belched. "Pardon. Compliments of the tai-pan."

Dmitri spooned a mouthful. "Last time I had cream was in Hong Kong, six months ago, goddam this's good. This a new Noble House exclusive?"

Malcolm smiled. "Our last clipper, a few days ago, sneaked in three cows. We unloaded them at night and with the help of the army quartermaster we've had them hidden amongst the horses—didn't want them hijacked or the Jappo Customs asking questions. Day and night guard now." He could not contain his pleasure at the effect of the cream after a lavish amount of beef, roast potatoes and fresh vegetables, local pheasant pie, French and English cheeses—with beer, Château Haut-Brion '46, a fine Chablis and port. "We're going to start a herd if they acclimatize here, and a dairy farm—as a subsidiary of our Hong Kong dairy farm—it was Jamie's idea originally, and of course the produce will be available to anyone."

"At the usual 'Noble' prices?" Norbert said sarcastically, plainly irritated he had had no forewarning of this new Struan endeavor.

"At a profit—but a reasonable one," Struan said. He had ordered the cows to be rushed from Hong Kong the moment he arrived here. "More, Dmitri?"

"Thanks, great pie, Malc!"

"How's the word from home?" Jamie asked, to break the tension between Struan and Norbert Greyforth.

"Lousy. Terrible. Both sides are mixing it and with rifles and long-range artillery—shit, the killings are the worst ever, afraid the New World's crazy."

"The whole world's crazy, old friend," Norbert said. "But war's good business, that's a fact, for the lucky ones," then added, just to rile Struan, "Brock's have all the Hawaiian sugar you'll need, at reasonable prices."

"It'd be a change for anything to be reasonable," Dmitri said lightly. He knew all about the huge losses Struan's were going to sustain because of Tyler and Morgan Brock's coup, but shrugged to himself. I'm not in their war, I've my own to worry about. Dear God in Heaven, how will it end? "War's never good for the people. Goddam, the cost's going to be huge—you hear that Lincoln's just got his goddam income tax through Congress to pay for the war?"

All the other spoons hesitated. "What's the rate?"

"Three cents on the dollar," he said disgustedly, and they all laughed.

"You're sure?"

"I just heard today by a special off the *Calif Belle.*"

"Three percent? You're bloody lucky, Dmitri," Jamie said, his plate almost empty. "I expected fifteen."

"You crazy? There'd've been a revolution."

"You're already in one. Anyway, three percent is the same as us, but yours is only for three years, that's . . . wait a minute," Jamie said, raising his voice, "that's what Lincoln promised, swore it was only for three years according to the last *'Frisco Chronicle,* if Congress passed it. Three years."

"True, but you know goddam politicians, Jamie, once they get a tax through Congress, or Parliament, they'll never take it off. Goddam Congress, shysters, all of them. Three percent's only the beginning."

"You're right there," Norbert began, equally sourly, then to Lun, "Yes, I'll have another slice, and a good dollop of cream. You're right about bloody taxes! Bloody Pitt, he's the bugger who first invented income tax and he promised the same and reneged like Lincoln will. Politicians are liars all over but Robert Peel should have been horsewhipped."

"Robert Peel, the same guy who started a police force, the Peelers?" Dmitri asked, and took another spoon of cream.

"Yes, that's him. The Peelers were a good idea—though it wasn't his idea alone, and we could use some here, no doubt about that, but income tax? Monstrous!"

Malcolm said, "Peel was a good Prime Minister. He—"

Norbert deliberately overrode him. "We only had that damned tax for two short periods during the Napoleon Wars, fair enough, but then it was repealed forever in '15, directly after Waterloo, forever, by God, but didn't piss-arsed Peel bring it back in '41 at seven pence in the pound, three percent like Jamie said? And only for three years. Didn't he renege, and all the other buggers who followed him? It'll go on forever and twenty guineas to a bent farthing Lincoln'll renege too. You're stuck, Dmitri old lad. We are too, because of Peel. Stupid bastard," he added deliberately to irritate Struan even though privately he agreed with his assessment of Peel overall.

Struan's good humor was evaporating fast. "Brandy, Lun, then close door!" Lun Two poured generous snifters and left with the other four liveried servants.

Norbert belched. "Cream was good, young Malcolm. Now, to what do we owe the pleasure of such a feast?"

The mood at the big table changed. Deepened.

"What concerns all traders. Sir William and us being excluded from the Shōgun and Bakufu meeting."

"I agree the bugger should be axed. Never heard anything like it in my life!"

"Yes," Struan said. "At the very least we should have had a representative there."

"Agreed," Dmitri said grimly, most of his mind on home. One brother already dead. Food riots nearby. "Our guy's nice enough but he's Yankee. I suggested he appoint me Deputy but he shat on that idea. What do you have in mind, Malc?"

"A joint deputation to make sure it won't happen again, an immediate complaint to the Governor an—"

"Stanshope's a berk," Norbert said and smiled thinly. "But he will do what your mama wants."

"He's not our puppet, if that's what you imply," Struan said, his eyes as cold as his voice.

Dmitri said, "Puppet or not, will he fire Wee Willie?"

"No," Struan said. "That has to come from London. My idea is if William won't agree that we're to be part of any negotiations in the future, then we advise Stanshope to make it policy—he can certainly do that, after all it's we who pay taxes, it's we who negotiate with the Chinese, why not here? Jointly we could accomplish that. Norbert?"

"That bugger will agree to anything for a simple life and it won't do a bit of good." His face tightened. "William's not our whole problem. It's the Admiral. We need a new Admiral. That's more important than shoving William aside. It's him who won't bombard the bastards like he should. It's him, not William—any fool can see that." Norbert finished his brandy and refilled his glass as he continued, pretending not to notice how his barb had rocked Struan and irritated McFay. "Again my compliments on the cream, but the brandy's not up to scratch. May I send you a barrel of our Napoleon?"

With an effort Struan kept his temper. "Why not? Perhaps it's better. Is your solution to our problem better?"

"My solution's well known," Norbert said harshly. "Demand they hand over Canterbury's murderers and the indemnity and if no action, three days later flatten Yedo. How many times do I have to say it? But the idiots we've got here won't take normal reprisals, which's the only action natives understand—any enemy, for that matter. And until the Navy act proper, every bloody one of us here is at risk, by God!"

The silence grew. McFay kept his thoughts off his face, concerned that Struan let himself be at loggerheads with this much older and more experienced man, and saddened that Norbert's reply had not been part of Struan's opening salvo, and disgusted that he had been kept unaware of the real reason for the meeting so had not had an opportunity to give some advice beforehand. "Be that as it may, Norbert, you agree that you, Dmitri and the tai-pan, representing the majority, should see Wee Willie as soon as he returns?"

"It's all right to see him, but it will mean nothing." Norbert drank more brandy, feeling better for the confrontation. "I know what Mr. Brock, a real tai-pan, and Sir Morgan would say: Tyler Brock would say, with a lot of blunt Anglo-Saxon, that the Admiral's the bleeder in the woodpile, William's an arrogant little bastard who won't change, that he'll see Stanshope personally who's an equal fool, and by the first post he'll write to our friendly Members of Parliament to raise holy hell." While he spoke, he lit a cheroot and said through the smoke, his voice sneering, "And he'll add, even though our friends are more powerful than yours and will do more than yours, meanwhile it's a bagful of fart because that'll take five or six months, so he'd say, 'Get thy arse out of thy godrotting chair, thee's responsible, by God, thee's to solve thy problem or I'll be coming to the Japans and break heads.' "

Struan felt the wave of anger, and wash of latent fear, that always occurred hearing Tyler Brock's name, or when he read about him in the papers or saw him on the streets of Hong Kong or at the races. "Then what's the answer?"

"I don't have one. If I had I would already have done it, by God."

Norbert belched rudely. "Like your secret Jappo and his mining concessions you'll never get."

Struan and McFay gaped at him.

Two weeks ago Vargas had excitedly whispered that he had been approached by one of their silk suppliers, acting as an intermediary for a Lord Ota, who wanted to meet the tai-pan secretly 'to discuss granting Struan's an exclusive gold-mining concession in his domain that included most of the Kwanto, the area covering most of the plains and mountains around Yedo—the concession in return for trade: armaments.'

'Perfect,' Struan had said. 'If this is bona fide it could be a major breakthrough for us! Eh, Jamie?'

'If it's real, absolutely!'

'Here, look, here's their authority.' Vargas showed them the sheet of fine-quality rice paper covered with columns of Chinese-style characters and sealed elaborately. 'This seal is Lord Ota's, and this the seal of one of the *roju*, Lord Yoshi. There are two conditions: that the meeting is to take place in Kanagawa, and that everything is kept secret from the Bakufu.'

'Why? And why Kanagawa? Why not here?'

'They just said that is where they have to meet, though they did say they would come by night to the Kanagawa Legation. The meeting could take place there.'

'It could be a trap, Tai-pan,' Jamie said. 'Don't forget Legation Lun was murdered there, and those assassins . . .'

Malcolm's excitement shriveled, being reminded. But he put that away. 'There are soldiers there to protect us.'

Vargas said, 'They guaranteed their officials would be unarmed, stressing only the need for secrecy, senhor.'

'It's too risky for you, Tai-pan,' Jamie said. 'I'll go with Vargas, who can interpret.'

'Sorry, Senhor McFay,' Vargas said, 'but they want to talk to the tai-pan personally. It seems there's no need for an interpreter—they would supply one who could speak English.'

'It's too dangerous, Tai-pan.'

'Yes, but too good an opportunity to miss, Jamie, nothing like this has ever been offered to any one of us. If we can make such a deal, in secret all the better, we'll have made a giant step forward. What are the terms, Vargas?'

'They did not say, Tai-pan.'

'Never mind. Accept their invitation and we'll meet as soon as possible. One condition: I also bring Mr. McFay. Jamie, we'll go by boat, arrange a palanquin for me at Kanagawa.'

The meeting had been quick and untoward direct. Two samurai. One, calling himself Watanabe, spoke a mixture of English and American slang, his accent American: 'Lord Ota wants two prospectors. Experts. They kin go anywheres in his lands—wiv guides. No arms. He guarantees safe conduct, gives 'em good dry lodgings, food, wiv all the saké they kin drink and women to spare. One-year contract. You's to keep half the gold they finds, you's to supply free all mining gear and overseers for to train his men if they makes a strike. You's to handle sales. If successful, he renews second year and third, and more—if Noble House plays fair. Agreed?'

'They're to prospect only for gold?'

'Of course gold. Lord Ota says he has one small mine, maybe more nearby, eh? You's to handle sales. Men must be good, must've been to Californi or Australi fields. Agreed?'

'Agreed. It will take time to find the men.'

'How long?'

'Two weeks if there are any in the Settlement—six months if we have to bring them from Australia or America.'

'Sooner the better. Next: how many rifles you's for sale in here right now?'

'Five.'

'Lord Ota buys 'em, and all the Choshu rifles you's agreed, when they arrives. Same price.'

'Those are already promised. We can supply others.'

'Lord Ota wants them Choshu rifles—he wants 'em. He pays same price. All Choshu guns, unnerstand? And all others you kin get. You sell to him only in Nippon, him only, unnerstand? Same wiv cannon and ships—all you kin get. He pays in gold. More you finds, more is yourn.'

Neither Malcolm Struan nor McFay could shift the man's position in any way. At length Struan had agreed and they had fixed another meeting in a month when Struan's would present a simple contract specifying their guarantees and also dossiers on the two men. After the samurai had left they had congratulated each other and, 'Jamie, you'll find them in Drunk Town. For God's sake hurry, and be careful, before Norbert finds out.'

'Leave everything to me.'

In days McFay had found two qualified men, an American and a Cornish tin miner, both of whom had worked the gold fields near

Sutter's Mill in California and the Anderson's Creek discoveries in Australia. Tomorrow the miners were to finalize their equipment needs and arrange the details of their contracts and now Struan and McFay listened appalled to Norbert saying, "I've done that deal, young Malcolm, it's done, you can forget it—and those mining scallywags too, they're contracted to Brock and Sons for five years."

"You've what?" Struan gasped.

Norbert laughed. "Early bird gets the wriggles, old son. I bettered your deal and I've already shipped them off to Yedo to samurai Watanabe. Where'd that bastard learn American English? Did he tell you? Never mind. Fifty-fifty on any gold we find is a good deal." His laugh became even more scornful. "As to William, I'll see him soon as he's back, no skin off my nose. Dmitri, you're welcome, I'll make the arrangements." He looked at Struan, his upper lip curling. "As you won't be here I'll take Jamie along."

"What?"

Norbert belched again. "Didn't I hear your mother ordered you back to Hong Kong on the next boat?"

Jamie flushed. "Now look here, Nor—"

"Keep out of this, Jamie," Struan snarled. "Norbert, I'd advise you to choose your words more carefully."

"Is that so, my fine young feller? Didn't I hear correct that she wants you back, ordered you back right smartly, that your Captain was under orders to do just that?"

"That's none of your damned business! I advise you—"

"Everything that goes on in Yokohama's my bloody business!" Norbert slammed back at him. "And we don't take advice from anyone in Struan's, least of all a young puppy not yet dry behind the ears!"

McFay jumped to his feet and Struan jerked up his glass of brandy and threw the contents in Norbert's face.

"Christ Almighty—"

"Retract that, Norbert," Struan shouted, Dmitri and Jamie McFay stupefied by the suddenness of the escalation. "Take it back or I demand satisfaction, by God!"

"Pistols at dawn?" Norbert jeered, the action even better than he had hoped. Abruptly he yanked half the tablecloth away to dab his face, sending the glasses clattering. "Pardon for the mess, but you two are witness I said nothing but the truth, by Christ!"

"Do you apologize—yes or no?"

Norbert put both hands on the table, glaring down at Malcolm Struan who glared back, white with rage. "You *were* ordered back, you

are twenty so still a minor before the law and that's hardly dry behind
the ears. It's the truth and here's another: I could blow your head off or
cut it off with one hand tied, you can't even stand straight so how you
going to fight, eh?" he said, his voice jeering and heavy with scorn.
"You're a cripple, young Malcolm, and that's the God's truth! Another
truth, your ma runs Struan's, has for years, and she's running it into the
ground—ask Jamie or anyone honest enough to tell you! You may call
yourself tai-pan but you're not, and you're not Dirk Struan, you're not
the tai-pan and never will be! Tyler Brock's *the* tai-pan and, by God,
we'll be Noble House before Christmas too. Duel? You're mad, but if
that's what you want, any time." He stalked out. The door slammed.

"I'd—I'd like you both to be my seconds," Malcolm said, trembling with rage.

Dmitri got up shakily. "Malc, you're crazy. Duelling's against the
law, but okay. Thanks for lunch." He left.

Struan tried to catch his breath, his heart hurting. He looked up at
McFay who was staring at him as though he were a stranger. "Yes, it's
mad, Jamie, but then Norbert's the best of Brock and Sons, he's
swamped you and—"

"I'm sorry th—"

"So am I. But more truth is I told no one about the miners, Vargas
knew nothing about them, so it leaked through you. You're the best
we've got in the company but Norbert will bury us here. A bullet in the
bastard's head is the best way to deal with him—or any of the God-
cursed Brocks."

After a pause McFay said, "Sorry I failed you—yes, I am, very
much, but . . . but sorry, I want no part of any duel, or your vendetta.
It's insane."

Struan's pallor increased. "Let's talk about you. Either you keep
your holy oath to support me, by God, or you're really finished. You've
three days."

Earlier this morning Settry Pallidar and a troop of mounted dragoons led the procession across the bridge that spanned the first moat
of Yedo Castle.

They clattered between ranks of impassive, uniformed samurai,
shoulder to shoulder—thousands of others had lined the route—over
the drawbridge, under the portcullis and through the massive iron-
sheathed gates. Ahead were their guides, massed samurai carrying ten-
foot-high banners bearing the insignia of the *roju,* three entwined
cherry blossoms.

Behind the dragoons were half a hundred Highlanders preceded by their twenty-man band and giant bandleader, pipes skirling, then the party of Ministers and their staff, all mounted, Ministers in court dress—cocked hats, ceremonial swords, cloaks or frock coats against the stiff breeze—except the Russian who wore Cossack uniform and cape and rode the best horse in Japan, a brown stallion that had a personal covey of twenty stablemen to cherish and guard him with their lives. Phillip Tyrer and Johann were in attendance on Sir William, André Poncin on Henri Seratard. A company of Redcoats brought up the rear.

Two small horse-drawn cannon with their camions and gun crews remained on the other side of the bridge. This had been the subject of days of wrangling, Sir William insisting that accompanying ceremonial cannon were an accustomed courtesy to royals, the Bakufu that any gai-jin arms were against the law and an insult to their revered Shōgun. The compromise, after a week of impatient dickering—by Sir William—was that the cannon would stay outside the bridge, that royal salutes would not be fired until the unanimous *roju* gave the promised formal permission. 'No ammunition to be landed, so sorry . . .'

This major hitch was resolved with the help of the French Admiral. During one of the interminable sessions he brought the flagship closer to shore and fired broadside after none too accurate broadside of shells and cannon balls that passed just beyond the Settlement to land harmlessly in the paddy beyond, but petrifying every Japanese within hearing.

'If we can't land ammunition,' Sir William explained sweetly, 'then we will just have to make salutes from the sea like this—we did ask him to use blanks but somehow I suppose he misunderstood, language you know—and so sorry if his range falls short and hits your city, it will be your fault. I will have to explain this in detail to your Emperor Komei as the cannonade, and carrying our rifles for full royal honors, is only a token of respect to honor your Shōgun and, when we see him, *your Emperor Komei,* which visit to Kyōto I have postponed three times to accommodate you, I will certainly reschedule the very moment my more powerful fleet returns from decimating most of the China coast inhabited by foul pirates who had the effrontery to pirate a small British vessel!'

Bakufu opposition crumbled. So all rifles were armed and all soldiers warned that though there might be a fight, under no circumstances and on pain of extreme punishment were any Japanese to be provoked. 'What about H.M.S. *Pearl,* Sir William?' the General had asked at the last briefing.

'She can deliver me and my party to Yedo, then return here, in case our hosts mount a surprise attack against the Settlement while we're away—she can cover an evacuation.'

'Good God, sir, if you think there's a chance of that, why put yourself at risk?' the General had said worriedly. 'The other Ministers, well, they'd be no loss but you, sir, if anything happens to you it would be an international incident. After all, sir, you represent the Empire! You should not risk your person.'

'Part of the job, my dear General.'

Sir William smiled to himself, remembering how he kept his voice flat, meaning it as a pleasantry, but the General had nodded wisely, believing it to be the truth. Poor bugger's a berk but then that goes with his job, no doubt about that, he thought cheerfully then dismissed everything to concentrate on the castle and the coming meeting that was the culmination of months of negotiating, that would, in effect, give legality to the Treaty and the opening of the Treaty ports. It was those few French shells that worked the miracle, he thought grimly. Damn Ketterer, but thank God his operation in China went well, according to dispatches, and that he'll be back soon. If he can bombard the coast of China why not here—damn him!

And damn this castle.

From afar it had not looked very imposing but the closer they got to it the more immense it became, with eight rings of barrack-like structures as its outer defenses. Then the castle itself, elegant and beautifully proportioned, he thought, its moat almost two hundred yards across, the towering outer walls thirty or forty feet thick and made of huge granite blocks. Even our sixty-pounders wouldn't dent those, he told himself, awed. And inside, God only knows how many fortifications surrounding the central keep. And the only way in through one of the gates, or over the walls, a frontal attack, and I wouldn't like to have to order that. Starve it out? God only knows how many storage places it would have—or how many troops could be billeted here. Thousands.

Beyond the gate the roadway angled into a narrow staging area dominated by bowmen massed in defensive slots or on the parapets thirty feet above. The gate was open and led to another confined courtyard that let out through another fortified gate into another, clearly to be repeated in a maze of passageways that eventually would lead to the central keep but would always leave a hostile force at the mercy of the defenders above.

"We dismount here, Sir William," Pallidar said, riding up and saluting. He was Captain of the escort. With him were samurai officers on foot and they were pointing at a vast door that was being heaved open.

"Good. You're clear on what you have to do?"

"Oh, yes. But I haven't a hope in hell of covering you or fighting our way out of here, even against bows and arrows."

"I don't plan to have to fight anyone, Captain." Sir William smiled. He turned in his saddle and gave the signal to dismount. "This's quite a castle, eh?"

"Better than anything I've ever read or heard about," Pallidar said uneasily. "Beats anything the crusaders had. It makes the great castle of the Knights of St. John in Malta seem tiny. Lovely to defend, I'd hate to have to attack it."

"My thought too. Phillip!" Sir William called out. "Ask someone where you pee around here."

Tyrer hurried over to one of the samurai officers, bowed politely, and whispered to him. The man grunted and waved at a casual screen. "There are buckets over there, sir, and I think he said there's a bucket in the corner of most rooms in case one is caught short."

"Good. Always best to do it before a meeting—even so, a strong bladder is a most important boon to a diplomat." After Sir William, mightily, and the other Ministers had relieved themselves, he led them through the door: Seratard, Count Zergeyev, von Heimrich, van de Tromp, Adamson and a newcomer by the last mail ship, Burgermeister Fritz Erlicher of the Confederation of Helvetia—Switzerland—a bearded giant from their capital Bern who spoke French, English, German, Dutch and many German dialects. Phillip Tyrer and Johann followed closely, André Poncin alongside Seratard.

The audience room was forty yards square with a massive, high-beamed ceiling, very clean, very drafty, and stone walls with arrow slits for windows. Impassive samurai lined the walls. Two rows of half a dozen chairs facing each other at the far end. Many doors. Only servants present to greet them. An elaborately garbed though low-rank Bakufu official motioned them to chairs without bowing as servants brought small trays, saying in Dutch: "Please be seated for tea."

Sir William saw that Johann was deep in conversation with his Swiss Minister so he said irritably, "Phillip, ask that fellow where the Council of Elders, the *roju,* are."

Hiding his nervousness and conscious that all eyes were on him and wanting to relieve himself again, Phillip Tyrer walked over to the official and waited for him to bow. The man did not, just stared at him, so he said sharply, *"Where are your manners? Bow! I am a Lord in my country and I represent these High Lords!"*

The man flushed and bowed low and mumbled his apologies and Tyrer was exceedingly pleased that he had had the foresight to ask Nakama for some key phrases. He interrupted the man even more imperiously, *"Where are your masters, the roju?"*

"Ah, so sorry, please excuse me, Lord," the man stammered, *"They ask that you wait here to, er, to take refreshment."*

Tyrer missed words but he caught the gist. *"And after refreshments?"*

"It will be my honor to conduct you to the meeting place," the man said, his eyes cautiously lowered.

Again, to Tyrer's enormous relief, he understood. As he told Sir William what had been said he could feel the cold sweat on his back and knew he had been lucky so far.

Sir William snorted and leaned towards the others. "Damned if we should wait, eh, gentlemen? They're overdue—it was agreed we'd go straight to the meeting—damned if I want to wait, nor drink their apology for tea. Good," he said, and added to general approval, "Phillip, tell the fellow we came to see the *roju.* That's what we want to do now. Now."

"How, er, how strong do you, er, want me to be, sir?"

"For God's sake, Phillip, if I wanted you to be long-winded and diplomatic I would have been long-winded and diplomatic. An interpreter's job is to translate what is said exactly, not to give his interpretation of what is said."

"The Great Lord says: he want see roju *now. Now!"*

The official was shocked at the impolite bluntness, an unheard-of affront, and was in a complete quandary. His instructions had been clear: The gai-jin will be kept waiting a suitable 'face losing' period, about half a candle, when we will send word and you may escort them into our presence. He said rapidly, *"Of course I will take you the instant you have had refreshment and everything is ready for your perfect reception, but oh, so sorry, this is just not possible for a little while as their August Persons are not yet in their correct attire so it is not yet possible to comply with your Master's unseemly request, Interpreter-san."*

"Please to say again, not fast," Tyrer said nervously, swamped. Another flood of Japanese. "Sir William, I think he's saying we have to wait."

"Eh? Why?"

"My Master say, why wait?"

More Japanese which Tyrer lost, so the man turned to Dutch, and Erlicher stepped into the conversation, further irritating Sir William and the others. At length Erlicher said, "It seems, Sir William, that the *roju* are not, how you say, ah yes, they are not quite ready, but when they are we'll be taken to the audience room."

"Please tell this—this fellow bluntly to take us there right smartly, that we are on time, that high-level meetings are always on time because both sides have other important affairs of State to deal with as I've explained fifty times! And tell him to hurry up!"

Erlicher beamed and said it plainly and however much the official twisted and turned and eventually begged, he bowed and, as slowly as possible, led them through a door, down a corridor—first sending a messenger ahead to warn the Council of the gai-jin's astounding impertinence.

Another corridor and then, ahead, samurai opened huge doors, the official went onto his knees and bowed his head to the floor. Four men in elaborate silk robes, swords in their belts, sat on chairs at the far end of the audience room on a slightly raised platform. The central chair was empty. In front of them, on a lower level—which all Ministers noted instantly—were six chairs for each of the Ministers and between the two knelt the official interpreter. A hundred or so samurai officers knelt in a half circle facing the door and as Sir William came in, all samurai in the room bowed. The four *roju* did not.

Sir William and the others bowed back politely, then approached the dais and took their seats: "Under no circumstances do Ministers of civilized nations get down on their knees and bow their heads to the floor," Sir William had said, "whatever your customs, whether you do it or no and that's the end of it!"

Phillip Tyrer, now an expert on bowing because of Nakama, noticed that each time an Elder bowed it was as superior to inferior. Never mind, he thought, awed and excited, we're in the inner sanctum. When does the Shōgun arrive to take the empty chair? A boy? I wonder what he'll look like and what—

An Elder began to speak. With a sudden start, Tyrer recognized him as the youngish official from their previous meeting at their Legation, and also the nervous, swarthy man sitting beside him who had said nothing then but had watched everything with his narrow eyes.

Why had two Elders come to meet with us without announcing themselves as such? he asked himself. Wait a minute, didn't the young

Official introduce himself as Tomo Watanabe, yes, certainly he did, 'junior official, second class.' Obviously a phony name. But why? And why the disguise?

Unsettled, Tyrer left that to be answered later and gave his attention to what the man was saying, understanding almost none of it, as he had been forewarned by Nakama would happen, who had told him that Court-oriented words would probably be used, most of which, as with most ordinary Japanese words and phrases, had different, often conflicting meanings.

His concentration wandered. The third Elder was rotund with a pudgy face and feminine hands, and the last truly elderly, greying and thin-faced with a bad scar on his left cheek. All were barely over five and a half feet, their winglike overmantles and wide-legged trousers and high-domed, lacquered hats tied under their chins and, above all their immobile dignity, making them imposing.

Now the Japanese interpreter spoke in Dutch: "The *roju,* the Council of Elders of the Shōgunate, welcomes the foreign representatives and wishes them to present their documents as has been agreed."

Sir William sighed, mesmerized by the empty chair. "All right, Johann, let's begin. Say to them, shouldn't we wait until the Shōgun honors us with his presence?"

This into Dutch into Japanese, much discussion, then again the young Elder, Yoshi, made a pronouncement, slowly and meticulously translated into Dutch, into English. "Basically, without the usual palaver, Sir William, the spokesman says the Shōgun wasn't expected in this meeting, this is with the *roju* only. The Shōgun was to be later."

"That was not as was agreed and I inform them again that Ministerial credentials are only presented to the Head of State, in this case the Shōgun, so we can't proceed."

Back and forth and then, to the Ministers' displeasure: "The Elder says the Shōgun had to leave for Kyōto urgently and regrets he will not have the pleasure of meeting you, etc., but you can give the *roju* your credentials as they have his authority to accept them."

Back and forth, Sir William's annoyance reddening into visible anger, more discussion on both sides and more time consumed, then a scroll, heavy with characters and sealed importantly and handled as though it were the Holy Grail, was presented by a kneeling official to Sir William. "Phillip, can you read this?"

"I . . . no, sorry sir."

"No need to worry." Sir William sighed and turned to the others. "This is most improper."

"Yes," von Heimrich said coldly.

"Unacceptable," Count Alexi Zergeyev agreed.

"A dangerous precedent," Adamson said.

"It's certainly most unusual," Seratard said in French, "and they did promise the Shōgun. We could, for just this meeting, agree to their request, eh, my friends?" He was careful to hide his own annoyance and kept his voice smooth and gentle as André Poncin, at his elbow, had suggested in a cautious whisper the moment they had entered the room, adding: 'Be careful, Henri, the *roju* spokesman is the same Bakufu official I . . . we made the offer to after the other meeting, to inspect a warship, remember? *Mon Dieu,* I thought he was important, but never one of the Elders! If we could get him on the side of France, it would be a marvelous coup . . . '

Count Zergeyev was saying, "Agreeing will create a deplorable precedent."

"It will only be for this meeting. Yes?"

"It doesn't matter, it's wind over a cow's arse," the Swiss, Erlicher, said. "Let's get on with it."

They argued. Tyrer listened but kept his attention on the Elders without being apparent, fascinated by them, wanting to take advantage of this rare opportunity to learn the maximum about them in the minimum time. His father had impressed on him from an early age: 'In any meeting, always watch your opponent's hands and feet, they are the giveaways, eyes too and faces, yes, but those are usually easily controlled. Concentrate! Observe, but cautiously, or the clues to tell you what he or she is really thinking will be obscured. Remember, my son, everyone exaggerates, everyone lies in some degree.'

The hands and feet of the swarthy, shifty-eyed Elder twitched constantly, little nervous movements, those of the young Elder hardly at all. From time to time, as in the other meeting, he saw the man he had dubbed 'Shifty Eyes' whisper to the young Elder, the spokesman—only to him. Why? Tyrer asked himself. And why does Shifty Eyes take no part in any of their discussions, seemingly dismissed by them, keeping his eyes constantly on the Ministers and not the interpreters?

Abruptly Sir William motioned at the empty chair: "If the Shōgun was not expected at this meeting, and there are five Elders in the *roju,* why is there an empty chair?"

Back and forth, forth and back and then: "He says the President of their Council, Lord Anjo, has just been taken ill and cannot be here, but that does not matter, they have his authority to proceed. Please proceed."

Von Heimrich said, in perfect French as a put-down to Seratard, "Doesn't this invalidate the meeting, didn't they keep harping on the 'unanimous' nature of this Council? Five men. This could be another deceitful ploy to be used in future to negate the whole proceedings." Again an argument began.

Only Sir William was silent. He was keeping his fury, and anxiety, off his face. Clearly we've been duped again. What to do? Then heard himself say in a firm voice: "Very well, we will accept this authority as bona fide from your Shōgun, for this meeting only. We will inform our governments that prior agreement was not adhered to and *we will proceed to Kyōto as soon as possible to present credentials properly to your Shōgun—and Emperor Komei—with a more than suitable escort."*

As Johann began to translate into Dutch, Count Zergeyev murmured, "Bravo—that's the only way to deal with the *matyeryebitz!"* Von Heimrich and van de Tromp, the Dutchman, quietly agreed, to the objections of Seratard, Adamson the American and Erlicher.

The Japanese interpreter gaped and said loudly he was sure that he had misunderstood. Johann told him there was no misunderstanding. During this lengthy back and forth, Sir William closed his ears to them, watching the faces of the *roju* intently as they listened to the interpreter. In varying degrees all of them became unsettled. Good, he thought.

"With the usual palaver, Sir William, but with a heavy load of polite apologies this time, he says it won't be possible to see the Shōgun in Kyōto, the weather is very inclement at this time of the year, but they will make sure the moment he's back, etc., etc."

Sir William smiled mirthlessly. "Say to them: Inclement or not, we will visit the Emperor in the very near future. Stress that, Johann. On that basis only we will proceed."

The *roju* received that in stony silence.

In turn, Sir William first, then the others, got up and bowed, spoke his name and rank and the country he represented, and offered his credentials. These were accepted with dignity. Each time the *roju* bowed back, respectfully.

"Now," Sir William said, his chin jutting. "To proceed with the second business of the meeting: Her Majesty's Government reaffirms that on Friday the 12th September, this Year of Our Lord, 1862, an English gentleman was foully murdered in daylight by samurai of the

Satsuma contingent under the command of their king Sanjiro. Two others were wounded. Her Majesty's Government demands the murderers be handed over or dealt with publicly according to Japanese law, that a reparation of one hundred thousand pounds sterling in gold be paid forthwith, an apology published and a public guarantee promulgated that this will not happen again. Next: the second and final payment of five thousand pounds sterling in gold as reparation for the murders of Sergeant Gunn and Corporal Roper in our Legation last year, weeks overdue, be paid in gold in three days or the amount is doubled every day thereafter . . ."

Sir William allowed time for Johann to translate word for word but allowing no discussion until he had finished the list, then Adamson had demanded reparations for the murder of the American official.

Last, the Russian Minister, Count Zergeyev, his multitude of medals and decorations clinking on his gold-braided uniform, said, "A Russian officer and one soldier off our man-of-war, *Gudenev,* were hacked to death in Yokohama on 16th of February, last year," then added to the consternation of the others, "For reparations, Tsar Alexander II of all the Russias demands the Kurile Islands."

During the translations, Sir William leaned over and whispered pleasantly in Russian: "A nice jest, Count Alexi, for of course Her Majesty's Government could never agree to such an intrusion into our sphere of influence."

"Perhaps, perhaps not. War is coming in Europe again. Soon we'll have to see who are our friends, and who enemies."

Sir William chuckled. "That's always a problem for certain countries. The United Kingdom has no permanent enemies, only permanent interests."

"True, dear friend, but you forgot to add 'no permanent friends.' Also now, with Vladivostok, we're a Pacific power."

"Power from sea to sea? The dream of the Tsars, eh?"

"Why not? Better us than some," Count Alexi said pointedly, then shrugged. "The Kuriles? If not them some other islands—merely to protect Vladivostok."

"We must discuss your 'curious' Pacific presence under more perfect conditions. My Government is most interested."

Seratard, not understanding Russian and furious that he had not been party to this exchange, said coldly in French, "I trust, Sir William, you are well aware of French interests."

"As always, Monsieur, the interests of gallant allies are forefront in the mind of Her Majesty's Foreign Office."

"Sir William," Johann said wearily, "the Elder says . . . he's only repeating their previous position that they've no jurisdiction over Satsuma, don't know who the murderers are, and think any reparation should be claimed from Satsuma itself, through correct channels, of course."

"What correct channels?"

Back and forth: "He says through them, that they'll pass on your request to Satsuma again."

"It's not a request, by God. We will try one final time—stress that, Johann, a different tack," Sir William said. "Say, Do they punish murderers? And tell the interpreter I require a yes or no. Only."

Back and forth: "He says, Sir William, that under some circum—"

"Murder, for Christ's sake. Yes or no! Phillip, say it in Japanese!"

Tyrer's stomach twisted. He had been watching the swarthy Elder whispering again but bravely he jumped to his feet. *"Honored Lords, please excuse my poor Japanese but my Master ask, please if when murder, you kill murder man, yes or no please."*

Silence. The Elders looked at Yoshi who stared at Tyrer, hands playing with his fan. The man alongside whispered to him and he nodded. *"The penalty for murder is death."*

"He says yes, sir. For murder, the penalty is death," Tyrer said, having learned those key words from Nakama who had also explained the Japanese penal code and its severity.

"Tell him thank you."

"My Master say thank you, Lord."

"Now ask him, Is it correct to demand a reparation for such a crime, yes or no?"

"Lord, please excuse me but is . . . is . . . I . . ." Tyrer stopped, his mind a sudden blank. "Sorry, Sir William, I don't know the word for 'reparations.' "

At once André Poncin leapt in with, "The word's *bakkin,* Sir William, and little known. May I try, please?"

"Go ahead."

"Honored Lords," Poncin said with a deep bow, and Tyrer blessed him for the rescue and saving his face. *"Please, my Master ask if correct, humbly ask for justice and head payment for family, for murder, a fine against Satsuma?"*

"Against Satsuma yes," Yoshi said with a fleeting smile.

André sighed with relief. "He says yes, Sir William, but the reparation should be demanded specifically from Satsuma." Before Sir William could ask another question, Poncin in his most perfect, rehearsed Japanese—and to Tyrer's astonishment—began to offer the face-saving formula he had devised: *"Honored Lord, on behalf of my Master, humbly suggest* roju *perhap consdir, ah please excuse, perhaps consider* roju *lend Satsuma first payment, one fifth. This you offer now, give time get rest Satsuma, collect rest from Satsuma. Please?"*

This time they all saw the young Elder's interest. At once he began a whispered conversation with the others. André saw Tyrer frowning at him so subtly shook his head, silently asking him not to interfere. In a moment Yoshi said, *"Perhaps it would be possible to offer a twentieth, paid in a hundred days against Satsuma's obvious debt."*

"Honorable Lords . . ."

"What the devil's he saying, Phillip, and the Elder?"

"Just a second, Sir William," André cut in pleasantly, wanting to crush him. *"Honored Lords, my Master would recommend a tenth, in sixty days. So sorry, please excuse bad pronouncing but humbly, very humble beg yes."* Greatly relieved, Poncin saw their discussion begin and gambled again. "Sorry, Sir William, but as Phillip will confirm, I suggested they consider advancing payment on behalf of Satsuma who they say, rightfully, should pay any reparations."

"The devil you did? They are?" Sir William stared at him, tiredness dropping away from him and all of them. "Well done—if they'd do that then I could compromise, eh? You agree?" For the sake of courtesy he turned to the others for their opinion. Behind him, Tyrer whistled tonelessly, having understood most of what Poncin had said in Japanese, the way he was manipulating the Elder and the Minister, and the slight, though important difference of the English translation. Clever of André. But what is he up to, is this his idea or is it Seratard's? Again Shifty Eyes began murmuring confidentially to the young Elder whose attention went to the Ministers. It's almost as though . . .

All at once it was as if cataracts had dropped from his eyes and he had become clear-sighted again. Even more than that, now he was seeing the Elders with straight eyes and not with the oblique and clouded gaze of a self-styled civilized man, seeing them as people, equally civilized, equally simple or complex but as people, and not as outlandish, mysterious or weird 'Jappos' that Nakama, Fujiko, even André, in their various ways correctly resented.

God Almighty, Shifty Eyes understands English, he wanted to shout ecstatically. That's the only answer, and another's that he's a *roju* spy and no more an Elder than I am, which is why the others pay no attention to him in their discussions. What else? He must be Watanabe's spy because he's the only one whispered to—must find out their real names and to ask Nakama about them. Watanabe is the most powerful of this lot, acting President. The absent President? Got to find out his real name too. What else? Where did André . . .

He concentrated as Yoshi addressed the interpreter. His voice had sharpened. Instantly the interpreter became more alert and his Dutch twenty times briefer. Johann translated, trying to contain his astonishment, "The *roju* agrees in this instance it is correct to ask for a reparation, from Satsuma, that yes, a hundred thousand seems reasonable for a nobleman though they can't say it will be considered so by the Lord of Satsuma. As a gesture of friendship to the British, and to outside nations, the *roju* will advance a tenth part in seventy days on Satsuma's behalf—while formal British requests are forwarded to the Satsuma. Concerning the request of the Russian Minister, as with his own Homeland, Japanese soil is Japanese soil and is . . . I suppose the word would be inviolate, or not to be bartered."

Without being obvious Sir William put a hand on Count Alexi's to stop the outburst, saying softly in Russian, "Let it rest, Alexi," then loudly to Johann, ready to negotiate the number of days down and the amount up, "Excellent. Johann, please tell them th—" He stopped as Tyrer whispered quickly, "Excuse me, sir, suggest you accept at once but you really should know their names."

It was almost as though Tyrer had not spoken for Sir William continued with hardly a pause and no change of expression: "Johann, please tell them their suggestion is acceptable to Her Majesty's Government in the same spirit of friendliness. Concerning the Minister from the Court of St. Petersburg, I am sure he will consult his government who will, undoubtedly, agree that a monetary settlement would satisfy." Without allowing Count Alexi any time to reply he rushed on: "Regarding our other pressing problem, the Shimonoseki Straits: all foreign Governments protest shore batteries firing on their ships when using those Straits peacefully." Sir William repeated the dates and the names of ships, already the matter of much heated correspondence.

"They say they will pass on the complaint, Sir William—with the usual, that they've no control over Choshu."

"Johann, say: In the friendly spirit of this meeting, may I suggest it is difficult, if not impossible, for Foreign Governments to deal with the Bakufu that apparently does not have authority over its various kingdoms or States. Therefore what should we do? Deal directly with the Shōgun who signed our Treaties—or Emperor Komei?"

"The legal government of Nippon is the Shōgunate, the supreme ruler of the Shōgunate is the Shōgun who rules on behalf of the Son of

Heaven, the *roju* are the supreme advisors to the Shōgunate whose officials are the Bakufu. In all cases Foreign Governments must deal with the Shōgunate."

"In that case, how can we ensure safe passage for all shipping using the Shimonoseki?"

More draining discussion and always variations of the same response that was an answer but not an answer however much Sir William probed. Bladders agitated the general impatience and fatigue. Three hours had passed since they began. Then a vagrant thought became a full-blown solution. Sir William smiled to himself. "Very well: say, presuming there are no further attacks and our serious remonstrations are delivered to the Choshu daimyo forthwith, we will, in the spirit of this new friendliness, accept their position for a future meeting in one hundred days."

An hour of added maneuvering. "The *roju* agree to a second meeting in a hundred and fifty-six days, here in Yedo, and wish to declare this meeting over."

"Good," Sir William said, satisfied, stifling a yawn. "Could we please have their names now, verbally, and then in correct characters on the paper that we will exchange within three days to confirm our formal agreements."

Back and forth, minor details changed, then finally: "Sir William, he says you'll have the paper in a week, the interpreter will give you their names and the meeting is ended." As each Elder was introduced the man nodded briefly and impassively: "Lord Adachi of Mito, Lord Zukumura of Gai, Lord Yoshi of Hisamatsu . . ." Tyrer was delighted to see that Shifty Eyes, last in the line, was sweating, his hands and feet squirming and his bow had nowhere near the imperiousness of the others: "Lord Kii of Zukoshi."

"Please give them our thanks. As previously agreed, I will now order royal salutes."

"Lord Yoshi says, unfortunately one of their members is missing. As previously agreed, unanimous approval of the *roju* is necessary to grant the firing of any cannon."

Abruptly Sir William's bonhomie fell away. All Ministers were shocked. "What about our agreements?" he asked sharply. "Do they require unanimous approval too?"

Back and forth amid much tension and muttered caution amongst the Ministers. Then Johann said awkwardly, "Lord Yoshi says that this gathering has the Shōgun's authority and the President's to accept credentials, to listen and recommend. They will unanimously recommend the settlement. As previously agreed, approval for firing cannon needs unanimous approval of all Elders, so regretfully this body cannot allow it."

The silence became unhealthy as Sir William and all of them realized the trap they had fallen into. No option this time, he thought, his stomach twisting. "Captain Pallidar!"

"Yessir?" Pallidar came from the back, heart suddenly grinding, knowing along with everyone else facing the *roju* that Sir William had no option now but to give the order to fire the salutes, whatever the cost, or the same excuse would surely be used to negate their settlement.

As Pallidar saluted perfectly, Seratard broke in with his smoothest and most diplomatic voice: "Sir William, I feel sure that the agreement is bona fide, will be implemented, and you can accept it. I recommend you do this, we all do, eh, gentlemen?" he said to general relief at the face-saver, "and also recommend under the circumstances we forgo the salutes. You agree, Sir William, on our behalf?"

Sir William hesitated grimly.

To further astonishment, Seratard added grandly, "André, tell them on behalf of France I will go surety for the first installment."

Before Sir William could say anything, André was bowing: *"My Master say, Honored Lords, he happy* roju *give paper in a week, agree lend Satsuma first money in seventy day. Say also France, as Nippon friend, honored give personal bond to British Minister against first payment. Also he honored greet all or one of* roju *any time personally, in ship or any place. Humbly thank you, Honored Lords."*

With narrowed eyes, Yoshi said, *"Thank your Master. The meeting is ended."*

A samurai officer called out, *"Kerei!"*—salute—and every samurai bowed, holding that position as the *roju* got to their feet and bowed back with measured politeness. Sir William and the others had little option but to follow suit as Yoshi led the way to an unseen door beside the dais, and they were quickly gone. At once the samurai straightened and resumed their staring, suspicious hostility.

"Very satisfactory, Sir William," Seratard said expansively in French, taking his arm, wanting to distract him again. "Well done."

"Your Masters in the Elysée will be very peed off with you when we ask for ten thousand in gold," Sir William said, a little piqued but not entirely—except for the firing of the cannon he had made a giant step forward. "Peed or not it was a grand gesture, Henri, however expensive."

Seratard laughed. "Twenty guineas says they'll pay."

"Done! Will you dine with us at the Legation?" They began walking out, careless of the arrogant, bellicose stares.

"Thank you, no. As we've concluded our business I think I'll start back for Yokohama now instead of tomorrow, there's time enough and the sea's calm. Why wait for *Pearl,* join us aboard my flagship, we can dine en route, eh?"

"Thanks but I'll wait till tomorrow. I want to make sure all our lads are back safely on our transports."

Behind them, unnoticed in the throng, Tyrer had waited for André who had knelt to adjust a shoe buckle, who then, not realizing Tyrer was watching, began a whispered conversation with the Japanese interpreter. The man hesitated, then nodded and bowed. *"Domo."*

André turned, saw Phillip scrutinizing him. For a split second he was nonplussed, then smiled as he joined him. "Well, Phillip, that went very well, didn't it? I thought you were excellent, and we certainly made the points."

"I wasn't and you saved the day. And my face, for which many thanks." Tyrer frowned, unsettled, following the procession. "Even so, though you brilliantly solved the impasse, what you said in English and what was said in Japanese was different, wasn't it?"

"Not that different, *mon ami,* not enough to matter."

"I don't think Sir William would agree."

"Perhaps, perhaps not. Perhaps you were mistaken." André forced a laugh. "It's never wise to agitate a Minister, eh? A closed mouth catches no nasties."

"Most times, yes. What did you say to that interpreter?"

"I thanked him. *Mon Dieu,* my bladder's killing me—how's yours?"

"Same," Tyrer agreed, sure that André was lying about the interpreter. But then why shouldn't he? he was thinking with his newfound point of view. André is enemy, if not enemy, the opposition, and every nuance was to benefit and ingratiate Seratard, France and André. Fair enough. What would he ask for secretly? To pass on a message, yes, but what? What secret message? What would I ask for secretly? "You asked for a private meeting with Lord Yoshi, eh?" he said, gambling. "For you and Monsieur Seratard."

André Poncin's expression did not change but Tyrer noticed his right hand on his ceremonial sword became white-knuckled. "Phillip," he said thinly, "I've been a good friend to you since you arrived, helping you begin Japanese, introducing you around, eh? I haven't interfered with your private samurai—Nakama, eh, though I've heard, secretly, he's got other names. Haven't . . ."

"What other names?" Tyrer asked, suddenly nervous and not knowing why. "What do you know about him?"

André went on as though Tyrer had not spoken: "Haven't tried to question him or you about him though I did warn you about Japanese, all of them, time enough for you to tell me about him if you want to, as a friend. Remember we're on the same side, Phillip, we're servants not masters, we're friends, we're in Japan where gai-jin really have to help each other—like I did introducing you to Raiko who led to Fujiko, eh? Nice girl, Fujiko. Best to have a little Gallic realism, Phillip, best keep private information private, best beware of your Nakama and remember what I've said a dozen times: In Japan there are only Japanese solutions."

Near sunset the same day, Yoshi hurried along a somber, drafty stone corridor in the castle keep. Now he wore his characteristic kimono with two swords, a cowled riding cloak over them. Every twenty paces were flickering oil torches, set into iron brackets beside bowman emplacements that also served as windows. Outside the air was cool. Ahead was a circular staircase. It led to his private stables below. He ran down the steps.

"Halt! Who . . . ah, so sorry, Lord!" The sentry bowed.

Yoshi nodded and went on. Throughout the castle soldiers, stablemen, servants were preparing for bed or for night duties, following the universal, worldwide custom of bedding down at nightfall. Only the well-to-do had light by night, to see, to read or to play.

"Halt! Ah, so sorry Lord." This sentry bowed, and the next, and the next.

In the stable courtyard a personal guard of twenty men was assembled at the heads of their ponies. Amongst them was Misamoto, the fisherman, the make-believe samurai and Elder. Now he was poorly clad as a common foot soldier, unarmed, and frightened. Two small enclosed palanquins, especially light and designed for rapid transport, were there. Each was slotted onto two shafts that fitted into a harness for two saddle ponies ahead and behind. All hooves were muffled and all this part of a plan he had devised with Hosaki days ago.

The spy window of one palanquin slid aside. He saw Koiko peer out. She smiled, nodding a greeting. The window closed. His hand tightened on his sword. Ready, he slid her door open enough to ensure she was who he thought she was and that she was alone. When he was very young his father had beaten the first law of survival into him, word by word: 'If you are caught unawares, betrayed unawares, killed unawares, you failed in your duty to me and to yourself. The fault will be yours alone because you failed to check personally and to plan against any eventuality. There is no excuse for failure except karma—and gods do not exist!'

A quick reassuring smile to her. He slid the door home and checked that the other palanquin was unoccupied and available for his use if he needed it. Satisfied, he gave the signal to mount. This was done in almost complete silence which again pleased him—he had ordered all armor and harnesses to be muffled. A last silent check but he could sense no danger. The new rifle was in a saddle holster, the ammunition pouch full, the other four guns slung over the shoulders of his most trusted marksmen. Noiselessly he swung into his saddle. Another signal. His advance guard and banner man carrying his personal standard led off. He followed, then the two palanquins and the rest fell into place as rear guard.

Their progress was quick and almost soundless. Up the passageway into the next fortification, directly away from the main gate and main thoroughfares. At each checkpoint they were motioned through without challenge. Instead of turning into the maze of the castle proper, they made for a large building on the north side set against one of the major fortifications. Outside it was heavily guarded. The moment Yoshi was recognized, tall doors swung open to let them ride through. Inside was a large enclosed and packed-earth practice riding ring with a high vaulted ceiling and a second tier for viewing. A few torches, here and there. The doors closed behind them.

Yoshi cantered to the head and led briskly through the far archway, past stables and harness rooms. All were empty. This area was cobbled, the air heavy with the smell of dung and urine and sweat. Beyond, the hard-packed earth began again and another arch let out to an inner, smaller ring. Across it was an archway, dimly lit. Yoshi heeled his surefooted pony faster, then reined in suddenly.

The surrounding upper tier was packed with silent bowmen. None had arrows in their bows but all those in the ring knew they were dead men—if the order was given.

"Ah, Yoshi-sama." Nori Anjo's harsh voice came out of the semi-darkness above and Yoshi had difficulty for a moment picking him out. Then he saw him. Armorless, he was sitting at the back of the tier beside the staircase. "At this afternoon's meeting you didn't tell us you were going to leave the castle with armed men like . . . like what? Like ninja?"

A rustle of anger spread through Yoshi's men but he laughed and this broke the tension, below and above. "Not ninja, Anjo-sama, though certainly as quietly as possible. It's a good idea to test defenses, without warning. I'm Guardian of the castle, as well as Guardian of the Shōgun. And you? To what do I owe this pleasure?"

"You are just testing our defenses?"

"I am killing three doves with one arrow, yes." The humor had left Yoshi's voice and all were chilled, wondering why three and what did he mean. "And you? Why so many bowmen? For an ambush perhaps?"

The coarse laugh pealed among the rafters, edging everyone further. Hands tightened on weapons though no one made an overt move. "Ambush? Oh no, not an ambush—an honor guard. The moment I heard you planned a patrol with muffled hooves . . . these men are just to honor you, and to show you not all of us are sleeping, that the castle is in good hands and a Guardian not needed." He barked a command. At once all bowmen hurried down the stairs and formed two lines the length of the ring, Yoshi and his men between them. They bowed formally. Yoshi and his men bowed back, formally. But nothing had changed, the trap was still ready to be sprung. "You need guns to test defenses?"

"Our Council advised all daimyos to arm with modern weapons," Yoshi said, his voice outwardly calm, inwardly furious that his plan had been betrayed and that he had not foreseen an ambush. "These are the first of my new rifles. I wish to accustom my men to carry them."

"Wise, yes, very wise. I see you carry one too. Lord Yoshi has to carry a gun himself?"

Seething at the jeer, Yoshi glanced down at the rifle in its holster, hating all guns and blessing the wisdom of his namesake in outlawing their manufacture or importation the day he became Shōgun. Hasn't that more than anything ensured our peace for two and a half centuries, he thought grimly. Guns are vile, cowardly weapons, worthy only of stinking gai-jin, weapons that can kill at a thousand paces so you may never see who you kill or who has killed you, weapons that any simpleton, low person, maniac, filthy robber, man or woman can use against anyone, even the highest lord with impunity, or most perfectly schooled swordsman. Yes, and now even I have to carry a gun—the gai-jin have forced us into it.

With Anjo's sneering jibe ringing in his ears, he jerked the rifle out of the holster, pushed the safety off as Misamoto had shown him, pointed it, pulled the trigger, immediately pumped shells into the breech, blasting five bullets deafeningly into the rafters, the rifle almost twisting out of his hands with unexpected force. Everyone scattered, even his own men, a few unseated by frightened rearing ponies. Anjo and his guards dived for the floor anticipating more firing, lethal this time, every man in the room unnerved by the rapidity of firing.

In utter silence all waited breathlessly and then, because there was no follow-up and they realized Yoshi was just demonstrating the rifle, the two ranks of archers hastily but warily re-formed around his own men who were sorting themselves into order. Anjo and his guards scrambled to their feet. "What was the meaning of that?" he shouted.

As nonchalantly as he could, his own heart pounding, Yoshi continued to gentle his pony and quietly pushed the safety catch on and laid the gun across his lap, concealing his delight with the success of his action and that he was as impressed as anyone with the rifle's power—he had fired muzzle loaders before and some old-fashioned duelling pistols at targets, but never a breech-loader with cartridges. "I wanted to show you the value of one of these. In certain circumstances they're better than a sword, particularly for daimyos." He was glad to hear that his voice sounded calm. "For instance, when you were ambushed a few weeks ago, you could have used one, *neh*?"

Shakily Anjo was controlling his wrath, quite sure that now he was in great danger, his life under immediate threat, and equally certain if he ordered Toranaga's arrest as he had planned bullets would pepper him—in the name of all gods where and how did that dog learn to shoot and why was I not informed he had become an expert?

And being reminded of the shishi incident was an added public insult, for it was well known he had not been brave but had had to scramble to safety, never duelling once with his assailants and then, after the wounded were captured, had ordered them to be killed in a dishonorable fashion. "Under some circumstances, Yoshi-sama, some, but I doubt if your gun or any others have value tonight. I doubt that. May I ask your purpose tonight? Is it to visit our outside defenses and return? Or is one of your 'doves' a departure for elsewhere?"

Both knew Yoshi was not answerable for his movements in or out of the castle precincts. "That depends on what I see outside," he said curtly. "I may decide to return to my own domain for a day or so, perhaps not—of course I would keep you closely informed."

"The Council would miss your presence, if only for a few days.

There's much to be done. If you're absent, we will have to make the decisions ourselves."

"As we decided this afternoon, there's nothing major to be decided, fortunately without five Elders nothing of major importance can be settled."

"There is the matter of the gai-jin agreement."

"That was also decided this afternoon."

The meeting of the Council after the gai-jin had departed, for once, had been happy and filled with laughter at the enemy's loss of face, that once again the gai-jin had been outsmarted, Anjo, Toyama, and Adachi congratulating him for his expert handling of the confrontation and understanding of gai-jin, Zukumura saying little except muttering feeblemindedly from time to time.

Anjo had chortled, 'Agreeing to advance a pittance to get rid of them and their ships from Yedo while we bring Satsuma to heel was very clever, Yoshi-sama. Very. At the same time we've indefinitely postponed their threat to go to Kyōto, and they agree that Satsuma is completely to blame.'

Toyama said, 'Then we declare war on Satsuma? Good!'

'No, not war, there are other ways to curb that dog.' Anjo was very confident with his newfound knowledge. 'You were right about the gai-jin, Yoshi-sama. It was vastly interesting to see how enmity among them all is so close to their revolting surfaces.' He and Toyama had witnessed the meeting from behind the dais, the wall there deliberately made see-through from the inner side. 'Revolting. We could even smell them through the screen. Disgusting. I've ordered that audience room washed out and the seats they sat in destroyed.'

'Excellent,' Adachi said. 'My skin crawled all the time I was there. Yoshi-sama, may I ask about that monkey Misamoto, did he really tell you what the gai-jin said, everything? I couldn't hear a word.'

'Not all of it,' he had told them, 'enough to give me some advance clues but only when they were speaking English. Misamoto said much of the time they were speaking another language, he thought French. This proves another point: we must have trusted interpreters. I propose we start a language school for our brightest sons at once.'

'School? What school?' Zukumura mumbled. No one paid any attention.

'I disagree.' Toyama's dewlaps shook. 'The closer our sons get to gai-jin, the more infected they'll be.'

'No,' Anjo said, 'we'll personally select the students—we must have trusted barbarian speakers. We will vote: the Bakufu will be ordered to form a language school at once. Agreed? Good, next, the gai-jin letter: we will continue Yoshi-sama's tactic, the day before it's due we tell them it will arrive "as soon as possible." Agreed?'

'Sorry, no,' he had said, 'we must do the exact opposite. We must deliver the letter on time, exactly, and give them the second blackmail payment on time too.'

They stared at him and Zukumura mumbled, 'Letter?'

Yoshi said patiently, 'The gai-jin must be kept off balance. They will be expecting us to delay, so we don't, and that will make them believe the one hundred and fifty-six days is also firm, which of course it isn't. *That* we certainly delay and delay and hope to send them all mad.' They had laughed with him, even Zukumura who did not understand why they were laughing had laughed anyway—and even more when Yoshi told them how many times he had almost guffawed during the meeting, seeing how their impatience was ruining their already illusory bargaining position. ' "Without the killer dog the master's as weak as a puppy against a man with a stick." '

'What? Man with a stick?' Zukumura asked, his dead codfish eyes peering stupidly. 'What dog?'

Much of Yoshi's good humor had left him, reminded that now he had to endure this feebleminded man forever. Nonetheless, he explained that without muscle to back up their complaints, and the will to use it, the enemy were helpless.

'Muscle? Don't understand, Yoshi-sama. What muscle?'

'Force,' Anjo said impatiently. 'Force! Their cannons and their fleets, Zukumura. Oh, never mind!'

Toyama, the old man, said fiercely, 'While they're without their fleet we should burn them out—they are unspeakably arrogant, with foul manners, and as for their spokesman . . . I'm glad I didn't have to be present, Yoshi-sama, I think I would have burst. Let's burn them out, now.'

'Who? Burn who?'

'Keep quiet, Zukumura,' Anjo said wearily, 'and just vote when I tell you. Yoshi-sama, I agree with your reasoning. We'll send the letter on time and the second part of their blackmail money when agreed. Everyone in favor? Good. Next: now that we've dealt with the gai-jin, and the Shōgun and Princess are safely on the North Road there's not much to do for the next week or so.'

'Allowing them to go was a misguided decision and will come back to haunt us,' Yoshi had said.

'In this you are wrong. Please prepare a plan, your ideas how to bring that dog Sanjiro and Satsuma to heel. I vote we meet in two weeks, unless there is an emergency . . .'

Later, going back to his own quarters, Yoshi had not been able to think of any potential emergency that would require his presence in Yedo—even the second covert, whispered invitation to visit the French warship that he neither accepted nor refused but left open for the weeks ahead was not urgent. So he had resolved to put into effect at once the plan he and his wife, Hosaki, had devised. Now Anjo and his bowmen were barring his path.

What to do?

"Good night, Anjo-sama," he said, making the decision. "As always, I will keep you advised." Covering his disquiet and feeling naked, he spurred his pony forward, heading for the far archway. None of the archers moved, waiting for orders. His men and the two palanquins followed him, feeling equally defenseless.

Anjo watched them go, enraged. But for those rifles I would have had him arrested as planned. On what charge? Treason, plotting against the Shōgun! But Yoshi would never have been brought to trial, oh no, so sorry, fools would have killed him as he tried to escape justice.

A sudden shaft of pain in his bowels made him grope for a seat. *Baka* doctors! There must be a cure, he told himself, then heaped more curses on Yoshi and the men who had disappeared under the far archway.

Yoshi was breathing better now, the fear sweat no longer chilling him. He trotted deeper into fortifications, along poorly lit corridors, passed more stables and harness rooms until he came to the end wall. The wall was sheathed in wood. Men dismounted and lit torches from those in wall brackets.

With his riding whip he pointed at a knob to one side. His aide dismounted and pulled it sharply. A whole section of the wall swung outwards to reveal a tunnel, tall enough and wide enough for two men to ride along, side by side. At once he heeled his pony into motion. When the palanquins and the last man were through and the door once more closed, he sighed with relief. Only then did he holster the rifle.

But for you, Rifle-san, he thought affectionately, I might be a dead man, at the very least a prisoner. Sometimes I can see a rifle really is better than a sword. You deserve a name—it was ancient Shinto custom to give names to special swords or weapons or even rocks or trees. I shall call you 'Nori,' which also can mean 'seaweed' and is a pun on Nori Anjo, to remind me that you saved me from him and that one of your bullets belongs to him, in his heart or head.

"Eeee, Lord," his Captain said, riding alongside. "Your shooting was a marvelous thing to behold."

"Thank you, but you and all the men were ordered to be silent until I gave you leave to speak. You are demoted. Go to the rear." The crestfallen man hurried away. "You," Yoshi said to his second in command, "you are now Captain." He turned in his saddle and went forward again, leading.

The air was stale in the tunnel. This was one of the many secret escape routes honeycombing the castle. The castle with its three moats and soaring donjon had taken just four years to build—five hundred thousand men had, at Shōgun Toranaga's suggestion and at no cost to him, proudly worked on it night and day until it was finished.

The floor of the tunnel sloped downwards and curled this way and that, the sides hewn out of rock in places and roughly bricked in others, the ceiling propped here and there but in good repair. Always downwards but without danger. Now water dripped from the sides and the air became cooler and Yoshi knew that they were under the moat. He pulled his cloak closer around him, hating the tunnel and almost sick with claustrophobia—a legacy from the time when he and his wife and sons had been close confined for almost half a year in dungeon-like rooms by *Tairō* Ii not so very long ago. Never again will I be confined, he had sworn, never again.

In time the floor sloped upwards and they came to the far end that opened into a house. This was a safe place that belonged to a loyal Toranaga clan vassal, who, forewarned, greeted him. Relieved that there was no further trouble, Yoshi motioned the advance guard to lead.

The night was pleasing and they trotted through the city by little known paths until they were on the outskirts and at the first barrier of the Tokaidō. There hostile guards immediately became docile seeing the Toranaga standard. Hastily they opened the barricade and bowed and closed it, all of them curious but none stupid enough to ask questions.

Not far beyond the barrier the road forked. A side road meandered northwards, inland, towards the mountains that, in a normal three or four days' ride, would bring him to his castle, Dragon's Tooth. Gladly the advance guard swung that way, heading for home—to their homes as well as his, most of them not having seen their families, fiancées or friends for the best part of a year. Half a league down the road, approaching a village where there was a fine watering place and a hot spring, he called out, "Guards!" beckoning them back.

The new Captain of the escort reined in alongside and almost said, Sire? but caught himself in time. He waited.

Yoshi pointed at an Inn as though a sudden decision. "We stop there." It was called Seven Seasons of Happiness. "No need for silence now."

The courtyard was neat and tidy and cobbled. At once the proprietor and maids and menservants hurried out with lanterns, bowing and anxious to please, honored with the majesty of their expected guest. Maids surrounded the palanquin to take care of Koiko, while the proprietor, a neat, balding, slim old man who walked with a limp, conducted Yoshi to the best and most isolated bungalow. He was a retired samurai called Inejin who had decided to shave his knot and become an innkeeper. Secretly he was still hatomoto—a privileged samurai—one of Yoshi's many spies that dotted the surrounds of Yedo and all approaches to Dragon's Tooth. The new Captain, conscious of his responsibility, and four samurai accompanied them, Misamoto and his two guards last.

Quickly the Captain made sure the dwelling was secure. Then Yoshi settled himself on the veranda, on a cushion facing the steps, the Captain and the other samurai kneeling on guard behind him. He noticed the maid offering tea was fresh-faced and well chosen, the tea tasting better for it. When he was quite ready he waved the maids and servants away. "Please bring them here, Inejin," he ordered.

In moments Inejin returned. With him were the two gai-jin prospectors. One tall, the other stocky, both gaunt, tough-looking, bearded men wearing grimy, rough clothes and battered caps. Yoshi studied them curiously, distastefully, seeing them more as creatures than men. Both were uneasy. They stopped near the steps, gaping at him.

At once the Captain said, "Bow!" and when they did nothing, just stared at him without understanding, he snarled at two samurai, "Teach them manners."

In seconds they were on their knees, faces in the dirt, cursing their stupidity at accepting such a perilous job: 'Wot the fuck, Charlie,' the stocky man, a Cornish miner, had said in Drunk Town a few days ago after their meeting with Norbert Greyforth, 'wot we's got to lose? Nuffink! We's starving and we's broke, we's no work, we's can put nuffink more on the slate, man—even with my cobber Bonzer, for Gawd's sake—there ain't a bar in Yokopoko that'll give us a beer, a bed or a bite of bread let alone some crumpet. Not a ship'll give us a berth. We's stuck and soon the Aussie Peelers'll land here, or yors from 'Frisco, then we's both be in chains, me hanging for bushwhacking a few poxy, claim-jumping miners and you for rustling and shooting some bloody bankers.'

'You trust that bastard Greyforth?'

'Where's yor honner, me old cock sparrer! We give him our markers, right? He done like he promise, a proper toff, right? He give we's twenty-two quid to pay wot we's owe to stay out of the brig, another twenty in the bank for when we's back, all shovels, powder and goods we's need and a sworn contract in front of the preacher that we's to gets two parts of every five we ships to Yoko, right? All like he promise, right? He's a toff but all toffs is slimy.'

The two men had guffawed, the other saying, 'You're goddam right.'

'Now we's the prospectors, right? It's we's who finds the pay dirt, right? In Jappo land, where's we's alone, right? We's kin hide a poke or two, eh? And sneak it out, right? All the grub, booze and dinkie-die for a year, our own bleeding Yoshiwara for not a penny piece, an' a first shot at Jappo gold? Me, I'm in if you isn't. . . .'

"Let them sit up, do not hurt them. Misamoto!"

Misamoto was on his knees at once. The moment the two men saw him, some of their concern left them.

"These are the men you met at the dock yesterday?"

"Yes, Sire."

"They know you as Watanabe?"

"Yes, Lord."

"Good. They know nothing about your past?"

"No, Lord, I did it all as you ordered, everything an—"

"You said sailors in Nagasaki taught you English?"

"Yes, Lord."

"Good. Now, first tell them they will be well treated and not to be afraid. What are their names?"

"Listen, you two, this's the Boss, this's Lord Ota," Misamoto said as he had been told to name Yoshi, his coarse slang American easily understood by them. "I tol' you bastards to bow and scrape or you'd hav' it done for you. He says you're to be well treated and wants to know yor names."

"I'm Johnny Cornishman and he's Charlie Yank an' so far we's nothing to eat or drink, for Christ's sweet sake!"

As best he could, Misamoto translated the names.

"You will tell them nothing about me or what you have done since I took you out of prison—remember I have ears everywhere and I will know."

"I will not fail, Lord." Misamoto bowed deeply, hiding his hatred, desperate to please and frightened for his future.

"Yes." For a moment Yoshi considered him. In the two-odd months since he had taken Misamoto into his service the man had changed radically, outside. Now he was cleanshaven, his pate also shaved and his hair groomed in samurai fashion. Enforced cleanliness had improved his appearance greatly, and even though he was deliberately kept in the vestments of the lowest class of samurai, he looked samurai and wore the two swords now as though they belonged. The swords were still false, just hilts with no blades within the scabbards.

Thus far Yoshi was pleased with his performance and when he had seen him robed and hatted as an Elder, he had been astonished, not recognizing him. A good lesson to remember, he had thought at the time: how easy it is to appear to be what you are not!

"It would be better for you not to fail," he said, then turned his attention to Misamoto's two guards. "You two are responsible for the safety of these two men. The Lady Hosaki will supply further guards and guides but you two are responsible for the success of the venture."

"Yes, Lord."

"As to this fake Watanabe," he said, his voice soft but no man mistook the finality therein, "he is to be treated as samurai though of the lowest rank, but if he disobeys correct orders, or tries to escape, you will tie his hands and feet and drag him to wherever I am. You are both responsible."

"Yes, Lord."

"I won't fail you, Lord," Misamoto muttered, grey-faced, some of his terror passing on to the two miners.

"Tell these men they are quite safe. And also that you will be their helper and teacher, there is no need for any of you to be frightened if you obey. Tell them I hope for a quick success to their search."

"The Boss says there's no need to be scared."

"Then why's yous pissing in yor pants?"

"Piss off yorself. I'm . . . I'm to be in charge, so mind yor goddam manners."

"Best watch yors or when we's alone we's feeding you yor balls. Where's the piss-arsed grub and where's the booze an' where's the doxies we's promised?"

"You be getting it soon enough, and best be polite around these . . . guys," Misamoto said cautiously. "They's like a cat with a bee up its ass. And the Boss says best find the gold right smartly too."

"If there's gold we's kin find it, Wotinabey, old cock. If it ain't there it ain't there, right, Charlie?"

"Excuse me, Lord, they thank you for your kindness," Misamoto said, not quite so frightened. He had suddenly realized that if he was to accompany them he would be the first to know about a strike. "They promise to try to find treasure as quick as possible. They respectfully ask if they could have some food and drink and when can they begin."

"Impress it on them it pays to be patient, pays to be polite and to be diligent. Teach them correct manners, how to bow and so on. You are responsible."

As Misamoto obeyed, Yoshi motioned to his aide, who brought out the two short overmantles that Hosaki had had especially made, like waistcoats with ties on them. On the front and back were panels of inked characters on pale silk that read: *This gai-jin is a personal retainer and prospector, under my protection, who is allowed, provided he has official guides with correct papers, to prospect anywhere within my domain. All are ordered to assist in this work.* Each panel bore his seal. "Tell them they are to wear it always and it will give them safe passage—explain what the writing says."

Again Misamoto obeyed without thought and showed the two men how to wear them. Cautiously now, they pretended a patience and humility alien to their nature and upbringing. "Charlie," the Cornishman whispered, adjusting the tie strings, hardly moving his lips to speak like most ex-cons—he had had four years' hard labor in the Australian outback for claim jumping: "In for a penny, in for a fuckin' quid."

The American grinned suddenly, more at ease. "I hope there's more than a quid's worth, old buddy. . . ."

Yoshi watched them. When he was satisfied he motioned to Misamoto. "Take them with you and wait in the courtyard."

Once they had gone, after bowing correctly without assistance this time, he sent everyone out of hearing range, except Inejin. "Sit down, old friend." He motioned to the steps where the old man could sit comfortably—his left hip crushed in a fall from a horse, making it impossible for him to kneel. "Good. Now, what news?"

"Everything and nothing, Lord." For three centuries Inejin and his forefathers had served this branch of the Toranagas. As a hatomoto he had no fear of speaking the truth but the obligation to do so: "The land has been worked diligently and manured properly, crops grow, but farmers say this year there will be famine even here in the Kwanto."

"How bad will the famine be?"

"This year we will need rice from elsewhere to be safe, and elsewhere will be far worse."

Yoshi remembered what Hosaki had already told him, and was very glad with her foresight and prudence. And also glad to have a vassal like Inejin—rare to find a man who could be trusted implicitly, even rarer to find one who would speak truthfully, the truth based on real knowledge and not for reasons of personal aggrandizement. "Next?"

"All loyal samurai are seething with impatience at the impasse between Bakufu and the rebellious Outside Lords of Satsuma, Choshu and Tosa, their samurai equally discontented, mostly because of the usual problem: rates of pay fixed a century ago are causing ever greater hardship, it being ever more difficult to pay the interest on ever-increasing debts, and to buy rice and food at ever-increasing prices." Inejin was deeply aware of the problem, as the majority of his widespread family, still samurai class, were suffering badly. "Daily the shishi gather adherents, if not openly, certainly undercover. Peasants are correctly docile, merchants not so, but all, except most merchants in Yokohama and Nagasaki, would like the gai-jin expelled."

"And *sonno-joi?*"

After a pause the old man said, "Like many things on earth, Lord, that battle cry is part right, part wrong. All Japanese detest gai-jin—worse than Chinese, worse than Koreans—all want them gone, all revere the Son of Heaven and believe His wish to expel them correct policy. Of your twenty men here tonight, I believe twenty would support that part of *sonno-joi.* As you yourself do, providing it is the Shōgunate who wield the temporal power to effect His wishes, according to procedures laid down by Shōgun Toranaga."

"Quite correct," Yoshi agreed, but in his innermost heart he knew that if he had had the power he would never have allowed the first Treaty, so never a need for the Emperor to interfere in Shōgunate matters, and would never have allowed mean-minded men surrounding the Son of Heaven to misguide Him.

Even so, contrary to *sonno-joi,* if he had power, now he would invite some of the gai-jin in while he had time. But only on his terms. And only for the trade he desired. It is only with fleets and guns like theirs, he thought, that we can deny them our land, expel them from our seas, and at last fulfill our historic destiny to place the Emperor on the Dragon Throne of China. And then, with their millions and our bushido, the whole gai-jin world will obey. "Go on, Inejin."

"There's not much more that you do not already know, Lord. Many fear the boy Shōgun will never be a man, many are disturbed by the less than wise Council, many are shocked that your prudent advice against his journey to Kyōto as a supplicant was overridden, many regret that you do not control the *roju* to force necessary changes: the Bakufu made corruptless, clever—and to stop the rot."

"The Shōgun is the Shōgun," Yoshi said curtly, "and all must support him and his Council. He is our liege Lord and must be supported as such."

"I completely agree, Sire, I merely report samurai opinion as best I can. Few want the Bakufu and Shōgunate cast out. Only a handful of numbskulls believe the Emperor could rule Nippon without the Shōgunate. Even amongst shishi few really believe the Shōgunate should be ended."

"So?"

"The solution is obvious: somehow a strong hand must take control and rule as Shōgun Toranaga ruled." Inejin eased his leg more comfortably. "Please excuse me for being long-winded. May I say how honored I am by your visit."

"Thank you, Inejin," Yoshi said thoughtfully. "No news of any daimyos collecting forces against us?"

"Not mobilizing, Lord, not in this area, though I hear Sanjiro has all Satsuma on a war footing."

"And Choshu?"

"Not yet, but Ogama has again reinforced his garrison troops holding the Gates, and increased the number of shore batteries on the Shimonoseki."

"Ah! His Dutch armorers?"

Inejin nodded. "Spies tell me they train his gunners, and make four cannon a month in the new Choshu arsenal. These are rushed to redoubts. Soon the Straits will be impregnable."

That's good and bad, Yoshi thought—good to have that option, bad that it is in enemy hands. "Ogama plans to step up attacks on shipping?"

"I am told for the moment, no. But he has ordered his batteries to destroy all gai-jin shipping and close the Straits permanently when he sends them a code word." Inejin bent forward and said softly, " 'Crimson Sky.' "

Yoshi gasped. "The same that Shōgun Toranaga used?"

"That's what was whispered."

Yoshi's mind was in a whirl. Does that mean, like my forebear, Ogama is going to launch an equally sudden and all embracing surprise attack—supreme power again being the prize? "Can you get proof?"

"In time. But that is the present code word. As to Ogama's real plan . . ." Inejin shrugged. "He has the Gates now. If he could persuade Sanjiro to pledge allegiance to him . . ."

The silence grew. "You've done very well."

"Another interesting fact, Sire. Lord Anjo has a disease of the stomach." Inejin's eyes lit up even more seeing Yoshi's immediate interest. "A friend of a friend who I trust tells me he has secretly consulted a Chinese doctor. The disease is the decaying disease and cannot be cured."

Yoshi grunted, part from pleasure, part from an ice pick of anxiety that he might contract the same—who knows how or from where—or have it already in his innards, waiting to fell him. "How long will he live?"

"Months, perhaps a year, not more. But you should be doubly on guard, Sire, because my informant says that while the body rots with no outward blemishes, the mind does not, just twists into dangerously implacable routes."

Like the stupid decision to permit the Princess to dominate, Yoshi thought, his head buzzing with what he had been told. "Next?"

"Next, Sire, about the shishi who attacked and assassinated Lord Utani and his paramour. They were led by the same Choshu shishi who attacked Lord Anjo—Hiraga."

"The one whose likeness was sent to all barriers?"

"Yes, Sire, Rezan Hiraga, at least that's what the captured shishi said the man's name was before dying. It is probably false. Another of his aliases is Otami."

"You have caught him?" Yoshi said hopefully.

"No, Sire, not yet, and unfortunately we have lost all trace of him so he must be elsewhere. Possibly Kyōto." Inejin dropped his voice even more. "Rumor has it there is going to be another shishi attack in Kyōto. Many are believed to be collecting there. Many of them."

"What sort of attack? An assassination?"

"No one knows yet. Possibly another coup attempt. The shishi leader with a code name, 'the Raven,' is said to have issued the summons. I am trying to find out who he is."

"Good. One way or another shishi must be wiped out." Yoshi thought a moment. "Could their venom be directed against Ogama, or Sanjiro, the Emperor's real enemies?"

"Difficult, Sire."

"Have you discovered who told the shishi about Utani? About his secret tryst?"

After a pause Inejin said, "It was the Lady's maid, Sire, who whispered to the mama-san who whispered to them."

Yoshi sighed. "And the Lady?"

"The Lady appears to be blameless, Sire."

Yoshi sighed again, pleased that Koiko was not involved, but deep inside, he was unconvinced. "The maid is with us now—I will deal with her. Make sure the mama-san suspects nothing, she will be dealt with when I return. Have you discovered the other spy, the one feeding gai-jin with information?"

"Not for certain, Sire. I'm told the traitor is, or his alias is, Ori. I don't know his full name but he's a Satsuma shishi, one of Sanjiro's men, one of the two Tokaidō killers."

"Inept to kill one when four were such easy targets. Where is the traitor now?"

"Somewhere in the Yokohama Settlement, Sire. He has become a secret confidant of both the young English interpreter and the Frenchman you told me about."

"Ah, him too." Yoshi thought a moment. "Silence this Ori at once." Inejin bowed, accepting the order. "Next?"

"That ends my report."

"Thank you. You have done well." Yoshi finished the tea, deep in thought. Moonlight cast strange shadows.

The old man broke the silence. "Your bath is prepared, Sire, and you must be hungry. Everything is ready."

"Thank you, but the night is good so I will go on at once. There's much to do at Dragon's Tooth. Captain!"

Quickly everyone assembled—Koiko and her maid hastily changed back into travelling clothes and she reentered her palanquin. With due deference, Inejin, his household, maids and servants bowed their guest on his way.

"What about all the food we prepared?" his wife, a round-faced, tiny woman, also of samurai descent, asked hesitantly, delicacies she had hastily but correctly bought at vast cost to tempt their liege lord on this sudden visit—more than three months of their profit for the single meal.

"We will eat it." Inejin watched the cortege trotting away through the sleeping village until it was gone. "It was good to see him, a great honor."

"Yes," she said, and dutifully followed him back inside.

The night was gentle, enough moonlight to see by. Beyond the village the dirt road twisted northwards through the trees, villages every few miles, all the land around well explored by Yoshi since childhood. It was quiet. No one journeyed at this time of night, except robbers, ronin or elite. They forded a brook, the land more open here. On the other side he called a halt, beckoning the Captain.

"Sire?" the Captain asked.

To their growing excitement, Yoshi twisted in his saddle and pointed east and south, back towards the coast. "I am changing my plan," he said as though it were a sudden decision and not one planned over many days. "Now we go that way, to the Tokaidō, but we bypass the first three barriers, then cut back onto the road just after dawn."

There was no need to ask where they were heading. "Forced march, Sire?"

"Yes. No further talking. Lead off!" A hundred and twenty leagues, ten or eleven days, he thought. Then Kyōto and the Gates. My Gates.

25

YOKOHAMA

In the late afternoon of the same day Hiraga ducked into the lee of a shack on the edge of Drunk Town where a small, grimy sailor waited nervously. "Gimme the money, mate," the man said. "You got it, eh?"

"Yes. Gun, p'rease?"

"One day you's a toff, now you's a poxy nuffink." The man was grizzly-faced and suspicious, a wicked knife in his belt, another in a forearm holster. When Hiraga had first talked to him on the beach, he had been wearing his Tyrer-arranged clothes. Today he wore a dirty laborer's woolen smock, coarse trousers and scuffed boots. "Wot's yor game?"

Hiraga shrugged, not understanding him. "Gun, p'rease."

"Gun, is it? I's the gun right enough." The shifty little eyes darted around, across the weed-infested, scrap heap strewn area between Drunk Town and the Japanese village—called No Man's Land by the locals—but could sense no alien watchers. "Where's brass?" he said sullenly. "The money, for crissake, the Mex!"

Hiraga reached into the pocket of the smock, everything feeling uncomfortable and outlandish, the clothes bought especially for today. Three Mexican silver dollars glittered in his hand. "Gun, p'rease."

Impatiently the sailor reached into his shirt and showed the Colt. "You gets it when I gets the money."

"Bu'rret, p'rease?"

A filthy rag from the man's trouser pocket revealed a dozen or so cartridges. "A bargin's a bargin and me word's me word." The sailor reached for the money but before he could take it Hiraga's hand closed.

"Not sto'ren, yes?"

" 'Course not stolen, come on, for crissake!"

Hiraga opened his fist. Greedily the coins were grabbed and examined carefully to ensure they were not clipped or forged, all the time the crafty eyes darting this way and that. When he was satisfied he passed over the Colt and bullets and got up. "Don't get caught with it, matey, or you'll swing: 'course it's stolen." He leered and scuttled away like the rat he resembled.

Hiraga hunched down as he went back to the comparative safety of the Japanese village—safe only so long as the riffraff and drunks did not decide to rampage. There were no police or sentries to protect the villagers. Only an occasional naval or army patrol passed along their main street and these men rarely took their side in any ruckus.

It had taken Hiraga many days to arrange the purchase—naturally he could not ask Tyrer's assistance. No one in the Yoshiwara possessed one. Raiko had said queasily: 'Only gai-jin have them, Hiraga-san, so sorry. Dangerous for civilized person to be caught with one.'

Akimoto said with a grin, 'If my cousin wants one, then get him one, Raiko! You can do anything, *neh*? For payment I will take you to bed without fee . . .' He ducked as she threw a cushion at him, laughing with him.

Raiko said, fanning herself, 'Ah, Hiraga-san, so sorry, I beg you to take this naughty man away, two of my girls have already demanded a day off to soothe their yin from the onslaught of his yang . . .'

When they were alone, Akimoto said seriously, 'Perhaps you should change your mind, forget the gun. Let me try and persuade Ori to meet us here.'

Hiraga shook his head, glad for the company of his good-natured cousin. 'Ori has a gun, he will use it against us the moment he sees us. I have tried every way to snare him out of Drunk Town and failed. If I ambush him with a gun there, it will seem a gai-jin did it. Any day he will try to get at that girl again and then I'm finished here.'

'Perhaps he will tire of waiting. Every man in the village has been told to watch out for him, and no one is to sneak him in by sea.'

'Who dare trust a villager?'

Akimoto said heavily, 'Then when you get a gun, let me do it.' He was much bigger than Hiraga, who had not recognized him when he arrived, since he too had cut his hair in similar fashion.

Eventually Hiraga had accosted the sailor on the beach, pretending to be a visiting Chinese trader from Hong Kong and had struck a deal, his only proviso that the gun should not be stolen. But of course it would be stolen . . .

Akimoto was waiting for him in their dwelling in a village alley they now rented by the month. "Eeee, Cousin, please excuse me," he said, laughing, "no need to ask if you got it, but you look so funny in those clothes, if our shishi comrades could see you . . ."

Hiraga shrugged. "This way I can pass for any of the gai-jin coolies, wherever they come from. All kinds of gai-jin and coolies dress like this in Drunk Town." He eased himself more comfortably, sore in the crotch. "I cannot understand how they can wear such heavy clothes and cramping trousers and tight coats all the time—and when it's hot, eeee, they're terrible, and you sweat a fountain." While he talked he checked the action of the Colt, testing its weight, aiming it. "It's heavy."

"Saké?"

"Thank you, then I think I will rest till sunset." He loaded the revolver, swigged some saké and lay down, pleased with himself. His eyes closed. He began to meditate. When at peace he let himself drift. In moments he slept. At sunset he awoke. Akimoto was still on guard. He looked out of the tiny window. "No storm or rain tonight," he said, then pulled out a scarf and tied it around his head as he had seen low-class gai-jin and sailors do.

Suddenly Akimoto was filled with dread. "And now?"

"Now," he said, hiding the gun under his belt, "now for Ori. If I do not return, you kill him."

Most villagers on the streets did not recognize him, the few who did bowed nervously as to a gai-jin and not a samurai, as they had been ordered. To most gai-jin eyes, in his European attire he would be just another Eurasian or Chinese trader from Hong Kong or Shanghai or Manila, the quality of his clothes and bearing foretelling his position and wealth: 'But never forget, Nakama-san,' Tyrer had warned him continually, 'however rich you appear, smart clothes won't protect you from harassment or insults from riffraff if you go alone into Drunk Town, or anywhere.'

The first time he had gone looking for Ori, the moment the shoya had told him Ori had disobeyed him, he had stormed into Drunk Town wearing his Tyrer clothes. Almost at once he had been cornered by a rowdy group of drunks who surrounded him, jeering and cursing him, then started to attack. Only his skill in karate, still an unknown art to gai-jin, had saved him and he had retreated, seething, two broken heads and another man crippled in his wake.

'Find out exactly where Ori is! At once,' he had told the shoya. 'What he's doing and how he's living!'

The next evening the shoya drew a rough map: 'The house is here, on this corner facing the sea, near some wharfs. It is a drinking-sleeping house for very low persons. Ori-san rents a room, paying double, I was told. Very bad that place, Hiraga-san, always full of evil men. You cannot go there without a special plan. It is important he is sent away?'

'Yes. Your village is at risk with him here.'

'*So ka!*'

Two days later the shoya told him that, in the night, the Ori house had burned down, the remains of three men had been found in the ruins. 'I was told "the native" was one, Hiraga-san,' the shoya said easily.

'A pity the whole foul area was not destroyed too, and every gai-jin in it.'

'Yes.'

So life became calm again. Hiraga continued to spend time with Tyrer, content to learn and to teach, unaware how vastly important and informative his knowledge was to Tyrer, Sir William and Jamie McFay. For half a day he had gone aboard the British frigate with Tyrer. The experience had shaken him and made him more determined than ever to find out how these people he despised could invent and make such unbelievable machines and warships, how such despicable people of such a tiny island, smaller than Nippon—if again Tyrer was to be believed—could have acquired the vast wealth necessary to possess so many ships and armies and factories and, at the same time, rule all sea-lanes and much of the gai-jin world.

That night, he had drunk himself to insensibility, his mind disoriented, uplifted one second, in the abyss the next, his kernel of belief in the absolute invincibility of bushido and the Land of the Gods badly mauled.

Most evenings he would spend with Akimoto in the Yoshiwara, or their village haunt, planning and sharing his gai-jin knowledge though keeping the extent of his disquiet hidden, but always strengthening his net around Tyrer, toying with him: 'Ah, so sorry, Taira-san, Fujiko contract take many weeks, Raiko hard trader, contract expensive, she have many c'rients, many, so sorry she busy tonight, perhaps tomorrow . . .'

A little over two weeks ago, to Hiraga's fury, the shoya had discovered Ori had not died in the fire: ' . . . and oh, so sorry, Hiraga-san, but I'm told now Ori-san has become suddenly wealthy, spending money like a daimyo. Now he has several rooms in another drinking house.'

'Ori rich? How is that possible?'

'So sorry, I don't know, Sire.'

'But you do know where his new house is?'

'Yes, Sire, here—here is the map, so sorry th—'

'Never mind,' Hiraga had said furiously. 'Tonight burn him out again.'

'So sorry, Hiraga-san, that is no longer easy.' The shoya was outwardly penitent, inwardly just as furious that his first and immediate solution to the mad ronin had not achieved the purpose he had paid for. 'It is no longer easy because this house is isolated and it seems he has many bodyguards, gai-jin bodyguards!'

Icily Hiraga had considered the consequences. He sent a honeyed letter to Ori by one of the villagers who sold fish in Drunk Town, saying how delighted he was to hear Ori was alive and not dead in the dreadful fire as he had heard, also that he was prospering and could they meet in the Yoshiwara that evening as Akimoto also wanted to discuss shishi matters of great importance.

Ori had replied by letter at once: 'Not in the Yoshiwara or anywhere, not until our *sonno-joi* plan is done, the girl is dead and the Settlement burned. Before that if you, Akimoto or any other traitor comes near you will be shot.'

Akimoto said, 'He knows the fire was not an accident.'

'Of course. Where would he get money?'

'Only by stealing it, *neh*?'

Other messages only brought the same answer. A poison plot had failed. So he had bought the gun and made a plan. Now it was time and tonight perfect. The last rays of sunset guided him across No Man's Land and along the fetid streets that were pocked with dangerous potholes. The few men who passed him hardly looked at him except to curse him out of the way.

Ori reached haphazardly into the small sack of coins on the table beside the bed and pulled one out. It was a clipped Mex, now worth half of its normal value. Though still five times her agreed price, he handed it to the naked woman. Her eyes lit up, she bobbed a curtsey, mumbling abject thanks again and again, "Yore a proper gent, ta, luv.'

He watched absently as she wriggled into her tattered old dress, astonished that he was here, repelled by everything about this room and bed and house and place, and the pallid, bony gai-jin body and slack buttocks he had fantasized would allay the fire maddening him, but had only made his need worse, in no way comparing with *her*.

The woman paid no attention to him now. Her job was done except to mumble the customary thanks and lies about his performance—in his case not lies, for what his organ lacked in size was made up with strength and vigor—and to get away and keep her newfound wealth without further trouble. Her dress hung on her thin, bare shoulders to trail on the threadbare carpet, partly covering the rough wooden floorboards. Torn petticoat, no drawers. Lank brownish hair and heavy rouge. She looked forty and was nineteen, a street urchin born in Hong Kong to unknown parents, and sold into a Wanchai House eight years ago by her foster mother. "You want me back termorrer? Termorrow?"

He shrugged and pointed to the door, his wounded arm healed and as good as it would ever be, never with the same strength, or quickness with a sword, but good enough against an average swordsman, and good enough with a gun. His derringer was on the table and never far from his hand.

The woman forced a smile and backed away, mouthing thanks, glad to get away without a beating or having to endure the foul practices she had feared. 'Don' you worry, Gerty,' her madam had told her, 'Chinermen're like any others, sometimes a bit picky, but this bugger's rich so just give 'im wot he wants, give it to 'im quick, he's rich so give it good.' There was little extra she had had to do, other than to endure his frantic battering with stoicism and necessary grunts of feigned pleasure.

"Ta again, luv." She went out, the Mex secreted in the soiled bodice that hardly covered her flaccid breasts, another coin, a twentieth of its value, clutched in her hand.

On the landing outside was Timee, a rough Eurasian seaman of mixed but predominately Chinese blood. He shut the door and grabbed her. "Shut yor gob, you poxy whore," he hissed, forcing her hand open to take the coin, then cursed her in Chinese and guttural English for the poorness of her earnings: "Ayeeyah, why didn't you please the Guv?" Then he cuffed her and she half stumbled, half fell down the stairs, but when safe, turned and cursed with even more venom. "I'll tell Ma Fortheringill 'bout yer, she'll do yer!"

Timee spat after her, knocked and reopened the door. "*Musume* gud, Guv, heya?" he asked unctuously.

Now Ori sat at an old table by the window. He wore a rough shirt and breeches with bare legs and feet, his short sword-knife in a belt holster. The money sack was on the table. He saw the narrowed eyes staring at it. Carelessly he found another Mex and tossed it. The heavy-shouldered man caught it expertly, touched his forelock and smirked,

his few remaining teeth broken and yellowed. "Thankee, Guv. Grub?"
He rubbed his big belly. "Grub, *wakarimasu ka*?" Their communication was with sign language and a little pidgin, and he was chief
bodyguard. Another watched downstairs in the bar. A third in the alley.

Ori shook his head. "No," he said, using one of the words he had
picked up, then added, *"Beer-u,"* and waved him away. Alone at last he
stared out of the window. The glass was cracked and fly encrusted, a
corner missing, opening on to the drab facade of another ramshackle,
wooden hostel opposite, ten yards away. The air smelt dank and his
skin felt filthy, and crawled at the thought of that woman's body in
sweating close contact, with no chance for a civilized Japanese bath
afterwards though he could easily have had one in the village, a couple
of hundred yards away across No Man's Land.

But to do that you risk Hiraga and his spies who will be waiting, he
thought, Hiraga and Akimoto and all villagers who deserve to be
crucified like common criminals for trying to prevent my grand design.
Scum! All of them. Daring to try to burn me to death, daring to poison
the fish—eeee, karma that the cat stole it before I could stop the beast
and, in moments, died retching instead of me.

Since then he had eaten sparingly, and only rice that he cooked
himself in a pot in the grate, with a little meat or fish stew made for the
other boarders and bar customers that he made Timee taste in front of
him as a further protection.

The food's foul, this place foul, that woman foul and I can only wait
a few more days before I go mad. Then his eyes noticed the money bag.
His lips moved from his teeth in a vicious smile.

The night of the fire in the other hovel he had been sleeping on a cot
in a tiny, squalid alcove in the back of the bar that had cost him the last
of his money. Long before others in the hostel awoke, his danger senses
honed in a score of fires since childhood had warned him, tearing him
out of sleep, to find flames were already licking the wooden stairs
above, and to see another gourd of oil with a burning rag in its neck
being hurled into the main barroom.

A hysterical dog bounded down the stairs and joined two cats
frantically seeking escape and the three animals began charging
around the room, crashing into bottles of spirits that, smashing on the
cobbled floor, nourished the blaze. Screams and uproar began from
the crowded floor above. Half-naked men started cascading down the
stairs in panic, flames licking at them as they fled into the street.

The stairs caught. Then a sudden tongue of flame soared upwards
along the tinder-dry walls and banister. The barroom was blinding hot,

the air seared as a heat-generated wind roared the fire into an implacable killer. The sides of the front door began to burn furiously, the flames almost barring it. More men rushed pell-mell down the stairs, screaming, tripping over one another in panic through the flames to the outside, some already with parts of their hastily donned clothes on fire. Only minutes had passed since the arson began but now the fire was in total command and the building doomed.

In his cubbyhole Ori was unafraid, fire drilled, safely out of the billowing smoke, hugging the floor, his mouth already covered with a beer-soaked rag, his emergency escape route automatically docketed the moment he had gone into the room. Safety lay always in refusing to panic, and this time through a small, shuttered window across the barroom, well away from the burning stairs that let out onto the back alley.

He was just about to sprint away when he saw the corpulent proprietor in nightshirt and tasseled hat with other terrified men fighting down the stairs, an iron safety box tight under his arm. Furiously this man shoved another out of his path into the flames only to have the same flames convert him into a screaming torch and tumble him with two others into the blazing ruins of the stairway as it collapsed, cutting off any further escape from above. The box flew out of his helpless arms to skeeter across the floor. One badly burned man staggered out of the fire for the doorway. Flames greedily consumed the proprietor and the two other men and seemed to reach for the box, equally greedily.

Without hesitation Ori rushed through the flames, grabbed it up and charged for the window, easily bursting the rotting shutters apart and was out safely into the fresh air and back alley. At once he ducked down and ran for the fence opposite, scaled it and, still keeping low, wormed through the trash and weeds of No Man's Land towards the abandoned well.

Once there, chest heaving, he looked back warily. Flames from the hostel soared into the sky. Men milled about, shouting and cursing. Two men jumped from the upper windows. Others with buckets of water were dousing adjoining shacks and buildings, bellowing for help.

He had not been noticed.

While the noise covered him, he found a broken crowbar and prized off the lid of the box, dismissing the swarming mosquitoes and night insects. The treasure inside made him throb. Quickly he stuffed two bags of coins into the pocket of his breeches, another into his smock shirt. With great care he buried the dozen or so other bags and, in a different place, did the same with the box.

The next morning he wandered Drunk Town until he found a more isolated rooming house that was far from the burned-out wreck. Ten Mex in the owner's hand, and the weight of the bag that remained, brought him immediate, unctuous service, a big room of his choice. The owner, a man with deep-set, brilliant blue eyes— just like *hers,* he had thought, a sudden shaft in his loins—had pointed at the bag: "You'll be bushwhacked wiv that lot, young woggeroo."

Ori had not understood the words. The man's meaning soon became clear and produced Timee. Also that if Timee was well paid, and the owner well paid, Ori would be safe here or on the street, and when out, his room would be sacrosanct. As an insurance, knowing the danger of putting his trust in these men, with more sign language and patience Ori had made it also clear that these two bags were only a small part of his wealth that was safely under guard in the village, which he was ready to spend lavishly for protection and anything else he required.

'Yor the Guv, you name it and you can 'ave it. Me name's Bonzer and I'm Australian.' Like almost everyone in Drunk Town, he scratched constantly at flea and lice bites, his teeth few and twisted, and he stank. ' "Guv?" That means *Ichiban!,* Number one. *Wakarimasu ka?*'

'*Hai, domo.*'

The door opened, dispelling his thought pattern. Timee brought him a tankard of beer. "Guv, I'm getting me grub now." He coughed. "Grub, food, *wakarimasu ka?*"

"*Hai.*" The beer quenched Ori's thirst but did not settle his mind or compare with beer of the village. Or at home in Satsuma or in the Yoshiwara, or at Kanagawa's Inn of the Midnight Blossoms. Or anywhere.

I must be going mad, he thought, bewildered. That gai-jin whore with her toad belly skin and fish smell was worse than the worst old hag I've ever had, yet I enjoyed the Clouds and the Rain twice and wanted more and more.

What is it about them? Is it their blue eyes and white skin and fair brown pubics—in those that whore was not much different from *her,* in all else, yes. Unconsciously his fingers toyed with the cross that he wore, half hidden around his neck. His lips curled in a crooked smile. In the tunnel he had tricked Hiraga. The piece of metal he had thrown was the last of his gold oban. I'm glad I kept her cross—to remind me constantly. And it has been more than useful in other ways, making these stupid gai-jin think I'm Christian. What is it about their women that sends me mad?

It's karma, he told himself with finality, karma that there is no answer, never will be any answer except . . . except to send her onwards.

The thought of her neck in his hands, his manhood deep within, made his flesh tingle and ached him anew as though the other had not happened. Once more the room began to swim and crush him so he swung his feet to the floor, pocketed his derringer, put on a leather jerkin and went downstairs.

"Guv?" Timee coughed and got up from a plate piled with rice and stew to go with him, but he waved him back and the other man to guard upstairs and went outside.

Hiraga saw him at once. He was on the other side of the busy dirt street, sitting on a bench outside a dingy bar. In front of him was an untouched gourd of beer and around were noisy men, drinking or standing or dead drunk on benches, or heading homewards for their dormitories or rooming houses, or favorite bar or gambling rooms that crowded together here in a slum as bad or worse than any in London town. The men were a polyglot of European, Asian and mixed-race laborers and workers, armed with at least a knife and dressed similarly to him, coming from their day's toil in sail-making shops or ship's chandlers, or mechanics from the machine shops, a new profession, or from any one of the dozens of services to do with ships. Along with beggars and bums were bakers and butchers and brewers and moneylenders and others who supported this part of Yokohama or fed off it, separate from the village and 'Nob Town' as they all called the traders' sector, by mutual consent.

'In Drunk Town,' Tyrer had explained to him, 'there are perhaps a hundred and fifty souls, most are drifters. They've few rules. It's every man for himself but woe betide anyone caught stealing, the immediate mob would beat him half to death. They've no law except army and navy patrols searching for deserters, or just trying to keep the peace between the services, breaking up fights or riots. Beer and gin parlors—gin's a rotgut that will kill if you're not careful—they're open as long as there're customers, so are the gambling dens. Don't try any of them or Ma Fortheringill's, she loathes Japanese because of our cut-rate Yoshiwara—bless it! At the far end, near the South Gate, off Hog Lane, is the worst part of Drunk Town. I've never been there, best stay away from it too, that's where the most depraved and lost try to survive. Opium, beggars, scum, male prostitutes. Abattoir. Cemetery. Disease. And multitudes of rats . . .'

The little that Hiraga had understood had made him want, even more, to see everything for himself. Tonight was his first opportunity. Except for a few absent curses that would apply to anyone, no one bothered him as he trailed Ori easily, just enough light in the darkening sky.

His prey meandered towards the shore, seemingly without purpose and without any of the bodyguards he had been warned against. His excitement notched higher. The revolver in his pocket felt good to his touch. His fingers ached to grip it and aim it and pull the trigger to end the menace to his future here, then to begin his controlled retreat to safety through No Man's Land, or along the beach to the Legation.

Now they were nearing the small main square beside the promenade and shore where bars and eating and rooming houses fought for custom. This was the far end of the Settlement, the narrowest part, and jammed between the sea and encircling fence where the South Gate was. As at the North Gate, the fence was strong and high and went into the surf. The only opening was the barricaded guarded South Gate.

The square was clogged. Mostly British soldiers, sailors, and merchant seamen with a few French, American and Russians, and Eurasians. Ori eased through them to stand on the edge of the promenade. He stared at the sea. The sea had a three-foot swell and was black and greasy. Northwards, half a mile away, he could see the lights of the trading houses coming on, and in the French Legation. And in the upper story of Struan's, which, with Brock's, dominated the waterfront.

Tonight? Should I try tonight?

His feet began to take him that way. A sudden rumbling and the sound like that of an express train just a few feet below the surface rushed at them, the earth heaved and with everyone else in the square, he tottered, nauseated, and went down on his hands and knees, holding on to the earth as it shook and rose and fell and stopped. A moment of silence that seemed to shriek to the skies. Now a few whimpers and shouts and curses that were cut short as another shock took them. Again the earth reared, not as bad as before but bad enough, and the shakes went on and on and heaved and shuddered and stopped. Tiles cascaded off a roof. People scuttled or crawled to safety. Silence again that was almost palpable, men silent, gulls silent, animals silent. Earth waiting, everything waiting. Hugging the ground, praying, cursing, praying. Waiting.

"Is it over, for God's sake?" someone called out.

"Yes . . ."

"No . . ."

"Wait, I th—"

Another rumble. Wails of fear. The noise peaked, the earth twisted and cried out and became still again. Several shacks collapsed. Shouts for help. No one moved.

Again everyone held their breath. Waiting. Moans and prayers and whimpers and supplications and curses. Waiting for the next one. The big one. Waiting, but nothing more.

Yet.

Moments that became an eternity of waiting. Then Ori sensed that it was over and got up, the first in the square, heart dancing that he was not dead this time, that he was alive and untouched and safely reborn but instinctively ready for the next danger, an immediate dash from fire that was a normal aftermath and the greatest hazard to be endured. Every earthquake was someone's nemesis, a rebirth for all others and, from time immemorial, to be treated as such by those who lived in the Land of the Gods that was also called the Land of Tears.

Abruptly Ori's stomach had a quake of its own and fell away. Across the square, above the mass of people still grounded, many retching and cursing, he saw Hiraga standing alone watching him. Fifty yards behind Hiraga most of the samurai guards were also on their feet—some studying the two of them curiously.

At almost the same instant that Ori had sensed the earthquake had ended and had jumped up, Hiraga and the samurai had spontaneously done the same, experiencing identical, ecstatic relief and rebirth, Hiraga not realizing he was on his feet until he saw Ori staring at him. His face closed. At once he started towards him, the square rapidly coming to life as men noisily scrambled or staggered erect. Blindly Ori took to his heels, but frightened, angry men, some laughing hysterically, others wailing thanks to God, barred his escape—and Hiraga's pursuit—with cries of "Wot the devil's up with you . . ."

"Who the hell're you pushing, for crissake … ."

"Hey, he's a bloody Jappo . . ."

Then someone bellowed, "FIRE! LOOK!"

With everyone else Ori looked northwards. At the other end of the promenade a building was on fire. He recognized it as the two-story Struan headquarters. Perhaps next door. Careless of anyone, Ori broke out of the throng in a rush.

Hiraga pushed forward after him but at that moment a nearby gin bar collapsed, scattering people into his path, sending him reeling and others trampling him. He fought to his feet amidst the uproar. In this part of the square men were milling around aimlessly, blocking him. For a second he caught a brief sight of Ori, then the ruins of the bar began to blaze and the crowd surged backwards again, engulfing him.

When Hiraga had recovered his balance, Ori was obscured, and as much as he tried to force a path in the direction of his last sighting, the less progress he could make and the more furious the crowd became: "Who you pushin', for crissake! . . . It's another bleeding Jappo . . . Give the bugger wot for . . ."

By the time he had placated them and retreated and circled, finding a path out to the edge of the square, Ori was not running down the promenade as he had expected, heading for the fire, nor was he going by way of the beach—but had truly vanished.

In Struan's, Jamie McFay was running up the stairs in the semi-darkness amid cries of alarm and "Fire!" an oil lamp swinging in his hand, only the chandelier alight in the whole staircase area and it still swayed drunkenly from the shocks. He gained the landing and ran down the corridor to burst Struan's door open. "Tai-pan, are you all right?"

The room was in shadow but for an ominous flickering glow that danced on the window curtains. Struan lay on the floor, dazed, half dressed for dinner, shaking his head to try to clear it, both oil lamps shattered, the open wick of one that was hidden by the bureau sputtered on the oil-drenched carpet. "Think so," he gasped. "Must have hit my head when I got knocked over. Christ Almighty, Angelique!"

"Here, let me help you . . ."

"I can manage, check her, Jamie!"

Jamie tried the handle to the connecting door. Bolted on the other side. At that moment the carpet ignited, Struan scrambled out of the way, cursing with pain, but before the blaze could spread Jamie had stamped it out. In his haste to help Struan out of the way, he dragged him up roughly.

"Oh, Jesus, watch it, Jamie!"

"Sorry, sorry, I didn't—"

"Never mind," Struan panted, a stabbing pain in his side where he had fallen heavily, more throbbing in his stomach where there was none before and the usual under the healed but angry scar. "Where's the fire?"

"I don't know, I was downstairs wh—"

"Later—Angelique!"

Jamie ran into the corridor, smoke from the far end of the corridor

making him cough. He banged on her door then tried the handle—
again bolted on the inside. His shoulder smashed into the wood near
the jamb and the door flew open. Her boudoir was empty, one oil lamp
was on its side still alight, oil dripping onto the curtained bureau,
another shattered on the floor, more oil everywhere. He doused the
burning wick and ran into the bedroom. She was propped in the four-
poster, as pale as her peignoir, eyes fixed on the swaying oil chandelier
that was incongruously, merrily alight.

"You all right, Angelique?"

"Oh, Jamie . . ." she said hesitantly, her voice sounding far away.
"Yes, I'm—I was just—just lying down before dressing for dinner
then the room started rocking. I—I thought I was dreaming then the
lamps shattered and . . . *mon Dieu,* it was the noise of the building
shifting that frightened me the most. . . . Oh, is Malcolm . . ."

"Yes, best get dressed quick as you can. Hurr—"

The fire alarm bell at the nearby Harbor Master's office began
tolling, startling them. With sudden apprehension she smelt the smoke
and heard the muffled shouts from outside and saw the glow through
the window curtains and gasped, "We're on fire?"

"Not to worry for the moment but best get dressed quick as you can
and come next door, I'll unbolt the connecting door." He hurried out.
She slid out of bed. Under her peignoir she wore pantaloons and a
boned chemise. Hastily she stepped into her crinoline that was already
laid out for her and picked up a shawl.

"She's all right, Tai-pan," she heard Jamie say as he unbolted the
connecting door. "She's getting dressed, let me help you downstair—"

"When she's ready."

Jamie started to say something, changed his mind, both of them still
conscious of their lunchtime clash and neither prepared to compromise. He opened the window. In the front garden and street below,
clerks and servants were milling around, Vargas amongst them, onlookers and others from the various Legations gathering, but no flames
that he could see. "Vargas!" he shouted. "Where's our fire?"

"We're not sure, senhor, we think it's just part of the roof. Men with
the fire captain are already there but Brock's upper story is alight."

Jamie could not see next door so he hurried back into Angelique's
boudoir and pulled the curtains aside. Fire had taken a good hold of the
front of Brock's—a two-story structure similar to Struan's—where the
main bedrooms would be. Smoke billowed from the open windows. He
could see teams of men passing along pails of water, trying to douse the
fire, Norbert Greyforth supervising—the Brock fire teams drilled as

often and as ruthlessly as he himself had drilled Struan's. Whipped by the breeze, flames were being dragged with the smoke to reach across the gap.

Just my luck to be burned out by their godrotting fire, he thought sourly then leaned out of the window. "Vargas," he shouted, "get men and water up here—douse this side! When we're clear, help Norbert." I hope the bugger burns and all of Brock's with him, that'd solve the stupid duel for all time.

There were no other fires that he could see from here, other than one far down the promenade in Drunk Town and two in the Yoshiwara. The smell of burning wood and oil and clothing and the tar that they used on the roofs overpowered everything, though there was a taste of sea salt on the breeze. Inexorably his attention went back to the flames from Brock's that sought them. The wind pushed the flames closer. He willed them to die, afraid of fire—the croft that he had been born in had burned one foul winter night when he was a child, his father dead drunk as usual and his younger brother consumed, he and his mother and sister barely escaping with their lives and little else, soon to go to the work house and vile years until they were rescued by Campbell Struan, kinsman of Dirk Struan, on whose land his father had toiled.

"Vargas! Hurry up, for Christ's sake!"

"Coming, senhor!"

Now the promenade was packed, everyone in the streets ready to help and give advice, others with much shouting forming a water bucket line from the huge fire tank of sea water that was within easy reach, army units from the tented barracks joining the throng. Samurai were running towards them from the North Gate to help—any fire a threat to them also. Southwards, and on the other side of the canal, one of the Yoshiwara Houses was burning brightly, more cries and alarm drifting on the wind, but that blaze seemed contained and not a major danger and, thankfully, nowhere near where Nemi would be.

The sweat was pouring down his back. He felt sick with relief that Malcolm was safe. Since lunch he had been brooding in his office, furious his search for prospectors had leaked, beside himself with worry over the duel, and his future. Never once had he conceived he would ever be involved in such a quarrel, or be forced to leave the Noble House, or Japan, except for ill health or an accident, before retiring in five years at the ripe age of forty-four after twenty-five good years of service, rung by rung. Now, with Malcolm alienated, and Tess Struan furious with him, his promotion, retirement—his whole future was in jeopardy.

What to do, he had been worrying, then the shocks turned the world upside down, his precarious mortality had been rammed home to him again and then, when the jolts had ceased and he could reel to his feet, his glands and the memory of the debts he and his family owed the Struans had sent him scurrying upstairs, petrified for Malcolm's safety—after all he was in charge and this youth little more than an invalid. Tai-pan? Sorry, Malcolm, Norbert's right, your ma's in command. If you hadn't been wounded you'd have rushed back to Hong Kong when she said, none of this would have happened, you'd be taking over the reins and in a year or so you'd—

"Jamie . . . could you do me up?"

Blankly he turned. Angelique was standing at the doorway, back towards him, the front of the off-the-shoulder crinoline held up and the back open. For a second he almost shouted at her, That bloody dress's crazy, for Christ's sake, we're on fire! But he did not, just hastily did up the top button and shoved a shawl around her and hurried her into the next room where she at once went into Struan's open arms. A team of men rushed past the open door with full buckets. "Best get out, sir . . ." someone shouted.

"Time to go, Tai-pan, all right?"

"Yes." Malcolm went for the door as quickly as he could. With his two sticks he was slow—disastrously slow had there been a real emergency, which all three of them knew, Struan most of all. Now there was tramping above them in the attics, men pounding, the smell of smoke worse, adding to their anxiety.

"Jamie, take Angelique out, I'll make my own time."

"Lean on me an—"

"For Christ's sake, do it, then come back if you must!"

Jamie flushed. He took her arm and the two of them hurried out, men overtaking them with empty buckets, others staggering in with a full load.

The moment he was alone, Struan groped back to his chest of drawers, rummaged under some clothes and found the small bottle that Ah Tok had refilled this afternoon. He swigged half of the brownish liquid, recorked it and put it in the pocket of his frock coat, sighing with relief.

Angelique swept down the staircase and out through the front doors. The clean air was welcome. "Vargas!" Jamie called out. "Look after Miss Angelique for a moment."

"Certainly, senhor."

"Please allow me, Monsieur," Pierre Vervene, the French official

said grandly. "I will escort Mademoiselle Angelique to our Legation—she can wait there in safety."

"Thanks." Jamie rushed back inside.

Now she could see that their roof was burning, not too badly at the
moment, but not far away from their suites, the flames from Brock's
still licking the side of their building. Well-trained samurai, kimonos
tucked out of their way and masked against smoke inhalation, had
ladders against one of the walls. Some scaled it as others with signs
and shouts motioned men to bring buckets that were quickly handed to
the topmost man who hurled them where they would do most good. An
angry shaft of flame sought him but he ducked, covered his face and
held on, then once more went back to fire fighting. She caught her
breath, thinking how strong and brave the man was and how helpless
Struan had become, how little he could do to protect her in an emergency, how he was more and more of a weight, more and more of an
invalid, every day more querulous and less and less fun. What of my
future? A tremor went through her.

"Nothing to worry about, Mademoiselle," Vervene said in French, a
tassled cap covering his bald pate. "Come along, you're quite safe.
Earthquakes are really quite normal here." He took her arm to lead her
up the promenade through the men swarming the front, watching or
fighting the fire.

Ori had seen her the moment she came into the street.

He was on the edge of the crowd in the neck of the alley beside the
French Legation near the North Gate. His laborer's clothes and cap
were not much different from those of many men around him, camouflaging him well. From this position he could see most of the promenade, the front of Struan's and the street beside it that came up from
the village main street.

He stopped staring at her and scanned all around, seeking Hiraga or
Akimoto, sure that they were lurking somewhere near or soon would
be, his heart still pounding from his frantic run through Drunk Town
and into the village. The moment he had seen the Struan fire and the
open length of the promenade he knew that he was doomed to be
caught if he tried that way or the beach—and no time to fetch Timee to
act as guard or rear guard.

Not that I could ever trust those dogs, he thought, his heart grinding
even more heavily at the nearness of her.

She was only twenty yards away.

Those who saw her doffed their hats and murmured greetings that
she absently returned. Ori could easily have gone deeper into safety but

he did not, just took off his hat like the others and looked. Short beard, strong face, curious eyes, his hair short but groomed. Her eyes flowed over him but she did not really see him, nor did Vervene who was chattering pleasantly in French.

They passed within a few yards. Ori waited until they had gone into the French Legation—no sentries there now, all had gone to join the fire fight—then he trudged away, down the alley. The moment he was sure no one was watching he scaled the Legation fence as he had done before and went into the previous ambush under her window. Tonight the shutters were unbarred and open. So was the inner door. He could see across the room into the corridor and caught sight of them going into a room opposite. The door was ajar.

Now that he was safe and unobserved Ori checked his derringer and made sure his knife was loose in its holster. Then he squatted on his heels, took a deep breath and began to think. From the moment he had seen Hiraga and, almost at once, the Struan fire, he had blindly allowed his instincts to guide him. That's no longer any good, he told himself.

Now I must plan. And quickly.

The open shutters were the magnet. He slid over the lintel into the room.

26

"WHY NOT SLEEP HERE TONIGHT, Mademoiselle, Monsieur Struan? We've plenty of room," Vervene said.

It was near dinnertime and they were in the main reception room of the French Legation having champagne and Jamie had just arrived to report that their fire was out, nothing serious except some water damage in her suite, a little in Struan's. "If you want you can have my rooms, Tai-pan," Jamie said. "I'll bunk elsewhere, and Miss Angelique can have Vargas's room."

"There's no need for that, Jamie," Angelique said. "We can stay here, no need to disrupt everyone. I was moving here tomorrow anyway. Yes, *chéri*?"

"I think I'd be more comfortable in my own suite. It's all right, Jamie?"

"Oh yes, hardly touched. Miss Angelique, would you like my rooms then?"

"No, Jamie, I'll be fine here tonight."

"Good, then that's settled," Struan said, eyes strange and feeling very tired, most of his pain still drowned by the opium, but not his deep-set rage over Norbert Greyforth.

"Monsieur Struan, you are certainly welcome to stay too," Vervene said. "We have rooms enough, as the Minister and his staff are at Yedo for a few days."

"Oh!" Angelique was openly shocked. Tomorrow André had to collect the medicine. They all stared at her. "But André told me, he told me they were all returning by the latest early tomorrow, after today's meeting with the Shōgun."

"It depends on the Shōgun's punctuality and how the meeting goes—and our hosts are international models for punctuality, eh?" Vervene chuckled at his own joke, adding grandly, "You never know how State Occasions will turn out. It may take a day, even a week. More champagne, Monsieur Struan?"

"Thanks, yes, tha—"

"But André said the meeting was this morning and they'd be back at the latest tomorrow." She fought the tears that threatened to spill down her cheeks.

"What the devil's the matter, Angel?" Struan said testily. "Does it matter when they come back?"

"It . . . n-no . . . but I—I just hate it when someone says something and it's not true."

"You were probably mistaken, ridiculous to be upset about such an unimportant matter." Struan took a large swallow of his refilled glass. "For goodness' sake, Angel!"

"Perhaps they'll be back tomorrow, Mademoiselle," Vervene said, ever the diplomat. Stupid cow, however delectable her breasts and kissable her lips, as if it matters. "Never mind," he said with his most oily smile, "dinner will be served within the hour. Monsieur McFay, you will join us, *bien sûr*?"

"Thank you no, I'd best be going." McFay hesitated at the door. "Tai-pan, shall I, er, shall I come back for you?"

"I'm capable of walking two hundred yards by myself," Struan snapped. "Perfectly capable!" And of pulling a bloody trigger tonight or any night, he wanted to shout after him.

Just before coming over here Norbert Greyforth had taken a respite, the Brock fire almost under control, and, unnoticed by him, had walked out into the street. Jamie, beside him, was directing Vargas and the fire fighters, Dr. Hoag and Dr. Babcott nearby, tending burns and a few broken bones.

Ah Tok's elixir had worked its usual magic and Malcolm was feeling fine and confident, though strange and wanting to sleep as always—he had been fantasizing, to sleep perchance to dream, to dream about loving, about connecting with the Japanese girl or Angelique with ever greater passion, their need as great as mine and ever more erotic. Then, abruptly, he had been jerked into the vicious present.

'Evening, Jamie. Proper bugger, eh?'

'Ah, Norbert,' Struan said, politeness helped by the euphoria. 'Sorry about your bad joss. I think th—'

Norbert pointedly ignored him. 'Fortunately, Jamie, no damage to our offices or warehouse, or trade goods or strong rooms, you'll be happy to hear—just in my sleeping quarters.' Then he feigned to see Struan for the first time and his voice became louder and taunting for others to hear. 'Well, well, if it isn't the young tai-pan of the Oh So Noble House himself. Top of the evening to you, laddie, you don't look so good—is your milk off?'

Struan's bonhomie had vanished. Through his opiate screen he realized he was confronting evil and his enemy was there in front of him. 'No, but your manners are.'

'Manners are not your strong suit, laddie.' Norbert laughed. 'Yes, we're not harmed, laddie. In fact our new mining ventures make us Noble House in Japan and we'll have Hong Kong by Christmas. Best toddle home, Malcolm.'

'The name's Struan,' he said, seeing himself tall, strong and omnipotent, not quite aware of others around him or that Jamie and Babcott were trying to intervene. 'Struan!'

'I like "young Malcolm," young Malcolm.'

'Next time you call me that I'll call you a motherless bastard and blow your head off without waiting for your seconds, by God.'

Now there was a pit of silence around them. The crackle of flames and the soft, baiting hiss of the wind only enhanced it. The news of the luncheon challenge had spread within minutes and all waited for the next move in the game that had been brewing since Malcolm's grandfather, Dirk Struan, died before he could kill Tyler Brock as he had sworn to do.

Norbert Greyforth's mind was working hard. Once again he measured his future and his position in Brock's, considering carefully what he should do—the stakes immense. He was well compensated—so long as he obeyed orders. Tyler Brock's last letter had opened a door to paradise, telling him bluntly to 'ride Malcolm Struan to the limit while he be sick, wounded, and unprotected by my hellcat daughter, God curse her to Hell! There be five thousand guinea a year for ten year if that stripling be crushed while he be in the Japans—thee be taking any measure thee be wanting.'

Norbert would be thirty-one in six more days. By forty, the normal retirement age, the average China trader was old. Five thousand for ten years was truly a princely sum, enough for him and all his generations, enough to buy a seat in Parliament, to become gentry, a squire with a manor house, married to a young bride with a fine dowry of good Surrey land.

It was easy to decide. He put his face close to Struan's and was happy to see the pain under the taut skin—of a height with him now that Struan hunched over his sticks. 'Listen, young Malcolm, you tossed brandy in my face for lunch, you can kiss my arse for supper.'

'You-sir-are-a-motherless-bastard!'

The older man laughed, a cruel jeering laugh. 'You're an even bigger motherless bastard, in fact y—'

Babcott moved between them, his great height and size dwarfing them. 'Stop it, both of you,' he said angrily, 'both of you! This is a public place and these quarrels should be settled in private as between gentlemen.'

'He's not a bloody gen—'

'In private as gentlemen, Malcolm,' Babcott said louder. 'Norbert, what's your pleasure?'

'A duel's not my choice but it's what this bastard wants, so be it! Tonight, tomorrow, sooner the better.'

'Not tonight, tomorrow, or any day, duelling's against the law, but I will be at your office at eleven.' Babcott looked at Struan, knowing that no one here could prevent a duel if that was their mutual wish. He saw the dilated pupils and was sad for him and furious with him. Both he and Hoag had long since diagnosed the addiction but nothing they did or said had made any impression, nor could they prevent access to the drug. 'I'll see you at noon, Malcolm. In the meantime, as the senior British Official still in Yokohama, you are both ordered neither to address each other nor attack each other, in private or in public. . . .'

Never mind about bloody Babcott, Struan was thinking now, even more confident, the champagne mixing nicely with the opiate. Tomorrow or the next day you'll send Jamie, no, send Dmitri to see Norbert—not Jamie, he's no longer to be trusted. We'll do it near the racecourse and the Noble House will give Norbert a noble funeral—and bloody Brock too if he ever comes here, by God! They've both forgotten you were the best revolver shot at Eton, and duelled that sod Percy Quill for calling you a Chinaman. Killed him too and was sent down for it, though the affair was hushed up and settled by Papa for a few thousand guineas. Norbert will get his comeuppance . . .

A stir in the room distracted him. Seratard had just come in and was surrounded and being greeted by the others, André Poncin behind him. Through his mist he heard Seratard saying the Yedo meeting had been concluded quickly after "we broke the deadlock and French compromises were accepted so no need to stay . . ."

His ears stopped listening as his eyes focused on André. The taut, sharp-featured, straight-backed handsome Frenchman was smiling at

Angelique who was smiling back more happily than she had for days. Jealousy began to swamp him but he put it away. Not her fault, he thought wearily, or André's, she's worth smiling at and I'm not good company and not myself, just sick to death of the pain and being helpless. God, but I love that woman and need her to death.

He struggled up, made his excuses and thanked them for their hospitality. Seratard was his usual charming self. "But surely you'll stay? So sorry about the fire—we felt none of the earthquake at sea, not even a swell of any sort. Don't worry about your fiancée, we'll be delighted to have her company, Monsieur, as long as necessary while your apartments are repaired, of course you are welcome anytime." He saw them to the door, Angelique insisting on taking Struan's arm to walk him home.

"I'm fine, Angel," Struan said, loving her.

"Of course, my love, but it's my pleasure," she said, bursting with goodwill now that André had returned. Only a few more hours and then I am free.

Dinner was a great success with Angelique radiant, Seratard full of himself at his success in Yedo, regaling them with his exploits in Algiers where he had been an official in charge of subjugation before this appointment, Vervene all the time vying for her attention to tell heroic versions of what he had previously achieved, all of them flushed by her company and abundant wine, a bottle of Burgundy per man, with champagne before to tickle the taste buds, and now again to settle the stomach. Then André Poncin began telling saucy tales of Hong Kong, Shanghai, and Kowloon where villagers from time to time really believed the Penis Plague was with them again when that appendage would disappear back into their bodies, so all the men would tie a string around it, anchoring it tightly to their necks to prevent the catastrophe.

"Oh, that's impossible, André, and naughty of you!" she said, her fan fluttering, amidst laughter and his protests that this was the absolute truth, sure it was now time for her to leave. She finished her second tall glass of champagne that went nicely with the previous three goblets of Château d'Arcins, more than mellow herself—her relief that André had come back when he had promised, and her pleasure at speaking French for the whole evening, had overcome her usual caution. "Now I will leave you to your cigars and brandy—and naughty stories!"

"But only for a moment," Seratard said. "André is going to play for us."

"Tonight, no," André said, too quickly. "If you don't mind, there are some papers I must ready for tomorrow, sorry."

"Everything can wait, pleasure before business," Seratard said as a genial order. "Tonight we must have music to finish the evening, something romantic for Angelique."

"Let him have some peace, Henri," she said, the wine making her cheeks rosy, delighted that André was clearly anxious to fetch the promised medicine. "You've taken him from his business long enough, after all he's not an official."

"André will adore to play for us."

"Ah, so André is always to be commanded, yes? Then I must command you, Monsieur le Ministre, to excuse him this once . . . and me too, it's time for my bed." She got up, her knees a little weak. They surrounded her, protesting loudly. "But I'm here tomorrow and for at least three days." She offered her hand to André with a special smile. "Now you are free to go, I command you to guard our interests."

"You may count on it, Angelique."

"A last glass . . ."

She allowed herself to be persuaded to take it with her and they escorted her to ensure the bolts on the windows and new shutters of the boudoir and bedroom were secure.

"We decided to replace all our shutters since you were last here." Vervene said again what he had already told her earlier, his sparse hair awry, beaming tipsily, "Even in last week's storm there were no rattles." All eyes noticed the filmy green peignoir and nightdress laid out on the bed that had been turned down invitingly by the heavyset maid who watched and waited balefully. Dimmed oil lamps and their alcoholic haze made the room all the more enticing and her more provocative.

More reluctant good nights and sweet dreams and then she was alone with Ah Soh, the door to the corridor bolted. The maid undressed her and brushed her hair and put her crinoline away in the deep hanging cupboard with her other clothes, lingerie in the chest of drawers, all the while Angelique humming happily, content to be here, safe for tomorrow, elated to be alone and that the fire and earthquake had not harmed any of them or interfered with her plan but had made it simpler.

I will make peace between Malcolm and Jamie, bad for them to be estranged, she thought exhilarated, still thirsty, but soothed and wine content. Thank God for André. I wonder what the Yoshiwara's like, and his girl. I'll encourage him to tell me about her and we can laugh together . . .

" 'Night, Missee" interrupted her. Ah Soh was walking ponderously for the boudoir couch. The last time her maid had slept there, even with the bedroom door closed, her snores had been deafening, further disturbing her.

"No, Ah Soh, no sleep here! You go, come back chop chop with coffee-ah, morning, heya?"

The woman shrugged. " 'Night, Missee."

Angelique bolted the door after her and in the warm light, completely and peacefully alone at last, lazily twirled to a hummed waltz. In a moment her ears caught the muted notes of the piano. Ah, it's Henri, she thought, recognizing his touch. He's a good player, better than Vervene but not to be compared with André. Chopin. Soft, delicate, romantic.

She swayed in time with the lovely melody, then caught sight of herself in the tall mirror. For a moment she studied herself, this way and that, then cupped her breasts higher as she and Colette used to do, pouting this way and that to see if that made them seem more desirable or less.

A sip of champagne, the bubbles tickling, the music and the alcohol nudging her. A sudden excited impulse and she let the peignoir fall, then slowly slid her nightdress higher and higher, coquetting the mirror image, admiring the legs and loins and hips and breasts and now full nakedness of the other person, posing this way and that, using the bunched nightdress to obscure or to reveal.

Another sip of champagne. Then she dipped a finger into it and put the liquid on her hardened nipples as she had read the great Parisian courtesans would do, sometimes using sweet Château d'Yquem there and in other places. Curious that our two most famous courtesans in the center of the world are English.

She chuckled to herself, possessed by the night and the music and the wine. When I have birthed one or two sons and am, say, twenty-one and Malcolm has a mistress and I am ready for my special lover, that's what I'll do—for his pleasure and mine, and before that for Malcolm's.

Another sip and another and then finished, languidly licking the last drop, then, watching her mirror, curling her tongue around the glass, toying with it. Chuckling again, putting the glass back on the dressing table, letting it fall unnoticed to the carpet, ears only tuned to Chopin

and his underlying passions—eyes fixed on the mirror, now the reflected image close, brazenly intimate.

Lazily she leaned forward and turned down the wick, shadows
kinder now, then moved back a little, the mirror person still there,
lovely, voluptuous. Fingers moving with a life of their own, straying,
caressing, heart picking up tempo, fluttering with growing pleasure.
Eyes closed now, imagining Malcolm tall, strong, very strong, sweet-
smelling, leading her into the bedroom, laying her on the coverlets,
lying with her, as naked as she, his fingers wandering, fondling.

Ori had eased the door of the cupboard open in the other room and
moved noiselessly and now stood in the deep shadows near the half-
open doorway watching her, heart pounding in his ears. It had been
easy for him to hide among the cases and hanging dresses and
crinolines, easy to slide further into hiding to become invisible when
the maid opened the cupboard door and closed it again. Easy to hear
the final bolts ring home and to judge when Angelique was truly alone.

In the bedroom half light she lay on the sheets, eyes closed, a little
shudder from time to time, face in shadow, body part in shadow,
shadows dancing as the small flame moved with the air currents. It
seemed to him he waited an eternity. Soundlessly, he stepped out of the
darkness to the threshold. The door clicked closed. The distant music
cut. Her eyes opened and focused and she saw him.

Some sense told her that this was *him*—the murderer from the
Tokaidō, father of the child that was never to be, who had violated her
but had left no memory of pain or ravishment, only erotic half dreams,
sleeping, waking—*and that she was defenseless and tonight he would
murder her.*

Both were hardly breathing. Motionless. Waiting for the other to
move. Still in shock, she saw his youth, not much older than she, a little
taller, sheathed sword-knife in his belt, right hand on the hilt, neat short
beard and hair, broad shoulders and narrow hips, rough shirt, flapped
breeches, strong calves and legs and peasant sandals. Face in shadow.

This's another dream, surely it's a dream, no need to be afraid . . .

Bewildered, she propped her head on one hand, motioning him to
move into the light.

Momentarily fused into the same unreal, dreamlike state as she, his
feet obeyed and when she saw the chiselled features, so different and
alien, the dark eyes so filled with craving, she opened her mouth to say,
Who are you, what's your name, but he thought she was going to
scream so he leapt forward in panic, the naked blade violently at her
throat.

"No, please," she gasped, backed into the pillow, and when he did not understand she shook her head, petrified, eyes pleading, every part of her shrieking, You're going to die, there's no escape this time! "No—please."

The fright slid off his face and, standing over her, heart thundering as hers was thundering, he put a finger to his lips, warning her to be silent and not to scream, not to move. *"Iyé,"* he whispered hoarsely, adding, "No!"

A drop of perspiration slid down his cheek.

"I . . . I won't—won't make a sound," she muttered, terror confusing her. She pulled the sheet over her loins. At once he ripped it away. Her heart stopped. But in that second she *knew,* a primeval instinct in mind had propelled her to a different plane and she felt herself possessed by a latent, newfound knowledge. Her horror began to slide away. Inner voices seemed to whisper: Be careful, we can guide you. Watch his eyes, don't make a sudden move, first the knife . . .

Heart pounding, she watched his eyes and put a finger to her lips as he had done, gently pointed at the blade and motioned it away.

He was like a coiled spring, expecting her to dart for the door any second and scream—he knew he could silence her easily, but that did not fit into his plan: she was to flee for the door in his time, not hers, and scream and scream to wake the enemy, then he would slash once and make sure and then he would wait and when they arrived he would shout, *"Sonno-joi,"* turning the knife on himself and, spitting in their faces, die. That was his plan—one of many he had considered: taking her wildly then killing her and then himself, or just killing her silently at once as he should have done before, however much he wanted her now, leaving the Tokaidō characters on the sheets as before, then to escape through the window. But she was not reacting as he had expected. Unwavering eyes, her hand motioning the blade away, sky-blue eyes asking, not begging, tension there, but no terror now. Uncanny half smile. Why?

The blade did not move.

Be patient, the voices whispered to her. . . .

Again she gestured the point away, unhurried, willing him. His eyes narrowed even more. With an effort he tore them away from hers to surge over her to be inexorably drawn back. What is she planning? Warily he lowered the dirk and waited, ready to lunge.

He was standing close to the bed. Leisurely her hands began to unbutton his shirt, then froze. The cross at his neck flickered in the light, *her cross.* The suddenness that the lost forever was miraculously found again, elated her strangely and, dreamlike, she watched her fingers touch it, trembling slightly, weirdly pleased that he had taken it to wear it, part of her around him forever as part of him was around her forever but even the cross, her cross, did not deflect her.

Gently she eased the shirt off, down his right arm, over the knife, tightly held and a constant threat. Her intent look drifted over him, the shoulder wound, freshly healed, muscled body. Again the wound.

"Tokaidō," she said softly, not as a question though he took it as such.

"*Hai,*" he muttered, watching and waiting and choked with lust. "*Hai.*"

Again the cross glittered. "Kanagawa?"

He nodded, hardly breathing, spellbound, and she was glad that she had been right in the first instant, and now that he was almost naked she was more secure with the plan that had swamped her mind. She reached out and touched his belt, always watching his eyes, and felt a tiny tremor. A current went through her at this victory.

Don't be afraid, the voices said. Continue . . .

His fingers found the buckle. It loosened. The belt dropped away, the scabbard with it. His breeches slid off him. Below he wore a loincloth. With a grinding effort he remained motionless, his weight balanced on both legs, slightly apart, and body throbbing with his heartbeat, eyes locked.

Continue, the voices whispered, don't be afraid. . . .

Abruptly, the image of him in the web that myriad generations of women before her—defenseless in the same mantrap—were aiding her to weave, caused her resolve to soar unexpectedly, heightening her awareness, making her part of the night and yet apart, to watch herself and him, and fingers untying the string and seeing him unadorned.

She had never seen a man thus. But for the wound he was without blemish. As she was.

For a moment he continued to dominate his lust, then his will vanished and he threw the knife on the bed and covered her but she closed like an oyster and twisted away and he did likewise, grabbing for the knife before she did but she had not made a move toward it, just lay there, watching him kneeling on the bed, blade poised, another phallus pointing at her.

In the waking dream, she shook her head, telling him to lay the knife aside, to forget it, to lie down beside her. "There's no hurry," she said softly, knowing he would not understand words, only gestures. "Lie here." She showed him where. "No, be gentle." She showed him how. "Kiss me . . . no, not so cruel . . . gently."

She showed him everything she wanted, he wanted, advancing, retreating, soon to be aroused and then, when at last they joined she imploded to carry him over the crest and them into the abyss.

When her panting had lessened and her ears could hear, the music was still playing but far away. No sounds of danger, only his panting matching hers, body light, fitting perfectly. Belonging. That was what she could not understand—how or why he seemed to belong. Or how and why she could be so thrilled, or consumed with such ecstasy. He began to ease away.

No, the voices told her quickly, hold him, don't let him move, beware, the danger's not over, stay with the plan . . .

So her arms tightened around him.

They slept for an hour or so and when she awoke he was lying beside her, breathing softly, his sleeping face young and untroubled, one hand tight on the knife, the other touching her cross that he wore so easily.

It was my first gift, Maman told me, the first day of my life and worn ever since, only the chain changing. Is it his now, or mine, or ours?

His eyes opened and a shiver went through her.

For a moment he was not sure where he was, or if it was a dream and then he saw her, still beautiful, still desirable, still beside him, the strange, half smile washing over him. Enchanted, his hand went to her and she responded, to coalesce again but now without anger or haste. Only to prolong.

Afterwards, barely awake, he wanted to tell her how vast the Clouds and the Rain had been, how much he admired her and thanked her— beset with a great sadness that he had to end her life, this life. But not sad that his own death was near. Now, because of her, he would die fulfilled, her death sanctifying the just cause of *sonno-joi.*

Ah, he thought with sudden warmth, in return for such a gift perhaps an equal gift, a samurai gift, a samurai death: no screams or terror, one moment alive the next dead. Why not?

Completely at peace, hand on unsheathed knife, he allowed himself to stray into dreamlessness.

Her fingers touched him. Instantly he was awake, on guard, fingers tight on his knife. He saw her gesture at the curtained and shuttered window, a finger to her lips. Outside whistling was approaching. The sound passed, then went away.

She sighed, then leaned over and snuggled close, kissed his chest, then, so happily, pointed at the clock on her dresser that read 4:16 A.M., again at the window. She slid out of bed and with signs, made him understand that he was to dress and to leave now and to return with the night, that the shutters would be unbarred. He shook his head, pretending to tease her, and she ran back, shadows and the sight of her delighting him, to kneel beside the bed and whisper, pleading with him, "Please . . . please . . ."

His spirit twisted. Never in his life had he seen that expression on a woman's face before, such an open depth of passion beyond his ken—no word for love, not in Japanese. It swamped him but did not deflect his decision.

Easy to pretend to assent, to agree to go, to return with nightfall. As he dressed she stayed very close, helping him, reluctant to let him go, wanting him to stay, completely protective. Finger to her lips, almost childlike, she moved the curtains aside, opened the windows soundlessly, unbarred the shutters and peered out.

The air was clean. A hint of dawn. Sky speckled with clouds. Sea calm and no sound or sight of danger, only the sigh of the waves on the sandy beach. Along High Street only threads of smoke remained of the fires. No one about, the Settlement was at peace, asleep.

He stood close behind her and realized this was the perfect moment. His hand angled the blade, knuckles white. But he did not strike for as she turned her tenderness and concern obliterated his resolve, that and the lust that still obsessed him. Quickly she kissed him, then she leaned out again and peered both ways to make sure it was safe. "No, not yet," she murmured anxiously, making him wait, her arm around his waist.

And when she was sure, she turned again and kissed him again, then she motioned him to hurry. He stepped silently over the lintel and the moment he was safe in the garden, she slammed the shutters closed and the bolt home and her screams tore through the night, "Helppppp meeee . . ."

Ori was paralyzed. But only for a moment. Blinded by rage he clawed at the shutters, her continuing screams and the knowledge he had been duped sending him berserk. Fingers now talons ripped a shutter open, almost tore it off its hinges. At that second the first of the French sentries hurtled around the corner, rifle armed and ready. Ori saw him and was faster and jerked out the derringer and pulled the trigger but missed with both barrels, never having fired a gun before, the bullets whining off the brickwork into the night.

The sentry did not miss the first time or the second time or the third and in the room Angelique cowered with her hands over her ears, exulted, forlorn, not knowing what to think, what to do, whether she was laughing or crying, only that she had won and now she was safe and revenged, all the time the inner voices rejoicing, You've won, well done, you were marvelous, wonderful, you followed the plan perfectly, you're safe, you're safe now from him forever!

"Am I?" she whimpered.

Oh yes, you're safe, he's dead. Of course, there's always a price, but don't worry, don't be afraid . . .

What price? What . . . Oh God, I forgot the cross, he still has my cross!

Amid the growing uproar outside and the hammering on her door, she began to tremble. Violently.

27

Friday, 7th November:

I N THE AFTERNOON H.M.S. *PEARL* returned from Yedo with all sails set and hurtled for her usual mooring in Yokohama's busy harbor. Sir William's flag was at the masthead, other flags demanded his cutter immediately but these were unnecessary as his longboat was already waiting in the roads, the Struan steam cutter beside her—Jamie impatient in the stern. All those ashore who saw *Pearl* watched to see if her Captain was up to his arrogant dash, the wind frisky and his speed under sail making the maneuver dicey. Her bow wave was high, the sea good. At the last second she spun into wind and stayed there quivering, her bowsprit perfectly over her buoy just alee. At once smartly dressed sailors dropped rope hawsers over the bollard and made her secure while others went aloft to furl all sails.

Not bad at all, Jamie thought proudly, then called out, "Full ahead, get alongside," needing to be first at the gangplank to intercept Sir William as Malcolm had ordered. "Hurry it up, Tinker, for Christ's sake!"

"Aye, aye, sorr!" Tinker, the Struan coxswain, beamed toothlessly, anticipating him with throttles full forward. He was an old hand, a pigtailed, tattooed, greying bosun's mate off one of their clippers and he zipped passed Sir William's eight-oared cutter to their chagrin, spat tobacco juice good-naturedly, gave them the finger and took possession of the slot. Jamie jumped onto the gangway. At the main deck he raised his top hat to the officer of the deck, a fresh-faced midshipman. "Permission to come aboard, message for Sir William."

The midshipman saluted him back. "Certainly, sir."

"What is it, Jamie, what the devil's wrong now?" Sir William called down from the bridge, Phillip Tyrer and Captain Marlowe beside him.

"Sorry, sir, the Settlement's in a bit of an uproar and Mr. Struan thought I should give you the details."

Marlowe said, "You can use my cabin, Sir William."

"Thank you. Best you come along too, after all you're 'Admiral in charge of our Naval Defense,' however temporary."

Marlowe laughed. "I could certainly use the salary, sir, if not the rank, however temporary."

"Wouldn't we all! Come along, you too, Phillip." They followed him, Marlowe last. Before Marlowe left the bridge, he beckoned his Number One. "Engine room to get steam up, all cannon cleaned, oiled and made ready, ship's company prepared for battle stations."

In the small, austere stern cabin, with a bunk, private head and chart table, they sat down. "Well, Jamie?"

"First, Sir William, the tai-pan and all traders want to congratulate you on a successful meeting."

"Thank you. What uproar?"

"There's been trouble: early this morning a Jappo tried to break into Angelique's bedroom in the French Legation, the sentries shot him, killed him. Dr. Hoag and Dr. Babcott w——"

"Christ Almighty, was she hurt? Touched?"

To their relief Jamie shook his head. "No, sir, she said she heard him fumbling with the shutters and began screaming bloody murder an——"

"Then it *was* someone, like last time!" Tyrer burst out. "Not the wind rattling the shutters!"

"We're inclined to think so." Jamie ran on quickly, "Babcott and Hoag were summoned—she was in shock, not hurt as I said but shaking. They took a look at the dead man and at once Hoag said he was the same bugger he operated on in Kanagawa . . ." Phillip Tyrer gasped and Marlowe looked at him quickly. "The same we suspect was one of Canterbury's murderers, same man who might have been at our Kanagawa Legation and Captain Marlowe and Pallidar tried to catch."

"I'll be damned!" Sir William glanced at Tyrer who had blanched. "Do you think you could identify him, Phillip?"

"I don't know, I don't think so. Malcolm might be able to, I don't know."

Sir William's mind had hurled him onwards: If this is the same man then both probable murderers are dead so how does this affect our demand for indemnity? "French Legation, eh? Astonished they shot the bugger, their security's abominable at the best of times and marksmanship worse. But why was the man there, was he after her or what?"

"We've no idea, sir. It also turns out he was Catholic—at least he was wearing a cross. Wh—"

"That's curious! But ... but wait a minute, Angelique there? I thought she had moved back to Struan's."

"She had but her quarters were fire damaged. I forgot to mention, after the earthquake, sir, we had a small fire, us and also Norbert. The—"

"Anyone hurt?"

"No, sir, thank God, nor anywhere in the Settlement far as we know. The French offered her accommodation but th—"

"Was Malcolm Struan staying there too?"

Jamie sighed at the continual interruptions. "No, sir, he was at our place."

"Then you can't have had much damage."

"No, sir, fortunately, and not much in the whole Settlement though Norbert lost most of his upper floor."

"Well, that should please you. So the girl wasn't touched, the assailant's dead, so what's the fuss about?"

"I've been trying to tell you, sir," Jamie said, then rushed on, refusing this time to be interrupted by Sir William's shocked questions. "Some of the morons in Drunk Town, aided I'm sorry to say by some of our more stupid traders, decided that every Jappo in the village was responsible so a couple of hours ago a mob of them started beating up anyone they could find, that brought samurai steaming in, troops and Navy fellows confronted them and now there's a standoff, both sides armed, reinforced and getting grimmer by the minute, some of our cavalry there, the General's in command and bristling to order a charge like the Light Brigade at Balaclava."

Bloody fool, Sir William thought. "I'll go ashore at once."

Marlowe said, "I'll send a detachment of marines with you, sir. Orderly!"

The cabin door opened instantly. "Yessir?"

"Marine Captain and ten marines with a signalman to the main deck gangway on the double!" Then to Jamie, "Where's the riot, exactly?"

"The south end of the village, near No Man's Land."

"Sir William, I'll be standing off, close in. Any trouble, use my signalman and you can order up a barrage."

"Thank you, but I doubt if I'll need naval support."

Jamie said, "Another problem is—"

"When we're in the cutter." Sir William was already halfway to the main deck. "We'll take yours, it's faster. Head for the Drunk Town wharf."

In moments the Struan cutter was at full speed, marines crowded into the stern, Sir William, Jamie and Tyrer in relative comfort in the midship cabin. "Now, Jamie, another problem?"

"It's Mr. Tyrer's not-so-tame samurai, Nakama." Jamie glanced at Phillip briefly. "Part of the mob attacked him but he broke away, somehow got some swords and fought back, cut one drunk, an Aussie, but not badly, and would have killed the rest if they hadn't fled. Some of them got guns, rushed back and nearly blew him away so he retreated into a village store, we think there may be some samurai with him—and there's a dozen or so maniacs surrounding the place, ready to lynch him."

Sir William gasped, "A lynch mob? In my jurisdiction?"

"Yes, sir. I tried to get them to leave him alone but they told me to piss off. Nakama wasn't at fault initially, Sir William, I saw him on High Street, that much I'm sure of."

"Good," Sir William said tightly. "Fortunately we've one law for the rich and the same for the poor, and the same for anyone under our protection. If he's lynched we will lynch the lynchers. I'm tired of Drunk Town and their rabble nonsense. Until we get our allotment of Peelers from London we'll form our own police force. I'm Chief. Jamie, you're temporary Deputy Police Chief with Norbert an equal Deputy—equally temporary."

"Not on your nelly, Sir Wil—"

"Then it's Norbert alone," Sir William said sweetly.

"God dammit, all right," Jamie said, not pleased at all, knowing that that job had to be a thankless task. "Norbert, eh? Did you hear about Norbert and the tai-pan?"

"What about them?"

Jamie told them about the quarrel and challenge. "The betting's five to one they sneak off one dawn and one of them will end up very dead."

Sir William's eyes looked to Heaven and he said wearily, "I'm away three days and everything's up the creek." He thought a moment. "Phillip, you'll order both of them into my office first thing tomorrow." His voice changed and the other two men winced at the venom therein: "Advise them both, in advance, that they had both better be wise, docile and better listen to, and be guided by, my gentle homily. Coxswain! Get a bloody move on, for God's sake!"

"Aye, aye, sorr . . ."

"Did you bring my briefcase, Phillip?"

"Yessir." Tyrer thanked Heaven he had remembered.

Hiraga was peering through the slats of the barricaded door of the shoya's shop-house at the shouting, angry men armed with pistols and muskets. Sweat ran down his face. He was choked with rage and not a little afraid though he hid it from the others. Blood from a slight wound in his back stained his shirt—he had discarded his frock coat the moment he had rushed in here to fetch some swords. The shoya stood nervously beside him, unarmed except for a fishing harpoon—only samurai could bear arms, on pain of death.

Trapped with them was a greying ashigaru, a foot soldier, who watched Hiraga with awe and confusion: awe for his fighting ability and because he was clearly shishi, confusion because he wore gai-jin clothes and grew his hair like them and seemingly lived in the Settlement with them, yet was also the subject of these unwarranted attacks.

Stinking gai-jin, he thought, as if a futile attempted burglary by a *baka* ronin mattered—of course the man was just a simple ronin thief and not after the girl, what civilized man would want one of them? The fool was correctly killed for his impertinence, no one was hurt, so why all the violence? *Baka* gai-jin! "Is there a way out the back?" he asked.

The shoya shook his head, his face ashen. This was the first time there had been a major disturbance with so many gai-jin on the rampage. And he was directly involved: had he not harbored this shishi? Even the maniac ronin had been in his house and he had not reported them as he was obliged to do—not only them but *any strangers*.

'There's bound to be a Bakufu investigation,' his wife had moaned an hour ago. 'We are bound to be called before them to testify. Enforcers are still at the guard houses. We will lose everything, including our heads, *Namu Amida Butsu*!' She and their eldest daughter had been shopping at the vegetable market when the first of the mob had rushed through the village shouting threats, upsetting crates, barging and jostling shoppers and causing them to run home in panic.

"So sorry, Sire," the shoya managed to say, "we are surrounded—there are more gai-jin in the back alley."

Apart from the dozen-odd men outside confronting them, most of the population of the Settlement was collected on both sides of No Man's Land. The majority had begun as onlookers out for a lark, but now many were well whipped up by a hard core of rioters wanting revenge. Behind those in the village street were twenty samurai from the North Gate guarding the village. In front were those from the South Gate. None of the samurai had their swords out but all had their hands on their hilts, officers to the fore. The same was true with the troops confronting them, rifles ready, the dozen cavalry sitting on their horses waiting for orders, the General nearby—everyone confidently and noisily spoiling for a fight.

Once again the senior Japanese officer shouted above the clamor for the gai-jin to disperse and once again the General shouted imperiously—to a following roar of approval—the samurai were ordered to disperse, neither side understanding the other, or wanting to understand.

Hiraga could just hear the General among the shouts and countershouts. Fool, he thought, seething, but he is not as big a fool as madman Ori. Good that he's dead, very good! Stupid to do what he did to achieve nothing but trouble, stupid! I should have killed him the moment I caught him wearing her cross—or in the tunnel.

When her warning screams had broken the night's quiet, immediately followed by rifle fire, he and Akimoto had been hunched down in the alley near Struan's, wearily lying in wait for Ori, hoping to intercept him—they had not seen Angelique go to the Legation so presumed him to be somewhere nearby, perhaps even inside the Struan Building.

In the confusion that followed, they had joined the growing mass of half-dressed men converging on the Legation, their laborer's clothes and caps camouflaging them.

In shock Hiraga and Akimoto saw the two doctors arrive and then, in a little while, Ori's body dragged out into the light. At once Hiraga motioned to Akimoto and they slid nervously into the night, and the moment they were in their village hideaway, Hiraga burst out, 'May Ori be reborn gai-jin filth, not samurai! This will stir up a hornet's nest. Sneak back to the Yoshiwara at once, use the tunnel and hide until I send word or come to find you.'

'And you?'

'I am one of them,' he had said with a twisted smile. 'Taira is my protector, so is the gai-jin leader, everyone knows, so I am safe.' But I was wrong, he thought bitterly, the mood of the men outside becoming even rougher.

A couple of hours ago, the moment *Pearl* was spotted on the horizon, he had left the village and walked along High Street, heading for the British Legation with a whole list of phrase translations Tyrer had asked to be done while he was away. He was lost in thought, more than a little anxious to hear firsthand about the Yedo meeting, when furious gai-jin faces jerked him out of his reverie.

'It's Tyrer's Jappo . . .'

'Isn't he samurai . . . ?'

'Hey, monkey, you-ah, you samurai, heya . . .'

'He certainly looks like the other bugger . . .'

'Jesus, that's a fact . . . same hairstyle . . .'

'We'll teach you lot to interfere with our women . . .'

Without warning someone shoved him in the back, knocking him down, sending his top hat rolling away to be stomped into the mucked roadway to roars of laughter while others began to kick him, banging into each other in their haste. This gave him a second's respite and, using his superior physique and youth, he had scrambled up and broke through the cordon with them in ponderous pursuit.

Down the alley by Struan's into the village area, samurai guards running in from both gates to see what was going on. More men blocked access to his hideaway where he had hidden his pistol so he darted into the shop of the shoya, grabbed some inadequate swords and whirled to the attack. His berserk charge caught his assailants unawares, scattering them, three went down, one wounded, and the others fled out of range. Somewhere down the street a man fired a musket, the bullet passed harmlessly, and more men with guns started collecting, and in the jumbled melee of samurai and gai-jin, he and the ashigaru had somehow retreated with him into the shop.

The three men ducked as a bullet came out of nowhere to shatter an ornate vase. From the back part of the house a child moaned only to be quickly hushed.

Outside, the shouting increased. Lunkchurch, well heated and in his usual afternoon brandy haze, bellowed, "Let's fire them . . . burn the buggers out . . ."

"Are you off your rocker? All Yokopoko could catch f—"

"Burn 'em out, by God! Who's got a match?"

When the Struan cutter swung alongside the Drunk Town wharf, everyone piled out and ran down its length into the square, marines in front. Ahead they saw the backs of the samurai confronting this portion of the mob. At once the Captain put their plan into operation. On his command his men formed into a wedge, rifles at the ready, and charged into the space between the two sides and wheeled, the point of the wedge threatening the Drunk Town people who began to give away and split into two groups, shouting and alarmed. Tyrer had rushed over to the samurai, who were equally alarmed by the sudden appearance of the disciplined soldiers, bowed and called out loudly in Japanese,

"Please, Sir Officer, all men to stay here safe. Please to salute my Master, Lord of Gai-jin."

Automatically the nonplussed samurai bowed back to Tyrer and as he straightened, Sir William, flushed from his unaccustomed run, stopped for a moment and faced the samurai. Immediately Tyrer bowed to him, calling out, *"Salute!"* The officer and all his men bowed, Sir William bowed back and now the samurai were back in control.

At once Sir William turned and went into the wedge, which was gaining ground, the people closest to the marines being shoved back by the rifles.

"Get out of the way! Get back . . . back!" the young Captain was shouting, his adrenaline pumping. He was just behind the point of the wedge, and when the way did not clear fast enough for his liking he shouted, "FIX BAYONETS!"

As one man the marines stepped back two paces, fixed bayonets, levelled them at the crowd, each marine picking a target, each becoming a graven, waiting cog of a killing machine that was famed and feared throughout the world. "PREPARE TO CHARGE!"

Sir William, Tyrer, and McFay stopped breathing. Along with everyone else. Immediate silence. Then the evil spirit that all mobs contain vanished and the men here became just a rabble that broke and fled in all directions.

The Captain did not wait. "Port rifles, follow me!" He led the way at a run towards the village where the majority of traders, soldiers, a dozen cavalry, and samurai were gathered, all of them still oblivious of Sir William and his marines.

Again the wedge formed but as they came up to the back of the shouting mass, they heard the General shouting, "For the last time I order you out or I will throw you out . . ." to be drowned under a roar from a crowd that was clearly ready to explode. The Captain decided there was no time to waste. "Halt! One round over their heads, FIRE!"

The volley blew away the noise and the fury and got immediate attention, even from the equally unprepared cavalry. Everyone had whirled or ducked and in the silence Sir William, red with rage, stalked into the space between the two sides. Further down the street Lunkchurch and the others were transfixed. He held a second burning rag in his hand, poised to throw, the first was already on the veranda against the wooden wall, flames spreading. Seeing Sir William and the marines, they evaporated into side streets, rushing pell-mell for home.

All other eyes were on Sir William. He settled his top hat more firmly and took a paper out of his pocket. In a loud grating voice he began: "I am reading you Her Majesty's Riot Act: If this unauthorized assembly does not disperse instantly, every man, woman or child is liable for arrest and . . ." His next few words were lost under general grumbling and curses but, instantly, the rabble began to dissolve.

The Riot Act of 1715 had been promulgated by Parliament after the Jacobite Rebellion that only ruthlessness had contained and obliterated. The new law was designed to stop any unauthorized dissension at its source. It granted all Magistrates or Justices of the Peace the right and duty to read the Act out to any group of more than twelve persons considered a threat to the peace of the realm, the onus on the rioters to hear and obey. Anyone who did not disperse within forty-five minutes was liable to immediate arrest, incarceration, and, if proven guilty, to either a sentence of death or to being sentenced to transportation for life at Her Majesty's pleasure.

There was no need for Sir William to finish reading. The village street emptied but for the troops and the General, and the samurai. "Phillip, deal with them, tell them to go home please." He watched for a moment as Tyrer went over and bowed and the officer bowed back. He's a good lad, he thought, then turned away to put a bleak eye on the General who was flushed and sweating. " 'Morning, Thomas."

" 'Morning, sir." The General saluted. Smartly—but only because of the soldiers around him.

Sir William did not raise his hat in reply. Stupid berk, he was thinking. "Pleasant day, what?" he said easily. "I suggest you dismiss the men."

The General motioned to the cavalry officer who was, secretly, more than a little pleased that Sir William had arrived when he did, knowing too that the Japanese were not at fault and he should have been walking his horses into the rabble of traders. What a bunch of ill-disciplined scum, he thought. "Sergeant!" he called out. "All the men back to barracks and dismiss them. Now!"

The soldiers began sorting themselves out. Tyrer bowed a last time to the samurai officer, feeling very pleased with himself, then watched them amble away up the street towards their North Gate.

"Damn good show, Phillip, you did very well," Jamie McFay said.

"Oh? Didn't do a thing really," Tyrer said, pretending diffidence.

Jamie McFay grunted. He was sweating, his heart thumping, he had been sure that someone would pull a trigger or jerk out a sword. "That was bloody close." He glanced over at Sir William who was deep in a one-sided conversation with the General, now even more flushed.

"Wee Willie's giving the bugger hell," he said softly, smiling. "Stupid clod!"

"He's . . ." Tyrer stopped as their attention was diverted up the street. Samurai were sprinting towards a shop on the east side that had caught fire. "Good God, that's the shoya's house. . . ." He was already running, McFay at his heels.

Several of the samurai had jumped up onto the veranda and began beating out the flames while the others hurried to the big water barrels with their ring of buckets that were kept at intervals everywhere against such emergencies. By the time Tyrer and McFay had reached there the fire was under control. Half a dozen more buckets and the last of the flames sizzled and died. The outer shop wall was gone. Inside they saw the shoya, beside him an ashigaru, a foot soldier. Both of them stepped out onto the veranda. The shoya knelt and bowed, the ashigaru bowed. They muttered thanks. To McFay's astonishment there was no sign of Hiraga, the man he and Tyrer knew only as Nakama. But before either of them could say anything the officer had begun questioning the shoya and the foot soldier.

"How did the fire start?"

"A foreigner threw a rag against the wall, Sire."

"Dog's shit, all of them! You will make a report and explain the cause of this disturbance. By tomorrow, shoya."

"Yes, Sire."

The officer, a pockmarked man of thirty-odd, peered into the shop. *"Where's the other man?"*

"Sire?"

"The other man. The Japanese who was chased in here by the gaijin?" he said irritably. *"Hurry up!"*

The ashigaru bowed politely, *"So sorry, sir, there was no one else here."*

"I distinctly saw him rush in here—he was carrying swords." He turned to his men. *"Who saw him?"* They stared back at him uneasily and shook their heads. His face reddened. *"Search the shop at once!"* The search was thorough and produced only the shoya's family and servants who knelt and bowed and stayed kneeling. They denied seeing anyone. A moment of silence then Tyrer and McFay were dumbfounded to see the officer suddenly lose his temper and begin raving at them.

Stoically the ashigaru and all the soldiers stood at attention, rigid, the villagers on their knees, heads to the ground, trembling under the tongue-lashing. Without warning he stepped up to the ashigaru and belted him backhanded around the face. The man stayed as impassive as he could under the flurry of blows and invective. At the officer's shrieked command the shoya was instantly on his feet and stood unflinchingly while the frenzied man beat him as cruelly around the face, the women and children trying not to wince at every blow, yet motionless.

As suddenly as the beatings had begun they stopped. Both men bowed deeply, their faces now welted. Again the shoya knelt. Formally the officer bowed back, all traces of the tirade gone. His men formed up and he led them towards the North Gate as though nothing untoward had happened. Tyrer and McFay stared after them blankly. In a moment, when it was correct to do so, the shoya got up, the women and children went into the house, and he began to supervise the repair to the wall. Village activity in the street picked up.

"What the devil was all that about?" McFay said.

"I don't know," Tyrer said, both of them shocked at the brutality and its impassive acceptance. "I only caught a word here and a word there—I think it was to do with Nakama, I think they all said he'd never been there."

"That's impossible—I know he was inside that hut. I saw him myself." McFay mopped his brow. "Apart from that, why take all that from that bastard? He was a lunatic. And look at them now, acting as though nothing happened. Why?"

"I don't know—perhaps Nakama can explain." Tyrer shuddered. "I'll tell you one thing, I'm damned if I'd like to be in their power. Ever."

"Hello, Angel, how are you?"

"Hello, darling, I'm—I'm much better, thank you." Angelique smiled wanly as Struan came in and shut the door. She was propped up by pillows in her bedroom in the French Legation, the late afternoon sun coming nicely through the window and the shadow of a guard now permanently stationed outside.

In the early hours of this morning when Struan had rushed—hobbled—to her side, she had resisted his entreaties to move, enough in command of herself to remember that she must stay here because tonight André Poncin would deliver the medicine that would deliver her from evil. No, not evil—yes, from evil, she had wanted to shout: André's going to deliver me from the evil I carry and from the evil I've done. *'Oh, mon Dieu,* Malcolm, I am all right and don't want to move!'

'Please don't cry, my darling, please.'

'Then leave me be, it's all right, Malcolm. I'm quite safe, I always was safe and Doctor Babcott has given me something to stop this shaking, haven't you, Doctor?'

'That's right, Malcolm,' Babcott had said, 'and please don't worry, Angelique's perfectly all right, she'll be right as rain when she wakes up. It would be better not to move her. Not to worry.'

'But I bloody do!'

'Tonight, perhaps she can move bac—'

'No,' she had whimpered, tears spilling, 'not tonight, perhaps tomorrow.'

Thank God for tears, she thought again as she watched Malcolm plod over to the bed, knowing that this Heaven-given weapon against men, thought to be a weakness, was a mighty shield. His smile was fine but she noticed the dark rings under his eyes that seemed strange and an air of weariness.

"I dropped by earlier but you were dozing and I didn't want to disturb you."

"You would never disturb me." His concern and love was so open and so deep that she had to fight to keep quiet and not helplessly scream the truth. "Don't worry, my dear one, everything will be wonderful soon, I promise."

He sat in a chair beside the bed, telling her about the near-riot and how Sir William had stopped it so quickly. "He's a good man in many ways," he told her, but he was thinking: not in others. He and Norbert had been forewarned about their summons into his presence tomorrow morning. At once they had met privately: 'It's none of Wee Willie's bloody business,' Norbert had agreed sourly. 'Let him concentrate on Japanners and getting the fleet back! Listen, the intruder, I hear you identified him as one of old Canterbury's murderers, the other Tokaidō bastard?'

'No, I didn't, I think he was a different man though he'd certainly been shot. Hoag said he was the same one he operated on at Kanagawa.'

'Why was he at her window, eh?'

'I don't know—it's weird. Just a thief, I suppose.'

'It's right weird. A Catholic too. Weird . . .'

Struan saw that Angelique was waiting for him to continue and he wondered if he should bring the subject out into the open, the why of that man, to ask for her ideas and give her his, but she looked so tiny and defenseless that he decided to wait for another time and another day—the sod's dead whoever he was and that's that. "When I come back after dinner I'll bring the latest *Illustrated London News,* there's a great article about the latest London fashions . . ."

Angelique listened with half an ear, avoiding the clock on the mantelpiece that tick-tocked the minutes delicately. André had told her he would return from the Yoshiwara about nine that evening, that she should have a pot of warm green tea ready, and something sweet to eat as the mixture might be foul-tasting. Also some towels, and it would be best not to take any more of Babcott's sleeping draft.

She glanced at the clock. 6:46. It's so long, the waiting, she thought, her anxiety increasing. Then the inner voices became alive again. Don't worry, they whispered, the hours will quickly pass and then you are free, don't forget you won, Angelique, you were so brave and so clever, you did everything perfectly—don't worry about anything, you lived and he died and it was the only way you, or any woman, could have lived—soon you will be free, of him, *of it,* and all that has gone before will be no more than a bad dream. . . .

I'll be free, thank God, thank God.

The relief surged through her. She smiled at him. "How handsome you look, Malcolm. Your evening clothes are perfect."

Her warmth jerked him out of his gloom, everything dreadful surrounding him—except her. He beamed. "Oh, Angel, if it wasn't for you I think I'd explode." Tonight he had taken much trouble to select the right silk evening clothes and the finest doeskin half-boots, pure white silk ruffled shirt and white cravat with a ruby pin that his father had given him on his last birthday, his twentieth, May 21st. Only six more months and then I am free, he thought, free to do whatever I like. "You're the only thing that keeps me sane, Angel," he said, and his smile banished the last of her devils.

"Thank you, my darling," she said. "Explode? Why?"

"It's just business," he said, matter-of-fact, avoiding the real issues. "Damned politicians are messing up our markets in their usual, obsessive pursuit of personal power, money and advancement, it never changes no matter what country, creed or color. Overall the Noble House is in fine fettle, thank God," he told her, sluffing over the crisis they were facing in Hawaiian sugar and Brock's increasing stranglehold over Struan's markets and borrowing facilities.

Yesterday an openly hostile letter arrived from the Victoria Bank, Hong Kong's central bank and Brock-dominated, a copy of one sent to Tess Struan, Managing Director, Struan's, his copy addressed, M. Struan, Esq., Yokohama, For Information Only:

Madam: This is just to remind Struan's it has ignoble debts, and too much paper supported by questionable assets and ignoble profits, the most of which paper becomes due January 31st, and to inform you, Madam, again, that repayment of all said highly unNoble paper the Bank owns is required on due date. I have the honour to be, Madam, yr obedient servant.

Never mind those poxy bastards, he thought with certitude, I'll find a way to outsmart them and all the Brocks. Killing Norbert will be a good beginning. Our managers and staff are excellent, our fleet's still the best and our captains loyal.

"Never mind the Brocks and the rumors, Angel, we can deal with them, we always have. The American civil war has boosted our profits enormously. We're helping the South to run cotton through the Northern blockade for our Lancashire mills and bringing back all the powder, shot, guns and cannon that Birmingham can make, half for the South, half for the North—with everything else our factories can invent and provide, machinery, presses, and shoes and ships and sealing wax. British output is gigantic, Angelique, more than fifty percent of the world's industrial goods. Then we've our tea trade and Bengali opium to China, a bumper crop this year—I've an idea how to buy Indian cotton to boost the American lack—and together with all our usual cargoes . . . England is the richest and most prosperous country on earth and you're beautiful."

"Thank you, kind sir! *Je t'aime*—I really do love you, Malcolm, I know I'm very difficult, but I do, and I'll make you a wonderful wife, I promise, an—"

He had heaved himself out of his chair and stopped her with a kiss—his strong cigar smell and pomade manly and pleasant. His arms embracing her were muscular and strong, one hand straying to her breast and she felt its heavy roughness, his lips hard with the faintest taste of brandy. Just the opposite to *him*.

Forget *him*, the voices whispered.

I can't, not yet.

Bending over her like this was a dreadful strain on his wounded back and stomach muscles so he straightened with an effort though he would have gladly taken her now—had he her acquiescence—whatever the pain. "The sooner we're married, the better," he said, sure that he had felt her lips and breast and body respond.

"Oh yes, please, yes."

"Christmas. That's only next month."

"Do you think . . . sit down, my darling, and rest a moment. Should we discuss . . . when should we return to Hong Kong?"

"I—I haven't decided." Much of his bonhomie went at the thought of having to face his mother.

"Perhaps we should go back next week an——"

"Not till I'm fit." And off the painkiller, he thought, his insides grinding, then I can deal with her and Brock and the bloody bank. Just before coming here he had had the second dose of the day, earlier than usual.

I'll have a last one before sleeping, then tomorrow start fresh. Once a day from now on. Couldn't start today—last night and the problem with Norbert and . . . well, yesterday was especially rotten. "Don't trouble your lovely head."

"But I worry over you very much. Malcolm, I'd never want to interfere with anything, but I do worry about you. And there is something that I feel I must mention," she said carefully. "The trouble between you and Jamie. Isn't there anything I—"

His sudden smile stopped her. "Jamie's all right now, my darling. That's today's good news. This evening I sent for him and he apologized for being difficult. He even renewed his oath to support me in everything. Everything."

"Oh, that's wonderful, I'm so pleased."

Just before coming here Jamie McFay had asked to see him. 'Sorry to interrupt you, but I wanted to clear the air and try to make a peace and try, a last time, to dissuade you from the duel: Norbert will surely try to kill you.'

'Sorry, but it's none of your affair, and I'll certainly try to kill him. I agree it's a good idea to clear the air, once and for all: Jamie, will you obey me as tai-pan or are you going back on your holy oath?'

'Yes, I will obey the tai-pan as I swore.'

'Good. After we see Sir William tomorrow, secretly ask Norbert if next Wednesday suits him—yes, Jamie, I know it's his birthday. The racecourse, behind the stands, first light. On your head keep it secret, don't even tell Dmitri.'

'If you kill him you'll have to leave Japan quickly.'

'I've thought about that. Our clipper *Storming Cloud* will be in the roads. We'll board her and go to Hong Kong. There I can, well, arrange matters whatever happens.'

'I hate this whole idea.'

'Yes, but never mind. You remember your oath and will stick by it?'

'Yes.'

'Thank you, Jamie. Let's be friends again . . .'

Through his haze of excitement, he heard Angelique saying, "Oh, how happy that makes me," and had to make an effort not to burst out with the news that he had set a date for the duel, when his own revenge on the House of Brocks, at long last, would begin. Angel will know soon enough and be proud of me, he thought confidently. "No need to worry about Jamie, my darling, or about Hong Kong. Or anything."

"Malcolm, dear, may I please write to your mama?" she asked, knowing that she must begin to bring the enemy to battle. André had warned her that Tess Struan's power within the company was immense, and influence over Malcolm, his brother and sisters, equally vast—reminding her that he was a minor, therefore without Tess's approval the marriage could not take place for months, and without her benevolence might never happen. As if I needed reminding, she thought. "I want to assure her of my undying affection and my promise to become the best daughter-in-law in the whole wide world."

He beamed at the idea. "Excellent! I'll write one too and we'll send them off together." He took her hand. "No woman so stunning as you should also be so thoughtful and kind. I know she's going to love you as much as I do."

Again Hiraga said, "When gai-jin run away, shoya say me to go quick'ry—he very 'fraid of the samurai, very 'fraid."

"I can believe that." Tyrer shifted in his chair, Hiraga opposite him, uncomfortable too. The sitting room of the small bungalow in the Legation grounds that Tyrer shared with Dr. Babcott was sparsely furnished, with a few chairs, two desks and the smell of ointments and salves from pots of medicaments on shelves lining one wall. Windows were open to the night and though it was not cold Hiraga shivered, still unsettled by his near capture. The moment the rioters had rushed away and he could escape the back way he had told the shoya and ashigaru 'You know what'll happen if I'm caught here! Better silence . . . better silence and a quick beating that will soon be forgotten than a trek to prison which none of us—or your wife and children—will survive. *Sonno-joi!*'

Tyrer was saying, "But I don't understand why one moment that officer was sane, the next a brute, and the next sane again with everyone pretending nothing had happened."

Hiraga sighed. "All so simp're, Taira-san. The captain sure ashigaru 'ried . . . sure not say truth, and shoya not say truth, and men not say truth so he beat them to save face—not say truth to samurai is very bad, against 'raw, so very bad. Punishment correct so everyone happy, no more prob'rem."

"Maybe for them," Tyrer said gloomily, "but we have lots of problems. Sir William isn't at all happy, either with the rotter who was killed—or with you."

"I no prob'rem, I not attack, men attack me."

"Sorry, Nakama, that's not the point. He says you are an irritant, an unnecessary complication. Sorry. But he's right. The authorities will soon know you're here, if they don't already. Then they'll demand that we hand you over—we can't avoid that and eventually we'll have to comply."

"P'rease? Not understand."

It took Tyrer several attempts with simpler words to make his meaning clear, then he added, "Sir William told me to tell you it's best you sneak off, disappear while you can."

Hiraga's heart almost stopped. Ever since he had escaped the trap in the village he had been frantically trying to devise a way to negate the inevitable results of the riot, and of being seen—the samurai officer would surely realize a shishi was loose in the Settlement. No solution had occurred except that he must remain in hiding here. To attempt flight now was even more dangerous. Samurai vigilance would be vastly increased, and if they realized he was Hiraga of the poster . . .

He wanted to scream aloud, his mind disarrayed by the rushing events and the depths of the panic and fear he had endured since Ori's betrayal. Then his ears focused and he heard a key word in Tyrer's rambling on about 'how sorry he was to lose such a valuable ally in his search for Japanese knowledge but there seems to be no way of avoiding it . . .'

His head cleared. "Have idea, Taira-san," he said softly. "Bad for me go now, I sure die. Want he'rp Ing'erish friends, want to be *va'ru'ber a'rry*, very va'ru'ber friend. I know about Satsuma daimyo, know Satsuma secrets. Shoya give me mandy . . . sorry, give me many informations. I can exp'rain how make Satsuma obey, perhaps even Bakufu obey. I want to he'rp. Ask Sir W'rum: I give informations to keep gai-jin safe, you keep me safe and give me informations, fair exchange. Friends, *neh*?"

Excitedly Tyrer thought through the offer: Sir William will surely agree, but only if the information is truly valuable, and only if it comes direct from questioning Nakama himself. That means . . . oh God, I can't! "I'd have to let Willie in on the secret that you speak English. No way to avoid that, and I just can't blurt out that I've been hiding such vital info, I'd get sacked for certain. Can't risk that, not when Willie's in such a foul mood!" Better Nakama leaves before my head's on the block and he's an international incident. "Sorry," he said, in despair. "It's not possible."

"Ah, so sorry, perhaps have way," Hiraga said, and made a final gambit to give himself time. "Have message from Fujiko—eeee, Taira-san, you make great mark on her, now she thinks you very best friend. Mama-san say, so sorry, but Fujiko yesterday begin woman's sick, month'ry sick, so cannot receive you for one, two days." He had seen Tyrer's immediate disappointment, followed by resignation and anticipation in quick order.

Weak with relief, he relaxed slightly, at the same time once again astounded that any man, let alone an important official like Taira would allow himself to show his inner feelings so openly to anyone, let alone to an enemy. These barbarians are beyond belief.

"Here," he continued, offering him the fan with the calligraphy on it he had had prepared. "It poem, Fujiko writes: 'Counting hours, very sad. Hurry hours when your sun shine on me, then no sad, stop time.' " He watched Tyrer take the fan reverently, pleased with his choice of words though disgusted with her inadequate writing skill. Still, he thought, the effect seems to be perfect. "About Chief Gai-jin, have p'ran but first, meeting with Shōgun, Taira-san, the meeting was good, yes?"

A gust of laughter took Akimoto, so infectious that Hiraga joined in. "Eeee, Hiraga-san, brilliant to manipulate the gai-jin like that! Brilliant! Saké, bring more saké!"

They were lolling in their isolated room in the grounds of the Three Carp, shoji windows closed against the night insects. Sprigs of autumn maple in a green vase decorated the alcove. Oil lamps. Their swords on racks beside them, and when the maid had left and they had refilled their cups and quaffed them, Akimoto said, "What happened next?"

"After little fish Taira swallowed the bait, we went to bow before the Great Grouper who gorged on both. I told him that unbeknownst to Taira I spoke some English that I had learned from Dutchmen from Deshima . . ."

"And that's no lie," Akimoto said, and replenished their cups. He had gone to the same school for gifted Choshu samurai at Shimonoseki but had not been selected for the language classes, instead he had been ordered to specialize in Western naval affairs, taught by a retired Dutch sea captain. "*Baka* that I never learned Dutch or English. What did the gai-jin leader say?"

"Not too much. Taira pretended to be equally astonished as we had agreed. It was easy to divert the man with unimportant information about Satsuma, about Sanjiro and his fortress at Kagoshima, some of their history and so on," Hiraga said easily, although the meeting had not been easy at all. The questions had been probing and he had found it difficult to convince the leader his pretended sincerity was genuine. In his anxiety to get permission to stay he had told more than he wished, both about the political situation of the outside lords of Satsuma and Tosa but also about his own fief of Choshu, and even about the shishi.

He felt a new heaving in his stomach, remembering the cold blue, fishlike eyes staring at him that somehow had squeezed knowledge out of him, and the final, curt: 'I will consider allowing you to stay a few more days. We will talk again tomorrow. Meanwhile you will move back into the Legation for safety.'

'Better I to stay shoya, Sir W'rum-sama.'

'You will move into the Legation tonight and stay with Mr. Tyrer, leaving only with his permission or mine. When you are on the streets you will be most careful to avoid inflaming any of our people. You will obey without question or you will be marched to the North Gate . . . at once!'

Again he had feigned a meekness and most abject thanks but inside he had seethed at the man's lack of manners and was still seething, and more determined than ever to implement Ori's plan to burn the Settlement—at a time of his own choosing. All gods, if there are any, curse all gai-jin.

"Saké?" Akimoto asked, a dribble sliding down his chin.

"Yes, thank you." His face twisted with anger. "Ori! *Baka* that he's dead before I could kill him."

"Yes, but dead, so is Shorin. Nothing but trouble, both of them, like all Satsumas. The men," he added hastily, remembering Shorin's sister, Sumomo, "not the women."

"Satsumas are trouble, I agree," Hiraga said darkly. "As to Sumomo, I don't know where to send for news of her, where she is or if she reached home safely—that could take her weeks, and more weeks for Father to send word here. News would take two, maybe three months."

"You asked Katsumata to watch for her. He will have spies out from here to Kyōto. She can take care of herself, that one. You'll hear soon." Akimoto scratched his crotch irritably. To see Hiraga so unsettled was disturbing. "You know we're almost locked in here. The Bakufu

Enforcer patrols have been reinforced and they wander in and out at random. All the mama-sans are nervous and after the riot today, Raiko . . . she will not let us stay much longer."

"As long as we pay we will stay. And as long as the tunnel is safe we can escape by sea if necessary. Curse Ori!"

"Forget him," Akimoto said impatiently. "What should we do?"

"Wait. The gai-jin will provide us with cover—Taira will see to it."

"Because of Fujiko? Eeee, he is mad. What does he see in that drab? I cannot fathom that. She is nothing but a drab." Akimoto laughed and ran his fingers through the stubble of his hair. "Think I will try her one night, just to see if anything is special—even though she's polluted."

"Try her tonight if you want, Taira won't be using her."

"Raiko will already have given her other clients—she's rapacious."

"Yes, but Fujiko's already paid for."

"What?"

"My new arrangement is that Raiko will not offer Fujiko elsewhere unless she and I agree first—so I can keep her available for Taira at a moment's notice, in case I decide. Try her if you want, she is cheap enough."

"Good, I need all the cash I have left. Raiko squeezed a down payment out of me, rumbling about the extent of my credit." Akimoto grinned and drained the flask into his cup. "I want to bribe one of the fishermen to take me out to the frigate—perhaps I can talk myself aboard one of the warships, pretending to sell fish. I must see inside an engine room, one way or another."

Hiraga's stomach heaved, thinking about his own visit. "Perhaps I could get Taira to take me again, with you this time. I can pretend you are the son of an important Choshu merchant, a shipbuilder, anxious to do business with them, but any business must be kept secret from the Bakufu."

Secret? How long will we be secret here? A tremble went through him. "It's cold tonight," he said, to cover his fear, which once again Akimoto politely feigned not to notice.

A few metres away in her own quarters Raiko had finished her makeup and was dressing for the evening. She decided on the new pink kimono. A large heron decorated the back, embroidered with gold filaments. For many months she had coveted it. Now it was hers, paid for with part of the profit garnered from the hugely successful sale of the pearl earrings. They proved to be even more valuable than she had estimated.

Eeee, she thought happily, the kami and gods that look after mama-sans were looking after me that day. A major business coup, all profit except for Furansu-san's part. Money for the medicine was hardly worth considering though she had put a substantial debit in her open set of books. She smiled to herself. The cost was nothing but the knowledge of which plant and who could harvest it, at what correct season and how to make the infusion, ah, that was worth whatever the market would stand.

"The gai-jin princess will be a marvelous, long-term asset," she murmured contentedly, pleased with what she saw in her full-length mirror. It was the only modern one in the whole Yoshiwara, imported especially for her from England, a present from a client. A small frown creased her forehead as she thought of him: *Kanterberri,* the gai-jin who was killed on the Tokaidō by those fools Ori and Shorin. *Baka!* He was a good client and most appreciative of my services in finding him the perfect mistress, Akiko, whose name is now Fujiko—very convenient for us that our Ing'erish gai-jin rarely share their women, prefer to fornicate in secret, with one woman, keeping her secret in our Floating World that is based on discretion and secrecy.

Taira none the wiser, Fujiko a new life and new lover. Good for everyone.

"Mistress? The gai-jin Furansu-san has arrived."

"Good." Raiko made sure the medicine was correct and put it beside the table. When she had kept André waiting the precise amount of time, neither too little nor too much, she sent for him. "Ah, Furansu-san, welcome to my humble House." She poured thimbles of her best saké and toasted him. "You're looking well."

"Health! Ten thousand summers," André replied politely.

She discussed the weather and the state of business and then came to the first point. "Your choice of earrings was more perfect than I thought, your share comes to a little over double what you asked."

His eyes widened, "Jésus, so much?"

"Yes." She poured more saké, filled with glee at her acumen on both their behalfs for, of course, once a business deal was finally agreed between them, it was a matter of face that it was honored exactly. "My bank, the Gyokoyama, found the client, a Chinese silk and opium merchant from Shanghai who was visiting Kanagawa." Another smile. She added delicately, "He indicated that he would be in the market for as many such trinkets as I could offer."

His smile matched hers and he drained his cup and held it for a refill and toasted her, "To future trinkets!"

"Next, the . . ."

"Before next, Raiko. Why he pay so much?"

"In bad times a wise man puts part of his wealth into tiny things he can carry in his sleeve. He's no fool—I considered holding on to them myself for the same reason."

His interest quickened. "What bad times in China?"

"He said that all China was in revolt, famine everywhere, gai-jin business in Shanghai less than usual, though now that the English fleet laid waste the Mirs coast and sank many of the White Lotus pirates, the sea-lanes would be safe for a while and trade up and down the Yangtze would pick up in the spring. Eeee, Furansu-san, I hear they sank hundreds of junks and massacred thousands, many villages now in ashes." Her fear was open. "Their killing power is terrible."

She shuddered, knowing that though Japanese despised Chinese as weaklings, they shared the same great phobia: fear of gai-jin and an obsession to keep them forever out of their lands. "Will gai-jin fleets come against us when they return?"

"Yes, Raiko, if Bakufu not pay reparations money. War, yes. Not here, not Yokohama. Yedo."

She studied her cup for a moment, wondering how she could further protect herself and turn this to profit, more than ever convinced that she must, somehow, quickly rid herself of Hiraga and Akimoto before it was discovered that she was implicated in the Ori disaster by harboring him and them, however righteous *sonno-joi* was. A wave of apprehension went through her and she fanned herself, complaining about the strength of the saké. "Karma," she said, and shrugged off what 'might be' for what 'is.' "Now, some more good news: There is a girl I would like you to meet."

André's heart seemed to skip, and then, when it started again, it was more weak than before. "Meet when?"

"Do you wish to see her before we discuss business matters, or after?"

"Before, after, no difference. Will pay what ask, if like." Again a Gallic shrug and the stark, naked desperation.

It touched her not at all. Why should it? she was thinking. The Yang's hunger for the Yin is the essence of our world and without it our Floating World would float no more.

Strange that the Yang's obsession to join with the Yin—in and out, battering at the gate, more pain than pleasure, desperate to end, desperate to continue, if to end never enough, if not to end moaning in the night—is all so transient, the Yin never so grasping. In that women are blessed, though the gods, if there are gods, have dealt all mortals a cruel hand.

Three times I have tried to go onwards, always because my Yin craved the possessor of a particular Yang—when a Yang is always more or less the same—always useless choices that brought nothing but misery, with no future and twice my passion unrequited. How foolish! Why? No one knows.

Never mind. Now the yearning of the Yin can be quenched so easily, and for a mama-san, toyed with. Easy to employ a Yang, or harigata, or to invite one of the Ladies to your bed. Fujiko, for example, who seems to enjoy the diversion and whose kiss can be celestial.

"Raiko know me, yes?" André was saying, and she thought, Indeed I do. "I know Raiko." Indeed you do not. "We old friends. Old friends always help old friends." True, true, but you and I are not old friends—not in its special Asian sense—and never will be. You are gai-jin.

"Furansu-san, old friend," she said. "I will arrange a meeting, you and this Lady."

He felt weak and tried to hide it. "Yes. Thank you."

"It will be soon. Last, the medicine." She reached down beside the table. The small package was carefully tied in a square of russet silk as invitingly presented as an expensive gift. "Listen carefully." Again her instructions were explicit. She made him repeat them until she was sure he understood.

"Raiko-san. Please, say truth, medicine dangerous, yes, no?"

"Eeee, truth? Am I not a serious person? I am Raiko of the Three Carp. Have I not already told you? Of course it could be dangerous and of course not dangerous! This is an ordinary problem that happens all the time to all girls and the cure is rarely a problem. Your princess is young and strong and so it should be easy, with no problems."

"Princess?" His features hardened. "You know who for?"

"That was easy to guess. How many women are there in the Settlement, special enough for you to help? Never worry, old friend. The secret is safe with me."

After a pause, he said, "What problem possible?"

"Stomach pain and no result, just very sick. Then we must try a second time, with stronger medicine. If that does not work then there is another way."

"What?"

"Time enough for that later." Confidently Raiko patted the silk. "This should be all that is necessary."

28

"Yᴏᴜ ᴜɴᴅᴇʀsᴛᴀɴᴅ, AɴɢᴇʟɪQᴜᴇ?"

"Yes, André," she said, her eyes on the silk-wrapped package. Her salvation sat on his desk. They kept their voices down though the office door was closed against unwanted ears.

His clock chimed 10:00 P.M.

He looked back at her uneasily. "The mama-san told me it would be best if you had your maid with you."

"That's not possible, André, it's not possible to trust Ah Soh, or anyone—didn't you tell her that?"

"Yes, but that's what she said." From across the corridor they could hear the muted sounds of men laughing over the dinner table that she had just left—Seratard, Vervene, Dmitri and a few French officers— saying she was tired and wanted an early night. Going to her suite, by prior arrangement, she had happened to see André in his office. "We'd . . . we'd best check that everything's there."

He made no move to undo the silk. Instead he toyed nervously with a corner. "If Ah Soh's not there to help, who . . . who will dispose of . . . of the bottles and herbs and . . . you can't leave them around, and who will clean up?"

For a moment her brain became addled for, foolishly, she had not considered this problem. "I—I won't need help, there won't be . . . nothing except the bottles and herbs . . . and towels. I can't trust Ah Soh, obviously I can't trust her, or anyone, only you. I won't need help." Her anxiety to begin the treatment and have done with this forever capped all the worries that swirled about her. "Don't worry, I'll bolt my door and . . . and tell her that I'll sleep late and not to disturb me. I . . . it should all be over in a few hours, by dawn, yes?"

"God willing, yes, that's what the mama-san told me. I still think you should risk Ah Soh."

"You're not thinking clearly, no, not at all. You're the only one I can trust. Knock on my door early, like this." She rapped the table thrice, then once. "I'll open it only to you." Impatiently she untied the silk. Inside were two small corked bottles and a packet of herbs. "I drink one bottle at once and then . . ."

"*Mon Dieu,* no," he said, wearily interrupted her, his nerves as taut as hers. "You must do everything in the correct order, Angelique. First you put the herbs to infuse in the pot of hot water you've arranged. When that's done drink one bottle, drink it quickly and don't worry if it tastes foul, use the honeyed green tea or a sweet to take away the taste."

"I've some Swiss chocolates Monsieur Erlicher gave me, will those do?"

"Yes, of course." He used a handkerchief to wipe the sweat off his hands, his imagination taking him down all kinds of lurid passages. "When the infusion is tepid, say after half an hour, sip half of the brew—it won't taste good either. Then relax and wait, go to sleep."

"Will there be a reaction, will I feel anything yet?"

"No, I already told you, no! The mama-san said that normally nothing happens until some hours later—it should be like a—a strong stomach cramp." The more he talked about it the less he liked being involved. What if something goes wrong? *Mon Dieu,* I hope there's not a second time, he thought queasily and tried to push the bad away—and embarrassment—and be clinical.

"It should just be like a stomach cramp," he said, sweating even more. "That's the beginning, Angelique, a cramp. I'll start again: Drink the first bottle, then sip *half* the infusion, half of it, remember you must do everything in the correct sequence—relax and try to go to sleep, the more relaxed you are the easier it will be. When the—the cramps begin, gulp the last bottle, take some honey or sweet, then sip the last of the infusion—sip it, don't swig it down. The cramps will increase and then—then it should begin to . . . the mama-san said it would be like a heavy monthly, so . . . so be prepared with a . . . a towel." Again he used his handkerchief. "It's close in here tonight, isn't it?"

"It's cold and there's no need to be nervous." She uncorked one of the bottles and smelt the contents. Her nose wrinkled. "Worse than a Parisian street toilet in August."

"You're sure you remember the sequence?"

"Yes, yes. Don't worry, I'll—"

A knock on the door startled them. Hastily she scooped up the two bottles and packet of herbs and put them in her bag. "Come in," André said.

Dr. Babcott dwarfed the doorway. "Ah, Angelique, the servant told me you were here. I just popped in on the off chance of seeing you a moment. 'Evening, André."

" 'Evening, Monsieur."

"Ah, Doctor, I'm really all right," she said, a sudden twinge of disquiet under his penetrating gaze. "No need t—"

"Just wanted to take your temperature, count your pulse and see if you needed a sedative. Always best to check." When she began to protest he added firmly and kindly, "Best to check, Angelique, always safer to check, won't take a minute."

"Come along then." She said good night to André and led the way down the corridor to her suite. Ah Soh was waiting in her boudoir. "Ah Soh," Babcott said politely in Cantonese, "please come back when I call you."

"Certainly, Honorable Doctor." Obediently she left.

"I didn't know you spoke Chinese, George," Angelique said as he sat beside her and began to count her pulse rate.

"That was Cantonese, Chinese don't have one language, Angelique, but hundreds of different languages, though only one form of writing they can all understand. Curious, what?"

How stupid to tell me what I already know, she thought impatiently, wanting to scream at him, Do hurry up! As if I haven't been in Hong Kong, as if Malcolm and everyone else hasn't told me a hundred times—as if I've forgotten you're the cause of all my misfortune.

"I picked it up while I was in Hong Kong," he continued absently, feeling her brow and the pulse in her wrist, noting that her heart was racing and there was the slightest sheen of perspiration on her forehead—nothing to worry about considering her ordeal. "A few words here and there. Spent a couple of years at the General Hospital—we could certainly use such a fine place here." He kept his fingertips lightly on her pulse. "Chinese doctors believe there are seven levels of heartbeats, or pulses. They say they can sense them probing deeper and deeper. It's their main diagnostic method."

"And what do you hear from my seven hearts?" she asked, impulsively, enjoying the warmth of his healing hands and, in spite of her hatred, wishing she could trust him. She had never felt such hands or the good sensation that seemed to radiate from them to calm her.

"I hear nothing but good health," he said, wondering if there was any truth to the seven pulses theory. In his years in Asia he had witnessed remarkable insights and cures by Chinese doctors—along with an abundance of superstitious nonsense. The world's strange, but people are more strange. He looked back at her. His eyes were grey and very direct and kind. But there were shadows there and she saw them.

"Then . . . then what troubles you?" she asked, suddenly frightened that he had diagnosed her real condition.

He hesitated, then reached into his pocket and brought out a piece of tissue paper. Inside the tissue was her little gold cross. "This is yours, I think."

In violent turmoil she stared at it, her lips dry and not moving though her head had conjured up an immediate denial and shrug that were replaced in the same nauseating instant with: "I—I certainly . . . lost one like it. Are you sure it's mine? Where did you find it?"

"Around the neck of the would-be interloper."

"His neck? How . . . how odd," she heard herself say, watching herself as though she were another person, her voice another person's, forcing herself to be controlled even though she wanted to screech aloud for she knew she was again in the vise—her brain frenzied to concoct a plausible reason. "Around his neck?"

"Yes, I took it off the body. Thought nothing of it at the time, except that the man was a Catholic convert. Quite by chance, I saw the inscription—it's hardly noticeable." A short nervous laugh. "My eyesight is better than Hoag's. 'To Angelique from Mama, 1844.' "

Her mouth said, "Poor Mama, she died birthing my brother just four years later." She saw her fingers pick up the crucifix and examine it, squinting in the oil light, unable to read the tiny writing clearly—cursing the writing. Then her instinct committed her and she said, "I lost it, or thought I lost it at—at the Tokaidō, perhaps at Kanagawa, the night I went to see Malcolm, remember?"

"Oh, yes. Bad night, very bad . . . bad day too." Babcott got up hesitantly. "I, er, I thought you should have it."

"Yes, yes, thank you, I'm glad to have it back. So very glad, but please sit down, don't go yet," she said, much as she wanted him to go. "Who was he, that man, and how would he have found it? And where?"

"We'll never know, not now." Babcott watched her. "Did Malcolm tell you we think he was one of the Tokaidō murdering devils, though neither he nor Phillip are sure?"

In spite of her dread as she squirmed in this new trap, she had an overwhelming impulse to laugh hysterically and say, He wasn't a devil, not to me, not the first time, he left me alive the first time, and not a devil after I changed him. He didn't kill me though I know he was going to, I know he was going to just before I made him leave. . . . Devil, no, but even so he deserved to die, had to die. . . .

Mon Dieu, I still don't even know his name, I was so enmeshed I forgot to ask . . . I must be going mad to think such things. "Who was he?"

"No one knows. Yet. The Satsuma king could name him now that he's dead, but it would probably be a false name. They're such liars—that's not quite true, it's just that what we call lying seems to be a way of life with them. Probably the man found the cross at Kanagawa. You don't remember exactly when you discovered it had gone?"

"No, I don't. It was only when I got back here . . ." Again she saw his probing, questioning eyes and her mind screamed: Did my pulse or pulses tell him my real condition? "It's found. Good, thank God. I can't thank you enough but why should he wear it or keep it, that's what I can't understand."

"I agree, very odd."

The silence grew. "What does Dr. Hoag think?"

Babcott looked at her but she could not read what he was really thinking. "I didn't ask him," he said, "didn't discuss it with him, or with Malcolm." His eyes went back to hers and seemed to take on a deeper color. "Hoag's a Struan man and he, well . . . his rice bowl is with Tess Struan. I don't know why, but I thought I should talk to you first."

Again a silence. She looked away, not trusting herself, wishing she could truly trust him, wanting to trust someone other than André—his knowing was bad enough—but sure beyond sure it was impossible. She had to keep to the plan: she was alone, she must save herself alone.

"Perhaps . . ." she said, "no, surely he must have found my crucifix at Kanagawa, must have seen me there and—and perhaps. . . ." She stopped then hurried on, leading him on, inventing as she continued, "perhaps he kept it to remind him of me, to . . . I don't really know, to what?"

He said awkwardly, "To obviously do you harm, my dear, to possess you, one way or another, kill you. Sorry, but that must be the truth. At first I thought, like everyone else, that he was just one of these outlaws called ronin, but your crucifix changed all that. The moment I discovered it was yours . . . It must be as you say, he saw you at the Tokaidō, he and the other man must have followed Malcolm and Phillip Tyrer to

Kanagawa to finish them off, probably to avoid identification. Then he saw you again, found the crucifix and kept it because it was *yours,* pursued you here and tried to break in to, sorry again, to possess you, whatever the cost. Don't forget it would be easy for such a man to be infatuated by such a person as you, to be, to be obsessed."

The way he said it made it clearer than ever he too was within her spell. Good, and good that he's realized the truth, she thought, faint with relief that another hazard had been eliminated. Her mind strayed to the little bottles and to tomorrow when she would be cleansed, to start her new life, the future wonderful.

"Japanese are a curious people," he was saying. "Different. But different in one major way, they're not afraid to die. They almost seem to seek it. You were lucky, so lucky to escape. Well, I'll be off."

"Yes, and thank you, thank you." She caught his hand and pressed it to her cheek. "You'll tell Malcolm and Dr. Hoag? Then that will end it."

"I'll leave Malcolm to you." For a second he considered asking her help with Malcolm's opium addiction but decided it was not yet urgent, and anyway it was his own responsibility, not hers. Poor Angelique, she has enough to deal with. "As to Hoag, what does it matter to him, or to busybodies and wagging tongues in Yokohama? None of their affair, or mine, eh?"

He saw her clear eyes in the radiant face smiling up at him, pellucid skin, all of her emanating youth and health together with the magnetic, unconscious sensuality perpetually surrounding her that had, against all medical expectation, increased in power. Astonishing, he thought, filled with wonder at her resilience. I only wish I knew her secret and why some people thrive on adversities that would break most others.

Abruptly the doctor part of him fell away. I can't blame that ronin, or Malcolm, or anyone being mad for her, I want her too. "Curious about your cross," he said throatily, not a little ashamed. "But then, life's a collection of curiosities, isn't it? 'Night, my dear. Sleep well."

The first cramp clawed her out of a crooked sleep that was sated with prison hulks and sloe-eyed, raving demons, the women bloated with child, the men horned and grasping her away from Tess Struan, who stood guard over Malcolm like a malevolent ghoul. A second cramp followed quickly and brought her awake to reality and what was happening.

Relief that it had begun obliterated the previous hours of trepidation, for it had seemed an eternity before she had slept. Now it was just past

4 A.M. The last time she looked at her clock it was almost 2:30. Another cramp, rougher than before, went through her and concentrated her on the sequence.

Trembling fingers uncorked the second bottle. Again she gagged on the putrid taste and almost brought the liquid up but managed to keep it down with a spoon of honey, all the while her stomach churning with revulsion.

She lay back gasping. Fire seemed to spread from her stomach. In moments sweat poured out of her. Then the sweating passed leaving her limp, soaked and hardly breathing.

Waiting. As before, nothing. Just a bilious, sweet-sick disquiet that had, after hours of anxiety, drifted into troubled sleep. Her dismay crested. "Blessed Mother, let it work, let it work," she murmured through her tears.

More waiting. Still nothing. The minutes passed.

Then, unlike before, a startlingly different cramp almost doubled her up. Another. Just bearable. More, still bearable. She remembered the second half of the infusion and she sat up and began to sip it. The taste was bad but not as bad as the liquid in the bottles. "Thank God I don't have to take more of that," she muttered, and sipped again. Another sip. After each sip a taste of chocolate . . .

More cramps, stronger now. An increasing rhythm to them. Don't worry, everything's happening, she thought, just as André forecast. Her stomach muscles were beginning to feel stretched and angry. More sips and more cramps and then the last drop was down. Honey jar almost empty—last of the chocolate but now even its sweetness could not mask the bilious aftertaste. A draft from under the boudoir door swayed the flame of the lamp on the side table, making the wall shadows change and dance. Stoically she lay back and watched them, her hands holding her belly against the shafts of pain, the muscles tightening and loosening, becoming more tight, knotting under her fingers.

"Watch the shadows, think good thoughts," she whispered. "What do you see?"

Ships and sails and the roofs of Paris and brambles and, look, there's the guillotine, no, not the guillotine but a bower covered with climbing roses, why it's our country cottage near Versailles where we would go in the spring and summer growing up, my brother and I, darling Maman dead so long ago, Father gone only God knows where, Aunt and Uncle loving us but no substitute for darlin—

"Oh, *Mon Dieu!*" she gasped as the first of the violent spasms slashed her, then cried out at the next, frantically crammed part of the sheet into her mouth to stop the shrieks that burst out of her and would have brought all the Legation pounding on her bolted door.

Then the chills began. Ice picks into her guts. And more violence, twenty times worse than the worst monthly cramps. Her body heaved against the strain, limbs twitching in time with the waves of torment that ripped from her loins and into her head. "I'm going to die . . . I'm going to die," she moaned, her teeth grinding on the sheet, muffling the screams that followed with more spasms and chills and more, on and on and on and then stopping. Quite suddenly.

At first she thought she had truly died but soon her senses focused and she saw that the room had ceased spinning, the flame of the lamp was low but still burning and she heard the tick of the clock. The hands of the clock pointed to 5:42.

She struggled up in the bed, feeling awful. A glance in her hand mirror frightened her. Ashen features, hair lank with sweat, lips discolored by the medicine. She rinsed her mouth with some of the green tea and spat into the chamber pot and pushed it back under the bed again. Grimly she fought out of her soiled nightdress, used a damp towel to clean her face and neck as best she could, combed her hair and lay back exhausted but feeling better for the toil. It was only then that she noticed the red smear on her nightdress, thrown carelessly onto the threadbare carpet.

A quick examination confirmed that blood was seeping. She arranged a clean towel between her legs and, in the dawn, lay back once more, almost sinking into the mattress with fatigue. Warmth spread through her tired limbs. The flow increased.

29

Sunday, 9th November:

"Illustrious Chen said to tell you anything that might affect the tai-pan, Elder Sister," Ah Soh began uneasily. "The night before last Golden Pubics started her monthly and sh—"

"Ah, that's why she took to her bed and would not see my son," Ah Tok said. They were in her room at the end of the corridor, safe from prying ears. "He was like a teething child all day, worse this morning, it's time we went home."

"Yes. But listen further: she says it's her monthly but I know her dates like my own. It seems not possible. Normally she is like any young civilized virgin, regular, though . . ." Ah Soh toyed nervously with her smock, "though now that I remember it her last one was sparse, almost as if she missed it."

The older woman belched and used a toothpick. "To miss, or to be little, or irregular with all the anxiety over my son's wounds and the vile, murdering barbarians surrounding us here is ordinary news, not unusual." On the table between them were various bowls with the remains of her lunch: sweet and sour soup, stir-fried mixed fresh vegetables, a ginger-basted fish with soy, pork slivers in black bean sauce, garlic prawns, and rice. "It's ordinary, Younger Sister."

"What is un-ordinary is that yesterday morning when I went to bring her tea, and hot water to bathe, I had to bang several times to awaken her and she would not let me into her room, just shrieked rudely, 'Go away!' through the door in that vulgar voice of hers, and then"—Ah Soh dropped her voice dramatically—"just minutes later, Big Pointed Nose, that other sort of foreign devil our foreign devils call Frogs, he knocked softly like this." She rapped three times, then a fourth. "She let him in at once!"

Ah Tok blinked. "At once? Him? The Frog? She let him in but not you? You saw him?"

"Yes, but he did not see me."

"Ayeeyah! That was clever. Go on, Younger Sister!" Ah Tok said, now hanging on every word. "Go on."

"He stayed a few minutes, then came out carrying things wrapped in a brown piece of silk. Like a thief in the darkest night. But he did not see me spying on him." Ah Soh paused again, loving—like all Chinese—to be the purveyor of gossip and secrets. ". . . Or even when I followed him."

"By all gods great and small, you did?" Ah Tok poured two glasses of the Madeira wine they savored. "Long life, Younger Sister, may your Jade Gate never trouble you. Go on, go on!"

"He went down to the shore and got into a rowing boat and rowed out to sea. After a while I saw him drop whatever it was over the side into the sea."

"No!"

"Yes. Then he rowed back. But he didn't see me, never."

"What could it have been?"

Ah Soh leaned closer. "When Missee let me in I looked around carefully. Her bed and nightdress were soaked with sweat, and she looked as though she had had a Happy Valley fever. Her personal towels were soaked, heavier than usual. She told me to clean everything, to bring hot water and not to let anyone in—even the tai-pan. As soon as I had done what was necessary she flopped back in bed and went to sleep."

"That's not strange, but Pointed Nose is!" Ah Tok nodded sagely. "This is like donkey dung, shiny on the outside but still all dung. Clearly he disposed of something for her."

Ah Soh hesitated. "Your Honored Son, is there a chance he has lain with her?"

Ah Tok cackled. "I am sure he has tried but Golden Pubics will not let his Celestial Stem relish the breaching of her Gate, though she flaunts it every chance she gets. I've heard him moaning her name in his sleep, poor man. Disgusting, if she was a civilized person we could arrange the price and that would end it."

Ah Soh watched Ah Tok thoughtfully pluck a piece of the decimated fish head with her chopsticks, suck the bone clean and spit it into her bowl. The younger woman would gladly have partaken of the leftovers, their cook not as good as Ah Tok's. "How's your cook these days?" she asked innocently.

"Improving. The dog comes from my village so he had promise. I'm training him, of course." Ah Tok grimaced. "Baffling, Younger Sister. How is the Empress today?"

"Irritable as usual. The flow continues, stronger than normal. Medicine Man Giant came to see her this morning but she would not see him, told me to send him away. There's someth—"

"Has my son seen her yet?"

"She will see him this afternoon."

"Good, today his tongue's like an asp to his old mother over her. Pointed Nose and Pubics in a secret plot? Smelly, smelly indeed. Keep your eyes and ears open, Younger Sister."

"There's something else." Ah Soh's eyes rolled with excitement. She reached into her pocket and put the cork on the table. The lower part was stained purple to black. "I found this under the bed when I was reaching for the chamber pot."

The wrinkled face became even more wrinkled with puzzlement. "So?"

"Smell it, Elder Sister."

Ah Tok obeyed. The odor was pungent, slightly familiar. "What is it?"

"I cannot be sure . . . but it smells to me like Dark of the Moon. I think the bottle this corked contained Dark of the Moon . . . with other herbs."

The older woman gasped. "The expeller? To cause a miscarriage? Impossible! Why should she want to do that?"

"Very bad face for your son to be named a father before marriage, eh? You know how foreign devils carry on about marriage and scandals and virginity, no fornication before the wedding— the man always blamed, how foolish! Bad face for your son. Then there's Tai-tai Tess to answer to, as well as her foul and vengeful foreign devil god."

Both women shuddered. Ah Tok sniffed the cork again. "You think Pointed Nose threw the bottle into the sea?"

"I'm missing a teapot too, that could have been for the accompanying herbs, she wanted hot water and honey too."

"To take away the taste! Ayeeyah!" Gravely Ah Tok said, "My son is . . . is quite unbalanced about that woman."

"What should we do?"

"You were right to tell me. We will write at once to Illustrious Chen and send him the cork in the first mail. He will know if you are right, and then what to do." Shakily Ah Tok poured another glass of wine for each of them. "Keep your eyes wide, be like a clam, I will do the same—not a word to her, my son, or anyone until we hear from him what to do."

Malcolm Struan was hobbling across the High Street heading for the Struan Building, leaning heavily on his sticks. The sky was overcast, a slight wind off the sea, the afternoon chilly and his crushing worry had dropped away. Seeing Angelique, convinced that she was all right, more lovely than ever, though pale and drowsy, had done it. He had stayed only moments, not wanting to tire her.

A group of mounted traders reined in politely to allow him to pass, raised their riding crops in salute. " 'Day to you, Tai-pan," Lunkchurch said, grim-faced like the others. "Will you be at the Club at sundown?"

"What's amiss?" Struan said.

Lunkchurch jerked his thumb at the squat, black-hulled, two-masted steamer anchored in the bay near Marlowe's frigate. She flew the flag of Brock and Sons. "Her and her news. Norbert's called a meeting: just traders, not Sir William."

"I was going to do the same. Sundown, good, I'll be there," Malcolm said tightly. *Ocean Witch*—all Brock's major vessels were surnamed 'Witch' as Struan's used 'Cloud'—had unexpectedly arrived late yesterday evening with news, mails and the latest Hong Kong papers. "Bloody stupid!"

Major editorials in all papers were about Admiral Ketterer and the fleet's highly successful attack on Chinese pirate nests in and around Mirs Bay and that now he was en route to Shanghai for coaling. The *Guardian*, using big, angry type, summed up the problem:

In a dispatch to the Governor, Admiral Ketterer wrote that they had suffered some casualties caused by Chinese shore batteries being armed with modern cannon—cannon made in Birmingham, emanating from Hong Kong, and acquired through fair means or foul by Wu Sung Choi, leader of the White Lotus fleets who, regrettably, was not captured or killed.

Astonishingly, because of this minor incident (the cannon were spiked by a landing party of marines) the Admiral recommended that

all sales of all arms—and all opium—be declared illegal and embar-
goed throughout Asia at once, particularly to China and Japan, with
the stiffest penalties for any infraction.

This unwarranted interference with legitimate trade, this uncon-
scionable imputation of blame on all China traders—renowned for
their fair-mindedness, their intrepid Empire-building capabilities, their
loyalty to Her Majesty, God Bless Her, and of putting the Mother
Country before profit—must be protested in the strongest terms.

The Editors would like to ask the Admiral: Who provides the taxes to
pay for the greatest navy the world has ever seen (of which he is
undoubtedly an admirable member though clearly misinformed on vital
matters of interest to the Crown) without which our Empire ceases?
Only and always hard-working traders and their trade . . .

"Ketterer's a bloody fool," Struan said. "Norbert's right in that. Perhaps now Sir William will see the light and ask for a replacement at once. We've got to deal with the Jappos here ourselves and Ketterer won't move without crossing the t's and dotting the i's."

"We certainly needs a bugger with balls," Lunkchurch said. "Ketterer's a damp fart."

One of the other men said, "Hey, Charlie, he smashed the pirates when he'd the order, he'll do the same here. Wot's an extra few months, eh? Tai-pan," he asked anxiously, "can we know how Miss Angel is?"

"She's fine, she's fine now."

"Thank God for that!"

News that she had taken to her bed had flashed around the Settlement yesterday and when it was learned she had refused to see Babcott, Hoag or even the tai-pan concern escalated: "Christ, it's the Frog cooking, she's poisoned." . . ."No, she's caught their plague." . . . "Frogs don't have plagues, for God's sake, just lice. . . ." "We all got lice . . . I heard it was cholera. . . ."

Universal relief permeated Yokohama at noon today when Minister Seratard had put out an official bulletin that she was in perfect health, merely suffering from a temporary indisposition—quickly whispered it was just her period.

"My fiancée's fine," Malcolm said again. Proudly.

"That's a relief," Lunkchurch said. "You hear *Witch*'s leaving on tonight's tide?"

Malcolm glanced out to sea, much of his disquiet returning. Last night when he had first heard of the ship's arrival he had been filled with a nauseating, sudden panic that Tyler Brock or Morgan Brock were aboard. It was only when Jamie reassured him they were not that he could think clearly.

Why the hell does Tyler Brock terrify me, even now? he asked himself again. I can understand it when I was small but now Tyler's not much taller than me, though ugly as ever, rough-visaged and foulmouthed, with his big belly and his one eye always bloodshot. What does that matter? There are many men in Hong Kong like him, many uglier. Many such enemies. But they don't frighten me. He's always been our enemy and we've contained him every time—Dirk did, my father did, Mother did, has, and I must, but . . . Christ Almighty, I hate that bugger for all the grief he's caused Mother and the family.

He took a deep breath and concentrated on *Ocean Witch*. "She's not due out for two days."

"That's the rumor."

"But why? Why so fast a turnaround?"

"Don't know, but that's the poop."

"We'll soon find out. 'Day!" Malcolm cast off his foreboding and continued across the road. Ahead was the Struan Building where he was heading and beyond that the spire of Holy Trinity. He had been to the early service this morning and had prayed for Angelique and for strength and afterwards had felt better. But God curse all Brocks forever, let me kill Norbert quickly an—

"Tai-pan!"

Startled from his reverie he looked up, around. Phillip Tyrer was hurrying from the British Legation. "Sorry, but we all just wanted to know how Miss Angelique was."

"Fine, she's fine," Malcolm said. Now, behind Tyrer, he saw Sir William peering at him out of one of the ground floor windows. He waved a stick and gave an awkward thumbs-up and saw the Minister wave back. Just before Sir William retreated into the room he caught a glimpse of another man beside him. "Oh, that your tame samurai, Nakama?"

"Who? Oh yes, yes, it was. Is she really all right?"

"Everything with her was *very* good, thank you."

"Thank God for that, we were all worried to death!" Phillip Tyrer beamed down at him, a picture of health, ruddy, strong, taller than Struan but only because now he walked, and stood, hunched over. "You're looking much better yourself."

"Wish that were true, Phillip." Abruptly Malcolm's envy prompted him to say sharply, "I hear Nakama's been giving you all sorts of information, you and Sir William?"

Tyrer's smile faded. "Yes, I suppose he has."

"The arrangement was that you were to keep Jamie and me informed. Everything. Eh?"

"Well, yes, yes, it was. But Sir William . . . he's trying to find out the politics of Japan an—"

"Politics of a country and business are like a pair of gloves, Phillip. Perhaps you'd drop by tomorrow, before tiffin? I'd appreciate knowing what's new." He forced a smile. "Please give my best to Sir William, see you tomorrow."

He limped down the street, angry at himself for being so caustic, sick to death of walking like this, then climbed the stairs of the Struan Building heading for his suite. His back and stomach ached alarmingly. No more than usual, he thought irritably, and that's no cause to snap at Phillip. He was just trying to be pleasant. Never mind, a little of Ah Tok's elixir and I'll be fine again. I'll ask Phillip to dinner an—

"Tai-pan!"

"Oh, hello, Jamie." Malcolm stopped halfway up the staircase. "Did you hear *Ocean Witch* is leaving early? Perhaps on this evening's tide?"

"Ah! I was just going to tell you. Heard the rumor, tried to get it confirmed by Norbert but he's busy at the moment—how's Angelique?"

"Fine," Malcolm said absently. "We'd better be ready with our mails in case the *Witch* sails early."

"I'll be all set. I'll collect yours as soon as I hear if it's true." Jamie frowned, seeing how distracted Malcolm was.

"Send someone to Angelique, she has mail too." Her letter to his mother, written and rewritten until both were satisfied. It's a good letter, he thought.

"She was really all right, Tai-pan?"

"Gorgeous." Malcolm smiled, aches momentarily forgotten, the *Witch* forgotten. She had looked spectacular in bed, fresh though wan, happy and attentive and so pleased to see him. "She said by tomorrow evening she'll be fine, Jamie. Why don't we arrange a grand dinner, here, eh? Us, and say Dmitri, Babcott, Marlowe if he's free, and Pallidar, they're both good sorts though they fawn on her like puppies."

"What about Phillip and Sir William?"

"Phillip, yes, but not Sir William . . . no, best leave them both out. How about Count Zergeyev? He's always good for a laugh or two."

"If you invite him you should really include all the Ministers—can't very well leave Sir William out then."

"You're right. Make it simple, them another night."

"I'll make the arrangements," Jamie said, glad that they were on friendly terms again. Together they walked into his suite. All damage from the fire had been repaired though there was still the slight smell of smoke. "What about Ketterer?"

"He has to guard our interests or he's out." Malcolm sat at his desk, began to stack the mail he wanted to send. "Mother will have already seen the Governor and sorted him out."

"Yes."

Malcolm looked up sharply, hearing a strangeness under the voice. After a moment he said, "Curious how confident we are she'll do that, and not at all confident I can persuade her to approve my marriage."

"Don't quite know how to answer that, Tai-pan," McFay said sadly, "if it's a question."

Malcolm nodded slowly, seeing the strong, well-used face and strong, tough body and wondering if he would be as strong when he was thirty-nine—in nineteen years. "You got another letter from her?"

"Yes. 'Fraid no good news at all from *Ocean Witch*."

"Oh? Sit down, Jamie. What did she say?"

"Sorry, but, well, she reiterated her order I assist Dr. Hoag to see you back to Hong Kong at once, confirming I'm sacked at the end of the month."

"You can forget that. You wrote her, as I told you, that you're under the tai-pan's orders, my orders, not hers?"

"Yes."

"Good, so did I and that's the end of it. Your letter and mine must have crossed hers." Malcolm lit a cheroot and noticed his fingers were shaking. "You've never smoked?"

"No, tried once and didn't like it."

"Forget the sacking nonsense. What other bad news?"

"I've got all the correspondence and cuttings for you when you're ready. Business is rotten all over. We've lost *Racing Cloud*—she's too long overdue in San Francisco."

"Bloody hell!" *Racing Cloud* was one of their clipper fleet, twenty-two ships. Clippers, three-masted queens of the sea, were much faster on long ocean runs than cumbersome steamers that had to carry and conserve coal. Her cargo was tea, silk and spices, all highly prized goods and now, because of the American war, astronomically valuable— particularly if diverted to the South. "Insurance won't cover us, will it?"

" 'Fraid not. Never does, even Lloyd's. They may even claim an Act of War. It is a war zone."

"Ayeeyah! That'll cost a pretty penny. Damned shame about the crew. Her Captain was Caradoc, wasn't he?"

"Yes. They must have run into a hurricane—several were reported off Hawaii though they're late this year. Her Second Mate was my cousin, Duncan McGregor."

"Oh, sorry about that." Even more depressed, Struan glanced at his bureau where the elixir waited. I wonder if the same storms swallowed *Savannah Lady,* along with young Pedrito Vargas and our order for five thousand rifles, he thought absently. That reminded him. "Those cannon at Mirs Bay—they weren't sold through us, were they?"

"Not to my knowledge," Jamie said, the normal response to such a question. Both were aware of major arms sales to Chinese traders, who always represented the Manchu government. What happened on delivery at Canton or Shanghai was another matter.

Malcolm was thinking, I'll bet fifty Mex to a dollar they were from us, one way or another. He was party to one of Struan's inner secrets: a tenuous friend-enemy relationship existed between the Noble House and the seaborne White Lotus Wu Sung Choi's, begun by his grandfather and continued by his father. What about me? What do I do about them, he asked himself, suddenly sick to death of Yokohama and violently anxious to assume all the mantle and secrets of his grandfather—and to confront his mother. "In a week or so," he muttered.

"Tai-pan?"

"Nothing. What else, Jamie?"

Jamie went through a litany about the falling price of goods they sold and escalating price of goods they had to buy, of demands for increased danger wages for their seamen, many of whom were of English-American heritage and were being forcibly pressed aboard roving, marauding warships of both North and South. "I could go on forever, Tai-pan. Russia and France are spoiling for a fight, so Europe's a tinderbox. All over India, Moslems and Hindus are killing, murdering each other, burning crops. Whole world's crazy." He hesitated. "More urgent, the Victoria Bank wrote again about the paper they carry on us here. The notes are due . . . ."

"I know all about that and they can rot. The Bank's Brock-controlled, they've dropped us in the sewer financing Brock's takeover of Hawaiian sugar and they're out to bankrupt us. They can all rot, by God." Malcolm's voice had thickened. Pain was shafting from his belly. "Think I'll finish all this paperwork in case the *Witch* sails on the tide. Why should she turn around so fast?"

After a moment Jamie shrugged. "Don't know, but I agree: any news to do with Brock's is bad news."

The Club meeting had quickly gravitated into the usual shouting, cursing, angry mass of men, increasingly heated, with plenty of drinking, talking and no one listening, with a single theme locking them all together: "God curse all governments, all bleeding tax collectors, all fat-arsed Admirals and Generals wot don't know their poxy place, wot don't do wot they're supposed to do which is listen to the business community, do wot we bloody say and Bob's your bloody uncle!"

"Good on yer, Lunkchurch. I proposes . . ."

Whatever the man proposed was drowned in the uproar as several shouted, "Let's impeach Wee Willie. . . ."

Exasperated, Norbert Greyforth pushed his way through the crowd from the corner of the bar where he had begun the meeting and headed for Malcolm Struan who sat beside the door, Jamie nearby. Dmitri called out, "No conclusion, Norbert?"

"What do you expect, Dmitri? It's up to tai-pans as ever was. Come along. Jamie, would you and . . ." Norbert was going to needle Malcolm by calling him young Struan but he remembered Sir William's very blunt and sour threat not to provoke him in public or else. Even more he could feel Tyler Brock's letter burning in his pocket. He looked down at Malcolm and said politely, "Would you two please join me—a private chat, eh? Dmitri, you too?"

Malcolm had expected Norbert just to pass by with a curt nod. "Certainly. Where? Outside?"

"In my office, if it pleases you."

The three men followed him. All on guard. "Is *Ocean Witch* leaving on the tide?" Malcolm asked.

"Yes."

Dmitri said, "Why the fast turnaround, Norbert?"

"Tyler's orders." Norbert noticed the sudden shadow cross Struan's face and he smiled to himself.

His temporary office was on the ground floor while repairs were being done to the fire-ravaged upstairs. The central staircase was blackened, the roof off in places but covered temporarily with sail canvas. "Proper bugger, the fire, but there you are, happens to everyone sometime. Fortunately, as I said, the safes weren't touched, nor the books and warehouse." He motioned to leather easy chairs. "Make yourself comfortable."

On the sideboard were glasses and drinks, whisky, brandy, gin, vintage wine, with champagne already on ice. His Chinese Number One Boy stood waiting to serve them. Their caution increased. "What's your pleasure?"

"Champagne," Malcolm said, the others echoing him. He was feeling fine now, the elixir as always encouraging him to seem inviolate as well as deadening the pain. When all glasses were filled, Norbert jerked his thumb at the servant who bowed and left them. "Health!" They returned the toast mildly. He sat on the edge of the desk, tall, lean and confident.

"We're safe from ears here," he said. "First, we, us'n, we represent the three biggest companies, we should jointly write a complaint to Wee Willie, not that it'll do much good, and to the Admiral—we all agree he's an impediment. No reason, Dmitri, why you shouldn't have at him too: Cooper-Tillman's got a lot to lose here as well as us. At the same time we should mount a campaign, Struan's and us, in Parliament to settle Japan once and for all—either we smash the Jappos and put them in their place or we quit."

"We're not quitting Japan," Malcolm said, and McFay relaxed a little.

"Nor are we," Norbert said thinly, "that's only our ploy for those miserable bastards in Parliament." He picked up a file from the immaculate desk and selected a single sheet of paper. "This's a secret dispatch from London via *Ocean Witch* from one of our watchdogs there, dated September 16th."

"That's damn fast," Jamie said for all of them.

"We keep abreast, Jamie. Tyler says to share part of it with you three. I'll read it: *Yesterday the Prime Minister and Chancellor of the Exchequer privately agreed in the next Budget to up the tax on tea by 4 pence the pound, a penny a pint on beer, shilling on all brandy and imported wines, doubling the tax on tobacco*"—they all gasped— "*doubling the import tax on cotton—*"

"Goddamn!" Dmitri exploded. "That's crazy! That and tobacco are the only cash crops we've got in the South! They do that, what happens to our war and what happens to your goddam Lancashire mills?"

"We don't have cotton mills, though Struan's have. There's more: *To muzzle certain powerful factions on both sides of the House they're going to order all our opium plantations in Bengal torched and tea pl—"*

"Jesus Christ!" Struan was aghast, Jamie purple and Dmitri in shock. "Then how do we trade in China, for God's sake? Opium to silver to . . ."

"Parliament don't give a tinker's fart for our Heavenly Triangle," Norbert said grimly, "or Asia, or China, or trade, only staying in office. They want to replant with tea." He replaced the paper in the folder and sat back on the desk, knowing full well the others would dearly love to know the veracity of the document, and what else was in it. "The Old Man said to tell you we've an informant close to the P.M.'s office, his whispers have always been true in the past, and that's the God's truth. He says, rightly, we've got to get this bloody pair out, fast. Dmitri, you've got to pressure them from your side. Tyler says whatever's necessary we'll do and asks you to do the same. Agreed?"

Dmitri said, "Agreed. Jesu, I can't believe it."

"I do." Struan raised his glass, wondering where Tyler Brock's trap was. "May they burn in Hell."

Solemnly they drank with him. Norbert refilled their glasses. His face had hardened to focus on Struan. "Next: we're all party to our duel. I don't need seconds and we agreed Wednesday dawn. Sorry, I'm on *Ocean Witch* tonight, sorry, Tyler's orders—so Wednesday's off. I sugg—"

"Why put it off, there's light enough now." The words were out before Malcolm could stop them and he was pleased that he had reacted so quickly and firmly though suddenly his brain seemed stretched. The silence intensified. Jamie had blanched.

"Not now." Eyes glinting and hiding his amusement, Norbert turned to Jamie and Dmitri, the formal seconds. "I suggest we postpone, gentleman's agreement, till I get back, about three weeks, eh? Then it'll be next day, whenever."

Jamie said, "That's a better idea, Tai-pan. Yes?"

After a moment the tightness in Struan's head seeped away. "Fine," he said, neither pleased nor disappointed but content that he had thrown down the gauntlet again. He did not notice Jamie and Dmitri cover their relief. They finished their drinks and left.

When he was quite alone, Norbert took out Tyler Brock's letter and reread it, his palms sweaty. The first part dealt with their spy's information. The letter ended: 'Get thy arse aboard *Ocean Witch* and leave on first tide—just thee, no other passengers, mind. Bring thy inner books, the Jappo gold-mining contract, and all bullion in thy control. We's to meet in Shanghai, secret—that's *Witch*'s first port of call though manifest says direct to Hong Kong—Morgan, me and thee, fast as possible and secret, no one to be wiser. When thee returns to Yokohama, mayhaps thy bed'll be in godrotting Malcolm Struan's room, ay, with his doxie's tongue fawning all over thee if that's thy pleasure—soon she be for sale too. We's just heard her dad's fled Bangkok, like Hong Kong, more fraud and swindles, Frog officials this time. They be catching him, trying him and then the guillotine—Frogs bain't like our lily piss-arsed Peelers. Missus sends best wishes.'

30

KYŌTO

Sunday, 16th November:

WELL AFTER DARK, YOSHI AND HIS
guard, muffled and disguised in nondescript clothes as ordinary soldiers, wearily picked their way through the deserted streets of the sleeping, ancient capital where Emperors and the Imperial court had lived for centuries.

The city had been constructed in Chinese fashion with straight streets, the cross streets at right angles, with the sprawling Forbidden Palace and grounds central to it. Only the roofs could be seen behind its tall walls—six Gates in the walls. Yoshi avoided it carefully, wanting to elude Ogama's patrols and samurai guarding the Gates, and when he arrived, unheralded, at the Shōgunate barrack complex, he went to his own quarters and soon sank gratefully into a steaming bath that could easily hold eight.

"How many fighters do I have in Kyōto, Akeda?" he asked, the aches of his days of forced march beginning to seep away.

Grim-faced, the old general lowered himself into the water beside him, the bath a metre deep. The bathhouse was within the inner redoubt, all maids had been dismissed and sentries posted outside.

"Eight hundred and two, of which eighty are sick or recovering from wounds, all sworn to you, all trustworthy, all mounted. Plus the eighteen you brought with you," he said in his gravelly voice. The moment Yoshi had arrived, Akeda had doubled all guards. He was a tough, hatomoto retainer whose family had served the Toranaga clan for generations and now he commanded their Kyōto garrison. "Not enough to protect you."

"I'm safe here." By Legacy law, this was the only defensible complex in Kyōto, capable of billeting five thousand men if need be, all other daimyos restricted to a maximum of five hundred men—with no more than ten daimyos in Kyōto at any one time, their comings and goings strictly controlled. Time and weak Councils of Elders had whittled Shōgunate numbers to under a thousand. "Do you doubt that?"

"Inside our walls, no. So sorry, I meant outside."

"Allies? How many daimyos can I count on?"

Akeda shrugged irritably. "It was totally wrong to put yourself at such risk travelling with so few guards, even more dangerous to come to Kyōto. If I had been warned I could have met you and escorted you in. If your father were alive he would have forbidden such dan—"

"But my father's not alive." Yoshi's lips set into a hard line. "Allies?"

"If you raised your own standard in Kyōto, Sire, your very own, most daimyos and most samurai would rush to your side, here and throughout the land, more than enough to enforce whatever you wanted to enforce."

"That could be construed as treason."

"Ah, so sorry, but truth is usually treasonous at your level, Lord—and very difficult to obtain." The weathered old face broke into a smile. "The truth: If you raise the Shōgunate banner, the daimyos here will not combine against Ogama of Choshu, not while he holds the Gates."

"How many samurai does Ogama have here?"

"They say over two thousand, handpicked men, all well placed in fortified guard houses around the palace, close to nominal guards on our Gates." Akeda smiled mirthlessly, seeing Yoshi's eyes narrow. "Oh, everyone knows it's against the law, but no one reminded him and no one has stood up to him. He's been sneaking them in in tens and twenties since he threw out that old fox Sanjiro, Katsumata and his Satsumas. You know they escaped by boat to Kagoshima?" He slid deeper into the water. "Rumor has it Ogama has another two to three thousand Choshu samurai within ten *ri*."

"Eh?"

"His grip tightens on Kyōto, every day a little more, his patrols control the streets, except for an occasional shishi band who pick a fight with anyone they fancy does not honor *sonno-joi,* particularly us and anyone allied to the Shōgunate. They are fools because we are equally opposed to gai-jin, their foul Treaties and want them out."

"Are shishi here in strength?"

"Yes. Rumor is they are getting ready for some mischief. A week ago some of them picked on an Ogama patrol, openly calling Ogama a traitor. He was furious and has been trying to hunt them down ever since. There is—"

A knock stopped him. The Captain of the Guard opened the door. "Excuse me, Lord Yoshi, an emissary from Lord Ogama is at the gate, requesting an audience with you." Both men gasped.

Yoshi said angrily, "How could he know I have arrived? For the last fifty *ri* we have been disguised. I waited outside Kyōto till dark, we bypassed the barricades and met no patrols. There must be a spy here."

"There are no spies inside here," Akeda grated. "On my head, Sire. Outside they are legion, everywhere, for Ogama, shishi, and others— and you are not easily disguised."

"Captain," Yoshi said, "say that I'm asleep and may not be disturbed. Ask him to come back in the morning when he will be received with due honor."

The Captain bowed and began to leave. Akeda said, "Order the whole garrison on full alert!"

When they were alone, Yoshi said, "You think Ogama would dare attack me here? That would be a declaration of war."

"What he dares doesn't concern me, Sire. Only your safety. Now you are my responsibility."

The water's heat was into Yoshi's joints now and he lay back, letting the warmth take him for a moment, glad that Akeda was in command, reassured by his presence, although not swayed by his opinions. He had not anticipated being discovered so soon. Never mind, he thought, my plan is still good. "Who is Ogama's running dog, his Court go-between?"

"Prince Fujitaka, a first cousin of the Emperor—his wife's brother is the Imperial Chamberlain."

The air hissed from Yoshi's mouth and the General nodded sourly. "Difficult to break that link, except with a sword."

"Unthinkable," Yoshi said shortly, and thought, Unless it were possible. Either way very stupid to say such a thing out loud, even in private. "What news of Shōgun Nobusada and Princess Yazu?"

"They're expected in a week an—"

Yoshi looked over sharply. "They are not expected for two or three weeks."

The old man's voice rasped, "Princess Yazu ordered them to cut back to the Tokaidō and take the short route, clearly anxious to see her brother, to guide her husband to kowtow to him against all tradition— the sooner to bury the Shōgunate and give it to Ogama."

"Even here, old friend, you should guard your tongue."

"I am too old to worry about that now—now that your neck is in Ogama's vise."

Yoshi sent for maids who brought towels and dried both men and helped them into fresh yukatas. He picked up his swords. "Wake me at dawn, Akeda. I've much to do."

Just before dawn in the southern outskirts where the river curled south towards Osaka and the sea, twenty-odd *ri* away, where the lanes and streets and alleys were haphazard, so different from the straight-lined rigidity of the city, where the smell of feces and mud and rotting vegetation was heavy, Katsumata, the Satsuma shishi leader and confidant of Lord Sanjiro, awoke suddenly, slid from under the coverlet and stood in the darkened room, listening intently, sword ready.

No sound of danger. Below were the muted noises of maids and servants lighting the day's fires, chopping vegetables, preparing the foods of the day. His room was on the second floor, under the rafters, in this, the Inn of Whispering Pines. A dog barked in the distance.

Something is wrong, he thought.

He opened the shoji silently. Along the passageway were other rooms, three occupied by other shishi, two per room. The last was for the women of the Inn.

To one side was a small window overlooking the forecourt. Below nothing moved. Again his gaze ranged the area and the gate and the street beyond. Nothing. Again. Nothing. Then a glint, more felt than seen. At once he slid doors aside and hissed the code word. Instantly the six men leapt to their feet, sleep vanished, and rushed after him, swords in hand, down the rickety stairs, through the kitchen area and out the back door. At once over the fence and into the next garden in a carefully rehearsed retreat, into the next, over that fence and into the alleyway, down it, quickly diverting into a passage between the low hovels. At the end of this cul-de-sac he turned left and eased a door open. The alert guard's spear menaced his throat. "Katsumata-san! What's wrong?"

"Someone has betrayed us," Katsumata panted, and motioned to a Choshu youth, spare like himself, steel hard but half his age, nineteen. "Circle, see, then come back. Do not be observed or get caught!"

The youth vanished. The others followed Katsumata across the messy entranceway into the hovel itself. Within were many rooms, this building discreetly connected to others on either side, and more shishi. Twenty, all armed, most captains of shishi cells, now awake and ready to fight or retreat—one of them, Sumomo, Shorin's sister, Hiraga's fiancée. Silently they gathered, waiting for orders.

When they were escaping the Inn not one of the servants or maids had acknowledged them or their headlong departure, continuing their labors as though nothing had happened. All froze a few seconds later when an Ogama patrol burst through the front door and started to go through the sleeping rooms, waking guests and girls and the mama-san while others leapt up the stairs to search the rooms aloft. Wails of surprise and fright and protest and squeals from the women now occupying the four rooms above, that, moments ago, had housed the shishi—again all part of Katsumata's careful planning.

In the ensuing uproar of cries and outrage from the mama-san, and as much as the enraged Ogama officer cursed and demanded to know where the ronin outlaws had gone, bashing a few of the male servants around the face, it was to no avail. Everyone trembled and loudly protested innocence: "Ronin? In my respectable, law-abiding House? Never!" the mama-san cried.

But when the patrol had departed and they were all safe, the mama-san swore, her acolytes swore, and servants swore, everyone cursing the spy who had betrayed them.

"Katsumata-san, who was it?" Takeda asked, a heavyset, almost neckless Choshu youth of twenty—a kinsman of Hiraga—his heart still racing from their narrow escape.

Katsumata shrugged. "Karma if we find him, karma if we do not. It only proves what I hammer into you: be prepared for betrayal, instant flight, instant fight, trust no man or woman except a blooded shishi and *sonno-joi*." Everyone in the crowded little room nodded.

"What about Lord Yoshi? When do we go for him?"

"When he's outside the walls." News of Yoshi's sudden arrival had come in the night, too late to intercept him.

"But, Sensei, we've adherents inside," Takeda said. "Surely that would be the place to surprise him, when he feels safe and his guard is down."

"Yoshi's guard is never down. Never forget it. As to our people with him and inside his walls, they are ordered to remain calm and hidden, their presence and information is too valuable to risk. In the unlikely event that Shōgun Nobusada escapes our ambush, then they will be even more necessary."

Many grim smiles and hands tightening on weapons. The ambush was planned for dusk, in five days at Otsu, the last way station before Kyōto. Only a few Inns on both the North Road and the Tokaidō coast road were considered fitting resting places for such august persons with their multitudinous guards, maids and servants, so their night stops were easy to know. And to set spies in place.

Ten shishi had been assigned the suicide mission and were already at Otsu, preparing. Every one of the hundred and seven shishi now gathered in various safe houses throughout Kyōto had begged to be on the attack team. At Katsumata's suggestion they had drawn lots. Three Choshu, three Satsumas and four Tosas gained the honor and were already around their target, the Inn of Many Flowers.

"Eeee," the girl, Sumomo, whispered excitedly, "only five days, then *sonno-joi* will be a fact. The Bakufu will never recover from that blow."

"Never!" Katsumata smiled at her, liking her, the best of all his women students—as Hiraga was best amongst the men, except for his Ori—admiring her bravery and strength and skills. She too had volunteered but he had forbidden it, considering her far too valuable a weapon to cast away on such a high-risk endeavor. He was glad that he had told her to wait here, overruling Hiraga's order to her to return to his father's home. She had brought the latest intelligence from Yedo: confirming rumors of the negotiated détente between Bakufu and gai-jin, the failed attack on Chief Minister Anjo but the successful killing of Utani and firing his mansion. And importantly, confirming the growing rift between Anjo and Toranaga Yoshi. 'Where this information came from,' she had whispered to him, 'I do not know but the mama-san said it was from the source you would know about.'

Also she reported the facts of the manner of Shorin's death. But knew nothing further of Ori or Hiraga, other than that Ori's wound was healing and both were hiding out in the Yokohama Settlement, with Akimoto—Hiraga, somehow, miraculously a confidant of a gai-jin official.

"You are right, Sumomo, the Bakufu will never recover," Katsumata said. "And our next hammer blow will end the Toranaga Shōgunate forever."

Immediately following the successful elimination of Shōgun Nobusada—at all costs leaving Princess Yazu unharmed—shishi would launch a mass attack on Ogama's headquarters to assassinate him, simultaneously Katsumata and others would seize the Gates, raising the banner of *sonno-joi,* declaring power had returned to the Emperor, at which time all true daimyos and samurai would flock to make obeisance.

"Sonno-joi," she murmured, exultant like all of them.

Except Takeda, one of the Choshu shishi. Uneasily he shifted in his place. "I'm not sure about killing Ogama. He is a good daimyo, a good leader—he stopped Sanjiro seizing power, stopped the Tosa seizing power, he is the only daimyo enforcing the Emperor's orders to expel gai-jin. Isn't he closing the Shimonoseki Straits? Only our cannon oppose the gai-jin ships—only Choshu forces are in the front line, eh?"

"That's true, Takeda," a Satsuma shishi of renown said. "But what did Sensei Katsumata remind us? That Ogama has changed now he has sole control. If he honored the Emperor, now that he controls the Gates, simple for him to declare *sonno-joi* and return all power to the Emperor. That is what we will do when we have the Gates."

"Yes, but . . ."

"Simple for him, Takeda. But what has he done? Only used his power to twist the Court to his whims. He wants to be Shōgun. Nothing less."

There were murmurs of agreement and then Sumomo said, "Please excuse me, Takeda, but Ogama is a major threat. You all know I am Satsuma, so is Sensei Katsumata, we agree Sanjiro also has done some good, but nothing for *sonno-joi.* So he must relinquish power, gladly or unhappily, and will go . . . *will go.* The same for Ogama. Yes, he has done some good, but now he does bad. The truth is no daimyo who has the Gates and is so close to being Shōgun will ever go willingly."

Takeda said, "Perhaps if we petitioned Ogama?"

She said, "Please excuse me but a petition will be of no value. When we possess the Gates, to prevent civil war and the possibility of any daimyo being tempted ever again, when we possess the Gates we must go further, we must request the Emperor to abolish the Shōgunate, Bakufu *and all daimyos.*"

Amid sounds of surprise at such a radical proposal, Takeda burst out, "That's mad. Without a Shōgunate and daimyos, who will rule?

There'll be chaos! Who pays our stipends? Daimyos! The daimyos own all rice koku an—"

Katsumata said, "Let her finish, Takeda, then you can have your say."

"So sorry, Takeda, but this is Hiraga-san's idea, not mine. Hiraga said that, in future, daimyos will be figureheads only, the good ones, that power will be exercised through councils of samurai, of all ranks, equally, who will decide everything, from stipends, to which daimyo is worthy and who will succeed him."

"It will never work. It's a bad idea," Takeda said.

Many disagreed with him, the majority for her, but Takeda was unconvinced. Then she said, "Sensei, is it a bad idea?"

"It is a good idea, if all daimyos agreed," Katsumata said, well pleased that his teachings were bearing such fruit, that correctly they were arriving at the future by consensus. Like the others he was squatting on his heels, saying little, his mind on his close escape, inwardly seething at the new attempt on his life and narrow escape.

Too near this time, he thought, bile again in his mouth. The net is closing. Who is the traitor? The traitor has to be in this room. No other shishi units knew I was spending the night at the Whispering Pines. The traitor has to be here. Who is he—or even she? Who? "Continue, Sumomo."

"I just wanted to add . . . Takeda-san, you are Choshu, so is Hiraga-san, others from Tosa, the Sensei and others and me Satsumas, others from other fiefs, but first we are shishi with duties above family, above clan. In the New Order this will be the law—the First law for all Nippon."

"Well, if that's going to be the law . . ." One of them scratched his head. "Sensei, when the Son of Heaven has power again what will we really do? Us? All of us?"

Katsumata glanced at Takeda. "What do you think?"

Takeda said simply, "I will not be alive, it matters not at all. *Sonno-joi* is sufficient and that I tried."

"Some of us must survive," Katsumata said, "to be part of the new leadership. More important for now: Toranaga Yoshi. How to eliminate him?"

"Whenever he comes out of his sanctuary we must be ready," someone said.

"Of course," Takeda said irritably, "but he will be surrounded by guards and I doubt if we can get near him. The Sensei said not to activate our men inside. It has to be outside but that will be very difficult."

"Half a dozen of us with bows from rooftops?"

"A pity we have no cannon," another said.

They sat there in the growing light, each within his own mind: Yoshi a prize. But the next five days were foremost, then the attack on Ogama—the only way to take the Gates.

Sumomo said, "It could be easier for a woman to infiltrate the Toranaga bastion, *neh*? Once inside . . ." She smiled.

Now clouds covered the sky. The afternoon was gloomy. Even so, the wide streets outside the walls of the Shōgunate barracks were crowded with townspeople, buying and selling in the market opposite the main entrance, along with orange-clad Buddhist priests, their inevitable begging bowls outstretched, samurai strutting along, singly or in groups. Ogama patrols were prominent, each with the insignia of their fief embroidered on their clothes. Katsumata, Sumomo and half a dozen shishi strolled amongst the crowds, disguised and wearing large conical hats. Housewives, maids, servants and street sweepers and night soil collectors, porters and hawkers, moneylenders, letter writers and fortune-tellers, palanquins and ponies for samurai and highborn and never a wheeled vehicle.

All who passed the Shōgunate gates, open now but heavily guarded, bowed politely according to rank and hurried on. News that the Guardian of the Heir had arrived unbelievably without pomp had flashed through the city—and this, coupled with the never-in-historical-memory imminent arrival of the awesome Shōgun himself, arbiter of the Land, his personage shrouded with almost as much mystery as the Son of Heaven, and who, rumor had it, was even married to one of the Deity's sisters, was almost too much to bear.

At once samurai worriedly began checking the readiness of their weapons and armor, daimyos and their most trusted counselors trembled at the news, assessing their own positions and what to do and how to avoid taking any decisive action when the inevitable happened: Lord Yoshi clashed with Lord Ogama.

Activity on the street outside the Shōgunate barracks ceased as a heavily armed cortege began to come out of the gates, Yoshi's banners to the fore, soldiers surrounding a closed palanquin, with more soldiers bringing up the rear. At once everyone within seeing distance put their heads to the earth, all samurai stood still, then bowed deeply until the cortege had passed. Only when Yoshi and his men had vanished did a semblance of normality return. Except that Katsumata and the others were cautiously following.

Half a mile away a similar armored cortege began snaking out of the main Choshu barracks, Ogama's banners to the fore, to even greater obeisances. Inside the palanquin was Ogama. For days he had been forewarned of his enemy's arrival, just as he had been monitoring the progress of Shōgun Nobusada. His advisors had recommended waylaying Yoshi and destroying him outside Kyōto but he had refused. 'Better he becomes my pawn. Once he's here, where can he hide, where can he run?'

Details for the urgent meeting he had requested had been settled between their advisors. It was to take place in the courtyard of an empty, neutral barracks, equidistant between their headquarters. Each side to have a hundred guards. Only twenty would be mounted. Ogama and Yoshi would ride in protected, armored palanquins. One counselor each. They would arrive simultaneously.

Within moments spies were hurrying the news to the palace, to shishi groups, and to daimyos that the two most dangerous men in Nippon were, astonishingly, on the streets in armed columns at the same instant. Quickly a spy found Katsumata and whispered the where of the meeting, and by the time Ogama and Yoshi's samurai marched through the neutral gates, Katsumata and thirty men were stationed nearby—in case an opening for a suicide attack presented itself.

The courtyard was a hundred metres square with light wooden walls, easy to breach, the one-story barracks and extensive stables also of wood, dark with age. Opposing guards took up their positions, while others brought four folding chairs and placed them carefully in the center of the space.

The two men got out of their palanquins together and strode to the chairs and sat down. Then General Akeda and Basuhiro, Ogama's chief counselor, sat beside them. Basuhiro was in his forties, a narrow-eyed, scholarly samurai, his family hereditary heads of the Choshu bureaucracy for generations. Formally they bowed. Then the eyes of the two leaders locked.

Yoshi was two years younger than Ogama—twenty-six—and tall where Ogama was short and thickset, his face clean-shaven in contrast to Ogama's heavy blue-black beard. His blood line was more regal though Ogama's was equally ancient, equally renowned, both of them balanced in ruthlessness, ambition, and secretiveness.

Leisurely they went through the obligatory compliments and polite questions, fencing, waiting to begin—hands easily on their sword hilts. "Your arrival is a pleasant surprise, Lord Yoshi."

"I had to come myself to make sure the wild rumors I heard were not true."

"Rumors?"

"Amongst them that Choshu forces inhibit Shōgunate representatives, legal representatives from their positions around the Gates."

"A necessary measure to protect the Deity."

"Not necessary and against the law."

Ogama laughed. "The Deity prefers my protection to the traitorous Council of Elders who signed gai-jin Treaties against his wishes and continue to treat with them against his wishes instead of expelling them as he has asked." He motioned to Basuhiro. "Please show Lord Yoshi."

The scroll, signed by the Emperor, 'requested the Lord of Choshu to assume command of the Gates until the distressing matter of the gai-jin was settled.'

"It is not within the Deity's sphere to dictate matters temporal. That is the law—I must ask you to retire."

"Law? You refer to Toranaga law, Shōgunate law, all of which the first of your line implanted by force which disavowed the ancient, Heaven-granted rights of the Emperor to rule."

Yoshi's lips set into a thin, hard line. "Heaven granted the Emperor rights to intercede between us mortals and the gods in all matters spiritual. Matters temporal were always in the sphere of mortals, of Shōguns. The Emperor granted Shōgun Toranaga and his line perpetual rights to deal with all matters temporal."

"I repeat that the Emperor was forced to agree an—"

"And I repeat this is the law of the land that has kept the land at peace for two and a half centuries."

"It is no longer valid." Ogama waved the paper. "What a previous Emperor was forced to concede, this Emperor has freely cancelled."

Yoshi's voice became softer, more deadly. "A temporary mistake. Clearly the Son of Heaven has been given misguided advice by self-seeking malcontents, as he will soon realize."

"You accuse me?" The grip of all four men tightened on their hilts.

"I merely point out, Lord Ogama, your piece of paper was obtained by false information, and is not according to the law. The Presence is and always has been surrounded by ambitious men—and women. That is why he granted perpetual rights to Shōgun Toranaga and the following Shōgunate to guide him in all matters an—"

A bellow of laughter cut him off and set everyone within the walls even more on edge. "Guide? Guide did you say? The Deity's to be guided by Anjo Nori, Toyama, Adachi and now that slobbering half-wit Zukumura? By incompetent fools who overrule you at their leisure, make stupid agreements with vile gai-jin, against all daimyo, advice that lay the Land of the Gods and all of us open to destruction?" His face twisted with anger. "Or is he to await guidance from the child Nobusada to pull our nuts from the fire?"

"You and I, we need not wait, Ogama-dono," Yoshi said smoothly, knowing that his major strength was in his calm. "Let us discuss this in private—the two of us."

Ogama stared at him. A slight breeze picked up and rustled the banners. "When?"

"Now."

Thrown off balance a moment, Ogama hesitated. He glanced at Basuhiro. The small man smiled with the front of his face. "I would have thought that important matters should be discussed openly, Sire, not that my poor advice would be of value. Private agreements can sometimes be misinterpreted, by either side—that was your honored father's rule."

Ogama's eyes went back to Yoshi. "This Shōgun visit to the Emperor, to kowtow, to 'ask advice,' the first time in the whole Toranaga period, this negates the very kernel of your Toranaga structure, eh? Worse, it clouds any future settlement between the Son of Heaven and . . . future leaders, for of course mortals will rule, eh?"

"In private, Ogama-dono."

Ogama hesitated, dark eyes recessed in the weathered face. In spite of himself, in spite of knowing that this man was potentially the only one in the Land who could perhaps gather enough opposition to prevent him reaching the prize he sought, he enjoyed the clash, enjoyed meeting face-to-face. He waved his hand, dismissing Basuhiro, who obeyed at once though clearly disapprovingly. Akeda bowed and also moved away, even more watchful for the expected treachery he had warned against.

"So ka?"

Yoshi bent forward slightly and kept his voice low, his lips hardly moving in case Basuhiro, who had placed himself out of earshot, could lip-read. "The Council vote was four to one against me in favor of the Shōgun visit. Of course the visit is a major mistake, Anjo cannot and will not see that. The present Council will vote as he wishes, on any subject. Nobusada is a puppet until he is eighteen, in two years, when formally he can create many changes and problems if he so wishes. Does that answer all your questions?''

Ogama frowned, astonished that his opponent would be so open. "You said, 'in private,' Yoshi-dono, what do you want to say in private that of course I will tell my advisors afterwards and you will tell yours?''

"Some secrets are better kept between leaders, than. . ." Yoshi added deliberately, "than with certain retainers."

"Eh? What does that mean?"

"You have spies—retainers—within my gates, *neh*? How else did you know I arrived when I did? Surely you don't think I don't have men here, and spies within your walls?''

Ogama's face became grimmer. "What secrets?"

"Secrets we should keep. For example, Anjo is very sick and will die within a year—or at the very least will have to resign." Yoshi had seen the flicker of immediate interest that Ogama could not totally contain. "If you want proof I could tell you how your spies can confirm it."

"Good, thank you," Ogama said, docketing that for immediate action without waiting for guidance. "I would like the means to prove such pleasant news. So?''

Yoshi pitched his voice lower. "Within this year—if we were allied—it will be easy to ensure you are appointed an Elder. Then jointly we would approve the other three.''

"I doubt if we could ever agree, Yoshi-dono," Ogama said with a twisted smile, "neither on a Council, or which of us would be *tairō*, the Leader.''

"Ah, but I will vote for you.''

"Why would you be so stupid?" Ogama said blankly. "You must know I would at once demolish your Shōgunate."

"As it exists, yes. I agree we should. I would like to do it now. If I had power I would do it now and make reforms together with the advice of a council of all daimyos, including Outside Lords." He saw Ogama's astonishment increase and knew he was gaining. "But I can't, I must wait until Anjo resigns or dies.''

"Why not sooner than later, eh? If he's the boil on your balls, lance it! You are both in Yedo Castle, eh?''

"That would precipitate the civil war I do not want, no daimyo wants. I agree the Shōgunate and Bakufu must be reorganized radically—your views and mine are very similar. Without your support I could not achieve reform." Yoshi shrugged. "It is difficult to believe but it is an offer.''

The other man said, "With Anjo out of the way you could do whatever you wanted. You could tempt Sanjiro and the fool of Tosa, perhaps both together, eh? If you three allied against me, perhaps I am a dead man and my fief ended. Then you divide them and you are the power." His lips curled into the smile that was not a smile. "Or more likely they stay together and divide you."

"Much more likely. So why not choose power to us and not them. First, together we crush Tosa."

Again the short, hard laugh. "Not easily, not with Sanjiro and his Satsuma legions ready to go to Tosa's aid at once—he could never allow us to smash Tosa, because then he is isolated and we would turn on him. He would never allow me to smash Tosa, which I could do in time, let alone allow an alliance between us. Not possible to split them although they hate each other. At length we would beat them but neither of us can easily sustain a lengthy war—and certainly never while the gai-jin are on our shores and ready to exploit us."

"Leave the gai-jin for the moment, except to say that I oppose the Treaties, want all gai-jin expelled, want—with all my strength—to fulfill the Emperor's request, want the Elders replaced and most of the Bakufu dismissed."

Again Ogama stared at him, hardly able to believe his ears. "Such private thoughts, lethal thoughts, so openly spoken will not remain secret for long. If true."

"They are true. They are spoken privately, between us. I gamble with you, yes. But there is purpose: Nippon. I propose a secret alliance: together we could control all power. You are a good leader, you possess the Shimonoseki Straits, your cannon cannot stop the gai-jin ships until we can buy or build an equal fleet and modernize our armies— gai-jin ships, cannon and firearms are all we need. And you are strong enough and clever enough to understand the problems confronting us."

"They are?"

"Five main ones: a weak, stupid and out-of-date Shōgunate supported by an even more stupid Bakufu; second, the nation is divided; third, the gai-jin and the need for us to modernize before their ships, cannons and rifles enslave us like they enslaved China; fourth, how to obliterate all shishi whose influence grows in spite of the smallness of their numbers. And then fifth: the Princess Yazu."

"Four, I agree. But why is she a problem?"

"Nobusada is a child, querulous and simple, yes, and I think he will remain one. On the other hand, she is strong, educated, and cunning, cunning beyond her years."

"But a woman," Ogama cut in irritably, "with no army, no purse, and once she becomes a mother all her energies will be expended on her sons. You see fire in a bowl of water."

"But say her husband is impotent."

"What?"

"That is what his doctors whisper to me. Say also he is totally within her spell—believe me this girl has all the wits and devilment of a wolf kami! This visit is her idea, the beginning of her plan: to put him and through him the Shōgunate into the clutches of Court sycophants who have no temporal experience, who will misguide the Deity and wreck us all."

"She could never do it," Ogama said sourly, "however clever; no daimyo would accept such madness."

"Step one: the visit, step two: the Shōgun takes up permanent residence in the palace. From then on, supported by the Emperor's requests, her brother's requests, decisions come down through her cronies, one of whom is your Prince Fujitaka."

"I do not believe that!"

"Certainly he will not admit it. I can give you proof in a little while that he is not really working for you but against you." Yoshi kept his voice down and filled with sincerity. "Once Nobusada is permanently inside the walls, she rules. That is why she is a problem."

Ogama sighed and sat back, again weighing what his adversary had been saying, much of which was true, wondering how far he could trust him. Certainly a secret alliance had possibilities, if the price extracted was high enough.

"The answer to her is to break the marriage," he said thinly. "The Emperor was asked to approve it, eh? Perhaps the Emperor would be happy to request the annulment. At once you neutralize her, gain back support from the many who detest the Toranaga connection as a gross impertinence . . . not my opinion," he added hastily, seeing a momentary flush, not wanting an open clash yet, so much yet to hear and to decide.

After a moment, Yoshi nodded. "A good idea, Ogama-dono. It had not occurred to me." Indeed it had not. The more he thought about it, the more titillating the offshoots became. "That should have priority. Excellent."

Across the square a horse neighed restlessly and skittered. Both men watched while the soldier holding the bridle gentled her, Ogama wondering in his most secret heart if, when he had eliminated Yoshi—and then, without a hiccup, Nobusada, the rest of the Toranagas and their allies—and became Shōgun, if he should then inherit this Imperial Princess. No woman would ever give me a problem, she would be spawning sons so quickly even gods would smile.

"So what is your proposal?" he asked, his head reeling with the wonderful avenues a temporary alliance might open.

"We make a secret agreement from today to join forces and influence and formulate plans: first to smash the shishi; second to neutralize Anjo and Sanjiro of Satsuma; third, a surprise attack on Tosa being a priority. The moment Anjo is dead or resigns, I will propose you as Elder in his place and guarantee your appointment. Simultaneously Zukumura will resign and a replacement, agreed in advance by both of us, put in his place. Three to two. Toyama I keep, Adachi is replaced by your appointee. I vote for you to be the Council Leader."

"With the rank of *tairō*."

"To be Chief Minister of the Council, that is enough."

"Perhaps not. In return for what?"

"From today Tosa and Satsuma are considered enemy. You will commit all necessary force for a joint, surprise attack on Tosa the moment it is feasible. We divide his fief."

"As he is an Outside Lord, his lands should go to an Outside Lord."

"Perhaps, perhaps not," Yoshi said easily. "You agree never to ally yourself with Tosa and Satsuma against me, or the Shōgunate. If, I should say when, Satsuma and Tosa separately or together attack you, I bind myself to support you at once with massive force."

"Next?" Ogama asked impassively.

"You agree not to take sides against me, as I agree not to take sides against you."

"Next?"

"From today, quietly, each in our own way, we work to annul the marriage."

"Next?"

"Last: the Gates. You agree that legal, legitimate Shōgunate forces take back control from dawn tomorrow."

Ogama's face closed. "I already showed you I am the legal and legitimate representative of the Deity."

"I already pointed out, though the document is certainly signed correctly, the signature was, regretfully, obtained by misrepresentation."

"So sorry, no."

"The Gates must come back into Shōgunate control."

"Then we have little left to talk about."

Yoshi sighed. His eyes slitted. "Then, sadly, there will be a new request from the Emperor—for you to leave the Gates and leave Kyōto with all your men."

Just as coldly Ogama stared back at him. "I doubt it."

"I, Toranaga Yoshi, guarantee it. In six or seven days Shōgun Nobusada and his wife are within the palace. As Guardian I have immediate access to him—and to her. Both will see the correctness of my argument—about the Gates and much else."

"What much else?"

"The Gates should not be a problem for you, Ogama-dono. I would give guarantees not to flaunt this in your face, would 'gratefully accept your kind invitation to assume control,' would not fortify them against you. What is so difficult? The Gates are mostly a symbol. I advise you formally, to continue the peace and ensure order in the Land until Anjo is onwards, the Shōgunate should have their place there."

Ogama hesitated, in a quandary. Yoshi could easily have such another 'request' sent to him, that he would have to accept. "I will give you an answer, in a month."

"So sorry, noon on the sixth day from now is the limit."

"Why?"

"In five days Nobusada reaches Otsu. By the dusk on the sixth day Nobusada will go through the Gates. I require possession, temporary possession, before that." It was said so gently and so politely.

Their eyes locked. Noncommittally, but equally politely, Ogama said, "I will think about all of this, Yoshi-dono." Then he bowed, Yoshi bowed, both men walked to their palanquins and everyone in the square sighed with relief that their ordeal was over and the expected bloodbath had not happened.

31

Friday, 21st November:

THE WAY STATION OF OTSU HAD
been bustling all day in a crescendo of excitement, anticipation paired
with fear over final preparations for tonight's stop of the impossibly
august visitors, Shōgun Nobusada and the Princess Yazu. For weeks
the citizens had been brooming streets, cleaning all dwellings, hovels,
outhouses—roofs, walls, wells, gardens manicured—new tiles, shojis,
tatamis, verandas, with the Inn of Many Flowers, the best and biggest
in the whole of Otsu, still in a state of near panic.

It had begun the moment it was known the Hallowed Travellers had
declined to stay in the nearby Shōgunate castle of Sakamoto that had
graced the area since before Sekigahara, selecting the Inn instead:
"Everything must be perfect!" the Patron wailed, awed and at the
same time petrified. "Anything not perfect will merit beheading or at
the very least a whipping, man, woman or child! Tales of the honor
done to us this one night will be remembered through the ages—our
successes or failures! The Lord High Shōgun himself? In all his glory?
His wife, a sister of the Deity? *Oh ko.* . . ."

Late in the afternoon, veiled, surrounded by guards and counselors
and well screened from being observed, Shōgun Nobusada hurried
from his palanquin through the gates into the isolated section of the Inn
reserved for him, with the Princess and their entourage of personal
bodyguards, servants, her ladies-in-waiting and maids. There were
forty traditional raised bungalows of four rooms each, surrounding the

inner sanctum of the Shōgun's sleeping quarters and bathhouse, many of the covered verandas interlocking in a maze of pleasing walks and bridges over delicate pools and streams that came down from tiny mountains and all self-contained within a high, thick hedge of manicured hemlocks.

The room was warm and spotless, with new tatamis and polished charcoal braziers. Nobusada threw his veiled hat and outer clothes aside, tired and querulous. As always the palanquin had been uncomfortable and the ride bumpy. "I hate this place already," he said to their Chamberlain, whose head was touching the floor beside those of an echelon of maids. "It's so small and stinks and I ache all over! Is the bath ready?"

"Ah, yes, Sire, everything is as you require."

"Otsu at long last, Sire," Princess Yazu said gaily, sweeping in with several ladies-in-waiting. "Tomorrow we arrive home and everything will be marvelous." She dropped her huge, also veiled, hat and outer clothes. Maids scrambled to gather them up. "Tomorrow we will be home! Home, Sire! Bypassing a few way stations will be well worth it, neh?"

"Oh, yes, Yazu-chan, if you say so," he said, smiling at her, quickly caught up in her exuberance.

"You will meet all my friends, cousins, aunts, uncles, elder sister and baby sister, my dear stepbrother Sachi, he's nine this year——" she twirled with happiness——"and hundreds of less close relatives and in a few days you'll meet the Emperor and he will greet you as his brother too and solve all our problems and we will live in tranquility ever after. It's cold in here. Why isn't everything ready? Where is the bath?"

Their Chamberlain—a portly, greying man of fifty with few teeth and heavy jowls—had already been here a day with an advance party of special maids and cooks to prepare their quarters, and particular foods and fruits, with an abundance of polished rice, which the Shōgun's delicate stomach required and the Princess demanded. Superb flower arrangements by a Master of *ikebana* abounded. Again he bowed, inwardly cursing her. "Extra charcoal heaters are ready, Imperial Highness. The bath is ready, your light meal just as you and Shōgun Nobusada ordered, dinner the same. It will be the most sumptuous——"

"Emiko! Our bath!"

At once her chief lady-in-waiting led her out and down the corridor, cocooned by other ladies and maids like the queen bee she was. Nobusada glared up at the Chamberlain and stamped his tiny foot.

"Am I to be kept waiting? Show me the bath and send for the masseuse, I want my back rubbed now. And make sure there is no noise—I forbid noise!"

"Yes, Sire, the Captain issues the order daily and I will send the masseuse to the bathhouse, Sire. Sako will b—"

"Sako? She's not as good as Meiko—where's Meiko?"

"So sorry, she's sick, Sire."

"Tell her to get better! Tell her to be better by sunset. No wonder she's sick. I feel sick! This foul journey! *Baka!* How many days on the road? It should be at least fifty-three and it's less than . . . why all the haste . . . ?"

The Captain of the Escort waited for the Chamberlain in the garden. He was in his thirties, bearded, highly trained, a renowned Master of Swords. His adjutant hurried up.

"Everything is secure, sir."

"Good. It should all be routine by now," the Captain said, his voice weary and edged. Both wore light travelling armor and hats and two swords over Shōgunate tunics and pantaloons. "Only one more day— then our problems get worse. I still cannot believe the Council and Guardian would allow such a dangerous venture."

His adjutant had heard the same thing said every day. "Yes, Captain. At least we will be in our own barracks, with hundreds more men."

"Not enough, never enough, we should never have left. But we did and karma is karma. Check the rest of the men and make sure the evening roster of guards is correct. And then tell the horse master to look at my mare, to take a look at her left foot, she may have split her hoof . . ." Shoeing horses was unknown in Japan at this time. "She almost shied passing the barrier, then come back and report." The man hurried away.

The Captain was more satisfied than usual. His tour of the Inn and its grounds within the high, giant perimeter bamboo fences, and particularly this sector, the hedged area with a single gateway, had reassured him that the Shōgun's cluster of bungalows was easy to defend, that all other travellers had been forbidden the Inn for this night, that the watch knew the password and were clear on their prime duty: no one was allowed within five metres of the Shōgun or his wife uninvited, and no one, ever, with any weapons—except the Guardian, the Council of Elders and himself, and any guards accompanying him. The law was well known, the punishment for an armed approach death, for both the armed man and the unalert guards—unless pardoned by the Shōgun personally.

"Ah, Chamberlain! Is there any change of plans?"

"No, Captain." The old man sighed and mopped his brow, his jowls shaking. "The August Ones are bathing as usual, then they will rest as usual, take their real bath and massage at sunset as usual, after which they will dine as usual, play *Go* as usual and go to bed. All is in order?"

"Here, yes." The Captain had a garrison of a hundred and fifty samurai at any one time within the compound that measured about two hundred metres square. A unit of ten men guarded the only entrance, a pleasing bridge over a stream that led to tall decorative beams and equally ornate gates. Around the whole perimeter hedge a samurai was stationed every ten paces. These would be relieved by fresh units from the six hundred samurai lodging in barracks just outside the main gate or nearby in other Inns. Patrols would scour the garden and fence line discreetly, as noise and an obvious samurai presence infuriated the Princess and therefore her husband.

Above them the clouds were thickening, a bleak, misted sun not yet on the horizon, a high wind toying with the clouds. It was cold and promised to be colder. Servants were lighting lanterns amongst the shrubs, their light already reflected in the pools, and glistening off rocks that had been moistened for that effect moments ago.

"It's beautiful," the Captain said. "Easily the best, though most of the other Inns have been good." This was the first time he had ever made such a journey. All his life he had been within or near Yedo Castle, with or near Nobusada, or the previous Shōgun. "Beautiful, yes, but I'd rather have the Lord Shōgun and his wife in Sakamoto Castle than here. You should have insisted."

"I tried, Captain, but . . . but she decided."

"I will be glad when we are in our own barracks, when they are within the palace walls and even gladder when we and they are safe at home in Yedo Castle."

"Yes," the Chamberlain said, privately weary of his Master and Mistress and the constant fault finding, nagging and petulance. Still, he thought, his back aching, wanting a bath and massage too, and the attentions of his youthful friend, I suppose I would be the same if I were as exalted as them, so mollycoddled from birth, and only sixteen. "May I ask the password, Captain?"

"Until the middle of the night it is 'Blue Rainbow.' "

Two hundred metres away on the eastern outskirts of the village, an old broken-down farmhouse huddled at the end of an alley not far from the Tokaidō and the Otsu barrier. Inside, the leader of the shishi attack team, a Choshu youth called Saigo, glowered at the farmer, his wife, four children, father and mother, brother and a maid who knelt petrified, crowded into a corner. This was the only room and it served for living, eating, working, sleeping. A few scrawny chickens in a rafter cage clucked nervously. "Remember what I told you. You know nothing, have seen nothing."

"Yes, Lord, certainly, Lord," the old man whimpered.

"Shut up! Turn your backs, face the corner and close your eyes, all of you. Tie your sashes around your eyes!"

They obeyed. Instantly.

Saigo was eighteen, tall and strongly built, with a rugged handsome face and he wore a short dark tunic and pantaloons similar to the samurai at the Inn and two swords, straw sandals, no armor. When he was satisfied the peasants were blind as well as docile, he sat beside the door and peered out through rips in the window paper and began to wait.

He could see the barrier and guard houses clearly. It was not yet sunset so the barrier was still open to latecomers. It had taken him and his men many days to find this place, ideal for their purposes. The back door led to a maze of alleys and paths, perfect for a sudden retreat. This afternoon, the moment the Shōgun's party had passed through the barrier, he had taken sudden possession.

Footsteps. His hand readied his sword, then relaxed. Another youth came in silently, to be followed by another from a different direction. Soon seven more were within. Outside one stood guard, another at the corner of the alley that joined with the Tokaidō, with an eleventh man, hiding in the village, to act as courier to gallop the glad tidings of success to Katsumata in Kyōto that would signal the attack on Ogama and the Gates. They were tough young men, dressed as he was without armor and identification, formerly goshi—the lowest rank of samurai—now ronin, all more or less the same age, nineteen to twenty-two. Only Saigo, eighteen, and Tora, seventeen, his Satsuma second in command, were younger. Drafts through rents in the window shivered them—that and their tension.

With signs he motioned them to check their swords, shuriken and other lethal weapons—no need for words during the whole operation. As much as could be planned had been decided over the days. They all agreed it was to be conducted in silence. A glance out of the window. The sun was touching the horizon, sky clear. It was time.

Solemnly he bowed to them and they bowed to him.

He turned his attention back to the peasants. "Three men will be outside," he said harshly. "One rustle out of any of you until I get back and they'll fire the farm."

Again the old man whimpered.

Saigo gestured to the others. They followed him. So did the outside guard and the one on the corner. No turning back now. Those who were Buddhist had said a final prayer before a shrine, those who were Shinto had lit a last stick of incense and so joined their spirit with the thread of smoke that represented the fragility of life. All had written their death poems and sewn them to the breast of their tunics. Proudly they had given their correct fiefs; only the names were false.

Once in the alley they split up into pairs, each taking an independent route. Soon they were in position, crouched down in the tall weeds and coarse vegetation beside the perimeter fence at the back of the Inn, within sight of each other, Saigo at the southeast corner. The fence was three metres high and strongly made of giant bamboo and spiked at the top. By now shadows were losing form in the fading light.

Waiting. Heartbeats heavy in their chests, palms sweaty, the slightest rustle an enemy patrol. Strange, strong taste in every mouth. Stabbing pains in the loins. Somewhere nearby a cricket began its urgent mating call, reminding Saigo of his death poem:

> *A cricket with its joy-filled song,*
> *Dies quickly anyway.*
> *Better to be joy filled than sad.*

He felt his eyes mist as the sky was misting, So beautiful to be so happy yet so sad.

From inside the fence they could hear voices of servants, maids, occasionally samurai, and the clatter of metal dishes, for the kitchen area was not far away. In the distance a samisen and the singer. Waiting. Sweat fell down Saigo's face. Then he heard the approaching, barely perceptible rustle of a kimono and a girl whisper, "Blue Rainbow . . . Blue Rainbow." Then silence. Again sounds of the Inn.

At once he motioned to Tora, beside him. Silently this youth hurried to the other units and gave them the words and came back again. At Saigo's signal each pair found the ladders they had made, camouflaged and hidden in the wild undergrowth so carefully, set them against the fence. Again he watched the sky. As the last thread of sunlight went, another signal and they went up and over the fence as one man, jumping to the ground that was soft and tilled, crouching motionlessly in the meticulous shrubbery but ready for an instant frontal attack.

Miraculously, no alarm yet. They looked up, warily. Ahead, sixty metres away, was the Shōgun's section, the thatched roofs showing just above the tall, thick hedge of hemlock, the roofs of the central sleeping section and bathhouses a little higher. The main entrance was well away from them, its doors still open. Everything exactly as they expected. Except for the guards, many more than planned for. Bile jumped into their mouths.

To their right were the main kitchens with great steaming cauldrons and massed staff—more guards there. Left and all around the compound were a scattering of guest cottages, in other gardens with streams and bridges, each with a well-tended entrance path curling through the shrubs. Silence there and no lights within, just one lantern at the front veranda. More anguish, they had expected them to be occupied and to serve as cover and a necessary diversion.

Karma, Saigo thought. Even so our positions are as we predicted, so are those of the enemy, the plan is good and we know the password. During the previous two weeks, disguised as an ordinary samurai traveller, he had found the correct courtesan and inveigled his way into her emotions so that soon he had been taken on a secret guided tour of the grounds—even to the places where the Hallowed Travellers were to rest.

'Why not?' he had whispered. 'Who will know? They're not due here for days—ah, you are so beautiful. Let us join where a Shōgun and a sister of the Son of Heaven will join—that will be something to whisper to our grandchildren, eh? I think I shall never leave you. . . .'

It had been equally easy to find a bathhouse maid who was secretly fanatic for shishi, and to pursuade her there was no risk to listen and whisper a few words into the night.

He felt Tora touch his arm. Anxiously the youth pointed. A patrol had come through the far gates. It began to circle the grounds. Small pools of light were beneath the lanterns. Inevitably the patrol would come this way and be very close. His signal, the call of a night bird, gave the order.

At once they sank deeper into the foliage and kept their heads lowered, hardly breathing. The patrol approached, and then passed without seeing them—just as Katsumata had forecast when he had suggested their attack plan: 'Initially it will be easy to be missed in the dark. Never forget surprise is with you. Your infiltration will be totally unexpected. Who would dare to attack the Shōgun when he is surrounded by so many men? At a way station? Impossible! Remember, with stealth, surprise and ferocious speed two or three of you will reach the kernel—and one is enough.'

Saigo watched the enemy marching away. A marvelous glow pervaded him and all his confidence returned. Another short wait until the enemy patrol had turned the corner, then he motioned for the attack teams to move into their predetermined positions. Protected from view by the shrubbery, four men slithered away to his right, two to his left. When all were in position, he took a deep breath to help slow his heartbeat. His signal, again the call of a night bird, gave the order to begin.

At once the pair on his far right eased out of the shrubs onto the path, adjusting the ties on their pantaloons, and began strolling away, their arms around each other as lovers will. Within moments they had been noticed by the guards at the nearest hedge. "You two, halt!"

The two youths obeyed and one called out, "Blue Rainbow, Blue Rainbow, Lord Sergeant," and both laughed, pretending to be shy at being seen, then continued to stroll away, hand in hand.

"Halt! Who are you?"

"Ah, so sorry, just friends on a nightly stroll," the youth said in his softest, most gentle voice. "Blue Rainbow, have you forgotten our password?"

One of the samurai laughed and said, "If the Captain catches you 'strolling' in the bushes around here you'll get more than a Blue Rainbow and both pairs of cheeks will know another type of beating!"

Again both youths pretended to laugh. Unhurried, they walked away, ignoring more strident calls to stop. Finally the Sergeant shouted, "You two. Come here, at once!" They faced him a moment, calling out plaintively there was no harm in what they were doing. Saigo and the others, covered by the diversion, had been crawling into final positions. Taut with excitement that they had not been noticed, they rested a second, knowing this diversion was almost over. The sound of the night bird Saigo made this time was loud enough to reach the two youths.

Without hesitation, they pretended to laugh and ran off gaily, hand in hand, directly away from the guards as though playing a game. Their path carelessly took them through a pool of light and allowed them to be seen clearly for the first time. With a shout of rage the Sergeant and four men charged in pursuit. Sentries at the far main gate peered into the darkness to see what was happening, and those guards at the hedge who could see beckoned others nearby, all of them alert.

The two shishi were quickly surrounded. Back to back, swords ready, they stood silently at bay under a barrage of questions, nothing effeminate now in their stance or the way their lips were drawn back from the teeth.

Enraged, the Sergeant stepped forward a pace. The youth opposing him readied. His right hand darted into his sleeve and came out with a shuriken and before the Sergeant could duck or move aside the five-pointed circle of steel was embedded in his throat and he fell burbling, choking in his own blood. Both shishi leapt to the attack but neither could break out of the net and though they fought bravely, wounding three of the samurai, they were no match for the others who, though wanting to disarm them and capture them alive, could not do so.

One of the youths took a sword thrust through the lower part of his back and cried out, severely wounded but not enough to kill him immediately. The other whirled to his aid and in that instant was mortally wounded and crumpled, dying. *"Sonno-joi,"* he gasped. Aghast, the other heard him, made one last impotent attempt to close with an attacker, then abruptly turned his sword on himself and fell on it.

"Find the Captain," a samurai panted, blood streaming from a sword slash in his arm. One of the others ran off as the rest collected around the bodies, the Sergeant still gurgling though dying fast. "Nothing we can do for him. Never seen a shuriken so fast." Someone turned the two dead men over. "Look, death poems! Shishi all right—eeee, both Satsumas! They must have gone mad."

"Sonno-joi!" another muttered. "That's not mad."

"It's mad to say that aloud," a hard-faced ashigaru warned him. "If an officer hears you . . ."

"Listen, these motherless dogs had the password, there's a traitor here!" More nervously they looked at each other.

Over on the right the kitchen staff were transfixed, not knowing what was going on. Many samurai had been drawn away from the hedge and stood gaping at the bodies, creating the opening Katsumata and Saigo had planned.

Again Saigo signalled. His two strongest fighters broke out of the bushes on his extreme right and ran for the far southeast corner. Almost at once they were spotted. Cursing, the two nearest samurai rushed to intercept as others ran to their aid. Violent hand-to-hand combat began again, darkness helping the attackers immeasurably. One defender screamed and went down clawing his half-severed arm. More samurai were drawn away from the hedge immediately in front of Saigo and just before the samurai overwhelmed the two fighters, in a coordinated maneuver the two shishi broke off the battle and pretended to flee pell-mell for the fence near the kitchens, well away from Saigo and the three final teams. As they fled they unwound ropes from their waists with small grapples on the end. Nearing the fence, they threw them deftly, caught the top, and began to climb, their pursuers redoubling their efforts.

By now all attention was on these two. Guards near the entrance and the far side of the Shōgun's complex, still not knowing exactly what was happening other than that two ronin were loose in the compound and were now trying to escape over the fence, hurried to intercept them. Others ran out and down the perimeter fence to catch them on that side.

One of the shishi reached the top of the fence but before he could scramble over it a knife impaled him and he fell backwards into the shrubberies. The other man abandoned his rope, leapt beside his friend and just had time to see him bury his own knife in his throat to avoid capture before he went down under a flurry of blows. He twisted and turned and fought with great strength but was soon disarmed and pinioned to the earth by four samurai.

"Now, who are you?" a samurai asked, out of breath. "Who are you and what's your game?"

"*Sonno-joi*. . . . obey your Emperor," the man panted, and again tried to fight out of their grip but could not. Others were collecting around him and he was confident he had done his part in the attack and could continue his diversion for a little while longer, unafraid of capture, because there was a poison vial in the neck of his kimono within reach of his teeth. "I am Hiroshi Ishii of Tosa, and demand to see the Shōgun."

From where he was hidden Saigo and the five men with him could hear their compatriot but their attention was fixed on the hedge facing them and on the far entrance. The few remaining guards left it to gather around the doomed man and now, at last, the target was open. "Attack!"

The six men leapt to their feet and charged, Saigo and Tora leading the wedge. They had covered perhaps half the distance before there was a warning shout and samurai surrounding the bodies of the first team began running back to head them off. At once Ishii redoubled his efforts to escape, shouting and raving to distract those holding him but a fist smashed him into unconsciousness.

"You two stay here," the samurai panted, sucking his bruised knuckles. "Don't kill the son of a dog, we'll need him alive." He got up painfully and limped off to join the others, a bad sword cut on his thigh.

Some of the defenders were gaining on the six shishi who still ran directly at the hedge that curled away in both directions. "Now!" Saigo ordered. Immediately the pair to his right turned back into defensive positions, shurikens in their hands. Warily the running samurai slowed, darted left and right, feinted, then attacked, the shurikens finding targets but not wounding badly enough and another hand-to-hand began, six samurai against the two of them.

Reinforcements were running from the main gate, others from the first diversion, all of them, defenders and attackers, converging on their lodestar—the gateway to the Shōgun's lair. When the men from the Inn's main gate saw to their horror that the hedges and entrance had been left completely unguarded—though the doors were closed—with Saigo and three others running fast and not far from the hedge, they swung away to position themselves between the shishi and the entrance, leaving others to attack them, and frantically raced to protect the gate. Behind Saigo and Tora the two fighters were attacking, retreating, still covering their rear. Both men had sustained wounds but two samurai were on the ground, writhing with pain. Four against two with others not far away.

"Now!" Saigo ordered, and the pair on his left broke away and stabbed for the entrance. No doubt they would reach it before the defenders and this caused others heading for Saigo also to change direction and make for the entrance as well. At once Saigo and Tora whirled and joined the fight behind them. Their ferocious charge dispatched two of the remaining four samurai and helped eliminate the remaining enemy—only Saigo and Tora, though breathing heavily, were untouched.

At once Saigo ordered, "Go!" the two men sang out, *"Sonno-joi,"* and, painfully, rushed to support the attack on the entrance, drawing off more samurai, leaving Saigo and Tora to resume their headlong charge for the hedge.

The first pair of shishi attacking the gateway reached the narrow path and ran for the doors. One man began to push them open. At that moment an arrow thwacked viciously into the wood and then both men were hit and shortly riddled with more arrows from bowmen amongst the reinforcements. They cried out, impotently tried to continue, and died on their feet. The second team gained the pathway. One rushed at the oncoming samurai, the other went for the gates, stumbled over his dead comrades, and died, pierced with four arrows. His friend hit the samurai head-on, and was quickly killed. Only minutes had passed since the beginning.

Now the way was open to the pathway. In moments the fleetest of the defenders would reach the entrance and then there would be no way that Saigo and Tora, almost at the end of their run and due to turn for the gateway, could reach their goal. So the pace of the defenders slackened, the bowmen took aim leisurely, confident of victory. To their astonishment, instead of wheeling along the hedge, Saigo and Tora kept the straight line of their rush and hurled themselves forward at the hedge, side by side.

Their momentum caused them to burst through it, that and the accuracy of their leap. Over preceding days, Saigo found that though the branches were tightly interwoven, the trunks of the trees were about half a metre apart, and, he had surmised, if judged correctly, a rush would carry them through.

It did, successfully, though the branches lashed them bloodily around the face and arms. The two men picked themselves up exactly where Saigo had planned—on the meandering path beside the veranda that led to the bathhouse. For a moment no one was in sight, then several terrified maids and servants gaped at them from a doorway and vanished. Saigo led the soundless dash down the path and up the steps and around the veranda corner. Two anxious officials came out of nowhere, unarmed and unprepared, one of them the Chamberlain. Saigo cut both down, killing the Chamberlain instantly, and wounding the other, and charged onwards. Tora finished off this man, jumped over the bodies and rushed in pursuit.

Along the veranda and around the corner and smashing through the light shoji screen. they burst into the bathhouse. Half-naked maids stared at them panic-stricken: swords bloody, faces scratched and bloody, kimonos ripped and bloody. The air was warm, sweet-smelling, humid.

Saigo bellowed with rage. The steaming, shallow bath, fed from a natural hot spring, was empty, so were the four wooden steam boxes, and so were the massage tables, except one. In an instant he saw every detail of the tiny naked girl lying there, the shock in her eyes, her half-opened mouth, teeth blackened, her plume of jet hair twisted into a stark white towel, more towels under her, small breasts and limbs and feet, dark brown nipples, all of her curved, inviting, golden skin now pinkish from the heat of the bath, oiled and fragrant—and the blind, half-naked masseuse, standing motionlessly over her, head cocked, listening intently.

So easy to kill the girl and all of them, but his orders were not to harm the Princess at all costs. Nonetheless his fury at being cheated— for their timing had been perfect, their intelligence perfect and the Shōgun's pattern never varying—made his head seem about to explode. The fury turned to lust and shivered him, all of him wanting her, now, fast, brutally, any way, the wife before the husband, death to both of them but first her splayed.

His lips came away from his teeth and he charged across the expanse. The maids scattered, one fainted, the Princess gasped and lay motionless, petrified. But his obsession with the Shōgun diverted him and his rush bypassed her and took him to the shoji door where again he crashed through and, once more, with Tora close behind, unerringly led the run along verandas towards the sleeping quarters and his prey, gardens to his right, rooms left—no longer a thinking man just a raging killing animal. Shoji doors were open, faces there. Maids and youths and ladies-in-waiting and servants attracted by the commotion, dressed or half dressed for the evening or for bed or for bath, gaped at them.

No guards in these rooms. Yet.

Still no opposition. Yet.

A few more rooms to pass, doors, faces, and then he would turn the last corner and last veranda. Saigo's anticipation crested, for this was a delightful covered walkway, gardens right and left, no more rooms with waiting guards to worry about, and at the end the Shōgun's sleeping quarters where he himself and the courtesan had secretly bedded.

All senses tuned for expected danger, Tora a few paces behind him, running as fast, sounds of men approaching, pounding feet. Another room passed. Only one more doorway, last danger. Faces at the door, a doctor and a coughing youth stared at him in shock, then he was around the corner, and together they began the last charge.

Both men skidded to a stop. Their hearts stopped. Ahead an officer and three samurai came out of the sanctuary door, swords drawn, to stand waiting for them. The barest hesitation, then Saigo rushed to the kill, his or theirs, Tora equally committed—only these four men between them and the Shōgun they protected. *"Sonno-joi!"*

The Captain held the first charge, parried the blow and locked sword to sword, then twisted and hacked at Saigo as two other samurai attacked Tora, the last staying in reserve as ordered. Saigo deflected the blow and slashed back but missed. Another ferocious flurry of blow and counterblow, Saigo supremely confident, so near to success, pressing the attack, feeling superhuman and that his blade, almost of its own volition, was seeking enemy flesh as it would in seconds destroy the boy Shōgun . . .'

There was a blinding flash behind his eyes, the pounding in his head soared and he suddenly saw that doctor again and that boy again and remembered someone telling him it was believed the boy Shōgun had a hacking cough—no portraits of him, of course, not one of the shishi ever having seen him, of course: 'If you do not catch him in the bathhouse,' Katsumata had said, 'you will recognize him by his black-ened teeth, the cough, his nearness to the Princess, the quality of his robes—remember, both he and the Princess detest guards nearby.'

With enormous, heightened strength, howling like a wild beast, Saigo hacked at the Captain, who slipped on the polished floor and was, for an instant, helpless. But Saigo did not deliver the death blow, instead whirled back for the boy—and the last samurai saw the open-ing he had been ordered to wait for. His sword went deep into Saigo's side but Saigo felt none of it and cut impotently at the Shōgun wraith in front of him, again and once again and slid to the floor stabbing, already dead but not knowing it.

The Captain had leapt to his feet and hurtled to the attack on Tora, impaled him, and then like an expert butcher withdrew the blade and beheaded him with a single blow.

"Do the same to him," he gasped, pointing at Saigo, his chest heaving as he tried to regain his breath, and rushed back up the veranda. At the corner, men from the entranceway came pounding up, headed by his second in command. He cursed him and them, shoved him out of the way and hurried past saying: "Every man on this shift ordered to the square outside the Inn, disarmed and on their knees. You too!"

His heart was still pounding and he was enraged and not yet over his panic. Just before sunset Nobusada had testily sent for him: 'Take all guards from inside the hedge. Ridiculous to have them here, the rooms so small and awful! Are you helpless, so inept you can't secure this nasty little Inn? Must we bathe with guards, sleep with guards, eat with them looking at us? Go away, tonight I forbid all guards here!'

'But, Sire, I must ins—'

'You will insist on nothing. No guards inside the hedge tonight. This meeting is ended!' There was nothing the Captain could do, but then there was no need to worry. Of course everything was secure.

When the first muffled sounds of the attack had reached him he was making a final, satisfactory circuit inside the hedge, four men with him—the hedge also acting as a fine sound barrier. By the time he had reached the gate doors and looked out, he had been appalled to see four men charging the hedge, two rushing for the gates. His first thought was for the Shōgun and he ran for the bathhouse but the Chamberlain had called out: 'What's going on?'

'Men are attacking us, get the Shōgun out of the bath!'

'He's not there, he's with the doctor. . . .'

Another panicked dash, bypassing the bathhouse to the inner quarters, finding them empty, a frightened maid saying that the Lord Shōgun was in one of the rooms on the next veranda and then coming out and seeing the two men charging, no way to protect the Shōgun now but thinking if these two were attacking here perhaps they had missed his liege lord. . . .

He knew he would not truly be alive until he found him alive. This took no time. Nobusada was coughing and raving, still in fright, others around him adding to the tumult. Quickly he learned the Princess was unharmed though also hysterical. His panic left him. He disregarded Nobusada's rage, his voice icy, and every soldier nearby quailed: "Get a courier and four men on the double to rush a report ahead and except for this present shift, all guards here on the double, every man within the compound, fifty men around the sleeping quarters, two men at each corner of every veranda. And ten men permanently in sight of the Lord Shōgun until he and she are safely within the palace walls."

In midmorning the next day, within the palace walls, Yoshi hurried through the outer rim of gardens in the light rain. General Akeda was beside him. "This is terribly dangerous, Sire," he said, afraid that every shrub or thicket, however carefully tended, might hide enemies.

Both men wore light armor and swords—a rarity here where all samurai and all weapons were forbidden, except for the ruling Shōgun and an immediate guard of four, the Leader of the Elders and Guardian of the Heir.

It was almost noon. The two men were late and noticed none of the beauty surrounding them, lakes and bridges and flowering shrubs and trees groomed and cherished over centuries. Whenever a gardener saw them, the man would kowtow until they were out of sight. Over their armor were straw overmantles against the rain. All morning there had been intermittent showers. Yoshi's pace quickened.

This was not the first time he had hurried to a clandestine meeting within the palace grounds—safe but never truly safe. So difficult to have a truly safe meeting anywhere, with a spy, informer, or adversary—in secret almost impossible—always afraid of ambush, poison or hidden bowmen or musketeers. The same applied to every daimyo. His own safety factor he knew was very low. So low in fact that his father and grandfather had taught him to accept the fact that death from old age had no place in their karma.

"We are as safe as anywhere on earth," he said. "It would be unthinkable to break a truce here."

"Yes, except for Ogama. He is a liar, cheat, he should be meat for vultures, his head spiked."

Yoshi smiled and felt better. Since the appalling news of the shishi attack had arrived in the middle of the night he had been more on edge than ever—more than when on the death of his uncle he had been passed over as Shōgun and Nobusada appointed instead, more than when *Tairō* Ii had arrested him, his father and their families and sent them to rot in foul quarters. He had made preparations to rush two hundred men to meet the entourage at the Kyōto barrier, and at dawn had sent Akeda secretly to Ogama to relate what had happened and why a large party of men equipped for war were leaving his stockade.

'Tell Ogama all that we have been told, and answer any of his questions. I want no mistakes, Akeda.'

'There will be none from me, Sire.'

'Good. Then give him the letter and request an immediate answer.' Yoshi had not told Akeda what the letter contained, nor did his general ask. And when Akeda returned Yoshi said, 'Tell me exactly what he did.'

'Ogama read the letter twice and spat, cursed twice, threw it at his counselor, Basuhiro, who read it with that stony, slimy, pockmarked face of his that gave nothing away, who said, "Perhaps we should discuss this in private, Sire." I told them I would wait, I did and then after a reasonable time Basuhiro came out and said, "My Lord agrees but he will come armed and I will be armed." What's this all about, Sire?'

Yoshi told him and the old man went purple. 'You asked to meet him alone? With only myself as guard? That is craziness, just because he says he will come only with Basuhi—'

'Enough!' Yoshi knew the risks were great but he had to gamble again, had to have an answer on his proposal about the Gates and then, when he was about to leave and one of the surfeit of Shōgunate spies reported certain conversations overheard between the shishi Katsumata and others at the Inn of Whispering Pines, he had been elated he had asked for the meeting. "There he is!"

Ogama was standing in the shade of a wide-branched tree where they had agreed, Basuhiro at his side. Both were clearly suspicious, expecting treachery, but not as visibly nervous as Akeda. Yoshi had proposed that Ogama come in through the South Gate, he would use the East Gate, leaving his palanquin and guards outside with their safe conduct guaranteed. After the meeting, all four would walk out of the East Gate together.

As before, the two adversaries walked towards each other to speak alone. Akeda and Basuhiro watched tensely.

"So!" Ogama said after their formal greeting. "A handful of shishi attack through hundreds of guards like a knife through dung—and almost in Nobusada's bath, naked wife and bed before they are caught. Ten men, you say?"

"Three were Choshu ronin, the two that got through the hedge were Choshus, one of them the leader." Yoshi was not over his fright at the attack, and wondered if he dared draw his sword at this rare opportunity to challenge Ogama alone—Basuhiro presented no physical threat, with or without Akeda.

I need Ogama dead one way or another, he thought, but not yet. Not when two thousand Choshu hold the Gates and me in thrall. "All of them died without doing harm, except to some guards, the survivors not long on this earth. I hear you have offered all your Choshu ronin an amnesty?" he asked, his voice edging, wondering again if Ogama had a secret hand in the planning, which had been impeccable and, if the truth were known, should have been successful. "If shishi or not."

"Yes," Ogama said, his mouth smiling. "All daimyo should do the same, a quick and simple way to control all ronin, shishi or not. They are a pestilence that must be stopped."

"I agree. Amnesty will not stop them. May I ask, how many of your ronin have accepted your offer?"

Ogama laughed roughly. "Clearly not the ones who were in the attack! One or two so far, Yoshi-dono. How many are there in all? A hundred? Not two hundred, of which twenty or thirty may be Choshu? Choshu or not, never mind." His face hardened. "I did not plan the attack if that is what is in your mind, or know about it." The mirthless smile returned. "Unthinkable to have such a treasonous thought. Eh? Easy to stamp shishi out if you and I wanted to—but their slogan is not as easy to suppress, if indeed it should be suppressed. Power should return to the Emperor, gai-jin should be expelled. *Sonno-joi* is a good slogan, eh?"

"I could say many things, Ogama-dono, but allies should not bait one another. We are allies? You agree?"

Ogama nodded. "In principle, yes."

"Good," Yoshi said, hiding his astonishment that Ogama had agreed to his conditions. "Within the year you are Chief of the Elders. From noon I garrison the Gates." He turned to go.

"Everything as you said. Except the Gates."

The vein in Yoshi's forehead knotted. "But I said I need the Gates."

"So sorry." Ogama's hand had not tightened on his sword though his feet had shifted into a better fighting stance. "Secret allies, yes, war with Tosa, yes, with Satsuma, yes, the Gates, no. So sorry."

For a moment Yoshi Toranaga said nothing. He looked at him. Ogama stared back unafraid, waiting, ready to fight if need be. Then Yoshi sighed, wiped raindrops from the edge of his wide-brimmed hat. "I want to be allies. Allies should help one another. I have a compromise, perhaps, but first I give you some special information: Katsumata is here in Kyōto."

The blood rushed into Ogama's face. "Not possible, my spies would have told me."

"He is here and has been here for some weeks."

"There are none of Sanjiro's men in Kyōto, least of all that man. My spies would have t—"

"Ah, sorry," Yoshi said softly. "He is here, secretly, not as Sanjiro's pathfinder and spy, at least not openly. Katsumata is shishi, a Sensei of shishi, and the leader of shishi here, code name the Raven."

Ogama gaped at him. *"Katsumata is the shishi leader?"*

"Yes. And a little more. Think for a moment: Is he not Sanjiro's most trusted, long-time counselor and tactician? Did he outsmart you on behalf of Sanjiro with his false pact and foil you at Fushimi and allow Sanjiro to escape? Does that not mean Sanjiro of Satsuma is secretly the real leader of shishi and that all of their assassinations are part of his general plan to overthrow all of us, you particularly, to become Shōgun?"

"That's always been Sanjiro's goal, of course," Ogama said, momentarily glazed, many hitherto unexplained occurrences now falling into place. "If he controls all shishi too . . ." He stopped, suddenly infuriated that Takeda had never told him. Why? Is Takeda not a spy for me, not a true secret vassal after all? "Where is Katsumata now?"

"One of your patrols almost ambushed him at the Inn of Whispering Pines a few days ago."

Again color came into Ogama's face and he almost spat. "He was there? We heard that shishi were sleeping there but I never knew . . ." Once again he choked with rage that Takeda had not forewarned him that his hated enemy was within his grasp. Why? Never mind, easy to deal with Takeda. First Katsumata. I have not forgotten Katsumata ruined my surprise attack on Sanjiro. But for Katsumata, Sanjiro would be dead, I would be overlord of Satsuma, and there would be no need to talk with Toranaga Yoshi—he would be on his knees in front of me. "Where is he now? Do you know where?"

"I know the safe house where he was last night, perhaps tonight too." Yoshi added softly, "There are over a hundred shishi in Kyōto. They already plan a mass attack on you."

Ogama felt chilled, knowing there was no true defense against a fanatic assassin not afraid to die. "When?"

"It was to be at dusk tomorrow—if the attack on the Shōgun had been successful. Then, once you were dead, with adherents amongst your troops, they would seize the Gates."

It took much of Ogama's strength not to tell Yoshi a secret meeting with Takeda was due at dusk tomorrow, a perfect moment for a surprise attack. "And now that it was a failure?"

"The information I have is that the leaders are meeting tonight to decide. Now, formally, you head their target list, after Nobusada and myself."

"Why?" Ogama spluttered. "I support the Emperor, support the fight against the gai-jin."

Yoshi kept the smile off his face, knowing very well. "Let us join forces tonight. I know their meeting place, where Katsumata and most of the leaders should be—there is a dawn-to-dusk curfew in that part of the city."

Ogama exhaled. "And the price?"

"First, here is more information that seriously affects both of us." To Ogama's further disquiet, Yoshi related the details of the Elders' meeting with Sir William and the other Ministers, about his spy Misamoto, about Sir William's threat to make an armed sortie here as soon as his fleet returned, and how the threat and payment had been finessed for the moment.

"Their fleet will not pass my Shimonoseki Straits—if I order it."

"They could take the long route around South Island."

"Long route, short route, it makes no difference. If they land in or near Osaka, I, or we, will destroy them."

"The first time. With great losses but, yes, gai-jin will be repulsed. However, two days ago I received a secret report from the department of the Bakufu here who deal with China information." He brought out the scroll. "Here, read it for yourself."

"What does it say?" Ogama snapped.

"That the Yokohama fleet sent to punish the sinking of just one British ship devastated twenty leagues of China's coastline, north of Shanghai, burning all villages, sinking all shipping."

Ogama spat. "Pirates. Pirate nests." He knew much about that area. In the past it had been historic, though secret Choshu—and Satsuma—policy to send raiders to the China coast to pillage ruthlessly from Shanghai, southwards beyond Hong Kong to the Taiwan Straits. The Chinese called them *wako,* pirates, hating and fearing them so much that, for centuries, Emperors of China had forbidden any Japanese from landing on their shores, and all trade between their lands was to be conducted only by non-Japanese.

"Pirates, yes, but those scum are not cowards. Not so long ago an army of these same gai-jin humbled all China a second time and burned the Emperor's Summer Palace and Peking at their whim. Their fleets and armies are awesome in power."

"This is Nippon, not China." Ogama shrugged, not prepared to be drawn out or to divulge his plans for the defense of Choshu. But he was thinking: my coasts are rugged and rock-infested, difficult to invade and very defensible, soon impregnable when all armed emplacements are in place, and bunkers for my fighters. "And we are not Chinese."

"My thought is that we need peace between all daimyos to gain time, to manipulate gai-jin, to learn their cannon secrets and gun secrets and ship secrets and how it seems this one foul little island, smaller than our land, has become the wealthiest in the world and rules most of it."

"Lies. Lies spread to frighten cowards here."

Yoshi shook his head. "I do not believe that. First we must learn, then we can smash them. We cannot now."

"We can. This is the Land of the Gods. In Choshu I have one cannon factory, soon there will be others. Satsuma has three small steamers, the beginnings of a shipyard, soon there will be others." His face twisted. "We can smash Yokohama and this fleet and by the time others return we will be ready."

Yoshi hid his surprise at the vehemence and strength of the hatred, secretly elated he had smoked out another weapon to use. "I agree. My whole point. There, you see, Ogama-dono," he said as though greatly relieved, "we think the same though perhaps from different points. We smash them but in time, we must choose the time, gain their knowledge and let them give us the means to spike their guns and their heads." His voice firmed. "In one year you and I control the Council and Bakufu. In three or four we can buy many guns, cannon and ships."

"Paid for how? Gai-jin are greedy."

"One way is coal for their ships. Another is gold." Yoshi explained his prospecting scheme.

"Clever," Ogama said, his lips twisted into a strange smile. "In Choshu we have coal, iron and trees for ships."

"And one armament factory already."

Ogama laughed, a good laugh, and Yoshi laughed too and knew he had made a breakthrough. "True, and my batteries increase monthly." Ogama shifted his overmantle under the increasing rain and added pointedly, "So does my resolve to fire on enemy shipping, when I wish. Is that all your information, Yoshi-dono?"

"For the moment. May I advise you to slacken your grip on the Straits—in any event they are yours to play with. Yes, that's all for the moment, but as an ally you will be given all kinds of privileged information."

"As an ally I would expect privileged information." Ogama nodded half to himself. He glanced back at Basuhiro then changed his mind about consulting him—Yoshi is right, he thought, leaders should have secrets. "We have talked enough. Katsumata: I asked the price. A joint attack tonight."

"What would a very particular ally offer?"

Ogama stretched to ease the grinding tension in his neck and shoulders, expecting that question—for all his bravado no fool. Time enough to vary an offer, he thought, though neither of us would ever deign to lose face by bartering like the despised Osaka rice merchants. "You can garrison the Gates for one month, twenty men only at each of the six Gates, two hundred of my men stationed nearby—" Ogama smiled—"not near enough to embarrass you. Any persons going in or out will receive permits from your officer of the Gates, as is correct—who will have quietly and previously consulted with my . . . my liaison officer before permits are granted."

"Consult?"

"Consult, as between privileged allies, so a consensus can easily be arrived at." The easy smile was gone. "If more than twenty of your men appear, my men take possession and all agreements are ended. Agreed?"

Yoshi's eyes had flattened. No need to make threats, obviously any trick on either side would end all agreements. "I would prefer forty men at each of the Gates—we can arrange details of how the guard changes without problem—and I garrison the Gates as long as Shōgun Nobusada and the Princess Yazu are inside."

Ogama had noted the change. "Shōgun Nobusada, yes. But not the Princess who . . . who may stay inside permanently, eh? Forty? Very well, forty at each Gate. Of course, her brother, the Son of Heaven, will not rescind his memorial, his request to me to hold the Gates against his enemies."

"The Son of Heaven is the Son of Heaven, but I doubt if a cancellation would be forthcoming while Shōgunate forces exercise their historic rights."

At once Ogama's expression was naked. "Let you and I forget this polite back and forth and speak plainly: I'll concede a face-saving device on the Gates in return for Katsumata and all the rest—your men become the honor guard, your banners can be there and I agree with a lot you said, yes, much of it, but I do not concede my opposition to 'historic rights' or to the Shōgunate or Bakufu"— he stopped, and because he really wanted what was offered, he made another concession—"to the present Shōgunate and Bakufu, Yoshi-dono. Please excuse my bluntness. It would be good to be allies—I did not expect it would be possible or that I could agree to anything."

Yoshi nodded, hiding his glee. "I am happy we can agree and I tell you bluntly too we can agree to major changes, and little ones. For example," he added lightly, "if such a memorial arrived from the Emperor, it would be a forgery."

Now Ogama's smile was genuine and he felt he had achieved a perfect compromise. "Good. And now Katsumata."

The attack on the shishi hideaway began a few hours before dawn. Surprise was perfect. Katsumata, all subleaders, and others were inside. And Sumomo.

The first moment the two lookouts became aware of danger was when, just down the alley, muddy from the rain, one of the hovels burst into flames to muffled cries of alarm from the occupants and close neighbors. At once these men and women—all secret Bakufu plants— began to crowd the alley in pretended panic, the diversion helping to cover the stealthy approach of the attacking force. As the sentries went to investigate, arrows came out of the night and cut them down. One of them howled an alarm before he died.

At once the main force swarmed out of the night to surround this whole section of slum dwellings. Most of the men were Ogama's, at his request—Yoshi had agreed, saying that he would send a token forty handpicked men, under Akeda.

In moments many of the assault group had lit torches. These partially illuminated the target hut, back and front, and a fusillade of arrows went into every opening and weak spot. Then, unexpectedly, the four Yoshi riflemen ran into position, two at the back of the huts and two in the front, and fired several volleys through the paper walls.

For an instant there was a stunned silence—samurai, shishi, and all nearby slum dwellers equally shocked—the sound of rapid firing unheard of. Then the silence broke as everyone but the assault group scattered for cover, and screams and shouts came from the wounded within. A hut adjoining the first blaze caught fire and this fire spread rapidly next door and next door and next door until both sides of the far end of the alley became an inferno, trapping many a family inside.

The Ogama captain leading the raid paid no attention to that hazard, which only threatened inhabitants, but ordered the first attack wave in, disregarding Yoshi's advice to torch the hovels and let his riflemen pick off the shishi as they broke from cover. Four Ogama attackers fell under a vicious shishi sally from the front door and side windows. A general fight erupted both here and in the back alley as another furious foray was contained, men flailing, hampered by the confined space and mud and semi-darkness. Two men breached the cordon to be cut down by others waiting in ambush. Another volley into the hovel was followed by another attempted breakout by a frantic group of shishi, a helpless mission as another circle awaited them beyond and then another. Smoke from the fires began to hinder attackers and the attacked.

An order from Akeda. His men with torches rushed close to the hovel and hurled them onto the roof or through the shojis, swiftly retreating to give a clear field to their comrades with rifles. More firing and more deaths as another cluster of shishi rushed out to join the shouting, screaming melee. The stench of smoke and offal and blood and fire and burning flesh and death began to fill the damp night. The rain turned to drizzle.

Well protected by personal guards, Ogama and Yoshi were watching from a command position away from the blaze and fighting. Both wore armor and swords and Yoshi had his rifle slung. Beside them were some Bakufu officials. In the raging confusion, they were surprised to see a shishi dart through the cordon and run up the alley, escaping into a side alley obscured from attacking Choshu samurai.

"Is that Katsumata?" Ogama called out, but his words were

drowned as, without hesitation, Yoshi had aimed and fired and loaded and fired again. The man went down screaming, Ogama and everyone nearby recoiling at the suddenness, not expecting Yoshi to become personally involved. Taking his time, Yoshi aimed again at the man squirming helplessly in the dirt. The bullet shoved the body backwards. A final tortured howl and it became inert.

"That is not Katsumata," Yoshi said, disappointedly.

Ogama cursed, his night vision not good. He pulled his eyes off the body and looked at the rifle, loose in Yoshi's hands, repressing a shudder. "You use that well."

"It is easy to learn, Ogama-dono, too easy." With careful nonchalance, Yoshi put another shell into the breech, fairly sure that this would be the first rifle Ogama had seen. He had brought it and his riflemen deliberately to impress him, to keep him off balance, and make him more wary about trying any assassination attempts. "To kill like this is disgusting, cowardly, dishonorable."

"Yes, yes, it is. May I see the gun, please?"

"Of course." Yoshi put on the safety catch. "It's American—the very latest breech-loader. I take delivery of five thousand shortly." His smile was thin, remembering he had usurped Ogama's order. "My ancestor was wise to outlaw all guns—anyone can use one of these to kill, close up or from a distance, daimyo, merchant, robber, ronin, peasant, woman, child. My ancestor was very wise. A pity we cannot do the same but gai-jin have made it impossible."

The rifle felt strange to Ogama, heavier than a sword, oiled and deadly, and this added curiously to the excitement of the raid, the killing and screams and battle and knowing that spies had reported Katsumata was truly inside so, soon now, his hated enemy's head would be on display. All this filled him with an untoward sick-sweet nausea.

Good to kill like that without danger to yourself, he told himself, his fingers caressing the barrel, but Yoshi is right again. In the wrong hands . . . all other hands would be wrong. Five thousand? Eeee, that would make him very difficult to fight. I only ordered two hundred and fifty—where is he getting the money, his lands are almost as debt-ridden as mine? Ah yes, I forgot, bartering mining concessions. Clever. I will do the same. What is his secret plan? Does he have a 'Crimson Sky' too? If Yoshi gets five thousand I must get ten. Tonight he brought forty men. Why forty? Was that to remind me I agreed to forty at each Gate? Forty riflemen could easily decimate my two hundred unless equally armed.

"You have more here?" he asked.

Yoshi decided to be open. "Not at the moment."

Thoughtfully Ogama handed the rifle back and turned his attention to the hovels.

The sounds of the battle were lessening, those of the fires increasing, more and more inhabitants trying to douse them in lines passing water buckets. Roofs of the target hut and those each side were burning now. There was another desperate hand-to-hand combat as more shishi left the burning hovel, many already wounded. Yoshi said, "Katsumata's not amongst them."

"Perhaps he tried to break out from the back."

There, out of their sight, five shishi were already dead in the dirt together with eight Ogama samurai, and six wounded. Another battle between three shishi and ten Ogama samurai was drawing to its inevitable conclusion. A final shout of *"sonno-joi"* and the three men rushed to their deaths. Thirty Choshu samurai were arranged in depth, waiting for the next breakout. Smoke billowed from rips in the shojis. Stench of burning flesh was on the air. No movement from inside. An officer motioned to one of the samurai. "Report to the Captain what occurred here and ask him, do we wait or go in?"

The man ran off.

In front, the skirmish ended as all the others had done. The three shishi died bravely. Twelve more of them dead here, seventeen Choshu Samurai and one of Yoshi's men scattered in heaps. Fourteen wounded, three shishi helpless, disarmed and still alive. The Captain listened to the report. "Tell the officer to wait and kill anyone we flush out." He called out to a group held in reserve. "Empty the huts while there is time. Kill anyone who will not surrender but not the wounded."

At once the men went for the door. Inside there were brief shouts and countershouts and then silence. One of the men came out again, blood pouring from a vicious cut in his thigh. "Half a dozen wounded, many bodies."

"Bring them out before the roof falls in!"

The bodies, and wounded, were lined up in front of Yoshi and Ogama, the officials nearby. Torches cast strange shadows. Twenty-nine dead. Eleven helplessly wounded. Katsumata was not amongst them.

"Where is he?" Ogama shouted at the chief official, enraged, Yoshi equally angry, no one knowing exactly how many enemy were within when the battle had begun.

The man went to his knees. "Sire, I swear he was there earlier and he never left."

Ogama stomped over to the nearest wounded shishi. "Where is he?"
The man glared at him through his pain. "Who?"

"Katsumata! *Katsumata*!"

"Who? I know no . . . no Katsumata. *Sonno-joi,* traitor! Kill me and have done with it."

"Soon enough," Ogama said through his teeth.

Each of the wounded was questioned. Ogama had looked into every face—no Katsumata. Or Takeda. "Kill them all."

"Let them die honorably, as samurai," Yoshi said.

"Of course." They both looked back as the roof of the hut fell in and the walls collapsed in a shower of sparks, carrying the adjoining hovels with it. The drizzle turned to rain again. "Captain! Put the fire out. There must be a cellar, a hiding place, if this piece of dung is not an incompetent fool." Ogama strode off, in total rage, believing somehow he had been cheated.

Nervously the chief official got off his knees and sidled nearer to Yoshi. "Excuse me, Sire," he whispered, "but the woman's not here either. There must be a h——"

"What woman?"

"She was young. A Satsuma. She has been with them for some weeks. We believe she was Katsumata's companion. I am sorry to say Takeda is not there either."

"Who?"

"A Choshu shishi we have been watching. Perhaps he was Ogama's spy—he was seen sneaking into Ogama's headquarters the day before our other attack on Katsumata failed."

"For certain Katsumata was in there and the other two?"

"Certain, Sire. All three, Sire."

"Then there is a cellar or secret escape route."

They found it in the dawn. A trapdoor over a narrow tunnel, just enough to crawl through that ended well away in a weed-covered garden of an empty shack. Furiously Ogama kicked the camouflaged cover. *"Baka!"*

"We will put a price on Katsumata's head. A special price," Yoshi said. He was as angry. Obviously the failure had bruised the relationship so agonizingly manipulated and begun. But he was too shrewd to mention Takeda, or about the woman—she had no significance. "Katsumata must still be in Kyōto. The Bakufu will be ordered to find him, capture him or bring us his head."

"My adherents will be ordered the same." Ogama was a little mollified. He also had been thinking about Takeda, wondering if his escape boded good or bad. He glanced at the Captain who had walked up. "Yes?"

"You wish to view the heads now, Sire?"

"Yes. Yoshi-dono?"

"Yes."

The wounded shishi were allowed to die honorably without further pain. They were ritually decapitated, their heads washed and were now in a formal row. Forty. Again that number, Ogama thought uneasily. Is that an omen? Nonetheless he hid his disquiet, recognizing none of them.

"I have seen them," he said formally, the dawn misted with the light rain.

"I have seen them," Yoshi said equally gravely.

"Put the heads on spikes, twenty outside my gates, and twenty outside Lord Yoshi's."

"And the sign, Sire?" the Captain asked.

"Yoshi-dono, what do you suggest?"

After a pause, knowing he was being tried again, Yoshi said, "The two signs could read: *These outlaws, ronin, were punished for crimes against the Emperor. Let all beware misdeeds.* Is that satisfactory?"

"Yes. And the signature?" Both of them knew this was highly important and difficult to solve. If Ogama signed it alone, that implied he was legally master of the Gates; if Yoshi, that would imply Ogama was subservient to him, legally true but out of the question. A Bakufu seal implied the same. A Court seal would be undue meddling in temporal matters.

"Perhaps we give these fools too much importance," Yoshi said, pretending contempt. His eyes narrowed as, over Ogama's shoulder, he saw Basuhiro and some guards come around the far corner of the mean, puddled alley at a run. He looked back at Ogama. "Why not just put their heads on spikes here? Why give them the honor of a sign? Those who we want to know will know soon enough—and be chastened. *Neh*?"

Ogama was pleased with the diplomatic solution. "Excellent. I agree. Let us meet at dusk an—" He stopped as he noticed Basuhiro hurrying up to them, sweating and out of breath. He went to meet him.

"Courier from Shimonoseki, Sire," Basuhiro panted.

Ogama's face became a mask. He took the scroll and moved nearer to one of the torches. All eyes were on him as he opened it—Basuhiro politely holding an umbrella over him.

The message was from the Captain commanding the Straits and dated eight days ago, couriered express, day and night, as highest priority:

> *Sire, yesterday the returning enemy fleet consisting of the flagship and seven other warships, all steamers, some towing coaling barges, entered the Straits. Following your instructions that we should not engage enemy warships without your written orders we let them pass. We could have sunk all of them. Our Dutch advisors confirm this.*
>
> *When the armada had passed, a steamer frigate flying a French flag arrogantly returned and fired broadside after broadside into four emplacements on the east end of the Straits, destroying them and their cannon, then steamed away. Again I refrained from retaliating in accordance with your orders. If attacked in future I request permission to sink the attacker.*

Death to all gai-jin, Ogama wanted to scream, blind with rage that a whole fleet had been within his grasp, like Katsumata, but had escaped vengeance—like Katsumata. Flecks of foam collected at the corners of his lips. "Prepare new instructions: Engage and destroy any and all enemy warships."

Basuhiro, still trying to catch his breath, said, "May I suggest, Sire, you consider 'if more than four at any one time.' You have always wanted to maintain surprise."

Ogama wiped his mouth and nodded, his heart pumping at the thought of so many ships he could have destroyed. The rain had increased and was drumming on the umbrella. Beyond Basuhiro he saw Yoshi and the other officers waiting, watching him, and he weighed whether to treat Yoshi as enemy or ally, the implications of the fleet, the arrogance, and his own impotence swamping him. "Yoshi-dono!" He beckoned him and, with Basuhiro, moved further into private. "Read it, please."

Yoshi read rapidly. In spite of his control the color left his face. "Is the fleet heading up the inland sea for Osaka? Or will they turn south for Yokohama?"

"South or not, the next warships in my waters get blown out of my waters! Basuhiro, send men at once to Osaka an—"

"Wait, Ogama-dono," Yoshi said quickly, wanting time to think. "Basuhiro, what is your counsel?"

The little man said at once, "Sire, for the moment I presume it is Osaka and we should, together, prepare at once to defend it. I have already sent spies urgently to discover the fleet's course as best I can."

"Good." Ogama shakily wiped rain out of his face. "Their whole fleet in my Straits . . . I should have been there."

Basuhiro said, "It is more important for you to guard the Emperor against his enemies, Sire, and your commander was correct not to fire on the single ship. Surely it was a decoy to smell out your strength. He was right not to give away your defenses. Now the trap is baited should you wish to close it. Because only one enemy warship sneaked back and bombarded some easy positions and left hastily, I surmise their fleet commander was afraid, was not prepared to attack or land troops to start the war that we will end."

"Yes, we will. A ruse? I agree. Yoshi-dono," Ogama said with finality, "we should have done with it and start the war. A surprise attack on Yokohama, if they land at Osaka or not."

Yoshi could not answer at once, almost sick with a sudden apprehension that he tried to hide. Eight warships? That's four more than sailed to China, so the gai-jin have reinforced their fleet. Why? To retaliate for the Satsuma murders, but more particularly, Ogama's attacks on their shipping. And they will do it as in China. The gai-jin ship was sunk in the Taiwan Straits, but they decimated China's coast hundreds of leagues away.

What is their easiest target in Nippon? *Yedo.*

Has Ogama realized this and his secret plan is just to provoke the gai-jin? If I were the gai-jin leader I would destroy Yedo. They do not know it but Yedo is indivisible from our Shōgunate. If Yedo ends, the Toranaga Shōgunate ends and then the Land of the Gods is open to rape.

Therefore this will be prevented at all costs.

Think! How to bottle the gai-jin, and Ogama, whose answer is to put our heads on their block—not his. "I agree with your wise counselor, we should prepare to defend Osaka," he began, his stomach churning. Then his anxiety for the safety of Yedo bubbled over. "Whether Osaka now or later, a war fleet has returned. Unless we are very careful war is inevitable."

"Enough of being careful." Ogama leaned closer. "I say whether there's landing at Osaka or not, we excise the boil on our balls and exterminate Yokohama. Now! If you will not, so sorry, I will."

BOOK THREE

BOOK THREE

32

YOKOHAMA

Saturday, 29th November:

"WE PASSED THE FLEET TWO DAYS back, Mr. Malcolm, Jamie," the clipper captain said genially, hiding his shock at the change in Malcolm, whom he had known since birth and had laughed and drunk with barely three months ago in Hong Kong—the drawn sallow features, strange haunted eyes, the sticks he needed to walk or even to stand with. "We were under full sail with a Force Six aft and going like the clappers, they were riding it leisurely, wise, for they surely wouldn't want to lose any of the coaling barges they towed."

His name was Sheeling and he had just come ashore from his ship, *Dancing Cloud,* her arrival unexpected. He was forty-two, a tall, bearded, weather-beaten man, twenty-eight years with the Noble House. "We just saluted them and kept going."

"Tea, Captain?" McFay asked, automatically pouring, knowing from long experience this was his preferred drink. During a voyage he always drank it ladened with sugar and condensed milk, day or night. They were in Malcolm's suite at the big table and, like the tai-pan, Jamie was hardly listening, his eyes also on the sealed mail pouch, embossed with the Noble House crest, under Sheeling's left arm.

Instead of a left hand Sheeling had a hook. When he was a midshipman on a voyage along the Yangtze River trading opium, pirates of the White Lotus fleet had surrounded their lorcha and in the fight his hand had been cut off. Afterwards he had been commended for his gallantry. His beloved idol, Dirk Struan, had brought him back from the brink, then put him with the fleet's chief captain, Orlov the Hunchback, with orders to teach him all he knew.

"Ta'," Sheeling said with a smile, and took a large swallow. "Excellent, Jamie! Of course I'd prefer a large whisky, as you know, but that'll have to wait until Honolulu—I plan to leave right smartly, just came t—"

"Honolulu?" Struan and Jamie said, almost in the same breath. This was not a normal call for their clippers racing across the Pacific for San Francisco, then to hurry back again.

"What's your cargo?" Malcolm said, almost adding 'Uncle Sheeley,' the name he had used in the good days of his youth.

"The usual, tea and spices for 'Frisco, but I've orders to first deliver mail to our agents in Hawaii."

"Mother's orders?"

Sheeling nodded and his grey eyes looked back at Malcolm pleasantly. He had heard the undercurrent and knew part of the problem existing between mother and son—Malcolm's engagement and her opposition the private talk of Hong Kong—but was under strict instructions not to mention it.

"How is business there, in Hawaii?" Malcolm asked, a new shaft of anxiety going through him. "Did she say?"

"No, Mrs. Struan just ordered me to stop there."

A gust rattled the office shutters. They glanced out of the window. In the bay the three rake–masted clipper was at anchor, taking the swell prettily, her sails ready to be hoisted again, soon to hurtle seawards and ride the wild winds or good winds or bad, whatever that lay ahead. The three men were filled like sails with pride and Sheeling felt warmed that he ruled such a queen of the sea. He turned his attention back to Malcolm and absently scratched an itch on his neck with his hook. "I was ordered here for the same reason: mail!" He gave him the pouch. "May I have a receipt, please?"

"Of course." Malcolm nodded to Jamie who began to write it out. "What's the latest from Hong Kong?"

"I'd say most would be in the pouch, but I've brought the latest papers, both Hong Kong's and London's—I left the bundle in your office downstairs." Sheeling gulped the tea, anxious to be on his way. This would be his fourth Hawaiian visit over the years and he knew the beauty of their girls and their rare, joy-filled loving nature, money hardly a consideration, so unlike Hong Kong, Shanghai or anywhere else he had ever been. This time I'll buy some land, secretly. Different name. It's Hawaii for me next year when I retire, that's where I'm going and no one any the wiser. The thought of sailing off for good, of leaving his wife, an accomplished nag, and rapacious children in London, Daddy buy me this, Daddy buy me that—not that he saw them often—pleased him.

"I meant local news in Hong Kong," Struan was saying.

"Oh. Well, first your family's in fine fettle—Mrs. Struan, your brother and sisters—though young Duncan had another bad cold when I left. As to Hong Kong, the races are as good as ever, so's the food, Mrs. Fortheringill's is still booming in spite of a recession, the Noble House stays on course as you'd know better than me, along with the usual rumors that all's not well, probably spread by the Brocks, but that's just more of the usual and never changes." He got up. "Thank you kindly, I best be going, must catch the tide."

"Won't you at least stay for lunch?"

"No, thanks, I'd better be off an—"

"What rumors?" Malcolm said harshly.

"Nothing worth repeating, Mr. Malcolm."

"Why don't you call me tai-pan like everyone else?" Malcolm said irritably, fear of what might be in the pouch eating him. "I am, aren't I?"

Sheeling's expression did not change, he liked him and admired him and was sorry for the burden he now carried. "Yes, you are, and you're right, it's time I stopped 'Mr. Malcolm.' But, begging your pardon, your father said exactly the same to me after he became tai-pan, a few days after the typhoon killed the . . . killed the tai-pan, Mr. Dirk. As you know he was very special to me, and I asked my captain, Captain Orlov, if I could talk to Mr. Culum and he said it was all right. So I said to your father that I'd always called Mr. Dirk tai-pan and as a special favor, could I just call him sir, or Mr. Struan. He said I could. It was a special favor. Could th—"

"I'm told Captain Orlov called my father tai-pan, and my grandfather was just as special to him, perhaps more so."

"That's true," the Captain said, standing straight. "When Captain Orlov disappeared, your father put me in charge of the fleet. I've served your father with all my heart, as I will you, and your son if I live that long. As a special favor, please, could it be the same as with your father?"

Sheeling was more than valuable to the Noble House. All three men knew it. And his inflexibility. Malcolm nodded, hurt even so. "Have a safe voyage, Captain."

"Thank you, sir. And . . . and good luck, Mr. Struan, in everything. And you, Jamie." As he strode for the door Malcolm broke the first seal on the pouch, but before the Captain touched the handle, the door opened. Angelique stood there. Bonnet, navy blue dress, gloves, and parasol. All three men caught their breath at her radiance.

"Oh, sorry, *chéri,* I didn't know you were busy . . ."

"That's all right, come in." Malcolm had clambered to his feet. "May I present Captain Sheeling, of *Dancing Cloud.*"

"La, Monsieur, what a gorgeous ship, how lucky you are."

"Yes, yes, I am, Miss. Thank you," Sheeling said, smiling back. By God, he thought, never having seen her before, who could blame Malcolm? " 'Morning, Miss." He saluted and left, not wishing to leave now, not for a little while.

"So sorry to interrupt, Malcolm, but you said to collect you for lunch, it's to be with Sir William—and you haven't forgotten I have a piano lesson this afternoon with André and I've arranged for us to have our daguerreotype taken at five. Hello, Jamie!"

"Our picture?"

"Yes, you remember the funny Italian who arrived on the last mail ship from Hong Kong for a season, he makes them, he guarantees we will look very handsome!"

Most of Malcolm's concern had left him and he felt all of her presence, doting on her, even though he had seen her an hour ago—coffee in his suite at eleven, a habit she had instituted and he enjoyed immensely. Over the last two or three weeks her loving disposition seemed to him to have blossomed even more though she spent much of her time riding, or at archery, or piano lessons, or planning soirees, and at her journal and letter writing—a way of life for all of them. But every moment she was with him she was as attentive and tender as any woman could be. His love and his need for her grew daily, overwhelming him with its power.

"Lunch is at one, darling, it's just after twelve," he said, and as much as he didn't want her to leave added, "Will you give us a few minutes?"

"Of course." With her grace, she seemed to dance over to him and kissed him and went to her suite next door. Her perfume lingered as a delicious memory.

His fingers trembled, breaking the last seal. Inside were three letters.

Two from his mother, one for him, one for Jamie. The third letter was from Gordon Chen, their compradore and his uncle. "Here," he said, handing Jamie his letter, his heart beating furiously, wishing that Sheeling had not arrived. His two letters were burning his fingers.

"I'll leave you to it," Jamie said.

"No. Bad news needs company." Malcolm looked up. "Open yours." Jamie obeyed and read rapidly. His face became red.

"Is it private, Jamie?"

"It says: 'Dear Jamie'—that's the first time she's used the old way of writing me for a long time—'you may show this to my son, if you wish. I'm sending Albert MacStruan as soon as I can arrange it from our Shanghai office. You are to make him your deputy and teach him all you can about our entire Japanese operation, so that, unless two things happen, he can adequately take over from you when you leave Struan's. The first is that my son is in Hong Kong by Christmas. The second is that you accompany him.' " Jamie stared at him helplessly. "That's it. Just a signature."

"That's *not* it," Malcolm said, his own face hot. "As soon as Albert arrives he can bloody go back."

"No harm in him staying a few days and letting him look over the place. He's a good fellow."

"Mother's . . . I never thought she could be so cruel: if I don't obey and kowtow, you get fired. Eh?" Malcolm's eyes strayed to his bureau. For the last few weeks he had made the immense effort to restrict his intake to once a day. Some days he had failed. 'Laudanum in moderation, Malcolm,' Dr. Babcott had said, 'is a panacea for pain.' He had insisted that Malcolm show him the medicine, not to take it away, just to check its contents. 'This is fairly strong. Remember, it's not a cure and with some people it is addictive.'

'Not with me. I need it for the pain. You stop the pain and I'll stop the medicine.'

'Sorry, my friend, wish I could. Your internal organs were badly damaged, not too badly, thank God, but even so will take time to heal.'

Too much time, Malcolm was thinking. Is it worse than Babcott will admit? He looked at his two letters, reluctant to open them. Filthy of her to use Jamie as another cudgel. "Rotten."

"She has certain rights," Jamie said.

"She's not tai-pan, I am. Father's will was clear." Malcolm's voice was dull, his thoughts untidy. "Guess old Uncle Sheeley was right, you have to earn that title, don't you?"

"You're tai-pan." It was said kindly though Jamie knew it was not true. "Strange he should bring up Orlov, haven't thought about him in years. Wonder what happened to him."

"Yes," Malcolm said absently. "Poor fellow was a marked man after he blew Wu Sung Choi's Number One Son out of the water. Orlov was stupid to go ashore alone in Macao. He must have been snatched by the White Lotus pirates. Macao's a deadly place, easy to go into China, and everywhere the White Lotus has spies. I'd hate to be on their marked list . . ." His voice trailed away. He looked down at the letters, lost in thought.

Jamie waited. Then he said, "Give me a shout if I can help. I'll be going through the rest of the mail." He left.

Malcolm did not hear the door close. There was the "I love you" postscript to his mother's letter, so no secret message:

> *My dearest but prodigal son, I had planned to arrive with* Dancing Cloud *but decided against it at the last minute as Duncan was poorly and has the croup again. Perhaps what I have to say is better in writing then there can be no mistake.*
>
> *I've received yr ill-advised letters about what you will and will not do, about yr "engagement," Jamie McFay, Miss Richaud, etc.—and about the five thousand rifles. I immediately wrote and cancelled the extravagant order.*
>
> *The time has come for open decisions. Since you are not here and will not do as I ask, I will make them. For yr private knowledge it is my right to do so.*
>
> *When yr father was dying, poor man, there was no time to wait for yr return so, almost with his last breath, he made me de facto tai-pan according to all the provisions in Dirk's Will and Legacy—some of them terrible—all of which have to be accepted, before God, sight unseen and must be kept secret from tai-pan to tai-pan. At the time it was our expectation that I would pass the mantle to you on yr immediate return. One of Dirk's Laws lays down: It is the duty of the tai-pan to swear absolute belief in the integrity of his successor. I cannot do this for you at the moment. All this, and the following, is again for yr private knowledge—it would hurt*

Struan's for it to be made public, so destroy the letter after reading it.

By today's mail to Scotland, I have offered the post of taipan to yr cousin Lochlin Struan, Uncle Robb's son, with four provisos: first that he comes at once to Hong Kong and spends three months in training here—as you know he is well versed in our company operations, better than you as far as Great Britain is concerned, though you are far and away better fitted and better trained; second, he agrees to keep this all secret; third, at the end of the trial period, before God, I will make the final choice between the two of you, my decision of course to be binding; fourth, that if you come to yr senses, he agrees that I must choose you but he will be next, should you fail to have sons, Duncan to be after him.

Coming to yr senses, my son, means returning to Hong Kong at once, the very latest by Christmas Day, alone but for Jamie McFay (and Dr. Hoag, should you wish to have his company) to discuss yr future plans, to take up pressing duties and prepare for the position you have trained all yr life for. Should you prove to be satisfactory, I will make you taipan on yr twenty-first birthday, May 21st.

I have shown this to Gordon Chen and asked him to comment where necessary—our compradore must, MUST, by Dirk's Law, be a party to the handing over of power. Yr devoted mother. P.S. I love you and an added P.P.S.: Thank you for your news from Parliament about more of their usual stupidity (via the curious channel of our archenemy Greyforth. Beware of him, he's up to no good, but then you know that better than I). Yes, we had heard the rumours, the Governor still denies any knowledge. I had already written to our Parliamentarians on the first rumour telling them to stop the nonsense if it was true, and to Bengal forewarning them. In response to your letter I have written again. It really is time you came home to apply yrself to your duty and our mounting problems.

"Duty!" Malcolm shouted at the wall, balled the letter and hurled it at it, hurting himself with his violence. He stumbled to his feet, lurched to his bureau. The little bottle contained his evening dose. He drained it, smashed it on the oak top cursing, and almost fell as he groped to his chair.

"She can't! Can't! That . . . that bitch can't do that . . . can't! 'Go back alone' only means without Angel 'to discuss' . . . I won't and she won't interfere . . ." and he continued to half think and half speak imprecations until the opiate entered his bloodstream and began its deadly solace.

In time he noticed the other letter from Compradore Gordon Chen—his father's stepbrother, one of many illegitimate children sired by Dirk Struan. "Three that we know about," he said aloud.

> *My dear, dear nephew: I've already written how sorry I was about your bad joss, the wounds and accident. I'm even more sorry to hear there is an estrangement between you and your mother that promises to become dangerous and could disrupt our Noble House—therefore it is my duty to comment and advise. She showed me her letter to you. I have not shown mine to her, nor will I. In mine I will confine myself only to the position of tai-pan, other than to give you my very private advice about the girl: be Chinese.*
>
> *Facts: though you are formally my stepbrother's heir, your mother correctly says you have not undergone the obligatory ceremony, attestations, oaths and signatures laid down in my Honourable Father's Will and Legacy that are necessary before you can be tai-pan, which, to be valid, must be witnessed personally and attested to in writing as properly executed by the current compradore, who must be of my branch of the House of Chen. Only then is the chosen one the tai-pan.*
>
> *Before your father died he did in fact appoint your mother tai-pan. It was correctly done in all details. I witnessed it. She is tai-pan legally and has power over the Noble House. It is true that your father and mother expected the position to be passed over to you quickly, but she is also correct that one*

*of the tai-pan's obligations is to attest before God to the
integrity of his successor, and also true the Noble House is
governed only by what the tai-pan, he or she, decides, particularly the choice and timing of any succession.*

*My only advice is: be wise, swallow your pride, return at
once, kowtow, kowtow and kowtow, accept a 'trial' period,
become again a dutiful son, honouring your ancestors, for
the good of the House. Obey the tai-pan. Be Chinese.*

Malcolm Struan stared at the letter, his future in ruins, past in ruins,
everything changed. So she is tai-pan! *Mother is!* If Uncle Gordon says
it then it's true! She's cheated me out of my birthright, she has, my
Mother has.

But isn't that really what she's wanted all these years? Didn't she
always cajole, beg, whine, plot, do whatever was necessary to dominate father, me and all of us? Her maddening family prayers every day
and church twice on Sunday, us trailing along when once on Sundays is
more than enough. And drinking! 'Drunkenness is an abomination'
and quoting the Bible all day long to the point of insanity, no fun in our
lives, Lent observed to the letter, fasting, forever carping on the brilliance of Dirk Struan, God curse him, always saying how terrible to
have died so young—never bringing up that he died in the typhoon
with his Chinese mistress in his arms, a fact that was and still is the
scandal of Asia—always sermonizing on the evils of the flesh, Father's weakness, the death of my sister and the twins . . .

Suddenly he sat up solidly in his high-back chair. Insanity? That's it!
he thought. Could I put her in an insane asylum? Maybe she is. Would
Uncle Gordon help me to . . . Ayeeyah! It's me who's mad. It's me
who's . . .

"Malcolm! It's lunchtime."

He looked up and saw himself talking to Angelique, saying how
pretty she was but would she mind very much going without him as a
few serious things had to be decided, letters to be written—no, nothing
that affected her, no really, just a few business problems—all the time
remembering 'return alone' and 'kowtow, she's tai-pan.' "Please,
Angelique."

"Of course, if that's what you want, but you're sure you're all right,
my love? You don't have a fever, do you?"

He allowed her to feel his forehead and caught her hand and pulled her into his lap and kissed her and she kissed him back and laughed gaily and straightened her bodice saying she would be back after her piano lesson and not to worry and for the picture he must wear his evening clothes and, oh, you'll be so impressed with my new ball gown.

And then he was alone with his thoughts again, the same words grinding his brain: 'return alone . . . she's tai-pan.' How dare she cancel the order for rifles—what does she know about this market?

Tai-pan legally. So she really does rule the roost, and me. Certainly until I'm twenty-one and ever afterwards. Until she's not. Until . . .

Ah, is that the key? Is that what Uncle Gordon meant when he wrote: *be Chinese*. Be Chinese how? Just be patient? How would a Chinese handle my whole predicament?

Just before he went into his special sleep, he smiled.

As it was Saturday and a pleasant afternoon a football match had been arranged on the bluff. Most of the Settlement was watching and with the usual fights and hysteria, on and off the pitch, when one side or the other scored a goal, Army versus Navy, fifty men per side. The score was Navy 1, Army 2, and the first half not yet over. Hacking permitted, brawling permitted, almost everything permitted and the only purpose to force the ball through the opposing posts.

Angelique, seated on the halfway line with Sir William and the General, was surrounded by the rest of his lunch guests—Seratard and other Ministers, André and Phillip Tyrer—who had decided to come en masse to watch. Crowding them and vying for her attention were British and French officers, Settry Pallidar and Marlowe, the only British naval officer, amongst them—Jamie nearby. When she had hurried back to Malcolm to tell him she was cancelling her piano lesson, which was another excuse not to have to sit with him, and to ask him if he would like to go to the game, he was still asleep. So she had asked Jamie to escort her.

'Yes, best to let him sleep—I'll leave him a note,' Jamie had said, welcoming any excuse to distract him from looming disaster. 'Pity he won't see the match—Malcolm was a sports enthusiast, as you know, a grand swimmer, a fine cricketer as well, tennis of course. Sad that he's, well, not his old self.'

She could see that he was as gloomy as Malcolm but that did not matter, she thought, men were generally serious and she was pleased to have company as a foil against the others. Since the great day when that which was growing had ceased to be, and her health and vigor had returned, better than ever, she had found it unwise to be alone with any of them. Except André. To her delight he had changed, no longer threatening or referring to the help he had given her, all of it she would like to forget, no longer looking at her with rough and heavy-lidded eyes, too easy to read the cruelty behind them, though sure the cruelty still lurked within him.

Important to keep him friendly, she thought, aware how vulnerable she was. Listen but beware. Some of what he says is good: 'Forget what happened before, it never happened.'

André's right. Nothing happened. *Nothing, except he's dead.* I really do love Malcolm, I'll bear him sons and be the perfect wife and hostess and our salon in Paris will be . . .

A roar distracted her. A mob of Navy players had forced the ball between the Army posts but the Army fought the ball away and now a general riot began, the Navy claiming a goal, the Army disputing it. Dozens of seamen swarmed onto the pitch to join the melee, then soldiers and soon there was a free-for-all, traders and others cheering and laughing and enjoying the spectacle, the referee, Lunkchurch, desperately trying to stay out of the fight and, meanwhile, get some order back on the field.

"Oh, look . . . that poor fellow's being kicked to death!"

"Nothing to worry about, Angelique, just horseplay, clearly it wasn't a goal," the General said confidently. The man was Navy, so of little concern. Sir William, on the other side of her, was as excited as any, nothing like a good brawl to lighten the spirits. Nonetheless, conscious of Angelique, he leaned over to the General. "Think we should get on with the game, Thomas, eh?"

"Quite right." The General motioned to Pallidar. "Break it up, if you please—reason with them."

Pallidar of the Dragoons went onto the pitch, took out his revolver and fired a salvo into the air. Everyone froze. "Listen, you lot," he called out, all eyes on him now. "Everyone off the pitch except the players. The General's order: another riot and the match is cancelled and those involved will be disciplined. Move!" The field began to clear, many hobbling, the injured dragged off by supporters. "Now, Mr. Referee, was it a goal or not?"

"Well, Captain, yes and no, you see . . ."

"Was it or not?"

The silence was strong. Lunkchurch knew whatever he said was going to be wrong. He decided the truth was best: "A goal for the Navy!"

Amid cheers and countercheers, threats and counterthreats, Pallidar walked back, tall and very pleased with himself. "Oh, Settry, what bravery!" Angelique spoke with such appreciation that Marlowe and others were riven with jealousy. "Good work, old boy," Marlowe said reluctantly as the game—the fight—began in earnest to cheers drowned by the boos and curses.

"Jolly good game, Thomas, what?" Sir William said.

"Clearly that wasn't a goal, the Referee's a—"

"Poppycock! Five guineas says the Navy will win."

The General's neck had gone a darker shade of red and this pleased Sir William and helped to get him out of his ill humor. Nothing but quarrels in the Settlement and Drunk Town, irritating letters and complaints from the Bakufu and Customs House, and he had not forgotten the General's stupidity at the riot.

Added to these woes, the last mails had brought more foul news and forecasts from the Foreign Office that lack of financial support in Parliament would herald major cutbacks of Diplomatic personnel: 'even though the coffers of the Empire are overflowing, there will be no salary increases this year. The American war promises to be the most savage in history because of the newly invented shell, bronze cartridge, breech-loading rifle, machine gun and breech-loading cannon; with the defeat of Union forces at Shiloh and the Second Battle of Bull Run the war is presently expected to be won by the Confederates, most pundits in the City having written off President Lincoln as weak and ineffectual, but, dear Willie, H.M.'s policy remains the same: to back both sides, keep our heads down and stay to hell out of this one . . .'

European news was also bad: Russian Cossack troops had again massacred thousands of Poles in Warsaw demonstrating against Russian rule; Prince von Bismarck had been made Minister President of Prussia and was rumored to be preparing for war against expansionist France; Austria-Hungary and Russia appeared to be on the verge of war again; inevitably more fighting in the Balkans . . .

And so on, ad nauseam, Sir William thought with a scowl. Nothing changes! And I'm damned if I believe the Bakufu will do what they've promised, which means I will have to show the Flag here. I'll have to teach the Japanners that a promise is a promise if it's made to the British Raj, by God, and to remind Zergeyev, Seratard and others the same thing.

Bombard Yedo would be the simplest and easiest solution, that'd bring them to heel quick enough. But then there's Ketterer—perhaps his foray into history books will have changed him. Ugh! What a hope . . .

"A ruble for your thoughts, Sir William," Count Zergeyev said with a smile, offering a silver flask embossed with his family crest in gold. "Vodka is good for thoughts."

"Thanks." Sir William took a swallow and felt the fire slide down his gullet, reminding him of all the wonderful times at the Embassy in St. Petersburg when he was in his twenties, a center of power, not an outpost like Yokohama, drinking and carousing, balls and ballet and dachas, night life and luxury—for the few—excitement and intrigues and marvelous dinners and Vertinskya, never far from his thoughts.

For five of his seven years there she had been his mistress, youngest daughter of a favored goldsmith to the Court, an artist like her father, her father benign about their liaison, William's own Russian mother doting on the girl and wanting him to marry her. 'Sorry, Mama dear, no chance of that at all, much as I'd like it, the Service would never approve. It's Sir Roger's daughter Daphne. Sorry . . .'

He drank again, the misery of their parting still with him. "I was thinking about Vertinskya," he said in Russian.

"Ah! Yes, the girls of Mother Russia are very special," Zergeyev replied compassionately in the same language. "Their love, if you are so blessed, is forever and then forever again." The affair had been smiled at in diplomatic circles and well documented by the Cheka, the Tsar's secret police, therefore part of Sir William's dossier that of course Zergeyev had read. Stupid of the girl to kill herself, he thought, never quite sure if William was aware of her suicide shortly after he had returned to London. That was never part of the plan, nor his duty to tell him. Why did she do it? Over this boor? Surely that's not possible, but for whatever reason, a pity, her usefulness, to both of us, would have lasted for many more years. "Perhaps your Foreign Office will post you there again—there are other Vertinskyas."

"Not much chance of that, I'm afraid."

"Let's hope. Another hope, *mon ami,* that your Lord Palmerston will see the logic that we should have the Kuriles. Like the Dardanelles— both should surely be Russian."

Sir William saw the glitter in his strange sloe eyes. "Not much chance of that, I'm afraid."

The halftime whistle sounded, the score still two all, to be swallowed by a roar of recriminations and praises and promises of dire punishment for the losers. At once Marlowe moved over to Jamie. "Do you think Mr. Struan and, er, and Miss Angelique would like to join me aboard *Pearl* for tiffin and a day's sail?" he asked, simulating a sudden thought. "Have to do some trials soon as the fleet's back and I'd be glad to have them aboard."

"I think they'd enjoy it, why don't you ask him?"

"When would be a good time?"

"Any day around eleven—or just before dinner."

"Thanks, thanks very much." Marlowe beamed, then noticed Jamie's pallor. "Oh, are you all right?"

"Yes, thanks." Jamie forced a smile and moved away.

He had been considering his future. Some weeks ago he had written to Maureen Ross, his fiancée, in Scotland, telling her to wait no longer for him—almost three years since he had last seen her, five years engaged—that he was sorry, he knew he had been abominable to keep her waiting so long but he was absolutely, finally convinced the East was positively no place for a lady, and equally certain Asia was his home, Yokohama, Hong Kong, Shanghai, anywhere but there, and he had no intention of leaving. Yes, he knew he had been unfair to her but their engagement was at an end. This was to be his last letter.

For days he had felt nauseated, before he wrote it, after having written it and after he had seen the mail ship put to sea. But he was sure. That chapter was ended. And now the Struan chapter that was so rosy, promotion next year for certain, will also end. God Almighty! No way Malcolm will go back, so I've only a few more weeks to decide what to do—and don't forget Norbert will be back before then. Then what? Will they really duel? If they do that's joss, but you've still got to protect Malcolm as best you can.

So a new job! Where? I'd like to stay here, there's Nemi, it's a good life with a wide-open future to build. Hong Kong and Shanghai are mostly built, the old-boy structure strong in place—great if you're a Struan or Brock or Cooper and so on but difficult to break through.

First choice would be here. With whom? With Dmitri in Cooper-Tillman? Could they use me? Yes, but not as top man. Brock's? Oh, yes, I considered that in the depths of her unfairness, but no chance of top man with Norbert—but if Malcolm killed him what a coup that would be, what revenge! Lunkchurch? Yes, definitely, but who'd want to work for that uncouth bugger? What about on your own? That'd be best, but the riskiest and who'd sponsor you? I'd need money—I've some put away but not enough. I'd need lots to begin, lots to cover the time agrowing, for letters of credit and insurances, time to arrange agents in London, San Francisco, Hong Kong, Shanghai and all over Asia, Paris—and St. Petersburg. Don't forget Russians are huge buyers of tea and will trade sables and other furs to great profit and there are all your contacts in Russian Alaska, and their trading posts on the American west coast south. A good idea but risky, such a long time between buying and selling and profit, too many hazards for the ships, too many lost at sea or to piracy . . .

A little farther away Phillip Tyrer was also staring into the distance. He was thinking about Fujiko and almost groaned aloud. Yesterday evening, with his friend Nakama—Hiraga—to help him, he had tried to begin negotiations for her exclusivity. Mama-san Raiko's eyes had soared and she shook her head, saying, Oh, so sorry, I doubt if it is possible, the girl so valuable and wanted by so many important gai-jin, *important gai-jin*, implying that even Sir William was an occasional client though never mentioning him by name, which had unsettled Tyrer and made him even more anxious.

Raiko said that, even before discussing financial and other details, first she would ask Fujiko if she would consider it, adding to his shock that it would be best for him not to see her again until and unless a contract had been agreed. It had taken him another hour to reach a compromise that Nakama had suggested: in the interim period, when seeing Fujiko, he would never mention the matter or discuss it directly with her, that was the mama-san's responsibility.

Thank God for Nakama, he told himself in another sweat, I nearly messed up everything. But for him . . .

His eyes focused and he saw Seratard and André Poncin deep in private conversation, and not far away from them, Erlicher, the Swiss Minister, was equally private with Johann, who was concentrating on every word.

What's so important and urgent to those men, he asked himself, that they would discuss it at a football match, reminding himself not to daydream, to be adult and aware that all was not well in Japan, to do his duty to the Crown and Sir William—Fujiko could wait until tonight when he might get an answer.

Damn Johann! Now that the wily Swiss was leaving his post as interpreter it had put a further burden on him, leaving him little time to sleep or to play. Only this morning Sir William had flared, unfairly, he thought bitterly, 'For God's sake, Phillip, put in more hours. The sooner you're fluent the better for the Crown, the sooner Nakama is fluent in English the better for the Crown. Earn your daily bread, stop slacking, lean on Nakama, make him earn his daily bread too or out he goes!'

* * *

Hiraga was in the Legation reading a letter aloud that Tyrer had written for Sir William which he had helped translate, that was to be delivered tomorrow to the Bakufu. Though he did not understand many of the words his reading was improving rapidly: 'You've an aptitude for English, Nakama, old boy,' Tyrer had said several times. This had pleased him, even though, normally, praise or criticism from a gai-jin was meaningless. Over the weeks most of his waking hours had been spent cramming words and phrases, repeating them over and over, so much so that the language of his dreams was mixed up.

'Why bash your head, Cousin?' Akimoto asked him.

'I must learn English as quickly as possible. There is so little time, this gai-jin leader is rude and ill-tempered and I have no idea how long I can stay. But Akimoto, if I could read who knows what information I could get. You cannot believe how stupid they are about their secrets. Hundreds of books and pamphlets and documents lie around everywhere. I have access to everything, can read anything, and this Taira person answers my most obvious questions.'

This was said last night in their safe house in the village and he had had a cold towel around his aching head. He was no longer confined to the Legation. Now he could stay in the village if he wanted to though many nights he was too tired to leave, and he would stay and sleep on a spare bunk in the cottage Tyrer shared with Babcott. Of necessity George Babcott had had to know about him. 'Marvelous! Nakama can help me with my Japanese too and my dictionary! Marvelous, I'll organize lessons and a cram course!'

Babcott's approach was quite radical. Learning was to be enjoyed and soon it had almost developed into a game, a hilarious game to see who could learn faster, an entirely new style for Hiraga and Tyrer, for whom schooling was serious, and education implanted by rote, repetition and the birch.

'How fast the lessons go, Akimoto. It becomes easier every day— we shall do the same in our schools when sonno-joi is supreme.'

Akimoto laughed. 'Teachers gentle and kind? No bashing or stick? Never! More important, what about the frigate?'

He had told Akimoto that Tyrer had promised he would ask a captain friend for permission to take the two of them aboard, explaining Akimoto as the son of a wealthy Choshu shipbuilding family, come to visit him for a few days, and a valuable friend in the future.

From the open window Hiraga heard cheering from the football match. He sighed, then reverently picked up Babcott's handwritten dictionary. It was the first dictionary he had ever seen, and the first

English-Japanese, Japanese-English ever. Babcott had built on lists of words and phrases gathered by himself, traders and priests, both Catholic and Protestant, with others translated from Dutch-Japanese equivalents. At the moment the book was short. But daily it grew and it fascinated him.

Folklore had it that, two centuries or so ago, a Jesuit priest called Tsukku-san had written out a form of Portuguese-Japanese dictionary. Before that no dictionary of any sort had ever existed. In time, a few Dutch-Japanese ones appeared, to be zealously guarded. 'No need to lock this up, Nakama,' Babcott had said yesterday to his astonishment. 'That's not the British way. Spread the word, let everyone learn, the more educated everyone is the better the country.' He had smiled. 'Of course, not everyone agrees with me. In any event, next week with the help of our printing presses, I'll—'

'Printing press, so sorry?'

Babcott had explained. 'Soon we'll start printing and if you promise to write a history of Choshu I will promise to give you a copy of my dictionary for yourself alone.'

A week or so ago, in wonder, Hiraga had shown Akimoto a copy of the *Yokohama Guardian*. 'It is the news of the day, from all over the world, and they prepare a new version every day, as many copies as they like—thousands if necessary . . .'

'Impossible!' Akimoto said. 'Our best block printers can't poss—'

'I've seen them do it! Machines do it, Akimoto. They showed me their machines! They set all the words in what they call type in lines, they read left to right, the opposite to us, right to left and down our columns of characters, column by column. Unbelievable. I saw the machine man make words out of individual symbols, called *"roman rett'rs"*—they say that all words in any language can be written with only twenty-six of these symbols an—'

'Impossible.'

'Listen! Each rett'r or symbol always has the same sound so another person can read individual letters, or words made out of them. To make this "news paper," the printer uses combinations of little pieces of iron with the symbol cut into the end of it—sorry, not iron but a kind of iron called *"stee'r,"* some name like that. This man put the rett'rs in a box that somehow was inked, paper run over it and here was a new printed page that contained something I had written a moment ago. Taira read it out exactly! A miracle.'

'Eeee, but how can we do that with our language, each word is a special character with as many as five or seven different ways of saying it and our writing's different an—'

'The Doctor Giant listens when I say a Japanese word, he writes it down in their roman rett'rs then Taira says the word just by reading them!'

It had taken Hiraga much more explanation to convince Akimoto. 'Eeee,' he said, exhausted, 'so many new things, new ideas, so difficult for me to understand myself, let alone explain. Ori was such a fool not to want to learn.'

'Good for us he's dead, buried and forgotten by the gai-jin. For days I thought we were lost.'

'So did I.'

Hiraga found the English word he sought, 'reparations.' The Japanese translation was: 'money to be paid for an agreed crime.' This puzzled him. The Bakufu had committed no crime. Two Satsumas, Ori and Shorin, had merely killed a gai-jin, both were now dead, two for the death of one gai-jin was certainly fair. Why should they demand 're-par-at-eeons,' he said aloud, the nearest his tongue could get to the word.

He got up from the desk to ease his knees, difficult to sit like a gai-jin all day long, and went to the window. He was wearing Western clothes but soft *tabi* on his feet, English boots still very uncomfortable for him. The day was still good, the ships at anchor, fishing boats and other vessels moving back and forth. The frigate beckoned. His excitement grew. Soon they would see into its bowels, see the great steam machines Taira had told him about. He caught sight of a reproduced photograph cut out of a magazine and stuck on the wall, of the Great Ship, an enormous iron ship being built in the British capital city, London, the biggest that had ever been, twenty times bigger than the frigate in the bay. Too enormous to conceive—even 'fo-to-gr-aff' for him impossible to understand, eerie, almost a form of evil magic. He shuddered, then noticed the door to the corridor was ajar and across from it Sir William's door. As far as he knew there was no one in the Legation, everyone at the football match and not expected until later this afternoon.

Soundlessly he opened Sir William's door. The elaborate desk had many papers on it, half a hundred books on untidy shelves, a portrait of their Queen and other paintings on the walls. Something new on a sideboard. A photograph in a silver frame. He saw only ugliness, a curiously dressed gai-jin woman with three children, and realized it must be Sir William's family. Tyrer had mentioned they were expected soon.

How lucky I am to be Japanese, and civilized, with a handsome father and mother and brothers and sisters and Sumomo to marry if it is my karma to marry. Thinking about her safe at home warmed him, but then, standing there in front of the desk, the good feeling quickly turned sour. He remembered all the sickening, uneasy times he had stood there before the seated gai-jin leader, answering questions about the Choshu, Satsuma, Bakufu, Toranagas, the questions inquiring into every aspect of his life and Nippon's life, now almost a daily occurrence, the fish eyes scouring the truth out of him, much as he would have preferred to lie and confuse.

He was careful not to touch anything, presuming a trap had been laid for him as he would certainly have done if he had left a gai-jin alone in such an important place. His ears caught an angry voice outside and he scurried back to peer out of Tyrer's window. To his astonishment Akimoto was at the gate, bowing to the sentry who had him covered with his bayoneted rifle and was shouting at him. His cousin wore gai-jin laborer's clothes and was clearly very nervous.

Hastily he went outside, put a smile on his face, and raised his hat. "Good day, sir sentry, this my friend."

The sentry knew Hiraga by sight, that he was some sort of interpreter, also that he had a permanent Legation pass. He replied caustically with incomprehensible words, waving Akimoto away, ordering Hiraga to tell "th's ere monkey t'pushawf or'e'll g't'is bloody 'ead shot awf."

Hiraga's smile never wavered. "I take him away, so sorry." He took Akimoto by the arm and hurried him into an alley that led to the village. "Are you mad? To come here y—"

"I agree." Akimoto was not over his fright at having a bayonet shoved within an inch of his throat. "I agree, but the shoya, the village elder, asked me to find you urgently."

The shoya motioned Hiraga to sit on the other side of the low table. These private quarters, behind his deliberately drab and untidy shop, were spotless, the tatami and shoji window papers the best quality. The tabby cat sat comfortably in his lap, her eyes malevolently fixed on the intruder. White-green porcelain teacups sat around a small iron teapot. "Please, some tea, Otami-sama, so sorry to cause you inconvenience," he said. pouring and using the name Hiraga used, then stroked the cat. Her ears twitched nervously. "Please excuse me for interrupting you."

The tea was aromatic and noteworthy. Hiraga mentioned it politely, feeling awkward in front of the shoya in his European clothes, difficult to sit in them, and uncomfortable without swords. After the customary courtesies, the shoya nodded, half to himself, and looked at his guest, eyes flinty in the mask of graciousness. "Some news has arrived from Kyōto. I thought you should have it at once."

Hiraga's disquiet increased. "So?"

"It seems that ten shishi of Choshu, Satsuma and Tosa, attacked Shōgun Nobusada at Otsu. The assassination attempt failed and all were killed."

Hiraga pretended to be uninterested but he was sick inside. Which ten and why had they failed? "When was this?"

The shoya had seen nothing to indicate if Hiraga knew of the attack or not. "Eight days ago."

"How could you possibly know in such a short time?"

To his astonishment the shoya reached into his sleeve and brought out a tiny cylinder. Inside was a roll of very thin paper. "This arrived today. Our Gyokoyama *zaibatsu* has carrier pigeons for important news." It had actually arrived yesterday but he had needed time to decide how he was to deal with Hiraga. "Important to have quick, accurate information, *neh*?"

"Were names mentioned?"

"No, no names, so sorry."

"Is that all your information?"

The eyes glinted. To Hiraga's shock he added, "The same night, in Kyōto, Lord Yoshi and Lord Ogama and their forces fell on the shishi headquarters, caught them unawares, destroyed it and them. Forty heads were spiked outside the wreckage." The older man kept the smile from his face. "Otami-sama, would forty be a big percentage of our brave shishi?"

Hiraga shrugged and said he did not know, hoping that the shoya could not tell if he lied. His head was hurting as he wondered who was dead, who survived, who had betrayed them, and how could it be that such enemies as Yoshi and Ogama were acting in concert? "Why are you telling me all this?"

For a moment the shoya looked down at the cat, his eyes softened and his fingers began scratching the center of her head and her eyes closed with pleasure, her claws moving in and out of their sheaths without menace. "It seems that not all those ambushed were caught," he said quietly. "Two escaped. The leader, sometimes called the Raven, his real name is Katsumata, the trusted advisor of Sanjiro of Satsuma, and a Choshu shishi called Takeda."

Hiraga was rocked to his core that so much could be known and his muscles coiled, ready to reach out and kill with his hands if need be. His mouth opened but he said nothing.

"Would you know this Takeda, Otami-sama?"

Anger rushed through Hiraga at this impertinence, he felt his face flush but he held on to a measure of control. "Why are you telling me this, shoya?"

"My Gyokoyama overlord ordered it, Otami-sama."

"Why? What is all this to me? Eh?"

The shoya, to calm his own nerves—though he had a small, loaded pistol in the pocket of his sleeve—poured some more tea for both of them, knowing this was a dangerous game and this shishi was no man to fool with. But orders were orders, and standing orders of the Gyokoyama *zaibatsu* were that anything unusual, in any of their hundred branches, must be reported instantly. Particularly the Yokohama branch, more important now than Nagasaki as it was the main gai-jin base, and so the main observation post on gai-jin—and he specially chosen for the senior post. Of necessity he had carrier-pigeoned news of this man's arrival, Ori's death, all subsequent events and the actions he himself had taken—all of which had been approved.

"The Gyokoyama . . ." he began, following instructions and using great care, for he could see Hiraga was seething and unnerved by the revelations, which was their purpose. His overlords in Osaka had written: *Put this shishi, whose real name is Rezan Hiraga, off balance quickly. Risks will be great. Be armed and talk to him when he is not . . .*

". . . my Masters thought that perhaps they could be of use to you, as you could be of great value to them."

"Use to me?" Hiraga grated, ready to explode, his right hand nervously seeking the sword hilt that was not there. "I can order no taxes. I have no koku. What use have I for parasites, that's what moneylenders are, what even the great Gyokoyama is! *Neh*?"

"It is true that samurai believe it and have believed it forever. But we wonder if your Sensei Taira would agree."

"Eh?" Again Hiraga was unbalanced and he stuttered, "Wh-what about Taira? What about him?"

"Maid! Saké!" the shoya called out, then to Hiraga, "I ask your patience but my superiors . . . I am an old man," he added humbly, with open self-deprecation, knowing his power in the *zaibatsu* was large, his yang still functioned perfectly, and if need be he could shoot this man or cripple him and hand him over to the Bakufu Enforcers who still guarded their gates. "I am old and we live in dangerous times."

"Yes, you do," Hiraga said through his teeth. The saké came quickly, the maid poured quickly and fled. Hiraga quaffed some and was glad of it though he feigned otherwise, accepted more and drained that too. "So? Taira? You better make sense."

The shoya took a deep breath, launching himself on what he knew would be the biggest chance of his life, with vast implications for his *zaibatsu* and all his future generations: "Ever since you have been here, Otami-sama, you have wondered and enquired how and why the Ing'erish gai-jin rule much of the world outside our shores when they are a small island nation, I understand smaller than ours . . ." He stopped, amused by the sudden blank look on Hiraga's face. "Ah, so sorry, but you must know you have been overheard talking to your friend who is now dead, and your cousin, so sorry. I can assure you your confidences are safe, your aims and Gyokoyama aims and shishi aims are the same. It could be important to you . . . We believe we know a major secret you seek."

"Eh?"

"Yes, we believe the major secret is their moneylending, banking and financ—"

He was drowned out as Hiraga was convulsed with a paroxysm of jeering laughter. The cat was torn from her tranquility and her claws dug through the shoya's kimono into his flesh. Gingerly he eased the claws out and began to soothe her, controlling his fury, wishing he could beat some sense into the insolent young man. But that would cost him his life eventually—there would be Akimoto to deal with, and other shishi. Doggedly he waited, the task his overlords had given him fraught with hazards: *'Probe this young man, find out what his true aims are, true thoughts, true desires and allegiance, use him, he could be a perfect tool . . .'*

"You are mad. It's only their machines and cannon and wealth and ships."

"Exactly. If we had those, Hiraga-sama, we could . . ." The instant he deliberately used the real name he saw all laughter vanish and the eyes focus, menacingly. "My superiors told me to use your name only once, and then only so you would know we are to be trusted."

"How do they know?"

"You mentioned the Shinsaku Otami account, the code name of

your honored father, Toyo Hiraga. Of course this is written in their most private books of record."

Hiraga was filled with rage. It had never occurred to him that moneylenders would have private books, and as everyone, from the low to the highest, needed their services from time to time, moneylenders would have access to all kinds of private knowledge, recorded knowledge, dangerous knowledge that they could use as pressure or a cudgel to gain all kinds of other information they should not have—how could they possibly have found out about our shishi except by foul means—as this dog is daring to use on me! Rightfully merchants and moneylenders are despised and distrusted and should be stamped out. When *sonno-joi*'s a fact, our first request to the Emperor should be an order for their destruction. "So!"

The shoya was prepared, aware the thread between a sudden, berserk attack and sanity was stretched to breaking, shishi never to be trusted, one hand not far from his sleeve pocket. He kept his voice soft, nevertheless there was no mistaking the threat, or promise: "My superiors told me to tell you that your secrets and those of your father, honored clients, though recorded, are private, completely private . . . between us."

Hiraga sighed and sat back, the threat cleansing his head of useless anger, and he considered all that the shoya had told him, the threat—or the promise—and all the rest, the danger of the man himself, the Gyokoyama and their like, weighing his choice, his heritage and training in the balance.

The choice was simple: To kill or not to kill, to listen or not to listen. When he was very young his mother had said, 'Beware, my son, and remember seriously: to kill is easy, to unkill impossible.'

For a moment his mind dwelt on her, always wise, always welcoming him, always with arms outstretched—even during the pains in her joints that were a way of life for her as long as he could remember, and twisted her a little worse every year. "Very well, shoya, I will listen, once."

In his turn the shoya sighed, a major ravine straddled. He filled the cups. "To *sonno-joi* and shishi!"

They drank. He replenished the cups from time to time. "Otami-sama, please be patient with me but we believe we can have all that the gai-jin have. As you know, in Nippon rice is a currency, rice merchants are bankers, they lend money to farmers against future crops, to buy seeds and so on, without the money most years there would be no crops, therefore no taxes to collect; they lend to samurai and daimyos for their living against future pay, future koku, future taxes, without this money there is usually no living until there are crops to tax. Money makes any way of life possible. Money, in the form of gold, silver, rice or silk or even manure, money is the wheel of life, profit the grease of the wheel an—"

"Come to the point. The secret."

"Oh, so sorry, the point is that somehow, incredibly, gai-jin moneylenders, bankers—in their world it is an honorable profession—have found a way to finance all their industries, machines, ships, cannon, buildings, armies, anything and everything, profitably, without using real gold. There cannot be that amount of real gold in all the world. Somehow they can make vast loans using the *promise* of real gold, or *pretend* gold, and that alone makes them strong, and, seemingly, they do it without debasing their currency, as daimyos do."

"Pretend gold? What are you talking about? Be clearer!"

The shoya wiped a bead of sweat off his lip, excited now, the saké helping his tongue, but more so because now he began to believe it was possible that this youth could solve the puzzle. "Excuse me if I am complicated but we know what they do, but not yet know how they do it. Perhaps your Taira, this gai-jin fountain of information you so cleverly drain, perhaps he would know, could explain to you how they do it, the tricks, the secrets, then you can tell us and we can make Nippon as strong as five Englands. When you achieve *sonno-joi*, we and other moneylenders can join to finance all the ships and arms Nippon will ever need . . ."

Cautiously, he elaborated on his theme, eloquently answering questions, guiding Hiraga, helping him, flattering him, judiciously plying him with saké and knowledge, impressed with his intelligence, over the hours snaring his imagination, and he continued until the sun was down.

"Money, eh? I will ad . . . admit, shoya," Hiraga said unsteadily, heavy with alcohol, his head bursting with so many new and unsettling ideas that conflicted with as many deep beliefs, "admit money never inter . . . ested me. Never really . . . really understood money, only the lack." A belch almost choked him. "I—I think I can see—yes, Taira will tell me." He tried to get up and failed.

"First may I offer a bath, and I will send for the masseuse?" The shoya easily persuaded him, called for a servant to help and gave Hiraga over to strong though gentle hands—soon to be snoring and oblivious.

"Well done, Ichi-chan," his wife whispered when it was safe, beaming at him. "You were perfect, *neh*?"

He beamed back, also speaking softly, "He is dangerous, always will be, but we begin, that's the important part."

She nodded, satisfied that he had taken her advice to send for Hiraga this afternoon, to be armed, and not to be afraid to use the threat. Both knew the risks, but then, she reminded herself, her heart still pounding from listening to the parry and thrust, this is an opportunity sent by the gods and gains are proportionate to risks. Eeee, she chortled to herself, with success we will be granted samurai status, our descendants will be samurai, and my Ichi will be a Gyokoyama overlord. "You were so wise to say two and not three escapees and not to reveal what else we know."

"It is important to keep something in reserve. To further control him."

She patted her husband maternally and again told him how clever he was and did not remind him that this too had been her suggestion. She let her mind drift a moment, still puzzled by the two shishi making for Yedo, thus surely risking capture or betrayal immeasurably. And even more puzzling was why the girl Sumomo, Hiraga's samurai wife-to-be, had joined the household of Koiko, Yedo's most famous courtesan, now the pleasure person of Lord Yoshi. Very puzzling indeed.

A vagrant thought blossomed. "Ichi-chan," she said delicately, "something you said earlier made me want to ask you: If these gai-jin are so clever and such magical bankers, would it not be wise for you to begin a careful venture with one of them, quietly, very quietly." She saw his eyes fix and the dawning of a seraphic smile. "Toshi is nineteen, the cleverest of our sons, and could be the figurehead, *neh*?"

33

Monday, 1st December:

N ORBERT GREYFORTH CAME ON deck of the mail ship just rounding the headland. She was from Hong Kong via Shanghai and now ahead was the Yokohama coastline. He was freshly shaven and wore a top hat and frock coat against the early morning chill and he saw the Captain and others on the bridge in front of the funnel with its plume of acrid smoke trailing aft, seamen preparing for port, sails furled on her three masts. On the foredeck, behind locked grilles separating them completely from the rest of the ship, were steerage passengers, the flotsam of Asia, remittance men and riffraff, huddled under canvas shelters. Grilles were standard on passenger ships against piracies attempted from this area.

The wind was brisk and smelt good to him and tasted clean, not like below where the stench of oil and coal smoke and the throbbing, headache-making engine noise permeated the closeness. *Asian Queen* had been under power for hours, battling the head wind. Much as he loathed steamers, Norbert was pleased, otherwise they would have been many more days late. He bit the end off a cheroot, spat it overboard and cupped his hands, lighting it carefully.

The Settlement looked the same as ever. Samurai guard houses and Customs House, north and south, outside the fence and over small bridges, smoke from various chimneys, men walking the promenade, horsemen exercising their ponies on the racetrack, Drunk Town its usual mess with little of their fire and earthquake damage cleaned up, contrasting with the disciplined tent lines of the encampment on the bluff where soldiers were drilling, the odd bugle call wafting seawards. As if peeping over the fence were the Yoshiwara roofs. He felt a halfhearted stirring, nothing like normal for he was still satiated from carousing in Shanghai, the richest, raunchiest, wildest city in Asia, with the best racing, gambling, whoring, bars and European food anywhere.

Never mind, he thought, I'll give Sako the bolt of silk and that'll make her toolie flutter and who knows?

His eyes passed the flagpoles of the various Legations, hardened as they saw the Struan Building, then centered on his own. During the three weeks he had been away he was pleased to see external repairs to the top floor had been completed, no sign of fire damage. He was too far away to recognize people going in and out of the buildings fronting High Street, then he caught a glimpse of a blue bonnet and hooped dress and parasol crossing to the French Legation. Only one like that, he thought. Angel Tits! It was as if he could smell the perfume surrounding her. Wonder if she knows about the duel.

Morgan Brock had guffawed when he told them. 'Thee's my consent to blow his head or balls off. 'Stead of pistols, make it fighting irons and really earn thy bonus.'

Tenders were already scurrying to meet the mail ship. Sourly, he noted that the Struan steam launch was waiting in the chop, first in line, Jamie McFay in the stern. His oared launch second. Never mind, won't be long before your launch's mine, your building, with you and all the bloody Struans beached or dead, though maybe I'll give you a job, Jamie, maybe, just for amusement. Then he saw McFay put binoculars to his eyes and knew he would see him. He waved perfunctorily, spat over the side and went to his cabin below.

" 'Morning, Mr. Greyforth, suh," Edward Gornt said with Southern charm. He stood at the door of the cabin opposite, a tall, though slight, good-looking young man from Virginia, twenty-seven, with deep-set brown eyes and brown hair. "I've been watching from the aft deck. Nothing like Shanghai, is it?"

"In more ways than you can think. Are you packed?"

"Yes, suh, and ready to have at it." Apart from the slight roll to the 'suh' his accent was faint, much more English than Southern.

"Good. Sir Morgan told me to give you this when we arrived." He took an envelope from his briefcase and handed it to him. The more he thought about his whole trip the more flabbergasted he became. Tyler Brock had not come to Shanghai. A curt note had greeted Greyforth instead, telling him to obey his son, Morgan, as though he was giving the orders. Sir Morgan Brock was a big-bellied, balding man, not as coarse as his father, but just as mean-tempered and bearded like him. Unlike him, he was London-trained in Threadneedle Street, center of the world's stock markets, and for all manner of international trade. As soon as Greyforth arrived Morgan had laid out his plan to break Struan's.

It was foolproof.

For a year he, his father and their associates on the board of the Victoria Bank of Hong Kong had been buying up Struan's debt paper. Now, with the whole board backing them, they only had to wait until the 30th of January to foreclose. There was no way Struan's could meet this deadline. On that date the bank would own Struan's, lock, stock and clipper ship, with Morgan cornering the Hawaiian sugar markets, cunningly excluding Struan's, who counted on their yearly profits from those markets to service their debts. He would make the killing certain. And another, even bigger coup: Morgan, with supreme cleverness, had bartered these crops forward to Union and Confederate importers for Union goods and Southern cotton for the huge British market that still, by law, could only be serviced by British ships—their ships.

'It's a genius scheme, Sir Morgan, congratulations,' Norbert said, awed, for it would make Brock's the wealthiest trading company in Asia, *the Noble House,* and guarantee his stipend of five thousand guineas a year.

'We be buying Struan's at ten pennies on the pound from the Bank, that be agreed, Norbert, their fleet, everything,' Sir Morgan had said, his huge belly shaking with laughter. 'Thee's to retire soon, and we be very grateful for thy service. If all goes well in Yokohama, we be thinking of another five thousand a year as bonus. Look after young Edward and show him everything.'

'To what end?' he had asked, that vast amount of money every year swamping him.

'To any end I want,' Sir Morgan had said curtly. 'But since thee asks, perhaps I be wanting him to take over Japan, take over thy job when thee goes, if he's worthy. Rothwell's be giving him a month's leave'—this was Gornt's present employer, one of the oldest Shanghai companies and associates of Cooper-Tillman, the biggest American China trader, for whom he had been working for three years, and with whom Brock's, as well as Struan's, had extensive business relations—'this be enough time for the lad to decide, perhaps he'll take over from thee, when thee retires.'

'You think he's experienced enough, Sir Morgan?'

'By the time thee leaves, make sure he is—that's thy job, teach him, toughen him. Don't break him, I don't want him scared off, broken— don't forget now!'

'How much should I tell him?'

After thought, Sir Morgan said, 'Everything about our business in the Japans, the gunrunning plan and opium smuggling if them bastards in Parliament get their way. Tell him thy ideas on opening up the opium trade and busting any embargo if there be one, but nought about provoking Struan, or about our scheme to smash them. The lad knows about the Struans, no love lost on them at Rothwell's, he knows what scum they really be and the devilment old Dirk did, murdering my stepbrother and the like. He's a good lad, so tell him what thee will, but not about sugar!'

'Just as you say, Sir Morgan. What about all the specie and paper I brought? I'll need replacements to pay for the guns, silks and this year's trade goods.'

'I be sending it from Hong Kong, when I returns, and Norbert, it were right clever to shove Struan's out of the way with the Jappo prospecting offer—if that pays dirt, thee will share in't. As to Edward, after the month send him to Hong Kong with a confidential report to the Old Man. I like the lad, he be highly thought of in Shanghai and by Rothwell's—and the son of an old friend.'

Norbert had wondered about 'what' old friend, and about the debt Sir Morgan owed the man to take so much trouble, unusual for him to be kind to anyone. But he was too shrewd to ask and kept his own counsel, happy that the problem of staying in Brock's good favor would not concern him much longer.

Edward Gornt proved to be pleasant enough, reticent, a good listener, more English than American, intelligent, and, rare in Asia, a nondrinker. Greyforth's immediate assessment had been that Gornt was totally unsuited to the rough, adventurous, hard-drinking China trade—a lightweight in everything, except at cards. Gornt was an exceptional bridge player and lucky at poker, a major virtue in Asia, but even this was academic for he never played for high stakes.

He was convinced that Edward Gornt would not suit the Brocks for long, and nothing on the voyage back had made him change his mind. From time to time he had seen a strangeness behind the eyes. The bugger's just wishywashy, out of his depth and knows it, he thought, watching him reading Morgan's letter. Never mind, if anyone can make him grow up I can.

Gornt folded the letter, pocketed it and the sheaf of money the envelope had contained. "Sir Morgan's so generous, isn't he?" he said with a smile. "I never thought he'd . . . I can't wait to begin, to learn . . . I like work and action and I'll do my best to please you, but I'm still not sure if I should leave Rothwell's and . . . well, I never thought he would ever consider I would maybe be good enough to head Brock's in Japan if or when you retire. Never."

"Sir Morgan's a tough master, difficult to please, like our tai-pan, but straight if you do what you're told. A month will be enough. Can you handle a gun?"

"Oh, yes."

The sudden directness surprised him. "What kinds?"

"Handguns, rifles, shotguns." Again the smile. "I've never killed anyone, Indians or the like, but I was second in the Richmond skeet-shoot four years ago." A shadow went over him. "That was the year I went to London to join Brock's."

"You didn't want to leave? Didn't like London?"

"No, and yes. My mother had died and—and my father, he thought it best I should be out in the world, London being the Center of the World, so to speak. London was grand. Sir Morgan very kind. Kindest man I know."

Norbert waited but Gornt volunteered nothing more, lost in his own thoughts. Sir Morgan had only told him Gornt had spent a satisfactory year with Brock's in London, with Tyler Brock's last and youngest son, Tom. After the year he had arranged the junior post at Rothwell's. "Do you know Dmitri Syborodin who runs Cooper-Tillman here?"

"No, suh. Only by reputation. My parents knew Judith Tillman, the widow of one of the original partners." Gornt's eyes had narrowed and Norbert noticed the strangeness in them. "She didn't like Dirk Struan either, loathed him in fact, blamed him for the death of her husband. The sins of the father do pass onwards, don't they?"

Norbert laughed. "They do indeed."

"You were saying, suh? Dmitri Syborodin?"

"You'll like him, he's Southern too." The landing bell sounded. Norbert's eyes glittered with anticipation. "Let's get ashore, there'll be action soon enough."

"Man wan' see tai-pan, heya?" Ah Tok said.

"Ayeeyah, speak civilized, Mother, and not gibberish," Malcolm told her in Cantonese. He stood at his office window, binoculars in his hand, and had been watching the mail ship unloading passengers. He had seen Norbert Greyforth and now he was feeling very good. "What man?"

"The foreign devil bonze you sent for, the foul-smelling bonze," she mumbled. "Your old mother is working too hard and her son won't listen! We should be going home."

"Ayeeyah, I've told you not to mention going home," he told her sharply. "Do that once more and I'll pack you off on the next dirty little lorcha where you'll puke your heart out if you have one, and at the very least the God of the Sea will swallow you up! Send the foreign devil in." A smile crossed his face and some of his good feeling returned.

She went off grumbling. For days she had been harping on a return to Hong Kong, as much as he told her not to. So much so, he was sure she had had orders from Gordon Chen to harass him into obeying.

"By God, I won't until I'm ready." He hobbled back to his desk, glad that his score with Norbert would soon be settled and his whole glorious plan put into effect. "Ah, 'morning, Reverend Tweet, kind of you to be prompt. Sherry?"

"Thank you, Mr., er, Tai-pan, bless you."

The sherry went in a nervous gulp though Struan had deliberately chosen a big glass. "Admirable, er, Tai-pan. Ah yes, thanks, I'll have another small one, bless you." The untidy sack of a man settled with an uneasy smile in the tall chair. Tobacco stained his beard. "What can I do for you?"

"It's about myself and Miss Angelique. I want you to marry us. Next week."

"Eh?" The Reverend Michaelmas Tweet almost dropped his glass. "Impossible," he stuttered, his false teeth chattering.

"No, it isn't. There's lot of precedent for condensing the banns that have to be read out on three succeeding Sundays in church into one Sunday only."

"But I can't . . . you're a minor and so is she, and worse, she's Catholic and there's no possible way. . . . I can't."

"Oh, but you can." Confidently he parroted what Heatherly Skye, nicknamed 'Heavenly,' the only lawyer in Yokohama as well as coroner and insurance agent, had told him. "The fact that I'm a minor applies only in the United Kingdom, not in the colonies or abroad, and only when the father is alive. That she's Catholic doesn't matter if it doesn't matter to me. That ends that. Tuesday the 9th is an auspicious day to be married on. We keep everything quiet until then and that's when it will be."

To Malcolm's amusement Michaelmas Tweet's mouth opened and

closed like a fish but no sound came out. Shakily, the clergyman groped to his feet, poured another sherry, gulped it, then collapsed into the chair again. "I can't."

"Oh, but I've taken legal advice and I'm advised you can. Also I intend to endow you and your church with an extra stipend—five hundred guineas a year." He knew the man was hooked, for the offer was three or four times his present salary and twice what the lawyer had advised: Don't spoil the old fart! "We'll be in church on Sunday to hear the banns read, Tuesday's the great day, the same day you get a hundred guineas advance for your trouble. Thank you, Reverend." He stood but Tweet did not move and he saw his eyes fill with tears. "What on earth's the matter?"

"I just can't do what you ask," Tweet spluttered. "It's—it's not possible. You see, your . . . even if that advice is correct, which I, er, I doubt . . . your mother wrote to me, she wrote formally, by the last post saying that . . . that your father had made her your legal guardian and you had been forbidden to marry." The tears were flowing down his cheeks, his rheumy eyes bloodshot. "Dear God in Heaven, that's so much money, more than I ever dreamed, but I can't . . . I can't go against the law or her, dear God no!"

"A thousand guineas."

"Oh God, don't, don't," the tired old man burst out. "Much as I want the money . . . don't you see, the marriage wouldn't be legal, it's against Church law. God knows I'm as big a sinner as the next, but I can't and if she wrote to me surely she wrote to Sir William, who must sanction any such marriage. God forgive me, I can't. . . ." He stumbled out of the room.

Malcolm stared after him. Speechless, his mind blank, his office suddenly a tomb. The plan, hatched with Heavenly Skye, had been perfect. They would marry quietly, just Jamie and perhaps Dmitri, then he would leave at once for Hong Kong after the duel to be there well before Christmas as his mother had asked and before the news could possibly reach her. Angelique would follow on the next boat.

'Those whom God hath joined together, let no man—or woman—cast asunder,' Heavenly Skye had intoned when he had consulted him.

'Perfect! That's perfect, Heavenly.'

'Thank you, Tai-pan. The fee's fifty guineas. Could I, er, could I have a down payment, cash, if you please?'

Fifty guineas was outrageous. Even so Malcolm Struan had given him ten sovereigns, with Noble House chits for the balance, and had walked home, feeling lighter than in weeks.

'You're in a happy mood today, Malcolm. Good news?'

'Yes, my darling Angel, but I'll share it with you tomorrow. Meanwhile, when do we see our picture? Your dress was really marvelous.'

'It takes such a time to develop whatever has to be developed. Perhaps tomorrow. You looked so handsome.'

'Wonderful. I think we should have a party. . . .'

But now, with the party arranged for tonight, it would not be wonderful. He was totally downcast. Perhaps there was a way to force Tweet? Should he have at him tomorrow when the shock had warn off? More money? Sir William? A sudden idea. He rang the bell. "Yes, Tai-pan?"

"Vargas, run over to the Catholic church and find Father Leo. Ask him if he could step by for a moment."

"Certainly, Tai-pan. When should he come?"

"Now, as soon as possible."

"Now, Tai-pan? But it's lunchtime——"

"Now, by God!" Malcolm shouted, so pent up was his frustration that he had to ask others to do the simplest jobs that he could have done himself before the Tokaidō—God curse those swine, God curse the Tokaidō—it's like B.C. and A.D. for me, except the bad is now, not the good. "Now. Hurry up!"

Vargas was white-faced as he rushed off. While he waited, Malcolm tried to think of ways to strong-arm Tweet, letting his mind brood and, as the minutes passed slowly, becoming ever more infuriated and ever more determined.

"Father Leo, Tai-pan." Vargas stepped aside and closed the door after him.

The priest tried to hide his nervousness. Several times he had begun to walk here to discuss with the Senhor his conversion to Catholicism, but each time he had stopped, promising himself he would go tomorrow but never had, afraid of making a mistake, stumbling over the words. In desperation he had sought out André Poncin to arrange a rendezvous and had been shocked at the way Poncin, then the French Minister personally—who rarely talked him—had reacted, telling him such a discussion was premature, advising him God's work needed patience and prudence, forbidding the approach for the time being.

" 'Morning," Malcolm said weakly.

This was the first time any of the Protestant traders had ever invited him into an office. Throughout the Protestant world, feelings against Catholics and their priests were seriously antagonistic, accusing them of bloody pogroms and religious wars, recent and never to be forgotten, reminding them of the iron control they exercised over their converts and countries they dominated—Protestants equally loathed by Catholics, and according to Catholic beliefs, heretic.

"The Blessings of God upon thee," Father Leo murmured tentatively. Before leaving his little bungalow adjoining the church he had hastily said a prayer that the summons was about what he had prayed so hard for. "Yes, my son?"

"Please, I want you to marry Miss Angelique and me." Malcolm was astonished that his voice sounded so calm, abruptly appalled that he was not only saying it but had actually sent for the priest, whilst understanding clearly the implications of what he asked—*Mother will have a fit, our friends and our whole world will think I've gone raving mad. . . .*

"God be thanked," Father Leo had burst out in ecstatic Portuguese, his eyes closed, arms lifted up to Heaven. "How marvelous are the ways of God, I thank Thee, thank Thee for answering my prayers, may I be worthy of Thy favor!"

"What?" Malcolm stared at him.

"Ah, senhor, my son, please forgive me," he said in English again. "I was just thanking God that in His mercy He has shown you the light."

"Oh. Sherry?" was all Malcolm could think of to say.

"Ah, thank, you, my son, but first will you pray with me?" At once the priest came nearer and went on his knees, closed his eyes and put his hands together in prayer. Embarrassed by the man's sincerity—though disregarding his prayers as meaningless—and unable to kneel anyway, Malcolm stayed seated and closed his eyes and said a small prayer to God, sure that God would understand this momentary lapse, trying to convince himself it was quite all right to have this man to do what was needed.

That the ceremony would probably be invalid in his world was unimportant. It would be valid for Angelique. She could join his marriage bed with a clear conscience. And once the initial storm in Hong Kong had settled and his mother won over—or even if she wasn't—as soon as he was of age next May a proper ceremony would correct any little wrong.

He half opened his eyes. Father Leo was lost in the jumble of Latin. The prayer dragged on, and the blessing. When it was over Father Leo got to his feet, the little coffee beans of his eyes sparkling in his swarthy jowls. "Please allow me to serve the sherry, to save you pain, senhor, after all now I am your servant too," he said jovially. "How are your wounds? How are you feeling?"

"Fair. Now . . ." Malcolm could not bring himself to call him 'Father.' "Now, about the marriage, I th—"

"It will be done, my son, it will be done marvelously, I promise."
How wonderful are the works of God, Father Leo thought. I have not
broken my promise to the French Minister, God has brought this poor
youth to me. "Don't worry, senhor, it is the will of God you have
asked me, and it will be done for the Glory of God." Father Leo gave
him a full glass, and poured one for himself, spilling a little. "To
your future happiness and God's mercy." He drank, then sat in the
chair with such friendliness—the chair that such a short time ago
had been occupied with such rejection—that Malcolm was further
unsettled.

"Now, your wedding, it will be the best, the biggest ever held," the
priest said, and rushed onwards, his enthusiasm vast, and Malcolm's
spirits drooped lower, for he wanted this temporary wedding to be kept
quiet. "We must have a choir and an organ, and new vestments and
silver goblets for Communion, but before those details, my son, there
are many wonderful plans to discuss. The children, for instance, now
they will be saved, they will be Catholic and saved from Purgatory and
the agonies of eternal Hellfire!"

Malcolm cleared his throat. "Yes. Now, the marriage should be next
week, Tuesday's the best day."

Father Leo blinked. "But there's your conversion, my son. That
takes time and y—"

"I . . . well, I don't want to convert, not yet, though I agree that—
that the children will be Catholic." They'll all be brought up properly,
and be intelligent, he reasoned, feeling sicker by the moment. They'll
be able to choose for themselves when they're adult . . . What am I
thinking about? Long before that we'll be properly married in a proper
church. "Please, next week, Tuesday, that's the day."

The eyes no longer smiled. "You're not going to embrace the True
Faith? What of your immortal soul?"

"No, no, thank you, not at the moment. I—I will . . . I will certainly
consider it. The—the souls of the children . . . that's important . . ."
Malcolm tried to sound more coherent. "Now, the marriage, I'd like it
private, a simple ceremony, Tuesday wo—"

"But your immortal soul, my son. God has shown you the light, your
soul is even more important than this marriage."

"Well, I'll certainly consider it, yes, I will. Now the marriage.
Tuesday would be perfect."

The priest set his glass down, his mind tangled with joys and hopes
and questions and fears and danger signals. "But, my son, that will not
be possible, no, not for many reasons. The girl is underage, no? Her

father's approval must be obtained, documents approved. You, the same, no?"

"A minor?" Malcolm forced a tentative laugh. "It doesn't apply in my case, not when your father is dead. It's—it's English law. I checked it with . . . with Mr. Skye." He just managed to stop using 'Heavenly' but cursed himself anyway for mentioning him at all, as he suddenly remembered Angelique telling him how Father Leo hated the man, hated the nickname, believing him, an open agnostic, to be an abomination.

"That person?" Father Leo's voice hardened. "His opinion will certainly have to be approved by your Sir William, he's certainly not to be trusted and as to the senhorita's father, he can come from Bangkok, no?"

"He's . . . I believe he's returned to France. He won't be necessary, I'm sure Mr. Seratard can act for her. Tuesday would be perfect."

"But, my son, why the hurry, you're both young, so much life ahead, your soul to consider." Father Leo tried a smile. "It's God's will you sent for me, in a month or two y—"

"Not, not in a month or two," Malcolm said, ready to explode, his voice strangled. "Wednesday or Tuesday, please."

"Reconsider, my son, your immortal soul should be y—"

"Forget my soul . . ." Malcolm paused to get a grip on himself. "I thought I would endow the Church, though it's not—not currently my Church, endow it handsomely."

Father Leo heard the 'currently' and the way 'handsomely' had been said, ever conscious that God's work on earth required practical servants and pragmatic solutions. And funds. And influence. And those two essentials came only from the highborn and the rich, no need to remind himself that the tai-pan of the Noble House was both, or that already today a giant step forward in the service of God had been made: he had been asked for a favor, and the children would be saved even if this poor sinner burned in the Molten Torment. A shiver went through him, appalled for this youth and all those who would needlessly suffer such horror for all eternity when salvation was so easy to obtain.

He pushed that problem aside. The will of God is the will of God. "The marriage will take place, my son, never fear, I promise . . . but not next week or the week after, there are too many barriers."

Malcolm felt his heart about to burst. "God Almighty, if it can't be next week or the latest the week after, then it's no good, it has to be then—or nothing."

"But why? And why private, my son?"

"It has to be then, or nothing," Malcolm repeated, his face twisted. "You—you will find me a good friend. . . . I need your help. . . . For God's sake, it's a simple thing to marry us!"

"Yes, yes, it is, for God, but not for us, my son." The priest sighed and got up. "I will ask God's guidance. I doubt if . . . but perhaps. Perhaps. I would have to be very sure."

The words hung in the air.

"I hate to pour feces on your bouquet of roses, Tai-pan," Heavenly Skye said, steepling his fingers. He was slumped behind his desk in his drab little office. "But since you ask my professional advice I'd say your Father Leo's not to be trusted, not a jot or tittle, unless you convert. There's no way that can be done in time and I wouldn't advise that, oh dear, no. He'll puppet you like a will-o'-the-wisp and your vital dates will pass and you'll be truly buggered."

"Then for Christ's sake, Heavenly, what do I do?"

Skye hesitated, blew his bulbous nose and cleaned his pince-nez, small spectacles, a favorite ploy to allow time to compose himself, or to cover a lapse, or, in this case, to prevent an all-pervading beam.

This was the first time anyone important had consulted him since he had hung up his own shingle, *H. Skye, Esq., late of Moodle, Putfield and Leech, Solicitors and Barristers, Inns of Court, London,* initially in Calcutta ten years ago, then Hong Kong, and recently here. At long last he had, potentially, a perfect client: rich, beset with anxiety, with a simple problem that could become ever more complicated, with long-term possibilities from the cradle to the grave. And grand fees, for a solution, of which there were many, some good, some violent.

"Can't think of a worse pickle to be in," he said solemnly, playing his part, liking and admiring the youth, not merely as a client, then offered a key. "The Gordian knot, eh?"

Malcolm was miserable. Obviously Heavenly was right, Father Leo can't be trusted. Even if I converted . . . I can't, that would be too much. . . . He looked up abruptly. "Knot? Gordian knot? That was solved! Ulysses hacked it in two. No, it was Hercules!"

"Sorry, Alexander the Great in 333 B.C."

"Whoever did it doesn't matter. My problem is . . . Heavenly, help me cut through my knot and you've my undying gratitude and five hundred guineas . . ."

The Harbor Master's signal gun echoed over the Settlement. They looked out of the mildewed window—Skye's office was in

Lunkchurch's building and godown, stacked with books, fronting the sea. To their joy the fleet was rounding the headland in line ahead, flagship to the fore, with flags overall. Pride filled them, and relief. Cannonade salutes thundered from shore and ships, H.M.S. *Pearl* the most exuberant, with replying salvos from the fleet.

Both men whooped, and Skye said, "Now we can deal with the Jappos and sleep snug in our beds." Obliquely, he returned to the matter in hand, envying him Angelique and determined to help. "Not difficult to solve Jappos, Willie needs to be simple and decisive, the old iron fist in the iron glove, or velvet, applies in most, if not all cases. As with you."

Malcolm Struan looked at him. "How? How? If you solve my problem you can ... you can name your own price." Tiredly he reached for his canes. "Within reason."

"A moment, Tai-pan," Skye said, exuberantly polishing his glasses. My price won't only be money, not from the Noble House, your influence can help me become a Hong Kong judge, ah, what joy that will be! My only dilemma is should I reveal the solution now, or wait and risk losing the initiative. Not on your Nelly! A bird in the bed is worth two in the Yoshiwara.

No longer solemn, he set his pince-nez back on the tip of his nose, now like twin doors dominating his pink, babyish face, which seemed to overflow them. "I had a sudden thought, Tai-pan. It could solve your problem, in the time you need. Why don't you do what your mother did?"

Malcolm was thrown for a moment, then the meaning became clear. "Oh, oh, you mean elope? I've thought of that, for God's sake," he said irritably, "but elope where and who's going to perform the ceremony? We're a million miles from Macao."

"What has Macao to do with it?" Skye asked.

"Everyone knows Mother and Father eloped and were married in the English Church in Macao, the ceremony performed quietly and quickly because of Grandfather's influence."

Skye smiled and shook his head. "That's the published story, but it's not true. Your Captain Orlov married them aboard your clipper *China Cloud* en route from Macao to Hong Kong—your grandfather had made your father Master for that short voyage, and as you know the tai-pan's law is that at sea the Master was the law of the ship."

Struan was gaping at him. "I don't believe it."

"The first attribute of a good lawyer, and I am a good lawyer, Mr. Struan, is to be a good listener, the second to have a nose for facts and secrets, the third to be discreet. It's very important to know as much as you can about your most important, potential clients—all the better to help them in adversity." He took a pinch of snuff, sneezed. "The Noble House is the first in Asia, the stuff of legends, so when I came to Hong Kong I wanted to sift fact from legend about the Struans, Brocks, the Americans Cooper and his partner Wilf Tillman, even the Russian Zergeyev. I think—" He stopped. The young man's eyes were glazed, staring into the distance, not listening, his mind surely on the solution as it surfaced and filled his firmament. "Mr. Struan!"

"Oh, sorry, you were saying?"

"I'm delighted to present you with your solution: there are difficulties of course, but you have ships, they have captains, and *captains of a British ship,* in certain situations, can perform a marriage. You are tai-pan so you-can-order-it! *Quod erat demonstrandum.*"

"Heavenly, you're fantastic," Malcolm burst out. "Fantastic! You're sure—sure about my mother and father?"

"Yes. One of my informants was Morley Skinner, owner of the *Oriental Times,* a contemporary of Dirk Struan, an old man who loved to gossip about the old times; another was Mrs. Fortheringill before she died, and—have you noticed how few people are interested in listening to old people who actually witnessed all kinds of events? Skinner died about eight years ago, did you know him?"

"No." Some of Malcolm's hope evaporated. "If that story's true, everyone in Hong Kong would know it."

"Dirk Struan decided to hush it, decided a 'quiet church wedding' was better face. He was powerful enough to do that, and even got the Brocks to agree. It's true."

"But if he . . ." Malcolm stopped—his face a delight to see. "But true or false, that doesn't matter, does it?"

"Yes, it does. The truth is vastly important because *it gives you a complete defense against your mother.* After all, you're only doing what she did, you're following her example."

"My God, Heavenly, you're right again." Then even more excitedly. "Do you have proof?"

Of course, silly boy, Skye thought, but you don't get everything at once. "Yes, in Hong Kong. I'll need expenses to go there at once—against my retainer. Shall we say five thousand, which includes proof . . . and always providing my solution cuts your Gordian knot. By the time you get there, after the wedding, I'll have all the proof you'll need."

"God in Heaven, and I thought I was lost!" Malcolm sat back in the chair. Now there was nothing to stop him. And this fact cleared his mind of many devils, devils of the night and of the day and of the future. "What other 'facts' do you know about me and the past?"

"Lots, Mr. Struan," Skye said with a smile. "But they're not for now, however precious."

Malcolm Struan was heading homewards, happier than he could remember, his sticks or the pain not bothering him as much as usual.

And why not? he almost sang. Married next week to the most beautiful girl ever, Mother finessed flawlessly—I can't wait to see her face—I've a party tonight that now will really be a celebration, and Norbert's back in perfect time to be sent onwards to meet his Maker. "Ayeeyah!"

Jovially he greeted and waved at those who passed by. He was popular as well as pitied, respected as tai-pan of the Noble House, and envied even more as the adored husband-to-be of the Settlement's darling.

The sun breaking through the clouds matched his mood and set the sea sparkling, while the fleet sorted itself out in the bay, Sir William's tender rowing out to the flagship, the mail ship clustered with other tenders. Their own merchantman, *Lady Tess,* which plied between Yokohama, Shanghai, Hong Kong, then all the major ports home to London and back again, was prepared for sea, outward bound this evening.

Her captain would do, he thought—Lavidarc Smith, big and blustery, many years with Struan's like most of our captains, but I've never liked him much, I'd rather have had old Uncle Sheely to marry and bless us. Pity I didn't know what I know now when he was here. Never mind. Joss! Anyway, I can't keep Lavidarc here and even tomorrow would be impossible, have to deal with Norbert first.

What about Vincent Strongbow, off *Prancing Cloud*? She arrives Sunday and turns around for Hong Kong Wednesday. That gives me plenty of time to kill Norbert and slip aboard her before Sir William creases me. I mustn't be delayed here, far safer to be in Hong Kong where we've real power and Angel ... *my wife* by then ... she can follow in two or three weeks.

So, everything's decided. And Heavenly's right again: I must be very careful and not tell anyone, not even Angel, until just before. I can trust him, he's sworn to secrecy and his fee will be spread over the year, which will ensure I have his devotion. Ayeeyah, five thousand! Never mind, he's given me the answer, he's really done it! Thank God!

Another decision: I'm going to cut down on the medicine, even try to cut it out altogether. I've a duty to Angel to get well and be strong without props. And be fit to take over the Noble House. With Angel beside me, I can . . .

Horses trotting past dispelled his reverie. He waved at the riders and saw that he was near the church, sun on the steeple, the smell of the sea and horses and earth and life in his nostrils. In sudden gratitude he began to go in to say a prayer of thanks when he noticed their steam launch heading for their wharf, Jamie in the stern, his head deep in a newspaper, and that reminded him of mail. He changed direction and was at the wharf head just before she came alongside.

"Jamie!" he called out above the noise of the engine, and waved as she nosed against the timbers, heavy with seaweed and barnacles. He saw Jamie squint against the wind, then wave back. One look at his face was enough. "I'll come aboard."

Awkwardly he stepped on deck, difficult to walk on a sloping surface with two canes, but he maneuvered his way aft and allowed Jamie to catch his arm and help him down the three steps into the cabin. The cabin was spacious and private, with benches around a sea table, lockers underneath them. On the table was the mail, in neat bundles, separated into letters, newspapers, magazines and books. At once he saw a letter from his mother atop his pile, her writing so distinctive. Another letter from her to Jamie was already open on the table.

"I'm—I'm glad to see you, Tai-pan."

"What's up now?"

"Here, read my letter for yourself."

For yr information my son may not marry until he has attained his majority, under any circumstance. I have already informed Reverend Michaelmas Tweet, Sir William (by this post), and made a careful announcement in this day's Oriental Times *(enclosed). Also all our captains of all our ships plying to and from your waters have been so informed and have ordered them to spread this information, and also advised Admiral Ketterer (by this post) in case a captain's ceremony tempts him. What my son does after his 21st birthday is of course up to him. Until that time, before God, I will protect his interests and ours as best I can.*

The air had rushed out of Malcolm's lungs and blood from his face. He ripped open his own letter. It was almost a copy of the other, except personal and addressed *My dearest son,* and ended,

> *This is really for yr own good, my son. I regret to say the girl's stock is bad—we have heard officials in French Indo-China now pursue her father for fraud, you already know an uncle is in Debtors' Prison in Paris. If you must have her, make her a mistress, much as I disapprove, but you will only store more trouble for yourself I am sure. I, of course, will never meet her.*
>
> *I trust I will have the pleasure of seeing you before Christmas when this sorry business can be behind us. I would write about the vile Brocks but that must be settled here and not in Yokohama. Yr loving mother*

The 'P.S. I love you' was there, so no secret message.

Slowly he tore the letter into pieces. This control pleased him, but did not take away the fury that she had checkmated him. "That woman," he muttered, unaware he was speaking aloud, "that woman's a hag . . . a devil-spawned hag, a witch, how could she possibly know . . ."

McFay watched and waited, gravely concerned.

When he could think straight, Malcolm said, "What's in the paper?" The article was brief:

> *Mrs. Tess Struan, acting head of Struan's, announced today that the Noble House would host a major celebration on the occasion of the 21st birthday of her eldest son, Malcolm, and his formal elevation to tai-pan on May 21st, next year.*

"Well, Jamie," he said with a bitter smile. "Not much more she can do to undermine me, is there?"

"No," Jamie said, his heart going out to him.

Malcolm saw the ships and horizon and beyond that Hong Kong and the Peak and all his friends there, and enemies. Now she was atop the list. "It's funny in a way. A few moments ago I was riding a crest . . ." Dully he told Jamie about his great idea, about Tweet's turn-down, and all about Heavenly's marvelous scheme. "That's garbage now."

Jamie was as much in shock as Malcolm. He could not seem to get his mind working. "Perhaps . . . perhaps Tweet could be persuaded. Perhaps a contribution to the Ch—"

"He turned that down. So did Father Leo."

"Jesus Christ, you asked him too?"

Malcolm related that meeting, shocking Jamie even more.

"God Almighty, Tai-pan, if you're so set on it to go to those lengths . . . perhaps . . . we'll find another captain."

"Not much chance of that, Jamie. Anyway Heavenly stressed to keep it quiet until it was over, particularly Sir William who could forbid it as Angelique and I are under age. And if she put him on formal notice, he'll have to tell Seratard. She's won . . . God curse her!"

Again he set his eyes on the horizon. In the past when a catastrophe happened, when the twins drowned, for example—while she never said it directly, he always thought that she blamed him, if he'd been there somehow it would not have happened—he would feel the tears welling, like now, but would force them back and that would make the hurt worse and the sick feeling terrible. He did that because 'A tai-pan never cries.' *She* had always drummed it into him. It was the first thing he could remember her saying, 'The tai-pan never cries, he's above that, he fights on, like Dirk, he never cries, he bears the burden,' repeating it again and again though tears always came easily to his father.

I never realized what contempt she had for him.

She never cried, never once that I can remember.

I'm not going to cry. I will bear the burden. I swore I'd be worthy of the tai-pan and I will. Never again will she be "Mother" to me. Never. Tess. Yes, Tess, I will bear it.

His eyes focused on Jamie, feeling so old, and so lonely. "Let's get ashore."

Jamie started to say something, stopped. His face was strange. Then he pointed to the seat opposite. More packets of mail there.

"What is it?"

"That's . . . that's Wee Willie's mail. Bertram, the Legation's new dogsbody, was sick so I said I'd . . . I'd fetch their mail for them." Jamie's fingers were as shaky as his voice. He picked up the large bundle of letters. Its crisscrossed string was government-sealed in the center but it was still easy to leaf through the corners and find her two letters. To Sir William and Admiral Ketterer. "We, with a little time, and . . . and luck you could, I . . . I might be able to . . . to get them out."

The hair at the nape of Malcolm's head seemed to stiffen. To rob the Royal Mail was a hanging offense.

34

THE TWO MEN STARED AT THE BUN-
dle of letters, in turmoil, consumed with dread. The cabin was claustro-
phobic. Malcolm said nothing and watched Jamie, who was silent, both
of them drained. Then, making the decision for him, Jamie's shaky
fingers ripped at the string, but this galvanized Malcolm into his own
decision and he reached over and grabbed the bundle and stopped him.
"No, Jamie, you mustn't."

"It's the—the only way, Tai-pan."

"No, it isn't." Malcolm straightened the string, relieved the seal was
not broken, then smoothed the letters out and put them back on the
other pile, the touch of them hateful. "It's just not right," he said, his
voice as weak as his knees, despising his weakness—was it weakness?
"I'd never forgive myself if you . . . if you were caught and . . . and,
well, I just don't have the courage—apart from that it's not right."

Jamie's face was wet with sweat. "Right or not, no one's to know. If
we don't, you've no chance. Maybe we can find a captain—even
Brock's, they've a ship next week."

Malcolm shook his head, his mind blank. A wave rocked the launch
against the pilings, screeching the rope fenders. With an effort he
forced himself to concentrate. All his life, whenever he was in quandary, he would ask himself what Dirk Struan, the tai-pan, would do—
but never a real answer came forth.

At length, wearily he said, "What would he do, Jamie? Dirk
Struan?"

At once Jamie's memory took him to that devil-may-care giant of a
man, the few times he had seen him, or been in his company for a few
minutes—he himself so junior and just arrived. "He'd . . ." After a

672

moment, a smile began. "He'd . . . Dirk would . . . yes, that's it. I think he would order us and the Bosun ashore and take the launch out himself 'to test her as something feels amiss,' and then . . . then when he was well away and in deep water, he would calmly open the sea cocks and, while she filled, he would make sure all this mail was well weighed and could not float free, then he'd go to the stern and light a cheroot and wait till she sank and swim ashore. Had he interfered with the mails? 'Perish that thought, laddie.' " Jamie's beam became seraphic. "Why not?"

Before Tokaidō Malcolm was a strong swimmer. Now he knew he would sink like an anchor. "I'd never make it ashore."

"I could, easily, Tai-pan."

"Yes, but this isn't your problem, Jamie, and even if you did, it would only buy me a week or so and that's no good. Joss. We can't interfere with the Royal Mail. Let's agree to forget this happened. Eh?" He held out his hand. "You're a real friend, best I've ever had. Sorry I was rotten to you."

Jamie shook warmly. "You weren't, I deserved what you said. No harm's done. Tai-pan . . . please, it would be easy."

"Thanks, but no." For the ten thousandth time, Malcolm knew he was not Dirk Struan and could never do what the tai-pan could do, in this case either blatantly remove the letters or sink them. Before Tokaidō, perhaps I would have dared, but now . . . now it's fifty times worse. Tokaidō, *always Tokaidō,* he thought, the word branded into his mind, so frustrated he could scream. "I have to face it alone."

He hobbled ashore and went to his own suite. The small bottle was full but he took none of it, firmly putting it back into the drawer. Painfully he pulled his chair nearer to the window and sank into it with relief.

I'm going to win, he promised himself. Please, God, help me. I don't know how but I'm going to win Angelique, I'm going to conquer the pain, the opium, the Tokaidō, Tess, and *I am going to win.* . . .

His sleep was deep and restful. When he awoke Angelique was there, seated near and smiling at him.

"Good afternoon, darling. My, but you slept well. It's almost time to change for the party!" Her eyes were sparkling. She came and kissed him and knelt beside him. "How are you?"

"Seeing you makes me so happy." His voice was filled with love but it did not hide his inner worry.

That decided her. It was important to take him out of his usual seriousness so he would enjoy tonight's party, which he had promised was a celebration. "I've a surprise for you," she said, mischievously.

"What?"

She scrambled to her feet and began to twirl as though dancing, her afternoon dress sibilant. Suddenly she chuckled and called out, "Look!" and lifted her skirts and petticoats, revealing the long length of her perfect legs enhanced by silk stockings, saucy garters under her knees, and garter belt and multilayered frilly panties. He had been expecting the traditional, all-concealing pantaloons. The sight of her took his breath away.

"Christ Almighty . . ." he spluttered.

"It's for your pleasure only, my darling," she said, flushed at her daring, laughing at his color, then coquettishly raised her skirts over her head for an instant, letting them fall as suddenly, and fanned herself, saying breathlessly, "It's the latest fashion, no more pantaloons! Pantaloons are finished. The columnist of *Le Figaro* says nowadays some of the most famous ladies of Paris don't even wear panties at the Opéra—on special occasions—for the secret pleasure of their lovers."

"Don't you dare," he said, laughing with her, swept up in her exuberance. He caught her hand and settled her into his lap. "The thought would drive me wild."

She buried her head in his shoulder, pleased that her stratagem had worked. "I think I'll whisper in your ear during dinner, sometimes, or when we're dancing, that I've forgotten them—just to tease my Prince Charming, but only when we're married and to amuse. You don't mind, *chéri,* do you—the new fashion, no pantaloons?"

"Of course not," he said, man-of-the-world, secretly not. "If it's fashion, then it's fashion."

"You said tonight's party was to be a celebration?"

Most of his lightness left him. "Yes, yes, it was. But . . . be patient with me, Angel. In a few days I'll be able to tell you the real reason—I just have to delay a little. In the meantime, know that I love you love you love you. . . ."

In the evening the weather became changeable but it did not dampen the spirit of Malcolm's party. The main Struan dining room had been built for this purpose and dwarfed the rest of the Settlement's private facilities except for the Club. Sparkling silver, crystal glasses, the finest Peking china, the thirty-odd guests in evening dress or dress uniforms. Hoag had declined as he had a fever.

Dinner was immense as usual and at length over. Now to roars of approval, the long table was set against the wall—a rare occurrence but almost obligatory whenever Angelique was present, all guests

wanting to dance with her. Except Jamie—but only tonight. By prior
agreement with Malcolm, Jamie had quietly left during the mayhem of
moving the table. 'Sorry, but I don't feel much like dancing. I'll slip
out, Tai-pan.'

'We both swore to forget about the launch today.'

'It's not that, just want to collect my wits.'

Tonight Angelique was the only lady present, the other two, like
Hoag, were regretfully sick, and she was squired to the heating tempos
of waltzes, polkas played by André Poncin on a grand piano, imported
to huge applause in the spring. One dance per guest was the rule, she
was allowed to rest after four dances and to stop whenever she wished.
Her face was glowing and she wore a new crinoline of red and green
silk, but without the full hoops of a crinoline, that dramatized her wasp
waist and swelling bosom, her nipples minimally covered in the fashion decreed by Paris, deplored by absent clergy, and devoured by every
man in the room.

"Enough, *mes amis*," she said after an hour to groans and pleading
from those who had not had a dance, and she went back to Malcolm,
fanning herself and exhilarated.

He was in a great, carved oak chair at the head of the table, gentled
by wine and brandy. He enjoyed watching her as much as any although,
as always, deeply frustrated that he had not claimed the first dance, or
would not claim the last as was his right. Normally he was an accomplished dancer.

She settled herself on the arm of his chair. His arm went lightly
around her waist, hers rested on his shoulders.

"You dance marvelously, Angel."

"None of them are as good as you," she whispered. "That's what
first attracted me to you and, Prince Charm—"

Cheers of anticipation stopped her. To her embarrassment and chagrin, André's fingers began the first slow, seductive chords of the cancan. Not a little annoyed, Angelique shook her head, and did not move.

To her surprise, and amid roars of delight, Pallidar and Marlowe took
center stage, towels wrapped around their uniforms as skirts, the rollicking music picked up tempo and the two of them began hilariously to
parody the dance that scandalized the civilized world, outside of Paris,
faster and faster, lifting their pretend skirts higher and higher, high
kicking to more cheers and jeers and roars, every table thumping to the
beat, faster and faster until the two men, red-faced and sweating in their
tight uniforms, tried valiant splits and collapsed in a heap to tumultuous
cheers and shouts of "encore, encore," the applause deafening.

Laughing with all of them, Malcolm graciously released her and she went over and helped them up, congratulating and praising their efforts.

Pallidar was panting and pretended a groan. "I think I've put my back out for good."

"Champagne for the Army, and rum for the Navy," she called out, linked arms with both of them and brought them back to Malcolm for more praise, smiling at him. "Not for me the cancan, eh, darling?"

"That would be too much."

"My word, yes," Marlowe said.

"Yes," Malcolm said, sharing the secret smile with her, nicely titillated.

When André began playing again, he chose a waltz. It was just enough to show her ankles as she swayed but not enough to reveal the daring lack of pantaloons. He had shown her the article in *Le Figaro,* encouraged her and shared the secret. All evening he had watched her and those fawning on her—Babcott towering over all the others, then resplendent Pallidar and Marlowe trying to ease him out of the inner circle—relishing his secrets and, for the moment, the life within a life that he led. Angelique was dancing with Sir William. Laughing to himself, he let his mind drift as his fingers played. What would they all do if they knew what I know? About the earrings, the abortion, and how I disposed of the evidence? They'd turn from her as if she were a leper, all of them, including lovesick Struan, he more than any.

If things were different and I were in Paris with her, backed by Noble House power and money and an adoring but invalid husband, what secrets I could obtain! She'd require expert training in the more feminine and not so gentle arts, her claws would need honing but then she would be a classic, any salon and any bed would welcome her, and once she had a taste of the Great Game this oh-so-cunning little chicken would feed on it with gusto.

And into my bed? Now or later, certainly, if I wanted to turn the screws, but I no longer want her and will not take her, except for revenge. She's much more amusing as a toy and there's little enough in this world to amuse . . .

"Wonderful idea, André!" Phillip Tyrer was beaming down at him. "Settry said you cooked the whole thing up with them."

"What?"

"The cancan!"

"Ah, yes," André said. His fingers continued with the waltz, then ended it. "Time for a break, let's have a drink," he said, deciding that now, being almost public, would be a perfect time to bring Tyrer to heel. "I hear a certain lady's contract is worth a Minister's salary," he said in French, and saw Tyrer's face redden with embarrassment and look around. "My God, as though I'd be so indiscreet. Phillip, don't worry, my friend, I have your interests in mind." He smiled, remembering their encounter at the Yedo Castle. "Affairs of the heart have nothing to do with affairs of State, though I believe France should share the spoils of the earth with Great Britain, no?"

"I . . . I agree, André. Yes, I . . . the negotiations are not so good, I'm afraid. Yes, at a standstill."

"Better to speak French, eh?"

"Yes, yes, you're right." Tyrer used his handkerchief as a dandy would to wipe away a sudden sweat. "Never thought it would be so difficult."

André beckoned him closer. "Listen, I can tell you how to fix that: Don't see her tonight even though you've an assignation for the night." He almost laughed aloud as Tyrer's mouth dropped open. "How many times have I told you there are few secrets here. Perhaps I can help . . . if you need help."

"Oh yes, yes, I do. I, yes, please."

"Then . . ."

Both of them glanced at a roulette table that had been set up at the other end of the room, where there was a burst of laughter and clapping as Angelique won on double zero—no gambling for money tonight, just worthless bronze Chinese coins called small cash. Vargas acted as croupier.

Tyrer sighed. "Lucky at gambling and lucky in love.".

"She works at it," André said thinly, irritated with her, "so should you. Listen, break tonight's rendezvous with Fujiko; oh, I know Raiko's set it up especially at your pleading—Raiko didn't tell me by the way, it was one of her maids. Don't go, and don't send word that you're not going, just go to another Inn, say the Inn of the Lily, take any girl there, their prettiest is one called Yuko."

"But André, I don't wan—"

"If you don't want to bed her, just make her please you in other ways, or get drunk, or pretend to get drunk, believe me you won't be wasting your money. Tomorrow, when Nakama mentions Fujiko, or anything about the contract or Raiko, act offhand, and tomorrow night, repeat the performance."

"But . . ."

"*Anytime* Nakama mentions anything, act casual, say nothing other than that the Inn of the Lily was many times more promising, telling him sharply not to mention it again, particularly to Raiko. All right so far?"

"Yes, but don't you think——"

"No, unless you want to be driven mad, and not have Fujiko at a relatively reasonable price—you're going to get stuck anyway, Phillip, but never mind, it's not fair you should be beggared, it's a matter of face. *Do not* discuss this plan with Nakama, and keep the pattern up for a week at least."

"My God, André, a week?"

"Three would be better, old friend." André was amused at Tyrer's miserable countenance. "I'm not only saving you enormous money but an ocean of aggravation. It's important you act as if you couldn't care less, that you were pissed at the delays and breaking appointments and Raiko's outrageous asking price—particularly to an important official like you! That's a good thing to throw at Nakama once or twice. But not more, he's a sharp fellow, no?"

"Yes, yes, he is, and very knowledgeable."

Yes, André thought, and soon it will be time to share all of it with me, both what he's told you and what I have gleaned for myself. Interesting that he speaks English—thank God my spies have their ears open as well as their eyes. That explains a lot, though I don't know why he won't speak English to me or even Japanese whenever I've caught him alone. I suppose because Willie ordered him not to.

"Now," he continued quietly, "Raiko will ask me a dozen times to intercede and arrange a rendezvous. After a week I'll reluctantly agree. Don't let Nakama do it or let him in on the game and when you see Raiko, act tough, and with Fujiko. You've got to be very convincing, Phillip."

"But . . ."

"Tell Raiko she was correct to consider her client's interests, *yours,* first—particularly as you are an important official, harp on that— giving you time to consider the matter carefully. You quite agree it's better to be prudent, that buying 'the woman's' contract now is not a good idea. Use that term and not Fujiko by name—don't forget from their point of view you're only discussing a piece of merchandise at this stage, not the lady you adore. Thank Raiko, and say with her help you have thought carefully and believe buying a contract would be a mistake. You'll just hire 'the woman's' services from time to time, and if 'the woman' is busy, *shikata ga nai*—it doesn't matter—life's too short, etc."

Tyrer had listened attentively and knew that André was right and groaned at the thought of not seeing Fujiko for a week, already imagining her suffering under the hulk of every gai-jin in Yokohama. "I . . . I agree with what you say but—but I don't . . . I don't think I can do it, I mean the acting."

"You have to and why not? They're acting all the time, all the time! Haven't you noticed they live lies as the truth and the truth as lies? Women have no option, especially in the Floating World. Men? They're worse. Remember the Bakufu, the Council of Elders, what about them and what about Nakama, especially Nakama? They're past masters at the game, and that's all it is. Why be a pigeon, why let Raiko humble you and at the same time thrust gold you can't afford—can never afford—into her hands just because you are trying to assuage a never-ending ache that God implanted in us?"

André shivered. He knew the trap too well. He was in it. Raiko had pressed him far beyond his own financial limit. That's not true, he told himself irritably. It's all right to twist the truth and lie with other people but don't do it with yourself, your secret self, or you are lost. The truth is I rushed to the limit and beyond, gladly. Seventeen days ago.

The instant Raiko first introduced me to the girl . . .

The instant I saw her, she of the raven hair and alabaster skin and alluring eyes, I knew I would give Raiko my soul and walk into the Everlasting Pit to possess her. Me, André Edouard Poncin, servant of France, spymaster, killer, expert on the vileness of human nature, me the great cynic, in an instant I had fallen in love. Madness! But true.

The instant the girl had left the room, me helpless and tongue-tied, I said, 'Raiko, please. Whatever ask, I pay.'

'So sorry, Furansu-san, this matter will cost more money than I care to mention, even if she agrees to be with you—she has not yet agreed.'

'Whatever money, I pay. Please ask, ask if agrees.'

'Of course. Please come back tomorrow, at dusk.'

'No. Please. Now ask—ask now, I wait.'

He had had to wait almost two hours. While he waited he fretted and prayed and hoped and died and died again. When Raiko returned and he saw her set face, he began to die once more but rushed to life as she said, 'Her name is Hinodeh, meaning Sunrise. She is twenty-two and she says yes, but there are conditions. Apart from money.'

'Whatever Hinodeh want.'

'Best to listen first.' Raiko was more somber than he had ever seen her. 'Hinodeh says she will be your consort, not courtesan, for a year and a day. If on that last day she decides to remain with you, she will give you her *inochi,* her spirit, and be with you for another year, and another, year by year until she decides to leave or you tire of her. If she wishes to leave, you swear to release her freely.'

'Agreed. When begin?'

'Wait, Furansu-san, there's much more. There will be no mirrors in your house, and you will bring none into it. When she disrobes, the room will always be dark—except once, the first time. Only once, Furansu-san, you may see her. Next, the moment any . . . any disfiguring mark appears, *or whenever she may ask you,* without hesitation you will bow to her and bless her, and be her witness and give her the poison cup, or knife, and watch and wait until she is dead to honor her sacrifice.'

His mind spun out of control. 'Dead?'

'She said she would prefer the knife but did not know a gai-jin's choice.'

When he could get his brain working, he said, 'I—I the judge if—if mark disfiguring?'

Raiko shrugged. 'You or she, it does not matter. If she decides to ask, then you must honor your promise. It will all be written into the contract. You agree?'

After he had sifted that, the horror of it, and made peace with it, he said, 'Then sickness her early, no mark yet?'

Raiko's eyes were unrelenting, her voice so gentle, so terribly final, the stillness in her room so vast. 'Hinodeh has no disease, Furansu-san, none. She is blemishless.'

His head seemed to explode with 'she is blemishless' echoing in the sky of his mind together with his all-pervading shriek to himself 'but you're Unclean!'

'Why? Why agree? Why? Why she . . . *she know . . . know my . . . my bad. Yes?'*

A maid, waiting on the veranda outside, frightened by his bellowing voice, pulled the shoji open. Then, waved away by Raiko, obediently closed it again. Delicately Raiko sipped her saké. 'Of course she knows, Furansu-san. So sorry.'

He wiped the saliva from the corners of his mouth. 'Then why . . . agree?'

Again the strangeness. 'Hinodeh will not tell me, so sorry. It is part of my agreement with her that I do not press her to know, as it must be part of your agreement with her. We are not to press her, she says she will tell in her own time.' Raiko had exhaled heavily. 'So sorry, but you must agree as part of the contract. That is the final condition.'

'Agreed. Please make contract . . .'

After an agony of time—only a few days—it had been signed and sealed and he went with Hinodeh, him Unclean and her Clean, in all her glory, and tomorrow he would again . . .

André almost leapt out of himself as a hand grasped his shoulder and he found himself back in Struan's great room. It was Phillip saying, "André, are you all right?"

"What? Oh, oh yes . . ." André's heart was palpitating, cold sweat making his flesh crawl, that and the memory of 'Blemishless' and 'First Time' and the horror of it—and dreading tomorrow. "Sorry, I . . . a cat was walking on my grave." All at once the room pressed down on him and he had to get out into the air. He got up, groped away, mumbling, "Ask . . . ask Henri to play, I . . . I don't feel . . . sorry, have to leave . . ."

Blankly, Tyrer stared after him. Babcott wandered over from the roulette wheel. "What's up with him? Poor fellow looks as though he's seen a ghost."

"Don't know, George. One moment he was all right, the next, mumbling and white as a sheet, sweat pouring off him."

"Was it anything you were talking about?"

"Don't think so, he was just advising me what to do about Fujiko and Raiko, nothing about him at all." They watched André leave as though the room were empty.

Babcott frowned. "Not like him, he's usually so debonaire." Poor chap, must be his affliction—wish to God I could supply a cure, wish to God there was a cure.

"Talking about debonaire," Tyrer was saying, "I didn't know you were such an accomplished dancer."

"Nor did I," the giant said with a booming laugh. "I was inspired, she'd inspire anyone. Normally I dance like a rhino." They looked across at her. "Extraordinary constitution that girl, and wonderful, infectious laugh."

"Yes, Malcolm's a lucky fellow. 'Scuse me, I'd best ask Henri to sub for André . . ." He wandered off.

Babcott watched Angelique. Curious that a doctor can examine a patient and not be aroused, he thought, even with someone like her. I wasn't, the times she consulted me at Kanagawa or here, though there was never any intimate examination, never a need except for the unusual heaviness of her period, a few weeks ago, when a careful examination was clearly necessary, though she never allowed it. I'd never seen her so pale or her lips so bloodless. Come to think of it, she acted strangely, wouldn't let me near her, just let me into her room briefly, almost as a stranger, when the evening before—the time I returned her crucifix—I had listened to her heart, tapped her chest and back and stomach and she had behaved like a normal patient. I remember her pulse was quite agitated, for no apparent reason. Curious behavior.

Have I missed something? he asked himself, watching her at the roulette table, bubbling with life, clapping her hands with childlike glee when she won Red or Black, Zergeyev and others teaching her the finer arts of gambling. Strange she doesn't wear her cross as most Catholics would, especially as it was a gift from her adored mother.

"Grand party, Malcolm," Sir William said, coming up to him, stifling a yawn. "Time for me to turn in."

"Another brandy?" Malcolm was sitting near the inglenook fireplace, the fire down to embers now.

"No, thanks, my back teeth are awash. Great lady, Malcolm, great sport."

"Yes," he agreed proudly, mellowed by the wine and brandies that deadened the pain and calmed his fluttering panic for the future. Not as strongly as the medicine, he thought. Never mind, it's a beginning.

"Well, good night." Sir William stretched. "Oh, by the way," he said, his voice easy, "could you drop by sometime tomorrow, any time that suits."

Malcolm looked up sharply, the thought of his mother's letter putting ice into his stomach again. "Say eleven?"

"Perfect, any time. If you want to change it, fine."

"No, at eleven. About what, Sir William?"

"It can wait, nothing that can't wait."

"About what, Sir William?" He saw pity in the eyes studying him, perhaps compassion. His discomfort increased. "It's about my mother's letter, isn't it—she said she was writing to you by today's mail."

"Yes, it was, but only partially, I had been warned to expect a letter. The first matter was Norbert, now that he's back. I hope this duel nonsense is out of both your heads."

"Of course."

Sir William grunted, unconvinced, but let it rest. He could do no more than warn both parties and then, if they proceeded, to enforce the law. "You're both warned."

"Thank you. Second?"

"Second was that I have been informed officially of the Government's plan to outlaw all trade in opium by British nationals, to forbid the trade in all British ships, to destroy our Bengal opium plantations and replant with tea. As you had led the delegation to ask and complain about the rumors I wanted you to be the first to know."

"That will ruin our Asian trade, our China trade, and completely upset the British economy."

"In the short run it will certainly cause a major problem for the Exchequer but it is the only moral course. Should have been done years ago. Of course, I understand the unsolvable silver-opium-tea triangle and the chaos of lost revenue it will cause the Exchequer." Sir William blew his nose, already weary of the problem that had harassed and aggravated the Foreign Office for years. "Think I'm getting a cold. I suggest you convene a meeting next week to see how we can minimize the confusion."

"I'll arrange it."

"Growing our own tea is a good idea, Malcolm," Sir William said. "Marvelous idea! It might interest you to know the first Bengal test plantations producing crops were grown from seeds smuggled out of China and brought back to Kew Gardens by Sir William Longstaff, Hong Kong's governor in your grandfather's day, when he returned home."

"Yes, I know, we've even tasted the tea, it's bitter and black with none of the delicacy of China, even Japanese tea," Malcolm said, impatiently. Tea could certainly wait until tomorrow. "Next?"

"Last, your mother's letter," Sir William added, more formally. "It's not the policy of Her Majesty's Government, or her officials, to interfere with the private life of her citizens. However, your mother points out you are a minor, she is your surviving parent and legal guardian. I am obliged not to approve any marriage without the legal guardian's consent, in this case of both parties. Sorry, but that's the law."

"Laws are made to be bent."

"Some laws, Malcolm," Sir William said kindly. "Listen, I don't know what the problem is between you and your mother, nor do I wish to know—she did draw my attention to the piece in the *Times,* which can be read in several ways, not all of them good. When you are back in Hong Kong I'm sure you can bring her to your side, and in any event, you are of age in May, which isn't far away."

"Wrong, Sir William," he said, remembering the same advice from Gordon Chen—advice from men who don't know what love is, he thought without malice, just sorry for them. "It's a million years away."

"Well, be that as it may. I'm sure it will all work out for you both. Henri's of the same opinion."

"You've discussed the matter with him?"

"Privately, of course. The French consul in Hong Kong is, er, aware of Angelique and her affection for you, your mutual affection. She's a wonderful person, she'll make a wonderful wife, whatever the problem with her father."

Malcolm reddened. "You know about him too?"

The lines in Sir William's face etched deeper. "French officials in Siam are most concerned," he said delicately. "Naturally they informed Henri, who rightly informed me, asking our assistance. Sorry, but it is an official matter of interest. You must be aware that, in fact, anything to do with the Noble House is a matter of interest." Adding sadly, for he liked Malcolm and regretted the Tokaidō as barbarism, "The price of fame, eh?"

"If—if you hear anything I would appreciate hearing first, privately, as—as quickly as possible."

"Yes, I can keep you informed. Privately."

Malcolm reached for the brandy bottle. "Sure you won't?"

"No, thanks."

"Is there an answer to my problem?"

"I've given it to you." Sir William kept his voice formal to hide a sudden wave of irritation. As if a few months really mattered—the girl's not dead as Vertinskya's dead, nor anywhere near as marvelous! "Your birthday's soon and Hong Kong only eight or nine days away. Of course you're welcome at eleven tomorrow, or any time, but that's all that I wanted to chat about. 'Night, Malcolm, and thanks again for the party."

It was past midnight. Malcolm and Angelique were kissing passionately in the corridor outside their adjoining suites. The corridor was dark, just a few night lights. She was trying to hold back but she was enjoying him, more every day, his heat warming her more than yesterday—tonight his need, and hers, almost crushing. *"Je t'aime,"* she murmured, meaning it.

"Je t'aime aussi, Angel."

She kissed him again, searching, then again stumbled back from the brink, and held on to him until she caught her breath. *"Je t'aime,* and it was such a lovely party."

"You were like champagne."

She kissed his ear, her arms around him. Before Tokaidō she would have to stand on tiptoe. She did not notice it, though he did. "I'm so sorry we sleep alone."

"Me too. Not long now," he said. Abruptly his pain soared but he bore it a fraction longer. "So," he said, looking at her deeply. "Sleep well, my darling."

They touched lips and murmured good night, many times, then she was gone. Her bolt slid home. He picked up his sticks and dragged himself into his own rooms, happy and sad and worried and not worried at all. The evening had been a success, Angelique had been content, his guests had enjoyed themselves, he had contained his disappointment over the wreckage of his plan, and he had faced himself over the mails, not allowing Jamie to decide for him.

That decision was right, he thought, though Dirk's would have been better. Never mind, I can never be him, but he's dead and I'm alive, and Heavenly has promised to devise a solution to her letters and the new twist in my joss: 'There must be an answer, Tai-pan,' Heavenly had said, 'there must be an answer. I'll come up with something before I leave for Hong Kong, you'll need that proof whatever happens.'

His eyes went to their communicating door, still bolted permanently at night by mutual consent. I won't think about Angelique or the bolt or that she's alone. Nor about my failure over our marriage. I made that promise early and I'll keep it. Tomorrow will take care of tomorrow.

The usual half carafe of wine was on the bedside table, with some fruit—lychee and mangoes from Nagasaki—English cheese, cold tea that he always drank instead of water, a glass and the small bottle. The bed was turned down, his sleeping gown laid out. The door swung open. "Hello, Tai-pan."

It was Chen, his Number One Boy, with his wide, toothed beam that always pleased him—Chen had looked after him as long as he could remember, as Ah Tok had been his amah, both totally loyal, completely possessive, and always at loggerheads. He was squat and very strong, his pigtail luxurious, his face round with a permanent smile though the eyes did not always. "Your feast was worthy of Emperor Kung."

"Ayeeyah," Malcolm said sourly at once, knowing what the old man meant. "May the great cow urinate on your immediate generations. Get on with your work and keep your opinions to yourself and don't act as though you were born under the sign of the Monkey." This was the Zodiac sign for clever people.

Chen's seeming pleasantry, like most in Chinese, had many meanings: Emperor Kung, who ruled China almost four millennia ago, was famous for three things: his epicurean tastes, the lavish banquets he staged, and for his 'book.'

In those days there were no books as such, only scrolls. He had filled a scroll with a detailed treatise, the first 'pillow book' ever, the source of all others that, by definition, dealt with the joinings of man and woman in all their possibilities and hazards, how to improve the climactic moment, names for the various positions and their minutiae, descriptions of devices, medicines, techniques—deep thrusts and shallow—how to choose the perfect physical partner, amongst other wisdoms saying,

> . . . *obviously, a man whose One-eyed Monk has the misfortune to be small should not be embattled with Jade Gate like that of a mare.*
> *Let it be known for all time, the gods have decreed that those parts, though appearing the same, are never the same but vary greatly. Extreme care must be used to avoid the trap of the gods who, while bequeathing man the means, as well as a need as strong and as permanent as the needle that seeks the North Star, to taste Heaven while on Earth—the moment of the Clouds and the Rain is such—at the same time, for their own amusement, they have set manifold obstacles in the way of the Yang's quest for the Yin, some easy to avoid, most impossible, all complex. As man should taste as much of Heaven while on Earth as he can— who knows if gods are really gods—the tao, the Path to the Gorgeous Gully must be scrutinized, examined, pursued and studied even more severely than the transmutation of lead into gold. . . .*

Chen bustled about the room, pained though pleased with his Master's knowledge. He was only doing his duty, drawing attention to the strength of the Yin, particularly tonight, the flaunting of it, her dancing and kissing, titillating the Master's Yang about which the Emperor had been very specific: *A nervous and unrequited Yang in any household, if it be the Master's, will upset the whole household, therefore all the household should make every effort to relieve the unrelieved.*

And our house is in turmoil, he thought disgustedly. Ah Tok is more difficult than ever, Ah Soh grumbling about the extra work and worry, the cooks complaining about his loss of appetite, the houseboys moaning that nothing pleases him, and all because this cowlike barbarian whore won't just do her duty. General opinion amongst the staff was that she must have one of those Rapacious Ravines Emperor Kung warned against:

> *There are some the gods have lined with demons, their magnetic force so strong as to send men mad, and make them forget an immortal truth that one Yin is like another when the need is great, and worse, when at last one such Ravine opens to receive the Yang, this Heaven becomes Hell for there is never enough.*

"Ayeeyah, Tai-pan," Chen said, aiding him to undress. "This person was only saying your banquet pleased everyone."

"Your Lord and Master knows exactly what you were saying." Malcolm struggled out of his shirt. His uncle, Gordon Chen, whom he treasured, had lectured him about the Emperor Kung's work, telling him this information, and other pieces of important knowledge about the Yang and Yin, was just between them and to be kept secret from his mother.

"You are an impertinent bugger," Malcolm said in English, his main defense with both Chen and Ah Tok. He could never seem to best them in Cantonese, but speaking English to them infuriated them. "And I know you were trying to be snide about the Mistress, but you'd better stop, by God."

The round face twisted. "Tai-pan," Chen said, in his best Cantonese, helping him into bed, "this person has only the interests of his Master before all else."

"Ayeeyah!" Malcolm scoffed. "Words from a forked tongue are as precious as mildewed fish bones to a starving man." He noticed an envelope propped on the bureau. "What's that?"

Chen hurried to fetch it, happy that the subject had changed from him. "A foreign devil arrived tonight to see you. Our shroff Vargas saw him. The foreign devil said the letter was urgent so the shroff asked this person to put it here in case our Illustrious Master wanted it."

The writing was not familiar. "Which foreign devil?"

"I don't know, Tai-pan. Is there anything else?"

Malcolm shook his head, yawned and put the envelope on the side table and dismissed him. The medicine bottle beckoned. "I won't," he

said firmly, started to turn down the oil flame, then changed his mind
and opened the letter with sudden expectation, thinking it was from
Heavenly, or even Father Leo.

> *Dear Mr. Struan: Perhaps I may introduce myself, Edward
> Gornt of Rothwell's, Shanghai, late of Virginia, presently
> here in Yokohama for training with Mr. Norbert Greyforth at
> the request of Sir Morgan Brock.*
>
> *Mr. Greyforth has asked me to act as his second in the
> private, though pressing matter of the duel you challenged
> him to. Perhaps I could wait upon you tomorrow? Would the
> morning be convenient, say noon or thereabouts? I have the
> honor to be, Sir, your most obedient servant, Edward Gornt.*

The signature was as neat as the copperplate writing.

35

Tuesday, 2nd December:

"'Morning, Mr. Gornt. May I introduce Mr. McFay, chief of Struan's, Japan. Please make yourself comfortable—Jamie, you too. Coffee, tea, sherry, champagne?"

"Nothing, thank you, Mr. Struan."

"Mr. McFay's one of my seconds. Details are supposed to be arranged by seconds, I believe. Yes?"

"Yes, suh. I've met Mr. Syborodin but didn't discuss anything with him, according to Mr. Greyforth's wishes."

The two young men studied each other. From the first instant both had experienced the same strange sensation: an intense attraction to the other. Each was thinking, How odd you could instantly like some people, for no apparent reason, while disliking others, loathing some, dismissing many. Even so, both were sure that however fierce their initial affinity, it would make no difference. Soon—today, tomorrow, even in the next few minutes—something would as quickly revert them to normality, to the comfortable historic enmity that bound their firms together and would reach down the ages, dismissing the first affinity as a peculiar aberration.

Malcolm said, "What can I—we—do for you?"

Gornt's smile was genuine, his teeth white, like Malcolm's. He was of similar height but built lighter, his clothes less elegant, dark hair against the reddish-brown of Struan, brown eyes against the blue. "Mr. Greyforth wanted to confirm dates, weapons, etc."

Jamie said, "You know this is all against the law, Mr. Gornt, and the duel formally forbidden by Sir William?"

"Yes, Mr. McFay."

Jamie shifted uncomfortably, detesting his involvement more than ever, and further unsettled by the curious mood in the room. He could not read it. Where there should have been ice and enmity, it seemed more a waiting moment, weirdly pleasant and preordained. "That being said, what did Norbert have in mind?"

"Today's Tuesday. Would a week from today be okay?"

"I'd prefer Wednesday, the 10th," Malcolm said at once. He had made a plan in the early hours. Sleep had eluded him. He had fought the dragon that was in the little bottle and had won, though the fight had taken its toll and this morning's measure had been a pathetic relief.

Prancing Cloud would arrive Sunday and was due to leave Wednesday evening. He would arrange secretly with her captain to sail the moment he could get aboard after the duel. Either he would have already smuggled Angelique aboard or would organize Jamie to escort her home in the next ship, to be decided at the last minute, the latest by Tuesday. It might be best to bring Jamie with Angelique, thus negating part of his mother's fury against Jamie by being obedient to one of her wishes and, hopefully, make her withdraw the termination order—he owed it to Jamie to try in every way to extricate him. If Angelique was aboard, perhaps he could find a way to persuade Captain Strongbow to forget his mother's orders.

It's a long shot, he thought, a very long shot but a faint heart never won a fair lady and it's the best I can do. Joss. "I'd prefer Wednesday."

"I imagine that will be all right, suh. As to the place, we suggest first light at No Man's Land twixt the village and Drunk Town, not the racecourse as that's too public with early morning riders and so on."

Malcolm laughed, not knowing why. "A good choice," he said before Jamie could answer. Much better for me, more secluded, closer to the sea, much easier to slip out to the clipper from the Drunk Town wharf than ours. "It's apparent you know a lot about Yokohama and you're here only a day."

"It was Mr. Greyforth's suggestion, but I did check out both early this morning. No Man's Land is better, safer."

"That's agreed. It will be difficult for me to walk my ten paces. I suggest we take our positions and on someone's order, yours if you wish, aim and fire."

"I will consult Mr. Greyforth."

"What else?"

Gornt hesitated, then glanced at Jamie. "We can arrange details later, how our principals arrive, by what routes, which doctor we can trust who should be present, etc. Lastly, th—"

"You seem to be very well informed about duels, Mr. Gornt," Jamie said thinly. "You've been involved in one?"

"Several, Mr. McFay. As a principal once, and twice as a second, while I was at the Richmond University." Again the smile, warm, kind and sincere. "We take matters of honor very seriously in the South, suh."

The pleasant unreality of the back and forth, and Jamie's belief that the tai-pan had been set up by Greyforth—notwithstanding Malcolm's stubbornness—broke his control. "Then you should know Norbert was in the wrong," he said angrily. "Norbert went out of his way to provoke the tai-pan, has done several times and there's no doubt he should apologize and then we could all stop this stupidity."

"Jamie!" Malcolm said sharply, and would have told him to leave but for yesterday. Yesterday's debt was vast and forever, so he just said, knowing the real friend that Jamie was, "This isn't your problem, and I know how you feel." He looked back at Gornt. "He is right, you know—Norbert has been personally very difficult." Gornt did not reply. Malcolm shrugged and smiled. "Joss. It's not your problem either, Mr. Gornt. So, you were once a principal and twice a second. Clearly you won. The other man?"

"I didn't kill him, suh, wasn't trying to kill him. I just wounded him."

Both men watched each other, weighing the other.

Jamie said nervously, "Then everything's settled."

"Yes, except weapons. Mr. Greyforth chooses swords." Malcolm gasped and Jamie blanched.

"Duelling pistols were agreed," Jamie said. "Agreed."

"So sorry, suh, it wasn't agreed. Mr. Greyforth as the challenged party has the right to choose weapons."

"But it was ag—"

"Jamie, let me deal with this," Malcolm said, astonished with his own detachment, expecting trickery from Norbert. "It was always presumed we were gentlemen and would use pistols."

"I'm sorry but those aren't my instructions, suh. As to gentlemen, my principal considers himself one, and chooses to defend his honor with a sword, which is quite customary."

"Obviously that's not possible."

"Mr. Greyforth also said—I must tell you I do not approve of this and told him so—he also said if you wanted, he would agree to knives, swords or fighting irons." Jamie began to get up but Malcolm stopped him.

"In my present state, that's impossible," Malcolm said, then gathered himself and said firmly, "If this is a ploy for Norbert to gain face, to humiliate me and call off the duel, then I spit in his eye and will continue to do so."

Jamie flushed at the bravado, admired it and hated it, then suddenly realized this could be a perfect face-saver for both men. "Tai-pan, don't you think—"

"No. Mr. Gornt, obviously I can't, now, even use a sword. Please ask Norbert to accept pistols."

"Well, suh, I will certainly ask, certainly the first duty of a second is to try to bring about a reconciliation and it seems to me there's room enough for both you gentlemen in Asia. I'll ask."

Jamie said, "Mr. Gornt, I'll be here. Anything I can do to help stop this insanity, just say the word."

Gornt nodded, began to rise, but stopped as Malcolm said, "Perhaps I could have a private word, Mr. Gornt? You don't mind, do you, Jamie?"

"Not at all." Jamie shook hands with Gornt, then said to Malcolm, "There's a meeting of all traders to discuss Sir William's bombshell at noon in the Club."

"I'll be there, Jamie, though there won't be much discussion, just a lot of shrieking and foul temper."

"I agree. See you later, Tai-pan." Jamie left.

In the fine office once more the two men watched each other. "You're aware of our Parliament's stupidity?"

"Yes, suh, I am. All governments are stupid."

"Would you join me in a glass of champagne?"

"A celebration?"

"Yes. I don't know why but I'm pleased to meet you."

"Ah, then you felt the same? Not right, is it?"

Malcolm shook his head and rang the bell. Chen appeared and when the champagne was opened and poured he went away, his little eyes darting from silent man to silent man. "Health!"

"Health," Gornt replied, savoring the chilled wine.

"I got the impression you wanted to speak privately."

Gornt laughed. "I did indeed. Dangerous for an enemy to be able to read your mind, eh?"

"Very, but we needn't be enemies. Rothwell's is a good client, the hatred and blood feud between the Struans and the Brocks needn't touch you, whatever Tyler or Morgan say."

Gornt put his eyes on the cut-glass crystal and the bubbles, asking them if he was correct in thinking that the time was now or if he should wait. The tawny eyes considered Struan. He decided to dismiss the danger. "You are reputed to like secrets, to be trustworthy."

"Are you?"

"In matters of honor, yes. Your reputation . . . do you like stories, legends?"

Malcolm concentrated, the unreality of the meeting and this man disorienting him. "Some better than others."

"I'm here under false pretenses." Gornt's sudden smile lit up the room. "Christ Jesus, I don't believe I'm truly here with the future tai-pan of the Noble House. I've waited and planned so long for this meeting and now it's arrived—before I came here I had no intention of saying anything now, other than what Mr. Greyforth asked me say. But now?" He raised his glass. "To revenge."

Malcolm thought about that, unafraid and spellbound, then drank and poured again. "It's a good toast in Asia."

"Anywhere. First: I need your word of honor, the honor of the tai-pan of the Noble House, before God, that what I tell you will remain secret between us, until I release you."

Malcolm hesitated. "So long as it's a story." Then he swore the oath.

"Thank you. A story then. Are we safe here? Can anyone overhear us?"

"In Asia, usually. We're aware doors have ears as well as walls, but I can fix that. Chen!" he called out. The door opened at once. In Cantonese he said, "Stay away from the door, keep everyone else away, even Ah Tok!"

"Yes, Tai-pan." The door closed.

"Now you're safe, Mr. Gornt. I've known Chen all my life and he doesn't speak English, I think. You speak Shanghainese?"

"A little, the same with Ning poh dialect."

"You were saying?"

"This is the first time I have ever told this story," Gornt said, and Malcolm believed him. "Once upon a time," he began, no lightness now, "a family went to England from Montgomery, Alabama—their home for generations—father, mother, and two children, a boy, and girl. She was fifteen, her name Alexandra, and her father was the youngest of five brothers. Wilf Tillman was the oldest."

"The co-founder of Cooper-Tillman?" Struan said, jarred.

"The same. Alexandra's father was a minor tea and cotton broker, an investor with brother Wilf in Cooper-Tillman, and he went to London to work with Rothwell's on a three-year contract to advise on cotton—Cooper-Tillman was their major supplier. They stayed just under a year. Unfortunately both parents had gotten very ill, no wonder, eh, with the fogs and that weather, I nearly died myself while I was there—I spent two years in London training with Brock's, one with Rothwell's. Anyway, the Tillmans decided to go home. Halfway across the Atlantic Alexandra discovered she was pregnant."

"Ayeeyah," Malcolm muttered.

"Yes. The shock, on top of her adored father's illness, killed him. He was thirty-seven. They buried him at sea. The Captain's death certificate just said 'brainstorm' but both she and her mother knew the real cause was the bad news. Alexandra was just sixteen, as pretty as a picture. That was in '35, twenty-seven years ago. Alexandra had a son, me. For an unmarried girl to have a child out of wedlock, to be a fallen woman . . . well, Mr. Struan, no need to tell you what a stigma and disaster that is, and Alabama's Bible country, our part, and the Tillmans were gentry. Earlier we talked about honor, it's true what I said, that we take honor seriously, and dishonor. May I?" Gornt motioned to the champagne.

"Please." Malcolm did not know what else to say. The voice was lilting, pleasant, uninvolved, just a storyteller relating a history. For the moment, he thought grimly.

Gornt poured for Struan, then for himself. "My mother and her mother were ostracized by society, and the Tillman family—even her brother—turned against her. When I was three my mother met a Virginian, a transplanted Englishman—Robert Gornt, gentleman, tobacco and cotton exporter, card-playing enthusiast from Richmond—who fell in love with Mother and she with him. They left Montgomery and were married in Richmond. The story they fabricated was that she was a widow, married at sixteen to a Yankee cavalry officer who had been killed in the Sioux Indian wars. She was nineteen then.

"Everything was more or less all right for several years. Until '42—the year after Dirk Struan practically single-handedly founded Hong Kong, the year before you were born. '42 was a bad year for Hong Kong with its Happy Valley fever plague, *mal-aria,* the Opium War with China, the great typhoon that obliterated the city there, and unholy bad for the Noble House because the same typhoon killed the great Dirk Struan." A sip of champagne. "He was responsible for Wilf Tillman's death and for ruining the Tillman family."

"I know nothing about that. Are you sure?"

Gornt smiled his smile, no animosity behind it. "Yes. Wilf Tillman was sick with the Happy Valley fever. Dirk Struan had cinchona bark that could have cured him, but wouldn't give or sell it to him, wanting him dead, like Jeff Cooper." His voice picked up an edge. "The Boston Yankee wanted him dead."

"Why? And why should the tai-pan want Tillman dead?"

"He hated him—he had different views than Wilf. Among other reasons, Wilf had slaves, not illegal at that time, or now, in Alabama. And to assist Cooper to take over the firm. After Wilf died, Jeff Cooper bought his shares for a pittance, and cut off my family's remaining money. Dirk was responsible."

Malcolm said, "We certainly have a joint venture with CooperTillman in cinchona bark, Mr. Gornt, and are old friends. As to the rest, I know nothing about it, or believe it. I'll check the story the moment I get back to Hong Kong."

Gornt shrugged. "Years later Cooper admitted he had never approved of Wilf Tillman. His exact words were, 'Listen, young man, Wilf deserved everything he got, he was a slaver and useless, never did a day's work in his life, your Southern gentleman was vile. Dirk was right to give the little cinchona he had to others who he judged deserved it. It's been my work, mine, that made the company that's paid for your mother, stepfather and you all these years . . .' "

Gornt's face twisted, then he was calm again. Outwardly. "He said a few other things, suh, that . . . that's unimportant now. But cutting off funds, our rightful money, was very important. It was then the rows between Stepfather and Mother began and we moved, downwards. It wasn't till many years later I found out he had married her for her money, his cotton and tobacco businesses were shams, he was just a gambler and card player, not a successful one, and she had continually covered for him. When Mother was dying she told me all this. But he wasn't bad to me, evil to me, just dismissed me. I've been dismissed all my life. Now it's time for revenge."

"I don't see why you should blame me."

"I don't."

Malcolm stared at him. "I thought 'fighting irons, or swords' was the beginning."

"That wasn't my idea, I told you. I told Mr. Greyforth it won't work. He'll be laughed at if he tries to insist."

After a pause Malcolm said, "It sounds as though you don't like him."

"I don't like or dislike him. I'm here to learn from him for a month and then take over when he retires next year. That's the plan—if I decide to join Brock's."

"You may have to take over sooner than you think." Malcolm's voice hardened. "Next Wednesday—hopefully."

"You're set on having this duel?"

"Yes."

"May I ask the real reason?"

"He's gone out of his way to provoke me, surely at Brock's direction. It will be better for Struan's if he's removed."

"Will you try to remove me when I go against Struan's?"

"I will oppose you, compete with you, stop you if I can—I wouldn't want to fight you." Malcolm smiled a good smile. "This is a mad conversation, Mr. Gornt. It's mad to be so truthful and so open but we are and that's that. You said 'revenge.' You're determined to have at us, because of what my grandfather supposedly did to Wilf Tillman?"

"Yes," Gornt said with a smile. "In due time."

"What about Jeff Cooper?"

The smile vanished. "Him too. In due time." Then, for a moment, Gornt's voice became thick with venom. "But that's not most of the revenge I seek. I want to destroy Morgan Brock, to do that I need your help . . ." He burst out laughing. "My God, Mr. Struan, suh, sorry, but if you could only see yourself."

"Morgan?" Malcolm spluttered.

"Yes." Gornt beamed. "I can't do it alone. I've got to have your help—that's ironic, isn't it?"

Malcolm groped to his feet and shook himself like a dog and stretched and sat down again, his heart in overdrive. He poured another glass and spilled some on his desk and quaffed it and all the time Gornt watched and waited, pleased with the effect his words had had. It took Malcolm a little time to respond. "Morgan? For God's sake, why?"

"Because he seduced my mother when she was fifteen and ruined her life and abandoned her. In the Bible it says killing your father, patricide, is an unholy deed—my mama made me swear I'd not do it when she told me the truth of my parentage on her deathbed. So I'm not going to kill him, just ruin him." The words were said flatly, without emotion. "To do that I need Struan's."

Malcolm took a deep breath and shook his head again. None of this made sense to him though he believed it all—even Dirk Struan's behavior. Ayeeyah, so much to learn, he thought, and listened intently as Gornt continued, saying that Morgan was twenty at the time, apprenticed to Rothwell's and living in their countinghouse-residence, so it was easy for him to sneak into her bedroom: "At fifteen what would such a girl know, the classic Southern belle, nurtured like a rare plant? When Rothwell found out, he fired him, of course, but Old Man Tyler Brock laughed and quietly and secretly bought a controlling interest in the firm an——"

Malcolm was shocked. "Brock controls Rothwell's?"

"He did, for a time, just enough to fire Rothwell and all their directors and appoint new ones. When Jeff Cooper found out, he had enough clout to force Old Man Brock to make it a hands-off deal, fifty-fifty. In return Jeff would run the company and keep it secret, particularly from Struan's. The deal's still in effect."

"Does Dmitri know?"

"No. Nor Mr. Greyforth. I stumbled on the details when I was in London."

Malcolm's mind was working hard. Struan's had been involved with Rothwell's over the years but no one had ever said they had been poorly treated, or cheated. Then something Gornt had said ran to the front of his mind. "Does Morgan know you know about him?"

"I wrote to him in London when Mama died. He replied it was all news to him and denied it, but telling me if ever I was in London to come to see him. I did. Again he denied it. Nothing to do with him, he told me, he'd been blamed for the mischief of some other apprentice, nothing to do with him. I was destitute at that time so he found me a job of sorts, then helped me get into Rothwell's." Gornt sighed. "Mama told me when Morgan had been confronted by Rothwell he had said that he would 'marry the slut if her dowry be ten thousand nicker a year.'" A shudder took him though his face did not change, nor the flatness of his voice. "I could forgive Morgan everything, maybe, but never that, never 'the slut.' That's in writing from Rothwell, he's dead now but his letter isn't. Thanks for listening." He got up and stretched and started for the door.

"Wait," Malcolm said, startled, "you can't finish there!"

"I don't intend to, Mr. Struan, but this sort of talk, confession is perhaps a better word, is good for the soul but exhausting. Also I can't spend too much time here or Mr. Greyforth might be suspicious. I'll arrange about the pistols, and about shooting from twenty paces, then come back."

"Wait a minute, for God's sake! What help do you need? Why should I help you anyway? What do you want from me?"

"Not much actually—you can kill Norbert Greyforth, but that's not essential," Gornt said with a laugh, then again became serious. "More important is what I can do for you. Before the end of January, the Brocks will crush Struan's, but that you already know, or should. I can stop them, for a price. As God is my witness, I can give you information that can turn their genius against themselves, to destroy Brock's forever."

Malcolm felt his heart turn over. If he could get Struan's off that barb his mother would concede whatever he wanted. He knew her too well. She'll give me anything I want, anything, he shouted silently, if I want her to become Catholic she'd even do that!

Whatever the cost, he knew he would pay it, and pay gladly. "The price—apart from revenge?"

"When I come back."

Malcolm waited all day but the stranger did not return. It did not worry him. That night he dined alone. Angelique had said she was tired, too many parties and late nights and an early night would do her good. 'So, my darling Malcolm, I shall just eat a snack in my room and do my hair and then into dream time. Tonight I love you and leave you . . . you are abandoned.' He did not mind. His brain brimmed with so much hope that he was afraid if she had stayed he would have to confide in her—and when Jamie dropped by early in the evening he had to stop himself blurting out the fantastic news.

"Heavenly found an answer?" Jamie asked.

"No, good Lord no, not yet. Why?"

"You seem so—so . . . as though the weight of the world has fallen off you. Haven't seen you looking so good in weeks. But you have had good news?"

Malcolm grinned. "Perhaps I've turned a corner and am really getting better."

"Hope so. Your accident on top of everything else . . . I just don't know how you do it. With all that's happened in the last few weeks, I'm truly tired, and that fellow Gornt's the last straw. Something about him frightens me."

"How so?"

"Don't know, just a feeling. Maybe he's not as harmless as he seems." Jamie hesitated. "Do you have a minute to chat?"

"Of course, sit down. Brandy? Help yourself."

"Thanks." Jamie poured a small measure from the sideboard, then pulled the other high-backed armchair beside the fire opposite him. The curtains were drawn against the night, the suite cozy. Nice smell of wood smoke and the sound of ship's bells from the fleet in the bay also comforting. "A couple of things: One way or another I want to go back to Hong Kong for a couple of days—before Christmas."

"To see Mother?"

Jamie nodded and sipped his brandy. "I'd like to be on *Prancing Cloud*. She'll dock . . . why the smile?"

"You're one jump ahead of me. I was planning to be aboard her too."

Jamie blinked, then smiled seraphically. "You've changed your mind and you're going to do what she says?"

"Not exactly." Malcolm told him his plan about *Prancing Cloud* and saw Jamie's euphoria evaporate. "Don't worry, I'm a much better shot than Norbert, and providing he agrees to shoot from twenty paces without the walk he's as dead as the dodo—if I decide to kill him. Forget Norbert. Angelique: if we can't smuggle her aboard, I say 'we' because you always were part of the plan, you bring her by the next ship, so one way or another you'll be in HK before Christmas."

Jamie hesitated. "Mrs. Struan will still be very irritated to find Angelique with us."

"Let me worry about that."

"I do. Which brings me to the nut: When I leave Struan's I was thinking of trying to start my own firm, that's really what I wanted to chat about. If you'd have any objections."

"On the contrary, I'd go out of my way, Struan's would, to help in every way. But that won't be for years yet."

"I think she's decided I am to go."

"I'll object like hell," Malcolm said, startled. "You're due for promotion, a raise and the company wouldn't want to lose you, she would know that. That's a shocking idea."

"Yes. But if it becomes necessary . . . bear with me, Tai-pan, if it's necessary would you object?"

"To you going off on your own? No. But I hate the idea and Struan's would be the loser, I swear to God. It won't happen, and if . . . if you asked to leave I'd find a way to make you stay—to persuade you to stay. I would."

"Thanks, thanks very much." Jamie took a large swallow and felt a little better. Not from the warmth of the brandy but from the way Malcolm had spoken. The last few weeks had been bad. Yesterday, because of Mrs. Struan's letter to him, he had been confronted with an immortal truth: however loyal you are to a company, however much service you give 'the company,' the company can and will spit you out at its whim, without conscience. And what is 'the company'? Just a group of men and women. People. Mrs. Struan, for instance.

People are 'the company' and those in charge can and always will hide behind that facade, that 'the company must survive,' or 'for the good of the company,' and so on, wrecking or promoting for personal reasons, enmities or hatreds.

And don't forget most companies these days are family companies. In the end it's 'family' that wins. Blood is thicker than competence. They may fight amongst themselves but in the end they usually unite in the face of the enemy who is anyone not family, so it's Albert Mac-Struan who has been positioned to take over Japan. Nothing I can do, will do about that. Maybe family businesses are more humane, can be better than impersonal bureaucratic, anonymous institutions but even there, perhaps more so, you're subject to the old-boy network. You lose either way. . . .

Last night, untypically, he had got very drunk in his little house in the Yoshiwara, finding no solace in Nemi. Every time he thought about the truth of 'the company'—adding it to the hanging crime he had almost committed, and Tess Struan's unfairness, Malcolm's stubbornness, and his own stupidity, knowing that if Malcolm had not stopped him he would have ripped the string off and torn the letters up and thrown them overboard—his head would spin and only another tumbler of rum would stop the motion until it created spinning of its own. Nemi couldn't help: "Jami, wot you matter? Jami, Jami!"

'It's Machiavelli who said it best,' he had said, his words slurred and incoherent. "Put not your trust in bloody princes, they can plead expedience." Bloody princes, tai-pans, mothers of bloody tai-pans, sons of Dirk Struan and their sons . . .' and then he had wept.

Ay, he thought queasily, that's the first time in years, last time was when I'd just arrived in Hong Kong, twenty years ago and heard Ma had died while I was on the high seas. She must have known she was dying when I left. 'Off you go, my bonny laddie, earn our fortune, and write every week . . .' If it wasn't for her we would have all died—only her strength kept us alive until the Struans arrived and our joss changed.

Cried my heart out. Like last night, though the tears were different. I was crying for my lost innocence. Can't believe how naive I was to believe in 'the company.' Would Dirk have let me down? Never. The tai-pan wouldn't have, couldn't have, but he's just a legend. I've got to find the courage to strike out on my own—I'm thirty-nine, old in Asia, though I don't feel old, only a ship without a rudder. And so is Malcolm . . . Is he?

He looked at him, still noticing the change. Malcolm's different, more like his old self, he thought. More adult, is that possible? Don't know, but either way his joss is fixed, like mine. "I'm glad we didn't tamper . . . I can't say how sorry I am she's blocked you."

"Me too." Malcolm had told Jamie what Sir William had said about expecting the letter, and about opium and their Bengal fields, the news of which this morning had erupted the Settlement into a frenzy. The noon meeting at the Club had been more violent than usual with the added motion, carried unanimously, that Sir William should be strung up or at the least impeached if he tried to enforce Parliament's stupidity. He saw how deeply unhappy Jamie was and once again was tempted to pour out the marvelous development called Gornt. But he remembered his oath. "I'm very confident now, Jamie. Don't worry. You're off to the Yoshiwara?"

"Not immediately though I've got to see Nemi." Jamie smiled ruefully. "I hung one on last night, going to take her a present. It's not necessary but she's a good sort, and lots of laughs. First I'm seeing Nakama, Phillip asked me to see him for half an hour. Seems he asked Phillip about business and banking, capital, things like that—Phillip asked me to explain the rudiments."

"That's curious."

"Yes. The bugger's got an enquiring mind all right. Pity he's not so forthcoming with us."

"Barter your knowledge for something we want to know. Tomorrow I think I'll have a chat with Phillip. Ask him to see me, will you?" Malcolm's voice hardened. "We were to share all information, wasn't that our agreement?"

"Yes, yes, it was." Jamie finished the brandy. "Thanks. And thanks for the chat." He stood up and said sincerely, "I hope with all my heart it works out for you, Malcolm."

"Yes, I know, Jamie. It will work for you too. 'Night."

In the quiet of his room, Malcolm contentedly stretched out his legs towards the fire, anxious for the morrow and more from Gornt. What could be the price? he mused, watching the coals. He could hear voices inside the building and outside on the *praia*. Occasional laughter and a few drunken songs. John Marlowe had come by this afternoon bringing a message from the Admiral, could he drop by the flagship tomorrow, or if not convenient, Sir William's.

'I could meet at Sir William's. What time?'

'Noon?'

'Good. What's it about?'

'Don't know,' Marlowe said. 'I'll bet it's not to pass the time of day.' Ever since Admiral Ketterer had returned from the engagement at Mirs Bay and Hong Kong he had been seething about adverse and critical reports in the papers, and was still furious that British-made cannon had fired on his ships. 'I don't think he took kindly to some of the more rude remarks at the meeting today.'

'Tough,' Malcolm had said, and laughed, still intoxicated with Gornt's information.

Marlowe had laughed too. 'For God's sake, don't say that on his quarterdeck, the whole ship would blow up! By the way, my trials are approved, Monday or Tuesday, weather permitting. Which would be best for you both?'

'How long would we be out?'

'Leave at dawn, or thereabouts, back latest by sunset.'

'Tuesday.'

A coal fell out of the fire onto the hearth but safely. He nudged it under the basket with the poker and stirred the embers. The blue-greened orange flames rose a little and died down again, making pictures for him. Positive pictures. About him and about her. He looked at their adjoining door. No sound ever came through it.

Gornt's the key to Tess.

Ironic that he needs me as I need him and we are enemies. I've a feeling we always will be. What's his price? It will be something I can deliver. He's wise enough to do that. Why are you so sure? Revenge is too strong a motive, I know.

In the Inn of the Lily, Phillip Tyrer was being massaged by a muscular Japanese woman with massive arms, her fingers of steel finding the pressure points, and she played them like a keyboard to his groans of pleasure. This House was not as delicate, or as expensive, as the Three Carp but the massage was the best he had ever had and took his mind off Fujiko and Nakama and André Poncin, and Sir William, who had been furious all morning, culminating at noon when the raging venom from the Club almost blew the roofs off Yokohama.

'As if it's my fault Parliament's gone mad,' Sir William had shouted at the lunch table, the Admiral equally furious. 'Is it, Phillip?'

'Of course not, Sir William,' he had said, co-opted to the lunch against his wishes, the General the third guest.

'Parliament's always been arbitrary and stupid! Why the devil don't they let the Foreign Office run the colonies and have done with all the heartache? As for the shower called traders here, enough to make you spit blood.'

The Admiral had growled, 'Fifty lashes with a cat-o'-nine-tails would make them toe the line, by God! Every man jack of them, especially journalists. Rotters, all of them.'

The General had said smugly, still smarting from the dressing-down Sir William had given him over the riot, 'What can you do, my dear Sir William, except take it like a man? And Admiral, old chap, you were really asking for it by making public political statements. First rule for Flag Rank or general's stars I always thought was to keep the old head down, be circumspect with public orations and suffer in silence.'

Admiral Ketterer's neck went purple. Sir William managed to interrupt the next broadside with: 'Phillip, I'm sure you have an abundance of work to do, for God's sake get the correspondence copied and the complaint to the Bakufu must go off today!'

He had escaped thankfully. Nakama had greeted him affably, 'Ah, Taira-sama, I hope you better feeling. Mama-san Raiko ask me ask how hea'rth is, as you not keep appointment with Fujiko who is tears . . . who was in tears and—'

'My health is fine. Last night I—I had a very pleasant time in the Inn of the Lily,' he had said, astounded André's predictions had been so accurate. 'Fujiko? I'm having second thoughts about her contract, yes, by God, second thoughts!' He had been delighted to see Nakama blink and was even more pleased that he could use his fright over Sir William's spleen during the morning and at lunch to act out André's plan.

'But Taira-sama, I th—'

'And we're not speaking English anymore today and no more questions about business. You can talk to Noble House McFay-sama and that's the end of that. . . .'

He groaned aloud as the masseuse probed deeply. Her fingers stopped at once. '*Iyé, dozo . . .*' No, please don't stop, he said in Japanese and the woman laughed, and replied, '*Don't worry, Lord, by the time I have dealt with this pallid, out-of-strength fishlike body of yours, you'll be ready for three of the best Lilies in the House.*'

He thanked her dully, not understanding but not caring. After three hours with Nakama in Japanese, and fielding more of the man's remarks about Raiko and her Inn—just as André had forecast—his head was spinning.

In time the woman began the soothing touches with knowing hands, fragrant with oil and she finished, wrapped him in a warm towel and left. He drifted off but woke as the shoji slid open and a girl came in and knelt beside him. She smiled and he smiled back and told her he was tired and please would she just sit there until he woke up, again following André's instructions. The girl nodded and smiled and was quite content. She would get her fee anyway.

André's a genius, he thought, equally contented, and went happily to sleep.

Tonight was the second time that André went to visit Hinodeh. It was exactly ten days and twenty-two hours and seven minutes ago that he had beheld her in all her glory, the night imprinted on him forever.

'Good evening, Furansu-san,' she had said shyly, her Japanese melodious. Their anteroom was off their small veranda and their house set in the gardens of the Three Carp, fragrant as she was fragrant. Her kimono's golds and browns of winter moved gracefully as she bowed and motioned to the cushion opposite. Behind her the shoji to their bedroom was ajar, just enough to see the edges of the futons and coverings that would be their first bed. 'The saké is as I was told you would like it. Cool. Do you always drink saké cool?'

'Yes, yes, I—I like taste more g-good.' He found himself stuttering, his Japanese harsh-sounding, his hands seemed to be in the way, and his palms were sweating.

She smiled. 'Strange to drink cold drinks in winter. Is your heart cold in winter and summer?'

'Eeee, Hinodeh,' he said, the pulse pounding in his ears and throat. 'I think my heart like stone for so long now, think about you, not know if hot or cold or what. You beautiful.'

'It is only for your pleasure.'

'Raiko-san told you about me, yes?'

Her eyes were slanting and calm in the white of her face, brows plucked with half-moons painted in their place, high forehead, widow's peak, raven hair piled high and pinned with tortoiseshell combs that he longed to loosen. 'What Raiko-san has told me I have forgotten. What you told me before the signing is accepted and forgotten. Tonight we begin. We meet for the first time. You must tell me about you, everything you want me to know.' Her eyes picked up a light and crinkled with amusement. 'There will be time enough, yes?'

'Yes, please. Forever, I hope.'

After all the contract terms had been agreed over days and had been set down and read and reread and put in simple terms that he could understand, he was ready to sign in front of her and Raiko. He had summoned all his courage: 'Hinodeh, please excuse, but must say, must tell truth. The bad.'

'Please, there is no need, Raiko-san has told me.'

'Yes, but, but please excuse me . . .' The words came haltingly, even though he had rehearsed them a dozen times, new waves of nausea washing through him. 'Must tell one time: I caught bad disease from my mistress, Hana. No cure possible, so sorry. None. You will, must catch if . . . if, must catch if become consort, so sorry.' The unseen sky had seemed to fly apart for him as he waited.

'Yes, I understand and accept that and I have had written in my contract that I absolve you of any blame, concerning us, any blame, you understand?'

'Ah, blame, yes, understand blame. Thank you an—'

He had had to excuse himself and rushed out and was violently sick, sicker than he had even been in his life, sicker than when he discovered that he had caught it, or after he found Hana dead. When he came back he did not apologize, nor would an apology be expected. The women understood.

'Before I sign, Furansu-san,' she had said, 'as you had importances, it is important to me to ask if you promise to give me the knife or poison as agreed in the contract?'

'Yes.'

'Thank you. Both important things need not be mentioned, or talked about again. You agree, please?'

'Yes,' he had said, blessing her.

'Then it is done. There, I have signed, please to sign, Furansu-san, and Raiko-san is our witness. Raiko-san says our house will be ready in three days. On the fourth day from now I will be honored to receive you.'

On the fourth day, sitting in front of her in their private sanctuary, he was consumed with her beauty, the oil lamps bright but not overly so. 'This house please you, Hinodeh?' he asked, trying to sound interested but only obsessed to have her unadorned.

'It is more important if it please you, Furansu-san.'

He knew she was only doing what she had been trained to do and her responses and actions would be automatic, trying her best to put him at his ease, whatever she felt within. With most Japanese men he could usually tell what they were thinking, with Japanese women almost never—but then it's usually the same with most Frenchwomen, he thought. Women are so much more secretive than we are, so much more practical.

Hinodeh looks so peaceful sitting there motionlessly, he thought. Is she volcanic or sad or terrified—or filled with so much fear and loathing that she's numb.

Blessed Mother, forgive me, but I don't care, not at the moment, later, perhaps later I will, not now.

Why would she agree? Why?

But that must not be asked, never. Hard to obey that clause, and yet it's an added spice, or the one issue that will destroy me, us. I don't care, hurry up!

'Would you like to eat?' she asked.

'At moment, I—I not hungry.' André could not take his eyes off her, nor hide his desire. The sweat trickled.

Her little smile did not change. A sigh. Then, with every movement leisured, long fingers untied her obi and she stood and let the outer kimono fall, all the time watching him, tranquil as a statue. Then the under-kimono, then the first slip and the second, and then the loincloth. She turned without haste, showing herself to him, and then again and stood before him. Perfect in every way.

Hardly breathing, he watched her kneel, pick up her cup and sip, then sip again, the pulse in his head and neck and loins pushing him to the limit of control.

He had planned over the days to be gallant with words and gestures and movements, so Gallic *and Japanese* and worldly and practiced, to be the best lover she had ever had, would ever have without regrets, to make their first joining a memorable and wonderful experience. It was memorable but not wonderful. His will snapped. He reached out for her and hurried her to the futons and there he was subhuman.

Since that night he had not seen her, or Raiko, avoiding them and the Yoshiwara. The next day he had sent a message to Hinodeh, saying that he would inform her when he next intended to visit her. In the interim he had had delivered another payment of gold to Raiko, his salary pledged for two years to pay the contract price—and then much more.

Yesterday he had said he would visit her tonight.

He hesitated on their veranda threshold. Shoji screens shut out the night. An inner golden light beckoned him. His pulse was pounding as before, throat choked. Inner voices overflowed with vile language directed at himself, shouting at him to leave, to kill himself—anything to avoid her eyes and the disgusting mirror image of himself that had been therein. Leave her in peace!

All of him wanted to run and all of him wanted to possess her again, in any way, every way, worse than before, whatever the cost, hating himself, better to die and end it, but first her. I must.

He forced his feet out of his shoes and slid the door aside. She was kneeling exactly as before, same costume, same smile, same beauty, same delicate hand motioning him to sit near her, same gentle voice: "The saké is as I was told you would like it. Cool. Do you always drink saké cool?"

He gaped at her. The eyes that had been filled with so much hate when he had stumbled away from her, now were smiling at him with the shy sweetness as in the first moment. "What?"

Again, as though she had never said it, she repeated in the same tone, "The saké is as I was told you would like it. Cool. Do you always drink saké cool?"

"I—I, yes, yes, I do," he said, hardly hearing himself over the roar in his ears.

She smiled. "Strange to drink cold drinks in winter. Is your heart cold in winter and summer?"

Parrotlike he muttered the correct responses, no difficulty in remembering every word and happening, indelibly recorded, and though his voice was erratic, she did not seem to hear it, just continued as before, her eyes slanting and calm.

Nothing changed. "Would you like to eat?" she asked.

"At moment, I—I am not hungry."

Her smile did not change. Nor the sigh. She got up. But now she turned down the oil lamps and went into the bedroom that he had defiled and doused those lights completely.

When his eyes had adjusted to the dark, he saw that the tiniest glimmer came through the shoji panels from the veranda lamp, barely enough to see her shape. She was disrobing. In moments he heard the sound of the coverlet being pulled back.

When he could stand he groped to his feet and went into the room and knelt beside the bed, long since realizing she had been trying to save face, his, to blot out that which could never be blotted out.

"From my mind, never," he muttered in misery, wet with tears. "I don't know about you, Hinodeh, but it never will. I'm so sorry, so sorry. *Mon Dieu,* I wish, oh, how I wish—"

"Nan desu ka, Furansu-sama?"

It took him a little time to adjust to using Japanese words, and he said, breaking, "Hinodeh, I say . . . just thank Hinodeh. Please excuse me, I so sorry . . ."

"But there is nothing to be sorry for. Tonight we begin. This is our beginning."

36

Wednesday, 3rd December:

HIRAGA CAUGHT A PASSING RE-
flection in the butcher's shop window and did not recognize himself.
Passersby on the High Street barely noticed him. He retraced his steps,
stared at his shadowed image—and new disguise. Top hat, high collar
and cravat, a broad-shouldered, waisted frock coat of dark broadcloth,
waistcoat of blue silk, stainless steel chain across it joining the toggle
to a fob watch, tight trousers and leather boots. All the gift of H.M.
Government, except the watch given him by Tyrer—for services rendered. He took off his hat and looked at himself, this way and that.
Now his hair covered his pate and was growing fast, nowhere near as
long as Phillip Tyrer's but certainly long enough to be considered
European. Clean-shaven. The quality and cheapness of British razors
had impressed him greatly, another stunning example of manufacturing prowess.

He smiled at himself, pleased with his masquerade, then took out his
watch, admiring it, noting the time, 11:16. As if sixteen minutes mattered, he thought scornfully, though pleased he had learned gai-jin
timekeeping so quickly. I have learned much. Not enough yet but a
beginning.

"Want 'ter buy a nice leg of frozen Aussie mutton, off the mail
ship's ice hold, me Lord, or wot'tabout some nice fat bacon, Hong
Kong smoked?" The butcher was big-bellied, bald, with arms like
cannons and a bloodstained apron.

"Oh!" Then Hiraga noticed the meats and offal and game hanging on the other side of the windows with their swarms of flies. "No, no thanks. I just 'rooking. Good day, sir," he said, hiding his revulsion. With a flourish he replaced his hat at a jaunty Tyrer tilt and continued down High Street towards Drunk Town and the village, politely raising his hat to other pedestrians or riders who replied in kind. This pleased him even more for it signified acceptance, by their standards, so different from Japanese customs—from civilized standards.

Fools. Just because I use their dress and begin to wear like them they think I am changed. They are still enemy, even Taira. Stupid of Taira to change his mind over Fujiko, what is the matter with him? That does not fit into my plan at all.

Hiraga caught sight of Struan hobbling out of his building with Jamie McFay, Ori's woman between them in animated conversation. This reminded him of his meeting with the Noble House Number Two man. His head was still reeling from Western facts and figures, and still limp from all the information McFay had extracted from him about moneylenders and rice merchants like the Gyokoyama. 'Jami-san, perhap possib'er you meet one of these men, if secret,' he had told him, in desperation, to escape. 'I interpret if keep secret.'

The shoya was waiting for him. Sensing the man's eagerness to learn what he had learned, Hiraga toyed with him, accepted the offer of a massage. Then, relaxed in a proper yukata, and over a delicate lunch of rice, dried squid, morning fresh sea bass sliced paper thin with soya, *daikon*—horseradish—and saké, he said he had had talks with important gai-jin and they had answered his questions. He sipped his saké and volunteered none of it. Important information needed encouragement. Reciprocity. "What news from Kyōto?"

"It is all strange," the shoya said, glad that the opening had been given him. "My Masters informed me the Shōgun and the Princess Yazu arrived safely and are inside the Palace. Three more ambushes by Ogama patrols of shishi . . . no, so sorry, no details yet of how many killed. Lord Ogama and Lord Yoshi hardly move from behind their walls . . . But Shōgunate samurai now guard the Gates, as in the past."

Hiraga eyes widened. "They do?"

"Yes, Otami-sama." The shoya was delighted that the bait was taken. "Strangely, a little distance from all Gates, there are secret pickets of Ogama samurai, and from time to time the opposing captains confer secretly."

Hiraga grunted. "Curious."

The shoya nodded and, like the good fisherman he was, struck hard.

"And, oh yes, not that it may be of importance to you, but my overlords believe the two shishi I mentioned before, Katsumata, and the Choshu shishi, Takeda, escaped capture in Kyōto and are travelling on the Tokaidō."

"To Yedo?"

"My Masters did not say. Clearly the news would be of no value." The shoya sipped some saké, hiding his amusement at Hiraga's attempt to cover his consuming interest.

"Anything to do with shishi could be of significance."

"Ah, in that case . . . although it's unwise to relate rumors," the shoya said, pretending embarrassment, judging the time ripe to land this fish, "they report there is a story around the Inns of Kyōto that a third person escaped the first ambush. A woman, a samurai woman skilled in the art of shuriken . . . what is it, Otami-sama?"

"Nothing, nothing." Hiraga struggled for composure, a thousand questions ricocheting in his mind. Only one woman samurai in Katsumata's school had ever gained that skill. "You were saying, shoya? A woman of samurai lineage escaped?"

"It's only a rumor, Otami-sama. Foolishness. Saké?"

"Thank you. This woman, was there anything else?"

"No. Such a silly rumor is hardly worth reporting."

"Perhaps you could find out if—if such nonsense has any truth to it. I would like to know. Please."

"In that case . . ." the shoya said, noting the big concession of 'please,' his voice honeyed with a trace of humility. "Any service to you and your family, valued clients, the Gyokoyama is honored to do."

"Thank you." Hiraga finished his saké. *Sumomo had been in Kyōto with Katsumata. . . .* Where is she now, why didn't she go on to Shimonoseki as I ordered? What was she doing? If she escaped, where is she?

In repayment, and with an effort, he put those and other questions aside for later, and concentrated. He took out a sheaf of notes and began explaining, partially parroting, what 'Taira' and 'Mukfey' had told him over the hours. The shoya listened intently, thankful that his wife was secretly overhearing them and writing it all down.

When Hiraga had rambled about loans, financing, and banking— unclear on most of what he had been told—the shoya, impressed with Hiraga's memory and grasp of what was so totally alien to him, said seriously, "Remarkable, Otami-sama."

"Another important matter." Hiraga took a deep breath. "Mukfey said gai-jin have a kind of market, shoya, a *stoku markit* where the only goods bargained for, bought or sold, are small printed papers called *stoku* or *sheru* that somehow represent money, huge amounts of money, each *stoku* being part of a *kompeni*."

He drank some tea. Seeing the shoya's lack of comprehension, he took another deep breath. "Say daimyo Ogama gave all Choshu, all land and produce of the land to a *kompeni*, the *Choshu Kompeni*, and decreed that the *kompeni* was to be split, by deed, into ten thousand equal parts, ten thousand *sheru*, understand?"

"I . . . I think so, please go on."

"Thus the *stoku* of the *Choshu Kompeni* is ten thousand *sheru*. Next, the daimyo, on behalf of the *kompeni*, offers all or any part or number of *sheru* to anyone with money. For their money the man or woman get this piece of paper saying how many *sharu* of the *Choshu Kompeni* he has bought. This person then owns that part of the *kompeni* and therefore the same proportion of its wealth. The money he and others pay into the *kompeni* then becomes its *kaipit'r*, I think this Mukfey gaijin said, the money needed to run and improve the wealth of the *kompeni* to pay stipends, or reclaim land or buy arms, or seeds, or improve fishing boats, to pay whatever is necessary to increase and make Choshu prosper, to make the value of the *Choshu Kompeni* higher.

"Mukfey explained that . . . He said in any market, Shoya, prices change, in famine times often daily, no? It's the same in this daily *stoku markit* with hundreds of different *kompeni*, buyers and sellers. If the Choshu harvest is huge, the value of each part of the *Choshu Kompeni* will be high, if famine, low. The value of each *sheru* varies also. Understand?"

"I think so," the shoya said slowly, understanding very well indeed, covertly afire with delight and questions.

"Good." Hiraga was tired but intrigued by these new ideas though at times lost in their maze. He had never, ever, bargained in a market, or an Inn, just paid what was asked, when asked, never in his life argued about the cost of anything or the amount of a bill—except since he became ronin. Bills were always sent to whoever received his stipend, if you were samurai. If unmarried, normally to your mother. Buying and handling money was the job of women, never of men.

You ate what she—mother, aunt, grandmother, sister or wife—bought from your stipend, you clothed or armed yourself in the same way. With no stipend you starved, you and your family, or you became ronin, or voluntarily had to give up your samurai status and become a farmer, laborer, or far worse, a merchant. "Shoya," he said, frowning. "Prices vary in a food or fish market. But who decides the price?"

The guild of fishermen or farmers, the shoya could have said, or more likely the merchants who really own the produce, having lent them the money to buy nets or seeds. But he was much too cautious, most of his energy spent trying to remain calm in the face of so much priceless information, however incomplete. "If there are lots of fish, they are cheaper than when there are few. If depends on the catch, or the harvest."

Hiraga nodded. Obviously the shoya was being devious, hiding the truth or twisting it. But that is only normal for merchants and moneylenders, he thought, suddenly deciding to keep any meeting between Mukfey and this man in reserve, and also to keep for later the last piece of *kompeni* lore that, for some reason he could not fathom, intrigued him more than the rest: that if you were the one who formed the *kompeni,* you decided how many *stoku* you reserved for yourself, without payment, and if the number amounted to fifty-one or more out of every hundred, you retained power over the *kompeni.* But why . . .

His head almost burst with sudden understanding: *With no outlay you became the kompeni shōgun, the bigger the kompeni the bigger the shōgun . . . with no outlay!*

When *sonno-joi* is fact, he thought weakly, we—the samurai council—we will recommend to the Emperor that only our council may form *kompeni,* then, at long last, we control all the parasites, the merchants and moneylenders!

"Otami-sama," the shoya was saying, not having noticed any change in Hiraga, his own mind agog with the marvelous information he had gleaned. "My overlords will be most grateful and so am I. When we have managed to sift all your brilliant thoughts and ideas, perhaps I could have an opportunity to ask a few insignificant questions?"

"Certainly," Hiraga said, exultant with the rosy future. The more questions the better—they will force me to understand first. "Perhaps when you hear more about Ogama and Yoshi, or the shishi, or that woman. Shuriken, you said?"

"I will do my best," the shoya answered, knowing a deal had been struck. Then his mind took him back to a missing, essential piece of the puzzle. "Please, may I ask, what is this *kompeni?* What is it, what does it look like?"

"I don't know," Hiraga said, equally perplexed.

* * *

"Good of you to be punctual, Mr. Struan," Admiral Ketterer said gruffly, "not normal for, er, traders." He was going to say 'tradesmen' but decided there was plenty of time to deliver the broadside. "Take a seat. Sherry?"

"Some dry sack, thank you, Admiral."

The orderly poured a glass, replenished the Admiral's port and left. They lifted their glasses, no love lost between them. The desk was clear of papers, except for an official document, an opened envelope and a letter in his mother's writing. "What can I do for you?" Malcolm asked.

"You know that some of my sailors were killed by Chinese pirates, firing shore-based British cannon during our Mirs Bay engagement. British cannon."

"I've read the news reports, but I don't know for certain if they were British manufacture."

"I do. Made sure myself." Sourly the Admiral picked up the document. "The Governor's initial investigation suggests the probable culprits were either Struan's or Brock's."

Malcolm looked back at the older, florid-faced man, unafraid. "He can suggest what he likes, Admiral Ketterer, but any formal accusation had better be backed by proof or we would be very upset, and the Brocks apoplectic. I know of no such deal and in any event sale of armaments are not forbidden by Parliament. Does Norbert Greyforth?" Jamie had warned Greyforth that he had also been summoned by the Admiral, at 10:30, but he had not appeared until 11:00 A.M. and that meeting had lasted barely three minutes.

Ketterer's neck reddened, remembering Greyforth's inflammatory response. "No. That—that impertinent fellow declined to discuss the matter. Do you?"

"I don't know what you want to discuss, Admiral."

"The matter of the importation and selling of cannon and armaments to the natives here. And warships. And opium."

Malcolm said carefully, "Struan's are China traders and we trade according to British law. None of those articles are forbidden by law."

"Opium soon will be," the Admiral snapped.

"When it is, then that trade ceases."

"It's against Chinese law now, and native law here!"

"Struan's are not, I repeat not, trading in opium here, even though it is not, I repeat not, against British law."

"But you do admit the trade's pernicious and immoral."

"Yes, but at the moment approved by Her Majesty's Government and unfortunately the only commodity we can barter for China's tea, from which Parliament derives huge taxes."

"I'm well aware of the China problem. I would like you and your company to anticipate the law now by agreeing voluntarily never to import opium into Japan."

"We're not trading in it here."

"Good. If I find any ships carrying opium I intend to confiscate the cargo and the ship."

"I'd say you do so at your legal peril, Admiral. Has Sir William agreed or approved your intention?"

"Not yet. I would like you and the other trades—other traders to do so willingly. The same with breech-loading rifles, cartridges, cannon and warships."

"Did Greyforth agree to such an astonishing proposal?"

The neck went crimson. "No."

Malcolm thought a moment. He and Jamie had reasoned in advance that this was what the Admiral had in mind. Apart from his mother's letter. "We have a meeting with Sir William in a few days," he said. "I'd be honored if you'd attend as my personal guest. All traders would hear you out."

"My views are already well known. You traders of all people should know which side of your bread is buttered, that without the fleet to protect you and your trade routes, you're helpless. If you supply natives with cannon you threaten the Royal Navy, you'll be helping to sink your own ships, murder your own countrymen and yourselves to boot!"

"If you take the example of India or any of the oth—"

"My whole point, Mr. Struan!" the Admiral slammed at him. "Without natives having our armaments the Mutiny would never have happened, revolts everywhere would be more quickly contained, savages all over the world could be more easily and properly educated, useful trade would be conducted in peace and world order would flourish in the benevolence of the Pax Britannica. And miserable, fornicating pirates would not have the means to fire on my flagship, by God! And without the Royal Navy ruling the seas, by God, there's no Pax Britannica, no British Empire, no trade, and we'll be back in the Dark Ages!"

"Confidentially you're quite right, Admiral," Malcolm said with abject, pretended fervor, following Uncle Chen's advice: 'When a mandarin is furious with you, for whatever reason, quickly agree *"confidentially"* he is right, you can always assassinate him later when he's asleep.'

Over the years he had been involved in the same argument with Army, Navy and government officials. And witnessed his father and mother quarreling, his father for free trade and his mother for morality, his father raging about the insolvable opium triangle, his mother vehemently against opium even so—and sales of arms—truth on both sides, both inflexible, the quarrel always ending with his father drinking himself into a stupor and his mother smiling with that fixed, infuriating smile that nothing would dislodge, his father's final barb always: 'my old man—and your Prince Charming—the Great Green-eyed Devil Dirk himself started the trade and we've flourished on it, so help us God!'

Many's the time he had wondered—but never dared to ask—if she had really been in love with the father and not the son, had settled for the son because the father would not. He knew he would never ask and if he did she would just smile that fixed smile of hers and say, 'Malcolm, don't be absurd.'

"Confidentially, you're right, Admiral," he repeated.

Ketterer choked on his port and poured some more. "Well, that's something, by God!" He looked up. "Then you'll make sure Struan's does not engage in arms sales here?"

"I will certainly take everything you said under advisement and consult with my fellow traders."

Ketterer took out a handkerchief and blew his nose, took a pinch of snuff, sneezed and blew his nose again. When his head had cleared his baleful eyes looked at the young man, irritated that he could perceive no weakening. "Then let me put it another way. *Confidentially,* you agree that helping Jappos to acquire cannon, British cannon, any bloody cannon, or British warships is stupid?"

"For them to have a comparable navy would be wr—"

"A disaster, sirrah! Total disaster and stupid!"

"I agree."

"Good. I would like you to persuade all other traders to your opinion: no arms here, particularly cannon, of course no opium. Confidentially, of course."

"I'd be glad to put forward those opinions, Admiral."

Ketterer snorted. Malcolm began to get up, not wanting to be cornered. "A moment, Mr. Struan—another matter, before you go. A private matter." The Admiral motioned at the envelope and letter on his desk. "This. From Mrs. Struan. You know what it's about?"

"Yes, yes, I do."

Ketterer moved the letter to the center of his desk. "Your Noble

House is supposed to be first in Asia, though I'm told Brock's are pulling ahead of you now. Never mind which, you could be a conduit for good. I would like you and your company to assist me in this just cause. Just, Mr. Struan."

Exasperated, Malcolm said nothing, considering he had answered at length and was not prepared for another lecture.

Pointedly Ketterer said, "*Confidentially,* between you and me, I don't normally acknowledge such letters from civilians. It goes without saying: Royal Naval rules and regulations belong to the Royal Navy." A sip of port and a subdued liverish belch. "Young Marlowe has invited you and . . . and your fiancée aboard *Pearl* during his trials. Tuesday. For the day." The eyes bored deeper. "Has he not?"

"Yessir," Struan muttered, his mind in spasm as his ears seemed to have betrayed him.

"Of course, my permission is needed." The Admiral let this float in the air, then said, "By the way, Mr. Struan, this intended duel is ill-advised, yes indeed." Malcolm blinked at the non sequitur, and tried to concentrate as the Admiral continued, "As much as that . . . that Greyforth fellow deserves to pass on as soon as possible, duelling is against the law and ill-advised, and mistakes can happen, bad ones. Clear?"

"Yessir, thank you for the advice, but you were say—"

"*Thank you,* Mr. Struan," the Admiral said smoothly, getting up. "Thank you for coming to see me. Good day."

In turmoil Malcolm groped to his feet, not sure if he understood correctly. "Do I understand you to mean that I ca—"

"I mean nothing more than what I have said, sir." The voice was withering, clear and from the quarter-deck. "Just as you have told me, in confidence, you will take what I have said under advisement, in return, I tell you, in confidence, that I will take what you say, and do, under advisement—before Monday, midnight. Good day."

Outside on the promenade the air smelt good and clean and uncomplicated, and Malcolm took deep breaths until its purity began to take the pounding out of his head and chest. Exhausted and elated, he slumped onto the first bench and stared at the fleet without seeing it.

Have I understood Ketterer correctly, Malcolm asked himself over and over, once again blinded with hope, that Ketterer might, just might be prepared to forget Mother's letter and give Marlowe permission to have us aboard *and not forbid Marlowe to marry us?*

" 'In confidence,' Ketterer had harped on that," he muttered, "and 'between ourselves' and 'in return.' " Does that mean he'll keep quiet if I do my part? he wondered. What in God's name could I do and say before Monday night to persuade the bugger, because that's what he is, a blackmailing sod with no morals!

Nonsense! It's a deal—he's offered a deal, a quid pro quo—a marvelous deal for me, and not bad for him. I'd have to be careful, the other traders won't take kindly to any voluntary embargo. I'll have to be aboveboard because that bugger's smart and won't be satisfied with just promises.

Who can I trust with this new twist in the tangle of my life? Heavenly? Jamie? Marlowe? Of course not him. Angel? No. Not her. If Uncle Chen were here he'd be the one, but as he's not, who? No one. You'd better tell no one!

You have to carry this alone—isn't that what Mother said Dirk always told Father about being tai-pan: 'It's the being alone and carrying responsibility alone, that's the joy and the hurt of it.' What can I do about cannon and gu—

"Afternoon, Mr. Struan."

"Oh! Oh, hello, Mr. Gornt."

"You looked so sad I just had to interrupt you."

"No, not sad," Malcolm said tiredly, "just thinking."

"Ah, sorry, in that case I'll leave you, suh."

"No, please sit down. You said, yesterday, there's a price?"

Edward Gornt nodded. "I apologize for not seeing you before, suh, but Mr. Greyforth wouldn't see the . . . the light. Now he agrees to pistols, double-barrelled duelling pistols, and one shot or two, as you choose, from twenty paces."

"Good. And?"

"And I tried to talk him out of the duel but he said, 'Not unless Malcolm Struan publicly apologizes,' words to that effect."

"Good. But the other matter, we've no walls or doors here." Malcolm motioned along the almost deserted promenade. "The price?"

"I thought this a perfect place but we can't spend too much time and have to be careful, Mr. Greyforth could have binoculars on us."

"Is he watching?"

"I don't know for sure, suh, but I'd bet on it."

"Then somewhere else? Later?"

"No, here's fine, but he's very wily and I don't want him to get suspicious. The price: If my information assists you to block Morgan's plan to sink you and bankrupts Brock's—"

"You know the details?"

Gornt laughed softly. "Oh yes, and much more, not that Morgan or Old Man Brock know I know, or Mr. Greyforth." He dropped his voice even more, his lips hardly moving. "This all has to be kept secret between us but the price is you break Morgan Brock, pursue him into bankruptcy, or prison if you can—if it's necessary to break Tyler it's all the same to me, but out of the wreckage you guarantee that I get their fifty percent interest in Rothwell's free and clear; that you assist me with the Victoria Bank to raise what's necessary to buy out Jeff Cooper's half; that for ten years you don't come after me other than a normal competitor, giving me favored nation status on any business dealings—all in a letter contract, written and signed by you. After ten years the gloves are off."

"Agreed," Malcolm said at once, expecting harsher conditions. "But the Victoria bastards aren't our friends, Brock started that bank and have excluded us always, so we won't be much help there."

"They soon will be, suh. Soon the whole Board will fart if you say fart. This all must be kept very secret, of course. What do you plan after the duel?"

Malcolm did not hesitate, finding it so strange that he could trust this man so immediately, telling him about going aboard *Prancing Cloud*. "This presumes I'm the winner and not hurt badly. Once I'm in Hong Kong I can simmer things down," he said confidentially.

"What about your shooting? I mean having to use sticks?"

"One is fine to balance with, for that amount of time." Malcolm smiled thinly. "I've been practicing."

"Now, I propose a deception to avoid legal repercussions that worked well in Virginia and should do the same here, in case either of you is killed: you each write the other a letter, dated and delivered the night before the duel, saying that you have mutually agreed to call the duel off 'at the No-Man's-Land rendezvous tomorrow, and you will both accept, as gentlemen, a mutual, simultaneous apology from the other.' " Gornt smiled. "We, the seconds, will testify that tragically, while you were showing each other your pistols, one went off."

"A fine idea. Has Norbert agreed?"

"Yes. I'll deliver his letter to you, Tuesday, send him his by Mr. McFay, but best keep it secret, that it's a device."

'Tuesday' kept echoing in Malcolm's head but he forced it aside. Gornt was saying, matter-of-factly, "After the duel—it would be best if you kill him, not wound him—I'll come out to the clipper with you. In exchange for the written contract, I'll lay out the details how you can utterly wreck Brock's financial safety net, with a package of authenti-

cated copies of letters and documents, enough for any court of law, and
others that hand you a cudgel to use with the Victoria."

Malcolm felt the glow deep within him. "Why not now, why wait
till Wednesday?"

"Mr. Greyforth might kill you," Gornt said calmly, "then the
knowledge would be wasted and I would have put myself at risk for no
reason."

After a pause Malcolm said, "Say he does, or wounds me badly,
how do you get the revenge you seek?"

"I'll approach Mrs. Struan, suh, at once. I'm gambling that won't be
necessary. I gamble on you, not her."

"I heard you did not gamble, Mr. Gornt."

"At cards for money, no suh, never—I saw the futility of that with
my stepfather. With life? To the limit." Gornt felt eyes on him and said
softly, "Someone's watching," and he glanced around. It was Angelique, coming out of Struan's, across the street. She waved. Malcolm
waved back and got up. The two men watched her approach.

"Hello, Angel," Malcolm said warmly, the Admiral's words
dancing in his head. "May I introduce Mr. Edward Gornt of Rothwell's
in Shanghai? My fiancée, Mademoiselle Richaud."

"Ma'am!" Gornt took her hand and kissed it gallantly.

"Mr. Gornt," she murmured, reading his eyes. There was an abrupt,
curious silence among the three of them, then for no apparent reason
they burst out laughing.

"What is it?" she asked, her heart picking up beat.

"Joie de vivre," Gornt said.

She looked up at him, liking what she saw, warmed by the smile,
then took Malcolm's arm, already relating the encounter in the letter
she had interrupted:

> *I confess, dearest Colette, I spied them on the promenade so
> put on my best bonnet and took them by surprise, and my
> Malcolm's arm (DEFENSIVELY) for this new arrival is tall and
> handsome with the naughtiest glint behind his eyes that I saw
> instantly, though Malcolm could not possibly be aware of, or
> he would have been more jealous than usual, poor dear! I
> wanted to meet this tall stranger casually. He has the slight-
> est of Southern accents, broad shoulders, narrow waist, a*

*fencer probably, and glorious dancer—I do hope he'll be a
friend, I need them here so much . . .*

"La, *chéri*," she said, fanning herself against the immediate and
pleasing internal heat, a subconscious feline reaction to Gornt's masculinity. "Excuse me, I didn't mean to interrupt an important conference . . ."

"You didn't, Angel," Malcolm said.

"I was just leaving," Gornt said. No need to conceal all of his
admiration. "I'm pleased to make your acquaintance, Ma'am." He
bowed. "Good day, suh, I shall be in touch."

They watched him walk off. "Who is this Mr. Gornt?"

He told her, but nothing in fact about the real Mr. Gornt. He was
fogged by the thought of Tuesday.

"More pork in black bean sauce, Younger Sister?" Ah Tok asked,
chomping on a piece of fish.

"Thank you." Ah Soh reached over with her chopsticks to replenish
her bowl, then snapped up the choice quick-fried prawn she had ogled.
"Please continue, Elder Sister."

The two women were in Ah Tok's room, their lunch spread out in a
multitude of dishes, a fresh pot of jasmine tea close at hand. "Ayeeyah,
it's very difficult. Illustrious Chen gave no clear instructions."

"That's not like him." Ah Soh took more of the succulent pieces of
beef in oyster sauce. "Not like him, not at all."

"I agree, but then his new concubine, the whore from Soo Chow, is
sure to be taking most of his concentration."

"Ayeeyah! Is it true she's fourteen with no pubics?"

Ah Tok took up another bony piece of fish head and sucked it
appreciatively. "It's only the Garlic People of Chosen who don't have
pubics." She spat the bones onto the floor and selected another part.

"Interesting. I wonder if it's all the garlic they eat? May I reread his
letter, Elder Sister?"

It said:

*Greetings, Ah Tok, Sixth Cousin Twice Removed, You did
very well to consult me at once. The cork of the bottle
revealed clear traces of Dark of the Moon which must be the
Expeller of Dog Land in the Eastern Sea. An abortion! The*

whore was wise and unwise to use it, the Master wise and unwise to advocate it. Until we know if he made the decision, or she did without his knowledge, you must do nothing. Cousin, listen to him sleeping—he's always muttered in his sleep since a child—perhaps he will tell you more. Instruct Ah Soh to do likewise and both of you be like bats. Unfailingly obey.

"Ayeeyah, what does he mean, be like bats?" Ah Soh asked irritably. "Bats are silent but they squeak. Bats can fly in the dark but are blind during the light, are invisible at night, helpless by day. Their droppings are valuable but stink to Heaven. What does he mean, heya?"

"Eyes and ears and nostrils open, like a bat, and watch where you drop droppings!" Ah Tok cackled. "Ten thousand summers to Noble House Chen, without him we would not have known her Jade Gate's hung on my son's door!"

"How do we know it was him?" Ah Soh said with a robust belch. "How do we know it was the Master and not someone else?" She dropped her voice and looked around as though expecting alien ears and Ah Tok's chopsticks hesitated in midair. "Someone like Long Pointed Nose, the same kind of foreign devil as she is, heya? Those two are as close as lice in a beggar's crotch. And didn't he sink the bottle, all the evidence in the sea, remember?"

The old Ah Tok was no longer laughing. *"Fang-pi!"* she said, using the rare expletive. "That's what Illustrious Chen must have been cautioning us about! Bats weave as they fly and don't alight on the first branch and even then they hang upside down. He's telling us to find out which Yang possessed that Yin! Ayeeyah, yes, I agree, it's possible . . . possible Long Pointed Nose made my son wear a green hat!"

"The Master cuckolded!" Ah Soh's eyes went to Heaven. "It's true Long Pointed Nose spent enough time in her room to . . ." She gasped. "Ayeeyah! Remember, weeks ago, when she sent me away and later screamed because she thought someone was climbing into her room from outside when it was only the wind banging the shutters? I remember now, I was quicker than a bat to her side but Long Pointed Nose was already there and both of them . . . now I think of it, both were whiter than a five-day corpse! Was that the time his Yang . . ."

"When was it, Young Sister? The day? When?"

"It was the day. . . . the day after the Master had that native whore from the brothel across the Canal."

Both women began calculating, minds abacus-fast. Today was twelfth month, fourth day. "That would be . . . that would be tenth month, eighteenth or nineteenth day, Elder Sister."

"Not enough, perhaps not quite enough time, unless this Dark of the Moon is swallowed earlier." Absently Ah Tok sucked more of the fish head, then spat out the bones with conviction: "They must have lain together earlier. The whore had plenty of chances, heya? She was always at that barbarian house, even before you both stayed there."

"You're right, you're right as usual, Elder Sister! We must inform Illustrious Chen at once."

"But why should she give her Jade Gate to such an ugly foreign devil when my son's panting over it?"

Ah Soh shrugged expansively. "Barbarians! Who knows what they think? You should tell the Master!"

Weak with excitement, Ah Tok looked at her bar. Madeira, whisky, brandy. "We need strength!" She selected the whisky and poured two large tots. "To work! We must plan, plot and think how to get the whore and her paramour to reveal the truth!"

"Good, very good! Together we'll do it!"

"But no hint to my son, unwise for us to carry dirty tidings. Until we are sure." They clinked glasses. "By all gods great and small, no one is going to cuckold my son, make him wear the green hat. He will live a long and happy life!"

"Good evening, Father Leo," Angelique said politely, knelt and kissed his hand, finding it hard to contain her revulsion against his strong odor. They were alone in the little church, the nave dimly lit, only a few candles burning, the dying sun coming through the small, poorly executed stained-glass window. There were few Catholics in the Settlement, the revenue miserly, even so the altar and crucifix were rich. Outside, in the sunset, Vargas waited to escort her back again.

"You wanted to see me?" she asked innocently, knowing she had missed Mass again on Sunday. Her pink bonnet had been chosen carefully, also the long Kashmir shawl over her most maidenly afternoon dress of somber silk. "How well you look, Father."

"I'm glad to see you, senhorita, my child," he said with his heavy Portuguese accent. "You are not at Mass again."

"It's the vapors, Father. I'm still recovering from the disorder . . . Dr. Babcott advised rest," she replied, her mind on what she would wear for tonight's birthday banquet for the Russian Minister, and what she could do to entertain Malcolm during the evening. "I am sure by next week I will be better."

I'm glad, my young and not so feeble teller of lies, Leo thought, disgusted with the perfidy of humanity. It's ungodly to dance at night and kick up your heels and show your unclothed nether parts. "Never mind, I will confess you now."

Angelique could have yawned, he was so predictable. Meekly she followed him into the confessional, knelt and went through the motions, glad for the screen between them, parroting her litany, comforted with the pact she had made with the Virgin Mary, repeating their code fervently, as always, ". . . and Father, I forgot to ask the Blessed Mother for forgiveness in my prayers."

Her absolution was quick, a modest penance of a few Hail Marys and she felt the better for it. She began to get up—

"Now, a private matter, my child. Two days ago Mr. Struan sent for me, privately, and asked me to marry you both."

She gasped, then smiled gloriously. "Oh, Father, how marvelous!"

"Yes, my child, yes, it is. 'Please marry us as soon as possible,' the young Senhor Struan said, but it is difficult indeed." Night and day he had wrestled with the problem. An urgent letter had gone the same day to the Bishop of Macao, Catholic spiritual leader in Asia, begging for advice, equally urgently. "Very difficult for us."

"Why, Father?"

"Because he is not a Catholic an—"

"But he has agreed our children are to be brought up in the True Church, he promised."

"Yes, yes, my child, he has—he has. He told me the same but he is not of marrying age, not without permission, nor are you, but I wanted to tell you secretly that, even so, I have asked His Eminence for permission to conduct the ceremony for the greater Glory of God, even so—with or without your father's . . . approval. I hear your father, he is missing, somewhere in French Indo-China or Siam, or somewhere." Particulars of her father's frauds and flight had raced around the Settlement, but in deference to her had been keep quiet, also from Struan. "If His Eminence agrees, I am sure Senhor Seratard, in loco parentis, he will agree, even so."

The tightness in her throat did not go away. "How long will it take for His Eminence to reply, to approve?"

"By Christmas, around Christmas, before then, if he is in Macao and not travelling, visiting the Faithful in China, and if it is the will of

God." As usual he sat facing away from the screen, ear close to it for whispered privacy, but now he glanced through the mesh and could see her vaguely. "The matter I would like to discuss, privately, is the conversion of the Senhor."

Again she gasped. "He said he would convert?"

"No, no, he has not yet seen the Light, that's what I want to talk about." Father Leo leaned closer to the screen, savoring her nearness, choked with a desire he knew to be unholy and Satan-sent, the same that, on his knees, daily and nightly he fought against—as, in equal torment, he had fought against for as long as he had been within the Church.

God give me strength, God forgive me, he thought, almost in tears, wanting to reach out and fondle the breasts and rest of her that was hidden by the screen and by her shawl and by her clothes and the wrath of God. "You must help . . . help him embrace the True Faith."

Angelique was as far from the screen as she could be. Painstakingly, she eased the curtains open to reduce the claustrophobia the boxlike structure gave her. Confessionals never used to be like this, she thought, shuddering. It's only since . . . since that which never happened. "I will help, Father. I will do as much as I can," she said, her nervousness increasing, and again began to leave.

"Wait!"

The violence in the voice shocked her. "Father?"

"Please . . . wait, please wait, my child," the voice said nicely now, but the niceness was forced and this frightened her for it was no longer the voice of a priest and sacrosanct in a sanctified place, but of a stranger. "We must talk about this marriage, and his conversion, my child, and beware of evil influences, yes, we must, conversion is a must . . . a must as preparation for . . . for Eternity."

" 'Must,' Father?" she muttered. "Were you about to say, 'must as preparation *for marriage*'?"

"For . . . for Eternity," the voice said.

She stared at the shadow behind the screen, sure that he was lying, appalled that she could even consider it, let alone believe it. "I will help all I can," she said, and got up and groped through the curtains for air.

But he stood in her path. She noticed sweat on his forehead and that he towered over her, in height and bulk. "It's for his own . . . his own salvation. His, my child. It would be better—better before."

"Are you saying, Father, his conversion is a must before you will marry us?" she asked, in dread.

"It is not to me the conditions, what His Eminence decides governs us, we are faithful servants!"

"In my fiancé's Church, he has not said I must become Protestant, of course I cannot force him either."

"He must be made to see the Truth! This is a God-sent gift, this marriage. Protestant? That heresy? Apostasy? Unthinkable, you'd be lost forever, doomed, excommunicated, your eternal soul consigned to everlasting torment in the Fire, to burn, to burn forever!"

She kept her eyes down and was barely coherent. "For me, yes, for him . . . millions believe otherwise."

"They're all mad, lost, doomed, and forever they'll burn!" The voice hardened even more. "They will! We must convert the heathen. The Malcolm Struan must con—"

"I'll try. Good-bye, Father, thank . . . I'll try," she mumbled, and stepped around him and hurried away. At the door she turned back a moment and genuflected and went out into the light, him standing in the aisle, his back to the altar, all the time his voice ringing in the rafters, "Be an instrument of God, convert the heathen, if you love God save this man, save him from purgatory, if you love God save him, help me save him from Hellfire, save him for the Glory of God, you must . . . before you marry, save him . . . let us save him . . . save him . . ."

That evening a samurai patrol came out of the guard house at the North Gate. Ten warriors, fully armed with swords and light battle armor, an officer at their head. He led the way over the bridge and passed the barrier into the Settlement. One man carried a tall, narrow banner with characters on it. The leading samurai held flares aloft that cast weird shadows.

The High Street and the seafront walk were still busy in the pleasant evening. Traders, soldiers, sailors, shopkeepers taking a constitutional or standing in groups, chatting and laughing, here and there, with a few singsongs and drunks and one or two wary male prostitutes. Down on the beach some sailors had lit a fire and were dancing a tipsy hornpipe around it, a transvestite amongst them, and from the distance came the noisy undercurrent of Drunk Town.

The ominous presence was noticed. People stopped in their tracks. Conversation hesitated in midsentence. Then ceased. All eyes turned northwards. Those nearest the patrol backed out of the way. Not a few felt for a revolver and cursed that it was not in the pocket or holster. Others retreated and an off-duty soldier near an alley took to his heels to summon the Marine night watch.

"What's the matter, suh?" Gornt asked.

"Nothing, yet," Norbert said, his face grim. They were amongst a group on the promenade but still well away from the samurai who paid no attention whatsoever to the silent crowd watching them, slouching along out of step as was their custom.

Lunkchurch sidled up to them. "You armed, Norbert?"

"No. Are you?"

"No."

"I am, suh." Gornt took out his tiny pistol. "But it won't make much of a dent in them if they're hostile."

"When in doubt, young feller," Lunkchurch said hoarsely, "take a powder, I always say." He stuck out his hand to Gornt before he hurried off. "Barnaby Lunkchurch, Mr. Gornt, pleased to meet you. Welcome to Yokopoko. I've seen you in the Club, hear you play bridge—anytime."

Everyone was quietly easing out of range. Drunks had suddenly become sober. All were very much on guard, the speed of a sudden samurai rush with flailing swords too well known. Norbert had already chosen a line of retreat should it prove necessary. Then he saw the Marine night watch come out of the side street on the double, rifles ready, a sergeant at their head, to take up a commanding, though not provocative, position and he relaxed. "Nothing to worry about now. Do you always carry that, Edward?"

"Oh yes, suh, always. I thought I'd told you."

"No, you didn't," he said curtly. "Can I see it?"

"Certainly. It's loaded, of course."

The pistol was tiny but deadly. Double-barrelled. Two bronze cartridges. Silver-sheathed hilt. He gave it back, hard eyed. "Neat. It's American?"

"French. My pa gave it to me when I went to England. Said he'd won it from a riverboat gambler, the only thing he gave me in his life." Gornt laughed softly, both of them watching the approaching samurai. "I even sleep with it, suh, but I've only fired it once. That was at a lady who was sneaking off with my wallet in the dead of night."

"You hit her?"

"No, suh, wasn't trying to, just parted her hair, to frighten her. A lady shouldn't steal, should she, suh?"

Norbert grunted and put his eyes back on the samurai, seeing Gornt in a new light, a dangerous one.

The patrol walked down the center of the road, sentries in front of the British, French and Russian legations—the only ones with permanent guards—quietly cocked their rifles, already warned. "Safety catches on! No firing, lads, till I says," the Sergeant growled. "Grimes, go warn his Nibs, he's with the Russkies, third house down the street, quietly now."

The soldier slid away. Streetlamps of the promenade flickered. Everyone waited anxiously. The strutting officer approached impassively. "Mean-looking bastard, ain' he, Sar'nt?" a sentry whispered, his hands slick on his rifle.

"They're all mean-looking bastards. Easy now."

The officer came abreast of the British Legation and barked a command. His men stopped and formed up facing the gate as he stomped forward and spoke guttural Japanese at the Sergeant. A sharp silence. More impatient, imperious words, clearly orders.

"Wot you want, cookie?" the Sergeant asked thinly, half a metre taller.

Again the ugly sentences, more angrily.

"Anyone knows wot he's saying?" the Sergeant called out. No answer, then Johann, the interpreter, carefully came out of the fringe of the crowd, bowed to the officer who bowed back perfunctorily, and spoke to him in Dutch. The officer replied in Dutch, searching for the words.

Johann said, "He's got a message, a letter, for Sir William, has to deliver it personally."

"Don't know about that, Mister, not with them bloody swords at his side."

The officer started towards the Legation gate and all safety catches came off. He stopped. A furious tirade at the Sergeant and sentries. All samurai eased their swords a quarter length out of their scabbards and took a defensive stance. Down the road the Marine patrol moved into riot order. Everyone waited for the first mistake.

At that moment Pallidar and two other dragoon officers hurried out from the Russian Legation just down the street, in evening dress uniform, dress swords. "I'll take charge, Sergeant," Pallidar said. "What's the problem?"

Johann told him. Pallidar, well rehearsed in Japanese customs now, went over to the officer, bowed, made sure the officer bowed equally. "Tell him I'll accept the letter. I'm aide-de-camp to Sir William," he said exaggerating.

"He says, Sorry, his orders are to do it personally."

"Tell him I'm authorized t—"

Sir William's voice stopped him. "Captain Pallidar—just a moment! Johann, who's this letter from?" He stood on the threshold of the Russian bungalow, Zergeyev and others crowding the entrance beside him.

The officer pointed at the banner and snapped more words and Johann called out, "He says it's from the *tairō* but I guess he means the *roju,* the Elders. He's been ordered to deliver it at once, personally."

"All right, I'll take it. Tell him to come over here."

Johann translated. Imperiously the officer beckoned Sir William to come to him but Sir William called out, even more sharply, with even less courtesy, "Tell him I'm at dinner. If he doesn't step up right now, he can deliver it tomorrow."

Johann was too practiced to translate exactly and only gave just enough emphasis to transfer the meaning. The samurai officer sucked in his breath with fury, then stomped over to the Russian gate, brushed past the two huge bearded sentries and stood before Sir William, clearly waiting for him to bow.

"*Keirei!*" Sir William barked. Salute!—one of few words he allowed himself to know. "*Keirei!*"

The officer flushed but automatically bowed. He bowed as to an equal, seethed even more when he saw Sir William just nod as to an inferior, but then, he thought, this foul little man is the leader gai-jin with a reputation for anger as vile as his smell. When we attack I will personally kill him.

He took out the scroll, went forward and handed it over, stepped back, bowed perfectly, waited until his bow was returned, however rudely, completely satisfied that he had bested the enemy. To rid himself of his anger, he cursed his men and strode off as though they did not exist. They followed, seething at the gai-jin rudeness.

"Where the devil's Tyrer?" Sir William asked.

Pallidar said, "I'll send someone to find him."

"No, ask Johann to join me, will you please?"

"No need for that, Sir William," Erlicher, the Swiss Minister said, "if it's in Dutch I can read it for you."

"Thank you, but it best be Johann as he knows some Japanese too," Sir William said, not wanting to share anything in advance with any foreigner, particularly one who openly represented a small but growing, highly specialized armament industry anxious for exports, with a reputation based on the extraordinary and unique quality of their watchmakers, one of the few areas where British manufacturers could not compete.

The dining room, largest room in the bungalow, contained a table for twenty ladened with fine silver and serving plates. All Ministers were guests, except von Heimrich who was still sick, Struan, Angelique at the head of the table, some French and British officers, with two liveried servants behind each seat and more to serve. "Can I use the anteroom, Count Zergeyev?" Sir William said in Russian.

"Of course." Count Zergeyev opened the door. They waited a moment until Johann hurried in and he closed it.

" 'Evening, Sir William," Johann said, pleased that he had been called. He would be the first to know what this was all about, and could continue to be useful, profitably, to his own country's Minister. He broke the seal of the scroll and sat down also. "Dutch and Japanese. It's short." Rapidly he scanned it, frowned, reread it and then again and laughed nervously. "It's addressed to you, the British Minister and says: 'I communicate with you by dispatch. By order of Shōgun Nobusada received from Kyōto, all ports are to be closed at once and all foreigners expelled and driven out, not nee—' "

"*Driven out? Driven out,* did you say?" The bellow went through the door. An uneasy pall fell on the dinner guests.

Johann winced. "Yes, sir. Sorry, sir, that's what it says: 'and driven out, not needing or wanting any dealings between foreigners and our people. I send you this before commanding an immediate meeting to make final particulars of your urgent withdrawal from Yokohama. Respectful communication.' "

"Respectful? God-cursed bloody impertinence, by God . . ."

The tirade continued. When Sir William paused for breath, Johann said, "It's signed 'Nori Anjo—*Tairō.*' As I understand it, Sir William, that's almost like Dictator—he's gone up in the world."

37

KYŌTO

Thursday, 4th December:

TORANAGA YOSHI WAS LIVID. "When was the *tairō* appointment confirmed?"

"The day before yesterday, Sire, by carrier pigeon to Lord Anjo at Yedo," Wakura, the Lord Chamberlain, head of the palace officials, said smoothly, untouched by his guest's open anger, and hiding his joy—he had been looking forward to this meeting that he had arranged in his quarters within the palace. "The formal scroll, signed by the Shōgun at the request of the Son of Heaven, was sent, I believe, for urgent delivery to Lord Nori Anjo the same day."

This made Yoshi even angrier. His ancestor, Shōgun Toranaga, had made carrier pigeons the exclusive property of the Shōgunate. Over two and a half centuries this method of communication had gone into decline as unnecessary, and now was only used to announce such vital occurrences as the death of a Shōgun or an Emperor. The Bakufu chose not to notice that for years certain Osaka *zaibatsu* moneylenders were surreptitiously using pigeons—leaving them open to punitive measures, extra taxes, or favors, if the Bakufu cared to enforce the law.

"And the fatuous ultimatum to the gai-jin? When is that to be delivered?" Yoshi asked.

"At once, Sire. The Imperial request was included in the same carrier pigeon message, Sire, confirmed by Shōgun Nobusada, and marked *Deliver at once*."

"The order is *baka*, the haste even more *baka*!" Yoshi pulled his padded over-mantle closer around his shoulders. The light rain that patted the gardens outside added a dampness to the chill. "Send another pigeon cancelling the order."

"If it were up to me, Sire, I would do so at once, since you suggest it. As soon as you leave, Sire, I will seek permission but I imagine your wishes will be too late, the gai-jin leader will already have received the command, it may even have been given to him yesterday."

Wakura happily kept his face and manner penitent. This was a culmination of years of intriguing in support of the Emperor's wishes—which matched the opinions of most daimyos, most court nobles, of Ogama who presently held power in Kyōto, though the Gates were ostensibly once again guarded by the loathed Shōgunate— but only with the permission of Ogama—also of the Princess Yazu— and, most important of all, in support of his own views.

His deft and sagacious timing a few days ago had delighted him. He had waylaid the Princess during her morning walk in the palace gardens and in one move had neutralized the Shōgunate, Bakufu, and Yoshi, most dangerous of his enemies. 'Imperial Princess, I hear some courtiers close to the Divine, with your interests in mind, whisper that the Lord, your husband, should appoint Lord Nori Anjo *tairō,* as soon as possible.'

'Anjo?' she had said in disbelief.

'People of wisdom believe, Princess, it should be done quietly and quickly. Plots in Yedo abound and this would avoid interference by . . . ambitious enemies,' he had said delicately, 'enemies who constantly try to undermine your revered husband, who must also have cursed shishi connections. Remember Otsu!'

'As if I will ever forget! But Anjo—not that I have any influence to arrange such a matter—is a dullard and a fool. As *tairō* he will become even more arrogant.'

'True, but raising him above the other Elders might be a small price to pay to make your Lord Shōgun more secure during his minority, and gag his . . . his only rival, Lord Yoshi.'

'Could a *tairō* remove his position of Guardian?'

'Probably, Princess. Another point in Anjo's favor, the wise whisper, is that he is the perfect instrument to use against gai-jin: simpleheaded but obedient to Imperial requests. The Divine would notice such loyalty and no doubt reward such service. If it was done quietly and quickly, I've heard the wise say, the better it would be.'

So easy to implant the seed that had blossomed like one of my hothouse orchids overfertilized—how wise I was to maneuver her marriage. Her words in that dull-witted youth's ears, some dependent nobles co-opted, my own advice quickly sought and quickly given, and it was done.

And now for you, Toranaga Yoshi, he thought happily, Yoshi the handsome, the cunning, the strong, the highborn usurper waiting and snuffling in the wings of power, ready to start the civil war that I and all but a few radical nobles dread, the war that will crush the resurgence of Imperial power and once more put the Imperial court under the foot of whatever current brigand warlord bestrides the Gates, who thus can strangle our stipends and makes us beggars again.

He suppressed a shudder. Not so many generations ago, the then Emperor had to sell his signature on the Kyōto streets to raise money for food. Not so many generations ago court marriages were arranged to ambitious, upstart daimyos, hardly samurai class, their only qualification for higher rank being success in war, and money. Not so many years ago . . .

No, he thought, none of that is going to happen. Once *sonno-joi* is a fact, our loyal shishi friends will disband and return to their fiefs, all daimyos will bow down to Him, we at Court will rule and our golden age will come again.

He coughed and settled the immense sleeves of his elaborate court dress more to his liking, watching Yoshi, his eyes narrowed in his heavy face that was made up according to court custom. "Surely the order to expel the gai-jin is good, Sire. The Emperor's wise and long-known aversion to gai-jin and the Treaties will come to pass, and our Land of the Gods rid of them forever. This should please you too, Lord Yoshi."

"If the order was meaningful, yes. If it would be obeyed, yes. If we had the means to enforce it, yes. But none of that will happen. Why was I not consulted?"

"You, Sire?" Wakura's painted eyebrows soared.

"I'm Guardian of the Heir by Imperial appointment! The boy is under age and not responsible for his signature."

"Oh, so sorry, Sire . . . had it been left to me of course your approval would have been sought first. Please, do not blame me, Sire, I can decide nothing, only make suggestions. I am just a servant of the Court, of the Emperor."

"I should have been consulted!"

"I agree, so sorry, these are strange times."

Yoshi's face was taut. The damage was done. He would have to extract the Shōgunate from their own dung. Fools! How?

First Anjo—one way or another . . . My wife was correct.

Ah, Hosaki, I miss your counsel. Thinking of his family, his eyes drifted outside and at once his fury seemed to dissolve. Beyond the shoji window he saw his guards waiting in the lee of the exquisite roof, the gardens behind them, the rain indulgent, sparkling the carefully orchestrated reds and golds and browns, making it all such a pleasing picture to eye and soul—so different from Yedo, he thought beguiled. Hosaki would enjoy it here, a huge change from our Spartan life. She appreciates beauty, she would like it here.

So easy to be swallowed up, by the weather and gardens, kind skies and tender rain, best music, poetry, exotic foods, abundant silks and clothes makers, exquisite carp and singing birds, the alabaster-skinned beauties of the Court, and of Kyōto's Floating World, the Shimibara, the most sought-after in all Nippon, without a care in the world except to seek the next pleasure.

Since coming to Kyōto, apart from his temporary peace with Ogama, he had achieved little except pleasure times—so rare for him. Pleasure with Koiko, daily sword practice and the martial arts, marvelous massage—Kyōto famous for it—banquets at every meal, playing *Go* and chess, writing poetry.

How wise of my ancestor to confine the Emperor and these over-dressed sycophants to Kyōto, and to build his own capital at Yedo, far from their seductions and twisted manipulations—and how wise to forbid a Shōgun coming into this honeyed trap.

I should leave. How can I without Nobusada?

The Court had all but excluded him. So had Nobusada. Twice the youth had cancelled a meeting at the last moment because of a chill. The doctor had officially confirmed the chill but his eyes agreed it was an excuse. 'But the Lord Shōgun's health does worry me, Lord Yoshi. His constitution is not strong and his manliness leaves much to be desired.'

'Is it the fault of the Princess?'

'No, no, Sire. She is vigorous and her yin ample and succulent enough to satisfy the most particular yang.'

Yoshi had questioned the doctor carefully. Nobusada had never been a swordsman or hunter or outdoor person like his father and brothers, preferring the easier sports of falconry and archery, or more often poetry competitions and calligraphy. But there was nothing wrong with that. 'His father is still as tough as an old saddle and his family known for longevity. You have no cause for alarm, Doctor. Give him one of your potions, get him to eat more fish, less polished rice, and less of the exotics the Princess enjoys.'

She had been present at the only interview he had had with his ward a few days ago. It had gone badly. Nobusada had refused to consider returning to Yedo, refused even to discuss a possible date, refused his advice in every other matter, taunting him with Ogama: 'The Choshu control the streets, Ogama's men are stamping out the vile shishi, Cousin. I'm not even safe surrounded by our warriors, I am only safe here under the Emperor's protection!'

'That is a myth. You are only safe in Yedo Castle.'

'So sorry, Lord Yoshi,' the Princess said sweetly and silkily, 'but it is so damp in Yedo, the weather is not to compare with Kyōto and my husband's cough needs protection.'

'That is right, Yazu-chan, and I like it here, Cousin, for the first time in my life I am free, not confined in that awful castle! Here I am free to roam and sing and play and feel safe; we are safe. I may stay forever! Why not? Yedo is a stinking, slimy place, to rule from here would be grand.'

Yoshi had tried to reason with them but to no avail. Then Nobusada had blurted out, 'What I need most of all, until I am of age—not long now, Cousin—what I need is a strong leader, a *tairō*. Nori Anjo would be perfect.'

'He would be very bad for you and the Shōgunate,' he had said, and patiently explained again but it had made no difference. 'Unwise to ma—'

'I do not agree, Cousin. Anjo listens to me, *to me,* which you never do. I said I wanted to bow before the Divine, my brother-in-law, he agreed and I am here, you were opposed! He listens to me! To me! To me, the Shōgun! And don't forget anyone is better than you. You will never be *tairō,* never!'

And he had left the two of them, never believing—despite Nobusada's derisive, infuriating laughter in his wake—that *Tairō* Anjo would ever become a fact.

But now it is a fact, he thought gloomily, conscious of the Lord Chancellor Wakura watching him. "I will leave Kyōto in the next few days," he said, coming to a sudden decision.

"But you have been here hardly any time, Sire," Wakura said, quietly congratulating himself. "Surely our welcome has not been so terrible?"

"No, not terrible. So, what other distressing pieces of information have you for me?"

"None, Sire. So sorry I related something that displeased you." Wakura rang a bell. At once a painted pageboy came in with tea and a plate of dates, his teeth also dyed black. "Thank you, Omi." The boy smiled back at him and left. "The dates are the sweetest I've ever tasted. From Satsuma."

They were large, honeyed and sun-dried. Yoshi's eyes narrowed. He took one, no coincidence they were from Satsuma. "They are excellent."

"Yes, they are. A pity the daimyo Sanjiro is not as sweet as the food and fruit his soldier farmers grow. Curious that samurai in Satsuma can be either, without loss of caste."

Yoshi chose another. "Curious? Just their ancient custom. A bad custom. Better that men should be samurai or farmers, one or the other, according to the Legacy."

"Ah yes, the Legacy. But then Shōgun Toranaga allowed that family to retain their fief and their heads after Sekigahara though they fought against him. Perhaps he liked their dates too. Interesting, *neh*?"

"Perhaps he was satisfied that they put their heads to the dirt in front of him, humbly gave him power over Satsuma, humbly swore perpetual allegiance and, even more humbly, thanked him when he gave Satsuma to them as fief."

"He was a wise ruler, very wise. But now the Satsuma under Sanjiro are not so humble."

"That is also true of others," Yoshi said thinly.

"As I said, we live in strange times." Wakura took time to select another date. "The rumor is, he prepares his legions for war, and fief for war."

"Satsuma is always on a war footing. Another ancient custom. You must tell me the name of your supplier of dates," Yoshi said. "We could use a supplier in Yedo."

"Gladly," Wakura told him, knowing he would never pass over his network of spies, never. "Some wise advisors suggest this time Sanjiro really will bring war to the mainland."

"War against whom, Lord Chancellor?"

"I presume those he considers enemies."

"And who are they?" Yoshi asked patiently, wanting to bring Wakura into the open.

"It is rumored the Shōgunate, so sorry."

"He would be so sorry if he did try war against the law of the land, Lord Chancellor. These wise counselors you mentioned, perhaps they should quickly counsel him not to be so stupid. Counselors can also be stupid, *neh*?"

"I agree." Wakura smiled with his mouth.

"I agree that Sanjiro is militant, but he is not stupid. Ogama of Choshu the same. And Yodo of Tosa. All the Outside Lords are militant and maneuvering, always have been—like some misguided, overly ambitious Court officials."

"Even if that were true, what could a few courtiers do against the great Shōgunate, Sire, when the entire Court possesses no armies, no lands, and no koku, all of whom depend on Shōgunate largess for stipends?"

Yoshi smiled with equal mirthlessness. "They spread discontent amongst ambitious daimyos. . . . Oh, yes, that reminds me," he said, deciding Wakura had gone too far and needed the whip. "Perhaps in this marvelous enclave you may not know it yet, but this year and next there will be famine throughout Nippon, even in my Kwanto. It is rumored the Court stipend will be cut, this year and next, I believe by half." He was glad to see Wakura's eyes almost cross. "So sorry."

"Yes, so sorry, it would be sorry, a sorry day. Times are hard enough now." Wakura fought back his impulse to shout and threaten, trying to estimate Yoshi's power to initiate and force through such a cut. He is not alone in wanting that, daimyos are always complaining, and of course the Council of Elders would agree. But *Tairō* Anjo would overrule them, why else is he there but to do our bidding. Ogama? That arrogant dog would approve the cut, so would Sanjiro, and all the others! Anjo had better overrule them!

Wakura put on his best smile. "The Prince Advisor asks if you would give him your views in a memorial on Satsuma, Choshu and Tosa, particularly the danger Satsuma poses, and how in the future the Court could help the Shōgunate—and avoid misunderstandings."

"I would be glad to," Yoshi said, brightening. This would be a wonderful opportunity.

"Lastly, I'm honored to tell you the Divine has invited you as His personal guest, Shōgun Nobusada, some daimyos and those of Tosa, Choshu, and Satsuma to the Festival of the Winter Solstice. The Tosa and Satsuma invitations have already gone, yours and the Lord Ogama's will be presented with due ceremony tomorrow, but I wanted the pleasure of telling you."

Yoshi was astonished, for such was an extreme honor for anyone outside the Inner Circle. The solstice was this month—Twelfth Month—twenty-second day. In sixteen days. The festivities would last at least a week, perhaps longer. He could leave afterwards, plenty of time to deal with Anjo then.

Wait! You have forgotten what the Legacy says: *Beware of camping*

*in the Lair of Heaven. It is not for us. We are men, they are gods, gods
are like people, jealous like people and closeness breeds their contempt. The death of our line would please these false gods very much. It
can only happen in their lair.*

Yoshi was filled with sudden dread. The invitation could not be
refused. "Thank you," he said, and bowed.

At midday the shishi lookout stationed opposite the Toranaga barracks watched idly as the forty samurai and banner men came out of
the gateway and went down the street towards the palace's East Gate.
This was the routine midday changing of the guard. Most carried
spears, all wore two swords, and rain cloaks and wide, conical rain
hats, all of straw.

The shishi yawned and pulled his own cloak around his shoulders
when a light shower began, shifting his stool under the awning of the
street stall that served noodles and soup and tea and was owned by a
sympathizer. Soon his own replacement would arrive. He had been on
duty since dawn. He was eighteen years old, his beard heavy. A
Satsuma ronin.

Before sneaking out of Kyōto their leader Katsumata had ordered a
constant surveillance on the Toranaga and Ogama headquarters. 'The
moment there is a chance to attack either man—it will have to be
outside their walls and must have a reasonable chance of success—
mount an immediate one-man assault. One man, no more. Shishi must
be conserved, but we must be ready. A random attack is our only
chance for revenge.'

At the gateway several porters carrying bales of fresh vegetables and
panniers of fresh fish stopped at the barrier. Attentive guards checked
them carefully, then gestured them through; everyone was inspected
with equal care.

The youth yawned again. No chance of sliding through the cordon.
He wondered briefly if the girl Sumomo had managed to get inside and
set herself in place as Katsumata had agreed. Eeee, a miracle those
three escaped through the tunnel, a miracle. But where are they now?
Nothing had been heard of them since their miraculous escape. What
does it matter? They must be safe, like us—we have important patrons.
We will regroup later. We will be revenged. *Sonno-joi* will happen.

He saw the guards turn the corner and disappear. Now he was tired,
but the thought of warm futons and his waiting lover took most of it
away.

*   *   *

The Shōgunate patrol reached the East Gate. A low barracks–guard house nestled against the walls and spread on either side of the Gate and could house five hundred men and horses if need be. The Gate was six metres high and made of heavy, iron-reinforced timber with a much smaller gate off to one side standing open. The perimeter walls were higher, ancient, and stone.

For a moment the new guards noisily intermingled with the old, all of them well muffled. Officers inspected men and arms, the old guard began forming up and an officer and an ashigaru, a foot soldier, from the replacement group trudged across the roadway. The shower stopped. A little sun broke through. The two men turned into another street and went into another barracks, similar to many all over Kyōto. Here two hundred of Ogama's samurai were housed—well away from the Gate, but close enough.

"Forty men, here are their names," the officer said to his counterpart, and bowed. "Nothing new to report."

"Good. Both of you come with me, please." The Ogama officer studied the list of names as he led the way down a corridor through a cordon of his men. Through a doorway into an empty room, across it to a closed door. The officer knocked, then opened it. This inner room was bare but for a low table and tatami mats. Ogama stood by the window, armed, wary but alone. Both officers stood aside and bowed.

The ashigaru took off his large hat and revealed himself as Yoshi. Silently he gave his long sword to his officer, keeping the short one, and went into the room. The door closed behind him. Both officers exhaled. Both were sweating.

In the room Yoshi bowed. "Thank you for agreeing to the meeting."

Ogama bowed, motioned Yoshi to sit opposite him. "What is so urgent and why such secrecy?"

"Bad news. You said partners should share particular information. So sorry, Nori Anjo has been made *tairō*!"

The news visibly shocked Ogama and he listened intently as Yoshi talked. When Yoshi spoke about the Imperial invitation some of his anger dissipated. "Such an honor, and recognition! Eeee, and none too soon."

"That is what I thought. Until I was out of the palace. Then I saw the depth of the trap."

"What trap?"

"To have the Lords of Satsuma, Tosa, you and me all in one place at the same time? In ceremonial clothes? Inside the palace walls? Without arms or guards?"

"What could Wakura do? Any one of them? They have no samurai—no armies, no money, no arms. Nothing!"

"Yes, but think: When we four are in front of the Son of Heaven together, that would be perfect timing for someone—Wakura, Prince Fujitaka, Shōgun Nobusada, or the Princess—to suggest 'as a gift to the Divine now is the moment for the four greatest daimyos in the Land to express their loyalty by offering up their powers to Him.' "

Ogama's brow darkened. "Not one of us would agree, not one! We would prevaricate, stall, even lie an—"

"Lie? To the Son of Heaven? Never. Listen further. Say the Prince Advisor, before the ceremony, in private, was to say to you something like: 'Lord Ogama, the Son of Heaven wishes to adopt you, to make you Prince Ogama, Captain of the Imperial Guard, Lord Chieftain of the Gates, member of the New Imperial Council of Ten who will rule instead of the usurping Toranaga Shōgunate. In return . . .' "

"Eh? What Council of Ten?"

"Wait. '. . . in return, you just acknowledge Him as who He is: the Son of Heaven, Emperor of Nippon, Possessor of the Sacred Regalia—the Orb, Mirror and Sceptre—descended from the gods and ascendant over all men; in return you dedicate your fief and your samurai to His service and His wishes that will be exercised through the Imperial Council of Ten!' "

Ogama stared at him, beads of sweat on his upper lip. "I would . . . would never give up Choshu."

"Perhaps, perhaps not. Perhaps the Imperial Mouthpiece says, in addition the Emperor will confirm you in your fief as Lord of Choshu, Conqueror of the gai-jin, Keeper of the Straits, subject only to Him, and the Imperial Council of Ten."

"Who else is on the Council?" Ogama said hoarsely.

Yoshi wiped the sweat off his own brow. The whole scheme had suddenly presented itself when he had reached his own barracks. General Akeda had precipitated it with a chance remark about how devious Kyōto thinking was, that it seemed to be in the very air they breathed, that what was considered a prize in an instant became a noose.

He had become physically ill because he knew he could be charmed as easily as anyone—he was today, a few moments before, lulled into a false sense of security until he would be isolated and then invited onwards.

"There, you see, Ogama-sama, you're already tempted. 'Who else is on the Council?' As if what they told you mattered. You would be one against their appointees, Sanjiro too. Lord Chancellor Wakura and his ilk would overwhelm and rule."

"We would not agree. I would n—"

"So sorry, you would agree—they could gear honors to tempt a kami—the great temptation being that they would pretend to replace the Toranaga Shōgunate with the Council of Ten Shōgunate! Of course I would not be offered a place on the Imperial Council, nor any Toranagas except Nobusada and he's already theirs because of that Princess, as I warned." Yoshi spat with rage. "Anjo is the first move."

The more the two men considered the ramifications, the more they could see the spikes of the limitless traps ahead. Ogama said hoarsely, "The festivities would go on for weeks or more—we would be obliged to give banquets to the Court and to each other. Slow poisons could be introduced."

Yoshi shuddered. All of his life he had carried a deep fear of being poisoned. A favorite uncle had died in great pain, the doctor saying 'natural causes,' but the uncle had been a barb in the side of a hostile Bakufu and his death a great convenience. Perhaps poisoning, perhaps not. The death of the previous Shōgun the year Perry returned, one day healthy the next dead, again so convenient to the *Tairō* Ii who hated him, wanting a puppet—Nobusada—in his place.

Rumors, never proof, but poison was an ancient art in Nippon, and China. The more Yoshi reasoned with himself—if death by poisoning was his karma—the more he made sure his cooks were trustworthy and took care where he ate. But that did not remove the panic that possessed him now and then.

Abruptly Ogama bunched a fist and smashed it into the palm of his other hand. "Anjo *tairō*! I cannot believe it."

"Nor I." When Yoshi had sent the messenger to arrange this secret meeting he had been thinking how ironic it was that now he and Ogama really had to work together if they were to survive. No longer could they survive alone. At the moment.

"How do we stop this happening? I can see they could tempt me." Ogama spat on the tatami in disgust.

"They can tempt anyone, Ogama-dono."

"They are like wolf kamis, I can understand that. We are trapped. If the Divine invites us, His befouled minions will destroy us. Let us round up those you spoke of, or . . . I'll send for Basuhiro, his mind is like a serpent's!"

"We are only trapped if we accept the invitation tomorrow. I propose we both leave Kyōto tonight, secretly. If we are not here . . . eh?"

Ogama's sudden smile was seraphic but it evaporated as quickly. Yoshi understood why, and said, "Such a move requires great trust between us."

"Yes, yes, it would. What do you propose to—to guard against any mistakes?"

"I cannot cover all alternatives but this is temporary: we both slip out of Kyōto tonight, agreeing to stay away for at least twenty days. I will go at once to Yedo and deal with or neutralize Anjo, and stay there until that is done. General Akeda will be in charge as usual and will say that I had to return suddenly to Dragon's Tooth, a sickness in the family, but I am expected back quickly. You go to Fushimi and spend the night there. By sunset tomorrow, the invitation has failed to reach you—because no one, not even Basuhiro knows where you are, eh?"

"Too dangerous not to tell him, but go on."

"I leave that to you but at sunset tomorrow you deliver a message to Prince Fujitaka inviting him to a private meeting the next morning, say at the Monoyama ruins"—a favorite sightseeing place for Kyōto people. "When you see him you express astonishment at the invitation and regret not being there to accept it. Meanwhile he had better ensure no more invitations arrive until you return. 'When will that be?' You are not sure. The gai-jin have threatened to land at Osaka imminently. You must visit there and make plans. Meanwhile make it clear to him that there better not be any more sudden Imperial Invitations—however much you humbly appreciate them—until you decide you will accept them."

Ogama grunted. He stared at the tatami lost in thought. Then he said, "What about Sanjiro, and Yodo of Tosa? They will be arriving, in ceremonial force, but still force."

"Tell Fujitaka to make sure their invitations are postponed—he should suggest to the Divine this solstice has bad omens attached to it."

"A good suggestion! But if they will not be put off?"

"Fujitaka will make sure they are."

"If it is that easy, why not stay, even with the invitations? I just tell Fujitaka to make the suggestion about the bad omens. The Festival is cancelled, eh? This supposes Fujitaka has the power to suggest or unsuggest."

"With Wakura he can. I believe Kyōto deviousness is in the air we breathe—we would be snared." This was the best he could do. It did not suit his purpose for Ogama to be here alone, and there were still the Gates to solve.

"I could stay at Fujimi, or Osaka for twenty days," Ogama said slowly. "I could not return to Choshu, that would leave my Kyōto . . . that would leave me open to attack."

"From whom? Not me—we are allies. Hiro will not be here, or Sanjiro. You could journey to Choshu if you wished. Basuhiro could be trusted to hold your position here."

"No vassal could be trusted that much," Ogama said sourly. "What about the shishi?"

"Basuhiro and my Akeda will continue to crush them—our Bakufu spies will continue to seek them out."

Ogama scowled. "The more I think about this the less I like it. Too many dangers, Yoshi-dono. Fujitaka is sure to tell me your invitation was not delivered either."

"You will be surprised; I suggest you can say my excuse about an illness must be a cover and that I must be rushing to Yedo to see what I can do to prevent the gai-jin from putting their threat to come to Kyōto into effect—and to ensure they quit Yokohama." His face hardened. "They will not."

Ogama said roughly, "Then we will make them."

"In due time, Ogama-dono." Yoshi became even harder. "Everything I forecast has happened. Believe me, the gai-jin will not be forced out. Not yet."

"Then when?"

"Soon. This problem must be left for the moment. First of importance is to protect ourselves. Two requests: We must leave together and return together. We stay secret allies until formally, person to person and alone, we decide otherwise." Ogama laughed but said nothing. "Last, while I am gone, our agreement over the Gates stays in place."

"Your mind jumps around like a cat with thorns in its pads." Ogama cleared his throat and shifted his knees more comfortably. "Perhaps I agree, perhaps not. This is too important to decide at once. I must talk with Basuhiro."

"No. Talk to me. I can give better advice because I know more and, importantly, in this your interests are mine—and I am not a vassal who has to seek petty favors."

"Only big ones. Like the Gates."

Yoshi laughed. "That is a little one compared to some you will grant me, and I will grant you, when you're *tairō*."

"Then give me one now while I'm not: Sanjiro's head."

Yoshi looked at him, hiding his surprise. He had not forgotten what Inejin, his innkeeper spy on the road to Dragon's Tooth, had told him about Ogama and 'Crimson Sky.' Inejin spoke of how, with Sanjiro in support, or neutral, Ogama would prevail against the Shōgunate with the historic tactic so favored by daimyos, a sneak attack.

"Would you settle for his balls?" Yoshi asked, and laid out the plan he had been refining for months.

Ogama began to laugh.

The column of guards that had been relieved trudged homewards, four men abreast, Yoshi still disguised as a foot soldier amongst them. Although they had been warned in advance to treat him as such, they were finding it difficult not to sneak a glance, or apologize when coming too close. One of the soldiers was a shishi informer named Wataki. He had had no opportunity to warn of this unique opportunity for an ambush.

Yoshi was tired but content. At length Ogama had agreed to everything so now he could leave Kyōto with the Gates safe in Shōgunate hands and the Shōgunate safe.

For a time—enough time, he thought. My gamble is great, and my scheme filled with holes that will worry Ogama if he sees them. It does not matter, surely he plans to betray me anyway. Never mind, it was the best I could do, and should be workable. Impossible for me to accept the invitation.

The day had improved now, the sun jousting with clouds for possession of the sky. He hardly noticed it or his surroundings, his mind occupied with all the details of his departure, who to tell, what to do about Koiko and General Akeda, who to take with him, and his overall concern: would he be in time to minimize the damage in Yedo?

First a bath and massage, decisions afterwards . . .

His eyes focused and he became aware of the streets as they marched along, the pedestrians, stalls and ponies and *kagas* and palanquins, the houses and hovels and stalls and children and fish sellers and hawkers and soothsayers and scribes and all the bustle of the markets. It was a completely new experience for him to be one of many, incognito in the column, and he began to enjoy this completely different perspective. Soon he was gawking like a country person at the sights and sounds and smells of the city he had never seen before, wanting to stop, to intermingle with the crowds, to experience them, what they thought and did and ate and where they slept. "Soldier," he whispered to the young man beside him. "Where do you go when you're off duty?"

"M-me, Lord?" the man stuttered, and almost dropped his spear, appalled at being talked to by the Most High, wanting to kneel at once. "Me, I . . . go and drink, Sire . . ."

"Don't call me 'Sire,'" Yoshi hissed, startled by the sudden confusion his question had caused in all those nearby, some of whom missed their footing and almost broke ranks. "Act normally—do not look at me! All of you!"

The soldier offered apologies, and those nearby tried to do what he had ordered, finding it almost impossible now that their Lord Yoshi had broken the spell of invisibility. The Sergeant glanced around and came back anxiously. "Everything all right, Lord? Is ev—"

"Yes, yes, Sergeant. Return to your post!"

Automatically the Sergeant bowed and obeyed, the soldiers picked up their step and continued onwards—their barracks a hundred metres ahead. To Yoshi's relief this minor confusion went unnoticed by the crowd alongside who had been bowing as the column passed.

But it had been noticed by two men further down the street. They were the shishi lookout, Ruru, and his replacement, Rushan, a young Tosa ronin, who had that moment arrived at the street stall not far from the Toranaga gateway. "Am I drunk, Rushan? A sergeant bowing to a foot soldier. A sergeant?"

"I saw it too, Izuru," the other whispered. "Look at the soldier. There, you can see him now, the tall one near the back, look how he carries his spear. He is not used to it."

"Right, but . . . What is it about him, eh?"

"See how the others watch him without watching!"

With growing excitement they scrutinized the soldier intently as the column approached. Though the soldier's weapons were the same and uniform and everything the same, there was no mistaking a major difference: in carriage, step, the physical qualities of the man, however much he pretended to slouch.

"Lord Yoshi," both men said simultaneously, and Rushan added at once, "He's mine."

"No, mine," Izuru said.

"I saw him first!" Rushan whispered, committed, so impatient he could hardly talk.

"Both of us, together we have a better chance."

"No, keep your voice down. One man one time, that was Katsumata's order and we agreed. He is mine. Signal me when!" Heart pumping, Rushan eased through the pedestrians and other customers to a better attack position. They bowed politely, taking him for one of the many, ordinary, low-rank samurai off duty from one of the ceremonial garrisons and gave him no more attention, preparing to bow to the approaching column.

Rushan's new position was on the edge of the roadway. A last look to place his quarry. Then he sat on a stool with his back towards the column, eyes on his friend Izuru, completely at peace. His death poem for his parents was in the hands of his village shoya, given years ago when he and ten other student samurai had rebelled. They were all goshi and had rebelled when they were refused entrance to the school for higher education—their parents could not afford the necessary bribes to local officials. They had killed the officials, declared themselves ronin and for *sonno-joi*, and fled.

Of the ten, he alone was still alive. Soon to die, he thought gloriously, knowing he was prepared, trained, at the height of his power and that Izuru would be his witness.

Izuru was just as ardent. He had already decided on his own attack plan if Rushan failed. Confidently, he moved into a better spot. His gaze left the patrol and went to the gateway. Guards were preparing for the ritual of checking the others back through the barricade. At once he noticed there was more bustling, and barking orders than usual, the men smarter and more nervous.

He cursed to himself. They know! Of course they know and have known since the column left! That explains why they have been so jittery and irritable all morning. They all knew Lord Yoshi was loose outside and in disguise. But why? And where's he been? Ogama! But why? Were they planning another ambush on us? Are we betrayed again?

All the time his eyes darted back and forth, never forgetting Rushan, gauging distances and timing. Already many pedestrians and shoppers close by were bowing. Any moment the officer would halt the column, the officer of the gate would come to meet him, both would bow, together they would inspect the incoming men and then they would all march away.

The officer held up his hand. The column shuffled to a halt. "Now," Izuru said almost audibly, and gestured. Rushan saw the signal and dashed for the tail of the column twenty metres away, his long sword poised in a two-handed grip.

He burst through the first two men, sending them sprawling before they or any of the soldiers realized they were being attacked, and hacked at Yoshi who stared at him blankly for a split second. Only Yoshi's honed instinct made him lurch towards the death blow, diverting it into a stupefied soldier beside him who screamed and went down.

Shrieking *"sonno-joi"* in the sudden shouting melee around him, Rushan jerked the blade out as soldiers fought for space, shoving each other out of the way, other guards rushing from the gateway, bystanders everywhere gaping and paralyzed, Wataki, the shishi informer, as surprised as any of the soldiers, and terrified he would become involved or betrayed by this shishi he recognized who had appeared out of nowhere.

Wataki saw Rushan strike again and held his breath. But Yoshi had recovered his balance though had no time yet to draw his sword so he used the haft of his spear against the blow. Rushan's sword sliced through it easily but the blade twisted and slowed slightly, giving Yoshi just enough time to lunge and grab the sword hilt left-handed.

At once Rushan's right hand flashed to his short sword, ripped it out and stabbed for the belly, a classic gambit in hand-to-hand fighting. Again Yoshi was prepared. He had let the spear fall and jammed his right forearm against Rushan's wrist to deflect the blade into his cloak to entangle it. Instantly Rushan let go and his hand, now a murderous weapon with fingers like rock-hard talons, and nails like claws, stabbed for Yoshi's eyes. The nails missed the eyes but sank in below them.

Yoshi gasped. A lesser trained man would have released his grip on his assailant's long sword hilt and would have died. Blindly he hung on, now with two hands, to the man who flayed impotently, out of control now. This gave a soldier behind Rushan the opening to grab him around the throat, and Wataki, knowing the fight was lost and petrified the shishi would be captured alive, thankfully drove his short sword into Rushan's lower back. The strength of the blow thrust the blade right through him. Rushan cried out. Blood seeped from his mouth, but he fought on, though blind with death as his life soared upwards and outwards and ended. Barely a minute had passed since the first attack.

Though his own glands generated panic, Yoshi felt the life go out of the man. And the sudden weight of the body against him. But he did not let go until he was completely sure the man was truly dead. Even then he allowed other hands to pull the corpse away and let it fall.

Blood covered him. He discovered quickly that it was not his. His good fortune did not dissipate his fury at the men nearby who had failed to be alert, failed to move into a protective screen, leaving him to do the fighting. He cursed them, ordering the whole troop inside, on their knees, their swords broken, except the two who had helped him. Then, panting, he looked around. The busy street was almost empty.

When the shouting, milling skirmish surrounding the lone attacker was seen to be what it was, and in seconds Yoshi's hat torn off and he was recognized, a hum of astonishment had gone through the common

folk. At once, two or three sidled away, heads averted. Others followed. The cautious dribble became a floodtide, no one wanting to be
held as a witness or even accused of being an accomplice.

Izuru was one of the first to leave when he saw there was no
reasonable expectation a second attack would succeed. Rushan mis-
handled the attack, he thought, walking down the predetermined side
street, well shielded by departing crowds. The fool should have hacked
the head off one of the first two as a diversion, then on the recovery
used the same fluid, brutal force to swing back on the prime target,
waist-high. No likelihood of Yoshi escaping that blow. None. Katsumata would be furious. He demonstrated it enough times, told us
enough times. A unique opportunity wasted! And as for allowing Yoshi
to catch his hilt and parry the belly thrust . . .

Rushan deserved to be captured alive and used for sword practice!
Wait, perhaps it was better this way. If Rushan was so inept in his
supreme duel, he probably would have broken and given away our safe
houses, the ones he knew about. You can't trust Tosa people, shishi or
not!

But why was Toranaga Yoshi taking such a risk?

There were shouts behind him. Soldiers were chasing the last of the
crowds to catch some as witnesses. No chance that he would be caught,
no need to hurry.

Rain began again. The wind picked up. He pulled his cloak around
him, glad for it and his hat. Down another puddled alley, into another,
across a bridge, the wooden slats slippery. Soon he was safe in a maze
of slippery little streets that led to a back entrance in the wall of a great
dwelling. The guard recognized him, let him pass, waving him toward
the secret shishi safe house lost in the vast gardens. The man's uniform
carried the insignia of Lord Chancellor Wakura.

In the street of the Toranaga Headquarters the stall keeper was being
hustled to the guard house, loudly protesting that he knew nothing, was
nothing and begged to be allowed to go—he had dared not vanish with
the others as he was too well known there. A few stragglers who had
been caught were shoved after him. The awning of the stall flapped
miserably in the wind and rain.

Koiko was putting the final touches to her makeup, helped by a hand
mirror of polished steel. Her fingers shook slightly. Again she made a
conscious effort to empty her mind and compartmentalize her fears, for
Yoshi and because of him, for herself and because of herself. The other
two women, Teko, her *maiko*—apprentice—and Sumomo watched

intently. The room was small and functional, like the rest of the suite adjoining Yoshi's quarters, sufficient for her when she slept alone, and one maid. Other quarters, for her attendants, were farther away.

As she finished she stared at her reflection. She could detect no worry lines and when she tried a smile the skin of her face crinkled only in the correct places, her eyes were white where they should be white, dark where they should be dark and showed none of the depth of her concern. This pleased her. Then she caught a glimpse of Sumomo. Not aware she was observed, Sumomo's face was momentarily open. Koiko's stomach twisted, seeing so many conflicts there.

Training training training, she thought, what would we do without it, and turned to face them. Teko, little more than a child, took the mirror without being asked, deftly touched a vagrant lock into place with a tiny hand.

"It's beautiful, Lady Koiko," Sumomo said, bewitched. This was the first time she had been allowed into Koiko's private quarters. The secrets of the beauty process had been a revelation, beyond her whole experience.

"Yes, it is," Koiko said, thinking she meant the mirror, the perfection of its surface making it almost priceless. "And it is a kind mirror too. Few are kind, Sumomo—vital in this life for a woman to have a kind mirror to look into."

"Oh, I meant the whole picture you make, not that," Sumomo said, embarrassed. "From your kimono to your hairstyle, your choice of colors and how you make up your lips and eyebrows, everything. Thank you for allowing me to witness it."

Koiko laughed. "I hope that with or without, the effect is not too different!"

"Oh, you are the most beautiful person I have ever seen," Sumomo burst out. Compared to Koiko she felt like a country person, unsophisticated, inept, bovine, all fingers and elbows and big feet, for the first time in her life conscious of a lack of femininity. What can my beloved Hiraga see in me, she asked herself dismayed. I'm nothing, unattractive, nothing, not even a Choshu like him. I bring him no face, no lands, no prestige and no money, I'm sure in truth his parents disapprove of me. "You are the—the most beautiful I'm ever likely to see!" she said, and she was thinking, Are all Ladies of the Floating World like you? Even the *maiko* will be stunning when she is grown, though not like her Mistress! No wonder men marry women like me just to control their houses and bear their children, because it is so easy for them to worship elsewhere, to enjoy beauty elsewhere and oh, so much more.

With the sincerity Koiko saw the unhappiness and envy that could not be hidden. "You are beautiful too, Sumomo," she said, long aware she had this effect on many women. "Teko-chan, you may go now but prepare everything for later . . . and make sure we are not disturbed, Sumomo and I."

"Yes, Mistress." Teko was almost fifteen. As with Koiko, her contract had been concluded with the mama-san of the House of Wisteria by her farmer parents when she was seven. Her earning life would begin when she was fourteen or fifteen. Till then, and as long as the mama-san wanted, the contract made the mama-san responsible for keeping her, clothing her, and training her for a life in the Floating World, and, if she developed the aptitude, in its various arts: as musician or dancer or poet or conversationalist, or all of them. If the *maiko* proved untrainable or difficult, the mama-san could resell the contract at her whim, but if her choice had been wise, as with Koiko, the mama-san's considerable financial outlay and gamble would be repaid abundantly in money and reputation. Not all mama-sans were considerate, or kind, or patient.

"Run along now and practice your scales," Koiko said.

"Yes, Mistress." Teko knew she had been blessed to be apprenticed to Koiko whom she adored and worked very hard to please. She bowed perfectly and, adorned by an irrepressible charm, went away.

"So." Koiko looked at Sumomo, uneasily fascinated by her, her direct look and manner and strength. Since she had agreed to allow her to stay five days ago, there had been almost no opportunity to talk alone. Now it was time. She opened a mental compartment: Katsumata.

Oh, my friend, what have you done to me?

He had waylaid her during her visit to the Kyōto mama-san who had, at the instigation of Meikin, her own mama-san in Yedo, arranged maids, hairdresser, masseuses while she was here. Only Teko and a maid had travelled with her from Yedo.

'I ask a lifetime favor,' Katsumata had said.

'No, you must not!' she had said, shocked to see him, shocked that he would endanger her with such a clandestine meeting and shocked that he would ask such a favor of her that surely must have dire consequences. Once granted, no other favor could ever be asked of the same person, the ensuing debt enormous. 'We agreed when Lord Toranaga Yoshi honored me, all personal contacts between us should cease, except in an emergency. We agreed.'

'Yes, hence the lifetime favor I ask.'

Seven years ago, in Yedo, when she was fifteen, Katsumata had been her first client. Quickly he had become a lot more: friend, guru and consummate teacher. He had opened her eyes to the world, to the importance of the real world, as well as the Floating World. Over the years he had taught her the tea ceremony, the art of debating, calligraphy, about poetry and inner meanings of literature, politics, and regaled her with his ideas and plans for the future, how his small band of acolyte samurai would dominate the land, would force through *sonno-joi,* and, in time, showed her how there was a vital place for her in the jigsaw called *sonno-joi.* 'As a courtesan of supreme rank you will be a confidante of the powerful, as wife of one of them, you'll marry one, never fear, and have samurai sons and be indispensable to the new future and a major part of its power, never forget it!'

Meikin, her mama-san, was an adherent so of course she had agreed, her imagination devoured by his bravery and daring and his band of shishi, the rise of their fortunes.

'Our fortunes have ebbed,' he had said, and told her about the ambush last night and his escape with two others. 'We were betrayed—I do not know by whom but we have to scatter—for the time being.'

'Forty shishi spiked?' she whispered, appalled.

'Forty. Most of them leaders. Only three of us escaped, another shishi and a girl—a ward of mine. Listen, Koiko-chan, there's not much time. The lifetime favor I ask is for you to guard this girl while you stay in Kyōto, take her into your household, even back to Yedo with you an—'

'Oh, but as much as I would like to, so sorry, that would be very difficult, the General Akeda is very particular about people. He would personally interview her—he did with all my other helpers,' she said as nicely as she could, inwardly horrified that he dared to make such a dangerous suggestion to her that she harbor a shishi escapee, however innocent. 'It would be very diff—'

'Of course it would be difficult. But you will be able to arrange this without having him see her.'

'I do not think that possible and then there is Lord Yoshi.' She had left that hanging, frantically hoping he would withdraw the request but he had continued softly, watching her with his intense, compelling eyes, saying that Sumomo would be safe with her, that she was samurai, the affianced of a very important shishi, a woman to be trusted: 'So sorry, but I ask you to do this for *sonno-joi;* she is to be trusted. Any problem, send her away. Any task she will do . . . sorry, Koiko-chan, I must go. A lifetime favor, as an old friend.'

'Wait. If . . . I will have to consult with General Akeda, but even if he can be avoided, certainly I must ask my household, I will have to consult them of course, but what am I to say about her? To the General or to them, I do not know these Kyōto people, or anything about them.'

'Their mama-san guarantees they are to be trusted,' he had said with utter conviction. 'I asked her and she approves of this, Koiko, or I would not suggest it. Tell them the truth, that Sumomo is simply a headstrong girl and her guardian—an old, old client—wants her curbed and trained in useful, feminine arts. I cannot take her with me and want her protected. I have an obligation to her fiancé. She will obey you in everything.'

Koiko trembled at the danger she had put herself into, as well as those she was responsible for, Teko and her attendants: four maids, a hairdresser, and a masseuse. Fortunately they had agreed to have this stranger in their midst and to help her to change her ways—and Akeda's scrutiny had failed to detect any flaw.

Ah, Katsumata, you knew I could refuse you nothing, she thought. Curious how quickly you went beyond needing my body, a few months, wanting instead to possess and expand my mind. I'm still bound by hoops of iron, deep in your debt. Without you and the knowledge you gave me I would not be at the pinnacle I am now—and able to beguile the greatest man in the land.

"Sit down, Sumomo," she said. "We have a little time now before I have to go. We cannot be overheard here."

"Thank you."

"My attendants are concerned about you."

"Please excuse me if I have not been correct."

Koiko smiled. "The maids wonder if you have a tongue in your head, all agree your gentility needs improving, and all can understand a guardian wanting you improved."

"I need improving," Sumomo said, smiling.

Koiko's eyes crinkled. The young woman opposite her was not unattractive, her body lithe and strong, the face without makeup, the bloom of youth and health making up for that deficiency. Her hair is in good condition but needs styling, she thought critically. The Kyōto style would suit her, lots of good oils on her hands and arms, some shading on her fine cheekbones, a touch of color on her lips. The girl has promise. We must bathe together and then I would know more though I doubt she could adapt to our life even if she wanted to adapt. "You are a virgin, yes?"

She saw the girl flush and laughed outright. "Ah, so sorry, of course you are, for a moment I forgot that you are not of our world. Please excuse me, but it is rare for us to meet outsiders, let alone a samurai lady, and to have one in your household however briefly, that is almost unknown."

"Is—is that what you call us? Outsiders?"

"Yes. Our Floating World sets us apart. Take little Teko. Soon her other life will have vanished and she will know only mine. That is my duty, to train her and keep her gentle and kind, to sacrifice herself for man's pleasure—not at her impulse." Koiko's eyes took on a sheen. "That is what keeps men happy and content, pleasure in all its manifestations, *neh*?"

"Sorry, I don't understand 'manifestations.' "

"Ah, so sorry, it means 'appearances, or qualities,' to show pleasure in all its degrees."

"Ah, thank you," Sumomo said, awed. "Please excuse me, I never knew that ladies of the—the Floating World were so . . . of course I presumed they were beautiful, but never, never as beautiful as you and never dreamed they could be so well educated and accomplished." In the few days she had been here she had heard Koiko singing, and playing the samisen and had been inspired by the peerless quality and her repertoire—she too could play the samisen, just a little, and knew how difficult it was. She had heard her teaching Teko the art of haiku and other poetry, how to caress a phrase, about silks, how they are made, the warp and the weft and other mysteries, the beginnings of history and similar wonders, her range of knowledge vast. She bowed in tribute. "You astonish me, Lady."

Koiko laughed softly. "Learning is the most important part of our work. It's easy to satisfy a man's body—such a transient delight—but difficult to pleasure him for any length of time, to intrigue him and retain his favor. That must come through the senses of the mind. To achieve that one must train oneself extremely carefully. You must begin to do that too."

" 'When there are cherry blossoms to admire, who would look at carrot tops'?"

"When a man is hungry he seeks carrots and not cherry blossoms and he is more hungry than not." Koiko waited amused. She saw Sumomo drop her eyes, at a loss.

"Carrots are peasant food, Lady," Sumomo said in a small voice. "So sorry."

"Cherries are an acquired taste, as are their flowers. Carrots can take on many flavors, if properly treated." Again she waited but Sumomo still looked down. "Not in riddles, so you will not be confused, it is not sex that is really sought by men in my World, but romance—our most forbidden fruit."

Sumomo was startled. "It is?"

"Oh, yes, for us. It is poisonous. Men seek romance in your world too, most men, and it is not forbidden you, is it?"

"No."

"Your future husband is no different, he seeks romance too, wherever it is available. Better you make as much available at home as you can, for as long as you can." Koiko smiled. "Then you can have cherries *and* fine carrots. The flavors can be acquired, easily."

"Then please teach me."

"Tell me about this man, your husband-to-be."

"His name is Oda, Rokan Oda," Sumomo said at once, using the cover name Katsumata had given her. "His father is a goshi . . . and he comes from Kanagawa in Satsuma."

"And your father?"

"It is as I said, Lady. He is of the line Fujahito," she said, using her new cover surname. "They are also from a village nearby and also goshi."

"Your guardian says this Rokan Oda is important."

"He is too kind, Lady, though Oda-sama is shishi and did take part in the attack on Lord Anjo at Yedo's gates, and also killed the Elder Utani." Katsumata had told her it was safer to tell the truth where possible, the fewer the lies to remember.

"Where is he now?"

"At Yedo, Lady."

"How long do you want to stay with me?"

"For me, Lady, as long as I can. My guardian said Kyōto was dangerous for me. I cannot return home, my father disapproves of me as he had told you, as Oda-sama's parents disapprove of him, so sorry, because of me."

Koiko frowned. "That will make life impossible."

"Yes. Karma is karma and what is to be will be. Though I am of no value to anyone and believe I am unknown to the Bakufu, Sensei Katsumata approves of my Oda-sama, accepted the responsibility. He said I'm to obey you in all things."

"Better to obey your parents, Sumomo."

"Yes, I know, but my Oda-sama forbids it."

A good answer, Koiko thought, seeing the pride and the conviction. Saddened, she glanced at the half-opened window. Surely this forbidden romance would end like so many others. In suicide. Together, if Sumomo was blessed. Or her alone when, as this Oda should, he obeys his parents and takes a wife acceptable to them.

She sighed. In the garden outside, twilight was becoming night. A slight wind. "The leaves are whispering one to another. What are they saying?"

Sumomo covered her surprise and began to listen. At length she said, "So sorry, I do not know."

"Listen while I am gone. It is important to know what leaves whisper. Tonight you will stay here, Sumomo. Perhaps I will return, perhaps not. If I do then we will talk some more, and you will tell me. If not we will continue tomorrow and you will tell me then. When Teko comes back to prepare the futons tell her I want you both to compose a haiku." She thought a moment and then smiled. "A haiku about a snail."

"Hello, Koiko," Yoshi said listlessly. His back was to the wall, his hand near his sword and he wore a yukata of purple silk. Outwardly he appeared calm but she saw through him and knew him to be lonely, frightened and in need of other skills.

Her smile was enough to brighten the blackest day. At once she saw his eyes soften. Good, first hurdle. "Now," she said, with pretended gravity, "I have a poem for you":

> *It is not easy*
> *To be sure which*
> *End is which of*
> *A resting snail!*

His laugh resounded around the room.

Good, second hurdle. "I'm so pleased you allowed me to come to Kyōto with you." His eyes took on the other glow and her soul warmed. Instinctively she changed what she was going to say, that he was so handsome in the flickering night lights. Instead she said what was deep within her:

> *Those were sad times*
> *When, without you,*
> *I watched days come up*
> *And go down again.*

She was kneeling opposite him and he reached out and caught her hand. No need for words. For him or for her. Now he was at peace, tension gone, loneliness gone and all fear. And she was at peace too. So much energy expended to take him out of himself. So much revealed. Unwise to reveal so much.

You are very important to me, he was saying without saying it, speaking as lovers will.

You do me too much honor, she replied with a tiny frown. Then her fingers, delicately caressing the back of his hand said, I adore thee.

Eyes locked with eyes. She raised his hand and brushed her lips against it. Silence gripping them, beginning to hurt, hurting and then in one swift movement, she slipped over to his side and embraced him tightly. Her laugh trilled. "Too much serious is bad for me, Tora-chan!" She hugged him again, nestling into his embrace. "You make me so happy."

"Ah, no more than I," he murmured, glad the tension was broken so nicely. "You are adored and so are your poems."

"The one about the snail was by Kyorai."

He laughed. "It is by Koiko the Lily! Is, not was."

Again she nestled closer, enjoying his warmth and strength. "I nearly died when I heard about this morning."

"Life," he said simply. "I should have been more prepared but I was fascinated by the street." He told her how different it had seemed. "It was a rare experience—the feeling of invisibility—too good not to sample again, however dangerous. Does the danger add a spice to it? I will experiment in Yedo. At night it would be easier and I will train special guards to accompany me."

"Please excuse me, but I would suggest you partake of that drug sparingly."

"I mean to." His arms held her, both of them comfortable. "It could develop into that, yes, easily."

The room adjoined his sleeping quarters. Like the whole barracks complex it was masculine, with minimum furniture, the tatami first quality but in need of replacement. I won't be displeased to leave this place, he thought. Their ears caught the pad of approaching feet, his hand snaked to his sword hilt. Both of them tensed. "Sire?" a muffled voice said.

"What is it?" Yoshi said.

"So sorry to disturb you, Sire, a letter has just arrived, from Dragon's Tooth."

Without needing to be asked, Koiko went to the side of the door out of the way and stood there on guard. Yoshi readied. "Open the door, sentry," he called out. The door slid open. The sentry hesitated seeing Yoshi in a defense-attack position, sword loose in its scabbard. "Give the scroll to Lady Koiko." The sentry obeyed then went away again. When he had reached the end of the corridor and had gone through that door, Koiko closed this one. She handed him the scroll and knelt in her place opposite. He broke the seal.

The letter from his wife asked after his health and gave news that his sons and the rest of his family were well and looking forward to his return. Then the information began:

> *The prospectors have been travelling diligently with your vassal Misamoto. As yet they have found no gold but report large—the word they used was 'huge'—deposits of high-quality coal, easy to mine and near the surface. I understand them to say this is 'black gold' and could be profitably bartered with the gai-jin for money. They continue to search. We hear Anjo has been made tairō and boasts that you will soon be invited to retire from the Council of Elders. Next, the confidant you visited on the way to Kyōto tells the following: The code word he gave you about an enemy is correct and that a similar plan is ready as the enemy's state policy.*

Crimson Sky. So a lightning attack is 'State Policy'! Will my agreement with Ogama hold?

He put that question aside for later and continued reading:

> *The ronin, Ori, who became a gai-jin spy, is dead in the gai-jin camp. The other ronin, Hiraga, is believed to be there also. Your spy says also he intercepted the 'maid' you sent back, as ordered, and sent her far north to a very poor brothel. Her ronin lover was killed.*

Yoshi smiled. This was Koiko's maid who had whispered of Utani's secret tryst to her ronin shishi. Halfway to Kyōto he had dismissed her, sending her back to Yedo on some imagined slight—of course Koiko had not objected. Good, he thought. Utani is revenged in some small measure.

*Next, the Gyokoyama: I have completed money matters.
May I use the coal possibility as a further pledge for any
armaments ordered? Perhaps we should try to deal with the
gai-jin direct, perhaps using Misamoto? Please give me your
counsel. Sire, your presence and wise advice are greatly
missed. Last, so sorry, famine has begun.*

Yoshi reread it. Knowing Hosaki so well, the way she had used
'further pledge' meant that the negotiation had been rough and the
price high. Never mind, next year there will be no famine and the
Gyokoyamas, if they live that long in lands I control, will be repaid.

He looked up at Koiko. She was staring into space, lost in dreams he
knew he could never share. "Koiko?"

"Oh. Yes, Sire?"

"What were you thinking about?"

"What leaves whisper to leaves."

Intrigued he said, "It depends on the tree."

She smiled sweetly. "A maple, a blood-red maple."

"In what season?"

"Ninth month."

"If they were watching us they whispered, 'Soon we fall, never to
return, But they are blessed. They grow on the tree of life. Their blood
our blood.' "

She clapped her hands, smiling at him. "Perfect. And if it was a pine
in spring?"

"Not now, Koiko-chan, later."

Seeing the sudden seriousness, she became serious too. "Bad news,
Sire?"

"No, and yes. I will leave at dawn."

"For Dragon's Tooth?"

He hesitated and she wondered if she had made a mistake in asking,
but he was wondering what to do about her. Earlier, weighing the need
for another forced march, he had decided to leave her and let her
follow as quickly as she could. Now, looking at her, he did not want her
to be away from him. Her palanquin would hold them back. She could
ride though not well enough and such a journey would be arduous.

Either way the plan he had agreed with Akeda would stay the same:
'The first party of forty men, with a double wearing a set of my light
armor, leaves just before dawn and heads leisurely and obviously for
the North Road. Halfway to Yedo they will turn back and return here,

my "double" vanished. The second party, mine, with the men I brought from Yedo, will leave shortly after the first and head rapidly for the Tokaidō. Forced march, under the same captain—I will be disguised as an ordinary cavalry samurai and will remain so until I am safely in Yedo Castle.'

'Very dangerous, Sire,' General Akeda said heavily.

'Yes. You will watch Ogama, and hope. It is to his advantage I succeed in curbing Anjo.'

'Yes. But you are an irresistible target outside, an easy one. Look at what happened today. Let me go with you.'

'Impossible. Listen, if Ogama decides to mount his strike he will attack here first—better expect it. You must repel him whatever the cost.'

'I will not fail in that, Sire,' the old general said.

And I will not fail to reach Yedo, Yoshi thought with equal confidence. As to the attack, it only reminds me it was not the first and will not be the last.

He saw Koiko watching him. It is easier to be balanced when she is near me. The lamplight was glinting on her lips and in her eyes, and he saw the curve of her cheekbones and column of her neck, the raven hair, the perfect folds of her kimono and under-kimonos showing slightly from her white skin. Smooth curves, her posture flawless, and her two hands held like flowers in her lap of azure silk.

She would have to travel light. No maids. And make do with whatever was available from Inn to Inn. That would displease her for she likes perfection. Perhaps she would balk at such inconsiderate and, for her, unnecessary haste. He remembered the first time he had suggested that.

It was not so long ago, just after he had decided to obtain her exclusivity and had told the mama-san, Meikin, to leave with her for Dragon's Tooth to make arrangements with his wife at once—Hosaki had, correctly, deemed it wise to see the mama-san and Koiko herself as the financial commitment would be huge.

Meikin had told him the journey would take at least a week to plan, Koiko would of course be taking her own hairdresser and masseuse and three maids.

'Ridiculous,' he had said impatiently. 'So many staff are not necessary for such a short journey and an unnecessary expense. You will both leave at once.'

They had obeyed at once. Without attendants. It had taken them three days to reach the first way station outside Yedo, three days for the second. Angry, he had easily ridden the same distance from dawn to dusk.

'Lord Yoshi,' Meikin had said, greeting him lavishly, feigning surprise. 'How pleasant to see you.'

'What is all the delay for?'

'Delay, Sire? We were ordered to leave at once. We are doing exactly as you ordered.'

'But why are you taking so long?'

'So long, Sire? But you did not order us to make a forced march.'

'You will hurry up,' he snapped, noticing how she belabored 'order.' 'Tell Koiko I wish to see her.'

The mama-san had bowed and hurried away to Koiko's quarters, leaving him seething. When at length she returned she said happily, 'Koiko-san will be honored to see you, Sire, instantly, Sire, the moment she can arrange a suitable maid to help her with her hair. She regrets it would be impertinent to receive you without the due preparation an honored, revered person such as you would expect, and adds, humbly, "Please be kind enough to wait, she will be as quick as she can when the maids arrive. . . ." '

Sourly he had glared at her, knowing that as much as he would insist, he would have to wait. His only recourse was to storm into Koiko's room and lose total face and destroy any chance that she would ever be available to him again.

Who does she think she is? he had wanted to bellow.

He had not. He had smiled to himself. When you purchase a rare sword, you expect it to be made of the finest steel, with the best cutting edge and a fire of its own. He nodded coolly. 'Send for her own maids—and hairdresser and masseuse—from Yedo very quickly indeed. It's your fault they are not here, you should have told me they were important to the Lady Koiko. She is correct not to see me improperly. I will expect this never to happen again!'

Meikin had flooded him with apologies and bowed him away abjectly, and he laughed all the way back to Yedo, having bested them, making them lose face and giving them both a firm warning: *Do not play games with me again.*

Koiko's eyes had never left his face, watching and waiting. "When you smile, Sire, it makes me very happy."

"What am I smiling about?"

"Me, Sire," she said simply. "I think because I help you laugh at life, and though Man's span on earth is but a quick hunt for shelter before the rains come down, you allow me to provide, from time to time, a shelter from the rain."

"Yes, you do," he said contentedly. If I leave her here I won't see her for weeks, and life is only a cherry blossom exposed to a vagrant wind that knows no master—my life, hers, all life. "I do not want to leave you here."

"It will be good to be home again."

In his secret heart, he thought about Meikin. I have not forgotten she is a shishi informant as your maid was. Stupid of the mama-san to risk you, risk me thinking you were also part of those murdering scum. "Do any of your maids ride, Koiko?"

"I do not know, Sire. I imagine at least one would."

"If you were to come with me you would have to ride too, with just one maid, and travel light, a palanquin would delay me. I can easily arrange for you to travel leisurely with your household if you prefer."

"Thank you, but since you would prefer me to be with you your preference is mine, of course. If I become a burden, then it is easy for you to decide. I am honored you asked me."

"But is there a maid, an acceptable maid who can also ride? If not then you must follow as soon as possible," he said, again giving her the opportunity to decline gracefully without offense.

"There is one, Sire," she said on a sudden impulse, "a new *maiko*, not quite a maid, but an apprentice and a little more. Her name is Sumomo Fujahito, daughter of a Satsuma goshi, ward of an old friend, a client who was good to me years ago."

He listened as she told him about Sumomo, and was too well versed in the customs of the Floating World to ask about the other client. Intrigued, he sent for the girl. "So, Sumomo, your father disapproves of your future marriage?"

"Yes, Lord."

"It is unforgivable not to obey your parents."

"Yes, Lord."

"You will obey them."

"Yes, Lord." She looked at him fearlessly. "I have already told them, humbly, that I will obey but that I will die before I marry any other man."

"Your father should have ordered you into a nunnery for such impertinence."

After a pause she muttered, "Yes, Lord."

"Why are you here in Kyōto and not at home?"

"I—I was sent here to be retrained by my guardian."

"He has done a very poor job, has he not?"

"So sorry, Lord." She bowed her head to the tatami, politely and with grace, but he was certain not with any penitence. Why do I waste my time? he thought. Perhaps because I am accustomed to absolute obedience from everyone, except Koiko who must be maneuvered like an unstable boat in a high wind, perhaps because it might be diverting to curb this young person, to train her to the fist like the fledgling peregrine she seems to be, to use her beak and claws for my purposes, not for her lord of creation, Oda.

"What will you do when this Oda, this Satsuma goshi, eventually decides to obey his parents as is his duty, and take another woman to wife?"

"If he will accept me as a consort, even without intimacy I will be content. As an occasional woman, I will be content. The moment he tires of me or dismisses me, so sorry, that is the day I will die."

"You are a stupid young woman."

"Yes, Lord. Please excuse me, that is my karma." She dropped her eyes and remained motionless.

Amused, he glanced momentarily at Koiko who waited for him to decide. "Say your liege lord, Sanjiro, orders you to marry another man and orders you not to commit seppuku."

"I am samurai, I will obey without question," she said proudly, "as I will obey my guardian and Oda-sama. But on my way to the wedding feast there may be a regrettable accident."

He grunted. "Do you have sisters?"

She was startled. "Yes, Lord. Three."

"Are they as stupid and difficult as you are?"

"They . . . no, Sire."

"Can you ride?"

"Yes, Sire."

"Well enough to journey to Yedo?"

"Yes, Sire."

"Koiko, are you sure she can please you if I agree?"

"I believe so, Sire. I am only afraid I may fail you with my lack of skill."

"You can never fail me, Koiko-chan. So, Sumomo, you are sure you will be able to please the Lady Koiko?"

"Yes, Sire, and I will protect her with my life."

"Will you also improve your manners, become less arrogant, more womanly and less like Domu-Gozen?" This was a famous woman samurai, mistress to a Shōgun, a vicious killer, who, centuries ago, rode into battle with her equally violent Shōgun lover.

He saw her eyes widen and she became even younger. "Oh, I'm not like her, Lord, not at all—I would give anything to be even a tiny little bit like the Lady Koiko. Anything."

He hid his laugh as Sumomo gorged on this first morsel he had tossed to her. "You may go. I'll decide later."

When they were alone again he chuckled. "A wager, Koiko? A new kimono that Sumomo will be trained by the time we reach Yedo—if I decide to bring you both with me."

"Trained in what way, Sire?"

"That she will contentedly agree to return to her parents and obey them and marry without seppuku."

Koiko shook her head smiling. "So sorry, whatever the wager I am afraid you would lose, Sire."

That she could consider him making an error of judgment lost some of his good humor. "A kimono against a favor," Yoshi said sharply, not meaning to be so sharp.

"I accept," she said at once with a laugh, "but only on the understanding that with the gift of the kimono, you accept the favor back from me that you would have asked."

His eyes crinkled with admiration with the way she had twisted his mistake into a pleasantry. It was a mistake to attempt a wager, any wager. And a mistake to be confident over the wiles of a woman—a certain path to disaster.

38

SAKONOSHITA VILLAGE

Saturday, 6th December:

ON THE TOKAIDŌ ROAD, SOME forty miles eastwards from Kyōto, in the mountains, was the Sixth way station, the village of Sakonoshita, and as dusk began to fall, the last of the travellers and porters, bent against a raw wind, were hurrying to pass the barrier before it closed. All were weary and anxious for hot food, hot saké and warmth, even the half-dozen barrier guards who stamped their straw-sandaled feet against the cold, checking identity papers at random. "It'll snow tonight," one grumbled. "I hate winter, hate the cold, hate this posting."

"You hate everything."

"Not everything. I like eating and fornicating. In the next life I want to be born son to an Osaka moneylending rice merchant. Then I can eat and drink and fornicate only the best, and be warm while my father buys me hirazamurai status, or at least goshi—not just a stinking pissed-on ashigaru."

"Dreamer! You'll be reborn a landless peasant, or a bending toy boy in a tenth-rank brothel. Close the barrier."

"It's not dark yet."

"Let any stragglers freeze or pay the usual."

"If the captain hears you, you will find yourself in the North Island where they say your cock freezes when you try to piss." The guard looked down the road that curled away to Kyōto, now empty, with a darkening, ominous sky above. A squall tugged at their straw over-mantles. "Hurry up, oaf," he called out impatiently at the last man, a half-naked porter staggering past with his heavy load. He lowered the first bar, his face chapped by the wind, and then the second bar, making the barrier firm, and turned away for shelter and hot soup.

"Hey, look there!" A phalanx of riders had trotted into view around the far corner. "Open the bars!"

"Let them wait. They're late." The guard used the back of his hand to clean away a persistent nose dribble, squinting against the squall. With the other guards he scanned the riders, thirty or forty he estimated, too tired to count. No banners, so unimportant. Travel-stained, their ponies lathered. They rode in a cluster around two women. The women rode astride, and wore heavy clothes and large hats with veils tied under their chins. He laughed to himself. They'll never get rooms tonight, nor sleep snug, not with the village full. Piss on them.

As they arrived, Captain Abeh in the lead called out, "Hey there, open up!"

"I'm coming, I'm coming," the guard growled, taking his time, and wished he hadn't. Abeh was out of his saddle in an instant. The blow smashed him senseless.

"Get this barrier open!" Abeh said, voice grating. Two riders had dismounted beside him, one of them Yoshi, a scarf around his face, the other Wataki, whom Yoshi had rewarded for helping to save his life. An officer stormed out of the guard house, gaping at his prone, unconscious man. "What's going on? You're under arrest."

"Get this barrier open!"

"You are under arrest."

Abeh strode around the barrier, no mistaking the danger. "Open the barrier. Hurry up." Guards rushed to obey but the officer blustered, "You will all show identity papers an—"

"Listen, monkey," Captain Abeh shoved his face at the officer, who froze, "important guests require important manners and no delays on a cold night and it is not yet sundown." With that he bashed him on the side of his head, the officer reeled, and a second savage blow collapsed him in a heap. To the stupefied sentries Abeh rapped, "Tell this fool to report to me at dawn or I will find him and use him for sword practice, and the rest of you!" He waved his party through then mounted and cantered after them.

Within minutes he had arranged the best quarters in the best Inn. Those who had reserved them bowed as they fled, grateful for the privilege of vacating them—rich merchants, other samurai, none of whom were prepared for a fight to the death that would have surely erupted.

Yoshi took off his hat and scarf when the shoji doors were closed. The rotund patron of this, the Inn of Pleasant Dreams, was on his knees beside the door, head bowed, waiting for orders. His mind was ringing with curses that he had not been forewarned about these late arrivals, cursing them for disrupting his tranquility as they would surely continue to disrupt it—whoever they were. He recognized none of them and found it extraordinary they flew no banners, wore simple Bakufu uniforms and symbols, used no names, noticing that even this samurai, now treated with so much respect in private by the vile Captain and given his most expensive rooms, was not addressed by name or rank. And who are the two women? A daimyo's wife and maid? Or just two high-class whores? The news of their arrival had sped around the Inn. At once he had offered a reward to the maid who discovered their identity.

"Your name, landlord?" Yoshi asked.

"Ichi-jo, Sire." He thought 'sire' the safest title.

"First a bath, then massage, then food."

"Instantly, Sire. May I have the honor of showing you the way myself?"

"Just a bath maid. I will eat here. Thank you, you may go."

The man bowed unctuously, heaved himself to his feet, and waddled away.

Captain Abeh confirmed security arrangements: sentries would surround this eight-room bungalow. Koiko's rooms were down the veranda, which would be guarded at all times. Between her quarters and Yoshi's would be a room with two more guards.

"Good, Captain. Now get some sleep."

"Thank you, but I am not tired, sir."

Yoshi had ordered that he was to be treated as an ordinary goshi, except in private, when the only honorific they would use was 'sir.' "You will get some sleep. I need you alert. We've many more days yet." Yoshi saw a flicker behind the young man's eyes, bloodshot from fatigue. "Yes?"

Uneasily Abeh said, "Please excuse me but if it is urgent for you to reach Yedo, it would be safer for you to be escorted ahead of the Lady."

"Get some sleep," Yoshi said. "Tired men make mistakes. It was also a mistake to crush the officer. The sentry was enough." Silently he dismissed him. Abeh bowed and left, cursing himself for his stupidity in volunteering something so obvious. Three times they had made unnecessary stops today, twice yesterday. He checked all the sentries and stretched out in his room. In moments he was fast asleep.

After the bath and massage and food eaten slowly though he was very hungry, Yoshi strolled down the corridor. The decision to bring Koiko had been easy. It had occurred to him that she would be a perfect decoy and had told Akeda to see that everyone knew he was just sending her under escort to Yedo, while he went separately.

'Perfect,' Akeda had said.

He went into her outer room. It was empty, the inner shoji closed. "Koiko?" he called out and settled himself on one of the two cushions. The shoji slid open. Sumomo was kneeling, holding it for Koiko, eyes on the tatami. Her hair was up in Kyōto style, her eyebrows plucked and a little makeup on her lips. A welcome improvement, he thought.

The moment Koiko saw him she knelt and both women bowed in unison. He noticed that Sumomo bowed perfectly, a pattern of Koiko's grace, and this pleased him too, no sign that the hard riding had affected Sumomo in any way. He returned the salutation. The beds of down futons were already made up.

As Koiko came smiling into this room and Sumomo closed the shoji behind her, she said, "So, Tora-chan, how are you?" Her voice was sweet as usual, her coiffure perfect as usual, but, as never before, the same kimono as the previous night.

Uneasily he noticed a flicker of discomfort as she settled herself. "The riding is too much for you?"

"Oh, no, the first few days are bound to be a little difficult but soon I will be as tough as . . ." Her eyes were merry. "As tough as Domu-Gozen."

He smiled, but knew he had made an error of judgment. Yesterday three way stations were covered, the same today, but on neither day had he made the distance he wanted. The riding was exhausting her. I made a mistake I should not have made. She will never complain and will go beyond her limit, may even do herself harm.

Do I need to hurry? Yes. Will she be safe in a palanquin with a ten-man escort? Yes. Would it be wise to reduce my bodyguard by that many? No. I could send for more men from Yedo tonight but that would cost me five or six days. My instinct tells me to hurry, the gai-jin are unpredictable, so is Anjo, so is Ogama—did he not threaten: 'If *you* don't deal with them, *I will.*'

"Koiko-chan. Let us go to bed. Tomorrow is tomorrow."

* * *

In the night Sumomo lay on warm futons and under coverlets in their outer room, one arm under her head, sleepy but not tired, and tranquil. From the inner room she could hear Yoshi's regular breathing, Koiko's hardly perceptible. Outside were night sounds. A dog barking somewhere, night insects, wind in the foliage, occasionally a guard muttering to another, pots and pans clattering from the early kitchen detail.

Her first sleep had been fine. The two days of exercise and vigorous massage and freedom had made her feel vibrant. And, too, the compliments from Koiko about the way she had arranged her hair tonight as Teko had taught her—and how to add color to her lips—had also pleased her.

Everything was succeeding better than she had dreamed. Her immediate objective had been achieved. She had been accepted. They were on the way to Yedo. To Hiraga. She was an innermost part of Yoshi's entourage, poised. Katsumata had said, 'Do not be impetuous. Under no circumstance put yourself at risk unless there is a chance of escape. Close to him you are of enormous value, do not ruin that or involve Koiko.'

'She will not know about me?'

'Only what I told her, the same that you know.'

'Then she is already involved, no? So sorry, I mean, because of her Yoshi may accept me.'

'He will make that decision, not her. No, Sumomo, she is not your accomplice. If she was to discover your real connection, particularly about Hiraga, and your possible purpose, she would stop it—she would have to stop it.'

'Possible purpose? Please, what is my prime duty?'

'To be ready. Better a waiting sword than a corpse.'

I have no sword, she thought. Perhaps I could grab one from a guard if I could surprise him. I have three shuriken, poison-tipped, hidden in my bundle beside me, and of course my obi knife always on my person. More than enough, with surprise. Eeee, life is very strange. Strange that I should prefer being on my own with my own mission—so alien to our normal way of life, always being part of a unit, thinking as one, agreeing as one in our culture of consensus. I enjoyed being with the unit of shishi, and yet . . .

And yet to be honest—'Always be honest to yourself, Sumomo-chan,' her father had said, over and over, 'that is your way to the future, for a leader.' To be honest I found it difficult to curb my urge to lead them, even shishi, and to bend them to the correct path and thinking.

Is that my karma, to lead? Or is it to die unfulfilled because it is truly stupid for a woman to wish to be a leader in the world of Nippon. Strange to want the impossible. Why am I like that, not like other women? Is it because father had no sons and treated us, his daughters, as sons, telling us to be strong and to stand up and never to be afraid, even allowing me, over Mother's advice, to follow Hiraga and his equally impossible star . . . ?

She sat up in the futons a moment, tousling her hair to try to clear her head and prevent her mind from so many new and untrammeled thoughts, then lay back again. But sleep would not arrive, only permutations of Hiraga and Koiko and Yoshi and Katsumata, and her.

Strange about Yoshi: 'We must kill him and the Shōgun,' Katsumata had said, over the years, so many times, and Hiraga, 'not for themselves but because of what they represent. Power will never return to the Emperor while they remain alive. So they must go, chiefly Yoshi—he is the glue that binds the Shōgunate. *Sonno-joi* is our beacon, any sacrifice must be made to achieve it!'

A pity to kill Lord Toranaga. Another pity that he is a good man and not vile, not vile like Anjo, not that I have ever seen him. Perhaps Anjo is also a kind man and everything said about him merely lies of jealous fools.

In this short time I have seen Yoshi for what he is: Dynamic, kind, strong, wise and impassioned. And Koiko? How wonderful she is, though how sad, so sad to be so doomed.

Remember what she said: 'The curse of our World is that as much as you bind and train yourself with all manner of defenses and resolves to treat a client as just a client, from time to time one appears who turns your head into jelly, your resolve into froth and your loins into a fireball. When it happens it is frighteningly, gloriously terrible. You are lost, Sumomo. If the gods favor you, you die together. Or you die when he leaves, or you allow yourself to stay alive but you are dead even so.'

'I'm not going to allow that to happen when I'm grown,' Teko had piped up, overhearing them. 'Not me. Have you been turned to jelly, Mistress?'

Koiko had laughed. 'Many times, child, and you have forgotten one of your most important lessons: to close your ears when others are talking. Off to bed with you.'

Has Koiko's head really been turned to jelly? Yes.

As a woman I know she considers Lord Yoshi more than a client, however much she tries to hide it. Where will it end? Sadly, so very sad. He will never make her consort.

And me? Will it be the same with me? Yes, I think so—what I told

Lord Yoshi was the truth: I will have no other husband but Hiraga. "It's the truth . . ." she muttered aloud, and that brought her out of the downward spiral. "Stop it," she murmured, following the method of her childhood, of her mother crooning: 'Think only good thoughts, little one, for this is the World of Tears soon enough, think bad thoughts and in a blink of the eye you are in the black pit of despair. Think good thoughts . . .'

She made the effort and turned her mind: only Hiraga makes life worthwhile.

A shiver went through her body as a new concept sprang at her with a shocking strength of reality: Foolish this *sonno-joi*! It is just a slogan. As if it will change anything. A few leaders will change, that is all. Will the new ones be any better? No, except yes, if Hiraga is one, perhaps yes, if Katsumata is one but, ah, so sorry, they will not live that long.

Then why follow them?

A tear slid down her cheek. Because Hiraga turns my head to jelly, my loins . . .

In the dawn Yoshi slid out of bed and padded through to the outer room, his sleeping yukata tucked up, breath visible in the cold air. Koiko stirred, saw that he was all right, and dozed off again. In the outer room Sumomo's futons and bedclothes were already packed away in the side cupboard, the low table already set for their breakfast, their two cushions neatly in place.

Outside the cold was sharper. He stepped into straw sandals and went along the veranda to the outhouse, nodded to the waiting manservant and chose an unoccupied bucket in the line of buckets and began to relieve himself. His flow was strong and that pleased him. Other men stood beside him. He paid no attention to them, or they to him. Idly he directed the stream at the swarming, ever present flies, not expecting to drown one of them.

When he had finished he moved to the other part and squatted over a vacant hole in the bench, men and some women either side, Sumomo one of them. In his mind he was alone, his ears and eyes and nostrils shut tight against their presence as theirs were against everyone else.

This imperative ability was painstakingly cultivated from infancy: 'You must work at this like nothing else, little one, you must, or your life will be unbearable' was drummed into him, as it was every child. 'Here where we live cheek by cheek, children and parents and grand-parents and maids and more in each tiny house, where all walls are made of paper, privacy has to be cultivated in your head and can only exist there, your own and also as the essential politeness to others. Only this way can you be tranquil, only this way can you be civilized, only this way can you remain sane.'

Absently, he waved at the flies. Once when he was young he had lost his temper at two or three that were plaguing him and had tried to smash them to pieces. It had earned him an immediate smack around the face, his cheeks burning with hurt, but more with shame that he had caused his mother grief, and her need to administer the punishment.

'So sorry, my son,' she said softly. 'Flies are like sunrise and sunset, inevitable, except they can be a torment—if you allow them to be. You must learn to dismiss them. Every day, for part of each day for as many days as necessary, please, stand there and let them crawl on your face and hands without moving. Until they become nothing. Flies must become nothing—use your will, that is what you are given it for. They must become nothing to you, then they'll not cause you to ruin your harmony or, worse, ruin the harmony of others . . .'

Now, sitting there, he felt the odd fly on his back and face. They did not offend him.

Quickly he was done. The rice paper was of good quality. Feeling very alive and well, he held out his hands for the servant to pour water over them. When his hands were clean, he doused water from another container onto his face, shivered, accepted a small towel and dried himself, stepped back onto the veranda and consciously opened his senses.

Around him the Inn was stirring, the few ponies being saddled and groomed, men, women, children, porters already eating and chatting noisily, or leaving for the next stage of their journey, to or from Kyōto. In the common area near the entrance gate, Abeh was checking men and equipment. When he saw Yoshi he joined him.

Because people were about he did not bow, finding that very hard. His uniform was smart and he was refreshed. "Good morning." He just managed to bite back the 'sir.' "We are ready to leave whenever it pleases you."

"After breakfast. Arrange a palanquin for Lady Koiko."

"At once. For ponies, or porters?"

"Ponies." Yoshi strolled back to his quarters and told Koiko she would not be riding today, that he would see how much progress they made and then, tonight, he would decide. Sumomo would ride as usual.

By evening they barely made two stations.

HAMAMATSU

Yoshi chose the Inn of the Cranes for the night, neither the best nor the worst in the village of Hamamatsu—a pleasing collection of houses and Inns straddling the Tokaidō, renowned for its saké, where the road curled down towards the sea.

After eating alone as usual, Yoshi went to join Koiko—if they ate together invariably, by custom, she would take almost nothing, having intentionally eaten beforehand so she could concentrate on his needs. Tonight it was his pleasure to play a game of *Go*. This was a complex game of strategy, played with counters and similar to draughts.

Both of them were good players, but Koiko was a virtuoso, so much so that she could, almost always, win or lose at whim. This made the game doubly difficult for her. He had ordered her never to lose deliberately, but he himself was a bad loser. If she won on a wrong day he would sulk. A win for him on one of his bad days would get him out of any ill humor.

Tonight he won. Narrowly. "Oh, Sire, you've destroyed me!" she said. "And I thought I had you beaten!" They were in her inner room, sitting with their legs in the small pit under the low table with a tiny charcoal brazier in it, and a thick padded cloth over the table tucked around them to keep drafts out and the heat in. "Are you warm enough?"

"Yes, thank you, Koiko. How are your aches and pains?"

"Oh, I have none. The masseuse was very good tonight." She called out, "Sumomo, saké and tea, please."

In the outer room Sumomo fetched the flask and teapot from another brazier, opened the shoji, and brought them in. She served both well and Koiko nodded with satisfaction.

He said, "Have you learned the tea ceremony, Sumomo?"

"Yes, Sire," Sumomo said, "but—but I am afraid I am sadly lacking in skill."

"Lord Yoshi is a master," Koiko said, and sipped the saké, glad for it. Her rump and back ached from the day's jolting in the palanquin, her thighs from the two days of riding, and her head from the effort of losing while appearing to covet victory. All of which she hid, and the fact that her spirits were down over the lack of progress today. Clearly this had disappointed him. But then, she thought, we both knew another forced march was not possible. He must go on and I will follow. It will be good to be without him for a while. This life is wearing, however wonderful he is.

They drank peacefully. Then he said, "Tomorrow, early, I will go on with thirty men, leaving ten with you, Abeh in charge. You will follow me to Yedo leisurely."

"Of course. With your permission, may I follow as quickly as possible?"

He smiled. "That would please me, but only as long as you arrive not aching, either in body or in spirit."

"Even if I was, your smile would instantly cure me. Another game?"

"Yes, but not *Go!*"

She laughed. "Then I must make some preparations." She got up and went to the outer room, closing the shoji after her. He heard her talking to Sumomo but paid them no attention, his mind occupied with tomorrow, Yedo and gai-jin.

Their voices died away as they went out. He finished his saké, enjoying it, then walked into the innermost room where the futons and padded coverlets were spread over impeccable tatami. Winter landscapes and colors were the dominant decorations. He took off his padded yukata, shivered, and slipped under the eiderdown.

When Koiko returned he heard her pottering in the outer room, then she came in and she went straight to the bathroom where there were containers for the night, should they be needed, jugs of water to drink, and others for washing. "I sent Sumomo to sleep in another room tonight," she called out to him, "and asked Abeh to post a guard outside with orders not to disturb you till dawn."

"Why did you do that?"

She came back into the room. "This is our last night for a time—I mentioned to him I would not be travelling with you tomorrow—and I wanted you totally to myself." Leisurely she stepped out of her kimono and snuggled beside him.

Though he had seen her naked many times, and felt her touch many times, and slept with her many times, tonight was many times better than it had ever been.

KYŌTO

In the palace in Kyōto, one of the Lord Chancellor's spies knocked on his bedroom door, waking him, and handed him the carrier pigeon message container. "This has just been intercepted, Lord."

The tiny cylinder was addressed to Chief Bakufu Palace Advisor, Saito, and bore the personal seal of *Tairō* Nori Anjo. He hesitated, then broke the seal with a manicured nail.

Anjo had sent the message at dawn:

The gai-jin leader has insolently rejected the Imperial command to leave Yokohama and they are preparing to invade us. Draft the Order for National Mobilization for the Emperor's signature which, with this document, I formally request the Emperor to sign at once. Then send copies urgently to all daimyos. Make arrangements for Shōgun Nobusada to return to Yedo at once to head our forces, the Princess Yazu can, preferably should, stay in Kyōto. Lord Yoshi is formally required to return at once.

The Lord Chancellor thought a while, smugly decided Saito would be overruled and the Emperor advised never to sign a mobilization order. With great care he replaced the message and resealed the tube with his secret duplicate seal.

"Put it back, make sure it is delivered," he said, and when alone, he chuckled. War! Good. Anjo was the perfect choice for *tairō.* They will all drown in their own urine, along with all gai-jin, and Yoshi, all of them.

Except the Princess. She will stay, to become a widow—the sooner the better.

39

HAMAMATSU VILLAGE

Monday, 8th December:

SUMOMO AWOKE WELL BEFORE first light. Her dreams had been bad. She was no longer on the Tokaidō with Koiko and Lord Yoshi but back in Kyōto, chased by Bakufu soldiers led by Abeh into the trap of the burning shishi house, screams everywhere, blood everywhere, guns firing, in panic squeezing down into the narrow tunnel after Takeda and Katsumata, the hole barely big enough, crawling after them, the sides encroaching, scraping her and becoming narrower. Not enough air to breathe, filled with dust. Takeda's feet ahead as he wriggled onward, gasping, someone or something just behind her, then Takeda becoming Yoshi, kicking at her, stopping her then vanishing—with nothing up ahead but an earth coffin.

When her heart slowed and eyes could focus in the shaded light of the oil flame, she saw one of the guards watching her from his futons next to hers. Last night she had accompanied Koiko to talk to Abeh and he had told her to sleep in this communal room, plenty of space for her to one side—a perfectly satisfactory arrangement. Four guards were using it, two sleeping and two on duty. There she had made a bed, not easily to sleep, her mind in turmoil for she had overheard Yoshi telling Koiko they would not travel onward with him, and overheard Koiko saying to Abeh, 'Lord Yoshi has decided from tomorrow I, and my party, will follow leisurely.'

'What arrangements does he want made, Lady?'

'I believe he said he wants to leave you and ten men to guide me to Yedo, so sorry to be a problem.'

'It is no problem for me, Lady, so long as he is safe.'

Safe, and out of reach, Sumomo had thought, dismayed by the change in plan. So much could go wrong between now and Yedo.

Eventually she had slept. To dream. Normally she did not dream. Last thing at night and in the morning she would always say a prayer, *Namu Amida Butsu,* just the name of the Buddha Amida, which was enough if there was a god to pray to. Last night she had forgotten. Now, silently, she said the words, and closed her eyes.

In moments she was again in the shishi hut.

That had been the worst experience of her life, the attack without warning, gunfire through the walls and in the same instant the head of the youth beside her exploded, no time for the lad even to shout but others did, partly in panic, partly in agony as random bullets poured at them, Katsumata paralyzed for a moment, then directing the defense, ordering some to charge out the front, others the back. Both charges driven back, she not knowing where to hide, knowing all was lost, fire beginning and more screams and more blood and this the end, *Namu Amida Butsu, Namu Amida Butsu,* then hands grabbing her roughly, shoving her down into the hole after the escaping Takeda—who, raving, had dragged another man out of the way, as Katsumata had torn someone else away—as her savior shishi, whose face she never saw, was murdered in his turn and a fight ensued that blocked the escape until it was too late.

Somehow out of that hate-filled darkness into the open air. Fleeing, their panic run going on and on until, chests bursting, Katsumata lead them tortuously to his haven of last resort. Iwakura's back door.

Immediately a council of war with the shishi there. 'I suggest we scatter for the time being,' Katsumata had said. 'We'll regroup and meet in the spring, third or fourth month. In the spring we will start a new offensive.'

'Why wait?' someone asked.

'Because we're betrayed, because there's a spy in our midst, or amongst our patrons. *We are betrayed.* We must conserve and scatter.'

And so they had. 'Sumomo, you'll go to Koiko . . .'

But before that her disorientation had been vast, unaccountable tears, rushing heartbeat, too easily in panic. 'It will pass, Sumomo,' Katsumata had said.

Again he had been right. He had given her a draft that had made her sleep, and calmed her. By the time she saw Koiko she was like before, almost but not quite. 'When you feel the fear returning, just take a little sip of the medicine,' he had said. 'In a week or two you will be perfect again. Always remember, *sonno-joi* needs you perfect. . . .'

She came out of her reverie, sweating again, the fear coming on again. It was still night. Her fingers reached for her bundle beside her head that held the small bottle. But the bundle was not there. She had not brought it with her when she had changed rooms. Never mind, she thought, I do not need it, I can do without it.

She repeated that several times, twisting in her bed, the quilts damp and clammy around her. Then she noticed the guard still watching her.

"Bad dreams, *neh*?" he whispered, his voice kind.

She nodded silently.

"I could give you good dreams." He moved his quilt aside, invitingly. She shook her head. He shrugged and turned over and forgot her, considering her stupid to reject such pleasure. Not offended she turned her back too, just a little amused. Her hand moved to her obi knife in its sheath at her waist. Its touch gave her the peace she needed. A last *Namu Amida Butsu*.

She closed her eyes and slept without dreams.

Koiko was pleasantly awake. It was not quite dawn. Yoshi slept peacefully beside her. It was nice to lie there, drifting, knowing she would not have to endure another day's discomfort in a palanquin, being bumped from side to side, because of unseemly haste. And also because her night had been tranquil. Yoshi had slept solidly. Occasionally a small snoring snuffle would tweak him but that did not disturb her. 'Train your ears, Ladies,' the retired courtesan would cackle toothlessly and endlessly to all *maiko* in the school, 'your working life will be spent with old men. All men snore, but old men really snore, but old men really pay—the young ones take your flowers and snore anyway.'

Of all the men she had slept with, Yoshi was the most serene while asleep. Awake he was the most difficult. To stay ahead of. To satisfy. Not physically. Physically he was strong and practiced and as much as she was trained to be uninvolved within an embrace, he would guide her so she too, most evenings, would gain the sheen of pleasure.

Katsumata was more of a magician. He caressed her imagination and thoughts, stimulating her beyond anything she could have imagined. He was delighted when she mastered a new skill—like training her ears to hear underspoken words: "That is where the golden knowledge is, the important parts, signs of danger, of safety, of what is within the secret heart within the secret heart. Remember, all of us here, men and women, have three hearts, one for all the world to see, one for their family, and one for themselves alone. Certain men have six hearts. Yoshi is one of these. He is your goal, the one for whom you must be the foil.'

She chuckled to herself, remembering how she had said that Lord Yoshi was completely beyond reach and Katsumata had smiled that smile of his and told her to be patient, 'You have time enough. You are eighteen, there is not much more I can teach you. You must begin to expand yourself. Like every serious student, follow the most important law for all students: repay your teacher by making it your duty to surpass him! Be patient, Koiko, at the correct time your mama-san and I will ensure the Lord Yoshi becomes aware of you . . .'

And they had. Within the year. The first invitation to the castle six months and five days ago. Racing heart and fearful she would fail, but not really. She was prepared and had done her duty to her teacher.

But am I guide enough for Yoshi? I know he enjoys me and my company and my mind. Where should I guide him? Katsumata never said, just told me that that will become clear. 'Sonno-joi sums it up. Bind Lord Yoshi to you. Help him change. Gradually you will help him move even more to our side. Never forget, he is not enemy, on the contrary, he is vital to us, he will head the new Bakufu of loyal samurai, as tairō—there will no longer be any need for a Shōgun or Shōgunate—with our new and permanent Council of Samurai helping him . . .'

I wonder what it will be like in the new era, if I will live to see it, she thought, lying there comfortably. Now, what about Sumomo?

It had been completely unnecessary to send her to another room—as if it mattered that she was next door, she would not be listening to their cries or thrashing about. That was not the reason. When Yoshi told Koiko quietly she would not be going on with him, she thought she had heard movements in the outer room, as though Sumomo had shifted closer and was actually trying to overhear what they were saying—an astonishing invasion of privacy, and bad manners.

Only a nasty busybody would do such a thing, she had thought. Or a spy. Ah! Is Katsumata dispassionately playing one of his intricate games within games, using me to wheedle a spy in to watch my Tora-chan and me? I will deal with her tomorrow, meanwhile she can sleep elsewhere.

When this had been arranged, telling Sumomo only that Lord Yoshi preferred to be alone, she came back and quickly searched Sumomo's bundle, not knowing why, for she was not certain the girl had actually tried to spy on them.

There was nothing unusual in there. A few clothes, a bottle of some kind of medicine, nothing else. The neatly folded day kimono was ordinary and merited only a cursory glance. Relieved, she had retied the bundle. As to the bottle . . . surely it could not be some kind of poison?

Before rejoining Yoshi she had resolved to make sure that it wasn't. Sumomo would take some. Never wrong to provide against a potential danger. Yoshi had said, 'That's what killed Utani. He did not post proper sentries.'

So sorry, what killed Utani was the news of the tryst whispered to my maid from the samurai barracks that I allowed her to pass on, to Meikin who told Hiraga. I wonder how Hiraga is? As a client, the two times he was a client when I was sixteen, he was no better or worse than the faceless others, but as a shishi, the best. Curious . . .

Yoshi snuffled in his sleep but did not awaken. Her hand touched him lightly, encompassed by his warmth. Sleep, my dear one, you please me more than I dare tell myself, she thought, then continued thinking about the past.

Curious that I remember only two faces amongst all the others: just Katsumata and Hiraga. Curious that I was groomed to be Lord Toranaga Yoshi's Lady—for a time. How fortunate I am. A year, perhaps two, no more than three and then I will marry. Tora-chan will choose him for me. Whoever he is he will be samurai. Eeee, how many sons shall I have? The old woman soothsayer said three sons and two daughters, the Chinese monk two sons and two daughters.

She smiled to herself. Oh, I shall be so wise ruling my husband's household and so good to my sons and so strict with my daughters, but, never mind, they will marry well.

She awoke a few seconds before Yoshi. He was up instantly, one moment asleep, the next completely ready for the day. She held his padded yukata for him, then clasping her kimono tightly around her, she opened the shoji door, then the other one, knelt and helped him into straw slippers. The guard began to bow, caught himself in time and watched all around again as Yoshi padded off to the outhouse area.

Sumomo was kneeling near the door, waiting patiently, a maid beside her with a brazier and hot tea and breakfast trays. "Good morning, Mistress. It's cold this morning, may I make you tea?"

"Yes, yes, please, Sumomo, quick as a wink. Close the door, it is chilly." Koiko hurried back to her inner rooms, calling out, "We will leave midmorning, Sumomo. We can change into travelling clothes then."

"Yes, Mistress." Sumomo was still standing at the outer doorway trying to contain her shock. She had seen at once that her bundle had been moved, the knot tying the square of silk holding it together not exactly as she did it. Her day kimono was still folded nearby but it too had been moved.

Hardly breathing, she waited until the maid left, then unfolded the kimono. When her fingers felt the hidden shuriken in the secret sleeve pocket her heart started again.

But wait, she thought, blood rushing into her face, just because they're still there does not mean that someone hasn't discovered them. Do not panic! Think! Who would search my bundle here and why? A thief? Never! Abeh? A guard? Koiko? Yoshi? If one of them, logically I would already be dead or at least roped and answering questions and . . .

"Sumomo, is the tea ready yet?"

"Yes, I'm coming, Mistress. . . ."

Quickly, and because of the cold, she put the kimono on over her sleeping yukata—she had already done her early first wash and brushed her teeth and her hair that was still in a conventional braid— tied her obi and replaced her sheathed knife, all the time her mind working at full speed: Was it one of them? Perhaps the searcher wasn't careful. He could have missed them, easy if not expecting them. Perhaps the searcher wasn't practiced? Koiko? Why should she search my possessions now ? Of course that had been done by the other maids when she had first arrived in Koiko's quarters—the shuriken had been on her person.

As her mind raced she set the rice gruel to keep warm, made the tea and took a cup into the bathroom where Koiko had finished bathing herself from the buckets of hot water made fragrant with extract of flowers. The water was delivered at dawn through a small trapdoor so that none would be spilled on the tatamis, and the guests not disturbed. Night containers were removed in the same way.

"I'll wear my brown kimono with the carp," Koiko said, sipping gratefully, the cold crinkling her skin however much she willed herself to pretend the cold did not exist. "And the golden-colored obi."

Sumomo hurried to obey, heart still grinding, and fetched the garments, helping her to dress.

When the obi was tied to her satisfaction, Koiko knelt on one of the futons. Sumomo knelt behind her to brush her lustrous, waist-long hair. "That's good, Sumomo, you're learning, but please make the strokes longer and smoother."

Outside, the tempo of the awakening Inn was increasing. Maids and soldiers and people calling to one another, Abeh's voice and then Yoshi's. The two women listened but could not distinguish what was being said. The voices moved away.

"Twenty more strokes and then I will eat and have another cup of tea. Are you hungry?"

"No, Mistress, thank you, I have already eaten."

"You did not sleep well?" Koiko said, noticing a nervousness about her.

"No, Lady Koiko. So sorry to tell you my problem, but sometimes I have difficulty sleeping, then when I do sleep I have bad dreams," Sumomo said ingenuously, still distracted. "The doctor gave me some medicine to calm me. I forgot to take it with me last night when I changed rooms."

"Ah, is that so?" Koiko hid her relief. "Perhaps you should take some now."

"Oh, but that can wait an—"

"Please, I insist. It's important you should be calm."

Obediently, and gratefully, Sumomo found the bottle. It had not been tampered with. She took a sip and recorked it. The inner warmth began almost at once. "Thank you, Mistress," she said, then continued brushing.

After the hot rice gruel and pickles, some cold roasted eel with a sweet and sour sauce, and rice cakes, Koiko said, "Please sit down, Sumomo, and pour yourself some tea."

"Thank you, Mistress."

"Lord Yoshi has decided I am not to accompany him anymore but to follow, by palanquin, at a more moderate pace."

"Some of the guards mentioned that while I was waiting for you. Everything will be ready whenever you wish to start."

"Good." Now that Koiko had discovered the truth about the bottle she was much more at ease but it had not changed her decision to be prudent—her duty to Katsumata already done. "You are safely out of Kyōto now," she said softly, and Sumomo's stomach twisted. But for the elixir she would have panicked. "It is time to part, Sumomo. Today. Do you have money?"

"No, Mistress." Sumomo wanted to sound matter of fact. "But would it be poss—"

"No need for you to worry, I can give you some." Koiko smiled, misunderstanding the fluster, and continued firmly, "Your papers, are they in order?"

"Yes, but may I st—"

"It is best for both of us. I have considered every possibility. It is best if I travel on alone. You may stay here or return to your home in Satsuma—I would advise that—or make your own way to Yedo."

"But please, may I stay with you?"

"It is wise if you go your own way now—of course you realize it was an extreme favor to your guardian that I accepted you. Now you are safe," she said kindly.

"But . . . but what will you do? You have no maid. I want to serve you an—"

"Yes, and you have been very good, but I can easily hire some-one. Please do not worry about that. Now, will you go back to Kyōto?" When Sumomo did not answer, just stared numbly, she said gently, "What did your guardian say you were to do, when you left me?"

"He—he did not say."

Koiko frowned. "But surely you must have a plan."

"Oh, yes, Mistress," Sumomo said, rattled—even more flustered—her mouth running away with her, "he told me I was to stay with you until Yedo. Then—then if it was your pleasure, I was to leave."

"To go where?"

"To—to go to Oda-sama."

"Yes, of course, but where in Yedo?"

"I am not sure. May I pour you s—"

"You are not sure, Sumomo?" Koiko's frown deepened. "Do you have another family to go to if he isn't there?"

"Well, yes, there's an Inn, they will know where he is or there will be a message for me, but I swear I will not be a burden during the journey, not at all, you teach me so much . . ."

The more Koiko listened as the girl rushed on—foolishly, she thought, for obviously she'd made up her mind—the less she liked what she was hearing, or Sumomo's agitation, the way she spoke and dropped her eyes.

She closed her ears to the reasons and used the time to gather her own thoughts. They became more ominous. "Your guardian, will he be in Yedo too?"

"I do not know, so sorry. Please, let me pour you some—"

"This Oda-sama is Satsuma—is he part of the Satsuma garrison?"

"No." Sumomo cursed herself. She should have said, I don't know. "The Sats—"

"Then what is he doing in Yedo?"

"I do not know, Lady," Sumomo said lamely, her mind not fast enough, more dismayed every moment. "I have not seen him for almost a year, that is . . . I was told he would be at Yedo."

Koiko's eyes bored into her. Her voice became edged. "Your guardian said this Oda-sama was shishi, so he . . ." Her voice trailed off as, saying the word aloud, the enormity of what she had done, and risked, by agreeing to have this girl with her, inundated her. "Shishi believe Lord Yoshi is their prime enemy." She moaned. "If he's enemy, th—"

"No, Lady, he is not, not him, only the Shōgunate, the Bakufu are enemy, he is above all that, he is not enemy," Sumomo said vehemently, the lie coming easily, then added before she could stop herself, "Katsum— my guardian impressed that on all of us."

"All of you?" Koiko's face went chalky. *"Namu Amida Butsu! You're one of his acolytes!"* Katsumata had told her that a few select young women were being trained by him to be members of his warrior band. "He—he trained you too?"

"I am just a humble loyalist, Lady," Sumono said, fighting for control, and to keep her face guileless.

Koiko looked around in disbelief. Her mind almost stopped, the blissful world she had been inhabiting fallen apart. "You are one of them, you are!"

Sumomo stared back at her, not knowing how to extricate herself from the pit that had suddenly opened in front of them. "Lady, please, let us think clearly. I—I am no threat to you, nor you to me, let us leave it like that. I swore to protect you and I will, and Lord Yoshi if need be. Let me travel with you. I swear I will leave the moment we reach Yedo. Please?" Her eyes willed Koiko to agree. "You will never regret the kindness. Please. My guardian asked a lifetime favor. Please, I will serve you . . ."

Koiko hardly heard the words. She watched her as a mouse would a poised cobra, no thought in her head but how to escape, how to make all this a dream. Is it a dream? Be sensible, your life is in the balance, more than your life, you must collect your wits.

"Give me your knife."

Sumomo did not hesitate. Her hand went into her obi and she gave her the sheathed knife. Koiko took the blade as if it were on fire. Not knowing what else to do with it, never having handled or owned or needed one before, all weapons forbidden in the Floating World, she thrust it into her own obi. "What do you want with us? Why are you here?" her voice barely audible.

"Just to travel with you, Lady," Sumomo said as though to a child, not realizing her own face was stark. "Just to travel with you, there is no other reason."

"Were you part of the assassins, the attackers on Shōgun No-busada?"

"Of course not, I am only a simple loyalist, a frien—"

"But you were the spy who whispered that my Lord was going outside the barracks to meet Ogama—it was you!"

"No, Lady, I swear it. I have told you he is not the enemy—that was a lone madman, not one of ours, I keep say—"

"You have to leave, you must," Koiko said in a tiny voice. "Please go. Please go now, please. Quickly."

"There is no need to worry or be afraid. None."

"Oh, but I am, I am terrified, and terrified that someone should . . . should denounce you. Yoshi would . . ." The words seemed to suspend themselves in the air between them. Their eyes locked, Sumomo willing her, Koiko helpless and wilting under their strength. Both seemed to have aged, Koiko torn apart that she could have been so naive and that her idol had used her so evilly, Sumomo furious that she was so stupid not to have agreed instantly the moment this meddle-some whore had proposed she should leave. Fool, fool, both were thinking. "I will do as you say," Sumomo muttered. "I will leave even though—"

The shoji opened. Yoshi strode in jauntily, heading for the inner room. Their trance shattered. They hastily bowed. He stopped in midstride, all his senses shrieking danger.

"What is it?" he asked sharply. He had noticed their instant of fear before their heads bowed.

"Noth . . . nothing, Sire," Koiko said, collecting herself as Sumomo hurried for the brazier to fetch fresh tea. "You will have tea, breakfast, perhaps?"

His eyes went from woman to woman. "What-is-it?" he said slowly, the words like ice needles.

Sumomo knelt humbly. "We—we were so sorry not to be going with you, Sire, it was just that . . . just that the Lady Koiko was so sad. May I serve tea, Sire?"

The silence gathered. His fists bunched on his hips, face set, bare legs planted. "Koiko! Tell-me-now!"

Koiko's mouth began to move but the words would not come out. Sumomo's heart stopped, then thundered in her ears as Koiko dragged herself to her feet, tears beginning and she stammered, "You s-see, she . . . it is true but she is not quite what . . ."

Instantly Sumomo was on her feet, her right hand darting into her sleeve and bringing out a shuriken. Yoshi set his teeth, seeing it. Her arm curled back for the throw—he was unarmed, an open target, his swords in the inner room. At once he ducked left, hoping the feint would confuse her, preparing to hurl himself at her, his eyes fixed on her hand. Unperturbed, she aimed for his chest and threw viciously.

The barbed circle of steel spun across the room. Frantically he arched his body and skewed around. One of the barbs caught the edge of his kimono and sliced through the material but touched no flesh and went on to disappear through the shoji and *thwackked* into one of the posts in the inner room as, jerked off balance by the supreme effort, he slammed into a wall and buckled into a heap.

For an instant everything seemed a slow dream . . .

Sumomo reaching endlessly in her sleeve for the next shuriken, seeing only the great enemy lying helpless and his dim-witted whore who had caused this unnecessary conclusion gaping at her, a pillar of fear—but feeling no fear herself, only elation, sure that this was her zenith, the moment she had been born for and had trained all her life for, and that now, invincible champion of the shishi, she would conquer and, dying, live in legend forever . . .

Koiko, standing paralyzed, aghast that she had been duped by the godlike guru who had betrayed her, told her nothing but lies, the girl equally a cheat, and because of them this monstrous conspiracy was happening: her Patron would die and even if he did not die, she was disgraced and would die, either by his hand or those of the guards, everything in this life wasted, never to marry her samurai, never to have sons, never in this life, better to end it quickly by her own hand than foully by theirs but how, how, and then she remembered Sumomo's knife . . .

Yoshi craned around from the floor, frantic to see the next throw, hauling his feet under him for the charge he had to make or die, everything taking so much time, his mind exploding that he had been nursing a viper in his embrace, then his eyes saw Sumomo's hand with the second shuriken—how many does she have?—her lips drawn back from her very white teeth . . .

The frozen instant ended.

Sumomo hesitated, exulting in the kill, but the moment was too long and she saw Koiko come out of her trance and the knife appear in her hand. Instinctively she shifted her aim, caught herself, wavered, aimed at Yoshi again and began the throw, but at that instant Koiko lurched forward, tripped over her hem and sprawled toward her.

The spinning shuriken embedded itself in Koiko's chest and she cried out, and that gave Yoshi time to lunge at Sumomo from the floor. He caught one of her ankles and brought her down, stabbed fingers for her throat but she was an eel and twisted away, trained in martial arts, her hand seeking the last shuriken. Before she could reach it, his iron fingers grabbed part of her kimono, tore half the sleeve off, inhibiting her. Again she squirmed from his grasp and was on her feet in a second, but now he was too.

At once she shrieked a nerve-racking battle cry, bunched her hand and threw again. He was transfixed, dead—yet her hand was empty, the throw only a feint, the last shuriken still caught in her torn sleeve.

As she groped for it the shoji behind her was jerked open by the guard. "Quick," she shouted, pointing at Koiko writhing and moaning on the floor, distracting and directing him. As he darted forward, she ripped his long sword out of its sheath, raised it and hacked, wounding him, and in the same movement turned for Yoshi. But he had leapt back a pace, jumped over Koiko's prone, squirming body and sprinted for the inner room and his swords, bursting through the closed shoji, Sumomo in fierce pursuit.

His sword hissed out of the scabbard. He spun, parried the first blow violently, and pivoted in the enclosed space. Fearlessly Sumomo attacked and was again parried while Yoshi measured her and she measured him. Another flurry of blows, she an impeccable sword fighter, as he was.

Now he attacked and was held and they broke off and circled, then she darted back through the shoji seeking more space, he close behind her and they circled seeking an opening. Outside there were shouts. Guards converged, the wounded samurai half blocking the doorway. Knowing there was little time Sumomo increased the pressure, lunged forward, then swivelled to put her back to the door and they hacked at each other, parry and blow, parry and blow. Yoshi twisted, forcing her around once more, but losing the initiative.

He saw Abeh rush for her back, sword raised, and he snarled, "*No!* Leave her to me!" and almost got decapitated, retreating in temporary disorder.

Obediently Abeh backed off. Another wild skirmish, Yoshi regaining his balance just in time. Both of them well matched, Yoshi vastly more strong though not as practiced.

Now their hilts locked. Quickly she disengaged, knowing he must beat her in such a clinch, stepped back, feinted then hurtled forward in a blind, unorthodox blitz, her sword edge cut into his shoulder. It would have disabled a less skilled fighter, but he had anticipated the blow and suffered only a minor wound, though he cried out and dropped his guard, pretending a great hurt. Carelessly she went in for the kill. But he was not exactly where she expected. His sword arched up ferociously from the ground, catching her unawares, the blow slicing through her left wrist and sending it flying with the sword, her fingers still gripping the hilt.

She stared at the stump of her arm, astonished, blood spurting up and out in a huge stream. There was no pain. Her other hand grabbed the stump and slowed the flow. Guards raced forward to seize her but again Yoshi cursed them away, his chest heaving as he tried to catch his breath, watching her so very carefully. "Who are you?"

"Sumomo Fujahito . . . shishi," she gasped, her courage and strength ebbing fast, then, with the last of her spirit, whimpered, "*sonno-joiiii,*" released her grip on her wrist, groped for the last shuriken, found it, dug one of the poisoned barbs into her arm and stumbled forward to jam it into him. But he stood ready.

The great blow took her perfectly where her neck joined her body and sliced across and through her to come out just under her arm. Those watching sucked in their breaths as one man, sure that they had witnessed a happening that would be passed from mouth to mouth for centuries and proved this man a worthy descendant of the great Shō-gun and bearer of his name. But all were rocked also, at the sight of so much blood.

Abeh recovered his voice first. "What happened, Lord?"

"I won," Yoshi said grimly, examining his shoulder, blood staining his kimono, an ache in his side and his heart still violent. "Get a doctor . . . then we'll leave."

Men raced to do his bidding. Abeh tore his eyes off Sumomo's corpse. Koiko was moaning and squirming pitifully, her nails clawing the tatami, gashing it. He went towards her, stopped as Yoshi said, "Careful, fool! She was part of the conspiracy!" Cautiously Abeh kicked Sumomo's knife to one side. "Turn her over!" He obeyed, with his foot.

There was only the slightest sign of blood. The shuriken had pinned her kimono to her flesh, stanching the seepage, more than half of the steel buried in her. Apart from the pulsating agony that twisted her face in waves, she was as breathtaking as ever.

Yoshi was filled with hatred.

Never had he been so close to death. The other attack was nothing compared to this one. How he had managed to withstand the onslaught and sneak attack, he could not understand. Half a dozen times he had been, knowingly, beaten, and the terror at the brink was not as he had imagined it to be. That terror will unman anyone, he thought, wanting to hack Koiko to pieces in fury for her betrayal, or to leave her to her agony.

Her hands were clawing impotently at her chest, at the huge pain centered there, trying to tear away the thing that was causing it. But she could not. A shudder racked her. Her eyes opened and she saw Yoshi standing there and her hands left her chest and went to her face, trying to make her hair neat for him. "Help me, Torachan," she sobbed, her words garbled, "please helllp meeee . . . it hurts . . ."

"Who sent you? And *her*? Who?"

"Helpppp me, oh please, it hurts, it hurts, I tried to save . . . save . . ." Her words trailed away and she saw herself again with the knife in her hand, him defenseless, heroically doing her duty, rushing forward to protect him, to give him the knife she could not herself use and to prevent the betrayer from wounding him with the flying steel, accepting it in his place, saving his life so he would reward her and forgive her, not that she was guilty of anything, only of serving him, pleasing him, adoring him . . .

"What shall we do with her?" Abeh was asking queasily, certain, with all of them, that the shuriken was poisoned and she would die, some poisons more cruel than others.

Throw her on a dung heap, was Yoshi's immediate thought, his stomach filled with sick bile, and leave her to her pain and the dogs. He scowled, tormented now, seeing she was still beautiful, even still desirable, only the dribbling moan underscoring his ugly, acid awareness that an era had ended.

Now and forevermore he would be alone. She had destroyed trust. If this woman on whom he had lavished so much affection could betray him, anyone could. Never again could he trust a woman or share so much. Never. She had destroyed that part of him forever. His face closed. "Throw . . ."

And then he remembered her silly poems and happy poems, all the laughter and pleasures she had given him, the good advice and satisfactions. Abruptly he was consumed with immense sadness at the cruelty of life. His sword was still in his hand. Her neck was so small. The blow was kind.

"*Sonno-joi,* eh?" he muttered, blind at her loss.

Cursed shishi, their fault she is dead. Who sent Sumomo? Katsumata! Must be, same sword strokes, same guile. Twice his assassins have almost killed me. No third time. I will wipe them out. Until I am dead Katsumata is enemy, all shishi are enemy. Cursed shishi—and cursed gai-jin!

It is really their fault, the gai-jin. They're a plague. If it wasn't for them none of this would have happened, there would be no stinking Treaties, no shishi, no *sonno-joi,* and no pussing sore of Yokohama.

Cursed gai-jin. Now they will pay.

40

YOKOHAMA

ON THE AFTERNOON OF THE SAME day, Jamie McFay came out of the office of the *Yokohama Guardian*, seething. He stuffed the latest edition of the newspaper under his arm and hurried along High Street. The breeze was salty and chill, the sea spotted with combers, grey and uninviting. His stride was as angry as his mood. I wish to God Malcolm had told me, he was thinking. He's off his rocker, crazy. It's bound to stir up trouble.

"Wot's up?" Lunkchurch asked, seeing the crumpled paper and perturbed by Jamie's unusual haste. He himself had been on the way to collect his own copy before his afternoon siesta and had stopped for a moment to urinate in the gutter. "Hey, the duel's in the paper, been reported, eh?"

"What duel?" McFay snapped. Rumors were rife that it was due any day now, though, as yet, no one had whispered they knew it was the day after tomorrow, Wednesday. "For Christ's sake, stop spreading that chestnut!"

"No offense, old lad." The big, florid man buttoned up, heaving his belt up over his paunch to have it slide down again. "Well, wot the eff's up?" He jabbed the paper. "Wot's effing Nettlesmith writ that's put your dingle out of joint?"

"Just more of the same," McFay said, avoiding the real reason. "His editorial claims the fleet's almost up to snuff, Army's sharpening their bayonets, and ten thousand sepoys are on the way from India to help us."

"Eff'ing balls, all of it!"

"Yes. Added to that the bloody Governor doing his usual, sodding up Hong Kong's economy. Nettlesmith's reprinted an editorial from the *Times* praising the plan to torch our Bengal opium fields, replanting with tea, a little item that'll cause heart attacks all over Asia—as if taste buds anywhere will be satisfied with Darjeeling muck! Stupid bastards will ruin us and the British economy at the same time. Got to run, see you at the meeting later."

"Eff'ing meetings! Waste of eff'ing time," Lunkchurch said. "Eff'ing government! We should go to the eff'ing barricades like the eff'ing Frogs. And we should be shelling Yedo right now! Wee Willie hasn't the balls, and as for eff'ing Ketterer . . ." He continued swearing long after Jamie had left. Others on the promenade nearby frowned, then quickened their pace heading for the newspaper office.

Malcolm Struan looked up as Jamie knocked. He saw the paper at once. "Good. I was going to ask if it was here yet."

"I fetched a copy. A dickybird whispered I should."

"Ah." Malcolm grinned. "My letter's in? It's there?"

"You might have told me so I could think of a way to lessen the impact."

"Calm down, for God's sake," Malcolm said, good-naturedly, taking the paper and turning to the section where letters were printed. "No harm in taking a moral position. Opium's immoral, and so is gunrunning, and I didn't tell you because I wanted you to be surprised too."

"You've certainly done that! This will incense every trader here and throughout Asia and it'll backfire—we need friends just as much as they need us."

"I agree. But why should my letter backfire? Ah!" His letter was in the lead position and headlined: NOBLE HOUSE TO TAKE NOBLE STAND! "Good caption, I like that."

"Sorry, but I don't. It's bound to backfire because everyone knows we have to use those trade goods or we're stuffed. You're tai-pan but you can't . . ." Jamie paused. Malcolm was smiling at him unperturbed. "What about the Choshu rifles, for goodness' sake? We've accepted their money though you agreed to pass them over to the other man, Watanabe, for Lord Someone or other—the order you increased to five thousand?"

"All in due time." Malcolm remained calm though reminded that his mother had cancelled the order that he had, promptly, reinstated by the fastest mail possible. Silly of her, she understands nothing about Japan. Never mind, only a few more days and she'll be curbed. "Meanwhile, Jamie, there's no harm in taking a public, moral position," he said airily. "We must bend with the times, don't you think?"

McFay blinked. "You mean it's a ploy? To confuse the opposition?"

"Bend with the times," Malcolm repeated happily. His letter advocated, at length, the phasing out of opium and guns, just as the Admiral wanted, and put him squarely behind the Admiral's vehement position and the Government's proposed new plan for Asia: *Ways must be found at once to put our trading approach on the most perfect footing, for the greater glory of H.M. the Queen, God Bless Her, and our British Empire. The Noble House is proud to lead the way* . . . he had written among other flowery effusions, signing it, *The tai-pan, Struan's,* as his father and grandfather had done with letters to the press. "I thought it was all put rather well. Don't you?"

"Yes, it is," McFay said. "You certainly convinced me. But if it's just a . . ." He was going to say 'sop,' but sop to who, and why? "But if it's just a ploy, why do it? Couldn't be a worse time. You're bound to be challenged at the meeting."

"Let them."

"They'll think you've gone mad."

"Let them. In a few weeks they'll have forgotten it, and anyway we'll be in Hong Kong." Malcolm beamed, filled with good humor. "Don't worry, I know exactly what I'm doing. Do me a favor, leave a message for the Admiral. I'd like to drop by and see him before dinner, and Marlowe when he comes ashore. They're both dining with us at eight, yes?"

"Yes, both accepted." McFay sighed. "So you're going to keep me in suspense over the why?"

"Don't worry, everything's perfect. Now, much more importantly, today we must settle on next season's order for silks. Make sure Vargas has the books up-to-date. I want to talk to the shroff about specie and funds as soon as possible—don't forget, tomorrow, Angel and I will be gone all day with Marlowe aboard *Pearl.*" He would have danced a jig if he could have, but his legs and stomach were aching more than usual. Never mind, he thought, tomorrow's the great day, I'm almost home, then the hell with everyone.

Jamie was finding him strange, not understanding him at all. Every ship from Hong Kong brought both of them another, ever more vituperative letter from Tess Struan and yet, for the last week-odd, Malcolm was completely at ease and as he had been pre-Tokaidō, good-humored, clever, attentive and dedicated to business affairs though still in deep discomfort and walking badly as ever. And then there was the overriding hazard of the duel set for Wednesday, the day after tomorrow.

Three times McFay had approached Norbert Greyforth to make an accommodation, even enlisting Gornt's help, but nothing would dissuade the man: 'Jamie, you tell the young bugger it's up to him, by God,' Norbert had said. 'He started this shit. If he apologizes I'll accept it—if it's public, and mighty public at that!'

McFay bit his lip. His last resort was to whisper the time and the place to Sir William, but he hated the idea of breaking his solemn oath. "I'm to meet with that bugger Gornt at six o'clock, to fix the final details."

"Good. Sorry you don't like him, he's a good fellow, Jamie. Really. I invited him tonight. 'Dinna fash yoursel'." Malcolm aped a heavy Scottish accent as a pleasantry.

McFay smiled, soothed by the friendliness. "Do y—" A knock interrupted him.

"Come in."

Dmitri strode in like a bad squall and left the door open behind him. "You gone crazy, Malc? How can Struan's back these assholes about opium and guns?"

"No harm in taking a moral position, Dmitri."

"There is, by God, if it's crazy. If Struan's take that position, the rest of us are fighting uphill, for crissake—goddam Wee Willie will use that to—" He stopped as Norbert Greyforth stalked in without knocking.

"Have you gone bloody mad?" Norbert snarled, leaning over the desk and waving the paper in Malcolm's face. "What about our bloody agreement to act together, eh?"

Malcolm stared up at him, hating him, instantly colorless. "If you want an appointment, make it," he said icily, but controlled. "I'm busy. Get out. Please!"

Norbert flushed, also on notice by Sir William to behave or else. His face twisted with anger. "Wednesday, early, by God! Just bloody be there!" He spun on his feet and stalked away. The door slammed behind him.

"Rude bastard," Malcolm said mildly.

Normally Dmitri would have laughed but he was too concerned. "While we're on that subject, I might as well tell you I'm not taking part in Wednesday's 'meeting.'"

"That's no problem, Dmitri," Malcolm said. Color was coming back into his face. "I still have your word, gentleman's honor, that nothing leaks."

"Sure." Then Dmitri burst out, "Don't do it, you could get seriously hurt."

"I'm seriously hurt now, old chap. Please don't worry. If Norbert keeps our date he's . . ." Malcolm was going to say, he's a dead man, and tempted to disclose Gornt's scheme to Dmitri—he had already explained it to McFay who had, reluctantly, approved it as workable—but decided not to.

Instead he said, "I've already offered Norbert a private accommodation but he spurned that. I'm damned if I'll crawl in public. Listen, while you're here, what about Colt Armaments? I hear Cooper-Tillman have a block of shares they want to sell. I'd like to buy."

"Eh? How d'you know about them?" Dmitri glanced at McFay, who was equally astonished but had managed to hide it. "Where'd you hear about that?"

"A dickybird told me." Malcolm hid his glee. Edward Gornt had given him the tip, amongst other inside tips about Brock's and Cooper-Tillman, to prove his sincerity about the major information he would pass over about the Brocks. 'Why wait to tell me, Mr. Gornt?' he had said. 'If the information is as good as you say it will need dealing with at once.'

'It will, yes, at once, Tai-pan. But let's leave it as we agreed: Wednesday's the day. Meanwhile, as we're going to have a long and happy relationship, why not let's drop the "Mister," you call me just Gornt, I'll stay with "Tai-pan" until we meet in Shanghai or Hong Kong—after Sir Morgan's ruined. Then, maybe, we could be on a first-name basis, eh?'

He watched Dmitri, his excitement increasing. So much good happening now. "What do you say, old chap? Is Jeff Cooper prepared to sell, and you have the necessary authority to deal?"

"Yes, I have his authority but."

"But nothing. The authority's in writing?"

"In writing and he might sell half but. At the right price—16.50 a share."

"Balls, that's nowhere near right—that's your Medicine Man approach coming out. 13.20, not a cent more. We can draw up a letter of intent, dated today. Forty thousand shares."

Dmitri gaped at him but quickly recovered—forty thousand was exactly the right number. 13.20 was low. He had offered the shares to Morgan Brock who had tendered 12.80, a fire-sale price, with a year payout which made the offer unpalatable, though to find a buyer for such a large block of shares was almost impossible. Where the hell did Malc get the information? "13.20's nowhere near good enough."

"13.20 today. Tomorrow it'll be 13.10, Wednesday I withdraw the bid." Gornt had told him Cooper needed to sell quickly to invest in a new U.S. venture making Ironclads—for either navy. "I've plenty of time, but old Jeff hasn't."

"What you mean by that?"

"Just that I have time and Jeff hasn't. Nor has the Union or even Confederate . . . navy," he added pleasantly, "with the war going badly for both sides."

"Crap on your spies," Dmitri said. "No deal. 15.20."

"Dreamer. 13.20, payment in gold from a sight draft on our bank as soon as it arrives in Boston."

Dmitri opened his mouth but Jamie McFay butted in hastily, "Tai-pan, it might be a good idea to conside—"

"Getting HK's approval," Malcolm finished the sentence for him. "Come on, Jamie, we've had that out and that nonsense is finished once and for all." His voice was level, and brooked no argument. "Right?"

"Yes, sorry, you're right."

Calmly Malcolm said, "Well, Dmitri, yes or no?"

Dmitri stared at him with renewed respect. The immediate payout had already clinched it for him. "It's a deal." He offered his hand. Malcolm shook it.

McFay said, "I'll draw up the paper this afternoon and have it for your signatures at 5:00 P.M. All right?"

"Good. Thanks for coming to see me, Dmitri, you're always welcome. Dinner's at 8:30."

After Dmitri left McFay could not stay quiet. "That's a lot of money."

"$528,000 to be precise. But Colt's got a new order for a hundred thousand rifles of a radical new design. By the time our letter of credit clears their shares will have doubled so we've just made half a million dollars."

"How can you be sure?"

"I'm sure."

"You'll sign the promissory note?"

"Yes. If you tell me I can't because I've no authority because of what my mother has or has not said, I will take no notice whatsoever and sign it anyway." Malcolm lit a cheroot, continuing, "If it's not honored that will backfire and ruin Struan's like nothing in our history. I'm tai-pan, like it or not, until I resign or until I'm dead, whatever she says."

They both watched a smoke ring rise and vanish and then McFay nodded, slowly, his misgivings overcome by Malcolm's strange surety and authority that he had never experienced before. "You know what you're doing, don't you?"

Malcolm's eyes lit up. "I know many things I didn't when I first came here. For example, if you insist on leaving . . . Come on, Jamie, I'm sure in your heart you've decided, and why shouldn't you? You've been treated shabbily—I know I haven't helped but that's all over, if I were you I'd do the same. You've decided, haven't you?"

McFay swallowed, disarmed. "Yes, I'm going to leave, but not until Struan's business here is optimum, six months or so, unless she fires me first. Christ, I don't want to leave but I must."

Malcolm laughed. "You've taken a moral position."

McFay laughed too. "Hardly. It's crazy."

"No, I'd do the same. And I'm sure you'll be a huge success, so much so a hundred thousand of the dollars I've just made—I have, Jamie, no one else—will be an investment in McFay Trading. For a . . ." He was going to say forty-nine percent share but changed that, to give McFay face, and thought, You deserve it, my friend, I'll never forget the mail you could have hanged for—Sir William would have caught us, I'm sure of that too. "A sixty percent share?"

McFay said, "Twenty-five," without even thinking.

"Fifty-five?"

"Thirty-five."

"Forty-nine percent."

"Done, if!"

They both laughed and Malcolm said what McFay had been thinking, "If the shares double." Then he added seriously, "And if they don't I'll find it another way."

McFay looked at him for what seemed a long time, his mind in a thought pattern of questions but no answers. Why has Malcolm changed? Heavenly? The business over the mails? The duel? Surely not. Why does he want to see the Admiral? Why does he like Gornt, who's a crafty one, all right?

And why did I blurt out, Yes, I'm going to leave, before I knew it, making the decision I'd been thinking about for months: to take a chance before I die. He saw Malcolm watching him, weak in body, but tranquil and strong. He smiled back, glad to be alive. "You know, I'm sure you will."

Angelique was taking her pre-dinner siesta, a coal fire merry in the grate. Curtains were drawn against the wind and she was curled under down covers and silk sheets, half asleep half awake, one hand comfortably between her legs as Colette had taught her in the convent when they would sneak into bed with one another after the nuns had left the dormitory and were snoring behind their curtained cubicles. Fondling and kissing and whispering and chuckling under the covers, the two young girls sharing secrets and dreams and wants, pretending to be grown-up lovers—as described in the romantic but forbidden street pamphlets that were smuggled in by the chambermaids and circulated from hand to hand amongst the students—all make-believe and healthy and amusing and harmless.

Her mind was on Paris and the wonderful future ahead, Malcolm softly content beside her, or already out in the Struan countinghouse, now headquartered in Paris, rich and tall, all his bad health a memory, her bad health not even a memory, a baby son in the nursery along the corridor of this their chateau, his own nanny and maids watching him, her body again strong and as well shaped as now, his birth easy. Then there would be visits with Colette to Struan's fabulously successful silk factory that she had persuaded Struan's to build after learning so much about the harvesting and growing of the silkworms:

'Oh, Colette,' she had just written,

> these little worms are extraordinary, eating mulberry leaves for food, and then you cure the cocoons and unravel the silk. . . . I never thought I could be so interested. Vargas is my secret informant and he sneaked the silk seller in to show me some, but I have to be so careful—I started talking about my idea for a factory with Malcolm and Jamie and they laughed. Malcolm said not to be silly, making silk was a highly complex business (as if I didn't know) and not to worry my little head about business. I do believe they want us to be cocoons, to use or abuse at their whim, and that's all. Colette, send all the books on silk you can find . . .

How lovely to have one's own countinghouse, and money, she thought. Living in Paris there will be visits to London, occasionally to Hong Kong, dinners and soirees and lavish balls for my Prince Charming and his special friends . . .

She glanced at the letter to Colette she had just sealed on the bureau. More secrets shared, at least, in part:

This Edward Gornt is becoming a real friend, so charming and attentive, a real friend, not like André. I'm sure, dear Colette, he will be a friend for life because my darling Malcolm seems to enjoy his company too. Isn't that strange—when Edward works for those awful Brocks I've told you about, and Norbert Greyforth who gets more venomous-looking every day, like the warlock he is! Tonight we are having another BIG soiree. Everyone will be there, André is playing, Edward, he is a dancer, light as a butterfly . . .

She had not written that the last time they had danced, at a dinner given by Sir William, he had held her hand differently, dangerously, with enough pressure to talk to her, once his little finger curled in his palm touching hers: the language of lovers, I want you in bed, yes or no and when—don't say no!

She had moved her hand, coolly and firmly. He had said nothing, his eyes smiling, and she knew that he knew she was not really angry, merely beyond reach, engaged.

Nor was she angry at André, really angry. A few days ago they had met by chance at the French Legation. 'You're looking well, Angelique, I'm delighted to see you. Can I have a word, privately?'

She had said of course, and when they were alone he had told her it was about the money he had lent her. 'I'm badly strapped, could you let me have it, please?'

'But I thought the . . . the other transaction covered that.' Her heart had skipped a beat being reminded of their stratagem over the lost earrings.

'Sorry, no, it didn't. That paid for the mama-san's advice and the medicine.'

Her flush had been sudden. 'We agreed never to mention the—the matter, *ever again,* don't you remember?' she said quietly, wanting to shout at him for disturbing their solemn agreement. 'It never happened, it didn't, that's what we agreed—it was just a bad dream!'

'I agree it never happened but you mentioned the transaction, Angelique, I didn't bring it up, just about the money. Sorry, but the money's pressing.' His face had gone cold.

Warily she had bottled her anger, damning him for disturbing her peace. She had convinced herself nothing had ever happened—except for the one man who could dispute it, nothing had. That was the truth. But for him. 'About the money, dear friend, I'll return it as soon as I can. Malcolm doesn't give me money as you know, just lets me sign chits.'

'Then perhaps we'd better arrange another "loss." '

'No,' she had said, her voice honeyed, and put a hand on his arm to soothe the flash of anger. 'That's not a good idea.' Though she purged the whole affair from her mind, for the most part, whenever it came back to haunt her, particularly at night, she was aware it had been a dreadful mistake. 'Perhaps I can think of another way.'

'I need it now, Wednesday at the latest. Sorry.'

'I'll try, I'll really try.' And she had. Yesterday she had seen Henri Seratard and tearfully begged and pleaded, saying she needed money for a surprise for Malcolm, that she would be always in his debt and signed another piece of paper, pledging her diamond engagement ring as surety.

Wisely she had borrowed twice as much as she owed. This morning she had repaid André. He had thanked her and thanked her. No reason to be angry with him. He's my good and trusted friend and I did borrow the money. What did I need it for? I forget. *Sans faire rien*, that's one debt repaid.

Half the rest she had taken to McFay. 'Jamie, would you send this to my dearest aunt in Paris for me. She's poorly and also, my dear uncle,' she had told him, pleased she at last could help them, and even more pleased that, as she had hoped, McFay had told Malcolm. He had asked her about it.

'Oh, I borrowed it from Monsieur Seratard, my darling. I didn't want to ask you for money and I can't send them a chit. I hope you don't mind but I pledged some jewelry.'

He had chided her, saying he would take care of the Seratard debt, that Jamie would have a revolving fund for her, the value of a hundred guineas which she could draw against as she wished, just give him a note of what it's for, and that he would double the amount she wanted sent.

So easy when you use your intelligence. A warmth went through her remembering how she had thanked him for his kindness, and kissed him so fondly, and how he had responded. She would have liked to have gone further, much further.

Her fingers distracted her. Their smoothly knowing sensuality pleased her and she closed her eyes and cast herself back with Colette but that did not last long. As always *he* loomed in the front of her mind, vivid and almost alive, and with him the details of their last time, the time she had been deliberately wanton and had done everything she had dreamt possible—to save her life, not realizing she would enjoy everything as much as *he* had.

Dearest Blessed Mother, we both know it was only to save my life—isn't that true? But also true—ah, how lucky I am I can talk openly, direct to You, and not have to go through that awful Father Leo—but also true, between us women, that somehow we must rid ourselves of *him,* and the memory of the two nights and the ecstasy before it drives me insane.

Raiko was irritable. "Furansu-san, I will accept this partial payment but our agreement was very specific, so sorry."

"I know." André loathed being in debt—a phobia—to her more than any, not only because meeting the payment schedule was giving him nightmares, but also because she controlled his Hinodeh completely and if he failed to conform she would end their relationship without hesitation. And then he would kill himself. "Soon can give big payment. Earrings."

"Ah, is that so? Excellent." She smiled. "Excellent. I presume Hinodeh is still to your liking, still pleasing you?"

His worry dropped from him for a blessed moment. "She . . . everything I dream of. More."

She smiled strangely at him. "It is unwise to be so open, my friend."

A Gallic shrug. "You make me lifetime favor. Cannot say thank you enough."

The eyes crinkled in her round face, puffy from drink even though it was only dusk. Her makeup was good and her kimono expensive, the evening chilly but her rooms were warm and the whole Inn inviting. "I hear your gai-jin Princess is as healthy as ever."

"Yes." For a moment André thought about her, and her ever-present sexuality. "Think she make good Lady of Night."

Raiko cocked her head to one side, unable to resist taking the remark seriously. "That would be interesting to me. I could get her the best prices—the best—many in Yedo would pay a price to sample such a gross person. I know one rice dealer, very rich, very old, no hard work for her to satisfy, who would pay huge money to be the first to examine such a Jade Gate, and it would be easy to show her how to become a virgin again, *neh*?"

He laughed. "I tell her, one day perhaps."

"Good. The best price, and secret. This rice dealer . . . Eeee, he would pay! She shows no other signs?"

"Signs? What sort of signs?"

Raiko said, "The medicine varies for different ladies. Sometimes it can make them much more . . . more passionate and more difficult to satisfy. Sometimes it increases her chance to become pregnant, sometime it destroys any chance. Strange, *neh*?"

The amusement left him. "You not tell me."

"Would it have made any difference?"

After a moment he shook his head.

She drank deeply. "Please excuse me for speaking about money, but a gold oban no longer buys what a gold oban should buy. Our officials have debased our currency and stink like eight-day-old fish mixed with fresh dog's droppings!"

"True," he said, missing words but understanding about officials and old fish and was equally disgusted. Seratard had refused to give him the advance on his salary he had expected, claiming poverty in Legation funds. 'But Henri, I'm only asking for what you have to give me over the year. It's just a few pieces of gold, Henri. Aren't I your most valuable aide here?'

'Yes, of course you are, my dear André, but you can't get wine out of an empty vat—only a migraine!'

He tried a different approach but did no better. So he had only two courses of action. Angelique, or this mama-san. "Raiko-san, you very clever, think. Must be way we both increase normal money, *neh*? What can we sell?"

She glanced down at the table to hide. "Saké?" she asked, and poured. In his honor the saké was cold. Her eyes were slits and she wondered how far to trust him. As far as a cat will trust a cornered mouse. "Information has a price. *Neh*?"

It was said matter-of-factly. He pretended to be surprised, delighted she had taken the bait so easily. Too easily? Probably not. Being caught by the Bakufu, or by his own masters, added up to the same penalty: an agonizing death.

Sir William would pay handsomely for the right information— Henri not at all—God curse them both to hell! "Raiko-san, what happening in Yedo?"

"More to the point, what's happening here?" she said at once, beginning the negotiation. "War, eh? Terrible! Every day more soldiers firing on the firing range, more cannons practicing, frightening my Ladies."

"So sorry, please speak slower, please."

"Ah, so sorry." Raiko slowed, saying how frightened the Yoshiwara was, painting an interesting local picture but nothing that he did not already know. And he told her things about the fleet and Army that he was sure she knew also.

They drank in silence. Then she said softly, "I think certain officials would pay much to know what the gai-jin leader plans to do and when."

He nodded. "Yes. Also think our Leader pay plenty know what Nippon samurai forces where, who leads, about this *tairō* who send rude messages."

She beamed gloriously and raised her eggshell cup. "To a new partnership. Much money for a little talk."

He toasted her, saying carefully, "Little talk, yes, but must be important little and real little for real money."

"Eeee," she said, feigning shock, "am I a third-class whore without brains? Without honor? Without understanding? Without connections, without . . ." But she could not keep it up and chuckled. "We understand one another completely. Tomorrow at midday come and see me. Now off you go and see your lovely Hinodeh. Enjoy her and life while we all have it."

"Thank you. But not now. Please say, I arrive later." He smiled at Raiko, liking her. "But you, Raiko?"

"I have no Hinodeh to go to, to dream about, to write poems to, to fill me with ecstasy. Once it was different, now I am more sensible, I enjoy saké and making money, and making money and saké. Off you go," she said with a hard laugh, "but tomorrow return. At midday."

When he was gone she ordered her maids to bring more of the wine, but hot this time, and not to disturb her. Seeing such friendliness on his face, mixed with the depth of his passion for Hinodeh, she had felt her sadness beginning and so had dismissed him.

She could not bear witnesses to her misery and the abject tears that poured from her, unable to contain them or the grief, at the same time despising the weakness within her that was a frantic longing for her youth, for the girl she had been, vanished such a short time ago, never to return.

It's not fair not fair not fair, she moaned, raising the cup. I'm not the old hag I see in my mirror, I am me, Raiko the Beautiful, Courtesan of the Second Rank, I am I am I am.

*   *   *

"Ah, Otami-sama," the shoya said, "good evening, please sit down, tea, saké? So sorry to disturb you again but I have just received a message from my overlords. Tea?"

Hiraga took the opposite cushion in the pleasant room, a hold on his impatience, thanked him and accepted the obligatory cup. "How are you?" he asked politely, his heart beating faster than he cared.

"Worried, Otami-sama. It seems the gai-jin are very determined this time, too many troop movements, too many ships cleaning weapons, many rumors of more ships coming here. Perhaps you have heard from your Taira gai-jin?"

Hiraga thought about that. Tyrer and the whole Legation staff had been in an uproar ever since the ultimatum from *Tairō* Anjo had arrived, Sir William bellowing more than usual, Johann the interpreter closeted for hours with Tyrer, rewriting letters to the Bakufu and only sometimes asking him to refine a phrase. 'Easier if see 'retter, Taira-sama,' he would always say, wanting to know what was being sent.

'Yes, well, but this phrase for the moment . . .' the Taira would always say, clearly uneasy, every day the same and this had increased his disquiet. Obviously they did not trust him as before, and this after working night and day to learn their language and giving them all manner of information. Despicable gai-jin dogs, he had thought, afraid that any day Sir William might order him out—his poster was still prominent in the samurai guard house, the Enforcer patrols malevolently checking all Japanese entering and leaving the Settlement.

Enforcer patrols should not be permitted. Gai-jin are so idiotic—with their sea power I would not allow 'enemy guards' within a league! Idiotic for Anjo to anger them with such vile manners and arrogance while their fleet is here. The Council of Elders is mad!

"The gai-jin officials tell me many things, shoya," he said, as though loath to be overheard. "Fortunately I am party to their inner secrets. It may well be I can warn you in time if any danger threatens you. Meanwhile I counselled them to beware of upsetting you and the village."

The shoya bowed to the tatami, thanking him and thanking him, then said, "These are terrible times, war is terrible and taxes are going to be put up again."

Good, Hiraga thought, his head aching, you can afford it, but it won't make you or any in the Gyokoyama eat less or drink less, or your wives and women dress less expensively, only your customers. Parasites! You're already breaking ancient laws of extravagance, allowing your women to wear forbidden dress colors, like red, as under-kimonos or in your homes that, stupidly, the Bakufu, do not enforce. When we are in power there will be a reckoning.

Come on, you old fool, get to the point. I cannot waste all evening and I am not going to lose face by asking. I have more studies tonight and another book to try to read. "I can perhaps guard your interests," he said pointedly.

Again the shoya thanked him. "The message I received concerned the girl you asked about. Four days ago Lord Yoshi left Kyōto secretly, just before dawn, with a small escort of soldiers and disguised as one of them. She went too. Also in the party . . . are you all right, Otami-sama?"

"Yes, please go on," Hiraga said, "go on, shoya."

"Certainly. Also in the party, mounted, was the courtesan Koiko, and the girl who is her new *maiko* an—"

"Her what?" Hiraga gasped, 'Koiko,' with everything that her name implied, pealing in all the corners of his mind.

"Please, may I give you some tea, or saké?" the shoya asked, seeing the impact the news was making. "Or a hot towel or may I order some—"

"No, go on," Hiraga said, his voice throaty.

"There is not much more. As you know, the Lady Koiko is the most famous of Yedo's courtesans and now Lord Yoshi's companion. The girl was sent to her ten days ago."

"By whom?"

"We do not yet know, Otami-sama," the shoya said, retaining that information for another time. "It seems the Lady Koiko accepted the girl as *maiko* after the girl was personally interviewed and approved by Lord Yoshi. She is the only other woman in the party. Her name is Sumomo Fujahito."

No mistake, Hiraga wanted to shout, that's the code name Katsumata gave her—so he sent her into that hornet's nest, but why? "Which way did he go? Lord Yoshi?"

"There are forty samurai accompanying him, all mounted but carrying no banners, and Lord Yoshi himself, as I said, was disguised. They slipped out of Kyōto just before dawn, three days ago, heading along the Tokaidō, a forced march, my masters presume for Yedo." The shoya hid his astonishment at the vehemence in the young man's face.

"Forced march, you say? They could reach Kanagawa when?" The last way station before Yedo. "In ten or twelve more days?"

"Ah, yes, you are probably right though with two women travelling . . . my message said both were riding—oh, I already mentioned that—and, oh yes, I forgot, Lord Yoshi was disguised as a common ashigaru, yes, I suppose it is possible to reach Kanagawa then.''

Dazed, Hiraga swallowed more saké, hardly tasting it, accepted another cup, thanked him for the information, saying they would meet tomorrow and left to go to the village hovel he shared with Akimoto.

Outside the village streets were quiet. Shops closed at nightfall. Lights behind shoji screens made the huts and hovels inviting. Wearily, and in turmoil over the news, he took off his top hat and ruffled his hair, scratching his scalp, still not completely accustomed to wearing his hair European style, though lately hardly noticed the discomfort of trousers and waistcoat, glad for them against the season's cold. Even scratching vigorously did not help the confusion and ache in his head so he sat on a nearby bench—squatting difficult in tight trousers—and stared at the sky.

Koiko! He remembered the two times he had been with her, once for an evening and once for the night. Eeee, both had been expensive, so expensive, but worth it. Katsumata had told him that never again would he perceive such texture of skin or silky hair or such fragrance, or such kind, gentle laughter in a woman's eyes, or experience the ultimate, exploding warmth that made you want to die, you had so much joy.

'Ah, Hiraga, to die then,' Katsumata had said, 'at such a high point, to carry that with you beyond—if there is a beyond—would be perfection. Or if there is no beyond, to be certain at the leap into nothingness you have experienced the best, to die at the zenith would surely be a totality of life.'

'True, but such waste. Why train her for Yoshi?'

'Because he is a major key to *sonno-joi,* for or against, because she is the only one I have ever known who might possibly enthrall him and so move him to our side, or be positioned to send him onwards. He may be the *key* to *sonno-joi,* for or against—that's our secret, yours and mine—of course, he dies at a time of our choosing anyway.'

Then has Katsumata sent Sumomo to be the dagger of the deed? Or is it to keep Koiko safe from betrayers, or even to guard Yoshi from a traitor within?

So many questions, so much unanswered.

He got up and walked off again, his head aching worse than ever. Tomorrow Akimoto was going with Taira aboard a warship. Hiraga had asked to go but had been refused: 'So sorry,' Tyrer had told him. 'Sir William said this friend of yours, Mr. Saito, may go, but only him. Of course no weapons. I understand his family is the biggest shipbuilder in Shimonoseki, eh?'

'Yes, Taira-sama. His father fami'ry.'

'But samurai are not allowed to be in business.'

'That is correct, Taira-sama,' he had said quickly, the man too apt a pupil, making the lie sound truthful. 'But many samurai fami'ries make arrangement with money'renders and boat makers to do work, *neh*? This man important sea fami'ry.'

A week ago he had introduced the subject of Akimoto, with that fiction, during one of his endless meetings with Sir William where he stood and answered questions, learning little in exchange. 'His name is Saito, Sir W'ram, fami'ry rich, he visit here want to see great British Navy ships, hear great stories about great British Navy. Perhaps you and he can make together, great ship-making factory.'

It was not altogether a lie. For generations Akimoto's forebears had lived in a fishing village, one of the three ashigaru families there who acted as a kind of policeman for Hiraga's father, head of the nearby hirazamurai-ranked family, also for generations. Akimoto, personally, had always been interested in the sea and warships. Hiraga's father had arranged for Akimoto to join the Choshu samurai school, ordering him to learn all he could from the Dutch seaman who was the sensei, because, soon, daimyo Ogama would need officers to captain Choshu ships, and to lead their navy.

'Eeee, Cousin,' Akimoto had said the day before yesterday, 'I cannot believe you persuaded them to let me learn their war secrets.'

Hiraga sighed. He had noticed that anything to do with 'business' got immediate gai-jin attention. Poetry, not at all, calligraphy nothing, sword-forging a little, politics, yes, but only as it affected trade, but an opportunity to make something to sell for profit—anything, a ship or cannon or cup or knife or length of silk—brought instant results. They're worse than rice dealers! Their food is money.

Last night Akimoto had been in his cups, rare for him, and started to ramble about money and gai-jin and being near them, 'You are right, Hiraga, that's one of their secrets: money worship. Money! How clever you are to smell that out so soon! Look at that dog of a shoya! Look how he is all ears when you start to tell him what Taira or that other gai-jin dog gleefully say about their dirty business methods, and how they extort money from others any way they can, calling it profit, as though profit is a clean word, feeding off each other like lice. When you talk about money does not that old fish head shoya bring out his best saké to encourage you to tell more and more? Of course he does. He is just like them, worshipping money, gathering it from us samurai, putting us deeper into debt every year when he creates nothing, nothing! We should kill him and do what Ori said, burn this stinking cesspool—'

'Calm yourself! What's wrong?'

'I do not want to calm down, I want action, a fight, attack! I am tired of sitting and waiting.' Akimoto was flushed, breathing heavily, eyes bloodshot and not just from the liquor. His huge fist pounded the tatami. 'And I am tired of you studying all night, your head in a book— if you're not careful you will ruin your eyes and ruin your sword arm and then you will be dead. Attack, that is what we are here for—I want *sonno-joi* now, not later!'

'Without knowledge and patience . . . how many times do I have to tell you? You become like Ori, or that fool Shorin, why be so anxious to put your head in the Enforcer's garrote?'

'I'm not and . . . Eeee, Hiraga, you're right, please excuse me, but . . .' The words had trailed off and he saw him swallow more saké.

'What is really troubling you? The truth.'

Akimoto hesitated. 'I heard from my father.' He began haltingly but soon the words were pouring out. 'A letter came through the mama-san at Kanagawa . . . there's famine in the village, in the whole area, your family is hurting too, so sorry to tell you. Two of my little cousins have died. Three of my uncles gave up samurai class and their swords— they sold them as part payment for debts to the moneylender, swords that were used in Sekigahara—to become fishermen, at least they are working the nets for boat owners, dawn to dusk, to get a little cash! Tomiko, she an aunt's widowed daughter who was living with us, she had to sell her little girl to a child broker. She was given enough to feed the rest of her family for half a year—her two sons and her invalid father. A week later she left the money in a teapot for my mother to find and threw herself off the cliff. Her note said her heart was broken having to sell her own child, but the money could help the family and not be wasted on another useless mouth . . .'

The tears were pouring down his cheeks but no sound of weeping was in his voice, only anger. 'Such a nice girl, such a good wife to my friend, Murai—remember him, one of our Choshu ronin who died in the attack on *Tairō* Ii? I tell you, Cousin, it is awful to be samurai when you have no face, no stipend, nowhere to go and to be ronin is worse. Even so, me . . . you're right again . . . I think we will have to imitate stinking gai-jin if we want warships, even I know they do not grow in a rice paddy, and must find ways to make stinking money and be like stinking rice-dealing moneylenders. Stinking money, stinking gai-jin, st—'

'Stop it,' Hiraga had said sharply, and handed him another flask. 'You are alive, you are working for *sonno-joi*, tomorrow you go on a warship to learn, that is enough, Cousin.'

Numb, Akimoto shook his head, wiping the tears away.

'Was there any other news? Of my father, my family?'

'Well . . . read for yourself.'

He read: *If Hiraga is with you tell him his family are in sad straits, his mother is sick, they have no money and no more credit. If he has any means to send any, or arrange any credit, it will save lives—of course his father will never ask. Tell him also his wife-to-be has not yet arrived and his father fears for her safety.*

Nothing I can do for them, Hiraga thought, nearing their village hideaway, again in misery. The night wind picked up, rustling the thatched roofs, and colder than before. Nothing I can do. Stinking money! Akimoto is right. We should put Ori's plan into effect. A night like this would be ideal. Two or three huts torched and the wind would jump the flames from house to house and whip it into a conflagration. Why not tonight? Then the stinking gai-jin would have to go back aboard their ships and sail away. Would they? Or am I deluding myself and it is our karma to be eaten up by them.

What to do?

Katsumata always said, When in doubt act!

Sumomo? On the way to Yedo? His pulse quickened but even the thought of her did not remove the remorse for his family. We should marry now, marry here, while there is time, impossible to go home, the journey would take months and it is vital to be here. Father will understand.

Will he? Is it vital, or am I just deluding myself? And why did Katsumata put Sumomo with Yoshi? He would not risk her for nothing.

Nothing! I am nothing. From nothing into nothing, famine again and no money and no credit and no way to help. Without *sonno-joi* there's nothing we can do—

All at once it was as if a skin covering part of his mind had shed and he remembered Jamie explaining some aspects of gai-jin business that had shocked him. In moments he was again tapping on the shoya's door and sitting opposite him.

"Shoya, I thought I should mention, so you can prepare, I believe I have persuaded the gai-jin business expert to meet you in his great mansion, the day after tomorrow in the morning, to answer questions. I will interpret for you." The shoya thanked him and had bowed to cover his sudden beam.

Hiraga continued blandly, "Jami Mukfey told me it was gai-jin custom that there would be a fee, for this and all the other information he has already given you. The equivalent of ten koku." He uttered the staggering sum as though it were a pittance and saw the shoya blanch but not explode as he had expected, telling such a lie.

"Impossible," the shoya said, his voice strangled.

"I told him so but he said as a businessman and banker you would understand how valuable his information was, and that he would even consider . . ." Again Hiraga controlled himself. "Would even help the shoya to begin a business, first of its kind, in the gai-jin fashion to deal with other countries."

Again this was not altogether a lie. McFay had told him that he would be interested in meeting and talking to a Japanese banker—Hiraga had inflated the shoya's importance and position in the Gyokoyama—that more or less any day at a day's notice would suit him, and that there were all kinds of opportunities for cooperation.

He watched the shoya, exhilarated at his transparency, clearly besieged by potential opportunities to use Mukfey's knowledge for profit, and being the first to do such a business: 'Very important to be first,' Mukfey had explained, 'your Japanese friend will understand that, if he's any sort of businessman. Easy for me to supply our business skills, easy for your Japanese friend to do the same with Japanese skills and knowledge.' It had taken Hiraga a blinding effort to understand what the man had been talking about.

He allowed the shoya to dream and to worry. "Though I do not understand business matters, shoya, I might be able to reduce that price."

"Oh, if you could do that, Otami-sama, you would please a poor old man, just a modest servant to the Gyokoyama, for I would have to beg their permission to pay anything."

"Perhaps I could bring it down to three koku."

"Half a koku would perhaps be possible."

Hiraga cursed himself. He had forgotten the Mukfey Golden Rule One, as he called it: 'When negotiating be patient. You can always come down but never go back up, and never be afraid to laugh or cry or scream or pretend to leave.'

"Asking ten, I doubt if Mukfey would reduce below three."

"A half is already very high."

If he had had a sword he would have gripped the hilt and snarled, 'Three or I will have your dirty head.' Instead he nodded sadly. "Yes, you are right." He began to get up.

"Perhaps my masters would agree to one."

Now he was almost at the door. "So sorry, shoya, I would lose face to try to bargain so cheaply an—"

"Three." The shoya was flushed.

Hiraga sat down again. It took him a little while to adjust to the new world. He said, "I will try to make it three. These are hard times. I have just heard there is famine in my village in Choshu. Terrible, *neh?*"

He saw the shoya's eyes narrow. "Yes, Otami-sama. Soon there will be famine everywhere, even here."

Hiraga nodded. "Yes," he said, and waited, allowing the silence to thicken. Mukfey had explained the value of silence in negotiating, that a closed mouth at the right time unnerves your opponent—for negotiation is a fight like any other—and snares concessions you would never dream of asking.

The shoya knew he was trapped but had not decided on the extent of the trap, nor the price he would pay. Thus far the information he had been given was worth ten times that amount. But be cautious . . . this man is dangerous, this Hiraga Otami-sama learns too fast, he may or may not be telling the truth, may or may not be a liar. Even so, better to have a cunning samurai with you than against you. "In bad times, friends should help friends. It might be that the Gyokoyama could arrange a little credit to help. As I mentioned before, Otami-sama, your father and family are respected and valued clients."

Hiraga bit back the angry words he would normally have spat out at being so openly patronized. "That would be too much to expect," he said, feeling his way in this new world of profit and loss—one person's profit is another's loss, Mukfey had explained many times. "Anything the great Gyokoyama could do would be appreciated. But speed is very important, could I be assured they would understand? Yes?"

"It would be at once. I will arrange it."

"Thank you, and perhaps they would consider along with a *substantial* credit, perhaps also an outright grant, a fee, of say one koku . . ." He saw the eyes flash with anger, which was quickly hidden, and wondered if he had gone too far. "For services rendered by the family."

Another silence. Then the shoya said, "In the past . . . and in the future."

Hiraga's eyes became as cold as the shoya's, though, like him, his mouth smiled. And, still in the new world, he did not take out the small revolver he always carried now and blow a hole in him for his rudeness. "Of course." Then he added sweetly, "Until the day after tomorrow, *neh?*"

The shoya nodded and bowed. "Until then, Otami-sama."

Once more outside and hidden by the night, Hiraga allowed his triumph to soar with his soul. One whole koku and credits and now how to exchange the three koku that the Mukfey gai-jin had not asked for, nor needed, into real rice, or real money, that he also could send to his father?

So much for so little, he thought, elated, and at the same time feeling soiled, in need of a bath.

"Ah, Admiral," Malcolm Struan said, "a private word?"

"Certainly, sir." Admiral Ketterer clambered to his feet, one of the twenty guests still at the table in the Struan great room, grouped around their port that Angelique had left them to. Ketterer was in evening uniform, breeches, white silk stockings and silver-buckled shoes, more florid than usual, having enjoyed a mulligatawny soup, barbecued fish, a double helping of the roast beef and Yorkshire pudding with potatoes roasted in the dripping and vegetables imported from California, chicken and pheasant pie, a few fried pork sausages, followed by Californian dried-apple pie with a lavish portion of the now famous Noble House cream, and to top everything off, a Welsh rarebit savory. Champagne, sherry, claret—a Château Lafite 1837, the year Queen Victoria came to the Throne—port and Madeira. "I could use a breath of air," Ketterer said.

Malcolm led the way to the side French doors, the good food and wine dulling the pain. Outside it was brisk, but after the stuffy inside refreshing. "Cigar?"

"Thank you."

Number One Boy Chen was hovering in the background with the box. After the cigars were lit he vanished in the smoke.

"You saw my letter in today's *Guardian,* sir?"

"Yes, yes, I did, much of it well put," Ketterer said.

Malcolm smiled. "If the hornet's nest of protests it stirred at the meeting this afternoon is any indication it put your point over rather well."

"My point? Damn, I do hope it's yours as well."

"Yes, of course, of course. Tomorrow—"

Ketterer interrupted sharply, "I was rather hoping, since you share a perfectly correct and moral position, a man of your undoubted power and influence would, at the very least, have formally led the way and outlawed all contraband on all Struan ships, and have done with it."

"All contraband is already proscribed, Admiral," Malcolm said.

" 'Slowly, slowly catchee monkey' is the way to go. In a month or two we'll be in the majority."

The Admiral just raised his thick eyebrows and puffed his cigar and turned his attention to the sea. The fleet looked grand under riding lights. "Looks as though there could be a storm tonight, or tomorrow. Not the sort of weather for a joy ride, for a lady, I would think."

Anxiously Malcolm looked up at the sky and sniffed the wind. No danger signs. As tomorrow's weather was a major concern he had gone to great lengths to check it. To his joy, as for the last few days the forecast had been for smooth seas and fair wind. Marlowe had confirmed it before dinner, and although he did not yet have final sailing approval—or was party to the real reason for Malcolm's need to be aboard with Angelique—as far as he was concerned their trip was on.

"Is that your forecast, Admiral?" Malcolm asked.

"My weather expert, Mr. Struan. He advised cancelling any trials tomorrow. Better to spend the time preparing to stand off Yedo. Eh?" Ketterer added with thin joviality.

"I'm against flattening Yedo," Malcolm said absently, his mind on this new and unexpected problem—the Admiral's snide refusal to accept his letter that he had been confident would be more than sufficient.

Everything's perfect except for this bugger, he thought, curbing his anger, trying to think of a way out of the dilemma. *Prancing Cloud* had arrived on schedule and was in the roads off-loading cargo, Captain Strongbow already apprised of the new secret orders for Wednesday's new departure time, and Edward Gornt equally primed to pass over the Brock information as soon as the duel was over.

"I'm also opposed," the Admiral was saying. "We've no formal orders for war. I'm curious what your reasons are."

"Using a hammer to kill a hornet is not only foolish but can give you piles."

Ketterer laughed. "Damn, that's a good one, Struan. Piles, eh? More of your Chinaman philosophy, eh?"

"No, sir. Dickens." He eased his back and leaned again on his sticks. "It would please me, sir, and Angelique, to be aboard *Pearl*, with Captain Marlowe, and out of sight of land tomorrow, for a short time." Heavenly had advised that as the precedent he was using, the marriage of Malcolm's parents, took place between Macao and Hong Kong out of sight of land, for safety he should do the same. "With your blessing, of course."

"It would please me to see the Noble House take the lead in the

Japans. Clearly you don't have enough time. I suggest ten days would be enough for practical steps. I believe *Pearl* and Marlowe are needed for fleet matters tomorrow." Ketterer turned to go.

"Wait," Malcolm said, panic rising, "say I make an announcement right now, to everyone here, that we're . . . that we're stopping all arms shipments into Japan from now on. Would that satisfy you?"

"The point is would it satisfy you?" the Admiral said, enjoying seeing the man who represented everything he despised wriggling on the barb. "Would it?"

"What . . . what is it, sir, that I can do, or say?"

"It's not up to me to run your 'business.' " The way Ketterer used the word, laced with scorn, made it a dirty word. "It would seem to me what's good for the Japans is good for China. If you outlaw guns here, why not do the same in China for all your ships—the same with opium?"

"I can't do that," Malcolm said. "It would put us out of business, opium's not against the law and both are legal—"

"Interesting." Again the word was heavy with sarcasm. "I really must thank you for a fine dinner, as usual, Mr. Struan. If you'll excuse me, I have lots to do tomorrow."

"Wait!" Malcolm said shakily. "Please, please help me, tomorrow's terribly important to me, I swear I'll support you in everything, I'll lead the way but please help me about tomorrow. Please."

Admiral Ketterer pursed his lips, ready to terminate this pointless conversation. That's what it is, though there's no doubt I could use support amongst these rotten bastards, if even a tenth of the slanders rumored at their bloody meeting are true. I suppose this one isn't so bad, if he could be trusted—compared to the others, compared to that monster Greyforth. "When's your duel?"

Malcolm was going to answer truthfully but stopped himself. "I'll answer that if you like, sir, and I remember what you said about duelling, but in matters of honor my family have been very serious for at least two generations and I don't want to be lacking. It's a tradition, like the Navy, I suppose. Much of the magic of the Royal Navy has to do with that, tradition and honor, doesn't it?"

"Without it the Royal Navy would not be the Royal Navy." Ketterer took another deep puff of the cigar. At least the young bugger understands, by God, though that doesn't tip the scales. The truth is the poor fool's mother is quite right to disapprove the marriage—the girl's pretty enough but hardly the right choice, bad blood line, typically French. I'm doing him a favor.

Are you?

Remember Consuela di Mardos Perez of Cádiz?

He had first met her when he was a midshipman on *Royal Sovereign* during courtesy calls at the port. Ultimately the Admiralty had refused him permission to marry, his father had been equally opposed and when, at length, he had won both their consents and rushed back to claim her, she was already betrothed. She was Catholic too, he thought sadly, still loving her after all this time.

Catholic, that sent everyone mad, like Struan's mother, I'll wager. As if it matters, though Consuela's family was good where this girl's isn't. Yes, I still love her. After her, no one. Never wanted to marry, not after losing her, somehow couldn't. Still, that let me put everything into the Navy, so life hasn't been a total sodding loss.

Has it?

"I'm going to have another port," he said. "That will take ten to fifteen minutes. What can you do to lead the way in ten or fifteen minutes, eh?"

41

GORNT HURRIED DOWN THE STEPS of Struan's into the night, following other guests leaving the party in animated conversation, bundled up and holding their hats against the wind. Servants were waiting with lamps to guide some of them home. After a polite but hasty good night, he went next door to Brock's. The guard, a tall turbanned Sikh, saluted, stared at him as he rushed up the stairs two at a time to knock on Norbert Greyforth's door.

"Who is it?"

"Me, suh, Edward. Sorry, it's important."

There was a sour grumble. Then the bolt jerked back. Norbert's hair was tousled. He wore a nightshirt, nightcap and bed socks. "What the hell is it?"

"Struan. He's just announced from here on he's committing the Noble House to embargo all guns and all opium in Japan and ordering the same in all Asia and the China trade."

"What's this, a joke?"

"No joke, Mr. Greyforth, suh. It was at the party—that's what he said in front of everyone a moment ago, Sir William, most of the Foreign Ambassadors, the Admiral, Dmitri—Struan's exact words, suh: 'I want to make a formal statement. Following my *Guardian* letter today, I've decided no guns or opium will be carried by our ships or traded by Struan's from now on, here or in China.'"

Norbert began to laugh. "Come in, this calls for a celebration. He's put Struan's out of business. And made us Noble House." He stuck his head into the corridor and shouted for his Number One Boy, "Lee! Champagne, chop chop! Come in, Edward, and close the door, it's drafty and cold enough to freeze the balls off a brass monkey." He

815

turned up the oil lamp. His bedroom was large with a vast four-poster, the floor carpeted, oils on the walls of Brock clipper ships—their fleet smaller than Struan's but their steamer fleet almost twice as large. Some of the paintings were fire damaged and the ceiling, too, was not yet completely repaired. Books were piled on the side tables and another opened on the bed.

"The poor bastard's really gone." Norbert chuckled. "First thing we do is to cancel the duel, got to keep him alive. Now this is wh—" His smile vanished. "Wait a minute, what am I talking about? It's all a storm in a pisspot, he's no more tai-pan of Struan's than I am. You're the fool, whatever he says means nothing and much as his Bible-thumping mother would like to do the same, she'd never agree, couldn't, it'd ruin them."

Gornt smiled. "I disagree."

Norbert glanced at him sharply. "Eh?"

"She'll agree."

"Oh? Why?"

"Secret."

"What sort of secret?" Norbert glanced at the door as it opened. Lee, an elderly Cantonese with a long, thick queue, wearing neat livery—white jacket, black trousers—waddled in with glasses, champagne in an ice bucket, a neat towel over his arm. In moments two glasses were served. When the door had closed, Norbert raised his glass. "Health, and death to all Struans. What secret?"

"You told me to try to befriend him. I have. Now he confides in me. First—"

"He does?"

"Up to a point but it's better every day. First, about tonight. The reason he wrote the letter and made the announcement was to curry favor with the Admiral, secretly."

"Eh?"

"May I?" Gornt motioned at the champagne.

"Of course. Sit down and explain yourself."

"He needs the Admiral's approval to get aboard *Pearl* tomorrow, that's the re—"

"What the hell are you talking about?"

"I happened to overhear them, talking privately—they went outside after dinner. I was looking at some of his paintings nearby—I'd noticed a couple of Aristotle Quances—and, well, their voices carried." Gornt related, almost word for word, their conversation. "Ketterer ended by saying, 'Let's see what you can do in ten or fifteen minutes.' "

"That was all? Nothing about what's aboard or what's so important about *Pearl*?"

"No, suh."

"Weird, that's weird. What could it be?"

"I don't know. The whole evening was strange. All during dinner I'd catch Struan glancing at the Admiral from time to time, but never once did he catch his eye. It was as though the Admiral deliberately avoided him without being too obvious. That's what prompted my curiosity, suh."

"Where was he sitting—the Admiral?"

"Next to Angelique, place of honor on her right, Sir William the other side, should have been the other way around—another curiosity. I was next to Marlowe, he was star-gazing at Angelique and talking boring naval talk, nothing about any trip tomorrow though I got the impression from what Struan had said, it had been planned for some time, pending the Admiral's okay. After the Admiral left I brought the conversation with Marlowe back to tomorrow but he just said, 'Might be doing some trials, old boy, if the Old Man approves, why?' I told him I enjoyed ships and asked if I could come along, he laughed and said he'd certainly arrange a future trip, then he left too."

"Nothing about Struan and the girl?"

"No, suh. He's all eyes for her though."

"It's her tits." Norbert grunted. "When Struan made the announcement what happened?"

"First there was a silence, then pandemonium, questions, some laughter, a few catcalls, Marlowe and the other naval officers cheered, and there was a lot of anger. McFay went white, Dmitri almost spat, Sir William stared at Struan, shaking his head as though the poor fellow was an object of pity. I'd concentrated on Ketterer. He made no sign one way or another, said nothing to Struan other than 'Interesting,' got up at once, thanked him for dinner and left. Struan tried to stop him, started to ask him about tomorrow but the Admiral either didn't hear him or pretended not to, and stalked out, leaving Struan shaking. At the same time, suh, everyone talking and no one listening, like in a Chinese market, not a few furious and shouting at Struan that he was insane, and how in the hell could we carry on trade—you know, the obvious and the truth."

Norbert finished his glass. Gornt began to pour for him but he shook his head. "Don't like bubbly too much at night, makes me fart. Pour me a Scotch—the bottle's over there." It was on a sideboard, oak, weatherbeaten, an old sea clock on it. "What's aboard *Pearl* he'd want so much?"

"I don't know."

"What did Struan do after Ketterer left?"

"He just sat down and took a large drink, stared into space, absently said good night as people began to drift off, paying no attention to Angelique, which again was unlike him. As to her, she just watched wide-eyed, not the center of attention for once, clearly not understanding what was going on so I guess not in Struan's confidence either. I thought I'd better give you the news so didn't stay."

"You said something about a secret? What's the secret, eh? Why that old bitch, Tess Struan, will agree to commit business suicide?"

"Because of Sir Morgan's plan, suh."

"What?"

"Sir Morgan." Gornt smiled broadly. "Before we left Shanghai he told me, privately, he and Mr. Brock had planned and were in the middle of executing some scheme to ruin Struan's and finish them for good. He told me it revolves around Hawaiian sugar, the Victoria Bank an—"

"Eh?" Norbert stared at him, remembering Sir Morgan had been specific that he had not given Gornt details of the coup, and did not want him to have them: 'Even though the lad's t'be trusted. Yes, an' there be no harm in letting him mix in the poxy Struan circle to see what he can spy out.' "Morgan told you the details? About the deal?"

"No, suh, at least he only told me what I was to pass on to Struan as secretly as I could."

"Jesus Christ," Norbert said, exasperated, "you'd better start from the beginning."

"He said I wasn't to tell you about my part until I'd accomplished it, until I'd done what he told me to do. I have, I'm in Malcolm Struan's confidence, so now I can tell you." Gornt sipped his champagne. "Very good wine, suh."

"Get on with it!"

"Sir Morgan told me to tell Struan a series of stories—he said it was near enough to the truth to hook Struan and through him the real taipan, Tess Struan. Suh, I can almost guarantee, the last of the Struan taipans is firmly hooked." Quickly Gornt gave him the substance of exactly what he had told Malcolm Struan. Ending it, he laughed. "I'm to give him 'the secret details' after the duel, en route to his ship."

"What're you to tell him?"

The older man listened carefully. Knowing the real details, he was fascinated to hear more of Morgan's craftiness. If Tess Struan acted on this false information, it would certainly buy Sir Morgan the extra few weeks he wanted. 'But Sir Morgan,' Norbert had said in Shanghai when the plan had been laid out, 'it's foolproof now, you don't need extra time, I can do my part in Yokohama before Christmas.'

'Yes, thee can, and will. But me an' Dad, we likes to be safer than safe, lad, and extra time will make sure our necks be away from any ropes and our arses out of prison.'

Norbert suppressed a shudder at the thought of being caught. No rope, but prison for fraud probably and Debtors' Prison a certainty. Sir Morgan's a crafty bugger all right, just like him to tell me one thing and Gornt another. He's saved me one risk, killing Struan. So it's England for me and five thousand a year but I lose the cream, the manor house and being rich. Better safe than sorry.

Norbert sighed. I was looking forward to putting a bullet into Malcolm and reaping the cream, he thought, Old Man Brock's words etched in his memory: 'Norbert, there be cream in thy retirement. Thy bonus be upped by five thousand guineas a year if thee kills him, a thousand bonus for a bad wounding, thee's beached if thee's humbled.'

"Morgan's clever, the plan's foolproof," he said with a smile. To make sure, testing him, added casually, "Isn't it?"

"Suh?"

"The small changes make all the difference, don't they?" He was watching him carefully.

"Sorry, suh, I don't know any details—other than what I've told you and he said to pass on to Struan."

"I'll have another Scotch—help yourself to wine," Norbert said, satisfied, then drank in silence until he had thought everything through. "You continue as if you haven't told me. Tomorrow I'll cancel the duel. Can't afford to kill or put the bugger out of action."

"Yes, suh, that was my immediate thought too." Gornt handed him Malcolm Struan's letter, the equivalent of the one Norbert had signed. "He gave me this for you, but I suggest you don't cancel tomorrow, that might make him suspicious—and we might find out what's so important about *Pearl,* if he goes or if he doesn't."

"All right, Edward, good idea." Norbert guffawed. "So Wednesday, young nipper Struan's on his way to disaster, eh?"

Gornt grinned. "On his merry way, suh. Their Noble House is finished and ours begins."

"Yes." The warmth of the Scotch mixed with the warmth of the future. "Then you've decided to join us?"

"Yes, suh, if you approve. Sir Morgan said you'd have to approve."

"You keep this up and you're approved. Tonight was a good night's work, tip-top. 'Night."

He bolted the door after him. Before he climbed back into the high bed he used the chamber pot and felt even better. His glass was on his side table, perched on a pile of books and magazines, still a quarter full. He settled himself against the high pillows he favored and picked up the half-opened book, *City of the Saints,* Burton's account of a stay among the mysterious, polygamous Mormons in Salt Lake City, Utah, another first for this, the most famous adventurer and explorer in the world, who spoke thirty or more languages, and whose exploits and idiosyncrasies were avidly followed in minutest detail.

He read a few paragraphs, then, distracted, tossed it aside. It's not as good as *Pilgrimage to El-Medina and Mecca,* he thought, or about discovering Lake Tanganyika.

Amongst all that Mormon snatch you'd think Burton, who openly favors polygamy, which any fool knows is the right idea, would describe his conquests—he's done it enough times in other books to raise the old hackles. Some papers reported he had a baker's dozen of 'em, all at the same time, presented personally by Brigham Young, head of their "Latter-day Saints" Church and Governor of Utah. What liars!

But, my God, what a man—he's done more and seen more than any Englishman alive, makes you even prouder to be English. And with all the freedom to go where he wants, live as he wants, how he wants, what's he do but go back to England and get married to a good Englishwoman like any normal man. Of course, he left after a month and now they say he's somewhere in parts unknown, the Hindu Kush or up in the secret land on Top of the World, living with the snow giants . . .

He sipped more of the drink, and thought about Gornt. That young bugger's not as smart as he thinks. Anyone can work out what's aboard *Pearl* and why. Ketterer can keep a secret, so can Wee Willie but Michaelmas Tweet can't, nor Heavenly when he's in his cups, so I'd heard about Tess Struan's letters and that she's boxed Wee Willie, blocked the Church, blocked all ship captains, and through Ketterer the Navy— 'cepting she's no power over the Navy! And aboard *Pearl* is Marlowe. Marlowe could marry 'em—if Ketterer allows it.

He chuckled.

But Ketterer hates Struan's because they sold cannon to the White Lotus pirates, like us, like we've been selling cannon to any God-cursed warlord who'll buy, and will continue to do the same even if

Struan's don't, and why not? They're legal and always will be. Parliament needs armament factories because armaments are great business and all governments like war—because wars are great business, and, most of all, because war covers up their own sodding incompetence.

To hell with governments.

Ketterer hates Struan's. For all his redneck arrogance he's no fool, he would want practical results for a favor. Those he can't get—announcements from that young fool mean nothing—so he's cat-and-mousing him. Maybe he'll let Struan and his doxy go aboard, maybe he won't, but either way Marlowe won't be allowed to marry them—Ketterer wants Struan to crawl. The sod would make me crawl too if he'd a quarter of a chance and give me a hundred lashes to boot.

A large swallow of the fine whisky put him into a better humor and he laughed. So young Struan's stymied: no *Pearl*-assisted marriage and back to Hong Kong, with or without his doxy, and into the sodding pit with his ma. Curious that I've got to leave the bugger alive when I'd planned to take the Old Man's cream: '. . . but Norbert, don't thee be a-telling Morgan, he's agin any killing, he be wanting to see young Struan in't shit, his ma too! Remember, or I'll have thy guts for garters.'

Must I stop the duel? I'll think about that. Careful. I need the extra bonus.

Just like Morgan to give Gornt secret instructions and keep me in the dark. What else has he told Gornt he hasn't told me? Never mind, Morgan's the clever one, with all of his Old Man's nerves but smooth with it, modern, no madness, and no risk—none of his dad's brutal, merciless obsessions. Morgan's our real tai-pan, and he'll be the tai-pan of the new Noble House. It's only taken twenty years to crush Dirk's company, the biggest that's ever been in Asia.

Satisfied, he finished his drink, turned down the wick, and settled himself with a yawn. Sorry I never saw the Old Man in his heyday, or the tai-pan, old Green-eyed Devil himself, whom only the devil winds of the Great Typhoon could kill. Lucky that young fool inherited none of his qualities.

Now the last guest had gone. Only Angelique, Jamie McFay, and Malcolm remained. The embers in the huge inglenook fireplace glowed as drafts came down the chimney and went away. Silently Malcolm was frowning at the fire, watching pictures in the coals. She sat on the arm of his chair, unsettled. McFay was leaning against the table. "I'll say good night, Tai-pan," he said.

Malcolm came out of his reverie. "Oh . . . Hang on a moment." He smiled up at Angelique. "Sorry, Angel, I've a few things to discuss with Jamie, do you mind?"

"Of course not. 'Night, Jamie." She bent and kissed Struan affectionately. "Good night, Malcolm, sleep well."

"Good night, darling, we should leave early."

"Yes . . . but Malcolm, please can I ask, what was all the shouting about? I didn't understand, could you explain?"

"It was jealousy. Nothing more."

"Oh! Of course, how strong you were and how modern! How right you are about guns and opium . . . oh la la, *chéri*, and wise. Thank you. Of course." She kissed him again. "What time do we leave in the morning? I'm so excited, the voyage will be such a *changement superbe*."

"Just after dawn. I'll see you're awakened in good time, but—but don't be surprised if . . . if there's a change of plan—Marlowe said the weather might change."

"But he swore the wind would drop and it would be a grand day for a voyage."

"I said 'might change,' Angel." He gave her a hug. "If not tomorrow the earliest possible day, he promised."

"I do hope it's tomorrow. *Je t'aime, chéri*."

"*Je t'aime*."

When she was gone the silence in the room congealed. Chen peered around the door again. Malcolm said, "Close the bloody door and don't come back." It closed with alacrity. Jamie began to talk but he held up his hand. "Don't say a thing about ships or cannon or opium. Please."

"Very well."

"Sit down, Jamie." Malcolm had thought all around the corners of the Admiral and devised a plan for each of the various possibilities: if the Admiral decided they could make the trip with his blessing, or if they could make the trip but Marlowe was forbidden to perform the ceremony, or if the trip was postponed till sometime in the future. For the moment he put countermeasures aside. "Would you have our steam cutter alongside *Pearl* just before dawn, the Bosun to find out from Marlowe if our trip's on or not. If it is or if it isn't, tell the Bosun to report to me here with the answer. All right?"

"Of course."

"I wrote the letter for Norbert and gave it to Gornt tonight, so that's done. Have I forgotten anything?"

"About Wednesday?"

"Yes."

"Nothing I know of. Routes and times you know about, the pistols are standard, no doctors will be present as both Babcott and Hoag are considered unsafe. The letters are your only defense. No witnesses except Gornt and me."

"Good. You're ready to leave with *Prancing Cloud*?"

"I'll send a valise aboard with our mails tomorrow, no one should notice. What about your trunks?"

"I'm only taking one. Sneak it aboard tomorrow—if anyone says anything it's some clothes I'm sending on ahead, pending my move back to Hong Kong for Christmas."

"Chen will pack for you?"

"He'll have to. I'll swear him to secrecy but that'll only work with our society, not with the Chinese. I'll have to take him with me. Ah Tok's a problem but she can stay here pending our 'real move.' I'll have to let Ah Soh into the secret. She'll come with us to Hong Kong."

"Angelique?"

"No need to tell her. If we go aboard *Pearl,* Ah Soh can pack a trunk of clothes and send that aboard with the same excuse, after nightfall tomorrow for safety. All right?"

"Yes."

"Wednesday morning we, you and I, will sneak out the back way as planned. A little later Chen, Ah Soh and Angelique, well cloaked, will go across the road to our wharf where you'll have the steam cutter waiting to take them to the clipper—"

"Excuse me butting in but if this is the final plan, better to use an oared cutter, less noise. For safety, the steam cutter should be waiting for us at Drunk Town wharf."

"That's better, Jamie. Thank you. An oared cutter then. After dealing with Norbert, we get aboard as fast as we can. Tomorrow tell Vargas to organize a meeting with our Japanese silk dealers for Friday, make it look as if we've a heavy schedule for the rest of this week and next, all right?"

"Yes."

"Anything else, Jamie?"

"May I make a suggestion?"

"Of course."

"After tomorrow's trip in *Pearl* . . ." McFay hesitated. "You said there might be a change of plan—because of weather? Weather's forecast as good, isn't it?"

"Yes. That was just in case Marlowe has to stay in port," he said easily. "With all the fleet preparations to savage Yedo, or threaten it, you never know what Ketterer or Sir William might decide. What's your suggestion, Jamie?"

"Actually I've a couple. After you come back tomorrow— Marlowe said you'd be back by sunset—why don't you and Angelique go aboard *Prancing Cloud* for dinner with Captain Strongbow, even stay aboard overnight. At dawn you and I could come ashore an—"

"That's a much better plan," Struan said at once, jumping ahead with a beam, "much better. Then Angelique's already aboard, so's her luggage, so we don't have to worry about her, and after Norbert we can come straight back. Great thinking, Jamie. Our stuff can be sent aboard with Chen and Ah Soh, no reason why they shouldn't stay aboard too, no one should suspect anything." His smile was fine and genuine. "You're very clever to think of that, you're very clever, which is why I don't want you to leave Struan's."

Jamie smiled ruefully. "We'll see."

"By the way, in case there's an accident," Malcolm said calmly, eyes level and without fear. "If I'm wounded but mobile enough to get aboard, that's what I want to do. If there's a real emergency, well, just fetch either Babcott or Hoag. Plan to bring Hoag aboard anyway, we'll take him back to Hong Kong."

"I checked their Kanagawa clinic but that's on Thursday so they'll both be here."

"You think of everything."

"No. Wish I could, and wish you'd cancel the duel."

"There won't be any accident."

"I pray you're right. But whatever happens it's better that I stay here until you get back, or you send for me."

"But Mother said in her letter th—"

"I know. Let's be honest, Tai-pan. I'm out, one way or another. It's best I'm here to cover your tail, if Norbert's all right or if he isn't, and to keep an eye on Gornt. Sorry, I still don't trust that fellow. My job's here not in Hong Kong. In the spring I'll quit. That's best, and we should agree on it now—but not before your twenty-first."

The two men looked at each other, eyes locked. Both broke off sharply as coals fell onto the hearth. The coals flickered and died without danger. "You're a wonderful friend," Malcolm said quietly. "Truly."

"No, just trying to keep my oath—to the tai-pan of the Noble House."

André and Phillip Tyrer were outside the British Legation. "Malcolm's idea of an embargo, however moral, would be a disaster for every trading company in Asia," Tyrer said, "including yours, not that you'd follow suit or the Germans or Russians or Yanks." The wind ruffled his hair but he was not cold, with all the alcohol he had consumed and the excitement. "Sir William doubts if the Governor in Hong Kong will approve, could approve whatever Parliament orders, he'd prevaricate, not that I can officially speak for either of them. Parliament's a law unto itself," he added with a yawn. "I'm beat, aren't you?"

"I have a date."

"Ah!" Tyrer had seen the flash of expectation. "Lucky man! You've certainly seemed a lot happier recently, a very lot happier. We were all quite worried."

André changed to French and dropped his voice. "I'm fine now, the best I've ever been. Can't tell you how happy I am and the girl, well, she treats me like a king—best I've ever had. No more wandering for me. I have an exclusive."

"Wonderful."

"Listen, talking of that, what about Fujiko? Raiko's getting nervous and so is she. I hear the poor girl's crushed, cries all the time."

"Oh?" Tyrer felt a shaft in his loins. "Then your advice was right," he said, hardly noticing that he replied in French—most of the evening he had been speaking to Seratard, Zergeyev and other ministers, English intermingled with French.

"I'd say you've been tough enough and it's time. No point in hurting anyone, they're nice people. They're both sorry for irritating you."

A few nights ago Raiko had intercepted him and again asked if he had his overdue payment. After he had put her off with the promise that he was expecting funds any day—gambling that Angelique would find the money—Raiko had questioned him about Tyrer. 'What's wrong with the man? It would be a service to him, to me, to Fujiko, and to you, old friend, to correct whatever needs to be corrected. Obviously he's been seduced by the whores at the Inn of the Lily. In these bad times it would help us, and you, if you would convince him to return. The poor girl is near suicide.'

He had not believed that but Raiko had been ready to twist the knife called Hinodeh.

"Phillip, you've played the game perfectly," he said. "I'll arrange a rendezvous and we'll reopen negotiations."

"Well, André, I don't know about that," Tyrer said. "I, er, I must say I did try another girl, once—the Inn you recommended is not bad at all—and I've been thinking perhaps having a permanent girl is not a good idea. I mean it's a large expense and, well, I need a polo pony . . ."

"There are good points and bad points to having your own girl," André said, hiding his angst. "Perhaps the best idea would be to shelve contract talks pending 'an improvement in relations.' "

"You mean have your cake and eat it?"

"Why not? They're all there for our pleasure, aren't they—though Fujiko and Raiko are very special." André was persuasive, not wanting Tyrer off the Fujiko hook any more than he wanted to be on Raiko's. To be secret partners with her was one thing. To be at her mercy was another. He would make the date, the rest would be up to them to seduce Tyrer back to his previous state of passion. "Leave them to me. How about tomorrow? I can promise your welcome will be enthusiastic."

"Oh, really? Well, all right."

"Phillip . . ." André glanced around again. "Henri is more than anxious to support Sir William in moves to rap this fool *Tairō* Anjo severely—the cretin went too far this time. Could Sir William have a private discussion tomorrow? Henri has a few ideas he would like to pass on, privately."

"I'm sure he would." Tyrer was at once attentive and pleasantly surprised, his tiredness leaving him. Usually Seratard would launch a French initiative and they would only hear of it when it was in full force. Like the secret invitation to Lord Yoshi to visit the French flagship that they had just heard about through their own sources—Chinese servants in the French Legation had overheard André and Seratard planning, they had passed it on to Number One Chen, who had told Struan who had told him who had told Sir William. "A council of war? The two of them?"

André said, "I suggest the four of us—they'll need assistants to put their ideas into motion, but the fewer involved the better. If later they wanted to bring in the Admiral and General, all right. But later, eh?"

"An Entente Cordiale! I'll take it up with the Old Man first thing in the morning. How about eleven?"

"Could we make it ten? I must keep a noon appointment." André had already cleared the idea with Seratard the moment he had returned from seeing Raiko: 'Henri, this meeting could be very important, the more secret we keep it from other Ministers the better. This time we've got to pretend to be a hundred percent with the British. They have the warships, we haven't. This time we must encourage them to go to war.'

'Why?'

'I gather from Tyrer who gets it from his tame samurai Nakama—Henri, Tyrer's Japanese is astonishingly good for the short time he's been here. He has a remarkable aptitude for it so we should seriously watch him, and befriend him. Tyrer has found out that there's no love lost between this Anjo and Toranaga Yoshi, who is a patrician like you, whereas Anjo is more of a commoner.'

It had amused him to see Seratard puff up at the flattery—no more a patrician than he was himself. 'We secretly encourage the British to smash Anjo while distancing ourselves at the last moment from the actual conflict, while cultivating Yoshi as urgent, secret national policy. We make him an ally, we must, then through him we'll dump the British back in their sewer and control the foreign presence here.'

'How do we do that, André? Cultivate him?'

'Leave that to me,' he had said, gambling again that, through Raiko and by providing her with first-rate intelligence, and money, he could make the right contacts to get close to Yoshi. 'He's going to be our key to unlock Japan. We'll have to invest some money, not much. But in the right pocket . . .' With a little wandering into mine, he had chortled 'I'll guarantee success. He's going to be our Knight in Shining Armor. We're going to help him become Sir Galahad to wreck Wee Willie's King Arthur.'

Why not, he told himself again, standing there on the promenade with Tyrer, another key piece on the chessboard of French dominance in Asia. Phillip will . . .

My God! He almost burst out as the wild idea jumped into his mind: If Struan gets killed in his duel and Angelique becomes a free card, could she become a Guinevere for this Jappo Yoshi? Why not? He might enjoy a different tidbit. Through Raiko, perhaps Angelique would—for she would be perilously without funds and therefore vulnerable.

He laughed and put the thought aside as too heady to consider seriously tonight. "Phillip," he said, wanting him to consider him to be his best friend. "If we can help our masters to arrive at a firm solution and put it into effect . . . eh?"

"That would be marvelous, André!"

"One day you'll be Ambassador here."

Tyrer laughed. "Don't be silly."

"I'm not." In spite of the fact they would always be on opposite sides and he needed to be able to influence him, he genuinely liked Tyrer. "In a year you'll speak and write fluent Japanese, you're trusted by Wee Willie, you've your wild card, Nakama, to assist you. Why not?"

"Why not?" Tyrer said with a grin. "It's a nice idea to end a night on. Happy dreams, André."

Almost no one in the Settlement was sleeping as contentedly as Angelique—Struan's bombshell tonight, coupled with anxiety over the coming war here and in Europe and the resultant hazards for business, kept most awake: "As if there's not enough to worry about with our own civil war," Dmitri muttered to his pillow in the deep darkness of his room in the Cooper-Tillman Building. News from home was getting worse and worse, whichever side you supported, and he had family on both sides.

Dreadful numbers of casualties on both sides, looting and burning and atrocities and mutinies and brutalities and corruptions and monstrous tragedies, again on both sides. An uncle had written from Maryland that whole towns were being burned and pillaged by Quantrill's Raiders for the South and the Jayhawkers for the North, and that, by now, most important men in the North had legally bought themselves and their sons out of the army draft: *The war's being fought by the poor, the undernourished, the ill-equipped and the half starving. This is the end of our country, Dmitri . . .*

His father wrote from Richmond the same: *There'll be nothing left if this goes on another year. Nothing. Terrible to tell you, my darling son, your brother Janny was killed at the second battle at Bull Run, poor lad, our cavalry was decimated, carnage . . .*

Dmitri twisted and turned in his bed, striving to put the pain for his nation away from him but could not.

In the Club a noisy, drunken row was still in progress amongst the few remaining traders at the bar. A few naval and army officers, Tweet and others were at tables scattered about the room, having final nightcaps.

Near the window, Count Zergeyev and the newly arrived Swiss Minister, Fritz Erlicher, sat at a table. The Russian hid his amusement and leaned over their glasses of port. "They're all fools, Herr Erlicher," he said above the hubbub.

"Do you think this young Struan means it?"

"He means it, but whether or not the policy is ever implemented remains to be seen." They spoke French, and Zergeyev explained the conflict of mother and son within Struan's. "That's the current rumor, she pulls the strings though he has the title quite legally."

"If it's implemented it would be good, for us both."

"Ah! You have a proposal?"

"An idea, Count Zergeyev." Erlicher untied his cravat and breathed easier, the air in the Club smoky and close, the smell of beer and urine heavy, and the sawdust of the floor in need of replacement. "We are a small, independent nation with few resources but plenty of courage, and skills. The British, for whom you have no love, monopolize most arms manufacturing and sales throughout Europe—though Krupp's factory looks promising." The bearded, heavyset man smiled. "We hear Mother Russia already has a substantial interest there."

"You astonish me."

Erlicher laughed. "I astonish myself sometimes, Herr Count. But I wanted to mention we've the beginnings of fine gun and cannon foundries, privately I can tell you we are negotiating with Gatling to make his machine gun under license, and can supply you liberally with any arms you might need on a long-term basis."

"Thank you, my dear sir, but we've no such need. Tsar Alexander II is a peace-loving reformer, last year he emancipated our serfs, this year he's reforming the army, navy, bureaucracy, the judiciary, education, everything."

Erlicher grinned. "And meanwhile he's presiding over the biggest land conquest in history, with the subjugation of more peoples in history, except for Genghis Khan and his Mongol hordes. Genghis rode westwards," his smile became a beam, "while your Tsar's hordes spread eastwards. Over the whole continent! Imagine that! Over the whole continent to the sea, through Siberia to the Kamchatka Peninsula. And that's not the end. Is it?"

"Isn't it?" the Count said, smiling.

"We hear the Tsar's hoping to pass through your new fortress of Vladivostok to the Japans, then north to the Kuriles, north again to the Aleutians, at last to join with Russian Alaska that rolls down to northern California. While the world sleeps. Astonishing." Erlicher brought out his cigar case and offered it. "Please—they're the best Cuban."

Zergeyev took one and smelt it and rolled it between his fingers, and accepted a flame. "Thank you. Excellent. Are all the Swiss dreamers like you?" he asked pleasantly.

"No, sir Count. But we are peace lovers, and good hosts to peace lovers, but we stay in our mountains, well armed, and watch the world outside. Happily our mountains are prickly to those who come uninvited."

Another burst of shouting distracted them for a moment, Lunkchurch, Swann, Grimm and others more vociferous than usual.

"I've never been to Switzerland. You should see Russia, we have many sights there to feast the eye."

"I've been to your beautiful St. Petersburg. Three years ago, I was in our Embassy there for a few months. Best city in Europe I think, if you are nobility, wealthy, or a foreign diplomat. You must miss it."

"I bleed for it, more than you can imagine." Zergeyev sighed. "Not long now and I'll be there. I'm told my next posting will be London—then I will visit your mountains."

"I would be honored to be your host." Erlicher puffed his cigar and blew a smoke ring. "Then my business suggestion doesn't interest you?"

"It's certainly true that the British monopolize all manner of enterprises, all sea routes and seas, all manner of wealths from subjugated lands"—now there was no warmth in Zergeyev's smile—"which should be shared."

"Then we should talk again, in quieter surroundings?"

"Over lunch, why not? I would certainly inform my superiors of any discussion. If there is ever a future need, where should I contact you, or your superiors?"

"Here is my card. If you ask for me in Zurich, I'm easily found." Erlicher watched him reading the superb calligraphy of the miraculous new printing process they had just developed. Count Zergeyev had elegant features, patrician in every pore, with perfect clothes where he knew his own were mediocre and that his forebears were peasants. But he did not envy him.

I'm Swiss, he was thinking. I'm free. I don't have to bow a knee or doff my cap to any king or Tsar or priest or man—if I don't want to. This poor fellow's still a serf in a way. Thank God for my mountains and my valleys, and my brothers and sisters and living amongst them, all free as I am free and will remain free.

Near the bar, half drunk and swaying, Lunkchurch was comically squaring off against another man, shouting at the top of his voice,

"That there effing Struan's blown his effing rocker wot ever way you effing want and no effing . . ."

"For goodness' sake, Barnaby, stop your foul language," the Reverend Tweet shouted, pushing through the crush for the door, his collar slightly askew and his face flushed and sweating. "When you think about it from a fair, English point of view you have to agree, morally, young Struan has the right approach!"

Lunkchurch drunkenly made a very rude gesture in his face. "Stuff your effing santimonio effing doodle do!"

Purple with rage, the Reverend Tweet bunched his fist and threw an ineffectual blow. Those near Lunkchurch jerked him out of the way as usual, as others surrounded Tweet and soothed his soaring tirade, and then Charlie Grimm, always ready to take up the gauntlet, any gauntlet, roared above the noise and through his own sodden haze, "Barnaby, prepare to meet thy Maker!"

Helpfully, those nearby gave them room and, to cheers, the two men began battering each other with abandon.

"Drinks on the 'ouse," the chief barman ordered for those still remaining. "Scotch for the Rev, port for the Count and 'is guest. Now you two, stop fighting!"

Tweet accepted the drink and tottered to a table well away from the fighters who were now rolling on the floor, their belligerence undiminished. The barman sighed, emptied a bucket of slops over them, walked around the bar, picked up one in each hand and, to more cheers, cast them into High Street. "Gents, it's time, gents, please!" he said to howls that were quickly muted. Everyone finished their drinks and began to leave. Zergeyev and Fritz Erlicher raised their hats politely to the clergyman.

"Rev," Swann said—he was the thin trader who acted as the deacon. "How about looking in on the sinners in Drunk Town?"

"Well, Mr. Swann, it is, how shall I say, on the way."

In her little house in the Yoshiwara, Hinodeh waited. Furansu-san had said he would arrive tonight but he might be late. She was dressed to undress, her night kimono and under-kimonos the finest, her hair shining, tortoiseshell and silver combs decorating the swept-up coiffure that showed the nape of her neck perfectly, the combs only there to take away—to allow her hair to fall to her waist, hiding the erotic.

I wonder what is so erotic about the nape of a woman's neck to men, she asked herself, and why is hiding it erotic too? Men, how strange! But she knew that letting her hair fall excited Furansu-san like any client and this was her only concession to their pact. This alone she would do in the light.

In the dark before dawn, when he was with her, her *maiko* would softly awaken her and she would dress in the dark, if he awoke or if he did not. Then she would move to the second room and close the door, her *maiko* guarding the door, and would sleep again if she was tired. He had agreed never to enter this sanctuary—after the first time she had insisted: 'In this way the privacy of the night may extend into the day,' she had said.

'Please?'

'In this way that which you saw once will never change, whatever the gods decree.'

A tremor went through her. Much as she tried, she could not cast out the sensation that the seed of the vile Sore God he had implanted within her was gathering strength, growing, readying to burst forth everywhere. Daily, she scrutinized herself. Minutely. Only Raiko was trusted to make sure those places she could not see herself were examined as closely and were, as yet, blemishless. 'Daily is too much, Hinodeh,' Raiko had said before she had agreed to the contract. 'Nothing maybe happen for years. . . .'

'So sorry, Raiko-san. Daily, it is a condition.'

'Why are you agreeing to this at all? You have a good future in our World. You may never reach first class, but you are educated, your mama-san says you have a long list of clients who are pleased with you, she said you could marry a well-to-do merchant or farmer or sword maker, that you are sensible and would never be wanting for a good match.'

'Thank you for your concern, Raiko-san, but you agreed with my mama-san that you would not question me or pry into my past, where I come from or to seek reasons. In return you share with her a percentage of the money I will earn for this year, and perhaps another. Let me say again, the reason I accept the possible contract is that I wish it.'

Oh, yes, I wish it and how lucky I am.

Now she was twenty-two. Born on a farm outside Nagasaki in the province of Hizen on the South Island, and when she was five, she was invited into the Floating World by one of the many women intermediaries who travelled the country, seeking children who could become possible geisha, art persons, those who would be trained, like Koiko, in the arts and not purely as a *netsujo-jin,* a person for passion. Her parents agreed and were given money and a promissory note for five yearly payments, beginning in ten years, the amount depending on the child's success.

As an art person she had not been successful—at the samisen or singing or dancing or as an actress—but as a person of passion from fifteen when she made her debut, better educated than her contemporaries, she soon became important to her mama-san and to herself. In those days her name was Gekko, Moonbeam, and though there were many foreigners in Nagasaki at that time, she knew not one of them, her House catering only to Japanese of the highest order.

One October, the Month Without Gods, she received a new client. He was a year older than her, eighteen, a goshi and the son of a goshi—an average swordsman, average soldier but to her her dream person. His name was Shin Komoda.

Their passion blossomed. As much as the mama-san tried to curb their mutual magnetism—the youth was poor, his bills remained unpaid—nothing she could say or do had any effect. Until the spring of the following year. Without telling Gekko, the mama-san went to the youth's home and bowed before his mother and, politely, asked for payment.

There was no money to pay. The mother asked for time.

The youth was forbidden to see Gekko again. Outwardly he obeyed his parents, but inwardly nothing they said or did had any effect. Within a week, disguised, they ran away together, disappearing into the sprawling port. There they changed their names and with some money she had saved, and jewelry she brought with her, they purchased passage in steerage on a coastal ship sailing that day for Yedo.

Within the week Shin Komoda was dishonored in his village and declared ronin. Again the mama-san went to see his mother. It was a matter of face, of honor, that their son's bills were paid. His mother's only possession of value and her pride, was her long and beautiful plume of hair. With her husband's agreement she went to a wigmaker in Nagasaki. Without hesitation the man bought. The money was just enough to pay their son's bills. So, for them, honor was satisfied.

In Yedo, at the limit of their money, Gekko and Shin managed to find safe lodgings in the slums of the city. And a Buddhist priest to marry them. Without papers, either of them, and their real past obliterated, life was difficult, almost impossible, but for a year they lived happily, keeping to themselves, on the threshold of poverty. That did not matter for they basked in each other's company and their love increased and was fruitful, and though her money dwindled to nothing,

however much she tried to be prudent and his pay hardly fed them—
the only work he could find was as a guard at a low-class brothel that
was not even in the Yedo Yoshiwara—it did not matter.

Nothing mattered. They were together. They were surviving. And
she kept their two tiny rooms spotless and made of them a palace and
sanctuary for him and the child and as much as she offered and offered,
he refused and refused. "Never! Never never never again will any
other man ever know you, swear it!" She swore it.

When their son was a year old Shin was killed in a brawl. With his
death the light went out of her.

A week later the brothel mama-san propositioned her. She thanked
her and refused, saying she was returning to their home in Nara. In the
market she bought a bright new candle, a red one, and that night when
the child was asleep, quietly she lit it, to watch it and to think what she
should do until the flame died, petitioning the gods, promising them
that when the last fluttering was gone she would decide what was best
for her son, asking for their help to make the decision wise.

The flame had died long since, the decision so simple, so correct:
She must send her son back to his father's parents. Her son must go
alone—she must pretend she and her husband had committed *jinsai,*
joint ritual suicide, in apology to his parents for the hurt they had done
them. To be accepted the child must have at least a year of money,
preferably more. He must be clothed well and travel well with a trusted
nurse, more money. Only in this way could he gain his heritage,
samurai. Last, there was no point obeying an oath to the dead when the
future of their living child was at stake.

In the morning she left her son with a neighbor and with the last
of her money bought the best kimono and parasol she could find in
the thieves market, then, penniless, went to the best hairdresser
near the gates of Yedo's Yoshiwara. There she bartered a month's
future earnings for the best up-to-date hairstyle and massage and
facial and manicure and pedicure and other intimacies—and information.

Information cost a second month.

That afternoon she sallied through the gates and went straight to the
House of Wisteria. The mama-san was a pattern of everyone she had
ever known, always degrees of perfection in their dress and coiffure,
always a measure too heavy, with makeup that veered on being
masklike, eyes so gentle to customers that could become granite hard
in an instant, eyes that could make her girls quiver with fear, and
always scented richly with best perfume she could afford that still

could never quite disguise the pervading smell of saké. This mama-san was spare, her name Meikin.

"So sorry, I don't take ladies without papers or history," the mama-san said. "We are very law-abiding here."

"I'm honored to hear it, Madam, but I have a history, and with your help we can invent another that will satisfy the most inquisitive Bakufu officials while satisfying the nosey toad's probe massively, when I can find it."

Meikin laughed. Her eyes did not. "What training have you had and where? And what is your name?"

"My name is Hinodeh. The where is unimportant." Gekko told her about the geisha teachers and failure to realize their expectations. Then her practical training, the sorts of clients she had and their numbers.

"Interesting. But so sorry, I have no opening here, Hinodeh," the woman said, overkindly. "Come back tomorrow. I will make enquiries, perhaps a friend could take you."

"So sorry, please, may I ask you to reconsider." Sure that tomorrow she would not be admitted on some excuse or other. "You are the best, and the most trustworthy." She gritted her teeth and, praying the information was correct, added delicately, "Even shishi know that."

The color left the mama-san's face though her expression did not change. "You and your lover ran away and now he has abandoned you?" she asked calmly.

"No, Madam."

"Then he is dead."

"Yes, Madam."

"You have a child or children, which?"

"A son."

The older woman sighed. "A son. He is with you?"

"He is with his father's family."

"How old is he?"

"A year and three months."

Meikin had sent for tea and they drank in silence, Gekko trembling inside, afraid that the threat had gone too far, sure that the other woman was wondering where the information came from, and how she, a stranger—dangerous enough in itself—came by the knowledge. Or if she was a Shōgunate spy. If a spy, Gekko reasoned, surely I would not have said that, not on the first interview.

At length the other woman said, "You may not stay here, Hinodeh, but I have a sister who has a fine House in the next street. There's a price for the introduction."

"In advance may I humbly thank you for helping me."

"First, you will swear to excise bad thoughts from your head. Forever."

"On my life."

"On your son's life is better."

"On my son's life."

"Second, you will be a model Lady of our World, calm, obedient and worthy of trust."

"On my life, and my son's life."

"Third . . . the third can wait until we see if my sister agrees to succor the person I see before me."

The third was a matter of money, the split between the two mama-sans. It was settled satisfactorily. She had made a financial arrangement with her neighbor to care for her son, visiting him secretly every two weeks in the morning of her day off, the lie she had told Meikin not really a lie as he was already committed to his father's parents.

Soon, once again, she was popular but not popular enough. The payment to the hairdresser became continuous, to the masseuse, to the costumer. There was never quite enough left over to save. By this time her son was an open secret with both mama-sans who, of course, had her watched, and followed. They never mentioned the son to her but understood with compassion. Then, one day her mama-san had sent for her and told her about the gai-jin who would pay enough, in advance, to send the child to his future, with money for two years of food, at least two, and enough left over to guarantee his safe delivery wherever he was to be sent.

She had accepted with alacrity.

After the first hideous night she had wanted to end her life, the man was so bestial. As much as she had wept and begged, Raiko had refused, implacably, for she had warned her in advance that this could not be done for at least a month. Fortunately there were days to recover and to plan a new defense between them. The defense had conquered the Beast, as she thought of him, and had changed him, temporarily. Now he was docile, and cried a lot, and required passion in all its aberrations, but underneath his meek and pleasant manner she could feel the violence still bubbling, ready to explode.

In the quiet and lovely surroundings Hinodeh waited, her nerves tangled. The moment he knocked on the street gate, her *maiko* would come running to alert her. She still had time, so she folded herself into the Lotus Seat position for meditation and sent her mind to Zen. Soon she was prepared.

Joining with the Beast was bearable. Curious how different he is, she thought, built differently than a civilized person, a little longer and larger but without any of a civilized person's firmness and strength.

So different from Shin who was smooth and sweet and so strong. Curiously, there had been no sign in her husband of his gai-jin ancestor, Anjin-san, who, two and a half centuries before, took the name Komoda for this second family in Nagasaki—his first family living in Izu where he built ships for his liege lord, Shōgun Toranaga.

Thank all gods for him. Because of him, eventually my Shin was born, and born samurai, and so is our son.

She smiled so happily. Her son was almost three weeks on his journey, the two servants trustworthy. In their safekeeping was a money instrument drawn on the Gyokoyama in the name of Shin's mother for almost three years of food and lodging money for her son, and for his grandparents.

Everything taken care of, she thought proudly. I've done my duty to our son, Shin-sama. I have protected your honor. Everything was in order. Even Raiko's final question before we agreed the final clause of the final contract with the Beast: 'Last, Hinodeh, what am I to do with your body?'

'Throw it on a dung heap for all I care, Raiko-san, it's already defiled. Leave it to the dogs.'

BOOK FOUR

42

YOKOHAMA

Tuesday, 9th December:

In THE PREDAWN LIGHT, THE Struan cutter sped away from the frigate *Pearl* and hurried for their wharf. Her bow waves were clean, she was at maximum speed and her plume of smoke jaunty. Wind was fair and offshore, with an overcast that promised to break up by noon.

The Bosun's binoculars were trained on Struan's windows. A light was on but he could not tell if Struan was there or not. Then the engine coughed, stopped, his balls seemed to hit him under the chin and all breathing on the boat ceased. After a couple of seconds the engine picked up but coughed again and picked up again but now it sounded off kilter.

"Christ Almighty, Roper, get below," he shouted to the engineer. "Rest of you buggers, get oars on deck in case we're stuffed . . . Jesus Christ, and McFay's got smoke out of his arse that we're up to scratch . . . Roper," he roared, "wot's the problem, for God's sake? Roper! Get the lead out!" Again he trained his binoculars on the window. No sign of anyone.

But Struan was there, his binoculars on the cutter, and he had been watching since it arrived at the frigate. He cursed for he could see the Bosun clearly now and the man should have known he would be watching and could easily give him a signal, yes or no. "Not his fault, for God's sake," he said, "you forgot to set the signal. Idiot!" Never mind, the weather's good enough, no harbinger of any storm at all

841

points, not that a small one would hurt *Pearl*. He refocused on the flagship. Her cutter was returning from visiting *Pearl*. She must've been delivering orders.

The door behind him swung open. Chen came in breezily with a steaming cup of tea. " 'Morn, Tai-pan. You-ah no slip heya, gud cha chop chop?"

"Ayeeyah! How many times do I have to tell you to talk the civilized tongue and not pidgin. Are your ears filled with the dung of your ancestors and your brains curdled?"

Chen kept the smile on his face but groaned inside. He had expected the sally to make Struan laugh. "Ayeeyah, so sorry," and added the traditional Chinese greeting, the equivalent of 'Good morning,' "Have you eaten rice today?"

"Thank you." Through the glasses Malcolm saw an officer get out of the flagship cutter and go up the gangway. Nothing to indicate one way or another. Damn!

He accepted the cup. "Thanks." At the moment he had no special pain, just the normal bearable ache, he had already taken his morning dose. For the last week he had managed to cut back on the amount. Now he had one in the morning, one in the evening, and had sworn, in future, it would be one a day if this day went well.

The tea was good. It was mixed with real milk, thick with sugar, and as it was the first of the day, it was laced with a small tot of rum, a tradition started by Dirk Struan, his father had told him.

"Chen, put out my heavy breeches and jersey and I'll wear a topcoat."

Chen was startled. "I heard the voyage was off, Tai-pan."

"In the name of all gods, when did you hear that?"

"Last night, Tai-pan. Fifth Cousin in the House of Chief Foreign Devil heard him talking with Big Ship Squashed Toadstool Nose who said no voyage."

Malcolm's stomach sank and he groped to the window. To his shock he saw the cutter was wallowing two hundred metres offshore. No bow wave. He began to curse violently and then he saw funnel smoke begin and the bow wave appear as the cutter picked up speed. His binoculars raked the deck but all he could see was the Bosun shouting, with oars on deck in case of a further breakdown. At that speed the cutter would be at their dock in under ten minutes.

With Chen's help he dressed. A quick check showed that the cutter was almost ashore. He opened the window and craned out as the Bosun climbed onto the jetty and began running as fast as his big belly would allow.

"Ho there, Bosun!"

The grizzled man was panting by the time he was near enough to the window. "Cap'n Marlowe's compliments," he said, gasping. "Will you and the . . . and the Lady please step aboard."

Struan let out a whoop of joy. He sent for Ah Soh, told her to wake and dress Angelique quickly. Then, quietly, he said, "Listen, Chen, and don't interrupt or I shall be like a firecracker . . ." and gave him instructions what to pack, and what to order Ah Soh to pack and to bring the trunks aboard *Prancing Cloud* at sunset. "Missy and I will dine aboard and sleep aboard and you two will stay aboard also, and return to Hong Kong with us . . ."

Chen was overjoyed. "Hong Kong! Ayeeyah, Tai-pa—"

". . . And both of you will keep your mouths shut tighter than a fly's anus or I will ask Noble House Chen to remove your names from the family book." He saw Chen go grey. He had never used the threat before. The family book was every Chinese male's connection to immortality, to their ancestors in the mystic past and to far-off descendants, when he himself would be considered a distant ancestor, and beyond. Wherever a Chinese was born in the world, he was written into his ancestral village records. Without that he did not exist.

"Yes, Master. But Ah Tok?"

"I'll deal with her. Fetch her."

Chen went for the door. She was outside it. He fled. She strode in. Struan said that he had decided she would follow in the next boat and that was that.

"*Oh ko*, my son," she said, her voice honeyed. "What you decide for your old mother is not what your old mother decides is best for herself and her son. We will go home. We will be silent. No stinky foreign devils will know. Of course all civilized persons will be interested in the plot. We will go home together. Do you take your whore with you?" She stood under his tongue-lashing, ordering her never ever to use that word again—or else.

"Ayeeyah," she muttered as she left, her words dying away gradually, "your old mother won't call that whore your whore again but all gods bear witness, if not whore what do I call her? Whore is the correct name. Is my son daft . . . ?"

When he saw Angelique his anger evaporated. "My word!"

She was wearing riding clothes, boots, long skirt, tight at the waist, waistcoat and cravat and coat and hat with a green feather, gloves but no riding crop. "I thought this best, darling, for boating," she said, smiling gloriously.

"Welcome aboard." Marlowe was at the head of the gangway, looking splendid in uniform.

Before stepping onto the deck, Malcolm awkwardly hung on with his left hand, Angelique holding his sticks, and raised his top hat formally. "Permission to come aboard?"

Marlowe saluted and grinned. "Welcome, you both are most welcome aboard. May I?" He took Angelique's arm, weak from the intensity of her smile and the cut of her jacket that dramatized her figure, and led the way to the bridge, forward of the funnel. He waited until Malcolm was settled in a sea chair. "Cast off, Mister Lloyd," he said to his Number One, Davyd Lloyd. "Quarter ahead and steady as she goes."

Pearl eased off her moorings under power. "Soon as we're clear we'll up speed," he said. "Admiral's ordered us to conduct steam trials in sight of the flagship."

Struan's happiness vanished. "In sight of him? We're not going out to sea, out of sight of land?"

Marlowe laughed. "I suppose he likes his 'children' on a short leash. It'll be fun, I promise."

Then we're aboard, but not aboard for the right reason, Struan was thinking—the bastard's a sadist! And if the Admiral had been aboard he felt sure he would have killed him quite happily. Well, not really, but I'd like the bugger dealt with. He'll wish he had helped me. When I get back I'll reverse everything and be a thorn in his nose he won't forget.

Meanwhile what do I do now?

There was so much going on that Marlowe and Angelique did not notice the despair he strove to conceal. The frigate was making way through the fleet, not a few sailors and officers from the other ships noticing Angelique, and, some of them, the fine way *Pearl* was being conned. Aboard the French flagship, the twenty-gun paddle steamer they passed close to, sailors whistled and waved, appalling the British officers.

Good God, Marlowe thought, what bloody bad manners and awful discipline! All the same he watched benignly as Angelique waved back, to a chorus of whistles and catcalls.

To distract her, Marlowe said, "We're going to make speed trials, Angelique, under steam first and then sail. Have to strain the new mast, test her, you won't remember but we lost our mainmast in the storm.

You see . . ." He chatted away, explaining this and that, answering every question she felt obliged to ask.

For herself she feigned interest, really wanting just to be quiet, to feel the sea wind ruffle her hair now that she had taken off her hat and was basking in the new freedom, wanting the wind to broom away the ever-present stench of Yokohama that was so much a way of life here, and in Hong Kong, as to be hardly noticed now, to gaze ahead and dream of the Channel and blue seas and the fine coast of home, going home. *We French desire our land so much, whereas the English seem to be able to make themselves at home anywhere and really don't need England, not like we need France. . . .*

"We'll hove to at noon," Marlowe was saying, so content to be Captain of *Pearl,* "and I've arranged tiffin in my cabin and there's a bunk if you wish to siesta. . . ."

The morning passed nicely. Every half hour the ship's bell rang the changes and even Malcolm was dragged out of his despair as the ship went from one end of the bay to the other, twisted and turned and rushed ahead and went into reverse. "In a moment, we'll stop steaming and it will be all sails ho!" Marlowe said.

"I do so prefer sail," Angelique said. "The engine noise is really so distracting. Sailing is so much more pleasant, don't you agree, Malcolm, *chéri*?"

"Yes, indeed," Malcolm said contentedly, his arm around her waist, holding her against the tilt of the deck.

Marlowe said, "I agree too, so does almost every man in the British Navy. Of course we still have to sail most of the time—can't carry enough fuel and coal's so filthy! But on a dirty night when safe harbor's just ahead in the teeth of the gale, or the enemy twice your size with twice the cannon but he's sail and you're not, you bless old Stephenson and British engineers for giving you the blessing of going against the wind. I'd take you below but as I said, there's coal dust everywhere and noise."

"I'd love to peek. May I?"

"Of course. Malcolm?"

"No, thanks—you two go ahead," Malcolm said. He had been over engine rooms of their own steamships since a boy and engines had never interested him, only their efficiency and cost and amount of coal they consumed.

Before leaving the bridge Marlowe checked the lay of his ship and the wind. They were three quarters of a mile offshore, well away from the fleet and the merchantmen. "Number One, you have the conn.

When we're abeam the flagship, stop steaming and all sails ho, course due east."

"Aye, aye, sir."

Malcolm watched Marlowe lead Angelique to the midships gangway with a light step, at the same time amused by the infectious charm he poured all over her. He relaxed in his chair. The sea and the sky and the wind and the space had taken his gloom away. It was good to be afloat, wonderful to be part of such an efficient, well-kept and proud fighting ship, grand to be comfortable and safe in a sea chair and his mind had given him different plans to cope with tomorrow and the days after.

Joss. I'm not going to worry about anything, he promised himself. Remember your oath and the new era!

After Gornt arrived in Yokohama like a gift from heaven, Malcolm had thanked God for the reprieve and had sworn, if Gornt's information was what he claimed, that forevermore he would just do the best he could, and be satisfied with that. With enough information to smash the Brocks, he was certain beyond all doubt his mother would rush to his side. Angelique was all that mattered—and being tai-pan, but not only in name.

That same night he had been impelled to look in the mirror. It had to be done. Some power forced him to regard himself for the first real time in years, to really study himself deeply, not only his face.

At length, he thought: This is what you are, you're still badly hurt inside, you can't straighten up too well, your legs don't work as they should, but you can stand and you can walk and you will improve. The rest of your body works, and your mind. Accept it. Remember what Mother and Father kept telling you since you were a child: 'Accept your joss, that's what Dirk would always say. Dirk had half a foot shot off and that didn't stop him; Dirk was shot and cut a dozen times, almost killed at Trafalgar as a powder monkey; almost destroyed by Tyler Brock half a dozen times. Accept your joss. Be Chinese, was Dirk's advice. Do your best and devil take the hindmost!'

His heart began pounding. Dirk Dirk Dirk. God damn Dirk Struan! You've loathed having him thrown in your face, you've always been petrified you'd never measure up to his impossible image. Admit it!

The reflection did not answer. But he did.

'I've his blood, I've his Noble House to run, I'm tai-pan, I do my best, but I'll never measure up to him, I admit it, God curse him, that's the truth! That's my joss.'

Good, his reflection seemed to say. But why hate him? He doesn't hate you. Why hate him like you've hated him all your life—you've hated him all your life. Haven't you?

'That's true, I hate him and always have!'

Saying it aloud had shocked him. But it was true—and all the love and respect a sham. Yes, he had hated him, but suddenly, there in front of the mirror, he no longer did. Why?

I don't know. Maybe it's because of Edward Gornt, maybe he's the good spirit who's unlocked me from my past as he wants me to unlock him from his. Hasn't Morgan poisoned his life and his mother's and father's? Not that Dirk poisoned mine, but his spectre came between Mother and Father and poisoned them—wasn't that their joss, that Father died hating him, and as much as Mother openly worships him . . . in her heart she hates him for not marrying her.

There on the bridge of the frigate, he remembered the cold sweat soaking him, then later drinking some whisky, but not the other stuff, rupturing that obsession there and then, knowing another truth: he craved it, and was addicted.

Too many truths faced. Not easy to face yourself, the most difficult—and dangerous—task a man can do, must do once in his life, to be at peace. I've done it, like it or not.

"Number One," the young signalman said to Lieutenant Lloyd, his telescope trained on his distant counterpart. "Message from the flagship, sir."

Two decks below, the engine room was a dungeon of heat and throbbing noise and dust and blackness and stench that was pierced with squares of blazing coals as half-naked stokers opened furnace covers under the great boilers to shovel in more coal or rake the embers to receive more coal, and then more.

Angelique and Marlowe were standing on one of the overhead iron grilles, the air swirling up filled with the smell of coke and fire and burning oil and sweat and steam. Bodies below sheened with sweat, big-bellied men with muscles bunched, their razor-sharp shovels screeching along the iron deck into the coal bunkers to come back full, a deft throw and the coal scattered in a level bed to fire at once and be replenished.

Aft, the pounding engine shone with care and oil, more men using long-nosed cans to squirt oil into joints, others cleaning with swatches of cotton waste, others tending dials and pumps and valves as the engine drove the propeller shaft against the crush of the sea. Jets of steam from valves, more oil and cleaning and constant attention to pistons and levers and cogs and more coal and Angelique found it vastly exciting—those below oblivious of them.

Proudly Marlowe pointed and explained over the roar and she answered with a nod and a smile from time to time, holding his arm lightly to steady herself, not hearing a thing or caring to listen, possessed by the engine room that seemed to her a masculine Valhalla where machines were married to men, now part of them, primitive yet futuristic, slaves tending their masters and not the other way around.

Unnoticed the signalman came up behind them and saluted. Not being heard he came forward, saluted again and broke her spell. He handed Marlowe the written message. Marlowe read it quickly, then nodded and shouted at the man, "Acknowledge!" He leaned over to Angelique. "Sorry, we have to go now."

At that moment signal bells from the bridge sounded below. The engineer officer acknowledged the order. Men rushed to close cocks and open others, leaning on levers and checking dials. As steam power came off the huge driving shaft and the engine began to slow, the noise lessened and the stokers leaned gratefully on their shovels, their chests gulping air heavy with coal dust and wrung out the towels they wore about their necks. One man turned on the bunker and cursed it, still drowned by the roar, and opened his trousers and pissed on the coals in a jet that ended in steam to the laughter of other men. Marlowe hastily took her arm and guided her away, up the gangway. One stoker noticed her, then another and before she had gone, they were all staring at her departing figure, silently. When she had gone out of sight, one of them made obscene movements to more laughter mixed with a sudden, sad silence.

On deck the instant lack of noise and breathing in the sea air made her feel quite giddy for a moment and she held on to Marlowe. "Are you all right?"

"Oh, yes," she said. "Thank you, John, that was, well, extraordinary."

"Oh?" Marlowe said absently, his attention on sailors in the rigging and on deck hoisting and adjusting sails. "I suppose it is, the first time. At sea, in a storm it gets rough down there. Stokers and engineers are a race apart." He took her over to Malcolm. "Sorry, have to leave you a moment."

He went below to his cabin that was aft. The Marine sentry saluted as he passed. The ship's safe was under his bunk. He unlocked it nervously. The message from the Admiral had read, "Activate sealed orders, 1/A16/12." In the safe were the ship's log, codes, money for pay, pay book, punishment book, manuals, manifests, receipts, Naval Regs and several sealed envelopes given him by Flag this morning.

His hand shook slightly, finding the correct one. Is it the Return to the fleet, prepare for War, he expected? He sat at the table that was surrounded by seats screwed to the deck, and broke the seal.

"It was extraordinary, down there, Malcolm. Ghastly in a way, all those men down there, astonishing—and if it's like that in a small ship like this, what would it be like on a big steamer—say like on the *Great Eastern*?"

"It's astonishing, Angel. I saw her launched on the Thames the last time I was in London, four years ago, when I finished school—my, was I glad to have done with schooling. She's completely of iron, four thousand tons burthen, the biggest in the world by far and built to carry emigrants, thousands at a time, to Australia. It took weeks to launch her—they did it sideways, a complete cock-up and she almost sank. Poor Brunel who designed and built her went broke many times, the companies he floated did. She was ill-fated, caught fire on her maiden voyage and almost gutted—and that killed him. Damned if I'd sail on her—ill-fated she is, and was, from the first plate laid ..." He saw Marlowe come on deck and frowned. Now there was no humor on the man's face.

The Bosun rang eight bells. Noon. "I have the conn, Number One," Marlowe said.

"Yes, sir."

"Why don't you take Miss Angelique for'rard, she might like to see some of our deck cannon close up."

"Gladly. Miss?"

Obediently she followed him down the gangway and along the deck. He was short, freckled and her height. "You're Welsh, Mr. Lloyd?" she asked.

He laughed, his voice singsong. "Welsh as the hills of Llandrindod Wells that is my home, look you."

She laughed with him and, leaning against the tilting deck, whispered, "Why am I being sent off like a schoolgirl?"

"I wouldn't know about that, Missy." She saw his deep-set brown eyes look back and then they were turned on her. "The Captain wants to talk about lunch, no doubt, or asking him, your man, if he wants to use the head, the toilet. Man talk," he said, and the eyes smiled.

"You like him, don't you?"

"The Captain is the Captain. Now, cannon, Ma'am!"

Her laugh trilled, the sailors nearby were warmed and Marlowe and Malcolm on the bridge heard her too and turned to look. "She makes a pretty picture, Malcolm."

"Yes, she does. You were saying. Tiffin?"

"Does that sound all right? The cook's first class on his apple turnovers." The menu was to be fish stew, chicken and salt-pork pie and dumplings, cold roast chicken, cheddar cheese and apple turnovers. "I've a couple of bottles of Montrachet '55, chilled, that I've been saving against a special occasion, and a Chambertin '52."

"You live rather well," Malcolm said, very impressed.

Marlowe smiled. "Not really, but this is a special day and, to tell the truth, I scrounged the Chambertin—it was my Old Man's favorite. The Montrachet, he gave me a couple of cases when I came out."

"He's Navy?"

"Oh yes." The way Marlowe said it expressed surprise that the question needed to be asked. "He's Commander in Chief, Plymouth." He hesitated, began to talk and stopped.

"What's the problem? We're ordered back?"

"No." Marlowe looked at him. "I was given several sealed orders this morning, along with written permission to bring you aboard and to be back by sundown, without fail. A few minutes ago Flag ordered me to open one of them. I wasn't told to tell you about it but I wasn't told not to. Perhaps you'd explain. The message said 'Should Mr. Struan ask a peculiar favor, you may, *if you wish,* grant it.' "

The world stood still for Malcolm Struan. He did not know if he was alive or dead and his head reeled and if he had not been sitting he would certainly have fallen over.

"Christ Almighty!" Marlowe gasped. "Bosun, fetch a tot of rum right smartly!"

The Bosun took to his heels and Malcolm managed to choke out, "No, no, I'm all right ... actually a rum would be ... would be grand." He saw Marlowe's lips moving and knew he was being shaken but his ears were not hearing anything above the pounding of his heart and then he felt the wind on his cheeks and the sound of the sea returned.

"Here, sorr," the Bosun was saying, holding the glass to his lips. The rum slid down his throat. In seconds Struan felt better. He began to grope to his feet. "Better take it easy, sorr," the Bosun said uneasily, "looks like you seed a ghost."

"No ghost, Bosun, but I did see an angel, your Captain!" Marlowe stared back blankly. "I'm not mad," Malcolm said, stumbling over his words. "John, sorry, Captain Marlowe, is there somewhere we can talk privately?"

"Of course. Here." Uncomfortably Marlowe motioned to the Bosun who left the bridge. Only the helmsman and signalman remained. "Signalman, go for'rard. Helmsman, close your ears."

Struan said, "My peculiar request is: I want you to sail out of sight of land for a moment, and marry Angelique and me."

"You what?" It was Marlowe's turn to be disoriented. He heard Malcolm repeat what he had said. "You're insane," he said.

"No, not really." Malcolm was in control now, his future in the balance, with the Admiral's words, *you may, if you wish, grant it,* carved on his brain. "Let me explain."

He began. A few minutes later the steward came up and went away and a little later came again with "Cook's compliments, sir, lunch is ready in your cabin," but again Marlowe waved him away, concentrating and not interrupting.

"That's the reason," Malcolm finished. "The why of the Admiral, me, you, my mother. Now, please, will you grant my peculiar favor?"

"Can't." Marlowe shook his head. "Sorry, old boy, I've never married anyone and I doubt if regulations'd allow it."

"The Admiral's given you permission to do what I ask."

"He put it rather bloody carefully, old boy: 'grant it if I wished.' My God, that's putting my head in the old yardarm noose, old boy," Marlowe said, his mouth running away from him as he foresaw all kinds of future disasters. "You don't know Ketterer like I know him, my God, no, any senior officer for that matter! If I choose wrong here he'll have my balls in the wringer, my career's up the bloody spout . . ." He paused for breath, shaking his head and mumbled on. "No way I could do that, no w—"

"Why not? Don't you approve of us?"

"Of course I approve of you, for goodness' sake, but your mother doesn't, I mean she says no to the marriage, Sir William's got his finger stuck in the pie, the Church won't, other Captains won't and, dammit, you're both legal minors, so if I did it wouldn't stick and she's . . . Damn it, you're a minor and so's she . . . Just can't risk it . . ." A sudden thought and he glanced shorewards. "Not unless I signal Ketterer. I'll ask permission."

"If you do that you'll lose face with him forever. If he wanted you to do that he would have said so."

Marlowe glared back at him. He reread the Admiral's exact wording and groaned. Struan was right. His future was in the balance. Christ

Almighty, why did I invite them aboard? The first thing in his life he remembered his father saying was, 'In the Navy you run your ship by rules and regulations, by the bloody book, except if you're bloody Nelson and there's only ever been one of him!'

"Sorry, old boy, no."

"You're our last hope. Now our only hope."

"Sorry, no."

Struan sighed and eased his shoulders, playing his ace. "Angel!" he called out. She heard the second call and came back with Lt. Lloyd and stood beside him. "Angel, how would you like to be married today, right now," he said, loving her so very much. "John Marlowe can perform the ceremony if he wants. How about it?"

The wonder spread over her and she did not hear Marlowe begin to say that he was so sorry he could not but he was stopped by the passion of her embrace and kiss, and then she did the same for Struan again and him again, "Oh, yes . . . oh, yes . . . John, how wonderful, you will, won't you? Oh, thank you, thank you, how wonderful, please please please," begging with another irresistible snuggle and he heard himself say, "Yes, of course, why not, glad to," saying his doom words as underplayed as he could, though inside feeling more heated than he had ever been and still meaning to say no.

The helmsman sealed the matter with a joyful shout, "Three cheers for Cap'n Marlowe, we've a weddin' aboard!"

Lunch was a hilarious prewedding feast, just two or three glasses of wine to test and taste the rare quality, not too much food, the rest put aside for later, all of them too excited and too anxious to begin. Once he had made the decision Marlowe ordered the ship out to sea under full sail and became their most enthusiastic supporter, wanting the ceremony to be memorable and perfect.

But before proposing a prenuptial toast at the end of the meal, he said gravely, "God knows if it'll really be legal, but I can find nothing in Naval Regs that says it won't be, or it can't be done. Nothing refers to the age of the persons, only that both must formally agree before witnesses that they freely give their consent, and they sign an affidavit that's entered by me in the ship's log. Once we get ashore, all hell and/or congratulations will break out and you may have to, perhaps should, go through a church ceremony—both Churches will scream bloody murder at our effort anyway."

Angelique heard an undercurrent. "But, John, it's all right, isn't it?

Malcolm's told me about oppositions and as to Father Leo . . ." Her nose crinkled with distaste. "You won't get into trouble, will you?"

"Perish the thought, Admiral's given permission," Marlowe told her more grandly than he really felt. "Enough said, here's to your healths, and to future generations!"

Angelique began to get up to drink too but Struan stopped her. "Sorry, darling, it's bad luck to drink your own health, just an old custom, and aboard Royal Navy ships you drink toasts sitting down."

"Oh, sorry." Her sleeve caught a glass, tapped it against another and a bell-like ringing began. At once both Marlowe and Struan reached over and stopped it.

Malcolm said, "Sorry, darling, just another old seafaring superstition. If you let the ringing of a glass die of its own accord somewhere in the world a sailor drowns."

"Oh." Her face lost its glow. "I wish I'd known, so many times in the past . . ."

"Not to worry," Marlowe said quickly. "If you don't know, then the superstition doesn't count. Right, Malcolm?"

"Yes, you're right again. I would like to propose a toast, Angelique, to John Marlowe, Captain, Royal Navy, gentleman and the best friend we have!"

The small cabin was filled with animated talk and laughter and then Lloyd announced that all was ready on deck. A last kiss, so tender between them, and they had gone aloft and stood there, hand in hand, both committed.

The ship was into wind, her sails and spars trembling. Those of the ship's company who could be spared were lined up, slickered and spruced, facing the quarterdeck where Malcolm and Angelique stood before the Captain. He was flanked by an honor guard of two marines. He opened Navy Regs to the right page and motioned to the marine bugler who sounded a clarion call, the Bosun blew on his pipe and the company came to attention. "We are gathered here as witnesses to the marriage of these two people in the sight of God . . ."

The swell of the sea did not touch them, nor the wind that was gusting more than before. Around the horizon were nimbus clouds, not yet threatening but potentially dangerous. Overhead the sky was still clear, and Marlowe wondered, briefly, if the weather was an omen. No cause for alarm yet, he thought. The ceremony was quickly over, strangely fast for all of them, for Struan almost an anticlimax. He had used the signet ring from his little finger as the wedding ring. It was too big for her but she held it solidly, staring at it with disbelief. "I now pronounce you man and wife."

As they kissed there were three rousing cheers. Marlowe called out, "Splice the mainbrace!" the order for a tot of rum for all the company, to more cheers.

"Mrs. Struan, may I be the first to congratulate you."

Angelique threw her arms around him passionately, tears of joy on her cheeks. "Thank you, thank you."

"Nothing," Marlowe said, embarrassed, then shook Struan's hand. "Congratulations, old man. Why don't we—" A short gust crackled the canvas. "Why don't you two go below and I'll join you in a moment," he said, then turned away and forgot them, tending his ship. "Let her fall off the wind, Number One. Set course for Yokohama, under sail until further orders. We'll steam to our moorings—we may be in for a wetting. Signalman, give me your pad. When we're in range of the flagship, send this."

Edward Gornt sat comfortably in the bay window of the Brock Building, his feet propped on a chair, idly watching the bay. The rim of clouds had spread and promised a storm, though at this time of the year they could as quickly evaporate. Behind him Norbert Greyforth sat at his desk, engrossed in paperwork. They had seen *Pearl* sail off over the horizon but put no special meaning on it. "Part of their trial, suh, I suppose," Gornt had said. "Still can't figure what could be aboard that's so important."

Norbert had nodded, secretly amused, and returned to signing and checking documents and manifests. A Brock freighter was in the harbor, due to sail in a few days and the last of her cargo from Japan had to be accounted for: fifty pounds of silkworm eggs for the French market—thirty to fifty thousand eggs to the ounce—bales of raw silk, and silk cloth for the London market, lacquer goods, barrels of saké they were trying to introduce into the English market, and also for Japanese in the Philippines, cheap pottery as ballast, coal—anything and everything that could find a market, together with the remains of her inbound cargo that had not been sold and would be traded on her return journey. Some guns and opium in special cases.

"Cigar?" Gornt asked.

"Thanks." They lit the thin cheroots, enjoying them.

"I've made a date with McFay to finalize arrangements for tomorrow, suh."

"Good." Norbert blew a cloud of smoke and signed the last of the documents. He rang a bell. In a moment his chief clerk and shroff came in. "This is the lot, Periera."

"Yes, Senhor." This small, fair man with slightly oriental eyes, was—as with most companies—Eurasian from Macao. "What about the specials, Senhor?"

"They stay off the manifest and in the Captain's care."

"There's a rumor that the Navy is going to board and check cargo at random."

"Let them. None of our specials are illegal, by God, whatever the hell the fool Struans do." Norbert dismissed him, then gave his full attention to Gornt. Something had made him suspicious. "Edward, perhaps I should call the duel off, tell Struan tonight I'll accept his compromise, the trap's baited, isn't it? I let him go to Hong Kong to get deeper in the shit, thinking he's won. Eh?"

"You could. But why spare him a night of fear? He has to be afraid—why comfort him? Would he comfort you?"

Norbert looked at him and saw the thin upper lip and how it seemed to curl slightly with malicious delight. He laughed to himself, thinking about how special tonight could have been for Struan if Ketterer were a different man, and that, now more than ever, thought of the duel will take away what remained of Struan's sleep. "I didn't think you'd fit in with us, the Brocks. Revenge is sweet for you too?"

"Me, suh?" Gornt's eyebrows soared. "I was thinking of you—I'm to serve you, wasn't that the idea?"

"It was indeed." Norbert hid his smile deep inside. "Tomorrow then, but now we'll . . ." His sharp eyes caught a smudge on the horizon through the window behind Gornt. "Is that *Pearl*?" He got up and went to the window, also training his glasses. It was the frigate all right.

"Steady as she goes," Norbert said softly, and Gornt wondered what he meant. *Pearl* was in the process of furling her sails, black clouds behind her. "Wind's picked up out there," Gornt said, and trained his own binoculars. Her smoke was pulled at right angles to her path.

In the bay the rest of the fleet and merchantmen were at anchor. A few whitecaps. Norbert's glasses went to *Prancing Cloud*. Nothing untoward there. Then the flagship. Nothing. Back to the frigate. They waited. *Pearl* was coming in quite fast, bow wave churning. Again the flagship, nothing. The frigate. Norbert could just discern Angelique standing next to a man who must be Struan.

"Look," Gornt said, his voice picking up excitement. "There. Can you see the signalman?"

"Where? Ah yes."

"He's semaphoring the flagship. First flags are the standard opening," Gornt said quickly. "Captain of HMS *Pearl* to Admiral. Message reads ... Message reads: A-G-R-E-E-D T-O R-E-Q-U-E-S-T." Perplexed, he stared at Norbert for a moment. "What does that mean?"

"Watch the flagship for any reply!" Gornt obeyed. "Where the hell did you learn to read Navy flags?"

"In Norfolk, Virginia, suh. When I was a kid I used to watch the ships, ours and the British. It became like a hobby. Then my pa acquired a book, one American and another British, with most of their standard phrases and some of their codes. I used to win bets for my pa when he would entertain officers, usually at cards. He, my mother and him, he used to entertain a lot, lavishly, that was before the cotton crash and he lost most of his money."

"Can you read any flags? Any codes?" Norbert asked quickly, wondering if he could use Gornt's knowledge. "Could you read Struan flags, ship to ship or ship to shore?"

"If they used standard international flag codes, but probably, like Brock's, they have special ... Just a moment, message from the flagship: Standard opening: 'To Captain of *Pearl* from Admiral Ketterer.' Next standard: 'Return to your moorings at once.' Next: 'When tied up and sea safe, report to the flagship at once,' adding the letters 'W-I-T-H H-I-M'. Last standard: 'Acknowledge.' " Gornt glanced back quickly. " 'With him,' Mr. Greyforth? Would that be Struan?"

"Bull's-eye."

"Standard acknowledgment." Gornt put down the glasses and rubbed his eyes, the concentration had given him a headache. "Bull's-eye? You know what it all means?"

"What's aboard *Pearl* that's so important? Captain bloody Marlowe, R.N." It took Norbert no time at all to explain.

"Married?" Gornt burst out. "You're brilliant, suh!"

"Never thought Ketterer would agree but it seems he has. Why? He gains nothing." Norbert was puzzled, then smiled spitefully. "Unless ... unless he's ordered Struan and Marlowe aboard to mat Marlowe and undo the deed right smartly—to jam the knife further into Struan, to torture him some more."

"Can he?"

"That bugger can do what the hell he likes, if the truth be known," Norbert said, and spat into the spittoon, then threw the butt of his cheroot into it as well. "Every man jack aboard the fleet's duty bound to obey him, and they would!"

"You mean he could order them to go against the law?"

"Let's put it this way: they're to obey immediately or suffer the consequences—which range from the cat to hanging to keelhauling. If he wanted he could hang you from one of his yardarms, then plead he'd been misled by juniors—he'd beat any court-martial. Meanwhile you're dead."

"Then how could you be so . . . so opposed to him, to his face, Mr. Greyforth?"

"Because Ketterer's law-abiding; they breed 'em like that for the Royal Navy, special, to obey orders from the next above, but mostly because we've Wee Willie—that feisty little bugger's the one above. He's our real protection from Ketterer, the General, Jappos and every other bloody enemy—but that won't protect young Struan from Ketterer's phlegm."

"So, Captain Marlowe, Mr. Struan's peculiar request was for you to go out of sight of land—and to marry him to Miss Angelique Richaud?"

"Yes, sir." Marlowe stood at attention unable to read the Admiral's face. Ketterer was flanked at the table in the great cabin aft by the flagship Captain. Behind them, his aide-de-camp, the Flag Lieutenant, stood equally frozen.

"And you did, knowing them to be minors?"

"Yes, sir."

"Please give me a report, in writing, by sundown, specifying your reasons, exactly, and what occurred, exactly. Dismissed." Marlowe saluted and began to leave as Ketterer turned to the Captain, a weathered, craggy, ugly man renowned for the toughness of his discipline and worship of Naval Regulations. "Captain Donavan, perhaps you'd research the legal position, eh?"

"Yes, sir." His blue eyes were merciless.

"Good, that's all then—for the moment." This was the last thing Marlowe heard before he closed the door and his heart seemed to begin again.

Struan was waiting in the anteroom outside. Two marines stood guard suspiciously. "Christ, did you get stick?"

"No, not at all." Marlowe tried to sound calm. "The Admiral, correctly, wants a written report, that's all. I'll be getting back to my ship. See you later." Before he could leave, the cabin door opened and he died a little more. Captain Donavan brushed past, hardly acknowledging him or his salute. At the doorway, the Flag Lieutenant said,

"Mr. Struan, Admiral's compliments, would you kindly step in, please."

Struan hobbled into the cabin. Flag did not follow, but closed the door and waited within shouting distance. Before leaving, Marlowe caught his eye but that told him nothing—of course neither would say anything in front of the marines.

Ketterer, now alone in the cabin, motioned Struan to be seated. "On the one hand may I congratulate you," he said with grim formality, and put out his hand.

"Thank you, sir." Struan shook hands, finding the Admiral's grip firm but his palm soft. "And on the other?"

"On the other it seems you are going to have your work cut out to keep your promises."

"Sir?"

"You seem to have stirred up a snake pit of venom amongst your fellows. Sir William is besieged with complaints."

"As I said, I'll do my best."

"You must do more than that, Mr. Struan."

"Sorry, but what does that mean, Admiral?"

"It means nothing more or less than what you've already promised to do."

In the small silence, Struan decided not to be overpowered, or crushed, or to lose sight of the fact that this man had made his marriage possible—no, not possible, he corrected himself, had 'allowed' it to be possible. John Marlowe had had the balls to take the initiative. "Captain Marlowe's not in any trouble, is he?"

"Captain Marlowe is subject to Naval Regulations."

"Yes, naturally, but I believe he married us within Naval Regulations, sir. I read the paragraph meticulously beforehand, and there was no age limit or mention of ages."

"Regulations also state that any such marriage is subject *to immediate review if feasible*. In this case it is."

"So I'm married but not, is that what you are saying?"

"I merely point out, Mr. Struan, as in all matters in the Navy, unusual happenings are subject to review."

Struan forced a smile. "Correctly so. My . . ." He almost used 'reading,' but judiciously changed the word. "My understanding of the order, sir, gave him permission."

Ketterer raised an eyebrow. "Captain Marlowe showed you a sealed order from me to him?"

"As I understood it, sir, the order gave him a qualified permission, sir—I confess I went out of my way to ask for the exact wording, and to persuade him that was the case."

"I rather thought you would," the Admiral said dryly.

"Then it was a qualified permission?"

"My order was stated clearly: If you should ask a peculiar favor, he might grant it *if he wished*. Last night, didn't you mention something about wanting to go out of sight of land? Your peculiar request might have been only that—his orders were to do his trials within sight of the flagship."

Struan was trying hard to keep his balance, feeling the coals of disaster beneath him. "Yes, sir. Yes, you might have thought that. If there was any misunderstanding it was mine, not Captain Marlowe's."

"I'll note that, Mr. Struan."

Malcolm had been watching the older man carefully and listening even more carefully, wanting to discern where the Admiral was heading, now afraid that this was a continuation of the cat-and-mouse game. Am I again in his claws—and will never be out of them?

"May I ask, Admiral, why you gave Captain Marlowe even a perhaps qualified permission that certainly I may have misconstrued?" Struan kept his face clear, not forgetting he was married until the ceremony was declared illegal. "I never thought you would, last night."

In the night Ketterer had been beset with Consuela. 'Give the young senhor a chance, Charles,' she had said with that lovely, liquid accent, as sensual in memory as the depth of her brown eyes in life. 'We were never given one, why not give him one—remember, you were not much older than him. You have from him a giant step forward, surely he will keep his promise. Why not be generous—as our parents and your foul Admiralty were not? He is so much in love, Charles, like you were, but unlike you, the young senhor has already been dealt a cruel hand at the whim of God . . .'

He had awakened, her words sounding in his ears, the way she pronounced his name still tugging at his heart after all the years. But this isn't the same, he had thought, hardening his heart. The Struans are opium smugglers and gunrunners—I will not forget my dead sailors. Sorry, my long lost love, the marriage will be declared illegal immediately—Struan will not be allowed off the hook. Duty is duty.

Now, looking at Struan, remembering the way he had hobbled in, determined to appear strong when Hoag and Babcott had both confirmed privately the youth was almost constantly in pain, doubting if he would ever run, or ride comfortably again, remembering, *Unlike you . . . at the whim of God.*

He sighed. "A sudden whim, Mr. Struan," he said, deciding to be lenient, "coupled with a belief that you will perform as promised." He got up, her smile etched on the back of his eyes, and went to the sideboard feeling curiously young. "Sherry?"

"Thank you." Struan started to stand, and wavered, weak with relief at Ketterer's admission.

"I'll bring it. Tio Pepe? Good. Health!" They touched glasses. Ketterer took a large swallow.

"Listen, young man," he said, his voice unusually quiet and kind, "I shall, of course, consult Sir William and will prevail on him to read Naval Regs. More than likely Captain Marlowe's report will be accepted, after due consideration—we must make sure our officers are always aware of the consequences of independent action, but he will not be 'in trouble' as you put it. This is to be another secret between us. Understood?"

"Yes, sir. Thank you. I will do what I promised." Struan took a deep breath. "Then my marriage is legal?"

"That depends on your point of view. As far as I am concerned, the Navy is concerned, that is my belief, therefore it should be in common law. As far as your two Churches are concerned, and the inevitable legal broadsides you will have to endure, I suggest you both batten down your hatches and prepare for the worst. Again congratulations, on the one hand. My compliments to Mrs. Struan—privately, of course."

43

By SUNSET, THE NEWS HAD SPREAD throughout the Settlement, Drunk Town and the Yoshiwara.

Speculation had been immediate, noisy, and argumentative as theories were put forth for and against such a marriage, some predicting the ceremony was totally illegal, others angrily denying it, many of the more quarrelsome traders—and all Drunk Towners—using foul language, obscene gestures, and bunched fists to support their positions, while a few of the wiser said: 'Ah, the canny young bugger, so that's why he sucked up to the Admiral! It was a deal! Clever—I'd do the same if I were Struan. Now that he's got her will he still be anti-opium, anti-armaments? No way . . .'

With the new topics, several fights began in Drunk Town and a bar burned down. Father Leo was rumored to have had apoplexy and was now prostrate in front of his altar. Reverend Tweet, at this very moment, was supposed to be raving at Sir William, and in the Club, Lunkchurch and Grimm, inevitably on opposing sides, had begun to battle and, as usual, were tossed into the street.

Malcolm and Angelique were in the cabin of their launch. Ahead was their jetty and, holding hands, they saw a boisterous group of well-wishers that had gathered there, headed by Jamie McFay. The promised bad weather had not materialized, with only a sprinkle late afternoon. The wind was still up, sky overcast, but this did not dampen the welcoming uproar.

"Here we go, Mrs. Struan," Malcolm said, and hugged her. She kissed him, whispering, "Yes, my darling husband. Oh, Malcolm, that sounds so funny, strange, so marvelous. This isn't a dream, is it?"

"No, though it feels the same to me."

861

The cutter twisted in the chop, throwing them together to more laughter, and swung alongside to cheers and shouts, the neatest docking the Bosun had ever made. "Lively on the ropes, lads," he ordered, but there was no need as eager hands twisted the towlines to bollards and sailors swarmed to help them.

"Congratulations, Tai-pan, Mrs. Struan," Jamie shouted amidst cheers that reached the interior of the Club across High Street. At once the room emptied and everyone began to gather, doffing their hats, even Mrs. Lunkchurch and Mrs. Grimm amongst them, equally festive.

Gornt and Norbert Greyforth watched from the upper windows of their building. Outside all houses Chinese servants stood around popeyed, and samurai were collecting at the North Gate, mystified. Ministers and their staffs were trickling out of their Legations: Sir William, hard-faced, flanked by a smiling Phillip Tyrer, and Michaelmas Tweet, black-browed and furious, Zergeyev beaming and cheering lustily, Dmitri shouting congratulations waving an American flag, and Seratard and André were torn between elation that the marriage was now achieved, and fury that they had not been consulted.

"André, bring her in as soon as possible. *Jésus*, the stupid *gamine* should have let us into the secret—it's your job to control her!" Seratard said with the side of his mouth, enthusiastically waving back as Angelique caught his eye and waved. "Struan must execute a will conforming to the Code Napoléon at once, see to it! Only God knows what dirty tricks William will try, for or against—whatever he says, our position is the marriage is legal, but we must insist it conform to French law! Get Father Leo, he will conduct their proper wedding next week . . . *Mon Dieu*, look at those cretins!"

Angelique and Struan were being mobbed. With increasing difficulty they tried to push a way through the crowd, all of whom wanted to kiss the bride, as their right, to be prevented by others, to more uproar.

She began to panic. This heightened the tension of those nearby. The crowd swirled and swamped her, Struan using his sticks to fight to her side as Jamie began shoving through roughly. Someone threw a punch, and an ugly skirmish began. Sir William called out to the marine sentries, "Go and clear a way for them, hurry up, for God's sake, or they'll be crushed!" The four men began running. "Phillip, supervise them, and get Struan into my office on the double."

The Sergeant roared, "Hey, you lot!" and the mob devil that sometimes appeared in a crowd for no apparent reason was gone. Quietly and firmly he began forcing a passage. "Behave yourselves, give the lady room!" He was obeyed as Struan reached her. "Are you all right, Angel?"

"Oh, yes, love." Now that she had room her panic had gone. She adjusted her hat. The feather had been broken. "Look at that!"

"Here let me help you," Tyrer said importantly, waving others away. "You, go on, move, you've frightened her to death. Are you all right, Angelique? Malcolm?"

"Of course," Malcolm said. Now that she was safe and he had his sticks, his happiness returned and he shouted, "Thanks for welcoming us! Drinks on the Noble House, the Club bar's open and stays open until further orders!"

There was a general rush in that direction. Soon only Malcolm, Angelique, McFay and Phillip Tyrer remained. And the sour presence of Michaelmas Tweet: "Mr. Struan, the ceremony is completely not legal and I must warn y—"

"You may be right, Reverend, but I'm advised to the contrary, sir," Struan said firmly, having already devised a plan for Tweet, another for Father Leo and another for Sir William. "Nonetheless I believe there is a happy solution. Perhaps you would come to my office at noon tomorrow? The House of the Lord will be satisfied, sir, you may rest assured!" Then he whispered to Jamie, "Divert him," and to the others, "Head for the office, fast as you can."

They had to run the gauntlet of a few stragglers and then Angelique whispered, "Phillip, hurry!" She ran on ahead with him to avoid Father Leo who was approaching from down the street as fast as his bulk and his cassock would allow. Once in the foyer, with most of the staff lined up there, Vargas in front, Chen smiling glassily, she laughed nervously. "I didn't want to have to talk to him!"

"Why not?" Phillip was beaming. "You're married and that's that—at least Sir William's been spitting blood since he heard, cursing the Navy, Ketterer, Marlowe—so I imagine you are married, but all I want to say is congrats and may I kiss the bride?" He did not wait and kissed her like a brother. She hugged him and breathed another sigh of relief.

Struan came through the door with McFay. "Lock it," he ordered. Helped by Vargas, McFay obeyed, politely but firmly shoving the few more persistent traders out and slamming the bolt home as Father Leo strode up, tried the handle, then hammered on the door as though it were a cathedral portal.

But no one paid any attention, all fleeing into the office like a group of mischievous children, where they collapsed into the chairs. All except Malcolm.

"Champagne, Chen. Thank you, Vargas, see you later, " he said over congratulations, and added to Chen, in Cantonese, "Open the wine, little mealymouth."

Jamie McFay shut the door and sank into the last chair.

"Ayeeyah," Malcolm said, bubbling like the wine. "I didn't think it would be like this. Phillip, thanks again for the good wishes, you too, Jamie. Are you all right, Angel?"

"Yes, Mr. Struan, wonderful, thank you."

Tyrer said, "It's all marvelous news, Malcolm, and by the way could you see Sir William as soon as possible."

The way he said it, so tentatively, so matter-of-fact, when they all knew he had been bellowed at, made a sudden silence which broke apart as they all laughed hysterically.

"Tomorrow afternoon, happily," Malcolm said.

Their glasses were soon full and even more quickly empty and again filled, conversation loud and not listened to. The door eased open. Vargas signalled McFay, then whispered to him.

Jamie nodded. "I'll be there in a moment. Tai-pan, can you excuse me? And there's a message for Ang—for Mrs. Struan: Mr. Seratard wants to add his congratulations personally at the Legation, soon as possible and the . . . the priest would like to see you both a moment."

"Jamie, first finish your drink. Vargas, send word to Seratard we'll put him on top of the list, but first tell Father Leo to be here tomorrow at 5:00 P.M., here, in my office." Vargas vanished. Malcolm saw the shadow on Angelique's face. "I'll see him, Angel, you don't have to, and by Sunday everything will be calm, I promise. Everything's in control. Soon as it's dark, we'll slip back aboard the cutter."

"Cutter? Why, Malcolm, what on earth for?"

"Another surprise, we're dining aboard *Prancing Cloud* and staying the night, then tomorrow there are more surprises, lots and lots, there's a honeymoon to plan. We'll leave in an hour and there's no need for you to change, I had Ah Soh pack some clothes for you and they're already aboard." To Jamie, "You have to leave? What's up?"

"I'd made a date with Gornt and forgot all about it in the excitement. He's waiting in my anteroom. He asked Vargas to give you both his congratulations, and Norbert's."

"Thank him for me, but don't go for a second."

"Thank him for me too, Jamie," Angelique said.

"Of course, Mrs. Struan." McFay was trying to get used to the sound of the words, finding it difficult and artificial, the two words conjuring up Tess Struan, and nowadays every time he thought of her he became bilious. The moment he had heard about the marriage, the reason for Malcolm's letter to the *Guardian* and last night's announcement had become clear—even the timing of the duel dovetailed neatly.

Married! Oh my God!

The implications for Malcolm were immense. For himself it did not matter now that he had made his peace with Malcolm and with himself. He doubted if he would ever have a peace with Tess Struan. Though she was a fanatic Struan, at the same time she had inherited her father's vindictiveness, his ruthless need for revenge. He had witnessed it falling on the Bosun in charge of the boat that had capsized, drowning the twins. She had had him charged with murder, demanding hanging. The coroner had found him guilty of negligence, causing manslaughter, and gave him the maximum ten years, hard labor, in the Hong Kong prison, which the man would never survive. Negligent? Not really, McFay and most had thought at the time, the storm sudden, as happens that season of the year, an unhappy accident. But she was Tess Struan of the Noble House. The Bosun's real mistake, he thought sadly, was that he lived and the children died.

"Angelique," Struan was saying. "Why don't you freshen up, I'm going to do the same and we'll leave within the hour—I've just a few things to settle with Jamie." They kissed and she left. In Cantonese he told Chen he should arrange hot water for his wife and for him, "Then we go aboard *Prancing Cloud*. Is everything prepared?"

"Yes, Master."

"Good, and you three better be quiet as bats, and contented as pigs in shit like never before!" To Tyrer, he added pleasantly in English, "Phillip, you'll excuse us, won't you? Starting tomorrow, there'll be major celebrations all over, wedding feast and so on with formal invitations. Please give Sir William my compliments, and please don't mention we'll be aboard *Prancing Cloud* tonight to anyone—even to Sir William. I don't want any drunken rowdies circling us all night, we want to be private, all right?"

"Quite understand, again congratulations." Tyrer was happy to leave. He still had to see Hiraga to finish another, curt dispatch for *Tairō* Anjo before he could cross the bridge to Fujiko. After this morning's council of war between Sir William and Seratard, aided by himself and André, where final details of the forthcoming bombardment and punitive Yedo campaign were agreed, André had whispered:

'Fujiko's panting to see you, it's all arranged. She's even insisting on serving you a Japanese feast, so arrive hungry and thirsty, but don't forget to act tough.'

Now alone, some of Malcolm's fatigue showed. "Jamie, pour me a glass, would you? Thanks. Everything's organized?"

"For tonight, yes, and tomorrow, yes. Ah Tok and Ah Soh are aboard with the trunks, Chen will go with you and Mrs. Struan. As far as I know no one except them, Strongbow, me, and now Phillip know you'll sleep aboard *Prancing Cloud*."

"Good. Phillip was a mistake, but never mind," Malcolm said. "I got too exuberant but it should be all right. He shouldn't blab. What does Gornt want?"

"Just to arrange final details." McFay looked at him. "Shouldn't your marriage make a difference now?"

"It could. But unless Norbert apologizes, it won't."

"Gornt wanted a private word, if you had a moment."

"All right. Tell him that's all it can be—and let me see him first, eh?"

Gornt's friendliness filled the room. To Malcolm he seemed like a very old comrade. "Champagne?"

"Thank you, Tai-pan. May I congratulate you?"

"You may. Health!"

"And yours, suh."

"Sorry, but we have to be quick, tomorrow there'll be more time, what's up?"

"I wanted to tell you, privately, Mr. Greyforth is going to accept your compromise tomorrow. No duel."

Struan smiled. "That's the best news I've had . . . no, the second best news I've had all day!"

"Yes." Gornt's face hardened. "If he means it."

"Eh?"

"I think you should be ready for treachery. Sorry to be a cold towel on a great day but I wanted to warn you. I know he'll change his mind."

Malcolm watched him, then nodded, undisturbed. "With Norbert, and all the Brocks, we expect treachery for breakfast." Their glasses touched. "Health—and wealth—and happiness!"

The room was warm for both of them, Malcolm noticing a curiousness about him that he could not divine. "You're still planning on tomorrow, giving me the information I need?"

"Oh, yes." Gornt got up. "And my contract?"

"It's ready. My signature can be witnessed tomorrow."

"Thanks. Until tomorrow, and again congratulations."

Again Malcolm sensed more than saw a strange humor in him. "You're looking forward to it as much as I am."

Gornt's eyes seemed to focus. "Yes. It will be another great day, an ending and a beginning."

Upstairs, Angelique was in front of her mirror, seeing nothing, unconsciously tinkering with the signet ring on her finger. She was alone for the first time today, in the privacy of her own room with the door locked, and the moment she sat down, the clamor of truths and paradoxes had abruptly possessed her: everything happening so fast, married but never really expecting it, never that way, not aboard a ship, hoping and praying but not believing it possible, so many barricades between them; married but not in the sight of God, married to a man I set my cap at, actively pursued, and encouraged to pursue me; the man I adore but have cheated—the rape not my fault, the casting out necessary, the earrings the only way, the secrecy the only means to protect my life but still a cheat—this man, who loves me to oblivion, risking all, I've stolen from, cheated, and go to my marriage bed soiled and yet . . .

Three times, coming back ashore, I began to tell him.

That's not true, I began to tell him part, the part about the earrings, but each time his elation overpowered me and stopped me as he poured out truths about his mother and her letters—and Skye and Father Leo and the English priest, the Admiral and Sir William—how he had been blocked but in the end he had won . . . *'I won, my beloved wife. I won you and now no one can take you from me. . . .'*

Embracing and rapturous tears in each other's arms.

As God is my witness, I know he would have been destroyed had I begun, and once begun I know the rest would have poured out. And then he would have died, poor lovely man. For that's what he is, truly, the most lovely man in my life. I know now I do love him, equally—no one could have tried so hard, casting so many barriers aside. I love him and yet . . .

What must I do?

She saw her face staring back at her. Not liking to see herself so unguarded, her eyes dropped. She saw her fingers twisting the ring, this way and that, the way André did with his signet ring. Malcolm's ring was gold, heavy, with the ingraved Struan crest: the Lion of Scotland entwined with the Dragon of China. Is that good with evil? she asked herself, and suddenly shivered.

To divert herself she brushed her hair vigorously but this did not help. Dark thoughts soared back, faster, ever faster, all of them—and *him*.

It all became like a foul vomit ready to pour out. She felt faint and pressed her hands against her temples. "Don't . . . you must be strong . . . you must be strong, you're alone, you must . . ." Her moaning stopped as another thought cleared the sick away. *"But you're not alone,"* she said aloud. "There are two of you now, there's Malcolm and he needs you . . . two of you—you and Malcolm, he needs you, Malcolm who is your husband . . ."

This image moved around her mind, filling it, and then she heard him calling from downstairs, so joyously, "Angel, hurry, it's time to leave . . . hurry!"

Unhurried she went and knelt in front of the little statue of the Blessed Virgin and gave all of herself: "Mother of God, forgive this sinner. I have sinned grievously, I beg Thy forgiveness. I have sinned grievously, and live a lie, but I swear I will be the best wife I can be, for as long as I am permitted, for I love this man with all my heart as I love Thee. . . ."

"How nice to see you, Raiko-chan," Meikin said with a smile, kneeling opposite her. "It has been too long." She was mama-san of the House of Wisteria and Koiko's mistress and they were in Raiko's most private sanctuary.

"Yes, thank you, you honor me," Raiko said, delighted to see her old friend, though more than a little surprised that Meikin had responded with such alacrity to her invitation for a business discussion. "Please help yourself to some snacks, the eel is particularly delicate. Saké or gai-jin brandy?"

"First saké, please." Meikin accepted it from an attentive maid. Business must be good, she thought, noting the expensive trappings of this isolated, secure dwelling within the walls of the Three Carp.

"Though times are hard, happily gai-jin have little idea of money values and, disgusting as they may be, reapings are high and the cost of hot water and clean towels and perfumes small." The two women laughed, watched and waited.

Meikin sampled the sushi—delicious—and began eating hugely for such a small woman. Her travelling kimono was deliberately mediocre. Anyone seeing her would presume she was a minor merchant's wife, not one of the richest mama-sans in Yedo, owner of the city's most expensive Pleasure House in the greatest Yoshiwara in the land—

recently entirely rebuilt and refurbished after last year's fire—mama-san to ten of the most gifted geisha, twenty of the loveliest courtesans, as well as contract owner of Koiko the Lily. She looked around Raiko's most inner sanctum, reserved for special occasions, admiring the unique silks and cushions and tatamis, chatting while she ate, wondering why the request for a meeting.

When food was finished, the maids dismissed, Raiko poured two cups of her best brandy. "Health and money!"

"Money and health!" The quality of the liquor was better than any Meikin possessed. "Gai-jin have their good points."

"In the world of wines and fortified spirits, yes, not in their appendages," Raiko said sagely. "Please allow me to give you a bottle. One of my clients is Furansu."

"Thank you. I am glad business is so good, Raiko-chan."

"It could be better, always."

"And Hinodeh?" Meikin asked—she owned half her contract-price. When Hinodeh first came to see her, she had placed the girl with a cousin, the mama-san of another House she owned. Later, by chance, she had heard of Raiko's curious and highly unorthodox request for a special kind of girl. It was easy to make the arrangements—Raiko was an old friend, known over the years and trusted over the years from the times they were *maiko,* then courtesans together. "The arrangement continues to be satisfactory?"

"I have another payment for you though the man is slow."

Meikin laughed. "I am not surprised. You are a marvelous negotiator." She bowed her thanks.

"He promises a larger amount in a few days. Possibly more earrings."

"Ah!" Meikin had disposed of the other set profitably. "This had been a most satisfactory business." The client's down payment on Hinodeh's contract had been more than enough to carry all costs for at least a year. "How is she?"

Raiko related the first and subsequent meetings to the other woman's breathless interest.

"She's correct to call him the Beast," Meikin said.

"He is not a bad man. I think this disease must send him mad from time to time. At least she knows the worst, and accepts that he is her karma."

"May I ask, there are no—no signs yet?"

"No, nothing. But every day she makes me examine the parts she cannot see herself or with a mirror."

"Strange, Raiko-chan." Meikin settled a hair comb more comfortably. "When, and if, anything appears that cannot be hidden—will she seek the knife?"

Raiko shrugged. "One never knows for certain."

"Has she told you why she accepted this karma?"

"No. Nothing. I like her and can help only a little. Yes, strange she will not tell us, *neh*?" Raiko sipped her brandy, captivated by the heat that slid inside, and the rare pleasure of entertaining her oldest and most trusted friend. They had been inseparable while *maiko,* lovers in their youth, and exchanged confidences always—safe confidences. "Tonight he visits her. If you wish you can watch them for a while."

Meikin chuckled. "I am long past being interested or excited by the thrashings of others, violent or passionate—even by well-endowed gai-jin." She was too happy to be with her old friend to tell the sadness of Gekko and Shin Komoda that she had insisted on knowing before sending her here.

When Hinodeh is dead, Raiko-chan, I will tell you and we can share a tear for the sorrows we women must endure. Until then Hinodeh's secret is safe as we agreed, the name of her son safe, and where he was sent.

A glow went through her, loving secrets and the game of life. "So Hinodeh is settled. Good. And now?"

"Now." Raiko dropped her voice. "I might have important information about gai-jin battle plans."

Color rushed into Meikin's cheeks and she became as tense as the other woman had become. "Against Yedo?"

"Yes."

"That might be valuable information but, so sorry, it would be dangerous knowledge—perilous."

"Yes, and even more dangerous to dispose of, though highly valuable to the correct person."

Meikin touched away a droplet of brandy that could have been perspiration. "And once such knowledge is bought, proved correct, or incorrect, heads have a habit of falling."

"True." Raiko understood the danger but she was more excited than she had been in years. She had never been in the mainstream of Yedo politics, but the proximity of Hiraga and learning about the shishi from him—and secrets about him and Ori from the shoya—had given her an appetite. That and her relationship with Furansu-san, through him learning about gai-jin, paradoxically the source of all her wealth at the same time the enemy of their sacred Land of the Gods. That and because of her disgust with the Bakufu and Anjo, who had murdered another old friend, Yuriko, mama-san of the Forty-seven Ronin, for harboring shishi.

She trembled at the thought of her own head adorning a spike, trembled in fear but in ecstasy. Yuriko was already immortalized in the *ukiyo-e* prints of the Floating World, her name the new favorite of geishas, and soon there would even be a Noh play with her as heroine.

"You are right," she whispered, "but certain information might be worth the risk. And if . . . if I had important secret knowledge of what . . . of what high officials were secretly planning against the gai-jin, I might be able to place it also to our mutual advantage." Sweat had gathered at the edge of her elaborate wig. She brushed it away with a tiny pink paper tissue. "It is hot, *neh*?"

"Not so hot as the fire we might put ourselves into."

"What would the beginning day of the attack be worth—and the gai-jin battle plan?" This morning Furansu-san had given her more than enough details to tempt even the most skeptical buyer to be lavish.

Meikin felt her heart thumping. She had hoped that Raiko's invitation would be for something like this. Over the last two years she had nurtured and obliquely hinted at the potential, prompted by Sensei Katsumata for whom any gai-jin intelligence was of value. And also because, recently, there had been covert instructions to all Bakufu spies with promises of rich rewards to focus on Yokohama, to discover gai-jin secrets, and who was feeding the enemy forbidden information about things Japanese. That Raiko had made the first open move was crucial—in truth the only person she herself would trust in such a gangrenous game. "How soon is the attack to be?"

"Would it be possible to have some important secret for the gai-jin as part of the trade?"

Meikin sat back and thought long and hard.

Yes, Raiko was to be trusted, completely—until her life was threatened. Yes, a channel for intelligence on a continuing basis would be valuable not only in money but also to the cause—*sonno-joi*—that she supported with all her being. And yes, because it could be used to supply gai-jin with carefully conceived false information as well.

She said softly, "Raiko, old friend, I have no doubt *Tairō* Anjo, or Yoshi, would pay dearly to know those dates, amongst other details, but, ah, so sorry, how to place it in either of their hands and the money in ours without compromising either of us, that is the difficulty."

"Brandy, Meikin-chan?" Raiko poured, weak with excitement. "If anyone could solve such a riddle it is you."

The two women measured each other and smiled. "Perhaps."

"Yes. And now perhaps that is enough for the moment. We can continue later, or tomorrow if it pleases you. May I plan your evening's entertainment, unless you are tired?"

"Thank you. No, I am not tired. The ferry from Yedo was comfortable and not at all full, the sea fair and my servants made sure the captain granted my slightest wish." Meikin had arrived at the village jetty just before nightfall. "May I ask what you suggest?"

"We have geisha, but not up to your standards. There are some youths who might prove adequate." Raiko's eyes crinkled with her smile, remembering the good times they had when they were young. "Or perhaps a *maiko*?"

Meikin chuckled and sipped her brandy. "That would be a pleasant diversion and would remind me of old times, Raiko-chan. She will help me think, help me see if I can provide you with what we need. Good. I agree we have had enough seriousness for now. Let us talk of olden days and how business is, and how is your son?"

"He is well, still climbing the Gyokoyama ladder."

"May I put in a good word with them—though surely unnecessary. An excellent bank, the best, I get the highest interest and my deposits are spread for safety—famine is coming so I have bought future rice heavily. Your son, he would be twenty-four now, *neh*?"

"Twenty-six. And your daughter?"

"Thank all gods rich and poor, I successfully married her to a goshi so her children are samurai, she already has one son, but eeee, her husband is expensive!" Meikin shook her head from side to side, then laughed. "But I should not complain, I only convert the worthless dribbles of a few rich old men into a heritage we never dreamed possible. *Neh?*"

The sound of footsteps mingled with their laughter. A tap on the shoji. "Mistress?"

"Yes, Tsuki-chan?"

The *maiko* slid the door aside a crack and, on her knees, peered up at them with an innocent smile. "So sorry, but Shoya Ryoshi, the village Elder, begs to see you and your guest."

Raiko's eyebrows arced. "My guest?"

"Yes, Mistress."

Meikin frowned. "Does he usually greet visitors?"

"Only the most important and no doubt you are most important, your presence honors us all. Certainly he would have been told of your arrival. His web of informants is far-reaching, Meikin-chan, he is absolutely to be trusted—and also head of the Gyokoyama in Yokohama. Shall we see him?"

"Yes, but only for a moment. I will pretend a headache then we can continue our chat until the evening meal."

"Little one," Raiko ordered, "bring the shoya here, but first tell maids to bring fresh tea and hot saké—and to take these glasses away and hide my brandy. Meikin-chan, if he knew I had such a source he would be a daily pest!"

It was quickly done and the table made clean and perfect, their breath cleansed with herbs, before he was bowed in. "Please excuse me, Ladies," he said with untoward anxiety, kneeling and bowing and being bowed to. "Please excuse my bad manners arriving without an appointment but I wanted to bow to such an august person and welcome her to my village."

Both were surprised that he appeared so forbidding, for this was not a serious occasion. Meikin had never met him before but her own Gyokoyama official had mentioned him and that he was a man of integrity, so her reply was as polite and enthusiastic as befitted an eminent person from the biggest city in the world, complimenting him on the state of the Yoshiwara, and the little she had seen of the village. "You are a man of great reputation, shoya."

"Thank you, thank you."

"Tea, or saké?" Raiko asked.

He hesitated, began to talk, stopped. The mood in the room changed. Raiko spoke into the silence. "Please excuse me, shoya, but what is the matter?"

"So sorry . . ." He turned to Meikin. "So sorry, Lady, you are a most cherished client for our company. I—I . . ." Shakily he reached into his sleeve and handed her the little piece of paper. She squinted at it. "What is it? What does it say? I cannot read writing so small."

"It's a carr . . . carrier pigeon message." The shoya tried to speak again, could not, numbly pointing at the paper.

Jolted, Raiko took it and moved to the light. Her eyes scanned the tiny writing. She blanched, wavered, almost fainting, and sank to her knees. "It says, *An assassination attempt on Lord Yoshi at dawn at Hamamatsu village failed. Lone shishi assassin slain by him. Lady Koiko also dead in skirmish. Inform House of Wisteria our great sadness. More information soon as possible. Namu Amida Butsu* . . ."

Meikin had gone sallow. She mouthed, Koiko dead?

"It must be a mistake," Raiko cried out in anguish. "Must be! Koiko dead? When did it happen? There's no date! Shoya, how did you . . . It must be lies, must be lies . . ."

"So sorry, the date is in code at the top," he mumbled. "This happened yesterday, near dawn. The Tokaidō way station, Hamamatsu. No mistake, Lady, oh no, so sorry."

"*Namu Amida Butsu!* Koiko? Koiko's dead?"

Meikin looked at her blankly, tears pouring down her cheeks, and fainted.

"Maids!"

They came running and brought smelling salts and cold towels and ministered to her and to Raiko as she tried to collect herself, groping to discover how this would affect her. For the first time she was uncertain if Meikin was now to be trusted or had become a hazard to be avoided.

The shoya knelt motionlessly. It had been necessary, and was still necessary for him to pretend to be frightened and aghast to be the bringer of bad tidings, but he was glad to be alive to witness these amazing happenings.

He had not given them the second slip of paper. It was private to him and in code and read: *Assassin was Sumomo. Koiko believed to be implicated in plot, wounded with shuriken, then beheaded by Yoshi. Prepare to close Meikin accounts. Avoid mentioning Sumomo. Guard Hiraga as a national treasure, his information is invaluable. Press him for more, his family is being refinanced as agreed. We urgently require gai-jin war plans at whatever cost.*

The moment he had received the message he had checked his books for Meikin's accounts that his branch owed her, even though he knew the amount to the hundredth part of a bronze coin. No need to worry. When she was moved onwards by Lord Yoshi, or if she wriggled out of the trap, either way the bank would profit. If she failed, another mama-san would take her place—they would use her residual wealth to sponsor the replacement. The Gyokoyama monopolized all Yoshiwara banking—an immense and permanent source of revenue.

How ironic life is, he thought, wondering what these two would think if they knew the reason for Gyokoyama's unbreakable hold. One of the most inner secrets of their *zaibatsu* was that their founder was not only a mama-san, but a woman of genius.

In the early 1600s, with the enthusiastic approval of Shōgun Toranaga, she designed a walled district where, in future, all of Yedo's Pleasure Houses, high and low, had to conduct their business exclusively—at that time brothels were spread all over the city— calling it the Yoshiwara, the Place of Reeds, after the area Toranaga had allocated to her. Next she created a new class of courtesan, geisha, those trained and qualified in the arts, who were not, routinely, available for pillowing.

Then she began moneylending, concentrating on Yedo's Yoshiwara, soon to spread her tentacles to all others as they were institutionalized throughout the land, Shōgun Toranaga wisely having foreseen that in such districts the purveyors, and their clients, would be more easily monitored, and taxed.

Lastly, incredible in those days, somehow or another—no one still knew how—she persuaded Shōgun Toranaga to make her eldest son samurai. In short order her other sons prospered: in shipbuilding, as rice dealers, saké and beer makers, their descendants today owners or silent controllers of a vast network of businesses. In a few years she obtained permission for the samurai branch to take the name Shimoda. Now the Shimoda were hereditary daimyo of the small but affluent fief of the same name, in Izu. It was she who coined the inscription over the Yoshiwara gateway: *Lust cannot wait, it must be satisfied.* She was ninety-two when she died. Her mama-san name Gyoko, Lady Luck.

"Shoya," Meikin said between broken sobs, "please advise me what I should do, please."

"You must wait, Lady, be patient and wait," he said hesitantly, still wearing his mask of disquiet, noticing, at once, though the sobs were loud and heart-breaking, her eyes were more pitiless than he had ever seen them.

"Wait? Wait for what? Of course wait, but what else?"

"We—we do not yet know—know all the details, Lady, of what happened. So sorry, but is there a chance the Lady Koiko would be part of the plot?" he asked, twisting a knife in the ready wound for the sake of twisting it. Though Gyokoyama had no proof, Meikin was suspected of dangerous *sonno-joi* affiliations and a connection with the Raven—against their oblique warnings—another reason why she had been advised to buy rice futures, not only as a wise investment but also as a bank-controlled hedge against her being accused and condemned.

"Koiko in a plot? My beauty, my treasure? Of course not," Meikin burst out. "Of course not."

"Meikin-san, when Lord Yoshi returns, surely as her mama-san, he will send for you. In case, so sorry, in case enemies have whispered against you, it would be wise to have . . . to have ready tokens of . . . of your respect."

There was no reason for either women to ask, What enemies? Success bred jealousy and secret hatreds everywhere—particularly in best friends—and in the Floating World, a world of women, more than anywhere. And both were successful.

Meikin was over her initial shock now, her mind concentrating on means of escape—in case Yoshi suspected, or Koiko had denounced her, or he had proof that both she and Koiko supported *sonno-joi*, shishi, and knew Katsumata. There was no real way to escape, not into another identity or to another place, Nippon was too well compartmentalized. Throughout the land, ten family heads formed the basic unit responsible for their own behavior and obedience to law, ten of these units formed another grouping equally responsible, ten of these the same and so on, up to the ultimate giver of law: the daimyo.

So she could run nowhere, hide nowhere. "What could I possibly give the great Lord Yoshi?" she asked her voice hoarse, feeling sicker than ever before.

"Perhaps . . . perhaps information."

"What kind of information?"

"I do not know, so sorry," he said with pretended sadness. Tomorrow could be different, tonight he must still pretend, to give them face, whatever he thought of their stupidity. Stupid to embrace sedition with a penis, particularly when the shishi possessors were few, most were being scattered or killed, and they continued to commit the unforgivable sin: failure. "I do not know, Lady, but Lord Yoshi must be worried, greatly worried what the vile gai-jin fleet will do. They prepare for war, *neh*?"

The moment he said it he saw Meikin's eyes become even more flinty and fix on Raiko, who flushed slightly. Ah, he thought gleefully, they already know—and so they should, bedding the loathsome gai-jin! By all gods if there be gods, what they know the Gyokoyama should of course be told quickly.

"That news might—would ease his pain," he said, nodding wisely as a banker would. "And yours."

Half a hundred paces away in a dwelling within the walls, snuggled into gardens, Phillip Tyrer was sitting cross-legged, bathed, replete with food and saké, naked under his yukata and in a state of rapture. Fujiko knelt behind him, her knowing hands massaging his neck muscles, finding the points of pleasure-pain. She wore a sleeping yukata, her hair loosened and now she moved closer, delicately bit the lobe of his ear, near the center, where the erotic sites lay. Her tongue increased his pleasure dramatically.

Fingers slid sensuously to his shoulders, never slowing, taking away his cares, the conferences with Sir William and Seratard, helping his chief to deal with that Frenchman and his constant, inbred devious attempts to gain a minuscule advantage when, let's face it, he had thought, the slimy rotter has only two mediocre ships when we have a fleet of ships-of-the-line, crewed by men, not sycophants!

Taking notes and then setting out two alternate battle plans into correct diplomatic English and French for their governments, and into more ordinary orders for the Admiral and General to carry out, the time slipping away and his headache growing. But André had been an asset at the morning meeting, well prepared, and all the time suggesting ideas and dates, maneuvering the two principals into agreeing and making decisions, all four of them sworn to secrecy.

Then, at last, slipping out of the Legation and across the bridge, knocking on the door, instantly opened by Raiko herself and being bowed in and through the garden and bathed and fed, but before that Raiko had at last begun to treat him as an important official should be treated.

About bloody time, he thought, more than a little pleased, every nerve tuned to Fujiko's fingers . . .

Most of her mind was concentrated on Raiko's warning: 'Some vile and hungry low-class person at the Lily has seduced our gai-jin lord away from us. At great cost I have tempted him here, granting many concessions to go-betweens. Do not fail tonight, this may be your last chance to bind him to us with ropes of silk. Use every trick, every technique. . . . even the Moon behind the Mountain.'

Fujiko flinched. She had never tried this before, even in the most heated embrace. Never mind, she told herself stoically, better a few queer moments of eccentric behavior—than no gai-jin pay tonight, and no pay for a year of leisure.

As her fingers moved closer and her soft murmurs began, daydream pictures of her farmhouse began to intrude, the children, her fine husband and their ripening fields of rice, so grand and kind and . . .

Firmly she put them away.

Until the client is asleep, she ordered herself.

Tonight you will snare the ungrateful dog forever! It's a matter of face for the whole of the House of the Three Carp! Waylaid by a low-class person from the Lily?

Ugh!

44

THE CLIPPER *PRANCING CLOUD* swung at anchor with a change in the evening tide. "She's snug, sir," the First Mate said. Captain Strongbow nodded and continued puffing his pipe.

They were on the quarterdeck. Wind creaked the spars and blocks above. Strongbow was a clear eyed, thick, tough man of fifty. "It'll be a fair night, Mister, crisp but not cold." He smiled, adding softly, "Good for our guests, eh?"

The First Mate, as tall and tough and weathered but half his age, was watching them too and grinned. "Aye, aye, sir."

Angelique and Malcolm were on the main deck below, leaning on the gunnel close together, staring at the lights of Yokohama. Malcolm wore a topcoat over casual shirt and trousers and soft shoes, and had, for the first time, without too much discomfort, used only one stick while aboard. She wore a heavy red shawl around her shoulders and over a long, loose dress. They were near a deck cannon. The ship carried ten thirty-pounders, port and starboard, and bow and stern chasers and their gunners were as good as any in the Navy. That was Strongbow's boast. It did not apply to all their clippers or merchantmen or steamers.

"Pretty, isn't it, my darling wife?" Malcolm said, genuinely happy for one of the few times in his life.

"Tonight everything in the world is pretty, *mon amour*," she said, nestling closer. It was after dinner and they were waiting until the stateroom, the cabin they were occupying, was cleared of dishes and prepared. The cabin was large and used the whole of the stern, normally the Captain's quarters, unless the tai-pan was aboard—one of the many laws laid down by Dirk Struan, thirty years ago, the fleet still governed by his dictates to the last detail: best pay, cleanliness, training, and fighting readiness.

Strongbow was watching the tide, gauging it. In these waters a change in the tide could herald the coming, hours later, of a tsunami, a giant wave generated maybe a thousand miles away by a sub-ocean earthquake that would engulf anything in its path at sea, and coastal cities when it hit land.

When he felt that the shift had been normal, he looked back at Struan. He was glad to have him aboard, and new orders to sail early tomorrow with all speed for Hong Kong, knowing, as they all knew, Herself had commanded the young man home weeks ago. But he was troubled to be carrying the girl.

My God, damned if I can call her Mrs. Struan—there's only one of them, he was thinking. Young Malcolm married? In spite of Her orders? In spite of Her opposition? He must be daft! Is the marriage legal? By sea law, yes, if they were adults but they're not. Will it be overturned? A broken penny to a golden guinea She'll have twenty ways to null it without as much as a how'd you do! Christ!

What about the girl then? What will happen to her? And young Malcolm? How in the hell can he win against Her? I'm glad I wasn't the one who married them, thank God for that. Would I if he'd asked me? Not on your Nelly! Never!

Herself will spit blood, right about them being under age, and about her being Catholic. It's going to cause a battle royal, this time mother against son, a fight to the death with no rules and we all know she's a hellcat when aroused—worse than my Cat—though young Malcolm's changed, tougher than I've ever seen him, more determined than he's ever been. Why? Because of the girl? Only God knows, but it'd be a welcome change to have a proper tai-pan again, a man.

No doubt in the world young Malcolm's overboard for her and who's to blame him? Not me! I'd wed her myself given the chance but, by God, this's one time I'm not going to hurry to report in, to rush off to drink and bed my Cat. He chuckled. Cat was his mistress of years, a Shanghainese girl whose temper and jealousy were legend but whose passion had no rival.

"What about our change of orders, sir?"

Strongbow shrugged. Certainly no need for Malcolm to rush ashore before dawn to rush back again, not with his walking so badly—one stick or two, never mind. Any problems, things to sign, could be brought aboard by McFay. Ah yes, Jamie, what's he hiding? Something smelly—why else the secrecy and all shore leave cancelled for the crew?

He had heard rumors of an impending duel. Just the sort of damn fool escapade Struan pride would precipitate, then to deal with it before leaving, anything to humble the Brocks when everyone knows we should be making a peace, the feud's gone on too long, they're in the ascendance and they've got our noses jammed in the bucket. Will we be flying their flag come Christmas? By God, I hope not.

The young idiot doesn't take after his father but his grandfather. Christ, what a man! Strongbow had sailed with him several times, trading opium up the China coast as midshipman, then gunner's mate, then as Third Mate under Stride Orlov the Hunchback—Master of the clipper fleet after the tai-pan.

He saw Malcolm put his arm around the girl and she pressed even closer and his heart went out to them. Tough growing up, tough to be tai-pan, or almost taipan of the Noble House, with such a grandfather—and such a mother. Pointedly he moved across the quarterdeck and looked seawards. The First Mate followed. Both gazed up into the shrouds as a few of the resting sea birds changed perches, cawing. Then one dipped off the top gallant spars and they watched him vaporize into the dark for night fishing. Another followed as silently.

Malcolm and Angelique had not moved, lost in their serenity. The half hour sand timer on the bridge emptied. At once the duty watch turned it and rang six bells, 11:00 P.M., echoed by other vessels in the bay. They came out of their reverie. "Time to go below, Angel?"

"Soon now, beloved. Chen said he'd tell us when our cabin's ready." She had thought about that ever since he had said, 'How would you like to be married today . . .' She smiled and kissed his chin, prepared, and at peace. "Hello, my darling husband, we're going to have such a wonderful life, I promise, no more pain for you and fitter than ever before. Promise?"

"A thousand times . . . my darling wife."

More sea birds dipping from the rigging, and Chen came up and said everything was as the tai-pan had ordered.

Malcolm added in Cantonese, "Remember now, don't wake tai-tai when you wake me." Tai-tai meant Supreme of the Supreme, First Wife—who was supreme and ultimate law inside any Chinese household, as the Husband was supreme outside.

"Sleep well, Master, ten thousand sons, Missee."

"Tai-tai," Malcolm said, correcting him.

"Ten thousand sons, tai-tai."

"What was that about, Malcolm?" she asked, smiling.

"He was wishing you a happy marriage."

"Doh jeh, Chen"—thank you, she said.

Chen waited until they had bid the officers good night, and were below—Malcolm using one stick, leaning on her. Ayeeyah, he thought, going forward to the fo'c'sle gangway, all gods great and small, protect the Master and give him a night worth all the pain—past and future—but first consider me and my problems and explain to Illustrious Chen and tai-tai Tess this marriage was nothing to do with me.

From the quarterdeck Strongbow watched Chen go below. "They're all bedded down? The servants?"

"We put hammocks in the starboard sail room. They'll be snug unless we run into a storm."

"Good. You want to have your tea now, Mister?"

"Yes, thanks, I'll be back smartly." Tonight the First Mate had the midnight to 4:00 A.M. watch and he ran down the gangway lightly. At the stern end of the corridor was the state room. The door was closed. He heard the bolt slide home. Smiling, silently whistling a jig, he headed for the galley.

Malcolm was leaning against the door, aching with anticipation, determined to walk unaided to his marriage bed. She had stopped near the bunk and was looking back at him. The stateroom was well ordered. And warm. The big dining table and sea chairs secured to the deck. So was the roomy bunk, easily enough for two, another of the tai-pan's laws. It was high and its headboard centered against the stern bulkhead, with roped canvas guards against the tilt of the decks when reaching to windward, or tacking under full canvas. Now these were sheathed. Port was a small bathroom and toilet. Sea chest for clothes to starboard. From the beams a gimballed oil lamp cast pleasing shadows.

Both of them hesitated, unsure.

"Angel?"

"Yes, *chéri*?"

"I love you."

"I love you, too, Malcolm. I'm so happy."

Still neither moved. Her shawl had fallen away slightly to reveal her shoulders and the pale green, high-waisted Empire-style dress, the folds of soft silk gathered under her bosom that rose and fell in time with the beating of his heart. The dress was the most advanced haute couture from the latest *L'Illustration* that Colette had sent, not yet in full favor, daring in its simplicity. When she had appeared at dinner, Strongbow, their guest, and Malcolm, despite themselves, had both gasped.

Her eyes were mirrors of his and now, unable to bear the waiting and his need that seemed to reach out and envelop and smother her, she hurried into his arms. Passionately. Her shawl dropped unnoticed to the deck.

A little dizzy, she murmured, "Come along, *chéri*," and took his hand—and part of his weight—said another silent prayer for help, annihilated the past and the future, abandoning herself to the present, she led him to the bunk—resolved to be all that he desired and expected. Ever since today's sudden and unbelievable ceremony she had been planning for this moment, her role, sifting her own ideas and what Colette had whispered how some of the great ladies of the court conducted themselves on the first night: 'It's important, Angelique, to be the guide, to control the stallion as a good rider should, with strong hands and tight rein, with firmness but gentleness to remove the initial violence from even the most docile of husbands—to lessen the hurt. Be prepared . . .'

His impatience was vast, big hands wandering, lips stronger. "Let me help you," she said huskily, also wanting to begin, and eased the coat off and then the shirt and flinched when she saw the extent of the scar at his waist.

"*Mon Dieu*, I'd forgotten how badly you've been hurt."

His passion went. But not the thundering of his heart. Every instinct made him want to pull the shirt or sheet around him but he forced himself not to. The scar was a fact of his life. "Sorry."

"Don't be sorry, *mon amour*," she said, her eyes spilling, and holding him close. "I'm sorry, so sorry for you and all that horror . . . so sorry."

"Don't, my darling. It's joss. Soon it'll only be a bad dream, all of it, for both of us, I promise."

"Yes, my darling, so sorry, so silly of me," she said, still holding on to him and, in a moment, when the anguish for him had lessened, angry at herself for her lapse, she brushed away her tears—and with them her momentary sadness—kissed him quickly, pretending it had never happened. "Sorry, my darling, how silly of me! Sit there for a moment." He obeyed.

Watching him with veiled but shining eyes, she undid the silk belt and then the back buttons and let the gown fall as she had planned. Only a half-slip and pantaloons remained. He reached for her but she chuckled and slid away and went to the sea chest where her mirror and salves and perfumes were, and, taking her time, put perfume behind her ears and then on each breast, teasing and tantalizing.

But he did not mind, consumed with her, enchanted, for she had explained many times, in different words, 'We French are different from you, my darling Malcolm, we are open about loving, modest but not modest, so opposite to the English. We believe loving should be like a marvelous meal, one to thrill the senses, all senses, and not the way our poor English sisters, and their brothers, are taught: that it should be done quickly, in the dark, believing somehow the act is squalid and bodies shameful. You'll see, when we're married . . .'

And now they were. She was his wife, she was coquettish for his delight and he was filled with joy and pulsating. Thank God for that, he thought, monumentally relieved—he had worried for weeks, reliving the Yoshiwara girl, when nothing had worked. "Angel," he said throatily.

Shyly she stepped out of her pantaloons and slip and walked over to the gimballed lamp and turned the wick down, leaving just enough light, more strikingly lovely than he had imagined—the sight of her naked body was like a dream, and at the same time achingly, vividly real. Without hurry she climbed into the other side of the bunk and lay alongside him.

Whispering words of love, hands touching, exploring, his breathing heavy, moving closer, breath catching painfully when he moved, lips hot and kisses passionate. Her own hands tentative, carefully controlled, all her mind concentrated on the picture of happy, innocent first love that she wanted him to have of her—desperate to please but a little frightened.

"Oh Malcolm, oh Malcolm . . ." Murmuring and kissing him deeply, loving him—praying that what Babcott had said in answer to her questions was true: 'Don't worry, *for a time* he won't be able to ride comfortably, or dance a polka brilliantly, but that doesn't matter, he can drive a coach-and-four, captain a ship, run the Noble House, sire many children—and be the best husband ever . . .'

Her need for him was strong now. But she modulated it, checking her own desire, sticking to the plan, helping and guiding and then a sharp gasp, never wavering, now holding him tightly, reacting and reacting until so soon he cried out, her whole body rocked by the contortions of his release and cries that went on and on and then his helpless, panting, dead weight crushing her—but not crushing her.

How odd that I can bear his weight so easily, everything fitting together, she thought, her mouth whispering sweet and tender words, soothing his panting whimpers, content that their first joining had been accomplished so pleasingly.

He was half conscious, lost in some strange plateau, weightless, empty, feeling nothing yet sated with love for this incredible creature who, nude, was all that he imagined and more. The smell and taste and being of her. Every part of him satisfied. Everything worthwhile. In euphoria. Now she's mine and I was manly and she was womanly and, oh Christ, I hope I didn't hurt her.

"Are you all right, Angel?" he asked huskily, his heart slowing but still hardly able to talk. "I didn't hurt you?"

"Oh, no, my darling . . . I love you so much."

"So, so do I, Angel, I can't tell you enough." He kissed her and began to lift his weight on to his elbows.

"No, don't move, not yet, please, I like you like th— What is it, my darling?" she said nervously, her arms tightening.

"Nothing, nothing at all," he muttered, dealing with the sudden pain from his loins that stabbed into the base of his skull as he had moved. Cautiously, he tried again; better this time. And he stopped the groan this time.

"Don't move, Malcolm," she said tenderly. "Stay still, rest, *mon amour,* I like you like this, please . . . please."

Gratefully he obeyed, starting to murmur how much he loved her, so comfortable, so possessed, so peaceful, so utterly satisfied, to drift into sleep, to sleep deeply. The ship's bell sounded one bell: half-past midnight but he did not stir, and she lay there, calmed and soothed and gratified, her future launched, enjoying the quiet of the cabin, timbers creaking sometimes, waves lapping the hull, savoring the sensation of fulfillment too.

Without waking him, she slid from under him and went to the bathroom and cleansed herself. She sighed and begged forgiveness. A nick with the small knife. André had said, 'It's difficult, almost impossible for a man to tell if the girl's a virgin or not on their wedding night if he has no reason to suspect. A little fear, a gasp at the right time, a little telltale blood the clincher, and in the morning all will be serene and as it should be.'

What an awful cynic André is, she thought. God protect me from him and forgive me my sins—I'm glad I'm married, and soon off to Hong Kong so I won't need to think about him ever again, just my Malcolm . . .

She almost danced over to the bunk. Softly into bed to hold his hand

and close her eyes, seeing glorious mind pictures of their future. I do love him so.

Suddenly she was awake, thinking she had felt another earthquake. The cabin was dark, just the barest flame of the gimballed lamp, swaying slightly. Then she remembered dimming it before she slept, realizing the sound that had awakened her was the ship's bell and not the pealing of the cathedral during the earthquake of her dreams, the earthquake only the ship's movement, none of the dream bad. Then, seeing him there beside her, she experienced a loving glow, unlike anything before, knowing they were married and that not a dream either.

Four bells? 2:00 A.M. Or 6:00 A.M.? No, silly, it can't be, or there would be light outside the portholes and Malcolm said he had to go ashore before we slip anchor for civilization to beard the Dragon in her lair—no, to greet a mother-in-law I will charm and beguile who will quickly love me and be the perfect adoring grandmother.

She watched him in the half-light. He was sleeping on his side, his head cradled in his right arm, his sleeping face without care lines, breathing soft, his body warm with his good, clean manly smell. This is my husband and I love him and am only his and the other never happened. How lucky I am!

Her hand began to touch him. He stirred. His hand reached for her too. Not quite awake he said, "Hello, Angel."

"Je t'aime."

"Je t'aime aussi."

His hand sought her. She responded. Caught unawares he flinched and turned to her, held his breath as a pain leapt to the back of his eyes, and then, as it passed, exhaled.

"Je t'aime, chéri," she said, and leaned down to kiss him, and between kisses whispered, "No, don't move, stay there, stay still," and added with a little laugh, her voice husky with need, "Lie still, *mon amour.*"

In moments passion swamped him. Aroused and throbbing, everything forgotten, now sensuality shared and now moving slowly and slowly and then quicker and slow again and deeper, her voice throaty, urging him, him reacting, on and on, stronger and stronger, all his glands and muscles and yearning centering, centering until she was near and very near, and going and near again, holding her, helping her, thrusting until she sensed her body vanish, her weight vanish, everything vanish and she collapsed on him, her spasms and cries pulling him further into her, his muscles stretched to the limit by his final thrust. Then and then and then he too cried out and was weightless, his body grinding of its own accord, pumping of its own accord, until the last, frenzied, so welcome spasm passed and all movement ceased.

Only panting breaths mixed, sweat mixed, hearts mixed.

In time he became conscious. Her sleeping weight on his chest was as nothing. He lay there in wonder, vibrantly aware, euphoric, one arm holding her safe, knowing she was comely as ever a wife could be. Her breath cooled his cheeks, long and slow and deep. His head was cleansed and future clear, without a shred of self-doubt. Utterly sure that he had been right to marry her, certain that now he could end the conflict with his mother and that together they would end the Brocks, as he would end Norbert, end opium sales and cannon sales, and persuade Jamie to stay, and he would rule Struan's as it should be ruled—as the tai-pan would want it ruled. Until, with the fullness of time, he would have done his duty and made the Noble House first in Asia again, to pass it on to the next tai-pan, the firstborn son they would name Dirk, first of many sons and many daughters.

How long he lay there he did not know, supremely confident, joy-filled and in ecstasy, his arms around her, loving her, breathing her breath, more happy than he had ever been, could ever be, his lips telling her he loved her, his mind easing him into sleep in blissful warmth and away from the memory of that awesome, marvelous, agonizing, writhing, ultimate burst of immortality that had seemed to him to tear him apart.

45

Wednesday, 10th December:

IN THE GREY DAWN JAMIE MCFAY
hurried up from the Drunk Town jetty and turned the corner. Around it
he saw Norbert and Gornt in No Man's Land, waiting where they
should be waiting, noticing without interest the small bag in Gornt's
hand that would contain the duelling pistols they had agreed on. Apart
from the three of them—and acres of flies—the foul, weed-covered
dump was desolate. He had passed no one except drunks huddled and
snoring in the corners of shacks, sprawled on benches or in the dirt. He
had not seen them.

"Sorry," Jamie said, out of breath. Like them he wore a topcoat and
hat against the morning air, heavy and damp. "Sorry I'm late, I ha—"

"Where's the tai-pan of the Bloody House?" Norbert asked rudely,
shoving his chin out. "Is he yellow or what?"

"Go fuck yourself," Jamie snarled, his face as grey as the dirty sky.
"Malcolm's dead, the tai-pan's dead." He saw them gaping at him and
he still could not believe it either. "I've just come back from the ship.
Went to fetch him before dawn and . . . well, they . . . he'd spent the
night aboard *Prancing Cloud*. He was . . ." Words failed him. His tears
welled and again he relived the going there and seeing Strongbow at
the gangway, pale and frightened, yelling out long before he had come
alongside that young Malcolm was dead, that he'd sent their cutter for
a doctor but, for Christ's sake, he's dead.

Then charging up the steps. Noticing Angelique huddled in the corner of the quarterdeck, wrapped in blankets, the First Mate nearby but rushing past them, praying it was not true but a nightmare, then going below.

The stateroom was bathed in light. Malcolm lay in the bunk on his back. Eyes closed, calm in death, no cares, sheets drawn up to his chin, it suddenly hitting Jamie that his friend was as he had never seen him, exquisitely at peace.

'It were . . . it were Chen,' Strongbow was saying in a flood, distraught, 'his servant Chen, Jamie, he'd come to wake him ten, fifteen minutes ago, he's the one that found him, Jamie, he found him—you can unbolt the door from the outside like most sea cabins—and he did and they were sleeping, he thought. She was but Malcolm weren't and he shook him and saw and near died himself and ran out and fetched me and by that time, she was awake. She was awake and shrieking, poor thing, desperate, shrieking enough to put your teeth on edge so I took her out and told the First Mate to look after her and came back but there were no mistake, poor laddie, he's just as you see him 'cepting I closed his eyes but look . . . look here . . . '

Trembling, Strongbow pulled the sheet away. Malcolm was naked. The lower part of his body rested in a pool of blood. The blood was dried and caked now, the mattress soaked. 'He . . . he must have hemorrhaged, only God knows why but I suppose . . .'

'Christ Jesus,' Jamie had said, and lurched for a chair and cursed and cursed and cursed again, numb. Malcolm? 'What the hell do I do now?' he asked himself helplessly.

The voice of God ricocheted around the cabin answering him: 'You pack it in ice and send it home!'

Frightened, he leapt to his feet. Strongbow was staring at him perplexed and, all at once, Jamie realized it was the Captain who had answered him, unaware that he himself had spoken the question aloud. 'Is that all you can bloody say, for Christ's sake?' he shouted.

'Sorry, Jamie, didn't mean . . . I didn't mean to be . . .' Strongbow wiped his forehead. 'What do you want me to do?'

After another age, ears still pounding, head scourged, he muttered, 'I don't know.'

'Normally we—we would bury him at sea, can't keep . . . You could bury him ashore . . . What do you want me to do?'

Jamie's mind seemed to be in slow motion. Then he noticed Ah Tok squatting near the bunk, tiny, now an old crone, rocking on her heels, mouth moving but no sound coming out. 'Ah Tok, you go upside, nothing here, heya?'

She paid no heed. Just rocked back and forth, mouthing, and did not answer. He tried again but it was no use. To Strongbow he said, 'You'd just better wait. You wait for Babcott or Hoag.'

Aloft again to kneel beside Angelique, in the still dark, not yet dawn. But she would not answer him, however tenderly he talked to her, saying how sorry he was, how very sorry, trying to succor her. Momentarily she looked up, without recognition, great blue eyes in the whiteness of her face, then huddled back in the blankets, staring sightlessly at the deck.

'I'm going ashore, Angelique, ashore. You understand? It's . . . it's best to tell Sir William, you understand?' He saw her nod dully and touched her as a father would. At the gangway he said to Strongbow, 'Put the flag at half mast, all hands to stay aboard, your sailing orders are cancelled. I'll be back as soon as I can. Best . . . best not to touch anything till Babcott or Hoag arrive.'

Going back to the shore he had been violently sick and now he saw Norbert and Gornt in front of him. Gornt was shocked, Norbert's eyes glittered and, through his misery, he heard him say, "Malcolm's dead? How dead, for Christ's sake?"

"I don't know," he said, choked. "We—we—we've sent for Babcott but it looks like he hemorrhaged. I've got to tell Sir William." He turned to leave but Norbert's jeering laughter stopped him.

"You mean the young bugger died fucking? Died on the job? I come to kill the bugger but he's done fucked his way through the Pearly Gates? Old Man Brock will laugh fit to b—"

Blind with rage McFay lashed out, his right fist smashing into Norbert's face, sending him reeling, and missed with a violent left uppercut, overbalanced, and fell to his knees. Norbert had twisted like a cat and leapt to his feet, bellowing with fury, face bloody, nose ugly, and kicked violently for Jamie's head. The toe of his boot caught Jamie's collar and that deflected and deadened the impact slightly or it would have broken his neck instead of sending him tumbling. Norbert wiped the blood off his face as he rushed forward and again kicked savagely. But this time Jamie was ready and he twisted aside before Norbert could reach him and scrambled to his feet, his fists bunched, his left arm momentarily useless.

For a second they squared off, pain obliterated by hatred, Gornt trying to stop them but at the same instant the two men charged, amok, brushing him aside like a leaf. Fists, feet, gouging, street fighting, knees into the groin, nails clawing, tearing cloth or hair anything to crush the other—the enmity of years exploding with surpassing ferocity. They were the same height but Jamie was thirty pounds lighter, Norbert tougher and more vicious. His knife appeared in his hand. Both Jamie and Gornt called out as he lunged, missed, recovered, slashed again and drew blood this time, Jamie awkward and losing and tortured by the damaged shoulder. With a victorious battle cry Norbert thrust forward, to maim but not to kill, but the same moment Jamie's fist crashed into the bridge of his nose, smashing it this time, and Norbert went down whimpering and stayed down, on his hands and knees, sightless with pain, beaten.

Jamie stood over him panting, Gornt expecting him to finish the other man with a kick to the groin and another to the head, then perhaps to use the heel of his boot to mash his face forever. That's what he would have done—not gentlemanly to pull a knife or jeer at the death of another man, even an enemy, he thought with satisfaction at McFay's victory.

But Malcolm's death had not pleased him at all. It was the one option he had not planned for, not today. Now his scheme would have to be revised, and quickly. In God's name, how? Could this brawl be used, he wondered, sifting possibilities while waiting to see what Jamie would do next.

Now that he had won, Jamie's rage dissipated. His chest was heaving. Bile and blood filled his mouth. He spat it out. For years he had wanted to humble Norbert and now he had, and had his measure once and for all time—and had taken revenge for Malcolm who had been provoked deliberately.

"Norbert, you bastard," he croaked, astonished how bad his voice sounded and how awful he felt. "You say any—anything against my tai-pan, anything, by God, or laugh about him again behind his back, I'll smash you to pieces."

Roughly he stumbled past Gornt, hardly seeing him, to go to the jetty. Ten or fifteen yards away his foot caught in a rut and he fell cursing, and remained there on his hands and knees, oblivious of the others, spent.

Norbert was coming around, spitting blood, his nose ruined, a mass of hurt, sick with rage that he had been beaten. And petrified. Old Man Brock won't forgive you, his brain was screaming, you'll lose your bonus and the stipend he promised, you'll be the laughingstock of Asia, beaten and pulped and marked forever by that son of a bitch Jamie who's nowhere near your size, a Struan bastard . . .

He felt himself helped to stand. Unsteadily he forced his eyes open. Gasping for air and confused, his face and head on fire, eyes puffed and mostly closed, he saw McFay groping to his feet a few paces away with his back towards him, Gornt half in front of him, still carrying the double-barrelled duelling pistol.

Half mad with pain, a tangle of thoughts rushed at him: Can't miss at this distance, Gornt's the only witness, at the inquest we'll say, 'McFay went for the gun, Sir William, we'd been fighting, yes, a struggle, yes, but he'd hit me first, didn't he, Edward, tell the God's truth, then terrible, Your Honor, terrible it was, somehow the gun went off, poor Jamie . . .'

Norbert grabbed the pistol and raised it.

"Jamie!" Gornt called out in warning.

McFay turned, startled, gaped at the pointed gun as Norbert jeered and pulled the trigger, but Gornt was ready and with another warning shout deflected the shot upwards and now, with his back towards McFay, covered the pistol with his body, holding it in both hands with surprising strength, simulating a momentary struggle with Norbert for possession. And all the time he stared into Norbert's eyes who saw, appalled, only death. He twisted the muzzle into Norbert's chest and squeezed the second trigger. Norbert died instantly. Then, pretending to be aghast, Gornt let the body fall. It had taken a few seconds.

"Christ Almighty," Jamie gasped. Appalled, he stumbled over and sank to his knees beside the body.

"My God, suh, I didn't know what to do. Oh, my God, suh, Mr. Greyforth, he was going to shoot you in the back and all I did . . . oh, my God, Mr. McFay . . . you saw him yourself, didn't you? I shouted a warning but . . . he was going to shoot you in the back . . . isn't there anything we can do? He was going to kill you . . ." Easy to convince McFay, who blearily staggered away to fetch help.

Once safely alone, Gornt exhaled. Pleased with himself. Delighted he had, in that instant, foreseen what Norbert would do and had gambled his life on it.

'When you're gambling, timing and execution must be perfect,' was one of his stepfather's litanies when teaching him the art of cards. 'Sometimes there comes a chance, young Eddie, a gift from the Fates. They give you something special, you take it and make a killing. You win the big pot, you can't fail if they've really offered it, their timing's perfect. But don't be fooled by the Devil—he'll screw you to the cross, his deal's like the other but different, you'll recognize the difference once it comes your way . . .'

Gornt smiled crookedly. His stepfather hadn't meant a killing literally though it had come to pass that way for him. His gift from the Fates was Norbert.

Perfect timing, perfect killing, perfect alibi.

Norbert had to be sent onward for many reasons. One was because Norbert might have been able to deflect part of the Brock disaster, turning it back against Struan's. Another that Old Man Brock had ordered Norbert to kill Struan any way he could, another—the most important—that Norbert was common with no manners, no finesse, no sense of honor, and not a gentleman.

Flies were already swarming around and on the corpse. Gornt moved away and lit a cheroot. His eyes searched No Man's Land, looking through the mist. Still no alien eyes, no one stirring. Dawn barely breaking the overcast. While he waited he removed the blanks from the other pistol, Malcolm's pistol, that Norbert had insisted on. He smiled to himself. He would have switched them, giving Norbert the duds, if Norbert had decided to fight the duel, instead of cancelling as agreed.

What a bastard Norbert was, he thought. Good riddance. But I'm sorry about Malcolm. Never mind, now I'll go to Hong Kong and make my deal with his mother—safer and better. Norbert was right, she's the real tai-pan. I barter what I would have given Malcolm, real means and evidence to destroy Brock and Sons—to crush Morgan, the devil incarnate.

Vengeance is mine, saith the Lord. But not with me. Not me, Edward Gornt, Morgan's son. Ah, Father, if you only knew how glorious revenge will be, how correct patricide is! In payment for 'I'll marry the slut if . . .'

It's ironic, Morgan, you've spent your life trying to ruin your only sister and her family—your father the same with his only daughter—and I'm your only son, and nemesis, protecting her to ruin you.

Safer dealing with Tess than Malcolm, better. She'll deliver Rothwell's in Shanghai, and underwrite the Victoria Bank loans I'll need, and get me a seat on the Board. No, not that, rightly she'd consider that a threat, the seat will come later. Meanwhile, next on the list, Cooper-Tillman.

Meanwhile, what to do? Off to Hong Kong soon as possible. Curious, Norbert's gone, and Malcolm. Strange.

Dying on the job? I wonder. What a way to go!

By removing Malcolm the Fates dealt me another prize. Angelique. She's free and rich now, Noble House rich. Six months would be perfect, time enough for mourning, and me to get organized. By then

Tess Struan will be glad to have her out of Hong Kong, and out of her hair. And married. Say she's pregnant? I'll worry about that, if. Makes no difference either way, I'll get the Noble House quicker than already planned.

His low laugh mixed with the hum of the flies.

"Dr. Babcott's outside, Sir William," Tyrer said.

"Send him in, for God's sake! George, 'morning, what the hell happened to the poor fellow—terrible news! What about Angelique, how is she, did you hear about Norbert? Miserable bastard tried to shoot Jamie in the back couple of hours ago!"

"Yes, yes, we heard." Babcott was unshaven and clearly upset. "Hoag's taken Angelique to the French Legation, we all came ashore together—she wouldn't go back to Struan's."

"I can understand that, don't blame her, how is she?"

"In shock, of course. We've given her sedatives. Dreadfully sorry for her—she's had a rotten time here, the Tokaidō, then that bloody ronin thug and now this. Rotten luck, the worst luck. She's hurting badly."

"Oh. Will it . . . will it turn her mind?"

"Hope not. You never know. She's young and strong but . . . you never know. By all that's holy I hope not." The two men were gravely concerned. "Such a shame for both of them. Rotten business, feel so damned useless."

Sir William nodded. "Must confess I was bloody angry about their marriage, but then, when I heard this morning, well, I would have given anything for it not to have happened." His face hardened. "Did you see Norbert's body?"

"No, Hoag will do that once he's settled Angelique. I thought I'd better come straight here and report."

"Quite right. Now, what happened to Malcolm?"

In spite of his anguish, Babcott became clinical. "Hemorrhage. An artery or vein ruptured or burst. In the night, while he was asleep, without any pain or contortions or he would have awakened her, life seeped out of him. I'll do an autopsy, have to for the death certificate."

"All right, if that's what you recommend." Sir William turned his mind off that macabre business, finding it distasteful, not liking, either, to be close to the doctor, any doctor, their clothes always bloodstained here and there, and always the faint odor of chemicals and carbolic surrounding them, however clean they were in themselves. "Poor young Struan. Terrible. He just bled to death?"

"Yes. For what it's worth, Malcolm . . . he was the most incredibly peaceful man I've ever seen in death, as though it was welcomed."

Sir William toyed with an inkwell on his desk. "George, would he, would coming—I mean finishing—would that . . . would that do it? I mean if he was hugely excited?"

"That's probably what happened. Not the climax itself but the uncontrollable straining it generates could easily tear weakened tissues or cause a rupture. His genitals were in perfect shape but his stomach cavity generally weak. I'd repaired part of the large bowel and sutured a couple of arteries, there were some nasty lesions and he wasn't healing as I would have liked, his liver was—"

"Yes, well, I don't need the details now," Sir William said squeamishly, already feeling slightly sick. "My God, young Struan! Seems impossible—then there's Norbert! If it weren't for Gornt we'd also have a murder on our hands. That fellow deserves a medal. He said, by the way, Jamie was provoked and Norbert deserved to get pasted. Did you know Malcolm and Norbert were meeting in Drunk Town to duel?"

"Not till a moment ago. Phillip told me. Madmen, both of them. Damn it, you warned them!"

"Yes, I did. Damn fools, though Gornt swore both had agreed to accept the other's apology, but he also said Norbert told him this morning he had changed his mind and was going to kill Struan. Miserable bastard!" Uneasily Sir William shifted things on his desk, straightening papers and the small, silver mounted portrait. "What do we do now?"

"About Norbert?"

"No, Malcolm, what about Malcolm first?"

"I'll do the autopsy today, this evening. I've taken the liberty of arranging to have the body taken to Kanagawa—it'll be easier there. Hoag will assist and you'll have a report in the morning. We'll sign the death certificate, it'll all be quite normal."

"I meant with the body," Sir William said testily.

"You can bury him at your leisure. In this weather there's no hurry, the body will keep."

"Will it . . . is there time to send *Prancing Cloud* to Hong Kong to find out what his, what Mrs. Struan wants to do? I mean she might want to bury him there an—"

"My God, I wouldn't like to bring her that news."

"Nor would I." Sir William tugged at his collar. As usual it was chilly in the office, the coal fire tiny and miserable, with a strong draft from ill-fitting windows. "Hoag's the family doctor, he could go. But,

George, I mean, will he, will the body keep that long? To send word to her, come back, then take the body back—if that's what she wants?"

"You'd better make the decision, to bury him here or to send him back at once. We'd keep him on ice, surround the coffin with ice, on deck under canvas, he'll keep very well."

Sir William nodded, revolted. "Phillip," he shouted through the door. "Ask Jamie to come by at once! George, I think the wisest course, provided he will, er, he'll keep would be to send him back. What's your advice?"

"I agree."

"Good, thank you, keep me advised about Angelique and don't forget supper tonight. What about our bridge game?"

"Best postpone both till tomorrow."

"All right, fine, that'll be fine. Thanks again . . . damn it, I forgot. What about Norbert?"

"A quick burial, soon forgotten and not regretted."

"I'll have to hold an inquest, Edward Gornt's American, a foreign national—he's preparing a signed statement. Just as well Adamson's on leave or he'd want to be involved. He's a lawyer isn't he, as well as U.S. Chargé d'Affaires?"

"Doesn't matter either way. Hoag and I can give medical evidence." Babcott got up and added coldly, "But the 'shooting in the back'? Not a very good advertisement for Yokohama."

"My whole point." Sir William's face screwed up. "My whole point. Wouldn't like that breezed about."

"You mean to our hosts?"

"Yes. They'll have to be informed, that's required. Can't formally tell them exactly what happened, in either case. Obviously Norbert's an accidental death. But Struan?"

"Tell them the truth," Babcott said, enraged by the waste and furious with himself that his work had not been good enough, and that, not as a doctor, he had desperately wanted to take Angelique in his arms to protect her from it all. "The truth is this unnecessary, early death of that fine young man was attributable directly to wounds sustained in his unprovoked attack on the Tokaidō!"

Sir William added bitterly, "By murdering bastards who still haven't been brought to justice. You're right."

He let Babcott out, waved Tyrer away, then stood at the window, upset with his present impotence. I've got to bring the Bakufu to heel quickly or we're finished, and our vision of opening up Japan is lost. They won't do it for themselves so we have to help them. But they've got to behave like civilized, law-abiding people ... meanwhile the clock's ticking, I know in my bones they'll fall on us one night, put us to the torch and that will be that. Sure as God made little apples!

Oh yes, retribution would fall back on them—with great loss of life. Meanwhile I will have failed in my duty, we'll all be dead and that's a very boring thought indeed. If only Ketterer wasn't so pigheaded. How the hell do I turn that obstinate bastard to my will?

He sighed, knowing one answer: First you'd better make a peace with him!

Their stormy meeting late last night over the Admiral's blatant disregard of Mrs. Struan's request and his own advice, having had no suspicion of the real reason until he had wrung it out of Jamie McFay earlier, had deteriorated into a shouting confrontation: 'It was ill advised to allow Marlowe to—'

'I thought it best! Now you listen to me—'

'Best? God damn it, I've just learned you thought it best to stupidly interfere in political and trade matters by trying to barter a nonenforceable agreement with the pretender to the Struan throne and so alienate the true head forever more!' he had said furiously. 'Didn't you?'

'And you, sirrah, you interfere in matters that are the sole prerogative of Parliament—declaring war—and the real reason you are so ill advised with your language, sirrah, and so upset, is because I will not begin a war we cannot win, cannot sustain with our present forces, if at all, and in my opinion any attack on the capital will rightly be considered an act of war by the natives and not an incident. Good night!'

'You agreed to assis—'

'I agreed to rattle a few sabres, fire a few practice rounds to impress the natives but I haven't agreed to bombard Yedo, nor, for the last time, will I until you show me authority in writing, approved by the Admiralty. Good n—'

'The Navy and the Army are subject to civilian control and advice, by God, and I'm the control here!'

'Yes, you are, by God, if I agree,' the Admiral bellowed, neck and face purple, 'but you're not in command of my ships and until I get orders to the contrary, approved by the Admiralty, I will run my fleet as I think best. Good night!'

Sir William sat back at his desk. He sighed and picked up a pen and wrote on his headed paper:

Dear Admiral Ketterer, Much of what you said last night was correct. Please excuse my ill-advised use of some words in

*the heat of the moment. Perhaps you would be kind enough to
stop by this afternoon. You will have heard of young Struan's
sad death that, according to Dr. Babcott, is "directly attributable to wounds caused by the unprovoked Tokaidō attack." I
will have to make another, most serious complaint to the
Bakufu about the demise of this fine English gentleman and
would be very pleased to have your advice how this should be
couched. Most sincerely, my dear Sir, I remain yr obedient
servant.*

"What I do for England," he muttered, then shouted, "Phillip!"
signed the paper and powdered it to dry the ink.

"Yessir?"

"Make a copy, then send it to Ketterer by messenger."

"Jamie's just arrived, sir, and there's a deputation asking that you
make this 'Angel Day,' a day of mourning."

"Refused! Send Jamie in."

Jamie was very bruised, his shoulder strapped up now.

"Jamie, you're feeling better? Good. George Babcott gave me a
report." He told him what had been said about Malcolm's body. "What
do you think?"

"We should send him home to Hong Kong, sir."

"Good, my thought too. You'll accompany the . . . him?"

"No, sir. Mrs. Struan . . . afraid she doesn't approve of me anymore,
and if I went back it would only worsen a really rotten situation for her,
poor lady. Between us, I'm dismissed at the end of this month."

"Good God, why?" Sir William was shocked.

"Doesn't matter, not now. Angelique, our Mrs. Struan, will of course
go, and Dr. Hoag—did you know she changed her mind and decided to
stay in her old apartments with us, and not at the French Legation after
all?"

"No, oh well, I suppose that's best. How is she?"

"Hoag says as well as can be expected, whatever the hell that
means. We'll send *Prancing Cloud* soon as you and he give me the
word. When's that likely?"

"George said he'd do the autopsy today and sign the death certificate, I'll have that tomorrow. The clipper could leave tomorrow, only
problem would be Angelique, when she's fit to travel." Sir William
looked at him keenly. "What about her?"

"Don't know, not really. I haven't seen her since . . . since being aboard. She didn't speak to me, not once, not lucidly. Hoag's still with her." Jamie tried to hold back his grief. "We can only hope."

"Rotten luck. Yes, no doubt about it. Now, Norbert. We'll have to have an inquest, of course."

"Good." Jamie touched his face, brushing away a nagging fly that sought the dried blood. "Gornt saved my life."

"Yes. He'll be commended. Jamie, when you leave Struan's what will you do? Go home?"

"This's home, here or China," Jamie said simply. "I'll . . . somehow I'll start my own firm."

"Good, I wouldn't like to lose you. Bless my soul, I can't imagine the Noble House here without you."

"Nor can I."

As the day wore on, the pall over Yokohama thickened. Shock, disbelief, anger, war fears, general fears—the Tokaidō remembered—mixed with many whispered snide remarks, but careful who you said them to because the Angel had violent champions and any raunchy remark or laugh implied disrespect. Malcolm was not so fortunate. He had enemies, many were glad to sneer and happy another disaster had fallen on Dirk Struan's progeny. And both priests in their several ways were sternly satisfied, seeing retribution from God.

"André," Seratard said at the lunch table in the Legation, Vervene a third man. "Did he make a will?"

"I don't know."

"See if you can find out. Ask her, or Jamie—he would probably know more."

André Poncin nodded bleakly, worried sick. Struan's death had disrupted his plan to get more money from her quickly to pay Raiko. "Yes, I'll try."

"Very important we should continue to stress her French citizenship to protect her when her mother-in-law tries to break the marriage."

Vervene said, "What makes you so sure that will happen, that she'll be so antagonistic?"

"*Mon Dieu,* it's obvious!" André answered for Seratard, irritably. "Her attitude will be that Angelique 'murdered' her son. We all know she hated her before, how much more so now? She's bound to accuse her of God knows what deviations because of her twisted Anglo-Saxon sexual dogma, in private if not in public. And don't forget she's a fanatic Protestant." He turned to Seratard. "Henri, perhaps I'd better see Angelique." He had already intercepted her and whispered that she should go back to Struan's and not stay here at the Legation: 'For God's sake, Angelique, your place is with your husband's people!' It was so obvious that she must strengthen her position with Struan's—at any cost—that he had almost shouted at her, but his sudden anger turned to pity seeing the depth of her despair. Now he said, "I'd better go."

"Yes, please do."

André closed the door. "What the devil's the matter with him?" Vervene said with a sniff.

Seratard thought before answering, decided it was time. "It's probably his illness—the English disease."

His deputy dropped his fork in shock. "Syphilis?"

"André told me a few weeks ago. You should know, only you amongst the staff, as these explosions may become more frequent. He's too valuable to send home." André had whispered he had made a brand-new, high-up intelligence connection: 'The man says Lord Yoshi will be back in Yedo in two weeks. For a fairly modest sum, he and his Bakufu connections guarantee a private meeting aboard our flagship.'

'How much?'

'That meeting would be worth whatever it costs.'

'I agree, but how much?' Seratard asked.

'The equivalent of four months of my salary,' André had said bitterly, 'a pittance. Speaking of that, Henri, I need an advance, or the bonus you promised months ago.'

'Nothing was agreed, dear André. In due course you will have it, but sorry again, no advance. Very well, that amount, after the meeting.'

'Half now and half after. He also told me, for no money, *Tairō* Anjo is sick and may not last the year.'

'Has he proof?'

'Come on, Henri, you know that's not possible!'

'Get your contact to make this *tairō* ape see Babcott for an examination and . . . and I'll give you a fifty percent raise.'

'Double salary from today, double salary, and I'll need to give my contact a hefty down payment.'

'Fifty percent from the day of the examination and thirty Mex in gold, five down and the rest after. And that's all.'

Seratard had seen André's hope escalate. Poor André, he's losing his touch. Of course I understand a large part of the money will stick to his fingers, but never mind, dealing with spies is dirty business, and André is particularly dirty though very clever. And unfortunate.

He reached over and took the last slice of the one Brie cheese that had arrived, on ice, at fantastic cost, with the last mail ship. "Be patient with the poor fellow, Vervene, eh?" Every day he was expecting to see signs of the disease, but nothing, and every day André seemed a little younger, losing his previous harassed expression. Only his temper had deteriorated.

Mon Dieu! A private Yoshi meeting! And if Babcott could examine this cretin Anjo, perhaps even cure him, at my instigation—never mind that Babcott's English, I'll barter this coup with Sir William for some other advantage—we will have made a tremendous step forward.

He raised his glass. "Vervene, *mon brave,* the pox on the English and *Vive la France!*"

Angelique was lying listlessly in the four-poster bed, propped against piled-up pillows, never more wan or more ethereal. Hoag was in a chair by the bed, dozing, on and off. The late afternoon sun broke through the clouds for a moment to brighten a dull, windy day. In the roads ships tugged at their moorings. Half an hour ago—to her a minute or hour the same—the signal gun had announced the imminent arrival of the mail ship, waking her, not that she had really been asleep, wafting instead from consciousness to unconsciousness, no border between. Her eyes drifted past Hoag. Beyond him she saw the door to Malcolm's rooms—not his rooms, nor their rooms, just rooms now for another man, another tai-pan . . .

The tears returned in full flood.

"Don't cry, Angelique," Hoag said softly, tenderly, every fiber concentrated, watching for telltale signs of looming disaster. "All's well, life will go on and you're fine now, truly fine."

He was holding her hand. With a handkerchief she brushed away the tears. "I would like some tea."

"At once," Hoag said, his ugly face filled with relief. This was the first she had spoken since this morning, properly, coherently, and first moments back were vital indicators. Almost cheering, he opened the door, for though her voice was a thread, there was no hysteria in it or under it or behind it, the light in her eyes was good, face no longer puffy from tears, and her pulse he had counted while holding her hand was firm and strong at ninety-eight counts per minute, no longer jumping around nauseatingly.

"Ah Soh," he said in Cantonese, "bring your Mistress fresh tea but not a sound, say nothing and then leave." He sat near the bed again. "Do you know where you are, my dear?"

She just looked at him.

"May I ask a few questions? If you're tired, tell me and don't be afraid. Sorry, but it's important for you, not me."

"I'm not afraid."

"Do you know where you are?"

"In my rooms."

Her voice was flat, eyes blank. His concern increased. "You know what happened?"

"Malcolm's dead."

"Do you know why he died?"

"He died on our marriage night in our marriage bed and I'm responsible."

Warning bells sounded in the back of his mind. "You're wrong, Angelique, Malcolm was killed on the Tokaidō, months ago," he said, his voice calm and unshakable. "Sorry, but that's the truth and he'd been living on borrowed time ever since, not your fault, never your fault, it was the will of God, but I can tell you this with all my heart, we, Babcott and I, we have never seen a man more peaceful, more at peace in death, never, never, never."

"I'm responsible."

"The only part you're responsible for was the joy in the last months of his life. He did love you, didn't he?"

"Yes, but he died and—" She almost added, *and so did that other man, I don't even know his name but he died too, he loved me too and he died too and now Malcolm's dead an—*

"Stop it!"

The snarled harshness jerked her from the brink. Hoag began breathing again, but he knew this had to be done and done quickly or she was lost, like others he had seen. He had to rid her of the devil lurking somewhere in her mind that was waiting to break out, waiting to pounce, to turn her into a gibbering lunatic, at least to harm her radically. "Sorry. You've got to get this correct. You are only re—" In panic he just caught himself before using that word, changing it to "answerable for his joy. Repeat it for me. You are only ans—"

"I am responsible."

"Say it after me: I am only answerable for his joy," he said carefully, more of an order, noticing with alarm her abnormal pupils. She was brinking again.

"I am resp—"

"Answerable, God dammit," he said with pretended anger. "Say after me, I am only answerable for his joy! Answerable for his joy! Say it!"

He saw the sweat break out on her forehead and again she said the same and again he cut in, repeated the correct word, "answerable, answerable for his joy!" and again she said the other and again and during this Ah Soh brought the tea but neither saw her and she fled in terror as again and again Hoag ordered Angelique and she refused until suddenly she shrieked in French, "All right, I'm only answerable for his joy but he's still dead dead dead . . . my Malcolm's deaddddddddd!"

He wanted to hold her and tell her that all was well and that she could sleep but he didn't, judging it was too soon. His voice was hard but not threatening and he said in his good French, "Thank you, Angelique, but now we will speak English. Yes, I'm terribly sorry too, we all are that your lovely husband is dead, but it's not your fault. Say it!"

"Leave me alone. Get out!"

"When you say it: not your fault."

"Not . . . not . . . Leave me alone!"

"When you say it. Not your fault!"

She stared at him, loathing the tormentor he was, then again shrieked at him: "Not my fault, it's not my fault, it's not my fault, not my fault. Now are you satisfied? Get out, *gettout*!"

"When you tell me you understand your Malcolm is dead but you are in no way responsible!"

"Gettout!"

"Say it! God dammit, say it!"

Suddenly her voice became like the howl of a wild beast. "Yur Malcolm's dead yur Malcolm's dead he's dead, he's dead he's dead but yu're not not resp not responsible in no way any God-cursed way not resp in any way any way not responsible . . . not respon . . . not . . ." As abruptly as she had begun her voice changed to a whimper, "Not responsible, I'm not, I'm truly not, oh my darling, I'm so sorry, so sorry, I don't want you dead, oh Blessed Mother, help me, he's dead and I feel so terrible, so terrible, oh Malcolm, why did you die I loved you so much, so very much . . . oh Malcolm . . ."

This time he held her quiet, tightly, absorbing the tremors and weeping and the racking sobs. In time her voice trailed away, the sobbing lessened, and she sank into fitful sleep. Still he held her, gently but firmly, his clothes stuck to him with sweat and did not move until the sleep was deep. Then he eased away. His back was sparking with pain and he stood carefully, tortured, his muscles in spasm. When he had managed to ease his shoulders and neck he sat to regain his strength.

That was a near one he thought, the pleasure that he had won this time eliminating part of his pain, seeing her as she was, young and beautiful and safe.

His memory rushed him to Kanagawa to that other girl, the Japanese sister of the man he had operated on, as young and beautiful but Japanese. What was her name? Uki something. I saved her brother to wreak more havoc on this poor child. But I'm glad she escaped. Did she? Such a beautiful woman. Like my own darling wife that was. How terrible and thoughtless of me, how insane to take her from India to an early London death.

Dharma? Fate? Like this child and poor Malcolm. Poor them, poor me. No, not poor me, I've just saved a life. You may be squat and ugly, old boy, he thought, taking her pulse, but Christ Almighty, you're a bloody good doctor, and bloody good liar—no, not good, just lucky. This time.

46

Thursday, 11th December:

" 'AFTERNOON, JAMIE," PHILLIP
Tyrer said sadly. "Sir William's compliments, here are three copies of
the death certificate, one for you, one for Angelique, and one for
Strongbow to go with the body. The original he thought should go by
diplomatic pouch to the Governor's office for the Chief Coroner Hong
Kong, who'll register it, then pass it on to Mrs. Struan. Ghastly, isn't it,
but there you are."

"Yes." Jamie's desk was piled with incoming mail, and documents
concerning affairs to be arranged. His eyes were red from tiredness.

"How's Angelique?"

"I haven't seen her yet but Hoag was here first thing. He said to
leave her alone until she made the first move, that she was better than
expected. She slept for fifteen-odd hours. He thought she should be
well enough to travel tomorrow and recommended the sooner the
better. He'll go, of course."

"When's *Prancing Cloud* rescheduled for?"

"Tomorrow. Evening tide. Strongbow will be here any moment for
sailing orders. You'll have mails to go with her?"

"Definitely. And a pouch. I'll tell Sir William. Still cannot believe
Malcolm's dead. Dreadful. Oh, by the way, the Norbert inquest's been
fixed for five. Would you like a bite of supper afterwards?"

"Thanks, but not tonight. Let's do it tomorrow, all being well. We'll
confirm after breakfast." Jamie wondered if he should tell Tyrer about

the machinations of his samurai friend, Nakama, and the meeting with the local moneylender—that Nakama wanted private from Tyrer and Sir William. Nakama's suggestion had intrigued him and he welcomed the opportunity of talking direct to a local businessman, however minor.

Yesterday's meeting had of course been cancelled. He had considered putting it off until next week, but had decided to meet the man tonight—it might divert him for a moment or two from the tragedy.

It's none of Phillip's business—and don't forget Phillip and Wee Willie have been hiding all sorts of information when the arrangement was for everything to be shared. "See you later, Phillip. And thanks for these."

"See you later, Jamie."

The death certificates were signed by Babcott and Hoag. The autopsy confirmed what had already been said about death *being caused by internal bleeding of a damaged artery that had ceased to function correctly, its weakened condition being directly attributable to wounds sustained during the unprovoked Tokaidō incident.*

Jamie nodded to himself. The doctors had skirted the matter of what had caused the rupture. No reason to be more specific, unless someone required a specific answer. Like Tess Struan, he thought, a twinge in his stomach. She's bound to ask and then what will Hoag say? The same he told me this morning: 'In Malcolm's condition, Jamie, such a rupture could be caused by any one of a dozen sudden motions, like sleeping awkwardly, then turning suddenly because of a bad dream, even the strain of a constipated bowel.'

'Or particularly during intercourse?'

'Yes, that's only one of many possibilities. Why?'

'You know Tess Struan, for God's sake.'

'I'm not going to damn Angelique, if that's what you're asking. It takes two to bed—we both know he went out of his way to marry her and was madly in love.'

'I'm not asking anything, Doc. Tess will damn her whatever the certificate says.'

'I agree, Jamie, but she will get no help from me. Nor from George. That a violent climax caused the hemorrhage, and their subsequent euphoric sleep masked the fault for both of them is logical, but not provable, and even if it did, she is in no way to blame, no way, dammit . . .'

Poor Angelique, she'll be blamed, like I'll be blamed. Doesn't matter in my case. "Yes? Come in? Oh, hello, Edward!"

"Do you have a second?" Gornt asked.

"Come in, of course." Since yesterday his relationship with Gornt was different. He had insisted being on a first-name basis. My God, he thought, how wrong I was about him. "Sit down. Listen, I've said it a dozen times but thanks again—you certainly saved my life."

"Nothing, I was only doing my duty."

"Thank God you did. What can I do for you?"

"The rumor is that you'll be sending Malcolm's remains back to Hong Kong for burial, and I wondered if I could have passage on your ship?"

"Of course." Jamie hesitated. "To report to Tyler Brock and Morgan?"

Gornt smiled. "We can't avoid the truth, Jamie. I'll take the result of the inquest with me but it's up to me to tell them direct, man to man."

"Yes, you're right." Jamie's sadness swooped down again. "I'm sorry Malcolm's not alive to know what you did for me, sorry that he won't be around to be friends with you, I know he admired you greatly, sorry too that you work for them."

"After I see them I probably won't, I was only loaned by Rothwell's, so it's of no consequence. I'll go back to Shanghai after Hong Kong."

"You know, if I can help in any way, I will."

"You owe me nothing, I was just doing my duty but a man always needs a real friend. Thanks, if I get lost I'll ask. A cabin's all right then on *Prancing Cloud*?"

"She'll leave tomorrow evening."

"I suppose Mrs. Struan will accompany him? Difficult to think of him as dead, isn't it?"

"Yes. Dr. Hoag says she'll be fit to travel then."

"Rotten luck. Terrible. Thanks. See you later."

Jamie watched him leave, curiously unsettled. Nothing he could articulate. Guess I'm just so disoriented that anything and everything seems odd. My God, even Hoag acted peculiar, again nothing in particular.

He forced himself to work for a while, then, needing some documents from Malcolm's desk, got up and went out along the corridor to the tai-pan's office, automatically raising his hand to knock. Grimly, he didn't, and opened the door only to stop in midstride. Angelique was sitting in Malcolm's chair, behind Malcolm's desk. Seated in front of her Heavenly Skye was saying, "As far as I know and . . ." He looked around.

"Hello, Jamie," Angelique said quietly. Her dark dress set off the alabaster texture of her skin, hair up off the nape of her long neck, eyes clear, the faintest natural color to her lips. "How are you?"

"Oh, er, fine," Jamie said, nonplussed by her poise and new beauty—different from before, now somehow distant, unattainable but even more attractive. "Sorry, I didn't expect . . . Dr. Hoag told me not to disturb you until you called me. How are you?"

"I asked him to do that. I'm . . . I'm fine, thank you. There were some things I wanted to arrange this morning. I was sorry to hear about your—your ill luck with Norbert Greyforth. Poor Jamie, you're very bruised, are you all right?"

"Yes, thank you," Jamie said, even more off balance. Her voice was calm, too calm, and there was a dignity about her that he could not for the moment isolate. "Edward Gornt saved my life, did you hear that?"

"Yes, he told me about it a few minutes ago—actually that's not right, he came here a few moments ago to add his condolences and I saw him. Mr. Skye told me about his bravery. And about the duel."

"Oh." Jamie wanted to curse Skye for his interference.

"Poor Malcolm," she said. "I'm awfully glad I didn't know about that foolishness. If I had I would somehow have stopped it. But Edward, how lucky he was there, but how awful, how awful some people are."

"Yes, but more important, how are you really?"

"Not good and not bad. I'm nothing, and, well, empty."

"That's the right word, empty. Me too." Jamie looked at Heavenly who smiled noncommittally. The silence gathered. Discomfited, he knew they both wanted him to leave. "Anything I can do for you?"

"Not at the moment, thank you, Jamie."

Jamie nodded thoughtfully. "I need a few papers."

"Please help yourself." She sat back in the chair that dwarfed her, composed and in control.

Uncomfortably, he began to sift through the ladened In and Out trays, decided to take them as they were and put one on top of the other. "If there's anything . . . just call."

"After Mr. Skye and I are through, perhaps a few minutes if you're free."

"Whenever, of course. Just ring that bell."

Skye said, "Jamie, did you get the death certificates yet, by chance?"

"Yes, I did."

"Could I see a copy, please?"

Jamie stared at him. "For what purpose?"

"To check it."

Angelique said, "Mal . . . my husband had retained the services of Mr. Skye—I believe you knew that, Jamie?"

"Yes, I did." Jamie had noticed the way she had changed Malcolm to my husband and saw Heavenly nod approvingly and a danger signal went through him. "So?"

Skye said smoothly, "When I heard the disastrous news I felt beholden to offer my services to his widow . . ." the word was imperceptibly accented ". . . which she has kindly accepted. The tai-pan had asked me to undertake certain research for him which I thought Mrs. Struan might wish to continue."

"Good." Jamie nodded politely and began to leave.

"The death certificate, Jamie?"

"What's your pleasure, Angelique—Mrs. Struan?"

"Mr. Skye is my solicitor now, Jamie. He understands these things, which I don't, and he has agreed to act for me," she said clearly in the same unemotional way. "I would like you, please, to give him whatever help he needs."

"Of course. If you'll follow me, Heavenly." Jamie walked out and went into his office and stood behind his desk, pretending to look for the papers that he had put into his drawer for safety. "Would you shut the door, there's a terrible draft." The small man obeyed. "Listen," he said, keeping his voice down but there was no mistaking the undercurrent, "if you bamboozle her, or play silly buggers or overcharge her I'll kick the shit out of you."

The little man came closer, his pebble glasses cracked and fogged. "I've never done that to a client in my life," he said, puffing up like a cobra. "A few big bills, yes, but never more than the market could stand. That woman needs help, for God's sake. I can give it to her, you can't."

"I can and will, by God."

"I don't agree! Malcolm told me the other Mrs. Struan, the woman in Hong Kong, fired you, true or false? And true or false that you as well as Malcolm have been getting angry, even threatening letters from her for weeks, paranoiac against my client and her engagement with all sorts of unfounded accusations? True or false, for God's sake, that that girl needs friends?"

"I agree she needs friends. I don't object to her having a solicitor, I just want to be sure you'll act correctly."

"God dammit, I've never buggered a client in my life. Jamie, I may be a hungry lawyer but I'm a good one, and we're on the same side. She needs friends, Malcolm loved her, you were Malcolm's friend, for God's sake—he told me about the letters you would have risked hanging for."

"Never mind that wh—"

"I'm not arguing with you, Jamie, she's my client and I swear I'll do my best for her. The death certificate, please."

Seething, Jamie opened the drawer and gave him a copy.

"Thanks . . . ah three, eh? One for your files, one to go with the body and one for her, quite correct, though I'm surprised they bothered to think of her, original by special to Hong Kong." Heavenly scanned the paper. "Christ Almighty!"

"What's the matter?"

"Hoag and Babcott," he said. "They may be good doctors but as defense witnesses they're a disaster! Shit, I should have been told before they issued this—any fool could have given them better wording!"

"What the devil are you talking about?"

"Murder, or at least a charge of murder."

"You're mad!"

"It wouldn't be the first for Tess Struan," the little man hissed. "Remember the Bosun? Everyone in Hong Kong knew it was an accident but he was charged with murder, found guilty of manslaughter and given ten years!"

"The jury found him guilty, not Tess, by God an—"

"But she was the one who pressed for the charge!" Skye slammed back at him, keeping his voice down. "And she'll press charges here. If this was read out in court in a criminal or civil case, our opposing barrister would claim he died fucking—please excuse my vulgarity— 'and the other half of the act sits in the dock there, ladies and gentlemen of the jury, whose father is a felon on the run, whose uncle is in a French jail, who herself is a penniless adventuress, a Jezebel who knowingly seduced this poor young man, a minor, into marrying her and then—and then, ladies and gentlemen of the jury—with malice aforethought seduced him into an early death—*with malice aforethought*—knowing only too well his wounds would do the job for her!' True or bloody false?"

Jamie sat down, paler than before. Hoag's words had jumped into his mind. "What're you going to do?"

"First I'll try to get this wording changed, don't think they will but I have to try. Do you have his will? Malcolm's?"

Jamie shook his head. "He never mentioned one to me."

"I told him it was important he should have one drawn up when he first came to see me—that's routine. You're sure?"

"I know I don't have one, not in our safe." Jamie frowned. Would Malcolm have made one? If I was getting married, I would. Wait a minute—I was engaged to Maureen for years and never had one. My God, I wonder how she is, what she thought when she got my letter. "He never mentioned a will to me. Did he to Angelique?"

"No, that was my first question. Perhaps he made one without your knowledge. Did he have a safety box or a special place for his private papers?"

"No, not really, I suppose that would be in Hong Kong, except there's a small safe in his rooms."

"Let's go and look." Skye started out of the room.

"Wait a minute, I don't think we can do that."

The words came back sharp, and formal: "Mrs. Angelique Struan was his legal wife and is his widow therefore his immediate heir and inheritor of all his worldly goods unless his will states otherwise. If there's no will then she inherits, after probate and all legal fees and taxes are paid. Let's look in his safe."

"I don't think that we can presum—"

"Now, quietly, between the three of us as friends, or I'll get a formal court order through Sir William today to sequester all, I repeat, all his papers, and all Struan papers in Yokohama and Hong Kong, for a will search *to which my client is entitled*." His look was inflexible. "Sorry, old boy. Well?"

"Let's go and ask Angelique." Unsure of himself and knowing he could never allow an outsider to go through Noble House papers and records, Jamie followed Skye back to the tai-pan's office. Dammit, why do I think of it as that, he thought irritably. I suppose because it is the tai-pan's office. Who's the new tai-pan? Christ, what a mess!

Angelique was sitting where they had left her. Impassively, she listened to Skye. "There's no need for you to accompany us, Mrs. Struan, rest assured I act for you."

"Thank you, but I would like to be there."

They followed her up the grand staircase, the first time for Skye who tried not to be visibly awed by the wonderful chandelier and valuable oils. Jamie opened the door of the tai-pan's suite. A coal fire burned pleasantly. The four-poster was made up and waiting. Desk tidy, no papers on it. In a near corner of the room Ah Tok squatted mumbling, in despair, somehow tiny now, ugly and ancient. She paid no attention to them. Angelique shuddered then followed the two men and sat in Malcolm's high chair facing them. Watching them intently.

The little iron wall-safe was concealed behind an oil painting, another Aristotle Quance. Skye smiled thinly. The painting depicted a pretty young Chinese girl carrying a fair-haired, fair-skinned child with a pigtail, a boy, against a Hong Kong landscape. He had heard about the painting but had never seen it. Quance was the dean of the artist-chroniclers of Macao and early Hong Kong, an Irishman who had lived there for many years, and died a few years ago in Macao and was buried there. He was also a voracious drunk, gambler, libertine but old friend and devotee of Dirk Struan's. Rumor had it the girl was the fabled May-may, Dirk's Chinese mistress, the one who was killed with him in the typhoon of '42, in his arms, and the child their firstborn.

He glanced at Angelique, who watched Jamie impassively searching through a bunch of keys, and wondered if she knew about Malcolm's Eurasian cousins and his uncle, Compradore Gordon Chen—Dirk's son by another mistress—who, according to Hong Kong gossip, 'knew more secrets and had more taels of gold than an ox had hairs.' The mantelpiece clock chimed three.

"Who else has keys, Jamie?" Skye asked.

"Just me . . . me and the . . . the tai-pan."

"Where are his?"

"I don't know. I presume still with . . . still aboard."

The safe door swung open. A few letters, all in Tess Struan's writing, except one in Malcolm's apparently unfinished, a small chamois leather bag and a wallet. The wallet contained a faded daguerreotype of his father and mother peering self-consciously at the camera, Malcolm's personal chop, a few chits—IOU's and a list of debts and debtors. Heavenly leafed through them. "Would these others be gambling debts he's owed, Jamie?"

"I've no idea."

"Two thousand four hundred and twenty guineas. A tidy sum for a young man to lend or be owed. Do you recognize any of the names, by chance?"

"Just this one." Jamie looked at him.

"Madame Emma Richaud? Five hundred guineas."

Angelique said, "She's my aunt, she and Uncle Michel, they brought me up, Mr. Skye. Mama, I called my aunt that for she was mother to me, my own died when I was young. They needed help and Mal . . . Malcolm kindly sent them that. I asked him to."

"Jamie, I'd like a copy of these, a list please." The solicitor was talking again. "You are required to hold them in safekeeping." He reached for the half-dozen letters but Jamie was there before him: "I'd say these were private."

"Private to whom, Jamie?"

"To him."

"I will get a court order to see them and have them copied if I consider them to be valid."

"You certainly may do that," Jamie said through his teeth, cursing himself for blurting out about the safe until he could get Sir William's advice.

Angelique said, "May I see them, Jamie, please? I suppose they are part of my husband's effects. At the moment they seem so few."

Her voice was so gentle, so sad, no shred of begging, that he sighed and said to himself, Laddie, you're in so deep now it doesn't matter. Sir William will have to decide legalities. Then, suddenly, he was back at yesterday eventide, on the jetty, the three of them so lighthearted, laughing, confident, with any future Hong Kong stormclouds seemingly so far away, seeing the two of them off in the cutter for their wedding night, Malcolm saying, 'Thanks, my bonny friend, guard our tail, it's going to need guarding. Promise?'

He had promised, sworn he would do that, and guard her equally, wishing them long and happy lives, and waved, last on the shore. How right Malcolm was. Poor Malcolm, did he have a premonition? "Here," he said kindly. Without looking at the letters she put them in her lap and again folded her hands, again motionless. A draft waved a vagrant strand of hair near her temple. Otherwise she was quite like a statue.

The chink of coins attracted Jamie's attention. Skye had opened the little bag. It contained Bank of England golden guineas, and notes. He counted them aloud. Angelique's eyes did not move from the maw of the safe.

"Two hundred and sixty-three guineas." Skye put them back in the leather sack. "These should go to Mrs. Struan at once—she will of course give you a receipt."

Jamie said, "Perhaps it's best that we, you and I, Heavenly, we go and see Sir William. I've never been involved in this kind of matter before and I'm out of my depth—Angelique, you do understand, don't you?"

"I'm out of my depth too, Jamie, adrift too. I know Malcolm was your friend and you were his, as you are mine too. He told me many times. Please do whatever you think best."

Skye said, "We'll see him now, Jamie, sooner the better, he can decide on the ownership of these. Meanwhile . . ." He walked over to give her the little bag but she said, "Take it with you, take everything, and these too." She handed him the letters. "Just leave me the photograph. Thank you, Mr. Skye. And thanks, dear Jamie, and I'll see you when you return."

They waited for her to get up but she made no move. "You're not going to stay here, are you? Surely not?" Jamie said, perturbed—it seemed so macabre.

"I think I will. I spent so much time here, in this room, that it's—it's sympathetic to me. The door to my suite is open if I . . . if I need to rest. But please, would you take Ah Tok away, poor thing, and tell her not to come back. Poor woman, she needs help. Ask Dr. Hoag to see her."

"Do you want the door closed?"

"Door? Oh, it doesn't matter, yes, if you wish."

They did as she asked and made sure Ah Tok was handed over to Chen who himself was still distraught and in tears and went out into High Street, both of them relieved to be in the open again but lost in their own thoughts. Skye was planning and sifting the quicksands that lay ahead, Jamie unable to plan yet, his planning brain devoured by the tragedy and, he did not know why, concern for the Noble House.

What is it about her? he was asking himself, unaware of the promenade, or gusting wind, surf grinding up the pebbled beach, or the smell of rotting seaweed. Sadness suits her. Can it be that . . .

She's a woman now! That is what's different, she has a depth and poise that wasn't there before. She's a woman, no longer a girl. Is it because of the catastrophe, or because she's no longer a virgin—the mystic change they say happens, or is supposed to happen at the transmutation? Or both, with perhaps the finger of God helping her to adjust?

"Christ," he said, despite himself, thinking aloud, "what happens if she has a child?"

"For her sake, I pray she does," the little man said.

When they left, Angelique closed her eyes and breathed deeply. Soon she was soothed and got up and bolted the door, then opened hers. Her bed was made up, fresh flowers in a vase on her dressing table. She went back into Malcolm's suite, bolting her door, and sat back in his chair.

Only then did she look at the photograph—the first of his parents she had seen. On the back was *October 17th, '61*. Last year. Culum Struan appeared much older than his years, forty-two, Tess neither old nor young, pale eyes gazing directly at Angelique, the thin line of her lips dominant.

Tess turned thirty-seven this year. What will I look like when I'm her age—in nineteen years, more than twice my age today? Will I have the same hard cast to my features that shout an unloving marriage and crushing family burdens—hating her father and brothers, them hating her, both sides trying to ruin the other—that began in her case so romantically, eloping and married at sea, like we did but, oh my God, with what a difference.

Her eyes looked out of the window and to the bay and the ships there, a merchant steamer leaving port—captain and officers on the bridge, the mail ship surrounded by tenders, the Struan cutter there, and *Prancing Cloud*. Elegant, straining to up anchor and up canvas to sail the wild winds. That's what Malcolm always said about their clippers, she thought, that clippers sail the wild winds.

She closed her eyes and rubbed them and looked again. No mistake. All day her eyes had an unexpected, startling clarity of vision. She had noticed it the moment she had awoken this morning, every detail of the room in focus, curtains, dead flowers in a vase, flies circling, four of them. Within seconds there had been a knock and Ah Soh's voice, "Missee? Med'sin man wan you see-ah, heya?" as though, her hearing also more acute, the sound of Ah Soh's footsteps had brought her smoothly out of sleep.

What was even stranger was the clarity of her mind, all the weight seemed to be gone, not the sadness but how clearly it considered problem after problem without consternation, never mixing them, suggesting answers, and never the usual heart-hurting fear, not even a little. Concern, yes, that was only sensible, but no more nauseating panic and indecision.

Now she could remember that day and that night in all its details without a crushing, inhuman, insensate blankness. Have I been numbed? Forever? Is what Dr. Hoag said this morning correct: 'Don't worry, you're cured of any problem. So long as you can cry from time to time, and not be afraid to go back in time if that's what your mind wishes to do, then your life will be fine, better every day. You have youth and health, your life is before you . . .'

Mon Dieu, such platitudes they talk, doctors. After Hoag, Babcott. More of the same. He had been gentle and tall and tender, a tenderness that could turn into heat if she would allow it. No more heat, she thought, not until I am free. And safe. Safe and free.

Her body was rested. No blinding headache, not even a little one, no screams inside. Knowing at once where she was, who she was, and why she was here, and why alone, and what had happened. Experiencing it again, watching herself in the daymare, conscious of it all but not involved, not truly involved: watching herself being wakened by Chen's wailing shriek, torn out of sleep, seeing herself in panic trying to shake Malcolm awake too then glimpsing blood on her lower limbs, horrified for a moment she had cut herself too deeply and then realizing that it was him, his blood, and that he was dead, dead, dead.

Leaping out of bed naked, not aware of it, terrified and shrieking, disbelieving what her eyes and ears told her, praying it was a dream, others rushing into the cabin, Ah Soh, Ah Tok, someone covering her, voices and shouting and screams and questions and more questions until the cabin smashed her into blackness and terror. Now on the bridge, freezing and burning and questions and no answers, her mouth locked, head afire, stench of blood, taste of blood, blood on her loins and on her hands and in her hair, stomach rebelling.

Ah Soh helping her into a bath, the water cool, never enough hot to clean away his death, more sickness and then the blinding poison filling her, drowning her until she saw herself shrieking at Hoag, a picture of ugliness, oh, so ugly.

She shivered. Must I look like that when I'm old? How old is old? Not very for some. What exactly she had said to Hoag, even now she could not recall, only that the poison had gushed away and with the torrent, good sleep came to pass.

I've much to thank Hoag for, and Babcott to loathe for—his sleeping draft began my sink into despair. I'm no longer afraid, no longer in despair, I don't understand why but it's true—thanks to Malcolm and Hoag, to that smelly little lawyer with his foul breath, and to André. André is still wise, still my confidant and will remain so, so long as I pay. Yes, he's a blackmailer. That doesn't matter. To help himself he has to protect me and then, well, there is a God in Heaven and the mills of God grind slowly but they grind exceedingly small.

I can deal with my life now, I think, if I'm careful.

Madonna, we agreed so long ago that I had to help myself and could not be dependent on a man or men, like the rest of my poor sisterhood. I know I'm a sinner. Malcolm was truly the only man I've ever met I really wanted, really loved and really wanted to marry, loved as much as a silly teenager could love. Is first love true love? Or is love an adult emotion? I'm adult now. Was my love for Malcolm adult? I think so, hope so.

But my darling is dead. I accept that. And now?

Tess? Hong Kong? André? Gornt? Home? Tess?

One at a time.

First my darling must be put to rest. Properly.

She saw the safe, its door shut but not locked. She got up and opened it fully, reaching into the back, touching a small, concealed indentation. Part of the left wall swung open. In the cavity were some papers, another personal chop, another bag of coins and notes. A bottle of his medicine. A small box.

A week ago Malcolm had shown her the secret hollow, smiling at her. 'There's nothing much to hide yet, all the important stuff's in Hong Kong with Mother, papers about being tai-pan, a copy of Father's will, Mother's will and so on, the tai-pan's chop. This is for,' he shrugged, his eyes alight, 'for odds and ends and secret presents I might give you, if you're very good and love me to distraction . . .'

She opened the box. A gold ring, set with rubies. Not very valuable, but valuable enough. The papers were business papers she did not understand, lists of figures.

And no will.

Damn, she thought without anger. It would have made the future more simple. André had pointed that out.

He had been summoned this morning by Vargas at her request from the list of people who had called and left cards. 'Monsieur Vargas, first my tailor, I must have mourning clothes urgently, after him, Monsieur André, then Mr. Skye—no need to disturb Mr. McFay until I send for him. To anyone else I'm resting, and Monsieur,' she added carefully, 'please treat all this with the discretion my husband told me you possess. I'll see everyone in the tai-pan's office.'

She had seen a flicker in Vargas's eyes at 'tai-pan,' but he had said nothing, so no need to be firm. The office had been chosen with care and when the old dressmaker arrived with Vargas she said, 'Please ask how long it would take to make a mourning dress, black, like this.' The one she wore was long-sleeved, high-necked, dark blue.

'He says three days. Mourning, senhora? The color for mourning in China is white.'

'I want it in black. Silk. And tomorrow.'

'Three days.'

'If he takes my other dress, the pale blue one he made for me and dyes it black, how long?'

'He says two days.'

'Tell him the widow of the tai-pan of the Noble House requires such a black dress tomorrow. Tomorrow morning.'

The old Chinese had sighed and bowed and went away. Then Vargas announced André Poncin. 'Hello, André.'

'Hello. I've never seen you more beautiful.'

It was a statement, not a compliment. 'I need advice, quickly, privately. We must be very quick, very wise. My marriage is legal, yes?'

'We think so, yes, according to British naval law; we're not sure about French law. Both are grey areas.'

'I don't understand.'

'Subject to argument. If there was an argument between French and British lawyers, British law would prevail. The reality of him being a minor, both of you in fact though in this he's the important one, sorry, and his disobedience of the written dictates of his legal guardian means that the marriage ceremony will probably be challenged.'

'Where? Here? By whom?'

'By Tess Struan. Who else?' he said mockingly.

'Malcolm's death is meaningless to you, isn't it?'

'On the contrary, it has complicated my life immeasurably, Madame,' he added, the first time using the title. 'It is a serious complication for both of us.'

She had chosen to sit behind Malcolm's desk, in Malcolm's office, for her future was at stake and she had to have a hundred percent of this man's cunning, and then more. In her suite she would be less confident, though ordinarily at her best in her boudoir. Is that why men have offices, and women are limited to the chaise and the femininity of a semi-bedroom? 'How can this be made uncomplicated, André?'

'The first complication you've already uncomplicated.'

When she had fled in misery to the Legation he had intercepted her, almost dragged her into his office, cursing her once the door was closed, shaking her angrily, saying, 'You stupid bitch, are you mad? Get back to his house and stay there and don't move, you can't hide here or you'll ruin yourself! Go back there, you fool, we'll talk later and, for God's sake, don't sign anything, don't agree to anything. Go on, get out!'

'You were quite right, André,' she said, not resenting his venom, or violence, understanding clearly. 'Thank you for telling it to me so it got through to me, got through my anguish. That was the first. Next?'

The lines in his forehead deepened. This was a new Angelique, an unknown quantity, unexpected. He had seen such a change twice before in men, never a woman. Both had been enemy spies released after extreme torture. The doctors had no explanation other than to say, the men no longer feared, or feared more torture, or feared dying. They had been dragged to the brink and had survived, and were now convinced, beyond doubt, they would survive again whatever was done to them, or they would die and that no longer mattered. The doctors had said that death itself wouldn't matter until the day, weeks or months or years ahead when the terror raised its vile head again as it was bound to do.

Poor Angelique sitting there so confident, so grand. There'll come a day when it will all spill out, will tear you asunder. Will you conquer it or end up in the madhouse?

For himself he would have bet that so many calamities would prove too much for such a young girl: the flight of her father, theft of her dowry, rape and pregnancy, the shooting of the rapist, and now this new and ghastly death that he and all the Settlement knew in its most graphic details. He and Seratard had expected her mind to be turned, at least for months, still expected it to happen, neither believing Hoag whom they had cross-questioned closely.

If Hoag can work this miracle, he thought angrily, why can't doctors cure the God-cursed English disease? It's not fair. 'Life isn't fair, is it?'

'No,' she said. 'Not fair at all.'

'Did he leave a will, naming you his heir?'

'I don't know. Malcolm never mentioned one.'

'Angelique, in future refer to him as your husband, and yourself his widow.'

'Why?'

'To establish, to help establish your claim to his estate.' He saw her nod to herself, awed at her control. Is it an Act of God that she can appear so tranquil?

'If there's no will, does that make a difference?'

'We're trying to find out. It would be best if there was one that named you. That would be best. Next, you must go back with . . . with his remains to Hong Kong. Be prepared for his mother to be hostile— in public try to be her friend. You should be at the funeral, dressed correctly of course.' Then he added, 'Possibly Henri could give you a letter to our Ambassador, you've already met him?'

'Yes. Monsieur de Geroire. Henri "could"? What sort of letter could he write for me?'

'If Henri could be persuaded, with his strong recommendation you could be put under de Geroire's protection as ward of the State. It's my conviction you're legally the widow of the late tai-pan, Malcolm Struan. If Henri supported us strongly, this could possibly become State policy.'

'Then I need serious protection?'

'I am sure of it. Henri isn't.'

She sighed. This was what she had concluded too. But State policy? This was a new idea, a possibility she had not thought of. State policy would mean the protection of France. Anything was worth that—no, not anything. 'What could I possibly do to persuade Henri?'

'I could do that for you,' he said. 'I'd try.'

'Then please start at once. This evening tell me what I can do in return. Would before dinner be suitable, or tomorrow morning—just as you wish.'

There had been no need to say more. Tomorrow would be better, André had told her, and had left, and before her next guest, Skye, had arrived she sat back in the chair and smiled at the ceiling, wondering about the price.

Ward of the French State? She had liked the sound of that, for she knew she would need all the help she could have to combat the ogre of Hong Kong . . .

And now, curled up in Malcolm's other chair in the tai-pan's suite upstairs, the door bolted on the inside, she liked the idea even more and, again, wondered about the price. It will be expensive. The secret gold coins will be enough to begin with, then the ruby ring and now I have a chop, Malcolm's chop.

She replaced everything and shut the secret compartment.

Content with the headway made on the first day of her new life, she closed her eyes and slept dreamlessly until a knock on the door brought her back. It was almost four-thirty. "Who is it, please?"

"Jamie, Angelique."

A current of expectation went through her. Be calm, she cautioned herself as she unbolted the door, the ice you traverse is exceedingly thin and the waters below lethal. "Hello, Jamie, dear, please come in." Again she sat in her husband's chair, motioning him to the chair she had always used. The change pleased her. "You look so harassed, so sad."

"I still can't get used to the idea and, well, all the changes, Angelique."

"No. It's very hard."

"You've changed too. May I . . . may I say how marvelous you are being, so strong and, well, you know."

"That's the problem, dear Jamie, I don't know. I only know what has happened and can accept it, have accepted it. My tears . . . I think I must have cried all the tears of my life away. So, for the moment no tears. You saw Sir William?"

"Yes. Skye said he would come back around six, if that's convenient." He saw her nod absently.

"You don't like him, Jamie, do you?"

"Don't like any lawyers, they always mean trouble, though he's not a bad man. I think he'll be all right for you. If you get worried, tell me at once. Mal . . . Malcolm liked him and you should have someone to represent you."

"I find it hard to say his name too, Jamie—'husband' is equally hard. Harder. Don't be embarrassed."

Jamie nodded bleakly and took out the letters. "Sir William said these were part of Malcolm's estate, like the money. He could not rule on the legalities—he would write posthaste to the Solicitor General in Hong Kong—but he saw no reason why you shouldn't have these if you promise not to destroy them. As to the sovereigns, you should keep them—I told him I didn't think you had any money of your own at the moment—but he asks, please, to give him a receipt for them."

"Whatever he wants. Did he read them?"

"No, no one did." Hesitantly he put them on the mantelpiece. "There are a couple of other things, we've made some arrangements— would you like me to tell you now or . . . I can easily come back later."

"No, I'm fine. What arrangements, Jamie?"

He took a deep breath, hating to have to say all this but it was his duty. "In consultation with Sir William, Babcott and Hoag, we've arranged to send the body back to Hong Kong tomorrow for burial, we all agreed, we jointly agreed that would be best. Everything possible will be done and is being done to make this easy for you and the trip as tolerable as possible. Dr. Hoag will go with you to make sure you're in good hands." Jamie's smile was empty and his face a mirror of unhappiness. "Can't tell you how sorry this all makes me. Ah Soh can pack for you in good time, Chen will help if necessary and will pack things to go with the ship, sailing on the evening tide, meanwhile if you need anything, say the word."

He saw her look down at her hands, her fingers twisting Malcolm's signet ring on her marriage finger. Poor Angelique, she doesn't even have a proper wedding ring.

"Well, that's all for the moment—would you like company at dinner tonight?"

"Thank you, but no, I'll eat here, or in the dining room or my rooms, but please sit down. Sorry, that's not all for the moment. My husband is not going to be taken back to Hong Kong for burial but will be buried here. Neither my husband nor I will ever go aboard *Prancing Cloud* again."

She saw his look but that did not divert her from what she had decided this morning: the confrontation must happen at the very first mention of *their arrangements.* "Would you like me to tell you the funeral arrangements now, or would you prefer them later?"

"But everything's done," he said, "arrangements are already made. It's best, we all felt it would be best and we . . . we know it would be the best for you and everyone. Mrs. Struan would certainly approve and would of course want him buried at home in Hong Ko—"

"Mrs. Struan? I'm Mrs. Struan. You refer to the other Mrs. Struan, Tess Struan, the other Mrs. Struan?" She spoke without emotion. "She doesn't have precedence in this matter. I'm his widow and take precedence over his mother."

"My God, Angelique, just because Skye says you are—"

"This has nothing to do with Mr. Skye, Jamie, he didn't suggest this, nor have I consulted him. Yet. But I do know my rights, and my husband's wishes, and they will be carried out."

"But . . . but . . ." Jamie was in such shock he could not get the words out, then they came with a rush, "but you can't override what Sir William and . . . and what Doc Hoag and Babcott and I think is best for you and him, what we're sure is best for you and everyone. You're overwrought, Angelique. It's best, Angelique, it really is."

"Overwrought? Me? How silly you are, Jamie." She allowed a small glacial smile. "I'm not overwrought at all. I'm merely going to put my husband's wishes into effect."

"But everything's arranged, *Prancing Cloud*'s ready to leave and the . . . everything's arranged."

"I'm glad the clipper's ready. By all means send her at once, his mother should hear the terrible news as soon as possible—you should do that yourself, Jamie, go with *Prancing Cloud*, you're the senior here, you should. I beg you don't wait until tomorrow, go tonight, you can break the terrible news to her, it will lessen her hurt. You must."

"Of course I'll do that if it's necessary," he said, hating the idea. "But Angelique, this is ridiculous, you can't be serious, you must see it's best! Good God, Angelique, you must see this is—"

"Best for you and others perhaps but not for my husband and therefore not for me. He has a right to be buried as h—"

"You must allow us to do what's best, his body will—"

"My husband's body will not, *will not* go back aboard that ship, nor will I," she said quietly. "Tell me, old friend, if I was to go with him as you suggest, where would I stay? In the state room?"

He stared at her, that problem not having occurred to him. "No, of course not," he said quickly. "Of course you have the pick of the cabins. I guarantee everything will—"

"I guarantee every little thing will be done as my husband wished."

Jamie wiped his forehead, his mind working like never before, slightly sickened and out of balance whereas it was obvious she was nothing if not in control. A sudden idea. "Perhaps you're right. *Prancing Cloud*'s wrong, perhaps. We'll charter another ship—wait, the mail ship's due to leave day after tomorrow, we'll get space aboard her for you, Hoag and . . . and him, and I'll persuade her captain to sail early. Tomorrow . . . That'll solve everything, right?"

"No." She sighed wearily. "Sorry, Jamie, no." Now there was the barest edge to her voice that cut through plainly. "Please understand me, no. No! He will be buried here as he would wish. The day after tomorrow."

"You can't. Mrs. Struan must . . . I mean Tess Struan must be given time. We'll send *Prancing Cloud* for her. She would want to be at the funeral, must be."

"You can do what you like but my husband will be buried the day after tomorrow in the way he would want—I don't think there would be time to do what you suggest. I'm not going to argue with you. Sorry, old friend, it's you who are overwrought and I can well understand it. Please ask Sir William and Mr. Skye to come by together now, as soon as possible, and I will settle the matter formally."

"For God's sake, the family crypt in Happy Valley is where his grandfather, father and brothers and sisters are buried."

"Jamie, I tire of repeating. Please ask Sir William and Mr. Skye to come here as soon as possible. Together."

He did not know what to do so he shrugged helplessly and went out.

For a few minutes she sat still and breathed deeply. That wasn't so bad, she thought, then stretched and got up and went into her own room. There she selected a clean dress, conservative, dark grey, put it on the bed. The wind rattled the windows but did not chill her. Her mirror beckoned her. She studied herself. Critically. No smile. What she saw pleased her. And the new person she had become also pleased her. It was like fitting into a new dress—no, a new skin. "I hope it lasts," she said to her reflection. "We must work to make it last. This me is better than the other one."

Then she took up the first of the letters, Tess Struan's letters. She wanted to leave his to last.

Sir William was stony-faced. So was Jamie. Doctors Hoag and Babcott were frowning. Heavenly Skye had a glint in his eyes. All were sitting on chairs in front of Malcolm's desk. She faced them from his tall chair, tiny but secure in it. Darker dress than before, three-quarter sleeves, square neckline, her back straight, coiffure perfect. Without makeup and somehow regal. "The day after tomorrow?" Sir William asked.

"Yes, please," she said. "My husband should not be laid out for long for people to pay their last respects, if they wish to. Isn't three days normal, Doctor?"

"Normally, yes, Angelique," Hoag said. "But we've already made arrangements for the preservation of the body during the voyage home. Everything will be fine, you've no need to worry." He added gently, "He should be buried there, he really should. We all agree."

"You've embalmed him? Already?"

The men shifted uneasily. Hoag said, "No, that's not usual. You, er, you use ice to ensure the preserv—"

"Would you relish being packed in ice and sent to Hong Kong like a carcass of mutton from Australia?"

The tension in the room spiraled, the men more embarrassed than before. Her voice remained quiet, firm and friendly, which tended to further infuriate them. Except for Skye for whom she was taking on a very new dimension.

Sir William said, "That's not the point, Madame. We feel for his sake and his family's sake that burial at home is wise."

"He admired his grandfather, the tai-pan, didn't he?"

"Indeed he did," Sir William said. Abruptly, he relaxed, no longer concerned, for now he had the answer to the conundrum, whatever she said. "Everyone knows that. Why?"

"Many times, in various words, Malcolm said he wanted to live like him, be remembered like him and be buried like him. And that's the way it will be."

"Very correct, and wise." Sir William added crisply, "His grand-father's buried in the family crypt in the cemetery in Happy Valley."

He added kindly, "Angelique, I agree it should be the same for him. Now I unders—"

"But Dirk Struan wasn't buried in Hong Kong," she said, startling them. "Oh, I know his name's carved into the stone, but he was buried at sea. My husband will be buried at sea, in the same way."

"Sorry, Angelique, but you're wrong," Jamie said. "I was there, I'd just joined Struan's, an apprentice China trader fresh from England, and went to the funeral. It was an immense affair, all Hong Kong went. There was even a huge, separate procession in Chinatown organized by Gordon Chen."

"Sorry, Jamie, but you are wrong. An empty coffin was interred in the crypt, he was buried at sea with his mistress, May-may, in international waters off Hong Kong." She felt tears near. No tears, she ordered herself, not yet. "He was buried at sea. It was a Christian service, done correctly as he wished, and the witnesses were Culum and Tess Struan, Gordon Chen and Aristotle Quance."

"That's not possible," Jamie said.

"Oh, yes it is, and that's what happened. Your Church hierarchy refused to allow them to be buried together, refused them a Christian burial in hallowed ground in Happy Valley."

"But, Angelique, I saw the funeral. He was buried there, I don't know where May-may was buried but I agree, she wasn't with him."

"You saw a sham, Jamie, the coffin was empty."

"This is nonsense," Sir William said.

"The hierarchy were adamant against a joint burial," she said as though he had not spoken. "It was unheard of. They had been scandalized by Dirk Struan for many reasons, as you know only too well, Sir William, but the idea was too much for them. In his will, part of his Testament that's handed down from tai-pan to tai-pan, he had written two weeks before he died that if he and May-may died together, they were to be buried together, that it was his intention to marry her and—"

"He actually wrote that? He was going to marry her?" Sir William said, the others equally shocked, for even today, marriage to a Chinese was unthinkable—ostracism would be permanent, even for Dirk Struan. "He actually wrote that?"

"Yes," she said, seeing that Hoag alone did not share Sir William's consternation.

The English, the British, are such awful people in many ways, she was thinking. Such hypocrites, bigots, uncivilized and different from us, only too aware of their antagonism to marriage of Protestant to

Catholic, let alone their detestation of intermarriage with peoples of their Empire.

Why consider intermarriage a heinous sin, she wanted to shout, while you have native mistresses and children by them openly, such hypocrisy! It's never been like that with us, in our French colonies or Empire. If a Frenchman marries a native woman she becomes not only his wife but French with all the protection of French law. We even encourage intermarriage, correctly. A man is a man, a woman a woman whatever the color of her skin, but not to you people. God protect me from becoming English, thank God I can never give up my French citizenship whoever I marry . . .

What am I saying, she thought with a jolt, bringing herself back to the room and these enemies of her husband. Time enough for such luxury later.

"I find some British attitudes difficult to understand, Sir William, about intermarriage, but then I am French. That aside, with the funeral of my husband's grandfather there was an impasse: your Church was outraged and would not agree to joint burial. The new tai-pan, his son, Culum, was insisting on it—anything other than a proper Christian burial for Dirk Struan was unthinkable, Culum more so than Tess who was very disturbed by Dirk's wishes and his flouting of conventions that were the bedrock of all her beliefs. Her father, Tyler Brock, now the most powerful trader on the island was vehemently opposed, so was Tess's mother, so were most traders publicly, whatever they felt in private. The Governor supported the Church."

"Quite right," Sir William muttered.

"Yes," she said. "If Hong Kong had been Catholic my Church would have been equally hostile. So the scandal threatened the Colony, and this when most of Hong Kong lay in ruins after the typhoon—with no ice," she added thinly.

They shifted in their seats, except Skye who slouched in his chair with the same slight smile.

Babcott said gently, "It's normal, correct medical practice for important people in these circumstances, Angelique. Your husband was and is important to us. You must believe that."

"I do." She took her eyes off him and addressed Sir William as before, continuing in the same matter-of-fact way: "To break the impasse, a compromise was arranged. The compromise was arranged by Aristotle Quance and Gordon Chen, it was oral, nothing in writing. Quietly—the word should be 'secretly' because that was what it was—the bodies were put aboard *China Cloud*. The Church of England ceremony was officiated at by a Naval Chaplain and Captain Orlov. It was a proper Christian burial. Dirk Struan and his mistress, May-may Sheng were buried together as he had desired."

"If it was so secret, how do you know this's true?"

"It was recorded in the ship's log, Sir William, which was at once put into the tai-pan's private vault and all witnesses, Culum and Tess Struan, Aristotle Quance, and Gordon Chen, and of course the minimum crew aboard, were sworn by holy oath to secrecy. The Naval Chaplain, who he was I don't know, was sent back to England at once. The other funeral took place with all the pomp due the tai-pan of the Noble House."

The silence stayed in the room, broken only by the breath of the wind against the windowpanes, the afternoon outside fair. Sir William said, "Have you seen the log?"

"No, nor spoken to . . . to his mother about it."

Jamie said, "Tess Struan could corroborate it, or Gordon Chen—if they would agree to break their oath—and if they wanted to."

Skye straightened in his chair. "This morning Mrs. Struan asked me if this story her late husband had told her was true. Happily I was able to corroborate certain details."

"And you know it's true because . . . ?"

"I happened to meet one of the crew who was less susceptible to secrecy than the others. A seaman, Hennery Fairchild—I've no idea if he's alive or dead now—but when I first came to Hong Kong, Sir William, I made it my business to learn all I could about the Noble House, the Brocks, Quance, about the founding of Hong Kong, and the . . . the various corruptions that took place in high places."

Sir William nodded sourly, finding his bad breath and bad teeth more overpowering than usual, knowing some of the dirty scandals that had been kept from public view and had preceded him. "That's hearsay evidence."

"It would not have much weight in court, Sir William. But it is true."

What to do? the Minister asked himself. Have to do the right thing, by God. The judgment of Paris? No, this is all a typhoon in a wineglass. "Very well, Madam, by all means let us respect his wishes. Jamie, send the body at once to Hong Kong for burial at sea," he said crisply, and thought, Once there, Tess Struan can have at Angelique Struan and I'm damned if I'm going to get between them. What the devil's come over Angelique, never seen such a change! "Quite understand you are loath to go by *Prancing Cloud*. We'll arrange the mail ship."

"Thank you," Angelique said calmly, "but no, Sir William. My late husband will not be sent like a carcass, in ice, to Hong Kong. He will not."

"By God, Madame, if I order it, it will happen."

"True, if you order it. But, Sir William . . ." She glanced at Skye. "What is the legal position?"

"Legally the wishes of the husband, supported by his widow, would take precedence."

"Before I answer that where is there any proof? There's none. As to preference over whom?" Sir William said testily, "Over Mrs. Struan, Tess Struan, is that what you are saying? We should disregard any consideration of her?"

Skye began to answer but Angelique motioned him to stop, and said, "Not at all. If *Prancing Cloud* went at once. A fast time to Hong Kong is ten days there and ten days back, in fair weather. A few days to turn around. Dr. Hoag, is there time for your . . . your ice," she said distastefully, "to preserve my husband's mortal remains properly over that time for his mother to be brought here—if she wished to come?"

Hoag was thinking about Dirk Struan and his legendary May-may, his beloved beauty, and about intermarriage and how he himself wished he had not killed his wife, love of his life. He often felt he had. His love for her should have been great enough not to have married her, not to have taken her out of her safe, serene Indian life into the disaster he knew would be their lot. And was.

Once again your future is in the balance, Hoag old man. Do you help this girl or Tess Struan? Don't forget it was your fault that bloody assassin lived to frighten her, near to death. "Medically it might be, but I would advise against it," he said with a sideways glance at Babcott, cautioning him not to interfere. "The decision, Sir William, is really whether he should be sent back or not. If not, I think he should be buried as . . . as his wife wants."

Sir William hesitated, irritated that his solution was not accepted. "Angelique, why are you opposed to going with the body to Hong Kong, if not by *Prancing Cloud,* by mail ship?"

"I am opposed because then he will not be buried in the way that he wishes, like his grandfather—his mother would never admit the other story, could not. I am his widow and I tell you his wishes are my wishes, with all my heart."

Sir William was unsure of his legal grounds for assenting or dissenting, and massively concerned about Tess Struan, her position now as de facto head of the Noble House, her written opposition to the marriage, and what she would do if the body was not sent back.

She'll scream bloody murder for one thing, he thought, almost wincing. Obviously she'd want the burial there, it should be there, at sea or not at sea, whatever the truth or untruth of the story, and fifty pounds against a bent farthing in any event she'll try to overturn the marriage, with a fair chance of doing it. So you, poor lady, like it or not, are on a very dicey wicket. "I'm afraid you are making an already tragic happening even more complicated than it need be. The poor fellow can be buried at sea just as easily from Hong Kong as here. So the best thing . . ."

"Excuse me for butting in, Sir William," Skye said, then added as a brilliant Queen's Counsel cross-examining would, "but unless you are formally challenging the legality of my client's marriage, she does have certain rights. May I therefore ask you to approve that her late husband's wishes and hers prevail in this matter and let him be buried here." Then, the same Queen's Counsel finishing his summation for the defense, he said so softly, kindly: "Malcolm Struan was ours, Yokohama's, as much as theirs. His tragedy began here, it should end here."

In spite of her resolve, Angelique felt the tears begin. But she gave no sound of crying.

47

FOR AN HOUR AFTER SIR WILLIAM and the others left Skye and Jamie argued. She listened. Nothing they said made any difference. She had lost. Following Skye's impassioned appeal, Sir William pronounced: "I regret I've heard nothing here this afternoon to change my mind. The body should go back to Hong Kong for burial, either with *Prancing Cloud* or the mail ship. As you choose, Madame. This meeting is over."

Skye said bitterly, "If we were in Hong Kong I could apply for a writ on a dozen grounds, but here Sir William is court, judge and jury. There isn't time enough to go there and back whatever we do."

"Then there's nothing more to be done." Jamie was grim, rocked by her story. "You have to accept it, Angelique. There's nothing more to be done, God rot it."

"I cannot go to Hong Kong—I must be at the burial."

"I agree," Skye said, nodding.

"Why? What's to stop you, Angelique?" Jamie asked.

"Tess Struan," she said.

"What can she do? She can't stop you going to the funeral and she can't break the marriage. Nettlesmith's afternoon editorial says it's perfectly legal even though you're both minors. Go with the mail ship, I'll get her to sail at the same time."

"No. Sorry, Jamie, Mr. Skye already said the editorial is only an opinion. I know Tess Struan won't bury him at sea as he wanted, I'm sure she won't. And she will attack me in any way she can. Here, read her letters to Malcolm."

Both men were jolted by the intensity of venom. Skye said queasily, "Pity, there's nothing actionable in them. She'd claim they were private letters from a mother to a son, desperately warning him against marriage as is her right, even to forbid it—as is her right. And the threats against you—you as a person, Mrs. Struan, there's nothing we could attack her with."

"That's not fair," she said.

"Heavenly, what about 'if that woman ever steps foot in Hong Kong I'll make sure . . .' eh?" Not wanting to hurt Angelique further, Jamie did not read all of what Tess Struan had written: *I'll make sure every decent person in Hong Kong knows her history, her father's, uncle's and that her aunt was an itinerant actress in a travelling group of players, gypsies and mountebanks, and about her own personal finances.*

"I'm not ashamed that my mother was an actress," she had said sharply, "even though most English consider them harlots. She wasn't, ever. And they weren't mountebanks. I'm not responsible for the sins of my father—I wasn't penniless, he stole my money, not only other people's."

"I know." Jamie wished he had not mentioned the letter. "Heavenly, can you get proof of Dirk's burial with May-may?"

"Oh, yes, from Compradore Chen and Tess herself. But neither would volunteer, or admit it, would they? We would be jeered at and never get a court order to open the family crypt." Skye coughed and coughed again. "Mrs. Angelique Struan must go with her husband's remains, if she doesn't she'll immeasurably hurt her position, both legally and publicly. But to go to Hong Kong? Dangerous." He had asked Babcott and Hoag to smooth the wording of the death certificates but was told, as expected, it could not be done. "In my considered opinion, Mrs. Angelique is right not to take that risk at the moment, Jamie. I'm concerned she'd be more defenseless in Hong Kong than here."

"You'd go too, you can provide any shield necessary."

"Yes, but there's bound to be a scandal and I want to prevent that at all costs, for everyone's sake. Including Tess Struan's. She's not a bad woman if you look at her position from a mother's point of view. My considered opinion is that there's bound to be a stink—how to avoid it or minimize it, that's the question."

"Perhaps it can be contained," Jamie said. "Tess isn't an ogre, she's always been fair in her way."

"She won't be fair, not with me," Angelique said. "I understand her. Only a woman can really understand. She'll believe I've stolen her eldest son and killed him. Malcolm warned me against her."

"To contain her we need time," Skye said. "We need time to negotiate, and there's not enough before a burial."

When the two men left her, nothing had been resolved.

Never mind, she thought. I will bury my husband as he wished; I will inherit his worldly goods, if any; I will beat Tess Struan. And I will be revenged.

The letters had hurt, but not as much as she expected. Her tears were not tears as before. They had not racked her as before. Nor am I as before. I don't understand. I'm really very strange. Will it last? I surely hope so. Oh, Blessed Mother, how stupid I was.

Through the window she saw that day would soon be night, and in the bay, ships' riding lights, port, starboard and at their mastheads, blinked with the rise and fall of the swell. In the fire bucket coals settled noisily, flames flared briefly drawing her attention back. What to do?

"Missee?" Ah Soh stalked in.

"*Tai-tai,* Ah Soh! You deaf, heya?" she said curtly. Malcolm had explained tai-tai to her, and on his last night Malcolm had made Ah Tok, Ah Soh and Chen address her as such in front of him—and Skye had also reminded her to make the servants use it.

"Missee wan' my pack chop chop?"

"*Tai-tai. You deaf, heya?*"

"You wan' my pack, chop chop . . . tai-tai?"

"No. Tomorrow. If at all," she added quietly.

"Missee?"

She sighed. "Tai-tai!"

"Missee-tai-tai?"

"Go away!"

"Med'sin man wan' see-ah."

She was going to say "Go away" again, then changed her mind. "Medicine man what?"

"Med'sin frog, missee tai-tai."

Hoag. Yes, he is froglike, she thought, and was surprised to find that she was smiling. "Yes. See now," and when he came in she said, " 'Evening, Doctor. How are you? I'm fine, thanks to you."

"Are you?" His eyes were red from fatigue, face pasty and puglike as ever but still a warmth about him that was comely. He peered at her. "Yes, I can see that. Be cautious, don't press yourself. Take it easy, Angelique, be wise."

"I will, I promise."

"You were marvelous this afternoon."

"But I lost."

"Yes. George Babcott and I were sorry about that, outraged after your story and Heavenly's appeal. George's seeing Wee Willie for dinner and will try again but I—we . . . we don't hold out much hope." He saw her shrug, just a small gesture, and continue watching him, eyes enormous in the paleness of her face. "Do you need anything? To sleep or to calm—no, I can see you don't need any calming. I'm glad, so glad. I wanted to talk to you, chat, do you mind?"

"Of course not, please sit down. How did the inquest go? Oh, there's whisky or other drinks there if you want."

"Thanks." On the sideboard Waterford glasses and cut-glass decanters were lined up like soldiers in silver holders, with silver labels around their necks, the silver Georgian: Whisky, Cognac, Sherry, Port. He chose whisky and poured himself half a glass. "The inquest went as expected, Edward Gornt was exonerated of any blame and commended for bravery. The coroner, Skye, found that Greyforth's death was accidental and Gornt perfectly correct in trying to stop what could have been a brutal murder. We were surprised he used such strong words even though it was the truth." He sat facing her, raised his glass. "Health!"

"*Salut!* I'm glad for Edward. He deserves much praise."

"And so do you. Your story touched me deeply," Hoag said.

"It's true. Don't you believe me either?"

"I believe it. That's what I wanted to talk about. You see, I understand it only too well." Then, eloquently, Hoag told her his own story, of his days in the Indian Army and falling in love and marrying against all conventions, the ostracism immediate, awful, then going home. Nothing better there. "It was worse in fact. Arjumand died, that was her name, the same as the beloved of Shah Jahan, who built the Taj Mahal," he said, his eyes locked into the fire, telling the story to the fire as well, seeing pictures of her there, her and him in the grand days before marriage. "I'm so sad and yet glad that she didn't linger in the hatred, that she caught cold and died quickly like a gorgeous hothouse plant in an icy draft—that's what she was, you can't believe how exquisite, any more than I can believe she loved me—I know how ugly I look. I loved her to madness, and killed her."

"When you speak of her your face changes. You didn't kill her. It was fate. You weren't responsible." There's that word again, she thought.

"I was, marrying her and taking her home. May-may would have died too, forlorn, lonely and desperate for home. Even the great Dirk

Struan himself couldn't buck public opinion, not if they'd married. They were both lucky to have died like that." '

She watched him, his eyes misty. "Was Malcolm lucky to have died, like he died? I mean, you said he was so peaceful. Was he dying anyway?"

Hoag said, "I'm afraid so. He could have gone any day, any hour. He was on borrowed time and I think he knew it."

This rattled her. "Why wasn't he told, why didn't you warn him, warn us?"

"It was an Act of God—we didn't know, not for certain as we do now, impossible to know or we would have."

"I—I don't understand. Tell me the truth, please, I need to understand."

Gently Hoag said, "His insides, under and near the wound were worse than we'd thought. George couldn't probe around the wound much when he was brought in, that would have killed him anyway. The autopsy showed he was rotting away."

"The operation, it was well done?"

"Oh, yes, first class. George's repair job was admirable, as good as anyone could do," he said, and she believed him. "You see, Angelique, we can't replace, we can only repair, there was sepsis in pockets—the reason for all the pain, poor fellow—and bad lesions that prevented him from straightening up." He added sadly, "He was on the last of borrowed time. Even so I'm certain you made his last days the happiest any man could have."

A coal fell into the hearth. Her eyes went to it. The flame flared and flickered and died—just like my Malcolm, poor man, poor love. "Sad," she said to the fire, "so sad."

Hoag was weighing her, weighing himself and the memory of Arjumand—whom Angelique had reborn for him. Easy to decide now, after sharing Arjumand, he thought. Nervously he finished the drink. "May I?"

"Of course. Please."

Hoag replenished his glass, not so amply. "About the burial, that's what I really wanted to see you about. You could, possibly, still do what you and Malcolm wanted."

"What?"

He sat opposite her again. "Bury him at sea like his grandfather, like he wanted, like you want. I can help you."

"How?"

He mopped his brow. "You go to Sir William, say you'll bow to the inevitable and as much as you deplore his decision, you will allow the body to be sent to Hong Kong. Tomorrow, we—Babcott and I—we officially put his coffin aboard *Prancing Cloud* from Kanagawa where it is at the moment. You see the coffin off, officially, saying you could not bear to go with it on *Prancing Cloud* but you'll go by mail ship the day after tomorrow when she sails for Hong Kong. Everyone's satisfied."

"But the coffin is empty?" she said excitedly.

He shook his head, his brow and jowls glistening in the firelight. "No. There'll be a body in it but not his, a fisherman, a Korean, who died in Kanagawa this morning, at the clinic. Meanwhile Malcolm's remains are in the other coffin, still secretly at Kanagawa. If Jamie was with us, he could bring the cutter there tomorrow evening, we go out to sea and if we could get Tweet to officiate, Malcolm can be buried as you wish. The next day you catch the mail ship and no one's the wiser—if we can swear everyone to secrecy."

"So many 'ifs,' " she muttered, her heart thumping.

"Many more than I've thought of," he said, drying his forehead, throat tight. "It was just . . . The idea jumped into me a little while ago. I haven't thought it through, I may be quite off the mark, but I wanted to help. With or without George I can do the first part. Substituting the bodies. You have to do the other things. Perhaps I can help, I don't know," adding lamely, "I'm not good at keeping secrets. Sorry, we have to decide now if . . . I'll have to get back to Kanagawa tonight while George is dining here. What do you think?"

She was out of her chair in a flash and put her arms around him, embracing him in a perfumed envelope of softness and gratitude. "Let's try . . . and thank you, thank you."

"You wanted to see me, Ma'am?" Gornt said.

"Yes, please come and sit down." Angelique sat by the bay window of the tai-pan's office where lounging chairs, an oak table and sideboard were. Chen stood nearby.

"May I say again how sorry I am about all this. If there's anything I can do, you only have to ask, Ma'am."

"I know, thank you. Yes, you can help, we all need friends. I'm glad the inquest went properly—you should get a medal. It was very brave of you, I'd like to thank you for Jamie, I don't know what I would do without him." A good fire burned in the hearth and fine Thai silk curtains shut out the night. Chen went over to the ice bucket with the opened bottle. "My husband said you liked champagne?"

"Sure, yes, Ma'am, yes, I·do," Gornt said, thinking of the inquest and the heavenly verdict that put the dangerous Norbert chapter to bed. The coroner, Heavenly Skye, was well named.

She motioned to Chen who poured two tall glasses.

"Doh jeh"—thanks, Gornt said, accepting his glass.

Chen gaped at him as though he had not understood, despising this impertinent foreign devil even more for daring to speak a civilized dialect.

Angelique said, "Chen, you wait outside. If want, I use bell, heya?" She indicated the silver bell on the side table.

"Yes, Missee."

She glared at him. *"Tai-tai!"*

"Yes, Missee-tai-tai." Chen left, pleased with small victories. The servants had requested a conference that he had chaired. Ah Tok, her mind wandering, had wanted them to employ a soothsayer to put the Evil Eye on this 'Possessor of a Death-filled Duct,' but he had said, 'No, we can't—and it isn't. The Master's death was not her doing. The Master married her and made us call her tai-tai in front of him and her. Our compromise is to call her "Missee" first, then "Missee-tai-tai" until the matter is decided by Illustrious Chen, to whom my urgent, detailed report is already aboard *Prancing Cloud*.'

"Salut, Edward."

"Your health, Ma'am!"

She took the tiniest sip, he drank with enjoyment.

"Champagne's a source of life for me," he said, immediately wishing he had not said it that way. "I've never been able to afford it, except on festive occasions."

"I like champagne too, though not tonight. But soon you'll be able to afford all you want, no? My husband told me your affairs were going to improve, tremendously, and that you had many secrets to share with him—for mutual profit."

"He did?" Gornt was caught off guard, for he and Malcolm Struan had agreed to tell no one else. Norbert? Norbert didn't count, that was just more of the plan to confuse the enemy and Norbert had always been enemy. "Secrets, Ma'am?"

"He told me he liked you, trusted you, as I do, that you were a man who could keep secrets as well as know them, and who understood the value of old friends—in the Chinese sense."

"That part's true. I liked and trusted him too."

"Jamie said you've booked passage on *Prancing Cloud*."

"Yes, that's right, Ma'am."

"My husband said you were going to give him special information about how to ruin the Brocks. You were going to tell him yesterday morning after . . . was it only yesterday? It seems a lifetime ago—for Malcolm it was, poor Malcolm."

He sighed, sad for her. "Yes. May I say you've changed, Ma'am? You're different. Without wanting to be impertinent, or callous, may I say the change suits you very much."

"I would prefer ten thousand times to have my husband alive, and not to have changed." Her openness surprised her, though like Malcolm, she had always found Gornt easy to talk to. "I'm not yet sure about the change, if I like it. Growing up so fast is, I don't know the right word, is aching, scare-making." She got up and refilled his glass, then put the iced champagne bucket on the table, closer to him.

"Thanks," he said, aware of her more than ever before.

"I've decided not to go to Hong Kong by the clipper."

"Ah, yes, Ma'am. I'd heard the rumor, something about you not wanting to go aboard her again—or your husband's remains—that you'll go by mail ship." As soon as he had heard, for safety he had seen the agent to reserve passage also but all cabins were taken. Cursing, he had tried to find Jamie but Jamie was not in the building. "I can understand you not wanting to go on the *Cloud*."

Her hands were tranquil in her lap, her voice quiet and as controlled. "These secrets you were going to tell my husband, will you tell them to me?"

He smiled his nice smile, fascinated by her, and shook his head. "Sorry, Ma'am, no—even if I had any."

She nodded, not offended. "I didn't expect you to, I'm sure I wouldn't understand them if you did, and then, I could never put them into effect anyway, could I?" He smiled. "But Tess Struan can, no?"

"Ma'am?"

"My husband told me you said if anything happened to him, you would go at once to Hong Kong to deal directly with his mother, to make the same arrangement with her you had made with him. He said you were doing this because you hated the Brocks—he didn't tell me why you hated them." She reached up and toyed with the stem of her glass. "Tess Struan could certainly use the information, if what you claim is true, no? This was Tuesday, before we were married."

Again, he just watched her, a pleasant expression on his handsome face.

"I can understand why my husband liked you, Edward, why you'd be a dangerous enemy, and even more dangerous a friend."

This made him laugh outright and the tension between them broke. "Not to you, Ma'am, never, I swear it. Never."

"We'll see. We have many bridges to cross, you and I, for, by God, as my husband would say, I am embracing his hopes and dreams as my own: that you can help Struan's destroy the Brocks, once and for all. Perhaps your hopes and dreams too."

"Mine?"

She opened her bag and took out the paper she had found in the safe's inner compartment, held it closer to the light to see better and read aloud: " 'This is my solemn agreement with Mr. Edward Gornt, gentleman, of Rothwell's in Shanghai: if information provided by him assists Struan's to break Brock and Sons, causing them to go under within the next six months, on behalf of Struan's I guarantee that he will receive from their wreckage, the Brock fifty percent interest in Rothwell's free and clear, that we will assist him in good faith, as best we can, with the Victoria Bank to raise the necessary loan to purchase the other fifty percent belonging to Jefferson Cooper, that from this date, for twenty years, Struan's grants him, or any company he personally controls, favored nation status on any mutually agreed business dealings.' "

She held it for him to see but did not hand it over. "It's dated the day before yesterday, Edward, signed but not witnessed."

He made no move to take it. His eyesight was good. While she was reading it he had recognized the signature. Without the witness it doesn't have its real value, he thought, his mind moving rapidly from plan to plan, from question to question, to answers. "So?"

"I could witness my husband's signature."

His mind stopped churning with a jolt. "A wife witnessing her husband's signature isn't usually valid."

"Say I witnessed it the same day—before we were married."

Where the devil's she getting all this from? he was thinking frantically. Jamie? Heavenly? She's like one of Stevenson's new steam rollers. "Even if . . . even if the paper was witnessed, it wouldn't bind the Noble House."

"Yes, but it would carry weight with Tess Struan—it would be an agreement with her son. Doesn't it confirm you were working with my husband, clandestinely, to deliver her the greatest ambition of her life?"

"Perhaps, perhaps it would, Ma'am." He hesitated. "Jamie approves of the document?"

"He doesn't know about it. No one does except me," she told him, believing it. Why else would Malcolm hide it?

Thoughtfully, he poured some wine—he noticed she had not touched hers further. "I imagine," he said delicately, "such a favor would require one in return, Ma'am."

"I would like you to hurry by *Prancing Cloud* with all speed, as you planned, and see Tess Struan. And deliver a letter from me."

His eyes widened with disbelief. "That's all?"

"Not exactly. When you arrive in Hong Kong—the clipper will be there long before the mail ship—you must get to her before she hears the tragic news of my husband's death from anyone else. It is essential that you get to her first, telling her you bring her terrible news but also secret information, *vital information that guarantees the ruin of Brock's forever, that will put them out of business forever quickly.*" She took a deep breath. "It will, won't it?"

"Yes," he said softly, no longer a need to deny it.

"Next, tell her the Brocks had planned to murder Malcolm, using Norbert Greyforth. Third, that . . ."

"They what?"

"Isn't that true? Wasn't that part of Tyler Brock's plot? Or Morgan's? Certainly Jamie is of that opinion—he would swear to it. Mr. Skye told me about the duel, the rest I forced from Jamie—why there was a duel. Wasn't Norbert just a pawn for murder?"

"Maybe," Gornt said, overwhelmed by her. "Probably. Next?"

"Next." Her voice became quieter but oddly, clearer: "Please tell her it's because of me you're bringing her the evidence to destroy Brock's—you must keep stressing that."

"Because of you?"

"Because of me. Yes. Emphasize that. It's important to me, not much to ask, and you will get what you want anyway."

"You're sure?"

"Yes. You tell her you were going to forget this written contract you had with her son, believing it to be valueless now. But because I asked you, pleaded with you to see her in his stead, you decided to rush to Hong Kong to see her." She leaned closer. "The information, must it be acted on quickly?"

"Yes," he said.

"Then emphasize that. But most of all, keep stressing it was I who persuaded you to go to her, my pleading persuaded you to see her to give her the evidence to destroy Malcolm's enemies and hers . . . that I assured you she would honor the contract, or give you an equivalent. And she will. Tess Struan will, I guarantee."

"With your signature?"

"That's the first thing she will notice, so mention it in advance. Say Malcolm asked me to witness his signature, saying only it was a business contract between you two, which I did in front of you, without thought—on Monday, before the party. I didn't read it, nor ask about it. Last, say you have an urgent letter from me, and give it to her." Angelique picked up her glass. "If she reads it in front of you, she probably won't, but if she does, I'd like to know what she says or does."

Now she took a second sip, leaned back, waiting, her eyes locked on his.

Her face still told him nothing. "What's in the letter?"

"You may read it, if you wish, before I seal it." She added lightly, without spite, "It will save you the bother of opening it."

His mind was pondering the conundrum of her. "And the news of his death, your marriage and his death, how do I tell her that and all the rest?"

"I don't know, Edward. You will know how to do that."

He grunted, astounded by the gall—no, not gall, more by the cunning. Obviously, her goal was to slide into Tess's favor out of the existing enmity, and to forestall any action, civil or criminal, that a mother such as Tess Struan, torn apart by the agony of her loss, might, will, unleash against her—the current betting five to one Tess Struan would, two to one she would win.

Never mind that, this strategy could squeeze Angelique into the winner's circle—*could*. With care, not quite as she had suggested it, much more subtly than that, he could do what she proposed without harming his own position and make his deal with Tess, who would certainly give him everything he wanted—once the shock of her son's death had lessened and she could appreciate the enormity of what he had to offer.

Better for me to ease Angelique off the Tess Struan barb, much better. What should I ask in return? Her signature, of course, but what else? What else do I want from her? There are all kinds of gambits I co—

Angelique was reaching for the pen. Her face was grave as she signed her name as witness, dating it the day before yesterday. Silently she powdered it dry, blew the excess away, and placed it in front of him, her eyes still downcast.

"Whatever you decide, this is yours now, freely," she said, gambling on his well-advertised sense of honor. "As for the rest, if you help me, Edward," now she looked up at him, something inside of him stirred deliciously, "you would also have my gratitude, my undying gratitude, forever."

Inside the shoya's dwelling, Jamie sat cross-legged on the tatami, shoeless, Hiraga opposite him. At the head of the table was the shoya, and saké and tea.

For an hour or more Jamie had answered and asked questions, Hiraga translating, hesitating over the strange words, wanting further explanations to understand clearly. Jamie was tired, not because of the time spent here, a fascinating and a welcome relief from all his other troubles, but because there seemed to be no solution to them. He had been upset by Sir William's refusal to be swayed over the burial, though understanding perfectly—he would have done the same in his position. Poor Angelique, poor Malcolm, poor Noble House. Even poor bloody Tess.

Something has to give. It won't be Wee Willie. It has to be Angelique—there's nothing she or anyone can do. This time I think it will break her.

As simply as he could he had laid out his idea for a joint venture, the shoya and his contacts supplying the goods on consignment they agreed on, Jamie supplying the European know-how, a six-month leeway for payment, which would give time for the goods to be sold and the money either to come back or to be reinvested in mass-produced goods that they, in return, would advise the joint venture to import. This led into a discussion of quantities, then into mass production methods that could make them all rich.

"Shoya ask: What cost your *massu produk'shun* machine?"

"It depends what the machines are to make," Jamie said.

"Jami-sama, he ask you, p'rease, you say what goods to make to se're in Ing'rund. Not now, in three day, p'rease. If shoya agree, perhaps make *stoku kompeni* and bring *massu produk'shun* machine to Nippon."

Jamie smiled. "Mass production is initially expensive to set up, machines and factory. It's not like the joint venture I suggested. There's no way I could raise that much money."

"Jami-sama, you not worry, not worry about money. Gyokoyama can buy-se're Yedo if want." Hiraga smiled grimly as Jamie blinked. "Shoya thank you and I thank you. P'rease, in three days, you say what to make and price. I see you home."

"No need for that, thanks."

Hiraga bowed, the shoya bowed, Jamie bowed back equally and went into the evening air.

"Tea, Sire?" the shoya asked.

Hiraga nodded a yes, preparing to leave, needing a bath and massage, but pleased with himself, everything done now except to collect Jami Mukfey's supposed fee of the three koku.

The shoya ordered fresh tea. When the maid had gone, he said, "I have some news. By carrier pigeon, Otami-sama, about Lord Yoshi, and about the shishi you might like to hear."

"Stop playing games! Of course I wish to hear." Now that he was alone with the shoya, Hiraga became imperious and samurai without noticing it. "What news?"

"There's been another attempt on Lord Yoshi."

"He's dead?" Hiraga said hopefully.

"No, Otami-sama, here, please read for yourself." With pretended meekness the shoya offered the sliver of paper, the same he had previously shown to Raiko and Meikin: *An assassination attempt on Lord Yoshi at dawn at Hamamatsu village failed. Lone shishi assassin slain by him. Lady Koiko also dead in skirmish. Inform House of Wisteria our great sadness. More information soon as possible.*

Hiraga read it, and gasped. "When did this happen?"

"Five days ago, Otami-sama."

"Nothing further?"

"Not yet."

Reading the message, his headache seemed to become even worse, his thoughts jumbled. Koiko dead, another shishi dead! Who? If she's dead, what about Sumomo? "You've informed the House of Wisteria?"

"Yes, Otami-sama."

"What did Meikin say?"

"She was distraught, Otami-sama, naturally."

"What else do you know, shoya?"

"What I know that affects you and shishi, I tell you."

"What about Katsumata and Takeda?"

"The word, Sire, they were still travelling towards us, as, supposedly, Lord Yoshi is."

"When does he arrive back? Has he changed his plans now?" he asked, his mind tumbling. If Koiko was killed in the skirmish, was it by accident, or had Yoshi discovered Koiko had tentacles to us, as Meikin has? "Eh?"

"I don't know. Perhaps about eight days, Otami-sama." The shoya studied Hiraga's concern and thought that, yes, this youth should be concerned, for obviously he is in great danger, but eeee, how valuable he is! I agree he is a National Treasure, or should be. *Joint-u ven'shur!*—a godlike idea! My son will go to work with this Jami gai-jin starting tomorrow, to learn barbarian ways and then I will not need Hiraga, who represents nothing but trouble to me directly, and so sorry, is doomed. Like we all are, if we are not very clever. "Otami-sama, there are many troop movements around us."

"Eh? What kind of movements?"

"The Bakufu have reinforced the three nearest Tokaidō way stations to us. Also, there are five hundred samurai straddling the road north and south of us." A bead of sweat slid down his cheek. "We are in a box of *Tairō* Anjo."

Hiraga cursed and, too, felt the pressure increase. "What do you hear, Shoya? Is he planning to attack us here?"

"I wish I knew, Otami-sama. Perhaps telling the Taira about the troops might help to find out what is the gai-jin plan."

"They'll bombard Yedo, any fool knows that." Hiraga felt sickened at the thought of the inevitable gai-jin victory though it would serve *sonno-joi* like nothing else. "There's nothing the *tairō* can do to prevent . . ." His heart skipped a beat and he stopped.

"Except, Otami-sama?"

"Except history's answer, the usual answer: a sudden, brutal, surprise attack to destroy the fleet's base." Hiraga was astonished he had shared his thought, and been so open with such a lowly person, even though the shoya was intelligent, a valuable ally, and soon to be a business partner.

Eeee, he told himself through the throbbing of his headache, there's so much I do not understand, the world is turning upside down, everything different, I am different, no longer samurai yet totally samurai. It is these filthy gai-jin with their tempting, sickening, awesome, greed-making ideas. They must be thrown out—*sonno-joi sonno-joi sonno-joi*—but not yet. First *massu produk'shun,* the first to make rifles.

"Shoya, send out all spies in case that is Anjo's plan."

"Spies, Otami-sama?"

Hiraga said, "The time is now to stop playing games, Shoya. You understand? No-more-games!"

"I obey in everything, Otami-sama. As usual, as I ha—"

"You did very well tonight, Shoya. The moment you hear anything about Yoshi or shishi, send me word, please." Hiraga added the 'please' as a major concession.

"As quick as a hunting sea bird, Sire."

"Good night then—ah, so sorry, I forgot, there is the gai-jin's fee. He asked me to remind you."

The shoya's stomach turned over. From his sleeve he extracted a small bag—it would have been very bad manners to give it to Jami-sama direct. "Here is the equal in gold oban for one and a half koku, Otami-sama, the rest in ten days."

Hiraga shrugged and casually put it in his own sleeve, but the weight of it and the joy of it astonished him. "I will tell him, and see he is here in three days."

"Thank you, Otami-sama. These troop movements, terribly worri-some. War is coming. My Masters say if they could have advance warning of gai-jin plans . . . they would appreciate deeply any help. Perhaps your Taira-sama . . ." Hopefully, he left the name hanging.

Another message from Head Office in Osaka had arrived today, more urgent than the last. As if I cannot read? the shoya thought angrily, as if I'm uncaring and disloyal. I do everything I can. It is those two cursed mama-sans. Two days and still nothing from them!

Before he had left Raiko and Meikin he had impressed on them his urgent need to know everything they knew, or could find out, quickly. His anger began to increase, not only because the two women had pretended to know nothing however much he cajoled them, even though he was sure that they already had an inkling, but also because his precious gold oban were in this rapacious samurai's sleeve, fees, however well earned for an equally rapacious gai-jin. And where will all my lovely oban end up? Of course in some whore's Golden Gully.

"Thank you so much, Otami-sama," the shoya said unctuously, as Hiraga left, keeping his head on his tatami to hide the gnashing of his few remaining broken teeth, wanting to humble Hiraga, make him sweat, telling him, not sorry at all: oh, so sorry, your late whore Koiko was implicated in the plot, so was your trained female assassin and wife-to-be Sumomo who had her head chopped off too, and your shishi supporter Meikin, mama-san to the most important men in Yedo—even Gyokoyama leaders—is not long for this earth because we sur-mise Yoshi knows all this too.

And though you're the cleverest samurai I've known, you're doomed doomed doomed, and yet my illustrious superiors expect me to treat you as a National Treasure and keep you alive as well. *Oh ko!*

Tonight I shall get drunk, but not before congratulating myself on

the imminent formation of the *Ryoshi Joint-u Ven'shur Stoku Kompeni!*
Eeee, an idea worthy of gods!

Walking home, Jamie McFay loosened his topcoat though the evening air was cold. He was warm. The knowledge gained was substantial and his concentration had driven away his cares. All very
interesting, he thought, but neither of those two have any idea of the
initial costs of mass production. And yet the way Nakama said
Gyokoyama could buy and sell Yedo if they wanted, for the moment I
really believed it. The shoya will go for a joint venture, I'm sure of it.

His step was brisk and he greeted others walking the High Steet and
went up the Struan steps, into his domain. It's mine again, he thought,
with pride. Perhaps Tess will change her mind now—she's no fool and
I've done a good job.

Vargas was waiting.

" 'Evening, Vargas, time to lock up?"

"Yes, but first, senhor, sorry, these came in yesterday's mail but,
somehow, were in my In tray."

Both letters were marked Personal and Confidential and addressed
to him. The first was in Tess Struan's writing. His stomach heaved. The
other was from Maureen Ross, his erstwhile fiancée. His unease doubled. "Thanks," he said. In spite of his resolve to wait, he could not
and tore Tess's letter open. *This is to inform you formally that Mr.
Albert MacStruan is transferred from Shanghai, arriving by steamer,
Wayfong, on the 17th. Please acquaint him with all Japanese operations. Subject to your noncompliance with previous letters he assumes
control at the end of December.*

His dismissal from the Noble House, now that it was in effect, did
not anger him as he expected. In fact he was relieved. Weird, just a few
moments ago I thought it was my . . .

He looked up at Vargas who was watching narrowly. "What else,
Vargas?" He folded the letter and put it on his desk with the other one.

"Mrs. Angelique is in the tai-pan's office. She asked if you could see
her for a moment?"

"What's up now?"

"Nothing that I know of, senhor, the evening has been peaceful. A
message arrived from your Nemi, asking if you would be visiting
later. One other small matter, Captain Strongbow again asked for
sailing orders. Again I told him to be patient. It will be on the evening
tide?"

"Yes. I think so. Send word to Nemi: Perhaps."

"At once, senhor. Then it's decided? The tai-pan's remains will go with *Cloud*? And of course the Senhora?"

"Either by clipper, or the mail ship, one or the other," he said, walked along the corridor, knocked and went in.

She was curled in Malcolm's chair, which Jamie was coming to think of as her own, reading the *Guardian* by oil light. "Hello, Jamie."

" 'Evening. I've decided to go with you and the mail ship." He tried unsuccessfully not to sound blunt. "It's my job to explain to Tess Struan." Having said it, he felt better. "It's my job and I think Mal— I think he would like me to do that, and it might spare you a little."

"Yes," she said with her sweet smile, "I'm sure he would. Close the door, Jamie, and sit down a moment." When he had obeyed, she dropped her voice and told him Hoag's plan. "Can you bring the cutter to Kanagawa with the rest of us tomorrow evening?"

He was staring at her stupidly, completely off guard. "You're crazy. That plan's crazy."

"No, not at all. Dr. Hoag thinks . . ."

"He's over the moon too—you'd never get away with it."

"Why?" she asked calmly.

"Fifty reasons," he said. "So many reasons I'm not even going to mention any. Whole idea's ludicrous, insane, Willie will have you in irons."

"There's no law against what we would be doing, Mr. Skye says. The burial would be quite legal, he says."

"Mr. Bloody Know-it-all says that, eh? And what else's Heavenly going to do," he asked, "put his collar on backwards and read the bloody service?"

"Mr. Skye believes we can persuade the Reverend Tweet to do that," she said as though he were a child in a tantrum.

He threw up his hands. "You're both crazy and Hoag is stupid, off his head to have suggested it. We'll leave on the mail ship, you, me, and him." He stalked for the door.

"Jamie, can you handle the cutter by yourself or will we need a crew?" He turned back and stared at her. She smiled, determined, but nicely so. "Would we need a crew?"

"Two men at least. Bosun and engineer, at least."

"Thank you. If you don't wish to help, may I ask the Bosun, yes?"

"I can't seem to get through to you. This idea is foolhardy, extremely foolhardy."

She nodded ruefully. "You're probably right and we won't be able to do it, but I'm going to try, and then try again. I can't seem to get through to you either, dearest Jamie. I promised to love, honor and obey my husband and your friend—he was your friend—and I don't feel parted from him, not yet, nor do you. Tess Struan won't give him his wish, will she?"

All the time he had been looking down at her, not seeing her and at the same time seeing every detail of her, remembering all the years of Tess Struan and what she and Culum Struan had meant to him, and Malcolm Struan had meant and Dirk Struan had meant and the Noble House had meant. All gone and all wasted and all at an end, our Noble House no longer noble, no longer first in Asia. Well, not quite wasted and not quite over but its glory's gone and my friend's dead and that's a fact. I was his friend, but was he mine? God above, what we do in the name of friendship.

He said, "Tess wouldn't bury him as he wanted. I suppose that's the least a friend could do. I'll arrange the cutter."

He walked out. In the gathering quiet of the room she sighed, picked up the paper and, once more, began to read.

That night, when Dr. Hoag arrived at the Kanagawa Legation, part of the Buddhist temple, Towery, the Sergeant-in-charge, smart in his Guards uniform, tall hat, scarlet tunic, white trousers and black boots, met him. "Didn't expect you till morning, Doc."

"I just have to make sure everything's ready. We want an early start."

Escorting him to the part of the temple used as a morgue, Towery laughed. "If you left him ready, Doc, he's ready, 'cause he ain't about to've gone walkies." He opened the door. The room was large, with a dirt floor and access to the grounds through shutter doors. Towery sniffed the air. "They don't 'niff yet. Never did like corpses. You want a hand?"

"No, thank you." Two empty coffins were on trestles, lids beside them, others standing upright against the wall. The bodies were on marble slabs covered with sheets. At the far end were big barrels containing ice. Water seeped from them, discoloring the beaten earth floor. "What about the native? How long we've to keep him?"

"Tomorrow." Hoag felt faint, suddenly realizing, by custom, the body would be claimed for cremation according to Shinto ritual but now there would be no body . . .

"Wot's up, Doc?"

"Nothing, just a . . . thank you, Sergeant." His heart started again as he remembered the man was Korean, one of some shipwrecked fishermen who eked out a pathetic existence, no way to sail home, unwanted and despised by locals. Babcott had agreed to have the body cremated in the Buddhist crematorium. "Actually, you could help, Sergeant."

Malcolm's corpse had been cleaned and dressed after the autopsy by their Japanese trainee assistants. With the help of the Sergeant, who took the feet, they placed him in the coffin. "He looks right pretty for a corpse." Malcolm's face was serene in death. "Let's do t'other one, Doc. No need t'give yourself a hernia, eh, not that this little bugger weighs but a stone or two."

"We'd better wrap him in his sheet."

The Korean was skin and bones. Dysentery had killed him. Together they put him into the coffin.

"Thanks, I'll just tidy things up, then turn in."

"All right, Doc. I'll make sure your room's ready."

Once alone Hoag bolted the door. With Angelique's agreement, they had decided that there would be no traditional laying-out, with the coffin open for people to pay last respects to the dead man. With care he slid the lid into place. It took no time to nail it tight.

Now the other one. There would be a great difference in weight. What to use? Earth. There was a shovel belonging to the gravediggers to one side—not every body was cremated. Outside the earth was soft, the night cold with a slight wind that rustled the vegetation. He dug swiftly and brought shovelfuls back, scattering the earth on and around the corpse, packing it tightly. A few branches filled up the gaps. Satisfied, he levered on the lid and hammered the nails in. He leaned against the coffin, his breathing heavy, sweaty and dirty and even more concerned than when he started. Heavenly's right, he thought, washing his hands in a bucket. We'll never get away with it.

'You're off your rocker, Doc,' Skye had said with his wheezing cough, 'and so is she and so am I to say all right, I'm in. Wee Willie will have kittens but never mind, tomorrow night it is.' This was in the Club a few hours ago, noisy and argumentative as always. 'Have another whisky.'

'I'll have a coffee, thanks, then I'd better be off.'

'Her story reminded me of my Nellie, Doc. Married I was when I was an articled clerk, sixteen, she was fifteen, at least we pretended we were married and lived in a garret off Fleet Street, near the Old Cheshire Cheese Pub, Sam Johnson's place. She died in childbirth and the nipper, he would have been a boy, he died too.' He offered a cigar and lit one for himself. 'Pauper's grave, a couple of pence to the nightly barrow, bring out your dead, and that was the last of them.

Cholera was bad that year, dysentery too, cemeteries full to overflowing.' Heavenly spat in the spittoon. 'Haven't thought of little Nellie for years. You been married, Doc?'

'Yes, once, she died in London too.'

'Another coincidence, eh? Never felt like getting married after Nellie—swore I'd not be that poor again no matter what—always on the go, travelling too much. Had lots of girls but never did get the pox. Did you, Doc?'

'No.' Hoag had crossed his fingers. 'Not yet.'

'Hey, you're superstitious too, like me?'

'Yes. You're sure of our legal position in this?'

'As sure as can be, sure as shit—but if Wee Willie wants he can trump up a dozen charges, never fear. Listen, whatever happens, Tess Struan will bust her knickers and that's your stipend gone and you into the creek without a paddle.'

'No. I'm going back to India . . .'

Strange how bad leads to good or good to bad. All this has really decided me. I really am going back this time, going back to Cooch Behar in Bengal where I was stationed and where she came from. I'm going to find her family and . . . and then we'll see. I've enough cash for that and a few years left, our son and daughter are grown up now, part of the tapestry of London, educated as best I could, paid for as best I could, my sister and her husband their real parents—both sterling and the stuff of England.

I'm a good doctor and God knows they need doctors in India, even bad ones, so who knows, maybe I can find some happiness. . . . I don't even expect that, just some peace from the full-blooded horror of the killing of her.

Tired now, he studied the two coffins. A last look to check that everything was as it should be. Taking the oil lamp, he went out, bolting the door after him.

A baleful moon cast a shadow through the open windows. Silently another shadow moved. Sergeant Towery peered into the morgue. He was puzzled. Why should Doc Hoag arrive in the dead of night, and then why dig in the garden like a foul grave robber to pack the dead native's coffin with earth?

Curiosity killed the cat, me lad, but not Yours Truly, not when I'm in charge. Tomorrow you'll take a closer look afore the good Doctor's awake, and afore Lord God Almighty Pallidar arrives for inspection. He can find the answer.

48

KANAGAWA

Friday, 12th December:

PALLIDAR SAID ICILY, "WELL, Doctor?"

Hoag had just been summoned. He sat on the edge of a chair, uncomfortable and pale. Stiff-backed and uniformed, Pallidar was imposing even though he had a bad cold. On the desk was his plumed hat, his sword beside it, the early morning light glinting off the braid. Behind him stood Sergeant Towery. Bells from the temple toned ominously.

Hoag shrugged meekly. "Ballast."

"For Christ's sake, Doctor, this isn't a court-martial and personally I don't care if you pack coffins with cow shit, kindly tell me why you did what you did last night."

"I—I . . . thought . . . thought it was a good idea."

"I want to know, now . . ." A cough stopped him. Exasperated, Pallidar blew his nose and coughed, cleared his throat, and coughed again.

Hoag said brightly, "I've—we've some special, new cough mixture in the clinic, it'll get rid of that cold in a jiffy, it's got quinine in it, opium." He began to get up. "I'll get some an—"

"Sit down! The coffin, for Christ's sake, not my cold! The Sergeant saw you. Rightly he told me. Now you tell me why!"

Hoag had twisted and turned but knew he was trapped. Cursing the

949

Sergeant silently, he said, "Can . . . can I . . . can I talk to you alone, Settry, old boy, please?"

Pallidar glared at him. "All right. Sergeant!" Towery saluted and marched out. "Well?"

"Well, you see . . . you see . . ." Although Hoag had decided to tell him sharply to please mind his own business, that he wasn't subject to military discipline anymore, thank God, you bloody officers trampled on me before but you're not going to do it again . . . he suddenly found himself pouring out the story in detail, ending, "So you see, Settry, it was the weight, the difference in weight, earth was perfect. . . . Listen, George Babcott is due any moment but he's not to know, no one is—you know nothing—we just send the wrong, the right coffin aboard the clipper and tonight when the cutter arrives, God willing, we bury him as he wanted and Angel wants." Hoag fanned himself, feeling better, at the same time weak with guilt. "You know nothing. Now—now I'll get that cough mixture."

"Will you sit down." Pallidar glowered at him. "You're a bloody fool. First: have you looked out of the window?"

"Eh?" Hoag did as he was bidden. These windows faced seawards. The sea was grey, swell heavy and nimbus clouds had closed out the sun, dominating the sky. "Oh!"

"Yes, oh! There'll be a bloody storm before dusk so no cutter burial even if it was possible, and you know Sir William ordered a Hong Kong burial so, by God, that's where it will be."

"But Settry, don't—"

"Not for you, Angelique, anyone—" Pallidar broke off with a new fit of coughing, then added hoarsely, "Sir William's in charge, he made a decision and that's it. Clear?"

"Yes, but . . ."

"No bloody but, for Christ's sake. Kindly fetch some cough medicine and stay to hell out of the morgue. Sergeant!"

Towery stuck his head in. "Yessir?"

"Put a sentry on the morgue, no one to go in without my approval. I don't want the coffins touched."

Hoag went off cursing himself for leaking Sir William's decision, cursing Pallidar, the busybody Sergeant, but mostly himself. Fuck it, he thought. I've botched it. In the clinic he found the cough mixture, was tempted to add some castor oil but decided not to. "Here, Settry, this will do the trick."

Pallidar took some, choked. "Filthy stuff, you sure you didn't pee in it just for badness?"

"I was tempted." Hoag smiled. "Sorry for being a perfect bloody idiot. You can still close your eyes—you could, you know, Nelson did."

"Yes, but he was Navy, we keep our eyes on teeth marks."

"Settry. Please?"

Thoughtfully Pallidar sipped the medicine. "You should comply with Sir William's order, best in the long run."

Hoag's attention focused on the care lines on the good-looking face. "What's up?"

"With me, nothing, except this lousy cold and cough. Plenty's up in the Settlement."

"What now?"

"Last few days lots of enemy movement all around us, samurai patrols, most of them covert—just for safety we've been patrolling to the Tokaidō and Settlement limits, so we spotted them. Coming here samurai were stacked ten-deep in places. They didn't interfere with us except for the usual gibbering. I counted almost four hundred armed bastards."

"*Tairō* Anjo trying to harass us, scare us?"

"Probably." Pallidar coughed, took another gulp of the medicine. "This is dreadful, I feel worse already. Ugh! I'm recommending we withdraw all personnel from here for a while."

Hoag whistled. "We wouldn't want to close the clinic."

"I wouldn't want to have you dead without a coffin. These bastards love surprise attacks. Like poor bloody Malcolm. Someone's going to pay for him."

Hoag nodded. "I agree." Idly he was looking out towards Yokohama, the countryside flat and uninteresting in winter—hate the cold, always have, always will. His eyes took him to *Prancing Cloud,* the steamer mail ship, the merchantmen, warships and tenders all busy, preparing for the coming storm or preparing to leave. Warships had smoke trickling from their funnels—fleet orders, well publicized, so that the Bakufu and their spies would be aware that the whole fleet could sail on a war footing within an hour.

Stupid, all the killing, but then what can we do? Those responsible must pay. Then he saw the smoke from the Struan steam cutter chugging this way, bobbing through the troughs, spray from the bow wave drenching the glass of the bridge and main cabin. His anxiety crested.

"Settry, don't you think—" He aborted another fervent plea, suddenly realizing that even if tonight was out for the actual burial, with luck he could still keep the first part of the plan and have the wrong coffin put aboard *Prancing Cloud*.

I'm the only one who knows which coffin is which, except perhaps the Sergeant and I've a hunch he won't notice the difference. No one can, unless a coffin is opened. "Don't you think life in Yokohama is weirder than other places, living on a powder keg as we do?"

"It's the same everywhere. Just the same," Pallidar said thoughtfully, watching him.

YOKOHAMA

Jamie, Angelique and Skye were grouped around the bay window in the tai-pan's office. Rain splattered the glass. It was near midday. "Tonight will be too dangerous."

"Then it will storm, Jamie?"

"Yes, Angelique. Enough to stop us."

"Will *Cloud* sail tonight as planned?"

"Yes, no storm will stop her. The cutter's gone to Kanagawa to collect the other coffin. You still want it put aboard her and not the mail ship?"

"That's Sir William's order, not mine," she said firmly. "He wants to send my husband against his wishes and mine, he says it should go as quickly as possible and that's by clipper. A coffin will go as he wishes. Jamie, our ruse, I think our ruse is fair. As to the storm, it will be a little storm. If we can't bury my husband tonight, then we'll try tomorrow. Or the next day."

"The mail ship will sail tomorrow around noon."

"Could you delay her, in case?"

"I think so. I'll try." Jamie thought a moment. "I'll talk to the captain. What else?"

Angelique smiled sadly. "First we have to see if Dr. Hoag was successful. If not . . . perhaps I must go with the clipper after all."

"More than likely Hoag will come back with the cutter, then we can decide." Jamie added, not believing it, "Somehow it'll all work out. Don't worry."

"What about asking Edward Gornt to join us?" she asked.

"No," Jamie said. "The three of us are enough with Hoag. I've arranged berths on the mail ship, for Hoag, you and me."

Skye said, "Angelique, it's much wiser for you to stay here. Everyone here knows Wee Willie made the decision against your wishes, and that takes some of the heat from you."

"If we cannot bury Malcolm, then I will go. I must be at his funeral, have to." She sighed. "We should have a captain for our venture. Jamie, it should be you."

"I agree," Skye said. "Meanwhile, we wait for Hoag."

Jamie began to speak, stopped, then nodded and went to his own office. A big pile of mail waited for action. He began to deal with it, working diligently but his concentration was disturbed by his drawer. In it was Maureen's letter. At length he threw down his pen and took the letter out and reread it. There was no need, for he had read it twenty times before.

The key sentence was: *As there has been no reply to my fervent requests and prayers that you return and take up a normal life at home, I have decided to put my trust in our Maker and venture to Hong Kong, or the Japans, wherever you are. My beloved father has advanced us the money which he borrowed against a mortgage on our home in Glasgow—please leave word for me with Cook's in Hong Kong for I sail tomorrow, a second-class berth, on the Cunard* Eastern Mail . . .

The letter was dated over two and a half months ago.

He groaned. She'll be in Hong Kong any day. My letter arrived too late. Now what do I do? Grin? Hide? Flee to Macao like old Aristotle Quance? Not on your life. It's my life and there's no way I can support a wife, want a wife . . . I can't just write the same letter again and have it meet her there. I'll have to—

A knock interrupted his thoughts. "Yes?" he bellowed.

Tentatively Vargas poked his head around the door. "Can I see you a moment, senhor?"

"Yes, what is it?" Jamie asked.

Vargas said distastefully, "There's a man here to see you, a Mr. Corniman—some name like that, I think he said."

The name meant nothing to Jamie. Vargas opened the door a crack. The short, ferret-like man was strangely dressed, part in European clothes, part Japanese. Shirt, trousers and thick padded overcoat, clean-shaven, hair clean and tied in a queue, a knife at his belt and well-worn boots. Jamie did not recognize him but here strangers were often not what they seemed. On an impulse he said, "Come in, please sit down." Then he remembered the mail ship. "Vargas, ask Captain Biddy to stop by a moment, will you? He should be in the Club. Sit down, Mr. Corniman, is it?"

"You's grog, mate?"

"Who are you and what do you want?"

"Johnny Cornishman, remember I seed you wiv' the tai-pan, me and my mate, Charlie Yank, we's prospectors, right?"

"Prospectors? Oh, yes, I remember you." Now the man was clean and tidy where before he had been a hairy, filthy, foul-smelling beachcomber. His malevolent, furtive little eyes had not changed. "We made you a deal but you went with Brock's," he said sharply, "you sold us out."

"Ay, that we did. We's biznessmen. Norbert give us'n more brass, didn't he? Forget him, he's dead. First, some grog, eh? Then talks."

Jamie kept his interest hidden. A man like this did not come without pay dirt. He unlocked his sideboard and poured half a tumbler of rum. "You've made a strike?"

The little man quaffed half the glass, choked and bared his gums, toothless but for two twisted brown teeth. "Grog's better'n saké, by God, but never mind, the little sheilas is making up for th' lack o' grog." He belched and grinned. "Just so long as you barf. Jesus they's pekulier about water and barfing, more'n in our Yoshiwara, but when you's barfed then they's waggles theys bums till Kingdom come!" He roared at his own joke, then said toughly, "We's got best quality steamer coal, tons, mate, 'nuff to coal our whole effing fleet. At half Hong Kong price, th' ton."

"Where? Delivered where?" Jamie said, brightening. Steamer coal was extremely valuable and in short supply, especially for the fleet, and a local supplier would be a godsend as well as a constant source of revenue. At even twice Hong Kong price he could sell all he could get, let alone half. "Delivered where?"

" 'Ere in Yokopoko, for Christ's sake, but sixpence a ton you's puts in't bank for Johnny Cornishman." He gulped the rum down. "You's to pay in gold or silver Mex an' you's pay this bugger." He handed over a piece of paper. The bad printing read: *Yokohama Village, Shoya Ryoshi, Gyokoyama merchant.* "This sod know wot's wot, the ropes, knows wot to do. You's knows the bugger?"

"Yes, he's the village headman."

"Good. Me Guv sayed you'd know him."

"Who's your Guv?"

Cornishman grinned. "Lord 'igh Muck hisself. You's doan' need names. Doan' waste time. We's a deal, yes or no?"

After a moment Jamie said, "Where's the seam?"

"Me strike's me own, mate, not yorn." The little man laughed nastily. "It be close but in enemy lands. Listen, me first seam's open, wiv a mountain of coal nearby an' a thousand of the yeller buggers to dig'n carry, 'nuff for twenty fleet for twenty year, by God."

"Why me? Why ask me to deal with you?"

" 'Cause Norbert's bloody dead an' you's bloody kingpin now the tai-pan's dead. Yokopoko's proper bloody dangerous, eh?" Cornishman held out the glass. "I's enjoy more grog, if you please, Mister godalmighty Struan's."

Again Jamie poured and sat down again. Cornishman noticed half the last measure and grunted. "Wot's this?"

"We'll pay a fifth of Hong Kong price, less customs, delivered here, first delivery in thirty days. No side deal."

The little man's eyes darted around the room like a rat's. "Any customs you's pay, mate. Me side deal stays. Tell you wot: day after tomorrow you's send a coaling barge near Yedo, where I says. Day after termorrer. We fills her up, you's to pay a fifth when full and brings her here to Yoko, you pays that geezer the rest, th' one of the paper. Sixpence a ton in bank in me name, Johnny Cornishman. Can't be fairer, eh? You get coal before you pay an' at half price Hong Kong."

"A fifth of Hong Kong price overall."

The little man's face twisted with anger. "At harf Hong Kong price you's making a big profit, for Christ's sake, the coal's here, not in effing Honkers. You's saves shipping, 'surance, and Christ knows what—we ain't chicken-shit bushwhackers, this's spectible trade!"

Jamie laughed. "Tell you what: first barge I'll pay a third Hong Kong price. If the quality's what you say and you guarantee delivery a barge a week or whatever you can do, I'll up it over the year to half Hong Kong less fifteen percent. Threepence a ton on the side to you. What about your partner, what was his name, Charlie Yank?"

"Sixpence or nuffink." Again the glance darted around the room and came back to rest on him, glittering. "He's dead like yor tai-pan but he didn't die like that lucky bugger."

"You'd better watch your tongue about our tai-pan."

"Go stuff yourself, mate. That were no disrespekt, we's all like to meet old Boney with a doxy chomping on our dingle." He finished his drink and got up. "Two days, at high noon. Pick up be here." He offered a small hand-drawn map. The X was on the coast a few miles north of Kanagawa, south of Yedo proper. "You's brings tenders, we gives labor."

"Can't do two days, that's a Sunday. Make it Monday."

" 'Course, Lord's day's the Lord's day. Three days."

Jamie studied the map. An unprotected coal barge, with tenders and crew, might be a tempting bushwhack. "As the barge would be naval, and the coal for the Navy, I imagine they'll send a frigate to stand offshore."

"They's can send the whole effing fleet for all I cares." Cornishman tried to be dignified. "I's made a bonzer strike an' we's proper, by God, very proper."

"I'm glad to hear it."

"It be sixpence a ton or nuffink!"

"Fourpence."

Cornishman spat. "Sixpence, by God, I's knows worth of coal, and worth to effing fleet, an' wot you's can make off 'em. Maybe I's deal direct."

"You could try," Jamie said, gambling. "Tell you what, fourpence first ten barges, rest sixpence."

The little man glowered at him. "Now I's knows why you's Noble bloody House." He stuck out his hand, rough and horny. "Yor word as Struan's gent." They shook. Then he said, "Oh yus, you's any mercury?"

Jamie's attention soared back. Mercury would be used in the extraction of gold. "Yes. How much do you need?"

"Not a lot for starters. You's put it on the tab?"

"All right. You're staying at the Yokohama Arms?"

"Not effing likely—no Drunk Town for me," Cornishman said with a sneer. "I's on me way back right smartly, an' you's to keep supply secret, deal secret, no names, no pack drill—I's wanting no bleeding bushwhackers jumping me claim." He started to leave.

"Wait! Where are you going? How do I contact you?"

"I's going back to me claim, mate." Again he bared his gums in his evil smile. "Me samurais and me palanquin's outside th' North Gate, I snuck in private like. Next time I's come back, I's come back as gent, no effing Drunk Town no more. An' you's doan' contact me no more, you go's to the geezer. I's 'spektible trader now and doan' you's forget it. Put mercury on't barge." He walked out.

For a long time Jamie stared at the walls, sifting what had been said. A reliable coal supply would be wonderful but bound to vanish when the fleet flattened Yedo. And why mercury? Has that rotten bugger hit real pay dirt? And who's the real boss? Come to think of it, who's mine?

Tess until the end of the month. How much loyalty do I owe her? All of it. Till the end of the month.

Rain battered the window. He got up and looked around the bay critically. The sea was a dirtier grey than before, the sky lowering. No doubt the storm would be bad for the cutter but not for a ship. Ah, there she is!

Their cutter was a couple of hundred yards or so off their wharf, making way carefully against the waves, shipping some water but not badly, spray from the bow wave substantial, the Struan flag at half-mast—as the flag above their building had been since the death of the tai-pan. His binoculars were on the window ledge. Now he could see Hoag and Pallidar clearly in the cabin, the flag-draped coffin lashed securely to one of the benches as he had ordered. A twinge went through him seeing the entwined Lion and Dragon around Malcolm's coffin—a sight he had never expected to see. Then he remembered that it was not his friend's coffin but some unknown native, at least he hoped so.

"Vargas!"

"Yes, senhor."

"Take this lot of mail, copy it and seal it—I'll deal with the rest this afternoon. I'll be back later."

"Captain Biddy wasn't in the Club but expected, senhor. I left a message."

"Thanks." Unhurried, he put on his coat and hat and went out, leant against the rain-filled wind. He was almost alone on the High Street. At the North Gate, Cornishman was nowhere to be seen. A few samurai guards huddled in the lee of their Customs House. Some traders were scuttling for the Club and a late tiffin. A few waved. One of them stopped and urinated in the gutter. South Drunk Town seemed even more squalid under the overcast. This's no place for a woman, he thought.

"Ahoy, Jamie!" Hoag called from the cutter.

"Hello, Doc. Hello, Settry." They clambered onto the rough, tarred planks, the piling timbers sunk deep in the seabed, creaking with the thrust of the waves. One look at Hoag was enough to know that the switch had been successful, however much the squat man pretended nonchalance. So we're committed, he thought. Pallidar was having a coughing fit. "Settry, you'd better get that fixed before it turns into something worse."

"It already has," Pallidar said sourly. "This so-called doctor gave me a potion that's bound to kill me. Doc," he said, coughing again, "if it does, when it does, the hell with you."

Hoag laughed. "A double-strength toddy and you'll be right as rain tomorrow. Jamie, everything's all right?"

"Yes."

Pallidar said, "I'm turning responsibility of the coffin over to you, Jamie. It goes aboard *Cloud* at once?"

"About half an hour. Angelique wanted to . . . to say good-bye. Reverend Tweet will add a few words."

"Then she's definitely not going by the clipper?"

"I don't know, Settry, not positively. Last I heard she was going by the mail ship, but you know how women are."

"Don't blame her. Going back aboard the clipper would give me the creeps too." Pallidar blew his nose and huddled deeper into his great-coat. "If you want I'll get Sir William to send the coffin by mail ship, then they'd arrive together."

"No," Hoag said, too quickly for Jamie, then recovered, "no, Settry old boy, I wouldn't recommend that, medically. Best leave arrangements as they are, coffin by *Prancing Cloud*. Angelique's all right now but a sudden shock could shove her back into a nightmare. Better she goes by mail ship and the coffin by clipper."

"Just as you want. Jamie, I'm recommending to William we shut down Kanagawa at once—that's why I came back."

"Christ Almighty, why?"

Pallidar told him about the patrols and numerous samurai around. "Not to worry. We can blow 'em all to hell. Mind, if I have the cutter take me back, it'd save me time."

"Why not go with her to *Prancing Cloud,* and she can take you direct after that. Are you overnighting at Kanagawa?"

"No, I've seen enough and just have to get my lads," Pallidar said to their relief. "The clerks and guards can evacuate over the next few days. See you later." He walked off, coughing.

Before he was hardly out of hearing distance Hoag said, "It went perfectly, Jamie."

"Not now, for Christ's sake." In spite of the cold and wet Jamie was sweating. He led the way back to the High Street to the lee of a bungalow, safe from other ears. "What happened?"

"It worked like a charm. This morning as soon as the cutter arrived we went to the morgue an—"

"Who's we?"

"Settry, Sergeant Towery, the Bosun and two crew. We draped and secured the flag to the coffin and they put it aboard the cutter. The other one is waiting for us tonight or whenever—supposedly waiting for cremation." Hoag peered seawards, against the rain. "No chance tonight, eh?"

"No. But it'll blow itself out by morning. I think."

"Good." Hoag rubbed his hands against the cold. "Everything worked like a dream. One small problem, the native was tiny, just skin and bones so I packed his coffin with earth to make up the difference in their weights."

"God Almighty, of course! I'd forgotten about that. That was clever."

"Did that last night, no trouble—no one said a thing when they put the coffin aboard the cutter, not a sausage."

"My God, this is all so dicey," Jamie said uneasily. "How are we going to get the other coffin out of the Legation with the clerks and soldiers there?"

"Already taken care of that." Hoag chortled. "I told our Japanese assistants to put it in the shed by our Kanagawa jetty, it's not far from the crematorium. They can do it without arousing any suspicion. George told me he puts coffins and bodies there when he has an overload. It's routine."

"Marvelous! How far is it from the jetty?"

"Fifty yards or so. Three of us can carry it easily and we'll have the Bosun, won't we?"

"Yes. You've done damn well. Damn well." Jamie squinted into the rain. "Pity we couldn't do it tonight and finish it."

"Never mind. Tomorrow will be fine." Hoag was very confident and pleased with Jamie's praise. No need to tell about being spotted and about Pallidar. This morning they had had breakfast together and when he said: 'Settry, about last night . . .' Pallidar had interrupted him: 'Forget it, just forget it, Doctor, that's the best thing for you to do.'

That is best, he thought, beaming, forget it ever happened. "Shall we fetch Angelique? How is she?"

Within the hour they had reassembled beside the cutter. The rain was heavier and the wind squalling. Spray came over part of the jetty. The cutter, well moored, dipped and fell with the waves, ropes creaking. Angelique wore black, a black cloak raincoat over her dyed black dress, black hat with a heavy black veil, and an umbrella. The umbrella was sky-blue, a startling contrast.

Surrounding her were Jamie, Skye, Dmitri, Tyrer, Sir William and other Ministers, Captain Strongbow, Gornt, Marlowe, Pallidar, Vargas, André, Seratard, the Reverend Tweet and many others, all bundled against the rain. In the background Father Leo stood bleakly, hands in his sleeves, peering out from under his cowl. Jamie had invited Tweet to say a blessing: 'It would be odd if we didn't, Angelique. I'll make sure there's no real service, or speeches, that wouldn't be correct, just a blessing.'

The inclement weather helped to make the blessing brief. For once, Tweet was curiously eloquent. When he finished, self-consciously they all looked at her. Overhead, gulls cawed as the wind swirled them past, riding the currents joyously. Sir William said, "Again, Madame, my deepest condolences."

"Thank you." She stood straight, rain spattering off her umbrella. "I protest that I am not allowed to bury my husband openly as he and I wish."

"Your protest is noted, Madame." Sir William raised his hat. The rest filed past, saying their condolences and raising their hats or saluting if in uniform. Strongbow saluted and stepped into the cutter, Pallidar boarded after him as Marlowe stopped in front of her, still upset. "I'm so terribly sorry," he said, saluting, and walked off.

Father Leo was last. Somberly he made the sign of the cross, saying the Latin words, his face mostly hidden.

"But he's not Catholic, Father," she said gently.

"I think he was one of us, senhora, in his heart." Father Leo's accent was thickened with grief, his night spent in prayer, asking what should he do, should he attend or not. "He would have seen the Light, you would have helped him, I'm sure of it. *In nomine Patris* . . ."

Unhappily he ambled away. Now only Jamie, Hoag and Skye stood with her on the jetty. "What now, Jamie?" she asked, a deep melancholy swooping over her.

"We wait a minute," he said.

Like the others he was feeling that he was part of a cheat, at the same time deeply moved and not a cheat. This is just to help a friend, he told himself. You promised to guard his tail, and hers. That's what you're doing. Yes, but it's cheating and I hate it. Forget that, you're their leader, act like one. "Captain Strongbow, cast off! Godspeed!"

"Aye, aye, sir, thank you." The cutter eased away, dipping in the troughs, then picked up speed. Sea gulls mewed in her wake. They watched her go.

"It feels so odd," she murmured, weeping silently. "It is, and it isn't. We're not wrong, are we? Are we?"

Again Jamie made the decision for all of them. "No," he said, and took her arm and walked her home.

* * *

Just before sunset, Vargas knocked on the tai-pan's office door. "Mr. Gornt to see you, senhora. Monsieur André left a message that Monsieur Seratard would be honored if you would dine with him."

"Thank them but say no, perhaps tomorrow, perhaps. Hello, Edward. Come in." Again she sat in an easy chair by the windows, the day dark and rainy. A white wine was opened and waiting in ice. One fine glass was upended in the ice and chilling. "Please help yourself, you're boarding now?"

"Yes, the tender's ready. Your health, Ma'am."

"And yours. Are you the only passenger?"

"I don't know." He hesitated. "You look wonderful, ethereal, and unobtainable, Ma'am."

"I will be sorry to see you go. Perhaps everything will be better when you return," she said, liking him as before. "Will you come back or first go to Shanghai?"

"I'll know better in Hong Kong. Where will you be staying? On the Peak in the Struan Great House?"

"I've not decided—finally—even if I'll go."

"But . . . you won't be at the funeral?" he asked, confused.

"I'll decide tomorrow," she said, wanting to keep him off balance, him and everyone, even Jamie. "Mr. Skye strongly advises me to stay here, and I don't feel well." She shrugged. "I'll decide tomorrow, I've a berth reserved. I desperately wish to be with him, I need to be there, and yet, if he's not buried as he wishes and I wish, then . . . then I've failed."

"You haven't failed him, Ma'am. Everyone knows that."

"You won't fail me, will you, Edward? You'll deliver my letter to her, everything, as we discussed?"

"At once. A promise is a promise. A matter of honor, Ma'am." He looked at her directly.

"And I promised too. Didn't I? A matter of honor. Eternal friendship."

The way she said the two words was a promise and not a promise. For the life of him he could not read her as he had before. Earlier he would have known how far that promise would take him. Now there was a barrier. I'm glad, he thought, for if there's a barrier for me it will exist for every man. Six months is still not much to wait and a perfect time.

So she may not be in Hong Kong. How does that affect me? "My plans, Ma'am? They depend on Tess Struan." He wanted to tell Angelique his real plan, but was far too shrewd to indicate that, even obliquely. "I'm hoping she'll act on the information I'll give her. That will take a month, at least. If she wishes I'll wait the month and help— she'll need help, Ma'am. It all depends on her. If you arrive by mail ship we can talk more there. If not, may I write?"

"Of course, yes, please. I would like that. By every mail. I promise I will keep you advised of my plans." She opened the drawer and took out an envelope. It was addressed to Mrs. Tess Struan. And unsealed. "You may read it."

"Thank you, Ma'am, but that's not necessary."

Angelique took it back, did not seal it but just tucked the flap into the back. "This will save you the trouble of steaming the flap open, Edward."

He laughed. "What makes you so sure I'd do that?"

"I would. It would be too much of a temptation. But please seal it before you give it to her."

He nodded. "You once said, now you knew why your husband liked me, why I would be a dangerous enemy, an even more dangerous friend. Perhaps that applies to you, Angelique."

"Perhaps it does," she said simply. "I'm feeling my way in this new world, Edward. It's fraught with difficulties, and with quicksands. But you will find me very dependable once I've given my word, as I have. Do not forget I am French." A little smile. "Read it."

The letter read:

Dear Mrs. Struan, by now you will have heard the terrible news about Malcolm—sorry that I cannot tell you in person but I have been advised by Dr. Hoag not to travel by Prancing Cloud *or the mail ship.*

I cannot tell you how distraught I am and have been. Let me just say simply I loved him with all my heart and tried to do the best I could while he was alive, and, too, after his death have been desperately trying to bury him as he wished, at sea, like his adored grandfather. But that was forbidden me. Please, I beg you, please do for him what I failed to do.

But I have not failed him in a further duty. The bearer of this letter was your son's friend. He brings information of great importance—that he had promised to give Malcolm the day he died, that he, Malcolm, was rushing to give you by

*Prancing Cloud: the means to destroy your everlasting ene-
mies, Tyler and Morgan Brock. Mr. Gornt has sworn to me he
will give every last detail to you. I beg you to implement it if it
is what he purports it to be. The successful conclusion to that
feud, and the elimination of that agony from your head is, I
know only too well, all the epitaph Malcolm would wish.*

She had dated it, and signed it Angelique Struan, Yokohama. There
was a P.S.: *Strange, isn't it, we who have so much in common—I hate
my father too, he tried to destroy me too—have been so far apart, so
unnecessarily.*

Edward Gornt sealed the envelope thoughtfully. He put it in his
pocket and raised his glass. "A long life—you're a remarkable
woman, remarkable."

"How so?"

"You ask for nothing, give everything," he said with genuine admiration, and did not add, And you do not mention thirty days when, as
women, that will be uppermost in both your minds—for if you are
carrying his child, the Struan empire is mostly yours whether daughter
or son, though a son would be perfect! And even if you're not, an
immodest claim on Struan's is just as perfect and unassailable. In either
case you will still marry me! "You are a great woman," he said calmly.
"I hope I may be allowed to share an everlasting friendship."

He got up, gallantly kissed her hand and did not linger.

Alone again she nodded to herself, content, then poured wine into
his glass—there were other glasses within easy reach but she chose his
deliberately and sipped with added enjoyment. Then grimly raised the
glass seawards: "Godspeed, *Prancing Cloud.*" Another sip. And she
smiled.

"Phillip!"

"Yes, Sir William?"

"Here, take these. Are the rest of our dispatches ready?"

"Yes, sir. I've done extra copies of both the Inquests, the death
certificates, etc. I'll get your 'private and confidential' to the Governor
from the safe and that's the lot. Best if I take them aboard *Cloud*
personally."

"Yes, that's wise. I've one more. Give me a couple of minutes."
Weary from all the writing and the stress of the last few days, and
grinding awareness of how exposed Yokohama was, Sir William shook

off his headache, thought a moment, made sure the nib was clean, chose his most official letterhead and wrote firmly:

Dear Mrs. Struan. I'm sending this by special dispatch via Prancing Cloud *for special reasons, both formal and personal.*

First, I would like to offer my deepest condolences on the unhappy demise of your son whom I numbered amongst my friends as well as colleagues. Second, the circumstances and facts of his marriage and death were established under oath in an official Inquest, a copy of whose findings are enclosed.

To the best of my belief the shipboard marriage is legal—I have asked the Solicitor General for a formal ruling.

To the best of my belief Mrs. Angelique Struan had nothing whatsoever to do with the death of her husband, and was in no way responsible—a fact supported by medical evidence of Doctors Hoag and Babcott (and part of the Inquest documents) that you will no doubt receive in person.

To the best of my belief your son died as a result of wounds suffered during the unwarranted attack on the Tokaidō and was, in effect, murdered then. The King, or daimyo, who ordered these attacks has not yet been brought to justice. I assure you he will be.

To the best of my belief, and personal observation, your son was in love with Mademoiselle Richaud to the point of obsession, and pursued her for marriage in every way he could conceive. She reciprocated his affections in exemplary, ladylike fashion. She is a brave young woman and anything to the contrary are lies spread by scoundrels.

Lastly, to the best of my belief, your son wanted to be buried at sea like his grandfather. His . . .

Sir William hesitated a moment, continuing to be careful in his choice of words. He formulated his thought, then continued with his firm strong hand: *His widow pleaded strongly that this should be done, here, wanting to grant him his wish (we have found no will yet, nor a formal letter to that effect) but it is my belief that this was what he wanted. I overruled his widow's request and decided his remains should be sent to Hong Kong to you.* Again he hesitated as variations presented themselves, then wrote, *I strongly recommend this request be granted. I am, Madam, yr obedient servant.*

For a moment he reflected, then went to his sideboard and poured a brandy, drank, and sat down again. Now he read the letter carefully. Twice.

He made a couple of edits and changes and rewrote the letter, signing it Her Britannic Majesty's Minister to the Japans. Again he reread it. Now he was satisfied. The key changes were: after *She is a brave young woman* he had cut out *and anything to the contrary are lies spread by scoundrels* as inviting the question 'What lies?' adding, in its place, *and I commend her strongly to your benevolence.* After *buried at sea* he eliminated *like his grandfather,* not knowing the truth of that claim.

"Much better," he said aloud. "Takes the sting out of it." Rather like that, I commend her to your benevolence, he thought, though what those two will finally do to each other only God knows. A week ago I would have wagered it was no contest but now I'm not so sure.

Thankfully he opened his desk diary and added the name Tess Struan to today's long list of letters sent by *Prancing Cloud.* An entry on Tuesday, 9th, leapt at him: 'Malcolm Struan married Angelique Richaud aboard *Pearl* with Ketterer's connivance.' It was written in Russian as was the whole diary—a lifetime habit insisted on by his Russian mother—both to keep it private from most eyes, and also to maintain his fluency. That reminded him. His fingers opened his new, 1863 diary and he put a question mark on January 11th, adding a note: *We should know about now if A is carrying or not.* Malcolm's child would simplify her life considerably, he thought gravely.

He had decided to do what he could for Angelique because of her dignity yesterday, and at the wharf today, because of the pleasure she had given him with all the dancing and laughter and the lightness she had brought to Yokohama, and because she was French, with all the latent panache that Frenchwomen had above all others.

He smiled. Indeed, Angelique, you're French. And we're British, and no fools—and that is why we rule the earth and the French don't. "Phillip!"

Seratard and André were at the window. *Prancing Cloud* let go fores'les, tops'les and topgallants and royals and now, with full sail and the wind aft, she raced into the deep. Many others were watching too, envying her, jealous of her, wanting to sail or to own or to captain such a craft. Many wondered about her cargo, about the Angel who would leave tomorrow and what life here would be like without her, and about the fate of the letters aboard.

André said, "Will Ambassador de Geroire agree, Henri?"

"Yes. He owes me many favors, our mission here becomes more effective every day, and the private visit you've promised with Yoshi, that I've promised him, is arranged. Isn't it?"

"I am assured so," André said, his throat abruptly dry. Raiko had sworn that he could count on it, that the secret battle plans he had passed over to her were already in the heads of trusted go-betweens in Yedo for negotiation and rewards. "First Yoshi has to arrive back, Henri, then we can make a date. I'm promised he'll come aboard the flagship. I've a meeting tonight, and the down payment will fix it."

"I've changed my mind about advancing the money. It's best to . . ." Seratard raised his voice as André started to protest. "It's best to wait. I've decided it's best to wait!" He went and sat at his desk and motioned André to sit opposite, not angrily but with a smoothness that invited no opposition. "As soon as I know for certain he's back you can pay these . . . these go-betweens."

"But I promised them the money tonight, you agreed."

"So explain I don't trust them," Seratard said with a deprecating smile. "Let them prove themselves. I was saying, de Geroire will make her a ward of the State, André, and so becomes part of State policy, eh?"

Tonight André hated Seratard, hated him because he was dangerous and devious and knew too much, remembered too much, and was without feeling. At breakfast this morning Seratard had peered at him. 'What is it, Henri?'

'Nothing, there's a spot on your neck that wasn't there before and I wondered if . . . How are you, André?'

This had sent him into a panic to his bedroom mirror, petrified that the first sign of his disease had manifested itself. Ever since he had begun with Hinodeh he had become achingly sensitive to the slightest mark or twinge or fever. Most evenings she would undress him in the light, telling him how much she enjoyed looking at him, touching him, massaging or caressing, her fingers and hands always sensuous, but, even so, certain she was seeking telltale signs. 'None yet, not yet, thank God,' he had muttered to his reflection, wet with relief that the slight abrasion was only an insect bite.

"André," Seratard was saying, "tonight at dinner, we must make plans with her. I recommended that once she's a ward of the State she should stay in the Embassy and . . ." A knock interrupted him. "Yes?"

Vervene opened the door. "A message from Vargas, Monsieur. Madame Struan regrets she is not well enough for dinner."

Seratard snapped, "If she's well enough to see a coffin off she could certainly spare us time. Thank you, Vervene." Then to André, "We must see her before she leaves."

"I'll see her first thing in the morning, don't worry. But there's a rumor she might delay. Hoag's supposed to have advised against a sea voyage, for medical reasons, and certainly Heavenly Skye is openly opposed."

Seratard's lip curled. "I detest that man, he's so uncouth, boorish, and quite revoltingly British."

Angelique was watching the departure of the clipper from the tai-pan's suite, upstairs. A few passersby saw her at the window, then hurried on, wet and chilled, wondering what would happen to her. One of these was Tyrer, ashore after delivering the dispatches. She looked so lonely there, so funereal in her black, never black before, only the colors of springtime. For a moment he stopped, tempted to see her, to ask if he could help in any way but decided not to, there was still so much to do before his rendezvous with Fujiko, a monthly payment to Raiko for 'past services pending the conclusion of the contract,' and then there was his lesson with Nakama that had had to be postponed because of all the work for Sir William.

He groaned at the thought of all those phrases and words that he still wanted translated, and the new note to Anjo that Sir William had deliberately wanted Nakama to translate, not exactly not trusting him, but to gauge a Japanese reaction to a short, undiplomatic Anglo-Saxon harangue. Even worse he was behind in his journal and had had no time to write his weekly letter home. It had to catch the mail ship, whatever happened.

In the last mail his mother had written that his father was ill:

. . . *nothing serious, dear Phillip, just a chest flux that Doctor Feld treats with the usual bleeding and purging. Sorry to say, as always, it just seems to weaken him even more. Your Father has always hated Camomile and Leeches. Ugh!*
Doctors! Illness and agony seem to follow in their wake.

*Your cousin Charlotte took to her birthing bed four days ago,
as healthy as ever could be. We had arranged the midwife but
her husband insisted on having the doctor deliver her and
now she has Childbed Fever and isn't expected to live. The
baby boy is ailing too. So sad, such a nice young lady, not yet
eighteen.*

*News from London: The new Underground Railway, an-
other first in the world, will open in four or five months!
Horse-drawn Trams are all the rage and the Christmas Season promises to be the best ever though there are riots in
some of the Factory Towns. Parliament is debating and will
pass a law prohibiting horseless carriages from going more
than 2 miles per hour and they must have a warning Flagman
walking in front of them!*

*Measles is Everywhere, many deaths, Typhoid's not too
bad this year. The* Times *reports that Cholera is raging again
in Wapping and the dock areas, brought by an India merchantman.*

*Phillip, I do so hope you are keeping your chest wrapped
and wear woolens, and woolen underwear, and keep windows closed against the terrible Fluxes that abound in the
night air. Your Father and I wish you would come back to
Sensible England, though from your letters you seem to be
pleased with your progress in Japan's language. Does the
Penny Post (what a joy!) work for you from the Japans as
well as for us to go there?*

*Your father says this Government is Ruining our country,
our morals, and our Glorious Empire. Did I tell you, now
there are more than eleven thousand miles of railway track in
Britain. In barely fifteen years stagecoaches have vanished . . .*

The letter went on for pages, enclosing all kinds of cuttings she felt
interesting, and they were. Wonderful for Phillip, keeping him in touch
with home. But between the lines he read his father's illness was not an

easy one. His anxiety intensified. For all I know he's already dead, he thought, gravely concerned.

Standing there on the promenade in the rain, a tweak of pain came up from his stomach. Sweat abruptly wet his forehead, perhaps it was the rain, he didn't know for certain, only that he was sure he was feverish. Maybe I've really caught something—the pox or something! Oh, my God, perhaps Babcott's wrong and it's not just the White Man's Burden—Gippy Tummy or normal squitters or some such rheum. Oh, my God, even though André swore by all that's holy, Raiko too, that Fujiko was as clean as clean, perhaps she isn't!

'Oh, for goodness' sake, Phillip,' Babcott had said this morning, 'you don't have the pox, you've just eaten or drunk something bad. Here, here's some of Dr. Collis's tincture. That'll cure you by tomorrow and if it doesn't, we'll give you a good burial, not to worry! For Christ's sake, how many times do I have to tell you: drink only boiled water, or tea.'

He mopped his brow, the light fading but no letup in the wind. Certainly he felt better than in the night when he had the runs. Wasn't for Babcott, or Collis's magic, I would have to have missed the funeral—not the funeral, Malcolm's sending-off. How bloody awful! Poor fellow! Poor Angelique! What will happen now, he asked himself, perturbed, took his eyes off her and hurried for the Legation.

Angelique had seen him. When the clipper was swallowed by the dark she drew the curtains and sat at the desk. Her journal was open. Three letters were sealed and ready for the mail ship: to her aunt, enclosing a sight draft on the Bank of England for fifty guineas, the second to Colette with a ten-guinea money order, both of which Jamie had arranged for her, using part of the money Sir William had allowed her to keep. She had considered using one of Malcolm's chits that were in the desk, backdating it, using the chop from the safe, but thought that unwise for the moment. The money for her aunt was just to help, to Colette to buy the best medicines against her lying-in time.

I may or may not be there in time, she thought. Hope so.

The last letter was to be delivered by hand. It said: *My dear Admiral Ketterer, I know it was only through your kindness that we were married. I thank you from the depths of my heart and swear, whatever power this poor woman may have in the future, that I will use it in or out of Struan's to wipe out all sales of opium and equally dastardly arms sales to natives, as my husband had sworn to do. Again, with all my heartfelt affection, Angelique Struan.*

Signing Angelique Struan pleased her very much. The two names went well together. It was enjoyable to practice the signature, the swirl of the 'S' somehow helping her to think.

My scheme with Edward, where on earth did all those lovely ideas come from? It's excellent—if he does it as I want. That should convince Tess I'm not an enemy. But her son was her son and I wouldn't forgive, not if he had been my son, I don't think I would.

The way ahead's fraught with disaster, so much to go wrong, can go wrong, André's still a slavering dog waiting to be muzzled, or put down—yet, in truth, so many ways to go right—the correct coffin is en route, Malcolm's ready and waiting for tomorrow, I can still go to Hong Kong by mail ship if I want, I'm sure Edward wants to marry me and he of all people understands a rich wife is better than a poor one, I have Malcolm's blank chits and his chop that no one knows about— and twenty-eight days to go and not like last time, Blessed Mother, thanks be to Merciful God—I pray for his child.

Ah, Malcolm, Malcolm, what a good life we would have had, you and I. I would have grown up without all the awfulness, I swear I would have.

Making an effort she shook off her melancholy and rang the bell on the desk. The door opened without a polite knock, any form of knock. "Missee?"

"*Tai-tai*, Ah Soh!" she snapped, ready for her.

"Missee-tai-tai?"

"Send Chen here, chop chop."

"You eat here, down'stair, Missee? Er, Missee-tai-tai?"

Angelique sighed at the permutations Ah Soh could find to avoid calling her tai-tai. "Listen, you piece of donkey dung," she said to her sweetly, "I'm stronger than you and soon I'll be paying the bills and then you will sweat," and was happy to see the dark eyes in the flat face cross. As Malcolm had explained, speaking directly at Ah Soh in correct English, not pidgin, that the maid could not understand would make her lose face. Such twisted logic these Chinese, Angelique thought. "Chen, chop chop!"

Ah Soh shuffled off sullenly. When Chen came in she told him she wanted a letter delivered to the British Embassy. He nodded without comment. "Chen, Ah Tok sick, not sick, heya?"

"Ah Tok sick. Ah Tok gone Hong Kong." Chen waved a hand seawards. "All same along Master."

"Oh!" Angelique was greatly relieved and wished she had thought of that first. Several times she had seen her skulking in the shadows, her black eyes filled with hatred, saliva dribbling from the corner of her mouth. She gave him Ketterer's letter. "Go Big House, now."

He glanced at the name, pretending to be able to read the barbarian. "Eat all same this place, heya?"

"Tai-tai eat all same this place, heya? *Tai-tai!*"

Chen's eyes flickered. His mouth smiled. "Tai-tai, eat all same this place, heya? Tai-tai Missee?"

"You're a piece of donkey dung too. Perhaps I'll dismiss you—no, that would be too kind. I'll think about you later." She smiled. "Eat downstair'. What food have?"

"Wat you wan', tai-tai Missee, Missee-tai-tai?"

This made her laugh and she felt better for it. "Missee-tai-tai, tai-tai Missee, all same good. What food? Your food, Chinese food," she said suddenly, not knowing why. "All same you-ah, Chen. China food, Number One food. Best, heya!"

Chen gaped at her. This was most unusual. In the past she would just pick at the dishes the Master enjoyed to please him, and eat European dishes, meats and potatoes and pies and bread that he and all Chinese considered fit only for animals. "Master's food, heya?" he asked tentatively.

"Tai-pan food for Master's tai-tai!" Imperiously, aping Malcolm, she waved him away and turned her back.

Chen, unsettled, went off mumbling. "All same tai-pan, have got, yes Missee-tai-tai."

I must develop a taste for Chinese food and knowledge of it, she thought, grasping a new idea. In case I stay part of the year. Jamie said he likes Chinese cooking occasionally, Phillip's enthusiastic and Edward eats it all the time . . .

Ah, Edward, Edward-of-so-many-faces, and possibilities. I'm not sure about him. If . . .

If I bring forth a son I will be so happy that I've part of Malcolm forever. I'll go back to Paris, for then I'll have plenty of money, plenty. Tess Struan will be glad to have me leave and our son will be brought up part French, part British, and be worthy of his father. If a daughter, I'll leave too, with less, but there will be more than enough. Until I meet a title worthy and a man worthy.

If I'm unlucky and there's no child, then I may consider Edward, while negotiating with that woman for my widow's mite, all this subject to Heavenly Skye being wrong.

Wrong about how vindictive and ruthless that woman is.

49

Saturday, 13th December:

THE NEXT DAY THE SEA WAS THE
same grey, the sky the same grey but the storm had blown itself out.
Rain had stopped. Angelique, Skye and Hoag were waiting in the cabin
of the cutter, still moored to the Struan jetty and long overdue to leave
for Kanagawa. Beyond the bay they could see whitecaps. Gloom, fed
by the sharp wet wind, made waiting harder. Jamie and the Reverend
Tweet were half an hour late.

"I wish they'd hurry," she said, nervousness creeping into her
resolve. "What's keeping them?"

"We won't have to go too far out so we should still be all right,"
Skye said queasily, the cutter heaving gently. The men wore top hats
and sweaters and heavy topcoats—Angelique her dark green riding
clothes and boots as more suitable for shipboard travel.

Above the cabin was the small, glassed-in wheelhouse. Bosun Tinker leant on the sill of one of the opened windows, puffing a pipe, too
seawise to ask questions. Jamie McFay had simply said, 'Have the
cutter at the wharf early with a full load of coal, just you and a
dependable stoker.' That was enough for him. The rest would come
soon enough, like why sensible people wanted to put to sea on a day
when sensible seafarers were best ashore.

"Look, there he is!" Skye said, and cursed without noticing he had
done so.

Jamie was alone, hurrying along High Street towards them. Passersby greeted him, frowned and went about their business. He jumped aboard and closed the cabin door. "Tweet's changed his mind," he said, his chest heaving like the deck.

"God damn the fellow, why? He agreed." Skye was disgusted. With Jamie they had decided the best story was to say that a Christian fisherman had died in Kanagawa and had begged to have a sea burial, would he officiate, the rest could come later. There would be a contribution for his trouble.

"He said not in this weather," Jamie said, panting from his haste and frustration. "I tried every way to convince him but he only said, 'The fellow's dead, tomorrow or the next day will be just as good, weather's dicey, we probably wouldn't be back before dark—I'd forgotten Lunkchurch's dinner party. After service tomorrow, or even better Monday.' Rotten bastard!" He took another breath. "Rotten after he'd agreed."

Angelique felt sick with disappointment. "Father Leo! I'll go and ask him. He will do it."

"There's no time, not now, Angelique, and anyway Malcolm wasn't Catholic, that wouldn't be proper."

"Damn Tweet," Hoag said, fuming. "We'll have to postpone. Sea's not the best, perhaps it's just as well. I suppose we have to try tomorrow?" They all looked at her.

Jamie said, "Tweet's not dependable, he may want to put it off till Monday—either way there's the problem of the mail ship, she won't wait beyond noon." He had asked her skipper to delay but, already behind schedule, the man had said that was the best he could do.

Hoag said, "We absolutely should go aboard, no doubt about that. Angelique should absolutely be at the Hong Kong funeral."

"I'm opposed," Heavenly said. "But if she goes, I'll go."

"Father Leo," Angelique persisted. "I'll ask him."

Jamie said, "It wouldn't be proper. Listen, there's one solution, Angelique. A sea burial doesn't require a chaplain, a ship's captain can do it just as Marlowe marr—"

Her hope soared. "We'll ask John! Quick, let's—"

"Not possible, I've already checked, he's aboard the flagship and busy with Ketterer." Jamie continued in a run, "Angelique, I'm captain of this craft, I've a mariner's ticket, albeit an old one, I've seen enough sea burials to know what to do, I've never done it before but that doesn't matter. We have witnesses. If you like I can officiate . . . it'd be legal." He saw her confusion and looked at Skye. "Heavenly, legally that's right? Well, isn't it, for God's sake?"

"It'd be legal." Skye's nervousness increased as a larger than usual wave slapped the side of the boat, Hoag also feeling squeamish.

Jamie took another deep breath. "Angelique, this whole idea, the whole burial is bizarre to say the least, a little more won't harm Malcolm. I brought a Bible and Naval Regs, I had to fetch them, that's why I was late. What do you say?"

In answer she put her arms around him, the tears wetting her cheeks. "Let's begin. Please, Jamie, quickly."

Jamie McFay held her and found the closeness pleasing.

Skye said, "What about the Bosun and stoker?"

Jamie snapped, "I already told you I'll deal with them." Gently he loosed himself and slid the door back. "Bosun," he called out. "Cast off! Head for Kanagawa."

"Aye, aye, sorr." Glad that some decision had been made, Tinker took the craft to sea and turned northwards for the far shore. Waves made her bob and weave but not too badly, wind still well within limits, the sky promising no worse than before. Humming a sea chanty made him feel better.

Soon Jamie joined him. "You head for the Legation jetty. We're going to take a coffin aboard . . ." He saw the Bosun's bite harder on his pipe. "A coffin. Then we're going out to sea a league to deep water and we're going to bury him. We'll have a ceremony and you'll be part of it, you and our stoker." Jamie looked at him. "Any questions?"

"Me, sorr? No, sorr."

Jamie nodded tautly and went below again. The others said nothing, watching the coastline and Kanagawa, dead ahead.

In the wheelhouse, the Bosun picked up the metal voice tube, beside the helm, unhooked it and bellowed to his stoker down in the engine room. "Get the lead out, Percy!"

The warehouse shed was where Hoag had said, within easy distance of the jetty. The coffin was on a wooden bench. Skye, Hoag, the Bosun and stoker each took a corner and lifted it easily. After they left, Jamie closed the door, following them. He had thought it best for Angelique to stay in the cabin. A few fisher folk and villagers passed by, bowed and hurried away, not wanting to be anywhere near gai-jin.

To maneuver the coffin aboard was more difficult. The rise and fall of the deck, slippery with salt water, was hazardous. "Wait a sec," the stoker gasped, "lemme get aboard."

He was a short man wearing a tattered woolen skullcap, with heavy shoulders and immense forearms. Once on the deck he spread his feet wide and grasped the coffin mid-center and heaved it aboard and partway into the cabin, almost by himself. The vein-stretching effort made him fart involuntarily and loudly. "Pardon, all," he said gruffly, then hauled the box farther to safety. One end was in the cabin, the other projecting aft onto the poop.

"We'll lash it there," Jamie said.

"Aye, aye, sorr."

"Afternoon, Doctor Hoag." The voice was dour.

Startled, they all looked around. Sergeant Towery and another soldier were watching them balefully.

"Oh! Oh, good aft—hello, Sergeant," Hoag said, his voice strangled. With the others he stood stock still. Towery came closer and looked at the coffin. "Well, now, what have we 'ere? Taking the bugger, begging your pardon, Ma'am, taking the coffin to Yokohama, eh?"

"We—we . . . he asked to be buried at sea, Sergeant," Hoag said. "He, Mr. McFay kindly loaned his cutter, so here we are."

"At sea, eh?" Sergeant Towery looked at them, one at a time, as though wanting to etch their faces on his memory. "Very commendable, I'll be bound." Another wait while they died a little more. Then he said, "At sea, eh? Best not waste time or you'll be feeding fishes too. Ma'am." Politely he saluted her and marched off, the soldier falling into step.

They did not move for a moment. "Christ," Hoag muttered.

"What do you make of that?" Jamie asked.

"Trouble, sorr." Shakily, the Bosun took a swig of rum from his hip flask, passed it to Jamie who took a swig, Hoag shook his head, so did Angelique. The stoker was last. To Tinker's disgust, he swallowed most of it, belched. "Pardon."

Jamie's stomach was churning. "Bugger appeared from nowhere, as though he was waiting for us. Did you see him walking up?" They all shook their heads. "We'd best be going."

While they secured the coffin, the Bosun conned the cutter out to sea. She rode the waves well with only spray coming aboard, just enough to be irritating to those on deck. Below, the cabin was noisy but snug, the air clean and well ventilated, keeping out the smell of smoke from the coal-fired engine. Ahead, eastwards, where the deep was, the sky appeared meaner—and nothing beyond, between here and America.

"Best be fast, sorr," Tinker said quietly to Jamie in the wheelhouse. "We've no more than an hour or two of light."

"You sense something, Bosun?"

"Best be fast, sorr."

Jamie looked eastwards again. The sky seemed darker. "I agree. Hold your course." He turned to go.

"Sorr, that Sergeant, he's bound to snitch, right?"

"Yes."

"We've to make a funeral, right?"

"Yes."

"What's so important about this 'ere?" Tinker jerked his callused thumb at the coffin, "to risk all that there?" He pointed at the weather.

"We're burying the tai-pan, Malcolm Struan."

The old man laughed. "His coffin's aboard *Prancing Cloud,* sorr, we both knows that."

"Yes, we both know that. This is, well, a symbolic, a token, a make-believe burial to conform with his wishes—and his widow's wishes—to be buried at sea. She doesn't think that will happen in Hong Kong." Jamie knew the risk he was taking but there was no other way. So far he had been able to tell the truth.

"Make-believe, sorr?"

"Yes. That's all. There's nothing to hide and nothing to be afraid of."

Tinker nodded, unconvinced, and thought, There's a body inside, must be with all that weight. But, 'nuff said, don't go asking nobs questions you might not like answered, less you know the better, and let's hope to Christ the weather stays friendly and not shitty as she smells. "Thank you, sorr."

Jamie looked back at the bay that now was far behind. "Just go out of sight of land, Bosun." A last look at all compass points, then he went back to the cabin. "Not long now."

Angelique leaned closer. "What will that soldier do?"

"Report us, bound to. It doesn't matter."

"They can't do anything to us, can they, Mr. Skye?"

"I really can't forecast what . . . what Sir William might or might not do," Skye said, his stomach sickly conscious of the rise and fall of the deck.

Jamie reached into one of the lockers and brought out the large British flag he had put there, and the Lion and Dragon. Helped by Hoag, he secured them both around the coffin. The cutter was rising and dipping more severely than before and they had to hold on to steady themselves. Angelique sat near the open door. The sea air was wet and cold. She felt the tears beginning so she let the dark veil fall and pretended to look back at the land. "Not long now," Jamie said.

By the time land was just a thread on the horizon, the light was still fair, the sea heavier, waves white-flecked, wind stronger, but everything within limits. No rain. Jamie called out, "Bosun, slow ahead, just enough to give us way."

"Idle it is, sorr!"

Cutting the high-powered thrust of the engines created a sudden pool of near silence, pleasant to their spirits, a welcome relief to the grinding noise and apprehension at being so far out—both Hoag and Skye increasingly queasy. Only the whine of the wind now, and lapping sea, the comforting ticking over of the engine, felt through the decks more than heard, just enough to keep her bow into wind. The wind was firm, easterly, from the ocean, stronger than before. Jamie took a deep breath. "We'd best begin."

"Yes. What shall we do?" Angelique asked.

"Come on deck, here on the poop, but hold on. Bosun, lay aft, stoker too."

"Best I stay here on the conn, with yor permission, sorr." He bellowed down the voice pipe, "Percy, lay aft."

It was colder now. They grouped themselves as best they could, holding on to steady themselves. Jamie positioned himself near the stern, the others facing him. "Hats off," he ordered, removing his own. Skye, Hoag, the stoker and Bosun Tinker obeyed. He opened Naval Regs at the marked appendix.

Reading, and improvising he said, "We are gathered here in the sight of God to cast the remains of our friend Malcolm Struan, husband of Angelique Struan, tai-pan of the Noble House, into the deep, granting him the sea burial he wished and she wishes, acting as friends should act. . . ."

At the mention of the name the stoker's eyes had widened and he glanced back at the Bosun who shook his head, cautioning him to keep quiet. Muttering to himself, hating funerals, he pulled his jacket closer against the chill of the wind, wanting to be below in his warm engine room. The wind picked up a knot. They all felt the change. Jamie hesitated, then continued, "Now we say the Lord's Prayer. Our Father . . ."

Each in his own way prayed and said the words, the increased surge of the deck dominating most of their minds. When the prayer was finished Jamie squinted down at the book for a moment, not that he needed to for he had read the service in the wheelhouse coming here, needing time to slow his heart and gather his own thoughts away from the sea. While the others had had their eyes closed, he had not. With the Bosun he had seen the approaching squall line behind them, the waves beneath churning and ugly.

"As Captain of the Struan cutter *Cloudette*," he said, a little louder than before to carry over the wind, "it is my duty and privilege to commend this man's spirit to the Keeping of Almighty God, asking Almighty God to forgive him his sins, not that we knew he had any, not real sins, casting him into the deep from whence . . . from whence we came here from England, from home across the seas. He was a good, fine man. Malcolm Struan was a good, fine man and we miss him, we miss him now and we'll miss him in the future. . . ." He glanced at Angelique, who was holding on to a gunnel stanchion with both hands, her knuckles white. A gust hit her, pressing her veil against her face. "Do you want to say anything, Ma'am?"

She shook her head, the silent tears streaming. Spray came aboard to starboard, slightly lower in the water because of their weight and that of the coffin.

Bleakly he motioned to the stoker and Skye. Awkwardly, their footing precarious, they loosed the ropes binding the coffin to the bench and eased it laboriously towards the starboard gunnel to project out over the sea. With one hand, Jamie helped them. And when the coffin teetered on the brink, he said loudly, his own unhappiness cresting, "Dust will go to dust, and the sea and the sky will claim its own, and the wild winds will whisper one to another that this good, fine young man has gone to join his Maker too soon, too soon . . ." With the other two men, he gave the coffin a last shove and it tipped over and went into the ocean.

The cutter heeled, correcting for the loss of weight, a waiting gust caught the exposed hull and heeled her more. The port gunnel went into the sea. They all grabbed for handholds except the Bosun and stoker, who rode with it. Angelique, weak from tears, lost her grip and skidded away. She was almost overboard when Jamie lunged and caught her, frantically dragged her back, holding on with his other hand. Wind tore her hat and veil away and sent them swirling, then the stoker, with strong sea legs, slid down to her and lifted her and scrambled back into the safety of the cabin, tumbling after her.

Temperature dropped. Rain began. The squall fell on them. Jamie shouted, "Bosun, go home!"

"Best stay below, sorr!" Tinker shouted back, already decided what to do and how to do it. He waited until the stoker, mouthing violent curses, had scuttled to the engine room hatch and closed it after him and Jamie, Hoag and Skye were safe in the cabin. Rain became slashing. The sea violent.

Tinker signalled 'Slow Ahead,' swung the wheel to port and eased off the wind. Her bow dug into a comber. She broke free bravely, water cascading along her deck to smash into the glass of cabin and wheel-house, and continued to turn. "Easy now," he said, pipe firm in his mouth, "we're friends, for God's sake, we just give you old Green-eyed Devil's grandson."

Coming around was foul. Waves pushed by the wind heeled the cutter over, retchingly, and as she tried to correct herself they allowed almost no respite and dragged her over further. In the cabin the four of them hung on as best they could, anything loose cascading. Again Angelique lost her balance but the others held her, for the moment none of them thinking about much else than the storm. Hoag had gone dirty grey. With a bile-filled groan he lay down.

"It's just the turn," Jamie shouted over the noise and wind, the boat corkscrewing, and Angelique buried her head in his shoulder, fright-ened. "It'll ease off in a moment." He saw that the sea was bad but not revolting. Yet. Added to that he had complete confidence in the Bosun and craft—so long as the engine continued to provide power. "Not to worry!"

Bosun Tinker had decided that, too, and to scurry for a lee shore, plenty of time, if need be, to swerve back into wind, put out a storm anchor—a bucket on the end of a rope to keep her head firmly into the wind—and ride it out. "If she'll bloody ride out wot she weren't never to bloody be in," he said, fighting the wheel against the press of the waves.

The cutter came around and righted. Her bow dipped as the follow-ing wave went past, pushed faster by the wind, then the craft climbed sickeningly, crested and slammed down into the trough. All aboard winced. Again the same, and again the crash with plenty of water aboard this time. Down down down then up up up ever higher, then *crashhhhh* and foaming water swirled past the windows, decks awash. Angelique let out a little moan. Jamie had one arm around her, the other locked to a handhold. Rain slashed into the stern windows and door. Over in one corner now Skye had his head down and was retching, Hoag, prone and equally helpless.

Aloft in the wheelhouse the Bosun swayed from side to side, riding the pitching deck easily. He had his craft under control. Rain and spray

were heavy on the windows but he could see well enough and he did
not allow the waves to take her directly stern-on but gave them a little
way so that the up and down did not have the full force of the sea but
muted it, the craft sliding a little—vile for the passengers but "They're
safe, ain't they?" He beamed, enjoying himself, too many storms
conquered, time enough for fear over three or four hot toddies ashore in
front of a toasty fire in an hour or two. Happily he resumed his
rollicking chanty.

Then his heart skipped a beat. "Christ Almighty!" he burst out. The
coffin was alongside to starboard, still afloat, level in the water, dipping
and climbing with them, the two flags still around it. From the cabin
Jamie had seen it too and knew, equally shocked, if a big wave varied
course it could easily wash the coffin back aboard, or worse, use it as a
battering ram against the fragile superstructure, or, worst of all, punch
a hole in their unprotected hull.

The more Tinker eased away, the closer it came. Once it bashed
against the side, then swirled off, spinning like a top in a vortex, but
staying parallel and Jamie cursed that he had not had the foresight to
weight it with an anchor chain—air or the buoyancy of the wood was
keeping it afloat.

It was difficult for Jamie to watch it, holding Angelique as he did.
But he was glad her head was deep in his shoulder. Again he craned
around and caught sight of it, slightly aft and lying flat in the water,
now seeming to him like the ghoulish craft of a sick mind. The wind or
a current turned it and now, parallel to the waves, it began to tumble but
righted itself and was stable for three or four waves and then another
comber came that overturned it and to his joy it went under. He
breathed again, seeing it had gone for good, then it surfaced, the next
whitecap surrounded it, lifted it and hurled it directly at them. Involuntarily he ducked. It did not come aboard, just smashed broadside
against the hull, sounding as though they had hit a reef.

Momentarily, Hoag lifted his head. His brain was reeling in his skull
worse than the boat, so he saw nothing and fell back groaning into his
seasick miasma. Angelique too looked up but Jamie held her close,
caressing her hair to take the fear away. "Just some flotsam, nothing to
worry about . . ."

His eyes were on the coffin, a few yards away, parallel to them, its
lines clean and deadly, torpedo-like, both flags still intact. He flinched
as a frothing comber approached but it went by and over it and when
the wave had gone the coffin had vanished.

Breathlessly he waited, searching the sea. Nothing. More waiting.

Still nothing. The squall lessened slightly and no longer howled around the cabin. The waves were still high and bullying but Tinker was doing a masterly job, using every piece of seamanship to lessen the threat, the engine shrieking as the propeller shaft came clear of the water from time to time. "Come on," Jamie murmured, "keep going, nice and easy."

Then his eyes focused. The coffin was fifty yards away, a little aft, the nose pointed directly at them. It was keeping station with them, rising and falling as though attached by some invisible hawser. Ugly and deadly. He counted six waves and never a change. Then the seventh appeared.

The seventh wave was bigger than the rest. It took the coffin, made it into a missile and hurled it at them. Jamie knew the impact point would be dead center amidships on their starboard side and their roll would expose the hull for maximum damage. His breathing stopped.

Tinker must have seen it too for at the last moment the cutter veered crazily into its path, dipping slightly to starboard, the gunnel awash now, and the violent coffin-missile reared up the wave and over the prow to tangle itself in the bowsprit hawsers, hanging there half in, half out of the water, pulling the craft against the rudder.

The Bosun was hauling on the wheel with all his strength but the waves and wind had seized on the coffin and used it to make the craft unstable. In minutes the Bosun knew they would founder. There was nothing he could do to stop it. The voice whistle shrieked. With difficulty he answered it, "Yes, Percy . . ." but he was drowned out by the stoker's curses and saying what the bleeding hell was he doing up there, so he slammed it back into its holder, redoubled his effort on the wheel as the bow was inexorably being forced to disaster.

Then he saw the cabin door open. Jamie shoved his way on deck. Hanging on for his life, he groped forward. At once the Bosun stuck his head out of the nearest window bellowing and pointing: "The fire axe, fire axe . . ."

As though in a dream, Jamie heard him and saw the axe in its red holders on the cabin roof. The deck was heaving and shivering, the soul of the boat knowing she was in a death spasm. One foot skated away from under him but he collided with the gunnel and found he had the axe in one hand and was for the moment safe. Water came over the bow and swallowed him. Again he survived, but in its wake was a nauseating premonition. Involuntarily his stomach heaved and the foulness passed out of him. He lay there in the scuppers, cold and frightened, his fingers dug into holds, then more water swamped him.

When he could breathe, he coughed and spat the salt water from his mouth and nostrils and this helped shock him into action.

Up ahead the nose of the coffin was held tight by the mess of hawsers and twisted stanchions, the bulk of it shoved this way and that as the waves roared past or sucked at it. He squinted up at the Bosun against the wind and rain and saw him motion to hack it away, ". . . for the love of God, watch out . . ."

No axe will cut that bastard away, he thought helplessly, and hugged a stanchion as a violent wave came over the side at him, slammed him against the coffin then sucked him back to the gunnel again, choking and half drowned. When it subsided he was astonished to find himself still aboard. Don't waste time, his brain was shrieking at him, the next one or the one following will take you and drown you.

So he left his safe place and went forward until he was over the coffin, hating it and being here and that he had allowed himself to be part of this stupidity, risking her and the others for nothing, but mostly hating his own fear. The next wave tore at him but he survived it and hacked down two-handed with all his strength, slipped and grabbed the side of the cabin roof as another wave reached for him, battered him against the coffin's side. Gasping, he fought his way up and hacked again, this time at the coffin itself, hating the evil thing that it had become.

The blade sliced through one of the rope hawsers but made no impression on the wired ones, a tangled mess, and buried itself into the beflagged lid or bottom—he did not know or care which—and split it. But still the coffin hung there. Using all his strength, he could not move it, shoving and kicking and cursing, the main length of it dangling overboard and in the water dragging them, twisting them under the sea.

Another blow and another and another, using the head of the axe now as a sledgehammer to batter the coffin to pieces, raging at it, cursing it. The wood splintered but held, then a howling blow crushed the side and top and he slipped and fell sprawling. The axe skittered out of his grasp and went overboard and the next deluge bashed him against the coffin, then pulled him away again. When the spume had gone and he could breathe he forced his eyes open. Still the same. Still firm as ever. Again he groped forward but his strength had gone and his hands could hardly hold him safe.

Then he saw a single frayed hawser part. The mess of wires and ropes screeched under the tension, twisted and untangled a little, then more, then the whole coffin slid away tail first and as it hit the ocean began to break up. For a moment its head held the surface, then it went under, froth and bubbles in its wake. A piece of cloth that was the Struan flag surfaced. The next comber broomed the sea clean and came aboard and grabbed his legs from under him, dragged him against the bowsprit housing, then sucked him back along the deck, Tinker fighting for control again.

Astonished to be alive, Jamie found himself gasping in the stern. At the limit of his strength he groped for the door and fell into the cabin.

Skye was still in his corner retching, half-conscious, Hoag lying on his stomach, unconscious, Angelique curled up on a bench where he had left her, hanging on grimly, moaning and sobbing slightly, her eyes tightly closed. Shivering, he slumped beside her, chest heaving, mindless, knowing only that he was still alive and they were still safe.

After a while his eyes cleared. He saw land a mile or so away, and noticed that the rain had lessened and so had the sea. Now only the occasional wave came aboard. In a locker below the seat he found blankets and wrapped one around Angelique, the other around himself.

"I'm so cold, Jamie, where have you been?" she sobbed like a frightened child, only half aware. "I'm so cold, so lonely, and feel awful but so glad we did it, so glad. Oh, Jamie, I'm so cold . . ."

When they came alongside the Struan jetty a few misted stars were out. It was still early, at the edge of nightfall. The sky had cleared and promised a good day tomorrow. Merchantmen and the fleet lay safe at anchor, quiet, riding lights on—only the mail ship still being worked under a multitude of oil lamps like so many fireflies.

Nimbly the stoker jumped onto the wharf with a hawser and tied the craft, then helped the others. Angelique first, then Skye and Hoag. Jamie climbed the steps easily, still wrapped in his blanket, chilled but not badly. Skye and the doctor were pasty grey, their stomachs and heads ill at ease, legs weak. Now Angelique was much better. Her headache had gone. She had not been sick nor felt seasick. Once again she had cried herself out. The last half hour she had been on deck, away from the sick tainted air below, and had joined Jamie on the poop. There she faced the salt-sweet wind and let it wash her brain clean again.

Behind her Hoag coughed up a wad of phlegm and spat it into the water lapping the pilings. "Sorry," he muttered, needing a drink badly. Then he noticed the mess on the prow, some timbers crushed, the fore hatch stove in, bowsprit vanished, halliards gone, most of the gunnel. "What the hell happened?"

"Some flotsam was washed aboard, looked like a crate. Gave me a fright for a moment," Jamie said.

"Thought I heard a crash . . . I . . . think I'll . . . think I'll vis't the Club before turning in."

"I'll join you," Skye said, needing more than one drink to settle his stomach. "Jamie? M'ss Angelique?"

She shook her head and Jamie said, "Off you go, nothing more to do tonight. Don't forget the plan." They had agreed nothing was to be said other than, if asked, they had conducted a symbolic sea burial, nothing more.

Fortunately none of the others had seen the coffin come aboard or his struggle with it—except Tinker. As soon as he could, he had gone aloft to the wheelhouse. 'Bosun, about the coffin, the others below saw nothing, so on your head, by God, you saw nothing and you say nothing either. It's our secret.'

'Whatever you say, sorr.' Tinker handed him the flask and touched his forelock. 'Thanks. Weren't for you we'd be below, all of us—along with him.'

There was barely a swallow left but it helped. 'I thought I'd never make it. We forget it. Your oath, eh?'

'Whatever you say, sorr, but afore we forget it, when the box sank an' broke up an' he come out of it, he didn't half give me a turn, by God. I thort he were trying to bloody come back aboard.'

'Jesus Christ,' Jamie had gasped. 'You're imagining it, I saw nothing—you're imagining it.'

'Oh, no, I weren't, sorr, my eye line's higher 'an yors, right? An' I saw the bugger, begging your pardon, I saw him come out and flail for the surface afore he were sucked down.'

'You're imagining things, for Christ's sake. What an awful thing to say!'

'It's the God's Truth, sorr, so help me! 'Course it were only for a moment and sea spume were all around him, but I seed him right enough!' Tinker had spat to leeward, touched wood, and made the sign against the Evil Eye and the Devil, and pulled the lobe of his ear to make his point. 'God's truth, sorr, an' strike me down if I lie, made my balls jump to Kingdom come. Struck out for the surface he did afore Davy Jones sucked him down, naked as a babe.'

'A lot of bloody cobblers! Nonsense!' Jamie remembered how he had shivered and touched wood himself just in case. 'You're imagining it, Bosun, though I swear to God that bloody coffin seemed to have a mind of its own, an evil one at that.'

'My whole point, sorr, it were possessed by Old Nick hisself.' Again Tinker spat to leeward, sweating. 'Flailed for the surface he did, different like, eyes open and all, and I thort he was coming at us for good.'

'For Christ's sake, give over! Malcolm wouldn't do anything bad to us,' he had said, ill at ease. 'It was a trick of your mind.'

'My eye line, sorr, was high—'

'Forget your bloody eye line. Have you any rum left?'

Tinker coughed and reached into a hidden locker and pulled out another flask. It was half empty. Jamie took a large swallow, choked, and took another.

'There'll be ten cases of rum in our warehouse for you to draw against, Tinker, with my thanks. You did a fine job, so did the stoker— four cases for him.' Tinker thanked him effusively. The grand rum heat in his stomach had swamped all his chill. He looked at the old weathered face and shrewd blue eyes. 'I was never so bloody scared, never, in my whole life. I thought I was a goner three or four times.'

'Not me, sorr,' the Bosun said with a grin. 'Not with you aboard, but I was right happy when the bugger and his box were overboard and him sucked down cursing us all the way . . .'

Though safe ashore, again Jamie shivered, thinking of it. Angelique said, "You should get out of those wet clothes."

Hoag said, "Well, I'm off."

She put her arms around him and kissed his cheek, closing her nostrils to the smell of vomit. "Thank you so much, see you tomorrow." She did the same to Skye. The two men went off unsteadily. "Will they be all right?"

Jamie said, "Nothing that a few whiskies and a night's sleep won't cure."

"They're not in shape to discuss anything, are they?"

"No. What do you want to discuss?"

She took his arm in hers and hugged it. "Just to decide about tomorrow."

"We can talk as we go." They said good night to Tinker and the stoker, both men again thanking McFay for the rum. Then they walked off arm in arm. "Angelique—before you say anything, I'm glad we did it."

"Oh, so am I, dear Jamie, you are a dear and I truly am so glad and so happy nothing went wrong, no one was hurt." A wan smile. "Just a little sick."

"Nothing to worry about. Tomorrow?"

"I've decided not to go with the mail ship, no, please don't say anything, I've decided. I'm safer here. Until I hear from Tess formally. Really, Jamie, I am, I'm safer here. And I'm sure Hoag and George would agree that medically it would be wise. I don't think you should go either."

"It's my job to tell Mrs. Struan, Mrs. Tess Struan."

"You can call me Angelique, you always have and I, well, I've only been Mrs. Struan for a moment." She sighed, continued walking towards the Struan Building. "It's better I stay. She'll have to declare herself, better by letter here. Malcolm's buried and that's all that I wanted. Do you have to go?"

"In this wind," he said, thinking aloud, "*Prancing Cloud* could make fifteen to seventeen knots, day in day out, and be tied up in Hong Kong in five days—she'll have the bit between her teeth with such important news and important cargo." They had all agreed that publicly and now privately they would consider that coffin the tai-pan's. "The mail ship will average eight knots if she's lucky so she'll take the usual ten-odd days. By the time I got there the funeral will have been done, Tess will know everything from dozens of different points of view—my report's aboard, so is Sir William's and fifty others no doubt. She's dismissed me at the end of month and the new fellow arrives in a few days and I was told to show him the ropes." Then there were reasons he decided not to say aloud: he should be canvassing other hongs—as the major companies were sometimes called—for a job. The only real, suitable job available and up to his experience and surely on offer would be Brock and Sons. Then he had to decide about Maureen, and then there was Nemi. He smiled at Angelique sadly. "It adds up to no reason to go, doesn't it?"

She hugged his arm, oblivious of those passing. "I'm glad. I won't feel lonely if you're here."

"Jamie!" Phillip Tyrer had called out from the British Legation doorway, hastily putting on his topcoat and hat, hurrying towards them. " 'Evening Angelique, Jamie," he said in an uneasy rush. "Sir William's compliments, would you two and the—the rest of the—the passengers and crew of the cutter kindly see him tomorrow morning before church, before you both board the mail ship? She sails at two o'clock now."

"For what purpose, Phillip?" Jamie said.

"I—I think he'd like to . . . dammit, oh, excuse me, Angelique, obviously he'd like to ask what on earth you were doing."

"Doing?"

The young man sighed. "Sorry, old boy, it's not my idea. You're on the mat, I've delivered the message, that's all. Don't pick on me, I'm just the nearest dogsbody."

They both laughed, tension leaving them. "Ten o'clock?"

"Thanks, Jamie, that should be plenty of time." Tyrer looked down the way at the cutter. "Looks as though you had a rough crossing, what on earth happened to the prow?"

Jamie glanced back. The damage was clearly visible under the lamp at the head of the jetty, and, he knew, easily observable with binoculars for miles from the Legation windows. "Flotsam," he said readily. "A crate, what looked like a crate was washed aboard, then carried away again. No great problem."

50

"I DON'T AGREE, JAMIE. WE HAVE a distinct problem." Sir William sat behind his desk, facing them. Phillip nearby, the mood in the drab office inquisitorial. "Let's start again. You seem to be spokesman so I'll address myself to you. I specifically said no funeral here, the body was to go back to Hong Kong an—"

"It's already gone, Sir William, on *Prancing Cloud,*" Jamie repeated, his jaw set. They had been arguing for half an hour, he and Sir William, the others answering guardedly, all of them instructed by him and by Skye, only to respond when questioned directly and even then not to volunteer anything, just to answer the question as simply as possible: Hoag, Skye, Tinker, the stoker, and Angelique. Hoag was definitely the weakest link in the chain and twice had almost blurted out the reason. Angelique was heavily veiled, wearing black and dressed for church. "We had a make-believe funeral."

"I know that and as I have asked repeatedly, repeatedly, if it was merely symbolic why use a real coffin with a real corpse, albeit with a native therein, and shove him over the side with a form of a Christian's burial at sea?"

Jamie shrugged, stumped by that inevitable question. This morning Skye had said weakly, 'We'd best shrug it off, brazen it out, keep our heads down, nothing much he can do but spit blood.'

"The coffin was there, I thought it a good idea."

"Ah, this was all your idea then?"

"Yes," Jamie said stubbornly, glaring at Hoag who started to open his mouth. "I suggested it and . . . and the others were good enough to go along with it. It was the tai-pan's wish—it was Malcolm's wish and Mrs. Struan's. No harm was done."

"I most assuredly disagree. The whole idea's macabre. You deliberately went against my considered opinion; there seems to be an astonishing breakdown of reasonable thinking and a desire of all assembled here to avoid telling me the truth, the simple explanation, and you have colluded to hide . . . to hide what? Don't you agree, Phillip?"

Tyrer jerked in his chair. "Er, yes, sir, if you say so."

"Why the use of a real coffin and real body?"

Hoag shifted uncomfortably in his seat. They all knew that any moment he would break. Angelique decided that now was the time and she began to cry. "Why don't you just leave us alone? We did no harm, just did what we thought best, what my husband wanted, what I wanted for him . . ."

"Angelique, *please* don't cr—"

"That he wanted and you forbade. It's your fault, Sir William, I thought you were our friend, if you were our friend and you'd been . . . been reasonable we wouldn't have had all this trouble, of course it wasn't nice to do anything underhanded, even though I think you were quite wrong and . . ."

"Mrs. Struan, I on—"

"Of course that wasn't nice, none of us wanted to do that, but at least we did it in good faith, before God, at least these friends, real friends helped to do properly what my husband and I . . . it wasn't much to ask . . ."

For a moment she was going to flee the room but wisely did not, realizing that that would solve nothing and leave the others at his mercy so she stayed where she was, dissolving into ever more heartbreaking sobs, knowing she had not lied and had said nothing more than the truth: it *was* his fault!

In seconds they were all around her, trying to calm her, all feeling terrible, except Skye who was awed by the brilliance of her timing, and Sir William who was privately amused though, for face, pretending to be equally upset. He watched and waited, still disgusted with all of them for whatever machinations they had jointly conceived. What had possessed them and who was the real culprit? Surely not Jamie? Bloody stupid to do what they did. Ridiculous. Stupid to risk their lives like that.

People are no damned good. Even Angelique. Ah, but what a lady, and what a treasure and what an actress—where in the name of God does she get it all from? Like most girls of her age, her education is minimal, in her case convent, which is a bloody sight worse. Is Heavenly coaching her for the trial of the century? Or am I just a cynical old fool? Either way, I really will be sad to lose her.

His mantelpiece clock chimed quarter to the hour. Time for church, he thought, time to stop—he was reading the lesson and had not yet had time to skim through it.

"There there, Mrs. Struan," he said, as a good though stern father would. "No need for tears, we've all had enough of them recently. I must confess I still totally disapprove of the escapade, very poor show, but under the emotional circumstances I think we'll let it rest there, for the moment." Again he pretended not to hear their audible relief, or to notice the subsidence of her sobs. "Now it's time for church, and then the mail ship and our wishes for a bon voyage and a long life will go with you. Truly we will be very sorry and very sad to see you leave our shores."

"I—I'm not leaving yet, Sir William."

"Eh?" Sir William and Tyrer were flabbergasted.

Between sobs, her head bowed, she said, "Dr. Hoag has advised me not to travel for at least a week."

Hoag said quickly, "That's right, medically not a good idea, Sir William, not a good idea at all, no, not at all." This morning Skye, supported by Jamie, had insisted that it was best she did not go for a time. 'A medical certificate is what she needs, Doctor, one you can attest to with Tess Struan. With all this emotion, surely she shouldn't travel or have any confrontations until she's stronger?' Hoag had readily agreed, and said to Sir William, "As you can see she's easily upset, and I've given her a certificate, not that it's necessary."

For a moment Sir William did not know what to think. On the one hand they had not lost her, on the other the irritant that she already was, and the thorn she was bound to become when Tess Struan's wrath fell on her and all of them, would still be in his jurisdiction. "You really should go, Ma'am. I would have thought it very important to be at the funeral."

"I want to go but . . ." Her voice broke and a fresh sob racked her. "Dr. Hoag is—is going in my place, I really don't feel up to . . . it's best . . ."

"But Jamie, you'll be going too?"

"No, sir. There are things I've been ordered to do here by Mrs. Tess Struan."

"Bless my soul." Halfheartedly Sir William tried to dissuade her, then sighed. "Well, if Dr. Hoag says so, that's the end of that, he is the Struan doctor." He got up. Openly relieved, they thanked him and began to leave. "A moment, Dr. Hoag, a word if you please." He hid his pleasure seeing Jamie and Skye blanch and said pointedly as they hung back, "G'day Jamie, Mr. Skye. Phillip, no need for you to stay."

The door closed. Hoag was like a rabbit before a cobra.

"Now, Doctor, quietly tell me the truth, how is she?"

"She's very well, on the surface, Sir William," Hoag said at once. "It's a surface cure. What's underneath no one knows. It could last days, weeks, a year or more—then the nightmare will return. What will happen then . . ." He shrugged.

"You'll be seeing Tess Struan?"

"Yes, as soon as I arrive." Hoag waited shakily, dreading the questioning, knowing he would fail.

Thoughtfully Sir William got up and poured a whisky and gave it to him. The liquor vanished. "You won't be coming back here for a time, if ever. I need to know, in confidence, what medically are the chances of her carrying Malcolm's child?"

Hoag blinked, the liquor and the unexpected gentleness calming him and putting him off balance, not expecting this line of questioning. He said with great sincerity, "Of course that's up to God, sir. But Malcolm was healthy and so is she, both fine people, unfortunately both star-crossed—so sad. I'd say the chances are very good, for this was no idle fancy, their lovemaking must have been very passionate, as near a true love as I have ever seen."

Sir William frowned. "Good. When you see Tess Struan . . . I think our Mrs. Struan will need all the help she can get. Eh?"

"You may rest assured I'll intercede for her."

Sir William nodded and reached into his drawer. The envelope was sealed and addressed Personal, Confidential and Private, by hand, to Sir Stanshope, Governor of Hong Kong, from Sir William Aylesbury, Minister to the Japans. "I have an official commission for you, a secret one. I want you to deliver this personally to the Governor, as soon as you arrive."

He scrawled on the bottom 'Delivered by hand by Dr. Hoag' and had decided to use him the moment he had heard Jamie would not be on the mail ship, there being no one aboard *Prancing Cloud* he could trust. "It must be given over personally, to no one else, no one is to know you are a Queen's courier. Clear?"

"Yes, sir, of course, Sir William," Hoag said proudly.

He knew that now Hoag was putty and he could extract anything he wanted from him. Who began the escapade, what was in their minds at sea and why they did what they did, what really happened at Kanagawa. He smiled to himself, enjoying his position and for his own reasons let the matter rest. "Have a safe voyage, and I look forward to seeing you in Hong Kong."

"Thank you sir."

Hoag fled, ecstatic to have escaped with his honor intact. Jamie and Skye were waiting anxiously on the High Street. "Nothing, honestly," he said excitedly, "he just wanted to ask medical questions, private ones."

"You're sure?"

"Cross my heart and hope to die. Hurry up, time for a quick one before church. I still feel washed out." They went off happily, not noticing Sir William watching from his window.

I wonder how happy those rotters would be if they could read my letter to the Governor, he thought, scowling. They're not off the hook yet, none of us are. As if one coffin mattered when the whole world's falling apart, Russia teetering towards war again, Prussia licking her chops over the intestines of central Europe, the French with their militant, overblown pride, our Indian Empire and Asian colonies at risk because of misguided fools in Parliament, and us awaiting imminent Japanese liquidation.

On the surface the letter was innocuous. Decoded it read: *Urgently request all fleet and army reinforcements possible as I expect the Settlement to be attacked any day by Bakufu samurai legions and may have to abandon our base here.*

The Catholic church was candle-lit, the altar glinting, the congregation sparse and Father Leo was bringing the singsong litany of Mass to a close, his deep baritone voice melodious amidst the familiar perfume of incense that drifted over them—the service shorter than usual as a few had to catch the mail ship.

Angelique knelt at prayer in the front pew, Seratard beside her, André some rows behind, Vervene at the back with the rest of the Legation staff, a few traders, Eurasian Portuguese, and some officers and men from the French ships who had shore leave. The main body of French sailors had other services, earlier or later. Thankfully for all ships companies, there were no priests with the fleet—to have one aboard always considered bad luck, on any ship of any flag.

Father Leo bowed to the altar, prayed and then blessed the congregation. Angelique took a deep breath, leisurely finished her prayer, waiting for Seratard to move.

She had already been confessed. In the little box she had said, 'Forgive me, Father, for I have sinned.'

'What sins have you committed this week, my child?'

She had heard the barely disguised impatience to learn every thought and deed that had happened, this being the first time she had been to Confession since the troubles began. 'I forgot to ask the Blessed Mother for forgiveness in my prayers one night,' she said with perfect calm, continuing her pact, and the plan and words she had devised, 'and had many bad thoughts and dreams, and was afraid, and forgot I was in God's hands with never a need to fear.'

'Yes, and what else?'

A little smile settled, hearing the impatience. 'I sinned in that, though my marriage is legal in the sight of my husband's people and his law and his Church, there was no time for us to make it conform to the True Church.'

'But . . . but that . . . that, senhora, that is not . . . not of itself a sin, you were not responsible for that, he was taken from us. What . . . what other sins did you commit?'

She kept her nostrils closed as much as she could to the stench of garlic and stale wine and unwashed clothes, using a pomaded kerchief. 'I sinned in that I could not persuade Sir William to allow me to bury my husband as he wished and therefore I wished.'

'That . . . that in itself is not a sin, child. What else?'

'I sinned in that I could not persuade my husband to become Catholic before we married.'

'Nor is that a sin, senhora. What else?'

Now he was beginning to sound exasperated. As she expected. How odd I'm no longer petrified of him and can hear the nuances he seeks to hide. Is this another gift of God?

'Have you, did you commit sins of the flesh?'

Her eyes narrowed, the smile froze and she despised him even more, at the same time forgiving him some of it because of his magnanimity in blessing the other coffin. 'I have been a correct wife in accordance with the teachings of the Church.'

'Yes, but, but did you cohabit with him, not being prop—'

'I was properly married according to my husband's law and acted in accordance with the teachings of the True Church,' she said, adding with an even sharper edge, 'and now I would like absolution, Father.' This was contrary to accepted practice and she waited, holding her breath, ready to sweep out if he probed further against accepted practice.

'As . . . as you are leaving today, it is necessary to ensure, senhora, to give absolution th—'

'I am not leaving by mail ship, Father. Not today.'

'Oh, not leaving?' She heard the elation and relief. 'Then—then we can talk, my child, talk at length for the Glory of God. Oh, how wonderful are the ways of God.' He had given her absolution and a modest penance and she had left to join the service.

Having overcome that hurdle she enjoyed it. Her mind wandered but that was normal. Now she could relax and was pleased with herself. She had achieved what she had set out to achieve: Malcolm buried here, as she wished, Gornt launched, Hoag on his way, Tess neutralized—with the help of God.

God is on my side, I'm sure of it. *He* approves, I'm sure of it. Except for Malcolm, ah, Malcolm, my love, my love . . .

"May I escort you home, Angelique?" Seratard asked, interrupting her daydreams.

"Thank you, Monsieur," she said formally, "but I am not very good company and would rather stroll quietly by myself."

"There is a lot to discuss before you leave."

"Oh, I thought you would know already I'm not leaving with the mail ship—Dr. Hoag forbade it, which saddens me."

His smile broadened. "Magnificent! That is the best news I've heard in many a day. Would you care for dinner at the Legation tonight, just two or three of us—quietly?"

"Thank you but again, no. Perhaps the end of the week, if I feel better."

"Thursday or Friday, whenever you wish." Seratard kissed her hand, and she walked into the open air.

The wind had freshened again. She was glad for the veil that camouflaged her, no need to hide behind the front of her face. Those who passed greeted her sadly, Nettlesmith among them. "We will truly be sorry to see you go, Ma'am."

"Thank you, Mr. Nettlesmith, but I'm not going by the mail ship, not today." Again she saw the face light up the moment she said it and was amused. "Dr. Hoag has forbidden me to travel, which saddens me."

"Oh! Of course it would. Not going, eh! Oh! Well, yes, I can see that

. . . oh, will you excuse me, Ma'am?" He rushed for the Club. Within minutes the news would be around the Settlement and there would be no need to say it again. Down the praia she saw André. He was waiting for her. "Hello, André."

"I'm glad you're not going," he said simply.

"Ah. News travels fast."

"Good news. I need to talk privately."

"About money?"

"About money. How you've changed, Angelique."

"For the better, I hope. How are you, old friend?"

"Old." André was feeling drab today, and tired. He had seen Hinodeh last night and there had been shadows between them. And violence. While she was massaging him he had lifted up and reached into the neck of her kimono to kiss her breast, loving her to distraction, but she had jerked away and closed her kimono against him. 'You promise not to . . .' she had gasped, and his fury at himself for forgetting—any such trespass sent her into a pathetic, hangdog sorrow that would craze him further—turned into fury at her and he had snarled, 'Stop looking like that, *stoppit*! *Baka!*'

There were never any tears when he was there, just the constant, abject muttering, '*Gomen nasai*, Furansu-san, *gomen nasai gomen nasai gomen nasai*' on and on until the words maddened him and again he shouted, 'Shut up, for Christ's sake!' She had. And stayed kneeling, eyes downcast, hands in her lap, immobile except for an occasional tremble like a whipped dog.

He had wanted to apologize and hold her in his arms, his love unending, but that would not help him, only make him lose further face so he just got up sullenly and dressed and without a word left their home. Once he was out of the Yoshiwara and across the bridge he went down to the shore and kicked the nearest fishing boat and cursed it until he was spent. Then he sat on the cold pebbles, choked with frustration, knowing that she would be weeping and equally angry that she had not managed his mistake more cleverly, knowing that tomorrow they would begin again as though nothing had happened, but he was sure, not far below the sweet and gentle demeanor was a vast reservoir of hatred. For him.

"And why not?" he muttered.

"Why not what, André?" Angelique asked.

"Oh! Nothing, just wandering."

"Look, there's an empty seat. We can sit there and talk."

The bench faced the sea. The mail ship beckoned her attention and she wondered what would have happened if she had decided to go aboard. I'd only have gone into the Lioness's den earlier than necessary, she thought. No need to worry about that, no need to worry about anything—merely to ease into my new being, testing its limits, and wait. The smoke plume began trickling upwards. The mail ship was getting up steam. Only a few tenders remained at her gangway. "I'm not very good company, sorry," she said.

"Could you let me have some money?"

"I have only a little. How much do you need?"

"A thousand guineas."

"What on earth for?"

He took a deep breath. "Her name is Hinodeh," he said, and told her a story of falling in love and wanting her for himself and nothing about the real reason, his sickness. "It's difficult to tell everything, of course I can't, but I cannot live without that woman and the money is needed for her contract. I've got to have it. I must."

"There's no way I could find that amount, André," she said, genuinely shocked but moved. "What about Henri, surely he could provide you with a loan?"

"He's refused, and refused to advance me anything on my salary, I think he enjoys my dependence."

"If I was to talk to him an—"

"No, you mustn't, that would be the worst thing to do." He looked at her in a new way. "When you get your marriage settlement, I pray it's fast, I'll work to make it fast, I want you to lend it to me, a thousand."

"If I can, I will, André."

"Can you let me have some now? A hundred, that will keep the mama-san off my back for a week—she was the one who helped you," he added, driving in a nail.

She let that pass, well aware of the many ways he had helped her, or had promised never to mention any of them, her mind jumping forward to new conclusions: this Hinodeh is an added security for me. "I'll ask Jamie for an advance."

"There's the money Sir William said you could keep, two hundred and sixty-three guineas, wasn't it, from the safe."

"Yes, there's some of that left." She looked out to sea to avoid his eyes, their disturbing intentness, wondering how he knew and to mask her abhorrence of this different André with his underlying, searing edge of hysteria. Foolish to be like that, doesn't he realize our Fates are locked together? But then he is in love so I can forgive him. "I sent some home."

"I'm working on your behalf, Angelique, every day with Henri. The ward of the State, he's sure of it. Henri's important to your future, he and the Ambassador will be your champions in the coming fight, I guarantee it. You're wise to stay here and wait, it's safer, better," he said, and she remembered how, not so long ago, he had told her it was vital for her to go.

He was watching her, hard to see her clearly through the veil, remembering the signed affidavit he had deposited with his will in the British Minister's safe, not trusting Seratard—against any 'accident' happening to him. The affidavit that told about the Tokaidō assassin's lovemaking and the abortion—when and how it was achieved and the evidence buried—and about the death of the assassin. Then there was the second page of the letter her father had written her months ago that he had torn up in front of her but had put back together, the page that would damn any marriage settlement that Tess Struan might agree to when the screws were really turned on her—all of it to use, when necessary, Angelique his only passport to possession of Hinodeh and a comfortable future.

Raiko and Meikin and selling secrets and buying secrets? A pipe dream, he told himself bitterly. I've given them the whole campaign plan and what have I in return? Promises—and no chance to offset those against my other debt. "A hundred," he said, too tired and angry to say please.

She did not take her eyes off the sea. "How long will we have to wait? For Tess to act."

"It depends how Tess receives the news, or Hoag, what she does at the funeral. She will wait your thirty days—are you carrying or are you not—before deciding," he said in the same matter-of-fact voice, ramming back the past, wanting her dependent again. She looked back at him, glad for the veil. He thought her eyes were friendly—perhaps afraid, perhaps not. "Add ten days for that news to reach her. Ten to think, ten to send a message back. About two months, perhaps less."

"What will the message be?"

"Venomous." His own eyes slitted. "But I've a few ideas, plans. I can help to make you a rich woman. We have to wait, nothing to do for a while, just wait. Patience, Angelique. Patience and a little luck . . . I've ideas."

And so have I, André Blackmailer. Many. And plans. For you, Tess, and for the future.

Tenderly she leaned over and touched him. "I'm so glad you have a love to cherish. You're blessed," she said, meaning it. Then, as only a woman could, she put that tenderness aside forever, and her plans back in place. "The money will be waiting for you at six, André—I'm glad you're my friend."

"I'm glad too . . . thanks for the loan."

"So again we must be patient, both of us, and wait? That is what we must do, yes? A little luck and patience? I can be patient. A little luck and patience. Good. So be it."

He watched her walk away, straight and confident and, for all her splendid petiteness, somehow tall.

BOOK FIVE

51

YEDO

Thursday, 1st January 1863:

TORANAGA YOSHI HAD ARRIVED back in Yedo Castle from Kyōto eight days ago, tired and angry, the journey from Hamamatsu way station a forced march.

The lines in his face were etched deeper. Where men were afraid of him before, now they were petrified. His anger would turn on them like a lash. During the journey he had driven himself and them, sleeping only a few hours, demented by any delay, dissatisfied with the Inns, the baths and food and service and the future. Captain Abeh bore the brunt, all of them knowing it was only frustration and grief over the death of Koiko, the beloved.

Abeh had arranged her cremation, and that of Sumomo, and then they were in the saddle galloping the leagues, all aware such a gallant fighter deserved a courteous bow from the conqueror in front of the fire—particularly as the fighter was shishi and a woman who soon would be the subject of songs and legends, as would the blow that had sliced her in half. And Koiko the Lily too, she who threw herself in the way of the first shuriken and so had saved the life of their Lord, to whom he had then given the gift of painlessness.

But Yoshi, Guardian of the Heir, had said coldly, 'Their death poem is this':

> *From nothing into nothing,*
> *A corpse is a corpse,*
> *And nothing—*

Mine, yours, even theirs.
Did they exist? Do we exist?

Onwards, under the lash, then gaining the castle. But still no rest there, the castle and Yedo and the whole Kwanto in uproar over gai-jin preparations for war—precipitated by the *tairō*'s ultimatum, as he had expected.

"It was inevitable," Yoshi said at the meeting of the Elders he had immediately called for, adding, to give Anjo a way to extract himself, "You were given ill advice—remove the fool who suggested it and drafted the letter."

"It was the Emperor's command, and the Shōgun's, that all gai-jin be expelled," Anjo said angrily.

"Command? The Shōgunate commands, not an underage boy who mouths the words the Shōgunate puts into it—or the Emperor, who can only *request* us to do something!"

"As *tairō* I considered the ultimatum necessary."

"And again I ask, what do you propose we do when the fleet comes here?"

"They will not, we attack first," Anjo had said, then winced as a pain stabbed him, holding his side. "I have them surrounded, Yokohama is like a dead fish waiting for gutting. The attack force is almost ready."

"And their fleet?" he had asked, furious that all his advice had been discarded and once again they were in a trap of their own making. No point in reminding Anjo, and the others, of the plan he had meticulously set up to provide months of time for further delaying tactics against the gai-jin, while the Shōgunate gathered strength and more particularly dealt with the vital, pressing problem of smashing the hostile coalition of Tosa, Choshu and Satsuma that would destroy the Shōgunate if allowed to prosper.

"First we surprise Yokohama, burn it—I suggested it months ago," Toyama said, shaking with excitement. "Burn them!"

"And how do you sink the fleet?" Yoshi snarled. He had noticed Anjo's pain and was glad of it, remembering his pact with Ogama of Choshu that must be instituted quickly to keep that enemy off balance and neutralized.

Toyama said fiercely, "The gods will sink their ships, Yoshi-dono, like they did against Kublai Khan and his Mongols. This is the Land of the Gods, they will not fail us."

"And in case the gods are away, or sleeping," Anjo said, "we are going to send out fire ships—I have hundreds already under construction, hundreds. If the enemy break through this barrier to bombard Yedo, only peasants, tradesmen, artisans and parasitic merchants will die, our legions will be intact."

"Yes, they will be intact," Toyama said gleefully.

Anjo rushed on, "Once Yokohama is gone, the gai-jin fleet must sail away because they've no base where they can regroup. They must sail far away to their colonies in China, there will no longer be a foothold here. If they come back we'll . . ."

"When they come back," Yoshi had said.

"All right, Yoshi-dono, when they come back with more ships we will sink them in the Shimonoseki Straits, Ogama will, or elsewhere, for by that time we will have more cannon, fire ships, and we never allow them to land in force: they will never be able to land in force and set up a base, never again. No more Treaties to protect them! None. We close our land like before. That is what I plan," Anjo said triumphantly. "I have torn up the Treaties as the Emperor wants!"

"You are godlike, *tairō*, the gods will protect us with a Divine Wind," Zukumura chuckled, wiping saliva off his chin.

"The gods won't protect us from gai-jin shells," Yoshi said, "nor fire ships. If we lose Yedo we lose our Shōgunate citadel, then every daimyo in the land will join against us to carve up the spoils—led by Ogama of Choshu, Sanjiro of Satsuma and Yodo of Tosa. Without Yedo our Shōgunate is over, why can you not understand that?"

Anjo had twisted under another pain and flared, "I understand very well you think you are the Lord of the Land and the gods' gift to Nippon but you are not, you are not, you are under my orders and my command, I am *tairō*, I AM!"

"You are *tairō* and . . . but why are you in pain?" he asked with a pretense of concern—as though he had just noticed—wanting to stop the confrontation. "How long has this been going on? What does the doctor say?"

"Say? He . . ." Again Anjo sipped some of the bitter extract of herbs. The medicine allayed his pain hardly at all. The pains had been getting worse, with this new Chinese doctor useless like the others, so much so he was even considering a clandestine examination by the famous gai-jin doctor giant of Kanagawa. "Never mind my pain. *I know you.*"

Yoshi saw Anjo's hatred, knowing the hatred was because of his own youth and strength—little does the fool know how tired of life I am. "Can I—"

"You can do nothing. We will attack when I order the attack and that is the end of it! The meeting is over." Anjo stormed out. Now that he was *tairō*, Anjo ruled imperiously and treated all others with olympian disdain.

In a fury Yoshi prowled the castle like a caged tiger. After that first awful day he had compartmentalized Koiko and locked it tight. Even so from time to time she would peep out smiling. Angrily he would thrust her back—no way to find out now if she had really rushed forward to save his life, as Abeh assured him, no way to find out why she had employed a shishi assassin, Sumomo Fujahito, of course a false name but certainly one of Katsumata's acolytes.

And where is Katsumata now?

He had already issued orders to find him, wherever he was, and had put a large reward on his head, and orders to hunt down and destroy all shishi and their protectors. Then he had sent for Inejin, his spymaster.

The old man had limped in and bowed. "It seems, Sire, the gods guarded you like one of their own."

"By allowing a shishi assassin, shuriken-armed, to be in the inner sanctum of my courtesan," he exploded, "allowing my courtesan to be a traitor and part of the plot?"

Inejin shook his head, and said easily, "Perhaps not a traitor, Sire, nor part of a plot, merely a woman. As to the shishi, Sumomo, she simply exercised your fighting ability, which proved to be perfect—for which you were trained."

The singular strength of his old retainer sent his rage to China. "Not perfect," he said ruefully. "The cat clawed me, but the wound healed."

"Shall I drag Meikin, the mama-san, here, Sire?"

"Ah, the pivot. I have not forgotten her. Soon, not yet. You still watch her?"

"Like her second skin. You sent for me, Sire?"

"I want you to find Katsumata, alive if you can," he had said. "Did you remove the traitor ronin working for the gai-jin as I ordered? What was his name? Ori Ryoma, a Satsuma, yes, that's it."

"That man is dead, Sire, but it seems he was not the traitor. Gai-jin killed Ori some weeks ago. They shot him trying to break into one of their houses. The man supplying them with information, still, is a Choshu ronin named Hiraga."

Yoshi was startled. "He of the poster? The shishi who led those who murdered Utani?"

"Yes, Sire. For the moment I cannot remove him, he is under the protection of the Chief Ing'erish and stays close to their building. I have a spy in the village and can tell you more in a few days."

"Good. What else? All this talk of war?"

"I hope to have more news in a few days."

"Make it fewer than more," he said curtly, dismissing him. "When you have serious news come back."

Inejin won't fail me, he thought, sorry that he had been short-tempered. *Spies must be cherished like no others . . . on them depends your ability to move . . .* Ah, Sun-tzu, what a genius you were—but even my intimate knowledge of your precepts does not tell me what to do about the gai-jin, about that stupid boy and my archenemy, the Princess Yazu—both still gorging on the honeyed gruel served by Court sycophants obeying that dog, the Lord Chancellor. What would you do to destroy the enemies that surround me? Anjo, the Elders, the Court, Ogama, Sanjiro—the list endless. And impossible. And atop them all, the gai-jin.

Then he had remembered the invitation to go aboard the Furansu—French—warship. The coaling venture that his wife, Hosaki, had positioned in conjunction with the Gyokoyamas and the gai-jin prospector, made it easy for him to send Misamoto, his make-believe samurai, the fisherman interpreter, to make the arrangements. This had taken place yesterday.

He had slipped away from Yedo by oared galley to a sea rendezvous without fanfare, just beyond sight of land—with Abeh, twenty guards and Misamoto. The experience had been awesome. The size and power of the ship's engines, and cannon, the amount of powder and shot and coal carried, and the stories they told, lies or truths he could not yet tell about the extent of their Furansu Empire, its wealth and power, the leagues of travel such a ship could cover, numbers of warships and cannon, and size of their armies, as they stated them, were beyond belief. Misamoto interpreted, with the interpreter who called himself Andreh Furansu-san. Though they had their own language this meeting was conducted mostly in English.

A lot of what he was told, Yoshi had not understood. The words used were strange and much time was spent explaining miles and yards and powder and pitch and pistons, paddle steamers against screw power, breech blocks and flintlocks, factories and firepower.

Yet all of it was illuminating and certain pieces of information of major importance: the vital necessity of coaling facilities and safe harbors, *without which steamer warships were so many hulks*—unable to carry all the coal needed for the voyage out, for naval operations, and then the voyage back. And second, as he had witnessed at the Council meeting with gai-jin in Yedo Castle and found it difficult to believe the true extent, any mention of Ing'erish gai-jin brought sneers to Furansu gai-jin faces, who had no hesitation in showing the extent of their hatred.

This delighted him and enhanced what Misamoto had said earlier, that Ing'erish were hated by nearly every other nation on earth because they had the biggest Empire, they were the strongest and wealthiest nation, with the greatest, most modern fleets, the most powerful, disciplined and best-equipped armies, as well as enjoying their gains by producing more than half of the world's goods. With, best of all, an impregnable island redoubt to guard it all.

Of course they are hated. Like we Toranagas are hated. And therefore, he thought with an ache in his bowels for his past mistake, these Ing'erish gai-jin are the ones to be fawned on, to befriend, and handle with the most exquisite care. Best fleets? And arms? How could I tempt them into building me a fleet? Providing me with one? Would coal pay for it?

"Misamoto, say to them that I would like to learn more about these marvelous Furansu devices," he said blandly, "and yes, I would like friends amongst gai-jin. I am not opposed to trade— perhaps I could arrange my coal concession to go to the Furansu and not the Ing'erish."

This caught their immediate interest. At this time they were below decks in the largest cabin in the stern, which he found cramped and foul-smelling, with odors of oil and coal smoke and human waste, with a fine coating of coal dust everywhere. They sat around a long table, half a dozen officers in gold-braided uniforms and their leader, Seratard—*Serata* as it was correctly pronounced—in the center. Abeh and half his guards were at his back, the rest on deck.

The moment he had seen Seratard and heard his name he liked him immediately—totally different from the tall, sour-faced Ing'erish High Leader with the unpronounceable name. Serata, like Furansu-san Andreh, were easily pronounceable. In fact the names were Japanese. Serata was a miraculous omen.

Serata was the name of his family's ancestral village in which their ancestor, Yoshi-shigeh Serata-noh Minowara, had settled in the twelfth century. In the thirteenth, the warrior daimyo Yoshi-sada Serata raised an army against his overlords, the Hojo, obliterated them and captured their capital Kamakura and made it his own. Since then his direct descendants, the Yoshi noh Toranaga noh Serata, still ruled Kamakura—Shōgun Yoshi Toranaga being buried there in his great mausoleum.

"So we are related," he had joked, after explaining the coincidence to Seratard. Seratard had laughed and, with the others who chattered like so many monkeys in outlandish uniforms, then had explained that his own family was an ancient one in Furansuland too, but in no way as illustrious.

"My Master," Andreh said with a bow, "my Master, he greatly honored be friend and gai-jin part of your great family, Sire."

"Tell him that I consider his name a good sign," he had said, noting this man seemed much more than just an interpreter.

"My Master thanks and says what Ing'erish promise, Furansu promise better."

Misamoto said, obsequiously, "Lord, he means they will make a better deal—money arrangement. The Furansu make cannon as well as Ing'erish, though not as many."

"Tell them I will consider a proposal to give them the coal concession. They must tell me how many guns or cannons, with powder and shot, and when I can have them, for how much coal. And I want a steamer, a steamship with officers to train my officers and sailors. In fact," he added innocently, "perhaps I could grant Furansus the sole right to build, sell and train a navy. Of course, I would pay. If reasonable."

He saw Misamoto's eyes widen, but before Misamoto had time to begin, the gai-jin Andreh who had been listening equally carefully said, "My Master sure King of Furansuland, greatly honor assist Lord Yoshi Toranaga in ships." Fascinated, he watched Andreh turn to Leader Serata and begin talking, the naval officers listening and nodding, quickly becoming as excited. Astonishing how easy to manipulate these men with trade and the future promise of money, he had thought. If the Furansus react so quickly, surely the Ing'erish leader will do so also. Two fish fighting for the same hook is better than one.

They had talked of other matters, not enough time to cover them all, but he learned enough to want to learn more. One detail Andreh Furansu-san had mentioned had rocked him. They had been discussing modern medical knowledge, and how easy it would be to train and equip a hospital: "Chief Medicine Doctor in Kanagawa good, Sire. Hear *Tairō* Anjo sick. Hear maybe *tairō* see Chief Doctor-sama."

"When and where is this meeting to take place?"

"My Master say: not sure if arranged yet, Sire. Perhaps Chief Medicine Doctor help *tairō*."

"If a meeting is arranged, tell me. Tell Serata also that a hospital is an interesting possibility."

He decided to let it go at that. For the moment. But that was another piece of information that Misamoto had better forget. How can I get a personal interpreter I can trust? I must have one. Perhaps I should train Misamoto, he is my running dog, dependent and in my grasp. So far he has been obedient. Certainly he handled the prospectors well. Pity he was away, detailing progress to Hosaki, when they fought—like wild beasts, the samurai reported, how apt! Had Misamoto been at the mine, perhaps he could have stopped them. Not that it matters, one dead is one less to worry about, and surely the survivor is not long for this world. Coal! So we have an abundance of coal, Hosaki says, and that for these gai-jin coal is as good as gold.

Deliberately, he changed tack. "Ask Serata-san why gai-jin fire cannon and rifles and send warships up and down to disturb the peace of this Land of the Gods? Do they prepare for war?"

There was a silence. The mood reversed.

"My Master say, no prepare war." He saw Andreh gai-jin was translating meticulously. "Prepare defend only. So sorry, *tairō* say all gai-jin must leave."

"Why not leave for a month or two and then return?" He laughed inwardly, seeing the consternation this generated.

"My Master says, Treaty signed by Lord Shōgun and made true by Bakufu leader *Tairō* Ii, and Most High Emperor, allow us Yokohama, Kanagawa, Kobe soon. Treaty is good treaty for Nippon, gai-jin. *Tairō* Anjo, so sorry, wrong to be angry."

"Many daimyos do not think so. *Tairō* Anjo is the leader. You should do what he orders. This is our land."

"My Master says Furansu want help Nippon be great nation in world . . . as here too."

"Say to Serata-sama, the *tairō* is the leader, what he says is to be obeyed, though sometimes," he said delicately, "even the *tairō* may change if given the correct advice." He saw this register. "So sorry, we have explained a dozen times that Satsuma matters may only be resolved by Sanjiro, the Satsuma daimyo."

"My Master say hope someone can give correct advice to *tairō*. Satsuma daimyo must say sorry, pay indemnity agreed in Yedo meeting, punish killer openly."

He had nodded as if gravely concerned. Abruptly, he got up to more consternation—no point in further talk with these underlings who were valuable in other ways, the Ing'erish Leader must be approached.

This suited him perfectly. And while he kept his demeanor haughty and stern, he showed some friendliness and agreed, with pretended reluctance, to another meeting. "Misamoto, tell them we can meet in ten days, in Yedo. They may come to Yedo for a private meeting."

Just as he was leaving the warship, the gai-jin Andreh said, "My Master wish you Good New Year." Dumbfounded, he learned that the gai-jin world had its own calendar, totally different from the Japanese—and Chinese—lunar calender that had been the way to count the days and the months and years since the beginning of time.

"The first day of our year, Serata-sama," Misamoto explained, "is between 16th day of First Month and 22nd day of Second Month depending on the moon. This year, the Year of the Dog, First Day, which begins our season of festivals, is the 18th of First Month. That's when all China says Kung Hay Fat Choy."

All the way back to Yedo in the galley Yoshi had wondered about these men. Mostly he was appalled—gai-jin were like monsters in the shape of men who had come from the stars, their ideas and attitudes the wrong side of yin and yang.

Yet for us to survive as a nation, Nippon has to have bigger ships and guns and more power to protect ourselves from this alien evil. And for now, he thought, feeling nauseated, the Shōgunate must make an accommodation with them.

They will never go away, not all of them, of their own accord. If not these, others will come to steal our heritage, Chinese or Mongols or Hairies from the Siber Ice lands who eye us like slavering dogs from ports stolen from China. And always the Ing'erish will be around us. What to do about them?

That was yesterday. Last night and in this dawn he had been deep in thought, hardly eating, hardly sleeping, conscious too of the emptiness of his bed and of his life—the seams of Koiko's compartment leaking—like Anjo's, and Ogama's and the others. Many times during the journey here from Kyōto he had thought of the clean sword, the cleanliness and peace of death, the minute and the hour and the day chosen with godlike power—to choose your own death time made you a god: from nothing into nothing. No more sorrow grinding you to petals of pain.

So easy.

The first ray of dawn came through the shutters, touching his short sword. It was beside the bed with his long sword, both within perfect reach, his rifle there as well, loaded, the one he had named Nori. The short sword was an heirloom made by the Master Swordsmith Masumara and once possessed by Shōgun Toranaga. He saw the old used scabbard and through it, in his mind, the perfection of the blade. His hand stretched out, caressing the leather, then moved up to the hilt to rest on the small toggle secured to it. His father had instructed their swordsmith to attach it before presenting the sword to him, formally, in front of their inner circle of retainers. Yoshi was fifteen then and had killed his first man, a ronin who had run amok near his family castle, Eagle's Nest.

'This is to remind you of your oath, my son: that you will carry this blade with honor, that you will use only this blade to commit seppuku, that you will only commit seppuku to avoid capture on a battlefield, or if the Shōgun orders it and the Council of Elders confirms the order unanimously. All other reasons are insufficient while the Shōgunate is in jeopardy.'

A terrible sentence, he thought, and lay back on his bed, safe for the moment in this room high up in his castle quarters where he had had so much pleasure. His eyes went back to the short sword. Today his need was very great. In his imagination he had rehearsed the act so many times that it would be so smooth and kind and releasing. Soon Anjo will send men to arrest me and that will be my excuse . . .

His sharp ears heard footsteps. Marching feet. His hands took up the short sword and the long sword and he was in defend-attack position.

"Sire?"

He recognized Abeh's voice. That did not mean safety, Abeh could have a knife at his throat or Abeh could be a traitor—after Koiko everyone was suspect. "What is it?"

"The man Inejin begs to see you."

"Have you searched him?"

"Seriously."

Yoshi used the rope he had had rigged, allowing him to slide back the bolt on the reinforced door without moving.

Inejin, Abeh and four samurai waited there. He relaxed. "Come in, Inejin." Abeh and the others of his personal guard started to follow. "There's no need, but stay within calling."

His spymaster came in and closed the door, noticed the bolt arrangement but did not comment, and knelt ten paces away.

"You've found Katsumata?"

"He will be in Yedo within three days, Sire. His first place of calling will be the House of Wisteria."

"That den of scorpions?" Yoshi had not closed the trap on mama-san Meikin to learn the real extent of the plot against him before taking vengeance—vengeance best savored calmly. And he did not yet feel calm. "Could we take him alive?"

Inejin smiled strangely. "I doubt it, but may I tell the story in my own way, Sire?" He settled his aching knee more comfortably. "First about the gai-jin: a development hoped for and encouraged since the beginning has happened. A gai-jin spy has offered their battle plans for money."

His attention soared. "Not false ones?"

"I do not know, Sire, but it was whispered they contained troop and ship movements. The price was modest, even so the Bakufu official did not buy at once and began to haggle and the seller became frightened. With Anjo at the head . . ." The cracked leather lips twisted with disgust at the name. "*He's baka, unworthy!*—if the head is rotten the body is worse."

"I agree. Stupid."

Inejin nodded. "They forgot Sun-tzu again, Sire: *To remain in ignorance of the enemy's condition, begrudging the outlay of a few hundred ounces of silver is the height of inhumanity.* Fortunately an informant whispered about it to me." Inejin took a scroll from his sleeve and put it on the table. Yoshi sighed, pleased. *"So ka!"*

"With the help of my informant, I bought it for you, a gift, Sire. Also at great risk to my informant, I substituted a false scroll the Bakufu eventually will buy cheaply."

Yoshi did not touch the scroll, only looked at it with anticipation. "Please allow me to reimburse you," he said. Inejin covered his vast relief, for he had had to pledge their Inn to the Gyokoyama to obtain the money. "See my cashier today. Is the information to be trusted?"

Inejin shrugged. Both knew another of Sun-tzu's precepts: *An inside spy is the most dangerous, one who sells secrets for money. It takes a man of genius to penetrate such.* "My informant swears that the information is to be trusted and also the spy."

"And it says?"

"The gai-jin plan is frighteningly simple. On Battle Day, ten days after their ultimatum is delivered—if not complied with—their whole fleet moves against Yedo. The first day the attack area is farthest from the coast, Sire, the extreme range of their heaviest cannon, designed to pulverize all bridges and roads leading out of Yedo—these are pinpointed, more knowledge given them no doubt by the traitor Hiraga. That night, by the light of the fires they have begun, they bombard the castle. The next day the coastal areas are decimated. On the third day they will land a thousand rifle soldiers and drive for the castle gates.

There they will mount siege mortars and smash the gates and bridges and as much of the castle as they can. On the fifth day they retreat and sail away."

"To Yokohama?"

"No, Sire. The plan says they will evacuate all gai-jin the day before Battle Day and retreat to Hong Kong until the spring. Then they will come back in force. The cost of the war—as with their Chinese wars, and is their custom—will be doubled, and demanded as reparations from the Shōgunate and the Emperor *as well as complete access to all Nippon, including Kyōto* and an island ceded in perpetuity, to cease hostilities."

Yoshi felt a chill. If these barbarians could humble all China, Mother of the World, eventually they would humble us, even us. *Complete access?* "This ultimatum? What further impertinence is this?"

"It's not in the scroll, Sire, but the spy promised details, as well as the Battle Date and any changes."

"Whatever the cost, buy them—if true these could make a difference in the outcome."

"Possibly, Sire. Part of the information is about gai-jin counter-measures. Against our fire ships."

"But Anjo told me they are secret!"

"It's not secret to them. The Bakufu is a rice sieve for the interested, as well as corrupt, Sire."

"Names, Inejin, and I'll spike them."

"Begin today, Sire. Begin at the top."

"That's treason."

"But the truth, Sire. You enjoy truths, not lies, unlike any leader I have ever known." Inejin moved his knees, the ache intolerable. "The matter of this spy is complicated, Sire. It was Meikin who told me about him . . ." Yoshi grunted. "Yes, I agree. But Meikin told me, Meikin who diverted the intermediary from the Bakufu to me, Meikin who will substitute the false document, at great danger, for she must attest to its truth, Meikin who desperately wishes to prove her loyalty to you."

"Loyalty? When her House is a sanctuary for shishi, a meeting place for Katsumata, a training bed for traitors?"

"Meikin swears the Lady was never part of a plot against you, never. Nor was she."

"What else can she say—the maid was, eh?"

"Perhaps she speaks the truth, perhaps not, but perhaps, because of her grief, she now sees the error of her past, Sire. A converted spy can be most valuable."

"Katsumata's head would make me more sure. If caught alive, more so."

Inejin laughed and bent forward and dropped his voice. "I suggested she should quickly provide you with details about the traitor Hiraga before you request his head."

"And hers."

"A woman's head on a spike is not a pretty thing, Sire, old or young. That is an ancient truth. Better to leave it on her shoulders and use the venom, wisdom, cunning or simple rottenness that such a woman possesses to your advantage."

"How?"

"First by giving you Katsumata. Hiraga is a more complex problem. She says he is the intimate of an important Ing'erish official close to the Ing'erish Leader, named Taira."

Yoshi frowned. Another omen? Taira was another Japanese name of significance, an ancient regal family related to the Yoshi Serata line. "So?"

"This Taira is an official, an interpreter-in-training. His Japanese is already very good—the Ing'erish must have a school like the one you proposed and the Bakufu 'consider.' "

"Consider, eh? Taira? Is he an ugly young man, tall with blue eyes, huge nose and long hair like rice straw?"

"Yes, yes, that would be him."

"I remember him from the meeting of Elders. Go on."

"Meikin has heard his grasp of our language improves rapidly, helped by a whore called Fujiko, but more because of this Hiraga, who has cut his hair in gai-jin style, wears gai-jin clothes." The old man hesitated, loving the telling of secrets. "It seems this Hiraga is the grandson of an important Choshu shoya who was permitted to purchase goshi status for his sons, one of whom, this Hiraga's father, is now hirazamurai. Hiraga was chosen to join a secret Choshu school where, as an exceptional student, he learned Ing'erish." He suppressed a smile, seeing his Lord's face.

"Then the spy is not gai-jin, but this Hiraga?"

"No, Sire, but Hiraga could be a serious secondary source of intelligence. If he could be tapped."

"A shishi helping us?" Yoshi scoffed. "Impossible."

"Your meeting yesterday, aboard the Furansu ship. It was profitable, Sire?"

"It was interesting." Impossible to keep those ventures secret. He was glad Inejin was so well informed so quickly. Abeh and half a dozen of his men had been present at the meeting. Who had spoken in their cups? It didn't matter. It was to be expected. Nothing compromising was said by him.

"Abeh!" he called out.

"Sire?"

"Send a maid with tea and saké." He said nothing more until it had been served and accepted gratefully by Inejin, sifting the information, sorting it and coming up with new questions and answers. "What do you propose?"

"It would not be for me to propose what you have already surely decided, Sire. But it did occur to me, when and if the Ing'erish Leader sends his ultimatum, you alone would be the perfect person to mediate—alone, Sire."

"Ah! And then?"

"Amongst other things you could ask to see this Hiraga. You could weigh him, perhaps persuade him to be on your side. Turn him to your advantage. The timing could be perfect."

"That could be possible, Inejin," he said, already having discarded that for a much better thought, one that fitted the plan he had discussed with Ogama in Kyōto, and his own need to begin the grand design. "Or an example might be made of this Hiraga. Catch Katsumata, he's the head of the shishi snake—if Meikin is the means to deliver him alive, so much the better for her."

A few miles away on the Tokaidō Road, at the Hodogaya way station, Katsumata scrutinized the crowds from a Teahouse window. "Be patient, Takeda," he said, "Hiraga is not due till midmorning. Be patient."

"I hate this place," Takeda said. The village was in open country with few places to hide and barely three miles from the Yokohama Settlement. They were in the Teahouse of the First Moon, the same that Katsumata and daimyo Sanjiro had stayed at after Ori and Shorin had attacked the gai-jin on the Tokaidō. "And if he does not arrive?" The youth scratched his head irritably, neither his chin nor his pate shaven since their escape from Kyōto and now covered with stubbled hair.

"He will arrive, if not today, tomorrow. I must see him."

The two men had been hiding here for a week. Their journey from Kyōto had been arduous, with many narrow escapes. "Sensei, I do not like this place or the change of plan. We should be in Yedo if we're to carry on the fight, or perhaps we should turn around and go home."

"If you want to go on, go. If you want to walk back to Choshu, go," Katsumata said. "The next time you complain you are ordered to leave!"

Takeda apologized at once, adding, "It's just that we lost so many men in Kyōto, we do not even know how shishi have fared in Yedo. So sorry, yes, but I keep thinking we should have gone home like those who survived, me to Choshu, you to Satsuma, to regroup later."

"Hodogaya's perfect for us and this Inn is safe." Warned that Yoshi had put a heavy price on his head, Katsumata had decided to be prudent and not continue. "Tomorrow or the next day we'll go on," he said, glad for the youth's value as a shield to his back. "First Hiraga."

It had been difficult and dangerous to contact him. Few people here had access through the Yokohama barriers, or to the gai-jin Yoshiwara. New passes were continually being issued, new passwords. Enforcer patrols wandered at large. Covert pockets of samurai swarmed around Yokohama, almost cutting it off from the rest of the land.

Then three days ago Katsumata had found a maid whose sister was a midwife who went to the Yoshiwara from time to time. For a golden oban the midwife agreed to carry a message to the mama-san at the House of the Three Carp.

"Takeda, stay here and keep watch. Wait patiently."

Katsumata went down into the garden and strode through the front gates onto the Tokaidō, bustling with morning travellers, palanquins, porters, soothsayers, scribes, samurai, and some ponies carrying women or ridden by samurai. Talking, shouting, screeching. The morning was cold and everyone wore padded jackets and warm head scarves or hats. A few samurai eyed Katsumata but not rudely. The way he walked, the filthy thatch of hair and beard, the long sword in a back scabbard, another in his belt, shouted caution to the inquisitive. Clearly he was a ronin of some kind and to be avoided.

On the outskirts of the village, inside the well-guarded barrier, where he had a good field of view towards the sea and Yokohama, he sat on a bench at a roadside eating stall.

"Tea, and make it fresh and see that it's hot."

The frightened stall owner rushed to obey.

At the Settlement, a group of mounted traders clattered over the bridge, raised their hats politely or saluted the North Gate guards with their riding crops in return for perfunctory bows. Other traders, tradesmen, soldiers, sailors, Drunk Town riffraff were on foot, all of them on a holiday morning outing. Today was New Year's Day. Horseraces were scheduled for this afternoon and then, later, an interservice football match. It was cold though fine, the wind slight but sufficient to take most of the smell of winter and decaying seaweed and human waste further inland.

One of the riders was Jamie McFay. Close beside him was Hiraga, a scarf covering most of his face, his riding cap down over his eyes, his riding clothes well cut. This outing was not approved or even known to Tyrer or Sir William, the gift in return for interpreting between Jamie and the shoya, and also for providing him with business information.

Yesterday Hiraga had said, 'I answer more question during ride, Jami-sama. Need go, to go Hodogaya, meet cousin. P'rease?'

'Why not, Nakama, old chap?' McFay had not visited the village for months though it was within the agreed area of the Settlement and was glad for the excuse. Few traders ventured that far now without military escort, Canterbury's murder and Malcolm Struan's fate never far from all their thoughts.

Today McFay was feeling good. In the last mail a statement from his bankers in Edinburgh had led him to discover he was in better shape than he had thought, more than enough to start on his own in a small way. The Noble House was in good hands and that pleased him. Struan's new manager, Albert MacStruan, had arrived from Shanghai. He had met him in Hong Kong three years ago when MacStruan had first joined the company. Six months training in Hong Kong under Culum Struan, then to Shanghai where he had quickly become their Deputy Director.

'Welcome to Yokohama,' Jamie had said, meaning it, liking him though knowing little about him except he was good at his job and his branch of the clan was black Highlander—a Scots and Spanish bloodline from one of the thousands of Spaniards of the Armada who had been shipwrecked in Scotland and Ireland and survived, but never to return.

Here he would be taken as Eurasian though no one challenged him. Legend whispered that he was another of Dirk Struan's clandestine, illegitimate children whom Dirk had secretly sent home to Scotland with a stepbrother, Frederick MacStruan, both heavily endowed by him, shortly before he died.

'Dreadfully sorry about seeing you under these rotten circumstances, old chap.' MacStruan's accent was patrician, Eton and Oxford University, with a trace of Scots. He was twenty-six, a chunky, darkhaired man, with golden skin, high cheekbones, dark sloe eyes. Jamie had never asked him about the legend, nor had MacStruan volunteered anything. When Jamie had first arrived in Hong Kong, almost twenty years ago, it had been made clear to him by Culum Struan, then tai-pan, that here you don't ask questions, especially about the Struans—'We've too many secrets, too many black deeds to forget, perhaps.'

'Everything's in order, and don't worry about me, Mr. MacStruan,' Jamie had said. 'I'm ready for a change.' And though now no longer formally with the Noble House, he was still helping him, bringing him up-to-date on projects and deals, introducing him, with Vargas, to their Japanese suppliers. The books were in good order, the coaling venture with Johnny Cornishman had begun perfectly and should be highly profitable, the quality of the coal first rate, and further arrangements made to fill a barge a week for the next three months as a trial period.

Generously, MacStruan had given him a twenty percent share of the profit for the first year, and then approval to deal on his own account with Cornishman: '. . . should that little bounder still be alive,' he had said with a laugh.

Thanks to Hiraga, Jamie's secret dealings with the shoya had blos-somed and the first company formed in principle: I.S.K. Trading—*Ichi Stoku Kompeni*—the shoya's wife considering it prudent not to use their own name. The stock was split into a hundred parts: the shoya had forty, McFay forty, Ryoshi's wife fifteen, and Nakama—Hiraga—five.

Last week he had registered his own trading company, tomorrow he was open for business in temporary offices in the same building that housed Nettlesmith's *Guardian*. For a week now, Ryoshi's eldest son, shy, nervous and nineteen, reported for work at 7:00 A.M. daily and left at 9:00 P.M., there to learn everything. Particularly English. And in the last mail, an unexpected three-month severance pay arrived with a polite note from Tess Struan thanking him for his services. Three months isn't bad for nineteen years, he thought with grim amusement.

No word yet from Hong Kong, too early though *Prancing Cloud* would have arrived ten days or more ago, Hoag about a week. Four or five more days at the earliest to hear anything, perhaps longer, a huge storm rumored to be in the south China seas might delay that even further. No point in trying to forecast times and weather.

One day we'll have a telegraph to Hong Kong, and one day, perhaps, the wire will go all the way to London. My God, what a fantastic boon to everyone to be able to get a message to Hong Kong and a reply back in a few days—and to London and back in what, say twelve to sixteen days—instead of four months! Won't be in my time but I bet the wire reaches Hong Kong in another ten to fifteen years. Hooray for Nakama and my partner Ryoshi, hooray for my new company, McFay Trading. And hooray for Angelique.

Notwithstanding deep mourning, on Christmas Day she had agreed to join the dinner he gave for Albert MacStruan to which Sir William, Seratard, André and most of the Ministers had come. It had been a quiet success. Though she had none of her previous gaiety, and was little like her former self, she had been gracious and sweet and everyone remarked how even more beautiful she had become in her new maturity. Tonight there was to be a grand soiree at the French Legation to which they were invited. André would be playing. It was doubtful she would dance—betting was ten to one against. On whether or not she was carrying, betting was still evens. Hong Kong no one mentioned. Since their sea adventure and her successful finesse of Sir William, they had become firm friends and dined privately most evenings.

Hooray for the New Year, which will be marvelous!

In spite of his good humor a twinge went through him. Actual business was dicey, civil war around Shanghai brewing again, plague in Macao, the American civil war dreadful, famine in Ireland, rumors of famine here, riots in the British Isles over unemployment and factory wages. Then there's Tess Struan.

Damn it, I promised myself not to worry about her from January 1st, 1863, onwards! Or about Maureen . . .

To escape his anxiety he used his spurs. At once Hiraga did likewise, both men riding well. This was Hiraga's first ride in a long time, his first opportunity to move semi-freely outside the Settlement. He drew alongside Jamie, then went ahead. Soon they were happily galloping. Soon too they were alone, the others having turned off for the racecourse. They slackened pace, enjoying the day.

Ahead they could see the twisting Tokaidō, broken here and there with rivers in flood and fords, porters either side waiting to ferry or carry waiting goods and people over the waters. Southwards was Hodogaya. Its barriers were open. In the good old days before the murders, during spring and fall, traders would visit the village for saké and beer, taking their own picnic meals with them, laughing and flirting with the coveys of maids who would seek to drag them into their bars or restaurants. They were not welcome in the many brothels.

"Hey, Nakama, where are you meeting your cousin?" Jamie asked, reining in on the outskirts, not far from the barrier, more than conscious of the travellers' hostility. But not worried. He was armed, openly, with a shoulder-holstered revolver—Hiraga was not, so he thought.

"I 'rook for him. Best I go 'rone other side barrier, Jami-sama," Hiraga said. He had been overjoyed to get Katsumata's message, at the same time filled with misgivings: it was dangerous to leave the protection of Sir William and Tyrer. But he had to have news of Sumomo, and the others, and find out what had really happened in Kyōto, and what was the new shishi plan. Daily the shoya had shaken his head, 'So sorry, Otami-sama, I've no news yet about Katsumata or Takeda—nor about the girl Sumomo, or Koiko. Lord Yoshi remains in Yedo Castle. The moment I have news . . .'

Still well muffled, Hiraga motioned Jamie to lead. "P'rease, then I find good p'race for you to wait."

The barrier guards watched them suspiciously, bowing slightly and accepting their salutes. Hiraga winced, seeing a poster of his likeness attached to a wall. Jamie did not notice it and Hiraga doubted if he, or others, would recognize him with his European haircut and mustache.

Hiraga stopped at the first Inn. Using poor Japanese and imitating the gruffness of other traders, Hiraga found a table in the garden and ordered tea and saké and beer, some Japanese foods and told the maid to make sure they were not disturbed and she would get a good tip. The maid kept her eyes down but Hiraga was sure that she had seen his eyes and knew him to be Japanese.

"Jami-sama, I back in few minutes," Hiraga said.

"Don't be long, old chap."

"Yes, Jami-sama."

Hiraga sauntered out onto the roadway, heading toward the far barrier. The general hostility and ill manners infuriated him, a few belligerent samurai and some travellers forcing him to step aside and let them pass. At the same time he enjoyed the fact that everyone took him for gai-jin, and his scrutiny of every eating place and bar as rude gai-jin curiosity. Katsumata's coded message had said, 'Come to Hodogaya, any morning over the next three days. I'll find you.'

Feeling conspicuous, as indeed he was, he walked past people loitering, or at benches and tables or hunched over braziers who glared insolently at him. Then he heard the low, signal whistle. He was too well-trained to acknowledge it or turn around. It seemed to come from his left side. With pretended tiredness he chose a bench well away from the street at the nearest eating house and ordered a beer. The maid brought it quickly. Nearby, peasants stooping over and slurping bowls of morning rice gruel and hot saké eased away as though he had plague.

"Do not turn around yet," he heard Katsumata say quietly. "I did not recognize you, your disguise is perfect."

"Yours must be too, Sensei," he said as softly, hardly moving his lips. "Twice I scrutinized this place carefully."

The low, well-known and admired laugh. "Drop something and when you pick it up, look around briefly."

Hiraga obeyed and when, momentarily, he saw the only man within hearing, a wild-looking, bearded, venomous ronin with the filthy thatch of hair glaring at him, he turned his back once more. "Eeee, Sensei!"

"No more 'Sensei.' There is little time, Hodogaya crawls with Enforcers and spies. Where can we meet safely?"

"Our Yoshiwara—the House of the Three Carp."

"I'll be there in two or three days—it is vital to create an incident with the gai-jin, quickly. Think about it."

"What sort of incident?"

"A serious one."

"Very well," Hiraga said. "I was relieved to hear from you—we had no idea you were coming here. There have been wild rumors about fighting in Kyōto—Akimoto is with me but we are on our own and we lost many shishi in our Yedo attacks. There is much to tell about Yedo and the gai-jin. Quickly, what happened in Kyōto? Sumomo, how is she?"

"Kyōto was bad. Before leaving I assigned Sumomo to Koiko, who was returning here with Yoshi, to spy on him to find out who was betraying us—must be one of our men—too good an opportunity to miss and it got her out of Kyōto safely," Katsumata said, his eyes constantly raking; the other men in this eating place, even though they were not near, avoided looking at him. "We mounted two attacks on Yoshi, both failed, our safe house was betrayed, Ogama and Yoshi working together ambushed us. We—"

"Eeee," Hiraga murmured, gravely concerned. "They have become allies?"

"For the moment. We lost many leaders and men, I'll give you particulars later but we—Sumomo, Takeda, I and some others—fought our way out. I'm glad to see you, Hiraga. Leave now."

"Wait. Sumomo, I ordered her back to Choshu."

"She brought me valuable information about the situation here and about Shorin and Ori. I suggested she continue on to Choshu but she wanted to stay, thinking she might help you. How is Ori?"

"Dead." He heard Katsumata curse—Ori had been his favorite pupil. "The gai-jin shot him trying to break into one of their houses," he said hastily, his nervousness increasing. "There's a rumor there was a shishi attack on Yoshi at Hamamatsu, that Koiko was killed in the melee, a shishi also. Who was he?"

"Not he, she. So sorry, it was Sumomo." Color drained from Hiraga's face. "Koiko betrayed her, the whore betrayed her to Yoshi and so betrayed *sonno-joi* and us. But she died with Sumomo's shuriken in her chest."

"How did Sumomo die?"

"As a shishi, she will be remembered forever. She fought Yoshi, with shuriken and long sword and almost killed him. That was her mission—if she was betrayed."

So Sumomo had a mission, Hiraga thought with sudden insight, his whole being a volcano—*you expected her to be betrayed,* and even so, sent her into the pit. There was a tightness in his throat. He forced himself to ask the essential question: "How did they bury her? Was it with honor?"

If Toranaga Yoshi had not honored her after fighting and dying bravely then he would hunt him to the exclusion of all else, until one or the other of them was dead. Hiraga was leader of Choshu shishi, the strongest contingent. Sumomo, though from Satsuma, had declared her allegiance to him and to Choshu. "Please, I must know, was it with honor?"

Still no answer. He glanced around. Katsumata had vanished. Hiraga's shock was open. The other customers stared at him silently. To one side a group of samurai stood watching him. The hackles on his neck rose. He threw a few coins on the table and, his hand on his concealed derringer, went back the way he had come.

That afternoon, throughout Yedo Castle there was an air of premonition. Yoshi was hurrying after the Chinese doctor along a corridor, Abeh and four samurai guards followed. The doctor, tall and very thin, wore a long gown and his grey hair in a queue. Up some stairs and along another corridor and then the doctor stopped. Hostile guards stood in the way, hands on their swords, all their eyes on Yoshi and his men.

"So sorry, Lord Yoshi," the officer said, "the *tairō*'s orders are that no one should pass."

"And my orders," the doctor said, his fear giving him false courage, "were to fetch Lord Yoshi."

"Lord Yoshi, you may pass," the officer said grimly. "So sorry, your men may not."

Though heavily outnumbered, Abeh and his men went for their swords. "Stop," Yoshi said calmly. "Wait here, Abeh."

Abeh was sick with worry, adrenaline pumping, dreadfully aware of rumors in the castle that his master was about to be arrested, rumors that Yoshi scoffed at. "Please excuse me, Sire, but this may be a trap." The opposing samurai stiffened at the insult.

"If it is you may kill all these men," Yoshi said with a laugh. No one else laughed. He motioned the doctor onwards having decided that if they attempted to disarm him they might as well fight and die now.

They let him through unmolested. The doctor opened the far door and bowed Yoshi through. Yoshi's hand was not on his hilt but he was ready for an assassin behind the door. There was none. Just four guards around the futons in the big room. On the futons, crumpled with pain, was Anjo. "So, Guardian of the Heir," he said, his voice weak though spiced with venom, "you have information?"

"For your ears."

"Wait outside, Doctor, until I call for you."

The doctor bowed and left, glad to go. This patient was impossible, he despised him, and as he was slowly dying, only a few weeks or months left, there would be no fee. In China such was the custom—no cure, no fee—and it applied here.

The guards had not moved. Nor would they. The four were noted fighters and completely loyal. Some of Yoshi's confidence left him. He knelt and bowed politely. This morning, after Inejin had left, he had sent Anjo a message asking for an urgent meeting to give him important information.

"Well, Yoshi-dono?"

"Yesterday I went on one of the gai-jin warships an—"

"I know that, do you think I am a fool and that I do not know what you are up to? You said medical information."

"The gai-jin doctor at Kanagawa. The Furansu said he has made miraculous cures, with your permission I will have him brought here."

"I do not need you for that." In agony, Anjo raised up on one elbow. "Why so solicitous when you want me dead?"

"Not dead, in good health, *Tairō-dono*. It is important to have you in good health." Yoshi kept a tight hold, loathing this man and this room with its stench of death and diarrhea and vomit—at the same time afraid he had miscalculated: This could easily be his death trap should the sick man give the order. "Why be sick if you can be cured? Also, I wanted to tell you I have learned the gai-jin battle plan, not on the ship but early today."

"What plan, eh? How did you come by it?"

"It does not matter, except I know, so now you know." He told him the substance of the plan, accurately, but left out the part about the ten days of grace after the ultimatum.

"Then we must leave!" The voice became shriller. The guards shifted nervously. "The *roju* must leave secretly at once, we will take up residence in . . . in Hodogaya. When we're safe we burn the Settlement by night and catch them in their beds. What dogs! They deserve to die foully, without honor. We burn them out, kill all who escape, and return here when the fleet's sailed away. In the spring we will be prepared. We fire Yokohama tomorrow." Anjo's eyes glittered, a string of saliva wet his chin. "You have the honor of leading the assault. Organize it, lead the attack tomorrow or the next day."

At once Yoshi bowed in thanks. "I accept the honor, gladly, and while I organize it, I have a notion: first your health. Bring the gai-jin doctor here, ours are useless and the Furansu swore the man is a miracle healer. I can fetch him quickly and quietly, tomorrow if you permit it. Why be in pain needlessly? The gai-jin doctor will cure you," he said firmly. "A few extra days will not interfere with your wise attack strategy. Until you are well enough to command, we must keep the gai-jin off balance. I can do that while arranging the attack."

"How?"

"By putting myself into their trap."

"What?" The slight movement Anjo made to see Yoshi better caused him to bite his lip to prevent a cry of pain.

"I will risk putting myself in their power, meeting with them with only one or two guards. On the ship I found out they are on the point of lashing out at us, senselessly. We must prevent this at all costs, *Tairō*. They are as dangerous as a pack of starving sharks." This was said with all the sincerity at his command. He believed the opposite: that gai-jin were ready to negotiate and compromise, never really wanting to war unless pushed too far . . . like foolishly attacking them.

"It will be my risk," he said, dangling the bait with a pretense of fear. "If they hold me hostage, that will cause all daimyos to rush to your support. If they do not, never mind, in either event, you forget that I am hostage and attack them—all this, of course, with your permission, *Tairō*."

The silence became heavy. Another spasm. Then Anjo nodded agreement and waved a hand in dismissal. "Fetch the gai-jin doctor at once, prepare the attack at once."

Yoshi bowed humbly, and with difficulty, stopped himself from shouting with glee.

52

KANAGAWA

Friday, 2nd January:

As Yoshi rode up to the Kanagawa Legation gateway leading the small procession, Settry Pallidar, officer commanding the honor guard, bellowed, "Present aaarrmms!" and saluted with his sword. The soldiers brought their rifles off their shoulders, presented arms and stayed motionless: thirty Guardsmen, thirty kilted Highlanders, his mounted troop of Dragoons, equally smart.

Yoshi returned the salute with his riding crop and hid his anxiety seeing so many enemy soldiers with so many spotless rifles. Never in his life had he been so unprotected. Only Abeh and two guards, also mounted, in attendance. Following were a groom on foot and a dozen sweating, nervous porters carrying heavy bundles on poles swung between them. His other guards were waiting at the barricade.

He was dressed all in black: bamboo armor, light helmet, wide-shouldered tunic, two swords—even his stallion pony was jet. But the tasseled trappings and reins and blanket were deliberately scarlet, enhancing the black. As he passed Pallidar, turning through the gates, he noticed the cold blue eyes reminding him of dead fish.

On the steps above the beaten earth courtyard he saw Sir William, flanked by Seratard and André Poncin on one side, the Admiral, Dr. Babcott and Tyrer on the other—just as he had asked. All were dressed in their best, with top hats and warm wool coats against the damp morning, the sky overcast. His gaze flicked over them, paused a moment on Babcott, staggered by his great height, then he reined in and saluted with his crop. They bowed as, casually, the Admiral saluted.

At once Sir William, with Tyrer close behind, came down to greet him, smiling—both covering their surprise at the smallness of his guard. The groom rushed to hold the head of his pony. Yoshi dismounted on the right side as was customary in China and therefore here.

"Welcome, Lord Yoshi, on behalf of Her Britannic Majesty," Sir William said. Tyrer translated at once, carefully.

"Thank you. I hope I am not putting you to any trouble," Yoshi said, beginning his share of the ritual.

"No, Sire, our honor. You give us rare, great pleasure." Yoshi noted an improvement in Tyrer's accent and vocabulary and was even more determined to neutralize the traitor Hiraga, who, Inejin had found out, went under the pseudonym of Nakama. "Please, Lord Yoshi, will you take tea?"

Both men had already closed their ears to the meaningless phrases, concentrating on the other man, seeking clues that might help them. "Ah, Serata-dono," Yoshi said pleasantly, though he was irritated to be standing, having to look up at them, their height—usually more than a head taller—making him feel inferior, though amongst Japanese, he would look down on most. "I'm please to see you again so soon. Thank you." He nodded to André, then Seratard who bowed formally, André interpreting.

"My Master Seratar' greet you, Sire, on behalf of his friend, Emperor of Furansu, High King Napoleon III. Honored to be of service."

The moment Yoshi had left *Tairō* Anjo, he had sent Misamoto with a letter to Seratard asking him if he would arrange an urgent, formal though very private meeting with Seratard, Sir William, the Chief Officer of the Fleet, the doctor of Kanagawa, and interpreters André and Tyrer only—no one else. He would arrive informally, with minimal escort, and asked that ceremony be minimal.

'What do you make of it, Henri?' Sir William had asked when Seratard had hurried to see him the moment André had translated the letter.

'I don't know. He's an impressive man. He was aboard over four hours so we had the opportunity of studying him carefully—perhaps you'd like a copy of my report.'

'Thank you,' Sir William said, knowing it would be revamped with all interesting information excised—no more than he would do. He had a slight cold and sneezed. 'Excuse me.'

'As Guardian of the Heir, one of the Elders, of an ancient Japanese royal family—even connected to the Mikado, the Emperor, whose function you may not know is religious—this man is extremely well connected and important in the Shōgunate. Why don't we see him?'

'I will,' Sir William had said dryly, well ahead of Seratard's information, having spent many hours grilling Nakama for details of important rulers and their families, Toranaga Yoshi particularly. 'We'll do as he asks. Interesting that he wants Ketterer there, eh? That's smelly. We'll go by boat and take some crack troops, dress them up as an honor guard and have H.M.S. *Pearl* cruising offshore.'

'*Mon Dieu*, you suspect a trap?'

'It might be a cunning way to risk a knight to sweep our command structure off the board. Easy to sneak in samurai—Pallidar says they're holed down both sides of the Tokaidō from here to Hodoyama and beyond. I don't smell a trap but just in case we'll put a round in the chamber. No French troops, old man. Sorry, no. No, Henri! But why should he want Babcott?'

'On behalf of France I proposed we set up a hospital for them, to cement ties. He was delighted . . . never mind, William, you can't think of everything. We discussed Babcott who has a modest reputation. Perhaps Yoshi wants to consult him.' Seratard had seen no reason to divulge the intelligence André had uncovered about the *tairō*'s ill health.

Japanese tea was served in the big audience room. They seated themselves as protocol dictated and prepared for the interminable politenesses that would go on for an hour. One sip of tea and they were flabbergasted to hear Yoshi say, "The reason I called this private meeting, with the help of Serata-dono . . . naturally on behalf of the *tairō* and Council of Elders . . . is because it is time to make progress in our good relations." He stopped and said curtly to Tyrer, "Please translate that first and then I will continue."

Tyrer obeyed.

"First, the Doctor-sama, the rest of our meeting does not concern him." Yoshi had intentionally waited the three days to seek the doctor. No need to hurry, he had thought cynically: Anjo said he did not need me to arrange it, let him ache!

Abruptly a crick soared from his own stomach at the thought of the unnecessary risks he had taken, putting himself at the mercy of Anjo, who every day became more dangerous. Stupid to agree to lead the attack and plan it—that part done, too easy—for he would have to do it unless he could finesse the barbarians into doing his will today: "Would the doctor please return to Yedo with me to examine an important patient who may not be named. I guarantee him safe passage."

Sir William said, "An important person such as Doctor-sama could surely not go about without an escort."

"I understand that, but in this instance, so sorry, it is not possible," Yoshi said, and now, sitting as he was on eye level with them all, except Babcott, he was more at ease. "I guarantee him safe passage."

Sir William pretended a frown. "George? What about it?"

They had already discussed this possibility. 'I'd agree to go alone, Sir William. One of my assistants told me the *tairō* is rumored to be sick. It could be him.'

'My God, if you could cure that bugger—or poison him—I don't know which is best. Joking, of course.'

'It's no risk, not to me. I'm only valuable alive and no use as a hostage. To cure a V.I.P. would be terrific for us.'

'I agree. We'll play it by nose. Talking of that, I heard Angelique consulted you yesterday.'

'Ha! The whole Settlement seems to have heard, you're the eighth who has sidled into that one! She had a cold, in this weather everyone has a cold, you have a cold, and even if she had consulted me for any other reason, it is and always would be private, so give over.'

Sir William smiled to himself remembering how he had sniffed and protested he was not enquiring about private matters, like her possible pregnancy. Not many days to go and the whole Settlement nervous, no one ready to put down big money yet on what would be "P-Day," or if there would be none—and less than five days for the first blast to arrive from Hong Kong about Malcolm, the funeral and what Tess Struan was going to do.

Sir William pulled his mind back to the issues at hand. Babcott was saying to Yoshi directly in halting Japanese, "Yes, go Yedo, Lord Yoshi. When go, please?"

Yoshi said slowly, "When I leave, Doctor-sama. Thank you. I am responsible for you. I will ensure you come back safely. You will need an interpreter, yes?"

"Yes, please, Lord Yoshi," Babcott said, not needing one. He looked at Tyrer. "You're elected, Phillip."

Tyrer grinned. "I was going to volunteer."

"Ask him how long I'll be there."

"He says: however long it takes to make an examination."

"Then that's settled," Sir William said.

"I'll leave you to it. I've a clinic going on so you know where I'll be." The doctor bowed to Yoshi, who bowed back, and then he was gone.

Choosing his words carefully and trying to talk simply, Yoshi said, "Porters outside have cases of silver coins to the value of one hundred thousand pounds. This is offered by the Shōgunate in full settlement of the indemnity you have demanded from the responsible daimyo. In principle, the Shōgunate considers this a correct amount." He concealed his amusement at Tyrer and André's shock. "Translate exactly what I said."

Again Tyrer obeyed, not exactly word for word this time, but gave a credible précis, helped here and there by André. There was a stunned silence in the room.

"Sire," Tyrer said weakly, "my Master ask, he answer now, or Yoshi-sama say more?"

"More. The Shōgunate advances this money on behalf of Sanjiro of Satsuma. He alone is responsible. As previously explained, he is not subject to Shōgunate control—in all things. Translate."

Again this was done. He saw the two leaders were off balance as he had planned. This was pleasing, but did not allay his anxiety. "We cannot force Sanjiro of Satsuma to cancel any orders he may or may not have given his men about gai-jin—or even to apologize—or make him repay the money we are advancing to settle this matter *without waging war on him*. This we are not prepared to do."

This translation required time to get it accurate, André again assisting, aware of the tension and the way everyone was concentrating.

"Sire?"

"Say this exactly and carefully: wanting to be friends with the Ing'erish and Furansu, the Shōgunate has solved what the Shōgunate can solve . . . *without going to war*." Yoshi sat back, wondering if the bait was succulent enough.

His last remarks were received in silence. He noted Sir William was impassive now except for an almost inaudible grunt. But Seratard nodded and glanced at André.

Inwardly a ferment of glee, Sir William waited for Yoshi to continue. When he didn't, he said, "Phillip, ask Lord Yoshi if he wants to go on or may I now respond."

"He says he does not wish to continue for the moment."

Sir William cleared his throat and spoke grandly—to Tyrer's private dismay: "Lord Yoshi, on behalf of Her Majesty's Government, and the French Government, may I thank you and the Shōgunate for obliterating part of the problem between us. We thank you personally, wishing to make our stay in your land happy and profitable for your country, the

Shōgunate and ourselves. This gesture surely begins a new era of understanding between our two countries—and those others represented in Japan."

He waited as that was translated, both Tyrer and André apologizing and begging Yoshi's forbearance, putting the message in simpler terms, as accurately as possible. When they had finished, Sir William said, "With his permission I would like to take a short break. Phillip, or André, please ask his indulgence, apologies and all that, but explain my bladder needs assistance. It's my cold."

The two interpreters hastily translated.

"Of course," Yoshi said at once, not believing him.

Sir William got up and Seratard made his excuses and once in the corridor heading for the pot that neither needed, Sir William whispered excitedly, "My God, Henri, did you read him like I did? He's saying we can go after Sanjiro ourselves."

Seratard was equally elated. "It's a complete reversal of their policy that everything must go through the Bakufu and Shōgunate. *Mon Dieu,* is he giving us carte blanche?"

"Pas ce crétin," Sir William said, switching to French without noticing it. "If we can do it against Sanjiro, it's precedent to go against any other daimyo—the Shimonoseki Straits bugger, for one. But what the devil's the quid pro quo, eh?" He blew his nose loudly. "There's got to be one."

"I've no idea. Whatever it is it'll be rare, *mon brave.* Astounding that he put himself in our power, never thought he'd arrive with so few men, surely he must have realized we could take him hostage against Sanjiro's performance?"

"Agreed. My Lord, what a step forward! Unbelievable that he came to the point at once, no fart-arsing about, never thought I'd see the day. But why, eh? Something's smelly."

"Yes. *Merde,* pity he's not *tairō,* eh?"

Ha! My thought entirely, old boy, way ahead of you, Sir William told himself. A little push here, a little pull there and like in India we could be off to the races!

He had unbuttoned, and now, idly watching the flow, his ears closed to Seratard's further prognosis, he composed his thoughts, considering what he could barter, how far to go, and how to get Ketterer to agree without Admiralty or Foreign Office approval. God damn the fellow!

And God damn Palmerston. I asked for urgent approval to enforce civilized law, so why hasn't he replied? He probably has, he told himself. London's coded message went by telegraph to Basra and is now somewhere on a mail ship in a diplomatic pouch. His flow ceased. He shook himself, as always remembering the schoolboys' admonition at Eton: 'If you shake it more than three times you're playing with it.' Quickly he stepped aside for Seratard, buttoning up, noticing Seratard was like a small horse in quantity and power. Interesting. Must be the wine, he thought, returning to the conference room.

The rest of the meeting went breezily. With skill and diplomatic care Sir William, ably assisted by Seratard, established in a very oblique way that "if a force happened to proceed against someone like Sanjiro, for instance, against his capital, for instance, it would be an extremely unfortunate occurrence even though such action could possibly be merited because of some unacceptable act of murder committed against foreign nationals. This act would precipitate a flurry of protests from Yedo and would merit a formal apology if such an inconceivable action was taken. . . ."

Absolutely nothing was said directly, nothing to imply that permission had been given or sought. Nothing would be in writing. Such a possible major hostile act, 'a special case,' could be contained only if protocol was carefully followed.

By now, Tyrer and André both had splitting headaches and were inwardly cursing their Masters for the near impossibility of translating the necessary obliqueness.

Yoshi was silently ecstatic. Sanjiro was as good as dead and the first barrier removed at no cost. "I think we understand one another and can move to other matters."

"Yes, quite clearly." Sir William sat back, and girded his loins for the quid pro quo.

Yoshi took a deep breath and launched the next assault: "Translate the following, sentence by sentence. Explain this is for accuracy. Say also for the moment this conversation must be considered a State secret between us." Seeing Tyrer's blank stare, he added, "Do you understand State secret?"

After consulting with André, Tyrer said, "Yes, Sire."

"Good, then translate: Are we agreed this is to be a State secret between us?"

Sir William thought, In for a penny, in for a pound. "Agreed." Seratard echoed him.

Tyrer mopped his brow. "Ready, Sire."

With an even firmer grip Yoshi said, "It is my wish to modernize the Shōgunate and Bakufu. Translate. To do this I need knowledge. Translate. Ing'rand and Furansuland are the most powerful outside nations.

Translate. I ask you to draw up various plans to help the Shōgunate form a modern navy, dockyard and modern army. Translate."

Admiral Ketterer jerked upright, his neck pulsating fire. "Keep quiet," Sir William muttered carefully from the corner of his mouth, "and don't say a word!"

"Also a modern banking system and experimental factories. One country cannot do everything. You are rich, the Shōgunate is poor. When the plans are accepted I will agree to a fair price. This will be paid for in coal, silver, gold and yearly leases of safe harbors. I would like a provisional answer in thirty days if this is of interest. If yes, is one year enough time for detailed plans to be approved by your rulers?"

It was difficult for Yoshi to maintain outward poise, and he wondered what they would say if they knew he had no authority to make this offer nor any way to implement any of it. The offer was made to seduce them into a year's reprieve from outside conflict, a delay he needed to stifle internal opposition to the Shōgunate and to deal with his prime enemies, Ogama of Choshu and Yodo of Tosa, now that Sanjiro would be removed.

At the same time it was a jump into the future, into the unknown, one that frightened him and elated him in a way he did not understand. All of the ideas were based on information Inejin's spy had obtained from the unsuspecting shoya Ryoshi about gai-jin methods, and driven home to him by what he had seen and heard on the warship that was immensely impressive but nowhere near as big or as deadly as the Ing'erish flagship.

Hating the reality but accepting it, he had realized, in self-defense, the Land of the Gods had to become modern. To do this he had to deal with gai-jin. He loathed, despised and distrusted them but they had the means to destroy Nippon, at the very least to put them back into the kind of civil wars that had existed for centuries before Shōgun Toranaga had tamed bushido, the warrior spirit of the samurai.

He watched the two leaders talk amongst themselves. Then he saw the Ing'erish Leader speak to the young interpreter, Taira, who said in his quaint though understandable Japanese, "My Master thank you, Sire, for . . . for conf'dence. Need one hundred twenty day send message to 'Queen Parliament' and 'Furansu King' fetch . . . to fetch, bring back answer. Both leaders sure answer is yes."

A hundred and twenty days was better than expected. "Good," he said, grim-faced, inwardly weak with relief.

Now for the better part, he thought, seeing them preparing to close the meeting. An eye for an eye, a death for a death: "Lastly, I am sure

W'rum-sama does not know the man he shelters, called Nakama, is a renegade samurai, a ronin and revolutionary whose real name is Hiraga, sometimes called Otami. I require him at once. He is wanted for murder."

At that moment, across the bay in the Yokohama's Yoshiwara, Katsumata said, "Hiraga, have you thought how we can infuriate the gai-jin, a hostile incident to set them against the Shōgunate?" The two men were sitting opposite each other in a secluded little house in the garden of the Three Carp.

"Torching one of the churches would be easiest," Hiraga said, keeping his anger buried, for Katsumata was very perceptive—he had just arrived, summoned from his village hideaway by a sleepy servant. Except for a few cookhouse skivvies tending fires and cleaning, no one was about. Raiko and her Ladies were still sleeping—few would be up before midday. "That would madden them, but first let me tell you what I've achieved here an—"

"Later, first we must make a plan. A church? An interesting idea," Katsumata said, his face cold and hard, no longer disguised as he had been in Hodogaya.

Now he appeared to be a bonze, a Buddhist priest, clean-shaven but for a mustache. The thatch had been a wig and was gone. His head had the stubble of a bonze, he wore the orange Buddhist robe and sandals and a belt of prayer beads. His long sword in its back scabbard was beside him on the futons and the *mon,* the five insignia on his robe proclaimed he was a member of a militant, monastic Order.

These virtual military Orders were made up of samurai who had relinquished their samurai status to serve Buddha, permanently or temporarily, to preach and roam the land doing good works, singly or in bands, purging robbers and bandits and protecting the poor from the rich and the rich from the poor—and some monasteries. The Bakufu, and most daimyos, tolerated them so long as they kept their violence within bounds.

At dusk last night he strode arrogantly through the barrier, his false papers perfect. He was a day late, unheralded, at once to be given the best available bungalow by Raiko. Unlike other shishi, unique amongst them, his family was rich and he always carried numerous gold oban with him.

"A church," he repeated, relishing the idea. "I would not have thought of that—we would leave a message claiming it was done by the order of Yoshi, *Tairō* Anjo and the *roju* as a warning for them to leave our shores. We need revenge on Yoshi very much." A fleck of foam gathered at the corners of his mouth and he brushed it away angrily. "Yoshi is the archenemy. One of us must go against him, he killed too many of our fighters in Kyōto, shot some personally. If I could ambush him I would. That, too, later. So, the church will be burned. Good."

Hiraga was unsettled, finding Katsumata strange, and different. Now he was impatient, and acting as though he were a daimyo and Hiraga one of his goshi to be ordered about. I'm leader of the Choshu shishi, he thought with more anger, not a student under orders of a Satsuma Sensei, however renowned. "That would turn the whole of Yokohama into a hornet's nest. I would have to leave, which would be bad at the moment, my work important for our cause. The situation here is very delicate, Sensei. I agree we must plan, for instance where do we escape to, if we are to escape?"

"Yedo." Katsumata stared at him. "What is more important, *sonno-joi* or your safe haven amongst enemy gai-jin?"

"*Sonno-joi*," he said at once, believing it. "But it's important we learn what they know. *To know your enemy like—*"

"I do not need quotations, Hiraga, but action. We are losing the fight, Yoshi is winning. We've only one solution: to turn these gai-jin violently against the Bakufu and Shōgunate. This will advance *sonno-joi* as nothing before and takes precedence over everything. We desperately need this, then we'll regain support, and *face,* fighters will flock to our standard, meanwhile the spearhead of shishi regroups here and in Kyōto. I will call for reinforcements from Satsuma and Choshu and again we will attack the Gates to release the Emperor. This time we'll succeed because Ogama, Yoshi, and the stinking Shōgunate will be distracted dealing with hostile gai-jin. Once we have the Gates, *sonno-joi* is a fact." There was no doubting his confidence.

"And if we agitate the gai-jin, what then, Sensei?"

"They bombard Yedo, the Shōgunate retaliates by attacking Yokohama—both lose."

"Meanwhile all daimyo will flock to support the Shōgunate when the gai-jin return as they will."

"They would not return before Fourth or Fifth Month, if then. Before that we will have the Gates, at our suggestion the Emperor will be pleased to give the gai-jin the culprit, Yoshi, or his head, Nobusada, Anjo, and any other heads they need to slake their thirst for revenge. And at our further suggestion the Son of Heaven will agree to allow them to trade, without any more war, but only through Deshima in

Nagasaki harbor as they did for centuries." Katsumata was sure. "That's what will happen. First the church—what about a ship?"

Hiraga, startled, said, "What about one?" he asked, his mind stuffed with arguments against what Katsumata surmised, certain it would not happen that way, at the same time trying to think of a way to divert Katsumata, to make him go on to Yedo and come back in a month or two—things were going far too well here with Taira and Sir W'rum, Jami-sama and the shoya to want to jeopardize that. Plenty of time to enrage the gai-jin later with the church when a safe retreat was th—

"Sinking a warship would inflame them, wouldn't it?"

Hiraga blinked. "Like . . . like nothing else."

"We use the church as a diversion, while we sink a ship, their biggest one."

Dumbfounded, Hiraga watched Katsumata open a backpack. In it were four metal tubes, bound with wire. And fuses. "These contain explosive, cannon powder. One of them, fused, through a porthole or gun port, or attached to the side of the ship would blow out the side, two would be fatal."

Hiraga was transfixed, all else forgotten. He reached for a tube. In his hand the bomb seemed to pulsate with life. At the top was the small hole for the fuse and in his mind he saw the fuse spluttering and his arm slip the bomb quietly through the lowest gun port, then another—then ducking back quickly into the boat that was largely hidden by sea mist, silently away, and then, safe, the vast explosion as the bombs ignited other charges and then the great ship slipping under the water.

And with it all his own plans.

"It's an enormous idea, Katsumata," he said, feeling sick. "We'd need to pick the correct time of the moon and the sea carefully, and plan carefully. Spring or early summer would be best. After that I could not remain here and . . . There's so much to tell you about what I've discovered." He almost blurted out that he could speak English well now but stopped. "Just a few more weeks and I'll be done. Then the church and the ship."

"We burn the church and sink the ship tomorrow night."

"Impossible!"

Katsumata was coldly amused by his shock and thought what a shame Ori was dead and Hiraga alive—Ori was so much more superior. But then he, too, was Satsuma, not Choshu. "How many times must I say surprise is our shishi's best weapon. That and decisive speed. Where is Akimoto?"

"In the village. I thought it best not to bring him now," Hiraga said, his mind flooded. Since he had come back from Hodogaya he had not shared his innermost thoughts with his cousin, only that Katsumata had told him Sumomo was dead, betrayed by Koiko to Yoshi, not that he believed both had been thrown into the pit by chance. Like we would be thrown away uselessly in this wild-eyed scheme and all my work will have been in vain. "Tomorrow is too soon. I suggest we ma—"

"The church will be easy for one man. Akimoto. We will need a dinghy or small fishing boat. Can you get one?"

"Perhaps," Hiraga said, answering automatically, fogged with myriad questions and dreads. "Perhaps I could steal one. Sensei, I th—"

"You are not thinking clearly. Fishermen always remove the oars when the boat is not in use. No need for that. Buy one." Katsumata took out a small silk purse and put it carelessly on the table. "Hiraga, concentrate!" he said, his voice hardening. "Has living with gai-jin infected you so much with their evils that you've forgotten your oath to *sonno-joi*? Concentrate, the plan is good, the timing is perfect. *Could you buy a boat*?"

"Yes—yes, but—but, Sensei, where do we retreat to?"

"Retreat is simple. Three of us, you, Takeda and me, we sink the warship. Then we beach the boat as near Yedo as possible and lose ourselves in the city."

"What about the other man, the one who fires the church?"

"He will escape on foot."

"We need more shishi in support, this is a major task. This whole area will become lethal."

"That makes escape easier. Four men is enough. I will lead the attack on the ship and if tomorrow there's a wind the burning church may torch all Yokohama, a further gift. Come back tonight, bring Akimoto and I will make final plans."

"But—where's Takeda?"

"I left him at Hodogaya. He will be here this afternoon. Until dusk, Hiraga." Curtly Katsumata bowed a dismissal.

In turmoil Hiraga bowed back, too many years an adoring, awe-struck student of the Sensei, master swordsman and tactician, not to accept the dismissal. He went out and stumbled back across the bridge to the Settlement, along the village street, later turned to the promenade and walked back along it, seeing nothing, his head a mess of dark thoughts and impossibilities, his future in tatters all because this Satsuma outsider was determined to shove destiny forward.

But the Sensei is right, he brooded. Those two acts would drive the gai-jin berserk, the fleet would invest Yedo, Yedo would burn,

Yokohama would be decimated in revenge. In a few months fleets would come, this time with armies. By then shishi will not control the Gates, but all Nippon would be up in arms. And it would make no difference to the gai-jin.

One way or another we will have to open to their world. Gai-jin have decided. So they will have a base at Yokohama and other places—because they have the power to decimate our coasts and close our ports, forever if they wish, and no Divine Wind will help us.

" 'Allo, mate, where you goin'?"

"Oh." He was standing in front of the Legation. " 'Morning, Sir Sentry. I go Taira-sama."

"He's not 'ere, mate," the sentry said, yawning. "Mister Tyrer 'n the Guv, they's at Kanagawa."

"Oh?" Hiraga looked across the bay. The seascape was wintry. He could just discern Kanagawa. A frigate, he recognized it as the *Pearl*, was steaming slowly offshore, against the wind, neat, and deadly. In the roads the flagship with its forty 60-pounders, was at anchor into the wind. "I come back 'rater," he muttered.

Disconsolate, he wandered back to the village. To buy a dinghy. However much he disapproved, he was shishi first.

Early that afternoon in the wardroom aboard H.M.S. *Pearl* Seratard clinked glasses with Sir William, congratulating the other again on the meeting.

"A marvelous step forward, Henri, old chap," Sir William said jovially. He took up the bottle and rechecked the label. "Not bad for a '48. Excellent repast too." On the table were leftovers of the picnic lunch provided by Seratard's chef: cold pigeon pies, quiche, crumbs of the French bread, and a few slivers of a devoured Brie that had arrived on the last merchantman from Shanghai. "Still can't believe Yoshi offered what he offered."

"I agree. Marvelous is the word. We'll train the navy, you take the army, we'll take banking and customs and—"

"Dreamer!" Sir William said with a laugh. "But we're not going to quarrel about partitions, London and Paris will do that." He belched contentedly. "It'll come down to 'how much' in the end, for obviously we'll have to lend the wherewithal to buy our ships, factories or whatever—however much they say they'll pay."

"Yes, but there'll be the usual safeguards, customs revenues, etc." Both laughed.

"There'll be more than enough for both our countries," Sir William said, still not quite believing it. "But do me a favor, Henri, please don't bait the Admiral, I've enough trouble as it is."

"All right, but he's so . . . never mind. What about this Nakama? Astonishing. I think you were lucky he didn't kill you by night, you are their number one enemy. What possessed you to take such a risk?"

"He wasn't armed, he was helping Phillip with his Japanese," Sir William said. As far as he knew only four of them, Tyrer, McFay, Babcott and himself, knew the man could speak English and there was no reason to share that secret. "He was well watched," he added, matter-of-factly, though another pang went through him at the thought of the danger they had been in.

"What are you going to do about him?"

"What I told Yoshi."

They had all been shocked at Yoshi's revelations—Sir William almost as much as Tyrer—particularly that Nakama was wanted for the murder of Utani, one of the Elders, amongst other killings. At once he had said, 'Phillip, tell Lord Yoshi as soon I get back to Yokohama I will begin a formal enquiry, and if the facts are as he says I will return him at once to the authorities. Phillip!'

But Tyrer, speechless with disbelief, was staring blankly at Yoshi. André recovered quickly and translated for him, they jerked as Yoshi snapped at him.

'He, er, Lord Yoshi says, You question my words?'

'Say, Not at all, Lord Yoshi.' Sir William had kept his voice level, for he had seen the eyes narrow. 'But as you have your laws or customs, for instance your not being able to order this daimyo Sanjiro to obey you, I also have to comply with our laws, which the Treaty specifies clearly is Yokohama's dominating law.'

'He says, Sir William, ah yes, the Treaties. In this new spirit of friendship he agrees to . . . to allow you the duty of giving up the . . . the assassin. He'll send men to take custody tomorrow. About the Treaty, sir, he says, he said exactly, some changes are necessary, we can discuss them in twenty days.'

Tyrer said quietly, 'Excuse me, Sir William, about Nakama, may I suggest that—'

'No, Phillip, you may not. André, say to him exactly: We would be honored to discuss matters that affect our mutual interests at any time.' He had chosen the words very carefully and breathed a sigh of relief when the reply came back, 'Lord Yoshi thanks you and says, we meet in twenty days if not before and now will return to Yedo with Dr. Babcott.'

When the politenesses and bows were done and Yoshi had left the room, Seratard said, 'William, I think you slid out of that trap cleverly. He's cunning, that one. Congratulations.'

'About the navy,' the Admiral began hotly.

Sir William said, 'First let me get Babcott and Tyrer on their way. Come along, Phillip!' and when he had got him outside he hissed, 'What the devil's the matter with you?'

'Nothing, sir.'

'Then why is your face around your ankles? Why do you forget your job is just to interpret and not make suggestions?'

'Sorry, sir, but about Nakama, sir—'

'I know it's about him, for God's sake, you practically shat all over the conference table! Do you think our wily host didn't notice? Your bloody job is to translate what's said and be impassive and that's all. This is the second bloody time I've had to caution you!'

'Sorry, sir, it's just that Nakama's important and—'

'You mean Hiraga, or whatever other name he's using at the moment? Jesus Christ, he's accused of murder. I agree he's been a fund of information but God Almighty, a renegade outlaw? We're lucky he didn't kill us in our beds when you think he's had the run of the Legation and your quarters.'

'What do you plan to do, sir?'

'Damn it, what I've already said: investigate and if it's true, as I suspect it is, we are honor bound to turn him over.'

'Couldn't you consider him a political refugee?'

'Oh, for goodness' sake! Have you taken leave of your senses? We demand reparations and the murderers for the murder of our nationals, so how the devil can we refuse to return to them one of theirs who's accused and probably guilty of murder of one of their rulers? Yoshi promised him a fair trial.'

'He's a dead man, that's all the trial he'll get.'

'If he's guilty that's all he deserves.' He had held on to his temper, for Tyrer had done a good job today and he had noticed the growing friendship between the two of them that had worked to his advantage: 'Phillip, I know he's been tremendously valuable but he has to be turned over to them—after I've seen him. I warned him in the beginning that he would have to go if they asked for him. Now forget Nakama and make sure you learn all you can about Babcott's patient. With any luck it'll be the *tairō*.'

He led the way to the forecourt where Yoshi was mounting. Babcott waited beside a horse Pallidar had lent him, another for Tyrer. The honor guard was on alert surrounding them. At Yoshi's order the porters stood away from their poles with the bundles attached, then he beckoned Tyrer who listened, bowed and came back.

'He said you can, er, count the money at your leisure, Sir William, please give him a receipt tomorrow. That man,' Tyrer pointed at Abeh, 'will come for Nakama tomorrow.'

'Thank him and say it will be done as he wishes.'

Tyrer obeyed. Yoshi waved Abeh forward. *'Ikimasho!'* They trotted off, the porters and groom trailing.

'You all set, George?'

'Yes, thanks, Sir William.'

'Off you go then. Phillip, you did well today, a few more conferences like this and I will recommend you be upgraded to full interpreter.'

'Thank you, sir. May I be present when you see Nakama?'

He had almost lost his temper. 'How the devil can that happen when you're going to Yedo with George. Use your brains! George, give him an emetic, the poor lad's witless!'

Babcott said, 'I don't really need Phillip. I thought it might be important for him to meet this "unnamed person." '

'You were quite right, this meeting could be very important—Nakama, or Hiraga, whatever his name, isn't. Phillip, has that got through to you yet?'

'Yes, sir. Sorry, sir.'

Babcott leaned closer. 'It might be a good idea not to hand over Nakama until we get back, just in case.'

Sir William had looked up at him, this thought jumping the medical consultation to a possible new level. 'You mean they might try to keep you? As a hostage? Both of you?'

Babcott shrugged. 'Nakama's important to him. No harm in being wise, eh?'

Sir William frowned. 'I'll expect you back tomorrow.' He had waited until they were out of sight and then went back to the conference room.

At once the Admiral exploded. 'Never heard so much poppycock in my life! Build them a navy? Have you taken leave of your senses?'

'That's not up to us, my dear Admiral,' he had said calmly, 'that would be up to Parliament.'

'Or much more likely Emperor Napoleon,' Seratard interrupted sharply.

'I doubt that, my dear sir,' Ketterer said, his face and neck puce.

'Foreign naval matters are the prime concern of the Royal Navy and any French interference in areas of British influence will be dealt with right smartly.'

'Quite right,' Sir William said loudly, overriding both of them as Seratard's face matched the Admiral's and he volubly began to disagree. 'In any event it would be a political decision. For London and Paris.'

'Political be damned,' the Admiral said, jowls shaking with rage. 'A dozen of our best warships in the hands of those scallywags when you see what they can do with a couple of swords? I'm totally opposed!'

'So am I,' Sir William said smoothly, 'totally, and will so recommend.'

'What?'

'I totally agree with you. Such a major decision is entirely up to the Admiralty, assisted by the Foreign Office. Paris likewise. Not a thing we can do but report to our superiors. You should do likewise. Thank God Japanese authorities at long last approve our right to proceed against guilty parties ourselves. Don't you agree, Admiral?'

'If you're talking about your proposed, ill-advised punitive strike, here, there or anywhere, it's not yet approved by the Admiralty so it's not approved by me. I suggest we go back aboard *Pearl* before the rain starts. . . .'

Sir William sighed and looked out of a wardroom porthole. The rain had stopped temporarily, the sea was still leaden but his spirit wasn't. He had the indemnity money, there was no immediate need now to flatten Yedo, and through this Yoshi we'll help modernize Japan, he thought. We'll make a happy place for it in the family of nations, happy for them as well as us. Far better we do it and instill British virtues than the French implant French ones, though their wines and attitudes to food and fornication are far superior to ours.

Yes. Except in fornication the Japanese will benefit. In that their attitude is without doubt superior. Pity we can't import that into our society but the Queen would never stand for it. Dreadful shame, but that's life. We'll just have to bless our luck to be living here—once we've civilized them. "Henri, let's get some air."

He was glad to be back on deck. The wind was sea-salt heavy, sharp and wholesome, the frigate under sail now, making way nicely. Marlowe was on the bridge—officers and men on deck or in the shrouds, achingly aware of the Admiral who sat in the bridge sea chair, sourly hunched into his greatcoat. "For God's sake, Marlowe, take her closer to the wind."

"Aye, aye, sir."

Sir William was not an expert but that seemed to be a pedantic and unnecessary order. Bloody man! Still, can't blame him for wanting confirming orders, it's his neck if anything goes wrong.

When the frigate swung onto a new tack his grip tightened on the gunnel. He loved the sea and being on it, particularly on the deck of a British warship, proud that the ships of the Empire possessed the sea as much as any ships could rule the waves. Ketterer's right about not wanting to create another navy, he thought, not with these men—the French, American and Prussian navies are enough trouble as it is.

He looked aft.

Aft, over the horizon, was Yedo. Yedo and Yoshi spell trouble whichever way you look at it, whatever the rosy future he promised. Ahead was Yokohama. More trouble there but never mind, tonight Angelique's my dinner partner—I'm glad she didn't leave but still don't understand why. Doesn't that play even more into Tess Struan's hands?

Strange to think of Angelique without Malcolm Struan. Sorry he had such bad luck but he's gone and we're alive and he isn't. Joss. Who'll be tai-pan now? Young Duncan's only ten, last of the Struan boys. Terrible for Tess, more tragedy to bear. Wouldn't be surprised if this didn't finish her. Always admired her for her courage, carrying the load of Culum and the Brocks, not to mention Dirk Struan.

Well, I did my best for Tess, and for Malcolm—alive and dead. And for Angelique. When she leaves there'll be an emptiness that won't be filled easily. Hope she regains the youth she's lost, that's another sadness but she's got a whole life in front of her—if she has his child or if she doesn't. Betting's still evens.

Commands on the bridge attracted his attention for a moment but it was nothing urgent, just adding more sail. The wind was humming the shrouds. The frigate picked up speed. Their moorings were under an hour away. Sunset a good two hours. Plenty of time to bring Nakama to heel before dinner.

Sunset was just a lowering of light, the sun dying behind a blanket of clouds, regretting the loss of the day.

Hiraga said to the group of fishermen, "That boat will do—no fishing tackle, but oars and sail are included." He was on the beach near Drunk Town and he paid the owner what had been asked without bargaining, still unwilling to lose face by negotiating though he knew now—too well hammered into him by Mukfey—that he was being cheated and overcharged and that this man and his compatriots would laugh at him as soon as they were out of sight. He knew he was to blame because he was dressed like a gai-jin and not properly with swords.

Half of him wanted to scream and lash out at their bad manners and have them crawling on the beach, begging for the privilege of giving him the boat. The other half counselled patience: You have done what you must do, the boat is yours, tomorrow you die with honor in the cause of *sonno-joi*, these lice have no more value than the barnacles on the filthy little vessel they sell.

"Leave everything in the boat," he said. Unctuously the owner bowed and grovelled his way out of range, then, with his comrades, walked away, blessing their luck for a double profit.

The boat was an ordinary little fishing boat for one to three men with a small sail and single stern oar. Part of samurai training was the use of boats on short distances to traverse rivers or to reach offshore coastal ships or galleys, so they could all handle it. The news that he had bought one would fly around the village but that did not matter. By the time the shoya and others had worked out its probable use, the revelation would be too late.

Satisfied the boat was safe, he began to walk through Drunk Town, through the crowded alleys, stepping over drunks and garbage, disgusted with the filth. Taira says his London is the cleanest, biggest, wealthiest city in the world but I do not believe him—not if so many of his kind live like this, with the rest of the Settlement not much better. Taking a shortcut he crossed into a smaller alley. Men passed by, beggars held their hands out, eyes peered suspiciously from doorways but no one bothered him.

No Man's Land was as always, weed-covered and stinking, the main refuse dump of the Settlement. A few ragged scavengers raked through the latest pile of trash. They glanced at him briefly. His eyes went to the rickety well head. The broken wooden cover that hid the secret passage to the Yoshiwara seemed untouched. Ori's face fleetingly came from his memory and the time they were below, when he was ready to kill him and Ori had thrown, pretended to throw, the golden cross into the depths. Ori was *baka* to waste his life over that woman. We could use him tomorrow. He shoved Ori out of his mind.

Now his whole being was committed to the attack. All reasoning against it had vanished. There was a consensus, Akimoto gleefully in favor, Takeda, and the Sensei. Therefore he was also. The boat was ready. Now he would collect Akimoto and they would go back and finalize the plan. In reality he was glad. He would die in a blaze of glory doing the Emperor's wishes. What more could a samurai desire from life?

With the suddenness of an ice bath he was shocked from euphoria and disappeared into a doorway. Three Redcoats stood outside the shoya's house, two more were emerging from the nearby hovel he and Akimoto rented. Akimoto was between them, calling out at the top of his voice one of the few English phrases he had learned: "So sorry, no unn'erstan' Nakama!"

"N-a-k-a-m-a," the Sergeant said slowly and loudly. "Where is he?" Then louder, "Where Nakama?"

"Nakama?" Akimoto's voice itself was loud, clearly trying to warn him if he happened to be within hearing. "Nakama no unn'erstan', so sorry," then in Japanese, "Someone's betrayed someone," then in guttural English again, "Nakama no unn'er—"

"Shut up!" the Sergeant said angrily, "Corporal, this fool knows nothing. Butcher, you and Swallow stay here until Mister bloody Nakama comes back and ask him—ask him nice-like to come along wiv you to see Sir Will'm but make sure you bring the bugger. You," he stabbed a rough, iron-hard finger in Akimoto's chest, "you come along wiv me in case the Guv wants you." Loudly protesting in Japanese, he went with them, then in English, "Nakama, no unn'erstan'," over and over.

When Hiraga had recovered, and it was safe, he slipped out of the doorway, jumped a fence and hurried back to No Man's Land. There he ducked down into the doorway, not safe yet to run for the well, too much light, the three scavengers too near, too malevolent. Must keep it secret.

Who has betrayed us?

No time to think about that now. He went deeper into the shadows as one of the scavengers moved nearer, muttering and cursing at the smallness of the pickings, a grubby sack in one hand. All three were skeletal and filthy. One came close to the opening but passed without noticing him. In half an hour light would be gone, nothing to do but to wait. Suddenly the doorway was blocked.

"Thort I didn't see you, eh? Wot'cher doin?" the scavenger rasped, heavy with menace.

Slowly Hiraga straightened. His hand was on the small pistol in his pocket. Then he saw the knife appear in the clawlike fist and the man thrust forward viciously. But Hiraga was faster and caught the hand and chopped at the scavenger's throat. He squealed like a gutted pig and went down. At once the other two looked up and hurried to investigate.

They skidded to a stop. Now Hiraga was in the doorway, the gun in one hand, knife in the other and he stood over the man who writhed, choking in the dirt. Knives came out and the two men attacked. Hiraga did not hesitate and lunged at one man who darted away, leaving him the opening he needed. He was through the slot quickly, running for Drunk Town, not wanting to waste time fighting. In moments he had reached a side street but in his haste his hat had fallen off. He looked back and saw one of the scavengers had grabbed it up with a shout. In seconds the other had a hand on it too and they began a cursing fight for possession.

Chest heaving, Hiraga left them to it. Another look at the sky. *Be patient.* When they've gone you can go to the well. You must not reveal it, it's essential for the attack. Be patient. Buy a hat or a cap. What's gone wrong?

"Well, where the devil has he gone?"

"Can't be far, Sir William," Pallidar said. "I've men at both gates and on the bridge into the Yoshiwara. He's probably in one of the Inns. A matter of time before he appears. You want him in irons?"

"No, just here, unarmed, under guard."

"What about this fellow?"

Akimoto was sitting, his back to the wall, a soldier nearby. He had already been searched.

"I'll decide that when I've talked to him. Ah, André, come in. Settry, no need for you to wait. I'm dining with the Russian Minister, when you've got Nakama come and fetch me." Pallidar saluted and went out. "André, sorry to bother you but we can't find Nakama. As Phillip's not here could you interpret for me, ask this fellow where he is?"

He watched while André began questioning Akimoto, trying to contain his irritation and wishing Phillip Tyrer were here and not with Babcott. Hope that goes well. Damn it, if Nakama's not caught Yoshi will be irritable indeed, rightly so.

"He says he doesn't know," André said. He had not taken off his topcoat. Sir William's office was always freezing; even on the coldest day, his coal fire was mean. "He seems dim-witted, mumbles Nakama who, Nakama could be anywhere, the Yoshiwara, perhaps Kanagawa."

"Eh?" Sir William was shocked. "He's not supposed to leave the Settlement without my express approval. Ask him . . . ask him when did Nakama leave?"

"He says he doesn't know, doesn't know Nakama, if he's left or where he is, doesn't know anything."

"Perhaps a night in the brig will refresh his memory. Corporal!"

The door opened at once. "Put this man in the brig overnight, or until I give orders to the contrary. He is to be well treated, understand?"

"Yessir."

"He is to be well treated."

"Yessir." The Corporal jerked a thumb at Akimoto who backed out of the room bowing. The brig, used for rowdies, and servicemen subject to military discipline, was down the street, a low brick building with a dozen cells, flogging triangle. After the Club, it had been the second structure built, a normal British custom for most Settlements.

"*Merci,* André."

"*De rien.*"

"Have you any idea where he could be?"

"No, Monsieur, other than what the man said. See you at dinner." André smiled and left and began walking down the High Street, the wind whipping the leaves and papers and debris. Not much light was left in the sky.

Glad we're not responsible for finding him, he thought. Where would he have gone? If he has any sense to Kyōto or Nagasaki, or stowed away on yesterday's merchantman to Shanghai if he knows Yoshi wants him. Surely he must have known—no secrets in the Bakufu, or here. Great meeting, good for us too for we have the edge with Yoshi but damn Phillip, he's getting too good. Surely the patient will be Anjo. He spat irritably. I should have had the chance—after all it was my idea, Raiko and Meikin must have planted the thought somehow. *Mon Dieu,* they've more power than I imagined.

An icy current went through him. Raiko had asked him to see her urgently tonight. What now? Had to be trouble.

"Evening, sir," the Struan guard on the front door said.

"I've an appointment with Madame Struan."

"Yes, sir. She's expecting you, in the tai-pan's office along the corridor. Excuse the mess in the hall, sir, but Mr. McFay's packing. Terrible he's going, isn't it?"

"Yes, but let's hope th—" The signal gun at the Harbor Master's cut him off. Astonished, both men glanced seawards, for no ship was expected or overdue. Movement on the crowded High Street stopped and then a murmur of excitement went through Yokohama. Rounding the distant headland was a clipper, all sails set and the bit between her teeth. They saw puffs of smoke from her cannonade salute to the flagship, then heard the following boom and the flagship's answer.

Too far distant to see her flag. "She's one of ours," the guard said proudly. "Has to be, like in the old days . . . oh, evening, sir."

Jamie McFay came out of the door fast and focused his binoculars. "Hello, André, just want to make sure . . . *Prancing Cloud!* Hallelujah!" The implications would be clear to everyone. She had been scheduled to sail on to London. Returning here, and so quickly, meant she carried urgent news—or passengers. Good or bad.

"Hallelujah," André echoed. He saw Seratard with a telescope on the steps of the French Legation, Sir William at his window with binoculars, and next door, Dmitri stood at Brock's entrance, a short telescope to his eye. As Dmitri lowered it he noticed Jamie, hesitated, then gave him a thumbs-up. Jamie waved back then refocused. The clipper was beautiful charging for her moorings.

André said softly, "Perhaps she's aboard?"

"I had the same thought. We'll soon find out."

"Signal her."

"By the time I get the Harbor Master to put up the flags the light will have gone. Anyway it's not up to me now, that's Mr. MacStruan's decision." Jamie looked at him. "We'll know soon enough. You're seeing Angelique?"

"Yes."

"No need to worry her, until we know. Eh?"

"I agree, *mon brave*." André looked back at the clipper. "You'll meet her?"

"The ship?" The same hard smile. "Wouldn't you?"

They went into the foyer together. Coming down the staircase was Albert MacStruan, half dressed in evening clothes, tie undone but elegant. *"Prancing Cloud?"*

"Yes," Jamie said.

"Thought so." The strange eyes narrowed. " 'Evening, André. How are you?" MacStruan said.

"Fine, thank you. See you later."

Jamie waited until André had knocked and gone into the tai-pan's office that was now MacStruan's. "You'll meet her?"

"Oh, yes." MacStruan walked down the last step but now the bounce had gone from his stride. "Please join me."

"Thanks, but that's your privilege now. I've sent Vargas for the Bosun, the launch will be ready in five minutes."

MacStruan said kindly, "Come aboard with me, meet the ship like you used to, should still be doing."

"No, time to move on, it's all yours now. But thanks."

"I hear Zergeyev's banquet tonight will be grand, as Angelique's accepted. Change your mind, join the party."

"Can't, not tonight, I'm still not finished packing." Jamie smiled at him, then motioned down the corridor. "Angelique cleared using your office with you?"

"Oh, yes, glad to oblige, and better than having visitors upstairs in her suite, especially him. Can't say I like him."

"André's all right, his music is the best, certainly the best we have here. Hope *Prancing Cloud*'s news is good."

"Me too. But I doubt it. Do you think Tess is aboard?"

"The thought had occurred to me." Jamie grinned, no longer her servant. "It would explain *Cloud*'s changed schedule. That's what Dirk would have done."

"She's not Dirk, she's much more cunning—more's the pity, my dear fellow." There was no love lost between the stepbrothers and Tess Struan, but a codicil in Dirk's will had laid down that should the two boys prove themselves in schools and scholarship, they were to be used in the Noble House to the limit of their ability. Both were smart, their connections with highly placed Etonian and university friends scattered throughout the gentry, the City and in Parliament where his stepbrother, Frederick, had just won a seat, made them even more valuable. Even so both knew Tess Struan would dismiss them, but for the codicil. "Hope she hasn't come a-visiting—that's a boring thought."

McFay laughed. "We'll just batten down the hatches."

"Hello, André."

" 'Evening, Angelique."

She was in her favorite chair near the bay window, the curtains open to the harbor. *"Prancing Cloud?"*

"Yes."

"Good. Is she aboard?"

André smiled crookedly. "It would explain the clipper."

"It doesn't matter either way," she said evenly but her stomach was twisting. "Would you like a drink?"

"Thanks." He saw the bottle of champagne opened in its bucket of ice and a half-full glass on the table. "May I?"

"Please."

It was becoming her custom to watch the sun go down, or the gloaming and the night arrive, with champagne. Just one glass to prepare for the long evening and then the long night. Her sleep pattern had changed. She no longer put her head on the pillow and drifted off to wake at dawn. Now sleep eluded her. At first she had been frightened but Babcott had convinced her that fear only made insomnia worse.

'We don't need eight or ten hours, so don't worry. Use the time to your profit. Write letters or your journal and think good thoughts—and don't worry. . . .'

> *Dearest Colette,* (she had written yesterday)
> *His advice works but he missed the best opportunity and that is TO PLAN, so important because that woman is plotting my downfall.*
>
> *God willing, I will be in Paris soon when I can tell you all. Sometimes it's almost as though my life here is a play, or a Victor Hugo story, and Malcolm, poor man, never existed. But I enjoy the quiet, am content with the waiting. Only a few more days, and then I will know about the child, if it is to be or not. I so hope and hope and hope and pray and pray and pray I carry his child—and also that your birthing will be smooth, and give you another boy.*
>
> *I have to be wise. I've only myself to rely on here. Jamie is a good friend but he cannot help much—he's no longer with the Noble House and this newcomer Albert MacStruan is kind, a perfect gentleman, highborn British, and tolerates me only for the moment—until SHE orders otherwise. Sir William? He's government, British Government. Seratard? God knows if he'll truly help, but it will only be for what use I can be to him. Mr. Skye? He does his best but everyone hates him. André? He's too clever and knows too much, and I believe the trap he's in is driving him mad. (I can't wait to hear what YOU THINK!!!) My only hope is Edward Gornt. He will have arrived in Hong Kong and will have seen her by now. My prayers, and I know yours, for his success are abundant and daily.*
>
> *So I use my night waking time to plan. Now I've so many good plans and thoughts how to deal with every possible contingency—and plenty of strength to deal with the ones I haven't dared consider, for example if Edward fails me or, God forbid, he never arrives—there are rumors of terrible storms in the China seas, normal at this time of the year. Poor*

Dmitri's Cooper-Tillman lost another merchantman. Poor sailors, how terrible the sea is and how brave the men who sail her.

André, says, rightly, I cannot leave here nor make a move until SHE *declares herself. I am Malcolm's widow, everyone says so, Mr. Skye has registered all sorts of papers with Sir William and has sent more to Hong Kong and more to London. I have enough money and can stay here as long as I want—Albert MacStruan has said I can use Jamie's office when it is vacant and I have ten more chits that Malcolm chopped for me but left the amount blank—wasn't that thoughtful—that Jamie and now Albert have agreed to honor, up to a hundred guineas each.*

When SHE *declares herself I will join battle with her. I feel it will be to the death but I assure you, darling Colette, it won't be mine—this will be her Waterloo, not mine, France will be revenged. I feel very strong, very fit . . .*

She was watching André, waiting for him to begin. His face was hard, the skin pale and stretched, and he was thinner. The first glass had been gulped. And the second. Now he sipped the third. "You're more beautiful than ever."

"Thank you. Your Hinodeh, how is she?"

"More beautiful than ever."

"If you love her so much, André, why do your lips tighten and your eyes pop out with rage when I mention her name—you said it was all right to ask about her." A few days ago he had told her about their agreement. Part, not all. It had burst out when despair had overwhelmed him. "If you're so adamant about not making love in the dark and the huge price this Raiko demanded why did you agree in the first place?"

"I . . . it was necessary," he said, not looking at her. He could not tell her the real reason—it had been enough to see Seratard's lips curl and see him avoid making contact ever since, careful never to use the same eating utensils or glass even though it was only caught from a woman or a man—wasn't it? "I just took one look at her and, *mon Dieu*, don't you understand what love is, how . . ." The words died away. He poured another glass, the bottle almost empty now. "You cannot believe how crushingly desirable she was that once." He gulped the wine. "Sorry, I need money."

"Of course. But I have only a little left."

"You have paper, with his chop."

"Oh?"

His smile was, if anything, more crooked. "Fortunately shroffs talk to shroffs, clerks to clerks. Fill in another tomorrow. Please. Five hundred Mex."

"That's too much."

"Not half enough, *chérie*," he said, his voice barely audible. He got up and closed the curtains to the last of the sunset, then turned up the oil lamp that was on the table and reached for the bottle. The dregs went into his glass, and then he slammed the bottle back in its ice bucket. "Do you think I like doing this to you? You think I don't know it's blackmail? Don't worry, I'm reasonable, I only want what you can presently afford. A hundred Mex, or the guinea equivalent tonight, two hundred tomorrow, a hundred the next."

"That's not possible."

"Everything's possible." He took an envelope out of his pocket. The envelope contained a single sheet of paper that he unfolded carefully. Dozens of shreds of green paper were pasted meticulously on it to complete a perfect jigsaw. He laid it on the table, well out of her reach. At once she recognized her father's handwriting. The second page that she had seen André tear up so long ago.

"Can you read it from there?" he asked softly.

"No."

"Your loving father wrote, he signed and dated it, 'and hope, as we discussed, that you will arrange an early betrothal and marriage by whatever means you can. It's important for our future. Struan will permanently solve Richaud Frères. Never mind th—' "

"Never mind, André," she said as softly, no need now to disguise the venom. "The words are indelibly written on my brain. Indelibly. Am I buying it, or is it a permanent threat?"

"It's an insurance," he said, folding it and replacing it with care. "Now it goes back to a safe place, with details of the Affaire Angelique, in case anything nasty happens to me."

Abruptly she laughed, unbalancing him. "Oh, André, do you think I'd try to murder you? Me?"

"It would wreck any financial arrangement Tess might offer, may be forced to offer, and put you in the dock."

"How silly you are." She picked up her glass and sipped her

champagne and he noticed, disquieted, how steady her hand was. She was watching him placidly, thinking how foolish he was, foolish to let her know he had done what he had done and was a total cheat, but even more foolish to rile against Hinodeh for preferring the dark—perhaps he looks awful naked—and more foolish to scream about the price he paid, because both are insignificant if she's everything he says she is. "I'd like to meet this Hinodeh. Please arrange it."

"Eh?"

Amused at his expression, she said, "What's so strange about that? I have an interest in her, I'm financing her, the love of your life. Yes?"

Shakily he got up and went to the sideboard and poured brandy. "Would you like some?"

"No, thank you." Only her eyes had moved.

Again he sat opposite her. A draft played with the flame and made her eyes glitter. "A hundred. Please."

"When do I stop paying, André?" she asked pleasantly.

The brandy tasted better than the wine. He faced that question. "When she's paid for, before you leave."

"Before I leave? You mean I can't leave until then?"

"When she's paid for, before you leave."

She frowned and went over to the desk and opened a side drawer. The little purse contained the equivalent of about two hundred Mex in gold oban. "And if there's no money?"

"It will come from Tess, there's no other way. She'll pay, somehow we'll make that happen."

" 'We' will?"

"I promised," he said, the whites of his eyes bloodshot. "Your future is my future. At least on that we both agree."

She opened the purse and counted half. Then, not knowing why, put them all back and handed it to him. "There's about two hundred Mex there," she said, smiling strangely. "On account."

"I wish I understood you. I used to."

"Then I was a silly young girl. Now I'm not."

He nodded slowly. Then took out the envelope and held it to the flame. She let out a little gasp as the corner caught and then it flared and he put it into an ashtray and together they watched it curl and twist and die. He crushed the ash with the bottom of his glass.

"Why?" she asked.

"Because you understand about Hinodeh. And like it or not we're partners. If Tess doesn't pay you I'm a dead man." He stuck out his hand. "Peace?"

She put her hand in his and smiled. "Peace. Thank you."

He got up. "I'd better check on *Prancing Cloud*. If Tess's aboard, it will speed things up."

After he had gone she sifted the ashes but not a single word could be seen. Easy for André to forge a copy and tear it up and present it as the original and burn it—and still have the restored original secreted away for later use. That's just the kind of stratagem he would adore. Why burn the false one? To make me trust him further, to forgive the blackmail.

Peace? The only peace from a blackmailer is when the deadly exposure he threatens you with no longer needs to be hidden. In my case that's when SHE has paid, and the money banked. And after André gets what he wants—Hinodeh, perhaps. What is it she wants? She hides from him in the dark. Why? Because of his color? To titillate? For revenge? Because he's not Japanese?

I know now that the act of love can go from terror to ecstasy to delusion, with every variation in between. My first time with Malcolm was in the light, the second in darkness and both were beautiful. With *him* of the other life always in the light and he was beautiful and deadly, his color beautiful, everything beautiful and deadly and terrifying and blindingly powerful, nothing like my husband, Malcolm, whom I truly loved. And honored—and honor still, and will forever.

Her sharp ear caught the toot of the cutter's steam whistle. She opened the curtains and saw the launch hurrying away from their jetty, port and starboard lights clear, Albert MacStruan in the cabin. In the roads *Prancing Cloud* was scarcely visible, downing sails and easing for moorings.

Her mind swirled aboard and in her mind she saw her enemy—as ever, thin-lipped, pale-eyed, tall and stiff-backed, bony and badly dressed—then sped away to the outer harbor and Malcolm's burial and she smiled, glorying in that victory, the sound of her heart pulsing in her ears. Then she curled up in her chair again—*his* chair, their chair, another victory—and watched the dark become darker, only riding lights to be seen, hardly able to contain her excitement.

Surely Edward would be aboard.

THE DOOR TO JAMIE'S OFFICE
swung open and Vargas rushed in, out of breath, "Launch's left *Cloud,*
senhor," he said, his heavy street clothes still on, hat and head scarf
wrapped around his face, telescope in hand. "Four or five passengers."

"Is she aboard?" Jamie did not look up from the packing case he
was filling with papers. When there was no immediate answer his voice
edged, "Damn it, is she aboard?"

"I . . . I'm . . . I think so."

"I said to let me know when you were sure, not before!"

"I'm—I'm sorry, senhor, I was at the end of the jetty and looked
through the spyglass and thought I'd better report and ask what—what
I should do."

"Go back and meet her, but first make sure all servants are ready,
make sure there's a fire in the tai-pan's suite, she'll take that, Mr.
MacStruan's sure to move out."

"But that will mean she'll be next door to Mrs. Angeli—"

"I know that, for God's sake, but that's the tai-pan's suite and that's
the one she'll have!"

Vargas fled. Unable to resist, Jamie hurried to the window. The cutter
was nearing shore. Just riding lights outside and dancing in the chop. He
focused his binoculars. Vague shapes in the cabin but positively one a
woman. No doubt about the bonnet, and no mistaking her tall, erect
carriage and the way she rode the pitch and toss and tilt of the boat.

"Shit!" The breath sighed out of his mouth. To steady the image, he
leaned against the window. Not much better. One of the shapes he
identified as Captain Strongbow more by his height and bulk than
anything else. Two other men, no three—one of them MacStruan.

The cutter came in fast, the storm damage on the prow still easy to see, not yet completely repaired. Curious bystanders waited under the swinging lantern on the dock, everyone muffled against the dreaded winter flux with hats and head scarfs that were now obligatory. Difficult to see faces but he thought he recognized André there, and . . . ah yes, Vervene, Heavenly and, yes, and Nettlesmith. The vultures gathering, he thought, though like me, the main ones are watching from their windows.

Tonight the dark oppressed him. In his room his fire was good but now seemed to have lost its warmth. His throat felt tight and his chest hurt. Control yourself, he thought. She's not your problem.

Captain Strongbow was first onto the wharf in his heavy sea coat. Still difficult to see clearly but no mistaking him. Then, ah yes, MacStruan. They turned and helped her up. She was wrapped against the cold, stiff-backed, dark clothes, dark bonnet tied with the inevitable heavy scarf. *Her* size. Shit!

The other two passengers climbed onto the jetty. He recognized them. A moment's hesitation then he went out and along the passage to the tai-pan's office. Angelique was peering into the dark through a crack in the curtain, her fire glowing nicely, lamps lit and the room cozy. "Ah, Jamie. I can't see them clearly. Is she there?"

"Afraid so, yes." He saw no change in her expression. "Here." He offered her the binoculars. "I thought you might like these."

"No need for me to look, or be afraid, Jamie. Who else?" Her voice was the thinnest it had ever been. "Who's with her?"

"Strongbow, Hoag and Gornt."

She turned back to the window to hide but for an instant he had seen the joy that flooded her face. Never mind if Jamie saw, she was thinking, dizzy with excitement. That woman and Edward together? The two of them together, Hoag as well! Doesn't that portend success, Edward's success, that he convinced her? "I'll be upstairs, dressing for dinner. If anyone wants to see me, I'll come down again. Thanks, dear Jamie." Impulsively, she hugged him. And left.

He stared after her. Why the joy? If Tess is with Hoag, the heavy guns have arrived. Haven't they?

He went back to his office perplexed, leaving the door ajar, and continued to pack papers and books, his fingers doing the work, his mind elsewhere: on Tess, the future, the shoya, Nemi tonight, the Noble House that he had given twenty years to—Be honest, you don't really want to leave and know it's a bad time to go out on your own— thinking about Angelique's grim future, tomorrow's meeting with the

Swiss Minister and possible imports from their armament-watch facto-ries, all mixed with the news of the incredible Yoshi meeting, Babcott and Tyrer now in Yedo, the bullion the Bakufu had advanced already counted and accurate—and about Nakama, poor fellow.

Poor fellow? He's an assassin, the worst kind. I never felt that, never once did I feel threatened. He must be in Drunk Town or somewhere in the Yoshiwara. If the news flashed to us, someone must have whis-pered to him and he fled. Damn it! Now I'll have to cut Tyrer in or Johann . . .

Voices in the foyer broke into his reverie. A polyglot of voices: MacStruan, Vargas, Hoag, servants bustling around.

No need to greet them. I'll be summoned soon enough. Depressed, he continued with his work, almost done now.

"Jamie!"

He looked around. And was paralyzed. Maureen. His Maureen in the doorway! Maureen Ross. Navy blue winter bonnet, blue eyes peeping out above the folds of her heavy woolen head scarf. Navy blue topcoat over a dark blue dress. Maureen Ross, twenty-eight. Tall, a fraction taller than Tess—the average height nowadays a little over five feet, Queen Victoria four feet eleven. "Christ almighty," he said, voice strangled, mind gone.

"Hello to you, Jamie McFay." She stayed in the doorway, standing straight like her father, her voice lilting. "Can I come in, please?" She unwound the scarf and smiled tentatively.

Now he could see her. Same clear face, not pretty but strong and curiously appealing, hazel freckles, and just as he had last seen her just over three years ago—the dock at Glasgow—though then there were tears at their parting. He had forgotten how her eyes . . . "Hello, Sparkles," he muttered without thinking, using his nickname for her. "Jesus Christ . . . Maureen?"

Her laugh trilled. "I take that as a yes and you'll no' be blaspheming anymore, laddie. Once is fair, me coming like a wraith from the night, wanting to surprise you." Her smile and the lilt to her voice made her more attractive than she really was, and the light that danced in her eyes and the love that she wore like a shield. She closed the door and looked at him again. "You look grand, Jamie, a little tired, but you're as bonny as ever."

He had straightened up but still stood behind the desk, his mind jumbled with My God it's you, not Tess, it's you, easy to mistake in the dark, almost same height same stiff back—remembering his half-hearted, negative letters over the last year and the final one breaking their engagement, his soundless voice saying, Sorry, Maureen, I wrote you, we're not getting married, sorry, don't want to get married, can't now, now that I'm on my own, worst possible time and why didn't . . .

"Och, Jamie," she was saying from across the room, watching and waiting, her smile deepening, "you canna know how happy I am to see you, to be here at last, aye, the adventures I've had will fill a volume." When he didn't move or reply, a small frown wrinkled her forehead. "Will you no' get your wits about you, laddie?"

"Tess!" he croaked. "I—we thought you were Tess Struan."

"Mrs. Struan? No, she's in Hong Kong. Such a lady, she arranged for me to come here, didn't charge me a penny piece. 'You go see your Jamie McFay with my compliments,' she said, and introduced me to Captain Strongbow—who gave me a cabin to mysel'—and to fine Dr. Hoag and Mister Smartypants Gornt."

"Eh?"

"That laddie thinks he's God's gift to womanhood but not to me. I'm affianced, I told him, affianced before God to Mr. Jamie McFay. He said he was your friend, Jamie, and Dr. Hoag told me he saved your life so I was nice but kept a distance. Och, laddie, there's so much to learn, so much to tell."

"Christ," he muttered, not hearing her, "easy to make the mistake with the scarf around your face, you and Tess're both the same size, stand the same way . . ."

"Huh!" Maureen said, her eyes suddenly fiery. "I'll thank you no' to take the Lord's name in vain, and she's a mite shorter and much thicker and much older and her hair is grey, mine's brown and even in the dark I'm not like her!" When her sudden smile at her own pleasantry did not get through to him, she sighed. Exasperated, she looked around the room. She saw the decanter. At once went over to it, sniffed to make sure it was whisky, crinkled her nose with distaste but poured him a glass, and a dribble in another.

"Here." She looked up at him, close for the first time, a sudden beam covering her. "My Da' always needed a wusky when the shock of Scotland being part of the British Isles hit him."

The spell broke. Jamie laughed and took her in his arms and hugged her, welcoming her, and the glasses almost spilled out of her hand. "Watch it, laddie," she gasped, managed to put them down and hugged him desperately—all the waiting and standing there, seeing his shock and not the welcome she'd hoped for, trying to be strong and adult, not knowing what to do or how to say that she loved him and could not bear the thought of losing him so she had gambled, gambled and left her sanctuary, she had put her trust in God, took her prayerbook and Bible and her father's derringer in her purse and set out blindly on ten thousand miles of fear. Inside. But not outside—oh no, never, that's not the Ross way!

"Och, Jamie laddie, laddie . . ."

"It's all right," he murmured, wishing her trembles away.

In time the shuddering stopped and she released herself, untied her bonnet and let her long plait of red-brown hair uncoil. "That's better," she said. "You're a bonny man, thank you." She handed him his glass and took hers and touched glasses. "Scotland forever," she said as a toast, and sipped. "That tastes dreadful, Jamie, but I'm powerful pleased to see you, I canna say it any better."

Her smile was more tentative now, some of her confidence gone. His embrace had been like a brother's, not a lover's, oh God oh God oh God.To hide from him she looked around as she took off her coat and gloves. Her dress was warm and well cut, another shade of blue and showed off her curves and hourglass waist. "Your Mr. MacStruan says you can use your suite and I can have the rooms next door until we have a place of our own. Have you packed up your rooms yet, Jamie?"

"No, not yet." Confused, not knowing how to start but start he must. Soon. "This . . . all my papers and books were first, I was starting upstairs tomorrow. Everything, the furniture here and upstairs, belongs to Struan's."

"Never mind. We can buy our own." She sat in the chair opposite the desk and looked at him. Hands in her lap. Waiting. Sure that now she had to bite her tongue and wait for him to begin. She had done her part by arriving. Perhaps done too much, arriving unannounced, but she had thought about that carefully and done the best she could by writing the letter, and had imagined this meeting hour after hour in the nauseating months at sea, during the storms and once, in the China seas off Singapore, during a mutiny of Chinese steerage passengers, pirates amongst them, that had been put down bloodily. Jamie was her lodestar and now the time of reckoning had arrived.

'He's a bad man, this Jamie McFay,' her mother had told her when she announced her decision. 'I've said it and said it, and he'll do you no good, lassie. His letters are anything but encouraging, just the reverse.'

'I mean to go, Ma darling. Will Da' lend me the money?'

'Aye, if you ask him.'

'I mean to go. I must. I'm twenty-eight. I'm old. Past normal marriage age. I've waited so long and would wait another three years if need be but . . . it's now or never. I've decided. Do you understand, Ma?'

'Aye. I understand. But . . . well, at least you'll be with him, you'll be with your man, if you marry, not like me.'

She had seen the tears and listened to advice never given before, secrets never whispered before, and then her mother said, 'Bless you, lassie, go with God, lassie. Let's tell thy da'.' He was a Major, Indian Army retired, twenty-five years service, eighteen of those with the newly formed Gurkha Regiment, home on leave only every two or three years, before being forced to retire from wounds a decade ago, loathing retirement.

'Aye lassie, go wi' my blessing on two conditions,' he said. 'If he spurns you, tell him I'll find him and kill him, second, if ever he rapes you, hurts you, cut off his balls—I'll lend you my kookrie, young Duncan won't need it for ten years yet.'

'Yes, Da'.' The kookrie, the Gurkha knife, was his most prized possession. She was the eldest of three sisters, with a brother of eight, and the first to leave home—children of Britain were children of the Empire.

Jamie put more coal on the fire and moved his chair closer before he sat down. He took her hand. "Maureen, three months ago I wrote to you."

"You wrote many a letter, not enough," she said lightly, to give herself more time to prepare.

"In all my letters for the last year I tried to point out as best I could that this is no place for a lady, it's not India where there's a regimental life an—"

"I've never been to India, as you know, Jamie, my ma only went once and never again." She held his hand in both of hers. "Dinna fash yoursel', this place can be bonny, never fear. That's the job of a woman. I can make it bonny."

The tightness in his throat was choking him. No way to ease into this, his brain was shouting at him, do it or you'll never do it, do it now! Of course it's not fair but you've not been fair to her at all, not fair for years, you're rotten to have taken advantage of her all these years, my God, you've been engaged three and knew her two before that and you're rotten . . . admit it and say it quickly. Now!

The flood commenced: "Three months ago I wrote you that I felt, it must have arrived after you left, I thought it wise we should break off our engagement and you should forget me and that I was terribly sorry but it was the best for you and I won't go home and live there and work there, I won't leave Asia until I have to, if I get sick or . . . I won't leave, can't, I love Asia, love my job and there's no hope for a happy time for you, I'm not worth it and I admit I've taken advantage of you but we can't marry, not possible and now that I'm going out on my own . . ." He stopped for breath then added throatily, "I don't know what else to say, there's nothing more to say except again to apologize . . . there it is."

He had taken his hand away. His stomach was churning. Out came his handkerchief to mop his brow. "Sorry," he said lamely, and got up and sat down, then toyed with the glass. "Sorry."

Her hands lay in her lap. Her eyes were concentrated and open and had never left his face. "Dinna be sorry," she said gently with the barest frown. "These things happen, laddie."

His mouth dropped open. "Then you agree?"

She laughed. "Of course, to part of what you said, no' to all, of course—you're a man and I'm a woman and we see things differently."

"Eh? How?"

"Well, first about jobs," she said. "A woman's job, her work, is to look after a man, to make a home, that's what I've been trained for, home and family are the most important things in the world." She saw Jamie about to interrupt so she added quickly, "My da' thinks the Empire comes first but he's a man. Men have jobs to go to, to work at to bring home the porridge, a little meat, and aye, some wusky. But there has to be a home to bring it to. Without a woman there's no home. It's very important for a man to have someone you can trust to share the burden while you work, or seek a job or start your own business. You can trust me. Of the two, trying to start your own business is best for you. Mr. Gornt wants to do the same."

"He does?"

"Aye, sometime in the future, he says. Now he's back here to take over Brock and Sons an—"

"He is?" Jamie blinked, diverted.

"Aye. He says he's taking the job of this man who tried to kill you, Mr. Greyfifth."

"Greyforth. Norbert Greyforth." Jamie's mind slammed back into gear: I must be losing my wits with you appearing like a ghost, I'd forgotten about Hoag and Malcolm and Hong Kong. "What happened in Hong Kong? About Malcolm Struan? Did Gornt say anything about Morgan Brock or Tyler Brock?"

"Patience, my bonny laddie, that comes later. Back to you and me since you brought the subject up as you did. We'll make a grand team, the best, I promise. We're engaged. I promise I will make the best wife ever, I promise."

"But don't you see, lassie, it won't work," he said, hating himself, but totally sure. "This place is rough, the life rough, there are few women here, you'll have no friends, nothing to do."

She laughed. "Jamie, Jamie, you hav'na heard a single word I've said. Now this is what w—"

A knock on the door stopped her. She called out, "Won't be a second!" She got up, continuing in the same gentle but firm voice, "That'll be Dr. Hoag, he was urgent to see you but I begged a couple of minutes first, I could'na' wait to see you. Now I'll leave you to him." She collected her hat and gloves and coat and scarf. "Dinna concern yourself about me, I'll be changed and ready in good time. I'll knock on your door. Dinner's at nine, dinna forget now."

"Eh?" he asked blankly.

"This Russian Count, Zerevev, some name like that. We've accepted for dinner, Mr. MacStruan told me all about it."

She swept out, thanked Hoag, and before Jamie could say anything, Hoag had closed the door and had rushed up to him and said breathlessly, the words tumbling out: "Hong Kong went like a dream, Jamie, Malcolm was buried with full honors, *at sea* like he and Angelique wanted!"

"He was what?"

Hoag chortled, "You could have knocked me down with a feather too, Tess arranged it off Shek-O, one of his favorite places in all the world, a few days before I arrived. Full honors, Jamie, all flags at half mast, ships dipping their flags, cannonade salutes, pipers, everything, the funeral of the tai-pan, though he never was. The papers covered everything, I've the cuttings, month's mourning for Hong Kong, Governor ordered a special service in our church on the knoll in Happy Valley of Culum fame, Gordon Chen threw the biggest, most explosive procession and wake in Chinatown's history—except for the one he gave Dirk—of course starting the usual bloody fires on the slopes and they say a few thousand squatter shacks went up in smoke, not only that, when I saw Tess . . . can I have a drink, I'm parched!"

"Of course. Go on, don't stop," Jamie said, and poured for both of them, his own glass long since empty. He noticed his fingers were shaking. Christ, why would Tess do that, a sea burial, and what the hell is Maureen doing accepting for dinner when we've got to talk? "Go on, for Christ's sake!"

First Hoag drank. "My God, that's good!" He took off his coat and sat down, took a deep breath and felt better. "My God, I'm pleased to see you. Where was I? Oh, yes! When I saw Tess the first time I was so upset for her. It was awful. I met her in Culum's old office and she said, 'Ronald, tell me the bad, all the details, tell it as it happened.' She was standing by the huge desk, straight as a spar, pale, never so pale, Jamie—the painting of Dirk on the wall, staring at you with that green-eyed challenge, daring you to lie. I told her as best I could, of course she'd heard bits and pieces from Strongbow—you remember I'd told him to tell her I was on the mail ship and sorry I couldn't come by *Cloud* because there was an operation I had to perform.

"She never wavered, she never *wavered,* Jamie, just listened as I told about the Tokaidō, engagement, marriage and death as best I could, as gently as I could, the duel, Norbert, you and Gornt. It all came out, don't remember my exact words but I told it as it happened." He stopped a moment, less nervous now. "You know how she is, always holding back, always hiding, the stiffest upper lip in Christendom. She just thanked me, told me she had the death certificate and inquest papers from Strongbow. Remarkable woman. Uncanny. That's about all—oh yes, she thanked me for taking care of the coffin with the undertaker, which went perfectly, thank God."

"Eh?"

Hoag's eyes brightened. "Naturally I didn't want the coffin opened up. I'd told Strongbow to send it directly to Blore, Christenson, Herberts, Herberts and Crink, do lots of business with them, and ordered them 'for medical reasons' to put our coffin directly into one of theirs, top quality, silver handles, and to screw it tight at once, no lying in state or opening it, I recommended against that due to decomposition etc. and had advised Tess by letter to that effect in the strongest terms. Glad to say it went perfectly from our point of view, and Malcolm's." Hoag refilled his glass. "Glad I went. Otherwise all's well that ends well."

"Did you tell her about the other, about our burial?"

"Christ, no, am I that stupid? You're witless, Jamie."

Jamie said, "I just asked to make sure," not pleased to be reminded that Maureen had used the same word. I think I really am losing them. What the hell am I going to do with her? "Did Tess say anything about Angelique?"

"What she planned to do? No, though she asked dozens of questions. How is Angelique?"

"Fine—outwardly. Calm, stays to herself, occasionally comes to dinner. Tonight she's going to Zergeyev's, at Sir William's request. Nothing like her old sparkle"—there's that word again, he thought miserably—"but, well, lovelier than ever. What did Tess ask?"

"Nothing much, only about the facts as I knew them, that yes, I believed they were in love, that Malcolm pursued her, not the other way around, that she was a lady about him, she accepted his proposal and agreed to be married on *Pearl*."

"But nothing about what she plans to do?"

"No, that's the strange part. I thought she'd fume about her, ask my advice, give me a clue but she didn't, after all I'm their family doctor for years, employed by her, by Struan's, and I know her better than anyone. She didn't comment on anything, volunteer anything, the questions were just to cover details I'd forgotten to mention. Weird."

"Yes," Jamie said. "She'll have a plan."

"I agree. Of course the story was in the press from the gutter to the Peak in lurid details, 'TAI-PAN DIES ON WEDDING NIGHT,' that kind of headline though she had tried to bury it—sorry, no pun intended. I've all the cuttings for you, and this." His eyes took on a different glow. He gave Jamie an envelope. Tess's handwriting. *Mr. J. McFay, Personal by Hand.* "Before you ask, I don't know what's in it. She just said, Please give it to Mr. McFay as soon as you arrive."

Jamie put it on the desk. "Why did you come back?"

"Before I forget, something else. Old Man Brock and his equally vile son, Sir Morgan, turned up at the funeral."

"What, uninvited?"

"Created a furor! It happened like this. Tess arranged the funeral on *China Cloud*. Gun carriage to the clipper along the promenade. Forty guests invited aboard, Governor, all the nobs, Admiral Sir Vincent-Sindery, General Skaffer—the new Commander in chief of Asia, very pukka and Indian Army—all tai-pans and Gordon Chen. No press. Just as *China Cloud* swung into wind off Shek-O place, the service about to begin, Old Man Brock and Morgan arrived in his clipper, *Hunting Witch*. She stood off, a few chains away, dressed overall, his flag at half mast, him and Morgan on the quarterdeck dressed in funeral finery, top hats, ruffled shirts, and when the coffin went into the sea, the bastard fired a cannonade salute and opened champagne—everyone aboard said they heard the cork go. They drank a toast, threw the glasses and bottle into the sea, raising their toppers as they sailed off noisily."

"Bastards! Bloody bastards!"

"Yes! Later they claimed 'it were to honor the poor dead laddie!' The Governor was standing next to Tess. He told me she did nothing, said nothing, just stayed like a poker, except he heard her breath hiss out and the violence in it shocked him, said it made his balls jump, you know the feeling. . . . Oh, I forgot to mention, Gornt was also on Brock's quarterdeck."

"Maureen said he was taking over Brock's here."

"Yes. Even so he's a nice young man, I think. Even so. He told me he was ordered aboard *Hunting Witch* and . . . By Jove, I forgot to mention Maureen! Jamie, you're a lucky man."

"Thanks."

"Very lucky." Hoag stuck out his hand. "Congratulations."

"Thanks." Jamie shook hands and pretended to be pleased, filled with gloom. "We thought . . . I thought she was Tess. Through the binoculars, the dark and being muffled up, easy to make the mistake."

"Eh? Nonsense, she's nothing like her at all!"

Aggravated Jamie said, "I know that but they're about the same height, and it's the way she stood, just like Tess, you know, stiff."

Hoag frowned, then grunted. "Never occurred to me. Now that you mention it that's true, but she's nothing like Tess to look at, she must be at least ten to fifteen years younger and that red-brown hair of hers and sparkling personality."

"Christ, give over! I know that! It was an easy mistake."

"A lucky one." Hoag felt queasy. "Wouldn't have enjoyed the trip with Tess, my God, no! Your Maureen's a smasher! She said she'd written that she was arriving."

"Yes, at Hong Kong, not here. And no arrival date there."

"Ah, obviously there was no time as *Prancing Cloud* was leaving imminently and she'd just arrived." Hoag chuckled. "Best watch her or you'll lose her. Gornt was quite taken."

Jamie flushed, jealous in spite of himself. "Thanks for the tip. How're Tess's kids? Did you see them?"

"Oh, yes. They're all healthy, though Duncan had another rotten cold. They'd all been to the funeral—I heard it was so sad, young Duncan trying to be brave, Emma and Rose crying, Tess veiled, heavily veiled—everyone knowing it was the end of an era, the end of Dirk's direct line except Duncan, and he can't inherit for years, the lad's just ten. Doesn't augur well for the Noble House. The hottest rumor in Hong Kong is that Brock's have got the Noble House on the run."

"No way!" Jamie tried to sound convincing. "The new tai-pan will come from Robb's line, Robb Struan, Dirk's stepbrother. One of his sons or grandsons will be tai-pan."

"I suppose you're right, but it won't be the same. Bloody awful about Malcolm, he was Tess's hope. All the time I was in Hong Kong, I was thinking about our burial, so unnecessary, eh? It's best if we put that away forever. Malcolm was buried there, off Shek-O."

"I wish he had been, as Sir William and we all wanted." Last night Jamie had another nightmare about what the Bosun said he had seen, the corpse clawing for the surface, eyes wide open. He felt chilled again. "We did the best we could. Now," he said, "why are you back?"

Hoag got up. "Tess asked if I'd, er, deliver mail to MacStruan, you and . . . and see Angelique and give her a letter." He saw Jamie's eyes. "I don't know what's in them."

"Them?" Jamie said sharply. "You said a letter."

Hoag reddened. "Oh, er, yes. Yes, well, a letter. I don't know what's in it. Well, I'd better be go—"

"Come on, for God's sake!"

"Tess asked me to give her a . . . a letter, that's all."

"Come on, I know you!"

Hoag said irritably, "I think I'd better go and see her, she'll want to know—"

"Sit down! What letters, for Christ's sweet sake?"

"I don't know ab—"

"Don't give me that shit! What letters?"

Hoag hesitated, then blurted out, "If you'll swear on your mother's head I'll . . . I'll tell you."

"Done!"

The Doctor sat down. "She, Tess, she just said, 'Give that woman this letter, wait a week or so and then give her one of these two letters.' She gave me three in all, I don't know what's in them, I swear to God I don't."

"A week? You mean until Preggers Day? One of two letters, eh? One if she's preggers, one if she isn't?"

"The 11th would—would be the first day but it's not possible to tell then, have to wait at least two weeks after that and even then, safer to wait the month and see if she . . . if she does or doesn't menstruate. The date may be off, it's difficult to tell sometimes, in her case because the poor girl has gone through a tremendous amount of stress—Tess asked me to wait until I could be sure." He exhaled. "There, now you know everything."

"Tess asked you to wait until you've examined her?"

"Well, yes, until I'm sure."

"Then it's one letter if she is, the other if she isn't?"

"Yes . . . I told you. Yes."

"Who else have you told?" Jamie's eyes burned into him.

"No one."

"Who?"

"Go to hell!" Hoag shouted, then spat out, "Gornt!"

"Jesus Christ, why him?"

"I don't know, he seemed to know, jumped to the same conclusion as I suppose everyone will. I agree it's fairly obvious now I'm back—I told Tess that but she said nothing, just looked at me with those eyes of hers. It's easy for you, Jamie," he said, seething. "It's easy for you and the Gornts of the world, you're strong and used to business and isn't business lying most of the time? Well, doctors aren't." Disgusted with his inability to keep secrets, Hoag blew the breath out of his mouth. "Can't change after all this time. Tess said to tell Sir William why I was back, Albert and you, and no one else."

"Don't worry, you're right, there won't be a man in Yokohama who won't realize why you're here, for Christ's sake. Poor bloody Angelique! Who else have you mail for, from Tess?"

"I . . . Sir William."

"Who else? Who else, for Christ's sweet sake?"

"Heavenly Skye."

Pretending a tranquility he did not feel, Hoag handed Angelique the envelope that was sealed with the chop of the Noble House. Her stomach had been churning ever since Jamie had told her who had arrived with *Prancing Cloud,* however much she had tried to be detached. Even Vargas's almost immediate news that the woman was Senhor McFay's fiancée and not Tess Struan had not settled her. Nor had Hoag's rambling story about Malcolm's funeral, which had confused her even more. The writing on the envelope was copperplate: 'Angelique Richaud, By Hand.'

"Why don't you read it while I'm here," he was saying, concerned at her sudden flush.

"You mean in case I faint?" she asked sharply, sitting up in the tall chair beside the fire, Malcolm's chair that she had taken from his suite before vacating it for Albert MacStruan.

Hoag said kindly, "I mean you may want to talk. I'm a friend, as well as a doctor." He had rushed upstairs directly from Jamie, glad to leave the inquisition, had greeted and hugged her and brushed aside her immediate, What happened in Hong Kong, saying, 'Just a second, let me look at you.' He had scrutinized her as a doctor, then as a friend. In both cases what he saw had pleased him. "Just a suggestion."

"The letter's not addressed correctly. It should be Mrs. Angelique Struan, or Mrs. Malcolm Struan." Awkwardly, she returned it.

"Tess said you would do that." It was said gently.

"If she's so wise why didn't she address it properly?"

"It's difficult for her as it is difficult for you. She's a mother who's lost a son. Be patient, Angelique."

"Patient? Me? When I'm under siege for marrying and loving a fine man who . . . You're on her side. Struan's pays you."

"True, but my side is what I think best, that's not saleable, even to you." Hoag sat amiably in his chair. The room was warm and feminine and filled with tension. He saw the vein in her neck pulsing hard, fingers twitching ever so slightly. "I helped you, and Malcolm, but only because I thought it best. For your private knowledge I resigned while I was in Hong Kong. This is my last task for the Noble House."

She was startled. "Why did you do that?"

Again the same strange smile. "I'm going back to India, I'm going to try to find that which I lost. Soon as I can."

"Ah! Arjumand." That made her feel better and she leaned over and touched him. "Sorry. Sorry I said what I said, it was wrong. Sorry. It's just—sorry."

"Think nothing of it. Don't forget I'm a doctor, I do really understand the stress you're under. I was prepared for worse." He broke the seal and opened the letter. "She told me to do this." Inside was another envelope. This was addressed simply: Angelique. "A compromise, eh? A suggested compromise."

"Yours?"

"Yes."

"Do you know what it says?"

"No. God's truth. Do you want me to leave?"

Her gaze locked on to the letter. In a moment she shook her head so he went to the window to give her space, moved the curtains aside and watched the night, his own heart pounding.

She hesitated, then opened it. No greeting. No name.

I cannot forgive you for what you did to my son.
I truly believe, at your father's behest and encouragement,
you set your cap for my son to snare him into marriage, any

*form of marriage. Your 'marriage' to my son is invalid, I am
assured. This 'marriage' hastened his death, I am assured—
the death certificate indicates this, I am assured. To that end
Struan's solicitors are drafting writs for the case to be
brought expeditiously before the High Court in Hong Kong.
If you carry my son's child this will not divert the course of
justice or avoid declaring the child illegitimate.*

*I cannot thank you enough for the invaluable information
given me, at your instigation, by a mutual acquaintance.*

*If, as I believe will be the case, his material proves to be
valid, I and the Noble House will be indebted to you, and to
this person in a manner beyond price. That he named a price,
reasonable considering its value, is not your affair, you asked
for none and will get none. But your gift to my son's memory
and the future of Struan's deserves consideration.*

How to resolve this impasse?

*The resolution, if any can be found, must be private be-
tween us foes—we will always be that—and as women.*

*First, I ask that you cooperate with Dr. Hoag, allowing
him to examine you at the correct time to establish if you are
bearing a child or not. Of course Dr. Babcott or any other
doctor you wish can be consulted to corroborate the diagnosis.*

*Second, let us wait for the second month to be sure, then
we can proceed. By that time the legal brief will be complete
and ready for court submission—this is not meant as a
threat, only as fact. By that time, the evidence of our acquaintance will have been put to work, partially. At present I do not
see how it can fail. That you persuaded him to see me has, as
said above, obligated me and the Noble House to you.*

*Perhaps, by then, with the help of God, the impasse may be
solved. Tess Struan, Hong Kong, December 30th, '62.*

Angelique's mind was hacking between happiness and terror, victory and defeat. Had she won or had she failed? Tess Struan promised
nothing, but had she waved an olive branch? Legal brief? Courts?

Witness box? Ashen now, she remembered Skye's words about how easy it would be for the opposition to paint her as a penniless Jezebel, daughter of a felon and other horrid twisted truths. 'Impasse' and 'resolution'? Didn't that mean she had won, at least a partial victory?

Edward! Tonight or tomorrow Edward will tell me! And Mr. Skye, he's clever, he'll know. Oh, God, I hope he'll know.

She looked up and saw Hoag watching her. "Oh! Sorry, I'd forgotten . . ." Numbly she twisted the material of a sleeve, her foot tapping restlessly. "Oh, did you want a drink, I can ring for Ah Soh, I . . . sorry . . . I don't seem to . . ." The words were difficult to form and he heard the change and wondered if this was the beginning of the breakdown he had forecast. Signs were there, fingers and toes working unnoticed, face white, eyes wide, pupils changed.

"What did she say?" he asked easily.

"I . . . well, nothing except to—to wait until . . ." The words drifted away and her gaze went to the distance.

"Until?" he asked, to bring her back, hiding his concern.

But she was swept up in what she had read. So the battle lines had been drawn. She knew the worst, or the best. Her enemy had made the first move and declared herself. Now she could join battle. On her own terms. The nausea slid away. In its place came fire. The thought that SHE had laid out the foul and possible so icily was making her sting with rage—nothing on her side, no concern for her, no tiny concession for all the love and agony and pain over Malcolm's death, nothing. Nothing. And worst of all *illegitimate,* when they were married properly according to British law . . . *I am assured*!

Never fear, she seethed, that's branded on my memory in molten steel, and she looked at Hoag again, quivering. "She said she wants to—to wait . . . to wait until we—you and I—we know if I'm carrying Malcolm's child or not. She wants to make sure, that's what she wants."

"And then?"

"She doesn't say. She—she wants to wait and me to wait. There's a vague . . . I think she says perhaps there can be a peace, a resol—" The quivering stopped as a decision washed it away and her voice became sibilant, sizzling with venom. "I hope there will be a peace, because . . . because, by the Blessed Mother, I am Malcolm Struan's widow, and no one, no court, not even Tess Goddamned Struan can take that away from me!"

He covered his nervousness, saying cautiously, "We all believe you are. But you've got to be calm and not worry. If you break, she wins, you lose, whatever the truth. No need . . ."

The door swung open. Ah Soh waddled in. "Missee-tai-tai?"

"*Ayeeyah!*" Angelique flared. "Get out, why you no knock?"

Ah Soh planted her feet, secretly pleased that the foreign devil had lost her temper and so lost face. "Mess'ge, you wan', heya? Mess'ge, Missee-tai-tai?"

"What message?"

Ah Soh shuffled up, offered the small envelope, sniffed and went away. Gornt's writing. Angelique came down from the mountain of her fury.

Inside was a card, engraved E.G. The message said, 'Warmest greetings. A most intriguing Hong Kong visit. May we meet tomorrow morning? yr most obedient servant, Edward Gornt.'

Abruptly she felt whole again. Strong, filled with determination and hope and fight. "You're right, Doctor, but I won't break, I swear I won't, I won't for Malcolm and I won't for me, and for you and Jamie and Mr. Skye. You're a dear friend and I'm all right now. No need to discuss that woman anymore." She smiled at him and he knew the smile was both good and bad—more danger signals. "We'll wait . . . we'll wait and see what the future holds. Don't worry, if I don't feel well I'll call at once." She got up and kissed Hoag on both cheeks. "Thank you again, dear friend. Will you be dining at Count Zergeyev's?"

"Perhaps. I don't know. I'm a little tired," he said, and left, hiding his foreboding.

Again she read the card. Edward's circumspect, another good sign, she thought. If the card was intercepted or read, it gave nothing away. 'Intriguing' was a good word to choose, and 'obedient servant' again chosen carefully. Like the words of *that woman*, God rot her.

What to do?

Dress for dinner. Gather your allies. Bind them to you. Put the plans you've contrived into place. And make Yokohama your impregnable bastion against *that woman*.

"Ignore the gai-jin soldiers trying to find you, Hiraga, and forget Akimoto," Katsumata said, disgusted with the unexpected snag in his plan. "Three of us are enough. We attack tomorrow, burn the church and sink the ship. Takeda, you take the church."

"Gladly, Sensei, but why not use Ori's plan and burn Yokohama? Hiraga is right, forget the ship, he is right, so sorry," Takeda said, inclined to his side—after all, Hiraga was the Choshu leader and wise to consider how to retreat. "He is correct that it would be difficult to get close to a ship in this sea and wind unobserved. Why not use Ori's plan instead, burn the whole gai-jin nest?"

Hiraga said, "Ori's plan needs time, and a south wind. I agree it's a better plan. We should wait."

"No," Katsumata said harshly, rudely, "with courage we can do both, with courage! We can. Both! With shishi courage!"

Hiraga was still rocked by the unforeseen soldiers, his mind slow. That he believed he had killed the scavenger bothered him not a bit—the man was motionless in the dirt when, later, he had slunk for the well head, groped down it, then blindly through the meanness of the tunnel and freezing water.

"Impossible with only three of us," he said, "and tomorrow night is too soon, whatever we decide. If the plan's to burn the Settlement we need three days to place the flamers, and fuses. I advise against haste."

He was wrapped in a quilt, naked but for a loincloth—maids were drying his clothes, sopping wet from the tunnel water. The little bungalow was cold, the wind whining around the shojis and it took much of his will to keep from shivering openly. It was hard to concentrate. He still could not understand why soldiers were searching for him. The moment he had arrived here, Katsumata had angrily asked Raiko to send spies into the Settlement to find out what had happened and the three of them made plans to escape the Three Carp in case searchers came into the Yoshiwara.

Now he was watching Katsumata pour more saké. Anger had tightened his already sharp features, making him seem even more dangerous: "Hiraga, my opinion is we attack tomorrow."

"My opinion," Hiraga said with equal firmness, "is we move when we have a chance of success and not before—always your advice—unless caught in the open and face death or capture. Takeda, what is your opinion?"

"First I'd like to know what would be your plan? You know the target like no one else. What would you do?"

Hiraga drank his hot tea, pulled the quilt closer again, pretending to think, thankful that Takeda was teetering towards his position. "If I had my normal access, Akimoto and I could have all the flamers into place in three days—I have four already prepared and hidden in my village house," he said, embellishing the story. "We need about six, eight would be best: one in each of both the two-story buildings, they're wood and tinder dry and almost burned up in the last earthquake; the gai-jin leader's house; the house next door; three or four in

Drunk Town; one in each church. In the confusion we can make an escape by our boat to Yedo."

"Now, how much time would that take?" Katsumata asked even more rudely and the two men shifted uneasily. "How many days, now you do not have 'normal access'?"

"I can tell you that as soon as I know why the soldiers search for me," Hiraga said narrowly. Katsumata's swords were beside him, his own swords within easy reach. The moment he had arrived he had asked Raiko for the swords she had hidden for him—in the event they had to make a sudden escape over the walls and into the paddy behind the Yoshiwara. All of them had decided it was too dangerous to hide in the tunnel. "Takeda?"

"I propose we wait until we know what your trouble is. Then we can agree on a final plan, Sensei—but if we could do as Hiraga says I would be for that."

"We must attack tomorrow. That is our final plan."

Thinking better now, Hiraga threw out a bait. "If we could do both, sink a ship and fire the Settlement that would be best," he said, to placate Katsumata. "It would be possible if we planned it, but we need more men. A few men more, Sensei," he added, using the title of respect he had so far avoided, to further flatter him. "We could get three men from Yedo. Takeda could go, he's not known, he could bring them back in three or four days. I am marked and cannot move until the attack. You will lead us against the ship—I can tell the others where to place the flamers, can still guide them where to go and how to do it."

"It is good plan, Sensei," Takeda said, having seized on the chance of escape by boat—never one for a suicide attack. "I will go to Yedo, and find the men."

"You would be caught," Katsumata said, his lips a thin line. "You have never been there and do not know the alleys or where to go. You would be caught." His rage was near exploding for he could not attack by himself and needed these two, or other men, and without consensus nothing would be achieved. If anyone should go it must be him. That thought did not displease him for he did not like this place, not enough exits, not enough places to hide—he only felt safe in Kyōto or Osaka or Yedo, or at home in Kagoshima. Eeee, it would be good to see my home and family again. But they must wait, he thought and hardened his heart: "*Sonno-joi* must go forward, Yoshi must be humbled . . ." Simultaneously the three men had their hands on their swords. Shadows came on the shoji door.

"Katsumata-sama?" It was Raiko. "I have a maid with me."

"Please come in." When they saw it was she they relaxed. She bowed, the maid did the same, and they bowed back.

"Tell them, Tsuki-chan," she said to the maid.

"I went to the house of the shoya, Sires. He said that Akimoto-sama was taken to the gai-jin leader and after a short time taken to their prison. It has not been possible yet to talk to him but with his first meal, which one of our people serve, we can find out more."

"Good. He been beaten and was dragged?" Katsumata asked.

"No, Lord, neither, Lord."

"Not beaten, you're sure?"

"The shoya was also surprised, Sire. Akimoto-sama was whistling and singing and heard to say, as though it was part of the country song, 'Someone's betrayed someone.' "

Hiraga said darkly, "That's what he called out in the village. What else did the shoya say?"

"The shoya says, So sorry, he does not know yet why soldiers search for you. Guards are still there. As soon as he knows the reason he will send word."

"Thank you, Tsuki-chan," Raiko said, and dismissed her.

Katsumata said, "If he hadn't been beaten, he must have given them the information they want and they jailed him to protect him from you?"

"No. He would not tell them anything," Hiraga said, his mind elsewhere: Who's the betrayer? His eyes flicked to Raiko.

She was saying, "Perhaps I can find out. A gai-jin client who might know is arriving any moment. He might know, certainly he could find out."

André came into her room with a forced smile. " 'Evening, Raiko-san," he said, disgusted with his weakness. She greeted him coolly and offered tea. When the tea had been taken he handed her the small bag of coins. "Here another payment, sorry not all but enough for moment. You want see me?"

"Waiting a little is fair, Furansu-san, amongst friends," she said, annoyed. Feeling the weight of the bag, she was secretly content with the amount—for the moment—and that the first important matter had been settled. Then she added, to keep up the pressure, so important with clients, "A little is fair between friends, but a lot is not correct, not at all."

"I promise more in day or two."

"So sorry your payments are far behind."

André hesitated, then jerked off his gold signet ring. "Here."

"I do not want that," Raiko said. "Should I release Hinodeh and allow her to leave, then you—"

"No. Please, no . . . Listen, I have information . . ."

André was not feeling at all well, both because of her cool reception and also because of a migraine acquired during the Yoshi interview that would not go away. And because of Angelique. And because Tess Struan was not aboard *Prancing Cloud,* for surely that would have made it easier for him to negotiate a settlement and so get the wealth he required. He had no wish to go to Hong Kong, to challenge her there, in the lair of the Noble House.

Angelique's still the only chance you've got, his brain kept hammering at him. Seratard had again consulted Ketterer, Sir William, and even Skye about the validity of the marriage. They were all convinced it should hold up in a court. 'In Hong Kong? I'm not so sure,' Ketterer had sneered, the others saying the same with different words, in different degrees—except Sir William. 'Too many scallywags there, judges aren't like they are in London—they're colonials, plenty of corruption, plenty of hanky-panky. A few taels of silver . . . don't forget Struan's are the Noble House . . .'

Raiko leaned closer to André. "Information, Furansu-san?"

"Yes." It was now or never with Raiko—and Hinodeh. "Special. Secrets about secret Yoshi meeting with gai-jin."

"So ka!" she said, all attention. "Go on, Furansu-sama."

He told her what had happened, in detail, to her intense interest, much sucking in of breath and hissed exclamations. And when, abruptly, he slid in the part about Yoshi wanting Hiraga, she blanched. His anxiety evaporated, he hid his joy and closed the trap: "So Hiraga friend of you?"

"No, not at all, he's a client of a friend," she said hastily, fanning herself, mind humming with the wonderful pieces of intelligence to pass on to the shoya and the Gyokoyama that would put him and them totally into her debt—and to Meikin. Ah, Meikin! she thought in passing, how long will you stay alive? So sorry, you and yours will have to pay, one way or another, Yoshi invested too much in your late Koiko, but then you know that. Which brings me to my pressing problem, how in the name of all gods and the Amida Buddha, do I rid myself of Hiraga, Katsumata and the other two, they've become far too dangerous and . . .

Then she heard André's different voice. "So Hiraga client of mama-san friend in Yoshiwara. Hiraga with friend now. *Neh?"*

Her guard dropped back into place. "I would not know where he is. I imagine he is in the Settlement as usual. Lord Yoshi wants him? Why?"

"Because Hiraga is shishi." André used the word for the first time, aware of what it meant from Yoshi's revelations. "Also for kill daimyo. Daimyo Utani. Other killings too."

She kept the fear off her face. "Terrible. Shishi, you say? I've heard of them. About this information, old friend, may I ask about th—"

"Hiraga dis'ppear, Raiko. No in Settlement. Many soldiers search. Gone, Raiko. Search all places. He gone."

"Eeee, vanished? Soldiers? Vanished to where?"

"Here. To your friend. Where's your friend?"

"Ah, so sorry, I doubt he would be there," she said with perfect sincerity, and shook her head emphatically. "Probably he was warned and has run off to Kanagawa or some such place, and so sorry, old friend, but that is not a good question to ask. Your information is very interesting. Is there more?"

André sighed. He knew she knew. Now she was at his mercy. For a time. "Yoshi samurai come tomorrow for your Hiraga," he said, no longer afraid because one word from him and patrols, Japanese or British, would tear the House of the Three Carp to pieces—after Hinodeh was taken to safety. "If gai-jin not have Hiraga tomorrow, much trouble, Raiko. For gai-jin, Yoshiwara, all." The way he said it sent a tremor through her. "Perhaps gai-jin put Enforcers here, there, all places." He let that hover in the air.

"So?" she asked, a bead of sweat forming on her upper lip, frightened of what was coming, all else forgotten.

"Have idea: if you . . . so sorry," he said sweetly, "if your friend hide Hiraga few day, secret, safe place. Then, at right time give gai-jin leader Hiraga . . . perhaps get much money, enough you, and Hinodeh, neh?" He was watching her and she tried not to flinch. "Or your people give Hiraga to Yoshi. Hiraga is shishi—valuable—better than earrings," he said again, and saw a shudder take her. "Shishi valuable, neh?"

When her heart had stopped thundering enough and she could trust her voice, she mustered the best smile she could, for clearly he believed she knew Hiraga was here, and therefore he could, if provoked, put her and the Three Carp in lethal jeopardy. "I will ask my friend if she has seen him, or knows where he is, then we can talk, quickly," she said, voice conciliatory, deciding that it was better to hurry all shishi out of her life as soon as possible. Preferably tonight. "What wonderful information you have discovered, how valuable, how clever to know so much, it will bring some profit no doubt! Ah, Furansu-san," she said as if a sudden thought to further distract him, "we hear that a gai-jin lady has arrived from Hong Kong tonight. She is the famous mother of the tai-pan?"

"Eh? No." André said absently. "No, she—she promise in marriage to trader. Why?"

"Would he be one of my clients, old friend?"

"No, think Inn of Succulent Joy for year, perhaps more, Jamie McFay."

"Jami-san? Jami-san of Stru'n?" Eeee, she thought like quicksilver, Nemi will need to know quickly. She must prepare to present herself to this lady in the Struan big house, to bow before her and welcome her, and assure her in sharing his bed she had been looking after Jami-san expertly—very important to have good relations between *nee-go-san*—second lady, a consort—and *oku-san,* wife—because the wife pays all bills, and then to invite her to a return visit to the Jami house in the gardens of the Succulent Joy. Eeee, that would be grand, then we could all get a good look at her. "Furansu-sama, there is a rumor the gai-jin put a Japanese in prison tonight."

"What? Don't know about that. Maybe find out later. Not important. Listen, about Hinodeh."

She interrupted brightly, "Hinodeh was asking me earlier if you were honoring her tonight. She will be so pleased you are here—she honors you greatly."

André's chest felt tight. Now that he had Raiko in his grip he would ask her, no, tell her to make Hinodeh forgo the condition of the light. Suddenly he was afraid to do so.

"Yes?"

"Nothing," he muttered. "I go Hinodeh."

After he left she drank some brandy to steady her nerves, chewed some fragrant tea leaves to take away the smell then, worriedly, went to the three shishi and told them part of André's information about Yoshi demanding Hiraga, and that his men would arrive tomorrow to take possession. "So sorry, it would be best if you left tonight, much safer for you," she said, her voice heavy with dread. "Katsumata-sama, this client swore Enforcers and gai-jin soldiers were due any moment, coming to search everywhere."

The three men were silent. Hearing of Yoshi's secret dealings with the gai-jin, Katsumata was more determined than ever to create trouble between them. "Thank you, you have been of great service, Raiko-san.

We may leave, we may need to stay, either way you will be well rewarded."

"I really believe it would be better to leave an—"

Katsumata's voice rasped, "Either way you will be well rewarded. Meanwhile we will discuss how best to protect you."

She did not want to go but she bowed, thanked him and went out into the night, and when safely away cursed him and them and André, at the same time deciding who would be the trustworthy messenger to speed André's intelligence to Meikin.

"Light the lamps," Katsumata said. All had guttered and most extinguished as she had opened and closed the door and the wind had invaded the room. With the door closed again the few remaining flames settled but for an isolated draft. "Listen," he said, so that no one outside could hear: "Hiraga, I will get more men and return in three days. Hide here, safer than coming with me, use a new disguise and hide in the tunnel. If you are clever you will be safe."

"Yes, Sensei."

"In three days we gut Yokohama, sink the ship, kill as many gai-jin as possible, and escape. I will bring Bakufu uniforms. Takeda, help Hiraga with the incendiaries. They must be ready by the time I get back."

Takeda said, "Better if I come with you, Sensei. I can protect your back in case you are seen or intercepted."

"No. Stay with Hiraga." Katsumata did not want to be encumbered, exceedingly uncomfortable inside the Yoshiwara fence. "I'll leave the moment the barricades are open."

"It is the best plan. *Sonno-joi,*" Hiraga said.

He was feeling nauseated and light-headed at the same time, aghast at the thought of Yoshi's men arriving tomorrow, or Enforcers, and being caught—inevitable now that Yoshi, personally, was after him— knowing, too, the Sensei was right again: the walled Settlement and fenced Yoshiwara were traps.

At the same time he was marvelously relieved. Now that his end was inevitable there was no reason not to hurl himself whole-heartedly into the attack.

Three days is a lifetime. With Katsumata gone, who knows what may happen? In any event, I won't be taken alive.

"My God, Jamie, look there!" Dmitri said.

Jamie glanced at the doorway. So did the twenty other guests scattered around the reception room in the Russian Legation. Conversation died then picked up. Angelique was coming in on the arm of Sir William. A long-sleeved and simple black dress that showed off not only the paleness but the glow of her skin, and set off the column of her neck to perfection, the cut perfect, her tiny waist and swell of her breasts presented modestly, perfect for mourning, but no doubting their hidden magic. Hair swept up. No jewelry except a thin gold necklace and wedding ring—Malcolm's signet ring now cut to fit.

"She's twenty-four karat."

"Yes," Jamie said. Then, feeling a new stir, looked around. Across the room Maureen was smiling at him, surrounded by men, Pallidar amongst them. He smiled back, liking what he saw, still dumbfounded by her arrival, and courage, making such a formidable journey alone. What the devil am I going to do?

"Incredible about Hong Kong and Malc's funeral, huh?"

"You're right, Dmitri. I'd have bet Tess would never do that." What's she up to, he asked himself again, and what was in her letter to Angelique? No chance to ask yet, no clue from her appearance. His own had been illuminating.

> *Dear Jamie, Mr. Gornt has told me in detail what a good friend you were to my son. I thank you with all my heart. But I still cannot forgive you for not complying with my wishes— company policy—for not diverting my son back to his duty and persuading him to give up his attention to that woman or, at the very least, to put her in proportion and to return here; cannot forgive you aiding and abetting him in his foolishness, particularly as I pointed out at length his minority and that while tai-pan in name he did not exercise those powers until formally installed, and that, to my regret, I did, temporarily.*
>
> *I understand from Mr. Gornt you intend to try to form yr own business. I wish you luck and thank you for yr many years of fine service. In business Struan's will never be hostile. I enclose a sight draft on London for five thousand guineas. Please give my best wishes to yr fiancée. I enjoyed meeting her. Tess Struan.*

He beamed at the thought of all that money. It made his company possible, small to be sure, but it gave him the time he needed, and also to ease forward with the shoya though how those ventures would prosper without Nakama/Hiraga he did not know. He pitied him. And Tess. In her case he understood, and forgave her, not because of the money. "What, Dmitri?"

"You've every right to be smug. Your Maureen's great."

"Oh! Yes. Yes, she is."

"What about Nemi?" Dmitri asked.

Jamie's smile vanished, his discomfort returned, and he turned his back to the door. "A bloody problem, Dmitri. I'd made a date to see her tonight."

"Jesus, in Struan's?"

"No, thank God. In our . . . in her place."

"Jesus, that was lucky. Are you going?"

"Yes, why not? Christ Almighty, I don't know . . . When Maureen arrived out of the dark . . . It's not that I don't like her, I'm still in a state of shock."

"Sure, but a good one—you're lucky. Listen, we're old buddies and can speak straight. If you . . . if you decide to stop with Nemi, to pension her off, call it a day, whatever, may I ask that you let me know? She's a good sport, good fun and she speaks enough of our lingo."

"All right, but . . ." Laughter from the men surrounding Maureen attracted their attention there. Then to Angelique. "Smashing, isn't she?" Jamie said. "Angelique, I mean."

Angelique and Sir William were waiting for Zergeyev to join them. Tonight's dress and coiffure had been decided on earlier—selected specifically for Tess and this soiree, which was to have been their first battleground. Though her enemy had not arrived she resolved not to alter her plan, the effect was so pleasing. She had considered wearing the Imperial Jade ring that Malcolm had ordered from Hong Kong and had been delivered by mail ship a week after his death, causing her another flood of private tears. If Tess had been here she would not have hesitated. Without that reason the ring was wrong.

Actually I'm glad *she* isn't here, she told herself. Thank God Vargas warned me. I need more time to prepare for that joust, person to person—ah, time, am I or am I not bearing Malcolm's child . . . "Good evening, Count Zergeyev," she said with her gentle smile. "Thank you for inviting me."

"You're so welcome, you've already made the evening a success. 'Evening, Sir William. You both know everyone, except a new guest." In a sudden hush, everyone watching, comparing, Zergeyev beckoned

Maureen from the circle of admirers, Marlowe amongst them now. "Miss Maureen Ross, from Edinburgh, Jamie's fiancée. Madame Angelique Struan."

The moment Angelique had come in she had seen Maureen, instantly scrutinized her from nice head to neat shoe and decided she was no threat—noticing Gornt in passing, but leaving him for later. "Welcome to the furthest British outpost in the world, Mademoiselle Ross," she said pleasantly, wondering how old she was, and thinking, Yes, at night, in a muffler, this one could easily be mistaken for *that woman*— same tall, imposing way of standing; same direct gaze. "Jamie is very lucky."

"Thank you." The moment Angelique had come into the room Maureen had scrutinized her from shining head to tiny foot, recognized her beauty, and while instinctively liking her, decided at once she was a threat—her eyes had switched to Jamie to see his open admiration, and the men around him, no way of missing the general hum of appreciation—and she readied for battle.

"I'm so pleased to meet you and was awful sorry to hear about your tragedy, I'm so . . . everyone's so sorry." With genuine feeling, she leaned down and touched a cheek against Angelique's. "I do hope we'll be friends." A special smile. "Please, let's be friends. I'll need a friend, dinna fear. Jamie said what a good friend you've been to him."

"No need for 'please,' Maureen—may I call you Maureen, and would you call me Angelique?" she said with a special smile, acknowledging and understanding the warning put nicely and without claws, that Jamie was personal property and not to be flirted with. "Good, it would be very good to have a girl friend. Perhaps we could have tea tomorrow?"

"Och, I'd enjoy that. Angelique, what a pretty name and pretty dress." Too severe, yet too hourglass for mourning.

"And so is yours, that color goes marvelously with your hair." Green silk, expensive, but English not Parisian and the cut old-fashioned. Never mind. That can be improved, if she becomes an intimate. "Jamie was a great friend to my husband, and to me when I needed one badly. You are very lucky," she said truthfully. "Now where is your handsome fiancé? Ah, there he is!"

Watched by all eyes, she linked arms with her. Everyone beamed at the Entente Cordiale and, still the center of attention, she guided Maureen to him. "Be careful, Jamie, it's easy to see this lady is very precious—there are too many pirates in Yokohama."

Those around laughed and she left them and went back to Sir

William, greeting Ketterer en route—a special compliment and smile to him, and later to Marlowe—as well as Settry Pallidar, resplendent and rivaling Zergeyev in his Cossack uniform. "La, Sir William," she said. "How lucky we are."

"To be . . ." Zergeyev stopped himself in time. He almost said, To be alive? Instead he took a glass of champagne from a silver platter held by a liveried manservant and said, "To be in the presence of two such lovely ladies, we are lucky! Your healths." Everyone drank, and continued to compare. Zergeyev was too worried to follow suit, much more concerned with what other foul news had arrived with *Prancing Cloud,* particularly for the other Ministers.

An urgent, coded dispatch from St. Petersburg—three months old—had arrived. First, it related the usual trouble with Prussia, troops massing on their Western borders, six armies sent there; trouble expected soon with the Ottoman Empire and Moslems to the south, three armies sent there; famine everywhere, with intellectuals such as Dostoyevsky and Tolstoy advocating change and liberalization. Second, it ordered him to press the Japanese to remove their fishing villages from the Kuriles and Sakhalin under threat of 'serious consequences.' And third, much trouble for him personally: *You are appointed Governor General of Russian Alaska. In the spring the warship* Tsar Alexandre *will arrive with your replacement for the Japans, and then carry you and your entourage to our Alaskan capital Sitka where you will be in residence for at least two years to expedite Friendship.*

"Why so glum, friend?" Sir William asked in Russian.

Zergeyev saw that Angelique was again surrounded, so drew him aside and told him about his new posting. But not about 'Friendship.' This was the code name of a top-secret State plan to facilitate enforced, massive immigration of hardy Siberian tribes into their vast Alaskan-American territories that spread hundreds of miles inland, adjoined Canada and hugged the coast southwards to end not far from the American-Canadian border. Hardy, tough, warlike peoples who could, and would, over a generation or three, trickle southwards and eastwards to the vast prairies and warm exotic lands of California, eventually to possess America. The plan had been proposed by an uncle twenty-five years earlier. "Two years! A fornicating prison sentence!"

"I agree." Sir William felt equally uncomfortable with the vicissitudes of his own Foreign Office, their aptitude for sudden postings, equally olympian. "Alaska? Ugh! Know nothing about it—have you ever been there? Last year, the ship I was on stopped at Vancouver, in our colony there. It's just an outpost, and we went no farther north."

"Sitka's not much farther. I was there as a youth once. Now we've permanent settlement, lots of traders, a few hundred shacks," Zergeyev said sourly. "Furs, freezing, lawlessness, illiterates, Indians, drunks, and no society. The place is a foul wasteland, discovered by Bering and Chirikov a hundred-odd years ago . . . at first they thought it was just part of our northern territories, fifty-odd miles across an inlet, not realizing it was a Strait they named after Bering. Sixty-odd years ago, one of my granduncles helped form the Russian American Fur Company, our fur-trading monopoly, and appointed an imperious son of a whore—a cousin called Baranof—to be Director, who moved the capital to Sitka. It's on an island off the coast, totally miserable, and called, guess what, Baranof Island. Unfortunately my family made Alaska a special interest. Hence the posting. *Matyeryeybitz!* Both of them."

Sir William laughed and Angelique turned back to them. "May I share the joke?"

"Er, it wasn't well, very funny, my dear," he said, docketing the highly interesting data for transmission to London, "just a Russian vulgarity."

"English humor, Angelique." Zergeyev laughed. "And on that happy thought, it is time for dinner."

Gallantly he bowed, went over and took Maureen into the dining room, Sir William and Angelique followed, then the others. Abundant silver on the refectory table, liveried menservants behind each chair, others to bring in huge quantities of meats and borscht and beets and pies and jugs of iced vodka, champagne and French wines and sorbets. Gypsy musicians from the Russian warship, then later Cossack dancers from his entourage for entertainment.

Conversation buzzing and all of them still comparing: tiny and tall, French against one of us, delightful French accent, comfortable Scots. Both beddable, Angelique much more so, both eligible, and marriageable, Maureen much more so.

54

Saturday, 3rd January:

"Mass'r down stair, Missee-tai-tai."

"Master Gornt?"

Ah Soh shrugged, standing in the doorway of Angelique's boudoir. "Kwai-loh Mass'r." With her hand she indicated someone tall, and closed the door with a customary bang.

Angelique glanced quickly in the mirror. Her suppressed excitement was all the makeup she needed. A moment while she locked her journal and put it away. A final check and she swept out. Black silk dress with many petticoats, hair tied with a neat chiffon scarf, also black. Signet wedding ring. Down the staircase, oblivious of the servants at their early morning chores.

Into the tai-pan's office. Gornt stood by the window, looking out at the bay. Chen waited lugubriously.

"Good morning, Edward."

He turned and smiled a welcome. " 'Morning, Ma'am."

"Can I order coffee, or champagne?"

"Nothing, thank you, I've had breakfast. Just wanted to tell you about Hong Kong, and your shopping list. Hope I'm not disturbing you."

"Thank you. Chen, wait outside, heya."

The moment they were alone she said softly, "This is Albert's office now, I'm borrowing it while he's in the counting office with Vargas so we may not have much time—it's hard to have somewhere to talk privately. Let's sit here, Edward," she said, motioning to the table in the window, the curtains open. "Passersby can see us, that should be safe, you were Malcolm's friend. Please quickly, what happened."

"May I say first how marvelous you look?"

"So do you." Her anxiety was open now. "Please?"

"It went very well, I think," he said quietly. "Tess would make a great poker player, Angelique, so I can't be sure. At our first meeting I told her about my Brock information, as we agreed, saying several times in different ways it was because of you I was seeing her. Not th—"

"Were you the first to see her from the ship?"

"Yes, I'm quite sure because I went ashore on the pilot boat before *Prancing Cloud* docked, with Captain Strongbow. After I told Tess about the Brocks, there wasn't much of a reaction, she listened intently, asked a few questions and then said, 'Please come back tomorrow, with your evidence, shortly after dawn. Use the side door in the alley, it will be unlocked, and be muffled up and careful, the Brocks have spies everywhere.' The next day . . ."

"Wait! Did you tell her about—about Malcolm dying, and about our marriage?"

"No, I let Strongbow do that," Gornt said. "I'll start from the beginning. We went ashore together on the pilot boat, at my suggestion, keeping quiet about it, and Hoag out of the plan—he's a loose mouth. I had volunteered to support Strongbow and help because I was a witness to part of it . . . the poor fellow was scared to death though it really was his duty to tell her. When he blurted out that Malcolm was dead she went white. In a few seconds she had recovered her composure, astonishing how fast, but she did and then she asked, her voice flat, she asked him how Malcolm had died. Strongbow was distraught and he stut²tered, 'I brought the death certificate, Mrs. Struan, and inquest findings and a letter from Sir William and it was from natural causes and happened aboard *Prancing Cloud*. We found him dead in the morning, after the night he was wed' . . ."

"She shot to her feet like an arrow and screeched, 'You married my son to that woman?' Strongbow almost died and gabbled out the story as fast as he could, about *Pearl*, about the duel, me saving Jamie's life by killing Norbert, finding Malcolm, telling everything he knew, how you were in shock. The sweat was pouring off him, Angelique. I must admit I was sweating too—after the first screech Tess just stood there, eyes on fire like a Medusa. Then he gave her some letters, I saw one was from Sir William, mumbled sorry but it was his awful duty to tell her and he stumbled away."

Gornt took out a handkerchief and dried his forehead, and Angelique felt weak, nauseated at the strength of her enemy—if Tess could make Gornt sweat like this, what might Tess do to her? "She just stood there and then her eyes turned on me. Astonishing how such a woman could seem so . . . so tall. And tough. Tough one minute, soft the next, but never her guard down. I had to force my feet not to back off and looked around pretending to be afraid of being overheard, and said in a rush that I was dreadfully sorry too, Malcolm really was my friend, that you were her friend too and it was because of you I was there, as I had information that would bankrupt Tyler and Morgan Brock. The moment I said 'bankrupt Tyler' the madness left her, at least the scary fire left her and she sat down, still didn't take her eyes off me, sat down and after a long time said, 'What information?' I said I'd come back tomorrow but she said with a voice like a knife, *What information?* I gave her the bare bones . . . Sorry, Angelique, could I have a drink? Not champagne—whisky, bourbon if you have it."

She went to the sideboard and poured for him, water for herself as he continued, "The next day I brought half of the evidence and left it with her. She—"

"Wait, was she the same as the day before?"

"Yes and no. Thanks, health, a long one and a merry." He took a deep swig and gasped as the spirit caught his throat. "Thanks. When I'd finished she looked at me and I thought I'd failed. That's one hell of a scary woman, I wouldn't like to be her enemy."

"But I am? *Mon Dieu,* Edward, tell me the truth."

"Yes, you are, but that doesn't matter for the moment, let me go on. I—"

"You gave her my letter?"

"Oh, yes, sorry, forgot to mention it, I did that the first day, before I left, just as we agreed, again stressing this was all your idea, telling her then that as my arrangement was with Malcolm, the taipan, and he was dead, I had considered the deal was off and was going back to Shanghai to wait for a new tai-pan. But you sought me out and begged me to come to see her, saying I owed it to my friend Malcolm, that he had mentioned my proposal to you in secret—with none of the details—and you were certain it would be his wish to pass the information on to his mother as soon as possible, that I must do it urgently. At first I didn't want to, but you pleaded with me and persuaded me. So I was there because of you and you had asked me to give her a letter. I passed it over."

"Did she read it in front of you?"

"No. That was the first day. The next day at our dawn meeting, after

I'd given her part of the info, she asked lots of questions, intelligent ones, and said to come back after sunset, the side door again. I did. At once she said the dossier was incomplete. I told her yes, sure, no point in showing everything until I knew how committed she would be—was she truly interested, like Malcolm, in wrecking the Brocks? She said yes, and asked why was I after them, and what was my interest.

"I told her bluntly. The whole story of Morgan, the truth. It was Morgan I wanted to break, if his father went too, that was fine with me. I didn't mention that this made her my step-aunt, not once in all the meetings, nor did she. Never. Nor did she mention your letter to her. Not once. All she did was ask questions. After the Morgan revelations I expected her to say something, how sorry she was, or that that was typical of Morgan—after all he is her brother. But nothing. She didn't say a word, asked details of my deal with Malcolm and I gave her the contract." He finished his glass. "Your contract."

"Your contract," she said, on edge. "How you must hate her, Edward."

"You're wrong, I don't hate her. I think I understand, she was living on her nerves. Malcolm's death had torn her apart, much as she tried to hide it and rise above it. I'm sure of it. Malcolm was the future of the Noble House, now she faces chaos. Her only ray of hope was me and my scheme—barely legal, by the way, even in Hong Kong, which stretches rules like nowhere else. May I?" he asked lifting his glass.

"Of course," she said, wondering about him.

"She read the contract carefully then got up and stared down at Hong Kong harbor, looking frail in a way, like spun steel in another. 'When do I get the rest of the evidence?' she asked, and I told her now, if she agreed to the deal. 'It's agreed,' she said, and sat down and signed her name, and chopped it in front of her secretary as witness, then told her to lock up and leave. She—"

"She never mentioned my signature as witness."

"No, though as you forecast she sure as hell noticed it first thing. To continue: I stayed with her perhaps four hours, guiding her through the maze of papers and copies of papers, not that she needed much guiding. Then she put them in a neat pile and asked me about the Tokaidō affair, Malcolm, you, McFay, Tyrer, Suh William, Norbert, what Morgan and Tyler had told me in Shanghai, my opinions of you, of Malcolm, did he pursue you, did you pursue him, volunteering nothing, questions and more questions—avoiding mine—her mind as sharp as a samurai's sword. But I swear to God, Angelique, every time Morgan or Old Man Brock's name came up, every time I mentioned another quirk that the papers allowed, or suggested another barb that would rip into their empire, Tess almost salivated."

She shuddered. "Is—is there a chance for a peace with me, do you think?"

"I think so, let me finish in sequence. She asked again if the deal Malcolm had signed was still an agreeable reward. I said yes. She said, 'Tomorrow I will replace it with a more legal document chopped and signed as the other. Now to the last matter tonight, Mr. Gornt. What should I give this woman?' Angelique, I had told her you had asked me for nothing, you only wanted to put your husband's wishes and hopes before her, and that, if they proved fruitful—I had told her you knew nothing of their contents—that that would be reward enough."

"You used that word, 'husband'? And she let it pass?"

"Yes, but she said at once, 'I am informed that "marriage," whatever she claims or Sir William says, is not valid.' "

Angelique began to bridle but Gornt said, "Not so fast, honey, be patient. I'm telling you what she said. Be patient, time enough to make our play. After that meeting she wanted another the following evening. To keep everything on the table, I told her I had seen the Brocks and told them the same Yokohama story, particularly about the duel, and had given them a copy of Norbert's inquest. Old Tyler was mad as a pit bull terrier but Morgan calmed him, said that shooting Jamie McFay in the back would have hurt them more than the loss of one easily replaceable manager."

Angelique watched him collect his thoughts, her heart thumping, so many questions unanswered yet. "She'll act . . . act on the information?"

"On my evidence, yes. Oh, yes, and quickly. I'll have my revenge and you'll get a settlement."

"Why are you sure?"

"I'm sure, Ma'am, never fear. It's taken years of biting my tongue, kowtowing, but soon . . . you'll see! When I told her about my meeting with the Brocks—she kept asking about them, what was Tyler's reaction to the marriage and death of her son and so on, and never once used the term 'father.' I told her frankly how they both guffawed over your naval marriage and going against her wishes: Old Man Brock had said, 'Pays the bitch back, for goin' agin mine!' I told her straight how both gloated over Malcolm's death, Morgan saying, now they've no tai-pan and come February 1st Tess will be out of Jockey Club, busted in Hong Kong, Tyler adding, An' I'll be the *tai-pan,* Dirk's nose be in't shit an' Noble House an' his name forgot forever!"

"You said that to her?" Angelique's head reeled.

"Yes, Ma'am, but that's what Tyler said—he really did. And he's the engine to send her mad, so I thought I should report it accurately and when I did, Lordy, Lordy, Ma'am, her head was shaking so much her eyeballs had a hard time catching up and I thought the Medusa was coming back. But it didn't, not this time. This time the fiend's fire was confined—it was still there, oh yes, Ma'am, yes indeed. But she corked it, she kept it inside, even so I sure as hell . . . sorry, I sure as shooting sweated. Not proper for a woman to have that amount of rage, but after Tyler and Morgan it's easy to see where she gets it from.

"When she'd cooled down a bitty, I told her Tyler had eventually agreed to Morgan's suggestion I should come back here as manager, on trial for a year, with plenty of dire threats for nonperformance. She asked my salary. 'Excellent. Publicly we will be enemies, secretly we will be close allies, and if Brock and Sons goes under forever, which I pray to God happens, your Rothwell-Gornt will take their place.' That's about it, Angelique, except she had decided to send Hoag back here and was writing you a letter."

He sipped his bourbon, the taste turned smooth. "I didn't ask what was in it or make any defense of you other than continuing to say in various ways, if my scheme helped her destroy Brock's, she had you to thank too. What was in her letter?"

She had given it to him.

"A lot of dung with the bales of cotton," he had said, handing it back. "It's her first bargaining position—and clear from this I kept my bargain: she's convinced she has to thank you as well. You'll win."

"Win what? No legal harassment?"

"That and a stipend. She admits she's in your debt."

"Yes, but nothing more, just threats."

"We hold a few trumps."

"What?" They heard voices outside.

"Time, among others, Angelique. Tonight I'll invite you to a casual supper, we can talk safely there an—"

"Not in Brock's, and not alone. We must be careful," she said hastily. "Please invite Dmitri and Marlowe. We must be very careful, Edward, must pretend not to be too close—that would make that woman suspicious and she's bound to hear; Albert is totally on her side. If we can't talk tonight I'll promenade tomorrow at ten and we can continue. . . ." To forestall the embrace she had felt imminent she had kissed him quickly on the cheek and offered her hand, thanking him effusively.

When alone once more in the privacy of her boudoir, she let her mind roam. What trumps? What aces? And why that strange smile? And what had he really agreed with Tess? Is he hiding something from me? It's true from her letter he convinced her of my help and that's important. Or am I just being oversuspicious? If only I could have been there!

Then the Am-I-or-am-I-not took possession of her, racking her. Once, frightened, she had mentioned it to Babcott who said, 'Be patient, don't worry.' For a moment she wondered if Babcott and Phillip Tyrer would return from Yedo out of the enemy net they had gone into willingly, sent by Sir William.

Men with their stupidities of patience and mendacity and wrong priorities, what do they know?

In Yedo Castle, Yoshi was anxious and irritable. It was midmorning, he was in his quarters and still had no word how the gai-jin doctor's examination of the *tairō* had gone. When he came back to Yedo from Kanagawa yesterday with Babcott and Tyrer, he had installed them in one of the daimyo's palaces outside the castle walls that he had carefully chosen, staffed and ringed with trusted guards for further security, and at once invited Anjo for the examination.

The *tairō* arrived in a nondescript closed palanquin, protected by his own bodyguard—the assassination attempt on him had happened barely a hundred yards away. This, together with the mass shishi attack on Shōgun Nobusada and the various attempts on Yoshi had increased the Elders' sensitivity and security needs.

Yoshi, with Babcott and Phillip Tyrer beside him, met the clandestine palanquin in the courtyard. They bowed, Yoshi making the lowest bow, laughing to himself as, painfully, Anjo was helped out. '*Tairō*, this is the gai-jin doctor, B'bc'tt, and interpreter Firrup Taira.'

Anjo gawked up at Babcott. 'Eeee, the man really is as big as a tree! So big, eeee, a monster! Would his penis be in proportion?' Then he looked at Phillip Tyrer and guffawed: 'Straw hair, a face like a monkey, a pig's blue eyes and a Japanese name—that is one of your family names, Yoshi-dono, *neh*?'

'The name has almost the same sound,' Yoshi said curtly, then to Tyrer, 'When the examination is completed, send these two men for me.' He pointed at Misamoto, the fisherman, his spy and false samurai, and Misamoto's constant guard, the samurai whose orders were never to leave him alone with any gai-jin. 'Anjo-dono, I believe your health is in good hands.'

'Thank you for arranging this. The Doctor will be sent to you when it pleases me, no need to leave these men here, or any of your men . . .'

That was yesterday. All night he had worried and this morning, worried and hoped. His room was changed. It was even more austere. All traces of Koiko had been removed. Two guards stood behind him and two at the door. Irritably he got up from his writing table and went to the window and leaned on the lintel. Far below he could see the daimyo's palace in the inner circle. The *tairō*'s men were standing guard there. No other signs of activity. Over the rooftops of Yedo he could see the ocean, and smoke trails of some merchantmen and a warship out at sea inbound for Yokohama.

What do they carry, he asked himself. Guns? Troops, cannon? What mischief are they planning?

To settle his nerves he sat back at his table and continued practicing calligraphy. Ordinarily the exercise soothed. Today it brought no peace. Koiko's exquisite brushstrokes kept forming on the paper and, try as he could, he could not stop her face rising to the forefront of his mind.

"Baka!" he said, making a false stroke, spoiling an hour of work. He threw the brush down, splattering ink on the tatami. His guards shifted uneasily and he cursed himself for the lapse. You must control your memory. You must.

Since that evil day she had beset him. The smallness of her neck, hardly feeling the blow, then rushing away instead of lighting her pyre, the nights worst of all. Lonely in bed, and cold, but no wish for a female body or for succor, all illusions gone. After her betrayal, her treason introducing the dragon woman Sumomo into his inner chambers—no excuse was acceptable for that, none, he told himself again, none. She must have known about her. No excuse, no forgiveness—not even, as he now believed, for her sacrificial charge to receive the shuriken that would have impaled him. No woman could be trusted again. Except his wife, perhaps, and consort perhaps. He had not sent for either of them, only written, telling them to wait, to guard their sons and keep their castle safe.

He felt no real joy even in his victory over the gai-jin though he was certain it was a superb step forward, and sure that when he told the Elders, they would be ecstatic. Even Anjo. How sick is that dog? Unto death I hope. Will the giant do his magic and cure him? Or is the Chinese doctor to be believed, he who Inejin says has never been wrong and whispered an early death.

Never mind. Anjo, sick or not, will listen to me now, the others will listen at last, and agree to my proposals. Why not? The gai-jin are boxed, no threat now from the fleet, Sanjiro almost done to death by gai-jin, Ogama satisfied in Kyōto. Shōgun Nobusada will be ordered back to Yedo where he belongs, once he explained the part the boy should play in the great plan. And not only returning, but returning alone, leaving his hostile wife, the Princess Yazu, to 'follow in a few days,' never to follow if Yoshi had his way—no need for the others to be in his confidence. Only Ogama.

Not even Ogama to know all of it, only the part to enmesh the Princess and have her divorced by Imperial 'request.' Ogama would see to it that she stayed out of the way until she was safely and permanently neutralized, content to live forever within the palace quagmire of poetry competitions, mysticism, and other world ceremonials. And a new husband. Ogama.

No, not Ogama, he thought, cynically amused, though of course I will propose the union. No, someone else, someone she will be content with—the Prince to whom she was once promised, and still honors. Ogama will be a fine ally. In many ways. Until he goes onwards.

Meanwhile there is no need to share an immortal truth I have discovered about gai-jin—with Ogama, Anjo or anyone: *Gai-jin do not understand time as we do, they do not consider or think about time as we do. They think time is finite. We do not. They worry about time, minutes, hours, days—months are important to them, exact appointments sacrosanct. Not to us. Their version of time controls them. So this is one cudgel we can always use to beat them with.*

He smiled to himself, loving secrets, dreaming of a thousand ways to use gai-jin time against real time to dominate them, and through them the future. Patience patience patience.

Meanwhile I still have our Gates, though Ogama's men control my men who guard our Gates. That does not matter. Soon we will possess them entirely, and the Son of Heaven. Again. Will I live to see that? If I do, I do, if I do not, I do not. Karma.

Koiko's laugh sent a chill down his spine: *Ah, Tora-chan, you and karma!* Startled, and he looked around. It wasn't her. The laughter came from the corridor, mixed with voices.

"Sire?"

"Come in," he said, recognizing Abeh.

Abeh strode in, leaving his others outside. The guards relaxed. With Abeh was one of the household maids, a cheerful, middle-aged woman, carrying a tray and fresh tea. Both knelt, bowed. "Put the tray on the table," he said. The maid obeyed, smiling. Abeh stayed kneeling near the door. These were new orders: no one was to come within two metres without permission. "What were you laughing at?"

To his surprise she said merrily, "At the giant gai-jin, Sire, I saw him in the courtyard, I thought I was seeing a kami—two in fact, Sire, the other one with yellow hair and blue eyes of a Siamese cat. Eeee, Sire, I had to laugh. Imagine, blue eyes! The tea's this season's, as you ordered. Would like something to eat, please?"

"Later," he said, and dismissed her, feeling calmer, her warm nature infectious. "Abeh, they are in the courtyard? What is happening?"

"Please excuse me, Sire, I do not know," Abeh said, still furious that yesterday Anjo had ordered them all away. "The Captain of the *tairō*'s bodyguard came a moment ago and ordered . . . *ordered me* to conduct them back to Kanagawa. What should I do, Sire? You will of course want to see them first."

"Where is *Tairō* Anjo now?"

"I only know that the two gai-jin are to be taken back to Kanagawa, Sire. I asked the Captain how the examination went and he said insolently, 'What examination?' and left."

"Bring the gai-jin here." Soon there were heavy, foreign footsteps. A knock. "The gai-jin, Sire." Abeh stood aside and motioned Babcott and Tyrer forward, knelt and bowed. They bowed standing, both unshaven and clearly tired. Immediately one of the door guards angrily shoved Tyrer to his knees, sending him sprawling. The other guard tried the same with Babcott but the Doctor twisted with uncanny speed for such a huge man, grabbed the man by his clothes near his throat, one-handed, lifting him off his feet, slamming him back against the stone wall. For a second he held the unconscious man there, then gently let him crumple to the floor.

In the shocked silence, Babcott said carelessly, "*Gomen nasai,* Yoshi-sama, but these twits shouldn't pick on guests. Phillip, please translate that, and say I haven't killed him though the ill-mannered sod will have a headache for a week."

The other samurai were coming out of their trance and going for their swords. "Stop!" Yoshi ordered, furious with the gai-jin and furious with the guards. They froze.

Weakly, Phillip Tyrer had picked himself up, ignored the inert guard and said in his quaint, halting Japanese, "Please excuse, Yoshi-sama, but Doctor-sama and I, we bow as foreign custom. Polite, yes? No mean harm. Doctor-sama say, Please excuse, man no dead only . . ." He searched for the word, could not find it, so he pointed at his head, "Pain, one week, two."

Yoshi laughed. Tension left the room. "Take him away. When he wakes bring him back." He waved the others to their places and motioned the Englishmen to sit opposite him. When they had settled themselves awkwardly, he said, "How is the *tairō*, how did the examination go?"

At once Babcott and Phillip replied with simple words and gestures that they had agreed in advance, explaining that the examination went well, that the *tairō* had a bad hernia—a rupture—that Babcott could help relieve the pain with a truss and medication, which would have to be made and fetched from the Settlement, that the *tairō* had agreed he should return in a week to fit it and bring the results of tests. Meanwhile, he had given him medication that would take most of the pain away and help him sleep.

Yoshi frowned. "This 'hern'ah,' it is permanent?"

"Doctor-sama say that—"

"I know the doctor is talking through you, Taira," Yoshi snapped, displeased with what he had heard, "just translate his words without ceremonial titles!"

"Yes, Sire. He says damage is per'man'nt," a new word for him. "*Tairō* Anjo need . . . need medicine always stop pain, all time, sorry, each daytime, and also use each daytime this 'truss.'" Tyrer used the English word and with his hands, explained the belt and pressure point. "Doctor think *Tairō*-sama good if has care. No can . . . cannot fight use sword easy."

Yoshi scowled, the results not heartening. "How long . . ." He stopped and waved his guards out. "Wait outside." Abeh stayed. "You too." Reluctantly his Captain closed the door. Yoshi said, "The truth: How long will he live?"

"That only God says."

"Huh, gods! How long Doctor *thinks tairō* will live?"

Babcott hesitated. He had expected the *tairō* to order him not to speak to Yoshi but once he had told him about the hernia and medicine, and had given him some of his laudanum tincture, which had relieved the pain almost at once, the *tairō* had chuckled and encouraged him to relate 'the good news.' But the hernia was only part of the problem.

His fuller diagnosis, one that he had not told Anjo, or Phillip Tyrer, wanting to reserve judgment until he had made an analysis of urine and stool samples, had consulted with Sir William and made a second examination, was that he was afraid there could be a dangerous deterioration of the intestines from unknown causes.

The physical had only taken an hour or so, the verbal probing many hours. At forty-six, Anjo was in bad condition. Teeth rotten, surely septicemia from those sooner or later. Bad reactions to delicate probing of stomach and organs, obvious constrictions inside, very enlarged prostate.

Most of his diagnostic problem was due to his and Phillip's lack of fluency, because the patient was impatient, did not trust him yet, and was not forthcoming with symptoms or clues. It had taken much diligent questioning for him to *probably* establish the man experienced difficulties with bowel movements, passing urine and an inability to hold erections—which seemed to concern him the most—though Anjo had shrugged and would admit none of the symptoms outright.

"Phillip, tell Lord Yoshi I think he will live about the average for a man in his condition of the same age."

Tyrer's headache had returned, aided by his desperation to do a good job. "He live about same as man of same age."

Yoshi thought about that, also understanding the difficulties of probing delicate matters in a foreign language with inadequate interpretation. Therefore he must keep the questions simple. "Ask: two years, three years, one year?" He watched Babcott closely, not Tyrer.

"Difficult say, Lord. In one week perhaps know better."

"But now? The truth. One, two or three, what think?"

Babcott had realized before he left Kanagawa that his function here was not only as a doctor. Sir William had said: 'To put it bluntly, old chap, if the patient turns out to be Anjo, you're also an important representative of Her Majesty's Government, me, the Settlement, and a bloody spy—so, George, please don't pong on this golden opportunity . . .'

For himself he was first and foremost a doctor. With doctor-patient confidentiality. No doubt that Yoshi was the enemy of the patient, a powerful enemy, but also a potentially powerful friend to H.M.'s Government. Balancing the two, Yoshi was the more important in the long run. Anjo had issued the ultimatum to evacuate Yokohama, he was the head of the Bakufu who would, unless there was a violent end to Yoshi, certainly die before him. If forced what would you answer? he asked himself. Within a year. He answered instead: "One, two or three, Yoshi-sama? Truth, sorry not know now."

"Could it be more?"

"Sorry, not possible say now."

"Can you say next week?"

"Perhaps say can, not more than three year next week."

"Perhaps you know more than you say, now or next week."

Babcott smiled with his mouth. "Phillip, tell him politely I am here at his invitation, a guest. As doctor, not magician, and I don't need to return next week or any week."

"Damn it, George," Tyrer muttered guardedly, "we don't want trouble. I don't know what 'magician' is, and damned if I can cope with these nuances. For God's sake, make it simple."

"What did you say, Taira?" Yoshi asked sharply.

"Oh! Sire, that . . . difficult translate words of High Leaders when . . . when many meanings, and not know bet word . . . best word, please excuse me."

"You should study harder," Yoshi said testily, infuriated that he did not have his own interpreter. "You do well but not well enough, study harder! It is important you work harder! Now, what did he say, exactly!"

Tyrer took a deep breath, sweating. "He say, he doctor, not like god, Yoshi-sama, not know exact about *tairō*. He . . . he here Yoshi invite. So sorry, if not want come Yedo, Doctor-sama, not come Yedo." He died a little more seeing Yoshi smile the insincere way Babcott had, no mistaking that meaning, and he cursed the day he decided to be an interpreter. "So sorry."

"*So ka!*" Grimly Yoshi weighed his next move. The doctor had proved useful though he was hiding facts from him. If that was the case, he deduced the real facts were bad, not good. That thought pleased him. A second thought pleased him. It was based on an enlightened idea Misamoto unknowingly suggested months ago. Yoshi had at once initiated the practice through his spymaster, Inejin, for future use: one way to control barbarians was through their whores.

Inejin had been diligent as usual. So now Yoshi knew a lot about the gai-jin Yoshiwara, which were the most popular Inns, about Raiko and the whore of this strange and so ugly youth, Taira, the old one of many names now called Fujiko. And about the strange whore of Furansu-san. The gai-jin leader, Sur W'rum, had no special whore. Serata used two sporadically. Nemi was named as the consort of the chief gai-jin trader and an especially good source of information. The doctor did not visit the Yoshiwara. Why? Meikin will find out . . .

Ah yes, Meikin the traitoress, you are not forgotten!

"Tell the doctor I look forward to seeing him next week," he said, his voice flat. "And thank him. Abeh!"

Abeh was in the room, kneeling, in an instant. "Escort them to Kanagawa. No, take them to the gai-jin leader personally, at Yokohama, and bring back the renegade Hiraga."

*   *   *

"Hello, Jamie! It's lunchtime! Last night you said to call for you at one o'clock!" Maureen smiled at him from his office doorway, bonnet and dressed nicely, her cheeks rosy from her brisk walk along the promenade from Struan's. "One o'clock, you said, for lunch at this Club of yours."

"Be right with you, lassie," he said absently, finishing the letter to his banker in Edinburgh about the joint venture with the shoya, enclosing Tess Struan's sight draft for deposit. Got to talk to Nakama-Hiraga somehow as soon as he's found, he was thinking. Where the devil is he? Hope to God he hasn't fled as everyone thinks. "Take a seat, Albert's joining us." He was so engrossed he missed her disappointment.

This new office was in the *Guardian* building, near to Drunk Town, on the High Street. It was much smaller than the one in Struan's but it had a pleasant view of the bay, so important for the trader to be able to follow the coming and going of ships. Unfurnished except for a desk and three chairs, half a dozen filing cabinets. Piles of books and boxes, sheaves of blank paper, pens and new ledgers that he had scrounged until his order from Hong Kong arrived, were scattered everywhere. Heaped on his desk were more papers, letters, orders and a big mailing announcing the launch of his new company and requests for business. All had to be made ready for *Prancing Cloud*'s departure. "Did you sleep well?"

He sealed the letter, hardly hearing her. "Yes, thank you, did you?" and picked up another of the mailings.

These were being copied by two Portuguese clerks in their office down the corridor, next to the printing shop. The clerks had been lent by MacStruan until he could make permanent arrangements. "Albert's a good fellow, isn't he? I said we might be late," he remarked absently. If it had been up to him he would have skipped the Club and asked one of the clerks to make him a sandwich, or ordered some of the Chinese food that they ordered daily from Drunk Town. Half an hour later he put down his pen. "All set?" he asked brightly.

"Aye."

"What's up?" he asked, seeing her look.

"Weel, laddie, I'd hoped we could be alone for lunch, there's a lot to talk about—obviously there was no time last night. It was a bonny party though, wasn't it?"

"Yes, it was. The Cossack dancers were stunning. We've lots of time to talk—sorry, didn't think it was important."

"Angelique was stunning too, aye, and many of your friends, Marlowe and Settry!" She laughed lightly.

Relieved, his guard came down and he picked up his hat and coat and opened the door. "Glad you enjoyed it."

"You went out last night, after we'd said good night."

His guard came up too late to prevent the guilty flush. "Yes, er, yes, I did."

"I knocked on your door but there was no answer—I just wanted to talk, I wasn't tired. You said you were tired."

"Well, yes, I was, but then I wasn't. Shall we go?"

"Aye, I'm hungry." They went out onto the promenade. Few people were about. The day was not the best, sea choppy and wind cutting. "It's no' as bad as Glasgow at this time of the year," she said pleasantly, taking his arm.

"That's true, but the cold won't last, soon it'll be the best time, the spring and autumn are best." He was breathing better now that the subject had been dropped. "Spring and autumn are the best."

"You went to the Yoshiwara?" she asked pleasantly.

An ice pick leapt from his testicles to his heart and back again and a thousand answers presented themselves, the best of which was, If I want to go to the Yoshiwara, by God, I will go and we aren't married and even if I was . . . and I told you I didn't want to be married, at least not yet, not now that the new business has a chance. Confidently he opened his mouth to say all that but for some reason his voice came out strangled and limp: "I, er, yes, I did, but th—"

"Did you have a good time?"

"Look, Maureen. There's some—"

"I know about the Yoshiwara, laddie, and about men," she said matter-of-fact and kindly. "Did you have a good time?"

He stopped, rocked at the gentle voice and manner. "I, well, I suppose . . . but you see, Maur—"

"It's too cold to stop, Jamie, dear." In a friendly fashion, she took his arm again and forced him to walk on again and continued, "Good, so you had a good time. Why did you no' tell me? And why tell a fib about being tired?"

"Well, because . . ." Again a dozen answers, but his mouth only issued, "Because it's obvious, for goodness' sake. I didn't want . . ." He couldn't say, I didn't want to hurt you because I'd made a date, wanted to see Nemi yet didn't want to, didn't want you to know about her and actually I had a dreadful time.

When he had walked into their little house Nemi was dressed in her best sleeping kimono, their little sanctuary pristine, food and saké prepared and she was laughing and happy and completely attentive:

'Heya, Jami-san, good you see, ah! Hear good news from boat. You to marr'iage 'rady from Scut 'rand, marriage, heya?'

He had been flabbergasted at how quickly the news had travelled. 'How do you know?'

'All Yoshiwara know-ah! 'Portant, *neh*?' Nemi bubbled. ''Two day I at Great House kowtow meet soon *oku-san* you.'

'EH?'

' 'Portant, Jami-san. Wen marr'iage? 'Portant, for *oku-san, nee goh-san'* frien', *neh*?'

'Are you touched?' he had burst out.

She had stared at him without understanding. 'Wat for mad, Jami-san? *Oku-san* pay now. *Oku-san* pay, Jami-san, *iyé*? 'Portant *oku-san nee*—'

'That's not the way things are done, for God's sake.'

'No unn'stan' . . . 'Portant Nemi go *oku-san* . . .'

'You're crazy!'

'No unn'stan',' she had said sullenly, appalled at his bellicose manner, deciding flight was the best defense from this incredible behavior— but flight of course in tears.

She was gone before he could stop her, the mama-san could not convince her to return and so, furiously, he had stomped home to bed and to little sleep. God Almighty, Nemi coming to Struan's to see Maureen? Maureen's to pay Nemi in future? Important for mistress and wife to be good *friends*? God in Heaven! I must have misunderstood.

No, you bloody didn't. That's what she bloody said.

Eventually, he had come to the office. Before dawn. Bloody hell, he had thought all morning and now he had two bloody women to contend with. "Look, Maureen, I'm sorry I lied," he said lamely, "but . . . well, I don't quite know what else to say."

"Dinna' fash' yoursel', these things happen." She smiled.

"Eh? You're not pis—sorry, you're not angry?"

"Nay, laddie, no' this time," she said so nicely, "no' till we've had a wee chat."

There was no threat in her voice or manner that he could detect, she still held his arm tenderly, yet his innermost being screamed danger, and for God's sake hold your tongue, say nothing. "Wee chat?" he heard himself ask.

"Aye." Then there was a deafening silence even though the wind was clattering roof shingles and shutters, church bells, steam whistles from the harbor, dogs barking.

Hold your tongue, two can play in this negotiation, he cautioned himself. "Aye? What's that mean?"

Maureen was feeling her way carefully, enjoying the learning—and teaching—process. This was merely the first of a never-ending series of confrontations.

'All men are dreadful, Maureen,' her mother had said, amongst other counsel. 'Some worse than others, they're all liars though a canny wife can always see through her man's lies. In the beginning husbands are sweet and send your head to the stars, their warmth and lovemaking, and silly little kindnesses. In the beginning.

'Then come the bairns, the children, and looking after the home, most always wi' out enough money. By this time you're inclined to let yoursel' go in dress an' your hair and person. It's awful difficult with bairns, and lack of sleep an' being mortal tired, so soon thy man turns his back in bed, begins to snore, aye, that's na' a wee difficulty if you canna' learn to close your ears tight. Then they go awenching . . . but dinna' fash' yoursel', it's a temporary game for them an' willna' last, and if you're a canny wife, thy man will always come back—you've always got the bairns, and you've got God. Remember it's no' an easy task to earn the daily bread, as he should remember it's also no' an easy task to raise bairns and keep the home cozy, but they never will remember.

'Thy father, he's nay different with his women or woman in India, but he's home now and his problem's different. I should have known he was already wedded to his Regiment when we wedded. At least this Jamie, he's no' in the Services, that's terrible hard for a wife to compete against.'

'How do you become a canny wife, Ma?'

'I wish I knew, lassie, I wish, but some rules are certain: choose thy man cannily, a good hold on thy tongue will help, a good stiff broom and a wild temper if used shrewdly will help, lots of understanding and forgiveness all the time, and a warm, soft bosom for the poor wee laddie to cry on . . .'

"*Wee chat?*" she heard Jamie say again, his voice choked, and she almost laughed aloud.

She kept her smile and demeanor forgiving, the broomstick and temper ready in case. "I learned about the Yoshiwara on the boat." She left that hanging and he snapped up the bait.

"Gornt told you? Or Hoag? It was him? That idiot."

"No, it was your fine Captain Strongbow—and Dr. Hoag's no idiot, lad. I asked Strongbow how you all managed to stop from going mad without lady friends, was it the same as in India, or China?" She laughed remembering how difficult it had been to get him to talk openly. Wusky's wonderful, she thought, blessing her father for teaching her to drink, when necessary. "I think your Yoshiwara's very sensible."

He was going to say, You do? This time he said nothing. Her silence tortured him. When she was ready she said, "Tomorrow's Sunday."

His head reeled, unprepared for the non sequitur. "Yes, I . . . yes, I suppose . . . yes, it's Sunday. Why?"

"This afternoon I thought we could go to the Reverend Tweet, I hope he's not as silly as his name, and we should ask him to publish the banns."

He blinked. "What?"

"Aye, banns, Jamie." She laughed. "You've no' forgotten banns must be read three consecutive Sundays, have you?"

"No, but I told you I'd written and said th—"

"That was when I was there, I'm no' there anymore. I'm here and I love you," she said, and stopped and looked up at him and saw he was fine and what she desired in life and, all at once, her control went with the wind. "Jamie darlin', we're engaged and I believe we should marry because I will make the best wife a man ever had, I promise I promise I promise and no' just because I'm here, I've loved thee from the first moment and now is a grand time to marry, I know it, I'll go back, back to Scotland and never . . . if you want me to go back I will, by the next boat, but I love you, Jamie. I swear I'll leave if you want me to." Tears sprang into her eyes and she brushed them aside. "Sorry, it's just the wind, laddie." But it wasn't the wind, all guile vanished, her spirit open and naked for him to see. "I just love you, Jamie . . ." His arms went around her and she buried her head in his shoulder, feeling more terrible than she had ever been, desperate for his love, tears pouring.

When her terror had abated, pushed by his warmth, she heard him saying nice things to her, mixed with the wind and the surf, that he loved her and wanted her to be happy, and not to worry and be sad but this afternoon would be too soon, he had so much work to do for the company that it was going to be hard to start it and keep it alive.

"Dinna' worry about the new company business, Jamie, Mrs. Struan said that she'd—" She stopped, horrified. She had not intended to tell him but it was too late now as his arms tightened and then held her away from him.

"She said what?"

"It doesna' matter. Let's . . ."

"What did she say to you? What!" His face was grim, eyes penetrating. "She told you she was sending me money?"

"No, no, she didna', she said . . . she just said you were a good trader and you'd be a success. Let's eat, I'm starv—"

"*What did she say?* Exactly."

"I told you. Let's have lu—"

"Tell me what she said, by God. Tell the truth, exactly! She told you about the money, didn't she?"

"No, no' exactly." She looked away, angry at herself.

"The truth!" He held her shoulders. "Now!"

"All right." She took a deep breath and in a gathering rush said, "It was this way, Jamie, exactly. When I went to Struan's, to the Edifice on the promenade, to ask where you'd be, if you were in the Japans or where, I was told to wait and then she sent for me, Mrs. Struan did, to the great office overlooking all Hong Kong, but such a sadness to her and such strength, poor lady. Let me be a moment."

Again she dried her eyes and took out a handkerchief and blew her nose and then, not knowing what to do with her hands, put her arm in his and her hand found its way into his coat pocket. "Let's walk, Jamie, easier to talk walking, it's cold. Mrs. Struan asked me to sit down and told me you'd been dismissed and I asked why and she told me and I told her that was no' fair, no' your problem that her son was a wee devil and crazy in love with an unacceptable adventuress called Angelique—I don't know about adventuress but having seen Angelique, Jamie, I can understand why her son or any man would be in love with her, and having met his ma I understand why there was anger between them. . . ."

A gust pulled at their hats and they held on to them, then she went on, "We . . . we had a row, dinna forget this was days before we heard about his death. It was a terrible row, Jamie. Soon we were both on our feet and I'm afraid I lost my temper, you'd have been ashamed of me and I used some terrible words of my da'."

He stopped and gaped at her. "You had a row with Tess?"

"Aye, never in my life so bad, not even with my sisters and brother in secret. I was na' very brave about it, but her unfairness made me angry and it spilled out and I gave her . . ." Maureen's good nature and sense of humor returned and she laughed nervously. "Och, it was a Glasgow cat fight, like two fishwives at the docks, ready to tear each other's hair out. At one time someone came in and she threw them out and . . . So, Miss Ross? she said, lips like a gillie's dirk, both of us panting and no' at all friendly, What do you think I should do? Do? I said, First you give Mr. McFay a handsome parting bonus he's earned a dozen times over during his years of service, you give him business to start his business and you write him a nice note.''

"You said that? To Tess?"

"Aye, I did." She saw and heard the disbelief and dispelled that instantly. "I swear this's the God's truth, Jamie, I swear it. I was no' going to tell you but you insisted and I wouldna' lie. By the Lord God, I swear this's the truth!"

"Yes, sorry. Please go on."

"Dinna be sorry, laddie, I didna' believe it mysel' at the time. After I said my piece, not kindly at all, Mrs. Struan laughed—she laughed and said, sit down, all right, but no nice note. That's no' good enough, I said. What's fair compensation? I asked. Her smile vanished and she said, A thousand guineas. She spat it out just like Da' when he's in a rage. Poppycock, by God, says I. Ten thousand." Maureen stopped and looked at him searchingly. "I had to settle for five. Was that all right? I dinna' know if that was enough, is it?"

"You settled? *You* settled for five?"

"Aye, it took time and more curse words . . . that night I asked God's forgiveness for the curses, more of my da's words. I hope that was fair, Jamie, along with extra business . . . and she did agree no bad acts, to be business friends, I thought that important. After she agreed, she threw in a free passage with her icy smile, Go find your Mr. McFay, with my compliments." Maureen glanced at the surf a moment, collecting her thoughts. Another little nervous shrug, then she stared up at him, artlessly. "That's what happened, but it was for you, no' for me or for us, for you, I didna' mean to mention it."

"Jamie! M'ssross." Lunkchurch had reeled out of his office and was standing with them before they knew it. He greeted them effusively, nearly asphyxiating her with the smell of whisky, invited them to dinner that night and reeled away.

"He's always drunk by two o'clock, but he's all right," Jamie said. "He won't remember the invitation or our refusal." This time he took her hand and put it in his coat pocket for warmth and held it and walked on. "Maureen, I th—"

"Before you say another word, let me finish. I didna' mean to tell you about her and me, it slipped out. I'm deeply sorry, I swear to God I didna' mean to tell you, God's truth, no' when we were talking, serious, about . . . talking about us, you and me. Please believe that, God's truth."

"I believe you, I do, no need to worry on that score, and Tess wrote to me, kept her word, sent the money, more than I've had in my whole life, enough to start and all because of you."

Tears of remorse began. "No' because of me, Jamie. You'd been wronged and Mrs. Struan owed it to you—I would no' have told you but—but you wanted me to. And you were right to be angry, I was wrong to say, 'this afternoon,' please forgive me, it was just . . . you're right, this afternoon is too soon, you're right and I was wrong to suggest that. Can we wait, Jamie, please? Can we wait, say a week or two, a month, see how you like me? Please?"

"Now you listen," Jamie said, and gave her hand a squeeze. "I like you too much as it is and no, I don't want you to go and yes, we will wait a little while and no, I'm not angry, and yes, I believe you and thank you with all my heart and no, you weren't wrong to make a suggestion. Let's think about it and talk over dinner, Sparkles, just you and me, eh?"

Before she knew what she was doing she reached up and kissed him in thanks, the use of her nickname a harbinger of joyous portent. Her hand went back to his and both into his pocket. "You're bonny, Jamie, that's the truth and I love you and . . ." She was going to add, And you dinna have to say that until you're ready. But she did not. She withdrew from that precipice. "You're a bonny laddie."

"And you're a bonny lassie," he said, more calm about her than he had been for years, the ache and guilt no longer to the fore. What about marriage? he asked himself, for the first time without a shudder. Absolutely a man should be married and have children, at the correct time. I'm not opposed to marriage, far from it. When? When the business has settled and we're in profit? She's terrific, clever, good-looking, good family, patient and faithful and loves me, incredible that she stood up to Tess and did what she did, show's how smart she is. It might work. Do I love her? I like her enormously. . . .

I'm thirty-nine. And trim and fit, and should be married—should have married before. She's twenty-eight, young for her age too, so she must know her own mind, and there's no doubt she sparkles.

Last night Marlowe and Pallidar noticed too, noticed a little too much! That randy bastard Settry wouldn't leave her alone, not that I minded—one little jerk of my head and the darling came a-running. He squeezed her arm, liking that.

"What?"

"Nothing. I'm glad you enjoyed the party last night," he said, but he was thinking, in three or four months, no need to hurry, not a bad idea. "Here we are."

They turned into the clubhouse forecourt. MacStruan was talking to Dmitri on the steps and he saw them look up and Dmitri waved cheerily. The ice slammed back into his guts. Nemi! When Nemi gets the bit between her teeth . . .

God Almighty, he thought aghast, how the hell do I cope with Nemi, the Yoshiwara *and* Sparkles? Can't be done. Must be done. What was it she said about the Yoshiwara? She wasn't pissed off this time . . . 'no' till we've had a wee chat.' Chat?

"Are you cold, Jamie darling?"

"No, no, just fine."

"Phillip, tell Captain Abeh again, I'm sorry but Hiraga cannot at the moment be found." Sir William stood with his back to the fireplace in one of the Legation reception rooms, Tyrer, Babcott and Abeh just arrived from Yedo. It was dusk. "We're still looking everywhere. And Phillip, wipe that smug look off your face, do you really want to irritate him?"

Abeh was angered. So was Sir William. He had done everything he could, the Settlement had been combed and soldiers were again going through Drunk Town and the village. The Yoshiwara was more difficult. Weapons were not allowed, access to Inns was almost impossible without breaking and entering, a hideous idea and bound to create an international incident. If he did it, then samurai at their Gates would insist on the same right. In the beginning of the Settlement it had been agreed, so long as there was no rioting, the Yoshiwara was to be left alone to float and to serve.

"He says he cannot go back without Hiraga and Hiraga was promised to Lord Yoshi today."

Sir William bit back the oath. Instead he said sweetly, "Please ask him to wait. At the guard house. Surely Hiraga will be found soon, if he is still here."

"He says, Still here? If not here, where is he?"

"If I knew I would certainly fetch him for Lord Yoshi. Perhaps he has escaped, to Yedo or Kanagawa or somewhere." Even Sir William was shocked at the black rage in Abeh's face who spat out some Japanese, turned on his heel and stomped out.

"Rude bugger!"

"He said, Hiraga had better be found, Sir William." Tyrer rubbed his unshaven face, feeling filthy and anxious to have a bath, massage and siesta before Fujiko. Most of his fatigue had immediately dissolved by the joyous news that Hiraga was not locked up and in irons. "Have to feel sorry for Abeh, sir. He can't go back without Nak—without Hiraga, more than his life's worth."

"Well, that's his problem. Have you any idea where Nakama would be?"

"No, sir, if he's not in the village or the Yoshiwara."

"You might try and find out, obviously it's important." Sir William looked up at Babcott. "Now, more important. George, the patient? Was it Anjo?"

"Yes."

"Tallyho! Phillip, you look exhausted, no need for you to wait, we can talk later. George can fill me in. If Nakama-Hiraga appears you bloody clap him in irons at once. At once!"

"Yes, sir, thank you, sir. Before I go, can I ask what happened in Hong Kong?" The moment they had arrived both had asked, noticing anxiously that *Prancing Cloud* had returned, but Sir William had said, First Abeh.

"It's all quiet in Hong Kong, all quiet here, thank God." He told them about the funeral, Hoag returning and why. "The reason's supposed to be confidential but it's common knowledge. So it's a waiting game, Tess is waiting, it seems Angelique has agreed to wait, so Hoag says, not that she can do much else. She is, or she's not."

Babcott said, "If she's not she'll know in a few days. And so will we."

"Christ," Tyrer muttered. "What happens: if she is or if she's not?"

Sir William shrugged. "We have to wait too. Now off you go, Phillip. Whisky or brandy, George? Do you mind bringing me up-to-date now—you're not too tired?"

"No." The two men were alone. "Brandy, please. Yedo was very interesting."

"Health! And?"

"Health. Before Yedo, do we know more about Hong Kong?"

Sir William smiled. The men were old friends, and Babcott Deputy Minister. "It went perfectly. Yes. Tess wrote privately to thank me. Most of it I can tell you now: Hoag brought three letters for Angelique, she doesn't know this, by the way. One Hoag gave her at once and told me there was no noticeable reaction one way or the other, no clue, he presumed it was just asking her to wait. Tess confirmed the contents of that letter to me, that she proposed a lull until it was established if Angelique was pregnant or not. If Angelique has her period, he gives her one letter, if not he waits to the second month to make sure and he gives her the other. Hoag swore he does not know the contents, nor did Tess reveal them in her letter to me."

He sipped his whisky, his face set. "One issue Tess wrote that, I'm afraid, indicates her thinking: Struan's solicitors are drafting a brief to nullify in court the 'Ludicrous Ceremony'—she puts that in caps—whatever the legality or illegality, whatever the pregnancy result, and to contest any will if one is found there or in the Japans."

"My God! Poor Angelique . . . how awful!"

"An emphatic yes to that. My letter asking for forbearance had no effect. Bloody, eh?" Sir William stalked to his desk and brought out a dispatch. "This is what I really wanted to discuss—highly confidential, of course."

Babcott turned up the oil lamp. Daylight was fading fast. The Governor of Hong Kong wrote formally:

My dear Sir William, thank you for your dispatch of the 13th. I'm afraid it's not possible to send extra troops at the moment. I have just heard from London that all troops are needed elsewhere, that budgetary considerations preclude raising new levies in India or elsewhere so you will have to do with what you have. However, I am sending another 20-gun, sailing frigate, H.M.S. Avenger, on temporary loan. Rest assured if there is a major attack on Yokohama, in due course the attack will be punished.

I am instructed by London to inform you of the following directives for immediate prudent action: you will collect the indemnity demanded, together with possession of the murderers (or witness their trial and execution), you will punish and bring to heel the petty tyrant responsible, Sanjiro of Satsuma. I am to advise you further that the Naval and Army forces you presently have at your disposal are considered more than adequate to deal with one petty princeling.

Babcott whistled tonelessly. At length he said, "They're a bunch of idiots, the whole bloody lot."

Sir William laughed. "I rather thought the same. But having said that, what do you think?"

" 'Immediate prudent action'? That's a negation."

"Diplomatic verbiage to cover their tails, obviously."

"We have the indemnity, we . . ."

"The bullion was advanced on Sanjiro's behalf. It was a loan, not a payment by the guilty party."

"True. And both murderers are dead, probably."

"Yes, by chance and not one hundred percent certain and not as punishment for the crime."

"Well, yes. We . . ." Babcott looked at him and sighed. "What do I think? Between us I think you've already decided to launch a punitive strike against Sanjiro, probably at Kagoshima, particularly as Yoshi gave you tacit approval."

"Possible approval. Is the dispatch and are my answers enough to convince Ketterer a strike, if any, is authorized?"

"No doubt about that, they've given you directives. The dispatch clearly makes it obligatory, however stupid and however much I disapprove of it."

"Because you're a doctor?"

"Yes."

"If you ever have to take charge, George, I hope you'll forget that you are."

"You don't have to say that, William. I know on which side my bread is buttered. Meanwhile *Put not your trust in princes, bureaucrats or generals, they will plead expedience while spilling your blood from a safe distance.*" He raised his glass. "To London. Christ, I'm tired."

"Meanwhile remember that Machiavelli also said, *The safety of the State is the overriding duty of the ruler,* or some such platitude." His eyes crinkled. "Now Anjo."

Babcott told him. And being asked, gave his considered diagnosis. "Six months. A year, no more. Subject to my tests."

"Interesting." Sir William thought long and hard. Outside night had settled, the fleet bedding down. He closed the curtains against the drafts, went over to the fire and poked a blaze. "Putting that aside for the moment, my inclination is to order an immediate naval presence off Kagoshima, immediate bombardment if Sanjiro gives us no satisfaction— as much for Yoshi's benefit, Anjo and his Council of Elders as for scallywag Sanjiro, especially Yoshi."

"Sending the fleet there leaves the Settlement naked. What about the reports of samurai quietly surrounding us—we saw a great number around the Tokaidō."

"That's the risk."

Babcott looked back at Sir William steadily and said no more. The decision was not his. He would happily obey like everyone else, insisting on being part of the expedition. He got up. "Think I'll nap before dinner, didn't sleep much last night. By the way, Phillip did a cracking good job. I'll start my tests later and let you know."

"Do you want to have a late bite to eat? Nine o'clock? Good, and thanks for Anjo, that's very important. That makes Yoshi even more important. If he can be trusted. If."

"In this land that's a major problem." Then Babcott said, still sickened by Tess's attitude, "Rotten about the 'court case.' That's going to be messy for Angelique, so unfair, isn't it?"

"Has life ever been fair, old man?"

At dinnertime, Angelique knocked on the tai-pan's office door, dressed to go out. "Albert?"

"Come in! I say, I love your hat." It was an elegant dinner hat, discreet, still suitable for mourning, dark blue, yet made chic with a few silk flowers she had tucked into the band.

"Thank you. You're working late."

"Part of the job." Like everyone else he wondered what was in the letter Tess had written to her, wild rumors around the Settlement, from ordering her to get out of Asia to charging her with murder. There was no sign on her face, only a becoming melancholy.

In his own letter Tess had cautioned him to be wary about making commitments on armaments, and if proposed, to keep them very confidential. To use McFay if need be.

I have asked him to cooperate with you. Of course, his main interest will be to promote his own business but you are to treat him as friendly. Now that Mr. Edward Gornt has assumed control of Brock's in Japan, he is enemy—be careful of him, he's more cunning than we presumed. As to that other person, Dr. Hoag has agreed to assist me. I understand she still occupies quarters in our house granted by my son. You will be informed later of new arrangements.

"Where are you dining? French Legation?" he asked.

"I accepted to sup next door with Mr. Gornt." She saw his face harden. "It was a last-minute supper invitation with mutual friends, Dmitri, Marlowe. He asked me to ask you to join us to—to escort me if you would—are you free?"

"Sorry, can't, glad to take you to the door and to call for you, but that's Brock and Sons, he's the head of it and this's the Noble House."

"You should be friends, you could still be competitors. He really was my husband's friend, and mine, and Jamie's."

"Sorry, it's my problem, not yours." He smiled again. "Come on."

He took her arm, not bothering about a coat and they went into the cold. The wind tugged at her hat but did not displace it. She had secured it with a chiffon scarf.

" 'Evening, Ma'am." The guard on Brock's door bowed.

" 'Evening. Thank you, Albert, no need to come and fetch me, one of the others will see me home, off you go or you'll catch cold." He laughed and was gone. In the same moment Gornt was there to greet her.

" 'Evening, Ma'am. My, but you look smashing."

Now, as he accepted her wrap, her worries began to well up again. What trumps? A burst of laughter came from an inner room. She recognized Marlowe, saw that the guard had gone and there were no servants about and they were alone for the moment. "Edward," she whispered, her concern overcoming her caution, "why are you so sure I'll be all right?"

"Tess invited me back. Don't worry, it's in control. Better we talk during your promenade tomorrow—tonight is only for good conversation amongst friends, gentle pleasure. I'm truly honored you accepted my invitation—it's due to you I'm head here." Gornt took her arm and in a normal voice said, "Welcome to Brock and Sons, Angelique. Shall we go in?"

The dining room was as big as the one in Struan's, as lush, the silver as good, the wine superior, the linen richer. Liveried Chinese servants. Marlowe, Pallidar and Dmitri stood in front of a roaring fire, waiting to greet her. They kissed her hand, admired her hat that she kept on as was custom, Marlowe and Pallidar in their informal uniforms. And while she greeted them and listened with her quiet charm, her inner motor was sifting Gornt, what he had said and what was missing.

"Shall we sit now that our honored guest is gracing us?" Gornt settled her at one end of the table. He took the other. The table was small enough to be intimate, large enough to be impressive. "Suhs, a toast!" he said, lifting his glass of champagne, "To the Lady!" They drank and his eyes never left hers. An invitation, discreetly given. She smiled back, neither yes nor no.

Plenty of time, he thought, delighted to be the host and even more delighted with himself. So much left to tell. Perhaps the best part. But not to her.

On the last day in Hong Kong, Tess Struan had again sent for him, secretly. 'I've been through all the papers, Mr. Gornt. It's not absolutely certain the support the papers give your scheme will bring about the Brock crash.'

'I think they will, Ma'am,' he said, impressed that she knew so much about business. 'I truly believe you have everything needed to unlock Pandora's Box'— this was the code name they had agreed on. 'There's one last piece of the jigsaw that would complete the picture and guarantee success.'

'And that is?'

'Norbert's official chop. It's in his safe at Yokohama.'

She had sighed and leaned back in the carved chair. No need for either of them to articulate that this chop on almost any Brock letter-headed document, correctly couched and dated, validated it, commit-ting Brock's of Yokohama through him to whatever was on the paper.

No need to say aloud that all kinds of incriminating information could be written now, backdated, and found or slid surreptitiously into the pile. Who could challenge such a letter with Greyforth dead?

Both of them knew its value.

Morgan and Tyler Brock had speculated heavily on this complicated but incredibly ingenious scheme to corner the Hawaiian sugar market—in principle already accomplished—bartering the sugar crop forward for Southern cotton which they had presold legally to guaran-teed French interests—historic U.S. allies and not subject to Northern blockade *in this instance* through certain congressional help and safeguards—then to be shipped legally from France to Geneva, to be sent on legally to Lancashire cotton mills that were almost destitute and desperate for the raw material.

A tiny hazard: If the Union government discovered for certain the ultimate destination—Britain was formally neutral, most of the British were actively pro-Confederate—and this was made public knowledge, they would inhibit the export by interception. This was a minor risk because of high-level agreement to the French connection, which was, for the first time, proven by Gornt's papers to be a Brock company shell, and governmental noninterference more certain because a goodly pro-portion of the sugar, also desperately needed, was to be bartered for diverted Union armaments, which Brock's would promptly import to Asia. Projected profits were immense. Brock's standing in the Asia-America entente would become preeminent, whoever won the civil war. In Asia they would be supreme. And no possible way the plan could fail, because the Victoria Bank of Hong Kong was the underwriter.

The bank, biggest in the Colony, had eagerly underpinned the venture, approved by the Board of twelve of whom Tyler Brock was one, with Brock and Sons shares and liquidity as nominal collateral. For all intents and purposes the Victoria was a Brock preserve. Old Man Brock had been a founder in '43, he had chosen the other members—excluding any director of Struan's perpetually from the Board—had retained a forty percent interest and had permanent voting control of at least nine to three. And while backing Brock's on the international scene, the Board had meanwhile agreed to crush Struan's through repossession of all Struan's debt paper, due by January 30th—the timetable and questionable methods of the clandestine, long-term acquisition was also tabled in Gornt's evidence.

Gornt had excitedly pointed out that for the first time Brock and Sons were vulnerable—never before had they put up the control of their company as collateral. The Victoria was the key to the Pandora's Box. The key to the bank was the Board. It had to be subverted, turned around, and financial support withdrawn suddenly from Tyler and Morgan on the correct day, leaving them destitute without the necessary funds to oil the wheels. Meanwhile evidence of the scheme from Gornt's papers, and notice that the Victoria would not be supporting the deal any longer, had to be rushed by clipper to Washington to the right hands, which would make interception probable—without the Bank's backing there was no sugar to barter for cotton or for armaments. But this had to be done now, before rearranging the Bank's voting control.

How to turn the Board was the pivot of Gornt's plan.

The papers revealed highly embarrassing facts on the background of two pro-Tyler Brock Board members, so serious that their votes would go to whoever had the documentation. Seven to five. More facts about one other man, less damaging and questionable, were also there. A possible six to six.

Gornt's idea was that Tess should approach the chairman privately, give him the facts, tell him that details of the scheme were already en route to Washington, and propose 'that they pull the plug on Brock's and swing to you and Struan's, granting an extension of six months on Struan debts, two seats on the Board, take immediate control of Brock's and sell off the assets at bargain prices, enough to cover debts, leaving Tyler and Morgan Brock to drown in sugar they can't pay for. And last the Bank agrees to split Brock's forfeited forty percent bank holdings into four parts: one to the chairman, one to two Board members of his choice, one to the Noble House.'

'In return for what? Why should the Bank cross Tyler?' Tess had asked. 'Double-cross, isn't that the American word?'

'Yes, Ma'am, but this would be a triple-cross. Why should the Board gorge on the deal? Because they'll be huge winners, the chairman and all of them, because they hate Tyler privately and fear him, like everyone else. They don't hate you, you're the Noble House and no threat to them. Hate, not money alone, is the grease that oils the world.'

'I don't agree, but let that pass. Back to this mythical chop. What do you propose to do with it?' Her smile had been cynical. 'If you obtain it.'

'Anything you like, Ma'am.'

'Perhaps you should bring it here by *Prancing Cloud*.'

'No, sorry, that's too soon, unless you'll leave her to wallow for a week or two. I'll bring it in good time.'

'Why delay? Send it, Strongbow's trustworthy.'

'I'll bring it in good time.' He remembered how her eyes, so pale and seemingly so innocent most times, penetrated like molten iron. 'I promise.'

'Put that aside for the moment. The price, Mr. Gornt?'

'I would like to tell you that when I return, Ma'am.'

She had laughed without humor. 'I'm sure you would. I thought you knew me well enough by now not to try to squeeze me or Struan's. You could delay till the last moment, by which time I will have had to launch the assault, on both Tyler and the Bank, Struan's would be terribly exposed and I would have to agree, whatever you demand.'

'There must be trust on both sides. I've given you the evidence you need to crush Tyler Brock and Morgan, for a deal you promise me in the future, I'm trusting you to deliver, Ma'am. It's not much to ask to delay, I swear I'll be back in good time. What I would bring from Yokohama is the icing on the cake and the price will be fair.'

'I've never liked cake, or icing, Mr. Gornt—any liking was beaten out of me by my father, who disapproved of such vittles, when I was very young. The price?'

'May I assure you, Ma'am, it will be a price you will gladly pay, on my honor and my word as a gentleman.'

She had looked at him. 'May I assure you, Mr. Gornt, equally, if you cross, or double-cross or triple-cross me, I will see you will be an extremely unhappy man, apart from being persona non grata in Asia and throughout the Empire—*on my honor and my word as tai-pan of the Noble House . . .*'

Gornt went cold, remembering the way Tess's words had surrounded him, the pride with which she had said tai-pan of the Noble House even when she added, 'however temporary.' All at once he realized that this woman really was tai-pan now, realized whoever held the title soon would not hold the power. Realized with a stab of fear that he would have to deal with her for a long time, that by destroying Brock's perhaps he had created a monster for his own destruction.

God in Heaven, she can blow me to pieces at her whim! How do I make her an ally, keep her an ally? She's got to be my ally, whatever the cost.

Then laughter from Dmitri and Marlowe brought him back. His world came into balance again. Candlelight, dining table, fine silver, fine friends. Secure in Yokohama, the chop already removed from the safe and hidden away, a letter already written, backdated and chopped that corroborated the loose evidence against the key Board member, another letter implying collusion of the chairman. Without them the Board will collapse into our laps like a bent house of cards, has to, they won't resist their one and only chance of revenge on Tyler and Morgan Brock. And no need to fear Tess Struan. She's in my power as much as my future's in hers.

I've a lot to be pleased about. Here I am, twenty-seven, Morgan's head is almost in the basket, I'm tai-pan of Rothwell-Gornt's-to-be, head of a splendid table, servants waiting for orders. And she's there, beautiful, rich-to-be, and loving me however much she tries to hide it, my bride-to-be whatever the outcome—a child by Malcolm only makes the price higher to Tess, a sumptuous but bargain price she will gladly pay!

"Health and a long one," he toasted silently, raising his glass to Angelique and to himself and to them both together, sure his future was limitless.

His guests did not notice the private toast, too involved in chattering, vying for her attention. Comfortably he watched them. Mostly he watched her. Then he tapped the table.

"Angelique, gentlemen, your attention please. We have mulligatawny soup with sherry, baked fish with onions, olives and iced Pouilly Fuissé, sorbet and champagne, then the roast with potatoes and St.-Emilion—the cook 'found' a fine piece of Struan beef . . . Don't worry, Ma'am," he said with a laugh, "it was bought, not stolen. Then chicken pie and, to end, a surprise to end all surprises."

"And what's that?" Marlowe asked.

"Wait and see." He glanced at Angelique.

She smiled her enigmatic smile, the smile that excited him so much, like the Mona Lisa he had seen in the Louvre on a trip to Paris—never to be forgotten.

"I think we must trust our host, Captain," she said softly. "Don't you agree?"

55

Sunday, 11th January:

In the night Angelique awoke
in a cold sweat, back in time, back in the French Legation, the mama-
san's little bottles on the side table, one already empty, the other ready
to uncork and swallow as soon as the cramps began.

Finding herself warm in bed in her own suite, the fire coals still
glowing, her night light casting solid shadows, the terror left and her
pulse slowed and she waited for the indications. Nothing. No cramp or
stomachache. Waiting. Still nothing. Thank God, she thought, I must
have dreamed they had begun. She relaxed in the down mattress,
watching the fire, not quite awake, good pictures in the coals, happy
pictures of the roofs of Paris in the sunset, melding into the sum-
merscape of her dream house in Provence, her baby son contentedly
sleeping in her arms. "*Jésus, Marie,* please don't let it begin. Please."

Yesterday afternoon Babcott had arrived, 'Happened to be passing,
and wanted to see how you were.'

'No need to tell fibs,' she said sharply. 'Dr. Hoag said the same thing
this morning. The very same words.'

'Steady on, dear Angelique, I really did happen to pass by and I
really did want to see you. To reassure you.'

'Oh?'

'Yes, old Hoag said you were a little touchy. Rightly so.' He nodded,
smiling. 'And to tell you what you didn't give him a moment to say,
that it's quite possible for your monthly to be delayed, to have slight

period cramps that go away to return properly in a day or so. Or even never to return.'

'Why is it you doctors are so wise but know nothing, not really, not even about such a simple matter as having a baby or not having a baby, a process which has been with us a few years,' she had fumed, exasperated and weary of all the sidelong glances of the last few days and the sudden silences as she walked by. 'Kindly leave me be, both of you, I will inform you when I need to see you, if ever. Leave me alone!'

He had gone away, chastised, but she did not care. Since last Sunday's flaming row with Father Leo she had kept to herself as much as possible.

"I hate that man," she muttered, "hate him for upsetting me so much. He's vile, he's no man of God!"

During Confession he had said, 'Perhaps you should ask forgiveness for this sham marriage you took part in, my child—oh, I know you were cajoled, tricked. Even so, it's a sin.'

'I wasn't cajoled, Father, and it's not a sin or a sham,' she had said. 'It's perfectly legal according to law.'

'Heretic law? It's false. You blind yourself. Of course it is not lawful and not valid in the sight of God.'

'It is in the sight of English law,' she said, seething. 'It is in the sight of God, it is!'

'Ah, my poor child, it's not and you know it's not. The Church does not recognize a heretic marriage, let alone by a simple sea captain. You're not married in the sight of God.'

'I am, Malcolm's Church recognizes my marriage, his law does, my husband's law does. I'm married legally.'

'How foolish you are. Don't blind yourself. You're Catholic, the True Church does not recognize such a marriage. Repent, my child.'

'I'm married and that's the end of it!' She had got up.

'Wait! It's not the end, my child, to give you absolution you must admit your sins, to come before Him blameless! How can I give you absolution?'

'Their God is the same as our God, my God,' she had said, tears of rage and frustration blinding her. 'I can worship Him in their Church as well as here.'

'You risk damnation and Eternal Torment. Excommunication, the sacraments withdrawn from you. Beware, your mind has been taken by the heretics, pray for forgiveness . . .'

She had fled.

André and Seratard were in the congregation. Later André had asked what the trouble was and she had told him. He said, 'Thousands of Catholics are happily married under Protestant dogma, and vice versa, whatever Church hierarchies claim.'

'André, am I married or am I not?'

'You are, according to British law, and British naval law, until a British court says you are not.'

'But not according to the Church?'

'To their Church, yes, subject to the above, to ours, no. You already know the answer to that, no.'

'I hate that man.'

'He's a priest. Not all of them are good, we both know that too. Listen, Angelique, about your . . . your time, please, as soon as you know, one way or another, please tell me privately so we can begin to plan. Henri expects any day to have the French Ambassador's approval that you are a ward of the State. Don't worry, I promised we will guard you and your interests and we will,' he said, and left her to brood.

Not married according to the Church? Then to hell with the Church of Rome, she had thought, sick with apprehension. Beware! Never admit that openly, never. You are French, French people understand about Catholic Rome, its corruption and heresy and about misguided popes. Every night in her prayers she asked, implored, the Blessed Mother for guidance and succor.

Monday and all the other days dragged, always eyes and unspoken questions so she went out less and less. To pass the time she read and slept and read and wrote letters and began a story about a French girl who was cast ashore in Yokohama. This stopped abruptly and she burned the pages as she started to relive Kanagawa and *him* and the nights and days with Malcolm and their one night on *Prancing Cloud*.

Prancing Cloud had left. She had been glad to see that harbinger of ill wind disappear into the distance.

Since her promenade when she had talked again with Gornt—learning nothing new— by mutual consent they had decided not to meet for a few days. Twice she had invited Maureen Ross to tea, the second time deliberately receiving her in bed to encourage rumors that she had a fever. Their chats were gossipy, ordinary, about fashion, the problems in the Settlement, the life here, nothing serious. Later these visits would be fun when they could discuss more intimate matters and thoughts. Not now. But she liked Maureen who had brought welcome books and magazines and told about Jamie's new office, how he was working all hours, and, shyly, her hope that they would be married soon.

The only person she had enjoyed seeing was Phillip Tyrer. He had been sent by Sir William with best wishes for a quick recovery, bringing the latest London papers with him and presenting her with flowers he had purchased in the village. 'By Orders of Her Majesty's Government,' he had said in French with a flourish, his boyish grin and joie de vivre infectious.

For an hour or more he had chatted, mostly in French, relating the latest rumors. About his trip to Yedo, about Nakama-Hiraga who had vanished without a trace, creating a diplomatic problem for Sir William, and about his Captain, Abeh, 'who's still waiting and seething at the North Gate.'

'What's going to happen, Phillip?'

'Don't know. We hope the problem's going to go away. Pity of it is we had to describe Nakama, what he looks like now, so there's not much chance for him escaping. Damn nuisance, 'cause he was a fine fellow and he helped me greatly. I don't believe a word about him being an assassin. We didn't get a sausage of info out of the other fellow, Nakama's friend, whose family are shipbuilders in Choshu. I got him a look around one of our frigates. Nice enough fellow but fairly dumb. He knew nothing about Nakama or would say nothing. Sir William didn't want to give him to the Bakufu so he let him go. Damn nuisance, Angelique, Nakama aided me tremendously—not only with Japanese, and if it weren't for him . . .'

Later they had soup together and at her probing he had admitted, first swearing her to secrecy, that he had a girl, a special girl in the Yoshiwara. 'Oh, she's so beautiful and nice, Angelique, I think I can swing the money for the contract without straining the old Exchequer, the liaison is so comfortable . . .' and she had been amused by how young he seemed, envying him his simple love, and, compared to him, how adult and sophisticated she felt.

'One day I'd like to meet her,' she had said. 'I can easily sneak into your Yoshiwara. I'll dress up as a boy.'

'Oh, my God, no, you couldn't. Angelique, you mustn't.'

It might be amusing to do that, she thought, chuckling, and turned over in her bed, almost asleep. André will take me. I'd like to see this Hinodeh I've so much invested in. I wonder how she looks.

On the threshold of sleep her stomach spasmed.

Another cramp, different. Another. Wide awake now. Apprehensively she rubbed her stomach and loins to take the ache away but it did not go away and now she realized for sure it was the old familiar ache with the slightly bloated feeling.

It had begun. The bleeding followed. And with the flow all of her longing and worry and hoping burst. In abject grief she began to cry and buried her head in her pillows, "Oh, Malcolm, I had hoped so much, so much, now I've nothing left to give you, nothing left of you, nothing left to give you ... oh, Malcolm, Malcolm, I'm so sorry, so awfully sorry ... oh God, I'm so awfully sorry ... THY will be done ..."

Crying and crying; after an eternity, crying herself to sleep, no more tears to shed.

"Missee, wakee! Missee-tai-tai, cawfee, heya!"

In her waking mists Ah Soh banged the tray on the side table and Angelique smelled the warm, heavenly smell of fresh-brewed coffee—a present from Seratard and one of the few services Ah Soh would and could do properly—wafting around her, bringing her into the day without hurt.

She sat up in bed and stretched, astonished and delighted she felt so alert and so well. The cramps had gone, the ache had subsided into its normal pattern, better than usual, the bloated feeling less than usual.

And best of all, despair had left her. It's HER miracle, she thought, reverently. During the last month in nightly prayers to the Blessed Mother, talking, asking, pleading, one night exhausted by anxiety, she had listened. 'Leave it to me, child, it is MY decision not thine,' she heard, not hearing with her ears but with her innermost self, 'MY decision, all of it, rest in peace.' The anxiety had left her.

It was *her* decision, how wonderful! Angelique would accept HER verdict. The Will of God. And she had.

Impulsively she knelt beside the bed, closed her eyes and blessed Her and gave passionate thanks, and said again how sorry she was but thanked her for lifting the burden, Thy Will Be Done, then slid again under the covers ready for coffee and the world. Coffee at this time, nine, was custom on a Sunday, just enough time to bathe and dress for church.

Church! Why not? she thought, I must give proper thanks, but no Confession. "Ah Soh, bring my bath and ..." Ah Soh was staring at her, glazed. Abruptly she realized her maid must have seen bloodstains on the back of her nightdress.

Hastily Ah Soh said, "I get bar'f," and waddled for the door but Angelique was there before her and pushed her back. "If you tell anyone I'll scratch your eyes out!"

"Ayeeyah, no unn'erstan' Missee-tai-tai," Ah Soh grunted, petrified by the venom on her mistress's face and in her voice. "No unn'erstan'!"

"Oh, yes, you do! *Dew neh loh moh-ah.*" She spat out the Cantonese curse words as she had heard Malcolm use them at Chen once when he was angry with him, and had seen Chen go white. He had never told her what the words meant but they had the same effect on Ah Soh, whose legs nearly gave way. "Ayeeeeeyahhh!"

"If you talk, Ah Soh, tai-tai will . . ." Furiously Angelique stabbed her long nails to within a millimeter of her eyes and held them there. "Tai-tai do this! Understand?"

"Unn'erstan'! Sek'ret, tai-tai!" The frightened woman moaned some Cantonese, put fingers to her lips parodying a clamp. "Ah Soh no talk, unn'erstan'!"

Getting hold of her fury though her heart was still racing, Angelique pushed the woman towards the bed and got into it again. Imperiously she pointed at the coffee cup. "*Dew neh loh moh!* Pour my coffee!"

Saturated with humility and genuine fear, Ah Soh poured the coffee and handed it to her and stood there meekly.

"No talk, make all bed, clothes, clean. Secret!"

"Unn'erstan' tai-tai, no talk, sek'ret, unn'erstan'."

"No talk! Or . . ." Her nails slashed the air. "Bath!"

Ah Soh scuttled away to get the hot water but first, to breathlessly whisper the news to Chen, whose eyes would turn to Heaven and he would say, 'Ayeeyah, what will Tai-tai Tess do now,' on the run to speed the news on the fastest ship to Illustrious Compradore Chen who had commanded them to inform him at once, irrespective of cost.

The coffee was delicious. It soothed her stomach and spirit and took away the slight tumescence. One of Angelique's true joys in all the world was early morning coffee, most of all with croissants and Colette on the Champs-Elysées at one of the elegant street cafés, reading the latest Court Circular and watching the world stroll by.

First church. I will pretend that nothing has happened yet—Ah Soh won't dare to say anything. Who to tell first? Hoag? André? Edward? Mr. Skye?

She had already had a discussion with Heavenly Skye. His advice was that they had no option but to wait, to see what Hoag would do, and after that, what Tess would do. Tess's letter to him had been brief: *Dear Mr. Skye: I know my son had dealings with you. Cease and desist in our affairs, my son's and mine. No good will come of it.*

'Interesting choice of words,' he had commented.

'You sound afraid, as though we've lost already.'

'Not at all, Angelique. Our only posture can be to wait. She has the initiative.'

'By the next mail I want you to write to Struan's solicitors, asking for an accounting of my husband's estate.' This had been an idea André had given her, favoring opening of an immediate offensive.

'Gladly, if you want to fall into her trap.'

'What?'

'Your only posture is the aggrieved, wronged child-widow who was enticed into an early marriage by a strong-willed man—not the impoverished, rapacious widow of a rich husband, a profligate minor, who had gone against his mother's wishes in marrying an impoverished lady of questionable antecedents—please don't be angry, I only tell you what can, may and probably will be said. You must wait, dear lady, pretending to hope that Tess will behave like a human being should. If his child was, er, is en route, that would be a great assist.'

'And if there isn't?'

'Let us consider that when it happens, I mean when it doesn't. Lots of time to con—'

'I don't have lots of time. I will run out of money.'

'Be patient . . .'

Mon Dieu, patience! Men and their patience.

Now that Angelique knew beyond doubt she was not bearing Malcolm's child, she set aside all the ideas she had formulated in the event of a baby and concentrated on the other set.

An immediate onslaught on that woman? No, that comes later, Mr. Skye's right in that. I have to find out what she is going to do first. To do that I have to tell Hoag or Babcott. Hoag delivered her message so he will have to be the one. No need to have him paw me, either of them. I can tell him. At once or later? Is it worth asking André, or Edward? I don't think so.

Having no baby to contend with, to consider, makes my life simpler, my chances of remarriage better. Whatever happens, like every girl in the world, I must have a protector, the right husband—or, at length, any husband.

As to my prospects: I don't have money enough to get back to Paris to set myself up there. I've no prospects except through a settlement with Struan's—no, not with the company, with that woman. Even Edward is tied up in that. Especially him. Without a good settlement for me, and her benevolence on his deal, his marriage interest will evaporate. That's fair because mine will evaporate quicker. He's in love with me, I'm not in love with him though I like him a lot, but without mutual financial security the connection has no logic.

Always back to that woman, whatever idea comes up, Angelique thought, not a little pleased with the way her mind was working, coolly, logically, not worrying, simply examining all aspects as a prudent woman should.

I can last a month or two, no more—if I don't give any more money to André. Soon my chits will run out, any day Albert can get orders to stop my credit and throw me out. I can almost read her spiteful mind. Never mind, I can move to the French Legation. But they won't support me for very long.

Sir William? No reason for him to do more than he has. André is the only one outside her grasp who can help. Think clearly, Angelique, that's wrong! When André sees that the money is drying up or has dried up, no telling what he may do in desperation. He could sell Tess that awful paper, he could give her proof about the . . . about the past. He's a cynic, callous enough or clever enough to have kept proof I paid for the medicine with the earrings I lost. He'd settle for much less money than I would. Even so he's the only man here evil enough to combat her. Edward will go against her but only up to a point. He won't lose Rothwell-Gornt.

Should I get Edward to go back to Hong Kong at once? Or Hoag, he's a friend, a sort of friend, and he's the one she sent to me? Or André? Not him, for then I wouldn't sleep a moment knowing he was in Hong Kong with that woman, unwatched.

For her, church was a huge success, even with her melancholy. She had dressed as usual in black, a medium veil covered her hat and face. Prayer book in hand she had set out on the blustery day, and when she passed the Catholic church on the promenade, joined the throng that headed for Holy Trinity, and went up its path and entered the church and sat in the empty back row, at once going to her knees and beginning to pray, a current went through the nave, already half full, echoed by latecomers, the current gathering strength and swooping through the Settlement and into Drunk Town.

"God Almighty, the Angel's gone to church, our church . . ."

"Holy Trinity? Bollicks, she's Catholic . . ."

"Bollicks or not she be in't Holy Titties, bright as a berry, all dressed in red and no knickers on . . ."

"Oh, for God's sake, don't spread rumors . . ."

"That's no rumor, she don't never wears knickers . . ."

"In Holy Titties? Holy God! Is she become one of us'n?"

"Old Tweety'll wet hisself with glee . . ."

Maureen and Jamie had been behind her. They hesitated beside the last pew, readying to say, May we sit with you? but Angelique was still kneeling as if in prayer and did not acknowledge them though aware of their presence; and not a little envious of the joyous green of Maureen's dress and coat and matching hat, with its plume of yellow chiffon hanging down her back. In a moment they moved on, shoved ahead by the press of the others and not wanting to disturb her—which was what she wanted. After her initial passionate prayer of thanks for the strength to conquer her vast disappointment, she stayed on her knees, the hassock comfortable, and, protected by her veil, watched wide-eyed to see what would happen. This was the first Protestant service she had witnessed.

There was not as much reverence as in her own church but it was packed, braziers spotted here and there against the damp, and everyone mobile was in attendance. The stained-glass windows were rich, the altar and trappings throughout more stark than she was prepared for.

Others would have stopped to greet or to nod, filled with degrees of delight or bewilderment, ready to sit beside her. But they did not, again not wishing to interrupt. Gornt chose an opposite pew.

So she was left alone and soon the service began. First hymn and she imitated the others, standing when they stood, sitting when they sat, praying when they prayed but always to the Blessed Mother, listened to the sermon that the Reverend Tweet stuttered, completely undone by her presence. More hymns and chanting and the plate, an embarrassed moment as she fumbled for a few coins, another hymn and the blessing and then it was over to an audible, well-earned relief.

The congregation stood as the vicar went into the vestry preceded by an ancient altar boy. Most began to shuffle toward the exit, palates ready for the traditional Sunday lunch, the best meal of the week: roast beef, Yorkshire pudding, roast potatoes for the lucky ones who could afford a joint from the last shipment of ice-frozen Australian beef.

A few remained for a final prayer. Hers was for forgiveness that she had come to this church but she was confident that God would understand it was only a momentary, necessary protest to Father Leo. All eyes watched her as they filed out. Then she joined the last of them, nodding and saying ' 'Morning' to murmured greetings.

The vicar stood just outside the door, greeting some, glowering at others. When she came up he became both seraphic and stuttering,

"Oh, my, Miss Ang . . . oh, Madame, how wonderful to see you, welcome to Holy Trinity, may we see more of you . . . if there's anything I can explain . . . Oh! No? Well, I hope you enjoyed, well, please, please come again, wonderful to see you, you're welcome . . ."

"Thank you, Reverend," she said, bobbed a quick curtsey, hastily walked up the path and onto the promenade.

Sir William was waiting for her, Babcott with him, muffled like everyone against the gusts. "Glad to see you up and about," Sir William said sincerely, "particularly here. We're rather proud of Holy Trinity and you're very welcome, very, and we're all happy you're here. The Vicar was a bit off today, sorry about that, he's usually quite good and not too much fire and brimstone. Did you enjoy the service?"

"It was so different, Sir William," she said. "To worship in English and not Latin was exotic."

"Yes, I suppose it was. May we walk with you?"

"Please." They set off briskly, exchanging pleasantries and genial questions, avoiding the issue central to their mind with: the weather's shocking, isn't it? The football match yesterday afternoon was grand—may we escort you next week; have you seen the latest papers, or heard the Yokohama Players were putting on a performance of *Romeo and Juliet*—Mrs. Lunkchurch has kindly consented to play the starring role against Mrs. Grimm's Romeo. "Have you ever been on the boards, have you performed, Ma'am?"

"Only children's Nativity plays in the convent," she said. "And not very well . . . oh!"

A gust had seized Sir William's top hat and sent it twirling, Babcott just managed to hold on to his, she was not quick enough and hers went sailing away with hats all along the promenade to curses, wails, cheers and laughter. She joined the melee and scurried after hers, but Babcott retrieved it just before it went rolling down onto the beach. Sir William's was stopped by Phillip Tyrer who hurriedly handed it to him then charged after his own.

"My best beaver," Sir William said sourly, brushing off mud that looked suspiciously like manure. Her hat was undamaged and, smiling, she put it back on firmly, adjusted her hat pin. "Thank you, George, I thought it was going for a swim."

"So did I. Can we entertain you at lunch?"

"Thank you but no, I'm staying indoors today."

Soon they were at the Struan gateway. Both men kissed her hand and she disappeared inside.

"Lovely lady, good sort, good sport," Sir William said.

"Yes." Babcott was frowning, looking out to sea.

Sir William followed his intent look. Nothing amiss in the bay that he could see. "What's up?"

"Her period's begun."

"Christ Almighty, you've examined her? Or Hoag? Why the devil didn't you tell me?"

"We haven't examined her. I just know, that's all."

"Eh? How d'you th—" He stopped as MacStruan and Dmitri went by. " 'Morning, 'morning to you," he said impatiently, then took Babcott by the arm and started him down the street to the Legation. "How d'you know? Eh?"

"I'm a doctor, for God's sake. I saw her yesterday, and today when I saw her without the veil it leapt into my head. Her face was a little puffy and when she ran after her hat I noticed she ran awkwardly."

"Damned if I did! God Almighty! You're sure?"

"No, but a hundred guineas says so against a farthing."

Sir William frowned. "Will Hoag know just by looking at her too?"

"I can't say."

"In that case don't tell him."

"Why on earth not?"

"Let's leave it private between us, that's best." Then Sir William said kindly, "Let's leave Angelique to play her cards as she wants. It is her game, hers and Tess Struan's, not ours. It's ours no longer."

Four Bakufu Enforcers, including a sergeant, stomped through the Yoshiwara gateway. They were like any other patrol of samurai except the men were tougher, meaner and more alert. It was early afternoon. In spite of the weather, the traditional, leisurely procession of courtesans, trailing maids, paraded up and down, showing off their finery one to another and to the groups of gai-jin gawking and drinking at the cafés and Teahouse, laughing as the wind sent a few decorative umbrellas sailing.

From time to time one of the Enforcers would stalk up to the doorman of an Inn, or patron of a Teahouse, or restaurant maid. At once the person would bow and grovel and say, "No, Sire, the traitor Hiraga has not been seen. Oh, no, Sire, thank you, Sire. Yes, at once, Sire. No, I don't know him, Sire."

Almost all of them knew where he was but kept their peace, hating Enforcers, knowing, also, no reward was big enough to prevent shishi vengeance, or Floating World disgust, at a betrayal. In their world, secrets were the spice and currency of life, adding to the day's excitement.

The patrol's progress seemed to be haphazard. Then the Sergeant changed direction, turned into the alley of the Three Carp and hammered on the door in the fence.

Hiraga was trapped. Whenever patrols were in the vicinity, lookouts alerted him in good time to flee to his underground hideaway in the tunnel where he now had a rough bed, candles, matches, food, his swords and pistol, and Katsumata's explosives. Today when the alarm reached him, Hiraga discovered other samurai searching that garden, so there was no chance to reach the well.

In panic, he had rushed for the kitchen area and had barely enough time to assume a disguise, secreted there, that Katsumata had given him as, a few metres away, masked by a hedge, the Sergeant shoved past the bowing doorman, kicked off his sandals and stomped onto the veranda of the main house.

Unaware Hiraga was aboveground and so near, Raiko came out to greet the Sergeant, knelt and bowed, her face all charm, her insides fluttering, for this was the third day of searches—too many for comfort. "Good afternoon, Sire, so sorry the ladies are resting and not ready to receive clients."

"I wish to search."

"With pleasure, please follow."

"Go to the kitchen."

"Kitchen? Please, please to follow." She led the way pleasantly. When she saw Hiraga head down in the dirt amongst the dozen cooks and workers, her knees almost failed her.

Hiraga was filthy, his head covered by the matted wig Katsumata had worn in Hodogaya, and naked except for a soiled loincloth and ragged singlet. 'Tie a pebble under your instep, Hiraga,' Katsumata advised. 'Your walk as much as your face will give you away. Smear dirt on your face and armpits, dung is better, pretend to be a scullion, do not act, be one. Meanwhile make incendiaries, instruct Takeda how to do it, and be ready for when I return. . . .'

The leather-faced Sergeant stood with his hands on his hips in the silence and looked around. Painstakingly. Every corner, cupboard or storeroom was scrutinized. Rows of rare spices, teas, barrels of saké and bottles of gai-jin liquor and bags of the finest rice. He grunted to hide his envy.

"You! Head cook!" The portly, terrified man raised his head.

"Stand over there! Line up, all of you." In their haste to obey they stumbled over one another, Hiraga limping badly, dirty, shoved his way into line. Muttering curses, the samurai stared at each man as he went down the line. When he came up to Hiraga his nostrils wrinkled with disgust at the stench, then he moved to the next man and the next, vented his pent-up rage by shouting at the last man, who collapsed in a petrified heap. Then the Sergeant stalked back and stood in front of Hiraga, feet planted. "You!" he bellowed. "You!"

Raiko cried out and nearly swooned, everyone stopped breathing, Hiraga fell on his face, grovelling and moaning, bracing his feet against the wall to hurl himself forward at the Sergeant's legs. But the man began raving, "You are a disgrace to a kitchen, and you"—he whirled on Raiko, who backed against the wall, terrified, Hiraga just managing to stop his lunge in time—"you should be ashamed to have a dung-covered scum like this in a kitchen for the rich." His iron-hard toe kicked the befouled in the neck and shoulder joint and Hiraga cried out in real pain, the wig almost came off and he grabbed it in panic, hands over his head. "Get rid of him. If this lice bag is here or in the Yoshiwara by sundown, I will close you for filth! Shave his head!" Another kick and he stalked out.

No one moved until the all-clear came. Even then they started to pick themselves up warily, maids rushed in with smelling salts for Raiko, who tottered away leaning on them, while kitchen workers helped Hiraga to his feet. He was in pain but did not show it. At once he stripped and went out to the servants' area and washed himself, scrubbing and scrubbing, filled with revulsion—he had had only enough time to dig his hands into the nearest bucket of night soil and smear himself and rush to a place near the fires.

When he was partially satisfied he stalked naked for his house, to bathe again, this time in hot water, certain he would never feel clean again. Raiko intercepted him on the veranda, not fully recovered from her alarm.

"So sorry, Hiraga-sama, the lookout failed to warn us, but the samurai in that garden . . . Hot water and a bath maid is waiting for you inside, but now, so sorry, perhaps you should go, it's too dangerou—"

"I am waiting for Katsumata, then I shall leave. He has paid you well."

"Yes, but the Enforc—"

"*Baka!* You are responsible for the warning system. If there is another mistake, your head goes in the bucket!"

Grim-visaged, he stalked into the bathhouse where the maid knelt and bowed so fast she banged her head. *"Baka!"* he snarled, not yet over his utter fright, the foul taste of fear still with him. He squatted on the tiny stool, ready for the maid to begin scrubbing. "Hurry up!"

Baka, he thought, enraged. Everyone is *baka,* Raiko is *baka,* but not Katsumata—he is not *baka,* he was right again: without the shit I would be dead, or worse, captured alive.

YEDO

Dusk was a busy time for the inhabitants of Yedo's Yoshiwara, the biggest and finest in all Nippon, a maze of tiny streets and pleasant places on the edge of the city, covering almost two hundred acres, where Katsumata and other shishi, or ronin, could hide in safety—if acceptable.

Katsumata was particularly acceptable. Money was not a problem for him. He paid the waitress for his soup and noodles and strolled unhurried towards the House of Wisteria, still disguised as a bonze though now he wore a false mustache and was clad differently, his shoulders made wider with pads, his robe richer.

Colorful lanterns were being lit everywhere, gardens and paths given their last brushing, fresh flower arrangements finished. Inside the Teahouses and Inns of greater or lesser importance, geisha and courtesans and mama-sans were being bathed and dressed, chattering and preparing for tonight's entertainment. Kitchens abuzz, men chopping and dicing and preparing sauces and sweetmeats and decorations and cauldrons of the choicest rice, cleaning fish and caressing marinades into them.

Lots of friendly laughter. Misery here and there, some in tears thinking of clients allocated or strangers who must be received and welcomed with smiles and laughter, and satisfied—and not the young lovers many hearts yearned for, the yearning to be left alone and allowed to sleep. As always, mama-sans and older, more experienced courtesans gentled them, repeating the same dogma that Meikin was saying to Teko, Koiko's *maiko,* now in tears, who was to make her debut as a courtesan this night, "Dry your tears, Moonbeam, accept without thinking the sad impermanence of life, accept what lies ahead, laugh with your sisters, enjoy wine and song and your pretty clothes, gaze at the moon or at a flower and drift with the current of life like a gourd drifting downstream. Run along now."

I will not accept that Katsumata betrayed my Koiko with just cause, Meikin thought, her heart aching. He had no need or justification to compromise my precious with that woman shishi, however brave! Worse, he was *baka* to end such a marvelous source of influence and private information from Yoshi's shadow: stupid, stupid, stupid! But it is done. Finished. Take your own advice, Meikin: Drift, what does it matter, truly?

I accept that it matters. Koiko mattered to all of us, not the least to Yoshi, now pitilessly against all shishi.

Again the mama-san sat at her mirror. The reflection stared back at her. Her makeup, heavier than usual, no longer hid the shadows and sagging care lines.

I accept, too, that I have aged horribly since the shoya interrupted us, Raiko and me—Eleventh Day of Twelfth Month, Last Month, the last day of my life. Just thirty-three days ago. Only thirty-three days and I look like a crone, long past the normal span of fifty years. Thirty-three days of tears, a lake of tears when I thought I was safely beyond tears, sure that I had used up all my tears long ago, over lovers I can hardly remember, over one I can still feel and smell and taste and yearn for, my penniless young samurai who left without warning, without a word or letter, for another Teahouse and another woman, taking the little money I had saved and the broken pieces of my spirit that he cast into the gutter. And later then more tears over my baby son, dead in the house fire of his foster parents, his rich old merchant father wandering off like the other, my suicide unsuccessful.

Too many Floating years. Thirty-three years drifting, one for each of the harrowing days. Now I have forty-three years, forty-three years today I was born. What should I do now? Soon the Lord Yoshi will demand payment. Karma.

I accept that I trained Koiko, offered her, guaranteed her. What more can I offer in supplication? What can I do?

Her reflection did not answer.

A knock. "Mistress, Katsumata-sama is here, he is early."

Her stomach felt hollow. "I will be there instantly."

To calm herself Meikin drank some of the gai-jin brandy that Raiko had given her. When she was easier, she went out and along the exquisite corridor towards a guest reception room, all woods and tatami and shoji the most expensive. In wonderful taste. Bought and paid for with so much effort and heartache and cajoling but, because of Koiko the Flower, her House was immensely profitable and a pleasure for her bankers. Today she had a meeting. 'We notice, so sorry, your receipts are considerably down compared to last month.'

'It is the season, a poor time of the year for all Teahouses, and unseasonably cold. Business will pick up with the spring. We are in huge profit for the year, there's no need to worry.' But she knew, and knew the Gyokoyama knew, that most of her profit was because of Koiko, that now a gossamer curtain hung between her and ruin. If Yoshi decided.

Then why increase your risk, allowing shishi here, she asked herself. Particularly Katsumata—he's the first of Yoshi's enemies now. What does it matter? There must be bad with the good, the bad can be dealt with and the good enjoyed. Exciting to be part of the shishi, their bravery and *sonno-joi*, their fight for freedom from the yoke of centuries, laying down their lives for the Emperor in their tragic and hopeless quest, all of them so young and valiant, born to fail, so sad. And if they were to win, would those who next rule, would they free us from our yoke of ages?

No. Never. Not us, not women. We will be where we are now, in thrall to the yang.

Her eyes caught a glimpse of the moon breaking out of a sunset-reddened cloud, for an instant peerless, to be swallowed again, the red becoming more brown and then gold and into darkening flames—one moment alive, the next dead.

"Beautiful, *neh*?"

"Yes, Katsumata-sama, so sad and so beautiful, yes. Ah, they have brought tea, so sorry you are leaving us."

"I shall be back in a few days. Have you anything more from Raiko? Anything further about the gai-jin, their plans?"

Meikin poured tea for him, pausing a moment to admire the superb design of the cups. "It seems the Lord Yoshi has had a meeting with the gai-jin leader to make friends with them." She related Furansu-san's information that Raiko's envoy had whispered to her a few nights before, but had kept from him until now. "Also the gai-jin Kanagawa doctor secretly examined the *tairō* here the same day, giving him gai-jin medicines—I hear he is improved."

"*Baka,*" he said disgustedly.

"Yes. This doctor should be stopped. Raiko's source says he returns tomorrow or the next day to see the *tairō* again."

"*So ka?*" His interest doubled. "Where? In the castle?"

She shook her head. "No. This is the best part, outside the walls, in the palace of Zukumura the Idiot, as last time."

His face twisted. "So many choices, Meikin, rare choices. Just like Utani, *neh*? So much temptation. Utani's killing still resounds around all Nippon! Hiraga? Is he caught yet?"

"No, the chief gai-jin let Akimoto go and Takeda is still also safe." She watched him and wondered what he was thinking, then added softly, "Two last facts you should know. Lord Yoshi was at the meeting of doctor and *tairō*, also with only a few guards. I hear he will be there again." She saw his eyes glitter in the light that permeated the room and felt a sudden fear, sensing his restrained violence.

"Yoshi and Anjo together, those dogs outside the walls together? Eeee, Meikin, how rare!" Katsumata trembled with excitement. "Can you find out exactly when the doctor arrives?"

She leaned forward, almost sick with hope, and whispered, "Another courier is due this evening. I will know then. Raiko would understand what a vital chance it could be for us, for all of us, for all of us to settle many scores."

In truth it was a never-before opportunity, if it came to pass. He scowled. "I cannot wait here, or come back tonight. When was the other meeting, what part of the day?"

"Early."

The scowl deepened, then dissolved. "Meikin, all shishi will thank you. If the meeting's tomorrow, send me the time at once, the Inn of Blue Skies, near the bridge at Nihonbashi."

He bowed and she bowed, both satisfied, for now.

The bridge at Nihonbashi was considered the first stage of the Tokaidō, on the fringe of Yedo, and the Inn of Blue Skies one of dozens, rich and poor, that were scattered in the district. Tonight was black and cold, the sky solid cloud, midnight still hours away. The Blue Skies lay in a dirty little alley, one of the poorer establishments, a nondescript, ramshackle, two-story building with outhouses, kitchens and a few separate one-room bungalows in the garden behind the walls. On the veranda of one of these, Katsumata sat meditating, his robe padded against the chill, enjoying the garden that alone had had care lavished on it.

Colorful lanterns amidst choice plantings around a tiny stream, a bridge, the soothing, friendly sound of trickling water and *cloppp cloppp* of the pivoted, resonant bamboo cup falling against its stone, filling with water and emptying from the miniature waterfall as long as the water fell. His silent shishi bodyguard stopped momentarily, motioned that all was well, and continued on his roving patrol around the Inn.

Katsumata was content, his plans perfected: two shishi were to join him in the morning for Yokohama, this guard and one other. The sacrifice of these two with Hiraga, Takeda and Akimoto would ensure the burning of the Settlement and sinking the warship, and therefore the bombardment and obliteration of Yedo with all its consequent results. At the last minute he would take over the firing of the church as he had always anticipated, allowing Hiraga to lead the assault team against the warship, thus giving himself plenty of opportunity to escape whereas the others would have none.

His fingers fondled the hilt of a long sword in his lap, enjoying the touch of the fine leather, already imagining himself part of these acts of terrorism that would lift *sonno-joi* from the present apathy that surrounded it, making certain his leadership of the newly formed shishi cadres, from now on to be dominated by himself and Satsuma.

Next, Yoshi and Anjo, however tempting, were not as important as Yokohama, so he had left them to other shishi here. There were not enough men to mount a frontal attack, so he had devised an ambush. An ambush might succeed, probably would not, but its very audacity again would be uplifting. For this he needed to know the exact time of the doctor's return. If Meikin reported it was tomorrow, he would alert men already primed and waiting in a nearby Inn for this suicide mission, still leaving him his two for Yokohama.

It will be enough if the ambush is launched so close to the castle, he told himself, light-headed with anticipation. This, together with Yokohama, will assure *sonno-joi* and make my future sublime. If only there was more time to prepare! Ah, time! 'Time is a thought,' he had told his students in their Zen classes, opening and closing his fist for emphasis. 'Time exists but does not exist, is permanent and impermanent, fixed and elastic, necessary and unnecessary, to be held in the hand and wondered at: why?'

Solemnly he opened his palm and stared at it. Then chuckled. What nonsense! But, oh, how those youths used to rack their brains for meaning when there was none, Ori especially, and Hiraga, my best students, future leaders I had hoped. But Ori is dead and now Hiraga is tainted and treacherous.

The *cloppp cloppp* of the water mobile was comforting. And the trickling water. His being was filled with vitality and plans and ideas, the future once again balmy, no tiredness tonight, plenty of time for Meikin to send . . .

A shadow moved in the shrubs, another, slight sound at the back and he was on his feet, sword in hand, racing for the secret door that was hidden in the bushes but three ninja-clad men came out of the shadows and blocked him from it, swords raised. At once he twisted and charged another way, but more ninja were there, the whole garden filling, some moving at him, others rock still, waiting for him to come to them. At once he launched a berserk attack against an easy target, the four men closing on him from the left, killing one, the others evaporating as quickly as they appeared. A sudden blinding pain in his eyes from acid powder they had flung in his face. In agony he howled with rage, lunging sightlessly at the enemy, his frenzy at being ambushed and tricked lending him maniacal strength to his arms and wings to his feet.

His sword found flesh, the man cried out, armless, and Katsumata coiled and blindly lashed out again, darted left and right and right again, feinting, trying to wipe his eyes clean. Twisting, hacking, darting this way and that in panic, clawing at his eyes.

His sight cleared momentarily. An open path to safety and the fence lay in front of him. Berserk, he leapt forward, then an enormous blow on the back of his head sent him reeling. In desperation he reversed his sword to fall on it but another blow smashed it away, breaking his arm. He shrieked. His consciousness vanished.

The swirling black pit was an eternity of torment with red and green flashes behind his eyes, no sight there, no hearing but for a gigantic hammering, chest afire, heart pulsating, all openings out of control. Icy water drenched him and he gasped. Another deluge in his face and another. Coughing and heaving, he came out of the dark. Agony from his broken arm, the bone splintered and protruding, soared into his head and blew his sight back. He found himself spread-eagled on the ground, helpless, a ninja standing on each wrist and each ankle but they were not ninja. Now their masks were off. He recognized Abeh who stood over him. Then he saw Yoshi nearby, dark clad, but not as the fighters. Twenty or thirty others all around. Silent as the night and the area.

"So, Katsumata! Katsumata the Raven, Katsumata the shishi and leader of shishi and patron of women," Yoshi said, his voice so kind. "What a shame you are alive. Please, the truth. Koiko, she was part of your plot, *neh*?"

Katsumata was frantically trying to collect his wits and when he did not answer immediately, the samurai standing on his fractured arm twisted the protruding bone viciously and he screamed, the iron will he always presumed he possessed lost with his freedom. "Please, oh please . . ."

"Koiko, she was part of your plot?"

"Not my plot, Sire, hers and the mama-san's, hers, Sire." The broken man babbled, his head on fire like his arm, the pain intolerable. "Not . . . she was . . . it was her, her and the mama-san, not me, Lord, nothing to do with me. It was her and Meikin her mama-san, not me, it was them, not me . . ."

"*So ka?* And Sumomo, the shishi who escaped with you through the tunnel, the Kyōto tunnel, remember? You remember Sumomo? You blackmailed Koiko and without her knowledge secretly ordered Sumomo to murder me, *neh*?"

"Sum . . . momo, Sire? I don't know, who is—is she . . . nothing to do with me, noth—" The words trailed into another scream as the man standing on his arm shifted his stance.

Yoshi sighed, his face a mask. He motioned to Meikin who was standing to one side, out of Katsumata's eye line, Inejin beside her. "You heard your accuser, Meikin?"

"Yes, Sire." She came forward weakly, her voice small and shuddering. "So sorry, he is a liar. We were never part of any plot against you, never, he is a liar. We are blameless." She looked down at Katsumata, loathing him, glad she had betrayed him and that she was revenged—his cowardice and being caught alive better than anything she had dared hope for.

"Liar!" she hissed and backed off as he began raving, trying impotently to get at her until another of the men smashed him senseless and he lay back moaning fitfully, not one of them with any sympathy.

Her head was pounding like never before, her mouth tasted vile. "But, Sire, so sorry, it is also true I knew him, so did my treasure but only as an ancient client, only that. He was an ancient client and I did not know then who he was or what this"—she hesitated, trying to find a word that fit her loathing—"this thing really did."

"I believe you, Meikin. Good, at last the truth. Good. And because he is the liar you may have him, as I agreed."

"Thank you, Lord."

"Obey her," he said to Abeh, "then bring her outside."

He strode off. All the men went with him, surrounding him, shielding him, except for Abeh and the men restraining the spread-eagled man, now moaning into consciousness again. She waited, savoring the moment, for herself, for Koiko and all the Floating World, so rare to have revenge, so very rare.

"Please strip him," she said, quite calm. They obeyed her. She knelt and showed Katsumata the knife. It was small but sufficient for her purposes. "Traitor, you won't fornicate in hell, if there is a hell."

When at length the shrieks subsided into unconsciousness, she dealt with him as with a pig. "That's what you are," she murmured, and wiped the knife clean and slipped it into her obi, blood still on her hands and sleeves.

"I will take that, please," Abeh said, nauseated by her vengeance. Silently she gave him the knife and followed to the courtyard, men surrounding her. Yoshi was waiting. She knelt in the dirt. "Thank you, Lord. I believe he regretted he betrayed you, betrayed us before leaving. Thank you."

"And you, Meikin?"

"I never betrayed you. I told the truth. I have told you all I know and gave you the traitor tonight."

"So?"

Unafraid, she looked at him directly, not many eyes so unrelenting as his, and dismissed that, preferring to see him as a man, one of a thousand clients or officials she had had to brave in her lifetime, for money or favors, for herself or her House. "It is time to go onwards, Sire." She put her hand into her sleeve and brought out the small phial. "I can do it here if you wish, my death poem is written, the Gyokoyama possess the House of Wisteria. But I am of the Floating World," she said proudly. "It is not seemly to depart befouled, with unclean blood speckling me and on my hands. I would like to go onwards clean. I would like to go back to my House. A death wish, Sire: a bath and clean clothes. Please?"

56

YOKOHAMA

Tuesday, 13th January:

ANGELIQUE WAS AMONG THE riders exercising their ponies in the early morning light at the Yokohama racetrack, cantering alone, by choice, hardly noticing the others. The circuit was busy and all the riders watched her. A lot of money was riding with her that morning. She was overdue. At least a day.

"Edward, she is, isn't she?" Pallidar asked, riding alongside Gornt on the other side of the field. "Er, overdue?"

"Yes, suh, the figures add up that way. Gornt looked across at her and pondered what he was going to do. She was mounted on a black pony that Malcolm had given her, and wore a black riding habit, very snug, black boots and hat with a half veil. "Her tailor's good, never seen that outfit before."

"Yes, and she's got a good seat too," Pallidar said dryly.

Both laughed. "But she does ride like a dream, no doubt about it, pretty as any Southern belle."

"Seriously, what do you think? I mean, there are all sorts of rumors about dates, not many of us have ever had, I mean, not many of us know about the Curse, the intervals, and all that. Have you money on it?"

So much you'd never believe, Gornt thought. "Yesterday I asked Hoag point-blank."

"Good God, just like that? I'd never have had the balls, old boy."

1134

Pallidar leaned closer, his mount a dragoon gelding grey, and a hand bigger than Gornt's pony. "What did he say?"

"He says he doesn't know any more than we do. You know what he's like, so I believe him." Gornt hid his impatience, missing her company. They had agreed to keep up the pretense of avoiding each other until she was sure if she wasn't . . . nothing could begin until then—or until the second month. "The 11th or 12th are right though he did say she could be late but not much later to . . . start. If she doesn't, she's bearing."

"Christ! Makes you think, what? Tough for her if she is, poor lady, more than tough when you think of Hong Kong Tess and the problems. And tougher if she isn't, if you believe the rumors—don't know which is tougher." Bugles began sounding on the bluff above the racecourse where the soldiers' tented encampment lay—a thousand soldiers there. "Bloody hell," Pallidar muttered.

"What?"

"It's a 'Return to base.' The General's probably just got a hangover and wants to snarl at everyone."

"You going with Sir William tomorrow?"

"The Kanagawa-Yoshi conference? Suppose so. Generally I'm the dogsbody. I'd better go. Dinner in the Mess?"

"Thanks, I'd like that." Gornt watched Pallidar pirouette his horse impeccably to gallop off and mingle with other army officers streaming away. He noticed Hoag coming up from the Settlement to join the circuit. The Doctor rode well, easy in the saddle for such a heavy man. Deciding to intercept him he heeled his pony—a brown stallion, the best in the Brock stable—into a canter, then changed his mind. He had ridden enough for today. They would hear soon enough, Hoag would never be able to keep that news to himself once it was fact.

Before leaving the track he waved to Angelique and called out, " 'Morning, Ma'am, you're a joy to see on a chill day."

She looked up, pulled from her own private world. "Oh. Thank you, Mr. Gornt."

He saw her melancholy, but she smiled at him. Reassured, he trotted on, content, no need to rush her. First, is she or isn't she? Either way is fine with me.

Angelique had been pleased to see him, enjoying his open admiration and elegance and masculinity. The strain of the waiting, remaining alone, holding to her regimen of mourning, bottling up secrets, was beginning to tell—her early morning ride, occasional promenades, reading as many new books as she could find, talking to Vargas about silk and silkworms, trying to work up an enthusiasm, were the only luxuries she allowed herself. Then she saw Hoag.

Hoag! If she continued her canter she would catch up with him. A trot would avoid him, and even easier to turn and go home. "Good morning, *Monsieur le docteur,* how are you?"

"Oh, hello, you're looking well."

"I'm not," she said, "I'm piqued. But thank you anyway." A slight hesitation and she added casually, "A woman never feels well during that time of the month."

Startled, he jerked his reins and his mare bridled, neighed and shook her head, frightening Angelique's mount. In moments both were in tight control again. "Sorry," he said gruffly, "I'd . . . I'd expected the opposite." The suddenness and her nonchalance was so unsettling that he almost said, Are you sure? Must be getting old, he thought, irritated with himself for not seeing the obvious—obvious now that he looked at her. "Well, at least you know."

"I'm terribly disappointed, for Malcolm's sake, but somehow it doesn't seem to—to skewer me anymore. Of course I cried my heart out but now . . ." Her guilelessness made him want to reach out and comfort her.

"With all the rest, that's understandable, Angelique. Better that way. I told you before, so long as you can cry, none of it will damage you. May I ask when you started?"

There were more bugles from the bluff. "What's going on? I saw Settry and other officers rush off."

"The bugles are just recalling officers, routine, nothing to worry about." Hoag looked around to make sure no one was near. "Thanks for telling me," he laughed nervously, "if a little abruptly. Can we talk as we ride?"

"Certainly," she said, knowing full well why she had told him. It was seeing Gornt today and Hoag convenient. And because she wanted the fight to begin. "It began Sunday."

"I don't know whether to say you're lucky or unlucky."

"It's neither," she said. "It was the will of God, I accept that. I'm sorry for Malcolm, not for me. For me, it's the will of God. What do you do now, inform her?"

"Yes, but first I have to give you a letter."

It was her turn to be startled. "You had a letter all this time but didn't give it to me?"

"She asked me to give it to you if you were not bearing Malcolm's child."

"Oh." She thought about that, feeling slightly sick. "And if I were, what then?"

"That's a hypothetical question now, isn't it?" he said gently, her sudden pallor worrisome. *This young lady's not out of the woods yet, not by a long shot.*

"I want to know."

"I was asked to give you this letter if your period began, Angelique. Would you like to go back now? I'll bring it to your suite."

"Thank you, but I'll ... I'll wait while you collect it, I'll wait outside Struan's." She spurred ahead, finished this circuit, oblivious of the others—every one of them watching her. On a whim she wheeled to take the path for a short gallop to clear her head of fear. Spurs and knees and hands and the pony was smoothly flat out.

Ahead were two church spires and the perimeter fence, the Yoshiwara nestling outside but inside its own walls, the bridge and guard house. For a moment her mind took her back in time and it was as if she were galloping towards them panic-stricken, the bloody Tokaidō behind her, hat gone, clothes torn, frightened nearly to death. The vision evaporated as she reined in—how long ago that all seemed. A different kind of fear remained. She had cast the die.

Tess's letter read:

I'm sure you will agree there is no need for pleasantries that are meaningless between us.

I'm glad that you are not bearing my son's child. That makes the future simpler and less messy. I do not accept or acknowledge the 'marriage' or that you have any legal claims whatsoever against him—to the contrary.

By the time you read this the Noble House will have begun a new era, or be teetering on bankruptcy. If the first, it will be due in part to yr sending me that person.

Because of that, as a finder's fee, I will pay capital into the Bank of England, in trust, necessary to provide you with an income of two thousand guineas a year—if, in turn, you provide me within thirty days from today's date (when your period has been established), with an affidavit on the following conditions:

First, that you repudiate and relinquish forever any and all claims you or any representatives might dream up against my son's nonexistent estate—you realize that, as a minor and never accredited legally as tai-pan, he had no estate to leave.

Second, that you agree to relinquish all claims to, and agree no longer to use, the 'Mrs. Malcolm Struan' title or any version of it. (For face, yrs, I suggest you have regretfully decided to do this because, being Catholic, you accept you were not legally married according to yr faith and yr Church, not that I accept the ceremony was valid in any way.)

Third, that you will not set foot in Hong Kong again, other than to transship, nor seek to meet me, write to me or have any contact with me or my line in the future.

Fourth, that yr affidavit formally notarized by Sir William Aylesbury, H.M.'s Minister for Japan, be delivered to me here in Hong Kong, via Dr. Hoag as surety, by February 14th, a little over thirty days approximately from today (the date yr period has been established).

Last, that if you marry within the year the capital will be enlarged to increase the yearly stipend to three thousand guineas for the first ten years. On yr death the capital reverts to me or my heirs.

Within three weeks of reading this, please remove yourself from Struan premises. I have advised Mr. Albert Mac-Struan, by letter today, to that effect, and also that, from today, yr credit with Struan's is ended and that any chits given, or purportedly given, by my son and authenticated by his chop only are not to be honored— excepting those that are personally signed and dated by him, thus completely bona fide.

If, within three weeks, yr affidavit is signed and ready for Dr. Hoag, then Mr. MacStruan is authorized to give you at once credit to FIVE HUNDRED guineas on account of your guaranteed trust which will be erected within thirty days, the yearly amount to be paid quarterly.

Should you decline the above conditions (you have my solemn word they are not negotiable) or I do not see Dr. Hoag by said specified date, February 12th, the next day, Friday 13th, my solicitors will file court proceedings against you to the maximum I and they feel justified, the first of which is that with malice aforethought you caused the death of my son.

A piece of advice: Mr. Skye may twist and turn and scream duress, that these are threats against yr person. They are not. My solicitors advise me they are not, that this is a generous, legal way to remove a tiresome problem my son, for whatever ill-advised reasons, has caused.

Please ask Dr. Hoag to return as soon as possible with yr affidavit, or nonagreement. Tess Struan, 28th December, Year of our Lord, 1862, at Hong Kong.

Gornt looked up from the letter. "You don't accept."

"That's exactly what Mr. Skye told me." Some of Angelique's fury dissipated on the spot. She sat in her tall chair, stiff and setfaced, Gornt opposite her, and they were in her boudoir. "I'm glad you agree. I'll reply in kind to that—that woman this afternoon!"

"No, that would be wrong. I'm saying you don't fight, that's the worst you can do. You compromise."

She became ashen again, more than angry. "You say accept these . . . this foulness?"

"I'm just saying you can compromise in due course," he said, his mind working well and logically though his chest and throat felt tight. "I'm sure I can get you better terms."

"Terms? Then you do say accept this in principle? *Accept this?* I thought you were a fighter and my friend but you'll let her get away with dragging my face in the mud?"

"I know she said it's nonnegotiable, but I don't believe that. I can improve it. Her first offer, two or three thousand, already makes you comfortable, five and you'd be rich."

"That doesn't outweigh her vile manners, her evil threats, constant hostility and enmity! I was married legally. Legally!" Angelique stamped her foot. "Not to be Mrs. Struan? Not to set foot in Hong Kong, to be addressed in this way, how dare she? As though I am . . . I am a felon!"

"I agree. On your behalf I'll renegotiate."

"*Jésus.* I want her humbled, smashed."

"So do I, but now is not the time."

"What?"

"The great Dirk Struan really did ill-use my mother's family, the Tillmans—not as bad as Morgan, but bad enough." His smile was cruel. "If I can crush Brock's, why not Struan's? It's all the same to me. Revenge is a meal we can eat together leisurely, morsel by morsel."

"We can?" A sudden warmth went into her loins, he looked so confident and handsome and strong. "How?"

"First, what did Skye say?"

"He said at once to fight and showed me papers he has prepared for filing in Hong Kong, London and Paris an—"

"Paris? Why Paris?"

She explained about 'ward of the State.' "He says in Paris with ward of France as a fact we will win, the marriage will be declared legal according to French law, and then I can settle at my whim, not hers."

"Has he mentioned fees, Angelique?"

She flushed. "That has nothing to do with his advice."

"Nonsense," he said harshly. "Our only safety is to face the truth and understand the games being played. That little bastard, 'scuse me, but I use the term advisedly—he is by the way, I found that out in Hong Kong—that little bastard is only thinking of his future, not yours, imagining himself in various courts defending this poor but beautiful French widow, swaying various juries—and losing everything for you."

"I don't see . . . Why?"

"Malcolm has no estate."

"But . . . but, Mr. Skye says according to French law th—"

"Wake up, Angelique!" His voice was even harsher. It was vital to get her out of this stupid, useless rage.

The moment he had come into her boudoir and had seen her tight-lipped, seething, a letter shaking in her hand, he had realized that this was *the letter* Hoag had told him about, that therefore there was no child and now Plan A could be hurtled into place. His joy had crested.

Pretending to know nothing, he had begun cheery greetings but these were spurned, the letter shoved at him, her fury making her even more attractive—the passion good for both of them, he had thought contentedly. But now it must be channeled and refined, like his. "Skye's full of wind! Wake up!"

"I am awake, he is not, and don't think for a mom—"

"Stop it! Use your head, for God's sake! It's you who're at risk, not him!" For an instant he wondered again what Tess's second letter, the other letter, contained that, now, no one would ever know—Hoag had said part of the agreement with Tess was that, prior to delivering this one, he would burn the other unopened. Would Hoag really do that, or would he have read it before burning it though he had sworn a holy oath to abide exactly by her wishes? Wish I knew, but then that's only icing on the cake.

"Angelique, dear Angelique . . ." He tossed the letter on the table as though it were dirty, believing it to be wonderful, got up and sat beside her and took her hand. "Paris and French law and all the rest are only for Skye's benefit, not yours. Even if he won, I'd wager ten thousand to one against, their ruling would have no bearing on Tess Struan and Hong Kong. . . . Listen to me," he said louder as she started to override him. "We've not much time and you have to be sensible. While you borrow or pauper yourself or sell yourself to pay his costs, let alone the fees he needs, you'll lose this one chance. He hasn't got but a few dollars. How's he going to get to Hong Kong, let alone Paris or London? That's a pipe dream." Sullenly she pulled her hand away. He laughed. "You're like a spoiled brat and I love you for it."

"You . . ." She stopped. "You do?"

"Love you or think you're a spoiled brat?"

With a different voice she said, "Both."

"Both," he said in a different voice, and took her hand again and grinned when she tried to pull it away. This time he did not allow it. With equal, gentle firmness he pulled her closer and kissed her deeply. Her fight was immediate, soon to lessen, soon to enjoy. Both of them. When he released her he ducked at once, correctly anticipating her nails, which slashed at him. "Whoa, there," he said as though to a spirited horse, delighted he had the measure of her. "Whoa, there, Nelly!"

She laughed in spite of her anger. "You're a devil."

"Yes, but I'll make a fine husband, Ma'am."

Her smiled faded. The anger vanished. She got up and went to the window and stared out at the bay and the ships there. Lots of activity around the warships. He watched and waited, hoping that he had judged correctly. When she was ready, she said, "You say compromise, Edward. How?"

"I'd take the next, fastest boat to Hong Kong," he said. "I'll see her at once and make changes you and I agree on—and I think are possible. I'm sure I can up the stipend. Five instead of two or three thousand would be acceptable, yes?"

"She says those disgusting terms won't be changed."

"I will change them, some of them."

"Which?"

"We can discuss those today and tomorrow. I'm confident about the money."

"*Mon Dieu,* the money's not everything, and why so quickly? There's till the 14th of next month."

"I must be first with the news, to catch her off balance. That makes my bargaining position better. For you," he added.

She turned and looked at him. "Also for you too."

"Also for me," he said, these twists and turns and risks and gambles, a wrong word fatal, more thrilling than the best poker game he had ever been in, the stakes the highest. Her. Her and his future indivisible. And she holds most of the aces, he told himself, though she doesn't know it: her immediate agreement to Tess's demands, at his persuasion, would make Tess more keen than ever to be his ally, so vital to his future; her five thousand guineas would help to cement Rothwell-Gornt; and her venom would ensure Tess's end.

"I love you and want to marry you," he said. "Please."

"It's much too soon to answer that."

"I don't agree, you're footloose and fancy free."

"Because I'm not married and never was?" she snapped.

"Calm down, honey, think calmly! We're adults, I have a right to ask, to say I love you and to want to marry you."

She dropped her gaze and conceded, needing him, he alone could shield her from Tess. "Sorry, yes, sorry, the . . . the letter unsettled me. But, it's too soon to answer you, really."

"I don't agree. I believe you love me, the promise could be private, not to be advertised, between us. I love you, we would make a grand team," he said, meaning it. "The future's vast for us once this"—he motioned at the letter—"once this no longer threatens you. We've much in common and a common goal, to destroy your enemy and mine, at leisure."

"I don't love you, I like you, immensely, perhaps I could, perhaps I would love you in time and I would try if . . . if I was to marry you—no, don't move, let me finish." Her fingers were toying with a pearl buckle that she had bought in the village and that reminded her as MacStruan would not honor her remaining chits it was, apart from her engagement ring and the jade ring, the only jewelry she still possessed. And André would be around this afternoon again. She put that worry away for later and concentrated. Curious that Edward should have the same idea that I have. We think alike in many ways. "For the moment let me answer that later. When's the next ship for Hong Kong?"

"The best and fastest would be tomorrow night. Cooper-Tillman's *Atlanta Belle,* direct to Hong Kong then San Francisco," he said at once, arrivals and departures in the forefront of every trader's mind. "She'll be in Hong Kong before our clipper, *Night Witch*—she's not due here for three days."

"You'd want to be on her, the *Atlanta Belle*?"

"Yes."

"Then, Edward, let's discuss what you think can be bettered with that woman in the morning, that gives me time to think. If we agree, then please go quickly to Hong Kong . . . and hurry back, quickly."

"Good. But your answer to my proposal?"

"I will give you that when you return."

"I must have it before I leave."

"Why?"

"For my pleasure," he said.

She saw the same strange smile and wondered what was behind it. "Why? Seriously?"

He got up and stood over her. "Because it's vital to me. If you'll marry me the sky's the limit, you'll adore Shanghai, it's the greatest city in Asia, makes Hong Kong look like a backwater, you'll be the toast of the town and live happily ever after. I promise. Now, please promise."

"I promise to give you my answer when you return, there should be trust between us," she said, and he remembered saying the same thing to Tess. "When you return."

"Sorry, my dear Angelique, I need to know before I go."

"Or you won't negotiate for me, with Tess?"

He did not answer at once. "I'll negotiate for you. And I'd like to marry you tomorrow, tonight—nothing to do with Tess, but that's not possible." He went closer and held her shoulders in his hands, and kissed the tip of her nose. "*Jolie* Mademoiselle, an answer please? By sunset tomorrow? I'll have to board then. An answer before God."

That afternoon the news about Katsumata and Meikin's suicide reached Raiko in her private quarters. She fainted. When she had begun to recover, she sent a maid to ask Hiraga to find Akimoto and

Takeda urgently, there were terrible facts to report. They came quickly.

Weeping unashamed and wringing her hands, she told them about Yoshi capturing Katsumata, about his death and that of Meikin, Koiko's mama-san, but not that she had betrayed him. "This is the end . . . if Yoshi found out about Katsumata and Meikin, he knows about me, about you, we're all betrayed. Who's the traitor? It's only a matter of time . . ." Again her terror soared. "You must all leave at once before Enforcers discover you. . . . You must leave. . . ."

"Stop!" Hiraga hissed, face chalky, no longer disguised as a kitchen skivvy. He was wearing an ordinary kimono and was ready to rush for his tunnel sanctuary, the lookouts reliable now on pain of death. Akimoto and Takeda were also devastated. That Katsumata could die a coward was inconceivable.

I cannot believe the Sensei would allow himself to be caught alive, Hiraga thought. And for Yoshi to allow Meikin to do that to him was disgusting, however merited. *Baka* to be caught alive! "Leave us, Raiko. I will see you later."

"Thank you, Sire, so sorry but—"

"Leave us!"

She stumbled away, glad to be free of them, hating all shishi, wisely hiding the hatred.

Takeda spat in anger. "Yoshi has no honor to let that happen. Katsumata must be avenged!"

Akimoto glanced at Hiraga, sickened too. "What should we do, Cousin? That old crone is right, the search will be stepped up. We should slip away tonight, try to, eh?"

"You are *baka*! We are surrounded like rats on a carcass." In fact Hiraga, though pretending rage, was weak with relief. With Katsumata dead, now there need be no attack. Once again he was in charge of his own destiny. "We must not make a mistake."

Takeda said, "I agree we are rats in a trap here. So we attack as the Sensei planned. We've the bombs now. *Sonno-joi!*"

"No. We're safe for the moment."

Akimoto said, "Hiraga, if Yoshi gave Katsumata to this Meikin, it was a reward, *neh*? In return for betraying him? Raiko will do the same to us. Maybe she is the traitor who betrayed both of them to Yoshi in the first place, eh?"

Takeda scrambled up. "Let's kill her and begin."

"Sit down," Hiraga snarled. "We need Raiko. She has proved her worth in the past, and you forget, no mama-san is trusted wholly. Sit down, Takeda, be logical. She will not betray us—she is only a money-grubbing harridan, like any other mama-san who, if you let her, will charge you for a third-rank whore when the girl's only a streetwalker worth hardly a copper *momme*. Meikin gave us good information in the past, it was because of her we caught Utani the pederast. She herself was betrayed. Yoshi and Bakufu have thousands of spies."

"We're not safe here." Akimoto shuddered. "I hate this place. This gai-jin Yoshiwara is infected with their plague. I vote with Takeda. Attack, escape or die."

"Not yet. Let me think!"

Takeda watched him narrowly. "You knew this Meikin?"

"Many years ago . . ." Hiraga almost added, and Koiko, tempted to tell them the real reason for the betrayal, but decided not to, relishing the manner of Katsumata's death. Now Sumomo is revenged and so is Koiko. Now their spirits will become kami, or they will be reborn again on the thirty-first day as the gods decide—if there are gods. Now I can forget them though they will all live forever.

The Sensei begging for mercy? All those years idolizing him, listening to him? We were dupes, he thought, disgusted. Never mind, that coward will be derided and spat on in news sheets, and soon bards and plays will orate the story of how he betrayed Sumomo and Koiko and the mama-san's revenge—and death wish. Ah, what style she had!

Involuntarily he chuckled nervously and mimicked the high-pitched voice of an *onnagata*—a male actor who specialized in female roles, only men being allowed on the stage. " 'A bath and clean clothes. Please?' Kabuki and puppet theatres will fill houses with that for generations!"

"*Baka* on the Kabuki," Takeda said, fuming. "The Sensei will be revenged. Honor will be redeemed. Tonight we attack as planned, you take the ship, I take the church and the other church and kill every gai-jin I meet till I am dead. What do you say, Akimoto?" He got up and peered out of the window. Night was not far. Suddenly he noticed the wind rustling the shrubs. "Look! It's a sign from the gods! The wind is picking up. It's from the south!"

Akimoto leapt beside him. "It's true, Hiraga!"

For a moment Hiraga was thrown off balance. Was it a sign? "No attack, not tonight. No attack!"

Takeda whirled. "I say attack." He glared at Akimoto. "You agree? *Sonno-joi!*"

Akimoto was teetering. Both Takeda's rage and confidence were infectious. "Fire would cover our escape, Hiraga."

"A—a little one, perhaps," Hiraga said irritably, "not an attempt to burn all Yokohama." His brain was oscillating and he had no solution yet other than his final plan, and no way to effect that without Taira's help and purging Yoshi's grasp from around his neck. "Tomorrow or the next day, we cou—"

"Tonight," Takeda said insistently, his anger barely in check. "Tonight's a gift, the gods speak to us!"

"At this time of the year the wind will hold. We need more men to fire the Settlement. One of us should go to Yedo for them. Takeda, you could go."

"How? You said Enforcers are everywhere. How?"

"I don't know, Takeda." Shakily Hiraga got up. "Wait till I get back, then we can decide. I'll see Raiko, tell her we'll leave tomorrow—we won't but that's what I'll say."

"She's not to be trusted anymore."

"I keep telling you, she never was." Hiraga went and found her.

"All right, Hiraga-sama, you may stay." Raiko was over the panic, brandy in her stomach, dully allowing fate to be fate.

"Is Taira here tonight?"

"No, nor tomorrow. Furansu-san is. I know he is."

"Send for Taira. You can do that, can't you?"

"Yes, and when he arrives what should I tell him?" she said listlessly, then jerked awake as Hiraga ground the words through his teeth. "You tell him, Raiko, that Fujiko has decided she no longer wishes to sign a contract, that another gai-jin has approached you with a better business arrangement."

"But her contract price is fantastical good. He is no fool, he'll compare prices and I'll lose him to another House—he's already visited some. I'll lose him."

"You will lose your head if the turmoil you're in isn't solved," he said sourly, "and the rest of your well-fed corpse will be feeding fishes."

"Solved?" She became all attention. "There is a chance, Hiraga-sama? I've a chance? You know of a way?"

"Do as you're told and I may be able to save you. Send for Taira now." Coldly, Hiraga looked at her and went back to the other two. They were on the veranda watching the bushes bent by the wind. "We're safe for a day or two."

Takeda said with a sneer, "Little does she know she's dead, and tonight Yokohama will be dead, cleaned of vermin."

"We will delay one day. Tomorrow night is best."

Takeda's anger began to return. "Why?"

"Do you want a chance of escape? To deal the death blow but live to enjoy it? All of us? I agree with you it is time. You are right, Takeda. But tomorrow gives me time to plan."

After a moment, Takeda said, "Akimoto?"

"Let us agree to delay. To escape as well . . . Hiraga's wise, Takeda, *neh*?"

The silence grew immense. "Delay. One day. I agree." Takeda got up and left for his hideaway in the next Teahouse.

After a moment, Hiraga said, "Akimoto, in a little while, go and sit with him, reassure him."

"He's Satsuma, Cousin. Katsumata was Satsuma."

Hiraga glanced at the shrubs bent by the south wind. "Sit with him. Reassure him."

Tyrer was appalled. "No contract, Raiko-san?"

"No, so sorry, Fujiko has changed her mind and has a much better offer, so sorry, but she's adamant."

"Please?" he asked, missing most of her Japanese.

She repeated it, adding, "That's why I asked to see you urgently. So sorry, she won't see you, tonight or ever."

All of Tyrer's being plunged into a pit. He questioned her in his most polite and best Japanese but she shook her head. "So sorry," she said with finality, bowing a dismissal. "Good night, Taira-sama."

As if a drunkard, Tyrer went out onto the veranda. The shoji slid shut. He stumbled onto the garden path, cursed as he realized he had forgotten his shoes. In a daze he sat on the veranda and slipped them on. "What the hell's happened?"

Three days ago, when he had returned with Babcott from Yedo, all had been perfect, the contract agreed but for one minor point, payment was to be made within the week. His previous bill had been settled to smiles and bows, with Fujiko that night more loving and sweeter than ever before. This evening, when Raiko had sent a servant to the house he shared with Babcott, asking him to see her urgently, he had presumed, amused, it was just to sign the paper. He had left a message earlier that probably he could not come tonight nor would he be available tomorrow—he was due to go to Kanagawa.

And now this. "I don't understand." Gusts swirling more leaves around his feet. Miserably, he pulled his coat closer around him. The night seemed blacker than before. With a great sigh he got up and plodded down the meandering path, stopped abruptly as a samurai almost bumped into him.

"Christ Almighty, Nakama!" he burst out.

Hiraga went for his sword and Tyrer thought he was a dead man. But the sword stayed half in the scabbard and he saw the eyes staring at him on a hair trigger . . . "Don't," Tyrer said, his voice choked at the sudden apparition. "I'm . . . I'm not armed." He raised his arms in surrender, froze, cursing himself for his stupidity, almost died again as Hiraga slammed the sword back into its scabbard.

"Taira-sama, I not hurt you, I thought you enemy. You are friend." Hiraga smiled and stuck out his hand.

Blankly Tyrer shook it, then erupted, "What are you doing, we thought you'd fled to Yedo, what's this about being ronin? We have to turn you over to him, to Yoshi—you know Yoshi is after you, Lord Yoshi?"

"Not here!" Hiraga cautioned, and took his arm and Tyrer felt the iron grip. "Come with me." Motioning him to silence, he guided him down another path, into another in the maze of little pathways well screened from each other by hedges, until Tyrer had lost all sense of direction. Then this path ended at a bungalow. Wind tugged at the thatch, whining in the rafters.

Hiraga motioned him onto the veranda, kicked off his own shoes and waited until Tyrer had done the same then pushed him forward. "Inside, p'rease."

Wet with fear and powerless, Tyrer obeyed. There was no chance to run. He saw Hiraga look carefully to see if they had been followed. The shoji slid to. A shaded candle dimly lit the interior of the usual one-room house, a tiny bathroom adjoining. The flame guttered and almost went out in the draft.

"Sit! P'rease. Now, say again but not fast, keep voice down." Ominously Hiraga took his short sword out of his belt and laid it on the tatami beside him. "So?"

Trying to contain the shaking that mixed nauseatingly with his distress, Tyrer related about Yoshi and Abeh and the murder of Utani and how they all thought Hiraga had fled elsewhere. "We've got to turn you over to Yoshi, to guards at the gate—Captain Abeh went back to Yedo, Nakama, and . . . what should I call you, Nakama or Hiraga?"

"As you wish, Taira-sama."

"Hiraga then, that's your real name, isn't it?"

"I am caw'red that. But Japanese have many names, one at birth, another when age seven, another at manhood, and take another if want. I am Nakama, or Hiraga, your friend."

"Friend?" Tyrer said bitterly, forgetting his fear. "Why didn't you tell me you were an assassin? You killed Utani—you killed him, didn't you?"

"Yes, he a target, very bad man. Yoshi another. This not Ing'rand, Taira-sama, not Ing'rand. These bad men, the Bakufu, they thief power from the Emperor, they tyrants."

Solemnly, Hiraga explained as best he could about the shishi and their struggle to eliminate the despotic government—his sincerity obvious—explaining the greed of Utani and his rapacious taxes, how the Toranaga clans and daimyos possessed all the wealth of the land, the Toranagas most of all, about the corrupt Bakufu, and that the people were starved and powerless. "We want give Nippon back to Emperor, make govern fair for a'wre people."

By 'all people' Hiraga meant all samurai though Tyrer took it to mean all Japanese. And as he questioned Hiraga, fascinated with this unique window into the inner workings of Nippon—and Japanese mentality—he was more and more convinced there was merit on Hiraga's side. He had only to consider English history and the people's struggle to cast off the 'divine right of Kings' and the rule of tyrants, to become more and more sympathetic. Not hard to recall the huge cost in lives to create Parliament and the rule of the people for the people: a king's head, others humbled, revolution, riots, deaths before the British Raj and Pax Britannica had blossomed.

Remembering also the debt he owed this man, he said gloomily, "Even so, I don't see any hope for you. The moment you're seen you'll be captured, by your people or mine. There's nothing I can do to prevent that."

Hiraga took a deep breath and launched himself into the void: "One thing, yes, you can do to he'rp me. He'rp me onto ship—ship for Ing'rand."

Tyrer gaped at him. "Eh? You're mad!"

"P'rease, keep soft, many enemy here," Hiraga said quietly, passionately excited with this stunning, radical idea that had swooped out of the air at him, as if down from the Sun Goddess herself. "P'rease 'risten. Many times you say me 'rearn about gai-jin, your country best, *neh*? I go there with my cousin. We 'rearn best way to make govern, your Par'iment. We 'rearn your way. Yoshi right about navy and army, but I think more best to 'rearn banking and business and trading. We need knowing best way, *neh*? Your way, Ing'rish way, *neh*?"

Eloquently Hiraga continued to spin his web, his anxiety lending him extra words and soft cadences. This was his final plan, his only possible escape from Yoshi's trap. He was certain that a year or two spent with gai-jin, with the right introductions and help, would be of enormous value to *sonno-joi*.

It is the perfect answer to inevitable death if I stay, he had reasoned exuberantly. In a year or two we will return, perfect Ing'rish speakers, bursting with their secrets about *produk'shun* and *stoku markit*, rifles, cannon, tactics, strategy, the methods they used to conquer the outside world, even to humble China!

This is the Land of the Gods! China should be ours, not the gai-jin's. Before I leave I'll tell our Choshu shishi leaders of my plan, and somehow keep in touch through letters. "It's simp're, Taira-sama. You speak to Captain, we sneak aboard. No one need know."

"Sir William would never agree."

"Perhaps no need speak him." Hiraga leaned closer, giving him the option, unsure of himself. "Or if speak, I speak too, think he agree, *neh*? Very important for Ing'rish have Japan friend. I good friend. Jami-sama, he he'rp too if ask."

"Who?"

"Jami, big beard man, bigger as you. Jami."

"Jamie? Jamie McFay?"

"Yes, Jami Mukfey."

Now that the idea had sunk into him, Tyrer's mind began working better. There were tremendous long-term possibilities in doing what Hiraga suggested. It had ever been British policy to educate—re-educate—selected foreign students, the more important or princely the better. Many were radicals, or revolutionaries in their own country, India notably. Hiraga was very intelligent and if an enemy of Yoshi, important. Judge a man by his enemies, his father had said.

And while he chewed over Hiraga's suggestion he also wondered how his father and mother were, and his friends, sad that he could not see them or be in London soon—no home leave for two years. At the same time he was proud to be part of the Diplomatic Service and a cog, albeit very small, in the vastness of British empire building.

Hiraga's idea is good. It would work. But how to get him out and how to get Sir William to assist—Willie's the key.

The more he thought about it, the more his hopes sank, the more he had to admit he was stupid to even consider it, becoming more and more certain that Sir William would not, could not countenance such a ploy—not with this man, an admitted killer, not Hiraga who was a pawn in the far greater contest for Yoshi. There was no quid pro quo for Sir William—no compensation, no reason to risk Yoshi's enmity, the power of the future, whatever Hiraga claimed.

"I'll try," he said, purporting to be confident, not forgetting he was still Hiraga's prisoner, the sword too near. "Can't guarantee anything but I'll try. Where will you be?"

Hiraga was satisfied, his gamble immense though with room left to maneuver. He had convinced Taira, now again on his side. The gai-jin leader would be an ally. "You keep sekret?"

"Of course."

"Send word to Raiko. I can meet in vi'rage or here. You say where, Taira-sama. Think sooner is better, for ship, *neh*?"

"Yes. I'll send you a message tomorrow, or come myself." Cautiously Tyrer began to stand.

Hiraga beamed. "You go Fujiko?"

Gloom descended instantly. "There's no Fujiko anymore."

"What? What you mean, p'rease?"

Tyrer told him and he saw Hiraga's face flush.

"But you have promise, Taira-sama. Me, I t'awk, arrange with Raiko, *neh*?"

"Yes, but now the contract's off. Raiko says . . ." Tyrer stopped, frightened by the look on Hiraga's face.

"Wait, p'rease!" Hiraga stormed out. Tyrer peered out of a side window. No one in sight, only waving branches and the smell of sea salt in the air—run while you've the chance, he told himself but then, suddenly, desperately, he wanted to urinate. He used the bucket in the bathroom and felt better. Now he was hungry. And thirsty. He looked around. No teapot, no water jug. His hunger and thirst were grinding—like Hiraga's idea was grinding. No way to satisfy either. Without Sir William's benevolence Hiraga would be a child in the wilderness. Even Jamie couldn't help much, now that he was out of Struan's. Why should he or anyone help? There was no quid pro quo. Again he peered out of the little window.

Get out while you can, he thought, and went for the door. Then he heard footsteps. He rushed back to his cushion. The shoji was flung open. Raiko was shoved on her knees in front of him, Hiraga towering menacingly in the doorway.

"Oh, so sorry, Taira-sama," Raiko said, stumbling over the words in abject haste to apologize and placate him. "Oh, so sorry, I made a terrible mistake. . . ."

Her words were a fountain. Tyrer understood little of them though he got their message clearly. "Enough," he said firmly. "Bring contract now. I sign."

Meekly she brought out the scroll from her sleeve and offered it.

"Wait," Hiraga ordered. "Give it to me!"

She obeyed instantly and put her head down again. He scanned the short document, grunted. "This as agreed, Taira-sama, you sign 'rater," he said in English again. "This person . . ." he pointed angrily at Raiko, "says make mistake, says Fujiko begs honor to see you now, so sorry for the mistake. Her mistake. *Baka!*" he snapped at her, adding in Japanese, "Treat this lord properly or I'll destroy this Teahouse! Make sure Fujiko is ready, very ready. Now."

"*Hai, Hiraga-sama!*" Mumbling profuse apologies, she fled.

Once safely away, she chortled, delighted with her performance, with Hiraga's ploy, and that the deal was done.

Tyrer, elated, thanked Hiraga, too happy to worry about how his obvious friend had changed her so quickly. We'll never understand some things about these people. "I'll sign the contract and bring it back tomorrow."

"Take time, keep woman dog waiting." Hiraga smiled and gave him the scroll. "Now I take you Fujiko. *Ikimasho.*"

"*Domo arigato gozaimashita.*" Tyrer bowed as a Japanese would bow to someone owed a considerable favor.

"Friend he'rp friend," Hiraga said simply.

57

LATER THAT EVENING TYRER awoke, completely satisfied. His timepiece read 9:20. Perfect, he thought. He lay beside Fujiko who was fast asleep, the futons and feather coverlets as clean and sweet-smelling as she was, warm and comfortable—so much better than his bed, rough straw mattress and heavy woolen blankets with their dank smell. The sheen of her skin was golden in the candlelight, the tiny room golden and snug, with the wind worrying the roof and shoji walls and flames.

Another short nap, he thought, and then I'll leave.

Don't be silly. There's no need to go back tonight. All papers for tomorrow's Yoshi meeting are ready, a copy of the Treaty in Japanese and English in Wee Willie's briefcase and double-checked this afternoon. The agreed battle plan against Sanjiro of Satsuma is ready in the safe for his and Ketterer's signature. I'll be up with the dawn, bright as a mint-new golden guinea—after the Hiraga shock-u and Raiko's bigger shock-u I deserve a treat. He smiled, *shock-u*, sounding so Japanese. A contented sigh, good old Nakama, I mean Hiraga. He yawned and closed his eyes. And nestled closer. Fujiko did not awaken but opened herself to him.

In another part of the gardens Hinodeh waited impatiently for André, due any moment now, Raiko had warned, almost ill with anticipation.

Raiko was slouched in her own quarters, drinking saké. Soon she would turn to brandy and to oblivion, the drink swilling away all bad thoughts: her fear and loathing for Hiraga and her hopes for him, her terror over Meikin and esteem for her revenge intermingled with each emptied cup.

Across the garden, hidden in his safe house, Hiraga sat in the classic Lotus position meditating to clear the foul headache that the Katsumata news and Tyrer had caused. Soon Akimoto would return. Then he would decide about Takeda.

Over the next fence in a garden house of the Teahouse of Cherries, Akimoto was saké drunk. Lolling across from him, Takeda belched and quaffed his beer. Another saké flask was emptied blearily until it slid from Akimoto's fingers. His head drifted to his arms. He began to snore. Takeda smiled, not nearly as drunk as he had pretended.

When he was sure Akimoto was asleep, he slid the shoji open and closed it after him. The night was cold, the wind strong from the south. It whipped around him, ruffling his thatch of uncomfortable, stubbled hair. He scratched vigorously, checking the part of the gardens he could see. A maid with a tray hurried from a bungalow to the main building. In the distance he heard men singing drunkenly and a samisen. Somewhere a dog barked. When the maid had vanished, he put on his dark padded jacket, stuck his swords in his belt, stepped into his straw sandals and darted down the path, turned onto another, then another until he was near the fence. His cache was under a bush. Five bombs that he and Hiraga had made, with fuses of various lengths.

The bombs were constructed from two sections of giant bamboo tied together, a third of a yard long, half that wide, the hollows of one packed tightly with Katsumata's extra gunpowder, the other with oil, and plugged. Quickly he fused three bombs using the longest fuses he had, about a candle of time each—nearly two hours. The fuses were made of cotton rope, impregnated with a gunpowder solution and allowed to dry. He armed the remaining two with fuses for half that time.

A last look at the sky. Clouds raced with the wind. Good. He picked up two long-fused bombs and was gone, melding nicely with the night, through the secret fence door into the garden of the Three Carp that was south of the Cherries and headed for the southernmost garden house, like all of them, raised half a yard on low pilings. It was occupied and illuminated. Warily he crawled under it. He lit the fuse with a flint, the noise deadened by the wind. The fuse caught. A woman's footstep sounded above and he froze. Sound of the shoji being opened. After a moment it closed again.

Errant leaves heaped over the spluttering fuse concealed it almost completely and once more he was away, a shadow amongst shadows— to duck into the shrubbery, seeing a gai-jin coming down the path. The man passed without noticing him, then again he was in motion, running for the main Teahouse building. Another fire bomb was settled there neatly.

Now back through the fence, avoiding a servant, waiting for a portly old maid to trundle by, reaching the cache, there to collect the last of the long-fuse bombs and hastening away again. This he lit and placed under his own house, Akimoto's snores rumbling above. Takeda's lips drew back with his smile. A last time he darted back to the cache, sweating and euphoric. So far, all according to Ori's plan. Hiraga was gai-jin infected. So was Akimoto. He was not. He would do it alone.

With the remaining bombs he went across the garden and over the fence to the next and to the next and there was the secret well head. Quickly he went down into it, replacing the cover, no need to fear that Hiraga was below.

In the tunnel and safe he began to breathe again and lit the oil lamp. Scattered around were Hiraga's bed and few possessions. Katsumata's knapsack with the metal-cased bombs was under a blanket. He added his own two, shouldered the bag and hurried down the tunnel. Soon the water barrier was ahead. Quickly he was out of his clothes, tying them into a bundle.

The freezing water made him struggle for breath. When he reached the narrowest part where the roof sank toward the water, his head was just below it and the water not quite to his chin. With difficulty he managed to hold the lamp and knapsack above the surface. On the other side he dressed hurriedly, shivering and cursing, still so much to do. Never mind, he had begun. Soon he would be finished and then would live forever. His fervor warmed him and drove the cold away.

At the far end where iron bars led upwards and the well vanished below, he stopped to collect his breath. Now upwards. Once he slipped, almost fell but regained his hold and held on until his heart stopped racing. Up again. With great care he moved the broken cover aside and peered out. No Man's Land was empty. Drunk Town was busy with slavering and shouts and drunken singing, a few men reeling along alleys not far away, dogs barking at them.

Drunk Town was south of the village and the Settlement that hugged the coast on a south-north line, as the Yoshiwara was generally southwards of Drunk Town. Ori first, then Katsumata and Hiraga had planned where to plant the fire initiators so that a wind from the south would drive the flames before it to consume all in its path.

He left the knapsack in the weeds, and secreted one short-fused bomb against a rickety godown, the other behind a hovel. Rubbish covered the smoking fuses.

Hurrying back for the remaining bombs, he had to slump into hiding near a pile of rubbish. Approaching from the village a patrol of soldiers was making their nightly rounds. Their route went from the British Legation, along High Street, through the village, across No Man's Land, down through Drunk Town and back along the promenade again. Twice nightly. When they reached the alley, thirty yards from him, they stopped in the lee of the godown for a smoke and to relieve themselves.

Takeda cursed, pinned down.

More than three quarters of a candle had passed since lighting the first fuse.

"Good evening, Hinodeh," André said earlier when he had arrived at their garden sanctuary. "Sorry I late."

"Good evening, Furansu-san. You are never late. Whatever you do is correct." Smiling at him. "Will you take saké?"

"Please." He sat opposite and watched her pour, his legs in the space under the table where a small brazier warmed the air, the heat kept in by the eiderdown that was spread over the table and wrapped around them. Her grace was ever more pleasing, hair like glistening jet held with decorative pins, a touch of rouge to her lips, her long sleeves held delicately away from the flask.

Tonight she wore a kimono he had never seen before, a glorious shade of green, his favorite color, with cranes, the symbol of long life, embroidered in silver thread all over, the edge of a sheer under-kimono peeping out enticingly. With a bow she handed him the cup and then, to his surprise, poured for herself from another flask that contained warm saké—his was cold as he preferred. It was rare for her to drink.

With a special smile, she lifted her cup. *"A ta santé, chéri, je t'aime."* She copied his accent as he had taught her.

"A ta santé, chérie, je t'aime," he said, an ache in his heart, not believing that she did, how could she?

They clinked cups and she drained hers, choked a little, at once poured for him again and for herself. The same smile and she offered her cup to touch his. They drained them and again she poured.

"Mon Dieu, Hinodeh, you careful, yes?" he said with a laugh. "Not used to saké. Careful, no become drunk!"

She laughed, sparkling white teeth, voluptuous lips. "Please, Furansu-san, tonight is special. Drink and be merry. Please." She sipped this time, looking at him over the lip, her eyes alight and flashing in the dance of candle flames, eyes he always found fathom-less, always keeping him off balance—part of her fascination.

"Why special, Hinodeh?"

"Today is *Sei-ji-no-Hi,* Coming of Age Day—for all persons who have reached twenty years—you have reached twenty, *neh*?" she said happily, then pointed to the big candle on the table. "This candle I dedicated to my village god Ujigami for you." Then she motioned to the door shoji. Just above it was a bouquet of pine and bamboo. "That is a Kadamatsu, symbolizing stability." A shy smile and she poured and drank again. "I hope you approve."

"Oh, yes, thank you, Hinodeh," he said, warmed.

A few weeks ago he had discovered it was her birthday and brought iced champagne with a golden bracelet. She wrinkled her nose against the bubbles and said it was wonderful, but drank it only when he insisted. He had finished most of the bottle and that night his lovemaking had been frenzied.

Over their time together he had noticed that the violence of his thrusts did not disturb her, she responded equally whatever he did and, at length, lay back with him, as drained. But how much she really enjoyed their joining he could never fathom, nor could he savor her and leave it at that, leave her to her pretense if that's what it really was—and forget the enigma she had become. One day he would penetrate that enigma. He was convinced. It only required patience, that was all. He would wear away the shell of the enigma and then their loving and his frantic, insatiable passion would be calmed and he could live in peace.

She was still everything to him. Nothing else mattered. This after-noon he had humbled himself with Angelique and cajoled and begged and pleaded and menaced until she had given him a brooch in lieu of money. Raiko had accepted it.

Angelique's stupid. Why is she wavering? Of course she should accept Tess Struan's offer, buying her off, and quickly before it's withdrawn. The offer's generous, overgenerous, more than I expected considering her untenable position: no will in her favor and anyway no estate to claim against! Five hundred guineas as a down payment in three weeks! Wonderful—a gift from God! She can spare four hundred of that and I'll arrange moneylenders to advance another thousand against her trust, two thousand, whatever I need. Skye's a fool. She'll settle after I've talked to her, and gratefully accept any advance when I suggest it. I'm saved!

Looking at Hinodeh, he beamed, so joyously.

"What?" She fanned herself against the rising alcoholic flush, the tip of her tongue between her teeth.

In French he said, "I'm home free, my love, soon you're paid for and all mine forever."

"So sorry, I do not understand."

Reverting to Japanese he said, "Tonight I just happy, and say, you mine. You so pretty, you mine."

She bowed her head at his praise. "You are handsome too and I am glad when you are happy with me."

"Always." But this was not true. Frequently he was angry and stormed away. Always the same problem, a chance remark, leading to asking, then taunting, pleading, demanding, begging, shouting: 'We don't need darkness! We're lovers and we don't need the dark anymore, we're friends as well as lovers, I am committed to you forever. Forever! I love you, you can never know how much I love you, you can't know, I keep asking and asking and asking but you just sit there . . .'

Always the same patient, abject response, head to the floor, her voice soft, with or without tears, and absolute: 'Please excuse me but you agreed, so sorry, but you agreed.'

Again she drank and he saw the increasing blush in her cheeks, watched her pour again, her fingers unsure and a drop spilled. She caught her breath with a chuckle. "Oh, so sorry." His cup filled again, and hers, quickly drained, her tipsiness making her even more alluring. "Oh, that's very good, very very good, *neh*, Furansu-san?"

Long fingers with perfect nails shaking the flask and finding it empty, at once gracefully to her feet, the overlong kimono trailing, making her seem to glide to the brazier where other flasks sat in simmering water, and, on a ledge outside the tiny window, where others cooled. Wind came into the room momentarily, and with it an unexpected odor. Gunpowder smoke, faint but unmistakable. "What's that?" he said in French.

She looked at him startled. "Please?"

Now that the window was back in place the odor had vanished. "Nothing, I thought . . ." Tonight everything about her enticed him. "Nothing, please sit. Here."

Obediently she sat beside him, bumping him, chuckling. Unsteadily she poured again. Amused, he drank with her, the saké warming but not as she was warmed. Under the blanket her leg touched his. His hand went to her, the other around her waist and they kissed, her lips whisper soft and moist, her tongue sensuous. His hand went higher, she broke from the embrace, laughing. "Wait, wait, not here, tonight . . ."

Like an excited schoolgirl she pushed away, lifted herself and went for the bedroom and its single lamp, as always to blow it out and then, when she was ready in the darkness, to invite him in. But tonight she stopped at the doorway, steadied herself against it, then turned, eyes glowing. "Furansu-san."

Watching him, she hummed as she removed the long pins in her hair and let it cascade to her waist. Now she loosed her obi and let it fall. A chuckle. Then her kimono and let that fall. All at once he was breathless, transfixed. The gold of her under-kimono shimmered with the candle flames, the sheer silk revealed but did not. Again the tip of her tongue toyed with her lips. Coquettishly she loosed the ties and let the under-kimono open slightly. No underclothes beneath. Only the narrow line of her body revealed, from neck to tiny feet. And all the time the enigmatic smile and eyes beckoning, compelling him to wait, promising, tantalizing. Wind rustled the shojis but went unheard.

His heart was pounding as never before. He forced himself to remain seated. Now he could see her chest rising and falling, the nipples of her small breasts hard against the silk. Then she sighed. With perfect grace she let this covering slowly slide away and stood there in all her purity.

For him time stopped. Hardly breathing, he gloried in her gift, so unexpected and given so freely. When he could endure the waiting no longer he got to his feet. His arms were gentle and he kissed her with all the passion he possessed, strong against her, she limp in his arms. Easily he lifted her and laid her on the futons in the bedroom and tore off his clothes. And knelt beside her, gazing at her in ecstasy in the light. *"Je t'aime, je t'aime."*

"Look, Furansu-san," she said, lying there with her lovely smile. Her fingers were pointing at the inside of her thigh. For a moment he did not understand. Then he saw the abrasion. His heart almost leapt out of his chest, bile flooding into his mouth. "Look," she said again, so softly, smile constant, eyes so dark in the small light. "It has begun."

"It—it nothing," he said, his voice choked. "Nothing."

"It is everything." She looked up at him. "Please give me the knife."

His head reeled, his eyes blind but for the sight of the sore that filled the world. With a gigantic effort he shook his head to clear it. And forced his eyes to see. But this did not take away the vile, sick, sour taste. "It's nothing, it is just, it's nothing, nothing at all," he croaked.

The closer he looked the less important the blemish appeared. "Just a chafe mark, that's all."

"Please? You must speak Japanese, Furansu-san, so sorry."

"It . . . it not illness. Not that. Just—just tight loincloth, nothing worry." He reached out to cover her and blow out the light but she stopped him. Gently.

"So sorry, it has begun. Please. Give me the knife."

As always his knife was in the sheath on his belt. As always. With his clothes, behind him. "No, please, Hinodeh, no knife, knife bad, no need knife. That—that mark nothing."

Through his nightmare, he saw her shake her head, kindly, and repeat the request that had become a command. His limbs began trembling, his head to twitch uncontrollably, no way to stop them or the mumbling incoherent litany of French and Japanese that poured out, that begged and pleaded and explained that the little spot was a blemish, nothing more though he knew it was not nothing. It had begun. She was right. It had begun, it had begun. His stomach heaved. He just managed to stop himself vomiting, mumbling on and on.

She did not interrupt, worse, only lay patiently, waiting for the fit to pass. Then there would be a resolution.

He said brokenly, "Listen, Hinodeh, please no knife. Please. Cannot . . . That . . . it nothing. Soon go away. Look me, look!" Desperately he pointed at himself. "Nothing, nowhere. That little, soon go. No knife. We live. No afraid. Happy. Yes?"

He saw a shadow cross her face, again her fingers touched the abrasion, again the same sweetly monotonous "It has begun."

He fixed a smile and did not know it was grotesque, and as much as he cajoled and twisted and turned, she kept asking the same question, gently, politely, infuriating him more and more until he was near exploding. "It nothing," he said hoarsely. *"Understand?"*

"Yes, I understand. But it has begun. *Neh?*"

He stared at her, his face mean, then his rage broke, and he shouted, "For Christ's sake, yes! Yes, YES! *Hai!*"

Through a great silence, she said, "Thank you, Furansu-san. Then please, as you agree it has begun, as you have promised, please give me the knife."

His eyes were bloodshot, the corners of his mouth flecked with foam, sweat pouring off him and he was near madness. His mouth opened and his mouth said with finality what he always knew he would say: "No knife. *Kinjiru!* It-is-forbidden! Cannot. Cannot. You too value. Forbidden. No knife."

"You refuse?" Gently asked, no change in her.

"Hinodeh, you sun, my sun my moon. Cannot. Will not. Never never never. Forbidden. You stay. Please. *Je t'aime.*"

"Please, the knife."

"*No.*"

A long sigh. Docilely she bowed to him, a light gone out in her, and fetched a damp towel and a dry one and knelt beside the bed. "Here, Sire."

Scowling, sweat-stained, he watched her. "You agree?"

"Yes, I agree. If that is your wish."

He caught her hand. She let it lie in his. "Truly agree?"

"If you wish it. Whatever you wish," she said but sadly.

"No ask knife, ever again?"

"I agree. It is over, Furansu-san, if that is your wish." Her voice was gentle, her face in repose, different yet the same, shadows of sadness there. "Please stop now. It is over. I promise I will not ask ever again, please excuse me."

The weight came off him. He went weak with relief. "Oh, Hinodeh, *je t'aime,* thank you, thank you," he said, his voice breaking, "but please no sad, no sad. *Je t'aime,* thank you."

"Please do not thank me. It is your wish."

"Please no sad, Hinodeh. I promise all be very good now. Wonderful. I promise."

She nodded slowly. A sudden smile washed her face and all the sad away. "Yes, and I thank you, and yes, no more sad."

She waited while he dried himself then removed the towels. His eyes followed her, feasting on her and his victory. She padded across the tatami to the other room and brought back their two saké flasks. With a sweet smile she said, "Drink from the flasks, better than cups. Mine hot, yours cold. Thank you for buying my contract. *A ta santé.*"

"*A ta santé, je t'aime.*"

"*Ah, so ka! Je t'aime.*" She drained the flask, choked a little, then laughed, wiped some off her chin. "That was good, so good. Come to bed." Gaily she slid under the covers. "Come to bed, Furansu-san, you risk a chill."

The grand-tasting drink cleansed his mouth and took away the death feeling he had had. Slowly he moved the coverlet off her, aching for her. "Please, no more dark. Please?"

"If you wish it. No more dark. Except to sleep, *neh?*"

So gratefully, he bowed his head to the futon, reborn, and thanked her and lay beside her, loving her, craving her monstrously. His fingers reached for her.

"Ah, Furansu-san, may I rest first, please?" she asked tenderly, as never before. "So much passion has tired me. May I rest a little, please? Later we . . . later, *neh*?"

His flaring disappointment that almost turned to fury was difficult to contain. In a moment, as kindly as he could, he said, "Of course." No longer touching, he lay back.

"Thank you, Furansu-san," she whispered tiredly. "Please, can you reach the lamp? Turn the flame down, I wish to sleep a little, only a little while."

He obeyed and lay back, loins tormented with desire.

In the darkness, she was more content than she had been in years, content as in the days before her husband died and they lived in their little Yedo house with their son, the boy who was safe now, already with his grandparents, accepted, protected, and growing up samurai.

Bad of Furansu-san not to give me the knife as he promised. Despicable. But then he is gai-jin and not to be trusted. Never mind, I knew he would not keep his part of the bargain as I have kept mine—whatever Raiko promised. He lied when he signed, as she lied. Never mind, never mind. I was prepared for both of them, both liars.

Her smile broadened. The old herbalist did not lie. I tasted nothing, feel nothing, but death is coursing in my body and only a few minutes remain in this World of Tears.

For me and for the Beast too. It was his choice. He broke his promise. So the Unclean pays for cheating me. He will cheat no other lady. And goes to death unquenched!

He stirred, hearing her light, odd laughter. "What?"

"Nothing. Later we will laugh together. No more dark after tonight, Furansu-san. No more dark."

Hiraga slammed his fist on the tatami, tired of waiting for Akimoto. He went out into the blustering night and trudged the paths through the garden to the door in the fence. Through it to Takeda's house, missing the turning the first time. On the veranda he stopped. Snores came from within. "Akimoto, Takeda?" he called out softly, not wanting to open the shoji without warning, every one of them dangerous if surprised.

No answer. The snores continued. He slid the door aside noiselessly. Akimoto was slumped over the table, saké flasks and beer bottles strewn over the floor. No sign of Takeda. Angrily he shook Akimoto, cursing him. The young man came out of his stupor blearily, half awake. "What's the matter?" The words were slurred, Hiraga's face out of focus and swirling.

"Where's Takeda? Wake up! *Baka!* Where is Takeda?"

"Don' know, just we . . . just drinking . . ."

For a second Hiraga was transfixed, his whole world turned over, then he rushed out and through the garden to the fence and the cache.

His mind fogged. Then the plan they all knew, where the bombs would best be placed, surged at him. Panic lent speed to his feet. He peered under Takeda's house but could see nothing, then he caught a whiff of gunpowder smoke and ducked down and crawled between the low, stone supports but the fuse was too well hidden, its smoke dissipated by the stiff currents of air. Out again and up into the room to shake Akimoto. "Get up, wake up!" When the youth drunkenly tried to shove him away, Hiraga struck him across the face, openhanded, then again. Pain tore him back to slurring consciousness.

"Takeda's taken the bombs, he's firing the Inn, there's one below . . ." Hiraga dragged him roughly to his feet. Mumbling, leaning on him, Akimoto staggered out and fell down the steps onto the garden path, the sound of the wind fierce. At that moment the bomb exploded.

The blast was small, enough to knock them over and blow a hole in the floor, most of the noise muffled by floor joists, and by the wind. But the spray of ignited oil was deadly. Flames gushed up and outwards.

"Go into the tunnel and wait there," Hiraga croaked hoarsely, and ran. The shock of the blast and such near death blew Akimoto's stupor away. He started to run but the wind gathered some embers and threw them at him. Frenzied, he beat at his clothes and backed off and by the time he looked at the house once more it was an inferno—dry rice husk tatamis, dry oiled-paper screens, dry wood floor and beams and thatched roof. As he watched, the roof collapsed in a shower of sparks that were swiftly sucked up and driven by the wind to swoop on to the next dwelling. The thatch caught. Fire bells began sounding—maids, servants, clients, courtesans, guards on the gate beginning to respond.

Hiraga was racing down the path to the south-most house. A few metres away the bomb went off. The blast was smaller than before but it sent him sprawling into the bushes, crashing his body against a decorative stone dragon, causing a cry of pain, the explosion powerful enough to collapse a whole corner of pilings and a corner of the house, causing the dwelling to lurch and tip drunkenly. A wall burst into flames.

He forced himself up and without hesitation leapt onto the veranda and crashed through the burning shoji wall, the sprayed oil already working its mayhem inside, smoke choking. His hands went to his face against the scorching heat and he held his breath against the smoke.

He saw Tyrer blown to one side, helplessly trying to grope to his hands and knees, suffocating, surrounded by flames that in an instant turned the oil-sprayed shoji wall behind him into a sheet of fire. Other flames gorged on oil-drenched walls and supports and roof and licked at the remains of the futon and down coverlet Tyrer lay on. The hem of his ripped sleeping kimono caught fire. Hiraga jumped forward, stamped out the flame and pulled him up. One look at Fujiko was enough. The bomb had cut her in half. Already she was hairless and turning to cinder.

Half blinded by the smoke, Hiraga dragged Tyrer out onto the path. At that second the blazing roof collapsed, sending them reeling away to fall in a heap, the resulting gusher of sparks and embers turned into a flamethrower by the wind, blowtorching other houses, fences, and the next Teahouse. Shouts and screams and fire warnings, already lines of people were dashing this way and that with water buckets or fetching buckets, most now wearing dampened face masks against smoke inhalation that were always ready in abundance.

Astonished to be still alive, coughing and gagging, Hiraga beat out a smoldering patch on the chest of his kimono, his short sword still in his belt, the long sword vanished. As far as he could tell Tyrer was unhurt but it was impossible to be sure for he was not truly conscious, chest heaving, gasping and vomiting from inhaling the smoke. Painfully Hiraga stood over him to collect his breath and his reason, looking around against new dangers. The nearby dwelling burst into flames, then the next, cutting their escape route.

Katsumata was right, he thought. With this wind the Yoshiwara's doomed. And with it the Settlement.

On the edge of No Man's Land the patrol of soldiers stood stock-still—with everyone else in Drunk Town who was sober—and stared over the fence toward the Yoshiwara. Two columns of flames and billowing smoke reached skywards amid distant shouts and bells brought closer by the wind. Faintly a third explosion sounded. A third fountain of flames. Smoke began to surround them. A few embers swirled past.

"Christalmighty," the Sergeant said, moving out of the lee of the godown to see better, "was that a bomb?"

"Doan' know, Sarge, could be a barrel of oil exploding, but we'd better get back, that bleeder's heading our way an—"

The fire bomb that Takeda had planted against the far side of the godown detonated. Instinctively they all ducked. More smoke, fire crackling, bellowing from nearby Drunk Towners and cries for water buckets and "Fire! Fire! Hurry, for Christ's sake—*that's the lamp-oil depot!*"

Half-naked men dashed in and out of adjoining houses to save their valuables. Down the street Mrs. Fotheringill's was emptying, inmates and customers raving and swearing, climbing into their clothes. More warning bells. Looting began.

And down at the South Gate, disciplined samurai streamed in, racing for the Yoshiwara with ladders and fire buckets, wet smoke masks over their faces. A few diverted to fight the godown fire, the remainder rushed onwards. Flames from the blazing godown roof, fanned by the wind, jumped the alley to attack the next line of hovels. They caught instantly.

From his hiding place in No Man's Land, Takeda saw the soldiers in confusion and gloated with the success of the bombs, a large section of the Yoshiwara already ablaze. Time to make a run for it. Quickly he adjusted his face mask, the mask and the dirt and his soot-blackened, filthy kimono making him even more ominous.

In flickering alternations of night and light, he hurried for the well head, found the knapsack, stuck his arms through the straps and, as quickly as he dared, picked a precarious way through the dump. Warning cries behind him. He thought he had been spotted, but it was only about the building, as one wall caved in with a roar, showering more sparks and fire on scattering people and on neighboring property. Now the abundance of flames allowed him to see better. Elated, he began to run. Ahead was the village and safety.

"Hey, you!"

He did not understand the words but the shout jerked him to a stop. In front was another group of British soldiers with an officer who had come running from the village area to probe the danger and had stopped, startled. They blocked his escape.

"Must be a looter! Or arsonist! Hey, you!"

"My God, watch out, sir, it's a samurai an' he's armed!"

"Cover me, Sergeant! You! You there, samurai, what're you doing? What's that you're carrying?"

In panic Takeda saw the officer unbuttoning his holster, start towards him, soldiers unslinging their rifles and all the time the sound of the holocaust, flames chasing weird shadows. He whirled and ran. At once they gave chase.

On the other side of No Man's Land the godown blaze was totally out of control, soldiers impotently striving to organize a fire-fighting party to protect abutting dwellings and streets. The fire gave enough light to help Takeda dart through the dump, avoiding most obstacles, the knapsack banging against his back. His breath was coming in gulps. With a sudden gush of hope he saw safety in the empty alley beside the burning building ahead. He raced for it, easily outstripping the soldiers behind him.

"Stop or I shoot!" The words were meaningless to him but not the hostility. Onwards in his headlong dash, no need for evading action now, any moment safe. He had forgotten the light that helped him, aided them, etching him clearly against the flames.

"Stop him, Sergeant! Wound him, don't kill him!"

"Right, sir . . . Wait, God Almighty, it's . . . isn't he the bugger Sir William's after, Nakama, that bloody assassin!"

"Damn my eyes, you're right, that's him. Quick, Sergeant, cut him down, wound him!"

The Sergeant aimed. His target was escaping down the alley. He squeezed the trigger. "Got him," he shouted gleefully, and charged. "Come on, lads!"

The bullet sent Takeda sprawling. It had smashed through the knapsack into his upper back, piercing a lung, to come out from his chest cleanly, not a fatal wound if a man was lucky. But Takeda knew none of that, only that he felt destroyed and he lay in the dirt, howling with shock but without pain, one arm useless and dangling, the roar of the nearby fire drowning his cries. Terror dragged him to his knees, the heat from approaching fire ghastly, safety only a few paces ahead down the alley. He crawled forward. Then through his tears he heard the shouts of soldiers close behind him. No escape!

His reflexes took command. Using his good hand as a prop, he was driven to his feet and with a mighty shriek, he hurled himself into the flames. The leading young soldier skidded to a stop, scrambled back to safety, hands held up against the inferno, the structure due to fall any moment.

"Sod it!" The soldier said, and glared at the flames that sizzled, consuming his prey, the stench of burning flesh making him gag. "Another second an' I'da had the bugger, sir, it were him all right, the bugger wot Sir William . . ."

That was the last thing the youth ever said. Katsumata's bombs in the knapsack detonated violently, a piece of metal tore out the soldier's throat, strewing the officer and other men like ninepins, breaking a few limbs. As if in echo, an oil drum exploded as violently, then another and another with cataclysmic effect. Plumes of flames and embers shot into the air to be seized and used ruthlessly by the gathering force of the wind, now self-generating in ferocity because of its heat.

The first of the village houses began to burn.

The shoya, his family and all villagers, already masked against smoke and prepared within moments of the first alarm, continued to work with well rehearsed but stoic speed to pack away valuables into the small, fireproofed brick shelters that were in every garden.

Roofs all along the main street began to burn.

Less than an hour since the first bomb exploded, the Three Carp was no more, and most of the Yoshiwara burnt out. Only brick chimney stacks, stone house-supports, and brick, stone and earth fireproof shelters stood in heaps of ash and glowing embers. The odd cup or saké flask, most refired now, the glaze spoiled. Metal kitchen utensils. Gardens ruined, shrubs scorched, groups of dazed inhabitants huddled around. Miraculously the fires had missed two or three Inns but around them was stark emptiness, ash and embers, up to the charred encircling fence and the moat beyond.

On the other side of the moat was the village. It was blazing. Beyond the village, in the Settlement proper the roofs of three houses near Drunk Town were already alight. One of these was the *Guardian*, where Jamie McFay had his new office.

Nettlesmith and their clerks were hauling buckets for Jamie atop the ladder who used them to douse the roof flames, the next house well afire. Other men, Chinese servants, and Maureen bravely darted in and out of the front door, carrying armfuls of papers, printing dies, and whatever was most important. Burning wooden roof tiles cascaded around them. Billowing smoke from Drunk Town, causing them to cough and heave, hampered them. Above, Jamie was losing the battle. A gust shoved flames at him. He almost fell off the ladder, then shinnied down, defeated. "It's hopeless," he panted, his face black-smudged, hair singed.

"Jamie, help me with the press, for God's sake!" Nettlesmith called out, and ran back inside. Maureen began to follow but Jamie stopped her. "No, stay here! Watch your dress," he shouted above the noise, a shower of embers from the roof surrounding her, then he dashed inside.

Wisely she backed off to the sea side of the street, helping others stack what had been salvaged more safely. The whole roof was ablaze now and more embers showered Jamie and Nettlesmith as they stumbled out with the small, portable press. Then, seeing the roof was beyond saving and the building doomed, Jamie hurried back to help him rescue type, dyes, ink and some paper. Quickly the wooden building became too dangerous to enter. The two men stood outside and cursed, then stepped farther to safety as some rafters collapsed.

"Bloody sodding fire," Jamie said, angrily kicking a box of typeface, then turned, feeling Maureen take his hand.

"I'm so sorry, love," she said, awash with tears.

His arms went around her and he said fervently, meaning it, "Never mind, you're safe, that's all that counts."

"Jamie, dinna' worry, wait till morning, then we can think better and properly. Perhaps it's no' so bad."

At that moment samurai fire fighters trotted past. With signs Jamie asked one of them where he could get a fire mask. The man grunted, pulled a handful from his sleeve and rushed off again. Jamie doused them in a bucket of water. "Here, Maureen," he said, giving her the first one, another to Nettlesmith who sat on a keg, on the sea side of the promenade, cursing mutely. The roof collapsed, turning the building into a blazing mess.

"Terrible," Jamie said to Nettlesmith.

"Yes. But not yet a disaster." The lean, older man motioned along the promenade. The north end of the Settlement was still clean of fire, Struan's, Brock's and the Legations untouched. "With any luck it won't burn that far."

"This wind is killing us."

"Yes. We're safe enough on the shore side . . ."

More fire fighters with axes hurried up, Dmitri amongst them. He saw their wreckage. "Jesus, sorry about that," he said on the run, "we're going to try to cut a fire break."

Maureen said, "Jamie, go and help. I'm safe here."

"Nothing more you can do here," Nettlesmith said. "I'll watch her. We're safe here, and we'll retreat on Struan's if necessary." He took out a pencil and paper, licked the pencil thoughtfully, and began to write.

Their axes bit into the wooden shack, the buildings southwards ablaze, the wind hotter every minute and stronger than ever. They redoubled their efforts, then an ember-filled gust forced them back, then another, and they fled to safety. Dmitri said, helplessly, "Christ, you ever seen anything go up so fast? They're all tinderboxes, death traps. What now?"

"What about up there?" Jamie shouted. He pointed nearer to the fence. They all joined his rush. But the closer they got to the fence and the Yoshiwara, the worse the smoke and heat and fires became.

There was so little he or anyone could do. Nothing, in fact. The fires were spreading too fast, people running this way and that with buckets, but the moment one blaze was extinguished, ten others began nearby. Behind groups of dazed women and servants seeking safety, some with bundles, most empty-handed, the few remaining Teahouses flared in momentary blazes, so many moths around a candle, one moment alive, the next dead.

With almost everything of the Yoshiwara vanished under the blood-smoked sky, men mingled with the survivors, anxiously seeking their particular girl or mama-san and Jamie joined them, his eyes going from face to face seeking Nemi. He had not forgotten her. If anyone could escape, she would, he had thought. Suddenly he was not so sure. There were so few survivors here. Worriedly, Jamie sought a face he knew. None. *"Gomen nasai, Nemi-san, wakarimasu ka?"* he said, asking if they had seen her, but everyone said dully, or with degrees of bows and forced smiles, *"Iyé, gomen nasai"*—No, so sorry.

Dmitri reeled out of the smoke, coughing and gasping. "Samurai are damn good fire fighters, we could learn a thing or two, not that they can stop this shit. Have you seen Nemi?"

"No, I was just going to ask you."

"Maybe she's the other side, or over there," Dmitri croaked, his chest heaving for air, pointing towards the meadow that led to the racecourse, a few oil lamps there lighting the darkness. "Some of them are collecting there—some the other side. Listen, I'm going to work my way around, through the north gate and across the canal. You try the meadow. If I see her, what do you want me to say?"

"Just that I hope she's safe and I'll find her tomorrow."

They both ducked as fire jumped over them to fall on a village hut behind. In the confusion Jamie lost Dmitri and continued his search, helping where he could. Once Heavenly Skye rushed past, calling out, "Jamie, just heard Phillip's lost with the rest of the Three Carp."

"God Almighty, are you sure? What about . . ."

But Skye had vanished into the darkness.

The Legations that lay northwards were not yet directly menaced. Nor Struan's, Brock's, or nearby houses and godowns though the wind was strong and hotter by the minute. The promenade and streets were crowded, everyone preparing for a last stand, more soldiers and sailors coming ashore from the fleet that had first sounded the general alarm. Samurai poured into the High Street from their barracks outside the gates with ladders and buckets, fire-masked, and efficient. In groups they trotted along, heading for danger points.

Sir William, a greatcoat over his pajamas, had taken charge of the Legation defense. Down by the surf Pallidar was supervising dragoons connecting pumps to the sea through long canvas hoses. He looked back to see the General hurry out of the night, an engineer officer alongside, a detachment of soldiers with him, to stop in front of Sir William.

"I'm heading for Drunk Town and the village," the General said, out of breath. "Plan to blow up some houses to make a fire break—with your permission. All right?"

"Yes, do what you can, it might work. If the wind doesn't drop we're finished, hurry!"

"Happened to be watching from the bluff, looked like three of four fires started in the Yoshiwara, same time, different areas."

"Good God, you mean arson?"

"Don't know, but whether it was an Act of God or the Devil or a bloody arsonist, this'll burn us out!" With the engineers he raced into the night.

Sir William saw the Admiral trudging up the beach from the Legation wharf where more sailors and marines were landing. "Boats are ready to evacuate," Ketterer said. "We've stores enough for the whole population. We can assemble them along the beach, should be safe enough."

"Good. This could be dicey."

"Yes. Completely changes our plans, what?"

" 'Fraid so. Couldn't have happened at a worse time." God-cursed fire, Sir William thought angrily. Complicates everything—the Yoshi meeting tomorrow and bombardment of Kagoshima, and just when Ketterer had finally agreed to obey instructions. What the devil do we do, evacuate or what? Put everyone aboard the fleet and sail back to Hong Kong with our tails between our legs, or move everyone to Kanagawa and to hell with what the Japanese might do? Can't. Kanagawa's a worse trap, bay's too shallow for the fleet to be useful.

He glanced at Ketterer. The Admiral's face was hard and weather-beaten, the small eyes fixed in the distance. He'll plump for Hong Kong, he thought, sickened. Damn this wind!

Down the street MacStruan had ladders against the side of his building. Servants and clerks handed up buckets of water to others perched there dousing the shingles. Next door at Brock's, Gornt and others were doing the same.

"Christ, look!" someone shouted. Now fires blanketed the whole of the village and Drunk Town skyline. The wind was blistering hot and furious in their faces, rushing at them, taunting them.

"Mon Dieu," Angelique murmured. She wore a heavy coat over her nightdress, a head scarf, and had dressed hastily at the first warning and fled outside. It was evident the fires would reach them soon, so she scurried back indoors, up to her room. Rapidly she stuffed her brushes and combs and salves and creams and rouge into a bag, her best lingerie next. A moment of thought, and then, no longer frightened, she opened the window, shouted at Ah Soh below to stay there and began throwing dresses and coats to her.

Ah Soh sniffled and did not move. MacStruan, close by, cursed her into motion and pointed across the road to their jetty where clerks already guarded boxes of papers, stores and rifles, Vargas and others sweating more parcels into place, MacStruan having decided to chance leaving their specie, bullion and certain documents in their iron safe.

"You motherless whore, Ah Soh," he shouted in perfect Cantonese, "take tai-tai's things over there, guard them and stay there even if the fires of hell fall on you or I'll beat the soles of your feet to pulp!" She obeyed instantly. "Angelique," he called out with a laugh, "we'll get plenty of warning, stay in the warm until I call for you!"

"Thanks, Albert." She saw Gornt looking up at her from next door. He waved. She waved back. Now there was no fear in her. Albert would warn her in good time, safety lay across the road or in boats collecting on and near the shore. Her mind was clean of worry. Earlier she had decided how to handle André and Skye and the Woman in Hong Kong. And Gornt tomorrow, and what to do.

Humming Mozart, she took out her brush and sat in front of her mirror to make herself much more presentable for all of them. It was like old times. Now, what shall I wear, what would be best?

Raiko followed the burly servant amidst the remains of her Inn. He carried an oil lamp and led the way carefully, using stepping stones where he could, skirting bad patches of embers that glowed over-brightly, a warning in the dark, fanned by the hot, acrid air. Her face was blackened, hair heavy with ash and dust, her kimono scorched and in tatters. Both wore smoke masks, yet they coughed and wheezed from time to time. "Go more to the left," she croaked, throat dry, continuing her inspection, only stubs of stone supports, in neat square patterns above ashes, indicating where dwellings had been.

"Yes, Mistress." They plodded onwards.

Above the noise of the wind they could vaguely hear others calling, an occasional cry of pain and weeping, distant fire bells from the village and Settlement that were burning furiously. She was over her initial panic. Fires happen. They were the work of the gods. Never mind, I'm alive. Tomorrow I will find out what caused the fire, if it was an explosion, as some were claiming, though in the uproar this foul wind could play tricks with hearing, and the bang could easily have been an ill-placed oil jar falling into the kitchen fires and bursting where the blaze began. The Three Carp is gone. So are all the others, or almost all. I'm not ruined, not yet.

A group of courtesans and maids, many crying, appeared out of the night, a few of them scorched. She recognized women from the Green Dragon. None of her own girls. "Stop crying," she ordered. "Go to the Sixteen Orchids—everyone is collecting there. It's not badly damaged, there'll be beds for all, food and drink. Help those who are hurt. Where's Chio-san?" This was their mama-san.

"We haven't seen her," said one through her tears. "I was with a client, it was all I could do to hurry out with him to the underground shelter."

"Good, run along, go that way and be careful," Raiko said, satisfied, pleased with herself, remembering that when the Yoshiwara was being built, just over two years ago, and mama-sans had been selected by their Guild—with prior, expensive approval of that department of Bakufu—she had suggested that each Teahouse have a fireproof cellar built near the central structure, and for further prudence to put their brick fire-safes below ground level. Not all of the mama-sans approved, saying the added expense was not merited. Never mind, it's their loss. Let's see how many wail and beat their breasts tomorrow that they didn't follow my example.

She had just finished inspecting hers. Steps led down to the iron-sheathed door. The interior was unblemished. All valuables were safe, all contracts, indentures, debt papers, loans made to the Gyokoyama and bank statements, IOUs, best linens and dress kimonos—both hers and the Ladies' as good as new in their wrappers. From the beginning it had been her policy that all expensive linens and clothes that were not to be worn and used that evening, had to be put away underground, almost always to groans at the extra work. There won't be groans this dawn, she thought.

To her immense relief all her Ladies, staff and clients were accounted for, except Fujiko, Hinodeh, Teko, Furansu-san and Taira, two servants, two maids still missing. But that did not worry her. They were surely safe elsewhere. A servant had seen a gai-jin, perhaps two, running safely towards the Gate.

Namu Amida Butsu, she prayed, let them all be safe, and bless me for my wisdom making sure that my people were well rehearsed with fire drills.

The horror of Yedo's Yoshiwara conflagration, twelve years before, had taught her the lesson. That fire had almost killed her and her client, a rich rice merchant in the Gyokoyama. She had saved him by waking him from his drunken stupor, staying to drag him out at the risk of her own life. Escaping through the gardens, they had suddenly found themselves surrounded by fire and trapped, but they had rescued themselves from death by furiously digging a trench in the soft earth with her obi dagger, allowing the fire to pass over them. Even so, much of her lower back and legs had been badly burned, ending her career as a courtesan.

But her client had remembered her and when she had recovered enough to walk, he talked to the Gyokoyama who lent her the funds to open her own Teahouse and then he had gone on to another Lady. Their investment had been repaid fivefold. In that fire over a hundred courtesans, sixteen mama-sans, countless clients and maids had perished. More had died in Kyōto's Shimibara fire. Over the centuries hundreds in other fires. In the Great Fire of the Trailing Sleeves, a few years after the mama-san Gyoko had built the first Yoshiwara, fire erupted and obliterated it, and cost Yedo a hundred thousand lives. Within two years it was rebuilt and thriving, to burn again and be rebuilt again, endlessly. And now as before, Raiko swore, we will rebuild ours better than ever!

"The Sixteen Orchids would be that way, Mistress, *neh*?" The servant hesitated, unsure in the billowing smoke clouds. Around them nothing but embers and ashes, a few pathetic house supports, no outlines of meandering paths or stones to guide them. Then a gust broomed away ash and cinders to reveal cornerstones and a stone dragon cracked by the heat. She recognized it and knew where they were. Hinodeh's bungalow.

"We must go back a little," she said, then something caught her eye. A glint. "Wait. What's that?"

"Where, Mistress?"

She waited. Again the wind fanned embers and again the glitter, slightly ahead and to the right. "There!"

"Ah, yes." Taking care, he used a blackened, leafless branch to brush a path, stepped forward and raised the lamp and peered ahead. Another cautious step, to retreat hastily as a gust shoved embers at him.

"Come back, we'll look tomorrow!"

"A moment, Mistress." Flinching against the heat, he used the branch swiftly to brush away more ashes. He gasped. The two charred shapes lay side by side, the left hand of one in the right hand of the other. What glinted was a gold signet ring, twisted and partially melted. "Mistress!"

Aghast, like a statue, Raiko stood beside him. Furansu-san and Hinodeh, must be, she thought instantly, he always wore a signet ring—remember, he even offered it to me a few days ago.

And, as instantly, her spirit was uplifted with the sight of the clasped hands, the picture they made on their bed of living coals, seeming to her to be a cradle of precious gems, rubies, glinting and living and dying and being reborn by the air currents—as the two of them would be until the end of time.

Oh, so sad, she thought, tears brimming, so sad and yet so beautiful. How peaceful they are, lying there, how blessed, dying together, hand in hand. They must have decided on the poison cup and to go as one. How wise. How wise for both of them.

She brushed at her tears, murmured, *"Namu Amida Butsu,"* as a benediction. "We'll leave them in peace and I'll decide what to do tomorrow." She backed away, her tears bittersweet, but gladdened by the beauty she had seen. Once more they picked their way towards the gathering point.

A random thought took hold of her.

If those two were Furansu-san and Hinodeh, the gai-jin who escaped must be Taira. That's good, much better than the other way around. I lose a fine source of intelligence but gain more in the long run. Taira and Fujiko are more docile and have a future. Skillfully handled, Taira will easily become as informative, soon I'll be able to talk directly with him, his Japanese is improving daily and already good for a gai-jin. I must arrange extra lessons and teach him political phrases, not just the language of bedding and the Floating World that is all Fujiko is capable of—and with a peasant accent at that. Certainly my investment with him long term is much more promising and—

Both mistress and servant stopped at the same moment. They stared at each other, then abruptly at the southern sky. The wind had dropped.

58

Wednesday, 14th January:

"YOKOHAMA'S FINISHED, WIL-liam," the General said in the first light of dawn, his voice raw. They were on the bluff, overlooking the Settlement, Pallidar in attendance, all of them mounted. Smoke still wafted up to them. The General's face was bruised and filthy, uniform torn, cap ripped and the brim burnt. "Thought it best to ask you to come up here, gives you a better picture, sorry. Act of God."

"I knew it was bad, but this . . ." The words trailed off. Sir William was numbed. None of them had slept. The signs of fatigue and worry were in all their faces, their clothes scorched and dirty, Pallidar's ripped and the worst of all. As the sun rose slightly they could see the whole panorama to Hodogaya on the Tokaidō.

The Yoshiwara no longer existed, nor the village, most of Drunk Town, over half the Settlement including stables. No confirmed reports of casualties yet, but a richness of rumors, all bad. No confirmed reason for the catastrophe yet. Many shouted arson by Japanese, but which Japanese and at whose orders, no one knew, though destruction of the Yoshiwara and village would concern none of them to gain their ends.

"You'll order evacuation this morning?"

Sir William's head ached with a thousand questions and forebodings. "First an inspection. Thank you, Thomas. Pallidar, you come with me." He spurred his pony down the incline. At the Legation he reined in a moment. "Anything new, Bertram?"

"No, sir, no confirmed names or numbers yet."

"Send for the village Elder, the shoya, at once, ask him to find out how many casualties he has and to see me at once."

"I don't speak Japanese, Sir William, and Phillip Tyrer isn't here."

"Then bloody find him," Sir William bellowed, glad for the opportunity to rid himself of some of his pent-up anxiety, concern over Tyrer, and was rewarded to see the effete youth pale. "And bloody learn Japanese or I'll pack you off to Africa and you can burden them! Get all senior traders here in an hour . . . No, not here, the Club's better, and let's see, it's six-twenty now, make it at nine-thirty, and for Christ's sake, pull your finger out and start using your bloody head!" Idiot, he thought, and trotted off feeling better.

Under the lightening sky, the people of Yokohama were picking up the pieces of their places and their lives. At first Sir William, escorted by Pallidar, stayed on the High Street, greeting everyone, answering questions by saying, "First let me have a look. I've called a meeting at the Club for nine-thirty, by then I'll know better."

Nearer Drunk Town the stench of burned buildings worsened. This morning when the wind had dropped, about 2:00 A.M., the fires had died rapidly and no longer jumped firebreaks or from house to house. Only this had saved the Settlement from oblivion. All Legations were safe, as well as the Harbor Master's, the main traders and their godowns—Struan's, Brock's, Cooper-Tillman and others. Lunkchurch's was gutted.

The fire had stopped exactly before Holy Trinity, leaving it untouched, and he thanked God for a most suitable miracle. Farther down the street the Catholic church had lost most windows and roof, the maw of charred and smoking beams now like an open mouth of rotten teeth. " 'Morning, where's Father Leo?" he asked a man working in the garden, cleaning up.

"In the vestry, Sir William. Top of the morning to Yourself and that Yourself is safe, Sir William, sir."

"Thank you. Sorry about your church. I've called a meeting in the Club at nine-thirty, spread the word, would you? Father Leo's welcome, of course." He went on again.

Unlike the village and Yoshiwara where piles of clean ash were in drifts, like snow, the ravaged areas of the Settlement and Drunk Town were a mess of bricks, flagstones, twisted metal, the remains of machinery, engines, tools, guns, cannon, anvils and other manufactured objects, now junk. The festering sore of No Man's Land had been cleaned, except for metal, and that pleased him.

He meandered down to the South Gate. The guard house had disappeared. A temporary barrier had been erected in emptiness and samurai were on sentry duty. "Stupid clods," Pallidar said. "They're barricading against what?"

Sir William did not answer, too wrapped up in what he could see and what he could do. Ahead at the canal and moat he could see villagers and others wandering around, or squatting in dismal groups. The other side of the moat where the Yoshiwara had been, clusters of women and cooks and menservants sat or stood around the only partial structure still standing, canvas screens up as shelter. Samurai still doused fires here and there. A lot of crying and sobbing on the gentle wind.

"Terrible, sir," Pallidar said.

"Yes." Sir William sighed and again made an effort—it was up to him to give the example and, by God, he was going to act like Her Britannic Majesty's Minister for Japan should act. "Yes, it is, but look there, by God!" On the bluff the tented camp was undamaged. "All our soldiers are safe, cannon safe, artillery safe, all armaments and the munition depot as ever was. And look there!"

In the bay the fleet was unscathed, Union Jacks and ensigns flying proudly and with dawn passing into day, every available cutter plied back and forth, bringing men ashore or taking them aboard for food, drink, and sleep. "All the rest is replaceable, by Harry, except people. Get some soldiers, start counting heads and mounts. I need to know who we've lost by the nine-thirty meeting. Off you go!"

"Yes, sir. Most of the stables were opened and the horses bolted for the racecourse or bluff. I saw Zergeyev's stallion there with a couple of grooms." Suddenly Pallidar beamed, no longer as shattered. "You're right, Sir William, my God, how right. So long as the Army and Navy are safe, we're all all right, everything's all right. Thanks." He galloped off.

Sir William turned his attention inland. What to do, what to do? His pony jingled her bridles nervously and pawed the ground, sensing his disquiet.

" 'Morning, Sir William." Grey with fatigue, Jamie McFay was approaching from behind the remains of a building that now was a heap of twisted metal frames, the remains of bedsteads, furniture and charred wood. His clothes were tattered, burnt in places, hair matted. "How many lost? What's the latest?"

"Nothing for certain yet. Good God, is that . . . is that all that's left of the *Guardian* building and the presses?"

" 'Fraid so. But here." Jamie held the bridle and handed him a badly

printed sheet with a smudged banner headline that screamed:
YOKOHAMA TORCHED. ARSON SUSPECTED. STRUAN'S AND BROCK'S
UNTOUCHED, ARMY, NAVY AND ALL SHIPPING SAFE. FATALITIES EX-
PECTED TO BE HEAVY IN THE YOSHIWARA AND VILLAGE. Then a brief
editorial, with a promise that an afternoon edition would be out and
apologies for the bad printing.

"Nettlesmith's over there." Under a rough lean-to they could see
Nettlesmith, unkempt and filthy, laboriously working the press by
hand, his printer clerks sorting type into trays, still salvaging what they
could from the ashes.

"I heard you pulled a number of villagers out of a building, saved
their lives, Jamie."

It was still hard for Jamie to think straight. Vaguely he recalled never
finding Nemi, or news of her, but not about the others. "I don't
remember much about it, it was chaos everywhere—others were doing
the same, or helping folk to the hospital . . ." His head was swimming
with fatigue. "Last night I heard Phillip was lost. Is it true?"

"Don't know. Hope to God not, though I heard the rumor too." Sir
William exhaled loudly. "I heard the same and there are lots of rumors
but I've learned not to trust rumor. Zergeyev was reported dead in the
Yoshiwara, so was André, but I saw him a short time ago, Zergeyev. So,
as I said, best to wait." He indicated the tear sheet. "Can I keep this,
Jamie? Thanks. I've convened a meeting at nine-thirty, to discuss what
we should do, your opinion would be valuable."

"Not much to discuss, is there? I'm wiped out."

"There's lots to discuss, Jamie. We're really very lucky. The Army
and Navy . . ." Sir William glanced off, and raised his hat. " 'Morning,
Miss Maureen." She was still in the same clothes but clean and fresh
and wore a bonny smile.

" 'Morning, Sir William, glad to see you're safe and that the Legation's safe. 'Morning, love." Her smile became even more special. She
put her arm through Jamie's, careful not to be forward and kiss him
however much she wanted to—he looked so handsome in his charred
clothes, his face unshaven and etched with worry, nothing that hot
soup and hot whisky and a good sleep would not cure.

On the way here to find him, many had told her how brave he had
been during the night. Most of her night had been spent calming Mrs.
Lunkchurch and Mrs. Swann, their spouses and others at the Struan
outpost, doling out the demon drink, as her mother called all liquor—
though not in her father's presence—attending to burns or taking them

to Hoag or Babcott, who had set up field hospitals as near to the worst areas as possible. "You look fine, Jamie, just tired out."

"No more than others."

Knowing he had been forgotten—and not a little envious—Sir William saluted with his quirt. "See you later, Jamie. Miss Maureen."

They watched him canter away. Her arm and nearness felt good to Jamie. All at once his unhappiness and apprehension for the future surged and he turned and hugged her with the full measure of his misery. She melted against him, so happy, and waited, and gave him all of her strength.

In time he felt his wits revive, his courage returning and his sense of belonging easing back. "Bless you, I can't believe it but you've made me come alive again, bless you." Then he remembered Tess and the five thousand Maureen had wheedled out of her, and Maureen saying, Tomorrow things will no' be so bad, and his joy exploded. "By God, Sparkles," he said, hugging her again, "you're right. We're alive and lucky and everything's going to be fine and it's all due to you!"

"Now dinna exaggerate, laddie," she said with a little smile, head against his, not letting go of him yet. "Nothing to do with me." It's to do with God, she was thinking, that's His special gift to us women, as His gift to men is to do the same for women at special times. "It's just life." She used 'life' but she could have said, 'love' but did not though totally sure that's what it truly was.

"I'm proud of you, lassie. You were grand last night."

"Och, aye, but I did na do a thing at all. Come along, it's time to nap."

"No time to nap, I've got to see the shoya."

"A nap before the meeting, I'll wake you with a cup of tea. You can use my bed, Albert says it's our room for as long as we want and I'll throw everyone else out."

Smiling through his exhaustion, he said, "What are you going to do?"

She hugged him. "I'll hold your hand and tell you a bedtime story. Come along."

Tyrer opened his eyes and found himself in hell, every bone aching, every breath abrading his chest, eyes burning and skin tormented. In the acrid, smoky black he could see disembodied Japanese faces peering at him, two of them, their mouths twisted with cruel smiles and any moment they would pull up their pitchforks and begin to torture him again. A face moved closer. He backed, and let out a cry of pain. Through the mist he heard Japanese and then in English, "Taira-sama, wake, you safe!"

The fog enveloping his mind dissipated. "Nakama?"

"Yes. You safe."

Now he perceived the light was from an oil lamp, they seemed to be in a cave and Nakama was smiling at him. So was the other face. Saito! Nakama's cousin, the one interested in ships . . . No, this isn't Nakama, this is Hiraga the assassin!

He jerked up and fell back against the wall of the tunnel, his headache blinding him for a moment, and coughed and coughed, bile and a foul taste of smoke making him heave. When there was no more to come up and the spasm had passed, he felt a cup pressed to his lips. He drank the icy water eagerly, choking a little. "Sorry," he murmured. Again Hiraga wrapped the blanket around his half-burnt sleeping kimono. "Thanks."

In a minute he had caught his breath, mind slowly moving from blank to a kaleidoscope of images, coalescing into more pictures, blazing walls, Hiraga grabbing him out of a blaze and running, falling and being helped up, Teahouses collapsing around him, shrubs exploding in their faces, can't breathe, gagging, can't breathe, Hiraga shouting, "Quick, this way . . . no, this way, no back, this way . . ." something missing but picking himself up again, fleeing this way and that, guided through walls of fire in front and behind and to the side, women screaming, smoke, and then at the well head, the fire reaching for them, almost at them, "Down, down there, hurry," ducking into it, fire searing, a light below, an orb in the darkness, Saito's face, and then like a thunderbolt . . .

Fujiko!

'Where's Fujiko?' he had screamed.

Gasping for breath, Hiraga shouted above the roaring flames, 'Quick, go down, she dead in room, Fujiko dead when find you . . . quick or you dead!'

He remembered that part clearly now. He had leapt out of the well and began to rush back, the fire worse than before, certain death ahead but he had to reach her to make sure and then he was flat on his face, a blinding pain in his neck, he tried to scramble up, the heat monstrous, and all he remembered seeing was the edge of a rock-hard hand driving for the side of his neck. "You . . . I was going for her but you stopped me?"

"Yes. No way save. Fujiko dead, so sorry, I saw. She dead, you too if go back, so hit and carry here. Fujiko dead in room." Hiraga said it flat, still disgusted with Tyrer for risking both their lives on such a stupidity. He had only just had time to lift Tyrer onto his shoulder and clamber down, almost losing his footing to reach safety, saving his own life by a paper thickness from the flames. And he was thinking, fuming, even the most *baka* man must have known there was no chance to find her, no way to survive with the whole garden, entire Teahouses afire, and even if she hadn't been dead then, she was dead fifteen times now. "If no hit, you dead. Is dead better?"

"No." Tyrer's grief swamped him. "Sorry. I owe you my life again." He wiped his face to try, unsuccessfully, to stop the anguish. Fujiko dead, oh God, oh God. "Sorry, Nak—sorry, Hiraga-sama, where are we?"

"Tunn'er. Near Three Carp. It go to vi'rrage, under fence, moat." Hiraga motioned up the well. "It day now."

Tyrer clambered painfully to his feet. Once upright he felt a little better. Daylight at the well head was muted by billowing smoke, but he could see that it was about dawn.

"*Dozo.*" With a smile Akimoto handed him a loincloth and a spare kimono.

"*Domo,*" Tyrer said, shocked by the amount his own had been burned. There were some burn patches on his legs, nothing truly bad. Hiraga was climbing the rickety handholds to peer out, to be driven back by the heat.

Once more in the tunnel, Hiraga said, "No good. Too hot. Here." He offered him the water again and it was accepted gratefully. "Taira-sama, best go that way." He pointed down the tunnel. "You a'we right?"

"Yes. Fujiko, she was dead? You're quite sure?"

"Yes."

"What happened? I was asleep and then . . . was it a bomb? I can remember . . . I think I was blown the other side of the room from . . . from Fujiko. It felt as if a bomb went off below the house. Was it? And why the fire, everything on fire?"

Akimoto touched Tyrer with a smile and said in Japanese, "Taira-sama, you were lucky. If it weren't for Hiraga you'd be dead. Do you understand?"

"*Hai, wakarimasu.*" Tyrer bowed solemnly to Hiraga, adding in Japanese, "Thank you, Hiraga-sama, again in debt. Thank you for life." Sickness went through him. "Sorry, first rest little." Awkwardly he sat down. "What happen?"

"We speak Ing'erish. Why fires? Bad man have fire bomb. Set fire here, wind take fire to Yokohama and th—"

Tyrer was shocked into life. "The Settlement's gone too?"

"Don't know, Taira-sama. No time to 'rook but Yoshiwara gone, think vi'rrage too. Maybe Yokohama too."

Tyrer scrambled to his feet and went for the well.

"No, not up, this way." Hiraga lit another lamp. "You fo'rrow, yes?" In Japanese he said to Akimoto, "You stay here, I'll take him part of the way, I want to see what's happened, then I'll come back." Leading the way down the tunnel, he said again in English, "Bad man have fire bomb. Want hurt gai-jin. South wind make 'ritter fire big fire."

At once Tyrer understood the significance of the south wind pattern: "My God, everything's so combustible, it'll blaze like nothing on earth. My God, if . . ." He stopped, frantic with worry. Water was running down the tunnel wall. He scooped some up to cool his head. The cold helped. "Sorry, go on, a bad man? What bad man?"

"Bad man," Hiraga repeated darkly, but disoriented, of two minds: he was both filled with fury that Takeda had taken the initiative and demolished his own safe haven, and at the same time delighted with the success of the fire bombs that he had seen. With the south wind and the Yoshiwara fired, the village had to go and the gai-jin's houses too. And with their Yokohama base gone gai-jin would have to leave as Ori, first, and then Katsumata had predicted. *Sonno-joi* had been advanced.

An hour or so ago he had tried to peer out of the Drunk Town well head to see for himself but the heat was too much and had driven him back. Perhaps the bricks had cooled enough for him to see the extent of the devastation there. He held in his hope. Tyrer still had to be dealt with.

The success of his story depended on whether or not Takeda had been caught alive. It was a good gamble that Takeda had not been and then his version, mostly true, would be logical: "Bad man want destroy all gai-jin, drive away from Nippon. Man from Bakufu. Bakufu want all gai-jin away, Yoshi want all gai-jin gone. Pay spy to start fire, blame shishi, but man from Bakufu."

"You know this man?"

Hiraga shook his head. "A Satsuma man, mama-san say me."

"Raiko-san?"

"No, Wakiko, another Teahouse." Hiraga said, inventing a name. They had reached the water. "Best take off c'rothes. Safe." They stripped and, with the oil lamp held up, forded the barrier. And on the other side, while Tyrer painfully retied the loincloth and put on the kimono, Hiraga elaborated on the theme that the Bakufu were evil, they would cast the blame elsewhere, on ronin, the shishi, but they had planned and precipitated it, Anjo, the Elders and especially Yoshi.

To Tyrer it was very plausible. Very. Again a Satsuma, one of Sanjiro's devils.

At the lip of the well, Hiraga pointed upwards. "Same as other. First I see." He handed Tyrer the lamp and climbed to the top, the bricks still hot. Warily he peered out. What he saw made his head reel. Where once No Man's Land was hemmed in, now he could see clear to the sea, past the space that was once Drunk Town, past the other space that was once the village, right up to the north end. Many gai-jin buildings there were untouched but that did not worry him. All in all, Yokohama had ceased to be. He returned below.

"What's happened, Hiraga-sama?"

"You go see. I stay. You go now, friend. Hiraga not go, cannot— samurai still search, *neh*?"

Tyrer saw the brown eyes watching him, this strange alien who had certainly risked his life to save him. And had saved him for the second time. What more can a friend do than risk his life for his friend? "Without you, I know I'd be dead. I owe you a life. To thank you is not enough."

Hiraga shrugged, silently.

"What will you do?"

"P'rease?"

"If I want to see you, to contact you."

"I here. Taira-sama, not forget Yoshi price my head, *neh*? P'rease, not say about tunn'er. Bakufu and Yoshi want me bad. If Taira-sama say, soon dead, can nowhere to run."

"I won't tell anyone. How can I get you a message?"

Hiraga thought about that. "Sunset time, come here, speak down. I here sunset time. Understand?"

"Yes." Tyrer stuck out his hand. "Don't be afraid. I won't tell and I'll try to help." Hiraga's grip was as firm.

"Phillip! Phillip, my boy, thank God you're safe!" Sir William's face was alight with relief and he hurried towards him to grip him on both shoulders. "The rumor said you'd been swallowed up in the Yoshiwara, come and sit down, you poor chap." He helped him to the best chair in his office by the fire. "Good God, you look terrible, what on earth happened, you need a drink! Brandy coming up!"

Tyrer relaxed into the tall chair, feeling much better. After the initial horror of the damage and meeting a few people on the waterfront, seeing bandages and burns—no one spoke of deaths—seeing the Legations, Struan's and Brock's and important parts untouched—along with the army encampment and the fleet—all this took away most of his tension. No one seemed to know who was lost, or how many, so he had hurried here. He took a large swallow of the drink. "I was caught in the Yoshiwara all right. I was with, er, with my girl and, well, she died." His unhappiness rushed in again like a tidal wave.

"My God, sorry about that. Strange, your other friend, Nakama, Hiraga, whatever his real name is, he's dead too."

"Sir?"

"Yes," Sir William said, and sat in the chair opposite and ran on happily. "Definite identification. A patrol spotted him in No Man's Land at the beginning of the fire in Drunk Town, at first they thought he was a looter and gave chase but recognized him, shot the bugger, wounding him, to stop him, but can you imagine, the madman got up and hurled himself into a blazing building—the old oil depot. A few moments later the Sergeant said there was a terrific explosion and the place seemed to blow up."

"That's not possible be—"

"I agree it's unlikely, throwing yourself into an inferno, ridiculous, no one would do that. Sorry to say two of the lads were killed trying to catch him—caught by the explosions. Damned shame! Nakama certainly could have been the arsonist, if there was one, rather farfetched if you ask me. In any event, oil barrels were exploding all over." He saw Tyrer's agitation and pallor and felt bad for him. "Sorry for you, Phillip, sorry that he's dead, because I know you liked him, but not sorry otherwise—he was an assassin and it gets us out of a dreadful hole with Yoshi, doesn't it?" He waited expectantly for him to agree but there was only a hollow face in front of him. "Sorry, must be a shock on top of the . . . the other—it must have been awful."

Tyrer was unbalanced, difficult to assimilate Hiraga's mistaken death. "The Yoshiwara, yes—yes, it was," and just as he was about to correct Sir William he was overridden again.

"Have to tell you, Phillip, we've been incredibly lucky. Army's intact, Navy, only one of our community was lost so far, though we're still checking. Did you see any of our chaps last night in the Yoshiwara?"

"No, sir, not one of ours, no." Tyrer could not get his mind working properly. "Not a soul. You see I w—"

"Damn! Difficult trying to track everyone down, can't get an accurate count. Drunk Town's hopeless, but even there they say only half a dozen vagrants, no one with any name but Charlie or Tom or George. Glad to say Mrs. Fortheringill's young ladies are all safe. Astounding we all escaped—if the wind hadn't dropped . . . but then it did and thank God for that . . . Did you see Holy Titties escaped too? Of course, damages will run into hundreds of thousands of pounds. Thank God for insurance, what? Well, drink up and take a nap. When you think about it, you'll see how fortunate we were with Nakama, he was developing into a major diplomatic disaster. I'm off, just going to discuss a plan with the community. Why don't you lie down until I'm back an—"

A knock. Bertram said, "The shoya's here, Sir William."

"Perfect timing, show him in. Phillip, before you go you can translate for me. Come in, come in, Mr. Shoya."

The shoya bowed deferentially, on guard.

"My Master greet you, Shoya," Tyrer translated, still dazed, his mind elsewhere, desperate to lie down and think this all through. "Please to say how many lose in fire?"

"Please thank him for his kindness in asking but please do not be concerned about our problems." The shoya found the question astonishing for it was no business of the gai-jin. What trap are they setting for me? he wondered.

"My Master says want know how many lost?"

"Oh, so sorry, I am not sure of a final count, but five fishermen and two families have gone onwards," the shoya said politely, making up a figure as the gai-jin leader had asked pointedly, 'how many *lost*,' thus expecting figures. Actually they had lost none of their people or children or boats, having had plenty of warning.

"My Master say, so sorry. Can he help village?"

"Ah! Ah, yes—yes, please thank the Great Lord, the families could use some bags of rice and a little money, any help with food or . . ." The shoya left it hanging to allow them to make up their own minds. Is this another trap?

"My Master says that he send foods for village. Please say how fire start."

The shoya was thinking how totally mad of them to expect an answer to that. Dangerous to be involved in politics, even worse between shishi and Bakufu. While he greatly regretted the loss of all the profit when the gai-jin left their shores tomorrow or the next day, all was not lost because all his books and receipts and bullion were safe, and because of his agreement with the Jami gai-jin, which had become even more important now. I'm sure my *stoku kompeni* won't suffer.

At the same time he was pleased with shishi daring to drive them out, blaming the vile Bakufu. *Sonno-joi.* We're better off without gaijin here. Better they are locked up in Nagasaki's little Deshima as in the past. I will open a branch in Nagasaki and be ready for their return. If ever.

"So sorry, but probably oil in a kitchen," he said with a humble bow. "Only the Yoshiwara cooks at night, we do not, please excuse me, that is all I know."

"My Master say, this man Nakama, or Hiraga, the shishi Lord Yoshi want, he seen by soldiers who try catch him. He run away and dead in fire. You know him?"

The shoya's foreboding tripled, though the death, to his delight, had also been reported. "Please excuse me," he croaked, "I only know him as client, never shishi. Dead? How wonderful the assassin's dead. Wonderful!"

Sir William sighed, tired of the questions and answers. "Thank him and dismiss him, Phillip."

Thankfully the old man left. Sir William said, "Off you go, be ready to leave at noon."

"Sir?"

"For Kanagawa, the Yoshi meeting. You didn't forget?"

Tyrer was flabbergasted. "Surely he won't be expecting us now," he said weakly, the idea of a lengthy meeting translating the Treaty's nuances filling him with nausea. "Surely not!"

"That's why we're going." Sir William beamed. "Keep him off balance, eh? We're British, not a bunch of lily-white twits. We've just had a minor contretemps, a slight hitch." He put on his coat. "See you at noon, in best bib and tucker."

"But he won't turn up, not after this."

"Yes. If he doesn't, then he loses face, we don't."

"I can't, Sir William, not as interpreter. I'm . . . I'm just exhausted and just can't, not today, sorry."

" 'Fraid you'll have to. Stiff upper lip and all that."

Tyrer saw the thin smile, the coldness returning. And inflexibility. "Sorry, I can't, sir. I've had it. Please let André do it, he's better than I am."

"You have to do it," Sir William said, no humor in him now. "André Poncin's dead."

Tyrer almost fell. "He can't be . . . How?"

"In the Yoshiwara. I heard just before you came in, that's why I was so relieved to see you safe." Saying that suddenly reminded Sir William of the sealed envelope André had left with him in the Legation safe, to be opened in the event of his death. "Henri identified him, as much as one could identify such a corpse. His signet ring was still on. . . . Well," he said, sickened at the thought, "poor fellow was burnt to a cinder in his *garçonière*. I understand it's only a few yards from yours in the same Teahouse. I'd say you were ext nely lucky, Phillip. Be ready at noon."

He walked out and down the street, heading for the Club. Men were streaming from all directions. Passing Struan's he glanced at the building, thankful it was safe, with Brock's—a good omen, he thought, one of them's certainly the Noble House and Brock's is a bloody sight better with Gornt than with Norbert. He noticed Angelique at her window and waved. She waved back. Poor Angelique, wonder if Henri's told her about André. Then, hearing the tumult from inside the Club even this far away, the usual shouting, cursing and clinking glasses, he sighed and put his mind to the business of the Settlement.

Silence fell as he entered. The Club was crammed, an overflow on the steps outside. A narrow path opened up for him through the packed, sweating ranks and he walked to his usual place near the bar to greet the other Ministers, Seratard, Erlicher and Zergeyev, who had part of his face bandaged from burns and his arm in a sling. Anyone of importance was present, and many who were not, many bandaged, some with broken bones but all faces flushed. Already a few drunks were laid out.

" 'Morning. I'm happy to report we've been tremendously lucky—"

Catcalls interrupted him, shouts of "Balls, I'm ruined" . . . "Wot're you talking about, for God's sake" . . . "Let him talk" . . . "He's full of wind, hasn't he seen" . . . "Oh, for God's sake, shut up . . . !"

He waited and then continued, tougher in tone: "We really have been lucky, only André Poncin's been confirmed dead—" an audible murmur of grief, for his music was greatly appreciated—"no one else of the community. Mr. Seratard identified the body and the funeral will be tomorrow. Unfortunately we lost two soldiers, their funeral's tomorrow also. In Drunk Town a few are still unaccounted for but no one we know by name. Our Army's intact, all firearms, shells, munitions intact, Navy's intact—we are very lucky indeed and I propose we should give thanks to God." In the dead silence he added, "I'm asking the padre to hold a special evensong at dusk, all are invited. Any questions so far?"

"What about our firms?" Lunkchurch said. "I'm burnt out."

"That's what we all have fire insurance for, Mr. Lunkchurch." A bellow of laughter stopped him. "What?"

Heavenly Skye, Yokohama's forwarding insurance agent to Hong Kong, where all policies were accepted, said, "Sorry to say, Sir William, Barnaby's policy lapsed last week and, to save money, he refused to renew until the first of the month." The rest of what he said was again drowned in laughter and jeers.

"I'm sorry to hear that. In any event, by tonight's packet, to the Governor of Hong Kong, I'm formally declaring the Settlement a disaster area for all . . ." Roars of agreement and 'Good Old Willie' greeted that, for such a pronouncement made sure all claims would be dealt with expeditiously. ". . . a disaster area for all *legitimate claims, all of which must be substantiated, requiring my signature to be valid and . . .*"

Another roar, this time of fury, for he was known to be punctilious, unlike certain officials in the Hong Kong Government, and the fire had automatically been considered by many to be a Heaven-sent opportunity to inflate inventories.

When there was sufficient quiet, he added sweetly, "No exceptions will be considered and the sooner claims are on my desk the sooner they'll be approved, signed and dispatched . . ." A general movement for the door began and he bellowed with a voice huge for such a thin man, "I haven't finished, by God! Next, certain ill-advised, foolish people believe the wisest course is to abandon our foothold here. Her Majesty's Government has no intention of leaving. None-what-so-ever." Arguments to the contrary began but he overrode them coldly. "Next, you are required to assist each other like British gentlemen and . . ."

"Wot about the bloody Yanks?" someone shouted to jeers and cheers for and against.

"Them too," he called back, his humor returned. "A few of them are, and many more could be." More laughter. "So act like gentlemen and rebuild as fast as possible. That's important. We must confirm our position here because, last, most seriously, there are rumors the fire was arson."

"That's right, my *musume* said it were."

"One likely report is that the arsonist was the samurai, Nakama, the fellow wanted by the Bakufu as a revolutionary, though Mr. Tyrer and I—and Mr. McFay, I believe—found him pleasant, no threat and a vast source of information."

"That's right," Jamie said, refreshed by Maureen's tenderness. "I don't believe he could be an arsonist, least that's what I think."

"Be that as it may, we know for a fact he's dead and he was caught in suspicious circumstances. Everyone must be on their toes in case it was arson—personally I'm not convinced—but if the fire was an act of violence against us there will be others, if an Act of God, well, that's His privilege . . ."

"Amen," many said, so thankful to be alive.

"So be aware of possible danger but let us act as normal and get back to work. Thank you, good day."

"What about the Yoshiwara, an' Mrs. Fortheringill's?"

Sir William blinked. Good God, I must be getting old, he thought, the problem of the Yoshiwara had not occurred to him, when it was what made Japan bearable. even desirable to most men. "Mrs. Fortheringill's will certainly be well covered by insurance. As to the first . . . We'll start a fund right now. For one week. I'll open it with twenty guineas and, well, because it's part of our disaster area, Her Majesty's Government will match, pound for pound, all contributions."

To more cheers and backslapping he chatted briefly with the other Ministers, telling them, to their surprise, the Yoshi meeting was on, that he and Seratard would deal with Yoshi, but asked would they dine with him tonight for a private meeting. On the promenade he mopped his brow. Satisfied, he started for home.

"Hey, look!" someone called out behind him. He turned, and watched in wonder, and envy, with others leaving the Club.

In the desolate area where the village had been, now the whole location swarmed with industrious men, women and children, working and cleaning up with an antlike zeal towards the same goal; to re-create that which had disappeared. Two houses, roofed and shoji-walled, were already erected, others half up. Many were carrying new lumber and shoji walls from a pile already established outside the South Gate.

Pity our fellows aren't as quick off the mark, he thought, awed, and saw, on the other side of the moat, across the repaired bridge, the Bridge to Paradise, more activity, and a temporary gateway already up, swaying in the breeze.

From here he could read the cherished, well-remembered Chinese characters on it—the English translation already scrawled there too, looking somehow quaint in calligraphy: Lust cannot wait, it must be satisfied.

* * *

That afternoon, the sea fair, sky uneasy, the Struan cutter turned for her Yokohama berth, returning from the Kanagawa-Yoshi meeting. Sir William's pennant fluttered from the masthead. Those in the cabin, Sir William, Seratard, and Tyrer, dozed—Tyrer like a dead man. The Bosun tooted his whistle to ask cutters crowding their dock to move out of the way, but there were loud shouts of "Wait your bloody turn," with a variety of profanity as punctuation.

Sir William opened his eyes, called up to the Bosun, "Drop us at the Brock wharf," and when the Bosun suggested that Mr. MacStruan wouldn't like that at all, Sir William bellowed, "Do what you're told!" The others jerked out of sleep. Except Tyrer who mumbled and drifted off again.

Seratard stretched and stifled a yawn. "Grand lunch, William, good fish," adding in French without noticing it, "I would have preferred a garlic, butter and parsley sauce. Never mind, your chef is English, so what can he do?"

"He's Chinese," Sir William said good-naturedly.

The meeting had gone exactly as he had planned. There had been none. They had arrived on time, waited half an hour, then sent for the local Governor, Tyrer saying they could not understand where Lord Yoshi had got to: 'Is he sick?'

'Ah, so sorry I don't know Lord . . .'

'My Master says, Ask after the health of Lord Yoshi, say we here as asked. As soon as well, please make new day.' Deliberately Tyrer had dropped all real pleasantries. The Governor had flushed, bowed as to superiors, apologized again and hurried off disgusted that the gai-jin were still in place—naturally every civilized person from here to Yedo had seen the fires and presumed the gai-jin, those left, would be licking their burns, boarding their ships to join the exodus and sail away.

After the Governor and his entourage had left, Sir William had suggested a leisurely lunch, guiding Seratard to their substantial cellar. 'We deserve a celebration, Henri. What would you like to drink? We were truly lucky last night—apart from André, poor chap.'

'Yes. Pity. The will of God.' Seratard frowned, still looking at labels. 'Ah! Montrachet, '51. Two bottles?'

'At least two. George is joining us. Might as well taste a Margaux—I recommend the '48, Château Pichon-Longueville—and a Château d'Yquem with the pudding.'

'Perfect, shame we have no cheese. No chance Yoshi will appear now?'

'If he does we won't see him.'

'At the Club meeting you said dinner tonight. You want to discuss something special with the others?'

'Yes.' The cellar was cool and pleasant. A few glasses stood on a sideboard beside the racks. Sir William selected a half bottle of champagne and began to open it. 'I think we must pretend the fire is not the disaster it really is and press ahead against Sanjiro, and his capital Kagoshima.'

'Now?' Seratard was very surprised. 'But surely sending the fleet when we're so exposed is highly dangerous, isn't it? Tempting them?'

'Very, but that's my point. My proposal is that we send British warships only, keeping your flagship and the Russian here, with the armed merchantmen. We cancel sending army units for the proposed landing and send only marines. Simply make it a sea bombardment.' He popped the cork and poured. 'That'll make Ketterer's mission much easier, he never liked the idea of commanding a seaborne landing. Now he can stand off in the bay and pound the devil out of them. Health.'

The two men touched glasses, Seratard churning the proposal around to find the pitfalls, any places where his adversary had planted mines to disrupt French interests. There were none. On the contrary, this helped his long-term plan to ingratiate himself into Yoshi's confidence, making him realize the British were the barbarians, not the French, and that France, which he equated with himself, could be trusted to be more patient and far seeing. 'Marvelous vintage, William. *En principe,* yes, but I'd like to consult my Admiral.'

'Why not? Then that's what we'll do . . .'

Lunch had been pleasant. In good time they were aboard and now Sir William swung nimbly on deck as the cutter tied up alongside the Brock wharf, an unheard-of happening. He saw Gornt with a clerk beside some trunks near the jetty steps. "Hope you didn't mind, Mr. Gornt," he said. "I commandeered the cutter, it's under my flag, not Struan's."

"My pleasure, Sir William. How was the meeting?"

"Damn fellow didn't turn up. Didn't expect us, I suppose."

"He's lost face from here to Timbuktu."

"Quite." Which was the whole idea, Sir William thought with a secret smile, and pointed to the trunks. "You're not leaving, surely?"

"No, suh, but I am going to Hong Kong by tonight's packet to arrange building supplies for ourselves and others."

"Good idea. Have a safe journey and safe return." He raised his hat and walked off with Seratard. Tyrer, sick with tiredness, reeled after them, hardly acknowledging Gornt.

"Put these aboard, Periera," Gornt said. "Tell the Captain I'll be aboard in good time. Oh, hello, Doc." Hoag hurried up with some coolies bowed under a sea trunk and bags.

"I say, Edward, heard you're on the *Atlanta Belle* too." Hoag was out of breath and harassed, his clothes and hands bloodstained and filthy, eyes red-rimmed. "Could I prevail on your people to put these aboard for me, I've still a dozen or so arms and legs to set and burns . . . thanks awfully." He rushed off, not waiting for an answer.

"Put 'em aboard, Periera." Gornt frowned. Why is Hoag in such a hurry to leave? he asked himself.

Everything packed that should be, everything done to ensure Brock's would operate correctly while he was away: which traders to give credit to, which to deny; tomorrow or the next day Choshu representatives were due to discuss arms shipments—a nice business to acquire for himself when the Brocks went under and, as also planned, he acquired the premises and staff here at . . . well, fire sale prices. He laughed to himself at the joke. Next, the Yoshi coal concession that he had heard might be transferred from Struan's to Seratard through the late André Poncin's trading company, might still be available to offers. He had instructed his shroff to make such an offer secretly.

Periera was left in charge. Last night, hearing from Maureen that Jamie's new offices were gone, he had planned to appoint Jamie, but to his surprise this afternoon Jamie had thanked him and refused, saying he thought he would be able to restart his own business.

Jamie would be more icing on the icing, he thought. Doesn't matter, Jamie'll take over for me when this is all Rothwell-Gornt's. He felt in his pocket.

Norbert's chop was there and the two backdated letters for Tess. His money belt was heavy with more than enough Brock silver Mex and gold for expenses. Good. All done.

Now for Angelique.

"Hello, Edward," she said, her smile warm. This was the first time she had received him in her upstairs boudoir. Ah Soh stood by a wine cooler and he noticed the door to the bedroom was closed, curtains were drawn though the light had not yet completely gone, oil lamps lit, the room feminine, inviting, her manner demure, odd. His tension increased.

"White wine for a change," she said pleasantly. "La Doucette. Bourbon if you wish."

"Wine, please, Ma'am. I've never seen you look better."

"Nor you, my friend. Please sit here, by the fire." Her afternoon, blue-black mourning dress was new, the cut enhancing, the neckline square-cut and modest. But for his pleasure, and hers, she had draped a multicolored silk shawl around her shoulders, the effect startling, a breath of spring on this January day. "Ah Soh, wine," she said, and when they had the glasses, "Wait outside! I want, I call!" The maid shuffled out and carelessly banged the door closed.

Gornt said softly, "She'll have her ear hard against it."

Angelique laughed. "To hear secrets? What secrets could there be between us? To a safe journey, Edward!" She sipped and put her glass down. "You're all packed?"

"Yes, yes, I am. You look wonderful and I love you and would like an answer to my question."

Her fan slid open and she began using it as it should be used by a young lady of quality with an eligible man of quality—and ones of dubious reputation—to tantalize, flirt, to promise but not promise, to give answers, or avoid them, to questions that were dangerous to acknowledge openly.

The fan fluttered. "I admire you greatly, Edward."

"No more than I admire you. But a yes or a no?"

The fan snapped shut. Then she smiled and opened a box on the bureau, handed him an envelope. It was addressed: Mrs. Tess Struan. "Please read the letter. I am sending it by Hoag to Hong Kong in answer to hers."

Her handwriting was neat:

Dear Mrs. Struan, thank you for your letter, and generosity.
*   I agree to everything you requested: I solemnly swear and agree freely to relinquish all and any claims to your son's estate, I agree never again to use the title Mrs. Struan, I agree I am Catholic and was never married according to my Church, I agree never to set foot in Hong Kong except for transshipping, nor will ever try to contact you and any of your family, I agree to remove myself from these premises within the week, and accept, with sincere thanks, the offer of a trust of Two Thousand Guineas a year until I am dead.*

The space for her signature was blank and then below it: *Verified as a true signature by Sir William Aylesbury, Minister Japan,* and another space for his signature and date.

Gornt looked up. "You can't mean this. This gives her everything."

"Didn't you advise me to accept her conditions?"

"Yes, but to compromise—to renegotiate."

"Ah, yes, I remembered that. If you agree I'll ask Sir William to witness it now, before you leave. Dr. Hoag has promised to take it tonight on your ship, so it will be there when you arrive."

"But surely you know this yields everything—how can I, or anyone, negotiate for a second?"

"There's a second page." She took it out of the box, her fan slid open and began to move. Gently.

Again he concentrated. The writing was not so clear and here and there smudged—could those be tear stains, he asked himself?

Dear Mrs. Struan, for obvious reasons this part must be separate as it is just between us, and no concern of Sir William. Again I thank you for your generosity. The kind offer of a third thousand if I remarry, or marry as you would say, within a year, I cannot accept because I do not intend to remarry or marry, whichever you consider correct . . .

Again he looked up at her startled. "Is this my answer?"

The fan fluttered. "Finish it," she said.

Now his eyes flashed down the page:

Before God, I cannot avoid the belief I was married, though freely relinquish any public and legal pretension to that state as above. I will not take another. . . . I do not wish to hurt or offend you but to marry again . . . no. It is my intention as soon as possible to settle in London. I feel more English than French, my mother tongue English rather than French, my aunt was my real mother.

I will never use the Mrs. title, as I have agreed, but I cannot stop others here referring to me as such. Sir William will not accept Angelique, or Angelique Richaud, but insists that I sign as Mrs. Angelique Struan, née Richaud, to make the above binding, for, according to him, and his understanding of English law, that is presently my legal name until I remarry.

"Has he said that?" he asked sharply.

"No, but Mr. Skye says, if asked, he would have to agree."

"Ah." Gornt nodded thoughtfully, gulped some wine and went on reading, slower and more carefully:

Should any of the above be unsatisfactory, please draw up what you further require, give it to Mr. Gornt, who tells me he is going to see you again then return here almost immediately, and I will sign it. I commend him to you, he was a very good friend to your son, and has been kind to me—he advised me to accept your kind conditions, as Mr. Skye was against. Sincerely yours . . . Angelique.

Gornt sat back, exhaled and stared at her, awed. "It's marvelous. Marvelous. You agree to everything but still hold the sword of Damocles over her."

The fan stopped. "How so?"

"You plan to live in London, therefore under English law, a latent, obvious threat. Never once do you use 'husband,' but that threat is there, you put me squarely on center stage as friend to both sides and in a perfect negotiating position. And however devious she is, whatever she draws up for you to sign, you can shed more tears and sigh 'Duress,' and would win. Twenty-four-karat marvelous!"

"Then I should ask Sir William to witness my signature?"

"Yes," he said, enthralled by her, so clever and daring, and dangerous. Perhaps too dangerous. "This is checkmate."

"How so?"

"Tess is safe in only one way: if you remarry, and you've blocked that." Though the fan stopped, her eyes watched him over the edge. Then the movement began again and he handed her back the letter, thinking, Devilishly clever—for you, but not for me. "Skye advised you brilliantly."

"No one advised me, except you—something you said guided me."

His heart skipped. "No one else has seen this?"

"No. And no one else will. It can be a secret between us."

He heard the 'can be' and wondered where that led, despondent now but hiding it. The fire in the grate needed attention so he got up and used the poker to give himself time to think. The air was still strong with the smell of smoke and burning but he did not register it, only her.

How in the hell did she figure that all out? It's totally brilliant, all the pieces are on the board, for both of us. She's won, she'll beat Tess, but I've lost. I'll still have to negotiate for her, and now I'm surer than hell I can up her stipend, but Angelique's conceded nothing and left her game plan open. I've lost. I don't share in the big prize: Her. "So the answer to my question is No, must be No?"

Only the fan moved. "Why?" she asked, without emotion.

"Because the moment you do, you lose the game, you lose all power over Tess Struan."

"Yes, *I would*." She closed the fan quietly and let it rest in her lap. Her eyes never left his, nor their intensity.

For a moment he felt hypnotized, then his mind flared into action, and sudden hope spread through him. "*I would*, you said, meaning *you would*. But I wouldn't? I wouldn't lose power?"

Now she smiled. It was an answer.

The Mona Lisa again, he thought. Strange how her face changes, how I think it changes, how really devious she is, and how vigilant I'm going to have to be to tame this filly. I still don't understand but a faint heart never won a fair lady. It took all of his will to keep his feet planted where they were. "I love you for all the usual reasons, and I love your cleverness. Now, formally, please, will you marry me?"

"Yes," she said.

59

"HALLELUJAH!" GORNT SAID, light-headed, but did not move from the fireplace.

The fan stopped. "Hallelujah? Is that all?" she murmured, heart picking up tempo.

"Oh, no, but first tell me what are your conditions."

She laughed. "Should there be conditions?"

"I'm beginning to know the way your mind works—some of the time."

"When will you board *Atlanta Belle*?"

"At the last moment. There's much to . . . to talk about."

"Yes. Edward, would our children be brought up Catholic, and would we be married in a Catholic church?"

"Is that a condition?"

"A question."

He frowned, letting his mind race ahead and all around, wanting to be cautious in this rock-infested sea. "I don't see why not. I'm not Catholic, as you know," he said slowly, "but if that's what you want it would be all right—" The final piece of the jigsaw blinded him with its power. "Hallelujah!"

"What?"

"Just an idea. We'll talk about in a minute. Now, no more games, Angelique," he said, chiding her. "Conditions? What's in that magic mind of yours?"

She got up. On tiptoe she touched her lips to his in a gentle kiss. Her lips were soft and breath sweet. "Thank you for asking me, and for what you've already done for me."

He rested his hands on her hips. Both noticed that their bodies seemed to fit though neither acknowledged it.

"The conditions?"

"Tell me what they are, Edward."

Now that she had answered the main question, and had given him the keys, he was in no hurry. "I'll guess three," he said, amused. "If I'm right, you'll tell me the rest?"

"Agreed." His body, hard against hers, was pleasing to her. And so was her soft curving against him, diverting his concentration. Effortlessly. Careful, it's her major trump card and this game's now in its most dangerous stage—to settle the future. Goddam! Easy enough to make the kiss more serious, too easy, and easy then to whisk her off her feet to the bed in the next room and lose—whatever the result—even before you reach the door.

It was more exciting for him to hold back, to wait for the perfect moment—as with Morgan Brock—to accept the fact of his lust and put it aside and try to inject his mind into hers instead. Three conditions? I know at least five, he thought, wanting to win, needing to win as in everything.

"Not necessarily in this order," he said. "One is that I successfully renegotiate upwards, say at least to four thousand a year. Another that we spend time in Paris and London, say a month every two years—with travelling time, that'll be about a six months' trip. Next, that Tess's trust money, whatever it is, stays under your control, not mine." He saw her eyes dancing and knew he had won. "And another for good measure, that I must love you madly forever."

"You're so clever, Edward, I know we will be very happy." The strange smile returned. "Now, five would be better than four, and two months better than one."

"I'll try for five though I can't promise," he said at once, "and agree to two months in Paris, all other things being equal. What else?"

"Nothing important. We will need a house in Paris, but once you know it you will love it too. Nothing else, except you promise to cherish me."

"No need to ask that, but I promise." His arms tightened around her. She rested against him, fitting, feeling protected, though still not sure of him. "You're more desirable than any woman I've ever known," he said. "That's bad enough, but your mind is stunning too, and your scheming—no, that's a bad word—your flights of brilliance . . ." For a moment he held her away from him, looking at her deeply. "You're a stunner, whichever way."

She smiled and did not move out of his arms. "How so?"

"A Catholic marriage."

"Ah!"

"Yes, ah!" He laughed. "That, my clever young lady, is your dream solution because, together with your letter, it suddenly occurred to me what you'd already decided: a Catholic marriage removes you as a threat from Tess forever. For Tess, a Catholic marriage completely negates the Protestant, seaborne marriage, however lawful, before English law however lawful."

She chuckled, nestling against him. "If you were to say you thought you could persuade me to marry you, and then, you as a Protestant, were to offer to make such a deliberate sacrifice, surely that woman would be pleased to give you what you want, for both of us, if the requests are reasonable. No?"

"Yes." He sighed. "What request had you in mind?"

"Nothing much, but Malcolm explained to me once the importance of the Jockey Club, both in Hong Kong and Shanghai, how, together with the Shanghai and Hong Kong Councils, all business power is centered there. Her influence would get you a Stewardship of one and a seat on the other. No?"

He laughed and hugged her. "You're classic, Ma'am. For that I'd even become Catholic."

"No need for that, Edward."

"You're going to love Shanghai. Now I have conditions."

"Oh?"

He was glad to see a flash of concern behind her eyes, and hid his pleasure and made his face sterner. No need for me to make prior conditions, he thought amused: a husband has inalienable rights, like possessing all a wife's worldly goods. Thank God for this man's world. "First condition is that you love me with all your heart and soul."

"Oh, I will try, and try to be the best wife ever." Her arms tightened. "And?"

He heard the edge of underlying concern and laughed. "That's all, except you promise to let me teach you bridge, and mahjongg—then you'll never need pin money from me or anyone."

She stared at him a moment, then reached up. Their kiss sealed their bargain and then he eased off, too heated. "I can hardly wait, Angelique."

"Nor I."

"Now we must plan, there's not much time. First, get Sir William's signature, quick as a wink. My darling, I'm so happy you've accepted me."

She felt like purring. "I'm more happy than I can say. When you get back, do we stay here or leave for Shanghai?"

"Shanghai, as soon as possible—soon as the Brocks go under." He kissed her nose.

"Ah the Brocks. You're sure? You're sure about them? Our whole future, everything depends on that, doesn't it?"

"And Tess, but yes, my evidence is enough, and her venom will cement their ruin—she must realize it too or she'd never have made even this paltry offer. Even so, we must be careful, what we're like in private, that's different, but for six months—it'll take me that long to get you to Shanghai, your reputation blemishless, Rothwell-Gornt into place, your finances settled—we must act like good friends only. I adore you."

For answer her arms tightened again. Then she said, "Is it your custom to make a marriage contract?"

"No. But if you wish it, we will." He saw the smile that masked and promised and masked. "It's not necessary, is it? We're interlinked, our future's joined, we're one entity even now. Success depends on our joint performance, and on me for us. Never forget Tess is adroit, cunning and won't be cheated—a deal is a deal with her. Even so, I promise you'll get what you want."

Yes, I will, she thought.

In shock, Sir William put the last of André's pages onto the side table, all of them in French and in André's handwriting. "My God," he muttered, and shifted in his frayed, comfortable old chair. His anteroom was pleasant, a fire burning merrily, his curtains drawn against the drafts.

He got up, feeling very old, poured a drink, stared at the file of papers in disbelief, then again sat and leafed through them. The final part of Angelique's father's letter, carefully pasted together, clearly suggested a calculated scheme to snare Malcolm Struan, other pages set out dates and details of the ronin assassin's rape at Kanagawa and curious death at the French Legation, the name of the mama-san who supplied the medicine, how the 'lost earrings' paid for it, and how André had rowed out to sea to dispose of the evidence—some towels, the herbs, and one of the two bottles, the other left as proof, now waiting in his Legation desk drawer.

His covering letter had said,

Sir William, by the time you read this I am already dead. This evidence is to be used if I meet a violent end. I openly confess I used my knowledge to extract money from Angelique, yes, blackmail if you wish to put a word to it, but then blackmail is a diplomatic tool which you've used, as we all have. This information is given you as I may have been murdered, or my death made to look accidental, not necessarily by her but because of her, assisted by her—another truth is that quite a few would commit murder for her (Babcott, McFay, Gornt)—because of my unique knowledge and participation in her . . . 'crimes' is too strong a word . . . her manipulations makes me a target.

These pages give you evidence to catch the murderer and lay the blame where it eventually will lead. I bear Angelique no ill will, I used her as I needed though never bedded her. If my death appears accidental it may not be. If it is, so be it, I've made my Confession (though told none of the above to Father Leo) and go before you into the great adventure—as unclean as most, much more than most, God help me.

Why have I given you this, and not Henri? Why indeed?

It was boldly signed.

"Why me indeed?" Sir William muttered. "And how is it possible that that slip of a girl could hide all this for so long, hide it from Malcolm Struan, for God's sake? From George and Hoag, for God's sake? Impossible, surely impossible, André must have taken leave of his senses and yet . . ."

Apart from her father's letter—and even that, taken out of context, could be an exaggeration of the truth—the rest is just André's opinion, unless she's challenged and confesses. These stories could be fabrications of a demented mind. Of course he wanted her too, how many times have we all noticed him letching after her and there was that curious happening when Vervene found him in her room. And bloody curious he used 'unclean' like that, when he really was, poor fellow.

He shuddered. Seratard had whispered André's secret to him. Syphilis was endemic in all strata of society, in all cities, towns and villages, in St. Petersburg, London, Paris, in palaces as well as the vilest areas of the Casbah, it could lurk in any whorehouse or with any Lady of the Night, in China or in our Floating World here.

Ah, André, why give all this to me? Curious you died as you did, hand in hand with the girl you bought to destroy. How evil! Except she had a choice, so we are led to believe. Your death was an accident. Was it? Henri's not sure.

'It's all very curious, William,' Henri had said this morning. 'The bodies, skeletons would be more accurate, lay as though they were dead before the fire arrived, no sign of trying to escape by either of them. Just side by side, hands together. I'm bewildered, for all his faults André was a survivor, and in a fire it's instinct to try to escape, you don't just lie there, you can't, not possible.'

'Then what's the answer?'

'I don't know. It could have been a suicide pact that was concluded before the fire. Poison, nothing else would fit. It's true he was morbid recently to the point of insanity, and needed money desperately to pay for her. Apart from that, André a suicide? Do you believe that?'

No, not André, Sir William thought, disquieted. Was he poisoned, or both of them? Now, there's a motive for murder. Good God Almighty, is that possible? Yes, it is, but who?

Wearily, greatly troubled, he closed his eyes. The more he tried to answer that question the more distracted he became. The door opened silently. His Number One Boy padded in, began to greet him but seeing the paleness and age on his Master's face, frowned, presumed him to be sleeping, so poured a whisky and put it quietly beside him on the table. His eyes flicked over André's letters, which were atop the file, then, as silently, he went out.

A few minutes later there was a knock. Sir William awoke with a start as Babcott popped his head in. "Got a minute?"

"Oh, hello, George, of course." Sir William put the letters into a folder, grimly aware of the attraction they seemed to radiate. "Take a seat. Like a drink? What's up?"

"Nothing." Babcott was more tired than ever before. "Won't stay, just wanted to say I'm going to get a few hours' sleep. The count so far is three fellows from Drunk Town, one an Australian barkeeper and two vagrants, no papers—there may be other bodies in the wreckage but who knows when the cleanup will be finished. No one seems very concerned."

"What about the village and Yoshiwara?"

"We'll never get a count." Babcott yawned. "They seem to consider those sorts of statistics national secrets. Can't blame them, we're the outsiders. Not many casualties, I'd imagine. Same on our Yoshiwara, thank God—you heard that each Inn had an emergency cellar?"

"Damn clever. We'd better institute the same idea."

"Pity about André . . ." Babcott said, and at once another twinge went through Sir William. "We were terribly lucky more of our people didn't get caught—how Phillip got out with his life I just don't know. William, he's badly shaken up by the loss of his girl, why not give him a couple of weeks leave, let him go to Hong Kong or Shanghai?"

"Work's his best therapy, and I need him here."

"Maybe you're right." Another yawn. "God, I'm tired. You know Hoag's on the packet tonight?"

"He told me earlier, least he said he'd asked you and you didn't need him. I suppose Tess ordered him to report as soon as he knew—if she wasn't bearing."

"Yes. Part's personal, William, he's suddenly frantic to go back to India, thinks his happiness lies there. Hope he does, he's a grand doctor but talks too much." A frown and a stifled yawn. "Did he tell you what was in Tess's letter?"

"To Angelique? No. He said she didn't show it to him. Difficult to call that one, in more ways than you can shake a stick at," Sir William said, watching him closely. "Heavenly was here earlier, he said nothing about it either, only that she wanted me to witness her signature to a letter she was sending Tess."

Some of Babcott's tiredness went away. "I'd certainly like to know what's in it."

"I'll only be party to witnessing it. Rightly I don't need to know the contents."

Babcott sighed, yawned again. "I feel so terribly sorry for her, wish I could help, I'd do anything . . . such a nice girl and so unfair. For her and Malcolm. Well, I'm off. Glad she's not leaving us yet, she'll make someone a spectacular wife. See you in a few hours."

"Have a good sleep, and thanks for all the good work. By the way," Sir William said, not wanting him to leave, but afraid if he stayed he would be tempted to share André's evidence, to ask his advice. "When do you see Anjo again?"

"In a week or two, when the laudanum's used up—without that he'll be a most unhappy man."

"No hope for him?"

"No. He won't last but a few months, the tests are fairly accurate—his insides are in a mess. Yoshi's our man." Another aching yawn. "Do you think Anjo, or Yoshi, or both, ordered the arson?"

"Either or neither or both, we'll never know." He watched Babcott limp for the door. "George, medically, if a woman was sedated, could a fellow take her and she'd not know about it?"

Babcott blinked and turned back, fatigue fled. "What on earth made you ask that?"

"Just a sudden thought, you mentioned laudanum. A couple of days ago Zergeyev had some wild theories about drugs, the good and the bad of them. Could that happen?"

After a pause, Babcott nodded, not believing that excuse. He knew how subtle Willie's mind was, and wondered the why of the question but was too smart to ask again. "If the dose was strong and the man not savage, yes, no problem." He waited but Sir William only nodded thoughtfully, so he waved a hand and left.

Once more Sir William opened the file.

His fingers trembled as he reread André's covering letter. It's clear enough. The drug in Kanagawa started the chain of events, George's drug. If she'd awakened, the man would have killed her, no doubt about that. So she was saved but destroyed. But why didn't the man kill her anyway, why leave her alive? Doesn't make sense, any of it. And what happened in the French Legation that other night when he returned? If it hadn't been for George . . .

And what about George? If he could give her such a drug to help her sleep, to guard her sanity, surely he could easily do the same to André to remove a blackmailer from the woman he clearly loves. An overdose of the same drug . . .

George Babcott? Good God, I must be losing my wits. Impossible for him to do that!

Is it?

And Angelique, impossible for her to have done all that!

Is it?

What the hell do I do?

60

"EXCUSE ME, SIR," BERTRAM SAID. "Miss Angelique's here."

"Show them in. Then you can leave. Dinner's at nine. Make sure the *Belle* doesn't leave without my dispatches."

"Yes, sir. It's just her, Mr. Skye's not with her."

Sir William eased out of his old chair, tired and feeling bad, André's file facedown on his desk.

She came in, physically as magnetic as always, but different, her face set, and with an undercurrent he could not read. Topcoat, bonnet and gloves. Black suits her, he thought, sets off her fair skin, so pretty and young, younger than Vertinskya. Curious, has she been crying? "Good evening, how are you, Angelique?"

"Oh, all right, thank you," she said, her voice flat and unlike her usual, poised self. "Mr. Skye told you I needed you to verify my signature tonight?"

"Yes." He went to his desk, his concentration damaged by the pictures André had painted so vividly. "I . . . please sit down." She obeyed and as he looked at her another shadow went past her lovely eyes. "What's the matter?" he asked kindly.

"Nothing. I . . . this afternoon I heard about André, that he'd—he'd been killed. I would have come earlier but I . . ." With a visible effort she brushed that aside, took the envelope from her purse and laid the paper on the table. "How should I sign it, please?"

He steepled his fingers, unsettled that again, so soon, André's spectre had invaded the room—not at his whim. "I'm not really sure. I understand from Skye you have agreed with Mrs. Tess Struan, amongst other conditions, to renounce your 'Mrs.' title?"

1205

"Please, you may read the letter if you wish," she said dully.

"Thank you, but that's not necessary," he said, resisting his overwhelming impulse to read the short document. "What you agree with her is not my business, unless you need my advice?"

Numb, she shook her head.

"Well, then . . . Skye has a legal theory—I'm not certain if he's correct but I see no reason against it. You are renouncing the 'Mrs.' title for all time. But as he so rightly pointed out, only *after* you've signed so you'd best sign it, Mrs. Angelique Struan, née Angelique Richaud, and that should cover all possibilities."

He watched her concentrate, his mind filled with the appalling story André had related from a fiery grave—not possible for her to hide so much from us, not bloody possible.

"There," she said. "Now it's done."

"I feel obliged to ask: you're sure you're doing the right thing—no one's forcing you in any way to sign this document, whatever it contains?"

"I sign freely. She—she offered a settlement, Sir William. The truth is . . . the truth is, it is fair. Some of the clauses are badly put, and could be improved, perhaps will be, but Malcolm was her son, she has a right to be distraught." She got up, put the letter into the envelope and into her bag, wanting to leave quickly, wanting to stay. "Thank you."

"Don't go for a moment. Would you, perhaps you'd care to dine tomorrow, just a few of the fellows? I was thinking of asking Jamie and Miss Maureen."

"Well, yes, thank you, I think so, but I . . . They're nice, and she's sweet. Will they get married, do you think?"

"If he doesn't, more the fool him—she'll be snapped up if he doesn't." Before he could stop himself he said, "Sad about André, wasn't it? Did Henri tell you how they found him?" Abruptly he saw her eyes fill and her control disappear. "Sorry, I didn't mean to upset you."

"You didn't, I'm already so upset I . . . I still can't . . . Henri told me an hour or so ago, how André and she together . . . the Will of God for them, so sad and yet so wonderful."

She sat down, brushing at her tears, remembering how she had almost fainted and after Henri had gone she had rushed to the church and knelt before the statue of the Blessed Virgin—the church oddly changed, lofty without its roof, but the candles alight as always, the Peace there as always. And she had given thanks, desperate thanks for releasing her from servitude—and with a sudden, heartfelt understanding, for releasing him from torment too, André as much as her. 'I understand that now. Oh, Blessed Mother, thank you for blessing us, for blessing me and blessing him, he's with her and at peace when he knew no peace on earth but now they're safe in Thine arms, Thy Will be done . . .'

Her eyes could hardly make out Sir William through her sorrow and gratitude. "Henri told me about André's disease. Poor man, how terrible, and terrible to be so much in love, he was, you know, utterly. André was kind to me and . . . and to be truthful," she said, needing to say the truth aloud, "he was awful too but a friend. He was just madly in love with his Hinodeh, nothing else in the world mattered, so he should be excused. Did you ever see her?"

"No, no, never did, didn't even know her name." In spite of a resolve to leave well enough alone he said, "Why was he awful?"

She used a handkerchief to dry her tears, her voice sad and without anger. "André knew about my father and my uncle and . . . and used it and other things to . . . to put me in his debt and kept asking me for money which I didn't have, making wild promises and, to be honest, threats." Searchingly she looked at him, no guile in her now, open and so thankful to God and the Blessed Virgin for releasing her and him, the past consumed with him, and all the filth. "It was the Will of God," she said fervently. "I'm glad and sorry. Why can't we forget the bad and only remember the good—there's enough bad in this world to make up for our forgetting, don't you think?"

"Yes, there is," he said with untoward compassion, his eyes straying to Vertinskya's miniature. "Oh, yes."

This rare show of emotion in him triggered something in her and before she knew it she was telling her innermost fear: "You're wise and I have to tell someone, I feel cleansed like never before but it's my Malcolm that worries me, it's just that I've nothing left of him, no name, no daguerreotype—it never came out—no portrait, and I can't seem to find his features. Every day it seems a little worse.

"I'm frightened," she said, tears flooding silently, sitting there in front of him, him powerless to move. "It's almost as though he's never been and this whole journey and time in Yokohama is like a . . . a *Théâtre Macabre*. I'm married but not, accused of awful things that never happened or were never meant or never intended, innocent but not, I'm hated by Tess when I only wanted to do the best I could for my Malcolm—oh yes, I knew he was vastly eligible and my father not, and me not, I suppose not, but I didn't do anything to hurt him—he loved me and wanted to marry me and I tried my best, I swear I did, and now that he's dead I'm trying so hard to be sensible, I'm alone and he's gone and I have to think of the future. I'm frightened, I was a child when I arrived, now I'm different, it's all too fast, and the worst is I can't remember his face, it's slipping away and there's nothing. . . . Poor Malcolm."

61

In the twilight, on the edge of No Man's Land and in the lee of a half-completed village house, a shadow moved. Then another. Two men were lurking in hiding, waiting. Somewhere amid the temporary village of lean-tos and shelters and partially built huts, and subdued chattering, a child began to cry, to be quickly hushed.

Where once No Man's Land had been a series of hills and valleys of garbage and castaway junk, most had been consumed, the rest settled deeper into the earth, and over all, a thick mat of ash and threads of smoke. Only the brick well head was prominent. The first shadow became Phillip Tyrer and he rushed for the well head, keeping low, and ducked down beside it.

Cautiously he examined the surroundings. As far as he could tell he had not been seen. Across the way, Drunk Town was just smoking rubble and twisted remains, a few isolated fires still smoldering, temporary lean-tos, tarpaulin or canvas shelters. A few men about, quarrelsome, most of them hunched against the cold on upturned kegs, drinking looted beer and spirits.

Phillip carefully leaned over the edge of the well and whistled. From below there was an answering whistle. He ducked down again, stifled a nervous yawn. In a moment a hand reached the top bricks. Hiraga's head appeared. Phillip beckoned him. Silently Hiraga squatted beside him, then Akimoto. Both wore padded jackets and kimonos over loose pants and carried their swords camouflaged with spare clothing. Warily they ducked down as three men on the Drunk Town side began crossing near where the alley had been and went down it, picking their way over the remains of the godown. One was singing a sea chanty.

Long after they had disappeared his rolling baritone came up on the wind.

"Follow, but be careful!" Tyrer ran back to the village shadows and stopped beside the other man in the lee of the half-finished dwelling. Jamie McFay. When it was safe, Hiraga and Akimoto joined them, moving much more lithely, silently.

Jamie McFay said, "Here, quick." He opened the sack and handed them rough seaman's clothes and woolen balaclavas and shoes. They stripped and dressed and put their own clothes into the sack which Akimoto slung on his back. Tyrer saw Hiraga slip a derringer into a side pocket.

It had taken barely a minute or two. Jamie led the way along where the village main street had once been—and would soon be again. They could feel eyes everywhere. Above them the moon came out of the cloud briefly. Automatically Hiraga and Akimoto froze into shadows, both men ready to go for their weapons, mentally cursing the inept carelessness of the other two. The moon vanished, and they went on.

The shoya's dwelling was three-quarters rebuilt, the shop front empty but the living quarters behind were temporarily finished and livable. Jamie eased through a pile of beams and shojis and knocked on a makeshift door. It opened and he went in. The others followed into darkness. The door closed.

In a moment a match struck and the wick of the candle caught. The shoya was alone, grey with fatigue and a fear he tried hard to hide. On the low table were flasks of saké, and a little food. Hiraga and Akimoto wolfed the food and emptied two of the flasks in seconds. "Thank you, shoya," Hiraga said. "I will not forget you."

"Here, Otami-sama." The shoya gave him a small bag containing coins. "Here are a hundred gold oban and twenty Mex."

A brush was on the table, the ink tablet prepared beside the paper. Hiraga signed the receipt. "What about my cousin?"

"So sorry, this was all I could get so quickly," the shoya said, with a sidelong glance at Jamie the others missed.

"Never mind." Hiraga did not believe him but then Akimoto had no credit, nor anyone to repay the loan as he did. "Thank you. And please see my guarantor gets this safely." He gave him a small scroll. It was a painstakingly coded farewell note to his mother and father, telling them his plan, and giving them news about Sumomo. For safety it contained no real names. In English he said, "Taira-sama, ready. Here finish."

"Ready, Jamie?" Tyrer asked, feeling peculiar, nauseous, not knowing if it was caused by excitement or fright, tiredness or despair. Since the fire, every few minutes Fujiko's face would well up from his subconscious, screaming and in flames. "Best hurry, Otami-sama," he said to Hiraga. Both had agreed never to use Hiraga or Nakama again. "Pull your cap more over your face. *Domo, shoya, mataneh.*" Thank you, shoya, good night.

He went out on to the street again. When it was safe he signalled the others. "You lead, Jamie," he whispered. In sudden panic they slid into the shadows as a Grenadier patrol approached and passed by. Breathing once more, Tyrer muttered, "They're on the watch for looters, thieves, *wakarimasu ka*?"

"*Wakarimasu.*"

Once more Jamie hurried ahead, turned and twisted through the rubble towards the jetty on the other side of the promenade, near the site where the *Guardian* building had stood. Many men were wandering about, gawking at the damage to the village and Yoshiwara and Drunk Town, or just numb, too early to sleep yet. Recognizing some of them, he slowed his pace, not wanting to attract attention. Dmitri was amongst them, heading homewards, and he smiled wryly. This morning Dmitri, beaming, had sought him out to say he had found Nemi in the early hours and that she was all right, just a few bruises and hardly touched.

'Thank God for that, Dmitri.'

'The first thing she said was, Jami-san okay? I said yes and she gave me a hug for you. Then I gave her your message, that you'd find her as soon as possible.'

'Thanks, that's a load off my mind. I was afraid she was a goner. Eventually I found her Inn but it was a heap of ash, our house included. Never did find anyone . . . Thank God.'

'You remember what I—'

'I remember, but first I've got to talk to her. She's not a piece of furniture, for God's sake.'

'Hey, easy, old buddy, perish the thought, didn't mean to imply anything . . .'

Jamie sighed, picking his way through the wreckage of a saké still, now not far from the promenade. Dmitri's a good enough fellow, he thought, but Nemi was special and . . .

"Oh, my God, look!" He pointed. A group of weary samurai fire fighters were squatting around a bonfire beside the jetty, brewing tea. Quickly he weighed the alternatives. There were none. "Can't help it, come on."

As they reached the promenade Lunkchurch reeled out of the darkness. "Jamie," he said dully, "wot you going to do? You're wiped out like me . . ." He glanced at Phillip, hardly noticing the other two. They looked like ordinary Asian seamen of a type abundant in the merchant fleet. "It's a bastard . . ."

"Maybe it won't be so bad, Barnaby, I've a few ideas, I'll find you tomorrow."

Jamie brushed past and walked for the jetty, raised his hat politely to the fire fighters and their officer who absently acknowledged them. The rickety jetty pilings and its wooden walkway went fifty metres into the sea. His heart sank. No waiting cutter, and none approaching from the Struan jetty, to the north. Out in the bay *Atlanta Belle* was alight, swarming with rowboats arriving and leaving.

Earlier this afternoon Jamie had asked MacStruan if he could borrow the cutter for a quick trip this evening to see the captain of the *Belle*, Johnny Twomast, an old friend. Phillip, after leaving Sir William who had confirmed Hiraga's supposed death, had rushed over to see him. Stumbling over his words with excitement, Phillip told him, to his delight, that Hiraga was alive, hidden in a Drunk Town well, how the man had saved his life last night, laying out his scheme to save him. 'We just sneak him aboard the *Belle* and no one's the wiser.'

'He's alive? I'd heard about him dying in the fire—he's alive?'

'Yes. All we have to do is sneak him aboard.'

'I'll ask Johnny Twomast to hide them but only if you get Willie's approval. Hiraga is still a mur—'

'Hiraga's dead—Nakama, Hiraga, it's all the same, officially. Willie said it, the Sergeant confirmed his death in the fire. Nakama's dead and gone forever, so's Hiraga. Getting him out on a ship is the perfect solution and he's worth saving! We're only helping two samurai students to see the world, our world, for a year or so, one of them called Otami.'

'If we get caught, Willie will spit blood, our blood.'

'There's no reason we should. Otami is Otami, it's his real name and he's told me about you and the shoya cooking up all sorts of business deals, you'll be the winner when he comes back, we all will. We've got to help him!'

Finally Jamie had agreed and had seen the shoya to arrange the loan that he had also guaranteed. By then it was sunset. At sunset Tyrer had gone to the well to prepare Hiraga and Akimoto and now they waited on the jetty.

"Where's the cutter, Jamie?" Tyrer said nervously.

"It'll arrive." Feeling highly exposed, the four men waited at the end of the jetty near the wobbly, seaweed-slicked steps, all too aware of the nearby samurai, their captain idly swaggering up and down.

Hiraga whispered, "Taira-sama, that captain, remember? He Enforcer. Remember him, captain at gate?"

"What gate?"

"In Yedo. At your Big House in Yedo. When first meet."

"Oh, my God!" Now it poured back—the tough samurai who had insisted on searching the Legation when they had been surrounded and locked in before the evacuation, Hiraga escaping on a stretcher disguised as a smallpox sufferer.

"What's up now?" Jamie said. Tyrer told him. Over Tyrer's shoulder he could see the officer glance at them. His anxiety increased. "He's too bloody curious."

"I recognize him now," Tyrer was saying. "We'd better . . . Look, there she is!" The cutter was chugging out of the dark, her riding lights on but dim. The Bosun waved, they waved back. Waves against the pilings threw shards of spray at them.

"Get aboard, quick as you can," Jamie said, his excitement increasing. Phillip had convinced him Hiraga was not an assassin but a fighter for freedom, and, for himself, he already had seen how useful Hiraga had been. Now he was even more sure how valuable an English-speaking shishi and friend would be in the future, particularly one who had been guided and helped by him—he had prepared a dossier of people to meet in England and Scotland, where to go, what to see that he was going to explain before the ship sailed.

Phillip's a genius, he chortled, glanced back at him and drew in breath sharply. Behind Tyrer he saw the Japanese officer strolling towards their jetty. "My God, the bugger's coming for us!" They gaped at the man, took a quick look at the cutter. No way could she arrive before he did. "We're done for."

Hiraga had already decided the same. He tore at the kimonos covering their swords. "Akimoto, we kill him."

"Wait! Here!" Urgently Tyrer handed Hiraga a large envelope that contained letters of introduction to his father and uncle, also a solicitor, and to the dean of his university. "I was going to explain them on the cutter," he said hurriedly. "No time now—Jamie, you do it for me." He looked at Hiraga deeply a last time and stuck out his hand. "Thanks, I'll always be your friend, come back safely." He felt the strong grip, saw for an instant a smile, then turned and in a cold sweat went to meet the enemy.

The captain had already covered half the jetty when Tyrer planted himself in the middle of the planks and bowed with great formality. A grunt, the man hesitated, his hand on his long sword, then bowed back. When he tried to pass, Tyrer bowed again and said in his best Japanese, deliberately ponderous, "Ah, Sir Officer, I want say you how samurai men good fight fire. Remembering from Yedo, yes? Please excuse me, on behalf my Master, Head Gai-jin in Nippon, accept great thank for help save all houses ours."

"Yes, thank you, now I want to see th—"

"See? Look there, Sir Officer!" Tyrer pointed at the town and all around, his Japanese dissolving more and more into gibberish as each time the man tried to walk around him he moved into his path. "See what fire h—"

"Out of the way!" the samurai said angrily, his breath heavy with the stench of *daikon,* horseradish. "Move!"

But Tyrer pretended not to understand and flailed his arms to block him, trying to make it appear unintentional and careful not to touch him, saying how awful the devastation was and how well the samurai had performed—Jamie and the others were behind him so he had no way of judging how much time he had, then the officer snarled, *"Baka!"* he saw his face twist with rage and readied for the blow but at that second he heard Jamie call out, "Cast off, for Christ's sake!" and he was roughly shoved aside as the man ran for the boat.

Panting, Tyrer picked himself up and, wet with relief, saw the cutter swerving off at full throttle, the other three ducking into the cabin, Bosun in the wheelhouse, seaman at the prow, the cabin lights doused the instant the samurai reached the jetty's head, his bellowing shout, calling them back, drowned by the engine. The moment before the lights went out and Hiraga and Akimoto turned their backs, Tyrer thought he saw their faces clearly—if he did the officer must have done.

"Imagination," Phillip gasped, already hurrying away in the fastest walk possible. He raised his hat to the samurai around the fire who acknowledged him perfunctorily, and by the time he heard the Japanese shout of "You, come here," he was swallowed in the crowd. When it was safe he broke into a trot, and did not begin to breathe until he was safe in the Legation.

"Good gracious, Phillip," Bertram said, popeyed, "you poor dear, what on earth's the matter?"

"Oh, fuck off," Tyrer said, not over the close call.

"Why should he do that?" Sir William asked from his office doorway, his face taut and voice harsh.

"Oh . . . oh, sorry, sir, it was . . . just a pleasantry."

An irritable grunt greeted that. "Phillip, your brains are addled! Where the devil have you been? There's a note from the Bakufu marked urgent on your desk to translate, a dispatch for Sir Percy to copy that must go with *Atlanta Belle* tonight, four insurance claims to stamp—I've already signed and approved them. When you've done that come and find me. I'll either be here or at the jetty seeing the passengers off—well, don't just stand there! Hurry up!"

Sir William went back into his office and closed his door and leaned against it. Inexorably his eyes went to André's file neatly centered on his desk. Sadness welled up again.

When Angelique had left he had hardly moved for an hour or more, trying to decide, desperate to be correct, for truly this was a life and death issue. His mind had wandered into the byways of his own experience: to his boyhood in England, to the Paris Desk, to St. Petersburg, his house there and the garden and laughing with Vertinskya in spring and summer and autumn and winter, loving her; then back to England again, to missions in the battlefields of the Crimea, and into swirling, smoky dark passages that frightened him.

He was glad that Phillip's voice had drawn him back to normality. Again his eyes wandered over the room and the fire and to the file, past that to the lovely young face in the miniature smiling at him. His heart broke as it always did and then repaired itself. A little less each time.

He went over and picked the miniature up and studied it, every brushstroke already etched on his mind. If I didn't have her portrait, would I have forgotten her face as Angelique did her Malcolm? "No answer to that one, Vertinskya, my darling," he said sadly, near tears, setting it down again. "Maybe I would—your face—but never you, never never never you."

And much as he tried to go back to live again the time he had been most alive, André's file was an iron door between them.

God damn him!

Never mind that, make the decision. No more shillyshallying, he ordered himself. Back to work, deal with this problem so you can go on to more important matters like Yoshi and the coming war against Satsuma—you are Her Britannic Majesty's Minister. Act like one!

The correct and only proper way to deal with André's file is to seal it, to write a private report that relates what occurred and when, what was said and by whom, then to seal that and send it all to London and let them decide. Lots of secrets in their vaults and archives. If they want it to be secret, that's up to them.

Good, that's the correct, right and only course.

Confident he was making the right decision, he gathered the pages and, one by one, fed them to the fire, humming to himself, watching them curl and blacken and burn. This isn't ill-advised. They're not positive proof and anyway the poor girl was a victim, André was a dangerous and active undercover agent for an enemy power and if half the evils listed in his secret dossier are correct, he deserved to go over the moon a dozen times. Truth or lies, in this instance dust is going to dust.

When it was done he raised his glass to the miniature, feeling very good. "For you, my darling," he said.

62

I⟨T⟩ WAS GETTING TOWARDS MID-
night when Tyrer finally hurried out of the Legation and headed for the
Struan jetty. His head ached like never before, he had had no time for
supper, no time to think about Hiraga or Fujiko, no time to do anything
but work. He carried an official H.M. Government dispatch satchel and
in his pocket was the translation that he had done last and wished he
had done first. His pace quickened.

The jetty was thronged. A few people were there seeing off the last
of the passengers, but most of the men noisily surrounded the *Belle*'s
Purser, who was accepting last-minute mail for Hong Kong and Shanghai Head Offices—insurance agents, suppliers, shippers, banks—
anyone and everyone who needed to know about the fire and damage.
He saw Angelique chatting with Gornt. On the other side of the crowd
Pallidar was talking to some officers who were boarding as passengers,
and near the head of the jetty he spotted Sir William in conversation
with Maureen Ross. Seeing her immediately reminded him of Jamie
and Hiraga, and of his promise to Jamie to clear the 'students' with his
superior. He eased through the crowd.

"Evening, Miss Maureen, excuse me, Sir William, but you might
want to see this." He handed him the translation. "I'll make sure the
dispatches get safely aboard." Quickly he turned away from the Purser,
not wanting to stay close at hand for the inevitable explosion. The
Purser was a short, dyspeptic man and the haphazard queue of men
jostling for position around him was still long. Tyrer pushed his way to
the head, disregarding the "Wait your bloody turn," saying, "Sorry,
Sir William's orders, H.M.'s business. A receipt, please."

"All right, all right, wot's the bloody rush, eh?" While the Purser laboriously entered the shipment in his ledger, Tyrer peeked at Sir William who had moved under the oil lamp and was squinting at the paper. While he watched, the face contorted, the lips began to mouth profanities, men nearby backed off in shock, not because of the language but merely because it was so unexpected. He groaned and turned his back.

The document was from the *roju,* signed *Tairō* Nori, curt, without the usual flowery phrases, and addressed impudently *To the Leader of the Gai-jin,* so he had translated it as best he could in the same fashion, interpolating it where necessary:

> *The* roju *congratulates you and other gai-jin on your escape with your lives and little else from fires started by malcontents and revolutionaries. Tomorrow the Kanagawa Governor will send 500 coolies to assist in your evacuation of Yokohama in accordance with clear warnings from the gods, and according to wishes of the Emperor given to you many times. When you return, if you return, give us a long warning. Accommodation will be provided for selected gai-jin at Deshima, in the port of Nagasaki, from where, as in the past, all future gai-jin trade and business will be conducted. A cordial communication.*

"Tyrer!"

He pretended not to hear, kept his back to Sir William and accepted the receipt from the Purser, the impatient men in the line calling out with degrees of rudeness, "Hurry up, for God's sake, do you want all night . . . hurry, there she is!"

The empty cutter, returning from the *Belle,* was docking. Tyrer noticed Jamie was not aboard. The Bosun leaned out of his cabin and bellowed, "All aboard wot's going aboard!"

In the heightened bustle Maureen joined him. "Phillip, when will Jamie be back?"

"Certainly with the last ferry, if not before," he said, not sure if Jamie had told her of their scheme. "There's an hour or more yet."

"Tyrer!"

"Sorry, got to go. Yessir?" he called out, took a deep breath, mentally girding his loins, and hurried off.

"In half an hour, Phillip," Sir William began, almost cross-eyed with rage, "in half an hour I'll need you to translate a reply for me, extremely bloody accurately indeed."

"Yes, sir, by the way, s—"

"Go and find . . . ah, there he is, thought I saw him." One look at Sir William's face was enough to cause the crowd to fall silent and part for him instantly, all ears. "Pallidar, get the Dragoons, I want you to deliver *a cordial communication* to the Kanagawa Governor—at once."

"Tonight, sir?" Pallidar gaped at him, saw the expression on his face and added hastily, "Oh! Yessir. Sorry, sir. Right away, sir."

" 'Scuse me, Sir William," Tyrer said in a rush before Sir William could leave. "No time to tell you before but I helped two Japanese students aboard who wanted to travel, to visit England, they saved my life last night, hope that's all right."

"That they saved your life? I wonder." The eyes bored into him. "If you've turned travel agent on Her Majesty's time, I suppose there will be a satisfactory answer should I require one. Pallidar, arrive in strength in an hour and deliver my message rather rudely, by God!" He stalked off.

Pallidar blew his nose, his cold still bad. "What the hell's up with him?" Tyrer leaned closer and told him about the ultimatum. "My God, no wonder. What bloody cheek! Actually it's bloody good, now there'll be some action, all this hanging around inflames the General's neck along with his piles." He laughed, more from nervousness than the old chestnut.

At that moment, Hoag arrived puffing, still wearing his operating frock coat, the sleeves and chest stiff with ancient blood, and burdened with top hat, suitcases and packages. "I thought I was going to be late. What's the joke?"

"You've plenty of time," Tyrer said, and, with Pallidar, wondered what was in Angelique's letter that Sir William had witnessed, and Hoag carried to Hong Kong in reply to *the letter,* also still a mystery, given to Angelique when Hoag was sure she was not bearing Malcolm's child. Since the first day Hoag had arrived back, the outlines of Tess's ultimatum were common knowledge and the subject of heated, private debate. "Hope you have a safe trip. It's India next, isn't it?"

"Yes, I'll be there next month." The ugly face split with a smile. "Can't wait. Come and visit me, you'll love it."

Pallidar said, "India's my next posting, in fact I've just been told, the Frontier, Hindu Kush, Khyber Pass."

Though he spoke lightly Pallidar secretly hated the idea. Too many deaths in that special hell, too many killings, a bullet from nowhere, a dagger out of the night, wells poisoned, no glory there, only slog and kill and try to stay alive in that barren, festering rock landscape where nothing grew but death. And yet vital to the Empire, for there lay the historic invasion route to British India, for Mongol, Persian, or Russian hordes. A sick premonition swept through him and he could not resist adding, "No sea burials there, Doc."

"No, none, not at all," Hoag replied, and, misreading him, put a warm, friendly arm on him. "You're a good fellow, Settry. If I can help in India I'm easy to find. You'll love it, good luck!" He strode off to greet Angelique and Gornt.

"What was that about?" Tyrer asked. He had noticed the sudden change in Pallidar.

Pallidar shrugged, cursing his anxiety and lapse and abrupt envy of Hoag. "Doc Hoag told me he doesn't like sea burials, said he was glad to miss Malcolm's in Hong Kong." He smiled crookedly. After he had reported to Sir William about Hoag's curious behavior over the coffins at Kanagawa that the Sergeant had witnessed, on instructions and sworn to secrecy, unobserved he had switched the coffins after checking them. No difference between them that he could see. So the coffin sent by *Prancing Cloud* to Hong Kong had contained Malcolm Struan and the one Hoag, Angelique, Jamie and Skye had buried was that of the villager, as Sir William had ordered.

"Pity Malcolm got chopped," he said, his voice raw. "Life's curious, eh? You never know when it'll happen."

Tyrer nodded, Pallidar's depression unusual. Liking him, his own guard slid away. "What's up, old man?"

"Nothing. You were bloody lucky last night, weren't you, getting out of—"

Shadows rushed over Tyrer's face and Pallidar swore at himself for his stupidity. "Sorry, Phillip. Didn't mean to upset you, don't know what's got into me tonight."

"You heard about . . . about . . ."

For the life of him Tyrer could not say Fujiko's name, his grief scalding, driving him down in quantum depths where he had never been before. His mouth said, trying to sound brave, "When something like that, that something awful happens, my old man used to . . . I had a sister who got measles and died when she was seven, such a pretty little girl we all loved . . . my old man always used to say, 'These things are sent to try us. You cry and cry and . . . and you pick yourself up and say it was God's Will and try not to hate Him.'"

He felt the tears running down his cheeks and did not care. His feet took him away down to the shore and there, alone with the surf and the sky and the night, he thought about Fujiko truly, remembering her with all his passion, then put her into a little box and put the box safe beside his heart.

Aboard *Atlanta Belle* Captain Twomast was saying, "All right, Jamie, I'll give them passage, whatever Mrs. Struan decides, but you know her, she's not given to largess."

"Just give her my letter when you arrive in Hong Kong." Jamie had told Twomast the truth about Otami and his cousin, not wanting to get his friend into trouble, and had gone surety for their passage money, there and back, if Tess did not agree to his proposal: to advance it to them, with prudent introductions in England and Scotland—against a fifty-fifty joint venture he would form and run to take advantage of anything he could create from them on their return.

He had written:

I know it's a long shot, Mrs. Struan, but Otami is as smart as they come, well connected as far as I can ascertain and represents the future in Nippon. Should you not agree, please take their passage money out of the most generous golden gift you have given me. In the meantime Albert MacStruan is doing well, your property and buildings here were untouched in the fire, and all is poised for a good future—I will continue to help if he asks. Last, may I say be careful of Brock's new manager, Edward Gornt. He's a good, brave man but a dangerous rival.

"This is going to be expensive, Jamie," Twomast said. He was a lean, short, hard-faced seaman, with dark hair and brown eyes and leathery skin. "At least a hundred pounds. Is it worth the risk?"

"It's her ship, passage costs her nothing."

"It's still expensive and she looks after the pence as well as the pounds. Never mind, it's up to her. I'll cash your sight draft in London town if she doesn't foot the bill. You're sure your Jappos understand they're to obey me?"

"Yes. I've told them that on board you're king, a daimyo. They're to obey you and stay aboard until you disembark them in London. But Johnny, treat them like nobs. You'll be rewarded."

Twomast laughed. "Yes, but in Heaven. Never mind, I owe you one or two over the years past so I'll do it."

"Thanks." Jamie looked around the cabin. Small, a bunk, chart table, table to seat four, neat, tough, seaworthy—like Johnny Twomast, originally Norwegian, and a cousin of Sven Orlov, the Hunchback, who was Master of the Struan fleet after Dirk Struan. *Atlanta Belle,* a thousand-ton merchant steamer, could sleep four first-class passengers, ten second, fifty steerage with room for substantial cargo. "Where will they bunk?"

"With the crew, where else?"

"Can you give them a cabin? I don't mind how small."

"We've a full house and they'll learn fast with the crew, learn our ways, have to."

"Give them a cabin at least until after Hong Kong, I don't want either recognized."

Johnny Twomast said, "They can have the Third Mate's cabin, it's got two bunks. Are they armed, Jamie?"

"Sure they're armed, they're samurai."

"No arms, not samurai, by God."

Jamie shrugged. "Tell them, but please treat them as nobs, not natives, strange but nobs, important Japanese, they are, you know."

"Mister!" the Captain called out. "Send them in!"

Hiraga and Akimoto came in, well briefed by Jamie.

"Which one of you speaks English?"

"I do, Anjin-sama. I Otami-sama."

"Mr. McFay here is guarantor for you, Otami-sama, for your good behavior all the way to London. You agree to obey me, to stay aboard if I say so, to go ashore and come back as I say, until London town, obey me as if I was your chief, your daimyo?"

"We agree do what Anjin-sama say," Hiraga said carefully.

"Good, but no arms while aboard. I want all swords, guns, knives. They'll be returned to you." Twomast saw the flash of anger and marked it. "You agree?"

"But if men attack us?"

"If my men attack you, use your fists till I arrive. They'll be warned, fifty lashes for each man if they start it. You don't start it, understand?"

"No, so sorry." Jamie explained how the seamen would be tied to the rigging and flogged for disobeying. Appalled by the cruelty, Hiraga passed this on to Akimoto, then said, "But, Anjin-sama, you no fear? If man free on ship, after such insu'rt, no afraid this man assassin you?"

Johnny Twomast laughed. "He'd hang, sure as God made little green apples. Mutiny's punishable by death. I'll order the crew not to pick on you, you don't pick on them—that's important too, understand?"

"Understand, Anjin-sama," Hiraga said, understanding only partially, his head aching.

"Any trouble, come to me. No fighting unless you're attacked. Your weapons please." Reluctantly Hiraga gave over their bundled swords. And the derringer. "Mister!"

The cabin door opened. "Yessir?"

"These two'll have the Third Mate's berth, I'll show 'em."

Jamie got up and offered his hand to Hiraga. "Safe journey, you can write anytime you like, and to Phillip . . . to Taira-sama. As I told you I'll write you care of my bank, the Hongkong Bank in the Mall. It's all in the papers I've given you along with how to receive or collect mail. Don't expect a reply for four months. Good luck and safe return." They shook hands, Jamie did the same with Akimoto.

"You two come with me," Twomast said. He led the way down the corridor and opened a door. "You bunk here and stay out of sight, Mr. McFay doesn't want you recognized. After Hong Kong it'll be easier." He closed the door.

In silence Hiraga and Akimoto looked around. It was more of a cupboard than living quarters. Barely enough room to stand together. A gimballed oil lamp spluttered dully. Two dirty bunks, one above the other against a bulkhead, drawers below. Soiled straw mattresses and wool blankets. Stench. Gum boots, unwashed clothes scattered. Storm mackintoshes hanging on pegs.

"What are those for?" Akimoto asked, numbed.

"Some sort of clothing but so stiff, how would you fight in those? I feel naked without swords."

"I feel like death, not just naked." The deck rolled under their feet and they heard men shouting orders on deck and others chantying, preparing the ship for sea, the engine loudly vibrating the deck and bulkheads, increasing their discomfort. The smallness of the space, and unpleasant smell of coal smoke and oil, stale air and staler bedding bore down on them. Again the deck pitched as she swung on an anchor and Hiraga lurched against the bunks, and sat on the lower one. "Do you suppose we sleep on these?"

"Where else?" Akimoto muttered. Sharp-eyed, he moved the crumpled blanket aside. All corners of the mattress were splotched with colonies of bedbugs, alive and dead, the rough canvas streaked with old blood where generations had been squashed. He managed not to be sick. "Let's go ashore," he croaked. "I've had enough."

"No," Hiraga said through his own dread. "We have achieved a miracle, we have escaped the Bakufu and Yoshi, and we're launched into the enemy's heartland as guests, we can spy out their secrets and learn how to destroy them."

"Learn what? How to flog a man to death, how to live in this cesspit for months? Did you see how the Captain rudely walked off without returning our bow. Come on . . . even if I have to swim ashore!" Akimoto grabbed the door handle but Hiraga caught him by the shirt and dragged him back. "No!"

Akimoto snarled at him and broke free, to crash against the door, with no room even to struggle, then shouted, "You're not one of us, you're gai-jin infected! Let me go, better to die civilized than to live like this!"

Suddenly Hiraga was petrified. Time stood still. For the first time he completely understood the enormity of what he had launched them into: the outside, the barbarian world, away from everything civilized, leaving everything worthwhile behind, *sonno-joi* and Choshu and shishi and family, leaving no wife and sons—ah, my brave and so wonderful Sumomo, how you are missed, you would have made my leaving easier, but now . . .

His limbs began to tremble, heart hammering, breath choking, every part of him screaming at him to flee this hell that represented everything he detested. If London was like this, anything was better, anything.

He shoved Akimoto out of the way and lunged for the door. But stopped. "No," he gasped. "*I will bear this!* I will! I'll bear it for *sonno-joi*. We must for *sonno-joi*, Cousin, we must bear it but whatever happens we will die like samurai, we will make our death poems, that's what we'll do, we'll make them now, *now,* then nothing else matters in this life. . . ."

Ashore at the jetty the Bosun called out, "Last call for *Belle,* all aboard!"

"So, good luck, Edward, and a safe return," Angelique said, still consumed with melancholy, but with a little smile that lit up his being. "Take care!"

After leaving Sir William earlier, she had finished her tears in the privacy of her suite—so much to cry over these days, she thought, where do all the tears come from, and yet, when the heartache had passed, she was clear thinking and clearheaded again. Once more in control she had gone downstairs and, again in privacy, had met Gornt. They had said everything that needed to be said. The strength and confidence and love he radiated had pushed away the bad.

Edward is good for me, she thought, looking up at him—not that he will ever replace my Malcolm, that's different.

"You all right now?" he asked.

"Yes, thank you, my dear. Hurry back."

He kissed her proffered hand. "Take care, Ma'am." His glow made him even more boyish.

"Don't forget." She had asked him to tell Tess that she hoped one day they could meet as friends. "It's important."

"Yes, it is, and I won't forget and I'll be back before you know it." For those nearby he added louder, "I'll see that your shopping list is taken care of, never fear." A final little pressure on her hand and he leapt onto the slippery deck without a care, hung on with one hand, last aboard. The Bosun tooted, shoved the throttles Full Astern and backed into the chop. Gornt waved and then, not wanting to be indiscreet, went into the cabin.

"Pretty girl," Hoag said, thoughtfully.

"Yes, suh, a Belle to end Belles."

Both men watched the jetty recede. "Have you ever been to India, Edward?"

"No, never have. You been to Paris?"

"No, never. But India's the best place in the world, best life in the world for Englishmen, you're mostly that, aren't you?" In his mind Hoag could see himself arriving at her family house that was behind high walls, brown and dusty outside but inside cool and green, the sound of the water fountain mingling with laughter that permeated the main house and the servants' quarters, together with friendliness and the peace possessed by everyone because of their utter belief in birth and death and rebirth, in never-ending succession, until through the mercy of the Infinite they would reach Nirvana, the Place of Heavenly Peace. Arjumand will be there, he thought—oh, how I hope I can find my way there too.

His eyes focused on the jetty, on Angelique and others, all people he would probably never see again. Now Angelique waved a last time then strolled over to Maureen Ross who was waiting by the lamp. I hope they become friends, he thought, wondering about them. In a moment, they and the jetty became part of the night. Angelique's correct to bend to Tess, he thought, not that she had any option. Absently his fingers made sure her affidavit was safe in his pocket.

Sad about Malcolm, tragic. Poor Malcolm, diligently working all his life for something he would never have, would never be. Malcolm Struan, *the tai-pan who never truly was*—all his life like a snow-blind man in a blizzard searching for a white tent that was never there.

"Sad about Malcolm, don't you think?" But Gornt was no longer beside him. He looked around and saw he had gone on deck and, his back to Yokohama, was watching the *Belle* ahead, hatless, the wind ruffling his hair.

Why the smile, and what's behind it? he asked himself. So hard and yet . . . Something strange about that young man. Is he a king in the making or a man bent on regicide?

Most people on the jetty had wandered off. Angelique was beside Maureen near the lamp, watching the *Belle* and disappearing cutter. Soon they were alone but for Chen and Vargas who were talking quietly with one another, waiting to unload the cutter, should it be necessary and, unasked, to chaperone the two women.

"Maureen . . ." Angelique glanced at her. Her lovely smile faded, noticing how unhappy her newfound friend looked. "What's the matter?"

"Nothing. Well, no, it's . . . really, dinna concern yoursel'. It's . . . it's just that I haven't seen Jamie all day, he's been busy and, and I had something important . . ." The words trailed off.

"I'll wait with you if you like. Even better, Maureen, why not come with me? Let's wait in my suite and watch from my window. We'll see the cutter in plenty of time to meet her."

"I think I'd . . . well, I think I'd rather wait here."

Angelique firmly took her arm. "What is it? What's the matter, can I help?"

"No, I din'na think so, dear Angelique. It's . . . it's just that . . . it's just that . . ." Maureen hesitated again, then stammered, "Oh, God, I din'na want to burden you but his, Jamie's, his—his mistress, came to see me this afternoon."

"From the Yoshiwara?"

"Yes. She came to kowtow, to bow, she said, and tell me not to worry because she's looked after him perfectly and she wanted to ask in future should she present her bill to me monthly or yearly."

Angelique's mouth dropped open. "She did?"

"Yes." Maureen looked green under the oil light and stuttered, "She also said that if there was anything I wanted to know about . . . about . . . about 'Jami' as she called him, ugh!, about his bed habits, positions and so on, as I was a virgin and wouldn't know these things, she'd be happy to oblige in detail because she was a professional of Second Rank and promised to give me a picture book called a 'pillow book' and she would mark his—his specialties but not to worry because Jami was well practiced and his . . . his, she called it his One-eyed Monk was in perfect order. There, now you know it all!"

Angelique was flabbergasted. "*Mon Dieu,* you poor dear, how awful! But . . . but she speaks English too?"

"No, an almost incoherent mixture of gibberish and pidgin and some of Jamie's words but I understood her key points perfectly well indeed. It—it seems she's—she's been his doxy for a year or more. She was tiny, no' at all pretty, no' five foot and I said, I didna' know what to say so I remarked on her size, how small she was and the hussy—the hussy guffawed and said, 'P'renti big 'nuff, Jami tai-tai, on back fit awe' same, heya? You 'rucky womans.' "

"Oh, *mon Dieu!*"

"Quite. What do I do?"

Angelique found her own head buzzing. "You could . . . no, that wouldn't do . . ."

"Perhaps I could . . . no, I canna'. It's too much . . ."

"What if you . . ." Angelique shook her head. Impotently she stared at her and at that moment Maureen looked at her, each seeing herself in the other, the same shock, revulsion, repugnance, contempt, fury written clearly on both faces. For a moment they were frozen, then Angelique snickered, in a second Maureen did the same and then they were choked with laughter.

Chen and Vargas peered across at them, the peals of laughter mixing with the waves on the shore and those that battered the pilings. Angelique wiped away these, the first, good, laughter tears she had had in such a long time. "His One-eyed . . ." Again they were convulsed, shrieking with laughter until their stomachs hurt and they hung on to one another.

As suddenly as the laughing fit arrived it went away. An ache remained. "It's funny, Maureen, but not funny at all."

"Yes. Not funny," Maureen said heavily. "I feel . . . I want to go home now. I thought I could deal with the Yoshiwara—Jamie's no different from other men—but I canna', I know that now. I canna' face this life where . . . where the Yoshiwara is and will ever be and like it or no', Angelique, in a year or two the bairns, the children, arrive and a few years after he'll think us old, whoever he is—and we will be old, our hair will be grey and teeth fall out and whoever he is he will turn away. A woman's lot is no' a happy one. I wish I was aboard *Atlanta Belle* now, going home, no' here, no' here. I'm going home anyway, soon as I can. I've decided."

"Think about it, don't tell him tonight."

"It's better to say it tonight. That's . . . it's better."

Angelique hesitated. "I'll wait till we see the cutter, then I'll leave."

"Thank you. I'll be sorry to leave you, now that we've met. I've never had a real friend." Maureen put her arm in hers, and looked back at *Atlanta Belle*.

"Ayeeyah," Chen was whispering disgustedly in Four Village dialect that he and Vargas spoke fluently. "Why can't those two whores be sensible and wait indoors until the cutter arrives, then we don't have to wait in the cold either."

"Jami won't be pleased to hear you call her that!"

"Fortunately he doesn't speak this dialect, or even Cantonese, and anyway I wouldn't call her whore in front of him or any foreign devil—though that's what we call all their women, as you know—nor would I use such blunt words around them. I'd use 'Morning Flower' or one of a thousand other names which we both know means 'whore' but foreign devils think means 'Morning Flower.' " Chen chortled, warm in his long padded jacket. He looked up at the sky as the moon came briefly through the overcast. "That Morning Flower thinks she'll be Jami tai-tai." Again he chortled. "She never will be."

"No, not after today," Vargas said gloomily. "She's the right size for him, time he was married and it would have been good to have children here." Vargas missed his own, six of them, that he had left with his two wives in Macao until he could afford a house of his own here. "What about Missee-tai-tai and this Shanghai Gornt? Will he increase her money?"

"If he does it will be for his benefit not hers. What I want to know is what's in those papers?"

"What papers?"

"The ones Lun saw when Willum tai-pan was dozing by his fire. The ones from Long Pointed Nose. *Dew neh loh moh* that Lun can't read French. Willum tai-pan was in plenty shock, so Lun said."

"What would Pointed Nose send Willum from the grave?"

Chen shrugged. "Trouble for Missee-tai-tai. Perhaps it was about Dark of the Moon, eh?"

"That's only a rumor."

Chen said nothing, keeping that secret as Noble House Chen had ordered after Malcolm's death. "Whatever happens, Tess tai-tai will grind Missee-tai-tai and the Shanghai foreign devil into dust."

"Oh? What have you heard?"

Chen rolled his eyes. "Tess tai-tai is tai-pan now, that's what Noble House Chen says—he told us in the last mail and to beware. Did you ever hear of an Empress giving away power once she's got it? Any woman, for that matter? Never in all our five hundred centuries of history. She's tai-pan now, according to Noble House Chen, and he should know."

"I thought Shanghai Albert was to be tai-pan."

"Never. She'll grind him into dust too—Old Green-eyed Devil forced him and his brother on the Noble House. Rumor is Tess tai-tai hates them because they are secret bastards of that foreign devil missionary's daughter—the one of Many Lovers by Green-eyed Devil himself."

"Harbor Master Glessing's wife? Mary Sinclair? Never!"

"It could be true, she made One-Leg Glessing wear a green hat a dozen times."

"Made him a cuckold? That's another legend," Vargas said, guarding her reputation like all her ex-lovers. Now she was in her forties, used, but still as hungry as ever, he thought, the opposite to Tess Struan who abominates fornication and drove her husband Culum to drink and other women. "Tess tai-tai should have married the tai-pan—and not his son Culum. He could have lubricated her majestically, which was her real lack, and still have more than enough left for Second Wife May-may and Third Wife Yin Hsi as well."

"True," Chen said, "then we'd be strong with lots more sons to follow, and not weak and fleeing from One-eye Devil Brock." He added ominously, "Noble House Chen is worried."

"Sad that Number One Son Malcolm died as he did."

"The gods were out that day," Chen said wisely. "Listen, you kowtow to the foreign devil god, has he told you why gods spend more time out than watching over our affairs?"

"Gods are gods, they only talk to one another . . . look, *Belle*'s leaving . . ."

* * *

Maureen said, "*Atlanta Belle* on her way, Angelique."

Godspeed, Angelique thought, squinting against the slight wind, the ship only a vague shape.

"And there's the cutter."

"Where? My goodness, your eyes are sharp, I can hardly see her." Angelique gave Maureen's arm a friendly squeeze. "I'm sure you and Jamie will . . ." She saw the color had gone out of her. "Don't worry, Maureen, it will be all right, I'm sure." .

Maureen muttered. "I dinna think I can face him now."

"Then . . . then you run off, I'll say you had a headache and will see him tomorrow that will give you time to think, it will be better tomorrow."

"Tonight, tomorrow, my mind's made up," Maureen said.

Both women watched the cutter's riding lights becoming steadily more visible. In a little while they could make out the tall figure of Jamie in the cabin lights. He was alone.

Angelique said, " 'Night, Maureen, I'll see you tomorrow."

"No. Please stay, I canna' do it alone. Please stay."

The cutter was barely fifty metres from the jetty. They saw Jamie lean out of the window and wave. Maureen did not return the salute. Behind them the oil lamps were fine along the promenade, and in the big houses and warehouses that had remained untouched. Somewhere men were singing. Over at the French Legation Vervene was playing the flute. Maureen's eyes were fixed on the approaching man. Again he waved, then swung on deck. "Maureen!" he hollered, clearly so happy to see her.

Angelique glanced back at her and saw Maureen's eyes soften and knew she was forgotten. Rightly so, she thought, and smiled to herself. Maureen will weep and rave and swear she's leaving but she won't, she'll make him suffer, but she will forgive him and never forget and stay—she'll stay because she loves him—how silly we women are.

Quietly, unnoticed, she walked away, glad to be alone.

The night was pleasant. In the bay the bells were sounding the hour. Out to sea, beyond the headland her emissary was launched aboard *Atlanta Belle* on his voyage of conquest, a voyage of no return for both of them. And for the enemy, the Woman of Hong Kong.

Edward will squeeze that awful woman and we'll live happy ever after, we'll spend more than two months every second year in Paris, we'll summer in Provence and I will start a dynasty—with five thousand guineas of my own, I'm an heiress, and every sou I spend will remind me of *her*.

How silly of Edward to think I would ever, could ever be *her* friend, would ever want to be.

That woman's vile. I will never forgive her for the things she did and wrote. Illegitimate, eh? I will never forget that, and we will be revenged, my Malcolm and I, for all the anguish she caused us, him and me. We will be revenged on that hag.

I like that name, she told herself, smiling. That's one of my new secrets. That's what I knew she was from the first moment I met her, and during the few times we met and times we dined, barely talking to me, always disapproving of me, much as I tried. She's a hag. Even though she's thirty-seven. She is and always will be Hag Struan to me.

Angelique was eighteen and a few days over six months old and she walked into the Struan foyer under the entwined Red Lion of Scotland and Green Dragon of China and up the great staircase and into her own suite. There she bolted the door and then, so happily, went to bed—to sleep snug.

Seven days later, at his request, Yoshi met Sir William and the Ministers at Kanagawa and soothed them, content that Anjo had again fallen into his trap to use a big stick that was no stick at all—though equally astonished the gai-jin had not sailed away from the devastation. His salve was to be a meeting with the Shōgun, as soon as the Shōgun returned.

And when would that be? Sir William asked, and he replied, I will arrange it quickly, overruling the tairō if need be, he's so sick, poor man, though still tairō. Meanwhile I trust the information I require for our possible future accords will be ready soon and that my counsel will be considered?

Forthwith H.M.S. Pearl *was sent to Kagoshima with a formal demand to Sanjiro for an apology, reparations and the murderers handed over or identified. Sanjiro dismissed it as impertinent. The following week, with Sir William and his staff aboard the flagship, the battle squadron sailed—H.M.S.* Euryalus, *35 guns,* Pearl, *21,* Perseus, *21,* Racehorse, *14,* Havoc, Coquette, *and the paddle sloop* Argus, *9—and shortly anchored in the neck of Kagoshima Bay, out of range of the shore batteries that were protected in fourteen forts on both sides of the bay. The weather turned bad.*

As conditions worsened, Sanjiro vacillated. For four days. At dawn on the fifth day, the rain and storm heavy, three foreign-built Satsuma-owned steamers anchored off the town were seized and scuttled, and some soundings taken. At noon all shore batteries commenced firing and Admiral Ketterer gave orders to engage. In line ahead, the flagship leading, the fleet steamed into the uncharted waters. As each came into range of the forts the ships poured broadside after broadside into them, the returning fire much heavier than expected.

An hour after the battle had begun Euryalus *swerved out of line. Unwittingly she had been steered between a fort and a target area the shore gunners had ranged to a nicety, and a round shot had taken off the heads of her Captain and Commander on the bridge, standing beside Ketterer and Sir William, and a 10-inch shell exploded on the deck, killing another seven sailors and wounding an officer.* Pearl *led in her place. Near sunset* Perseus *went aground under the guns of a fort but* Pearl *dragged her off without loss.*

The engagement continued until sunset. Several forts had been damaged, many cannon destroyed, some magazines blown up and rockets fired into Kagoshima. No ships lost, the only deaths so far those aboard the flagship. That night Kagoshima burned as Yokohama had burned. The storm increased.

At dawn, with no letup in the foul weather, the dead were given their sea burial and re-engagement ordered. Euryalus *led. That night the fleet once more anchored out of range, all ships intact, morale high with plenty of ammunition in reserve. Kagoshima was gutted, most batteries damaged. At dawn, in gale-force winds and driving rain, to the disgust of most aboard and over Sir William's protests, Ketterer ordered the fleet to return to Yokohama. Though far out of range, a few shore guns still fired defiantly at their wake.*

Ketterer claimed it a victory, the city had been burned, Sanjiro humbled and, most important, the fleet was unharmed—weather had made his decision necessary, he maintained.

In Kyōto, the moment Ogama of Choshu heard that Kagoshima was destroyed—with Sanjiro reported killed— he launched a surprise night coup, code name Crimson Sky, to regain total control of the Gates, lured into another trap of Yoshi's design. At once Yodo of Tosa and all fence-sitting daimyos joined with the Shōgunate against Ogama— better a weak Shōgunate guarding the Gates than a single, all-powerful Ogama. So the coup was put down, Ogama forced out of Kyōto to retreat to Shimonoseki and his Straits, there to lick his wounds, swearing vengeance, particularly on his erstwhile ally Yoshi. And to prepare for war.

For Nippon nothing had been solved. Nor had Sanjiro been killed— more disinformation spread by Yoshi's spies. But that did not matter, Yoshi knew he had made a giant step forward towards capturing the future: now he had sole though tenuous possession of the Gates, Ogama was banished, Kagoshima destroyed, Shōgun Nobusada returning to Yedo, without his Princess, convinced that Kyōto was unsafe for his person, shishi were almost exterminated, Anjo not long for this earth—and, temporarily, the gai-jin tamed.

But a month or so later, Sanjiro's emissaries came from Satsuma to Sir William in Yokohama and sued for peace. Sanjiro admitted he was in the wrong, paid the indemnity, named the killers, swore to be friends to gai-jin, blamed the decadent Shōgunate for all problems, and invited gai-jin to his rebuilt Kagoshima to trade, to discuss modernization in all its facets and, amongst other matters, 'Lord Sanjiro wants you to know Satsuma is an ancient sea power and should have a navy such as yours. He is rich and can pay in gold or silver or coal what is necessary for Ing'erish ships and Ing'erish instructors . . .'

To his chagrin Yoshi heard about the offer almost at once from his spy Inejin and was utterly displeased. This was not planned for, never conceived and changed the balance of power.

Never mind, he thought grimly, that particular sunset. He was in his eyrie in Yedo Castle's keep, looking out over the city, the sky streaked blood-red, fires here and there lighting the coming of night. Never mind, gods play tricks on us, if there are gods. Gods or no gods, do not matter, that is what makes life what it is. Perhaps I will win, perhaps not. Karma. I will remember the Legacy. And have patience. That is enough.

No, never enough!

Deliberately he opened the compartment and recalled Koiko in all her beauty, all the good times they had had and all the laughter. This gladdened him and calmed him and the thought of her led at length to Meikin and her death wish: 'A bath and clean clothes. Please.' He smiled, happy that he had granted it—but only because of her good manners.

"In this life," he said with a chuckle to the evening air, "in this World of Tears, you need a sense of humor, neh?"

PRINCIPAL CHARACTERS

The Gai-jin
—

MALCOLM STRUAN, 20, eldest son and heir apparent of
CULUM STRUAN, 42, present tai-pan of STRUAN'S, the Noble House,
    son of DIRK STRUAN, founder of the company, and
TESS STRUAN, 37, his wife, daughter of TYLER BROCK
GORDON CHEN, 48, "Illustrious Chen," compradore of STRUAN'S in
    Hong Kong, an illegitimate son of DIRK STRUAN
JAMIE MCFAY, 39, manager of STRUAN'S in the Japans
MAUREEN ROSS, 28, his fiancée
DR. RONALD HOAG, 50, the STRUAN family physician

TYLER BROCK, 72, tai-pan and founder of Brock and Sons
SIR MORGAN BROCK, 48, his son, TESS STRUAN'S stepbrother
NORBERT GREYFORTH, 30, head of BROCK'S in the Japans

SIR WILLIAM AYLESBURY, 47, British Minister to the Japans
DR. GEORGE BABCOTT, 28, Deputy Minister and surgeon
PHILLIP TYRER, 21, diplomat and apprentice Japanese interpreter
ADMIRAL CHARLES KETTERER, 46, commander of the British Fleet
LT. JOHN MARLOWE, 28, captain of the 21-gun steam frigate, H.M.S.
    Pearl, presently aide-de-camp to KETTERER
SETTRY PALLIDAR, 24, Captain of the Dragoons
DMITRI SYBORODIN, 38, American trader of Cossack descent
EDWARD GORNT, 27, gentleman, Shanghai trader, from Virginia
HEATHERLY ("HEAVENLY") SKYE, 41, the only solicitor in the Japans
HENRI BONAPARTE SERATARD, 41, French Minister to the Japans
ANDRÉ EDOUARD PONCIN, 38, trader, secret spy for the French Legation

1235

COUNT ALEXI ZERGEYEV, 35, Tsarist Minister to the Japans

ANGELIQUE RICHAUD, 18, beloved of MALCOLM STRUAN, daughter of GUY RICHAUD, French China trader, ward of the French Minister

The Japanese
—

LORD TORANAGA YOSHI, 26, descendant of SHŌGUN TORANAGA, member of the Council of Elders, Guardian of the Heir, the boy Shōgun

KOIKO, 22, *Tayu*, the highest possible rank of geisha, his *ai-jin* (love person)

LADY HOSAKI, 29, his wife

INEJIN, 42, innkeeper and his spymaster

MISAMOTO, 33, fisherman, convict, a make-believe samurai, a secret American-speaking interpreter

SHŌGUN NOBUSADA, 16, the 14th Toranaga Shōgun

PRINCESS YAZU, 16, his wife, stepsister of Emperor Komei

LORD ANJO, 46, daimyo of Kii, head of the Council of Elders

LORD SANJIRO, 42, daimyo of Satsuma

KATSUMATA, 36, his most trusted advisor, also called the Raven, and secret head of the shishi

LORD OGAMA, 28, daimyo of Choshu

LORD HIRO, 28, daimyo of Tosa

WAKURA, 46, Lord Chancellor to the Imperial Court in Kyōto

MEIKIN, 44, KOIKO'S mama-san of the Yedo's House of Wisteria

RAIKO, 42, mama-san of Yokohama's House of Three Carp

FUJIKO, 31, courtesan, sought by PHILLIP TYRER

NEMI, 23, courtesan, JAMIE MCFAY'S *ai-jin*

HINODEH, 22, courtesan, ANDRÉ PONCIN'S *ai-jin*

the shishi (persons of courage), cells of revolutionary samurai idealists, fanatically xenophobic and anti–gai-jin:

HIRAGA, 22, leader of all Choshu shishi, also called UKIYA, NAKAMA, OTAMI

AKIMOTO, 24, of Choshu, his cousin

ORI, 17, leader of a Satsuma cell

SHORIN, 19, of Satsuma, his deputy

SUMOMO, 16, SHORIN'S sister, also shishi, HIRAGA'S wife-to-be